THREE GREAT NOVELS
April Grove Stories

Lilian Harry

Three Great Novels: April Grove Stories

Goodbye Sweetheart

The Girls They Left Behind

Keep Smiling Through

ORION

First published in Great Britain in 2003 by Orion,
an imprint of the Orion Publishing Group Ltd.

Goodbye Sweetheart Copyright © 1994 Lilian Harry
The Girls They Left Behind Copyright © 1995 Lilian Harry
Keep Smiling Through Copyright © 1996 Lilian Harry

A CIP catalogue record for this book
is available from the British Library.

ISBN 0 75285 659 6

Typeset at The Spartan Press Ltd, Lymington, Hants

Printed in Great Britain by Clays Ltd, St Ives plc

The Orion Publishing Group Ltd
Orion House
5 Upper Saint Martin's Lane
London, WC2H 9EA

Contents

Goodbye Sweetheart

'To my Mother and Father.
With all my love. Lilian Harry.'

1

The Budd brothers, Tim and Keith, came roaring up the garden path and in through the back door of number 14 April Grove as if the devil were after them. Their faces were grimy, their shirts hung half out of their short trousers and their socks were wrinkled round their ankles. They looked as if they had just fought in some historic battle and their eyes blazed with the triumph and delight of victors.

'We won!' Tim yelled as they burst into the small back room, jostling to be the first with the news. 'We won! We beat 'em hollow.'

Jess Budd, pregnant at forty with her fourth child, put out a hand to save her teacup from being knocked over. Her sister Annie, who lived at the top of the street, tutted and grabbed at the plate of biscuits that were about to be sent flying.

'Is that the way to come bursting in on your Ma of a Saturday afternoon?' she demanded. 'Can't she get any rest? And look at your boots, covered in mud – what've you been doing, mudlarking?' She touched her newly waved dark hair, cut to ear length in the latest fashion, and drew her skirt closer around her legs. She was wearing her new rayon frock today and wanted Jess to remark on it. So far, to her annoyance, she didn't even seem to have noticed.

'Certainly not,' Jess said sharply. 'Frank and me don't allow any mudlarking.' She looked at her sons. She knew quite well where they had been – down at the newspaper offices in Stamford Street, waiting for the football results, though how anyone could get that dirty just waiting in the street only boys would know. 'Quieten down, the two of you, and tell us what you're on about.'

'We told you – we've won,' Tim said impatiently. At almost ten years old, he was the elder of the two boys, though a childhood illness had left him the smaller. His curly hair was tousled and his hazel eyes sparkled. 'We beat 'em four-one. Four-one.' Forgetting his muddy boots, he began to dance a jig around the dining-table that took up most of the room, and chanted, 'Pompey's won the Cu-up, Pompey's won the Cu-up.'

Keith, nearly two years younger but chubbier than his brother, with a round face and dark brown eyes like his mother's, took up the chant too and Jess waved her hands at them for quiet.

'The Cup? You mean that football cup? Is that what all this fuss is about?'

3

Annie asked, knowing very well that it was, and the boys stared at her as if she had just come down from the moon.

'You must know it's the Cup Final today, Auntie,' Tim said. 'It's all people have been talking about. Portsmouth's been playing against Wolverhampton, at Wembley. The King's presenting it to the captain. You must know about it. Uncle Ted would know.'

'Well, maybe I did hear something about it,' Annie said offhandedly, and Jess smiled. It was one of Auntie's habits to ignore football completely, mainly because she didn't like the interest her husband took in it. 'Just like little boys,' she'd say scornfully when he and Jess's husband Frank came home for their tea discussing the latest match. And she didn't have much more patience with her nephews. 'You'll grow up just like your dad,' she told them now. 'Football mad.' She watched as the two boys, unable to keep still, grabbed a biscuit each and clattered out into the garden again. 'The whole town's gone crackers,' she went on, 'and for what? Twenty-two grown men chasing a ball around a field. Don't they have anything better to do?'

'It's not so much a question of have nothing better to do,' Jess said quietly. 'Seems to me too many people have got something worse to do these days.' She looked out of the window at her sons, now capering up and down the garden path pretending to be footballers, but her brown eyes were abstracted. 'And if the boys grow up to be like their dad, I'll be more than pleased. He's a good man, is my Frank, and so's your Ted.'

She pushed back a tendril of hair, the colour of beechnuts and almost untouched as yet by grey. She'd washed it after dinner and it wasn't properly dry yet. Perhaps Annie would do it up for her before she went.

'Oh, I know,' Annie said. 'I was just teasing them, that's all. You don't want to take any notice of me.'

She reached over and poured more tea, and Jess watched her fondly. Annie was a bit sharp sometimes but she was good-hearted enough, and a good sister. And she was right, in a way. There was more to life than football, even if Pompey had won the coveted Football Association Cup. The news everywhere else was bad – countries all over the world at each other's throats, it seemed, what with Italy invading Albania and Germany invading Czechoslovakia and now it looked as if Hitler was going to go back on his promise not to invade Poland. And only a few weeks ago, Britain and France had joined forces to protect Poland, so if he did . . .

Jess didn't want to think about what might happen if Hitler went ahead with his plan. But it was impossible to ignore, for the reminders were everywhere – trenches being dug up in the parks, talk of air raids, gas attacks, invasion . . .

For people like her and Frank, who had already been through the Great War, it was frightening. And they said this time it'd be worse.

Unconsciously, she covered her stomach with her hands and Annie's sharp eyes noticed the movement.

'How're you feeling today, Jess? Got over that heartburn?'

'Not really. The baby's riding too high – I had it right through with the others anyway.' She sighed and shifted a little in her chair. 'It's the sciatica really gets me down. Sometimes I can hardly sit comfortably, it's like toothache all down my leg. The doctor says the baby's pressing on a nerve and there's nothing he can do about it.'

'Well, I suppose you can't expect much else at your age,' Annie remarked, and Jess sighed. She knew a good many people disapproved of her having another baby at forty, but she and Frank had talked about it and agreed that they wanted one, while there was still time. Another two or three years and it could be too late. And when Mr Chamberlain had come back from Munich at the end of September last year, waving a piece of paper and declaring that it was 'peace in our time' the omen had seemed too good to ignore.

Peace in our time! A phrase full of hope for a world that had, after all, averted catastrophe. Along with twenty thousand others, she and Frank had gone to the Peace Thanksgiving Service in the Guildhall Square and sung hymns to the accompaniment of the Royal Marine bands. The sound of rejoicing had filled the air, bringing tears to the eyes of almost all who stood there, and on the Guildhall steps the Lord Mayor and the Bishop of Portsmouth had given thanks with the rest.

Jess and Frank had strolled home arm in arm, Jess with eleven-year-old Rose clinging to her other arm and the two boys walking in front, quiet for once. The October air was mild, with a hint of smoke in the air from the first fires of the autumn, and that night they had lain in bed, relief drawing them close. The world which had been teetering on the brink of disaster was once again a safe place.

What better time to have a baby?

And by the time the bitter knowledge had dawned that the 'peace' was no more than an uneasy respite, that war loomed blacker and larger than ever, it was too late. Jess was pregnant and the world a dark and dangerous place to be born into.

The boys came dashing back through the door.

'Mum! Mum! Can we go down the railway station, see the team come back? Bob Shaw next door says they'll be bringing the Cup. Can we, Mum?'

'Are you going to be with Bob?' Jess asked, and they nodded vigorously. 'All right, then, but mind you're back before dark. I don't want you roaming round the streets. And no mischief, mind.'

She watched as they tore away down the garden path. 'Bob Shaw's good to them. There's not that many lads of nineteen will bother with two boys like Tim and Keith, taking them swimming and fishing when their father can't spare the time. And Peggy and Bert are good neighbours too, always ready to give a hand.'

'Hm.' Annie pursed her mouth. Like Jess, she wore no make-up save for Pond's vanishing cream and a dusting of powder. 'I don't know about the girls, though – that Diane's altogether too flighty and knowing for a girl of fifteen, and Gladys thinks she's grown up now she's eighteen and been out at work a few years. And you know—' She broke off to pick up the brush and comb and start working on Jess's hair. 'I don't know why you don't get this lot cut off. It'd look ever so much smarter, it's got a nice wave in it.'

Jess smiled. 'Frank likes it this way. Go on, what were you going to say about Gladys?'

'Oh, nothing at all. Only that she took a fancy to our Colin before he went off to sea, you knew that, didn't you?'

Jess nodded. Her own daughter Rosemary was barely twelve and inclined to look up to the girls next door, and Jess had already had a few worries about what she might be learning from them. The Shaws weren't quite so strict with their daughters as Ted and Annie.

Annie was eight years older than Jess and had married at twenty. To Jess, she had always been 'grown up', more like a mother than a sister, and it was only when Jess had had her own family that they had drawn closer as friends. But Jess had always been a welcome visitor at Annie's home, and had helped with her sister's children from the time they were born. Olive and Betty and their brother Colin, now twenty-five and the pride of Annie's heart when he came swaggering down the street in his bell-bottoms, meant almost as much to Jess as her own three did.

'How's your Olive getting on with her Derek?' she asked. 'He seems a nice enough young chap.'

'He is.' Annie's mouth was full of hair-grips. 'She's asked him to tea a few times. Got good manners and no side to him, for all his dad's her boss.'

Jess leaned away for a moment to pour more tea. 'Think anything'll come of it? It'd be a good match for her.'

Annie pursed her lips again. 'Who can tell? They seem fond enough of each other, and I suppose she's old enough to get engaged. But you know what Ted's like. He won't have either of the girls getting serious too young. He didn't even like them going out with boys till they'd turned eighteen and I must say I think he was right. You don't know what they might get up to these days, not like when we were young.'

Jess nodded. Annie had had her share of suitors as a girl, but chose to forget them now. None of them had been 'serious' she would declare. And Jess had had no other boyfriends before she met Frank. If she had, she knew their father would have been every bit as strict as Ted. Home by ten o'clock unless they'd asked permission to be out later, and no string of boys knocking at the door. One at a time was the way he and their mother had believed in, anything else made a girl look 'cheap' and 'common', and got her a bad name.

That was the trouble with Peggy Shaw's two. Gladys was always out somewhere, often not getting home till gone eleven, and Diane spent far too much time on street corners, talking to boys. Jess was surprised at Peggy for allowing it, especially when they had the example of Nancy Baxter at number 10 before them . . .

'And what about Betty?' Betty had been a tomboy, wanting nothing more than to shadow her brother Colin whenever he was home on leave from the Navy, and had usually been found playing cricket and football with the boys in the street rather than joining the girls with their dolls and skipping. It was all right when she was a child but Ted and Annie had been worried that she might be turning into a flirt.

'Betty? I don't know – she doesn't let on much. Ted reckons she's getting too saucy, but I tell him she can't get up to much mischief working in the dairy at the top of the street. She keeps talking about getting something else – something more exciting, if you please!' Annie sniffed. 'Exciting! I asked her what she meant by that and she said she didn't know. She's all mixed up, that's her trouble. Doesn't want to be a boy any more and doesn't know how to be a girl.' She put down the brush and fixed the last grip in the knot on Jess's neck.

'Still, I daresay she'll sort herself out,' Jess said. 'Most girls are a bit here and there at her age.'

Annie nodded. 'Well, I'd better be going. I promised Mum and Dad I'd slip down and see them this afternoon. And then Ted'll be in for his tea, full of this Cup Final win, I daresay. I wouldn't be surprised if they've dressed the ferryboat overall in honour of the occasion!'

Jess laughed. Ted was a skipper on one of the boats which plied between Portsmouth and Gosport and as proud of his little craft as an admiral of his fleet.

'It'll be all over the front page of the *Evening News* too,' Annie went on. 'Well, I suppose it's better than talking about war, which is all we seem to get these days. Gas attacks, digging trenches in the parks – it's enough to turn you cold. Trenches! What good are they going to do us if war breaks out?'

'We're supposed to be getting shelters,' Jess said. 'Anderson shelters for the garden. And they'll be digging big ones in the streets for people who haven't got gardens.'

'And do you suppose they'll be any good if a bomb hits 'em?' Annie asked scornfully. 'They're expecting hundreds, thousands, every night. What use will a few tin huts be then?'

Jess was silent. Like her sister, she could remember the air raids over London in the last war – and they said this lot would be far, far worse.

That time, the Germans had used mostly Zeppelins, huge airships that looked terrifying as they loomed overhead but didn't do very much damage. This time, they had hundreds – perhaps thousands – of aircraft, able to fly faster and farther than ever before, carrying huge loads of bombs. Their navy had ships such as had never been seen at sea before and their army had been training for years, before they'd even begun to invade the other countries of Europe.

They want to take us all over, she thought with a jab of fear. And what can we do to stop them?

She felt the baby kick inside her and clasped her fingers together, as if in prayer, over the heaving bulge. Stay there, she begged it silently, just stay there inside me where you'll be safe. Don't get born.

But she knew that if war came, nowhere in Portsmouth would be safe. With one of the naval dockyards and harbours as target, she and Frank and the children would be in the front line.

Annie was watching her with concern.

'Are you all right, our Jess? You've gone dead white.' An expression of self-annoyance creased her face. 'That's me, I suppose, opening my big mouth and putting my foot in it as usual. Look, you don't want to take no notice of me. I don't suppose there'll be a war anyway, not when it comes down to it. The King can't be expecting it, after all – he wouldn't be going to Canada next week if he thought we were going to be at war.' She picked up yesterday's edition of the *Evening News*, which had been lying on a chair. 'Here – it tells you about their itinerary in Portsmouth on their way to the ship – arriving by train, they'll be, him and the Queen, and then walking through to the Guildhall and driving down to the Southern Railway Jetty. They reckon there'll be two thousand children lining the route. And the Princesses will be with them.' Annie looked down at Jess. 'Why don't we go and see them?'

Jess puckered her face. 'I don't know, Annie. Not in all those crowds, the way I am.'

'No, you're right, better not. But I might go. I could tell you all about it, what they were wearing and that. Be something to cheer us up a bit.'

'That's right,' Jess said, 'you do that.'

She took back the paper. Annie was easily enough cheered up. But she hadn't read the rest of the news. The mention of compulsory military training for all men over twenty years old. The plans for evacuating the city's children.

It all made war seem very close.

Annie was still watching her face. She put out a hand and touched her sister's knee.

'Hitler'll back off – sure to. You don't want to worry, Jess.'

Jess smiled at her. That was Annie all over, first letting fly and then remembering that Jess was her baby sister – even at forty! – and had to be petted and soothed. But no amount of petting and soothing was going to stop this war coming, and they both knew it, even though until it was properly declared everyone had to put on a pretence of hoping.

'I'm all right,' Jess said. 'Just a bit of a twinge . . . Thanks for popping in, Annie. Give Mum and Dad my love and tell them I'll be in on Tuesday, when I've been to the doctor's . . . And I like your new frock. It suits you. And the hairdo.'

Annie looked at her for a moment, then smiled. 'And I thought you hadn't noticed.'

'Go on with you,' Jess said, rising clumsily to her feet and gathering up the cups. 'Of course I noticed, the minute you walked in. I was just teasing you – like you teased Tim and Keith. Football, new frocks – we're all the same when it comes down to it, aren't we?'

Olive Chapman was spending Saturday afternoon walking along Southsea seafront with her young man, Derek Harker. They had gone out in one of the vans belonging to Derek's father, who ran the building business where Olive worked. She had been in the office for six months now, having moved there from her previous office job at a garage, and had been going out with Derek for three of those months.

She still couldn't quite believe her luck. Derek was one of the best-looking boys in the Copnor area, a good six foot tall with dark gold hair carefully combed into waves and shiny with Brylcreem. He dressed well too, with a suit for weekdays and a Fair Isle pullover and grey slacks for weekends. And he had a good job with a local firm of accountants as well as helping his father with the business.

'Of course, I'll take over one of these days,' he said carelessly as they strolled along. 'The old man's bound to want to retire before too long. And he deserves a rest – he's worked hard, building it up. There's not another builder in Portsmouth can touch him, you know.'

'I know.' Olive hugged his arm. It was cool today, with a wind blowing straight up the beach from the sea and whipping her chestnut hair around her face. She was glad she'd worn her new spring jacket. It was a light green tweed with a big collar and a wide belt and she'd put on a dark green skirt to go with it. It looked unconventional but Derek had given a little whistle when he saw her, and that was enough for Olive.

They stopped for a while to look across the Solent at the Isle of Wight. It was very clear, the buildings of Ryde and Seaview showing up sharply on the horizon, and the wind was tossing the sea into a thousand dancing white horses. Between Southsea and the island could be seen the Spithead Forts, the three grim-looking bastions that had been built there over a century ago to protect England's southern shores from invasion. Olive stared at them and shivered.

'Cold?' Derek slipped his arm round her waist and Olive felt a sudden thrill of excitement. Derek often put his arm round her, especially when he was walking her home at night, and sometimes in the pictures though she was always nervous of who might see them, but they'd had an unspoken agreement that he wouldn't do it in public in the daytime. But this afternoon, Olive felt reckless. They'd been going out together for three months, after all, and who was going to see them anyway?

'A bit. But I was just thinking about – you know. About the war. And those forts. D'you think they'd be any good, Derek? D'you think there is going to be a war?'

'Well, I reckon they'd stop most ships getting through. We've got better guns now than we had when they first built them, after all.' He frowned, remembering how his father and other men talked when they discussed the possibility of war. 'It all depends on what Hitler does next. If he goes into Poland—'

Olive shuddered and he held her more tightly. She leaned against him.

'Would you – would you go and fight, Derek?'

'If I had to. We'd all have to do our bit.'

'Even if it meant going away?'

'Well, it'd be bound to mean that, wouldn't it? We don't want Hitler coming here, do we?'

Olive pouted a little. 'You don't seem too bothered. P'raps you want to go away.'

'No, I don't.' Derek still had his arm round her. She felt his hand move a little on her waist, the fingers straying under her arm. 'I don't want to go away at all. It'd interfere with my plans.'

'Oh? What plans?' Olive felt another small tremor of excitement. She was very much aware of those fingers and glanced around, wondering if there was anyone about that she knew, but most of the other people on the beach that afternoon were children or young couples like themselves.

'Well, I want to buy a sports car. One of those little MG two-seaters. Red, if I can get hold of it. I know a bloke who's got one he's thinking of selling and he'd let me have it for fifty quid.' Derek's eyes gleamed. 'Think of it, Livvy – whizzing round the roads in a red sports car! Wouldn't it be fine? We could go anywhere – Brighton, Dover, even London.' His blue eyes gleamed and he hugged her close against him.

Olive gasped and giggled a little. At first she'd felt piqued and disappointed, but the idea of dashing about the countryside at Derek's side in a red sports car was too dazzling for her to continue to feel hurt. And Derek was obviously including her in his plans, which was the main thing.

'And have you got any other plans, Derek?' she asked coquettishly, her head on one side as she looked up at him. The sun was gleaming on his hair and his skin was already tanned. Just like a film star, she thought.

Derek looked into her eyes. His lids half-closed and he pursed his lips very slightly in the way that always made her heart turn over. Slowly, he smiled and drew her closer. He bent his head so that their lips were almost touching.

'Any other plans?' he murmured, and she could feel the warmth of his breath against her mouth. 'Well, I might have. But that'd be telling, now, wouldn't it?'

Frank and Jess Budd had lived in April Grove for nearly eight years. It was their first real house – before that, they'd lived in a couple of rooms in Frank's aunt's house, half a dozen streets away. Aunt Nell and Uncle Fred had been good to them, letting them stop while they saved up the money for a deposit on the little two-up, two-down terraced house, but it had been a relief to them all when Frank and Jess, together with Rosemary and Tim, had been able to move out at last with the few bits of furniture they'd collected, and set up in their own home.

Jess had been expecting Keith then, and Mrs Seddon, who ran the little corner shop just across the road, often said how she'd pitied the young woman moving into number 14.

'Two little ones under three and another on the way,' she would say to Jess as she weighed out sugar and biscuits, 'and only two bedrooms in that little house. I didn't know how you were going to manage.'

Well, we managed well enough, Jess thought as she moved heavily about getting tea ready, after Annie had gone. It was like a palace after living in two rooms, after all. It was the first time since Rose was born that she and Frank had had a bedroom to themselves, and the two children were still small enough to share the back bedroom. Later on, when the baby – as Keith continued to be called, even after he was long out of nappies – moved into the back bedroom, Rose was put downstairs in the front room on a camp bed. It wasn't ideal, but since they only used the front room on Sundays and when visitors came to tea, it didn't make much difference. And they'd always meant to move somewhere a bit bigger, once Frank was earning a bit more in the Dockyard.

But somehow the move never happened. Frank's wage went up a bit and they were able to afford a few more treats for the children – a bag of sweets on Saturday night, coloured ribbons for Rose's hair, a cap gun for the boys. But with war looming like a black cloud over everything, it didn't seem the right time to be thinking of moving.

Once 'peace in our time' had been declared, however, the idea cropped up again, and they began to look about for somewhere else to live.

'It needs to be near the allotments,' Frank said. 'I've just got that patch into good shape now, and there's all those vegetables and fruit coming along. I don't want to lose them.'

'Nor do I.' Jess had always liked the situation of April Grove, with the allotments running along the bottom of the narrow gardens. It was almost as good as being in the country, to be able to look out of the back window and see patches of green stretching away.

Frank's allotment wasn't actually close to the house, it was true – a good five minutes' walk, in fact – but seeing him off with his gardening tools over his shoulder made her feel good. It was satisfying, somehow, to know that he was going off to do something he really enjoyed, something out in the fresh air after the long hours spent in the boiler-shop, stoking up great furnaces and operating a huge steam-hammer.

Jess could barely imagine what Frank did all day long in the Dockyard, but when he was on the allotment she knew he was digging or raking, or hoeing. And she knew that when he came home he would be bringing a bucketful of potatoes, some carrots or a firm green cabbage.

It seemed the right thing for a man to be doing – feeding his family.

Frank grew more than vegetables on his allotment. He also grew soft fruit – currants, gooseberries, rhubarb and, as a special treat, a few strawberries.

The cupboard in the alcove beside the fireplace in the front room was filled with jars of jam and bottled fruit. There were pickles too, made from onions and the tomatoes that grew in the back garden because the allotment was full. Out in the shed were sacks filled with potatoes and root vegetables, and in summer there was always plenty of salad – lettuces, celery, cucumbers, spring onions and radishes.

He was a good provider, was Frank, and he worked hard. It didn't mean he was always easy to live with – tiredness and the frustration of his job made him short-tempered sometimes, and he'd never been one to suffer fools gladly anyway. But Jess knew he always wanted the best for her and the kids, and he was prepared to work all the hours God sent to make sure they got it.

Frank came in as she was slicing bread and spreading it with margarine. She paused for a moment to smile at him and he bent to kiss her. He was a big man, almost six feet tall and heavily built, his muscles developed by years of hard toil in the Dockyard. His hair, almost black like Rose's, was greying now he was in his mid-forties and beginning to recede a little but he didn't let it worry him. 'A high forehead's a sign of intelligence,' he would say, 'and I'm getting more intelligent every year!' Like Jess, he thought there were more important things in life than appearance, though he liked her and the children to look well cared for.

The cloth was on the table and he sat in his armchair, reading the *Evening News*, while Jess boiled the kettle on the gas stove out in the little lean-to scullery. She had made some rock cakes earlier that afternoon and she piled them on a plate and set them in the middle of the table, with a jar of home-made blackberry and apple jam and a pot of sardine and tomato fishpaste.

'Where are they all?' Frank asked as she came in with milk and sugar.

'The boys have gone down the railway station with Bob Shaw to see Pompey come back with the Cup. Goodness knows when they'll be home, but I told them to be back before dark. Rose is up at Joy Brunner's, she's stopping to tea. We might as well have ours now.'

Frank put down his paper and got up from the armchair. As always, he looked huge in the small room. He could strike terror into the hearts of guilty small boys (and in his eyes, small boys almost always were guilty) and command respect from most other men. His principles were rigid and sometimes harsh. Only Jess knew how soft his heart was in reality.

He sat down at the table. As usual, the family had eaten their dinner at one o'clock and there would be a supper later in the evening, a cooked snack of something on toast, or an egg. Tea was invariably bread and cake of some kind, usually home-made. The only cakes Jess bought were doughnuts or cream fancies, which they sometimes had on Sunday.

'So how's our Ted and Annie?' he asked, spreading his bread with fishpaste. At the sound of the jar being opened, Henry the tabby cat got up from the rag rug in front of the fireplace, stretched and came to sit beside Frank's chair. Frank cut a small triangle of bread and held it down to him, and the big cat reached up a paw and took it daintily. 'I thought Ted might walk over the allotment.'

'Ted was doing an extra shift on the ferry. Annie just popped in for a cup of tea on her own.' Jess poured him a cup of tea. 'Frank, d'you reckon there really is going to be a war?'

He shrugged. 'I don't know, Jess. Sometimes it seems as if there's no way of stopping it – sometimes it looks as if everything's going to be all right after all. How can we tell? We don't know anything, really – only what the papers and the wireless tell us. It's all up to the politicians, isn't it?'

'But why should it be?' she asked rebelliously, and her hands moved once more to protect her stomach. 'Why should they be able to mess our lives up? Nobody asks us if we want a war, and I don't suppose anyone's asked the Germans either – not the ones like you and me, who just want to live peaceful with their families.'

'I know, girl. But that's the way it's always been – them and us. People don't get any say in it, and it's no good expecting any different.'

Jess was silent. This was where she and Frank differed. He seemed to be able to accept his lot in life, unfair though she thought it had been, whereas she was always wanting something a bit better. If not for herself, for her children. She'd have liked to see the boys get on, do more in life than Frank, bless him, had had a chance to do. But he shook his head over her ideas.

'Doctors? Teachers? People like us don't do those sorts of things, Jess.

The boys'll do well enough at a trade, or maybe in the Army or Navy. That's the best sort of life for them.'

As for not having any say in the way the country was run – what was the point in having a vote if it didn't mean anything? Sometimes, though she never admitted it to Frank, she thought there might be something in the Labour Party's ideas. But Frank was a staunch Conservative and wouldn't hear a word in favour of Socialists.

Still, surely even he must agree in that it was wrong to force people into a war they didn't want.

'Didn't we lose enough men in the last war?' she asked. 'All those young chaps, not much more than boys most of them, cut down like a field of corn. And what for? Just so it could all start again twenty years later?'

'I know,' he said again, but Jess was not to be stopped.

'And it's going to be worse this time.' She stared at Frank, her brown eyes wide. 'Thousands of aeroplanes coming over, all dropping bombs . . . And where d'you think they're going to drop them, Frank? On Portsmouth, that's where. On us. You and me. The boys. Rose. And—' The baby kicked inside her and her voice shook with tears. 'Oh, Frank,' she whispered, 'what's going to happen to us all?'

Frank stared at her across the tea-table. Then he got up and came round to put his hands on her shoulders. She felt his big fingers kneading her flesh and turned to lay her head against him. He was so big, so solid. But he couldn't keep the might of Hitler's Germany at bay.

'I'll tell you what's going to happen, girl,' he said quietly. 'First smell of war, and you and the children are going into the country. You'll be evacuated, that's what, somewhere safe where there's green fields and trees, and nothing to bring aeroplanes dropping bombs. And then when it's all over – and it won't last long, not like the last one did – we'll find that new house and settle down together like we promised ourselves. Somewhere up Hilsea way, I reckon, don't you? You like it round there and it's not so far away from the rest of the family and our friends.'

Jess smiled shakily. 'It's a bit further for you to go to the Yard from Hilsea.'

'Well, I've got legs, haven't I? A nice walk never hurt anyone. Or I could go on me bike. And there's a good trolley-bus service for wet days, so no need to worry about that.' He held her close for a moment. 'I want you to have the home you've been looking forward to, Jess, even if we do have to wait a bit longer while they get this mess sorted out. So don't you go fretting that anything's going to happen to us – it isn't.'

Jess smiled again and fished for a handkerchief in the pocket of her pinafore. She dabbed at her eyes and Frank gave her a kiss and went back to sit down in his chair and go on with his tea.

It was only later that she realised that not a word had been said about the allotment. Hilsea was too far away from Copnor for Frank to be able to pop over for an hour's gardening as he did now. There were allotments at Hilsea, she was sure there were – but hadn't he always said he didn't want to leave the one he'd worked on for the past eight years?

So had he changed his mind – or did he, really and truly, think it was all no more than a dream, something that was never going to happen?

Fear jabbed her again. And the shadow of war crept a little closer.

Tim and Keith came back late that night, flushed with excitement and even dirtier than when they had gone out. The footballers had arrived at Fratton Station at 9.30, long after the boys' bedtime, but by then they were too caught up in the excitement to think of the trouble they would undoubtedly find themselves in when they got home.

Along with the thousands of other enthusiasts, cheering themselves hoarse, they followed the two coaches along Elm Grove and King's Road to the Guildhall. There they wriggled to the front of the crowd and scrambled up on the stone lions to get a good look at their heroes. They were swiftly dragged down by a policeman, but he was a football supporter too and did no more than give each boy a light cuff before allowing them to crouch down and peer between his legs.

'We saw Tinn holding the Cup over his head,' Tim reported when they finally reached home to a frantic, white-faced mother and a grim father. 'We actually saw the Cup!'

'And now you're going to see stars,' Frank promised, reaching for the thin cane he kept hung in a corner beside his razor-strop. 'Don't you realise your mother's been worrying herself sick?' He ignored the shock on his sons' faces and reached for them. 'Come here.'

'But Dad—' Tim protested in outraged tones. 'It was the Cup.'

'Cup or no Cup, I'm not having you roam the streets till eleven o'clock at night, worrying your mother half out of her mind.'

'Were you worried, Mum?' Tim turned his large, hazel eyes on his mother. 'We never meant to worry you. We were with Bob all the time. Well – up until we got to the Guildhall. But we know our way back from there, we wouldn't have got lost.'

'It's not a question of getting lost—' Frank began, but Jess interrupted. She laid her hand on his arm.

'Let's forget it now, Frank. They're back safe and that's all that matters. Don't hit them, not at this time of night. They're just boys, and it was something special. Portsmouth's never won the Cup before.'

'That's not the point,' Frank grumbled, but he was tired and thankful to see his sons and, though he'd never admit it, not nearly so angry as he made out. Looking at their faces, he'd seen an innocence, a childish excitement and absorption, that he'd missed in his own childhood. And when Jess begged him not to cane them at this time of night he was painfully reminded of Saturday nights from his own boyhood, when his father had come home the worse for drink and beaten not only him but his mother too.

Frank Budd was never the worse for drink, for he never took any. The scenes of childhood, when his father and uncles had come roaring home from the pub, had seared themselves into his mind like a brand. Ever since then, he had been afraid of violent anger – his own as much as that of others – and had fought to keep it in check. He knew all too well that his temper, once unleashed, would be formidable and that his strength was enough to do real damage. He dared not take the risk.

All the same, the boys had done wrong in staying out so late and must be punished. In Frank's view, children had to learn the difference between right and wrong, and the only way to teach them was by discipline.

'All right,' he said, lowering the cane. 'I'll let you off this time. But half-past seven's your time on Saturdays, and don't you forget it. And there'll be no going out to play for either of you next week, understand?'

'Yes, Dad.' The two boys went out to the scullery to wash. Their faces were downcast, but not unduly so. Not being able to go out to play would come hard during the next few days, but they were still too buoyed up by excitement to think of that now.

They had seen Pompey come home with the Cup. And nothing could take that away from them.

The Monday after the Cup Final win was also May Day, and the Portsmouth Labour Party led a demonstration which marched four miles through the city in pouring rain. Bob Shaw, who lived next door to the Budds, was still thrilling to the scenes as the footballers had returned home and enjoyed their own triumphal procession through the streets. He went along to hear Peter Paine, the Labour candidate for Parliament, speaking on conscription.

'If the government are asking young people to make sacrifices,' he declared, 'there ought to be a levy on the wealth of others.' And Bob and the rest of the crowd there in the rain, cheered and clapped.

'We lost enough youngsters last time,' a man near him said. 'Cannon-fodder, that's all they were. Send enough over the top and in the end a few got to survive. And they don't care which ones it is, so long as there's enough to keep firing at the other side.'

By 'they', Bob understood the man to mean the politicians and military top brass who ran wars from behind the scenes. The ones who went on aeroplanes to meet other politicians in other countries and came back waving pieces of paper and talking about peace; or directed events on a battlefield from hundreds of miles away, playing it out on a big table as if it were some kind of board game.

'Well, I reckon we ought to go over there, teach these Huns a lesson,' he said. 'I'd go, if they asked me. I'd join up.' His eyes burned with patriotic fervour in his thin face and he flicked back the lock of mousy hair that flopped over his forehead.

The man turned and looked at him. He looked old enough to have been in the last war and his face was scarred and pitted as if he had been burned. He shook his head.

'You wouldn't be saying that if you knew what it was all about. Months in the trenches, up to your knees in freezing mud, bullets like hail over your head. Mustard gas. Strong men breaking up with shell-shock, crying like babies. It's not pretty and it's not exciting. Most of the time it's dead boring, except that you might be killed at any moment.' He shook his head again. 'You ought to go down on your knees and pray it'll never happen, son. I do, every night.'

Bob stared and then turned away. His blood was still racing with the excitement of the Cup win on Saturday, and the speech he had just heard had filled him with frustration. The Labour Party were against war, against the government who were doing their best to avert it yet still making all the precautions they could. Of course they should bring in conscription – a country had to be ready with its army, didn't it? And there was going to be a war, make no mistake about it. The whole of Europe had been marching towards it for years.

The speeches over, the crowd dispersed and Bob roamed restlessly through the busy street. Even on a wet Monday, Commercial Road, the main shopping street of Portsmouth, was thronged with shoppers. Women mostly, crowding through the doors of the Landport Drapery Bazaar, commonly known simply as 'the Landport', or in and out of Woolworths, Marks & Spencer, Littlewoods and the British Home Stores. All much the same as one another, as far as Bob could see, apart from Woolworths, where you could at least get sensible things like tools and puncture repair outfits. He wandered in and stared at the counters for a while, bought a bar of chocolate and then wandered out again.

In the street, he encountered Graham Philpotts. The two had been at school together, though not special friends, until Graham's family had moved across the harbour to Gosport. But now they fell into step and turned towards the harbour. The rain had eased and a fitful sun poked through the scudding clouds, brightening Graham's red hair. He'd always been called Ginger at school and had been the ringleader in a good many escapades. Bob wondered if he had changed much. From the look of mischief in his bright blue eyes, it didn't look as if he had.

'There's a lot of ships in,' Graham said as they walked down Edinburgh Road towards Queen Street. 'Plenty of matelots about, too.'

There were always sailors in Queen Street. Long, straight and narrow, it led straight from the heart of Portsea to the Dockyard gate. The shops, cafés and pubs along its length were the sailors' Commercial Road, providing everything they required, from the 'worst drop of beer in Pompey' to a tattoo. There were several naval outfitters, where sailors would pay regular sums in order to be able to afford their uniforms when needed, and the two young men stopped to look at a window display.

'Look at the sword,' Bob said admiringly. 'I reckon I'd look a bit of all right with one of them slung round me waist, don't you?'

'Fat chance,' Graham sneered. 'That's a captain's sword – maybe an admiral's. Chief stoker's your limit, Bob, with a shovel to carry.'

Bob dug him in the ribs with his elbow and Graham swung a punch at his head. The two went on. A gang of matelots were coming along the road towards them, their bell-bottoms flapping round their ankles.

'First of May. They've got their whites on,' Bob said, looking at the white cap covers. 'D'you fancy their uniform, Ginge?'

'Me? Nah – when I join up, it'll be the RAF.' He spread his arms like a small boy pretending to fly an aeroplane and made a high whinnying sound. 'Bombers, that's what I'll fly. Or maybe fighters. The Spitfire they're building out at Southampton, that's what's going to win the war. I wouldn't mind flying one of those.'

'You definitely going to join up, then?'

'Well, we'll have to, won't we? All of us.'

'Not if it doesn't happen. Not then if we're in a – what do they call it? – "reserved occupation". If we get jobs.'

'What's the point?' Graham stopped to look in another shop window, where a few flyblown cardboard advertisements mysteriously extolled their range of 'rubber appliances'. 'They'll declare war the day we start and we'll have to down tools and go anyway. Here, what d'you reckon they really sell in these places, Bob? I mean, what are rubber appliances?'

Bob glanced in. The pictures on the advertisements seemed to be of male corsets. 'They're trusses, aren't they? For fat blokes with hernias, and that.'

'Yeah, I know that, but d'you think that's all they sell?' Graham nudged him and winked. 'How about going in to see, eh?'

Bob moved on quickly. He knew as well as anyone else the reputation Queen Street had. Leading from the Dockyard gate straight to the middle of town, every sailor who came ashore had to walk up here, and it was the natural haunt of prostitutes. Whether you could buy their services in a shop advertising rubber appliances, he didn't know, but he thought you probably could. There couldn't be that many sailors whose most urgent need was a corset.

He looked round nervously. As well as sailors, there were plenty of girls walking about, some respectable-looking enough, others heavily made up and wearing clothes that would have made his mother and Mrs Budd next door sniff. Were they tarts? How could you tell?

There was a woman in April Grove who was a tart, or so everyone said. Nancy Baxter, who lived at number 10 with her mother, Granny Kinch, and her son Mick, the same age as Tim Budd. Nancy Baxter was nothing to look at, thin with straight black hair and eyes like buttons, but she went out of an evening in a red coat that she wore unbuttoned, showing a blouse that revealed a lot of neck and a skirt that was always shorter than anyone else's. She wore a lot of lipstick too, bright red, the sort Bert Shaw would have gone mad over if he'd caught Gladys or Diane wearing it.

When Bob was about ten he and the rest of the boys round September Street used to snigger about Nancy Baxter. Preg-Nancy, they'd called her, and nudged each other knowingly when she'd appeared with baby Mick. There'd been no husband around, though Granny Kinch, who spent nearly all day standing at her front door watching all that went up and down April Grove and March Street, swore she was married to a sailor, just before they'd moved into number 10. 'He's away a lot,' she'd told the neighbours. 'Got posted the day after they were married. Nancy goes to meet him for weekends when he gets time, but he's a high-up and don't get much leave.'

'And the band played "Believe it if you like",' Tommy Vickers commented. He lived in the end house in April Grove and had something to say about everything, but like everyone else he was tolerant of Nancy Baxter and her mum. Granny Kinch, standing at her door with curlers in her hair, her beady black eyes missing nothing, was a good-hearted old soul and at least Nancy never brought her business home with her. The boy Mick was turning into a bit of a hooligan but what could you expect with no father to keep him in order?

Bob had wondered just where Nancy Baxter carried on her trade. Hanging round the Dockyard gates, he supposed, but perhaps she worked in Queen Street. He looked across the road. There was a girl now – not Nancy Baxter, but she was wearing a red jacket, unbuttoned over a slightly grubby white blouse. There was something about that blouse that made him feel uncomfortable, something loose and abandoned. And he knew his sister Gladys would never have walked about with her coat unbuttoned like that. Was this girl a tart? Were her unbuttoned coat and loose blouse signs?

She caught his eye and stared at him, lifting her eyebrows.

'Know me again, will you?'

Bob felt himself blush scarlet and looked away. Beside him, Graham sniggered.

'She looked a bit of all right. Reckon she's on the game?'

'I dunno,' Bob said shortly. 'She wouldn't be interested in us, anyway. They're after sailors down here.'

'Bosh. They're after money. Don't matter to them what kind of trousers a bloke wears, so long as he takes 'em off.'

'Well, I've got no money so they're out of luck. Anyway, I'm not interested. I'd rather have a proper girlfriend.'

'With the emphasis on proper? You won't find out what it's all about that way, Bob.' Graham jingled a few coins in his pocket. 'Reckon I might have a go one day. Where's the harm? It's what they're for.'

Bob said nothing. He was embarrassingly ignorant about sex and wasn't sure how much more Graham knew. Not many parents seemed to tell their children the facts of life, and the subject was never mentioned at school unless you were caught wanking in the lavatories. You were left to find out for yourself, from other boys, and how were you to know that what they said was true?

The only time Bob's dad had spoken to him about it was when they were walking down this very street on their way to the harbour a year or so ago. A couple of girls had passed them, skirts up to their knees, their frocks so tight they were almost bursting out of them, and Bob hadn't been able to help looking. Bert Shaw had given him a proper tongue-lashing and told him never to go with any of those girls. 'You'll get more than you bargained for,' he'd said grimly, and proceeded to explain in gruesome detail just what Bob might get. The graphic pictures of toes coming off in his socks and a brain rotting away in his head like putrefying meat, had kept Bob awake for a few good nights after that.

The thought of having a 'proper' girlfriend who refused sex until marriage, so could neither pass on these horrible diseases nor present him with the other nightmare, an unwanted baby, was much more attractive. Even though it didn't stop him wondering – just wondering – what it was like to go with a girl. Just once, to see . . .

But Dad hadn't minced his words. Just once was all it needed, he'd said with a glare so ferocious that he might have been suspecting Bob of having tried it already. Perhaps he did. He'd been eighteen himself once, after all, though it was hard to imagine it, so he probably knew just what kind of thoughts went through Bob's mind.

'That girl looks as if she knows you,' Graham said suddenly. 'Been having it off on the sly, have you?'

Bob glanced across the street and saw Betty Chapman, who lived at the other end of April Grove. She was coming out of a fish-and-chip shop, a newspaper packet in her hand. She came across, already unwrapping the parcel, and offered it to the two boys.

'Hullo, Bob.' Her short brown curls were tousled from the rain and her hazel eyes looked Graham up and down with interest. 'Want a chip? They're good ones, plenty of salt and vinegar.' She flicked her eyelashes saucily. 'What're you two doing down here on a Monday afternoon? Got no homes to go to?'

'Just having a walk round, Betty,' Bob said defensively, brushing back his hair with his fingers. Betty was only a year or so younger than himself and had joined him and his mates for a game of cricket or football in the street when they were younger. The boys liked her because she wasn't like most girls, never burst into tears because the ball hit her a bit hard or wanted extra turns just because she was a girl. He hadn't seen much of her since they'd all left school but just lately he'd thought once or twice of asking her to go to the pictures with him. 'Ginger says there's a lot of warships in, we thought we'd go and have a look. Anyway, I might ask you the same question – what're you doing down Queen Street? I thought you had a job in the dairy up September Street.'

'That's right. Mrs Marsh sent me down here on an errand and gave me some money for a bit of dinner.' Betty took a chip and gave Graham another bright enquiring glance. 'I've seen you before, but you don't come from round our way, do you?'

'I used to,' Graham said. 'I live in Gosport now but I used to sit next to Bob at school. And I remember you – you were in the class below us.'

'Oh yes,' she said, staring at him. 'You used to pull my pigtails.'

Graham grimaced and looked at the golden brown curls. 'You don't wear pigtails now.'

'I don't want 'em pulled, that's why,' she retorted with a toss of her head. 'But maybe you've grown out of doing that to girls.'

'Maybe I have. Maybe I've found better things to do.'

There was a brief silence. Bob, standing by, felt suddenly excluded. He shifted his feet and said rather more loudly than he'd intended, 'Well, are we going to look at these ships or not?'

'Sure.' Graham half-turned to move on, then looked back at Betty. 'Why don't you come too? Or d'you have to get back to work?'

'No, this is my dinner-break.' She shrugged carelessly. 'I might as well.' She walked beside Graham along the narrow pavement, Bob slouching moodily in their wake. He felt irritated but couldn't tell why. Maybe it was because he didn't want Betty tagging along, spoiling the fun he and Graham had been having. Or maybe it was because he'd rather have been the one walking with Betty.

He made up his mind that he would ask her out to the pictures. There was a good film on at the Odeon that week. He thought of taking her there, perhaps getting one of those double seats they had in the back row. Or was the first time out too soon for that? She might think he was going too fast. He watched the way she kept glancing up at Graham and giggling. What was he saying that was so funny anyhow? Bob had never found his jokes that hilarious.

Perhaps when they got to the Hard, Graham would go back over the ferry. That would leave him free to take Betty back to Copnor on the trolley-bus. The journey took a quarter of an hour, which should give him time to ask her out. Somehow it seemed easier to do that on a bus rather than back in the street where they both lived.

'You're too cheeky for your own good, you know that?' he heard Betty say as they neared the wider end of Queen Street and he was able to walk beside them again. She looked at Bob, her face full of laughter. 'Did you hear what he said to me? Well, it's just as well – it's not something I'd want repeated.' But it was obvious that whatever it was, she'd liked it and Bob sent a glowering look at his friend. 'I don't reckon any girl'll be safe once you get into bell-bottoms,' she told Graham.

'But he's not—' Bob began, and received a sharp nudge from Graham's elbow. 'I thought you said—'

'I haven't decided yet,' Graham said airily. 'I reckon there's a lot to be said for the Navy. After all, they say every nice girl loves a sailor, don't they – and I reckon I could be the sailor every nice girl loves.'

'Ooh!' Betty squealed. 'Well, count me out! I don't want to be one of a crowd.'

'Choosy, are you?' Graham challenged, and she tossed her head.

'I can afford to be, can't I? There's as many sailors in Pompey as there are fish in the sea.' She glinted a sideways look at him, her hazel eyes almost green now. 'I'm not interested in the ones who have a wife in every port.'

'Who said anything about wives? You were talking about fish a minute ago.'

'I was talking about sailors,' she retorted, 'but there's not much difference.'

Bob listened as the banter flew back and forth between them. He felt even more left out. He looked at Graham Philpotts. He'd been a weedy sort a chap at school, nothing to look at with that ginger hair and all those freckles. Now he was taller than Bob and not so thin, and anyone could see he thought a lot of himself. He wore a good raincoat that he'd left unbuttoned, like Humphrey Bogart in a gangster film, and underneath it was a Fair Isle pullover in about ten different colours. It had taken Bob all his time to persuade his sister Gladys to make him one in five colours.

By now, they were coming down to the Dockyard gate and in view of the harbour. As usual, it was thronged with craft. Alongside the Southern Railway Jetty lay the *Empress of Australia*, ready to take the King and Queen on their visit to Canada next week and, beyond that, a huge aircraft carrier, its wide deck overhanging its steep sides. A fleet of ships, grey and sombre in the shifting light, stretched into the distant recesses of the harbour, further than the eye could see. The docks, built on reclaimed land, were like a city in themselves and mostly out of sight from anywhere but the air. But it was from the air that they would be threatened.

There were plenty of other boats, large and small, crowding the harbour. At the end of the jetty, trains brought people from London to the paddle steamers that tied up there to make the journey across to the Isle of Wight. The *Whippingham* was there now, looming over one of the small launches operated by the two ferry companies which plied between Portsmouth and Gosport. They kept up a ten-minute service, from early in the morning until late at night, and when the Dockyardmen came out they were packed tightly with Gosport men going home.

They walked a short distance along the jetty and stood looking over the railings. The tide was out and although it was a school-day there were a few mudlarks wading waist-deep in the thick black mud under the long ferry pontoon, lifting up their arms to those who walked above and calling for pennies to be thrown down.

'That'll stop,' remarked a man standing nearby, watching the boys scrabble in the mud for the coins and putting them in their jamjars. 'They'll be treading on bombs and mines down there in a few months. Prime target, Pompey's going to be.'

Betty shivered. 'Don't! It scares me to death to think of it. I can't imagine what it'll be like – bombs falling out of the sky and blowing everything up. Nobody's going to be safe.'

'They're going to send the kids out into the country,' Bob commented. 'Your auntie'll be going too, seeing as she's having a baby.'

'There'll be hardly any people left,' Graham said. 'It'll be all women and old men. How're they going to keep the place going?'

The man chuckled. He had a straggly moustache and a big, bulbous nose. 'The women'll do that, same as they did in the last lot. Turned into bus drivers, ambulance drivers, went into the Navy – that's when Wrens first started – went on the land to do the farming – oh, the women were everywhere and a bloody good job they made of it too. That's why they had to give 'em the vote. Couldn't have won the war without 'em, see.' He grinned, showing broken teeth. 'Wouldn't have bin worth winning anyway, without them to come back to. And it'll be the same this time.'

'You really reckon there's going to be a war, then?' Bob asked. Like a lot of young people he was both anxious and fed up with hearing about war, but at least it was better than listening to Graham and Betty flirting with each other.

The man snorted and rubbed his nose with the back of a hairy hand. 'No doubt about it! I give 'em another two months – maybe three – to stop dragging their feet and make up their minds, and then we'll be in the thick of it. You'll get all the fighting you want, lads, and then some.' He looked down at the boys scrabbling beneath the jetty, their bodies plastered with thick, evil-smelling mud. 'I wouldn't be surprised if some of those poor devils do, too.'

'Go on,' Graham said, 'if we do decide to give Hitler a licking it'll be over by Christmas.'

'They said that last time.' The man watched the mudlarks for a few more minutes, then thrust his hand into his pocket and took out a fistful of small coins. 'Here you are, kids – fish for that lot,' he shouted, tossing them over the rail, and the boys cheered and made a dive, elbowing each other aside in their rush to retrieve the money. One of them fell and had to be dragged out. He stood upright, eyes blinking from a black face. The man chuckled but when he turned away his face was grave.

'I used to be in the Navy,' he volunteered. 'I was a chief cook.'

'Why aren't you scarred then?' Graham said cheekily, and then added, 'I suppose you were in the last war?'

'If it can be called that – the "last" one. I was, and I saw a lot of action. Got sunk twice, shelled more times than I can count. I tell you, I've seen men dying all around me, bits of bodies blown all over the decks, the bulkheads running with blood. It's no joke, war, and getting into uniform might get you the girls but it'll get you a lot else besides. And the next one—'

'I know,' Graham said in bored tones, 'it'll be even worse. Everyone tells us that. But that's not going to stop it happening, so we might as well make the best of it.'

Bob could see that Graham was growing restless. He whispered something to Betty and she giggled and smothered her mouth with her hand. They moved away a little along the railing.

'There's a Copnor bus up at the stop,' Bob said before Betty could move out of earshot. 'You'll be late back from your dinner-hour if you don't catch that one.'

Betty glanced at him, then looked back at Graham. He said something Bob couldn't hear and she nodded quickly.

'Well, I'll be off back to Gosport then,' Graham said loudly. 'Good to have seen you again, Bob. We must get together again, have a pint and another walk down Queen Street, eh?' He grinned and winked, and Bob flushed and looked away. He caught Betty's eye and felt his colour deepen. She was laughing, but at what he had no idea. Me, probably, he thought miserably, and then – But at least she'll be coming back on the bus with me. And then I can ask her out.

The man was still leaning on the railings. Graham was grinning, as if he could hardly wait to say something funny about him. But Bob wasn't in a mood to hear it. The expression on the man's face was one he didn't properly understand. But he knew somehow that when the stranger looked over the side of the jetty at the boys wading in the mud below, he was seeing something different.

Perhaps he was seeing other boys, from a distant past, who had found themselves scrabbling in a different kind of mud, who had been floundering not for pennies but for their lives. Or perhaps these boys in a future that no one could quite imagine, when the black, stinking mud of Portsmouth Harbour was no more than a nostalgic memory.

Bob remembered the words of the man he had met in the Guildhall Square. 'Cannon-fodder. Bullets over your head like hail. Men crying like babies . . .'

He looked up at the sky. If war came, it would be black with enemy aircraft, raining bombs instead of bullets.

Graham had turned away and was sauntering down the pontoon, on the way to catch the ferry back to Gosport. Betty, her face quivering with secret smiles, was waiting for Bob to go and catch the trolley-bus back to Copnor.

A quarter of an hour in her company, with no one else to interfere. They'd go up top, see if they could get the seat at the front. And he'd ask her to go to the pictures with him on Saturday.

Bob quickened his step. He forgot about the man at the railings and the man in the Guildhall Square. He forgot the mudlarks, lifting their doomed, mud-blackened faces and their arms in appeal. He forgot the glimpse he'd been given of the past and the vision of the future and thought only of Betty, snuggled beside him in a double seat in the back row of the Odeon on Saturday night.

Betty was ten minutes late back for work in the dairy that afternoon but Mrs Marsh said nothing beyond asking whether the trolley buses had stopped running and giving her the job of cleaning out the big refrigerator, which was the task Betty disliked most. It was pleasantly cool in the back room of the dairy on hot days, but the stone-flagged floor was cold to her feet and the air from the fridge chilly even when it had been turned off. And she didn't like being shut away from the front of the shop. Serving was what Betty enjoyed most, chatting with the customers and hearing all the latest gossip.

But she had plenty to occupy her mind today as she sponged round the inside of the fridge with a paste made from water and bicarbonate of soda. And the secret smile Bob had observed as Graham strolled away down the pontoon was permitted to tug harder at her mouth and even escape now and then as a small, hastily smothered giggle.

Two boys had asked her out, within half an hour of each other! Betty, at seventeen, had begun to despair of ever getting a boyfriend. All her friends had been talking about boys from the age of fourteen or fifteen and a lot of them were going steady by now. Whereas Betty, who had played with the boys more than the girls, had suddenly found herself out in the cold. Boys who had encouraged her to play football, climb trees and run races with them were no longer interested, and she didn't know how to make the transition from tomboy to girlfriend. She had given herself no practice in being a woman and the boys didn't seem to see her as a girl at all.

But this afternoon had restored her confidence. That boy Graham she'd met with Bob Shaw, was a smasher. Good-looking, with curly red hair and bright blue eyes, and cheeky with it – he'd made her laugh, and Betty liked anyone who made her laugh. And he'd seemed to like her too – enough to make a date with her for Saturday night. The Troxy, with Fred Astaire and Ginger Rogers in *Carefree*, that's what he was taking her to see. And Betty wouldn't mind betting he'd get seats in the back row – he was that sort, the sort who always did get what he wanted.

Not that he'd get too much of what he wanted, she thought as she stacked eggs in the clean refrigerator. Holding hands and perhaps a kiss at the end of the evening, that was all – none of this cuddling and necking a lot of boys seemed to want to do. Betty hadn't yet had any experience of that and wasn't at all sure she'd like it. Just for a start, it was good enough to be simply going out with a boy. Other things could come later.

Betty and her sister Olive had been told often enough not to bring 'trouble' home and she wasn't going to let any boy mess up her life. And he wasn't the only fish in the sea by any means. Hadn't Bob Shaw asked her out too, not fifteen minutes after Graham?

If Bob had asked first, she'd have accepted. He was one of the boys she'd played football and cricket with, but he seemed different now. More grown-up. He had a nice smile too – really, he was quite good-looking. But not as much as Graham. And because she'd known him all her life, not as exciting.

Betty finished restocking the fridge and went to the little back scullery to wash her hands. It was nearly four o'clock and time for the cup of tea Mrs Marsh allowed in the afternoons. She put the kettle on and stood gazing out of the window at the small backyard, thinking of Graham.

On Monday afternoon, in number 14, Jess Budd and her family were having tea. Tim and Keith were still bubbling over Portsmouth's win, but Rosemary wasn't interested. She was telling her mother about her friend, Joy Brunner.

'People are saying she's German. She's not really, is she?'

'Course she is,' Keith said. 'Brunner's a German name. It means Brown.'

'Why aren't they called Brown, then?' Tim asked, spreading his bread thickly with blackberry and apple jam.

'Because Mr Brunner is German,' Jess told him. 'He came from Germany a long time ago and married Mrs Brunner and they opened the shop.'

'You can hardly tell he's German now,' Rose said. 'And Joy doesn't sound a bit like a German.'

'She's not,' Tim said, eyeing the doughnuts.

'She is,' Keith contradicted him. He was looking at the doughnuts too. There was one which had jam already oozing out of one side and he wondered if anyone else had noticed it.

'She's not.'

'She is.'

'Stop it, you two,' Jess said. 'Joy isn't German because she was born in England. And Mrs Brunner isn't German either. She's lived in Portsmouth all her life. She went to Copnor School.' She looked at Rose. 'Are people being unkind to Joy?'

Rose shrugged. 'They're just saying she's German. It makes her cry sometimes.'

Jess tightened her lips. What did you say to children when this sort of thing happened? Mr and Mrs Brunner had run the newspaper shop at the top of the street for years. He knew everyone in the district, always had a friendly word and worked hard, as newsagents had to do. He was part of the little community of this network of streets. Most people had forgotten he wasn't English.

But there were always a few who were ready with spiteful gossip and now, with war looming, they were finding readier ears. Talk of spies and 'Fifth Column' was rife. There had been German spies in Portsmouth just before the last war started and it was only common sense to suppose that there would be more about now. An important naval dockyard, with a Marine barracks close by and who knew what secrets hidden in the great forts that lined the top of Portsmouth Hill and even stood out to sea in the Solent, between the mainland and the Isle of Wight – why, it stood to reason there would be spies about.

And who was more obvious than an actual German, even if he had lived amongst them for twenty years? Didn't that make him an even better choice? Didn't he have friends, even relatives, in the city who trusted him? Wasn't he a newsagent, handling papers every day, with all kinds of people coming in for a gossip and a chat? Wasn't it a newsagent that one of the German spies in the last war had enrolled as an accomplice?

The fact that the newsagent involved then had immediately reported his suspicions to the authorities was forgotten. The memory of the story was hazy in most people's minds, for it had never been officially told and no doubt there had been distortion over the years. But enough detail had survived to add fuel to the suspicions about the Brunners.

Jess had heard the gossip herself. *He was probably sent over specially, all those years ago, to worm his way in and make friends.* And, worse still – *she must have known. She's in it as much as he is. Look at the way they go over there every year, to see his mum. Mum! A likely story!*

Jess had known Alice Brunner all her life. They had attended the same schools, been in the same class. They had played hopscotch and five-stones on the pavements, walked out to Hilsea Lines to gather blackberries, learned to swim in Langstone Harbour. They had given birth to their daughters within weeks of each other and now those daughters were growing up together in the same way.

Jess and Alice had never been close friends. They were simply part of the crowd of children who lived in the little network of streets, who knew each other more or less casually, more or less intimately. They were on the same terms now – friendly, stopping for a chat whenever they met, interested in each other's families, but not close enough to pop in for a cup of tea or to go to the pictures together of an afternoon.

All the same, Jess would have been ready to go into court and swear on oath that Alice Brunner was no Fifth Columnist. Nor her husband, who was a gentle, kindly man with pale brown eyes peering short-sightedly through round glasses. He could be seen every Sunday evening at the little church at the top of Deniston Road, praying earnestly, and it was almost impossible to believe he could be a spy.

She felt sorry for him and Alice, and even more sorry for their daughter Joy, who was a nice girl with pigtails and her father's mild brown eyes and shy smile.

'Well, I hope you stand up for her,' she said to Rose. 'Joy hasn't done anything wrong and I don't believe her father has either. It doesn't help anyone to spread nasty stories like that about.' She looked sternly at the two boys. 'That goes for you two as well.'

'We don't tell stories about her,' Tim said indignantly.

'Well, see that you don't, then. All right, you can have a doughnut.'

She went out to the scullery to put more hot water into the teapot and stood for a moment gazing out of the window. There was no view to be seen, only the wall of Ethel Glaister's scullery next door, but she watched it and suddenly shivered.

It didn't matter where you went or who you talked to, it was war, war, war. She was still trying desperately to believe that it wouldn't happen, that her baby would be born into a peaceful world, that her boys would grow up without ever having to fight.

But the world wasn't peaceful. The whole of Europe was getting dragged into this horrible mess. And not just Europe – as far away as Russia, people's lives were being disrupted by the mania of one man.

Adolf Hitler.

He's mad, Jess thought. He's making a hell on earth for everyone else. And we're letting him.

And now it's spreading to our own doorsteps. A madness and a hell that can't be stopped, except by making it worse.

The baby kicked inside her and she put her hands over the bulge. What was going to happen to them all?

2

Portsmouth had been preparing for war for the past four years. Jess's uncle, John Bellinger, was on the City Council, and he had often told the family that when war came – if it came – Portsmouth meant to be ready for it. And Tommy Vickers, along the street, who worked for the council and seemed to have a finger in most pies, had nosed out a good deal more than Uncle John would reveal.

'Latest idea's doing a dustcart up as a fire engine,' he told Frank. 'Those big ones, used for squashing rubbish down small so they can shift huge amounts. They're watertight, see, so you can fill 'em with water and pump it out just like from a proper fire engine. What's more, they can be used to decontaminate gas.'

Everyone was afraid of gas attacks. Those who could remember the last war recalled the sufferings of soldiers returning home, not only their skin but their lungs as well, burned away by mustard gas. They never recovered. Some of them still survived, but they were coughing shells of the men they had once been, and those whose faces had been eaten away by the corrosive fumes were forced to become accustomed to looks of pity, shock and even repugnance.

In the 1914–18 war, only soldiers had suffered gas attacks. But now everybody was at risk, and before Jess's baby was born gas masks were issued to everyone in the country.

'They're horrible,' Rose exclaimed when she received hers. She took it out of its brown cardboard box and stared at the black rubber snout. 'Have we got to wear these?'

'If there's a gas warning, yes.' Frank was unravelling the straps on his own mask. He fitted it over his head and fastened them. The rubber clung to his face and he peered out through the transparent face-piece.

Rose gave a little scream.

'Oh, you look awful! Like some sort of monster.'

'A monster from outer space,' Tim said. He dragged his on and began to caper about the room, thrusting his black snout at his sister. 'Yaah! I'm a monster from outer space. Yaargh!'

'Stop it! Stop it! You're a horrible little boy.'

'Stop it, Tim,' Jess said, and Frank caught his son by the back of his collar and jerked him to a standstill. Tim stood turning his muzzle from one person to another like a dog wondering why it has been chastised.

Keith giggled and Jess felt a smile twitch at her lips. But Rose was looking sulky and Frank annoyed.

'It's not a toy,' he said severely. 'That mask is meant to save your life, not play with. Take it off – carefully – and put it back in its box. Rose, Keith, you'd better make sure you know how to put yours on. And then we'll have a practice every Saturday night. Apart from that, I don't want to see them out of their boxes.'

'Not even if there's a warning?' Tim murmured, and backed hastily out of his father's reach. Jess gave him a look which was intended to be reproving but, from the wink her son gave her when his father's back was turned, seemed to have failed. That was the trouble with Tim. Cheeky he might be, and forever up to mischief, but he could always win you over with that grin and those hazel eyes. And he was never rude or deliberately naughty.

'Dinner's ready,' she said, going out to the scullery. 'Put the masks away now. Rose, you lay the table.'

Later, she voiced her own fear to Frank. 'The children can put their masks on all right. But what happens to the baby, Frank? There's no masks for them. You couldn't get them to stay on.' She looked at him, her eyes full of fear. 'I couldn't sit and watch my baby die like that.'

'I know.' He laid his hand on her shoulder. 'They'll think of something, girl, don't you worry. They won't have forgotten about the babies.'

'I hope not.' She could feel the baby moving now, energetic little arms and legs pounding at the wall of her abdomen. If only she could keep it there, safe inside her. If only it didn't have to be born.

Children shouldn't have to suffer war, she thought with a sudden passion. Little babies, who can't understand – they shouldn't have to be born into a world of gas masks and bombs and air-raid shelters. It isn't fair, and they – the 'they' who sent troops marching on other countries, who signed pieces of paper with pledges they had no intention of keeping, who decided that young men should have to set aside their own lives and become soldiers when all they wanted was to live peacefully at home – they had no right to force it on them.

But there was nothing people like she and Frank could do about it. Like millions of others, they must just go where they were pushed.

'Air-Raid Precautions' became a familiar phrase, quickly abbreviated to ARP. The first appeals for volunteers for this part of Civil Defence were largely ignored; when several thousand men were requested in May, only seven hundred put themselves forward. But gradually more men and women offered their services, though they were still liable to be the butt of sneers from their neighbours, or – worse still – accused of warmongering.

'Never mind warmongering,' said Frank, whose working hours were too long to allow him to become a warden, but who agreed to be a fire-watcher should the need arise. 'It isn't people like us who do the warmongering. We just have to take the consequences of those who do.'

Once formed, the ARP personnel were trained. Most weeks found them engaged in various exercises simulating what the authorities expected to happen in war. Mock explosions were staged and emergencies of all kinds set up. The whole city was blacked out on several occasions and mock 'bomb damage', with craters, fractured gas and water mains and sewage pipes, and burning houses, prepared for air wardens, repair gangs and first-aid parties to deal with.

At first, a good many people preferred to turn a blind eye to these preparations. Others sneered. The ARP wardens, strutting about the streets in their uniforms and tin hats, looked faintly ridiculous. There wasn't going to be a war, was there? Not after the last lot. And who were folk like these wardens to set themselves up as something special anyway? They weren't nothing but greengrocers or coalmen, no better than the rest of us. Don't want 'em telling us what to do.

Their rebellion turned to glee when one of the newly appointed wardens was detailed to give a demonstration of fire-fighting in the local recreation ground, known generally as the 'rec'.

A small platform was set up as a stage on the grass and the warden, looking self conscious in his new dark blue uniform, placed a bucket of sand, a stirrup-pump and what looked like a replica of a bomb in the middle. As he did so, a desultory crowd gathered to watch, a sarcastic comment ready on everyone's lips.

'Fight fires!' one man murmured. 'Old Fred Stokes couldn't fight a fly.'

'What're you putting your mac on for, Fred?' someone else called out. 'Don't you want to get yer nice new uniform dirty, then?'

'Can't you see it's raining? What'll his mum say if he gets his feet wet?'

There was a roar of laughter. Old Mrs Stokes wasn't far off eighty but she was one of the characters of the September Street area, known for speaking her very tough mind, and it was generally agreed that she'd never allowed Fred to grow up.

'Leave the bloke alone,' Frank said sharply as more jeers rose around him. 'He's doing his best.' But he watched in embarrassment as Fred tried in the drizzle to set fire to the bomb, which sat sullenly refusing to ignite. Why didn't the man give up, for goodness sake, and put the demonstrations off till another day?

'What a farce!' someone snorted, and another sniggered and made some remark about Guy Fawkes Day. Frank glanced round in irritation and moved, intending to go and help Fred.

But before he could do so, his embarrassment turned to dismay as Fred, getting desperate, threw some paraffin over the weakly flickering flames. Instantly, fire leapt up, almost enveloping him, and he sprang back with a shout of fear. The watchers began to laugh harder than ever, but Frank saw that the sudden flare had actually set light to the warden's mackintosh and he dived forwards, shouting for help.

'He's burning! For God's sake, some of you – can't you see he's afire?' He pushed Fred to the ground and rolled him over and over. 'Stop that stupid jeering and help.' His own hands were stinging, but the flames were out now and he glowered up at the slightly shamefaced men who were coming to give him aid. 'Think it's funny to watch a man burn to death, do you?' he demanded savagely.

'Take it easy, mate. He ain't going to burn to death. He's just scorched hisself a bit.' Hands turned Fred over, examining him for damage. 'Look, all he's done is singe that posh mac of his. And get his face dirty. His mum'll soon wash that for him.'

'She'll want to know where his eyebrows have gone, though,' someone said, and the crowd laughed again. Fred, released from their ministrations, scrambled to his feet and brushed himself down. He looked miserably at his burned coat.

'Never you mind, mate,' one of the men advised him. 'Council'll buy you a new one. They got plenty of money for the ARP. Shelters, sandbags, posh uniforms, funny faces – you ask for it, they'll pay for it. And none of it a blind bloody bit o' good, if you ask me. If the Jerries come over here we'll all cop it, the whole bloody lot of us, and a few holes in the ground and rubber masks ain't going to help us, that's for sure.'

'Rubbish! There ain't going to be no war. It's all a waste of money.' The speaker was a thin, sandy-haired man who lived a few streets away. 'Didn't Chamberlain promise us peace in our time? Didn't he say? Well, then.'

'That's right,' someone else agreed. 'All this fire-fighting and stuff, it's all play-acting. It's to take our minds off the depression, that's what it is. Give people summat to do when there's no real jobs. Keep us in our place. War! What good 'ud all this be if the Jerries come over with their bombs? Old Fred Stokes and a bucket of sand ain't going to save us.'

There was a chorus of agreement. 'Government be better off giving us proper jobs, that's what.' 'Stop all this arsing about and get down to some real work.' 'Never mind what's happening in Czechoslovakia and them places – it's what's happening here we're interested in.' And, finally, 'You go back home to your mum, Fred, and tell her you fell down playing in the rec. She'll look after you when the Red revolution comes.'

The crowd dispersed, still making disjointed comments. Frank helped Fred Stokes gather up his bits and pieces and dismantle the platform. They stood for a moment looking at the faintly smoking remnants of the bomb, now smothered with sand.

'They're right, Fred,' Frank said at last, heavily. 'A bucket and a stirrup-pump aren't going to be much use if what they say about thousands of bombs is true.'

'It's all we've got, all the same.' Fred lifted the bucket. He had painted it red and scrawled 'SAND' on its side. 'And we've got to do what we can, haven't we, Frank? We can't just sit and let the city burn down around us without even trying.'

'Most people don't think it's going to, though. They're like ostriches – burying their heads in the sand.' He glanced again at the bucket and its smouldering contents. 'In fact, there's so many heads buried in the sand there won't be room for bombs as well.'

'Well, maybe they're right. I hope to God they are,' Fred said soberly. 'I've got a feeling we're all going to know soon enough, whichever way it goes.'

Olive told Derek about Fred Stokes and the bomb as they drove down the coast to Brighton. It was their first trip out in Derek's new car – the red MG he'd told her about. His father had given him the rest of the money he needed as a birthday present, and he'd come straight round to collect Olive.

The whole family had come out to admire the new acquisition, though Ted had looked down his nose a bit and asked Derek a lot of questions about his driving experience while Olive stood by squirming with embarrassment. But Derek hadn't seemed to mind. He'd answered politely enough, reminded Ted that he'd been driving his father's vehicles around ever since he was old enough to have a licence and some of them were vans and lorries, a lot bigger than this little red beauty. He stroked the gleaming bonnet as he spoke and Olive could see her father was secretly envious and would have jumped at the chance of a ride.

Annie made no secret of her admiration. 'It's lovely. But you won't go too fast, will you, Derek? Not while you've got our Olive with you.'

'Oh, *Mum*,' Olive protested, tying a bright green scarf round her chestnut hair. 'Derek's been driving for years. He's not going to have an accident.'

'Never you mind, *oh, Mum*,' Ted told her sharply. 'She's right to worry about you. Anyone can have an accident, specially when they get a bit too cocky.' He stood in the road, a short, stocky man with rough brown hair, glowering at the car. He still hadn't got used to his daughters going out with men – even young men like Derek, who lived only a few streets away – and to think of them going out in a car, out of Portsmouth, where he could have no control over them, had him in a state close to panic.

'Well, Derek isn't too cocky.' Olive put her hand on the door. 'Can we go now, if everyone's finished having their say? Or d'you want to have tea out here in the street, staring at it?'

'And there's no call to be cheeky either,' Ted began, but Annie touched his arm.

'Don't grouse at the girl, Ted. She's only going out for an afternoon with her young man – there's no harm in that, is there?' She gave Olive a smile. 'You go and enjoy yourselves. I know Derek'll be careful.'

They watched as the car roared away up the street – not that it could work up much of a roar just going up March Street, towards September, where it had to stop again for traffic. But she knew Derek was bound to let it out a bit when they got to the open road over Portsdown Hill, and she knew it wasn't a bit of use worrying about it.

'We've got to let them go their own way,' she said to Ted as they went indoors. 'Olive is old enough to make her own decisions now. And she's fond of young Derek, you can see that.'

'She's smitten by him, you mean,' he said. 'I just hope he's not going to take advantage of her. I don't like it, this jaunting round the countryside in a car. It's not our style, Annie. He could get up to anything, taking her miles away from home like that.'

'He could get up to anything anytime,' Annie said, but she knew what Ted meant. Out in the country, miles from Portsmouth, where no one they knew was likely to see them, it would be much more difficult for Olive to keep control. But there was nothing to be done about it. There came a time when you just had to trust your kids. Trouble with Ted was, he just didn't want them to grow up.

*

Olive, meanwhile, was apologising to Derek for her parents. 'They don't seem to realise I'm grown up,' she grumbled. 'Dad's the worst – treats me like a kid. D'you know he wouldn't even let me wear make-up till I was nearly seventeen!' She giggled. 'Not that I let that stop me! I used to put it on when I was in the bus on the way to work and wipe it off again on the way home. In the end, I got Mum to persuade him.'

'Shame,' Derek said, only half listening. He was nursing the car along the main road out of Portsmouth. Soon they would be on the coast road and then he could let her rip. He listened to the engine purring beneath the bonnet and looked forward to the moment when he'd hear it give that throaty snarl that meant it was gathering speed.

Olive sat close against his side. She too was looking forward to the moment when they'd be out on the open road. She pulled the green scarf more securely over her hair and wished she had sun-glasses, like a film star. Turning her head, she looked at the passers-by, wondering if anyone she knew had seen her. Well, the whole of April Grove and March Street must have known Derek had a new car, and if they didn't old Granny Kinch would tell them – she'd been standing at her front door as usual and her little black eyes had nearly popped out of her head when the sleek red motor had purred to stop outside the Chapmans' house.

The drive to Brighton was exhilarating. The road was almost empty, all the way through Emsworth, Chichester and Arundel. Olive's scarf slipped off and her hair streamed back in the wind. She laughed up at Derek, her dark eyes sparkling, and he grinned back, excited by the speed and the sense of freedom. 'No more buses for us, eh?' he shouted above the roar of the wind. 'We'll go where we like now, Livvy – Brighton, London, the New Forest. You name it!'

'I don't care where it is so long as I'm with you,' she answered recklessly, and he took his hand from the wheel and caught hold of hers, pressing it down firmly on his thigh.

Olive gasped. She'd never touched him so intimately and immediately experienced the sense of guilt that was her warning signal. Over years of delicate hints and oblique references her mother had, without ever making a direct comment, given her a full manual of instructions on how a 'nice girl' behaved when out with her young man. The main criterion, it seemed, was to avoid 'cheapness'. A kiss was permitted, but prolonged kissing was cheap. So was allowing any touching other than on the places where anyone at all might be permitted to touch – on the arm, for instance, or the shoulder, or the back provided the touch did not stray below the waist. Indeed, any touching below the waist was strictly taboo.

These strictures had the unintended effect of making any touch at all highly exciting. Derek might have been surprised to know that his casual stroking of Olive's dark hair, when his fingers brushed her neck, or the absent-minded movement of his fingers on hers as they sat holding hands in the cinema, were enough to have her melting with desire. But he did not know – at least, Olive hoped he didn't know – for she had also been schooled not to show her emotions, and her own fear of what might happen if she 'led him on' kept her cool and still in his arms when her body longed to respond with heat and vigour.

It was getting more difficult to remain cool lately, though. Derek's goodnight kisses were becoming more lingering and she'd found herself snuggling into his arms and wanting more. Why was it 'cheap' to let your chap kiss you more than once? Kissing was good – she liked the feel of his lips on hers, moving gently but purposefully. And she liked it when he hugged her close against him, so that she could feel the hard muscles of his body, so different from hers. Sometimes she felt a bit more than she'd expected and when that happened she gasped and tried to wriggle free, but Derek only grunted and held her closer. And really, she hadn't wanted to get away at all.

Afterwards, Olive would lie in bed thinking over every moment of their goodnight kisses, reminding herself of the feel of Derek's arms about her, the feel of his hands on her body. He'd never gone any further than she wanted him to, never tried to touch those forbidden zones. But she knew that each time he kissed her, he got a little nearer, and she had doubts about whether she would be able to stop him when he did try to go further. Or even whether she wanted to.

They spent the afternoon in Brighton, strolling along the front. Derek brought Olive a huge pink cloud of candy-floss and she buried her face in it, laughing. They watched some jugglers and a Punch and Judy show and played some of the machines on the pier, coming away with a fluffy white toy kitten and a watch that had stopped before they were back at the car. They bought some rock to take home to the family and had tea in a café on the front. They went down to the beach and chased the waves, regretting that they hadn't brought swimming costumes with them.

'We've never been swimming together,' Derek said. 'I bet you look smashing in a bathing suit.'

Olive blushed. 'I don't know. I look all right, I suppose.'

'All right? With a figure like yours?' Derek slipped his arm around her waist and squeezed her. 'You'd look gorgeous, I know you would.'

'Well,' she said breathlessly, 'p'rhaps you'll see sometime.'

'I'll take that as a promise.' He nuzzled her neck. 'It's been a good day, hasn't it?'

'Mm.' She glanced anxiously up and down the beach and then reminded herself that they were in Brighton. Nobody they knew was likely to see them here. She relaxed and let herself lean against him. 'Mm, it's been lovely. Thanks for bringing me, Derek.'

'It wouldn't have been any fun without you,' he murmured, and nuzzled closer. Olive felt her heartbeat quicken. 'So what d'you fancy doing now?' he went on. 'I reckon we've seen most of what there is to see in Brighton, don't you?'

'Well – go home, I suppose.'

'Just go home? Seems a bit tame.'

Olive looked at her watch. It was a small chromium-plated one, a present from her parents for her twentieth birthday.

'It's nearly six. It'll be getting on for eight o'clock by the time we get back to Portsmouth.'

'That's too early to be going home,' Derek said decisively. 'I mean, most

Saturdays we'd be going to a dance at Kimball's, or to the flicks. They won't be expecting you back that early, will they?'

'I don't know. I've never been out like this before – in a car, for the afternoon. Mum probably thought we'd be back for tea. I wouldn't like to worry her.'

'But she knew we were coming to Brighton.' Derek squeezed her again. 'Stop worrying, Olive. Let's go and have a drink and a sandwich in a pub somewhere on the way back, have a walk on the Downs perhaps. I'll get you back by ten, I promise.'

Olive laughed and gave in. Of course it didn't make any difference that they were in Brighton and not Portsmouth. And a snack on the way home in a pub would be fun. Dad didn't approve of girls going into pubs, though he wasn't as strict about that as Uncle Frank, but country pubs were different. Charabanc outings always stopped at pubs on the way back and all the women went into them and had a drink. Anyway, wasn't she old enough to decide for herself now?

What was even more important was that she didn't want Derek getting fed up with her. Derek, with his good looks, his dark gold hair and his sports car, wouldn't have any trouble at all in finding a new girl to go around with, one who wouldn't fuss about her parents or have to be home by ten.

'All right,' she said, 'let's do that. Mum and Dad'll just have to get used to it. It's time they stopped treating me like a kid anyway.'

'That's the stuff,' Derek laughed. 'Mind you, we don't want them to take against me, do we? So we won't take any chances – we'll be home by ten, like I said. This time, anyway.' He bent his head and gave her a quick kiss. 'I don't promise I'll always be so good,' he murmured wickedly. 'Not now we've got the car and can go just where we like.'

Olive giggled and gave him a push. 'Get away with you! Just because you've got a car, Derek Harker, doesn't mean to say you can do just what you want. I'm a respectable girl, remember? I don't want to go jaunting around dark country lanes late at night.'

'Why not?' he asked. 'Afraid I'll run out of petrol?' And when Olive squealed and giggled again, he drew her close, his face suddenly sober. 'Don't you worry, Livvy, and tell your mum and dad not to worry either. I think too much of you to do anything you wouldn't want. But just for now – let's have a bit of fun, shall we? We might not get many more chances if this war starts.'

Olive stared at him. His voice was as serious as his face and she felt a tremor of half excitement, half fear. He'd said he thought a lot of her, and said it as if he meant it. That was more than he'd ever said before. But then, even before she could begin to analyse what he had meant, he'd brought the war into it. And it was clear he wasn't joking.

War! she thought in disgust. Everlasting war – it gets into everything. She'd thought for once they could forget it, but here it was again, rearing its ugly head like some monster from the deep.

She looked out at the rippling sea and shivered. The bright afternoon was suddenly dulled, the glittering waves heavy and sinister. A few swimmers splashed in the water and a fleet of sailing dinghies swooped by like butterflies, their sails blue and white and brown wings of freedom against a wide and cloudless sky.

Over there was France, and beyond that Germany, where jackbooted troops were preparing to march on yet another helpless country. And if they did, men like Derek who wanted nothing but to sit on a beach with their girls, or take them driving in sports cars with the wind in their hair, would have to go and fight.

It's not fair, she thought with bitter anger. Just when our lives are starting. It just isn't *fair*.

'D'you think you'll ever have a car, Graham?' Betty asked wistfully. They were walking along the beach at Stokes Bay, over in Gosport, and she glanced about her with dissatisfaction, thinking of Olive on the way to Brighton for the afternoon.

'Course I will. Soon as I've got the money. But I'll have to get a better job first – working for old man Surrey won't make me rich.'

Andrew Surrey was a chemist and Graham had worked for him on and off ever since leaving school. He'd started as an errand and delivery boy and now served in the shop and sometimes mixed ingredients for Mr Surrey's potions and ointments. But he was restless, always looking for something better, and had tried several other jobs.

'Can you drive?' Betty asked, and he nodded.

'Been driving for old Surrey for the past three years. He took me out in his van a couple of times and then I taught myself. He says I can drive it better than him now.' He glanced at her. 'Here – I could borrow it of a weekend, take you out somewhere. That'd be a bit of all right, now, wouldn't it?'

'Oh, yes.' Her eyes lit up. It might not be an MG sports car but at least they'd be able to get away from Portsmouth. 'We could go down the New Forest, see the wild ponies.'

'That's right.' They turned away from the beach and began to walk along Jellicoe Avenue, back towards the town. Betty had come over to have tea with Graham and his parents. They lived in one of the streets off Carnarvon Road, barely fifteen minutes' walk from the bay.

Betty had not yet met Graham's mother and father. So far, Graham had come over to Portsmouth to meet her and they had gone to the pictures together or for a walk. But he'd been to tea twice with the Chapmans and Betty had made it clear she expected a return invitation.

After five or six weeks, Betty considered herself settled now as Graham's girlfriend. She was still thrilled to be going out with him and enjoyed boasting to her friends about her 'young man' but like her sister she drew very definite lines as to Graham's behaviour. Kissing had turned out to be pleasurable, and she enjoyed snuggling up to him in one of the shelters out along Southsea seafront, but she would quickly slap Graham's hand away if it roamed too far, and there was never any danger of her being 'carried away', as Olive sometimes feared she might with Derek. There were, as she had told Graham when she first met him, plenty of other fish in the sea, and one of them not a hundred yards from her own doorstep.

But although she knew now that Bob Shaw would ask her out any time she cared to give him the hint, Betty had no desire to break with Graham. He was cheeky and fun to be with; he made her giggle, and when she pushed his hand away he just laughed and kissed her, as if he'd known she would do that and had only been trying it on to tease her.

'You'll let me one of these days, Bet,' he said. 'You're no different from the other girls really. You'll like it just as much as anyone else.'

'Oh, and how would you know that? If anyone else had talked to her like that she'd have sent them packing, but Graham had a way of saying things you couldn't take offence at. 'I suppose you've had more girl-friends than I've had hot dinners,' she challenged him, wanting him to deny it.

'That's right,' he agreed equably. 'One every night of the week and two on Sundays. How else d'you think I know so much?'

'Oh, Graham! You're awful – I don't know why I go out with you.'

'Because you like me, that's why,' he said, and kissed her again, one of the lingering kisses that Betty liked in a queer, tingling way and remembered afterwards as she lay in bed, listening to Olive breathing a few feet away from her.

They were at Graham's gate now and he opened it and led her inside. The small front garden was rough and overgrown with weeds – Betty could imagine what her Dad or Uncle Frank would have had to say about that. The house itself looked neat enough on the outside, with a green front door and green-painted window-frames, but the step wasn't white and shining like her mother's – in April Grove it was almost like a competition to see whose step could be the whitest. It didn't look as if Graham's mother bothered about such competition.

Inside there was a passage, papered with dark red Anaglypta. The floor was covered with brown linoleum and a man's bicycle stood leaning against one wall. Graham and Betty squeezed past it. Graham tinkled the bell as he did so and a door at the end of the passage suddenly opened.

'Is that you, our Gray?' A big blowsy woman with unruly ginger hair appeared, filling the doorway with her bulk. She was wearing a flowery apron that stretched across a massive bosom and almost covered the blouse and skirt beneath. 'And is this Betty, then? Betty Chapman? Come here, love, let's have a look at you.'

'Well, move yourself out of the way so we can get through,' Graham said cheerfully, and pushed his way into the back room. 'Here she is. This is my mum, Betty, and you don't need to take any notice of what she tells you about me, it's all lies.'

'Hark at him!' his mother exclaimed. 'Lies, indeed! What a way to talk about your own mother, eh? I hope you don't stand no nonsense from him, Betty.'

Betty laughed and shook her head. Already she was feeling at home in this untidy household. It was plain to see where Graham got his cheeky, easygoing ways, she thought, and then noticed the man in the armchair by the fireplace.

'This is Dad,' Graham said as the man got up. He was smaller and thinner than his wife, with cautious blue eyes, but he smiled welcomingly enough and held out his hand.

'I remember your dad from when we lived up September Street. Ted Chapman, that's right, innit? Ferryboat captain.'

'That's right.' Betty could just remember Mr and Mrs Philpotts, though she wouldn't have known them in the street. They had moved to Gosport when she was about eight years old. Moving to Gosport was, to most Portsmouth people, rather on a par with emigrating to Australia. Once over the water they were liable never to be seen again. Of course, she knew other people who lived there – Uncle Frank had a brother there and she'd met him and his wife at family parties. But nobody went to Gosport unless it was to visit.

'Oh, I remember Ted Chapman,' Elsie Philpotts said, rolling her eyes. 'All us girls fancied him! He was a real bit of all right, I can tell you.' She laughed and dug Betty in the ribs with her elbow. 'Still, better not go telling tales out of school, had I? I don't want to cause no trouble.'

'Go on,' Graham said affectionately, 'you cause trouble wherever you go, can't help it.'

'Like mother, like son,' she retorted, and fixed her eye on Betty again. 'I hope you don't allow him no liberties. He needs a bit of keeping in order.'

'Oh – no. No, I don't,' Betty said, blushing scarlet as she remembered those moments when she'd pushed away Graham's straying hands. 'I mean, he doesn't – we don't—' She broke off in confusion as Elsie Philpotts roared with laughter.

'Don't tell me he never tries it on! Well, he doesn't take after his father then.' And she turned and dug her elbow this time into her husband's ribs. 'Does he, Charlie? My, we could tell 'em a thing or two, couldn't we? Maybe our Graham needs a few lessons!'

'Give over, Else,' Charlie said. His voice was mild and dry, like fine worn sandpaper on wood. 'You're embarrassing the girl.'

'Course I'm not. Am I, Betty?' Without waiting for an answer, she bellowed with laughter again, then hurried on. 'Well, it's time for a cuppa. I bet you two could do with one, couldn't you? I'll go and see if the kettle's boiled. Come and give me a hand, Charlie.'

Her husband looked startled. 'But I was just—'

'Never mind that. You come and give us a hand in the kitchen.' Elsie went through an elaborate pantomime of significant glances and jerking of the head. 'Come on. Don't stand there like a stuffed dummy. Can't you remember what it was to be young?'

Graham watched as his mother hustled his father out of the room, then turned to Betty and grinned. 'That's so we can do this,' he said, putting his arms round her. He gave her a smacking kiss then leaned back and grinned again. 'So we'd better do it, hadn't we? Wouldn't like to disappoint the old girl.'

'Graham! That's no way to talk about your mum. Old girl! Don't you have any respect?'

'Oh, she's all right. She wouldn't mind. She'd just laugh. There's not much that doesn't make my mum laugh, come to think of it.' He cocked an eye at Betty. 'She likes you.'

'Does she? How can you tell?'

'Easy. She wouldn't have left me in here with you if she hadn't. So that I could do this.' He kissed her again and Betty responded a little nervously, half afraid that Mrs Philpotts would come unexpectedly back into the room and catch them. But perhaps she wouldn't have minded if she had. Not like Betty's mother, who would have been embarrassed and probably disapproving.

That Elsie Philpotts was unlikely to come back unexpectedly was made clear by a rattle of teacups and an overloud voice outside the door a few seconds before it opened to admit her bulk. She carried a large tray set with cups and saucers and a big fruit cake, while Charlie followed with the pot and a jug of milk. Graham swept aside a pile of papers on the dining-table and his mother set the tray down and stood panting slightly.

'There. The cup that cheers. How d'you like it, love, as it comes? We like it strong in this house, strong enough to stand a spoon in as my old dad used to say, but I can easy put some more milk in if you want it a bit weaker.'

'No, that's just right.' Betty sat down in one of the armchairs and accepted a cup of tea and a slice of fruit cake. She looked around with interest. Her first impression had been of a large airy room, comfortably cluttered, and now she saw that this was true.

The room was bigger than the living-room in her own home, with french windows that opened on to the back garden. There were four armchairs – two by the fireside, two in the opposite corners. The dining-table stood against the wall opposite the fireside, piled with papers and bits of needlework, while beside one of the fireside chairs stood a sagging wicker basket filled with socks presumably awaiting mending. There was a big mirror over the mantelpiece, which was piled with letters, boxes of matches, pipe-cleaners and packets of cigarettes. In the middle of it was a large clock and on each end an alabaster figurine of a scantily dressed girl holding a torch above her head. Around the walls were gaudy pictures of seaside resorts or mountain scenes with shaggy cattle standing up to their knees in bogs under threatening skies.

'Now then,' Elsie Philpotts said, settling herself comfortably in the chair by the socks, 'tell us all about good old September Street and what's been going on there. How's your mum? I remember her from school, though we wasn't in the same class. I was more her sister's age – Jessie, wasn't it? She married Frank Budd.'

Betty nodded. 'That's right. Auntie Jess is having another baby soon.'

'No! She's not, is she?' Elsie leaned forwards. 'But how old's the youngest – what was his name, Kenny? Surely he's getting on for ten years old now?'

'Keith. He's nearly nine. The baby's due next month.'

'Well!' Elsie looked across the hearth at her husband. 'Did you hear that, Charlie? Jess Budd having another baby! Why, she's the same age as me.' She reached across and, being unable to dig him in the ribs, poked him sharply on the knee instead, so that his foot kicked upwards and he almost dropped his cup. 'Here, there's hope for us yet! How would you like a baby sister for Christmas, Gray?'

'Give over, Ma,' Graham said, turning red, and she squawked with laughter.

'Now I've embarrassed you! Well, I never thought I'd live to see the day.' She gave Betty a conspiratorial wink. 'Come out in the kitchen with me and we'll talk women's talk. It's no good with men around, they only want to talk about football and fishing. Here, pour yourself another cup of tea and bring it with you.'

Betty did as she was told. It struck her that probably most people did as they were told when Elsie Philpotts was around. Not doing so would be like arguing with a large, soft but very noisy bolster.

Anyway, she didn't mind. Graham's mum might be loud and even what Annie Chapman called 'common' but she was kind and good-hearted, and her house felt comfortable to be in. Already, Betty felt one of the family.

One of the family . . . The thought startled her. As she followed Elsie Philpotts into her cheerfully untidy kitchen, she wondered if she could be getting serious about Graham. No, she told herself decisively. It's too soon yet. Anyway, I don't want to settle down. I just want a bit of fun.

And to have fun, you needed a boy to go around with. But it needn't be any more than that.

To Jess, the winning of the FA Cup that summer seemed to be the last sign of peace. After that, there was talk of nothing but war. Trenches to be dug in public spaces. Shelters in your own garden or at the end of the street. Air defence. Evacuation tests – did they really mean to take the children away, to make them live with strangers far from everything they knew? She watched and listened with dread, and her thoughts were as much with the coming baby as with her living children. What had she and Frank been about, to bring another child into the world as it was today?

May passed into June and June into July. The news grew more serious daily. Frank bought a big map of Europe and pinned it up on the living-room wall, over the piano. He marked the advance of the Germans with pins and it was horrifying to see how they were spreading over the whole continent. How could anyone believe that they really meant to stop their ruthless invasions, when so many countries had already succumbed? How could they be trusted to let Poland stay free?

'We'll have to step in if they don't,' Frank said, frowning. 'We've signed a pledge. It's getting close, Jess.'

'I know.' She had been feeling unwell all day, her back aching and the baby squirming inside her. The midwife had come last night and said the birth was imminent; she was coming back this evening. 'I don't know what you've got in here, Mrs Budd,' she'd said, feeling the collection of knees and elbows that made protruding lumps on Jess's stretched abdomen. 'Feels more like a spider than a baby!' She'd laughed but Jess knew it meant a difficult birth. Not that she'd ever expected any different. They'd all been difficult and she was nine years older now than when Keith had been born.

'They're bringing Anderson shelters round now,' she said. 'Backbury

Road got them today and I could hear the clatter from the garden. There was talk about builders coming to install them but they never will, not that many. Only for old people and them that can't manage. You'll have to do ours.'

'That's no problem.' It just meant a few hours when he wouldn't be able to work on the allotment. Or sit and read the *Daily Express*, his one relaxation at the end of a long day. 'I'll do it at the weekend.'

'Perhaps the boys will be able to help you.' She sat quietly for a few moments, then put a hand to the small of her back. 'Frank—'

'Is it the baby?' He was at her side at once. 'The nurse said it'd be soon, didn't she?'

'Yes. I've been feeling a bit queer all day.' She looked up at him, her face distorted by sudden pain. 'Frank, the children—'

'It's all right. I'll see to them.' It had all been arranged weeks ago, that the children were to go to Annie and Ted, at the top of the street, for the night. None of them, not even Rose, knew that a baby was expected; like most of their generation, Frank and Jess didn't approve of children knowing too much about the 'facts of life' and avoided difficult questions. They'd find out soon enough, and they'd all been taught not to make personal remarks so had not even commented on their mother's size. Jess thought that probably the boys hadn't even noticed it.

Rose was up at her friend Joy's for tea and the boys had bolted theirs down and then rushed out to play again. When they came back, they'd be sent up to their aunt's. Meanwhile, Frank went next door to ask Peggy Shaw to come and sit with Jess while he hurried to the telephone box at the top of the street to call the midwife.

'I always have a bad time,' Jess said when the two women were alone. She was in bed now, everything put ready for the birth. 'I can't bear down properly, you see. The baby just has to manage by itself. I can't help at all.'

Downstairs, Frank waited to let in first the midwife, then the doctor. He had been through this three times already but the anxiety was never any less and now, with this one, Jess was so much older. Forty – a couple of weeks off forty-one – was old to have a baby, however you looked at it. And Jess had been so worried lately, so frightened by the threat of war. He knew she believed that the things she thought and felt could affect the baby, and her own fears had worried her twice as much on that score. Was she right? Would it make any difference to how things went tonight?

The children were up at Jess's sister's house now. They'd been surprised and a bit querulous to find themselves shoved off up there at a moment's notice, and Rose had wanted to know what was wrong with Jess, but he hadn't the time or patience to answer their questions. And Annie had taken them in cheerfully enough and put the two boys to sleep up in Colin's room, which was a treat for them. Frank had left them there, knowing they were in good hands, and hurried home again.

He could hear sounds from the room above. The nurse had told him as soon as she came that the doctor would be needed. It meant extra expense but he'd put the money by a few weeks ago – there were some things that had to be afforded. There was enough there for all the things the baby would need – a few clothes, for Jess had got rid of most of Keith's baby clothes years ago, a cot and a pram. Luckily someone in September Street had a toddler just growing out of both, so it had been arranged that they could be fetched as soon as Jess's baby was born.

Everything was ready. And by the grunts and groans now coming from upstairs, it sounded as if the baby was ready too.

Frank switched on the wireless. At times like this, he almost wished that he smoked or drank. A cigarette or a stiff whisky, wasn't that what helped men through these anxious hours? But he'd never been able to afford to smoke and he'd turned his face steadfastly against drink ever since he was a boy. He'd seen too much of it . . . But he wouldn't let thoughts of those times get into his mind now. He'd shut them away long ago, told only Jess what had happened when he was a boy, and never referred to it again.

The nurse came down for more hot water. It was the only thing Frank could do to help, keep the kettle boiling. He stared at her in mute misery and she gave him a cheery smile.

'No need to look so worried, Mr Budd. She's doing fine. The baby'll be born in good time for you to go to work, see if it isn't.'

Go to work! That was hours away. He looked at the clock that ticked on the mantelpiece, the clock he wound every Sunday morning. It was just past midnight and Jess was having a hard time of it up there. If only he could go and see her, hold her hand.

But the midwife was shocked when he suggested it. 'No place for a father, Mr Budd,' she said firmly. 'You're better off down here. Anyway, what with me and the doctor there'll be no room for you. We're bumping into each other as it is.' She gave him another professional beam and went upstairs with the bowl of hot water.

Frank sighed and filled the kettle again. No doubt she'd be back for more in a minute, and if not he'd make a cup of tea. He was sure they could all do with one. He set out cups, fetched milk from the meatsafe outside and got the sugar bowl from the cupboard.

The wireless had finished for the night. He'd barely heard it anyway – just gramophone records on the Light Programme and some sort of play on the Home Service. He could have done with something light and cheerful – *Band Waggon*, perhaps, with Arthur Askey and Stinker Murdoch. But it might have seemed a bit callous to sit down here laughing at their antics, with poor Jess going through the mill upstairs.

He sat down and picked up the *Daily Express*, stood up again, stared at the map on the wall. Things were looking bad, there was no doubt about it. The pins he had stuck in showed a steady, inexorable march across Europe. Czechoslovakia gone – what chance had Poland? Hitler had already denounced the 1934 pact of non-aggression. In May he had signed the Pact of Steel with Mussolini, agreeing on mutual support in any future war. He'd be sucking up to Stalin next, and the great Powers would be lined up, facing each other.

The great Powers . . . Could Britain really take on the might of Europe alone? The Dominions were there, of course – Canada, South Africa, Australia and the rest. But would they give their support? Or would they keep out of it, preferring to see it as Europe's battle? And what about America?

It was all of Europe. Turkey, Greece, Denmark – everyone was getting involved. But it's not just our fight, Frank thought. The situation's grim all over the world. Russia and Japan at each other's throats, Japan blockading the British at the Chinese port of Tientsin, it seems as if every country's got some quarrel, some score to settle. As if the whole world is a great festering boil waiting to swell and burst with its own poison.

And as if all that wasn't enough, there were the troubles that went on all the time. The IRA, who set off no less than thirty pillar-box bombs one day last month. And the loss of the submarine *Thetis* on the first of June.

Fourteen Portsmouth men had been aboard the *Thetis* when she dived during her acceptance trials in Liverpool Bay that day. She hadn't even been at sea – that was what seemed so cruel about it. She went down in one hundred and thirty feet of water and stayed there, her stern on the surface. And none of the desperate efforts with the salvage equipment was enough o save the men trapped inside.

Only four escaped. Of the rest, all hope was given up until tapping heard from inside the hull threw everyone into a frenzy of excitement and renewed bids to raise the stern. The country had held its breath, listening to the news on the wireless, scanning the front pages of newspapers . . . but in the end hope had died with the men who were even yet still trapped in their grim coffin. And only a week later, a memorial service had been held in the little church of St Ann in Portsmouth Dockyard, and Frank had seen the weeping mourners as he walked through the Yard and had felt a premonition of the future.

If war came – when war came – there would be many more ships sunk, many more men sent to a grim, choking death beneath the waves. And there would be others too. Soldiers, fighting a bloody battle in the mud and gore of the trenches, such as Frank himself remembered from the last Great War. Airmen, spinning from the skies in flames. And old people, women and children, blasted to death in their own homes, or huddled like animals in holes in their own back yards.

Babies, like the one Jess was struggling to bring into the world at this very moment, their lives smashed before they even knew what life was.

Footsteps sounded heavily on the stairs. He turned quickly as the scullery door opened and the doctor appeared tired and grey. At the same moment he heard – and knew that he had been hearing for some minutes without even realising it – the cry of a newborn baby.

When Jess and her sister Annie were fourteen they left school and went out to work. Annie went into service and learned how posh people lived, with jugs of water on the dinner-table and forks as well as spoons for 'afters' – which she called dessert or sweet. Jess, who had always been handy with a needle, was apprenticed to a dressmaker and learned a craft that would be useful throughout her life.

Most of her afternoons were spent in dressmaking, either for herself and Rose or for neighbours who would pay her to run up a frock or a blouse and skirt from a paper pattern. The children were accustomed to the floor of the front room being spread with tissue paper marked with strange hieroglyphics and fabric being cut into odd shapes. They were used to the rattle of the treadle sewing machine, which stood in a corner and could be employed to do duty as a horse when it had its wooden cover on. And Rose was delighted to be able to have clothes that were different from those of her friends.

During the fortnight after baby Maureen's birth, however, there was no dressmaking in number 14 April Grove, for Jess stayed in bed the whole time, not even allowed to put a foot to the floor. And with the children at school and Frank, after that first day, back at work, she had time for her other main spare-time occupation, reading.

Jess had always been a great reader. As a child, she read all of Dickens's novels – Dickens being a son of Portsmouth, this was almost obligatory, but Jess enjoyed them anyway. She read Jane Austen and Charlotte Brontë and when she went to the library she seemed to seek out the thickest, heaviest novels to bring home. Every evening, from eight until nine, she read. It was sometimes the only hour of relaxation of her day.

But for once, the library books lay on the bedside table, largely untouched.

'Look at these leaflets,' she said to Annie when her sister came in to bring her a bit of lunch. That was another thing about Annie – she always called the midday meal 'lunch', whereas to most of the other residents of April Grove and its neighbouring streets, lunch meant the sandwich or couple of biscuits you had halfway through the morning. Sometime between noon and one o'clock, depending on when men or children were home from work and school, you had dinner, and that was the main cooked meal of the day. Tea was bread and jam and cake at five o'clock, and most women, like Jess, turned to again at about nine in the evening and cooked supper – eggs and chips or something on toast, washed down with mugs of cocoa. During the week, for Frank and many other men who couldn't get home at noon, supper was the only freshly cooked hot meal they had.

Jess cooked for herself and all three children, for the school was near enough for them to walk home in less than ten minutes. She always saved a good plateful for Frank and covered it up in the meatsafe just outside the back door for the afternoon. At supper-time she would take out yesterday's empty plate from the box he carried to work, and put in today's, and he would heat it up to eat the next day. Where he heated it up, she wasn't quite sure, but there would be plenty of places in a boiler-shop.

But for this fortnight, meals were something she didn't have to worry about. Annie gave the children their 'lunch' every day and got dinner cooking ready for Frank when he got home. He was back before six, having arranged to do no overtime, and finished off the meal and served it. Jess imagined him downstairs, sitting at the head of the dining-table, keeping a stern eye on every plate. Every scrap had to be eaten and he was never soft like she was sometimes, going out to the scullery when Tim wouldn't eat his cabbage so that he got the chance to throw it on the fire. Otherwise he'd sit there for hours, staring miserably at it and refusing to eat, and neither of them would win.

Jess smiled, remembering the battles she and Tim had had over that cabbage. Once, he'd hidden it down the side of his father's armchair and it had been found several days later, black, soggy and stinking. Tim had been given a hiding for that and only narrowly escaped being forced to eat it anyway, after Jess had pointed out to Frank that it would probably make him really ill. Another time, caught halfway towards the fire with it in his hand when she had come unexpectedly into the room, he'd jumped and let it fly so it came to rest draped over a photograph of Frank's mother on the mantelpiece. She'd been hard put to it not to laugh outright that time and had gone hastily back out to the scullery, which had given him the chance to climb up on a chair and rescue it.

'He can't be allowed to get away with it,' Frank said sternly, but he wasn't the one who had to cope with Tim's next trick, which was to force himself to be sick whenever cabbage was put on the table. She'd kept him at home from afternoon school several times before she realised what was going on, and even took him to see the doctor, who examined Tim and pronounced him perfectly healthy. It was only later that she realised he was doing it deliberately, and she'd never told Frank. But, seeing that Tim really did hate cabbage, she'd decided not to force him any more. Instead, she gave him the opportunity to get rid of it in his own way – except on Saturdays and Sundays when, under his father's eagle eye, he dared not refuse and somehow swallowed the tiny portion she put on his plate.

'These leaflets,' she said. 'They're pouring through the letter-box every day now.' She picked them up and flicked through them. ' "Things You Should Know if War Should Come." "Your Gas Mask and Masking Your Windows." "Evacuation. Why and How?" "Your Food in Wartime." They must know it's coming, Annie. Otherwise why go to all this trouble?'

Annie shrugged. 'They have to, I suppose. I mean, we'd all look a bit silly if it came and we weren't ready for it. And I reckon it is coming, don't you?'

Jess shuddered. 'I've been trying not to think about it, with the baby on the way. But now – looking at all this . . . There doesn't seem any way of stopping it. It's as if it was some huge animal, getting closer and closer all the time. Or like a big cloud in the sky that's going to blot out everything.' She looked at her elder sister. 'Why is it happening, Annie? What started it all?'

'You mean who started it all,' her sister said grimly. 'And we all know the answer to that. It's that man – Hitler. He's mad and he's sending everyone else mad. That's what Ted says and I reckon he's right.'

' "Most of the injuries in an air raid are caused by flying fragments of debris or bits of shells," ' Jess read aloud. 'That's from bombs hitting buildings, Annie. And who are the people who are going to get injured? You and me – the children – old Mrs Seddon over the road. We never wanted a war, none of us. Why should we have to be treated like that? And what about the youngsters – your Olive, and boys like Derek Harker who're going to have to go and fight? All they want to do is get on with their own lives.'

'I know. It's unsettling them. I can see our Olive getting hurt whatever happens. Either they'll want to get engaged and she'll be miserable when he does go, or she'll want to and he won't.' Annie shook her head. 'It's pushing them too fast, Jess. Without the war they'd have been happy just to go out together and get to know each other properly. And there's our Betty with a young man too now, and only just turned eighteen.'

She sighed and got up to go. 'Well, don't upset yourself, Jess. It's bad for the baby. You don't want to lose your milk, do you?' She picked up Jess's empty plate and passed her a bowl of rice pudding, left over from yesterday with a bit of jam on top of it. 'I'll have to go now, the children'll be home any minute. You leave those leaflets alone and get a bit of rest. Forget it for a while.'

She went downstairs and Jess heard the front door open and close and her sister's footsteps hurry up the street. She ate the rice pudding slowly and then lay back on her pillows. Beside her, in a drawer pulled out from the dressing-table, Maureen lay fast asleep.

But Jess could not forget the war that loomed ever closer. She had not been allowed to. On 4 July, the very morning that the baby was born, the Anderson shelters had been delivered to April Grove and she had lain in bed, exhausted and wanting nothing but sleep, listening to the clatter of corrugated iron being dumped outside every house, to the shouts of the men and the exclamations of the neighbours as they peered at their new acquisitions. Then there had been the noise of the building – a deafening cacophony that echoed the worst of all from the gardens of October Street. For the first time, Jess had regretted the position of number 14, looking up the length of October Street's back gardens as it did. It seemed that she shared in every hammer-blow, in every yelled instruction, in every oath and curse, every blackened thumb. And now, after only a brief respite, came the leaflets. And she could not ignore them. They had to be read.

She picked them up, scanning through them again although she already knew most of them by heart.

There were going to be special anti-gas helmets for babies. That was something, anyway, though they weren't to be distributed before an emergency arose. That would be a bit late, surely? Perhaps they meant 'if war was declared'. And what sort of helmet could a tiny baby wear anyway?

Blackouts. There were to be no lights shining at night. No street-lights, no lights from cars or buses or trains, no lights from windows. Everyone had to make sure not the slightest gleam of light escaped, either by having specially thick curtains or by making blinds. Frank had already started. He'd been down to Bulpitt's at North End and bought several yards of blackout material – Italian cloth at tenpence-threefarthings a yard. This had been fixed to wooden frames which could be fitted into the windows as soon as it got dark. He'd tested it and reported that not a glimmer showed through.

The children were to be evacuated, she and Frank were agreed on that. The thought of Rose or one of the boys getting hurt in a raid was more than she could bear. But for herself . . .

'I'd rather stay here with you. How are you going to manage? You can't work long hours over the Dockyard and then come home and have to turn round and start cooking your own dinner. And what about your washing and ironing?'

'I'll manage,' he told her. 'I can cook my own dinner – haven't I been doing it while you've been laid up? And I can take my washing up to Mrs Brown's if I have to, she don't charge much. Your place is with the baby.'

The baby. Jess looked at the makeshift cot beside the bed. Maureen was fast asleep, one tiny fist curled under her chin, her downy hair a sheen of gold over her head. She was a good baby, never crying much, and the other children, after their first astonishment, adored her – although Jess had thought she detected, at first, a touch of resentment in both Rose and Keith. It had quickly faded, however, and now Rose was a real little mother to her baby sister while Keith would sit for half an hour at a time cradling her in his arms.

Tim took her, as he took everything else, in his stride. His first pleasure had been entirely unforced, but since then he accepted her very much as a natural development of the family. It was as if she had slipped into a place he had already prepared for her, as if they were friends from the start, so right that it barely warranted a mention.

But even though Jess now felt her family to be complete, she still couldn't help thinking it was a bad time to be bringing a baby into the world. Or a bad world to be bringing a baby into. And if it weren't for Maureen, she could stay at home with Frank when war came.

As if aware of the thought, Maureen stirred and began to whimper. And Jess, washed with guilt, reached down to pick her up. She cradled the baby close to her, whispering against the downy head, then bared her breast.

Frank was right. If war came, this precious little life must be protected. And she was the only person who could do it.

Once up and about again, Jess began her own preparations for war.

One of the leaflets dropped through the letter-box concerned food in wartime. It told how, during the past eighteen months, the government had been buying large reserves of essential foodstuffs – so they had been expecting it! What about that trip to Munich? she thought indignantly. What about that 'piece of paper'?

She resumed her reading. All ordinary householders were advised to lay in their own stocks – the quantity normally used in one week – to keep by them in case local shops ran out. Things like canned meat and fish. Flour. Suet. Dried milk. Sugar, tea, cocoa. Biscuits. And once having built up this reserve, to use and replace the items regularly, so they were always fresh.

It was something Jess did anyway. She had never had much house-keeping money and there had been times when the cupboard was almost as bare as Mother Hubbard's, but since Frank had been earning a little more she'd taken advantage of cheap offers in the shops and now kept a modest but complete little store-cupboard. And there were always the jars of home-made jam and the Kilner bottles of fruit from the allotment. And potatoes, carrots and turnips stored out in the shed all through the winter.

All the same, she didn't look forward to rationing. And Frank would need plenty of meat, doing the hard, strenuous work he did. It might be as well to lay in a few more tins of that, as well as make as much jam and bottle as much fruit as she could.

The family's clothes too needed attention. If the children were going to be evacuated, Jess was determined that they should look respectable. She wasn't going to have some countrywoman pursing her lips over torn trousers or frayed shirts. So there was a lot of sorting out to do, a pile of mending and darning, collars to be turned and cottons to be sewn on.

She discussed it over the fence with Ethel Glaister at number 15. She wasn't as friendly with Ethel as she was with Peggy, on the other side, but you had to be neighbourly and pass the time of day and they'd always managed to keep on reasonably good terms.

'Rose needs two new winter skirts. She's grown so much this past year, the ones she's got are up past her knees. And I'd better knit her a new cardigan for school.'

'How do you know she'll be going to school?' Ethel said, patting her hair. She had just had it permed by the new hairdresser at North End and Jess was certain she'd had it dyed too. It surely hadn't been that shade of yellow yesterday. 'Once they're evacuated their schooling'll go right down the drain.'

'Oh, I'm sure it won't,' Jess said. 'The teachers are going too. They had a rehearsal on Monday – we had to pack their cases just as if they were really going. All the teachers will be going with them.'

'But they won't have no schooling,' Ethel persisted. 'Look, it stands to reason. Country schools are only big enough for the children what are already there. How're they going to fit ours in? You only have to think about it.'

Jess stared at her. As well as newly permed hair, Ethel had a new blouse with a frilly neck. And she was wearing lipstick. Lipstick at her age! thought Jess, who never wore any make up at all.

'But how'll they get on, then?' she asked. 'Some of them will be leaving school before long. And the infants – how'll they learn to read and do their sums?'

Ethel shrugged. 'Don't ask me. Ask them as is getting us into this bloody war. Anyway, when it comes I don't reckon as that'll be our biggest worry. Staying alive'll be all we're interested in then.'

Jess was silent for a moment.

'What are you going to do about yours, then?'

'Well, what can I do? Joe and Carol are out at work now, they won't get evacuated. They can just get bombed, along with the rest of us, don't matter that there's rich people's kids the same age as them still at school, getting pampered out in the country. And I suppose I'll have to stay here to look after George, he's useless on his own.'

Jess listened to the whining self-pity in Ethel's voice and felt a twinge of irritation. 'What about your Shirley?' she asked. 'She's only seven – will you let her go?'

Ethel shrugged again. 'S'pose so. Can't say I've thought about it that much. I mean, we don't know it's going to happen for certain, do we? And I've had our holiday to think about.'

She had been talking about their holiday since Easter, Jess reflected, lording it over her neighbours who couldn't afford family holidays, even though she was only going to stay with relatives. But the relatives lived in Devonshire, which made it more special, and the way Ethel talked about them you'd think they owned half the county.

'You're still going, then?'

Ethel stared. 'Of course we are. Why shouldn't we be going?'

'Well, I thought with all that's happening – I mean, suppose you got stuck down there and couldn't get back home?'

'Stuck?' Ethel said. 'Why should we get stuck? D'you think the Germans are going to invade Pompey the first day, or something?' She laughed, a shrill, whinnying laugh that set Jess's teeth on edge. 'If they do, I won't be trying to come back anyway!' She tossed her permed hair and bridled a little. 'Oh, we're going all right. No German's going to stop me going on holiday, I can tell you that.'

Jess looked at the Anderson shelter, hidden now beneath a hump of freshly dug earth. In some places, there'd been a lot of complaints about flooding but April Grove was lucky and the shelters remained dry. So far, anyway – nobody yet knew just what would happen when winter came and there was a lot of rain or snow. But Frank was going to concrete the floor to keep it dry and clean, and he'd said he'd build bunks against the walls. He'd got a hurricane lamp too and made a stout door from old planking.

'I can't imagine sleeping down there,' she said. 'I can't imagine what it'll be like – all of us huddled in a hole in the ground, listening to the German aeroplanes. It's like being in a cave.'

'Better get evacuated, then,' Ethel advised her. 'You're lucky – you can go.' She nodded towards the pram where baby Maureen lay fast asleep. 'I must say, you've bin clever about it. It's not often I've thought kids could come in useful but I wish I'd thought of having one.'

Jess stared at her. A sudden fury welled up inside her and she turned abruptly and wheeled the pram up the path towards the house. How could Ethel Glaister suggest – how could she even *think* – such a thing? That she and Frank had foreseen all this and deliberately set out to manufacture a baby – that *anyone* could even think of bringing a baby into the world as it was today, just for the sake of saving their own skins – why, it was disgusting!

Did other people think that too? Did those who thought she was too old to have a baby think that she'd had little Maureen just so that she could get special treatment if there should be a war?

If there should be a war . . . Jess looked up at the sky and thought, if there's a God up there, please, please stop it now. Please don't let it happen.

But as she walked on up the path, past the tomato plants and the flower patch where she grew peonies and pansies and dahlias, past the coal shed and in at the back door, she knew that it could happen. And – failing a miracle – almost certainly would.

3

'Tomorrow,' Jess said, staring at the front page of the *Evening News.* 'They're going to start it tomorrow. September the first.' She raised her eyes to Peggy Shaw's face. 'It's really going to happen, isn't it?'

Peggy looked at her pityingly. She was a thin, wiry little woman about the same age as Jess, full of bustling energy, always the first to volunteer to run a street party or jumble sale for some good cause. Her hair had been fair once, like Ethel Glaister's, but it had faded now to pepper and salt and her skin had faded with it to a papery pallor. She looked, Frank said, as if a puff of wind would blow her away, but there was a stalwartness about Peggy that had earned her the gratitude of many a neighbour with troubles to be shared.

She had no children of evacuation age – not that that made things any better, she thought with a clench of her heart. They were calling up twenty-year-olds now. Bob would be for the Navy within the year, if he had his way, and sailing off to God knew what. But still, you couldn't expect Jess Budd to be thinking of that just at the present.

'It's only a precaution,' she pointed out. 'Look, the headline says "War not regarded as inevitable". You'll just go off for a bit of a holiday in the countryside and be back before you know it.'

Jess looked at the newspaper again, and shook her head. Her face was white. She put out her hand and touched the handle of the pram that stood on the pavement outside the front door, where the two women were standing.

'I don't know what to do. If I go, who's to look after Frank? He's working all the hours there are, he can't come home and have to start cooking his own dinner.'

'There's canteen dinners,' Peggy said, but Jess snorted.

'Canteen dinners! You know what they're like. Anyway, he needs a meal when he comes in, he needs a bit of comfort to come home to. How can I go off to the country and leave him on his own? I know Annie'll do her best – but there's Mum and Dad too, she'll have to keep an eye on them. I feel awful, going off and leaving her to do everything.' She looked again at the pram, where baby Maureen, now two months old, slept peacefully. 'But I can't keep her here, poor little mite, if we do get bombed . . .'

They stood silent for a moment, contemplating a future neither could really imagine. Both had memories of the last great war, the war of 1914–18.

49

There had been bombing then, of London and the east coast. But now it was expected to happen over the whole country. Every city was a target, but especially those which were important to the war. Places where aeroplanes or munitions were made, and military or naval centres like Portsmouth.

Already the serene blue August sky was full of barrage balloons, floating like silver cigars above the city. What would it be like when it was dark with enemy aircraft, when death rained from the clouds?

'The school had another rehearsal on Monday,' Jess said. 'Our boys were full of it. They think it's all some big game. Can't wait to see the fighting.'

'That's boys all over. Our Bob's as bad. Talking about joining up, never mind waiting to be called. Down at the harbour every day watching the ships. They don't seem to realise.'

'If it was women ran the world,' Jess said, 'there wouldn't be any wars.' She put both hands on the pram handle. 'Well, I haven't got time to stand here. I've got to get the boys' clothes washed and ironed.'

'There'll be plenty as don't,' Peggy said. 'I bet old Granny Kinch wouldn't bother.'

'Is Micky going, then?' Jess was diverted momentarily. 'I thought Nancy wouldn't let him. Mind, she could go herself – she's got that baby, only four months old.'

Peggy laughed. 'And how's she going to earn a living, with no Dockyard nearby and no sailors? They might send Micky, but I wouldn't want the billeting of him, would you?' She looked at Jess. 'D'you want me to give Frank his dinner in the evenings?'

'That's good of you, but I daresay our Annie'll offer. She mentioned it the other day but I changed the subject. Daft, I know, but I just didn't want to think about it.' She looked at the newspaper again and sighed. 'Can't avoid it now, can I?'

'I see her Olive's young man's got a smart new car,' Peggy observed. 'How does your Annie feel about her going out with him?'

Jess smiled. 'Well, you know our Annie. She's always wanted to go up in the world. It suits her to have a nice red sports car standing at the door! I don't think Ted's quite so keen though, between you and me. He's like Frank, thinks people like us ought to know their place.'

'Go on!' Peggy said. 'There's nothing special about the Harkers. I knew old man Harker when I was a girl – his dad started the business from nothing. Jobbing brickie, that's all he was.'

'Well, they're something better than that now. Did you hear young Betty's got a boy, as well? Graham Philpotts. Elsie and Charlie's boy – used to live in September Street before they went over the water.'

Peggy sighed. 'All growing up, aren't they? Our Gladys is off with a different chap every week and young Diane looks like going the same way. I can't make up my mind if it's better that way or the other. At least they don't get too serious, but you can't help worrying about them, can you?' A piercing whistle sounded from inside the house and she tilted her head. 'That's my kettle boiling, I'd better go and get on with it.'

She went back indoors and Jess eased the pram through her own front door. There was scarcely room for it in the narrow passage but there was nowhere else for it to go. Maureen was still asleep, thank goodness. She went through the back room and out into the scullery to start the washing.

Luckily, there wasn't much. She'd done a good big wash on Monday and it was all dry and ironed now. There were just the things the boys had been wearing during the week – she'd have to do today's as soon as they went to bed and hope to goodness she could get them dry by morning.

There was plenty to do to have the three children ready and at school for seven next morning. But Rose would be a help. And the boys could be trusted to behave properly when they had to – not like Micky Baxter, up the road, who was always in mischief. Jess hoped that if he did go he wouldn't be billeted with Tim and Keith. He was a bad influence.

For the next couple of hours she was too busy to worry much about the future. Washing on a Thursday afternoon meant getting the copper heated up, something she normally only did on Mondays, and turning to with the washboard to scrub the boys' shirts. It wasn't only their things, either. If she was going too, Frank must be left with as many clean shirts as possible. And there were those trousers of his to be mended, and a pile of socks to be darned, and she'd better make some cakes to start him off with.

But what was going to happen to him when the sheets wanted changing again? And he'd worn more holes in his socks? And run out of cakes?

Jess stood at the sink, the washboard held in her left hand while she scrubbed with the right, and the tears came into her eyes and dripped on Keith's school shirt.

What was going to happen to her boys, sent to live with strangers? To herself and Rose and the baby? What was going to happen to the family she and Frank had made?

She thought of their Sunday walks together. She and Frank, walking side by side with the pram in front of them, Maureen's downy head on the pillow. Rose, a new ribbon in her shining hair, one hand on the pram as if it were her baby that chuckled at the clouds. The two boys running ahead – Tim's fair curls glinting in the sun, Keith's darker hair cut short and smooth. For Jess, it was one of the best times of the week, when she could look at her family with pride and satisfaction.

When would they be able to walk together again?

For weeks the papers and the wireless had been talking about evacuation. The children had been rehearsing at school, lining up with their gas masks and parading round the streets. War was 'not inevitable' but nobody could doubt that it was on the way. And now, surely, it must be close. Evacuation was no longer just a word. It was real and happening this morning.

By seven o'clock the school playgrounds were filled with children, some excited, some bewildered, some crying, others with set faces. Each one had a cardboard box containing a gas mask and a small case or satchel packed with clothes. Each had a packet of sandwiches and to this was added a large bar of chocolate and a bag of biscuits.

'Don't eat them now,' Tim's teacher admonished him as his eyes widened in delight at this unexpected treat. 'It's for later on.' She fastened a brown luggage label to his coat.

'Here, I'm not a parcel,' he protested, but when he tried to remove it she stopped him.

'It's so that we know who you are.'

'But you already know who I am. *I* know I am who I am.' He was indignant at being treated like a small child. But Miss Langrish took no notice. She went round all the children, fastening labels, straightening coats, wiping eyes and noses and getting them to stand in lines. Small children were allowed to stay with their older brother and sisters, and clung tightly to their hands. Friends huddled together, anxious not to be parted. Necks craned and eyes peered for a last glimpse of the parents who stood on the pavement outside the playground, watching helplessly as their children were taken out of their lives for who knew how long.

Most of the children wore their winter coats, even though it was only the first of September. It was cool enough at this hour of the morning, for it had rained in the night and large puddles lay on the ground. But as Jess had said to Frank that morning as he stood looking at their sleeping faces before setting off for work, you didn't know how long the kids were going to be away and they'd need warm clothes before they needed light ones.

'We don't even know where they're going,' Jess heard one woman say. 'How am I going to sleep tonight, not knowing where my little Alan is? How do I know they'll look after him?'

Jess was almost too exhausted to answer. She had been up all night getting things ready, and the baby had been fretful, needing several feeds. Dawn had come too soon and she didn't feel ready to face the day and its partings. The first of so many partings.

'He's only four,' the woman was saying. Tears were running down her face and her hands were bunching her pinafore up in front of her. 'It can't be right, sending away little ones like that. They're just babies.'

'His sister'll look after him,' Jess comforted. She knew the woman. Her name was Molly Atkinson and she lived in September Street; her husband and father-in-law ran the greengrocer's shop. 'Wendy'll take care of him.'

'But she's only eight herself. And what if they split them up?' Molly Atkinson's voice was rising. 'What if he loses his label and nobody knows who he is?' She stepped forward, thrusting herself through the crowd. 'I've changed my mind. I don't want him to go – not my little Alan – he's too young—'

'So's Martin.' Another woman was joining in, as if the panic were infectious. 'It's not right, sending them off like this.'

'They'll be safer in the country.' Jess wished she could believe it. Who was to say that bombs and gas attacks wouldn't happen everywhere? 'The teachers will look after them.'

'They need their mothers.' Martin Baker's mother turned and stared at her with angry misery. 'It's all right for you, Jess Budd, you're going too. You'll be out there with your kids, you'll know what's happening to them. You don't know what it's going to be like for us.'

I do, Jess wanted to cry, but she knew that Mary Baker wouldn't believe her. How *could* she know? How could anyone know, before it had happened? But she could see the pain in these mothers' faces, she could feel her own distress at watching her children leave, and she could imagine very well what the separation was going to mean to them.

Outside the playground were the buses which were going to take the children to the railway station. Their arrival seemed to make it all the more real. There had been rehearsals before, with the children lined up just as they were now, but never buses.

Jess looked at them miserably. She could understand Molly Atkinson's distress all too well. In a few minutes, her own three children would be on those buses, being whisked out of her sight.

For her, it was only a day or two and then she'd be evacuated to the same place herself. But for most of the women here, there was no knowing when they would see their children again.

'Where d'you think they'll go?' someone else asked. 'It said in the paper they'd be going to the Island.'

'Some of 'em will. Some are going to the New Forest, or Salisbury or Winchester way. We'll find out soon enough. Once they're there they can send postcards home, see, then we'll know.'

'But my Alan can't write!' Molly Atkinson had been turned back from the school gates. 'How can he send a postcard?'

'Wendy will,' Jess said. 'Wendy'll look after him, you'll see. She's a sensible girl.'

She watched the crowd of children in the playground. They were growing restless and beginning to break out of the lines into which the teachers had formed them, shouting to make themselves heard over the hubbub. It would be better if they could just go now, she thought. This waiting was awful for everyone.

The crowd outside was constantly shifting as mothers tried to push nearer the railings for a last shouted message. Molly Atkinson was standing by one of the horse-chestnut trees that grew at the edge of the pavement. One hand clenched against the bark, the other pressed against her mouth.

Jess found herself next to a man. She recognised him as a milkman who would normally have been trundling his electric milk-cart around the streets at this times. She looked for his wife, then remembered she'd heard she was ill.

'Is your little girl going this morning?' she asked, and he nodded. His eyes were fixed on the crowd beyond the railings. Jess noticed his face looked puffy.

She racked her brains for his wife's name. She'd known her slightly at school, but she'd been several years younger. Margaret, was it? Maggie?

'How's Madge?' she asked as the name slipped back into her mind. 'I heard she was ill.'

He looked at her for a brief moment and she read the message a split second before he answered her. There was just time to wish she hadn't asked, to hope he wouldn't answer, but it was too late.

'She died on Monday,' he said flatly. 'The funeral's today.'

'*Today*? But—' She stared at the playground full of children, then looked back at the man's face. There was no expression there; it was as if he had been carved from stone. 'But—' And there was nothing to say. No words to express her feelings.

'She's better off out of it,' he said drearily. 'No mother to look after her. And I'm no good. Better out of it.'

His eyes were red with tears. Jess reached out and laid her hand on his arm. She wanted to offer comfort but felt totally helpless. What could you say to a man who had just lost his wife and was about to lose his child? What comfort was there for him?

She saw him peer again into the milling crowd of children, now being formed yet again into their ranks. Could he see his own daughter there? Or had she disappeared into the throng? Jess looked into his face, seeing the pain behind the stony mask, in the reddened eyes. From here he must go to bury his wife. How could he bear it?

A little girl broke free from her line and ran to the railing. She clutched one iron bar in each hand and peered through the gap. Her plaits, clumsily tied with inexperienced hands, were already coming undone and her face streamed with tears.

'Daddy! Daddy!' She saw the milkman and stretched both hands through in entreaty. 'Daddy, I want to come home. I don't want to go. *I want my Mummy!*'

The milkman stared at her. He took a step towards the railings. But before he could reach them a harassed teacher scooped up the child and carried her none too gently back to her place in the line.

'You just stand there, Susan Cullen, and don't dare move again. We're starting now and I don't want any more nonsense from any of you.'

The milkman stopped in his tracks. He stared, baffled, at the lines of children, at his weeping daughter. And then a whistle blew and the children began to move.

Suddenly silent, they filed out of the school yard and on to the pavement. The crowd of parents fell back to give them room. Led by their teachers, the children climbed aboard the buses and could be seen finding seats, arguing over them, squashing together and pressing their faces to the windows.

Susan Cullen had disappeared. So had little Alan and his sister Wendy. Jess saw Rose shepherd a group of smaller girls aboard, while Tim and Keith scampered up the stairs to the top deck. She found that her own hands were pressed against her mouth, just like Molly Atkinson's, and she felt her teeth dig into her knuckles.

Molly Atkinson suddenly let go of her tree and ran after the bus, screaming for her baby, her Alan, to be let off, he was too young to be sent away, too young to leave home. A few other mothers, crying themselves, caught her arms and held her back, huddling together to share their grief. Their weeping released the tears of others and there were few mothers in the crowd who did not have wet faces as they watched the buses move away down the road.

But Sam Cullen, the milkman, said nothing. His face grim, he turned away and marched from the school without glancing back, on his way to bury his wife.

*

Some of the mothers went to the station to see the children off on the trains, but Jess had no heart for it. The baby was due for a feed and in any case the buses were all being used to transport the children and blind people who were being evacuated that day. She could not walk with the pram all the way down to the Town station and she didn't think most of the mothers would get there before the trains left. Besides, as Frank had said, the more people there were milling about, the more difficult it was for those who were organising it all.

She went back to April Grove. The streets seemed unnaturally quiet now that the children were gone. It was eight o'clock and most of them would have been at home anyway, getting ready for school – but still you could tell somehow that they weren't there any more. It was like that old story of the Pied Piper of Hamelin, she thought. This is what it must have been like then. A town with no children in it. Dead.

She felt a sudden surge of bitterness towards the man who had made this necessary, the small, commonplace house-painter who wanted to take over Europe. What right had he to do this? How had he ever been allowed to grasp the power to ruin so many people's lives? Even if they come back tomorrow, she thought, the damage will have been done. Those tiny children, torn away from their mums and dads, without any idea why. The milkman's little girl crying for her dead mummy. Molly Atkinson's Alan, frightened and alone but for his sister – and she only eight years old herself.

There must be thousands like them. Little children, the first victims of a war they're still saying isn't inevitable. Their little minds and hearts have been hurt already and nobody will ever be able to make them better.

As she walked down October Street, she could see old Mrs Kinch standing at her doorway. Mrs Kinch wasn't really that old – probably in her early sixties – but she was known to most of the people along the street as Granny Kinch. Her house was number 10, looking straight up October Street, and she spent hours either sitting on a chair or standing in the doorway, watching all that went on.

'Gone off, have they?' she asked as Jess came nearer. 'I saw you going, not long after your Frank went to work.'

My God, Jess thought, does she stand there all night as well? 'Yes,' she said, 'the whole school's evacuated. I don't think many people have kept their children at home.'

'I suppose you'll be going too, seeing as you've got a baby,' the old woman said, looking at the pram. She was wearing a pinafore with a faded pattern of flowers, over a skirt and blouse of indeterminate brown, and her thin grey hair was as usual tightly wound in curlers. To Jess's knowledge, nobody had ever seen her without these curlers.

'She's saving her beauty for Nancy's wedding,' Tommy Vickers had once said and everyone had laughed, though the women tried to look disapproving.

'Will your Nancy be going?' she asked. Nancy's baby Vera had been born two months before Maureen, just after Portsmouth's famous football triumph. Nobody had asked who the father was, though it was known that Nancy had registered her in the name of Baxter. That was the name of the husband no one in the street had ever seen. He was supposed to be in the Navy, his ship based in Plymouth, and when Nancy went off for the occasional weekend Mrs Kinch let it be known that they were together.

'And the band played, "Believe it if you like",' Tommy Vickers commented again, sarcastically.

Once again the women tutted and tittered, but they all knew he was right. Where Nancy had got the name Baxter was a mystery – perhaps she had once been married and perhaps ten-year-old Micky really was legitimate – but where she got baby Vera was all too easy to see.

As Peggy said, how would she earn her living far away from the Dockyard gate?

'My Nancy?' Granny Kinch said. 'No – she wouldn't go and leave her old ma. She's not letting our Micky go either. No, we sticks together. We've got our shelter down the garden if the bombs come. We'll be snug enough down there.'

Jess looked at Granny Kinch, standing there in her old flowered apron and curlers. Some of the children called her a witch, but the old woman was good-hearted enough. She would bring out a bag of toffees sometimes and get the children to gather round before scattering them over their heads. It was a shame Nancy had gone the way she had, and that Micky was growing up a bad lot.

All the same, Jess envied her. War might come to Portsmouth but Granny Kinch wasn't going to be separated from her loved ones. She would have them with her in the house or in the shelter, day and night. She would know what was happening to them.

'You look done up,' the old woman said suddenly. 'Why don't you go and have a cuppa with your sister?'

'I was going to,' Jess said. 'But it's not long gone eight. I can't knock on her door at this hour. They'll all be getting ready to go to work.'

'Course you can,' Granny Kinch said. 'What's a family for? And she'll have a pot on the go, bound to. You go along and see.'

Jess thought of her own house, empty and too quiet. The old woman was right. Annie would welcome her and it didn't matter that the house would be in turmoil with the girls tripping over each other to get out.

'Well, if you don't want to go into your sister's yet,' Mrs Kinch said, 'why not come in and have a cup with me? Our Nancy's not back from work yet and I've had the kettle on this past half-hour, waiting for her. It's brewed and I reckon you could do with it.'

Jess hesitated. What would people say if they saw her going into Granny Kinch's house? What would Frank say? And suddenly she didn't care. She didn't want to go back to the empty house, with all its reminders that her children had left it. And neither did she want to go to Annie's – not just yet, with everyone scrambling to get ready for work. She needed somewhere to sit and catch her breath, with someone sympathetic, and as she looked up at Granny Kinch in her faded apron and curlers, she knew that this was her unlikely haven.

'All right, I will,' she said, and parked the pram outside the door.

Maureen would be all right there, fast asleep. She followed the old woman into the house.

Jess had never been in number 10 before. The residents of April Grove weren't given to popping in and out of each other's homes, unless they were friends or had some reason to call. And nobody called on Granny Kinch and Nancy. You didn't need to, after all – the old woman was always at her door.

The passage was dark and musty. The sun came up at the back of April Grove, filling the back rooms with light but leaving the fronts dim. In number 14 it would be pouring through a shining window, making the mirror and the polished wood of the piano gleam. But here in number 10 the sunlight was dusty, filled with drifting motes, and the room wasn't comfortably, if shabbily, furnished like her own, but almost bare, with no rug on the floor and only a couple of old armchairs with sagging seats, and four kitchen chairs round a table covered with American cloth.

An old pram stood in the corner and Vera, Nancy's baby, lay snuffling in her sleep. Jess stopped to peep in and was disturbed by the baby's appearance. She wasn't plump-cheeked and rosy like her own Maureen, but pale and wizened, as if she had been born old.

'Beautiful, ain't she?' Granny Kinch said proudly. 'And good as gold. Never keeps me awake at night while our Nancy's at work.' She busied herself in the little scullery, bringing the kettle to the boil again and making tea in a brown pot.

'Nancy's job's all right, then?' Jess hardly knew how to put it, but she had to keep up the fiction that Nancy had a proper job. The story was that she worked in a posh hotel at night, cleaning the shoes left outside rooms by the guests and polishing silver, but nobody believed it. Nancy Baxter had been seen too many times hanging around the Dockyard gates or walking up Queen Street on the arm of some sailor.

'Oh yes. She might be getting promotion soon. Reception work.' Mrs Kinch set out two cups and saucers. One of the cups was cracked and the saucers didn't match. She fetched a bottle of milk from outside and poured some into the cups, then filled them with strong tea. 'Here you are, duck, this'll make you feel better.'

Jess sipped the brew. It was hot and sweet and although she didn't normally take sugar she found it heartening. She smiled at Granny Kinch. Maybe they were all wrong about Nancy after all. Maybe she really did work nights in a hotel. She heard Tommy Vickers' voice inside her head. 'And the band played . . .' and stifled a sudden giggle.

Perhaps the truth was that it didn't really matter what Nancy did, so long as she wasn't hurting anyone else. After all, what was she doing other than giving a few poor lonely sailors a bit of comfort? Was that really so bad, when you thought of what other people were doing – marching into other countries, persecuting and killing people who'd never done any harm, sending little children away from their parents without even time to say goodbye . . . ?

Jess's face crumpled. She put her cup on the table and bent forwards, covering her face with her hands, and burst into tears.

Granny Kinch sat quietly beside her. She didn't tell Jess not to cry, she didn't tell her it was all for the best, she didn't say the children would be better off where they were going. She simply waited for the storm to subside, offering no comfort other than a touch on Jess's shoulder. Perhaps, thought Jess as she found a hanky and wiped her eyes, she knew that there was no comfort, for the wounds were too deep. And it wasn't only her own wounds she was crying for, but the wounds of the children, of little Susan Cullen with her clumsy plaits, motherless and now fatherless, of Alan Atkinson, still little more than a baby and his sister Wendy carrying responsibilities too heavy for an eight-year-old to bear.

Haltingly, she tried to explain some of this to the old woman, and the grey head with its tight steel curlers nodded.

'You're right. It shouldn't be happening. It ain't natural, sending little 'uns away from their mums. They oughter be in their own 'omes. 'Ow do they know they're ever going to come 'ome again? 'Ow does any of us know? Families oughter stick together, that's what I say.'

'I think so too,' Jess said, grateful to have found someone at last who understood and agreed with her. 'But my Frank says they'll be better off in the country and I must say I don't want them here if we're bound to get bombed.'

'But you're going too, ain't you? You've got a baby.'

'Yes. I'll be with Rose and the boys won't be far away. But it isn't the same as being at home. And Frank's got to stay here.' She looked at Mrs Kinch and her eyes filled with tears again. 'I don't want to leave him any more than I want to be parted from the children.'

'Well, it ain't going to be easy for none of us,' the old woman said. 'And we all has to decide for ourselves.' She lifted her head. 'Is that our Nancy coming? I'd better get the kettle on again.'

Jess wiped her eyes again and blew her nose. She felt suddenly embarrassed to be sitting here. Like most women in the street, Jess didn't have much to do with Nancy. She passed the time of day with her, of course, but she could never forget the younger woman's reputation, and the thought of the way she earned her living nagged at the back of her mind. It was as if she knew more than she wanted to know about Nancy's private life. And the arrival of baby Vera, with no father, confirmed her guilty knowledge.

Granny Kinch didn't seem bothered, however. Whatever she said to Nancy in private, she had outwardly accepted the baby as her legitimate granddaughter, the child of that mysterious, high-ranking naval officer, and even thought the wizened little creature beautiful.

She bustled about, making fresh tea and frying bacon and eggs. Jess's eyes opened wide. Bacon and eggs on a weekday! It was more than Frank and she could afford. But perhaps that was where Nancy's money went, instead of on furniture. And even if it wasn't Jess's way, who was to say it was wrong?

The door from the passage opened and Nancy came in. She grinned at Jess and shrugged out of her red jacket. She wore a bright yellow frock underneath, too skimpy for September and with half its buttons undone to show a lot of chest. She had no stockings on and there was still a smudge of lipstick on her thin lips.

'Hullo, Jess,' she said. 'I knew you were here, saw Maureen in her pram outside. She looks as if she's thriving.'

'So does your Vera,' Jess said politely, though privately she thought Nancy's baby a skinny little thing. But maybe she just took after her mother, for no one could call Nancy voluptuous. She was a thin, angular woman, who looked older than her thirty-odd years, with gaunt features and sharp bones. Not at all the sort you'd expect to find luring sailors up the primrose path. But as Tommy Vickers had once remarked, all cats were grey in the dark.

Nancy dropped her jacket on a chair and flung herself down in another. As her mother placed a cup of tea and a plate of bacon and eggs before her, she dragged a crumpled packet of Woodbines from her pocket and lit one. She smoked, ate and drank alternately, talking through whatever happened to be in her mouth at the time.

'Thought I'd never get home this morning, Ma. There's not a bus to be had anywhere. They're taking all the children off on this evacuation lark. Droves of 'em, full of kids, going to the railway stations.' She looked at Jess. 'Your lot gone?'

Jess nodded. She wanted to cry again but Nancy's casual talk wasn't like her mother's sympathy.

'I won't let Micky go. You don't know what'll happen to 'em, out there in the country. Farmers treating 'em like slaves, posh lah-di-dah women turning the girls into servants. I'd rather have him with me, where I know what's happening to him.'

'But what about school?' Jess asked. 'Is there anywhere for him to go? All the teachers have gone away.'

Nancy shrugged. 'School!' she said scornfully. 'What good's school ever been to my Micky? They've never liked him, they're always picking on him – anything goes wrong and it's my Mick gets the blame. He's well out of it. He knows as much as he's ever likely to learn from teachers and he'll be old enough in a few years to leave and start earning a living. Till then, he might as well make himself useful at home. He can always do odd jobs, run errands and that.'

'There's a couple of teachers left anyway,' Mrs Kinch put in. 'They're 'aving classes as someone's house. Coming once a week and giving the kids 'omework, for what good that'll do.'

Nancy finished her breakfast and leaned back, lighting another cigarette. She looked at Jess through the smoke and spoke again, her voice softened.

'I bet you're not feeling so good, sending your kids off?'

Jess was too surprised to prevaricate. 'No, I'm not. It's silly because I'll be seeing them tomorrow, but – well, it seems as if everything's crumbling away. I don't feel as if I can get hold of things any more.'

Nancy nodded. 'I know. It's a bad business.' She smoked for a minute or two in silence and then said, 'Look, if there's anything you want done while you're gone – I mean, for your Frank—' And before Jess could speak, she went on quickly, 'And I don't mean the obvious! I'm not after your man, that's not my style. I've got my work and it's just a job to me, and when I come home I don't want more of the same, no more'n anyone else. But I don't mind doing a bit of cooking or washing and I've got time to go in and clean up a bit if you like. But I won't do it if you don't. I'm not going behind your back.'

Jess was touched. It was clear that Nancy's offer was genuine and that she had no ulterior motive. Come to think of it, it made sense that she wouldn't have. As she had just said, she got enough of that sort of thing on her nightly excursions to the 'hotel', she wasn't likely to want to start all over again when she got home, and for nothing too!

'That's nice of you,' she said. 'I expect Annie will be keeping an eye on Frank. But I'll tell him you offered.'

Nancy nodded. 'We got to stick together in this lot,' she said. 'But I don't want no trouble. People writing letters to you and that sort of thing. It's got to be above board.'

She saw Jess to the door, then came back to her mother and poured another cup of tea.

'Jess Budd looks worn out.' She lifted the baby from her pram and rocked her for a few minutes. A half-empty bottle stood on the table and she stuck the teat in Vera's mouth, then picked up the Woodbine packet. 'Only one left! I'll have to go up the street, get some more.' She found the box of matches and lit up again. 'Mind, I reckon everyone is this morning. I've never seen anything like it – all them kids going off to God knows where. Half of 'em crying their eyes out, the rest looking as if they don't know what's happening to 'em. Don't reckon they do, either, poor little sods. I mean, how d'you tell a kiddy of four about the war? They must wonder what on earth it's all about.'

'You 'aven't changed your mind, then?' her mother asked. 'About our Micky, I mean?'

'Nah. Don't see no point. Anyway, he'd hate it in the country.' Nancy glanced around the room. 'Where is the little tyke, anyway?'

'Got up and went out early. Down to the station, I expect, to say goodbye to his pals. He might get a bit fed up 'ere on 'is own, Nance.'

'We'll find him plenty to do. And he can run errands for people – there'll be plenty who miss their own kids to send to the shops. Our Mick will earn hisself a bit of pocket-money.' Vera finished the milk and whimpered, a thin little cry. Nancy held her against her shoulder, rubbing the baby's back. 'Anyway, he's not the only one stopping. Young Joy Brunner from up the road, she ain't going either.'

'Well, I'm not surprised. Her dad must be worried stiff, and Alice too. I'm surprised he ain't bin took away already. Ain't they supposed to be putting all them whatjercallits, aliens, inside?'

'That's what I thought but he's still around. Still, war ain't bin declared yet, has it, and maybe it still won't be.' Nancy finished her cigarette and laid the baby back in the pram. She stood up, stretching her thin body. 'I'm just going up for some more fags, Ma, and then I'll get a couple of hours' kip. I feel proper done up. It upset me a bit, seeing all them kids being took off.'

Granny Kinch nodded. She found her brown coat and put it on to accompany her daughter to the door. It was well after breakfast-time now and the street would be coming to life. All the other women who had seen their children off on evacuation would be coming out again, their tears dried, ready to compare notes and share each other's troubles, and Granny Kinch didn't want to miss it.

'You go on,' she said. 'You needs your sleep. I'll take care of the baby and keep Micky quiet when he comes home.'

She stood at the door, watching her daughter walk up October Street. There were plenty of women about, standing in little groups, but none of them did more than give a brief nod of good morning. But Nancy's back was straight and she walked past them all like a queen, her head held high in the air.

That's right, Granny Kinch thought, you keep your head up, my girl. You're as good as them any day. And there's not a bloody one of them would do any different, if they'd been handed your plate of luck.

It was a pity they wouldn't be more friendly, though. They were, she knew, good enough at heart. It was just that they couldn't forget what Nancy did to earn her living.

Still, maybe this war would bring people together a bit more. Maybe it had already started, with Jess Budd coming in for a cup of tea this morning. Maybe number 10 would be what Granny Kinch had always wanted it to be – a place where people came for a talk, to get things sorted out in their minds, to let off steam and have a bit of a cry and a bit of a laugh.

That was what everyone needed, after all. It was as simple as that.

Meanwhile, Jess pushed Maureen's pram thoughtfully up the road to Annie's house. Once again, she wondered if they were right to look down on Nancy. She might not be much to look at and her way of life not what Jess would want but, like her mother, she was good hearted. And who knew why she'd started to live the way she did? It hadn't been easy these past few years to get jobs and earn a living, especially for a woman on her own with a baby.

Annie and Ted's address was really March Street, but their house was separated from the terrace. It was detached and had its own small garden all around it. It faced down April Grove and the side windows looked out over the allotments. But most interesting of all, it had a small tower at one side with a top just like a castle. The rooms inside this turret were not much more than cupboards but Annie's eldest, Colin, had had the upstairs one as his bedroom ever since they'd moved there, and had been the envy of all his friends. Jess could remember him as a small boy, spending hours on the top with a home-made bow and arrow, until he'd knocked a neighbour's cat off a wall. The neighbour had been furious, Ted had given Colin a good hiding and after that bows and arrows were banned from the turret.

Jess wheeled the pram along the side passage and parked it beside the back door. She could hear voices inside. The girls hadn't yet left for work.

'If I've told you once, I've told you a dozen times, our Betty,' Annie was saying, 'you've got to wash your stockings out yourself. I'm not doing them for you, a great girl of eighteen like you. And if you haven't got any clean, it's your own lookout. Who's that at the door?' She looked round, her morning face shiny under curlers and hair-net, as Jess knocked and pushed the door open. 'Here, it's our Jess. Come in, love, and sit down. Push the cat off that chair. Olive, get your auntie a cup.'

Her own cares were forgotten at once. She dropped the stockings she was holding and came over to her sister, enveloping her in a hug. Jess quivered for a moment. She'd thought she'd got over this at Granny Kinch's but the emotions she was feeling that morning were too strong to be dealt with so quickly, and once again she burst into tears.

'That's it, that's right,' Annie crooned, rocking her gently. 'You have a good cry, love. Let it all out. It'll do you good. Better out than in, that's what I always say. You'll feel better soon.'

Jess wept against her sister's breast. Annie hadn't held her like this since she was a little girl. But she was glad enough now to rest in the comforting warmth of her sister's arms and be a little girl again for a while.

'I don't know why I'm being so silly,' she said at last, sitting up a little straighter and finding her hanky again. It was still wet from the tears she'd shed in Granny Kinch's back room. 'I'm going myself tomorrow. I'll see them then. Some people don't know when they're going to see their children again. But – I don't know, watching them go off like that—'

'It's made it all seem real, all of a sudden,' Annie said. 'That's what it is. I mean, we've got used to all the talk – it's been going on for years. But lately, what with the Andersons coming and the shelters in the street, and the blackout—'

'The blackout!' Jess said. 'It took Frank and me hours to get the back bedroom one right. He's made wooden frames with blackout material on them, to fit in the windows, and try as we would there was a tiny chink of light showing through the back one. I didn't think it'd matter, being at the back, I mean, who's going to see it there, but no, it had got to be right. Germans might see it from aeroplanes, he said, and he had to take it all to pieces and start again.' She looked at her sister. 'D'you think he's right, Annie? Can they see little bits of light like that from aeroplanes?'

Annie shrugged. 'If they say so, I s'pose it must be right. Anyway, if everyone had a little bit of light showing—'

'That's what Frank says. There'd be no point in a blackout at all. We've all got to do our bit, same as everything else.' She sighed and sipped at the cup of tea Olive had put in front of her. 'I don't know, Annie. I don't know what the world's coming to. And when I think we've just had a baby – I mean, what a time to bring a baby into the world. What a time!' Her face puckered again. Olive and Betty, ready to go to work, hovered uncertainly by the table and their mother nodded at them.

'You two go off or you'll be late.' She watched them go and sighed. 'I know, Jess. It don't seem any time for young people now. You just wonder what they've got in front of them, don't you? Babies or girls like our Olive and Betty. And as for the boys—' She shuddered.

Jess was immediately filled with guilt. 'Annie, I'm sorry. Here I am, thinking only of myself and you must be worried sick. Where's Colin now?'

'Somewhere at sea, that's all we know. They don't tell you now and we don't get many letters. Thank God he's not on submarines like Cliff Barker round June Close, that's what I keep telling myself. When I think of those poor devils on the *Thetis* . . .'

The two women sat in silence for a few minutes. The sinking of the *Thetis* had been like a shadow from the future. In wartime there would be not one but many ships and submarines sent to the bottom. And what efforts could be made to save their crews while battle raged overhead?

'I'd better go,' Jess said at last. 'The baby's due for a feed and I've still got a lot to do if I'm going tomorrow.'

'You haven't changed your mind?' Annie looked at her anxiously. 'You ought to be out of it, Jess, with the baby.'

'I know – but I hate leaving Frank. He's got so much to do, and I'm afraid he won't feed himself properly or do his washing—'

'Well, that's no problem,' Annie said briskly. 'He can come here for his supper and I'll do his bits of washing along with ours. After all, I've got two great girls to help me and only Ted to look after now. You don't need to go worrying about Frank, Jess.'

'Oh, Annie.' Jess's eyes filled with tears. 'That takes a real weight off my mind. I didn't like to ask, what with Mum and Dad to look after as well, but—'

'You didn't have to,' her sister said. 'We're family, aren't we? Well, then, we help out. Frank'll be all right, you see. Now you go back and get yourself ready. A bit of country air'll do you good. You still haven't got over having the baby, you know.'

Jess smiled and went out to the pram. Maureen was beginning to stir and the two women bent over the pram.

'Look at her,' Annie said. 'Don't know a thing about it all. Best time of their lives, if they only knew it. Well, I'd better get on, I'm all behind like a donkey's tail and it's my day for cleaning the windows today.'

She went back indoors and Jess wondered just what it would take to persuade Annie to deviate from her routine. Washing on Monday, ironing on Tuesday, windows Friday . . . even Hitler would have his work cut out to stop Annie from keeping her house as she thought it should be kept.

She wheeled the pram down the back alley and up the narrow garden path. The tomatoes were ripening and spiders' webs shimmered between the rows. The few dahlias she liked to grow at the top of the garden glowed like jewels in the morning sun.

She parked the pram outside the scullery door and glanced into the little shed where they kept coal and the bits and pieces there was no room for indoors.

Keith's scooter was leaning against the wall. And beside it, looking rather soft, lay the football Tim had been given for his last birthday.

Without warning, the tears began to flow again. And as Jess fed the baby they dripped salt on to her breast and on to the baby's face, like a rain that would not stop.

For Tim and Keith, evacuation began like a holiday.

Their experience of travel was limited to a few day trips to London, where Jess had relatives. But even that was more than many of the children had. Some had never been on a train at all. And the reality of being suddenly taken away from home was beginning to sink in now that they had actually said goodbye to their parents. All at once, it was no longer a rehearsal.

They filed down the platform in subdued silence. A few mothers had managed to get to the station in time to wave goodbye, but the children were half-dazed by the suddenness of it all, by the early hour and the tears that had already been shed. They looked around uncertainly and those who did spot their mothers in the small crowd by the gates began to cry. The teachers ushered them through the gates and on to the trains. There was no time now for farewells.

Tim and Keith kept together. Rose, in the top class, had been told to look after some of the younger children. In any case, she wasn't likely to be put in the same billet as them. It had already been arranged that, if possible, she would be placed with someone prepared to take Jess and the baby as well. Nobody was likely to have room for the whole family.

'Why not?' Keith asked again as they stood on the platform. 'People have big houses in the country. Farms are big. We could sleep in a barn. I'd like that.'

Tim shrugged. 'I don't care where we sleep. It's going to be fun – milking cows, helping with the chickens and all. Like that day Dad took us over the hill and we met that farmer and helped make hay. We'll be farmers' boys.'

A red-haired boy standing nearby sneered.

'Farmers' boys! You couldn't milk a cow!'

Tim turned at once. Brian Collins was in his class, though nearly a year older, and never missed a chance to get at the Budd brothers.

'Bet I could, then.'

'Couldn't.'

'Could.'

The two boys scowled at each other and fists were being raised when Mr Wain, the headmaster, came along and separated them with a firm hand on their shoulders. 'Now then, boys, there's enough fighting already without you two starting your own private war. Get on the train and behave yourselves. Is that your gas mask, Tim?'

Tim looked at the cardboard box lying perilously near the edge of the platform and grabbed it quickly. The knot must have come undone – or been untied. He glared at Brian Collins but the red-haired boy was already on the train, and by the time Tim and Keith had scrambled aboard they found themselves crammed into a separate compartment. It was full of heaving bodies, but by dint of much pushing and shoving they managed to secure two window seats and sat back, well pleased with themselves.

The train pulled out of the station. The children stared out of the windows as the streets and houses of Portsmouth passed slowly by, looking oddly unfamiliar. Fratton. Copnor. Farlington . . . Somewhere was their own house, over the allotments, but it was gone before they could pinpoint it. They stared out, disappointed, and Tim realised that he had been hoping for a last glimpse of Mum, perhaps waving from the back bedroom window. His eyes blurred and he blinked rapidly and brushed his sleeve across his face, hoping no one had noticed.

They were in real countryside now, passing fields with cows in and small villages. His brief misery passing, Tim leaned forward for a better look.

'Where d'you think we're going?' Keith asked. He had already asked a dozen times, but no one had known, not even his parents. It seemed queer to think of going away somewhere, in a train, with all his clothes packed in a case and not even Mum and Dad knowing where he would sleep that night. How would they find out? he wondered. Would someone remember to tell them? Suppose they didn't? Suppose he and Tim got lost somewhere and nobody knew? Panic caught his breath and he looked wide-eyed at his brother.

'The teachers'll know,' Tim said. 'They'll tell us when to get off. And then people will come and choose us to go and live with them. Farmers and people like that.'

But his voice didn't sound quite so confident as it had before and Keith saw him look quickly out of the window again. His mouth looked tight, as if he didn't want to talk any more, and although Keith was longing to ask yet again where Tim thought they might be going, he bit the question back and stared out of the window too. His chubby face was pale and he wondered if he was going to have one of his tummy-aches.

The train was gathering speed now. It raced on through an endless succession of fields and woods. All at once, the country seemed to be a very big place.

Nobody was quiet for long, however. The first parting over, the children began to recover. Paper bags were opened and sandwiches, intended for dinner, quickly eaten. The bags of biscuits and bars of chocolate, which someone had told them were to give to their new families, were also broken into. Wrappers lay on the floor or were tossed out of the window, and scuffles broke out. Smaller children began to snivel and one was sick. Fortunately, one of the bigger girls realised in time and held the child up at the window, but the view was spoiled for Tim for the rest of the journey.

Shrugging, he took a crumpled copy of *Dandy* from his pocket and began to read. He was soon engrossed in a story of Desperate Dan, and oblivious of the noise going on around him.

Keith sat staring at the countryside. Most of the trees were still green but a few were beginning to show touches of gold and brown. He still felt peculiar in his stomach, half excited, half frightened. The vomit on the window made him want to be sick himself and he looked away from it. He wondered what Mum was doing now, and how the baby was.

Maureen's arrival had come as a complete surprise to all three of the Budd children. Nobody had even hinted to them that there was a new baby on the way. It wasn't the kind of thing that was discussed in front of children and although they'd noticed that their mother had grown rather fat, they had no idea what it meant.

The night before Maureen had arrived, they had all been sent up to Auntie Annie's to stay. Mummy was feeling poorly, they'd been told, and sure enough as they set off along the pavement carrying their pyjamas and toothbrushes, they'd seen the doctor's car come down the road. Rose had been frightened and wanted to go back home, but Auntie Annie had told them there was nothing to worry about. And Uncle Ted had taken them up on to the roof of the turret and let them play at castles.

Next morning, when they'd gone home and found Mum in bed with the new baby beside her, they'd been totally bewildered.

'But where did she come from?' Keith kept asking, but no one could tell him. Rose blushed and looked embarrassed and Tim was thoughtful for the rest of the day, as if trying to work out some difficult sum, but Keith could see they didn't really know. And the story that she'd been found under a gooseberry bush on the allotment sounded much too far-fetched. He'd gone to look and found the Dinky car he'd lost a fortnight before, still there, and the ground obviously not disturbed.

Having a new baby in the house was strange and exciting but he wasn't sure he really liked it that much. It was quite fun to see her being bathed but none of them, not even Rose who seemed to think the baby was hers as much as Mum's, liked the nappy-changing business. He liked cuddling her, especially now she'd started to smile, but he didn't like the way Mum kept disappearing upstairs to feed her. What was so secret about a baby being fed? Again, Rose looked embarrassed when he asked, but Keith was more concerned about himself than about actual information. Until now, he'd always been the 'baby' of the family and now he was supposed suddenly to be grown up. And Mum just didn't have so much time for him any more. Babies, it seemed, needed a lot of attention.

And now Mum was home alone with Maureen. He knew she was supposed to be coming next day, but suppose she didn't? Nothing seemed as safe now as it had once been, and he felt as if he was treading on the cakewalk he and Tim had once been on in a fairground, where the floor had shifted under their feet. It had been funny then but now all he wanted was to be on firm ground again, where you knew what was going to happen next, where babies didn't arrive overnight and families could stay at home together.

The train slowed down. It was running alongside a platform and after a moment it came to a halt. Teachers began to walk along the corridor, poking their heads into the compartments to tell the children to get their things ready, and there was a general scramble to collect up belongings.

'Keep hold of my coat,' Tim ordered his brother as they pushed their way off the train. 'Mum said we'd got to stay together. And try to get near Rose.'

It was only afternoon but the children were tired, hungry and thirsty. They had all been up early, most had eaten their sandwiches long before dinner-time, and they were grubby from the sooty smoke that had poured in through the open windows. They stood dispiritedly on the platform, waiting to be told what to do.

'Form up into twos,' Miss Langrish told them. 'We're going to the village hall. You'll be given your billets there.' She came along the platform, urging the children to line up. Some of the smallest were crying again but she had no time to comfort them. With the other teachers, she got them into some kind of order and they trailed out of the little station and down the lane.

Already, everything was strange. Tim and Keith had seen the countryside before, for Frank Budd was a countryman at heart and had taken his children out at weekends, but some of them had never even walked along a country lane. Two or three fell into the ditch before they had even turned the corner and they stared doubtfully at the hedges and even more uncertainly through the gates into fields full of cows.

Before they could comment, however, they were at the village hall and they found a gathering awaiting them. It seemed the whole village had turned out to welcome the newcomers, but the welcome was a variable one.

'They don't look too clean, do they,' one woman sniffed, giving Tim and Keith a disparaging glance.

'Well, they've come a long way, and you know what trains are.' Her friend was obviously more disposed to make allowances. 'The little fair-haired one's got a nice face.'

'Looks cheeky to me. Bet he's into everything,' Which Tim had to admit was true. He was insatiably curious and forever getting his fingers slapped for poking them into things that didn't concern him. But it was interesting to know how things worked, he argued when his father found him with the alarm clock strewn in bits over the dining-table. And he was still quite sure he'd have been able to put it together again, if he'd only been allowed.

The hall was set out with long tables on which stood big jugs of lemonade and plates of buns. The children's eyes brightened. Some of them made a dash for the tables and began cramming food into their mouths. Others, like Tim and Keith, held back a bit and then realised that if they didn't look out for themselves, no one else would, and joined in the rush.

'Manners!' A big woman in a tweed suit was standing arms akimbo at the head of the tables. 'There's no need to grab. There's enough for everyone.'

The children evidently didn't believe her and, from the way some were tearing at the food, it seemed they had justification. Brian Collins had already filled his pockets, and two thin, ragged little girls from Newbury Street who probably hadn't had any breakfast and no lunch other than the packet of biscuits and bar of chocolate that had been issued to each child, were fighting with a bigger boy over a whole plate of buns. The plate crashed to the floor as the tweedy woman spoke. Shards of broken crockery sprayed themselves about the children's feet and some of the buns were trampled on before they could be picked up.

'Children! Children!' Miss Langrish was amongst them, her face weary and harassed. 'How dare you behave like this. You're no better than a pack of wild animals. What would your mothers and fathers say? Now, calm down at once and get into your lines. At *once*.'

Mr Wain was there too, his face thunderous, twitching his cane against his thigh. The boys saw and understood at once, and all but the most rebellious fell back. There were not many boys in the hall who did not know the sting of that cane, and they knew from the headmaster's expression that any boy who came within its range this afternoon would feel more than a sting. Swiftly, they formed the lines they had rehearsed so often, and stood waiting. The girls joined them, subdued and suppressing nervous giggles.

After that, matters progressed in a more or less orderly fashion. Each child who had not already obtained one was given a bun and a glass of lemonade. The villagers, more reluctant than ever, it seemed, after the exhibition given by the evacuees, stepped up to the tweedy woman to be allocated the children who were being billeted with them. They went off together, giving each other cautious glances, and Miss Langrish heaved a sigh of relief.

The atmosphere in the village hall was now one of barely repressed anxiety. Children who had hardly spoken to each other in the streets and playgrounds of Portsmouth now felt an urgent desire to cling together. They stood in little huddles, feeling like slaves in a market as strangers looked them over, assessing, passing on, choosing. What was wrong with me? Rose thought, half hurt, half indignant. Don't I look clean enough? Aren't I pretty enough? But Miss Langrish, turning just in time to catch the expression on her face, slipped a comforting arm around her shoulders.

'We're waiting for someone who can take your mother and baby sister too,' she said, and Rose remembered that their request had been made right from the beginning. She had refused to be evacuated at all if she couldn't stay with Mum. She nodded and relaxed, confident that it would be all right.

Tim and Keith stood nearby, holding hands. They too wanted to be together. Tim watched the faces, trying to decide which one he liked best. There was a stout, comfortable-looking woman with rosy cheeks and a smiling face. She might be the sort who would be forever baking, producing cakes and scones and home-made bread from the oven at all times of day. Farmers' wives were like that, he'd heard. He gazed hopefully at her, but to his astonishment she chose Brian Collins.

'My husband said to be sure to pick a good strong-looking lad who'd be able to give him a hand on the farm.' She ran her smiling blue eyes over Brian's sturdy limbs. 'This one looks as if he could be useful.'

Brian looked cocky and flexed his arm. 'See them muscles?' he said proudly. 'Biggest in the school, they are.' He went off with the plump woman, looking pleased with himself.

Two elderly sisters were gazing along the lines of children. They wore identical dark-blue coats and hats, and their faces were pale. One wore tortoiseshell spectacles and had whiskers sprouting from a mole on her chin, while the other was small and timid with nervously blinking eyes. She reminded Tim of a white mouse.

'We'd like a nice little girl. We could take two, if they were sisters.' They looked at Rose, still shepherding the younger children. 'She looks quiet and clean.'

'Rose needs a place where she can be with her mother, who's coming tomorrow.' Miss Langrish looked at the children. 'Could you manage a brother and a sister? Wendy Atkinson and her little brother Alan want to stay together.'

'A boy?' They gazed doubtfully at him. 'Oh, we didn't really want a boy . . .'

'He's a very nice little one. He's only four years old,' Miss Langrish said coaxingly, as if at that age it would be difficult to tell the difference. 'And Wendy looks after him very well.'

'Yes, but she's very small too, isn't she.' Their eyes strayed again to Rose. 'That one looks much more capable.'

'Could you take her mother too? And a baby?'

'Oh no!' They recoiled at the very idea. 'No, we couldn't manage all that. Very well, we'll take the little girl and her brother.' They continued to gaze at little Alan with some doubt, as if he were of an alien species. 'Only four years old?'

'Almost five,' Miss Langrish said. 'His birthday is in October.'

'Will he be able to . . . see to himself?'

'He can dress himself, certainly, and I'm sure Wendy will be able to help with anything he can't quite manage.' Miss Langrish was beginning to look less sure of the wisdom of sending little Alan to live with two elderly spinsters. But there was no time to quibble. Other villagers were pressing forward, the billeting officer was growing impatient and Alan himself looked as if he might be about to cry. Hastily, she picked up his little case and handed it to one of the ladies. 'Here are his things. We'll be calling tomorrow to make sure everything's all right.' And before they could answer, she turned away to deal with the next child.

Tim scanned the faces of the remaining villagers, trying to pick out which he favoured. The two women who had first commented on the children's appearance caught his eye again. The one who had thought they looked dirty – and you try keeping clean on a train! he thought indignantly – was talking to Mr Wain about a tall girl with plaits, who had somehow managed to remain fairly tidy. It looked as if she was choosing her. And I hope you like her, he thought, knowing Penelope Tyson, who lived in October Street, for one of the most spiteful girls in the school.

He regarded the second woman and made up his mind she looked nice. She had yellow hair rolled up over her ears and a friendly smile. He grinned at her and she smiled back and went up to the billeting officer.

'I'd like to take that little boy. The one with fair curly hair.'

The billeting lady looked at Miss Langrish.

'That's Tim Budd. He's with his brother, Keith, they want to stay together.'

The woman looked at Tim and then at Keith. Keith gazed back at her, his brown eyes large in his round face. He rubbed his cheeks with his sleeve, hoping to make them cleaner.

'Well, that's all right. We've got room for two. We can easily make up another bed in the room.' Her voice was warmed by a soft burr. She held out both her hands. 'Would you like to come and live along with me?'

Suddenly shy, the two boys went forward. Keith reached out a grimy paw and laid it in her hand. Rather more awkwardly, Tim did the same. The young woman laughed and squeezed their fingers.

'So you're Tim and Keith. How old are you?'

Tim found his voice.

'I'm nearly ten. My birthday's in October. Keith's eight.'

'My birthday's in May,' Keith added.

'Are you the youngest, then? I'd have thought it was the other way, around, you being bigger.'

'No, I'm older than Keith. I had measles when I was five and they stopped me growing.'

'Oh, I see.' Her smile was sympathetic. 'Well, I daresay you'll start again before long. Anyway, I should say you're just about the right size for now. Well—' she squeezed their hands again '—let's go home, shall we? There's nothing else we have to do here, is there, Mrs Tupper?'

'No,' the billeting officer said. 'Just leave your name and address and the names of the children. Someone will be round to see you in the next few days to see how you're getting along. Oh, and the teacher said something about the boy's mother – she's being evacuated herself. I expect she'll want to come and see them too.'

'Bound to,' the young woman said comfortably. 'Well, we'll be pleased to see her, won't we? Have to make a cake specially. Come on, now.' She led them out of the hall. 'My name's Mrs Corner, by the way – Edna Corner. My husband's name is Reg and he works on a farm. Anything you want to know, you just ask. There's no need to be shy with Reg and me.'

The two boys trotted along beside her, still carrying their cases. Their gas masks, hung over their shoulders, bumped against their backs. They were tired, hungry in spite of the buns and a bit apprehensive. It was the first time they hade ever been away from home without their mother and the excitement of the train journey and the new sights and sounds were overlaid by apprehension. Mrs Corner seemed nice – but what was it going to be like, living with her? And with Mum just around the corner, too?

Tim stifled a nervous giggle. Fancy living round the corner from Mrs Corner. And there was a Mr Corner too. He wondered if they had any children. Would four Corners make a square? Or three a triangle? He looked at Keith, wanting to share the joke with him, but remembered Mum telling him it was rude to make fun of people's names and decided to keep quiet. Perhaps it wasn't so funny anyway. It couldn't be really, or why would he suddenly feel like crying?

The village street was straggly, hardly a street at all, just a few houses and cottages scattered beside the road. They passed two or three large ones, then came to one standing on its own. By Tim and Keith's standards it was big, with its front door set in the middle and windows on either side. That made it twice the size of number 14 to start with. And its front garden was as long as their back one, with the path going up the middle, a bit of lawn on one side and neat rows of vegetables on the other. Tim had been over to his father's allotment often enough to be able to recognise most of them. Runner beans, carrots, cabbages, Brussels sprouts, and a good patch of potatoes. Someone had already started to dig them. He wondered if Mrs Corner would be as strict as his own mother over eating things he didn't like, and felt the sudden ache of tears in his throat again.

'Here we are,' Mrs Corner said cheerfully, opening the front door. 'Home in time for tea. I expect you're hungry, aren't you?'

The two boys nodded dutifully but Tim wondered if he would be able to get anything past the lump in his throat. The day which had started out so exciting had suddenly changed. This morning, it had all seemed to be a big adventure, getting on the train to go somewhere so secret that not even his parents or the teachers knew, looking forward to weeks with no school, spent roaming the fields and woods and having adventures like those he'd read about in books. He'd imagined himself and Keith, leaders of a club, solving mysteries, catching criminals, perhaps even spies. That's what children did in books and everything that had happened just lately had seemed more like a book than real life.

But now it seemed very real. Frighteningly real. Here they were, he and Keith, miles away from home, with no one they knew close at hand. The other children and the teachers were in the village somewhere, but he had no idea where. If he went out into the street now he wouldn't know how to find them. And kind though Mrs Corner seemed to be, she was still a stranger. She wasn't Mum.

Suddenly, Tim wanted his mum very badly indeed. And when he looked at Keith, he saw in his brother's face the same desperate longing and knew that there was no comfort to be had there; nor had he any to give.

Rose found herself following a neat, motherly looking person in a brown coat through the lanes. She walked quietly, still wearing her best red coat and carrying the small new suitcase Mum had bought, her brown eyes noticing the bright red of the rose-hips in the hedgerows, the pink and golden fronds of honeysuckle that trailed through the leaves. There was no traffic other than an occasional horse and when they passed a gateway she could see cows and sheep grazing.

This was real country. Mum and Dad had brought them out for picnics to places like this sometimes. They'd caught a bus from the main road and gone up over Portsdown Hill and out to some quiet spot where they'd got off and gone walking, Dad carrying a bag with their tea in it. Sometimes Mum would take a big basket and they'd pick blackberries, and occasionally they'd found mushrooms gleaming like pearls in the dewy grass.

They hadn't done it this summer. Mum had started to get fat and didn't seem to want to go walking far any more. Rose knew now that this was because she'd been expecting a baby, but nobody had told her that and she hadn't even suspected it until that morning when Maureen was born. When she'd gone to school, full of the news, some of the bigger girls had stared at her and laughed. Hadn't she known! Didn't she know that's what happened when mothers were having babies? And Rose had felt angry and upset. She'd felt left out. She would have liked to know what was happening. She would have liked to be able to help get things ready, choose a name, speculate whether it might be a boy or a girl. Instead, all this had been denied her, everything done in secret, as if it were something to be ashamed of.

'We thought you were too young to know,' Mum had said when Rose had tried to tell her this. 'Little girls don't have to know about these things.' But Rose had gone on feeling angry. And to compensate and bury her feelings, she had almost taken over the baby for herself, dressing her, bathing her, playing with her, taking her for walks in the pram. The only thing she refused to do was change her nappies. If Mum wanted to have a baby without telling her, she could do that too.

The neat woman, whose name was Mrs Greenberry, opened a gate in the hedge at the side of the road and went in. Rose followed her into a garden that ran all the way round the house. A red brick path led to the door. On the left was a shady part, overshadowed by a tall tree, but the garden to the right was filled with afternoon sunlight. The brilliant colours of dahlias and chrysanthemums gave way to rows of vegetables very similar to those which, had Rose known it, her brother Tim was looking at not a quarter of a mile away across the fields. And close to the back door of the house, as Mrs Greenberry led the way up the red-brick path, was the raised circular wall and winding handle of a well.

Rose stared at it. Did they really get their water from a well? Hadn't they got taps in the house? But she had no time to ask questions, for Mrs Greenberry was already indoors, waiting for Rose to follow.

The room they were in was a kitchen, larger than any kitchen Rose had ever seen – as large, she thought bemusedly, as all their downstairs at number 14 knocked into one. There was a big table in the middle of the room and a tall dresser taking up nearly all of one wall, its shelves bright with plates and bowls and cups. Under the window which looked out into the garden was a low earthenware sink – with no taps, she noticed at once – and in the opposite wall was a big alcove with a range in it.

Rose knew what a range was. Auntie Nell had one in the house where she and Tim had lived before Keith was born. She still liked going round there, to sit in front of its glowing coals in winter and listen to the kettle purring gently on the hob. Great-aunt Alice would be there too, as often as not, and she would hold her palms out towards the fire and then take Rose's hands between hers and rub them gently to warm them.

The sight of the range in this kitchen brought a rush of homesickness. But at the same time, it held a promise of the same warmth, the same comfort that Rose always found in front of Aunt Nell's range. Almost involuntarily, she went towards it, holding out her hands.

'That's right,' Mrs Greenberry said approvingly. 'You just sit yourself down on that stool and get warm. There's a proper nip in the air today – be a frost tonight, I wouldn't wonder. Now, what do you say to a cup of tea, love, and then we'll get you settled in your room and you can help me get things ready for your mum when she comes tomorrow. And a new baby too, they tell me? Well, that'll be nice, won't it, having you all here together.'

Her voice murmured on as she bustled about the kitchen, taking cups off the hooks on the dresser, fetching milk from a cool pantry, pouring water from the kettle into a big brown teapot. But Rose hardly heard her. She was sitting close to the bars of the range, staring at the hot coals. Like her brothers, like every other child in the village, she was feeling the sudden immensity of what had happened. Like all the rest, she had been brought face to face with reality.

If war came, she might be living here for months – years. She might never go back to live in number 14. She might never live again with her brothers, her father, never see her family she had left behind.

Nobody really knew what the war would be like. They talked about bombs, about gas, about air raids and invasions . . . but nobody knew. Whole cities might be flattened, even villages like this one poisoned by a creeping fog of burning fumes. They might be starved, burned or shot to pieces. Nobody knew.

There might still, of course, not be a war. Every day they said it still wasn't inevitable. But if it wasn't, why were they here? Why had Rose and her brothers been torn from their homes, why had Wendy and Alan Atkinson been wrenched away from their mother, why little Susan Cullen taken from her father on the very day of her mother's funeral?

In any case, for Rose and her friends it was too late. Even if there was no war, if they were all simply given a holiday in the country and then sent home again, to go back to the lives they had lived until yesterday – nothing would ever be the same again. They would never be the same again. The shock had been too great, the impact too severe. The damage had been done.

All this, Rose sensed rather than thought as she stared at the burning coals in Mrs Greenberry's range. Her mind was too bemused to make shapes of the bewildered emotions that circled in her head. But she knew, without doubt, that something vital had happened to her and to all the others in the past few hours. Something vital and irrevocable.

As night fell over the village, the evacuees lay down in their unfamiliar beds and tried to sleep.

Wendy Atkinson helped her brother Alan to undress and made him say his prayers. The little ritual comforted them both, but when he was in his bed he turned large blue eyes on her and she saw the hopelessness in them and felt tears in her own eyes. He wants Mummy, she thought. He doesn't understand. And why should he, for she barely understood herself why they should find themselves in this dark mausoleum of a house with its furniture that mustn't be touched for fear of sticky fingerprints, its rugs that mustn't be trodden on, its delicate china that must be handled so carefully in case it broke.

The sisters, both confusingly called Miss Woddis, hadn't seemed to know what to do with them. They had given them tea – thin sandwiches and a slice of dry seed-cake which Wendy disliked and Alan had refused to eat – and then sat gazing helplessly at them. Finally, they had suggested that the children might like to go out into the garden – but had laid down so many strictures about flowerbeds and grass that Wendy and Alan had been afraid to do anything other than crouch on the path, staring at the grass and looking into an endless future of tiny sandwiches and seed-cake that couldn't be swallowed, and no mother to brush their hair or wash their faces or cuddle them to sleep at night.

All had been relieved when it was bedtime. But Wendy, lying uncomfortably in her own bed, missing the busy sound of night in Portsmouth and anxious about the strange noises and even stranger silence of the countryside, wanted morning to come. She wanted to see her friends, to reassure herself that there was still someone familiar nearby. She wanted her teacher. Most of all, she wanted to be at home.

A soft sound made her turn. Alan was sobbing under his breath, little heart-broken sobs. Wendy felt her own tears begin to flow.

She climbed out of bed and crept over the little strip of mat to Alan's. She slipped into bed beside him and felt his body shaking against hers. They wrapped their arms around each other and clung tightly, weeping out their fear and loneliness and terror. And as the darkness swept through the swaying trees outside and the owls called through the last few hours of peace, they fell asleep.

Tim and Keith fell asleep too, reaching out to clutch each other's hands. Their sister Rose, delighted as she was with her little bedroom under the eaves of Mrs Greenberry's cottage, warmed though she might be by the kindness of the neat, motherly woman and her big, cheerful husband, lay longing for tomorrow, when her mother would come with baby Maureen.

Even the biggest children, like Penelope Tyson and Brian Collins, felt their confidence ebb as they went to bed for the first time in their billets. And the little ones alone, without brother or sister to cling to, shed many tears that night. Some shed them quietly, unheard by foster-mothers and fathers; others wept noisily and refused to be comforted. Martin Baker, appalled by the privy at the end of the dark, tangled garden, lay clutching himself in the desperate hope that he could wait until morning. And Susan Cullen, to whom so many bewildering things had happened in the past few weeks, spent the greater part of the night on her knees beside her bed, praying to a God who seemed to have abandoned her, begging forgiveness for the sins she felt she must have committed to bring such retribution on her head, until she fell asleep where she knelt and woke in the morning, stiff and freezing, on the cold linoleum floor.

It was a night of anxiety and bewilderment for every child in the village, far away from home, and a night of anxiety too for those who had taken them in. How long would they have to look after these children, no kin to them and from a strange background? For how long must their homes be invaded, their lives thus disrupted?

And back in Portsmouth and the other cities from which children had been taken, mothers like Jess and fathers like Frank lay equally wakeful, wondering where their children were that night and who had seen them to bed. Had they been received grudgingly, or with kindness? Would they be cared for or neglected? Were they at this moment crying for a mother who had never been out of reach? Did they feel abandoned and betrayed?

'You'll be with them tomorrow,' Frank murmured to Jess, reaching out for her in the big feather-bed. But as she turned into his arms he felt the wet heat of tears on his shoulder and knew that she was crying.

'And I'll be away from you,' she wept, quivering against him. 'Oh, Frank, it's so cruel. Just when we were getting along so well. And where's it all going to end?'

He held her close, his big hands moving slowly over her back. It was a question that must have been asked in millions of homes that night, a question that neither he nor anyone else on earth could answer.

If war should come . . . Could anyone, now, doubt that it would?

4

'Everything I believed in has crashed into ruins this morning.'

The words that Neville Chamberlain, Prime Minister of Great Britain, spoke in the House of Commons at noon on 3 September 1939, echoed the feeling in the hearts of millions. For as they had listened to his wireless broadcast an hour earlier, their world too had crumbled and shattered about them. The lives they knew, the ordinary lives they had lived and expected to go on living, had come to an end. Their future was uncertain; for some of them, yet unknowing, there was no future.

Jess sat in the Greenberry's kitchen and listened to the wireless. In her arms, she cradled baby Maureen, while Rose sat on a low stool at her knee. Harold Greenberry was in his accustomed chair at the head of the big kitchen table, while his wife sat at his elbow. Nobody spoke as the solemn notes of Big Ben filled the kitchen, and they listened with dread as the Prime Minister began to speak.

'This morning the British Ambassador in Berlin communicated to the German Government that unless we heard from them by eleven o'clock that they were prepared at once to withdraw their troops from Poland, a state of war would exist between us.

'I have to tell you that no such undertaking has been received and that consequently this country is at war with Germany.'

Rose heard the sharply indrawn breath of the adults. She looked up into her mother's face, then at the Greenberrys. Their fear struck at her breast and she felt the tears spring to her eyes.

'You can imagine what a bitter blow it is to me that my long struggle to win peace has ended.'

'He tried,' Mrs Greenberry said. 'Nobody can say he didn't try.'

Her husband shushed her with a hand, lifted only a few inches from the table. The Prime Minister continued to speak. His voice was trembling slightly. He talked of his belief that, even to the last, an honourable and peaceful settlement could have been bought, but Hitler would not have it. He talked of joining together with France to go to the aid of Poland, even now bravely resisting a wicked attack upon her people. He talked of a clear conscience, of a situation which had become intolerable and must now be finished.

'May God bless you,' he concluded in a voice that sounded itself not far from tears, *'and may he defend the right, for it is evil that we are fighting*

against – brute force, bad faith, injustice, oppression and persecution, and against them, I am certain, right will prevail.'

The broadcast was over. Another voice began to speak, giving details of the plans that had been made and asking all engaged with the fighting force and in Civil Defence to report for duty. Mr Greenberry moved suddenly, making everyone jump. He stood up, scraping his chair back on the quarry tiles of the kitchen floor, and went to a cupboard. He took out a tin hat and his gas mask.

'I'm going down to the hall,' he said, and his voice sounded strange and creaky, as if it had not been used for a long time, and loud in the quiet kitchen, drowning the voice of the BBC announcer. 'They'll be wanting us down there.' He stood awkwardly for a few seconds, looking at the two women as if he felt that this moment should be marked in some way, by more than a few words. If he had been alone with his wife, Jess thought, he might have kissed her. But the presence of strangers held him back. Instead, he laid his hand on her shoulder and gave it a brief squeeze. Then he ducked his head at Jess, turned away and, as if he could no longer clearly see his way, blundered out of the kitchen door.

The two women looked at each other.

'That's dreadful,' Jess said at last, in a low voice. 'They've declared war.' She reached out an arm and drew Rose against her. 'What's going to happen now? What's going to happen to us all? What's going to happen to the children?'

Mrs Greenberry shook her head. 'I don't know, dear. I just don't know.' She stood up, resting her hands on the table as if she had suddenly grown old. Together, the three of them went out into the garden. They stared up at the September sky, so blue and innocent, the sky from which death would come. How soon would it arrive, the evil black rain they had been told about? Was it already on its way? Were Hitler's forces already unleashed, the bombers already in the air, their droning yet unheard but inexorably approaching?

'We're not ready,' Jess said in a sudden panic. 'We're not ready. I can't face it – not yet. Not with the baby and Rose, and the boys not even here. And my Frank, back there in Portsmouth, all by himself. It's wrong – all wrong. We can't . . .'

'We don't have no choice.' Mrs Greenberry's country voice was warm and her hand on Jess's arm intended to give comfort, but there was little comfort to be had. 'They don't ask us, do they? If it was left to us, there wouldn't be no wars. And I don't mean just us – I mean everyone like us, all over the world. There must be people like us in Poland and France, even in Germany, who just want to go on living their own lives, not interfering with nobody else. But we don't get the choice.'

'I know – and that's what's so wrong.' Jess's voice was passionate now. 'We don't get any choice at all. We just have to go where we're pushed. We have to leave our homes, that we've worked for and built up. You have to take strangers into yours. They take our children away from us just when they need their mothers and fathers most, and they take our boys away and make them fight, when half of them don't even know what they're fighting for. And they put hate into their souls. My sister's boy Colin – Bob Shaw next door – who've never hated anyone in their lives, nor ever would – they make them hate the Germans so that when they go to war they'll kill without even caring about it. Our Colin, killing people – it doesn't bear thinking of. But he will – he'll have to – if he lives long enough.'

'He'll have to if he wants to live,' Mrs Greenberry pointed out. 'But you don't want to go talking like that too much, my dear. People won't understand. And if it turns out to be a long war, like the last one—'

'I hope to God it doesn't! Four years, that was. Four years. We'd never stand four years of bombing, not the sort of bombing they've been talking about.'

'Well, let's hope we don't have to. Let's hope it'll be a short one – over by Christmas.' Mrs Greenberry touched her arm again. 'Let's go inside now, dear, and have a cup of tea. And then you walk over to Edna Corner's and see those boys of yours. Why don't you ask them over to tea this afternoon, eh? You didn't see much of them yesterday, what with being worn out after your journey and everything.'

Jess nodded. Suddenly, she felt overwhelmingly tired. It had indeed been an exhausting day yesterday, from the moment when she'd clung to Frank for their final goodbye as he set off for work at six, all through the struggle down to the school carrying Maureen and as much luggage as she could manage – thank goodness for Annie's help as she joined the other overburdened mothers, trailing along the streets in the sad exodus – and through the slow, dusty train journey with its many unexplained stops and their final arrival at the village hall.

It all seemed more like a dream now. Tim and Keith had been there with their foster-mother, who seemed a nice enough woman, and Rose with Mrs Greenberry. But Jess, after the first relief at being with them again, had been more concerned with the baby than anything else. Maureen had been fretful all day and was now crying a weary, hopeless cry that splintered Jess's heart. She must be hungry, yet seemed uninterested in the breast, and Jess felt its slackness and knew that there was little milk there. Fear stabbed her. It didn't take long for a baby as young as Maureen to lose weight and cease to thrive. And if she lost her milk . . .

'It'll come back,' Mrs Greenberry said reassuringly. 'It's only natural, after what you've been through. You'll be all right in a day or two, see if you're not. And there's always the bottle.'

Jess nodded. But she hated the idea of putting Maureen on to the bottle so early. She'd fed the others for at least six months each, and she'd wanted to do the same with this baby, the last she would bear. Feeding the baby yourself, with your own milk, was the right, the natural thing to do. It was finishing the job you'd started.

To put Maureen on the bottle would seem like failure. And another grievance to lay at Hitler's door.

Rose stayed out in the garden by herself while the two women went into the house. The big kitchen was too dim after the brightness outside. She wandered down narrow paths between the rows of vegetables and stared out over the rolling fields and woods.

It was hard to understand what was happening. She knew about the war, of course, had shared the anxiety as it approached. But now it was here. The Prime Minister had said so, on the wireless. She'd heard his words herself, seen the effect they had on the grown-ups.

Nothing would ever be the same again. And yet – nothing was any different.

She looked up at the sky. It was still blue, overlaid with the faint haze of early autumn. The trees were still green, just a few birches and horse-chestnuts beginning to turn with golden colour. The hedges were bright with hips and haws, and rich with glistening purple blackberries. At the bottom of the garden she found a gnarled, twisted tree with apples hanging like orange lanterns from its branches, and another that bore a few late plums.

The air was quiet, with no threatening drone of approaching death. Instead, she could hear the whisper of a breeze touching the long grass. A robin sang from a nearby bush and a flight of tiny birds with pink breasts and long tails skimmed past her head and settled in the apple tree. Mrs Greenberry's black cat, Tibby, emerged from the grass and came to rub himself round her legs, and she wondered suddenly how Henry would get along at home, with no one there all day.

Thinking of Henry made her think of her father, also alone at home. How was he spending this Sunday? Had he gone over to the allotment this morning? Had he heard the wireless? Did he know there was a war on?

She supposed he'd be going up to Auntie Annie's. What would they talk about, as Uncle Ted carved the joint? Were they worrying about Colin, away on his ship?

Rose sat down on the grass. She drew her knees up and rested her chin on them, her head bent so that her dark fringe fell forwards and made a little cave of darkness. She shut her eyes tightly and tried to imagine it all, feeling the fear, sensing the dark shadow of ominous clouds looming above. Her skin grew cold.

And yet when she opened her eyes again, the sky was still blue, the hips red, the trees green with a touch of gold. The robin sang from his bush and the breeze rustled the leaves. And Tibby rubbed his head against her legs with a mew, asking to be picked up.

It doesn't matter what they do, she thought, they can't stop this. Even Hitler can't stop the apples getting ripe or the birds singing. And no one can stop a cat from getting on your lap.

Frank listened to the King's broadcast in the afternoon and then went down to the *Evening News* offices in Stanhope Road to buy the special edition of the paper. With a crowd of other men and women, he stood in the street, scanning the front page with its dramatic headline.

'*This Country Is At War.*'

Frank stared at the words, his heart sinking. He already knew it was true. The Prime Minister had said so. The King had said so. But to see it, printed in black and white in Portsmouth's own evening paper . . .

He looked at the rest of the page. As well as a full account of the Prime

Minister's speech on the wireless, there was a report of his words to Parliament immediately afterwards. *'This is a sad day for all of us,'* he had said. *'For none is it sadder than for me.'* And then, striking the table with his hand, *'There is only one thing left for me, and that is to devote what strength and powers I have to forwarding the victory of the cause for which we have to sacrifice ourselves. I trust I may live to see the day when Hitlerism has been destroyed, and a restored and liberated Europe has been re-established.'*

Will he? Frank thought, folding the newspaper and pushing it into his pocket. Will any of us? That man has marched all over Europe, smashing and destroying wherever he's gone. What's to stop him doing the same in Poland, as he's already begun to do? What's to stop him doing the same in France? And then – with only a narrow strip of water to hold him at bay – what chance do we have against such might?

He wheeled his bicycle out into the road and swung his leg over the saddle. The street was full of people, standing in groups discussing the news. A few women were crying, while men were looking anxious, angry and, in some cases, even elated. 'Now we'll show the bastard,' one declared, waving his fists in the air. 'We can stop all the shilly-shallying about and do something about him. Get our boys over there, that'll wipe the silly smirk off his face. He'll find out he's bitten off more than he can chew.'

There was a murmur of agreement. Nobody was happy about the war, but at least, it was felt, they now knew where they stood. The suspense was over and the worst known. And, once known, could be faced.

'We showed Kaiser Bill what we thought of him in the last lot. We'll show this twerp too. A house-painter! Who does he think he is, trying to take over the world? A bloody maniac, that's what he is.'

'That's right. Well, he might be able to overrun some of those tinpot little countries in Europe but he won't be able to do it to Britain. He'll find we're a different kettle of fish.'

Frank cycled home. It had been a queer day right from the start. For the first time in their married life he had woken up without Jess beside him. He had lain for a while trying to pretend she'd just got up early and was downstairs getting breakfast ready, but it was no use. The house was silent without her and the kids, and he felt almost as if they had never existed, as if the past fourteen years were all a dream.

He'd got up eventually and got his own breakfast, then pottered about in the garden, waiting for the Prime Minister's broadcast at eleven o'clock. He'd listened to it by himself, sitting at the table – it didn't seem right to sit in his armchair while such an important announcement was made – and as soon as the grave voice had finished speaking he'd heard the doleful wail of an air-raid siren.

'My God – they haven't started already!' He'd run outside, and there were all the neighbours, staring up at the sky. There were no planes to be seen, only the glint of barrage balloons floating like huge silver fish above their heads. And after a few minutes the 'Raiders Passed' signal had sounded and they'd all sighed with relief. A false alarm. But they hadn't gone back indoors. They'd stayed outside for a while, talking across the garden fences to each other and wondering what was going to happen next.

Frank couldn't settle to anything. In the end, he'd got his tools and walked over to the allotment. He didn't know who was going to eat all the vegetables he'd grown, now that Jess and the children were away, but he couldn't let them go to waste. He'd take a few down to Jess's parents at North End.

After a couple of hours' digging, he felt better and went back to Annie's to have a bit of dinner, listen to the King's broadcast and then cycle down to the newspaper offices to get the special edition. Arthur and Mary were glad of the vegetables and he stopped to talk about the news for a while and have a cup of tea in their stuffy, overcrowded little back room.

'It's a bad job,' Arthur kept saying in his thin reedy voice. 'A proper bad job.' And Mary had nodded, her fingers plucking at a trembling lip. 'I don't know what the world's coming to, I really don't.'

It's not fair, Frank thought, cycling home again. They've been through too much already, old folk like them. They shouldn't have to face this, not at their time of life.

He entered the silent house and Henry, the cat, came to meet him, miaowing as if to ask where everyone was. Frank bent to stroke him.

'There, old chap, it's all right. We haven't deserted you. I'm still here. You'll still get your cods' heads for supper.'

But would he? When would Frank have time to buy them? Out in the mornings soon after six to walk down to the Dockyard, not home till seven or eight at night . . . It was another thing he'd have to ask Annie to do. And Annie had enough on her plate already, without Henry's cods' heads.

His mouth twitched, thinking how Jess would have laughed if he'd said such a thing. It was just the kind of inadvertent joke that amused her. And then he felt pain sweep over him, for Jess wasn't here to laugh and he didn't know when she would be here again. This war, that was supposed to be 'over by Christmas'. They'd heard that before, hadn't they? And last time, it had been four long years . . .

Four years in an empty house? Four years without Jess and the kids?

He looked at the newspaper again. Winston Churchill had made a speech in Parliament too. As always, he had spoken with force, using words in the way that was so inimitably his. *He* ought to be leading us, Frank thought. He's the man we need in this mess, not Chamberlain with his mealy mouthed talk of appeasement.

He read the words again, letting them roll around in his mind.

'*Outside the storm of war may blow and the lands may be lashed with the furies of its gales, but in our hearts this Sunday morning there is peace.*'

Yes, Churchill certainly knew how to use words. Frank could imagine him, speaking in slow, measured tones as he delivered his rousing message.

'*Our hands may be active but our consciences are at rest . . . There is another note which may be present at this moment, and that is a feeling of thankfulness that if these great trials were to come upon our Island there is a generation of Britons here now ready to prove itself not unworthy of the days of yore, and not unworthy of those great men, the fathers of our land, who have laid the foundations of our laws and shaped the greatness of our country.*

'*This is no war for domination of imperial aggrandisement, for material gain – no war to shut any country out of its sunlight and means of progress. It is a war to establish and revive the stature of man.'*

Frank laid down the paper. The stature of man. That was what they all had to hold on to. Forget some whipper-snapper of an Austrian house-painter, snatching other countries for his own greed. Forget the lust for power which had brought them to this brink on which the world now stood. Remember instead that people – men, women, children – were being persecuted, tormented, driven from their homes and treated like animals. It didn't matter what country they lived in, they should be free to walk with heads held high. It didn't matter what race they were, they were human beings.

The stature of man.

Henry jumped up on to his lap and began to knead Frank's thighs. Frank laid his hand on the furry head, grateful for the contact, for the warmth of another living being. He stroked the cat's back.

The war was, as Parliament had agreed, a right war, a just war. It must be fought for the sake of humanity.

To those who had thought that the war would start slowly, the sinking of the *Athenia* on its first day came as a shock.

The liner had left Liverpool on Saturday, bound for Montreal and carrying fourteen hundred passengers and crew. She had travelled two hundred miles west of the Hebrides when, without warning, the German torpedos struck. The captain told reporters later that the missile had gone right through the ship to the engine room. Most of those aboard were saved by nearby ships, who raced to the rescue, but a hundred and twelve died.

'The only good German's a dead German.' The phrase was on everyone's lips. Killing had suddenly become a part of the national mood. Even the games of the few children who had not been evacuated suddenly took on a new and sinister aspect. Instead of cowboys and Indians, the boys played at war. But nobody wanted to be the Germans, so the part of the enemy was given to the least popular boys.

'They said I was a dirty Jerry,' a small boy wept as he was taken home, bruised and grazed from a tumble in the road. 'They pushed me over . . . I didn't *want* to be a Jerry.'

'Don't know why they have to pretend anyway,' someone said to Frank. 'Not when there's real live Huns living in September Street.'

'The Brunners aren't Huns,' Frank said sharply. He made a point now of going in to buy his *Daily Express* at the little newsagent's shop instead of from the kiosk on the Hard, as he'd been accustomed to do. Custom had fallen off badly, Alice Brunner told him as he handed over his penny. People just didn't come in any more. It was as if they were ashamed to be seen coming through the door.

'They ought to be ashamed of walking past,' Frank said. 'They've known you and Heinrich long enough to know what sort of people you are. You're as good as anyone else round her. Better than a lot I could name.'

Alice shook her head. 'That's not what most of them think. They're saying Heinrich should be taken away.'

Frank stared at her.

'Taken away?'

'You know. Interned. Put into prison.'

'Prison?' Frank said. 'But he's done nothing wrong.'

Alice shrugged. 'He's a German. Isn't that enough?'

The papers were full of war news now. In the edition that reported the sinking of the *Athenia*, Frank read that Egypt had broken off diplomatic relations with Germany, Australia had declared itself at war and France had gone into action with all three forces. Anthony Eden had been made Dominions Secretary and Mr Churchill was back in the Cabinet as First Lord of the Admiralty. In Portsmouth, the offices at the Guildhall were being removed to the Northern Secondary School and the chimes of the Guildhall clock were stopped 'for the duration'.

That was another phrase that was on everyone's lips now. The children had been evacuated 'for the duration', and cinemas, theatres and dance-halls were closed 'for the duration', a move that was as unpopular with the younger members of the community as evacuation had been with others.

'It's not fair,' Olive said as she, Betty and Gladys Shaw walked home from work. 'Derek and me were going to see *Idiot's Delight* at the Ambassador. It's Norma Shearer and Clark Gable.'

'Clark Gable!' Gladys said, rolling her eyes. 'I think he's smashing. And Norma Shearer's gorgeous. I wouldn't mind looking like her.' She swaggered a little in her tight-waisted blue frock and passed a hand over her yellow hair, as if imagining herself as a film star. 'I'm thinking of doing my hair the way she does hers, I reckon it'd suit me.'

'Robb Wilton's supposed to be on at the King's,' Betty grumbled. 'Graham was going to take me.'

'Is that the chap I saw you with at Kimball's?' Gladys asked. 'Tall, with ginger hair?'

'It's not ginger,' Betty said at once. 'It's auburn.'

Gladys grinned. 'Thought it looked a bit carroty, myself. Why don't you go out with our Bob? He's been mooning about over you for weeks.'

Betty flushed scarlet. 'Don't be daft!' But she felt a quiver of secret delight. A boy – even if it was just Bob Shaw that she'd known since she was in her pram – mooning over her! 'How d'you know, anyway?' she couldn't help asking.

Gladys laughed. 'He's my brother, ain't he? We live in the same house. I can tell. Anyway, he's got your picture pinned up in the bedroom.'

Betty stared at her. 'My picture? Where'd he get that from?'

'Oh, sometime when we all went swimming last summer, I should think. You've got that striped bathing costume of yours on, anyway. He's cut off the other people in the snap and just left you – proper pin-up girl, you are.'

Betty tossed her head, the brown curls bouncing. 'What a cheek! I shall just tell him to take it down, next time I see him.'

'Don't do that. He's not doing any harm. I mean, it's not as if he was sticking any pins in it or using it for a dartboard, is it!' Gladys dug her in the ribs. 'He'll get over it.'

This, for some reason, irritated Betty even more. The idea of Bob Shaw keeping her photo on his bedroom wall was rather flattering, much as she might pretend otherwise, but the insinuation that it was no more than a passing fancy was an injury to her pride.

'Oh, I don't care whether he gets over it or not,' she said off handedly. 'Come to that, I don't care if he sticks life-sized posters of me on his wall. If he can't find anything better to do with his time—'

'Or his wall,' Olive interposed.

'—well, I'm sorry for him, that's all,' Betty finished with a scathing look at her sister.

'Well, don't be too hard on him, Betty,' Gladys said. 'He might be called up before long and have to go away. It's good for them to have someone at home to think about, someone to come back to. And he's never had a proper girlfriend, you know. He's too shy.'

'Well, going in the Forces would soon change that,' Betty remarked. 'Our Colin was shy before he went into the Navy but to hear him now you'd think the women were queuing up for him.'

Gladys looked at her. The fun had died from her face and she looked suddenly unhappy.

'There's no one special, is there?'

'No, of course not,' Olive said with a scowl at Betty. Honestly, wasn't she ever going to learn to mind her tongue? Had she forgotten that Gladys Shaw and Colin had started going out together just before he went off on the *Exeter*? It wasn't much more than that as far as Olive knew – Colin didn't even seem to be writing to her – but it was obvious that Gladys was carrying a torch for him. She was always asking if they'd heard from him. 'It's just talk. You know what sailors are.'

But that didn't seem to be the right thing to say either. Everyone in Pompey knew what sailors were. There were enough of them about, roistering around the Guildhall Square on a Saturday night. Only last week, on the way home from the pictures with Derek, she'd heard a couple arguing drunkenly in the darkness of the blackout. '*I'm looking after you.*' '*No . . . I'm looking after you . . .*' And neither of them fit to stand, by the look of their stumbling bodies in the dim light of a quarter moon.

But Olive didn't have too much energy to spare for Gladys and Bob Shaw, nor even for her sister. She was meeting Derek that night and, as usual, she didn't know whether she felt excited or scared.

Since their afternoon in Brighton, Derek had taken her out several times in his red MG. They had been down to the New Forest, where the wild ponies roamed freely through the trees and even into the little villages of Brockenhurst and Lyndhurst, and Olive had laughed to see one nose its way into the greengrocer's shop and steal an apple from the rack. The following Saturday they'd gone to Guildford and explored the Hog's Back and the Devil's Punchbowl, and last weekend they'd gone to Salisbury and wandered in the cathedral close, under the shadow of the tall, slender spire.

But wherever they went, there was no escape from the talk of war. Last Saturday, especially, the atmosphere had been particularly tense. Salisbury and its surrounding villages were filled with newly evacuated children and their schoolteachers, with a few mothers who, like Jess Budd, had small babies. Olive and Derek had seen them, wandering aimless and disconsolate, along the lanes, and it had taken the shine off the afternoon. They'd come home sobered, wondering like everyone else what Mr Chamberlain was going to have to say the next day.

Now, like everyone else, they knew. The country was at war and, as if to prove it, life was already beginning to change.

I couldn't bear it if Derek had to go away and fight, Olive thought miserably, hardly hearing her sister and Gladys Shaw sparring and giggling. I just couldn't bear it.

'I suppose Kimball's will be closing too,' Gladys said. She screwed up her mouth in disgust. 'What are we going to do with ourselves?'

The other two girls shrugged and shook their heads. The future looked bleak and grey. No pictures, no dancing. No lights at night, so you couldn't even go for a walk without fear of being run down by a car or bus. And the wireless seemed to play nothing but 'Sandy McPherson at the Theatre Organ' on the Light Programme or else talk endlessly about the war on the Home Service.

'Well, at least you've got your chaps at home,' Gladys said. 'I keep thinking about your Colin. I mean, they haven't dropped any bombs yet like everyone reckoned they would, but they're already fighting at sea. That liner that went down . . . And they don't tell us everything. My dad reckons it'll all be kept secret in case spies get to hear what's happening.'

'That's daft,' Olive said. 'People are going to know when their boys write home.'

'No, they won't be allowed to say where they are. D'you know where Colin is?'

'Well, not exactly. Going down the South Atlantic was the last we heard. He'll be safe enough there, anyway.'

'We hope,' Gladys said. 'What about your Derek? Is he going to be called up?'

Olive sighed. She'd been trying for the past few minutes to push her fears to the back of her mind. 'I don't know. He hasn't heard anything yet.'

'What'll you do if he is? Get married before he goes?'

'Fat chance of that! I'm not even twenty-one till next October.'

'Surely your mum and dad would stretch a point.' Gladys said. 'What's a few months?'

'Dad always said none of us would get married till we were twenty-one. Anyway, we're not even engaged. I don't know that Derek wants to get married.'

'They wouldn't let you get married quick anyway,' Betty said. 'Think what people would say!'

Olive blushed and dug her sister in the ribs. 'You shouldn't talk like that.'

'Why not? It's true. Look at Sheila Brown, round Carlisle Crescent. She got married in a hurry at the end of July and the old gossips haven't taken their eyes off her belly since.'

'Betty! If our Dad heard you say things like that!'

'Well, he won't. Anyway, it's better to know what's what. I'd hate to be like young Rose, no idea her mum was expecting till she saw the baby in its cot. I think children should be told the facts of life, not left to find out for themselves.'

'How did you find out, Betty?' Gladys asked curiously. 'Did your mum and dad tell you?'

'Them? Not likely! I heard about it from other kids, same as the rest of us. And then I found a book in the library.'

'What, in the children's library?'

'Don't be daft. In the big library, in the medical section. Diagrams and all. Mind, it puts you off a bit. I don't really fancy it myself. I mean, kissing's all right, but I don't think I'll bother with all that other stuff.'

'I bet that's not what Graham thinks!' Gladys said with a hoot of laughter. They had reached the Chapmans' gate now and she turned to walk down the back alley of April Grove to her own house. 'I daresay he's got a few ideas about what to do in the blackout.'

Olive and Betty went indoors. Their mother was out but Ted was there, reading his paper with Suky the cat on his lap. He looked tired and in need of a shave.

'Hullo, Dad. Had a good day?'

'Same as usual.' Ted's job as skipper of a ferryboat kept him plying back and forth across the harbour for the whole of his shift. The journey took a little over five minutes, with five to unload and load passengers at each side. It was never tedious, with the tides and currents changing all the time and ships coming in and out of harbour, but it was exhausting. You had to be continually on the watch, standing up on the bridge the whole time. And since the blackout, it was worse.

'You can't see a thing out there at night when there's no moon,' he grumbled. 'The other night I was halfway up to Whale Island before I realised it. And I'd got a boatload of Dockyardmen going home. I thought I was going to get lynched, they were that fed up.'

Betty giggled but her father gave her a glare. 'It's not funny, my girl. We could have run into anything. What it's going to be like with bombs dropping all round us, God only knows.'

'Anything from our Colin?' Olive asked, scanning the mantelpiece where letters were always put.

'No, there's not. Your mother's worried sick. I keep telling her no news is good news but she won't listen.'

The girls looked solemn. Olive went out into the kitchen and filled the kettle. There was a tin full of freshly made rock cakes and she set a few on a plate and carried it through to the living-room.

'Is Uncle Frank coming in for his dinner?'

'Supposed to be.' Ted reached out for a cake. 'I saw him on the boat this morning.'

'Must seem funny, with no one else in the house. Have the Glaisters come back yet?'

'Dunno.' The family in number 15 had been away on holiday, somewhere down in Devonshire it was believed, when war was declared. The two oldest children, Joe and Carol, were sixteen and fourteen, and both out at work.

Shirley, the 'afterthought', was seven and presumably would have been evacuated if they had come back in time.

'Perhaps they'll stay down in Devon. They've got family there, haven't they?'

'So Jess was saying. But George Glaister's an Army reservist, he'll probably be called up.' Ted looked at the clock. Annie ought to be back by now. He was starving for his tea, in spite of the two rock cakes he'd eaten. 'Can't you start getting a meal on, Olive?' he asked irritably.

Olive sighed and got up from her chair. She was tired after her day's work, but although her father had almost certainly been sitting in his armchair for the past hour, it did not occur to her to suggest that he might help.

'I'll do the potatoes, Bet,' she said. 'You do some carrots. I don't know what meat there is.'

Betty looked in the larder. 'Just some beef, left over from yesterday. And there's some veg too. We'll have bubble and squeak, shall we?'

The two girls prepared the meal. Both were feeling depressed. Nobody had been able to talk about anything but the war all day and although some voiced relief that a decision had been made at last, most were still clearly feeling the dread that had greeted the Prime Minister's announcement on Sunday. And the touch of excitement that many of the younger people, who had no memories of war, had felt, was soon dissipated as the sheer dreariness of their new life began to come home to them.

'No pictures, no dances, no nothing,' Betty groaned as she chopped leftover vegetables. 'What's the point of it all? People have got to do something. And what about the men, home on leave, aren't they supposed to have a bit of fun?'

'I suppose they think it's dangerous to have a lot of people crowded together. If a bomb dropped on a cinema—'

'It could just as easy drop on a church,' Betty argued. 'Or a bus or a train. Or an office. Know what I think? I think they're a lot of killjoys. Anything people like doing, they'll stop. Life just isn't going to be worth living.'

Olive went silent. Her brother was at sea, perhaps already fighting German ships, and Derek was likely to be called up any time. Would they think life was worth living when they came home, even if they couldn't go to the pictures for a while?

And Auntie Jess. She'd been really upset when she came in the other morning, after she'd seen Rose and the boys off. All she wanted was to be at home and have her family together again. She wouldn't care if the cinemas were open or not.

'Don't be selfish, Bet,' she said sharply, cutting in on her sister's moans. 'There's plenty would think they were well off to be where we are now. At least we've got a warm house and enough to eat and a wireless to listen to. You want to think about others for a change.'

Betty stared at her sister in astonishment. The two rarely quarrelled and Olive's angry retort took her completely by surprise. Defensively, she began, 'I only—' but Olive broke in again.

'I know what *you only*. You only think about yourself and what you want. Well, there's a lot of people worse off than you, and there's going to be more and more if this war goes on. You don't have any idea what it's going to be like, Bet. Mr Harker and some of the men at work were talking about it today. It's going to be horrible. People being killed, soldiers and sailors coming home without arms or legs, houses being bombed and smashed, little babies—' Her voice broke and she stopped and bit her lips hard. Then she said more quietly, 'It's going to be horrible, that's all.'

Betty mixed the chopped vegetables with beaten egg and tipped it into the frying pan. She could think of nothing to say. Olive was right, she knew, but did she need to bite her head off like that? And then she thought of Colin, somewhere at sea. Would he ever come down the street again?

And Graham, the first boyfriend she'd ever had. Would he be called up? Would he be taken away from her?

The chill of fear touched her heart and slid like a snake deep into her stomach, where it seemed to coil itself like some lurking monster. She looked at her sister and reached out a tentative hand. 'Livvy . . . ?'

The elder girl turned her head and their eyes met. But there was no anger in Olive's expression now, only a terrible, dark misery. And Betty, staring at her, felt the snake of fear lift its head and hiss.

Was this misery only the beginning? By the time all was over, would its blackness seem like a pale shadow beside what suffering lay waiting for them?

'Don't look so miserable, Livvy,' Derek said. 'It might never happen.'

She turned to look at him. 'They were sitting in the front room of Derek's parents' house, close together on the sofa. From the room next door came the sound of the wireless and the occasional murmur of voices.

Derek's open face was cheerful but there was concern in his eyes. She laid her head on his shoulder. She had brushed her hair loose this evening, with a bang over her forehead, and when he stroked it, it lay like a tawny web over his fingers.

'I can't help it, Derek. Ever since this war was declared I keep thinking about you having to go away.'

'Well, nobody's said I do have to go away yet, have they?' He squeezed her against him. 'Maybe it won't come to that. If it's over quick—'

'Dad says it won't be. He says they said that about the last war – that it'd be over by Christmas. And look how long that lasted. Years.'

'Well, this one's not going to,' he said. 'We've learned a lot since then. We can beat the Germans with one hand tied behind our backs.' His voice quickened with sudden enthusiasm. 'Tell you what I'd like – I'd like to fly a Spitfire. That's real fighting, that is, up there in a plane, dodging round the sky and—'

'*Derek!*' Olive lifted her head and stared at him. 'You see, you *do* want to go – oh, you're as bad as all the rest.'

He looked shamefaced but defensive. 'I'm sorry, Livvy. I don't really want to. But when I hear other blokes on about it – and see them in their uniforms . . . And when I think what's happening and how they really do need us . . . Well, it's natural for a chap to want to do his bit isn't it?'

'I suppose so,' she said drearily. 'And what are we women supposed to do? Sit and wait?'

'You can do your bit too,' he said. 'Look, Olive, it's no good ducking it. All right, so maybe it isn't going to be over by Christmas. So we've got to face it, haven't we? We've got to think what we can do. For us blokes, it's the Forces. For you girls, it's—'

'Factory work,' she said. 'Munitions. The Dockyard. Driving buses. Milking cows. All the jobs the men don't really want to do anyway. I reckon you're all pleased to be able to go off and play soldiers and sailors.'

'Some might be,' Derek said quietly. 'But not all of us, Livvy. I bet there's a hell of a lot like me who'd rather be staying home, taking their favourite girl out for a spin in their car. Specially when it's a little red MG sports like mine, and the girl's called Olive Chapman and has long chestnut hair and big brown eyes and a figure like Betty Grable's.'

Olive laughed and gave him a push. 'Oh, you! You'd talk anyone round, you would.'

'Well, it's too nice here to worry about me going away. Let's talk about staying instead. We don't really want to go out, do we?'

Olive hesitated. They had arranged to go for a drive and then a walk but the evening had turned dull and wet, and there was a spiteful breeze in the air. The idea of staying here in Derek's front room, cuddled together on the sofa, was much more attractive. 'But aren't your mum and dad going out?' she asked.

'Mm, they're going over to Southampton to see Uncle Percy. But that doesn't matter.' He pulled her close again. 'In fact, it's all the better,' he whispered. 'It gives us the house to ourselves.'

Olive quivered. 'Derek—' she began nervously, and he hugged her.

'Don't worry, Livvy. You know I wouldn't hurt you.'

It's not hurting I'm worried about, she thought, but said nothing. She was more and more aware lately that Derek wanted more than their goodnight kisses and their cuddles in the car or on the sofa, and she was aware too that her own body was urging her towards the same goal. She wanted to relax against him, to open her mouth to his kiss, to let him fondle her breasts and undo her blouse and her bra. Sometimes, her head swimming as they pressed close in the little MG, she had allowed him to touch her trembling body, to kiss her tingling bare skin, but the sensation of spinning and falling, the growing desire that throbbed through her, were too powerful and she'd been afraid and drawn back. And then, when they had parted and she'd gone to her own lonely bed, she'd lain in the darkness reliving every precious moment, excitement spiralling through her body, half thankful that she'd managed to resist and half regretful.

And each time Derek had taken his love-making just a little further; and each time she had let him, telling herself that she could keep control, that she could always stop, that she could always stop him.

Until now, time had always been on her side. There was always the need to go home by ten or risk her father's wrath. There was always haste.

But if they were alone for a whole evening in Derek's house . . . ?

'Will they mind us being in when they're out?' she asked doubtfully, knowing her own mother would never have allowed it.

'They don't have to know, do they? We can go out for a while – then come back. There's no harm in that, is there?' He grinned at her, then pulled himself out of her arms and went to the door, opening it to poke his head through to the other room. 'Olive and me are off now,' he said cheerfully. 'You're going up to Uncle Percy's, are you?'

Olive heard their voices reply and felt herself blush, even though there was no one to see. She looked at him with uncertainty as he came back and pulled her to her feet.

'Derek, I feel awful. It's – it's like telling lies.'

'No, it's not. We haven't told any lies. All I said was we're going now – and we are.' He picked her jacket up from a chair and wrapped it round her shoulders. 'Now, stop worrying and we'll have a spin along the front. And if we feel like having a drink, we'll stop and have a drink – and if we don't, we won't.' He gave her a quick kiss. 'There. Now d'you feel better?'

'I suppose so.' She gave him a wavering smile. But already the treacherous excitement was coiling and tingling in her stomach and she knew quite well that they would not stop for any drink and that within half an hour they would be back and ensconced once more on the big, comfortable sofa in Derek's front room.

Betty too was feeling the stirring of excitement as she and Graham said goodnight at the front door later that evening. She had been over to have tea at his house again and spent most of the time sitting beside his mother, going through an old family photograph album. Snaps of Graham as a baby, lying stark-naked on a rug, had made her giggle and his mother had said, 'Go on, there's nothing to laugh at – he was a fine little boy. Wasn't he, Charlie? All his bits and pieces present and correct – that was the first thing I asked the midwife when he was born, are all his bits and pieces there, and she said you don't have to worry about that, Mrs Philpotts, this little chap's going to break hearts wherever he goes!' She gave a squawk of laughter. 'Not that he has, not my Graham, he wouldn't hurt a fly, would you, love? You don't have to worry about my Graham, Betty, he won't lead you astray. Well, not if he hasn't already!' And she'd gone off into another peal of laughter and gone out to the kitchen to make a pot of tea.

Betty blushed and giggled again, giving Graham a sideways look with her hazel eyes. He wrinkled his freckled face at her.

'Don't take any notice of Mum. She shows all my girlfriends that album. Dunno whether she's trying to encourage them or put 'em off!'

'Go on,' Betty said, 'you're as bad as she is. Worse.' She got up to help Elsie Philpotts with tea. 'We'll have to go after this. I want to get home before it's dark. I hate being out in the blackout.'

'Oh, I know,' Elsie said, piling sugar into her husband's cup. 'There you are, Charlie, love . . . It's awful trying to find your way round the streets with no lights. And the cars, I know they're only supposed to go at twenty miles an hour but some of them dash about just as if it's broad daylight.'

'Twenty miles an hour's too fast anyway,' Mr Philpotts said, making one of his rare remarks. 'You can still get killed by half a ton of metal moving at twenty miles an hour. They ought to be banned altogether.'

'That wouldn't please our Olive,' Betty said. 'She'd practically live in Derek's car if she could. They're always out in it.'

'They won't be,' Charlie Philpotts said, 'when petrol's rationed.'

Olive and Derek were still out somewhere when Betty and Graham reached home. They stood in the shadow of the front door, watching the last of the twilight fade from the sky. Earlier on it had been raining but now the shower had passed and the cloud was thin and high, veiling the moon. The dark shadows of barrage balloons loomed like drifting monsters beneath the stars.

'D'you want to come in for a cup of cocoa?' Betty asked. 'Mum won't mind.' They had already seen Ted on the ferryboat. He'd given them a brief nod and told Graham to make sure he got Betty home before blackout time. Then, his face set with concentration, he'd mounted his little bridge and stayed there throughout the five-minute journey across the harbour. 'As if he was skipper of the *Queen Mary*,' Betty whispered with a giggle.

'All right,' Graham said, and Betty led him along the side passage to the back door.

They were drinking their cocoa when Olive and Derek came in. Olive looked flushed and bright-eyed and she avoided her mother's eyes. She showed Derek in and then went quickly back to the kitchen to make more cocoa. Derek lounged in Ted's chair and talked about his car, but Betty thought he looked as if he was thinking of something else, and a small grin kept pulling at the corners of his mouth.

'They've been up to something, those two,' she said to Graham as he kissed her goodnight. 'What d'you think it is?'

Graham sniggered. 'What do *you* think? Derek looks like the cat that's had the cream and your Olive is just as bad. I saw your mum looking at her once or twice as if she wanted to ask a few questions.'

'Oh no,' Betty said. 'Our Olive wouldn't do that.'

'Why not? She's human, isn't she? Like you and me?'

'Course she's human. But—'

'Well, then.' He held her closer and kissed her ear. 'Don't say you wouldn't like to do it, Bet. You and me. You know you would.'

Betty pulled sharply away. 'I don't know anything of the sort, Graham Philpotts, and neither do you. And I don't believe our Olive has been doing anything she shouldn't, either. Why, our dad would kill us if he thought—'

'Your dad doesn't have to know.' He put his hands against the wall, one on each side of her, and moved closer so that their bodies touched. Then he moved himself against her, slowly and sinuously. 'That's nice, isn't it. Go on, Bet, admit you like it. Go on.'

'Well, maybe I do,' she said, 'but that doesn't mean—'

'And this.' He took his hands away from the wall and ran them down her body from shoulder to hip. 'That's nice too. It feels nice to me – does it feel nice to you? Say yes.' His mouth was close to hers, his lips brushing her skin as he whispered the words. 'Tell me you like it, Bet.'

Betty shivered. Graham's hands were moving lightly over her body, tracing the contours of her shoulders, her breasts, her thighs. His palms cupped her buttocks and he lifted her towards him so that their bodies pressed together, hip to hip. Holding her there, he kissed her open mouth and she felt his tongue push against hers. He moved against her and she felt the shape of him and heard his breath quicken.

'Graham, don't. Suppose my mum came out and found you behaving like this? She'd never let you in the door again.'

'Well, we'll have to make sure we do it where she can't see, won't we,' he murmured, not letting go. He bent to kiss her again.

Betty wound her arms around his neck and closed her eyes. Her body felt as if it were melting. Graham's hands were splayed over her buttocks, his fingers moving in tiny circles on the softness. She quivered and Graham slid his mouth down her neck, into the hollow of her throat. He nuzzled there for a moment and she felt one hand slide up to cover her breast. Her head felt as if it were spinning. She wrapped her arms tightly around his shoulders, holding him firmly against her.

'You still out here, our Bet?' The front door had opened so suddenly they almost fell into the blacked-out hallway. Olive stood there, no more than a deeper shadow in the darkness and Betty sensed that Derek was close behind her. 'I thought you'd gone to bed.'

'Just saying goodnight,' Betty said defensively, but she hardly knew whether to be annoyed with her sister or grateful for her interruption. 'You can't get any privacy around here!'

'Strikes me you've had more than enough.' Olive stared through the darkness at her sister. 'What've you been doing?'

'I might ask you that,' Betty retorted. 'You came in tonight looking like you'd been dragged through a hedge backwards.'

'So would you if you'd been driving along the front in an open-topped car.' Olive gave her a push. 'Go on, you two've had long enough to say goodbye. Go in and give someone else a turn.'

'I'll have to be going now anyway, Bet,' Graham said. 'It takes a long time getting home in the blackout and I've got to be up early tomorrow morning.'

'All right.' Betty reached up and gave Graham a quick kiss. Maybe it was a good thing Olive had come out just then. Things had been moving a bit faster tonight than she'd meant them to. Another few minutes of Graham's kisses and the way he had of moving his hands, and she might not have been able to call a halt.

She went indoors, said goodnight to her mother and climbed the stairs to bed. Was that really what had happened to Olive tonight? Had things gone further than she'd meant, so that she'd been unable to stop them?

If so, she looked pretty pleased about it, Betty thought. And felt, mixed with her feelings of relief and half regret, a nagging curiosity.

What was it *like*? If only she could try it just once, just to find out, just to know . . .

The children who had been evacuated knew now where they were. It was Bridge End, a small village near Romsey, with a village hall and a school that had only two rooms. It was there that they had been marshalled on the first Monday and told what would be happening to them.

'School in the afternoons!' Tim crowed when his mother and Rose came over to see the boys at the Corners' cottage. 'We don't have to go in the mornings, that's when the village kids go. We can do what we like!'

'You'll do some extra schoolwork, that's what you'll do,' Jess said sharply. 'And help Mr and Mrs Corner. It makes a lot of extra work, having two boys to look after.'

Tim pushed out his lips. Now that his family was – except for Dad – with him again, he'd got over his homesickness and almost forgotten what it had felt like. Now he wondered whether it was so good having Mum nearby.

Some of the other boys had already begun to make plans about what to do with their spare time. Carts made from old pram-wheels, rafts to sail on the river, trees to climb, dens to be built – all this sounded far more interesting to Tim and Keith than doing extra schoolwork or helping Mrs Corner. What could they help her do anyway? There was only housework and cooking, and those were girls' jobs.

'You're lucky,' Rose said later, when Mum had gone indoors to feed the baby. 'You've got a good place here. So've we. Some of the others don't like where they are at all.'

Wendy and Alan Atkinson were among those who weren't happy. The two elderly sisters who had taken them in seemed to think that because the children were small they would also be both invisible and inaudible. It had not dawned on them that they would also need more care, nor that they might have problems older children had outgrown.

'Eleanor! The boy's wet his bed!' the younger of the sisters exclaimed that first morning, in tones of shock and outrage. And Alan, crying with misery and humiliation, had been made to have a bath while Wendy found herself faced with a pile of sheets to be washed.

'He's your brother, you must take care of him yourself. And the mattress will have to be scrubbed too.' She was given a brush and a large bar of yellow soap, both almost too big to close her small hands round. 'They didn't tell us we'd have to put up with this sort of thing,' Miss Millicent went on, going downstairs to her sister, and the two children, up in the bathroom, could hear the indignant voices in the kitchen below.

The bathroom was large and cavernous, its walls distempered a muddy green, and the bath stood in the middle of it on huge legs with clawed feet. It was more like an animal than a bath. At any other time it might have been fun, but now, in an atmosphere of disgust and disapproval, it loomed menacingly in the sludgy green cave.

At the head of the bath, fixed to the wall above it, was a large geyser. Wendy, whose home, in common with most of the others she knew, had no bathroom, eyed it dubiously. Miss Millicent had turned it on and started the hot tap, but there had been many strictures about not using too much hot water. It was gushing out now and clouds of steam were rising from the bath. Perhaps there was already too much.

'Have I got to get in there?' Alan asked fearfully. 'Won't I drown?' He was still sobbing.

'Of course you won't drown.' She spoke briskly, but the bath looked immense. Alan would need to stand on a stool to climb in. She peered over the top, wondering how deep the water was, but could see little through the steam.

'We'd better have some cold in as well.'

She twisted the big brass tap with both hands, but it wouldn't move. She struggled with it, wondering if she dared send Alan down to fetch one of the sisters up. But Alan was sitting shivering on a small, cork-topped stool, and he had nothing on. Wendy had already noticed how the sisters averted their eyes when confronted with naked bodies.

'I can't do it – *oh!*'

The tap suddenly loosened and cold water burst out as if a dam had been breached. The bath was filling rapidly. Wendy tried to turn the hot tap off, but now this one was too stiff.

'Oh dear. Oh, it won't shut. Oh, Alan . . .' Her voice rose in panic. 'I can't turn either of them off. You'll have to go and get one of the ladies.'

'I don't want to.' Alan had almost stopped crying but now his voice quivered and his face began to redden. Wendy gave him a despairing glance. She knew that he wasn't far off losing control, and if he did that he was capable of crying for hours.

But someone had to turn these horrible taps off, and if she couldn't do it herself . . .

'I'll go then. You stay here.'

She ran downstairs to the kitchen. The table was neatly laid, with a packet of cornflakes, a jug of milk, toast in a rack, butter and marmalade. The two sisters were eating.

'Please—' she panted, and they turned and stared at her. The hair sprouting from Miss Eleanor's mole quivered alarmingly.

'What is it, child? What are you doing down here? Have you washed those sheets yet?'

'Wendy shook her head. 'I can't. The—'

'What do you mean, you can't?' Miss Eleanor demanded ominously. 'Of course you can. It might help you to see that your brother learns to behave himself. Has he had his bath yet?'

'No. You see—'

'Why not?' Eleanor Woddis rose from her seat. She was tall, thin and angular, and in her black frock with a heavy silver cross hung round her neck she looked like some vengeful being from one of the stories Wendy had heard and only half understood at Sunday School. 'What are you doing up there?' She looked at her sister. 'I thought I told you to see that they cleaned themselves and the bedding properly.'

'I did, Eleanor. I took them into the bathroom and gave them everything they needed.' Miss Millicent spoke quickly, as if afraid of being blamed for the children's misdemeanours. Her pale lips trembled a little and her nose twitched like a rabbit's.

'Then why is the child down here?'

'I don't know, I'm sure.' The younger sister turned to Wendy. Go back at once and don't come down until you've finished.' Her voice was stronger when she addressed Wendy.

'But I can't—'

'And don't answer back, miss! The impertinence of it!'

'But—'

'Go upstairs at once!'

Wendy turned and fled to the door. But once there, the hopelessness of the situation overcame her. In the distance, she could hear the relentless gushing of water and knew that it must be near the top of the bath now, if not actually overflowing. Desperate, she turned and faced the two accusing women.

'I can't turn off the taps!' she yelled. 'It's not my fault – they're too big. And Alan's crying, he's frightened of that great big bath, he's frightened he'll drown. Oh, I wished we'd never come here, I wish we could go back home, I hate it here, I *hate* it!'

Without waiting to see the effect of her outburst, she dashed back upstairs. Her one thought now was to get her brother out of the bathroom before the bath overflowed and swept him away. Her mother had told her to look after him, and she would do her best – but she hadn't realised it would mean bathing him in that horrible room all by herself and washing the sheets.

Behind her, she could hear the feet of the two sisters, but Wendy was past caring now. She burst into the bathroom and grabbed her brother from where he was still sitting, naked and crying, on the stool.

The room was full of steam. The damp sheets were in a pile on the floor. Miss Eleanor Woddis entered behind her and gave a scream of horror.

'Whatever have you been doing, you naughty, naughty children? Look at this, Millicent. They've got both taps full on and the plug out. Have you ever seen anything so wilfully naughty in your life?'

With a rapid twist, she turned off both taps. Relief swept over Wendy as she saw that the bath had not overflowed. And, looking in, she realised that it probably would not have done, for Alan must have pulled out the plug and the water was running away almost as fast as it came in.

'Such a waste,' Miss Eleanor went on, rolling up her sleeve and plunging in her arm to replace the plug. 'I don't know what you can have been thinking of. No, don't answer me back again. I don't wish to hear your excuses.' She straightened up and looked at the two children in disgust. 'Now, perhaps, you'll do as you were told. And I don't want to see either of you downstairs until you have. Is that understood?'

Wendy nodded. Inside, she was seething with anger and misery. If Mummy was here, she thought, she wouldn't let them treat us like this.

But Mummy wasn't here. She was far away at home, where everything was comfortable and known, where the bath was made of tin and hung on a nail outside the back door, to be brought in and filled with buckets of hot water from the Ascot on Saturday nights. She was having her own breakfast of Weetabix and hot milk and sugar. Perhaps she was thinking about Wendy and Alan, wondering where they were and hoping they were all right.

Tears filled Wendy's eyes again. She helped Alan into the bath and soaped him all over. Then she got him out and wrapped him in a towel before heaving the sheets into the water.

How did you wash sheets? She swilled them about a bit, then pulled out the plug. Her small hands gathered the sheets in a bit at a time, squeezing them ineffectually. Vaguely, she knew that they ought to be rinsed, but she dared not turn the taps on again. She looked at the sodden heap lying in the bath and wondered what she was supposed to do with them now. Through all this, the tears had not stopped streaming down her cheeks. Alan, too, was still sobbing. The two children got dressed and then stared at each other.

'I don't like it here,' Alan whispered. 'I want to go home. I want my Mummy.'

'I do, too. But we can't.'

'Why can't we?' Alan asked, looking into her face. 'Why can't we go home? Doesn't Mummy want us any more?'

'Of course she does. It's because—' But Wendy could not answer him. Instead, she sat on the stripped bed, forgetting that she was supposed to scrub it, and cuddled him against her.

Why had they been sent here, to live in this strange house? Had they done something wrong? And why could they not go back home?

Wendy had heard little about the war. It had not been talked about in her presence at home and she'd only half understood the talk of other children. Just as children take for granted the world they find themselves in, accepting each new development as part of normal living, so she had taken for granted the digging of trenches in the parks, the arrival of the Anderson shelters, the blackouts and the sky full of barrage balloons. Evacuation had been just one more event, and it wasn't until it actually happened that she'd realised her mother's distress and connected it with herself.

Now, she felt totally bewildered. The only rock in this world that had suddenly turned upside down around her was the responsibility her mother had laid on her in those final moments of goodbye. Look after Alan. Take care of your little brother.

5

Since the day when he and Graham had met Betty Chapman down near the harbour, Bob had thought more and more about the girl who lived at the top of the street.

He'd always liked Betty Chapman. She was more fun than her sister – Olive was a bit toffee-nosed at times, as if living in a detached house made her better than everyone else. Her mum was a bit like that too, putting on airs because she'd worked in posh houses and talking about doilies and antimacassars, whatever they were. But Betty had always been ready, with a sparkle in her eye, for a game of cricket with stumps drawn in chalk on the side of the end house, or football in the wide bit where the road bordered the allotments. She wasn't forever fussing about with dolls or bits of ribbon and she could fight as well as any boy.

These attributes hadn't seemed so important when Bob was first beginning to take an interest in girls and, having seen Betty as a kind of surrogate boy, he found it difficult to think of her as female. But that day down at the Hard, hearing her voice with that new, flirtatious note in it, and seeing the saucy look she was giving Graham, he'd suddenly realised that she could be fun in a different kind of way. And since then, his days had been built around the chance of seeing and speaking to Betty.

'Our Bob's smartened himself up a bit lately,' Gladys Shaw remarked, coming across him as he smoothed Brylcreem into his hair at the kitchen mirror. 'Must be in love – nothing else'd make him clean his fingernails twice in the same week!' And she'd ducked and giggled as Bob rounded on her.

Peggy Shaw found her son suddenly keen to go shopping in September Street, especially if it meant a visit to the dairy. He would be gone for longer than she thought necessary, coming back sometimes depressed and taciturn, at others with a grin on his thin face. She sighed, knowing quite well what was happening, for she too had seen that photograph on the bedroom wall, and she knew from Jess Budd and Annie that Betty was going steady now with Graham Philpotts.

'You ought to look for some other girl,' she told Bob. 'Betty Chapman's not for you.' But he'd closed his lips firmly and buried himself in a copy of *Hotspur*.

'A job wouldn't be a bad idea,' Bert Shaw said caustically, but he knew as well as anyone else that jobs had been hard to come by in the past few years, and didn't pursue the matter. It wasn't Bob's fault he was unemployed, and with this war coming he'd be in demand soon enough, along with all the other youngsters.

Meanwhile, Bob lived for his snatched meetings with Betty. Sometimes days would go by without a word. The dairy would be full of women when he went in, or she'd be working at the back and Mrs Marsh would serve him instead. Sometimes she'd be on her own and he could linger, but although she was friendly enough she would never agree to go out with him.

'Sorry, Bob. I'm going out with Graham that night.' And when he suggested another evening, 'I can't. Graham wouldn't like it.' And she shook her head so that the soft brown curls danced around her face.

'You're not engaged to him, are you?' Bob said once and she blushed.

'I don't have to be engaged to be loyal. You wouldn't like it if your girl two-timed you, would you?'

'Not if she was you,' he said. 'I'd want you all to myself.'

And Betty had blushed a bit more and looked almost as if she liked that idea, but she'd only shaken her head again and said, 'Well, there you are, then.' And the door had opened to admit an old woman wanting a pint of milk, and at the same moment Mrs Marsh had come out from the back of the shop and glared at Bob, and he'd had to go.

After that, Betty hadn't been so ready to talk to him and the next time she'd seen him in the street she'd told him quite sharply to stop asking her out.

'If I've told you once, I've told you a dozen times, I'm going out with Graham. I don't want anyone else. And you're getting me into trouble with Mrs Marsh. She says I'm encouraging you and it looks bad. The other customers don't like coming in and finding you always hanging about.'

Bob stared at her. 'You mean you don't want me coming in any more?'

Betty avoided his eye. 'Can't stop you, can I? Not if you're doing your mum's shopping. Only don't make a meal of it, see? And don't keep on at me to go out with you.'

He bit his lip. He hadn't realised just how much his days depended on seeing Betty, having a laugh with her in the shop, and on the hope that one day she would relent and agree to go out with him. He felt cold inside, as if she'd driven a spear of ice deep into his heart. He didn't know how to deal with it. He clenched his jaw and turned away.

'Well, if that's the way you want it . . .'

'It is.'

'I won't bother you any more. I'm sorry I've been such a nuisance.' His voice was tight with misery. He scuffed with his toe at the loose gravel at the side of the road.

Betty looked at him. She put out her hand, then drew it back again. Her voice awkwardly gentle, she said, 'I'm sorry, Bob. It's just—'

'Oh, I know. It's just that I don't match up to Ginger Philpotts. Well, I wouldn't, would I? I'm not like him, I don't know how to talk to girls, I don't have money to flash around. Well, you go out with him, Betty, and good luck to you. I just hope you don't find you've bitten off more than you can chew, that's all.'

Betty stared at him. 'What d'you mean?'

'Oh, nothing,' Bob said. 'Nothing you won't find out for yourself. And when you do, when Graham Philpotts chucks you like he chucks all his girls, you'll know where to come, won't you? Except that I might not be here by then.'

He turned on his heel and walked away, back towards his own house. And Betty, left standing in the street, stared after him.

Bob had been really hurt, she thought in surprise. I didn't know he'd take it that way. I didn't know it mattered that much.

But there was nothing she could do about it. She was Graham's girl and that was that. And if Graham had chucked girls in the past, what did it matter? He'd just been waiting for the right one. And the right one for Graham was Betty Chapman.

On the other side of the Budd's house, silent and empty during the day now that all the family had gone, the Glaisters were returning after their holiday in Devon.

'I knew we shouldn't have gone,' Ethel said, pulling clothes out of suitcases and dropping them in piles ready for the wash. 'I knew it. It's as if we're fated. Our first holiday in years and they declare war in the middle of it. I said we shouldn't have gone.'

'It wouldn't have made any difference,' George said. He was a thin, lanky man with a mournful face. He was several inches taller than his petite blonde wife but had developed a stoop, as if he were trying to hide the fact. 'I don't suppose us staying home would have stopped them declaring war.'

Ethel glared at him. 'You know what I mean. We should have stopped home. Suppose we'd got stuck, down there in Devon? Suppose we hadn't been able to get back?'

'But we did get back,' he pointed out.

'We might not have done. And then what would we have done? Our Joe and Carol with jobs to go to, you supposed to report for Service . . . You could have had the Military Police after you for desertion.'

George sighed. Pointing out that they had managed to return home with very little trouble and that the trip had given them a chance to see his relatives for the first (and possibly the last) time in several years, as well as having enjoyed several days' holiday, seemed of little use. He performed the trick he had learned during the early years of his marriage to Ethel and closed his ears to her tirade, while still retaining enough awareness to be able to nod, shake his head and murmur 'yes' or 'no' at appropriate intervals.

'. . . now our Shirley's missed the evacuation,' Ethel was saying when he next tuned in. 'All the other children have gone to the country, you realise that? They're safe. I wonder if you'll ever be able to forgive yourself, George Glaister, if she gets killed by a bomb simply because you insisted on having a holiday in Devon.'

George's recollection was that it was Ethel who had insisted that they should have a holiday. His only stipulation was that it should be at the end of August, when he could take his annual leave. But that wasn't important now.

'I did suggest we should leave Shirley in Devon,' he reminded his wife. 'My sister would have been only too pleased—'

'Your sister's got enough to do, with that farm and all those hulking great boys to look after.'

'One more wouldn't have made much difference. She'll probably have to take an evacuee anyway. And the boys love Shirl, you know they do. They made a real pet of her.'

'I don't think it's suitable. Shirley's not used to boys.'

'Not used to boys? What about our Joe?'

'He's her brother.' Ethel picked up the washing and pushed past him to the scullery, which she dignified by the name of kitchen. Some time ago, she had bullied George into roofing over the area between their scullery wall and that of number 12. This was known as the conservatory and was the envy of the street, forming as it did another room, as well as making it possible to go to the lavatory without having to put on outdoor shoes. Ethel also kept the copper out there and did her mangling, another job that needed to be done under cover.

'So what are you going to do about Shirley?' George asked, when she came in again.

'What, are you still here? I thought you'd have gone over the allotment or down to the shed. There's plenty to be done, even if you are still on holiday.'

'I just wanted to know what you want to do about Shirl,' he repeated patiently. 'Now there's no school—'

'Well, you don't need to tell me there's no school! That's what I've been telling you all day. All the other children have gone and so have the teachers. There's nothing for her to do now and she'll be under my feet all day, not that you'll care when you're back at work—'

'I don't suppose I'll be going back to work,' George said, raising his voice slightly to make himself heard. Ethel stopped and stared at him. Her mouth hung open and he could almost fancy that he saw her unspoken words, teetering just inside.

'What do you mean, you won't be going back?'

'I'm a Territorial, aren't I? I'll have to report for duty. Didn't you hear what they said on the wireless on Sunday, what they've been saying ever since? Reservists and people like that, they all have to report at their centre for duty. Didn't you listen?'

'Of course I listened,' she said sulkily. 'I heard what they said. But it doesn't affect us—'

'Of course it affects us. I'm in the TA. I'll have to go.'

'Well, I know that,' she said impatiently. 'But you've only got to report – you won't be going away.'

'I might. I expect I will. That's what they were saying.'

Ethel stared at him. 'But what about us? Me and our Shirley? Joe and Carol? How're we supposed to manage?'

'Same as everyone else, I should think. There'll be plenty of families left on their own, Ethel.'

'Yes, but . . . What about your job? What about your pay? What are we supposed to live on?'

'I'll get paid by the Army.'

'And will they keep your job for you?' Her voice was rising. 'What are you going to do when you come out of the Army and your job's gone? Have you thought of that?'

'Of course I've thought about it. Mr Browning says my job'll be kept open for me. But even if it isn't . . . Look, we knew this might happen. God knows they've talked about it enough. Why did you think I joined the TA in the first place? What did you expect?'

Ethel did not answer. She turned away and began to fill the copper with water. She heard George go upstairs. When he came down again in his Territorial uniform she was standing at the sink, scrubbing his shirt collars. He stood behind her for a moment but she did not turn round, and she did not reply when he said awkwardly, 'Well, I'll be off then.'

Out of the corner of her eye, she saw him hesitate by the back door. Then he sighed, shrugged and took himself off down the garden path. She heard him get his bike out from the shed and close the gate behind him.

Ethel scrubbed furiously. Her eyes were blurred with angry tears. Just as if I don't have enough to put up with, she thought. Three children to look after, and all he can think of is getting away to play soldiers. That's all it is in the Territorials, just playing soldiers. A night a week out with his mates and weekend camps when he ought to be doing the garden – what good will all that be in a war? Why, he can't even swat a fly, let alone fire a gun. And never mind how I'm going to manage, left stuck here on my own. Never mind our Shirley, left behind when all the other children have been taken somewhere safe. The selfish beast!

She hadn't really minded when he'd suggested joining the TA, when they'd appealed for volunteers last year. It got him out of the house one night a week, out from under her feet. And she hadn't really minded him going off on the camps either, not at first. It meant she could get the house looking nice and keep it that way for the weekend, without his books and papers scattered all over the place. She could have Mum and Auntie Ellen over for tea for a good old natter. You couldn't do that with a man around. They always put a damper on that sort of thing, men did.

Still, she hadn't banked on him going quite so often as he did. And she wasn't too keen on the way he was when he came home, either. He'd looked really red in the face the last time or two, as if he'd been out in the sun too much – or in the pub. She was certain there'd been beer on his breath. And he'd had a silly grin, and kept grabbing hold of her and making – well, suggestions. She'd stopped that straight away. 'We're not a couple of newly-weds now, George Glaister,' she'd said sharply. 'There's time enough for that sort of thing at the weekend.'

'This is the weekend,' he'd said, fondling her, and she'd pushed his hand away quickly.

'It's Sunday evening. You've got to go to work tomorrow. And I'll have all the housework to do, so if you don't mind . . .'

She didn't really care whether he minded or not but she wasn't going to change their routine now, not after all these years, just because he'd been with a lot of men for a couple of days and got ideas.

But it wasn't just that, she thought, rinsing out the washing before putting it through the mangle. Men were all the same as far as that was concerned. What she didn't like was the way the TA was changing George in other ways, and not for the better in her opinion. He wasn't so easy to manage these days. Too inclined to argue when she wanted him to do something, and really snappy at times. And too set on having his own way – like today, going off to the hall in spite of what she said. As if he didn't care any more . . .

Ethel took the washing out and hung it on the line. Next door, Frank Budd had hung out a few bits and pieces. He must have done them last night, after getting home from work. They flapped dolefully on the line, looking rather pathetic. Jess's line was usually so full, with all the children's clothes and a row of white sheets.

Ethel looked at Frank's line thoughtfully. He was a fine figure of a man, Frank Budd, and it was a shame he had to do his own washing. He must be lonely too, there in that house all on his own in the evenings.

Suppose George did go away. It wouldn't hurt her to offer to do Frank's washing for him. Maybe a bit of cooking, too. And it'd be handy to have someone next door who could help with the odd job in return.

They'd always got on well enough, her and Frank, though she'd not had a lot to do with him, just the odd word over the fence. All the same, she'd often thought what a big, strong chap he was, and wondered what he saw in little Jess. And now Jess was away. For 'the duration'. Whatever that might mean . . .

Feeling suddenly more cheerful, Ethel picked up her basket and went back indoors.

Heinrich Brunner was having supper with his wife and daughter. They always ate together at six o'clock, after the shop was shut. Alice worked in the shop too, and spent the last hour or so dashing out to see to the cooking, but as Joy grew more capable she was able to leave more and more of it to her.

'She did all the supper tonight, didn't you, love?' she said tonight. 'She's getting to be a real little help, I don't know what we'd do without her.'

Heinrich looked across the table at his daughter. She was like him, quiet and anxious to please, with brown eyes and straight hair, but luckily she hadn't inherited his weak sight. He took off his glasses and polished the thick lenses on his handkerchief.

'Are you feeling lonely without the other children to play with?' he asked. His German accent had almost gone and sometimes people who came into the shop didn't realise he wasn't English. They thought he came from the north of England. 'If you would still like to be evacuated—'

Joy shook her head. 'I don't want to go away from home.'

Her parents looked at her doubtfully.

'But all your friends have gone,' Heinrich said. 'That nice little girl from April Grove – Rosemary Budd, Rosebud – has she gone away?'

'They've nearly all gone,' Alice said. 'There are only a few children left around here.' She pushed back her mousy hair. Since all the talk of war had begun, she had grown thin and pale. Her eyes were tired from waking in the night, worrying about what would happen to them all – about what would happen to Heinrich.

'It would be safer for you when the aeroplanes come,' Heinrich said.

But Joy shook he head again. 'I'd rather stay here.'

Heinrich sighed and looked troubled. Most parents, he knew, didn't give their children the option. But he and Alice had always treated their daughter almost as if she were grown up, as if she could make her own choices. And Joy was a thoughtful child, who would consider carefully before she made any decision. If she wanted to stay at home, she had good reasons.

'I wonder if we should tell her she must go,' he said to Alice as they went to bed that night. 'It's bad for her to be here, with so few children about. And when the bombs come . . . Why do you suppose she doesn't want to go?'

'I don't think many of the children did,' Alice said. 'They just didn't have the choice. But there's more to it than that, with Joy.' She hesitated, then said, 'I think it might be because of you.'

'Me?' Heinrich looked at her, then sighed and nodded. 'Yes. I wondered if it might be that.' He took off his trousers and folded them neatly over the back of a chair. 'Have the other children been making her unhappy?'

'Only some of them. She hasn't said much to me – you know Joy. But I think some of them have been teasing her.'

'Not little Rosebud?'

'Oh no – none of the Budds would do that. And Rose is a good friend of Joy. I've heard her standing up for her.'

Heinrich frowned. He struggled for a moment with his collar-stud, then said, 'But wouldn't it be better for Joy to be away? The other children would soon forget. And if there is any unpleasantness . . .'

'What sort of unpleasantness?'

Heinrich didn't answer. He had talked with his family during his visits to Berlin and knew what sort of unpleasantness there could be when a country turned against its inhabitants who were different in any way. Heinrich was not a Jew, but he'd heard what was happening to them there. Forced to wear yellow stars, to brand them as the butt of any lout who wanted a bit of sport . . . turned out of their homes, dismissed from their jobs . . . herded together into camps. Stoned in the streets, attacked for no reason, arrested on trumped-up charges. And if it were not these things, there were others. Dogs' excreta pushed through the letter-box, or even rags soaked in paraffin and set alight.

He'd seen the hate already in people's eyes. He'd noted the sharp fall in customers coming to buy their newspapers and cigarettes. And the war was not yet a week old.

'Joy would be better out of it,' he said, getting into his striped pyjamas.

'I don't think she'll go, all the same.' Alice was already in bed, her shoulders covered with the pink lace of the nightdress he liked best. 'She's afraid you'll be interned.'

'Interned? Oh, I don't think that's likely. I've lived here so long. Anyway, there's nothing for Joy to fear in that. It only means I'd go away for a while.'

'Does it?' Alice looked up at him. 'I think Joy's afraid that if you go away we'll never see you again.' Her voice quivered suddenly and she held out her arms. 'I'm afraid of it too, Heinrich. I dream about it at night. I don't want our family to be parted.'

Heinrich pulled back the sheets and climbed into bed beside her. She wound her arms around his neck and he drew her close. She could feel the warmth of his skin through the cotton and the lace that separated them, and the beating of his heart against her breast.

'We won't be parted,' he said softly. 'We'll stay together. If Joy wants to stay at home, she shall. And they won't take me away. What good would it do? Everyone knows Heinrich.'

Alice clung to him. Ever since she had known him, Heinrich had always been able to calm her fears and chase away the shadows that lurked cold and dark at the edges of her mind. Here in this small bedroom over the shop he had soothed her when her demons had grown too insistent, here he had given her love and reassurance.

Now the world was full of demons, and the shadows enveloped the whole of Europe. Heinrich was her only rock of sanity in the madness that was sweeping over them all. If she lost him, she would lose her rock.

Gladys Shaw went down the alley, between the gardens of April Grove and the allotments. Each garden had its hump of Anderson shelter down near the back gate, covered with earth. One or two people, who had lawns, had dug up turfs and laid them over the top, and others had put in a few stones or bricks in an attempt to make the shelter look like a rockery. But most of them had left the earth bare and weeds like groundsel and dandelions were already starting to grow.

Gladys hated the shelter. It was cold, damp and full of spiders. But her mother had tried to make it look homely, with a few magazine pictures stuck on the walls and a bit of old carpet on the floor, and Dad had made a couple of benches with planks laid over boxes and more carpet tacked on to them. All the same, the idea of spending hours down there – maybe whole nights – made Gladys shiver and she made up her mind that if the bombs did come she'd take her chance indoors. She'd heard people say you were as safe under the stairs as anywhere.

Bob was the only one home when she let herself in the back door. He was lounging back in his father's armchair, his feet up on the mantelpiece, reading *Hotspur*. As she opened the door, he lowered his feet guiltily and then grinned.

'You needn't look like that,' Gladys said, standing in the doorway between the back room and the scullery. 'I saw you through the window. Haven't you got anything better to do?' She looked at the sink, piled high with dirty dishes. 'Couldn't you even have done the washing-up?'

'That's women's work,' Bob said, returning to his reading.

'Oh yes? And I suppose you've been hard at it all day, slaving away to earn your keep.' Gladys marched in and snatched the comic from his hands. 'You're turning into nothing but a lazy slob, Bob Shaw. Why should you sit around all day doing nothing while Diane and me work fifty-two hours a week to keep you in fags? And Mum could do with a bit of help too. Women's work! You helped make those dishes dirty – you damned well make them clean again.'

Bob stared at her. 'Now look here—'

'No. You look here.' Gladys stood with arms akimbo, glaring down at him. 'I've just walked home with Olive and Betty Chapman. Olive's worried sick because her Derek's likely to be called up soon and *he's* got a job—'

'He words for his dad!'

'That's a job, isn't it? Anyway, he doesn't just work for his dad, he's an accountant. He works bloody hard—'

'You'd better not let our dad hear you talk like that—'

'I'll talk how I like to you. I'm telling you, Derek's got a job, he works morning till night doing something worth doing, and he's going to have to go and fight. While you sit here on your backside reading kids' comics and letting our mum run round after you and our dad pay for your fags. Don't you ever feel ashamed of yourself, Bob Shaw? Don't you ever wonder what it is makes you so special you don't even have to lift a finger to do anything for yourself? Why, you'll be calling out to have your bottom wiped soon!'

Bob leaped to his feet. 'Look here, our Glad—'

'Yes?' Gladys stared up at him. He was a good eight inches taller than she and, although thin, he was strong, but her eyes challenged him to use his strength against her. She pushed back her yellow hair. 'What are you going to do, then? Hit me? Go on, and see if it makes you feel better.'

Bob hesitated, then shrugged.

'You're not worth hitting,' he muttered, turning away. 'You're getting like all the rest of them, nagging a bloke just because he puts his feet up for a few minutes—'

'I bet you've had your feet up all afternoon.'

'I haven't.'

'So what else have you done? What time did Mum go out?'

'Just after two,' he mumbled.

'And where's she gone?'

'I dunno. Said something about the First-Aid Post up the school. They're getting it kitted out for when the raids start.'

'And she didn't have time to wash up. And when she comes homes, she'll have to run round and start getting a meal ready. Dad'll be in at six and you know what he's like – expects it on the table. And you've been sitting here ever since.' Gladys turned on the tap and rolled up her sleeves. 'Just tell me this, Bob Shaw, when and if you finally do get a job – just supposing anyone's daft enough or desperate enough to give you one – how're you going to know what work is? 'Cause I don't think you'll recognise it when it hits you in the face.' She took a piece of washing soda from the jamjar that stood on the windowsill and dropped it in the water.

Bob scowled. 'And what would you know about it, Miss Clever? For all you know, I've already got a job. There'll be plenty going now, you know, with men being called up. That Derek bloody Harker with his posh car and his fancy clothes—'

Gladys whirled. 'You'll never get Derek Harker's job! His dad's not going to give you his job while he goes off and fights to save your yellow skin.'

'Yellow? Who are you calling yellow?' Bob was as angry as she. He stared at her, his face white. 'You'll take that back, Gladys Shaw.'

'I won't.'

'You will.'

'I—' But Gladys was cut short by the sound of the front door opening. She closed her mouth abruptly, gave Bob a furious look, and turned back to the sink. Almost at random, she snatched a plate from the pile and plunged it into the water.

Bob grabbed a tea-towel. He took the plate from his sister and when Peggy Shaw walked through from the front room they were standing, apparently amicably, sharing the washing-up.

Peggy dropped her shopping bag on a chair and sat down, giving a sigh of relief.

'I thought I'd never get home. The things we had to do! And I've got to go for training two nights a week. I don't know what your father's going to say about that. They're looking for more volunteers too. I wondered if you might think about it, Bob.'

'Shan't be able to,' he muttered, avoiding his sister's eye.

'Oh? Why not?'

'Because I'll have other things to do.' He spoke reluctantly, still not looking at Gladys.

Gladys said sarcastically, 'He's got three months' worth of back *Hotspurs* to catch up on. Little Keith next door wants them back.'

Bob flung down his tea-towel.

'Oh, you think you're so ruddy clever, don't you, you and your posh job in British Home Stores and your posh friends with their flashy cars, and Olive Chapman with her Derek who's got a job and getting called up soon. I suppose you think he'll win the war single-handed? Well, he won't – he'll need a few other poor buggers to help him and shall I tell you who one of them's going to be? Well, shall I?' He stood glowering at her, his head lowered slightly and his chin pushed out.

'Bob!' his mother exclaimed. 'Watch your tongue – I won't have language like that in this house.'

But her words went unheeded. Brother and sister stared at each other. Then Gladys shrugged and turned away.

'Tell me if you like. Why should I care?' She swished a plate about in the water.

'No, you don't care,' Bob said bitterly. 'All you care about is your fancy friends. Well, you might be sorry for that one day – when it's your own brother marching out of here in uniform and getting blown up by a Ger—'

'Bob!'

Peggy was on her feet, staring at him, her face suddenly pale. Bob stopped abruptly and looked shamefaced. He glanced sidelong at Gladys, who was as scarlet as her mother was white.

'Now look what you've done, you idiot,' she muttered.

'What have you done, our Bob?' Peggy whispered. She grabbed him by the arms, shaking him so that he was forced to meet her eyes. 'What have you done?'

Bob looked down at her. He licked his lips and lifted his shoulders slightly. His glance shifted away and then back to his mother's face.

'I've joined up,' he said at last. 'I've been down the recruiting office and joined up. Well, isn't it what you wanted me to do?' he demanded, his voice suddenly loud. 'Don't you think I know what you're all getting at with your remarks about jobs and sitting on my backside all day? D'you think I want to have to ask for fag money and see other blokes getting all the kudos because they're in uniform? Well, I did something about it, that's all. I went and joined up, and on Monday I have to report to Hilsea Barracks and I hope you're all satisfied!'

He wrenched himself away and stared out of the window. Peggy and Gladys looked at his back, then at each other.

'What've you been saying to him, our Glad?' Peggy asked, her voice quivering.

'Me? I haven't said nothing. You're not blaming me for what he does.' Gladys's voice trembled. 'All I said was he ought to do a hand's turn about the place, that's all, give you a bit of help. I just came in to find him sitting here reading a comic, with all this washing-up staring him in the face. I never said he had to go and join up.'

'I'd already done it then,' Bob retorted. 'I just thought I was entitled to a bit of comfort, my last weekend in civvy street.'

'So why didn't you say?'

'Why didn't you ask?' he countered.

Gladys turned away with an exasperated sigh. She started to swish plates in the water again, but it was cooling now and the soda did little to remove the grease.

'I'll have to run off some more hot water now,' she said impatiently. 'That's waste, that is.'

'I never told you to—' Bob began, but Peggy shook him again and then sat down as if it were all too much for her. Her thin body sagged.

'Can't you two ever stop squabbling? There's a war on – and here's our Bob going off to fight in it. Don't that mean nothing to you, Glad?'

'It's only her stuck-up friends she cares about. She said so.'

'Stop it!' Peggy slapped her hand on the table and glared at them both. 'Stop it, the pair of you. You're behaving like a couple of kids.' She watched as they both bit their lips and glanced sideways at each other. It was just the same as when they'd been little. They used to get themselves into a squabble then and you could tell they really wanted to make it up, only neither of them wanted to be first to say so. They were too alike, that was their trouble.

'Say sorry,' she commanded, as she'd so often done before, and saw the unwilling grins pull at their mouths. They knew, then. They remembered the old formula. But would they comply with it, now they both reckoned they were so grown up?

To her relief, they turned to each other, still with those rueful grins on their faces, and said simultaneously, 'Sorry.' And then burst out laughing.

'Honestly,' she said, smiling in spite of herself, 'you two won't never grow up,' And then, the smile fading, 'But d'you really mean it, Bob? Have you really joined up?'

'Yes, I have. I've gone in the Army. Gunners.'

'But why?'

'Why d'you think? There's a war on. They're crying out for volunteers. And the pay's regular.'

'Oh, Bob.' Peggy shook her head. 'Why didn't you talk about it first?'

'What was the point? I've been all this time, since I left Mumby's, without a job. I'm not going to get one now – who's going to take on a chap my age, knowing he's likely to be called up any minute? So I thought I might as well just go and do it.'

'You mean you really did go and do it off your own bat?' Gladys said.

'Look, I'm not a little kid, I can make up me own mind—'

'All right,' Peggy said, 'don't start again. If this really is your last weekend, Bob, let's make the most of it. Get that washing-up finished, Glad, and let's have tea on the table ready for when your father and Diane come home.' She sighed. 'I'm proud of you, Bob, though I wish you hadn't done it. You could have waited . . . And I don't know what your father's going to say.'

'He'll say I did the right thing,' Bob said, but he didn't sound too sure and he picked up the tea-towel again and started to wipe the plates Gladys had dumped on the draining-board. Peggy went out to the shed and came back with the potatoes and carrots. It was too late to go and buy anything special for Bob's last meals at home, but she had a large tin of ham in the cupboard and she went to fetch that, and a can of peaches and Ideal milk for afters.

Gladys ran some hot water into the bowl. That was the third lot, and they were supposed to be saving fuel, but it wasn't every day your brother announced he was going to go for a soldier. She felt proud and upset and ashamed, all at the same time, and guessed that Bob probably felt much the same way, so that made them equal.

They'd always squabbled a lot, her and Bob, but they'd always been close, too. With only thirteen months between them, and Diane four years younger, they'd been more like twins. And they'd generally made their fights up quickly enough.

It was just that, coming in today and finding him there with his feet up as if he was lord of the manor – well, it had touched her on the raw. Especially after hearing that Derek was likely to be going away soon and seeing how upset Olive had been. If Bob had only said – but she supposed she hadn't really given him much chance. And now he was going too.

She wondered how much Betty Chapman had had to do with it. She'd been leading Bob on a bit, Gladys reckoned, for all she'd pretended she'd not known he fancied her. Girls always knew when a chap fancied them. Maybe she'd given him the cold shoulder and that was why he'd gone off and done it so sudden.

Gladys put the last plate on the draining-board and swilled the water round in the bowl before pouring it down the sink. What with that liner being torpedoed, all the kids sent away and the queues at the recruitment offices, this war seemed to have started with a vengeance. And they reckoned the air raids would start any day now.

She looked up at the bit of sky she could see through the scullery window. The tail of a barrage balloon drifted into view. They said the balloons would stop any low-flying aircraft. But that wasn't going to prevent others coming in higher up, and dropping their bombs, was it?

Betty Chapman didn't see Robb Wilton at the King's Theatre that week, but she did hear *Band Waggon* on the wireless on Saturday night, with Arthur Askey and Richard Murdoch. She was sitting in the front room with Graham, and they had switched the speaker on and now sat on the settee holding hands and laughing at the antics of the two comedians.

'That's a good idea, having speakers through from the other room,' Graham said when the programme finished. 'Did your brother do it?'

'No, it was Dad's idea. There's one up in the front bedroom too, so Mum could listen when she was poorly last winter. We wanted them put through to our rooms too but he wouldn't let us.'

'There's a new programme starting next week,' Graham said. 'On Tuesday night. It's Tommy Handley.'

'Oh, I heard about that. *It's That Man Again.*' Betty laughed. 'Everyone's been saying that about Hitler. Whatever goes wrong now, he gets the blame. Even when Mum spilt tea all over her new tablecloth and Mrs Marsh dropped a bottle of milk, we all said *it's that man again.*'

'Well, he's come in handy for something, then. It's useful to have someone to blame.' He sat stroking her fingers for a while. 'I'm glad I met you, Bet,' he said quietly. 'With all this going on – nobody knowing what's going to happen next – it's good to have someone special to think about.'

Betty leaned her head on his shoulder.

'Bob Shaw down the road's joined up,' she said. 'He's going Monday. Mum met Mrs Shaw in Mrs Seddon's shop. She'd gone in for a few rashers of bacon for Bob's last breakfast at home.'

She was silent for a moment. She had received the news with mixed feelings. One part of her was proud that Bob had volunteered. Even though she'd refused to go out with him, she still felt as if, in some way, he half belonged to her. But another part of her felt guilty – had he really joined up because of her? – and afraid that something might happen to him. Would his family think it was her fault? Would Diane and Gladys blame her?

'Old Bob joined up?' Graham said. 'What did he want to do that for? He could've hung on a bit, surely. I suppose he's gone into the Navy – he was talking about it the day we met you down Queen Street.'

'That's what surprised Mrs Shaw. They didn't know he was even thinking about it till today. And they thought he wanted to go into the Navy too, but he's gone for the Army. Gunners.'

'The Navy are a bit more choosy,' Graham remarked. 'Not that there's anything wrong with Bob Shaw, I don't mean that, but they just take longer to get around to taking people. If you go into the Army Recruiting Office you're lucky to be allowed home to fetch your toothbrush.'

Betty giggled. 'Fancy thinking about toothbrushes, when you're going off to war.'

'Well, you know what I mean. Mind, they're fussy about that sort of thing. I bet Bob'll spend the next six weeks learning to blanco his belt, before they even let him get near a gun.'

'D'you think you'll join up?' Betty asked.

Graham shrugged. 'Don't have any choice. I'm twenty-one in January.' He hesitated, then said casually, 'Matter of fact, my call-up papers came through today.'

Betty sat up straight. 'Oh, Graham! You never said anything.'

'I was waiting for the right moment,' he said with a grin on his freckled face. 'And then *Band Waggon* was on and you wanted to listen to that.'

'But not when you were thinking about your papers!'

'Well, I wanted to hear it too. And half an hour hasn't made any difference to my call-up. We all need a good laugh these days, Bet.'

'I know, but . . .' She turned suddenly and buried her face against his chest. 'Oh, Graham, I shall miss you.'

'I'll miss you too.' He stroked her hair, twining his fingers in the curls.

They were silent for a few minutes and then he said, 'Look, Bet . . . I know we've only been going out together for a few weeks, but – well, you're different, somehow. Different from other girls, I mean. You're special.'

'Am I, Graham?' she whispered.

'Yes.' He held her closer, his fingers moving gently on her waist. 'You're so special I think all the other blokes must want to go out with you.'

Betty laughed. 'Well, if they do, they haven't said so!'

'Bet they do, all the same.' He bent his head and kissed her ear. 'Will you say yes if I go away, Betty? Will you go out with other boys?'

Betty turned her face up to his and looked up into his eyes. 'Course I won't. Well, not unless—'

'Unless what?'

'Unless you don't want me any more,' she whispered.

Graham bent his head. She felt his lips touch hers. She stayed quite still as he let go of her hand and slipped his arm around her shoulders, drawing her closer. His lips moved against her mouth and she felt the strange excitement spiral in her stomach. His hand touched her breast and she quivered.

'Oh, Graham,' she murmured as he lifted his head again. 'Graham, I do love you. I don't want you to go away.'

'I love you too, Bet. I wish—'

'Wish what?'

'I wish there was something we could do before I go. So I could know you'd still be here, waiting for me.'

'Of course I'll be here,' she said, her eyes shining. 'You know that.'

'Well, we haven't known each other all that long. You might not feel the same way after a while. You might get fed up with waiting and want to go out with other blokes.'

'I shan't,' she declared. 'I shan't want to go out with anyone else.'

'I don't know,' he said. 'Girls say that when a feller goes away. But after a while . . . I don't blame 'em, mind. It's as bad for them as it is for the blokes. Being apart and not having anything to remember, to sort of hold on to.'

Betty said nothing for a moment. Graham's hands were becoming more persistent, more exploratory, and she was finding it difficult to think. She wanted him to go on, but she knew she ought to tell him to stop. It had never been difficult before – he'd been cheeky, knowing she'd pull his hands away when they went too far, and he'd just laughed and told her that one day she'd let him. But tonight was different. Tonight, she had the feeling he'd be really upset if she stopped him.

'If I could just be sure,' he whispered in her ear. 'If I could just know we really loved each other. If you could just *make* me sure, Betty . . .'

Betty's mind whirled. She knew what he meant. He wanted to make love to her – perhaps here, this very minute, in her mother's front room. Panic blotted out her other feelings. Suppose they did and Mum came in – or, worse still, Dad. And suppose something went wrong – suppose she got caught and fell for a baby. She remembered her parents' warnings, the tight-lipped disapproval of other girls who had found themselves in such a position.

Graham was kissing her neck, his lips nipping and tugging at the soft skin. Betty heard him make a sound deep in his throat. His hands were on both her breasts now, stroking and squeezing. If she didn't stop him soon, she wouldn't be able to.

'We could get engaged,' she said. 'Then you'd know. I'd belong to you then, Graham, and you'd belong to me and everyone would know it.'

'Get engaged?' He stopped kissing her and sat up a bit. 'But I thought you said your dad wouldn't let you get married till you were twenty-one.'

'That's what he's always said. But things are different now, aren't they? There's a war on. Anyway, I didn't say married, I said engaged.' She gazed at him, her eyes shining. 'Oh, Graham, wouldn't it be wonderful? Knowing we belonged to each other, that wherever you went I'd be waiting for you to come back. And when it's all over we'd be able to get married—'

Graham looked dazed. 'But suppose it's all over by Christmas, like people are saying?'

'Oh, well, then we'd just go on being engaged, I suppose. Two or three years isn't that long.' She looked at him. 'So are you going to ask him? Mind, he might take a while to come round to it.'

Graham was silent for a moment. Then he said, 'Course, if you don't think he'd let us . . . Well, we could be secretly engaged.'

'Oh, yes!' Betty sat up straight. 'We could, couldn't we? Nobody could stop that, could they?'

'And I'd still know you'd be waiting for me.'

'Yes. And when Dad sees I'm not interested in anyone else – well, maybe about Christmas, we could get engaged then. I'd like to get engaged at Christmas.'

'That's settled then.' He pulled her back into his arms. 'We'll be secretly engaged now and then ask your dad at Christmas. He should be used to the idea by then. I wouldn't mind betting your Olive'll be wanting to get engaged too. Or even married – she's not far off twenty-one, is she?'

'No. And if Derek goes into the Army—' She stopped and looked up at him again. 'Graham! You've never told me what you're going into. And when do you have to go? Is it soon?'

'Next week,' he said, his face suddenly serious. 'I'm going into the Navy. I'm going to be a writer.'

'A writer? What, books and things?'

'No, silly – it just means a clerk. Doing the office work and that sort of thing, like I do now.'

'Oh.' She gazed at him, relieved yet at the same time vaguely disappointed. 'So you won't be actually fighting, then. You won't be going to sea.'

'I expect I will. They still have office work to do, even on ships. Anyway, I'm reporting to the Naval Barracks next week so we'll know then. Once I'm in, I might be able to get transferred. I wouldn't mind being a gunner.' He felt obscurely irritated about Bob Shaw. He'd come tonight full of his own news, ready to be treated as a hero, only to find that Bob had got in first. And as a gunner too! You had to admit, it sounded a lot more exciting than a writer. But if the ship went down, it wouldn't make any difference what he was, he'd drown just the same.

'Oh, Graham.' Betty gazed at him. She felt a mixture of emotions. Fear, excitement, anxiety and pride, all surging together inside. And over all, the realisation that she was engaged.

Engaged! She'd actually had a proposal – and she was only eighteen! Betty felt a thrill of excitement. Of course, it was a secret engagement and she wouldn't have a ring to flash around – unless she could persuade Graham to buy her one to wear on a chain around her neck, under her blouse – but she could drop the odd hint, couldn't she? And although she didn't want Graham to go away, there'd be his letters to look forward to.

'When will you get your uniform?' she asked. 'Will it be bell-bottoms, like Colin's?'

'Yes. I'll have to learn how to do up all those lanyards and things.' He grinned at her a bit self-consciously.

'Oh, you'll have to come round here – we had to practically dress our Colin every time he went out at first. We're experts!' Betty realised suddenly how her words might have sounded and blushed. 'I mean—'

Graham laughed and hugged her. 'I know what you mean! At least, I think I do.' His smile faded and he held her tightly. 'Oh, Bet, it makes me feel good to know you feel the same way about me as I do about you. It'll make all the difference when I'm at sea, to know you're here waiting for me.'

Betty slid her arms around his neck. 'I'll wait, Graham,' she promised. 'It doesn't matter how long it is, I'll be here. And when it's all over . . .'

'We'll have a proper engagement,' he said.

'And a proper white wedding. And our own little home.'

'Yes.' But to Graham, these seemed too far into the future to be considered just yet. They were dreams, no more – dreams that he felt sure would come true, but much too distant to be real now. What was real now was his last week at work, reporting to the Barracks next week and starting a new life.

At the thought of going into the Navy, he felt both excited and scared. Service life had never appealed to him much, but when it looked as if war was coming he'd begun to feel differently. Like a lot of his friends, he wanted to 'have a crack at Hitler'. And the glamour of the uniform was undeniable. It was the boys in blue who got all the girls, no mistake about that. Go to a dance on a Saturday night and you could see them there, helping themselves to all the best lookers.

Of course, he wouldn't be interested in that sort of thing, not with Betty at home waiting for him. But a chap had to have a bit of fun when he was away from home, didn't he? Couldn't just sit in the mess, aboard ship all the time.

All the same, the idea of joining the Navy and going to sea was a bit overwhelming. What would it be like? He'd seen films, of course, and he knew a few blokes from school who'd joined up, but he still couldn't quite imagine it. Living with a lot of men, for a start – that would be different. It would be queer not to have his own room, to have a bunk in a mess below decks with everyone else. And he knew that there were cooks but did you have to do your own washing? How did you get it dry? And what about ironing? He'd never ironed so much as a handkerchief. And the Services were sticklers for being smart, at least the Army and Navy were – the Air Force didn't seem to bother quite so much.

Still, at least he'd have Betty to think about. He'd get her to give him a photo to stick inside his locker. And he could spend his time writing to her and reading her letters.

He just hoped he wouldn't be seasick. The only sea trip he'd ever had was on the Isle of Wight ferry, in one of the paddleboats. He'd been all right then, but it hadn't really been rough.

He glanced at Betty. She had a dreamy look on her face. She was really pretty, he thought, with that curly brown hair and those big hazel eyes. She didn't wear a lot of make-up but she had nice red lips and her face wasn't shiny. And she had a good figure, slim but not thin, with enough on her to make her nice and cuddly.

His arm was still round her and he tightened it a little. Perhaps now they were engaged, she'd be a bit more willing to let him make love to her. He was willing to bet she wanted it as much as he did – she was just scared. Girls usually were. But things were different now, weren't they?

He bent his head again and nuzzled his face against her neck. Betty made a little sound, half squeal, half giggle, and twisted slightly so that he could kiss her lips.

'Oh, Graham,' she whispered, and he felt a surge of excitement. He pulled her a little closer. Everyone knew that being engaged meant you could do more than just kiss, didn't they? And Betty hadn't really protested that much when he'd kissed her at the door the other night. Surely now she'd let him go a bit further.

There was a rattle at the door and Graham and Betty snapped apart. By the time the door opened, they were sitting side by side about six inches apart, staring straight ahead.

'Supper's on the table,' Annie said, putting her head round the door. 'Are you going to have a bit with us, Graham? I've made plenty of cocoa.'

The Shaws were up early on Monday to see Bob off to Hilsea Barracks. Gladys and Diane sat at the table, watching him eat his breakfast of bacon, eggs and fried bread. Gladys thought about the squabble they had had and the way she'd shouted at her brother, and the tears came into her eyes.

'Don't worry, sis,' Bob said. 'I'll be back before you know it, with a row of medals on me chest.' He winked at her and she gave him a scornful look.

'I wasn't worrying about you. I was thinking about something quite different.'

'Someone, you mean,' Diane said. 'That boy I saw you talking to down Charlotte Street the other day. I know him, his sister works in the laundry.'

'For goodness sake!' Gladys said, blushing. 'I was only talking to him. You don't have to make something of it.'

'Now then, you two,' Peggy said automatically, but her voice was subdued. 'It's time you were going, anyway. You don't want to be late for work.'

Diane made a face. 'I wish I could be joining up. Fancy having to work in a laundry. What sort of a job is that in a war?'

'People still have to keep clean,' Peggy said sharply. 'And if you don't get a move on, you won't have a job at all.'

Diane got up reluctantly and went to the door at the bottom of the stairs to fetch her coat. She looked at Bob and hesitated.

'Cheerio, little 'un,' he said, and stood up to give her a clumsy kiss. 'Mind what you get up to down Charlotte Street, now.'

'And you mind what you get up to,' she retorted. 'Just because you're getting a uniform won't mean you're God's gift to women.'

'Whoo! Hark at her,' he mocked. 'You'd better mind what you say to me from now on. Play your cards right and I might bring you home a nice soldier-boy for Christmas.'

'Bob!' his mother exclaimed. 'I've told you before, that's enough of that kind of talk. She's getting quite forward enough as it is. I sometimes wonder whether we did right, letting her go to work at that laundry,' she went on as Diane hurried out, still pushing one arm into her coat-sleeve as she went. 'They're a real common lot down there. I don't want her getting flighty.'

'Oh, our Di's all right,' Bob said. 'She's just lively. Better'n some of the girls I know, hardly got a word to say for themselves.' He drained his teacup. 'Well, it's me for the off now. I don't know if I'll get time to come in and say goodbye later on – well, I don't know where they're going to send me. So give us a smacker now, Glad, there's a good girl.' He held his sister for a moment, then turned to his mother. His face was suddenly serious. 'Bye, Mum.'

Peggy's eyes misted with tears. Bob's face swam before her eyes and for a moment she saw him again as he had been. A baby, her firstborn, asleep in her arms or suckling at her breast. A toddler, taking his first steps with a grin of delight on his round face. A small boy walking away from her on his first day at school. And now tall and straight, a man, leaving home for the first time on a journey whose destination nobody could know.

She put her arms round him and held him close. It was a long time since she'd touched his body like this. The Shaws were not a demonstrative family and hugs and kisses were reserved for going away, or coming back. Bob had not been away since he went to Scout camp four years ago, and he would not have welcomed such effusion then. It must be years longer than that since she had been so close to this body that had come from hers, which she had once known more intimately than her own.

'Bye, son,' she said, her voice creaky with tears. 'Look after yourself, now.'

'I will.'

'Don't let your feet get wet. You know how easy you catch cold.'

'I won't.'

'And make sure you eat your greens. Sailors used to get scurvy from not eating greens.'

'I'm not going in the Navy, Mum.'

'That doesn't make any difference,' she said, recovering herself a little. 'I don't want to see you come home with all your teeth dropping out.'

'I won't,' he said quietly. 'Don't worry, Mum.'

She gave his shoulders a pat and stepped away briskly. 'Well, off you go then. You don't want to be late, your first day.'

They went to the front door together. Bob hesitated, glancing up the street towards the Chapmans' house, and Gladys saw the look and understood what was going through his mind. She felt a sudden surge of bitterness towards Betty Chapman. Did she know she was responsible for Bob going off like this? If he gets killed, Gladys thought, it'll be her fault.

'Don't you worry,' she said to her brother. 'You'll find someone else a lot better than her. There's plenty of other fish in the sea.'

Plenty of other fish in the sea . . . Betty had said that to Graham, that first day. Bob remembered her, standing there on the Hard with the wind tossing her curls round her face, a paper of chips in her hand and her eyes laughing. It was the first time he'd seen that saucy look and it had turned his heart over. That's when it happened, he thought. That's when I knew I wanted her to be my girl.

But she'd chosen Graham. And now he was going away, to God knows what, leaving Graham a clear field because he just couldn't bear to see her any more.

'Cheerio then, Mum,' he said with a sudden gulp. 'Cheerio, sis. Write to me, won't you.'

They nodded, but neither could answer. Gladys stared at him for a moment and then threw her arms around him, holding him close. Peggy held them both, her face working with the tears she was trying so hard to hold back. And then he drew himself out of their arms and walked away.

He crossed over to the corner where Mrs Seddon had her shop and then turned to wave before disappearing up October Street.

'That's it, then,' Peggy said with half a sigh, turning to go back indoors. Her face was closed and grim. 'And you'd better get off too, our Glad. You've got your job to think about.'

Gladys looked at her mother. She saw the taut mouth, the reddened eyes. She thought of all the other young men, walking away from mothers and sisters, sweethearts and wives, the way Bob had just walked away, and saw a disturbed muddle of pictures of just what they might be walking into.

'I can go in late for once,' she said. 'They can manage without me for an hour. I'll help you clear up and have a cup of tea with you first.'

Peggy opened her mouth to protest and then closed it again. She went back indoors and sat down heavily at the table while Gladys filled the kettle and set it on the gas stove.

'He looked as if he'd turned into a man overnight,' Peggy said, looking at the tablecloth. There was a brown ring on it where Bob had stood his teacup. She was always nagging him about not putting it back in his saucer, but this morning she hadn't said a word. 'Yesterday, sitting here reading that comic, he was still a boy. But this morning . . .'

'I know,' Gladys said. 'And when we see him in uniform he'll look completely different. Not like our Bob any more.' Her eyes filled with tears and she stared at her mother. 'Is it going to change them all, Mum? Won't they ever be the same again?'

Peggy looked up and saw the fear in her daughter's eyes. Poor kid, she thought, this is hitting her real hard. It's hitting them all. All the young ones, the boys who've got to go and fight, the girls who've got to give up their boys, the wives who are going to end up as widows. And none of 'em have done anything to deserve it. All those lives ruined, just because of one crazy madman.

She reached across and touched Gladys's hand. It was easier to do than it had been with Bob, and maybe it was something they should do more often.

'Of course they won't change,' she said stoutly. 'They'll still be the same person inside. Bob'll still be our Bob. Nothing'll make any difference to that.'

But as they sat and drank their tea, both remembered Bob walking away up the street. He had looked different. Taller, bigger, more of a man. And if that was what one night could do . . .

It's going to change us all, Peggy thought. Every one of us. And how will we ever get back to normal once it's over?

6

'Goodness knows what sort of home they came from,' Miss Eleanor Woddis said disdainfully. 'The boy's not even house-trained. He – well, he relieves himself wherever he happens to be. And the girl's rude and sulky. I really don't know how we can be expected to put up with it.'

Mrs Tupper, the billeting officer, sighed. This was the twelfth house she had visited that morning and only three had been happy with their evacuee children. Bed-wetting was the most common cause of complaint, with refusal to eat a close second. In many homes, she knew the food offered was fresh and wholesome, but the children behaved as if they had never seen it before.

'Can't you use a rubber sheet on the bed?' she asked without much hope. The two spinsters really didn't look the type likely to welcome strange children into their immaculate home. But they had the room, and everyone who had room was expected to take in someone. 'Perhaps you'd prefer adult evacuees. Some of the male teachers—'

'Oh no!' Miss Eleanor said at once. 'We couldn't take men.' The hair on her chin quivered as if with indignation at the very thought.

'They're perfectly respectable.' But it was clear that the sisters would not entertain such a suggestion. It would have to be rubber sheets then.

'Of course we've put rubber sheets on the beds,' Miss Millicent said impatiently. 'We went out on the first morning and bought them from the chemist. And not a moment too soon,' she added. 'It seemed half the village was buying them. But it was extra expense. Are we supposed to pay for that? And all the other damage?'

'Has there been other damage?' Mrs Tupper tried to remember what the Atkinson children were like. Surely they were the two small, quiet-looking scraps that Miss Langrish had said were well-behaved and nicely brought up, just the kind that the Woddis sisters would be able to manage. Had there been some mistake?

Miss Eleanor held up her hands and counted on her fingers.

'Taps left running on the first morning and a whole tankful of hot water wasted. Water spilled all over the bathroom floor by sheets not properly wrung out – the floor's only just dry now. A broken milk jug. A stain on the carpet – that was the boy. I've already told you about his disgusting habits. And I've had to clean up after him myself. The girl seems quite incapable.'

'But surely—' Mrs Tupper referred to her papers '—she's only eight years old.'

'At eight years old,' Miss Eleanor said coldly, 'children used to work in factories. Or down the mines.'

'All we're asking,' her sister chimed in, 'is that she should help a little around the house. It's not much, surely? It would show a little gratitude for all we're doing for them.'

Mrs Tupper gathered up her papers. She still had a dozen families to see that day and had already spent too long with the Woddis sisters.

'Why don't you give them another chance?' she suggested. 'It's early days, after all. It's bound to take them time to settle in. They're very young, and they must be missing their mother.'

The spinsters glanced at each other. They knew that everyone with spare rooms was expected to take in evacuees. If it wasn't the Atkinson children, it would be someone else. Perhaps bigger children, even more difficult to manage. Or perhaps, as Mrs Tupper had suggested, a man.

And the billeting money was useful. Ten shillings a week for the two children was a sum that could make quite a difference to them provided they were careful with it. Two small children didn't need much to eat, after all – older ones might want much more. And men had dreadfully large appetites.

The little girl could probably be trained to be quite useful about the house, and once the boy had been properly disciplined . . .

'Very well,' Miss Eleanor said at last. 'We'll give them one more chance. But they must improve if they want to stay here. I hope someone can make that plain to them.'

'I'll ask their teacher to have a word,' Mrs Tupper said, and escaped. She walked down the village street, scanning her papers for the next address. Each child was supposed to be visited within the first few days of evacuation, but it was a slow job. Almost every home had a tale to tell and the billeting officer was expected to listen and do something to put the situation right.

'They don't ever seem to have seen proper food before,' one woman complained. 'I go to all the trouble to cook them a nice meal – lamb chops we had yesterday, and potatoes and carrots and cabbage – and what do they do? They turn up their noses and ask for fish and chips. Fish and chips! Well, there's nothing wrong with that but they want it every day. And not a nice piece of coley cooked at home and my own chips, oh no, they're not good enough. It's soggy chips in newspaper they want, and cod in batter from the shop.'

'But there's no fish and chip shop in the village,' Mrs Tupper said unwarily.

'Of course there's not! And even if there was, I wouldn't be popping round there every five minutes. Good home cooking's always been good enough for me, and if these little whatnames won't eat it, they'll just have to do the other thing.'

'I expect they're just missing their mother,' Mrs Tupper said, as she'd already said a dozen times. 'I'm sure they'll settle down.'

But as she went on her rounds and heard complaint after complaint, she began to doubt whether either the evacuees or their hosts would ever settle down. She heard of children who refused a good cooked breakfast and demanded bread and dripping instead; of others who wanted beer to drink rather than milk or tea; of some who had never seen stewed fruit or any other kind of pudding, and others who didn't know what to do with a bowl of soup.

'And if they've never seen it before, they won't even try it,' she was told. 'It makes you wonder what sort of homes they come from. Don't people eat proper meals in towns?'

Food was not the only source of complaint. Manners and 'dirty habits' brought problems too. Bed-wetting was the worst offence but apparently it didn't stop there. Like little Alan Atkinson, some children hardly seemed to know what the lavatory was for.

'I found him going in the cabbage patch the other night,' a cottager said indignantly. 'Said he was scared of the privy! I gave him a right walloping, I'll tell you!'

Mrs Tupper looked down at the little boy who was being held in front of her. Martin Baker, she thought consulting her notes. Six years old. No brothers or sisters here. He stared back at her and she saw the tears in his large blue eyes and felt suddenly sorry for him.

'Why are you afraid of the privy?'

He shook his head and his hostess snorted. She was a widow in her late fifties, her own children long since grown up and departed. Mrs Tupper could not recall their having visited her for several years.

'He's not afraid! It's just a way of getting attention. I know what children are.'

Martin's mouth trembled. Mrs Tupper bent to hear what he was whispering.

'Tell me. What is it you don't like?'

'There's nothing—' Mrs Hutchins began, but the boy was whispering and Mrs Tupper lifted her hand for quiet.

'Spiders? You don't like the spiders?'

'Spiders!' Widow Hutchins almost spat her indignation. 'Afraid of a few spiders? Don't tell me they don't have spiders in Portsmouth!'

'Perhaps there are more than he's accustomed to,' Mrs Tupper said mildly. 'He's only six, after all. If you could just sweep them out . . .'

'I see. So my house isn't clean enough for him, is that it? He can spread his filth in my cabbages but I have to clean the house to make it fit for him to live in. Well, I didn't realise I was having royalty to stay with me. Perhaps you should have said. I would have bought some satin sheets, specially.'

Mrs Tupper sighed. She opened her mouth to utter the words that were fast becoming a platitude – 'he's probably just missing his mother' – but she could see from the look on Mrs Hutchins's face that nothing she could say would improve matters. She could only mark Martin off on her sheet of paper as being in his billet and 'satisfactory', before moving on to the next.

Susan Cullen. Now here was a child who really was missing her mother. Mrs Tupper was aware that Madge Cullen had died only a few days before evacuation and she looked at the pale, red-eyed little girl with pity. Poor little mite, she thought, what can she be thinking in her little head? But there was no allowance made in the war for children who had lost their parents, and there'd be a good many more before it was over.

Susan's foster-parents were doing all they could, but it obviously wasn't easy for them, having to cope with a child who refused to talk or eat and did nothing but cry. Mrs Long looked almost as weary as Susan, and her husband just looked fed up. There'd be trouble there too, soon, Mrs Tupper thought, but what can we do? The child can't go back home to a father who's out at work from four in the morning.

'She'll get over it soon,' she said to the Longs, hoping it was true. 'Children are very resilient.' And she left the house, trying not to be haunted by the memory of Susan's stricken white face and the feeling that she'd somehow let the child down.

Not all children were unhappy in their new homes. Tim and Keith Budd had settled down without any trouble at all and were clearly as delighted with the Corners as Edna and Reg were with them. The four of them were playing Ludo when Mrs Tupper called and she felt heartened by the sight of them sitting round the kitchen table, mugs of lemonade and a plate of home-made biscuits at their sides.

'No need to ask if you've got any complaints,' she said, accepting Edna's offer of a cup of tea.

'Oh no, we're fine. These two scamps have really livened us up. I feel quite guilty, taking them away from their mother.'

'But she's in the village too, isn't she?'

'Yes, she and the girl and the baby are with the Greenberrys. They come over quite often, of course, or the boys go to see her, but I think she feels a bit awkward about it. You know, taking up our room, or all four of them being over there. It's not like being in your own home, is it?' Edna poured milk and tea into a cup and gave it to Mrs Tupper. 'She's a nice woman though. And Rose is a good girl. Always willing to lend a hand.'

'Well, it's good to hear of someone happy.' Mrs Tupper drank her tea. It was the first she'd been offered all morning. 'Not everyone's taken this as well as you.'

'How else can we take it?' Reg asked. He was a big young man with a thatch of yellow hair, straight and stiff as straw. 'We all have to do our bit.'

'That's not what everyone thinks, all the same. Some people don't seem to realise yet there's a war on.' Mrs Tupper nibbled a home-made biscuit. 'Mind, I don't blame some of them for complaining – they've got a lot to put up with. It's not easy taking strange children into your home, and when they wet the beds and break your things and won't eat – well—'

'The poor little mites are just missing their mothers,' Edna said, as Mrs Tupper herself had said over and over again.

'But what sort of mothers are they? Some of these children arrived dressed in nothing more than rags. Filthy dirty – not just from the train, either. At least six of the ones I've seen so far had nits and several have got impetigo. And they seem to live on the most peculiar food. One little boy said his mother gave him a penny every day to buy his own dinner. He bought a bag of chips or Oxo cubes. What kind of mothers have they got?'

Edna shook her head. 'You can't always believe what little children say.

But I agree it's a shame when they're not properly looked after. Still, it gives us a chance, doesn't it? Show them what life can be like.' She sat down beside Keith and cuddled him against her. 'You only have to give them a bit of love. It doesn't matter about the rest.'

Mrs Tupper departed looking more cheerful and the Corners finished their game of Ludo. Then Edna sent Reg out with the two boys for a walk while she got dinner ready.

'Take them over Hanger Wood,' she said, handing them each an old biscuit tin. 'See if you can find any blackberries.'

They set off along the lane, then went through a gate and began to cross the fields.

'Look out for mushrooms too,' Reg said, scanning the grass. 'Know what they look like?'

'Yes, we've collected them before. But Mum always tells us whether they're really mushrooms or not. Some of them are poisonous.'

'It's easy enough to tell the difference. There's others you can eat as well as mushrooms, but it's best not to pick them unless you're sure.' Reg suddenly dived across to a patch of dark-green grass. 'Look, here's some.'

The two boys followed him and helped pick the creamy cluster. Reg showed them how to recognise a mushroom by its pinky-brown gills and the collar of skin around its stem. Some of them were small and round, the collar not yet broken away, but you could still see that they were mushrooms. 'They'll make a nice breakfast,' he said, 'with a bit of bacon and an egg or two.'

They wandered on across the fields. Tim's biscuit tin was soon full of mushrooms and in the hedges they found blackberries, rich and sweet.

'Mum used to pick these to make jam,' Tim remarked, and this led to a discussion about fruit and vegetables generally and a discussion about Frank's allotment and what he grew there. And, from there, to the question of babies which had been puzzling the boys ever since Maureen was born.

'She was just there,' Keith said. 'Nobody seemed to know she was coming. And why did Mum have to stay in bed? If she came in the doctor's bag or they found her over the allotments—'

'I don't believe either of those things,' Tim interrupted. 'I think it had something to do with Mum getting fat. And our Rose knows something about it, I'm sure she does.'

Reg stopped and looked at them. 'Don't you know? Don't you know where babies come from?'

'Well, nobody will tell us.' Tim looked annoyed. 'They just say "Wait until you're older" and "don't ask questions". What's all the secret about?'

Reg laughed. 'It's no secret. Look, you know about flowers and vegetables, don't you? You know how they grow.'

'They grow from seeds,' Tim said. 'But—'

'And so do babies.'

The boys stared at him.

'Babies grow from seeds?'

'That's right. But the seeds aren't planted in the ground. They're planted in their mother's tummy. That's why your mum got fat. The baby was growing inside her from a tiny seed.'

Keith looked suspicious and Tim disbelieving. 'How did it get there, then?'

'Your dad put it there.'

'Dad did? But—'

'Where did he get the seed from?' Keith asked practically. 'Did he get it from a shop?'

'No, not a shop. He'd got the seed in his body. He keeps it in his willie.'

'In his *willie*?' Tim said, outraged.

'Yes. That's the right place for it, that's where it's always kept. And then, one day when he's feeling very happy and kissing your mum because they love each other, he puts his willie inside her and lets the seed out. And that turns into a baby.'

The two boys gazed at him.

'But where does he put it?' Keith pulled up his shirt and examined his stomach. 'Does it go in her tummy-button?'

'No, not there. That's where you were joined on to your mum when you were born.'

'So where does it go?'

'Well, you know girls don't have willies. They have a little hole instead. That's where he puts it.'

'But that's dirty!' Tim said. 'Our teacher said so. Ann Jenkins said she'd show me hers if I showed her mine and the teacher saw us and said we were being dirty. And Brian Collins told me—'

'Never you mind what Brian Collins told you. Or what your teacher said. There's nothing dirty about it, it's natural. But you don't need to do it until you're grown up. It doesn't work till then.'

'I wouldn't want to do it anyway,' Tim observed. 'Perhaps by then they'll have found some better way.'

Reg grinned. 'Perhaps.' He looked at the woods on the far side of the field. 'Let's see if we can find some chestnuts. Edna likes sweet chestnuts.'

The subject of babies was forgotten. The two boys, enchanted with their new life, wandered amongst the trees, filling their tins with nuts and berries until at last Reg told them it was time to go home. They returned with stained fingers and faces to find their mother in the kitchen, talking to Edna, and Rose sitting under a tree out in the garden. She was rocking Maureen in a pram borrowed from the Greenberrys' eldest daughter. Tim and Keith stopped and peered in at their baby sister. Her eyes were open and she was gazing up at the leaves that rustled above her. At the sight of their faces, she smiled and laughed, reaching out small hands to touch them.

'I still don't believe it,' Keith muttered. 'It's just another story, like the gooseberry bush.'

But Tim was looking thoughtful. He put his finger into the baby's hand and she clutched it, giving a gurgle of pleasure.

So far, he thought, everything Reg had told them was true. But seeds in willies? Babies planted like cabbages in mothers' tummies?

Maybe it's different in the country, he thought, and, satisfied, went indoors to have dinner.

In Portsmouth, the cinemas and dance-halls reopened after only twelve days and people began to think that the war wasn't so bad after all. No bombs had yet been dropped, most of the people had been saved from the *Athena* and the city seemed to be getting organised. There were First-Aid Posts in schools and hospitals, more wardens appointed and a Citizens Advice Bureau set up in the Girls' Southern Secondary School. The Northern Secondary School was converted into an office and over a hundred voluntary workers went there each day to fill in innumerable forms and prepare for the control of food and rationing that was expected to start soon.

'Everyone's going to have a ration book,' Annie, who was one of the volunteers, said as the family ate their dinner together. 'Even babies. There's meat on them, and butter, and sugar – everything.'

'How's it going to work, then?' Frank asked. He was still coming to Annie for his meals, though he missed Jess's cooking. Annie's tastes were too fancy for him. Tonight she'd done meat with rice. Rice! That was for puddings, in Frank's opinion. He'd rather have a few potatoes to fill him up.

'Well, there's pages for meat and other pages for the fats and things. They're all marked off into little squares with numbers on – coupons, they're called – and when you have your ration the shopkeeper cuts off one of the squares. And when you run out, that's it, you don't get no more.'

'But that's daft,' Ted said. 'Some people are going to eat it all in the first week.'

'No, they can't do that. The coupons can only be used in the right week. And you have to be registered with grocers and butchers, you can't go just anywhere. It'll depend what they've got in.'

'But how much are we going to get?' Olive asked.

'Some of it'll be done by weight and some'll be by price. So if your ration was a shillingsworth of meat a week, you could either have something cheap like sausages or liver and get a lot of it or something expensive like beef and only have a little bit. As long as the butcher's got it, that is.'

'Sounds complicated to me,' Ted said. 'It's going to take the poor buggers half the day to cut out all these little squares. They won't bother.'

'They'll have to,' Annie said. 'They'll get into trouble if they don't.'

Betty said nothing. Today was the day Graham was due to report to the barracks and she didn't know whether she was going to see him again before he went to sea. He'd promised to come and tell her what was happening if he could, and she was sitting with her ears pricked up for a knock at the door. The conversation passed her by.

'Anyway,' Annie went on, 'it doesn't matter about all that. Did Ted tell you, we've had a letter from our Colin?'

'No. That's good news.' Frank held his plate out for more rice and mince. Might as well eat the stuff if that's all there was, but he'd cook a few spuds as soon as he got back home, to take to work tomorrow. 'Where is he?'

Annie shrugged. 'Somewhere down South America way, that's all we know. Round the Falklands. That's where they've been lately. At least they're out of the way of the war there.'

'That won't last long,' Frank said. 'It's going to spread. The Jerries are sending their ships all over the oceans, trying to stop our merchant ships getting through. It's like putting us under siege. If they can stop us importing food and things, they reckon they can bring us to our knees. Some hope!'

'I've heard the *Graf Spee*'s on its way down to the South Atlantic,' Ted remarked. 'Remember seeing her at the Coronation Review at Spithead? Pocket battleship, they call her. More guns than a cruiser and armour a foot thick. She can do twenty-six knots and go nineteen thousand miles without refuelling.'

'I thought the Germans weren't allowed to have ships like that,' Annie said. 'Wasn't there some sort of rule about it?'

'That's right,' Frank said. 'They weren't allowed to build ships of over ten thousand tons. Battleships were always bigger than that, so they got round it by building these small ones. The *Graf Spee*'s loaded with guns. And now she's prowling round disguised as a French warship, ready to start picking off our merchantmen the minute Hitler gives the word.'

'But that's piracy!' Annie exclaimed.

'It's war,' Ted said grimly.

There was a knock on the door and Betty jumped to her feet.

'That'll be Graham!'

She ran through to the front door and flung it open. 'Oh, Graham – I was afraid you wouldn't be able to come.' She threw herself into his arms. 'You should have come to the back door and just walked in.'

'I wanted you to see me first.' He stepped back, a self-conscious grin on his face, and struck a pose. 'How d'you like my new uniform, then?'

Betty gazed at him. He was resplendent in new dark-blue serge, the tunic tight on his body and the trousers flaring widely about his ankles. His square rig collar was banded with white ribbon and his cap perched rakishly on his red hair.

'You look smashing. All these white lanyards. Come in and show the others.'

'In a minute.' He pulled her close again and kissed her. 'Bet, I've got to go away.'

'When?' She looked up into his face, suddenly afraid.

'Well – tomorrow. Not far,' he added hastily. 'I'm starting training on Whale Island. But I won't be able to get shore leave for the first couple of weeks. And then I expect I'll get a ship.'

'You won't be able to get leave from Whale Island? But that's just down the road.'

'I know. But nobody gets any leave at first, not even if they live near. It's the same for us all, Bet.'

'I suppose so.' She fingered his collar disconsolately. 'So when will I see you again?'

'I don't know. After I finish my training, I hope. It depends where I get drafted.'

'Are you going to shut the front door, Bet?' Ted shouted from the back room. 'Or are you going to stand out there all night?'

'All right, Dad.' She took Graham's hand and pulled him with her. 'Look at Graham. He's starting tomorrow.'

'My, you do look smart!' Olive said. 'Spanking new. D'you think you'll be able to undo yourself to go to bed tonight?'

Betty giggled. 'I told him, it took our Colin ages to learn what order to do it in.'

'That's what the training's for,' Frank said. 'Teach you to dress and undress. Once you can do that they reckon you're fit to handle a gun.'

There was a brief silence. Jokes that had seemed funny a few weeks ago were no longer so amusing. While the country was still at peace, it had been possible to pretend that even regular Servicemen would never fire a shot in anger. Now, a fortnight into the war, it was different.

'Well, I'd better be going,' Frank said after a moment. 'Got a lot to do this evening. It's still light enough to put in an hour's digging in the allotment.'

'You're never going over there now,' Annie said. 'You've been every night since our Jess went. You must have dug the whole patch twice over.'

'Wish I had. It could do with it. An hour a night's not much, Annie.' He pushed back his chair and stood up. 'Anyway, it gives me something to do. And they're telling us to Dig for Victory, aren't they? Thanks for the meal, Annie.'

He took his jacket off the hook on the back of the kitchen door and went out. Annie watched him go, her face soft.

'Poor Frank. He misses our Jess something awful. He's like a spare part without her, isn't he, Ted.'

Ted grunted. 'Wouldn't be surprised if she don't come back before long. There's already people saying the evacuation wasn't necessary. I mean, nothing's happening, is it. All that talk, all those preparations, and nothing's happening.'

'It is at sea,' Graham said. 'There's ships everywhere. And the Army's on the move too, going off to France and Belgium.'

Annie shuddered. 'Well, you can say what you like, I don't reckon we've seen anything yet. That man's going to come at us like a firestorm one of these days. What do they call it? The way he makes a rush on a country, attacking them from every side so they don't have time to look round, let alone defend themselves.'

'*Blitzkrieg*,' Ted said. 'The lightning war.'

'That's it. Well, that's what we'll get here soon enough, you see if we don't. *Blitzkrieg*.' She shivered again. 'It's a horrible word and it's going to be a horrible war.'

Frank collected a few potatoes from the shed and went into the house. He scrubbed them and put them in a saucepan, ready to cook when he came back from the allotment. Then he went down the garden path again to collect his spade.

Ethel Glaister from next door was out in the garden, looking at her runner beans. The Glaisters didn't have an allotment but grew a few vegetables in the back garden. Ethel had grumbled loudly when some had had to be dug up to make room for the Anderson shelter, but she was the first in the street to put stones over the top and start calling it a rockery.

She looked up as Frank came down the path and gave him a smile. As usual, she looked as if she was dressed up to go visiting rather than just for a walk down the garden.

'Hullo, Frank.'

'Hullo, Ethel. Got plenty of beans, then?'

'Some. They won't be as good as yours, of course. George doesn't put in the time you do. I'm always telling him, if you only put in the time and effort that Frank does, we'd eat a lot better than we do.'

Poor George, Frank thought. It's a wonder he doesn't hate me.

'Well, not everyone takes to it.'

'No, but you can turn your hand to anything, can't you? Not just the gardening. All the decorating and repairs about the place, making furniture, mending shoes . . . I hope Jess appreciates you, Frank.'

'Oh, I think she does.' Frank felt himself grow embarrassed. There was a funny look on Ethel's face, a sort of arch coyness. And surely she'd got lipstick on. 'And I appreciate her,' he added firmly.

'Oh, I'm sure you do.' Ethel had come a bit closer to the fence. She laid her hand on the top of it and gazed up at him. A waft of scent caught in his throat. 'You must feel really lonely in that empty house all by yourself. How are you managing, Frank?'

'Oh, pretty well, considering.' He took a step back. 'Annie gives me my supper most nights and does my washing. I get along all right.'

'Still, it can't be the same, can it.' She smiled. 'If there's anything else you want done, Frank – anything I can do . . . You don't want to impose on Annie too much, I'm sure. And it's not everything you feel you can ask family to do, is it?' She paused for a moment. 'I see Nancy Baxter's started calling.'

Frank flushed.

'She brought me in a bit of cake her mother had baked. I thought it was very good of her.'

'Oh, I'm sure it was. She's a very kind person, Nancy is. I mean, we all know that, don't we – how kind Nancy and her ma can be. Specially to a man who might be missing his home comforts.' She smiled at him and patted her hair, set in its golden waves. 'But you don't have to go to Nancy Baxter for home comforts, Frank. Not when I'm just next door, handy like.'

Frank stared at her. Didn't the woman realise what she was saying – how her words might be construed? And he a man on his own . . .

'I'd better be going,' he said abruptly, with a glance at the sky. 'Light's fading – I want to get a bit of digging in. Won't get the chance later on.'

'No, that's right. You go on.' Ethel was still smiling at him. 'We'll be getting long dark evenings soon. Have to find other things to do.' He was aware of her watching as he moved away down the path. 'Don't forget what I said, Frank,' she called after him. 'Anything you want done – anything – you've only got to say the word.'

Frank nodded and mumbled something. He unlatched the gate and went out into the alley. He was feeling hot and uncomfortable, and he looked back at the house and wished fervently that Jess was inside it, that he could see a light come on as he watched and know that she and the kids were there, that the warmth of his family would follow him over to the allotment and wrap itself about him on his return.

He looked up. The sun was throwing a faint glow of apricot high across the sky. It turned the barrage balloons, floating serenely above their moorings, to a shimmering russet. They looked strange and unearthly up there, but you couldn't deny they had a sort of beauty about them. And yet their purpose was anything but beautiful.

He shook his head and walked on. This war was a queer thing. All the preparations, all the expectations and fear, and yet what had happened so far? A few reports of ships caught up in pointless battle somewhere out at sea, an air strike here and there. The Army getting busy, spreading itself all over Salisbury Plain and places like that. People round the coast all staring out to sea in case Hitler decided to invade that way. And then – nothing.

Well, it was early days yet. Everyone had expected it to start at once, with aircraft screaming over, bombs dropping everywhere and maybe even gas attacks. But just because it was quiet so far didn't mean it was going to go on that way.

All the same, he couldn't help wondering if Jess and the kids had really needed to go away like that, so soon. And as he drove his spade into the earth, he felt a sudden hopeless misery.

Somehow, it all seemed so pointless.

Jess had finally decided to put Maureen on the bottle.

'She's not thriving,' she said to Mrs Greenberry. 'It's as if my milk's not good enough. Too thin. Perhaps it's because I'm too old, I can't make it so well.'

'That can't be true, my dear. You've made a lovely healthy baby, you ought to be able to make good milk. But you've had a lot of upset since she was born, what with the worry over the war and then the evacuation.' The country-woman's voice was warm and sympathetic. 'You don't want to go blaming yourself. It's the sort of thing can happen to anyone. I daresay there's a lot of mothers having the same trouble.'

Jess sighed and went to write to Frank. She wished he were here, so she could talk these things over with him. He'd say it was up to her, of course – decisions like that were women's decisions – but it always made her feel better to talk to him. Writing letters wasn't the same. And she didn't want to worry him.

Jess was missing Frank badly. She was missing home too, and the family – even though they were all around her. It didn't seem right, Tim and Keith living with the Corners, nice though they were, and she didn't like being in someone else's house. Mr and Mrs Greenberry were kindness itself and had soon become real friends but you couldn't do things your own way when you weren't in your own home. She felt uncomfortable when the baby cried at night and she was sure that all the washing was a nuisance. And what with feeding them all, the billeting money could hardly make up for what the extra food cost the Greenberrys.

'Don't you be silly,' Mrs Greenberry told her. 'Most of the veg come out of the garden, so don't cost nothing, and young Rose don't eat enough to keep a sparrow alive. Not like those two boys of yours – I'd rather feed them for a week than a fortnight!'

Jess smiled, but felt a fresh wave of guilt sweep over her. Were Tim and Keith eating the Corners out of house and home? Were they behaving themselves? Edna and Reg said they were, but were they just being polite?

'If they are, they're the only ones in the village,' Mrs Greenberry remarked. 'I've heard some real tales about some of the evacuees and how they're going on. I hear the Woddis sisters are having a dreadful time with the two they've got.'

'What, Alan and Wendy Atkinson? But they're like little mice.'

'Not according to Miss Woddis. I met her in the shop this morning and she was saying what trouble they've had. Mind, I don't think they're used to children.'

Jess thought of Molly Atkinson on the morning of the evacuation. She remembered the distress on the mother's face, the way she had clung to a tree and then almost run after the bus, weeping for her little boy to be kept back. How would she feel if she heard that the people who had taken him were finding him a problem?

'But Alan's a dear little boy,' she said. 'I know the family quite well – they live just at the top of our street. His mother keeps them really nice.'

'Maybe she's done too much for them. Miss Woddis says they don't seem to have any idea how to look after themselves. I've seen them myself – hair all tangled and it doesn't look as if the boy's washed his neck since he arrived here.'

'But he's not five years old yet!' Jess exclaimed. 'He should be having his neck washed for him.'

Mrs Greenberry pursed her lips. 'Well, I daresay it's six of one and half a dozen of the other. It can't be easy for two sisters their age to have strange children to look after. I expect they'll shake down together after a while.'

Alan and Wendy had no such hopes. To them, life had changed not only for the worse but for ever. Why they had not been allowed to go on living at home with their own mother, they did not understand, for they had been protected from talk of war at home and nobody bothered to explain it to them now. As far as Alan knew, this might be what happened to all children at their age. And Wendy knew only from listening to the talk of other children, that they'd been sent away because the Germans – whoever they were – were going to send bombs and gas and kill everyone in the cities.

She lay for hours in her lumpy bed, staring into the darkness and worrying about her parents. Were they going to be killed? Were bombs going to fall on them and blow them to pieces? Her vivid imagination showed her what this would look like, with arms and legs scattered over the streets. If so, why hadn't they come to the country with them? Why had they stayed at home?

These were not questions she could ask the Woddis sisters. Questions of any sort were discouraged, as was any conversation at all from the two Atkinsons. They were expected to be seen and not heard – and seen as little as possible. They understood very quickly that their presence was not welcome in the thin Victorian house with its dark, polished furniture.

'Fingermarks!' Miss Eleanor would exclaim. 'Have you been touching again, Alan?'

He shook his head at once, but Miss Eleanor grasped him by the ear, her fingers pinching painfully, and led him to the big mahogany sideboard with its carved drawers. 'Look at this! Fingermarks all over it. Do you know how long it takes to polish this?'

Again, he shook his head. In fact, neither sister polished the sideboard – Mrs Cherry, who came in every morning to clean and dust, did that. But her time had to be paid for, Miss Eleanor told Alan and Wendy, so it amounted to the same thing. 'I don't intend to pay her simply to clear up after you, you dirty little monkey.'

She produced a tin of polish and a cloth and handed them to the children. 'Now I don't want to see any fingermarks when you've finished, and perhaps it will teach you to keep your hands off the furniture.'

Wendy dabbed the cloth in the polish and rubbed it on the wood. It looked smeary and dull and she stared at it anxiously.

'Well, you'll have to do better than that,' Miss Millicent said sharply, coming into the room. 'It won't polish itself. Put some elbow-grease into it, child.'

Elbow-grease? Wendy looked doubtfully at the tin of polish. It said Mansion House on the lid. Miss Eleanor hadn't said anything about elbow-grease.

'I don't think we've got any,' she said timidly. 'Won't the polish be enough?'

Miss Millicent stared at her. Her nose twitched and two little spots of red appeared on her pale cheekbones.

'Don't be impertinent!' she said angrily. 'Just rub hard and then use the soft cloth. And see that your brother keeps his hands clean.'

Wendy sighed and went back to work. It seemed that everything she did was wrong and everything she said was impertinent. Cheeky, her mother would have said, but it meant the same thing. But what was so cheeky about asking questions? How else were you to find out things?

She couldn't even ask her teacher now. With only about two hours a day in the village school there just wasn't time for any more than a few lessons. The school only had two classrooms too, so they were all herded in together, the infants and lower classes in one and the two top classes in the other. The wall between was only a partition, so you could hear the other classes chanting their times tables when Miss Langrish was trying to explain proper sums, and it was very confusing.

It would have helped if they'd been able to bring books home, but that wasn't allowed. The books had to be used for the village children too. And there was enough bad feeling already over the sharing of desks, rubbers that disappeared and pencils that were left with newly sharpened points and were found next day broken.

The sideboard drawer was beginning to look more shiny now. She dabbed the cloth in the polish again and set to work on another bit.

It seemed quiet in number 13 now, without Bob. Gladys missed him more than she cared to admit, while Diane found tea-time dull without his teasing. And Peggy waited for the postman each morning, hoping there would be a letter or at least a card. 'We don't even know for sure where he is now,' she said to Alice Brunner when she went into the shop for the *Daily Mirror*. 'He went off that morning and just disappeared. I don't see why they can't tell us where they're going, do you? I mean, who's going to tell Hitler? Daft, I call it.'

'Why not ask one of the spiteful gossips around here?' Alice asked. She was looking tired, her thin face drawn and pale. 'They'll tell you who the spies are.'

'Oh, Alice! They're not still pointing fingers at your Heinrich, are they?'

'Of course they are. And me and my Joy too. I don't care for myself, but what's she ever done to deserve it? Downright cruel, I call it.' Peggy saw her face crumple as she said, 'Someone threw a stone at her yesterday.'

'Alice!'

'It was that Micky Baxter, from down your street,' Alice said, sniffing. 'As if he had anything to crow about, when you think what sort of family he comes from.'

'You don't want to take any notice,' Peggy said firmly, handing over the money for the paper. 'People like that aren't worth bothering about.'

'Maybe not,' Alice said, 'but the stones hurt just as much.'

Peggy went out of the shop. She called in at the dairy to buy some eggs. Betty Chapman served her. There was something a bit awkward in the girl's manner, Peggy thought, and it wasn't until she was at the door that Betty said, 'Have you heard from Bob at all? I hope he's all right.'

Peggy repeated what she had said to Alice Brunner. She wondered if what Gladys had said was true, and that Bob had only joined up because Betty had refused to go out with him. Well, if she had it was her right to do so, and Peggy wasn't going to take against her because of that. Any other time, he'd have just moped about for a while and then found someone else. But she had an idea that Betty was feeling guilty over it, all the same.

'Don't you worry,' she said. 'You've got your own troubles to think about. Your brother's at sea and your young man's gone too, hasn't he?'

'Yes, but he's only training on Whale Island, he hasn't gone away yet.' Betty hesitated. 'I think quite a lot of Bob,' she said at last. 'I wouldn't want anything to happen to him.'

Peggy's face softened. The girl really was upset. She gave her a smile, her mouth twisting with the tears that still caught her by surprise at times.

'I know, love. It's a hard time for us all.'

She left the dairy and walked back down October Street. The residents of these houses always thought themselves a bit posher than those in April Grove because they had a third bedroom built over the sculleries as well as a tiny front garden with a low wall topped with iron railings. The third bedroom wasn't all that much to write home about, Peggy thought, though she wouldn't have minded it herself. Like Jess and Frank next door, and the Glaisters, they had to shuffle about a bit to fit more than two children into the house. Her Bob had to sleep downstairs in the front room, on a camp bed, and the Budds had bought a Put-u-Up settee bed for Rose. It wasn't so bad when they were small, but it got difficult when they were older.

Granny Kinch was at her front door when she reached April Grove. She was wearing a brown herringbone coat, buttoned almost to her chin, with an inch of pinafore showing beneath the hem. It was only in the coldest weather that she didn't venture on to her doorstep, and then she sat in the window, still keeping an eye on everything. But she really liked to be outside, where she could talk to anyone who passed.

Like everyone else, she asked about Bob.

'We don't know,' Peggy said. 'We just had one postcard, from a place called Caterham. He didn't know whether they'd be staying there or going somewhere else.'

'How'd he sound?' The old woman seemed really interested. But I suppose she is, Peggy thought. Interested in everyone. Otherwise, why should she stand there? I suppose we always called it nosiness before.

'Well, he sounded cheerful enough. Talking about square-bashing and khaki and all that. But underneath – well, you can tell he's lonely really.'

'He must be homesick,' Granny Kinch said. 'He's never been away from home before, has he?'

'Well, only to Scout camp.' Peggy gazed along the street. 'I keep wondering what'll happen to him when he's finished his training. I mean, will he really have to go and fight?' She looked back at the wrinkled, none too clean face under the steel curlers. 'It don't seem possible, our Bob actually shooting at people – trying to kill them.'

'No, it don't. It's different when it's other people – but when it's your own boy, being made to kill other boys – lads he'd probably have played football with if they'd lived next door—'

'That's it,' Peggy said, grateful for the woman's understanding. 'I mean, Germans can't all be bad. Look at Heinrich Brunner. You couldn't wish to meet a nicer man. There must be others like him.' She shook her head. 'And he's still got family over there too. What must he feel like, watching boys like our Bob and Colin Chapman going off to fight. They might be killing his relations, for all we know.'

The old woman nodded. She had left her false teeth out this morning and her mouth was drawn in like a purse, lips folded back over the gums. 'It's wicked. Is your Gladys still carrying a torch for that young man?'

'What young man? Colin Chapman?' Peggy shrugged. 'Don't ask me, she don't confide in her mother. But I wouldn't be surprised. But our Bob's still hankering after young Betty, that I do know. Mind, it's his own fault she wouldn't go out with him. He never even noticed her till she started to knock about with that Ginger Philpotts boy. He had his chance and wasted it, and it's no use blaming anyone but himself. But it's the war again – it's made 'em all think if they don't get what they want straight away, they'll never get it.'

'Everything's bin turned upside down,' Mrs Kinch said. 'Bits of boys going off to the Services, the kiddies away in the country. Schools turned into First-Aid Posts, shelters in the gardens, the blackout . . .'

'Barrage balloons in the sky,' Peggy joined in. 'Air-raid sirens, gas masks . . . And when's it all going to end? When are they going to do what Mr Chamberlain said and bring Hitler to his knees?'

'I don't reckon they know what they're doing,' Granny Kinch said. 'Look at it. They've never run a war, not like this one's going to be. They don't know how to do it, no more than me and old Mrs Seddon over the road would know. They've got us into this mess, the whole lot of them from Hitler to Chamberlain, and now they don't bloody know how to get us out. And that's the truth of it.'

Peggy stared at her. It's true, she thought. It's all true. And it's people like us, ordinary people with sons who have to go off and get killed, and daughters who have to watch their sweethearts go away when they ought to have their lives before them, we're the ones who suffer.

Olive was late home that night. But for once, as she told Derek, her dad was going to have to put up with it. 'It's wartime now,' she said. 'Things are different. And I'm tired of being treated like a kid.'

They had walked out past the allotments and the brickworks, down to the shore of Langstone Harbour. It was a popular spot for courting couples and the grassy banks were dotted with young men and girls, sitting in pairs.

The tide was half out, leaving the mud rippled and shiny. Boats of all sizes and descriptions lay slumped on their sides, their masts teetering at acute angles. Gulls and wading birds tiptoed between them, probing for cockles and worms, and about fifty yards away a group of men were digging for bait.

'It all looks so peaceful,' Olive said. 'I can't believe there's a war on.'

'It doesn't seem to be going the way they thought it would,' Derek agreed. 'And now that they've opened the cinemas and that, you'd hardly know the difference except for the shelters and sandbags everywhere.'

'Which we don't need to use. Mind you, we do get a lot of things to read.'

Derek laughed. 'Those leaflets! They drive my old man barmy. He says he wonders how they think we've managed to get by all these years without being told what to do every five minutes. It's "do this, don't do that" wherever you look. We had one this morning that told us not to lie on our backs in the shelters in case we snored!'

Olive giggled. 'Perhaps they think it would help guide the Germans in. We'll hear the wardens shout "Stop that snoring" like they shout "Put that light out". But the worst one was the one that told us what to do with our pets. Did you see that one?'

Derek shook his head. 'Dad doesn't even bother looking at them now. He just chucks 'em in the bin. What did it say?'

'Oh, it's awful. It says to try to find a home for your pets – and if you can't, take them to the vet! Well, we know what that means. And what sort of home are you going to find that's any safer than your own? You can't evacuate cats and dogs to the country.'

'Aren't you supposed to take them in the shelter with you?'

'No. Not the public ones, anyway. I suppose they can't stop you taking them in your own.' She shook her head. 'Our Betty would go mad if we had Suky put to sleep. We've had her six years, ever since she was a kitten.'

'I don't believe most people will have their pets put to sleep,' Derek said. 'Not cats, anyway. They can look after themselves.'

They sat quietly for a few moments. The sun was going down behind them, casting long shadows over the drying mud. On the far side of the harbour a few windows reflected golden light.

'I can't bear to think of you going away,' Olive said at last in a small voice.

Derek tightened his arm about her waist. 'I know. I'm not looking forward to it much myself.'

'If only we were—' She hesitated, her fingers playing with a blade of grass. Her head was bent, the hair as brown and shiny as a conker falling across her face.

'Were what?'

'Well – engaged or something. I know it doesn't make any difference really – but people take a bit more notice. I mean, if they think we're just going out together they don't realise – they think—'

'They think it's not serious – you'll go out with someone else.'

'Well, yes.' She still wasn't looking at him. 'I don't want to go out with anyone else, Derek.'

'Nor do I. Only I wasn't thinking of getting engaged.'

'Oh.' She sounded deflated and he laughed and squeezed her more tightly.

'Don't sound so miserable. I was thinking of getting married.'

Olive's head flew round. Her brown eyes widened. '*Married?*'

'Why not?' He grinned at her.

'But – before you go away, you mean?'

'Well, it wouldn't be very easy afterwards, would it.'

'Oh, don't be so daft! You know what I mean.' Olive stared at him. 'My dad'd never let us.'

'Wouldn't he? Are you sure?'

'Yes, I am.' Her excitement disappeared abruptly. 'He doesn't believe in girls getting married too young. He's always saying so.'

'Well, what's too young? I don't reckon you're too young, Livvy.' He moved his hand caressingly on her waist.

'Dad would. And he wouldn't like you doing that, either.'

'Well, I'm not asking him.' Derek moved a little closer and nuzzled his lips into her neck. 'It's whether you like it that I'm concerned about,' he murmured, and let his fingertips stray over her breast.

Olive wriggled a little. 'Derek – don't.'

'Why not? You let me do more than that on our sofa the other night – remember?' He kissed her mouth, then her neck, nuzzling into the hollow of her throat. 'We're practically engaged now, anyway, whatever your dad says. We want to get married, don't we?'

'Yes, but—' Olive gave up and leant against him. 'Oh, Derek, if only we could.'

'Well, I don't see why we shouldn't. We've been going out for nearly a year now. He knows me, knows my dad. What's the problem?'

'He'll just say I'm too young. I know he will.' She sighed and turned her head towards him, offering her mouth for his kiss. 'Oh, Derek . . .'

'Look,' he said firmly after a moment, 'you're not too young. If I'm old enough to go off to fight and get killed – you're old enough to get married. And that's all there is to it.'

'It's not, though. We can't get married without Dad's say-so. And he can be very obstinate.'

'Well, then,' Derek said, 'we'll just have to persuade him, won't we? Show him we mean it.'

The sun had gone now, leaving the harbour in a deepening twilight. It was almost too dark to see the other couples along the banks, but Olive knew that they were mostly lying down together, kissing – perhaps more. She felt nervous and excited. What did Derek mean?

She remembered every detail of the evening they'd spent alone at his house. They hadn't gone all the way, but they'd got pretty near it. She knew that if they hadn't been expecting Mr and Mrs Harker back at any time, they might easily have got completely carried away. She'd wanted it and she knew Derek had wanted it even more. But nervousness and the fear of getting 'caught' had held her back, as it held her back now.

'Derek – you won't—'

'I won't do anything you don't want me to, Olive,' he promised, and drew her down close. She felt his fingers at the buttons of her blouse and trembled. Then he kissed her again and the darkening sky spun above her head.

'I love you, Livvy,' he whispered against her hair. 'I want to marry you. I want to go away knowing I've got a wife. I want to know what it's like to really love you. What's so wrong about that?'

'I love you too. But I'm scared.'

'It's all right,' he promised again. 'Nothing's going to go wrong. I'll take care of that.' He was stroking her breasts now. She felt his fingertips, cool against her flushed skin. His body was hard against hers and he was breathing quickly.

'No, Derek. Not until we're married. I can't.'

'You can. We can. Olive—'

'No.' She wriggled away and sat up, brushing her hair back from her face. 'You know what could happen. I can't take the chance.'

'I'll be careful—'

'I'm too scared. Dad would throw me out. And then what would I do?'

'You could go and live with my mum and dad, if we were married.'

'So let's get married first.' She looked down at him and put out her hand to touch his face. 'Please, Derek. I'd rather it was all above board.'

He sighed and sat up beside her. She could barely see his face in the darkness and wondered if he was angry, but when she touched him he turned and moved closer, taking her hand.

'All right, Livvy. We'll wait. But I want to get married before I go away. I want to know you're going to be safe at home, waiting for me.'

'I'll talk to Mum,' she promised. 'I'll get her round and then she can talk to Dad. That's the best way.'

'All right,' he said, and then turned and pulled her roughly into his arms. 'Only don't take too long about it. I don't think I can wait much longer.'

Jess wheeled Maureen's pram along the lanes. It was a fine afternoon and if Frank had been with her she would have enjoyed the warmth of the sun, the bright red of the hawthorn berries and rosehips in the hedges and the changing of the leaves. But Frank was in Portsmouth, sweating in a boiler-shop, and Jess was missing him badly.

All the same, she couldn't sit and brood. There were other people who were missing their homes, children who scarcely understood why they'd had to leave them, and this afternoon she had made up her mind to go round and see a few of them, just to make sure they were well and happy.

'I'll come too,' Rose said, and now she walked by Jess's side, her bright brown eyes observing everything. The boys were off with their friends, collecting nuts and blackberries, but although Rose had plenty of friends she seemed to prefer to be with her mother. It was as if she was afraid Jess would disappear if she took her eyes off her.

Jess had already met little Martin Baker in the village street. He had been tagging along behind Mrs Hutchins, his foster-mother, but she hadn't had time to stop for a chat. Jess had looked down at Martin and asked him how he was, and he'd stared mutely back, his eyes large and round.

'He don't talk much, I'll say that for him,' Mrs Hutchins said. 'Eats plenty, though. He knows what his mouth's for!' She was in her fifties, Jess guessed, and having to cope with a six-year-old boy must have come as a bit of a shock. She had a grudging face and small, pebble-like eyes, but she looked tidy enough and the basket she carried was full of vegetables and bread. It looked as if Martin would eat well.

All the same, Jess looked at him doubtfully. He was a quiet child, she knew that, but he looked paler than usual and a bit scared.

I suppose they all must feel a bit frightened still, she thought. It'll take time for them to settle down. And he looks clean enough, as if she's taking care of him.

Mrs Hutchins and Martin disappeared up the narrow track leading to her cottage and Jess watched them, still feeling vaguely uneasy but trying to stifle her doubts. What could she do, after all? The billeting officer, Mrs Tupper, seemed efficient enough and called regularly on all the children. It wasn't up to Jess to tell her her job.

She walked on. Susan Cullen was living with a couple near the church. When Jess knocked on the door, it was answered by a tired-looking woman of about thirty-five, with a baby in her arms and a toddler dragging at her skirt.

'Susan? Oh, she's all right, I suppose, all things considered.' The woman looked faded, as if she'd been left out in the sun too long. She pushed back lank, stringy hair and pulled the toddler's fingers away from Jess's coat.

'No, Billy, don't put your sticky fingers all over the lady's coat. Susan's out, if you wanted to see her. She's having tea with one of her friends.'

'It's all right,' Jess said, feeling embarrassed. It was as if she were checking up on these people – as, indeed, she supposed she was. 'It's just that I promised her father I'd keep an eye on her. She lost her mother just before she came away, you know.'

'You don't have to tell me that! She's hardly stopped crying since she got here.' The woman really did look exhausted, Jess thought, and no wonder. 'Mike and me, we've done our best, but there's no pacifying her sometimes. If you ask me, it was wrong to send her. She should've stayed at home.'

'But her father's a milkman, you see,' Jess explained. 'He has to go to work at four in the morning.'

'So Mrs Tupper said. Well, I can see there was no help for it, but you can see how we're placed. I'm sorry for the child, of course I am, but I can't keep on giving her all the attention. I've got my own kids to see to as well.'

'I know.' Jess looked at her helplessly. She really did look worn out. It must be very difficult, she thought, having to take in strange children and try to cope with their problems as well as your own. 'Well, if there's anything I can do to give a hand.'

'Ta, but I don't think there's anything much. You might get your two little boys to give an eye to her at school. But I don't really see what anyone can do. She's just got to get over it as best she can.' There was a sudden crash and a wail from inside the house and the woman threw a harassed glance over her shoulder. 'Oh lor', that'll be our Freddy pulled something over, I'll have to go,' and she disappeared indoors.

'Good heavens,' Jess said as she and Rose walked away. 'However many children has she got? I didn't realise there was another one indoors.'

Rose shook her head. It was difficult to get to know the village children when you were at school at different times of the day from them. And those below school age seemed to inhabit a different world anyway.

'Where are we going now?' she asked.

Jess consulted the scrap of paper on which she had written down the names and addresses.

'The Woddises. That's where the little Atkinsons are.' She looked up and a smile broke over her face. 'Look, there's Tim and Keith. They can come along with us, they know Wendy and Alan.'

The two boys ran up to their mother and gave her exuberant kisses. She hugged them tightly, feeling a sudden ache of tears in her throat. How lucky she was to have them so close, even though another woman was looking after them. At least she could see for herself how happy and well-cared-for they were. And if they were being looked after properly, didn't it make sense that so were most of the other children? It was natural enough, after all, that they were missing their parents – Tim and Keith, with their mother close by, didn't have that problem. They'd settle down soon enough.

Still, she'd promised Molly Atkinson that she'd keep an eye on the two little ones and although she felt rather intimidated by the tall, Victorian house that stood alone a little way from the village, she knew she must keep that promise.

With the pram and three children clustered around her, she marched up the path and pulled the old-fashioned bell.

There was a long silence. The door, painted a dull brown, stared forbiddingly back at her. Perhaps there's no one in, she thought, and was just turning away when it opened and a thin, elderly lady with a pale face and twitching nose stood gazing out at her.

'Yes? What is it?'

'Oh – hello.' Jess hesitated under the gaze. She fumbled for words. 'I'm Jess Budd. I've been evacuated from Portsmouth—'

'We can't take any more.' The gaze slid past to the children. 'We certainly can't take any more. We've got enough on our hands already.'

'I don't want – we've already got somewhere – I haven't come to ask you—'

'Then why have you come?' The voice was peremptory. 'Hurry up and tell me, please, the door's letting all the heat out.'

Jess could feel no heat. The passage stretching away behind the elderly woman looked cold, dark and uninviting. She wondered how Alan and Wendy were faring here. It looked so different from the warm, untidy greengrocer's shop.

'I just came to see how the children are. Wendy and Alan. I know their mother, you see, and—'

'Who is it, Millicent?' a voice called from inside, and Miss Woddis turned her head.

'It's a person, Eleanor. A person asking about the children. She says she knows their mother at home.' The twitching nose poked sharply at Jess. 'Did their mother send you? Is she not satisfied?'

'Oh, I'm sure she's satisfied,' Jess said hurriedly, though she couldn't help remembering Molly Atkinson's face as she'd stood with one hand pressed against a tree and the other at her mouth. 'I just thought I'd look in and make sure – I mean—'

'The children are perfectly all right.' The elder sister was at the door now, even taller than the first. Jess knew at once that the boys would be staring at the mole on her chin and prayed they would say nothing about it, at least until they were safely out of earshot. 'They're having their tea now. I imagine you'll take my word for that?'

'Yes – yes, of course,' Jess stammered. 'I don't want to be a nuisance. As long as they're well and happy—'

'Oh, yes. *They're* well and happy enough. Why shouldn't they be? Do you have some cause to doubt it?'

'No – none at all.' Jess wished she hadn't come. She began to turn the pram around. 'I'm sorry to have bothered you. Perhaps I could see Alan and Wendy another time. They could come and have tea with us—'

'I don't think so, thank you.' There was a smile, but it was so frigid that it could have been made of ice. 'We don't mix with the village people.'

Jess stared at her. She felt indignation creep red-hot through her body. She saw the woman's eyes move over the children, saw the distaste in the expression. Abruptly, forgetting the Atkinsons, she wheeled the pram around.

'I'm sorry,' she said again, but now her voice was as cold as Miss Woddis's. 'Perhaps I shouldn't have come. But Molly Atkinson and I are friends and I knew she would want me to see where Alan and Wendy were living—'

'And now you have seen. The children are perfectly happy and being cared for as if they were our own.'

Jess hesitated. Angry though she was, she couldn't let her temper rule her. And she had come to see Alan and Wendy – to see for herself that they were all right.

'If I could just see them for a moment—' she began, but already the two sisters were closing the door.

'Naturally, if their mother comes to visit, she'll be permitted to see her children. I don't think we're under any obligation to admit a procession of casual sightseers to our home. Now, if you don't mind—' And the door was closed firmly in Jess's face.

Jess stood absolutely still. She felt as if she had been slapped. Her cheeks burned and her breath, knocked momentarily from her body, came in a quick gasp. Abruptly, she began to march back down the path, her head up to prevent the angry tears from falling to her cheeks.

The children followed, subdued. Then Tim said loudly, 'I don't like that lady, Mum.'

Jess gave a quick glance back towards the windows. But what did it matter if they heard? They'd been just as rude. Ruder.

'No, Tim,' she said, 'neither do I.'

As they walked back to the Corners' house, to leave Tim and Keith for the night, she thought over her afternoon's expedition. Had it been any use? Martin Baker seemed all right, though even quieter than usual, and Jess hadn't much liked Mrs Hutchins. Susan Cullen was obviously miserable but the woman looking after her seemed sympathetic even though she was clearly worn out by her own family – and who was to say that Susan would be any less unhappy anywhere else? And the house where Alan and Wendy were living was a lot posher than that flat over the greengrocer's shop, even if the spinster sisters did think themselves better than anyone else.

What could you do? You couldn't choose different billets just like that. There just weren't any other places for the children to go. And as long as they were being fed and kept clean, what more could anyone ask?

Jess was uncomfortably aware that children needed a good deal more. But this was wartime, and nobody was getting what they needed. And it was better than being bombed, back home in Portsmouth.

7

'The Phoney War,' people were beginning to call it. A war of grinding
dreariness that Tommy Vickers said Hitler would win simply by boring
everyone to death. 'Not that he needs to lift a finger anyway,' he added.
'We're making a pretty good job of killing ourselves, without his help.'

By the third week in September, road accidents had trebled. More people
had been killed by being run over or in collision with other cars than by
enemy action. The blackout became more than an irritation and people
were forced to stay at home, or make visits to only their nearest neighbours.
With the evenings drawing in there was little social life and those families
that had stayed together huddled round their own fires, listening to the
wireless.

'If it wasn't for people like Tommy Handley and Arthur Askey we'd all
go mad,' Annie Chapman commented to Peggy Shaw one afternoon.
'They're the only ones as give us a laugh these days.'

'Oh, I like *ITMA*,' Peggy agreed. 'Ministry of Aggravation and Mysteries!
And that Mrs Mopp – "Can I do you now, sir?" Mind, we always listen to
the News as well. There's something about hearing Big Ben at nine o'clock.
You need to know what's going on, don't you?'

Annie nodded. Everyone listened to the Nine O'clock News on the
Home Service. The BBC had recently taken to letting the readers say their
own names too – *Here is the Nine O'clock News and this is Alvar Liddel
reading it.* 'It makes you feel you know them,' she said. 'As if they were your
own friends, just come in for a chat.'

'Mind, it's never very good news, is it,' Peggy continued. 'Petrol rationed
– not that that affects us! – income tax up to seven-and-six in the pound –
and now they've got anti-aircraft batteries out on Southsea Common. And
did you hear about that boy hit by a cartridge over Fratton way? Standing
watching a dogfight he was, and next thing he knew he was unconscious.'

'A dogfight?' Annie said, puzzled.

'It's what they call aeroplanes scrapping,' Peggy said. 'So the Germans
are getting here, you see. Our lads soon chased them off, though.'

Annie sighed. The three months since the war began seemed more like
three years. Still no bombs had dropped, the Andersons and street shelters
stood empty and people had begun to be careless about their gas masks.
Someone had reported a spot check done on the train from Portsmouth to
Waterloo one day, and two out of three people had sandwiches in their

carriers instead. The air-raid warnings sounded occasionally, but most people knew it was only practice and didn't even bother to look up.

There were, however, plenty of signs that the war was being waged elsewhere. Everyone in Portsmouth was shocked when the aircraft carrier *Courageous* was torpedoed and sunk off the Hebrides, the first naval casualty of the war. That ship had been moored in Portsmouth harbour, its sailors roistered about Portsmouth streets. Some, indeed, were Portsmouth men and there were grieving mothers and widows in the city at this moment.

On 14 October another ship had gone down – the *Royal Oak*, sunk in Scapa Flow. Again, there was shock in the city that had seen so many ships go to war and still sheltered Nelson's *Victory*, the most famous of them all, in its dockyard. The war came closer, touching everyone.

Olive and Betty Chapman were as restless as everyone else. With many of their entertainments denied them, they felt frustrated and anxious for something to do. For Olive, that something was marriage and she tackled Annie about it one evening as they washed up after supper.

'Derek'll be called up soon, bound to be,' she said. 'And then he'll go away and God knows when I'll see him again. What are we supposed to do, wait the rest of our lives?'

'Don't talk daft,' Annie said, holding a plate up to inspect. 'This lot's going to be over by Christmas, everyone says so. Hitler knows he's bitten off more than he can chew this time. He'll back down soon, see if he doesn't.'

'He's not backing down at the moment. Look at the ships he's sinking. Anyway, even if it is all over by Christmas, there's still going to be men killed – and my Derek could be one of them.' Olive stopped what she was doing, a tea-towel held in one hand, and stared at her mother. 'How would I feel if he got killed and I'd never – we'd never—' She stopped, feeling the blush creeping up her cheeks, aware of her mother's eyes. 'Well, we just want to get married before he goes, that's all,' she muttered.

Annie pursed her mouth. 'You don't know what you're saying. Getting married's for ever – not just a few months. There's plenty of people did that in the last war, and lived to regret it.'

'We wouldn't,' Olive said stubbornly. 'We love each other, Mum.'

Annie sighed. It was hard not to weaken when the girl gazed at her with those big eyes, just as it had been hard not to weaken when she was little and begging for another sweet or a new doll. And she wasn't far off twenty-one, after all. What was the point of refusing her?

'I'll talk to your father,' she promised. 'But I'm afraid he'll say the same as me, Livvy. He doesn't approve of girls getting married too young. Why don't you just get engaged?'

'Because we want to be *married*,' Olive exclaimed in exasperation, and Annie knew that there was no more to be said.

I think they really do love each other, she thought as she wiped the sink. I think they'd be all right, if they could only start off properly. But a man going off to war and his wife still living at home with her parents – that's not right. And what if it isn't over by Christmas? What if they start a baby?

And what's going to happen if Ted does agree to let them get married? What's our Betty going to say? It'll be her and Graham next, and that I *wouldn't* be happy about. They're not properly in love with each other, they're just in love with love.

But Betty had no thoughts of getting married. An engagement, even a secret engagement, was enough for her. In fact, she preferred it that way – she liked the feeling of hugging a romantic secret to herself, the feeling that she knew more than other people. And she didn't want to be tied down, anyway. Life was too interesting to be shackled to a kitchen sink and a pramful of squalling babies.

'They're asking for girls to join the Land Army,' she announced at supper one evening. 'I thought I'd go along.'

Annie paused in the middle of serving out helpings of shepherd's pie. 'You thought *what*?'

'I thought I'd join the Land Army. You know. Work on a farm. Milk cows and all that. It'll be fun.'

'*Fun*?' Ted stared at her. 'Look here, our Bet, this war isn't being fought for *fun*. It's serious, that's what it is. Not to give flibbertigibbet girls like you a bit of a holiday.'

'I'm not a flibbertigibbet! And I know it won't be a holiday – but I don't see why I shouldn't enjoy it, all the same.' Betty glared at her father. 'We don't all have to go around with long faces all the time. I don't see as that helps anyone.'

'And don't give me any of your cheek!' Ted was due to go on duty soon, for the last shift of the day and his least favourite. He still found it hard, taking his ferryboat across the harbour in pitch darkness, and was always more short-tempered when working this shift. 'You're not going in the Land Army, and that's that.'

Betty's face reddened and her eyes flashed. She and her father were always rubbing each other up the wrong way these days. It was as if she couldn't do a thing right, almost as if he was determined to object to everything about her. Wearing make-up – 'making yourself look cheap' – going out with Graham – 'that ginger boy from over the water', as if Graham were some kind of foreigner – and now decent war work being called 'a bit of a holiday'. It wasn't fair!

'And how are you going to stop me?' she demanded. 'The government wants girls like me – they're crying out for them. In fact, we'll probably *have* to go, like it or not, so I might as well volunteer.'

'If you've got to go, that's different. Conscription's conscription. But until then, you stay here, under my eye—'

'Why? What d'you think I'm going to do? What sort of girl d'you think I am?' Tears of anger threatened Betty's voice. Gulping them back, she faced her father, realising that for the first time in her life she wasn't afraid of his anger. 'All I want is to go and do some useful work, something I think I'll enjoy—'

'Yes, and that's just it!' He was as furious as she. How dare she answer back like this, his daughter, who ought to be meek and submissive and do as her father told her. 'It's *enjoyment* you're after. Fun. And I know just what sort of fun you've got in mind.'

'Oh yes?' Betty challenged him. 'What sort's that, then? Just tell me. It might be something I'd never have thought of for myself!'

'Betty!' Annie interposed. 'Stop it at once. You mustn't talk to your father like that—'

But Betty rounded on her. 'Why mustn't I? He can say what he likes to me – he can make out I'm some sort of tart—'

'*Betty!* I won't have that sort of talk in this house.'

'Well, It's what he meant, isn't it? It's what he was getting at.' She looked at Ted again and this time the tears overflowed and ran down her cheeks. 'You don't trust me at all, do you,' she accused him, her voice trembling. 'You never have. You've always treated me like dirt – as if I just didn't matter. I mustn't wear lipstick, I mustn't go out dancing, I mustn't have a boyfriend . . . You hate me, that's what it is, you always have, and shall I tell you something?' She was on her feet, her eyes wild and red, her face scarlet and wet with tears. 'I hate you too! I do – I *hate* you – and I'll tell you something else – I *am* going to join the Land Army and nothing any of you can do will stop me!'

'Betty—' Annie began, but Betty turned and rushed out of the room and they heard her feet pounding up the stairs to her bedroom.

Annie and Ted looked at each other.

'Now see what you've done,' Annie said heavily.

'What *I've* done? Annie, that girl's getting completely out of hand. She's been allowed too much freedom, that's what it is – been allowed to run wild. And this is the result.'

'Ted, all she wants is to do some war work. There's nothing wrong in that, is there?'

'Not if that's *all* she wants to do, no. But I'm not so sure, it is. She's always been one for the boys, you know that.'

'For goodness sake! That was when she was a child. She was a tomboy, that's all. It didn't mean anything. And if it was men she was after she wouldn't be talking about farm work – she'd be wanting to join the Wrens or something.'

Ted said nothing. He had to admit that Annie was probably right about that, but he wasn't ready yet to admit it out loud. Already, his temper was subsiding and he felt guilty at the sound of Betty sobbing just above their heads. He sighed and picked up his knife and fork.

'Well, I'm not going to let her spoil my supper,' he said, and looked at his elder daughter. 'And I hope you've been taking notice, Olive. Just because there's a war on don't mean I'm going to forget all the things I've said about you girls. You're still under twenty-one, both of you, and still under my authority, and don't you forget it.'

Olive looked at him. She had sat silent throughout the whole row, knowing that any contribution from her was likely only to make it worse and hoping that her father might forget she was there. But now all she could do was shake her head.

'No, Dad. I won't.'

Ted started to eat his shepherd's pie. Annie and Olive picked at theirs and Betty's lay untouched and cooling on the place. An uneasy silence hung over the house.

He'll never let me and Derek get married now, Olive thought miserably. He'll never back down, now our Betty's riled him so bad. She's ruined everything.

But she couldn't really blame her sister for what had happened. What was wrong with the Land Army after all? And why shouldn't people do as they wanted with their own lives?

He's just another Hitler, she thought rebelliously, pushing meat and potatoes about on her plate. He just wants to be in charge all the time. Captain of a ferryboat – huh! You'd think he was Admiral Nelson, the way he carries on.

It seemed strange in the street without Jess living in number 14. There were other families whose children had been evacuated too, of course, but it was Jess that Annie missed most. The sisters had lived near each other for nearly ten years now and Annie had to remind herself every morning that Jess was no longer there.

Instead, she found herself chatting more to Peggy Shaw, who loved next door to Jess. The two women had always been friendly, but it was Jess who had been Peggy's particular crony, and she missed her too. So it was natural that she and Annie should turn to each other for company instead.

Annie was still brooding over Betty's outburst when they met next afternoon, outside the newsagent's.

'Don't it seem quiet,' Peggy remarked. 'No kids about, not much traffic. It's hard to believe there's a war on, isn't it.'

'It is when you look round you,' Annie agreed. 'But there's plenty going on, all the same. It's these shortages that get you down most. Onions – they're like gold now. I've seen hardly any oranges this winter, and bananas seem to have disappeared altogether. My Ted likes a banana to take for his lunch, but they don't seem to have any anywhere. I tried Shepherds' and Atkinsons', neither of them had any.'

'They'll have to start rationing soon. I thought it would have started before this.'

'So did I.' Annie had seen the ration books at the school, stacked in bundles ready for distribution. She went back to the subject that had been on her mind all morning. 'Our Betty's on about joining the Land Army.'

'What! Going to work on a farm? D'you think she'd like it?'

'She seems to think so. Her dad doesn't like the idea, neither do I much. She's too young to be going away from home, to my mind, but she says she's going to volunteer and there's not much we can do about it.'

'It's daft, isn't it,' Peggy said. 'We can stop them getting married but we can't stop them going off to join the Services. I mean, they're just bits of boys, going off heaven knows where to fight and they don't have any idea what it's all about. They think it's just a game.'

'They'll find out different soon enough. How's your Bob?'

Peggy shook her head. 'I don't know, Annie. He writes home but he don't say much really. It seems as though it's as dreary for them as it is for us. Just sitting there, they are, waiting for something to happen. I mean, what's it all about? If no one wants to fight, why don't they bring them all home and forget it? Seems to me it'd make more sense.'

'Where is he now?'

'Somewhere in France, that's all we know. What about your Olive's young man?'

'He'll be out there too, soon by the look of it. He's waiting for his papers now. And that's another funny thing. He was in the TA, should have been one of the first to go, but he's still here, yet your Bob goes along to join up and he's in training before you can say Jack Robinson. It makes you wonder, doesn't it.' She paused. 'You've heard our Olive wants to get married, I suppose.'

'What does your Ted say about it?'

'Well, what d'you think? He's always said he wouldn't let either of the girls get married before they were twenty-one. Not that it's been mentioned outright, mind – though Olive had a word with me about it and Derek's all for asking him straight. But I know Ted'll just say no if they do that, and once he's said no he won't back down, he never does. No, I've told Olive, if they want to get round him they've got to do it slow and careful.'

'So you're in favour of it yourself, then,' Peggy said.

'Well, I'd rather they got engaged, but . . . you know how it is. They've known each other nearly a year. And if we don't let'em get married – well—'

Peggy nodded. 'Well, we all know what it is to be young – and with a war on and never knowing when they're going to see each other again—'

'It's not easy for them,' Annie said. 'It's different from when we were young, Peg. But it's getting the men to see it that's the hard part.'

'You'd think they'd see it more than we do – they're the ones who push, after all. But it's funny about men, they seem to forget what they were like when it's their own daughters.'

'Maybe it's because they don't forget what they were like,' Annie said shrewdly, and both women laughed.

Ethel Glaister, walking past at that moment, stopped and looked at them. She was wearing a pale blue costume neither of them had seen before, and a hat with a small veil. Annie stared at it jealously and Peggy was immediately conscious of her old coat and the scarf she had wound like a turban round her head.

'Well, it's nice to see someone's got something to laugh at,' Ethel said in her sharp voice. 'I suppose you've been in there.' She jerked her head at the newsagent's shop.

'And why not?' Annie demanded at once. 'It wouldn't do you any harm to go in and give Alice Brunner time of day, either.'

'Me? I don't go in there any more. I'd rather go down to the corner for my paper.'

'Well, it's the same paper, as far as I can see,' Peggy said, holding up her *Evening News*. 'I don't suppose it's got any better news in it for walking another quarter of a mile.'

'No, but it hasn't been handled by spies and traitors,' Ethel said sharply, and the other two women gasped.

'Alice Brunner could have you up in court for that.'

'Why? I never mentioned no names.' Ethel looked at them defiantly. 'There's spies everywhere, you know there are. Look at all the posters about it. Idle Talk Costs Lives. And pictures of Hitler hiding under railway seats. That sort of thing. You don't know what's getting reported back.'

'Well, nothing I say's likely to get reported back, wherever I say it,' Peggy said with a short laugh. 'And I don't believe either Alice or Heinrich's a spy. He's been here twenty years, for goodness sake.'

'And still goes back every year,' Ethel said darkly. 'Well, if I were you, Peggy Shaw, I'd be careful going in there. You don't want people thinking you're a sympathiser.'

'A sympathiser with what?'

'You know what I mean. A Fifth Columnist.' She stopped suddenly as Peggy lunged forward, waving her shopping bag.

'You'll take that back this minute, Ethel Glaister! Nobody calls me a traitor to my country.'

'I didn't. All I said was—'

'You as good as did. Calling me a sympathiser! Why don't you come straight out and say I'm a spy? Eh? Why not say what you think?'

'I never said you were a spy.' Ethel took a step back. 'All I said was you ought to be careful. You don't know who's listening. I'm only saying what we're all being told, only I don't go gossiping in the streets, that's all. I'd rather be doing something for my country.'

'And I suppose I'm not? Not with my Bob in the Army and likely to get killed any minute. Nor Annie here, her Colin's thousands of miles away on the *Exeter* and she doesn't know when she'll see him again. I suppose that doesn't count as doing something for your country. You'd better watch what you say, you spiteful little—'

'Peggy!' Annie grabbed her arm and dragged her back. 'Just ignore her – she's not worth getting upset over.' She gave Ethel a scornful look. 'When you've got someone serving like Peggy and me have, you might have call to talk, but until then you'd better keep a civil tongue in your head, see?'

'Well, pardon me for breathing,' Ethel said, putting her nose in the air. 'I didn't say anything about your Colin, nor about Bob Shaw. As for having someone serving, I suppose my George doesn't count? He's off next week, you might be interested to hear, leaving me all alone to manage with three children, so put that in your pipe and smoke it!'

She marched off, indignation in every line of her body, and the two women stared after her.

'George Glaister joining up! Well, did you ever?'

'Mind, you can't blame him, can you? I reckon any man'd be glad to go off and serve his country after a few years serving Ethel.' Annie giggled suddenly. 'I can't see him firing a machine-gun though, can you? I mean, if that's what we're depending on to win us the war—'

'It's going to be a long job,' Peggy finished. 'Well, I reckon I'd better get home and start cooking Bert's tea. He's a stickler for having it on the table the minute he gets in and our Diane won't have thought of doing the potatoes.'

145

They said goodbye and Annie walked back to her own house. Every time you went out, she thought, you heard of someone else going off to the war. George Glaister, of all people! He was such a quiet, meek little man. And although she and Peggy might laugh, there really wasn't anything funny about it. War meant people getting killed. That could mean George Glaister, her Colin and Peggy Shaw's Bob. And Derek Harker and Graham, and all the other men she knew who had joined up or would get their papers soon.

And not only them. She looked up at the sky, with the mannerism that so many people had developed in the past few weeks. Death had not yet come raining down from the stars, but there was really no reason to suppose that it wasn't going to. Perhaps in six months' time, perhaps tonight. It was going to come.

And not a thing we can do about it, she thought with sudden helpless anger. Not a single, bloody thing we can do about it.

She let herself in the back door. Ted was already home and she dropped her paper on the table and put the kettle on. The girls would be here soon, and then Frank, all of them hungry, and she liked to have a cup of tea ready for them when they came in.

'Ted,' she said, 'you won't go on at our Betty again when she come in, will you?'

He looked up and she saw his mouth set. 'Not if she apologises proper for what she said.'

'But what did she say that was so bad? She was upset—'

'She said she hated me. Isn't that bad enough? What does she have to say, for God's sake –?'

'Oh, Ted.' She took cups out of the cupboard and set them on the table. One of the saucers had got broken a few days ago and she pursed her lips and found an odd one. Ted wouldn't care, but Annie liked to have things nice and it irritated her. 'You know she didn't mean that. And you were a bit sharp with her. I mean, all she wants to do is help her country—'

'She can do that just as well by stopping at home and giving you a hand. And if that's not enough for her, there's plenty of other things she could be doing. They want people to knit things, don't they? And aren't they asking for women to sew sailors' collars and that sort of thing? She'd be better off doing that than slaving away on some farm.'

'Ted, a girl of eighteen isn't going to be satisfied with sitting by the fire knitting. She wants to be doing something more active.' Annie laid her hand on his arm. 'She only wants to do her bit. You know she's never been one for sitting at home, she likes being out in the fresh air and she's always been interested in nature and that. I think we ought to let her find out a bit more about it.'

'You mean give in to her? Let have her own way?'

'We've got to sometime, Ted. They've all got to live their own lives eventually.'

He was silent for a few moments and Annie saw that he was coming round. She sighed with relief. She hated rows in the family. She squeezed his arm and he looked at her and gave a reluctant grin.

'Well, all right, she can find out about it. Mind, that doesn't mean to say I'm giving in to her. But there's no harm in asking, I'll grant you that.' He grinned again. 'It might even put her off!'

'That's it,' Annie said with relief, 'that's the best way.' She paused, then took the bull by the horns and broached the other subject on her mind. 'Ted – while we're talking about the girls – you know our Livvy's getting serious about young Derek Harker?'

'I know they've been running round together a lot. I don't know about serious.'

'Well, she is.' Annie paused again. 'And it looks as if he'll be getting his call-up soon. I wouldn't be surprised if they didn't want to get married before he goes off.'

'Get married? But they're not even engaged!'

'Ted, you know we've talked about this before. It's the same as in the last war. Young people aren't going to want to wait – they're going to want to get married, and there's not much we can do to stop—'

'Until they're of age,' Ted said, 'there's everything we can do. They need my name on that consent from, and if I don't sign it—'

'If you don't sign it,' Annie broke in, 'there'll be more rows, and if Derek goes off and gets killed our Olive will never forgive you. Or me.'

'I'd rather that than have her tied up to a man she doesn't love for the next fifty years or so. I've seen it all before, Annie. And if you don't believe me, ask Frank. He'll tell you.'

'He won't. He never talks about it.'

'No, but he's told your Jess and Jess told you. And I knew Frank when we were boys, you know that. I knew his mum and dad and I knew what went on in that house. His dad coming home drunk every Friday night, taking a strap to poor Mrs Budd, and belting the daylights out of young Frank if he dared speak up. And all because they'd got married in a hurry and then found they hated the sight of each other.'

'But that wasn't because of the war.'

'It doesn't matter why it was,' Ted said. 'Ivy Budd was only nineteen when she got married and it ruined her life. I won't have the same thing happen to my girls.' He gave her a determined glare. 'All right, I might give in to Betty over the Land Army but she can always come home if it don't suit her. But getting married – that's another thing and I won't be responsible for it. That's something they've got to decide for themselves when they're of age, and not before.'

The kettle boiled and Annie got up to make the tea. She sighed. She knew that when Ted looked like that and spoke in that tone of voice, there was no shifting him. The world could be coming to an end next Saturday and he still wouldn't budge. If Olive wanted to marry Derek, she could do it on her twenty-first birthday, but she wouldn't be able to do it a moment before.

When Frank came in, Ted was sitting at the kitchen table, the *Evening News* spread out in front of him, reading a report that had come through that day.

'Dachau, they call it,' he said. 'It's full of Jews. Nearly twenty thousand of them. They arrested them and took them there in trains, all squashed in together. They made them look up at the light the whole way and if they couldn't, they shot them. They threw cold water over them in the night and made them stand ten hours in sleet and snow on the parade ground. Anyone they didn't like, they executed.'

'Anyone they didn't like? What does that mean?' Annie asked, shocked by the story.

Frank answered. He had read the story in his own paper.

'Anyone without blue eyes, I should think, wouldn't you?'

'But they were Jews,' Annie said. 'None of them would have—' She caught her husband's ironic glance and fell silent. 'Ted, that's terrible. People shouldn't be killed for the colour of their eyes.'

'That's why we're at war,' Ted said heavily. 'Remember? We heard all about this before, only no one believed it. And it's not the only place they've got. There's others at—' he looked down at the newspaper again '—places called Ravensbruck, Buchenwald and Sach – Sach-sen-hausen. And they reckon they're going to set up more in Poland.'

'Poland,' Annie said. 'We were supposed to be helping Poland.'

'I know. That's why we're in it.' Ted got up suddenly and screwed the newspaper up in both hands. He flung the crumpled ball down on the floor. 'And a fat lot of bloody use we are to them! What are we doing? Sitting around on our backsides while Hitler marches roughshod over the whole of Europe. What was Chamberlain playing at, sending him ulti-matums, declaring war? Did he think we'd frighten him? Nothing frightens that man – he's just impervious. He's laughing at us, that's what he's doing. Cocking a snook. He needs a good, sharp lesson, and I reckon that's what we thought we were going to give him. And instead – what?'

'He's just going on, doing what he likes,' Frank said. 'He's started labour camps in Poland now. The Jews are having to build them themselves before they've even got huts to sleep in. And the people aren't even allowed to walk on the pavements – they've got to be left for German soldiers to strut along like peacocks. They're turning them into slaves.'

'And it's what they'd do here,' Ted agreed. 'We had to go to war, Annie. I just wish we could get on and do something.'

'We will,' she said. 'We will, as soon as the time's right. Our boys aren't going to sit around for ever. They'll do something, if nobody else does. You see.'

'Well, I hope you're right.' Ted bent down and picked up the crumpled newspaper. He smoothed it out and looked again at the report of the German concentration camps. 'I just have a feeling it's going to take something big to pull people together now. But I don't reckon it's going to happen here. They're too busy over in Poland and Czechoslovakia. I don't think we're going to get the bombs after all.'

I don't think we're going to get the bombs after all.

The words were on many people's lips as autumn slipped into winter and still no aeroplanes came over with their dreaded load. And, inevitably, those with children in the country began to think of bringing them home.

'I've missed you so much,' Jess said to her husband when he came out on his first visit to her and the children. A new scheme had been started, allowing parents to buy cheap railway tickets to travel on one Sunday a month. 'It's very nice here – the Greenberrys have been very kind and Reg and Edna Corner have looked after Tim and Keith like they were their own – but I'd rather be at home.'

'I'd like to have you home too,' he said. He didn't mention Ethel Glaister, who had offered her services again – 'anything you want, Frank, anything, you just say the word' – but he suspected that he didn't need to. Jess had never liked their next-door neighbour much and probably had a very good idea of what Ethel might be up to. 'The house is like a morgue without you. And Henry's getting thin.'

'Oh, poor Henry.' Jess thought of the big tabby cat, sitting outside on the windowsill all day wondering where they all were. 'He won't even know who we are when we come back.'

'He won't forget.' *When we come back.* When would that be? he wondered. He knew a lot of the evacuated children had already begun to drift back. Their parents had decided there was no danger, or just couldn't bear to be without their kids. Or thought they weren't being treated right in their foster-homes.

It was better for the Budd children. They had their mother with them. But it wasn't better for him and Jess.

We need each other, he thought. I need to have Jess in the house. I need to know she's there when I go to work in the morning, and I need her there when I come home. And I reckon she needs me too. She's looking thin. I reckon that's why she's lost her milk.

'How's the baby?' he asked. Maureen had been asleep ever since he arrived and he was half afraid she'd still be asleep when he left. A few hours of a Sunday wasn't enough. The Greenberrys had gone off for a walk, leaving the family alone, but even so . . . He wanted to do so much with these few hours. He wanted to play with his sons and talk to them, he wanted to take Rose on his knee, he wanted to hold the baby and see her smile. Most of all, he wanted to be alone with his wife.

No chance of that, he thought wryly, and tightened his fingers over her hand.

'The baby's all right now. She smiles a lot.' But Jess didn't seem to want to discuss Maureen's progress. She looked at Frank's hand on hers, then lifted her eyes to his face and said again, 'Oh, Frank, I've missed you so much.'

'I know, love. I know.' But he didn't know what to do about it. I ought to be able to hold her and kiss her and love her properly, he thought with helpless anger. That's what we both need. But we can't. Not here in someone else's house, with the children all around. And in an hour or so the Greenberrys will be back and then we'll all have supper together, and at seven o'clock I'm going to have to go back. And it'll be another month before we see each other again . . .'

'Let's go for a walk,' he suggested. 'It's a nice afternoon and I haven't been out this way before. Show me the sights.'

Jess looked at him with understanding. Sitting in here was doing nobody any good. Rose was standing stiff and awkward, acting as if she'd never seen her father before, and the boys were showing off. She knew it was because they all felt uneasy in this strange situation, with their father a visitor, but it would be better outside. The boys could scamper about and let out some of their silliness and Rose wouldn't feel so shy. And maybe Maureen would wake up soon and create a bit of interest.

'Come on, then,' she said. 'Tim, Keith, get your coats on. Rose, bring the baby's blanket down from upstairs, will you? And you'll need your coat too.'

The children scrambled into their outdoor clothes, as thankful as their parents to have something positive to do. They ran outside and Frank and Jess looked at each other.

'Give us a kiss, love,' he said, pulling her into his arms. 'Give us a kiss, for God's sake. Oh, you don't know how I've been missing you.'

'I do,' she said, and pressed her mouth against his. She felt his lips move against hers, felt the hunger in them, felt the need in his arms that were like steel bands about her, in his body that was so hard against her. 'Oh, Frank, I do . . .'

Ethel Glaister also understood that Frank was missing Jess.

'It's the same for me,' she confided as she came out into the back garden the next Saturday afternoon to find him clearing out tomato plants. 'I mean, with my George away. Joe and Carol do their best, but they can't do everything, can they? I mean, there's some things a son just can't do for his mother.'

Frank straightened his back. If he'd known Ethel was in the house he wouldn't have come out in the garden. He'd made sure he'd heard the whole family go out only half an hour earlier. Ethel must have just walked up the street with them, perhaps to the shops, and then come back.

'We all have to make sacrifices,' he said. 'At least you've got your kids at home.'

'Oh, I know.' She touched her hair. It was even brighter these days and he wondered why she bothered. It wasn't as if George was here to appreciate it – not that Frank thought he appreciated it anyway. As Jess would say, there was no love lost between those two. So perhaps the trouble Ethel took with her appearance wasn't for her husband's benefit at all, but just to satisfy her own vanity.

'Mind, it's not easy, being a woman on your own,' she said. 'Not when there's kids to bring up. They need a father's hand, don't you agree, Frank? A man's hand.' Her voice lingered over the words and she gave him a coy look. 'I could say the same for myself sometimes!'

Frank felt his face grow hot. He wasn't used to this sort of talk. At work he was with men all day and at home he was with Jess and the kids, or relatives like Annie and friends they'd known for years. Nobody ever spoke to him like this, each word invested with double meanings.

He said, 'I'm sure your kids know how to behave, Ethel. You don't need to worry about them.'

'Well, I don't, most of the time. But just now and then – I need someone to advise me, Frank. Someone to talk to – you know?'

'Our Annie'd be glad to help, I'm sure. Or Peggy next door.'

'Oh, Peggy Shaw and me don't get on. And your Annie looks down her nose a bit, us being in a terraced house. Besides, it's a man's advice I need. And it's not just the kids – it's things about the house. There's something wrong with the kitchen tap, it won't turn off properly and I don't know what to do.' She looked up at him appealingly. 'You couldn't spare a minute to look at it, could you? I'd appreciate it ever so much.'

Frank hesitated. He could hardly refuse to help the woman with her kitchen tap.

'I'll just fetch my tools,' he said, and Ethel gave him a brilliant smile and turned to go indoors.

Frank had only been in the Glaisters' house a couple of times. He came up the garden path, feeling rather strange to see his own garden on the other side of the fence, and went in through the conservatory door. George hadn't made a bad job of it at all, he thought, looking at the neat workmanship of the wood and glass roof. It certainly must be a boon, having it all dry outside the back door and being able to get to the lavatory without going in the rain. When the war was over, he'd do the same at number 14.

Ethel was waiting for him in the scullery. The kettle was on the gas stove and, just as she had said, the tap was dripping.

Frank set to work. It didn't take long, changing the washer, and when he'd finished the kettle was boiling and Ethel made a pot of tea.

'I can't really stop,' he began, but she was already getting out the cups and saucers and putting a few biscuits on a plate.

'Oh, you've got time for a cup of tea, I'm sure. It'll do you good. You don't look after yourself properly, Frank, and you work too hard – oh yes, I know, I've seen you coming home tired from work, going straight off to that allotment of yours. You need a bit of relaxation and comfort.'

'I'm all right.' He followed her through to the back room. It was the same size as his own but looked different with Ethel's furniture. The armchairs were small and fussy, with lacy things on their backs, not nearly so comfortable-looking as his own and Jess's. On the walls were pictures made of some glittery material. There was no piano, which made it look bigger – Jess's piano took up nearly all of one wall, but he couldn't ask her to get rid of it and there was no space in the front room now that Rose had to sleep there. Instead, Ethel had a sideboard and, in the space under the stairs, a smart gramophone.

'Sit down, Frank. Make yourself at home. Milk and sugar?' She poured his tea and sat opposite him. Her skirt was up to her knees, showing legs that must surely be clad in silk, not the lisle that Jess wore most of the time. She saw him looking and crossed them, smiling, and Frank looked away, angry with himself.

'Is Annie feeding you well, then? I know you go up there for your supper every night.'

'Oh yes. Yes, she looks after me very well.'

'That's good. Mind, if you ever need a change or she can't manage for any reason, you know you're always welcome here, don't you? Always a chair at our table for you, Frank. The children would be pleased too. They think a lot of you, you know.'

Frank could think of nothing to say. He picked up his cup. It was a thin china one with roses all over the outside and a frilly little handle he couldn't get his big fingers around properly. He clutched it, hoping he wasn't going to drop it, and sipped cautiously.

'Still, I daresay I'm not the only one that's offered,' Ethel went on. 'I saw that Nancy Baxter down this end of the street again a few days ago. I hope Jess doesn't get to hear about it and put the wrong construction on it. I mean, she and Nancy Baxter have never been what you might call pally, have they?'

'Jess always used to stop and pass the time of day with them.'

'Oh, well, that's only common politeness, isn't it.' Ethel got up and came over the room. There was a dining chair next to his armchair and she sat in that, leaning down towards him. 'I've told you before, you don't need to go to Nancy Baxter for anything you want, Frank. Cake – a cup of tea now and then – any other home comforts. You've only got to say the word.'

Frank put his cup back in its saucer. His hand threatened to tremble but he kept it steady. It was difficult to stand up without brushing against Ethel, but he did so anyway. He heard her give a little gasp and she put her hand on his arm, as if to support herself. For a moment they stayed like that, both half standing, leaning close.

'Frank . . .' Ethel whispered, and lifted her face towards him.

Frank drew back. His sudden movement knocked against the little table on which Ethel had placed the cups, and he heard a rattle and then a small crash. He turned in dismay.

'Oh, my cups!' Ethel cried. 'My best cups!' She went down on her knees, scrabbling amongst the china and spilt milk. 'One of them's broken.'

'I'm sorry.' Frank watched as she gathered up the pieces. 'I'll mend it for you, Ethel. Give me the bits, I'll stick them together again.'

'Stick them together?' She glared at him from the carpet. 'How can I offer my friends tea in cups that have been *stuck together*? The whole set's spoilt now.'

'I'll get you a new cup then,' he promised desperately. He was at the door by now, anxious only to be out of there. 'Better still, you get one and I'll give you the money. I'm sorry, Ethel, but that's all I can do. I didn't mean to do it, you know that – it was an accident. But I'll pay for a new one.'

He escaped at last and went into his own house. Sinking down in his own armchair, he stared at Jess's empty place. He thought of last weekend and his longing for her, thought of the empty bed upstairs, the emptiness in his heart.

How could Ethel Glaister ever hope to fill any one of those places? How did she even dare to offer?

By December, most of the evacuees had received at least one visit from their parents and knew that home was still there, that it had not been swallowed up as some of them had feared. But for little Alan and Wendy Atkinson there had been no such relief.

Molly Atkinson wanted desperately to visit her children. But she was needed in the shop and when the first chance came she was in bed, suffering a bad attack of pleurisy.

'You go,' she begged her husband. 'Go and see that they're all right. I'm worried about them. Wendy's letters seem so queer and Alan can't write at all.'

'You're worrying too much,' he said. 'There's nothing wrong with Wendy's letters. You can't expect much from a child of eight. And if they weren't all right, their teacher would let us know.'

'Go anyway,' she said, but he shook his head.

'I can't, love. You know Dad's heart's bad. The doctor's told him he's got to rest, so he can't take over the shop. They're all right. In fact, they're probably better off left alone. Mrs Parish down October Street said some of the children are more upset when they've had a visit from their parents than they were when they first went away. It unsettles them.'

'But they need their mother.' Molly turned her head and wept tears of weakness into her pillow. 'They must wonder why I haven't come to see them. They must miss me so much.'

'Of course they miss you,' he said, cradling her in his arms. 'But children don't suffer long, love. They soon bounce back. I daresay they're having the time of their lives now, out there in the country. They won't even want to come home when this is all over.'

But that had been the wrong thing to say. Molly wept all the more and gave herself a relapse. The doctor said she must stay in bed for another two weeks at least, and even then must not go out in the cold. So the Atkinson children remained unvisited.

'Their parents obviously don't care a jot about them,' Miss Eleanor Woddis remarked to her sister. 'They're only too thankful to have them off their hands. And really, one can't blame them.'

'I blame them for not bringing their children up properly,' Miss Millicent retorted. 'I don't care what people say, a boy of almost five years old should be able to use the lavatory. I don't see why we should pay Mrs Cherry to clean up after him. And he's begun to steal now, you know. I found four biscuits gone out of the tin yesterday.'

Miss Eleanor clicked her tongue.

'I hope you gave him a good spanking. It's the only thing he understands.'

'I did something better than that. I shut him in the cupboard under the stairs for half an hour. I don't think he'll steal biscuits again.'

To Alan, the half-hour he had spent in the cupboard had seemed much longer. At first, he had been unable to believe it when Miss Millicent thrust him in and slammed the door shut. He had pushed back, trying to open it again, but already he could hear the key turning in the lock. And his hands, feeling the wood in the darkness, could find no knob to turn or rattle.

In panic, he began to scream and thump on the door with his fists, and then to kick. But nothing happened. And then, as he drew breath for another yell, he heard Miss Millicent's voice.

'Stop making that noise, Alan. And stop kicking. You'll only make it worse for yourself. I'm going out now, to the shop, so no one's going to hear you. You'll be let out when I come back – if you've been quiet.'

He heard her heels tap across the parquet floor to the front door, heard it open and close. The house was silent.

Alan took a deep breath. He wanted desperately to scream again, but he knew it would be useless. Wendy had been invited to another child's house for tea and Miss Eleanor was at something called a bridge club. The house was empty.

Suppose no one ever came back? Suppose something happened to them out there, and they never came back to the house? Nobody would know he was there.

Suppose something happened to Miss Millicent while she was out? He pictured her falling down in the street, like an old lady who used to live in September Street, and being taken to hospital. The old lady had died without ever speaking again. Suppose that happened to Miss Millicent.

Would anyone think to look in the cupboard? It was hardly ever used. Would anyone think that Miss Millicent had locked him in there before she went out?

He could be dead before anyone opened the door again. A skeleton, all bones, like pictures he'd seen in one of Dad's books.

That picture had given him nightmares for a week. Now he was in the middle of a nightmare.

Alan felt around him in the darkness. A few old brooms lived in here, their bristles like those of some long-dead animal. Perhaps some of them were dead animals. He crept down to the end of the cupboard, where the stairs met the floor. There were all sorts of queer things here, things that felt soft to the touch. He shuddered and scrambled back again.

There was no way out. Only the locked door.

Now that his eyes were used to the dark, Alan could see a thin rim of light around the edge of the door. He traced it with his finger and tried hopelessly to push the door open. It remained firm.

Alan sat down on the floor of the cupboard. It was cold and dusty. He wished he could see better, so that he could see if the brooms really were brooms. How did anyone know that what went into cupboards stayed the same once the cupboard was shut? The broom-handles were like thin, strong legs and the bristles like stiff, dead hair. Like very old giant spiders.

Spiders! He stood up suddenly and cracked his head on the stair above. The pain brought tears to his eyes but he dared not make a sound in case Miss Millicent had come back. If she heard him crying, she'd keep him there even longer. He rubbed his head, sobbing and hiccuping in his efforts to keep the tears back, and leaned against the door.

The cupboard must be full of spiders. And not only spiders – there might be all kinds of horrible, nameless things crawling on the floor and walls. Beetles, woodlice, earwigs – they all lived in cupboards. Perhaps even centipedes like the one he'd seen once in Dad's shop, a horrible, bendy thing with a hundred legs.

Alan imagined a hundred legs walking on his skin, and shuddered so violently that he banged his shoulder on something hard. He felt it cautiously and realised it was a step-ladder. As he touched it, something squirmed under his finger and he leapt back and cracked his head again.

It was too much. Miss Millicent's orders were forgotten. Fear and pain swept over him and he began to cry again, bitter sobs that welled up from deep inside and overflowed with tears that were for his mother as much as for himself; for his home, his family, for all things familiar. Would he ever see them again? Would he ever, ever be able to go back?

Too far gone in his grief to worry about spiders, dead or alive, Alan sank down on the floor. He huddled against the door and wept until his eyes and throat and head ached. And when at last he fell into an unhappy sleep, it was no better than slipping from one nightmare into another.

Betty Chapman volunteered for the Land Army, much against her parents' wishes, and found to her surprise that Graham was against it too.

'I wish you hadn't done that, Bet,' he said, sitting in the front room the first time he came to see her after his training on Whale Island. They had spent the first quarter of an hour kissing rapturously and were now taking time to exchange news. Graham had plenty, it seemed, and talked almost non-stop of the training he had received, of the way one of his mates had been sent halfway round the barracks for a pot of distemper to paint the Last Post white, of the way the 'lads' had to 'double' everywhere on the island in pairs. 'It's good for morale,' he told Betty when she raised her eyebrows, but was apparently unable to explain just why. And his conversation was peppered with naval jargon. The sea was no longer the sea, it had become the 'oggin', Portsmouth's rival dockyard Plymouth had become 'Guz' and the Navy itself was now the 'Andrew', while friends were suddenly 'oppos'.

He had also developed a casual arrogance that Betty had noticed in other sailors, which seemed to go with a rolling, swaggering gait that implied long hours at sea on a heaving deck. Graham had not yet been to sea; even Whale Island was reached by a bridge. But he talked of shore leave and liberty boats as if he had been arriving in foreign ports all his life. And Betty listened admiringly and thought how handsome he looked in his uniform.

'So what about you, Bet?' he asked at last. 'Have you managed to talk your old man round to us getting engaged yet?'

Betty shook her head.

'It's no good me mentioning it, Graham. He thinks the man should ask. Anyway, Mum doesn't think he'll let us. Maybe when I've been in the WLA a while—'

'The what?'

'The Women's Land Army. I've volunteered.' She grinned at him. 'I'll be in uniform next, Graham – what d'you think of that?'

He stared at her. 'You've volunteered? What did you want to do that for?'

'Why shouldn't I? I'm fed up, working in that stupid dairy. And I've always liked helping Dad in the garden. I thought it'd be a good idea.' She saw the expression on his face. 'What's wrong with it?'

'Nothing, I suppose.' He frowned at the fireplace. The Chapmans only had a fire in the front room on Sundays or at Christmas, but Annie had put the little electric fire in there for them and its bar glowed red against the reflector. 'I just – well, I wish you hadn't done it, that's all.'

'Why not?'

He scowled again and said nothing for a few minutes. His freckled face was sulky. Then he muttered, 'I thought you wanted to get engaged.'

'So I do. What's that got to do with it?'

'Well, you ought to stay here then,' he said. 'How d'you think I'll feel, going off to sea and not knowing where you are? And you might meet anyone, working on a farm. If we're engaged, you should stay at home and wait for me.'

Betty stared at him.

'Oh, should I? And what about you, going off to sea? I won't know where you are, will I? Or who you're meeting? If you don't trust me, Graham Philpotts, why don't you come right out and say so? Then we'll all know where we stand.'

'I never said I didn't trust you—'

'So it won't matter who I meet, will it?'

'I just don't want you working yourself to death on a farm, that's all,' he said. 'You don't know what it'll be like—'

'You don't know what it'll be like at sea, for all your big talk!'

'That's different. Men have to go away. Women should stay at home.'

'Not ·in this war,' Betty said. 'Women have to do the jobs men leave behind, or the country'll fall to bits. It was the same in the last war. Women had to take over and run the country. You want to listen to some of the older people, Graham.'

'Older people don't know it all.'

'And nor do you.' Betty sat up straight, moving out of reach of his arms. 'Listen, I'm not going to sit around on my backside when I could be doing something more interesting. Do you know what it's like, working in the dairy? Having to listen to customers complaining about the price of eggs as if it's all *my* fault? Standing about all day because I'm not allowed to sit down, not even when there's no one in the shop? What sort of a life do you think that is?'

'I should think it's a lot better than sloshing about in mud all day picking up potatoes,' he retorted. 'You don't know when you're well off, Bet, that's your trouble.'

'Maybe not. But I'm willing to give it a try. I'd rather work hard all day and know I was doing some good than stay warm and dry in a dairy, bored to tears. And it's a chance – a chance to get away from home, live my own life a bit and do something different.' She looked at him and her face softened. 'Graham, you look just like our Keith does when he can't have his own way. Come on.' She moved a little closer and put her arm round him. 'Stop pushing your lip out like that and give me a kiss instead,' she whispered coaxingly. 'It's not going to make any difference to us, me working on the land. I'll write to you just the same – and I'll have a lot more interesting things to tell you.'

'Oh yeah?' he sneered. 'All about picking potatoes and digging swedes and onions? I can't wait!'

'Well, it'll be better than measuring milk and patting butter,' she giggled, and shook his arm gently. 'Come on, Graham. Don't let's quarrel, the first night you're out. Give us a kiss.' She nuzzled against his neck while he stared woodenly ahead. 'Anyway, I don't know who you think I'm going to meet on the farm. There'll only be old men or boys too young to join up. I'm more likely to meet someone staying here in Pompey, with all you handsome sailors looking for girls!'

Graham grinned unwillingly. He turned his face and allowed himself to be kissed. Then he put his arms round Betty and held her close, the rough serge of his tunic rubbing against her thin blouse.

'Well, maybe there's something in that. But you mind you're here when I come on leave, Bet. I don't want to get engaged and then find my fiancée away whenever I come back to port.'

'I won't be,' she promised. 'And there won't be anyone else, Graham. You can bank on that.' She sighed and rested her head on his shoulder. 'There won't be anyone else for you either, will there?'

'No. But – I wish you'd talk to your old man, Bet. Or let me. I don't know how long I've got before I get a ship, you see. It could be any time. I'd like to get a ring on your finger before I go.'

'Oh, Graham, so would I.' She lifted her head and looked at him. 'But we can still be secretly engaged, can't we? I could have a ring and wear it on a chain, like we said before. And I could put it on at night or when I go out.' Her eyes sparkled suddenly. 'I could wear it all the time if I was away on a farm!'

A knock on the door announced that it was supper-time. If they didn't go at once, the door would be opened and Annie would poke her head round it. She believed in letting the young ones have their privacy, but not enough to feel they could take liberties. And she didn't want young Graham getting ideas about himself and Betty. She'd seen the look in his eyes, before he went off for his training and again when he came in tonight.

They'll be the next ones wanting to get engaged or married, she thought with a sigh. Like Olive, pestering them to let her marry Derek Harker. It was understandable enough, but they didn't realise what it meant. Getting tied down so young, perhaps a baby on the way almost at once, and nowhere to live. Most of the girls would simply stay on with their parents, but it wouldn't be the same. As married women, they'd expect more independence. If they had babies the house would be even more full, and if they didn't they'd as likely as not want to start going out . . . Either way, there'd be trouble of one sort or another.

No, on the whole it was better if they stayed single. After all, it wasn't going to be for long, was it? The war might not be over by Christmas, like they'd said at first, but it didn't look like getting any worse. It would surely be all finished with by Easter, and then everyone could settle down to a normal life again.

And there'd be no more silly talk of kids like her Betty and Gladys Shaw getting married, no more putting boys who'd hardly started to shave into uniform and sending them off to kill other boys who just happened to have been born in a different place. No more lads choking away their lives in the freezing depths of the Atlantic or catching their death of cold in trenches in France.

She pulled herself together. There had been no sound from the other room. What were those two up to in there? She'd heard their voices just now, sounded almost as if they were having a bit of a row. And then it had all gone quiet.

Annie knew perfectly well what might be happening if everything went quiet after two young sweethearts had a row. She gave the door another loud knock and opened it, rattling the doorknob hard as she did so.

Mrs Hutchins would have commiserated with the Woddis sisters if they had ever spoken to her, but the widow did not come within their social sphere. However, she knew them by sight, saw them at church and about the village, and talked to their cleaner Mrs Cherry.

'Sly, that's what I call them,' Mrs Cherry said, referring to the Woddises' evacuees. 'Specially the boy. Looks at you as if butter wouldn't melt in his mouth, then goes and does something dirty in a corner. The times I've washed his clothes out, you wouldn't credit.'

'Oh, I would,' Mrs Hutchins said. 'I have the same trouble with mine. Dirty little pigs, the lot of 'em. And give themselves such airs too, just because they come from Portsmouth. Portsmouth! I never did go much on the place, but if that's the way they live there they can keep it.'

She went indoors. Martin was at school but she had plenty of jobs for him to do when he came in, to keep him out of mischief. Six wasn't too young to give a hand around the place, and besides he ought to earn his keep. Eight shillings and sixpence wasn't much to feed and look after a growing boy, especially with all the washing she had to do. And she'd never be able to use that mattress of his again, not for respectable people.

Martin was late home. Some of the village boys had taken to lying in wait for the smaller evacuees and tormenting and chasing them on the way home. Martin had found a longer way, through the woods. Tim and Keith Budd went that way to their house and let him walk along with them for part of the way. When they arrived at the edge of the big field he stopped and looked at them.

'Go on,' Tim said, giving him a friendly nudge. 'That's the way you've got to go. We go across the field. See you tomorrow.'

They ran off across the stubble, obviously happy to be going back, and Martin stared after them. He felt very small and lonely, standing there on the edge of the meadow, watching as the two brothers zig-zagged away, their arms spread, making aeroplane noises. He wished he could have gone with them. Just to have tea, to see what it was like in another of the village houses. He wanted to reassure himself that they weren't all like Mrs Hutchins.

'There he is!'

Martin jumped violently and turned to see a small gang of boys approaching from the other end of the field. With a lurch of fear, he realised that they were the bullies who had been waiting for him on his normal way home, and he turned and ran into the woods.

'After him! Don't let him get away!' The boys were bigger than he and could run faster. They came to the trees and dived between them, racing between the big grey trunks, shouting and whooping like Indians. 'Catch him and we'll have a bit of fun.'

Martin's heart thumped and he felt sick. He often felt sick these days, but it was no good telling anyone. Mrs Hutchins would simply scold him and his teacher didn't have time to listen. Too many children were complaining about their food, and when the billeting office lady had gone to see them she'd found there was nothing wrong with it.

He ran blindly, his hands held out in front of him to ward off branches, but they whipped back across his arms, caught at his sleeves and slashed across his face. Sobbing with fright, he stumbled, righted himself, cast a wild glance behind him and stumbled again. This time he fell, grazing his knees, but he was up again, cannoning into a tree-trunk before throwing himself into a tangle of bushes and crouching there, breathing hard and peering wide-eyed through the undergrowth at his tormentors.

There were six of them. They were headed by Neil Miller, the biggest boy in the school, and Martin saw that Brian Collins, one of the evacuees, was another. Brian had quickly seen which side his bread was buttered and joined forces with the village boys. He and Neil Miller had recognised each other instantly as kindred spirits and now had the entire village school subject to their own reign of terror.

'Slimy little git,' Neil said as he passed within a couple of feet of Martin. 'He's got away. But we'll catch him tomorrow – now we know which way he comes.'

'That's right,' Brian agreed, standing on Martin's hand, which he'd burrowed under some dead leaves. 'We'll catch him. And then we'll have some fun.' He proceeded to describe in minute detail what they would do to Martin, and Martin lay shuddering under the bushes. His cheeks were wet with tears and he stuffed his other hand into his mouth and bit the knuckles hard to prevent himself from crying out at the pain of Brian's boot on his hand.

It seemed a long time before the two boys moved away. His eyes tight shut, he felt the pressure lift from his hand and then heard their laughter as they ran off through the trees. His blood was thumping hard in his ears but he could hear clearly enough what they were shouting, and he realised, sickeningly, that they had known all along where he was hiding, and were merely using their knowledge as just another form of torture.

'That had him scared!' 'I bet the little bugger just about shitted himself with fright!' 'He won't know which way to go home tomorrow . . .' Their voices faded and with them their raucous laughter, and after a long while Martin dragged himself up.

His hand was red and swollen, pain pounding through the fingers. His clothes were torn and covered in mud and his arms and face were scratched and bleeding. He felt sick and shaky, and his knuckles were sore and bruised where he had bitten them.

Slowly, he made his way through the woods. From the far side, he had to go down a long, grass-covered lane with hedges on either side. Anybody could be hiding there, he thought, glancing fearfully at the trees with their huge boles and creeping claw-like roots that stretched down the banks. Once or twice he heard a sudden rustle and jumped to press himself against the other bank, but it was only a blackbird fossicking amongst the dead leaves, or a squirrel gathering nuts. The third time, however, his courage failed him utterly and he took to panic-stricken flight and ran the rest of the way home.

'Well!' Mrs Hutchins exclaimed, opening the door. 'And what in God's name do you think you've been doing? Look at you! Covered in filth and your clothes ruined. No – you're not coming in here. Not until you're clean. Wait there.'

She disappeared indoors. Martin, by now crying bitterly, stood on the doorstep in the gathering dusk of a foggy December afternoon. How was he to clean himself out here? Would he ever be allowed indoors again, or would he be fed outside like the dog, perhaps even made to sleep in the kennel? He turned to see if there was room for him but before he could move, Mrs Hutchins was back.

'There.' To his dismay, he saw that she was holding a hosepipe. She fixed it to the garden tap and turned it on. 'That'll sluice you off like the dirty pig you are.'

The water hit Martin full in the chest, an icy jet that knocked him off his feet. He lay gasping and spluttering on the path then rose shakily to his feet as Mrs Hutchins turned off the tap.

'Now take off your clothes,' she ordered. 'All of them. You're as dirty underneath as you are on top, I'll be bound.'

With trembling fingers, Martin undid his buttons and laces and took off his clothes. She was right, he discovered, and so was Neil Miller. He dropped the stinking mass on the path and stood naked and shivering in the foggy air.

The jet of water hit him again. This time he stayed on his feet, his arms wrapped about his thin body, shuddering as Mrs Hutchins circled slowly around him, directing the hose at every part of his body. His skin was almost numb with cold, the water like spikes of ice stabbing at every pore. His sobbing had changed to a raw, hopeless retching that threatened to tear his heart and stomach from his body, and he felt the blackness of total despair as he stood at last, his head hanging down in utter subjection, waiting for Mrs Hutchins to tell him what to do next.

'All right, you dirty little Arab,' she said, as if disgruntled that she could not torture him further. 'Get inside and go to bed. I don't want to see you again today. And don't expect any supper – it's going to take me the rest of the evening clearing up after you, you and your filth.'

Martin moved stiffly, his legs blue with cold. He went indoors and up the stairs. At the top he hesitated, wondering if he dared ask for a towel, and then went into the tiny boxroom where he slept. He rolled himself about a bit on his blanket and then crept into bed and lay curled up, hugging himself, and tried to get warm.

But it was a long time before he could sleep. As a little warmth finally crept through his aching bones, his stomach began to make its own protest. Mrs Hutchins never gave him more than a cup of water and a bowl of lumpy porridge for breakfast. He'd been feeling sick all morning, and had eaten little dinner at school. Now his stomach was beginning to ache and he moved a bit and groaned.

When Mrs Hutchins came to wake him in the morning, thrusting a pile of damp clothes on to the bed for him to wear, she found him huddled in a corner, whimpering with pain and white as a sheet.

'I suppose you've wet the bed again,' she said furiously. 'Well, you can just do what Miss Woddis makes her boy do – wash the sheets yourself. I told you yesterday, I'm fed up with cleaning up after you, you filthy little shit!'

Martin looked up at her. His stomach hurt and he knew that if he ate anything at all he would be sick again. He dragged himself up and pulled on his clothes. There was no school in the morning, but he would go out anyway. Out in the damp, chilly lanes, where there were other children about, he might find some mean comfort. There was none to be had there.

Susan Cullen was also out in the lanes that morning. Her foster-mother had tired at last of trying to console her and sent her out for a walk. 'You've got to pull yourself together,' she said, helping the white-faced five-year-old into her coat. 'Think how lucky you are. There's plenty worse off than you.'

Her words had passed over Susan's head. She had no imagination to spare for those who might be worse off, nor the experience to understand it. All she knew was her own small world in the streets of Copnor, where she and her parents had lived in a small house together, and Daddy had got up at four o'clock every morning to deliver milk, and been home in the afternoon in time for the three of them to have tea together and play games.

It had been a warm, cosy world, a world that she had thought would go on for ever. And then it had fallen apart. Her mother had been ill, so ill that she'd had to be taken away from them, to hospital where Susan was not allowed to go and visit her. And then one day her father had come home with a strange, stiff face and told her that Mummy would never be coming back.

His face had screwed up as he told her this, and turned red, and she'd seen the tears drip from his eyes. Susan had been panic-stricken. Daddy crying! Mummy never coming home! Her world had crumbled and fallen away from her, leaving her swinging wildly in a dark, deep vacuum, and she'd clutched him in terror and screamed.

And then, only a few days later, she'd been sent away on the train, sent to live with the Longs. She didn't know why. She didn't know if she would ever go home. She didn't even know whether she would see her father again.

Perhaps, now that her mother was dead, he no longer wanted her.

Susan could not stop crying. She cried herself to sleep at night and in the first moment of waking in the morning, she remembered it all over again, the pain fresh in her mind, and began to cry again.

She was crying as she walked along the dripping lanes and met Martin Baker.

Susan and Martin knew each other well. They had been in the same class at school in Copnor, and sat near each other in the crowded village school. They had started on the same day and shared the same fears and pleasures.

They stopped and looked at each other, recognising the streak of tears on each other's faces. There was no need for questions.

'My tummy aches,' Martin said. 'I've been sick. I want to go home.'

'So do I.'

They stood a moment longer. Then they reached out their hands towards each other.

'Let's go now,' Martin said, and Susan nodded.

Feeling better than they had since the evacuation they turned and began to walk along the lane, towards the main road that they believed led back to Portsmouth.

8

Like all the other mothers in Bridge End, Jess was horrified to hear what had happened to little Susan Cullen and Martin Baker.

'Found on the Southampton road they were,' Mrs Greenberry told her. 'Trudging along hand in hand, worn out, crying their poor little hearts out. Lucky it was the rector that found them.'

Jess felt the tears in her eyes. 'What did he do with them?'

'Took them to the hospital in Southampton. He could see the little boy was poorly. Turned out he had appendicitis, so they kept him in and the rector brought little Susan back. But she's in such a state they've had to send for her father.'

'Oh dear. Poor Mr Cullen. And poor little Susan.' Jess thought of the tragic little face, pressed to the bars of the school playground the morning the children had been evacuated. And Martin Baker, stumbling along the village street behind Widow Hutchins. Jess had known neither of them was happy – but what could she have done? Mrs Hutchins seemed a respectable sort of person, and the young woman Susan had been billeted with just had too much to do to take care of the motherless little girl.

'Nobody seems to have thought about whether people were fit to look after children,' she said. 'It was all just done on spare rooms. If you had a spare room, you had to take an evacuee. But not everyone's as kind as you and Edna Corner.'

'And not everyone's as unkind as Widow Hutchins,' Mrs Greenberry consoled her. 'Most of the others have shaken down all right. And it's not your responsibility, Jess.'

It might not be Jess's responsibility, but she felt it just the same. She went out, pushing Maureen in the pram, thinking of the two children, trudging along the main road. It was a mercy they hadn't been run over. Or picked up by someone less kind than the rector. She shuddered at the thought of what might have happened.

How were the little Atkinsons getting along? she wondered. It was some time since she had called at the Woddises house, though she had seen the children about the village and often looked out for them at the school gates. They looked subdued and quiet, but then they always had been. Molly herself was pale, with mouse-coloured hair, so you couldn't expect Alan and Wendy to be much different. As far as Jess could see, they were clean and tidy enough, and they were at school every day, where their teachers would soon see if anything was wrong.

Well, they'll be going home for Christmas soon, she thought. Almost all the evacuated children at Bridge End were. And then Molly and her children would be together, just as she and Frank and their family would, and perhaps Hitler and the war would be forgotten for a while in happy celebration.

Christmas approached with a blast of bitterly cold weather. The hospitals reported an inundation of people with broken arms, collar-bones and ankles caused by slipping on icy pavements. Molly Atkinson, newly out of bed and determined to visit her children for Christmas, was one of the first. She slipped on ice only a few yards from the door of the shop and cracked two ribs, as well as twisting her knee so badly that she could not walk for a week and even after that could only hobble for short distances.

'Please go and fetch them home for Christmas,' she implored her husband. 'I can't bear to think of them there, wondering why we don't come. I know the shop's busy – but we could get someone in for a day or two. And I can serve if I sit in a chair.'

He hesitated and then gave in. Molly had been worrying herself almost out of her mind about the children, and since little Martin Baker had come home she'd been even worse. It was no use telling her that Frank Budd had been to the village and seen his own children, happy and healthy. She kept all Wendy's letters in her bag or her pocket and carried them about with her, taking them out half a dozen times a day to pore over them.

'She doesn't sound happy,' she said, but Dave read the letters and shook his head. 'You can't expect much more than this from a kiddy of eight. She tells you what she's done at school and what they had for their supper and that. What d'you expect, *Gone With the Wind*?'

Molly smiled but looked unconvinced.

'There's something wrong. I'm sure there is. It looks almost as if the envelope's been opened before.'

Dave turned the letter over in his hand.

'I don't think so, love. Look, you've been ill. Things have preyed on your mind. I know how much you've missed the kids but they're better off where they are, honestly. Why, I bet they're living the life of Riley, being spoilt to death by those two old sisters.'

'That's just it. Two old ladies. They're not used to children.'

Dave laughed. 'They might not have been when the war started – I bet they are now, after a few weeks with our two scallywags!' He put his arm round her and gave her a comforting squeeze. 'Don't worry, love – I'll go and fetch them back for Christmas, provided the bombing hasn't started by then. OK?'

'Oh, they won't start bombing over Christmas, surely,' she said, and gave him the happiest smile he'd seen for months. 'Give me a pencil, Dave. I've got to make a list. We'll need all sorts of special treats if they're going to be home. And we must think what presents to get them.'

'Presents!' he said. 'You've got a stack of toys and things in the wardrobe already, I've seen them.' But his face was soft as he handed her a piece of paper and a pencil. It was good to see Molly cheering up at last. Maybe he hadn't realised just how much she was missing the children.

Perhaps they ought to think about having them back permanently. It really didn't look as if there were going to be any bombs after all. And although he'd been firmly in favour of evacuation, he'd heard about little Martin Baker too and felt uneasy. You thought of children going to the country and being fed like fighting-cocks with eggs and fresh milk and cream. But Martin, from all accounts, looked as if he'd lived on bread and water. All country people, it seemed, weren't so hospitable as they'd been cracked up to be.

Frank Budd had said his seemed happy enough and were well looked after. He hadn't seemed to know much about any others. But he'd only managed to get to see Jess once or twice, and Dave didn't suppose they'd spent much time talking about other people.

He wondered if the Budds would be coming home for Christmas. Perhaps Frank would bring his Alan and Wendy along with theirs. That would save him a trip and save getting someone in for the shop, or having Molly sit in a chair to serve. If he knew her, she'd be working all the hours there were anyway, getting things nice for the kids. He made up his mind to talk to Frank next time he saw him.

Frank was getting ready to visit Jess and the children again. He made a pot of tea for his breakfast and sat with Henry purring on his knee, listening to the wireless, thinking of all the news he'd heard that week. So many things were going on now. So many countries had joined the war. It was difficult to keep track of it all, but he kept trying. If you knew what was happening, you could feel, if only slightly, that there was still some hope of control. Without knowledge, there was nothing.

The whole country was talking about the German pocket battleship, the *Admiral Graf Spee*. It seemed as if a worldwide hunt was on, to try to put a stop to her antics. She was like a firefly, darting round the ocean picking off merchant ships which were bringing essential goods to Britain. Now, everyone believed her to be on her way to South America.

'And if she is, we'll catch her,' Ted had told him with grim satisfaction. 'The *Ajax* convoy is down there, and our Colin's on the *Exeter*. She won't get away again.'

That wasn't the only thing happening, of course. The Russians were attacking Finland. They had bombed Helsinki and columns of soldiers were advancing along the frozen roads. But the Finns were fighting back. On skis, clad in fur-lined boots and reindeer-skin coats, they moved at night about the Russian camps, sniping, laying mines and tossing Molotov cocktails into tanks. Winter was on their side; when spring came, it might be a different story but until then they were putting up a magnificent battle.

Frank spread a piece of toast with margarine and some of Jess's marmalade. The house was bitterly cold. He hadn't lit a fire for a fortnight. Now that he was eating his supper most nights with his sister-in-law, there didn't seem much point in it. Without Jess here, it didn't seem like home anyway.

He thought of the last time he'd gone to see her. Their pleasure at being together again as a family was matched by their frustration at not having any time alone. He sensed the Greenberrys' embarrassment and knew that they realised this and just didn't know what to do about it. They can hardly offer us their bed for the afternoon, he thought with wry amusement, and anyway what would the kids think? As it was, he'd spent the entire afternoon being shown round the farm where Reg Corner worked, Rose clinging to his arm like a limpet the whole way, while Jess walked silently on his other side.

It would be the same today, he knew. And yet what else could they do? Families needed to be together, he couldn't tell the kids to get lost for an hour or so, and there was nowhere to go anyway. He thought of Jess, of her warm body in the bed, the way they would lie for an hour or more of a Sunday morning, just holding each other close. Just thinking like that made him ache with longing. And seeing her would make it worse. He almost wished he wasn't going.

'Can't we come home for Christmas?' she said that afternoon, as they walked through the lanes. 'We've been away all this time and there's not been a single bomb. Surely we could come back, just for the holidays.'

Frank sighed. He wanted her back – wanted them all back – badly, but when he thought of the map on the wall he knew that the battle had hardly begun. As yet, it was mostly a war of the sea, with thousands of tons of shipping lost already, but soon enough, surely, it would become a war of land and air as well. Soldiers were massing in France, aircraft were being built, munitions factories crying out for workers . . . And Hitler meant business too, you could see that. Strutting about in front of his troops, making speeches about what he meant to do with the 'new Europe' when he'd finally won. And threatening to bring Britain to her knees by the summer with his magnetic mines, which Mr Churchill had called 'the lowest form of warfare ever'.

No, Hitler wasn't on the point of giving in. And until he did, the country was the safest place for his children to be. But still – Christmas . . . What would Christmas be, without his family around him?

'You can always come and stay here, of course,' Jess said wistfully. 'Mrs Greenberry said we could make up a bed on the parlour floor. It'd be better than nothing. But – oh, Frank,' she turned and put her arms around him, laying her head on his broad chest, 'I really would like to come home. I want to see everyone else – Mum and Dad, our Annie and Ted and the neighbours. I'd even be pleased to see Ethel Glaister!'

Frank had to laugh at that. Jess had never had much time for Ethel, nor Ethel for her. They got along well enough as neighbours, helping out over the odd cup of sugar or taking in each other's washing when it rained, but they weren't friends, not like she was with Peggy Shaw on the other side. And she'd be even less friendly if she knew what Ethel was up to now.

Ethel hadn't given up her pursuit of Frank. A day or two after the teacup episode, she had called to him over the garden fence and handed him the pieces of broken china.

'I was a bit rude to you when we had that little accident,' she told him, all arch coyness and permed hair again. 'I'd be ever so grateful if you'd do whatever you can, Frank. And then we'll have another cup of tea together again, eh? Carry on from where we left off, like.'

Frank had mended the cup. But he'd made sure Ethel was out before he went to her door with it, and he'd left it on the step, wrapped in newspaper. Since then he'd managed to avoid her.

'I want us to be all together for Christmas,' Jess went on. 'Even if you come and stay, the boys will still be over with Reg and Edna. And I know they're looking forward to it – Reg and Edna, I mean – but they're our boys, not theirs. They should be with us.'

'Jess, there's a war on,' he reminded her gently. 'We can't have just what we want. We've all got to make sacrifices.'

Jess stopped and faced him. They were standing under a large beech tree, its trunk smooth and grey, its branches a mass of tracery against the grey sky.

'And you're making more than most,' she said. 'Look, I've been saying how much I'd like to come back – but what about you? I know what you're doing at home, Frank.' He stared at her, wondering if anyone had said anything about Ethel Glaister. Surely not. Not that there was anything to say, but some people had spiteful tongues and would make something out of nothing just for the hell of it.

'You're sitting there with no fire,' Jess continued. 'You're making do with tea and a bit of bread for your breakfast and you're not eating a proper dinner. Oh, I know Annie's giving you a meal in the evenings, and I know what sort of meal it is, too. No wonder Ted looks as thin as a rake! You need more than rice and stuff to keep you going, with the work you do. And you need a bit of warmth and home comfort to come back to of an evening.'

'We were talking about Christmas,' he began, but she stopped him with a finger against his lips.

'I know that. But now I'm talking about something else. I'm talking about coming back permanent, Frank, to look after you.'

He stared at her. 'But you can't do that.'

'Who says I can't?' She lifted her chin. 'Look, if it wasn't for the baby I'd never have been evacuated in the first place. Our Rose and the boys would have been, but I'd have stayed at home, where I belong, to look after you. Well, I think that's what I ought to be doing anyway.' She looked at him with serious brown eyes. 'Frank, it's not doing us any good being parted like this, and what doesn't do me any good doesn't help Maureen. I've already lost my milk through it. I'll be happier back with you, and she'll get on better too.'

'And what about when we're bombed? We're going to be, Jess. Don't make any mistake about that.'

'Then we'll be together.' She moved closer and slid her arms around his neck. 'Isn't that why we got married? Didn't we promise to stick by each other for better or worse? Then what am I doing out here, when you need me at home?' He shook his head. He was sorely tempted, but he looked at the children, who had run on ahead, shouting and laughing.

'They're better here.'

'They are, yes. They've got their lives in front of them. But we—' her voice shook suddenly '—we've only got each other, Frank. And being parted like this – it's wrong. Don't you see that?'

'But – what about the baby?'

'She'll have to come too. She has to be with me.' Jess looked at the borrowed pram. 'I don't want to put her in danger,' she said in a low voice. 'God knows, I don't want anything to happen to her. But I want to be with you more than anything else.'

The children had stopped and were walking back, puzzled and uneasy. Frank put his hands on Jess's shoulders and bent to kiss her.

'Come home for Christmas,' he said. 'And we'll think about it then.'

Annie was polishing a brass bell Colin had given her and listening to the News when Ted came in. Her face was white and he came over to her at once.

'What's the matter, girl?'

'They've just been talking about our Colin's ship,' she said. 'It's been in a battle.'

'A battle? The *Exeter*?'

'That's right. And two others – the *Ajax* and the *Achilles*.' She stared at him, her eyes frightened. 'Ted, I thought they were out of the way down there off South America. I didn't think they'd get caught up in any fighting.'

Ted sighed. He'd known Annie was hiding her head in the sand over this. There'd been news enough of Hitler's pocket battleships sneaking about all over the oceans, picking off British merchantmen. The *Graf Spee* was the most notorious, though the captain seemed a decent sort of chap for a German, taking their crews prisoner before sinking the ships. All the same, he couldn't be allowed to go on doing it, and that was why the three cruisers were off the east coast of South America – to protect the merchant ships and destroy the enemy marauder.

'The Battle of the River Plate, they're calling it,' she said, twisting the polishing rag between her fingers. 'It's been going on for days but they've only just started talking about it. Ted, our Colin's down there. He could be hurt, even killed, and us not know a thing about it.' She picked up the bell and stared at it. Colin had brought it home from his first trip abroad and it had pride of place on top of the sideboard.

He squeezed her shoulders. 'Don't talk like that, love. We'd know soon enough if anything had happened to him. No news is good news, remember.'

'No,' she said. 'No news just means they haven't got around to telling us yet. Or they don't know. There's no good news in this war, Ted.'

'Yes, there is. We've had no bombs here yet—'

'D'you think I care about bombs here, when our Colin's getting torpedoed on the other side of the world?' she cried. 'I wish we were getting bombs here. At least I'd know what was happening then. But this – hearing it on the News and then just having to wait and wonder . . .' She put her hands up to her face and began to cry.

The back door opened, letting in a blast of cold air. Olive burst in and dropped her bag on the table. She stood pulling off her gloves, one finger at a time, and stared with wild eyes at her parents.

'Have you heard the news?'

'About the *Exeter*? Yes, we have. But your dad says we're not to worry—'

'Not to worry? She's been sunk!'

'Sunk?' They came to their feet, staring at her. 'That wasn't on the News,' Annie said, her hand touching her throat.

'Granny Kinch told me.'

'Granny Kinch? What does she know about it?'

Olive looked embarrassed. 'She said her Nancy knows one of the sailors who used to be on the *Exeter*—'

'Only one?' Ted said ironically, and Annie gave him a sharp nudge with her elbow.

'He's over in Gosport now, at the *Dolphin*, working on submarines. He said there'd been a special signal through, saying the *Exeter* had been sunk with all hands.' Olive burst into tears. 'All hands, Mum! That means everyone. Our Colin – everyone.'

'Oh, Ted,' Annie whispered, putting out her hand blindly. Ted put his arm round her shoulders again and held her tight. His face was drained of colour, a dirty grey, the stubble like black pinpoints on his chin. His lower lip was trembling slightly.

'You sure about this, Olive?'

Olive slumped into a chair. The tears were streaming down her face. 'I only know what Granny Kinch told me.'

'It might not be true,' Annie said, her voice shaking. 'They'd have said on the News if it had been, surely. Her Nancy could have got it wrong. Who is this bloke she got it from, anyway?'

'I don't know. A sailor.' Olive buried her face in her hands. 'If our Colin's been killed—'

'Well, I wouldn't put too much credit on that,' Ted said. He was recovering a little now. 'Nancy Baxter knows plenty of sailors but I don't reckon they know any more about the war than you or me. I'd wait till we hear official. Or from the BBC.'

'It would have been on the News,' Annie repeated. 'They'd have said – wouldn't they?' She stared up at her husband's face, willing him to say yes, willing it to be true.

'I reckon so. They wouldn't keep us in the dark, not over a thing like that.'

'Maybe they didn't want Hitler to know,' Olive said through her sobs. 'Maybe the signal's only just come through—'

'And Nancy Baxter came home with it before they got it at the BBC?' Ted asked scathingly. 'Be your age, Olive. It's just a rumour, that's all, and Granny Kinch ought to know better than to go repeating it, specially when she knows our Colin's on that ship. Your mother's right. It would have been on the News if it was true. And I'm not going to believe it until I hear it from them.' He looked at his wife. 'How about a cup of tea? I'll put the kettle on.'

He went over to the sink and mother and daughter looked at each other in amazement. Ted seldom did anything so domestic as making tea. It was a measure of how serious he felt the situation was, in spite of what he said.

Annie saw the tears on her daughter's face and moved round the table. She put her arms around Olive's shoulders and held the girl's head against her body. The tears were hot in her eyes. She knew that Ted was right, whatever Nancy Baxter had got from some sailor wasn't likely to be the truth. All the same, the ship had been in a battle, the BBC had said so, and you just didn't know what that might mean. Perhaps the battle wasn't even over yet. She imagined the ships lined up at sea, firing their guns at one another. And torpedoes . . . They were terrible weapons, torpedoes. How could she be sure that Colin would survive?

Men had come home from the last war horribly maimed. There'd been one down Commercial Road for years, selling matches. He'd had no legs and had sat on a little cart on the pavement outside Woolworths. Ted had always bought matches from him and been quite sharp with Colin once when the boy had reminded him there were plenty of matches at home.

'He's one of the heroes of the Great War,' he'd said. 'One of the boys who went out to make Britain a land fit for heroes to live in and then found you had to be a hero to live in it. I'm ashamed to walk past that man on my two good legs, and know I've got a job and a home and family, and if all I can do is buy matches from him then I'll fill the house with 'em and be glad to do it.'

After that, Colin had bought matches from the man too, as soon as he was old enough. But the little cart hadn't been outside Woolworths for a long time now, and no one seemed to know what had happened to the legless man. Suppose Colin came home like that? Burned or disfigured, his arms or legs blown off? He was only twenty-five, so tall and strong, so full of life. Suppose he never came home again?

I couldn't bear it, Annie thought, still holding Olive. If he got killed – if any one of them got killed – I just couldn't bear it.

The whole street knew that Colin was on the *Exeter*. They followed the News with anxious interest, switching on the wireless for every bulletin. Frank stopped sticking pins in his big map of Europe and found an atlas with South America in it. He laid it open on top of the piano and looked at it as he listened to the News, tracing the place names with his finger.

Montevideo. It was thousands of miles away. The war was spreading everywhere. What did a little country like Uruguay have to do with Hitler's invasion of Poland? Why did Argentina and Brazil have to get dragged in? Weren't they neutral? Why were British ships having to patrol those faraway seas, when our own shores needed protection?

The *Graf Spee* had been a thorn in the British side for weeks, storming around the oceans and pouncing on vital merchant ships. Disguised as a French warship, she'd eluded the fleet sent to intercept and destroy her, and had slipped away, no doubt cocking a snook at the frustrated British battleships, cruisers and aircraft carriers that pursued her. She had stridden the world, swooping down the Atlantic to terrorise the seas of West Africa and darting around the Cape of Good Hope ('cape of some hope' cynical sailors called it) before sliding away towards South America.

It was here that she had been caught at last and, in the Battle of the River Plate, damaged and forced into the harbour of Montevideo.

'She's trapped now,' Frank said to Ted when his brother-in-law came in to bring a cake Annie had made. 'She's run into Montevideo for safety and our ships are waiting outside. They'll get her the minute she pokes her dirty little nose through the harbour entrance.'

'There's a three-mile limit of neutrality,' Ted said, studying the map. 'They can't do anything inside that. If she came out at night she could slip away before they knew she was there.'

'They'll catch her.' Frank spoke positively, convinced he was right. 'They won't let her get away this time.'

The two men were silent, thinking of what was going on out there, so far away. They had both seen war before, knew what exploding shells were like, could remember the screams of injured and dying men, the stench of fresh blood and festering wounds, gangrene and trench-rot. They could remember men who were brave and men who were not; men who did silently what had to be done, and others who panicked, who screamed and clawed the air and had to be shot by their own officers because they might infect the other men with their terror.

Was that what it had been like on the *Exeter* during the Battle of the River Plate?

Ted's own son must now have witnessed scenes such as those, and perhaps worse. Had he survived to tell the tale? Would he, one day, sit in this room and smile his merry smile, gently pull Rose's hair as he used to do and regale the wide-eyed Tim and Keith with stories of life at sea?

Or was he already dead – rolled over the side for a sea burial, drifting downwards through the waves to be eaten by crabs and end as a clutter of anonymous bones, wafted apart by the turbulence?

'If only we knew,' Ted said, breaking their silence. 'That's the worst of it – not knowing. Poor Annie's in a bad way, I don't mind telling you. She can't sit still, can't rest a minute. And if she's looked out of the front door once she's looked out a hundred times, hoping to see him come down the street.'

'But he'd never get back as quick as this,' Frank said. 'Even if he was sent home – and he wouldn't be.'

'She knows that. She just can't seem to help it.' Ted nodded towards the cake. 'That's why she made that. She's cooking for him to come home. I've told her, we can't afford it, what with shortages the way they are, but it seems to give her some comfort so I've given up. I don't know what she'll do if we don't hear soon, though.'

Frank was silent for a moment.

'It's harder on the women than it is on us, Ted. They still see the lads as their babies. They had to carry them and give birth to them – they take it hard when something happens to them.'

'I know. And our Olive is fretting her heart out now about that young man of hers – Derek Harker. He's expecting to be called up any time now and they're pestering to get married before he goes. Well, you know what I think about that, Frank – same as you do. Twenty-one's time enough for that, when they're old enough to take their own responsibility. We've seen plenty of people marry in haste and repent at leisure, and there's nothing like war for making them hasty.'

'Your Olive'll be twenty-one soon though, won't she?'

'Next October. And there won't be much I can do to stop her then. But I've told her, till then she's under my authority and does what I tell her. Mind, she's got a sensible head on her shoulders. It's young Betty I worry about. She's got proper headstrong just lately.'

He went home and Frank cut himself a slice of cake to take over to the allotment. Not that there was much he could do over there. The ground was frozen hard and he'd done all the digging anyway and sown what he could sow. The carrots he'd sown were wasted now, spoiled by the frost. But with the house empty and himself the only one at the table, there wouldn't have been any point in digging them anyway.

He'd stopped going to Annie's on Sundays. It didn't seem right to be taking up a place at her table every day, and he knew she liked to have Arthur and Mary along then. It gave him a chance to do things about the house and have his dinner when he liked. But it meant he didn't get a proper Sunday dinner – just whatever he could put together. And sitting there alone, he felt lonelier than at any time during the week.

Sunday dinner had always been his favourite meal. Jess always put on a roast, with plenty of vegetables. Her roast potatoes were crisp and golden, her Yorkshire pudding light and fluffy and when she cooked pork the crackling was as crisp as thin toffee. Frank would sit at the table, looking at the feast, most of it grown by himself, and then look at the three children – the two boys on one side of the long table, Rose on the other – and finally at his wife, and feel a warm glow spread through him. This was what life was all about. This was why he went to work in the Yard, slaving hour after hour in the sweltering clamour of the boiler-shop. This was why he went to the allotment in the evenings and at weekends. So that his family could eat food he'd grown and live in a house he'd worked for. And all he needed in return was to see their faces, clean and glowing, around the table, and see them grow into fine citizens who would do the same for their own families.

But now there was no family at the table, and the house was silent. And Frank was taking no pleasure in the work he did, not even in his allotment. There seemed to be little point in it now.

Frank moved impatiently, annoyed with himself for his misery. He had a lot to be thankful for, he reminded himself. His children weren't going off to war like Colin or Bob Shaw, nor likely to. And they were safer in the country than here. Wasn't that enough for him?

What's more, they would be home next weekend, for Christmas, all four of them and Jess too. They'd be together for the first time in three months. And the baby would be sitting up, taking an interest in all that went on.

Frank looked out of the window. There had been another hard frost following a bitter night. Perhaps he wouldn't go over to the allotment today after all. He'd look out the Christmas decorations instead and start getting things ready for next weekend.

By Tuesday, the world knew of the end of the *Graf Spee*, and those who had sons or husbands on the *Exeter* were waiting to know if they should grieve.

'Sixty-one dead,' Annie said, sitting with dry, aching eyes at the kitchen table. 'Sixty-one. And no one to tell us if our Colin's one.'

Ted sat beside her, his arm about her shoulders. He could think of nothing to say. His own thoughts were too painful to be expressed and he had no comfort for either his wife or his daughter.

'Remember when we first come here?' Annie said, still in that dry, painful voice. 'Remember how he thought we were coming to live in a castle? I could see then that blessed turret was going to be a devil to clean and the furniture would never fit in them round rooms, but Colin was so excited I couldn't bring myself to tell him we didn't want the house. He made up his mind right from the start, that upstairs room was going to be his, didn't matter how awkward or small it might be. And so it always has been.'

'I remember him playing the fool up on top,' Ted said. 'Him and his bows and arrows! I thought he'd killed old Mrs Henderson's Tibby, you know.'

'And I thought you'd almost killed him, you gave him such a hiding.' Annie realised what she had said and turned, clinging to her husband and weeping. 'Oh, Ted – Ted! If anything's happened to our Colin—'

He held her tightly. His own throat ached with tears, the first time he had wanted to cry since he was a small boy in his own mother's arms. But he could remember men in the Great War, men who had been injured, crying out in their pain, crying for their own mothers. Was Colin doing the same thing now?

'Put the kettle on, our Olive,' he said, and his daughter rose and went, red-eyed, to the kitchen.

Annie had stopped crying as suddenly as she had begun. She sat watching dully as Olive made the tea and poured out the first cup. When it was placed in front of her, she stared as it as if she did not know what it was.

'I've never let him down before,' she said at last in a dry aching voice. 'When he grazed his knees when he was a baby, he came running to me. When he fell off the wall and broke his arm, I took him to the hospital. When he had measles and mumps and chicken-pox I sat up with him at night. I've always been there, whenever he's needed me.'

'He's a man now, Annie,' Ted said. 'He has to manage without his mum.'

She turned her eyes in his direction but it was as if she did not see him, as if she were blind.

'Yes. That's it. They all do, don't they? All the mothers' sons out there, fighting each other for the sake of one nasty little German – they're all having to manage without their mums. And all the children like our Jess's boys and Molly Atkinson's little Alan and Wendy, and that poor little

Martin Baker. All of them, sent away from home, having to manage on their own.' Her face crumpled suddenly. 'It's not right, Ted, it's not right. It shouldn't be happening. There must be better ways than this – there must.'

Once again, the tears poured down her cheeks. She pushed her teacup out of the way and laid her arms on the table. She put her head down on them and wept.

Ted put his arm around her shoulders again. But there was nothing he could say. The tears were on his cheeks too and all he could do was lean his head on his other hand and suffer with his daughter and his wife.

Alan and Wendy Atkinson did not come home for Christmas. Just as Dave was preparing to go and fetch them – for Frank, with some apologies, had told him that he wasn't going to fetch Jess and the kids himself, he couldn't get the time off, and she wouldn't be able to manage Wendy and Alan as well as their four – his father had an accident and was killed.

'He only went down to the Harvest Home for a pint and a game of darts,' Molly told Annie. Molly's knee was still sore and her ribs caught her whenever she laughed or coughed, but with this latest disaster she was forced to come and help in the shop. 'He was crossing the road by the railway. You know what it's like there, with all those trees, you can't see even if there's a moon. And this car came along – and he must have just walked out in front of it. The driver swears he never saw him and I don't suppose he did. And you know Dad was hard of hearing, he probably didn't hear the engine.' Her eyes filled with tears. They were already red, as if she'd spent most of the past few days weeping. 'The doctor said he must have died at once, he couldn't have known anything about it, that's our only comfort.'

'I'm really sorry,' Annie said. Old Arnold Atkinson had been a bit cantankerous sometimes, which was why the shop wasn't as popular as Shepherds', with its genial proprietor who always had a joke and a laugh. But he'd been a good enough neighbour all the same, and part of the community for seventy years. He'd built the business up himself and handed it over to his sons a few years ago, but he was still very much a part of it, serving in the shop while they fetched the produce from the ships down at Camber Dock, or from market gardens round about.

'We'll miss him,' she said sincerely. 'It won't seem the same round here without him. And I reckon you'll miss him too.'

Molly nodded. 'We will. He wasn't always easy but his heart was in the right place. He'd never see anyone go in want if he could help it. And he loved the kids.' Her tears overflowed and ran down her cheeks. 'He missed them nearly as much as Dave and me these past few months,' she said shakily. 'He was just living to see them again at Christmas.'

'Oh, Molly,' Annie said helplessly. 'I'm really sorry. When are they coming home?'

To her dismay, Molly sat down suddenly in the chair that had been brought into the shop for her use. She covered her face with her hands and began to sob. Annie looked round. There was no one else in; it was almost closing time. Quickly, she went to the door and turned round the 'Closed' sign, put the bolt across and then went back to Molly. She laid her hand on the other woman's shoulder and waited for the storm to subside a little.

'That's it, girl,' she said after a moment. 'You cry it out. It'll do you good.' And then, after a further pause, 'Aren't they coming?'

Molly shook her head and felt in her apron pocket for a handkerchief. She blew her nose, wiped her eyes and said shakily, 'We decided it was best to leave them there after all. It's the funeral on Christmas Eve, see – we can't have them here for that. And the shop's so busy – with not having Dad here – Dave can't go, and the doctor says I can't, so—' She shook her head, the tears beginning again. 'I wanted them so bad,' she wept, 'and it just isn't fair. He was just walking down to the pub for a drink with his mates . . . Why did it have to happen? Why should he get run over like that?'

'It's this awful blackout,' Annie said. 'There's been more accidents these past four months . . . They won't let people shine any lights at all. And I know cars are supposed to go only twenty miles an hour, but how are they supposed to know how fast they're going when they can't see their speedometers?'

'There was a woman over in Gosport,' Molly said, 'put on the dashboard light, just for a quick look, and she got fined. Anyway, you can get killed by a car doing twenty miles an hour.'

They were silent for a few minutes. Molly slowly recovered herself and even gave Annie a watery smile. Annie squeezed her shoulder again and picked up her basket.

'Well, I'd better be getting back. I really am sorry about Dave's dad, Molly. And about the children. You let me know if there's anything we can do, won't you?'

'Yes. Yes, I will.' Molly opened the door for her, watched her go round the corner and then closed and bolted it again. She stood for a moment in the empty shop, looking at the sacks of potatoes, the bins of carrots and turnips and sprouts, the empty shelves where once they had stacked fruits like bananas and coconuts and pineapples, none of them available now.

It seemed very empty without Dad. And the flat upstairs seemed empty too, without the children. She thought of the presents she had bought, the decorations ready to be hung up, the little tree that Dave had managed to acquire.

All useless.

Oh, my babies, she thought, putting her fist to her mouth and biting the knuckles. What are you doing now?

When am I going to see you again?

A list of those killed in the battle with the *Graf Spee* was published at last in the *Evening News*, and Annie and Ted and the girls crowded round the table to read it, their fingers tracing down the columns of names. Once or twice, someone caught back a gasp as a similar name sprang to their eyes, but at last, having read the list at least three times, they drew back and gazed at each other.

'He's not on it,' Annie whispered. 'Our Colin's not on the list.'

'That means he's still alive,' Olive said. 'Oh, *Mum!*'

They flung their arms around each other. Once again, the tears flowed, but this time they were smiling and needed no comfort. Even Ted wiped his eyes a couple of times and blew his nose loudly, and then grinned rather self-consciously as Annie hugged him.

'Don't pretend you're not as pleased as we are, Ted Chapman!'

'Well, of course I'm pleased. He's my son, too, isn't he? Or so you've always led me to believe.'

'Ted!' Annie slapped his arm, glancing at the two girls and blushing. But Betty laughed and said, 'Go on, Mum, I bet you had your moments. And why not – it's human nature. And you don't have to look like that, we're not kids any more.'

'So you may not be, but I'll still thank you to keep a decent tongue in your head,' Annie said, but her accustomed sharpness had softened and she gave her daughter a hug too. 'Come on, Olive – give us a kiss. We're celebrating!'

Olive did so. But as she stepped away again, she glanced first at her father and then her mother, and said, 'Why not have something else to celebrate as well? Why not let me and Derek get married at Christmas?'

'Oh, Olive!' Annie sighed and looked at her husband. 'She's not going to let it rest, you know.'

'And I'm not going to give in,' Ted said grimly. 'Just because our Colin's safe doesn't alter my mind about that.' He looked at his daughter's face. 'But I'll tell you what. You can get engaged. How about that?'

Olive bit her lip. It was better than nothing, she thought. At least it showed that her father was willing to accept Derek into the family. But it wasn't what she really wanted.

I want to be *married*, she thought mutinously. I want to be able to let Derek love me without having to say 'no' all the time. I want to be able to have his baby with nobody pointing their finger at me.

And I will. Somehow or other, I *will*.

Jess came home for Christmas late one afternoon, bringing the boys, Rose and baby Maureen with her. She came down October Street with Maureen cradled in her arms, and felt close to tears.

It all seemed so cramped and narrow after the space of the countryside, the terraced houses crowded together and the tiny front gardens of March and October Street, which she had once thought so smart, meagre and useless. A snow-storm a week or so ago had left slush, frozen and dirty, in the gutters and the pavement was lumpy with ice. It had been scraped away from in front of some houses, while other people had thrown down ashes to make it less slippery. The afternoon was already growing dark, with thick, acrid smoke filling the streets as women lit fires to welcome men home from work. It was very different from the open fields and woods of Bridge End. But it was home, and Jess was overwhelmingly thankful to be back.

Granny Kinch came to the door of number to as she approached and threw up her hands.

'Mrs Budd! Well, this takes me back, it does really. It's just like the day I first saw you comin' down October Street, with two kiddies and another one on the way. Mrs Seddon was out'ere too and we said to each other, that poor woman, 'owever's she going to manage? And 'ere you are with another one – let's 'ave a look at the little dear. My, ain't she grown!' She put out a grubby finger and pulled the shawl away from the baby's face. Maureen, who had fallen asleep in the bus, stirred and whimpered a little as the cold air touched her skin. 'Why, she's twice the size of our Vera, and two months younger, ain't she?'

'She's six months old now,' Jess said proudly. 'Sitting up by herself. And weighs a ton!'

'You'd better get her inside,' the old lady advised. 'It's comin' in nasty. We've 'ad this fog now for the past three days, enough to choke a body to death. I've wondered once or twice whether to wear my gas mask, I 'ave really. And 'ow are the boys and Rose? 'Ow d'yer like the country, then?'

The children had been straggling behind, laden with bags and cases. They hadn't been able to bring much luggage and most of it was the baby's, but a lot of their clothes were still at home so it didn't matter. Tim and Keith came level and grinned at the old woman in her brown coat and curlers.

'It's smashing. We can milk cows.'

'Milk cows! Well, I never. You must be a real 'elp to the farmer, then.'

'Yes, we are,' Keith said. 'He didn't really want us to come home. He said we're too useful. But it's all right, we can go back.'

'Well, they seem to be 'aving a good time,' Granny Kinch said to Jess. 'And 'ow about Rose? D'you like being evacuated, love?'

Rose looked at her mother. 'Only if Mum's there too.'

The old woman laughed. 'A proper little mother's girl you are. I daresay you do a lot for your baby sister, don't you? You'll 'ave to pop in and see our Vera one day. 'Ow long are you staying, then?' she asked Jess.

'I don't know. We haven't decided yet. Over Christmas anyway.'

Jess shifted her feet. 'I'll have to go now, Mrs Kinch, this baby's getting heavier every minute. I daresay I'll be seeing you in the next few days.' Try not to, she thought with a little smile as she walked along the street. As Tommy Vickers would say, you'd need to be the Invisible Man to get past number 10 without being spotted. But the old woman had a good heart and Jess hadn't forgotten her kindness on the morning that the children had been evacuated.

Number 14 looked much as she'd left it, its windows dark and forbidding with the blackout curtains up. She rested the baby on one hip and felt for her key. But before she could fit it into the lock, the door of number 16 opened and Ethel Glaister came out with a shopping basket hung over her arm.

She gave a start of surprise at seeing Jess, and Jess knew immediately that she was 'putting it on'. Probably the woman had been looking out of the window and seen her talking to Granny Kinch, and now she wanted to get her oar in. She sighed. At this moment, all she wanted was to get indoors in her own home, lay Maureen down somewhere and have a cup of tea. But you had to be polite.

'Jess!' Ethel said with exaggerated astonishment. 'Well! So you decided to come home, then?'

She was looking as smart as ever, Jess thought, conscious all at once of her own shabby tweed coat and hair that had never seen a perm. How she managed to dress so well on George Glaister's money was a mystery.

'What d'you mean?' she asked sharply. 'Of course I've come home. Couldn't leave Frank on his own all over Christmas, could I?'

'Oh no, of course not.' Ethel gave a little laugh. 'Mind, I don't think he'd have lacked company. He's a very popular man, is your Frank. And how does life in the country suit you? You're looking well – cheeks like apples, you've got! But the natural look always did suit you best.'

Jess looked at Ethel, her hair waved and shining, her face carefully made up, and decided this wasn't intended as a compliment. But there was no sense in having words with Ethel Glaister the minute she got home, and anyway it was Christmas.

'The country's nice. I'd sooner be home with Frank, though.'

Ethel smiled. 'Course you would. He's a fine man, your Frank. I reckon there's a good many women'd like to be in your shoes. And some of 'em not a million miles from here either.'

'What d'you mean?' It was clear from Ethel's manner, her sideways glance and suggestive tone of voice, that she meant *something*. But then she always did like to pretend she knew more than other people.

'Oh, I don't mean nothing.' Ethel's gaze slid past Jess. Jess was suddenly aware of Rose, standing close beside her, of the boys fidgeting restlessly on the pavement, and of Maureen's weight bearing down on her arms. 'It's just that I don't think *I'd* be too pleased to find that a certain person had been in and out of my house while I'd been away, not if I was in your position.'

Jess sighed. 'Come on, Ethel. You might as well tell me what you're getting at. Otherwise I'll just have to go indoors, I can't keep the baby out in the cold much longer.'

Ethel turned pained eyes on her. 'I'm not getting at anything! I'm just saying, that's all – if I was away and my George here on his own, I wouldn't want Nancy Baxter in and out every five minutes. But each to his own, and if you don't mind—'

Jess felt a sudden fury. She forgot Maureen's weight, forgot the sighs and scuffles of the boys, forgot her good resolutions about Christmas. She lifted her chin and looked Ethel Glaister straight in the eye.

'I know all about Nancy Baxter coming down here. She told me before I went away that she'd be glad to do anything she could to give Frank a hand. She offered to do a bit of cleaning for him when our Annie didn't have time, and she's brought him a bit of cake now and then. *And that's all.* Anything else you might have heard is just spiteful gossip.' She paused and then added deliberately, 'And so is anything you might say, if it's about my Frank, so I'll thank you not to go talking like that to other people. And while we're on the subject, I might as well tell you that there's a few other people I wouldn't want in my house but anyone Frank invites is all right by me, because I happen to trust him. And now if you don't mind, I'll go indoors, I've got my husband's tea to get ready.'

Ethel tossed her head. 'Well! Pardon me for breathing! I'm sure I only wanted to be neighbourly, but if you're going to take it like that—'

Jess was no longer listening. Her key in her hand, she had turned once again to her own front door. But before she could open it, it was flung open and her sister Annie stood on the doorstep, arms held wide and a beaming smile stretched across her face.

'Jess! Our Jess! Come in, love, and have a cup of tea by your own fire. I bet that's what you've been looking forward to all day. Come in, all of you, out of the cold. My, you two boys have grown. And Rose – you've had your hair cut – I wouldn't have recognised you. Oh, it *is* good to see you again!'

Half laughing, half crying, Jess allowed herself to be led into her own house, her baby removed from her arms and her coat unbuttoned as if she were a little girl again. Aware only of the warmth of the room, she sank into her own armchair and smiled up at her sister.

'Oh, Annie, I've missed you all so much.'

'We've missed you too, Jess.' Annie poured cups of tea for them all. 'It hasn't seemed right, not having you down the end of the road. And poor Frank – well, he kept cheerful as best he could, but I could tell it's been a strain. Been right off his food, he has, this past week.'

Jess hid a smile. Frank had told her last week he'd begun to pop a few potatoes on the stove as soon as he came in of an evening, ready to fill up on when he got back from Annie's. But the smile was a tearful one. Her sister had been good to Frank and Jess hated to think of him sitting here on his own, cold and lonely.

Not that it was cold now. Annie had built up a really good fire and the room was warm and cosy. She had laid tea, with plenty of bread and marge, a pot of jam and home-made cake. And a plate of doughnuts too, Jess noticed, and felt tears in her eyes again. That was Annie all over, remembering how much the children liked doughnuts.

'Here!' she said. 'You've put up the Christmas decorations.'

Annie laughed. 'That was Frank. He spent all last Sunday doing it. Went out and got the holly and everything. I must say, he's made a nice job of it, and the fairy-lights look quite pretty strung around the walls like that, better than a tree really.'

'I suppose you can't get trees,' Jess said. 'They managed all right at Bridge End. You wouldn't know there was a war on there, Annie. I wish I'd been able to bring some more stuff back with me. Eggs, butter, cream – there's no shortages out there. Mrs Greenberry's put any amount of eggs into waterglass and they get milk from the house cow – you wouldn't believe it.'

'You'll see a difference here, then,' her sister said. 'We're all expecting the rationing to start soon. Most of the shops are half empty now, especially with Christmas coming – everyone's decided they're going to make it a good one in case it's the last chance.'

'It'll probably be a good thing when they do bring rationing in,' Jess observed. 'Some people are getting more than their share and others have to go without. It's the same even in the village, with things that aren't local. I haven't seen a tin of fruit in weeks.' She looked at Annie, suddenly remembering. 'Here! What about your Colin? Have you heard anything?'

Annie nodded and smiled. 'There was a list of the men killed in the paper. Colin wasn't one of them. And the ship's down in the Falklands now getting repaired, so they're safe enough there for the time being. Ted says they're learning to live posh, even the penguins wear evening dress!'

The two women laughed. Jess felt a wave of thankfulness wash over her. She'd heard little news, knowing only that the *Exeter* had been damaged, but she'd known that Annie and Ted must be worried.

She finished her tea and put the cup back on the table. The boys had dashed upstairs and could be heard thumping about in the bedroom. Rose was cuddling Maureen and giving her a bottle. Henry, who had been fast asleep on the rug in front of the fire, suddenly woke to the fact that his mistress was home, and stood up to put his front paws on her knee.

'It's so good to be home,' she said, and leaned back in her chair. 'You know, you don't really realise how badly you miss it all till you're back. I mean, I knew I was missing it – but not how much. I don't reckon I'll be able to bear to go away again, Annie.'

'I'm not sure your Frank'll be able to bear to let you,' her sister said shrewdly. 'He's been a different man this past week, getting things ready. And I reckon he'll be glad to have good reason to keep Ethel Glaister at arm's length.'

'Ethel Glaister!' Jess sat up straight. 'You don't mean she's been setting her cap at him!'

'Oh, I'm sure there's nothing in it,' Annie assured her hastily. 'Not on his side, anyway. But you know what she's like – and now George has gone away—'

'I know there wouldn't be anything in it as far as Frank's concerned,' Jess said grimly. 'He doesn't like her any more than I do. But if she thinks she's going to pester my husband while I'm away—'

'Well, I don't know that she has been. It's only one or two little things Frank's let drop – and knowing what she's like. She won't try anything now you're home, anyway.'

'She'd better not.' Jess remembered Ethel's malicious hints and repressed a small smile. So that was what was the matter with her! She'd tried it on with Frank and he'd given her the cold shoulder. Well, what else did she expect – she wasn't his type at all. And even if she was . . .

Jess got up out of her chair. Suddenly she was no longer the little sister, to be looked after, but a woman in charge of her own home.

'Well, thanks for coming round and doing everything, Annie. I'll get my pinafore and start Frank's tea. He told me he'd try to get home early tonight, if they'd let him off the overtime. And there's a lot to be done, with Christmas only a few days away.'

Annie recognised that Jess wanted to be alone with her family when Frank came in. She got up, leaving her own cup of tea half finished, and gave her sister a kiss.

'I'll be getting back too. I'll see you tomorrow, Jess – pop up whenever you like. And don't forget you're all coming to us for Christmas dinner.'

'I won't forget. Thanks, Annie.' But Jess's smile was absent-minded and she was already thinking of something else as she saw Annie out into the dark, foggy street.

Frank would be home soon. They'd be a proper family again, clustered around the table, warmed by their own fire. And then the children would go to bed. First the boys, in the iron bunks up in the back bedroom, then Rose in the Put-u-Up in the front room downstairs. And then she and Frank would be alone together, for the first time in three long months. She heard his key in the front door, then the tramp of his boots along the passage. Her heart thumping suddenly, she stood by the dining-table, facing the door. And then he was in the room, dirty in his working clothes, his lunch box in his hand and, held clumsily in the other, a straggly bunch of flowers from the corner shop.

Jess moved forward and found herself in his arms, pressed once more against that firm, broad chest, feeling his big, strong hands on her shoulders and back.

'Oh Frank,' she said, 'I've missed you so much!'

9

Bob Shaw was home for Christmas, proud to wear his rough new khaki uniform in the streets, but glad to take it off indoors and sit in his old grey flannels and the Fair Isle pullover Gladys had knitted him. He was still waiting to go to France – twice he had been expecting to go within twenty-four hours, only to be kept back at the last minute. He basked in the adulation of his sister Diane, who was getting on for sixteen now and missing the blue-eyed young delivery man at the laundry who used to stop and flirt with her. He had been called up and posted in November.

But it wasn't Diane's admiration Bob craved. All the time he'd been away, he'd been thinking about Betty Chapman. He still carried the photo of her in her bathing costume and looked at it every night before he fell on his camp bed in the hut and slept an exhausted sleep. At the first opportunity, he asked Gladys if Betty was still going out with Graham Philpotts.

Gladys snorted. 'Going out with him? She says they're "secretly engaged" – whatever that might mean! Far as I can see, it just means she don't get a ring and her dad doesn't know. I mean, how can you be engaged if you don't have a ring? It doesn't make sense.'

'I suppose if you say you'll marry someone, you're engaged,' Bob said, feeling depressed. 'But they can't get married without her dad knowing, can they.'

'Well, of course not. I don't think they're even thinking about it. If you ask me, Betty doesn't even care about being engaged, not properly, except that she'd like a ring to flash about. She just wants to be able to tell people she's got a boy in the Navy. But she's got no more idea of settling down than flying to the moon. You know she's going off to work on a farm, don't you?'

Bob stared. 'On a *farm*?'

'That's right. Land girl. Fancies herself in trousers, driving a tractor. I don't know what her "secret fiancé" thinks about that!'

Bob looked at his sister. 'I thought you liked Betty.'

'I do really.' Gladys grinned at him. 'But it riles me a bit to see her messing about. I mean, she could find she's bitten off more than she can chew, leading Graham on, letting him think she's serious when all she wants is someone to show off. I wouldn't like to see her in trouble.'

Bob said no more. But when he met Betty in the street next morning, he remembered all that Gladys had said and wondered if it was really true.

'Bob!' Betty exclaimed. 'My, you do look smart. And I reckon you've put on weight too. You look bigger. How d'you like being a soldier?'

'It's all right. I still wish I'd gone in the Navy though. I'd have liked to go to sea.'

'You ought to have joined the Marines, then.' She put out a hand and stroked the rough khaki. 'I bet that's nice and warm. Have you heard when you're going to France?'

'Pretty soon, I think. I've been on standby to go twice and kept back at the last minute.' He grinned self-consciously. 'They're saving the best for the last.'

'That's it,' Betty said. 'Our Olive's boyfriend, Derek Harker, he's waiting for a posting too. They're getting engaged at Christmas. They wanted to get married but Dad won't let them till she's twenty-one. Daft, I call it.'

They stood awkwardly for a moment and then Betty moved her feet as if preparing to go. Bob tried frantically to think of something to say, to keep her there, talking to him. He looked at her brown hair, shining in the wintry sun, at her clear skin and sparkling hazel eyes. If only she was my girl, he thought miserably, and wondered what it was she saw in Ginger Philpotts.

'Our Gladys says you're going in the Land Army,' he said, and Betty nodded vigorously.

'That's right – soon as they'll have me. Mum and Dad don't like it much but I told them, this is something you *can't* stop me doing. Not when there's a war on. I'm looking forward to it – being in the open air, working with the animals and that.'

'Well, I think it's a good idea,' Bob said, and she looked at him in surprise.

'Do you? Graham doesn't! He thinks I'll get off with some handsome young farmer.'

'He ought to trust you,' Bob said warmly. 'He ought to be *glad* you're doing something for the war. He ought to be pleased you're doing something you'll enjoy.'

Betty looked at him again. Her face softened and she put out a hand and touched his arm.

'Thanks, Bob. Thanks for saying that.' She hesitated and then said quietly, 'You know, if you'd asked me to go out with you before we'd met Graham that day – I would've done. I've always liked you, Bob.'

He stared at her, remembering the day he and Graham had walked down Queen Street and met Betty eating fish and chips from newspaper. He'd seen her then as if for the first time – bright-eyed, laughing, attractive, a girl he'd be proud to be seen out with. Before that, she'd just been good old Bet, a sport who didn't mind being wicket-keeper or goalie in the street games, who'd climb trees and fish for crabs without fussing about her clothes, who could use her fists as well as any boy and wouldn't go crying home to her mother if she got hurt.

Trust me to leave it too late, he thought bitterly.

'I wish I had asked you out,' he said. 'I think a lot of you too, Bet. And if – well, if things don't work out – you know, with you and Graham – well,

I'm always here. At least, I s'pose I *won't* be here, not once I've gone away, but – oh, you know what I mean.' He floundered to a stop and Betty laughed and squeezed his arm.

'I know what you mean, Bob. Thanks. I'll remember.' She tilted her head to one side and gave him a saucy grin that turned his heart over. 'And there's no reason why you shouldn't write to me once in a while, is there? Let me know how you are and all that. After all, we're friends, aren't we? There's no reason why we shouldn't.'

Bob thought Graham Philpotts would think there was every reason why they shouldn't, but he didn't say so. That was for Betty to decide. He nodded eagerly.

'I'll write to you every week. And you'll write back?'

She smiled. 'Course I will. That's what friends are for.' Then she flicked back her curls, gave him another heart-stopping smile and dropped her hand from his arm. 'Well, I've got to be going now, Bob. Have a smashing Christmas. And don't go away without saying goodbye.'

'I won't.' He watched her flit away up the street. His arm burned from the touch of her fingers. His mind went over everything she had just said, every expression of her face, every movement of her body.

'I've always liked you, Bob . . . If you'd asked me to go out with you, I would've done . . . I've always liked you, Bob . . . Write to me . . . Don't go away without saying goodbye . . . I've always liked you . . .'

He went back into number 13, forgetting why he had gone out in the first place, and sat for half an hour in his father's armchair, gazing at the photograph he always carried of Betty Chapman.

The Budds and Chapmans were in celebratory mood. Jess and Frank were thankful to be together again, the whole family under one roof. And although Colin was still down in the South Atlantic on the *Exeter*, he was safe and had written long letters home. Not about the Battle of the River Plate, or the *Graf Spee*, for that would have been crossed out by the censor, but about the unexpected summer holiday he was having on the islands, about soft blue skies, rolling moorland and penguins.

'To absent friends,' Ted said, holding up his glass of sherry at Christmas dinner. 'To absent friends, and especially our Colin.'

Everyone joined in. The whole family was there, including Arthur and Mary, Jess and Annie's parents, and all raised their glasses – even Frank was willing to break his rule and have a glass of sherry at Christmas – and responded to Ted's toast of 'absent friends'. And Frank thought gratefully how good it was to have Jess and the children at home again, and the house turned back into a home.

'And the toast to the engaged couple,' Ted said.

All eyes turned to Olive and Derek. Olive went pink and giggled, looking at the ring with its tiny diamond that flashed on her finger. Derek cleared his throat and grinned sheepishly. It wasn't really what they'd wanted – he'd have liked to be married to Olive by now – but it was all Ted would agree to, so they had to make the best of it. And surely he'd let them get married at Easter, if Derek was home again then.

Betty glanced down at her own hands. Graham had given her a ring too, a little gold one with her initial engraved on it, which she was wearing on her right hand. She'd swap it to her left hand as soon as she was on her own with him. But he wasn't even here at the moment – he was over in Gosport with his own family. Unless you were properly engaged, that was what you were expected to do.

Ted hadn't approved of Graham giving Betty a ring, but as Annie had pointed out, there wasn't much you could do about it. It wasn't a proper engagement ring – though she had a pretty good idea what Betty meant to do with it – and if Graham went away the whole thing would probably blow over and no harm done.

'Anyway, our Betty will be off on her own before long,' she said. 'We're not going to be able to keep an eye on her once she's on that farm.'

'I should hope the farmer would do that,' Ted said. 'He'll be responsible for her, after all. She's under age.'

'I daresay they'll look after her,' Annie said, hoping it was true. 'Anyway, that'd be one good thing about letting her get engaged – she wouldn't be wanting to go off with anyone else. Like our Olive.'

Watching the pair of them now, she decided that they'd done the right thing. Olive certainly had no eyes for anyone but Derek, and he was like a dog with two tails, sitting back in his chair with his arm possessively along the back of hers. And there was no chance of their getting married too soon – he'd be off before long and Ted had made it clear there was to be no talk of weddings until the war was over. And not then, if it was very quick.

'Twenty-one's old enough for that,' he'd said firmly, and with that Olive and Derek had to be satisfied.

Annie looked around the big table. It almost filled the room. They'd had to carry Frank and Jess's extending table up the road and put it at the end of Annie's. She sat at one end and Ted at the other. Jess sat near Annie, to be handy for the kitchen, with Olive beside her. Frank was opposite and had Rose on one side of him and Tim on the other. Derek was next to Olive, with Keith on his left and Betty sat on the other side of Keith, with her grandparents opposite.

'Twelve,' Annie said, dishing out the turkey. 'That's a good number for Christmas dinner. What d'you want, Mum, white meat or dark?'

'White, please.' At seventy-five, Mary still had a healthy appetite but her husband Arthur ate like a bird. He was a thin, fragile man of eighty who seemed to have shrunk over the past few months. He had spent his life in the Army, too old to fight in the last war but had seen action in Africa during the Boer War, and he spent most of his days reading the newspaper and trying to relate his own experiences to what was happening now. He was shaky and walked with two sticks, and he said little but turned his cloudy eyes from one to the other as the family chattered.

'You've got a good table,' Mary said appreciatively, cutting up Arthur's meat for him. 'You'd never think there was shortages, looking at this lot.'

'I was lucky, getting a turkey. I thought I'd have to do with two chickens but I got the last one. And I made my puddings early on, before the shortages really started.'

'The vegetables are all from the garden,' Ted said. 'It's a good thing I lifted them early. It's been so cold, you can't get them out of the ground now. We're going to lose a lot if it doesn't ease up soon.'

'I don't reckon it's going to ease up,' Frank said. 'I don't think we've seen the worst of it yet.'

'It's a nuisance not getting any weather forecasts.' Annie finished dishing out the turkey and took the big meat plate back to the kitchen. 'I don't really see what harm there'd have been in it, do you? I mean, the Germans must have their own weather forecasters. They don't rely on ours.'

'It might help them to know what we're expecting, though,' Derek said. 'And where the bad weather is. I mean, if they know we've got bad power cuts or the telephone lines are down, they'd know where to hit us. That's why it's not allowed to be reported.'

'Well, they haven't started hitting us at all yet,' Jess remarked. 'All this time and nothing's happened. Not here, anyway.' She looked at Frank.

They were still discussing whether or not she should return to the country after Christmas. Jess badly wanted to stay at home and Frank just as badly wanted her there, but he was still afraid of the threatened air raids. Just because they hadn't happened yet, didn't mean they weren't going to. We were making aircraft as fast as we could, weren't we, at Airspeed and the Spitfire factory near Southampton? Well, so were the Germans. It stood to reason. And one day – one day soon, if he was any judge – all hell was going to break loose.

But he wasn't going to start that argument again, not at Christmas dinner with all the kids listening in.

'Let's forget the war for a day or two,' he said, helping himself to roast potatoes. 'It's Christmas. After dinner I want a walk out to the shore.'

'Can we play some games?' Tim asked. 'We always play games at Christmas.'

'We'll play games after tea.' Traditionally, Christmas Day tea was salad and tinned salmon with trifle and fruit salad and small fancy cakes made by Olive, who was turning into what Annie called a 'handy little cook'. Rose had spent Christmas Eve helping her ice them. There was a large Christmas cake too, but nobody ever wanted it on Christmas Day, they were all too full.

A rather newer tradition was the King's Christmas broadcast on the wireless. George VI had been King for only a couple of years, after his brother's abdication, and had broadcast his message for the first time a year ago. His voice was slow and hesitant, for as everyone knew he suffered from a bad stammer, but in spite of that – perhaps, in a way, because of it – his short talk was moving, and brought tears to the eyes of most of his listeners.

'That was lovely,' Annie said, wiping her eyes. 'And I liked that bit of poetry he read out. The man who stood at the gate of the year – it's just right for now, isn't it?'

'Yes,' Ted said. 'He's a good man, King George, and he's been handed a packet of trouble by that brother of his. At least he knows what his duty is, and he'll do it.'

'I 'ad a lot of time for the Duke of Windsor,' Arthur said, in his piping voice, speaking up suddenly so that they all stopped and looked at him. 'He 'ad the common touch. Look 'ow 'e went round the mines that time and said something 'ad got to be done about the way working people lived. None of the others ever did that.'

'And did he ever do anything?' Ted demanded. 'No – he was too busy running around with that Mrs Simpson, who was no better than she should be. If you want my opinion–'

'We don't,' Annie cut in. 'We just want to enjoy Christmas.' She softened her tone a little. 'Don't get into politics now, Ted. Let's just forget all that and have a nice day with the family all together.'

The whole family, except for Arthur and Mary, went out in the afternoon. Rose pushed the pram with Maureen now sitting up inside, her face almost obliterated by a woolly bonnet that Annie had made. Her eyes turned solemnly from one face to another.

'She doesn't know us now,' Annie said. 'We're all strangers to her – her own family.' She took her sister's arm. 'I'm glad you came home for Christmas, Jess.'

'So am I. They're very nice at Bridge End, but it's not the same as being with your own, is it? Specially not at Christmas. And they needed the room too, they've got their own families coming.'

Tim and Keith ran on ahead, wearing the new scarves Jess had knitted them. They were chattering about the games that would be played later in the evening.

'Family Coach,' Keith said. 'Dad'll tell the story and we'll all be different parts. I'll be the lamps.'

'Yes, and I'll be the whip. And whenever he says our bit we have to stand up and turn round. I bet our Rose will want to be the horse, she always does.'

'Land, Sea and Air,' Keith said. 'We'll play that too. I can think of lots of things for land and air but there's only fish or whales in the sea.'

'You have to think of different fish. Cod. Herrings. Sprats.'

'Crabs,' Keith said. 'Lobsters, shrimps, sticklebacks.'

'Sticklebacks aren't in the sea. They're in the rivers.'

'It's the same thing. It's water.'

'It has to be sea, dopey.'

'It doesn't. Does it, Mum?' he appealed as the others caught up with them. 'If someone throws the ball of paper at you and shouts 'sea' you can say things that live in rivers, can't you?'

'So long as you get it in before they get to ten, yes.'

'But it's not sea,' Tim expostulated. 'Sticklebacks live in rivers. Reg showed us some.'

'Well, we'll say "water" then,' Jess said. They had arrived at the shore and she stood gazing out across Langstone Harbour. Rose had joined her brothers now and they were poking about amongst some rocks. Olive and Derek were lagging behind and Annie knew they were hoping to find some corner out of sight for a while. Betty was walking alone, her hands in her coat pockets, brooding about Graham.

'It looks just the same as always,' Jess remarked. 'So peaceful. You can't believe there's a war on, can you, Annie?'

'You can if you go down to Portsmouth Harbour,' her sister replied. 'There's plenty of activity there. Ships going in and out. The Yard working at full stretch. Ted says the ferry's loaded with men, from six in the morning till nine at night.'

'I know. Frank's worn out with overtime.' Jess stood silent for a moment. The air was bitterly cold and the shore, left muddy on an outgoing tide, was already covered with a thin film of ice. The sky was lowering, with heavy, yellow-bellied clouds like bruises. 'I don't want to go back to the country, Annie.'

Annie turned and looked at her. 'What does Frank say?'

'Oh, we've talked about it – but he thinks I ought to go.' Jess turned and spoke passionately. 'Annie, I hate thinking of him all by himself. It's not right, us being apart. I'm his wife – I ought to be here with him.'

'But what about the children?'

'Oh, I agree with him there. We've got to keep them as safe as we can.' She looked at the pram. Maureen had slipped down now and fallen asleep, and she bent forwards to tuck the covers in more securely about her. 'The baby'd have to stay with me, of course. But my place is with Frank.'

Annie nodded. She agreed with her sister that a woman's place was in her own home, by her man's side. It had never seemed right, Jess being away. But it would be hard to make up her mind to being away from the rest of the children.

'This war,' she said, looking out over the gleaming mud, at the little boats that lay keeled over waiting for the next tide, at the sullen, threatening clouds. 'This war . . . It's getting us all down, Jess. And it hasn't even got started yet – not here.' She shivered suddenly. 'It's too cold to stand about, Jess. Let's get home and have a cup of tea.'

They called the children and then turned and walked back along the path. After a few minutes, Jess said quietly, 'Frank was right. We shouldn't be thinking about the war today. It's Christmas. We ought to be making it a really good one. The best we can.'

Annie nodded. There was no need to say why. Everyone she knew had the same idea in mind. To make the Christmas of 1939 the best they could, for who knew what the next year might bring . . . ?

The Woddis sisters were regular churchgoers, and Christmas Day was no exception. Holy Communion at eight, matins at eleven. They would be at both services, sitting upright in their pew, dressed in their best navy-blue coats and hats, with gloves on and their own prayer-books.

They did not take Alan and Wendy with them. They did not take Alan and Wendy anywhere. That was not, as they saw it, their job. They had been compelled to take in two evacuees, to give them beds and feed them, but they were under no obligation to do any more than that. They would have been startled and indignant to be told anything different.

Their main concern, having done their duty by their country, was to ensure that their lives were disrupted as little as possible and that their home remained undamaged by the two children. At seven forty-five, therefore, they donned their navy-blue coats and hats and left Wendy and

Alan in bed, with strict instructions that they were not to get up until the sisters returned.

For a short while, there was silence. Then Alan said in a small voice, 'Didn't Father Christmas know we were here?'

'I don't think he did,' Wendy said miserably.

'We didn't write any notes.' They had asked a week ago if they could write their letters to Father Christmas and put them up the chimney but had been refused outright. That was the way fires started! In any case, it was all nonsense, there was no such person as Father Christmas and they were old enough to stop believing in such fairy-tales. Any presents that might come would arrive through the post, just like any other parcel.

Alan did not believe this. Since hearing Miss Eleanor tell a friend that he was a wicked little fiend and not even house-trained, he had not believed a word either of them said. He knew perfectly well that they had told him these lies because they didn't want him to have any presents. Perhaps they had even written their own note, telling Father Christmas that the children weren't here.

'Let's go down and see if he's been,' he suggested. 'He might have done. They haven't been in the sitting-room yet.'

Wendy considered this. She didn't want to disobey the sisters' instructions, since she too, by now, had experienced the cupboard, but on the other hand, if Alan was right . . . There could be presents down there now. Would the sisters give them their presents if they came home and found them first? Or would they keep them for themselves? Wendy couldn't believe that they would really want the Rupert Bear annual she always received, or the two new aprons, or the car that Alan was hoping for, but you never knew.

'All right,' she said, getting out of bed. 'But we'd better be quick.'

They crept downstairs, half afraid that the sisters had not gone out after all but were lying in wait in case their instructions were disobeyed, but the house was empty. They went into the sitting-room and looked at the fireplace.

It had been laid yesterday morning by Mrs Cherry and left unlit, so that it did not need to be cleaned and relit this morning. It was undisturbed, each piece of wood and coal still in place. Clearly, no one had come down there during the night.

They went into the dining-room. It was icily cold and again the fireplace was undisturbed.

'He didn't come,' Alan said sadly.

Wendy stood thoughtful for a moment. She was remembering past Christmases, when she had been given presents by her parents and had always done some little task in return, as her gift to them. Perhaps she and Alan should do something now for Miss Eleanor and Miss Millicent. You couldn't expect presents if you didn't do something for other people first, her mother had always said.

'I'll go and lay the breakfast table.' She looked around for something Alan could do. 'You could polish the sideboard.' At least it was something they'd done before, something he knew how to do. And there had been so much fuss about it last time, surely they couldn't help being pleased.

They went into the kitchen. It was warmer in here, for there was a stove that burned wood and coal, which the Woddis sisters were keeping alight most of the time in the cold weather. Wendy started to get things out of the cupboards and Alan looked around for the polish.

He found the cloth but no tin of polish. He went into the pantry and looked on the shelf where it was normally kept. There was a mixture of tins, for the sisters had a brother in America who had started to send parcels of food and anything else he thought might be useful. Alan had been there when the last one was opened and thought he could remember a tin of polish being amongst the items unpacked.

Perhaps this was it. It was quite a struggle to open it but he managed it and looked inside. It was yellow and waxy so he carried it into the dining-room and began work.

When the sisters came home, half an hour later, Wendy had the table laid and the kettle almost boiling. She waited nervously, hoping she had done everything right. She wondered how Alan was getting on; she had heard no sound from the dining-room.

The front door opened and a blast of bitter air blew through the passage to the kitchen. Wendy heard the two sisters come in discussing the service.

'. . . and did you see her hat, Millicent? Quite unsuitable for Holy Communion, in my opinion. Why, she looked as if she were going to a wedding. But then she never has had any sense of what's correct.'

'And can you be surprised, with a mother like hers? They say she was nothing but a common housemaid.'

'Common is the word!' Miss Eleanor paused by the hallstand. Wendy, peeping through the kitchen door, saw her give her navy hat with its little veil one last admiring glance before removing it. She turned her head and gasped.

'What is it, Eleanor?' Miss Millicent, also in the middle of taking off her hat and coat, stopped and gave her sister an enquiring glance. 'Is something the matter?'

'Something the matter?' Miss Eleanor was looking through the half-open door of the dining-room. She walked through, and Wendy heard an exclamation.

'What on earth do you think you're doing? Oh – you naughty, *naughty* little boy!'

'What is it? What have they done now?' Miss Millicent followed her quickly and Wendy, trembling with fear and dismay, came behind.

'Look at him. Just *look* at him.' Miss Eleanor was standing in the middle of the dining-room, her hands on her hips, quivering with anger. Her face was white, her cheekbones burning red. 'Oh, whatever will they do next? What will they do next?'

'What? What's he done?' There was a greedy note in Miss Millicent's voice as she pushed into the room, almost as if she gained some twisted kind of pleasure out of Alan's misdoings. Or perhaps out of what followed them. 'Let me see . . . Oh-h-h. You little *beast* . . .' She sounded almost awed.

Wendy peered through the door. The sisters were standing just inside and she had to hold Miss Millicent's skirt back to see past. For a moment or two she stared, puzzled. What was it that Alan was doing? Why were they so angry?

Alan was kneeling by the sideboard. He had a cloth in one hand and a flat, round tin in the other. He seemed to be frozen in the act of rubbing yellow grease from the tin into the ornate carving of the sideboard drawers. Much of the wood was already smeared and the tin was half empty. He was looking up at Miss Eleanor with large, frightened eyes.

'You . . . horrible . . . little . . . boy,' Miss Eleanor said, speaking very slowly. 'You . . . nasty . . . little . . . wretch. You little demon.'

'*Butter!*' Miss Millicent said, snatching the tin out of his hand. 'Our best butter, that Howard sent us. Nearly all gone—'

'Never mind that,' Miss Eleanor snapped. 'Look what he's done with it!! Oh, the sideboard will never be the same again. We'll never get it all out, never.'

Alan's terrified eyes went to his sister and Wendy stepped forward, trembling.

'It's not his fault,' she said. 'He thought it was polish. He wanted to—'

'Thought it was polish? Don't talk nonsense! Look on the lid, it says *Butter*, as plain as plain.'

'But he can't read—'

'Then it's time he learned to. And it's time he learned to keep his hands off other people's property.' Miss Eleanor lunged forward and grabbed Alan by the arm, jerking him roughly to his feet. 'And if his own parents won't teach him, I will! You'll spend the rest of the morning in the cupboard, my lad, and maybe that will give you time to think things over.'

'But that's not fair!' Wendy exclaimed. 'He didn't mean to do any harm. He was only trying to help. He wanted to do it for Christmas—'

'Stop it at once!' Both sisters turned on her. 'Don't you dare answer back. Trying to help, indeed! Trying to make a mess, that's what he was doing, it's the only thing he knows how to do. He's a naughty little boy and he has to be taught a lesson.'

'But he's not a naughty boy, he's *not*!' Wendy felt rage well up inside her. She stared at the two women. 'He's always been a good boy – everyone says so. It's only since we've been here – he doesn't know what you want – he tries his best – and we wanted to do something for you for Christmas, so I laid the table and Alan polished the sideboard, how was he to know it was butter and not polish, he can't read, it was on the same shelf in the pantry, it's not his fault!' She ran out of breath. The sisters stood staring at her. 'It's *your* fault he gets into trouble, *yours*!' she continued, her voice rising to a shout. 'He wets the bed because he's frightened of you and he's frightened of that horrible cupboard and the spiders in it, and he's frightened of the dark. And you're horrible to him. You're horrible to both of us, you don't give us any nice food or let us sit by the fire or anything and now we haven't even got any Christmas presents.' She burst into tears and stamped her foot.

'Well!' Miss Eleanor gasped. She stared at the furious little girl for a full minute. 'Well! You insolent little hussy. I think you'd better go into the cupboard too, along with your brother.'

Wendy glowered at her.

'I won't!'

'You certainly will,'

'I won't!' Overcome with her fury, she pushed Miss Millicent aside and marched into the room. She grabbed Alan's arm and pulled him towards the door. 'Come on, Alan. We won't stay here any longer. We'll run away. We'll go home – we can walk all the way, even if it takes us weeks – and we'll tell Mummy and Daddy what these horrible people have done to us.'

The Woddis sisters were transfixed. They stared as the two children ran through the door. And then they came to life, gave each other a swift glance and made for the passage, where Wendy was already turning the knob on the front door.

'Don't let her! Don't let her get out.' Miss Eleanor thrust past her sister and rushed to grab them. 'How dare you! How *dare* you try to run away. Showing us up like that – what would people think?' She hustled the crying children back along the passage. Miss Millicent had already opened the cupboard door. Together, they thrust the squirming, fighting bodies in and slammed the door against them. Miss Eleanor locked it and then stood with a hand to her side, breathing hard.

'Well!' she said. 'And I think that's the best place for them today, don't you, Millicent? Now let's go and have our breakfast. And by the time that's over it will be almost time for matins. Really! Such behaviour! On Christmas Day too, of all days.'

The two children, crouching in the dark and stuffy space amongst the coats and brooms and step-ladders, heard their voices fade as they went towards the kitchen. The last they heard, before the door closed, was Miss Millicent remarking on the kitchen table, laid for breakfast.

'Look at this, Eleanor. As if we'd eat breakfast in the kitchen on Christmas Day. Can you believe that they didn't even notice the dining-table was already laid?'

'It's just another piece of insolence,' came Miss Eleanor's voice. And then the door closed and they heard no more.

Alan and Wendy sank down, trying to find a space to sit on the cluttered floor. They knew from bitter experience that it was no use making a noise. They would be left here for hours, perhaps most of the day. And when they were let out, it would be only to go to the lavatory and then back to their bedroom, with a plate of scraps for their Christmas dinner.

Father Christmas had indeed forgotten them. And so, it seemed, had their mother and father. And as they clung together in that dark and foetid little space under the stairs, it was as if the whole world had forgotten that it contained two children called Alan and Wendy.

The Budds and Chapmans kept their party going until two in the morning. They always did this, staying up until they could barely keep their eyelids propped open. After their hearty tea they washed up and then played games. Some of these were noisy, hilarious ones, such as the Jelly Race, in which Annie provided a plate of jelly, kept back from supper, and a knife and fork. With the plate was a large pair of thick fur gloves, donated by

Grandma, Grandpa's cap and Tim's new scarf. The racers had to pass a dice to each other and the first one to throw a six ran forwards, donned gloves, scarf and cap and proceeded to try to cut and eat the jelly with the knife and fork. As often as not, they had barely got the clothes on when another six had been thrown and the scarf was being unceremoniously unwound and the gloves and cap dragged off. Sometimes there were three or even four people milling about by the plate of jelly, tugging at each other's clothes and howling with laughter while the rest screamed, 'Two! Four! Five! One! *Si-i-ix!*'

Other games were more restful. Pencil and paper games, such as Consequences or Telegrams. For 'Alibis', two people were sent out to fabricate some story of how they had spent a day together and then brought in one at a time to be interrogated. 'Scissors' involved the whole group lounging back in chairs passing a pair of scissors to each other and saying 'I pass these scissors to you closed' or 'I pass these scissors to you open'. This was a game that could only be played once, or with people who had not come across it before, for once you knew the secret there was no fun in it any more.

To the boys' delight, they were allowed a game of Murder, with the lights switched off and a bloodcurdling scream from the victim, and then it was time for Family Coach, with Frank telling the story of a disastrous family picnic and everyone else taking the part of some accessory. And then Annie and Jess went out to 'get a bit of supper ready', returning with trays laden with sausage rolls, cheese and biscuits and Marmite sandwiches, and everyone fell to once more.

After that, refreshed, they were all supplied with drinks of lemonade or squash, with beer for the men (except Frank), and settled down for a singsong. The room resounded to the strains of 'Tavern in the Town', 'Roaming in the Gloaming', and 'Hello, Hello, Who's your Lady Friend?' They went from old songs – 'Daisy, Daisy', 'Two Little Girls in Blue' – to the more modern songs from shows by Noel Coward or Ivor Novello, and finished up with songs that had been popular during the Great War – 'Tipperary', 'Pack Up Your Troubles in Your Old Kitbag', and 'There's a Long, Long Trail A-winding'.

There was a sadness in their voices as they sang these. Jess and Annie, who could remember when men had been forced to leave their homes then as soldiers and sailors, found tears in their eyes. And they both noticed Olive's face as Derek sang 'If You Were the Only Girl in the World', looking at her as if she were indeed the only girl in his world, and her sudden movement to cover her eyes when they began on 'Keep the Home Fires Burning'.

'I reckon that girl's had just about enough,' Jess murmured under cover of the words. 'Let's find something more cheerful, Annie.'

'. . . till the boys come home,' they sang, and there was a muffled sob from the corner where Olive was sitting.

Jess jumped to her feet. 'Let's have something a bit more jolly. *Old Macdonald had a farm—*'

'*Ee-I-ee-I-oh,*' they roared back.

'*And on that farm he had some pigs—*'
'*Eei-ee-i-oh!*'
'*With an oink-oink here—*'
'*An oink-oink there—*'
'*Here an oink—*'
'*There an oink—*'
'*Everywhere an oink-oink—*'
'*Old Macdonald had a farm—*'
'*Ee-i-ee-i-oh!*'.

They went through the entire farmyard, including chickens, ducks, turkeys, cows, sheep and (Tim's contribution) elephants, by which time Olive had dried her tears and was smiling again, though a little tremulously. The last verse finished with a trumpeting that could surely have been heard at the top of September Street, if every other house in the row hadn't been making exactly the same kind of noise.

'All right,' Annie said, 'and now let's have some nice carols to finish off with.'

Jess sat down again, breathless, and Keith, who had been recently discovered to possess a soprano voice, began to sing 'Once in Royal David's City'. His voice rose above the others and one by one they fell silent, listening to the sweet young tones. Faces grew abstracted and eyes looked at the carpet or into the fire. Olive's eyes filled with tears again and Jess felt for Frank's hand. He squeezed her fingers.

'I'm not going back,' she whispered to him as the carol came to an end and the others applauded Keith. 'I'm not leaving you again.'

'We'll talk about it tomorrow,' he said. 'Tomorrow. That'll be the best time.'

After that, nobody seemed to want to sing any more. They lolled in chairs or on the floor, leaning back against people's knees. Keith's eyes were closing and Rose was asleep with her head on Ted's knee. Olive and Derek were on the sofa, their hands entwined. Frank and Ted had the two big armchairs and Annie and Jess the smaller ones. Arthur and Mary had gone home soon after supper.

'Well, I think we'd better be getting off home,' Jess said with a yawn. 'It's been a good Christmas, Annie.'

'Well, we had to make it as good as we could, didn't we?' Annie said. 'We don't know where we'll all be this time next year. Our Colin still at sea, likely as not – Betty down on the farm, if she can stand the hard work. And the rest of us—'

'Still here holding the fort,' Frank said stoutly. 'It'll take more than a few bombs to bring us to our knees, Annie. We're not going to let old Hitler beat us, are we?'

'No!' they all shouted, and broke into laughter. And with that and several reminders that next day they would all gather again for tea at number 14, the Budds found their coats and wrapped themselves up for the short walk home.

Jess looked up at the sky. The surly clouds had drifted apart a little and stars were visible between them. With no city lights to dim them they looked large and bright, and so close that she felt she needed only to reach out her fingertips to be able to touch them.

'It's freezing cold,' she said, holding the baby close against her. She was wrapped in blankets and fast asleep. Jess looked down from the stars at her small, sleeping face.

'Your first Christmas,' she said softly. 'Well, my love, it was as good as we could make it. But what'll the next one be like? And what will you remember about Christmas when you grow up?'

Two days after Boxing Day there was a slight lessening of the bitter temperatures. And as if they had been waiting for it, the great clouds sighed and opened their bruised bellies to let the snow fall.

It came softly at first, then gathered power as the rising wind whipped the whirling snowflakes into a maelstrom of icy shards, their feathery softness sharpened like needles by the storm. All day they swirled through the air, coming to rest at last in great pillowy mounds, piled up against walls and fences and turning gardens and allotments into mysterious fairylands. By next morning, the streets were ankle-deep and few vehicles were moving.

Olive was at Derek Harker's house. His parents had gone to South-ampton to visit his married sister, and Derek had invited Olive to tea. She went, knowing that her mother and father would have disapproved had they known Derek was alone in the house. But Derek would be going away soon and they had had so little time together lately. What with the blackout and the bitter cold, it was impossible to go out at night, and indoors there just wasn't the chance of any privacy.

'Mind, I'll have to be home by ten,' she said. 'And – you know what we agreed, Derek.'

He nodded. He knew, but there was no harm in hoping, was there? Girls were famous for changing their minds, after all. And in an empty house, with just the two of them and a cosy fire – well, who knew what might happen?

The truth was that both he and Olive were tired of waiting to get married. They knew he was likely to be going away soon, and both were dreading the separation. Each time they parted, it was more difficult to say goodnight, more difficult to give each other that last kiss. They clung together, achingly aware of each other's bodies, miserably conscious that this might be the last time, that Derek could be called up at a moment's notice. And each time, Olive felt her resolution ebb a little more. Why not? she thought recklessly. Why shouldn't we love each other properly? It'd be Dad's fault if anything happened – he should've let us get married.

But she had never quite dared to say such things to Derek. Instead, she buried her face against his shoulder and held him tightly, unaware of the almost intolerable frustration this was causing him.

Derek, facing not only separation but a total disruption of his life, was almost desperate. To him, the future was like a deep black abyss, an almost unimaginable chaos of tumult, of fear, of killing and being killed. He thought of all he had ever heard about war and especially about the Great

War of 1914–18. The war to end all wars, they had called it – yet here they were, only twenty years later, starting the whole thing over again, with worse to come. And he and all the other young men like him were expected to throw up their whole lives, toss aside all they'd planned and give themselves up for a cause they barely understood. All right, so Hitler was marching across Europe, trampling over everyone and everything in his path, but who had allowed him to get into that position to start with? Politicians, that was who – old men who'd had their day. Wasn't it up to them to put right the wrongs that had been done, without involving people like him and Olive – people who were just starting their lives and had a right to live them as they chose?

Derek's thoughts were bitter. If he had known it was possible, he would have refused to serve. But he had heard about the 'conchies' of the Great War, and knew what had been done to them. Strapped to the wheels of gun carriages, forced into labour, even shot . . . He knew he did not have the courage to face such things and he dared not ask whether it would be the same again. They wanted people to fight. There would be no sympathy for those who thought it was no way to run the world.

His frustration, his bitterness and his fears found their outlet in his feelings for Olive. He lived now for the times when they would be together, when he could hold her in his arms and feel safe. He lived for her touch, her kisses, and he yearned for her loving. He knew that he could not go away without having at least once known what it was to lie in her arms, to feel the ecstasy of making her his. And he knew that Olive longed for it too.

Tonight, with his parents out for the evening and unlikely to return unexpectedly, might be their only chance.

He made his preparations carefully. Plenty of coal and wood in, and the fire alight early so as to warm the room. The Christmas decorations were still up and a few cards stood on the mantelpiece. There was a plate of sandwiches and some Christmas cake for tea and, for later on, some sherry or port and an unopened bottle of cider. He wondered if Olive had ever drunk gin, and put that out too with some orange squash. He brought down his mother's bedside lamp and set it on a low table, then turned out the main light. It made the room look quite different. Then he moved the settee in front of the fire, found some Glenn Miller records to put on the gramophone and checked that there was a packet of fresh needles.

Olive arrived, rather shy and nervous at finding herself alone with Derek in his parents' house. She stamped snow off her boots and came in, taking off her headscarf and shaking out her hair. They looked at each other, remembering the last time they had been alone here, remembering how close they'd come to losing control. What was going to happen tonight?

Olive closed the front door.

'My, it's wild out there!' Her eyes took in the room and she giggled. 'Goodness, you have made it look cosy!'

'Well, we don't often get the chance of an evening on our own.' He helped her off with her coat and kept his hands on her shoulders. 'I thought we'd make the most of it.' He dropped his head and nuzzled the back of her neck.

Olive quivered a little, then moved away. 'And just what d'you mean by that, Derek Harker? You know what you promised.'

'I meant it, Livvy. I won't do anything you don't want me to.' He pulled her into his arms again, hard enough to squeeze the breath out of her. 'But I'm sure you want me to give you a kiss!'

'Derek! *Derek!*' Laughing and protesting, she allowed herself to be kissed and then slid her arms round his neck, winding her fingers in his hair. 'Oh, Derek, it *is* nice to be on our own.'

'So let's enjoy it.' He led her to the settee. The fire was blazing. 'You sit there and I'll pour you a cup of tea. There's plenty to eat, look – I made the sandwiches myself. Well, I couldn't ask Mum to do it, could I? She'd have started to ask awkward questions.'

'Doesn't she know I'm coming then?'

'Does your mum know you're here with me, on our own?'

Olive blushed. 'No. Well, actually she doesn't know I'm here. She thinks I'm over at Iris Bentley's. I thought – well, I thought she might hear your mum and dad weren't here, and since she never actually asked—'

'You didn't tell her. And mine never asked either.' He sat down beside her. 'Don't let's waste time talking about them, Livvy. Let's just think about ourselves tonight. Pretend – let's pretend we're married.'

'Derek—'

'I don't mean that. I mean, just sitting here, looking at the fire and having our tea. Pretend it's our house and we've been married – oh, two or three years. Pretend we've got kids asleep upstairs.' He grinned and Olive blushed again.

'Derek! The things you say.'

'Well, what's wrong with that?' He took a sandwich. 'People do have kids when they get married. We will.'

'Yes, but not yet.' Olive sipped her tea. 'We're not married yet.'

'Nor don't know when we will be,' he said. 'Livvy, can't we get round your dad? I'll be going away soon. We don't know when we're going to be together again.'

'I know.' She looked miserably down at her hands, at the little engagement ring. 'But when I said I'd heard of lots of girls getting married before their boys went off, he said it was just a craze and they'd be sorry for it later. Like he did before. So I knew it'd be no use keeping on about it.'

'But we can't just leave it like that!' Derek took her empty plate and put it on the table. He put his arm round her and cuddled her against him. 'Livvy, it takes time to get married. You can't just walk in and out like buying a pound of sausages. You have to – to give notice of some sort. It takes nearly a month.' He stared at her. 'We've probably left it too late already.'

Olive began to cry.

'Oh, Derek! What are we going to do?'

Derek drew her head down on to his shoulder. He rested his cheek on her hair. If only Olive would agree to let him love her properly. It wouldn't be so bad, not being married, if she'd do that. After all, what difference would marriage actually make to them just now? They wouldn't have anywhere to live, they'd have to stay with either her parents or his – hers, he supposed, since she was the one being left behind. He'd be able to stay with her when he was on leave, all open and above board, that was true – but if she'd just let him love her as he wanted to, it wouldn't really matter that they had to wait. They'd belong to each other and that was what he really wanted. To go away knowing that his love for Olive was safe, that they'd been everything to each other if only for a little while.

It would be something to remember in the long, dark days that lay ahead.

'Don't worry,' he said. 'We'll think of something.'

They sat by the fire, watching the flames and listening to Glenn Miller. After a while, Derek got up and they cleared away the tea things together. They came back to the fire with a glass of gin and orange each, Olive giggling because she had never drunk it before, and Derek began to kiss her.

'I love you, Livvy,' he murmured, his hands moving gently over her body. They had evolved a pattern of permitted caresses. Derek was now allowed to touch Olive's breasts – even, sometimes, to undo her brassière and slip his hands inside. He could caress her anywhere above the waist, but was not allowed to go below it nor to touch her legs. He could kiss her as much as he liked, though Olive was nervous of him kissing her neck in case he left love bites which her father might see.

'Oh, Livvy,' Derek whispered. He had got her brassière off now, as well as her blouse, and she could feel the warmth of the fire on her skin. She shivered and clung to him, not wanting him to see her breasts, but Derek pulled his head down and kissed them, burying his face in their softness.

Olive gasped. Her arms tightened involuntarily about his shoulders. He was half lying over her now and she felt suddenly frightened and tried to push him away, but her efforts were feeble and she knew she didn't really want him to move. It was nice, feeling him there, feeling his body so hard against hers, feeling his lips on her breasts. She looked down at his head and stroked his hair.

Derek moved his head. He kissed her bare shoulders, then trailed his mouth all the way down to her waist. He nuzzled at the waistband of her skirt and Olive shivered again and tried to pull up his head. It was suddenly heavy, immovable and she glanced frantically at the clock.

'Derek – your mum and dad, they'll be back soon. Derek, please—'

'Not yet,' he murmured, lifting himself to kiss her mouth again. 'They won't be back for a long time yet. Oh, Livvy—'

'They will. It's half-past nine. And I've got to be in by ten, you know I have. Derek – please – you promised—' She pulled his head, trying to lift it away from her body, but again her arms were treacherously weak. 'Oh, Derek – Derek . . .'

He looked at her. His eyes were dark, the lids heavy. 'Olive, I love you. You know I do. I can't go away without loving you – I can't. And you feel the same, I know, I can tell. Olive, we'll never get another chance—' But his words were drowned by the sudden shrilling of the telephone.

Derek's house was the only one Olive knew with a telephone. It was needed for business, which was run from the house, but there was an extension indoors as well as in the office. It sounded loud and intrusive in the quiet room and Olive jumped. Derek, more accustomed to it, cursed briefly and went to pick it up.

'Hullo. Yes. Oh, hullo, Dad. What's happened?' He listened for a moment and Olive saw his eyebrows go up. He looked across at her and winked. 'Is it really? Gosh. No, much better not, specially with the blackout. It'd be lethal . . . No, everything's all right here. Yes, I can manage.' He smiled. 'Yes, I'm sure. Don't worry. See you tomorrow then.' He hung up the receiver and his face almost split in a wide, excited grin.

Olive gazed at him. 'Derek? What was that all about?'

'It was Dad,' he said. 'They're stuck over in Southampton. The trains have stopped because of the snow and they can't get home tonight. They're stopping there till morning.' He bounded across to the settee and leapt over the back of it, catching her up in his arms. 'Till *morning!*'

Olive stared at him. She tried to draw away. Panic fluttered like a trapped bird in her breasts. 'Till morning? But – that doesn't make any difference to us.'

'Doesn't it?' He snatched up her jacket and flung it round her shoulders, drawing her into the passage where it was dark. With a quick glance to be sure no light was showing, he pulled open the front door. The wind immediately gusted in their faces, half choking them with snow as if someone had thrown a bucketful directly over them. It caught the door, almost tearing it from its hinges, and ripped through Olive's hair. She felt it lift her skirt and swirl like icy water around her thighs. It struck her naked breasts and she pulled the jacket more tightly about her.

Derek slammed the door again and they stood in the darkness, breathing quickly. Olive could feel him very close. He slid his arms around her, pushing the jacket from her shoulders, and pulled her face round until his lips found hers. She gasped as he ground his body against hers, and felt her own excitement rise and with it, inevitably, her panic.

'Derek! No! I've got to go home—'

'Why? You told me, they don't know you're here.'

'No, but—' His hands were moving over her body, searching and insistent. 'Derek, please—'

'Please what?' he murmured against her ear. 'Please stop? Or please don't stop?' He cradled her breasts in both hands, leaning over to kiss her. 'Olive, this is the only chance we'll ever get – we can't let it go. You can't say no – not now. You can't.'

'They'll expect me back. I've got to be in by ten, you know that.'

'But you can't go out in this weather. You've seen what it's like. They won't expect you to – not in the blackout and everything.' He was holding her close again, moving his body against hers, and she moaned at the feel of it. One hand strayed down her buttocks, slid down her thigh and pulled up her skirt. She felt his fingertips on the bare strip of thigh between stocking-top and knickers. 'They'll think you've stayed with this – what's her name? Iris? Won't they think that? Wouldn't anyone, on a night like this?'

Olive was almost past speaking. Her head on Derek's shoulder, she whimpered as his fingers explored further, inserting themselves delicately into her knickers and stroking with the utmost gentleness along the deepest crease of her thigh. Her legs weak, she clung and leaned against him, squirming as he found a sensitivity she had not known existed. When he kissed her, her mouth was slack under his, her lips parted, and she felt her heart jerk and begin to pound rapidly in her breast.

'Stay with me, Livvy,' he muttered against her throat. 'Stay with me tonight. We'll never get another chance like this.'

'Derek—' She must, she knew, make one last effort. And if this one failed, as she already knew it must, she could make no more. 'Derek – you promised—'

'I promised not to do anything you didn't want me to.' He moved slightly away, but his arm was still about her and his fingers were still stroking, gently, firmly and insistently. 'Tell me you don't want me to, Livvy, and I'll stop.' He kissed her again. 'Tell me you don't want to – and mean it – and I'll stop straight away.'

There was a breathless pause. And Olive knew that it was too late. It had been too late from the moment she had stepped through the door.

'Oh, Derek,' she breathed, and turned her face for his kiss. 'Oh, Derek, love me. Please, please love me . . .'

The year ended almost without comment. Portsmouth was swathed in a blanket of snow, its traffic stilled, its lights dimmed. The New Year celebrations that normally filled the Guildhall Square with revellers were forbidden, the sirens of vessels in the harbour, which would normally have sounded at midnight, were silenced.

'It's as if we're all glad to say goodbye to 1939 but no better pleased to see 1940 instead,' Jess said, getting ready for bed. She and Frank had thought about stopping up and toasting the new year, as they usually did, but it seemed like a bad joke. 'The only good thing that happened to us in 1939 was Maureen,' she said, bending over the cot.

Frank looked at her. She was wearing a nightdress she'd made herself, white with some bits of lace at the neck. It had always been his favourite. He felt his heartbeat quicken.

He slid into bed beside her and slipped his arms around her, cradling her against his shoulder, thinking of the months she had been away, when he had come lonely night after night to this empty bed, cold without Jess's warm body. The past week had been like a honeymoon again, rediscovering each other after their parting.

A honeymoon, he thought with amusement, and us married for thirteen, fourteen years!

'What are you laughing at?' Jess asked, and he turned and smiled at her.

'Us. No, not us – I'm just laughing for happiness. I'm happy that you're staying an extra week. I'm happy that you're going to be here while I'm at work and every evening when I come home. And I'm happy you're going to be in bed at night.'

Jess laughed softly. 'Oh, you! You're like all the other men. You never think of anything else.'

'So I'm normal.' He squeezed her against him. 'And so are you, Jess –

thank the Lord. So – why don't we prove it, eh?' He kissed her and his hands and body began the pattern of love-making that was so familiar to them both. Each knew all the places to touch, to caress, to linger over and to savour. Each knew the other's response and when to proceed, when to hold back. And, at the end, each knew just how to bring the other to that soaring, satisfying climax that had reinforced their love so regularly for the past fourteen years.

Afterwards, Frank fell asleep at once. But Jess, in the few moments before she too closed her eyes, lay for a few moments listening to the house breathe.

It seemed so long since her family had been all together under the same roof. In the next room, Tim and Keith lay curled up in the old iron bunks, a web of cotton stretched across the ceiling where they had fixed up the small wooden aeroplanes they had carved with Reg Corner. In the room beneath, Rose lay sleeping in the Put-u-Up. Beside her, baby Maureen slumbered peacefully, one fist crumpled under her chin.

Soon they would be parted again and there would be fresh tears to shed. But for tonight, number 14 April Grove was a family house once more and she felt as though it had wrapped its arms about them all and was keeping them safe.

God keep them safe, she thought as she drifted into her dreams. God keep them all safe, wherever they might be.

10

The weather grew steadily worse. The day after the boys and Rose went back to Bridge End for the start of school, there was a blizzard. The snow blocked roads, stopped traffic and brought down telephone lines. The water in Langstone Harbour froze and people skated on the ice. For three days, no electric trains ran between Portsmouth, London and Brighton. Twice rain fell and froze immediately, coating ground, walls and trees with a glittering layer of ice. The city was in chaos, with almost all services no longer functioning and the roads turning rapidly to ice-rinks.

'It's as bad as 1881,' Arthur told Jess when she went round to make sure her parents were all right. 'My, that was a winter and no mistake! Railways blocked – the trains were just running into mountains of snow and getting stuck in it. There was seven foot of snow in Stubbington Lane, down North End, and a huge drift out at Portscreek. And Hilsea Pond was buried and gone.'

'Well, let's hope this one isn't going to be so bad,' Jess said, looking out of the window, but the sullen clouds seemed to snarl at her and she shivered and turned back. 'How are you managing for coal?'

'Oh, we've got enough so long as we're careful,' her mother said. 'Mind, there's not much about, is there? Some people have run out already, having to use the electric. But that's not much good when there's a power-cut!'

'I hope there's not one tonight,' Arthur observed. 'I want to listen to *ITMA.*'

Jess went back home, pushing Maureen's pram with difficulty along the slippery streets. She'd been planning to go to the sales at the Landport Drapery Bazaar and McIlroys today with Annie but the snow had stopped the buses and Jess didn't think many people would have managed to get down to Commercial Road anyway. That meant that those who did make it would have got all the best bargains, she reflected.

Well, it couldn't be helped. And it was time now to start Frank's supper. With only the two of them she'd started cooking in the evening, like Annie did. It meant he came in to a good hot meal and she could pack up his box afterwards so he could take another helping for dinner tomorrow.

Tonight she was making stew with dumplings. She'd managed to get a nice piece of shin and some kidney at the butcher's at the top of the street and it had been simmering on top of the stove all afternoon, along with some onions, carrots and turnips out of the garden. She'd made a bread-

and-butter pudding to go with it – not that it had seen much butter, but it would be hot and sweet and filling, and that was what Frank needed.

She was more than ever thankful that she'd decided to stay home for a few extra days and even glad of the bitter weather which was keeping her for longer. Annie had been good to him, but there was no getting away from it, he'd lost weight and he looked tired. Annie's meals weren't enough for a man doing heavy work. Jess didn't think they were enough for Ted either, standing up in all weathers on the bridge of the *Ferry King*, and she knew he sometimes got one of the lads to fetch him a penn'orth of chips or a pasty from the kiosk on the Hard.

Ted looked tired too. He hadn't said much, but he'd let drop a few things and Jess had gathered that he hated taking the ferryboat across the harbour in the blackout. She wasn't surprised. It must be nerve-racking, trying to feel your way across the water with buoys and moored boats floating about, more or less invisible, not to mention other ships going in and out.

'They're telling people to take cod-liver oil to help them see at night,' she said to Frank, reading the *Evenings News* after supper. 'Does it really help, d'you think?'

He shrugged. 'I suppose it might do. Can't do any harm, anyway. It's good for you, isn't it? Prevents colds, so they say.'

'Oh yes. I've always given it to the children when they were babies. I heard carrots were good too.'

'What, for babies?'

'No, silly – for helping you to see at night. Oh, look – Anna Neagle's on at the Odeon. In *Nurse Edith Cavell*.'

'My God,' Frank said, 'isn't there enough war without going to see it at the pictures?'

'I suppose so. I just like Anna Neagle.' Jess put down the newspaper and sighed. 'How long d'you think this is going to go on for, Frank?'

'How long's what going on for?' He was engrossed in the *Daily Express*.

'This war. I mean, it's so queer. We were told there'd be bombing right from the start and there hasn't been any at all. What's he waiting for? And there's more and more soldiers going over to France and nothing much seems to be happening there either. The Navy seems to be getting the worst of it so far.'

'They are.' Frank spent his days making or mending for ships. The boiler-shop was like an inferno, with furnaces going full blast day and night, and a never-ceasing racket of metal being hammered, drilled and welded. 'But I'll tell you why there's nothing happening on the ground or in the air, Jess, and you've only got to look out of the window to see it for yourself. It's too bloody cold. I mean, if it's like this here it must be like it over there, mustn't it? Stands to reason. They're just waiting for a thaw, that's all.'

Jess pursed her lips and nodded. It made sense. She remembered another piece of news. 'Derek Harker's gone.'

'Gone? Called up, d'you mean?'

'That's right. He came round to say goodbye to Annie and Ted last night. Olive is in a right old state about it, crying and going on like he's been killed already.' Jess stopped and bit her lip. 'He thinks he's going to France. And Peggy Shaw's in a panic about their Bob now, she thinks he'll be off any minute too.'

'Well,' Frank said, 'I think he probably will. They're getting themselves into position, see. Once the weather starts to get a bit better they'll start. And then we'd all better keep our heads down. And you'd better get back to Bridge End before it starts.'

Jess said nothing. The thought of bombs dropping on Portsmouth – perhaps on April Grove, on number 14 itself – made her feel sick with fear. But she still wished she could stay with Frank. We ought to be together, she thought miserably. It's not right, being apart like this, for months, perhaps even for years.

Upstairs, the baby began to cry and she got up to go to her. If it wasn't for you, I'd never have gone away at all, she thought, gathering the damp little bundle up in her arms. But you can't be blamed, can you? It's not your fault you were born at such a time. And we wouldn't be without you now.

Sighing, she went back downstairs. Perhaps it had never been easy for women, trying to be all things to all people, keeping the family going, to be both mother and wife. And in war, it was easy for nobody.

As Frank would say, everyone had to make sacrifices.

Olive was crying into her pillow and feeling a different kind of fear.

She had said goodbye to Derek this morning at the builder's yard. He'd come in, wearing his stiff new uniform, and shaken hands all round with the men, and then walked out with her and his father to the gate. They'd stood, the three of them, looking awkwardly at each other.

'You've seen your mother?' John Harker said at last, though it was difficult to see how Derek could have got out of the house without seeing her.

'Yes. She's a bit upset.'

John nodded. 'I'll go in for a bit. Make her a cup of tea.' He glanced at Olive. 'Or maybe you could do that. Women are better together at times like this.'

Olive was biting her lip, fighting back her own tears. She blinked hard and nodded. She would be quite glad not to have to go straight back into the office.

'Well, cheerio then,' Derek said at last, and shook hands with his father. He turned to Olive, 'Bye, love.'

Olive looked up at him. Her mouth was trembling uncontrollably. She wanted to fling her arms around him, hold him tightly against her as she'd done last night, keep him with her by force. She could not believe that he was standing in front of her now, still within touching distance, and that in a few minutes he would turn and walk away. When would she be able to touch him again? When would she see him again? What would she do if he never came back . . . ?

Derek dropped his case and put his arms round her and she clung to him, the tears flowing. For a long moment he held her close, and then he turned her face to his and kissed her on the mouth.

'Keep your pecker up, girl,' he said softly. 'I'll be back.'

'Oh, Derek,' was all she could say. 'Oh, Derek, Derek . . .'

Gently, he unwound her arms from about his neck and bent to give her a last brief kiss. Then he let her go, picked up his case and turned. She reached out both hands but he was already marching firmly away, and she stood there, leaning forward slightly, her hands held out towards him as if begging him to return while the tears streamed unchecked, unnoticed, down her cheeks.

'Go inside, girl,' John Harker said. 'Go and have a cup of tea with the wife. I reckon she'll appreciate it just now.'

That had been their final goodbye, taken in public with most of the men looking on. But as Olive lay in her bed that night, fresh tears soaking her pillow, she was thinking of their real goodbye – the one they had shared last night. And with her grief there mingled a terror that had nothing to do with war.

Since the night of the snowstorm, two days after Christmas, Derek and Olive had taken every opportunity to make love. As Derek said, once they'd started it seemed daft to stop – and he didn't want to stop. Olive didn't either. She spent her days dreaming of the night before and looking forward to the next one. Whenever she remembered the way he'd touched her, the way he'd kissed and caressed her, the way he'd finally come inside her, she felt her stomach tingle, as if someone had passed a tiny, fizzing electrical current through her body. It was a feeling she liked. She called it up as often as she could, by thinking and remembering.

They were never again able to enjoy the luxury of that first night. Olive remembered the warmth of the room, the flickering firelight, the softness of the big settee. Still shaking with nerves, she had allowed Derek to undress her and lain naked before him, the fire casting an apricot glow over her smooth skin. She had watched as he began to pull off his own clothes, then turned her eyes away in embarrassment.

'No need to be shy, Livvy,' he said. 'Look. See what an effect you have on me.'

She looked and blushed scarlet as she saw what he meant. 'But surely it's too big!' she said. 'It'll never—'

'Oh yes, it will,' he said with a grin, and stretched himself beside her on the sofa. She gasped as their bodies touched, his chest rough and hairy against her tender breasts, his flat stomach hard against the soft cushion of hers. His thighs were hard too, long and muscular as he twined his legs about hers, and his hands trembled a little as they moved almost reverently over her smooth skin.

He hadn't hurried her. He had taken his time, bringing every part of her to life with his kisses and with his touch. Here, the brush of his fingertips was as gentle as the brush of a feather; there, it was firm and decisive, leaving no doubt as to his confidence. As Olive's fears fell away his touch became more intimate, more demanding, until the pressure of his fingers had her twisting and crying out in his arms. Almost, she wanted him to stop. It was unbearable, it was too much, she couldn't go on feeling like this, she would be driven crazy . . . But Derek continued, his own breathing quickening as he murmured against her ear and held her close with his other arm.

'Livvy . . . Livvy, my sweet girl, you're lovely, you're beautiful . . . oh, Livvy, I've wanted you so much. I want you to be mine, mine . . . I want to go away knowing you're mine. Mine. Mine.' He was rearing above her now, thrusting into her with an urgency he could not hold back. Olive lay flat, staring up at him, but his head was flung back and he saw her no longer. What did he see? What did he feel? Her wild thoughts careered and tumbled through her mind as she held his shoulders and braced herself. He was pushing hard now, hard . . . it was hurting, hurting, hurting . . . and then there was a small tearing sensation, a sudden pain and a feeling of being given something she had wanted, needed always, and never ever understood the wanting.

Derek quivered and seemed to regain control. He looked down at her and she saw the darkness of his eyes. His face was almost stern, taut with emotion, and she reached up tentatively to touch his cheek. He leaned down and kissed her, and with the touch passion flared again, leaping through them so that they both gasped and clung to each other. Olive felt his tongue on her lips and in her mouth, and her mind reeled. She clutched his shoulders, lifted herself towards him and twined her legs about his body. And she felt Derek's stillness break in a fury of desire, a desire that pounded through him, a desire he had no choice but to fulfil, a desire that sliced through the last vestige of her fear and defeated it for ever.

Derek cried out and held himself above her, tense as a steel rod. And then he collapsed on to her body, moaning and breathing hard, and Olive put her arms around his shoulders and held him, moving her hands on his back almost as if she comforted him in some desperate extremity.

Later, they went upstairs and there, holding her close in his narrow bed, Derek made love to her again, differently this time, more slowly, luxuriating in each small sensation, savouring the steady rise of passion, until they were once more caught up in its tumult and strained together as if endeavouring to merge their bodies, to become one being, one world, one total universe.

'When we're married and this war is over,' Derek said, in the moment before he fell asleep, 'we'll be able to do that whenever we feel like it.'

He would have felt like it again in the morning, but Olive woke in a panic, imagining his parents at the door, and hers wondering all night where she was. Would they believe she'd stayed with Iris? Were they on their way there now, to find her? She ran naked down the stairs to collect her clothes, saw the chaos they had left last night – the settee pulled up before the fire, plates and glasses on the floor. Derek would have to see to that. She scrambled into her clothes and he appeared at the door and came over to take her in his arms.

'Don't worry, Livvy. It's early yet. I'll clear this lot up.'

Olive looked up at him, trembling. A new fear had struck her now and she wondered how she could possibly have forgotten. 'Derek – suppose there's a baby?'

'There won't be,' he assured her easily. 'It hardly ever happens the first time.'

'But it might—'

'No. It just doesn't. It'll be all right, Livvy. And I'll get something for next time – a french letter. You'll be all right.' He kissed her lingeringly. 'It was marvellous,' he murmured. 'You're marvellous, Livvy. And you're mine now.'

She leaned against him. 'I was anyway.' But she couldn't regret what had happened. 'I love you, Derek.'

'I love you. And now – you'd better go.' He pulled down the blackout curtain and looked out at the garden. 'Wow, it certainly did snow! You're going to leave your footprints all the way.' He laughed at her look of alarm. 'Don't worry – no one's going to trace them back here. Why should they?'

Olive had walked home through the snow in a dream. And she had stayed in that dream ever since. But now Derek was gone and the dream ended, and she feared that it could be all too easily replaced with a nightmare.

Was it true? she wondered as she lay weeping into her pillow after Derek had left in his khaki uniform.

Was it really true that you couldn't get pregnant the first time?

Food rationing began on 8 January and everyone got out the ration books they had been issued with and stared at them, trying to make sense of the little squares and the numbers on them.

'It's just butter, sugar and bacon so far,' Jess said. 'Four ounces of butter and bacon, and twelve ounces of sugar! Where's that going to go? And it surely won't be long before meat's rationed. You can hardly get any now, but I bet some people aren't going without. I saw Mrs Carter getting a big parcel from Hines's yesterday, he had it under the counter for her. She said it was some sewing his wife had done for her, but Mrs Hines can't be much of a needle-woman if she pricks her fingers that badly!'

Most of the young men were away now. Bob had gone off the same day as Derek and both were in the same unit. The wireless, which was the country's mainstay for information, was now broadcasting messages from someone called Lord Haw-Haw, who could be heard by switching to Hamburg radio after the Nine o'clock News. Lord Haw-Haw, whose real name wasn't known, would introduce himself with a plummy 'Jairmany calling, Jairmany calling' and spent a quarter of an hour giving more detailed news and sneering at the British. 'Where is your *Ark Royal* today?' he would demand. 'Ask your government. She has been sunk, along with many more of your ships.'

'I hate that man,' Jess said to Annie. 'I won't listen to him. If he's really a lord he's a traitor.'

'I don't believe he's a lord – he just talks that way. Ted says he's a traitor anyway, and ought to be shot. But he does seem to know what's going on, and he tells us more than our own people do.'

'That's if it's all true. The trouble is, you don't know what is and what isn't. That stuff about the *Ark* – I mean, we know that's nonsense. He's just trying to frighten us.'

'Well, he's taken on a big job, then,' Annie said staunchly. 'He's not going to frighten us in a hurry.'

These days, she was being determinedly cheerful, though she was worried about Olive. The girl was pale and had lost weight. She picked at her food and sat about looking miserable in the evenings. She spent most of her time writing long letters to Derek and refused to go out dancing or to the pictures.

'You ought to have a bit of fun,' Annie told her. 'It doesn't do you any good, moping about the way you do. And it's not helping Derek.'

'Don't keep on at me, Mum,' Olive said snappily. 'I don't feel like going out. I don't have to, do I?'

Annie looked at her closely. 'Are you all right, Livvy?'

'All right? Of course I'm all right. I've just had to send my feller off to war, that's all, and don't know if I'll ever see him again, but that's nothing to worry about, is it?'

'There's a lot of girls in the same boat,' Annie said quietly. 'And young wives with children—'

'And I could have been Derek's wife if you and Dad had let me!' Olive burst out. 'It wouldn't be so bad, if you'd just let us get married first.'

Annie stared at her. 'I hope there's no reason why you should have got married, our Olive.'

Olive blushed scarlet. 'No, of course there isn't. What reason could there be?' Her eyes, red from nights of weeping, mocked her mother. 'Only that we love each other and want to be married, that's all. But you and Dad wouldn't care about that, would you?'

She turned and flung herself out of the room and Annie heard her footsteps stumbling upstairs and then the creak of the bed as she threw herself down on it. She'd be up there crying till supper-time now, and then only come down to collect a cup of cocoa and take it back up with her. No wonder she was getting thin.

Annie sighed and went out to the kitchen to start peeling potatoes. She was still nagged by the thought of that night just after Christmas, when Olive hadn't come home. She'd said she was round at Iris Bentley's and had stayed the night when the snow came on, but was that true? She'd done it before, and Annie could have found out easily enough by mentioning it – just casually – to Mrs Bentley, but she didn't want to to that. To tell the truth, she thought, she didn't want to know.

She remembered the argument she'd had with Ted over Olive wearing make-up. She'd said then, if we don't let her do things she'll do them anyway, behind our backs. And told him how she'd done just the same when her father had forbidden her to go dancing with Ted himself. She'd smuggled her dancing shoes out in a bag, pretending she was going round to a friend's for the evening – just like Olive saying she was going to Iris's – and her dad had never known.

Nor had Ted until she'd told him, but it made him realise that he had to let Olive grow up. It hadn't been enough to persuade him to let her marry Derek, though.

Annie sliced the potatoes into thin, neat lengths for chips. Olive had wanted badly to get married and they'd said no. They'd wanted her to wait. But in times like these, no one wanted to wait. Life was too uncertain. They wanted happiness when it was within reach, not postponed to a time that might never come.

Would she and Ted have wanted to wait?

Tim and Keith woke on the first morning back at Bridge End to find the countryside swathed in a heavy white blanket of snow. They stared out of their bedroom window, marvelling at the shape of the trees and bushes, and then dragged on their clothes and rushed downstairs.

'It's snowed! It's snowed!'

'You don't say.' Reg grinned at them. The kitchen was warm and cosy and they could smell bacon frying. The shortages in the towns and cities had not yet reached the country. Edna was stirring a saucepan full of porridge and she smiled at them. She and Reg had missed the boys over Christmas.

'I suppose you want to go out and play in it. Sit up to the table, then. You're not going out without something hot inside you.'

The boys watched as she ladled porridge into four bowls and then dug a spoon into the golden syrup tin. She poured a gleaming pool of syrup on top of three bowls and handed them round. The fourth she gave to Keith, who took his own syrup and trailed it round the top of the porridge in circles.

'Don't forget you've got something to do before you start building snowmen and getting into snowball fights,' she said. 'You've got to go round and see Alan and Wendy Atkinson.'

Tim made a face. Mrs Atkinson had come down to number 14 the day before he and Keith had come back, bringing a parcel for them to give her children. She had already posted their Christmas presents but wanted to send them something else, to make up for not having had them home for Christmas. The parcel contained fruit and sweets, with a few groceries for the ladies who were looking after them.

'Do they live near you?' Edna asked. 'I thought they'd gone home for Christmas.'

'They live up the top of our street,' Keith said. 'In a greengrocer's shop.'

'They don't live in the shop, silly,' Tim corrected him. 'They live over the top of it. In a flat.'

'Well, Wendy's in my class at school,' Keith retorted, as if that clinched it.

'Never mind that,' Edna said. 'Did Wendy and Alan go home for Christmas or did they go somewhere else?'

'They stayed here,' Tim told her. 'Their grandad died just before we went home. Their mum's been ill too. That's why they couldn't go back.'

Edna glanced at her husband. 'I don't know what to do. You know what the Woddises are like. They'd be so annoyed if they thought I was interfering.'

'But if you're worried about the kids . . .' Reg said. 'I mean, if they're all right there's no harm done. But if they're not . . .'

'That's right,' she said. 'I'd never forgive myself if . . .'

There was a short silence, then Reg said, 'Kids come first, before offending old ladies.'

Tim and Keith listened, only half understanding the conversation. The Corners were worried about Alan and Wendy, they could see that, but why?

'D'you think they've been kidnapped?' Tim enquired at length.

The Corners gave him a startled glance.

'Kidnapped? Why should we think that?'

Tim shrugged. To him, it seemed obvious. Edna had asked him if the Atkinsons had gone home for Christmas, so they couldn't be in the village. What other conclusion was there?

Edna seemed to understand what he was thinking and smiled. 'No, Tim, I don't think they've been kidnapped. But I'm a bit worried about them all the same. They didn't go to church all over Christmas and they didn't go to the evacuees' party in the church hall. And nobody seems to have seen them since school finished. I just wondered if they were ill.' She hesitated, then said, 'Ask to see them when you take the parcel round. Ask them over to tea.'

Tim frowned, remembering the time he had gone to the Woddis sisters' house with his mother. The old lady with the mole frightened him and he didn't much like her sister either. He didn't want to go there again, especially on his own. But he knew this would be difficult to explain to the Corners.

'All right,' he said unenthusiastically. 'So long as Keith comes too. And then can we make a snowman and have a snowball fight?'

Edna smiled. 'Of course you can.'

The two boys set out half an hour later, wrapped up in coats and scarves, their wellingtons packed with as many pairs of socks as could be squeezed in and hats made from the tops of a pair of old socks of Reg's, cut down and sewn up at one end.

'We're soldiers,' Tim said, 'spying round the enemies' camp. Our leader's held hostage and we've got to get essential supplies to him or he'll die.'

'What's essential supplies?' Keith asked, clutching Mrs Atkinson's parcel against his chest.

'Food and gold and stuff like that. A rope ladder to escape with.' Tim had a parcel too. 'Anyway, we must make sure nobody sees us approaching the enemy camp.'

Keith looked doubtfully at their footprints. The snow was almost up to the tops of their wellingtons and they were making deep pits in its smooth, sparkling surface. They seemed to be the first people to make their way down the lane leading to the Victorian house this morning.

'Will we have to run away?' he asked a little fearfully. 'They won't shoot at us, will they?'

'They might.' Tim always threw himself wholeheartedly into such play, forgetting that Keith could not always sort out imagination from reality. 'I expect they've got guns trained on us at this very moment.'

The lane was silent. Even the birds seemed to have stopped moving and the snow muffled all sound from the village. Cattle had been taken in from the fields and all around the boys was an expanse of white. It was as if nobody else existed.

Tim was struck by the idea. Half abandoning his earlier scenario, he announced that they were in an unknown world completely covered in snow.

'Nobody knows what kinds of creatures live here,' he said. 'Probably monsters. We've got to rescue our leader before they freeze our world too.'

'What'll happen if we're caught?'

'We'll be frozen too. Like statues made of ice.'

They were almost at the house now. They stopped and stared at it. It looked dark and forbidding, its roof frowning over the windows.

'D'you think there's ghosts there?' Keith asked in a whisper. 'D'you think it's haunted?'

'Bound to be.' Tim crouched and then sprang up with a weird howl. He spread his arms and capered round his brother. 'Whoo-oo! I'm a ghost – I've come to hau-aunt you!'

Keith squealed and ducked away. 'Don't! It's horrible!'

Tim giggled, but there was a note of hysteria in his giggle. He was uneasily aware that he was almost as nervous as Keith at the idea of going right up to the house, summoning one of the sisters to the door and demanding to see Alan and Wendy. They hadn't let his mother see them, after all – why should they let him and Keith? And whatever Reg and Edna said, he still thought it possible that something had happened to the two Atkinsons. If not kidnapped, they might be kept in the house by force. Or worse . . .

Stories of children being eaten came into his mind and he felt sick.

They were almost at the house now and Keith stopped at the gate, looking nervously up at the dark hedge surrounding the house and garden. Anything might lurk behind there, he thought, and looked at his brother.

Tim returned his look. His stories had been intended to boost his own courage but now he felt it ebb away from him. He stared at the gate again and it looked forbiddingly back. The thought of opening it, entering the cold shadowed world beyond and then actually pulling on that stiff, old-fashioned bellpull brought a tremble to his lips. He wished he hadn't started to talk about enemy soldiers and monsters. He wished Keith hadn't talked about ghosts and most of all he wished he'd never thought about children being eaten.

'Go on,' he said to Keith. 'Open the gate.'

'You,' Keith said, shrinking back.

'You open the gate and I'll ring the bell.' Let's just get it over with, he thought. Let's get out of here and back to Reg and Edna.

Keith pushed the gate and it swung open slowly, creaking loudly.

It was the creak that did it. That and the sight of a pale face pressed against the window. It was Alan, his nose squashed flat as a pig's, but neither boy recognised him. For, worse still, there was someone behind him – a tall, indistinct figure, draped with dark, flowing clothes, that loomed waveringly like a shadow in water: a more realistically supernatural figure than any Tim could mimic.

With squeals of pure terror, they dropped the parcels on the path and turned to run. With the snow tugging at their boots and hampering every step, they lurched panic-stricken from the garden and along the lane. Slithering and sliding, occasionally falling full length in the snow, they ran along the lane and scrambled across the stile to cross the fields, not stopping until they were well out of sight of the lonely Victorian house and its cold, unhappy occupants and could see the first comforting glimpse of smoke from the Corners' chimneys.

By this time they were slightly ashamed of their panic. They glanced sideways at each other and grinned a little, then began to giggle. The sight of Alan's face, pressed piglike against the glass, struck them as hilariously funny and the glimpse of Miss Eleanor, towering behind him like a wavering shadow, as deliciously spooky. Pushing each other, snorting and holding their stomachs in exaggerated laughter, they staggered up the garden path, which Reg had by now cleared of snow, and tumbled breathless into the kitchen.

'And are Alan and Wendy all right, then?' Edna asked. 'Did they like their presents? When are they coming to tea?'

The two boys looked at each other guiltily.

'We didn't actually see them,' Tim admitted. 'But we left the presents.'

'Weren't they in?' Edna looked surprised. 'They must have gone out very early, then. We'll have to ask them another day.' She handed the boys a mug of cocoa each. 'Drink that and then you can go out and help Reg chop some wood. And then you can make a start on the snowman.'

The bitter winter continued and, with it, the war. The Navy were still in the forefront; on 19 January, three British submarines, the *Seahorse*, the *Starfish* and the *Undine*, were reported lost. The local weekly paper, the *Hampshire Telegraph and Post*, described them as having been engaged in 'particularly hazardous service' and published a list of the men still missing. Others were claimed to have been rescued by the Germans and would be kept as prisoners – bringing comfort to their families that they were still alive but fresh anxiety about their treatment and welfare.

'Cliff Barker from round June Close was on one of those subs,' Peggy Shaw told Annie when they met in the street. She and Bert had just had a letter from Bob, who was 'somewhere in France' with Derek. The two families kept each other in touch, sharing news and letters as they arrived.

Still talking about Cliff Barker, Peggy went on, 'His mother doesn't know whether to be thankful he's saved or worried sick about what they're doing to him. You hear such stories! Someone told me they're torturing the prisoners and using them in experiments.'

'They wouldn't do that, surely,' Annie said. 'I mean, they're not allowed to. They'd be in trouble when the war's over.'

'Not if they win the war,' Bert said with grim cynicism. 'Who's to take them to court then?'

'They're not going to win, Bert Shaw,' Peggy said sharply, 'and don't let me hear you say so.'

Graham had gone to sea and Betty was still waiting for her call-up papers from the WLA and looking forward to becoming a farmer's girl.

'Mind, I don't know how she'll stand up to the work,' Annie remarked. 'She turns dizzy if Ted asks her to hold a trowel. But she's set on it and it's war work, so what can you do?'

'It's better than going in the Services, anyway,' Peggy said. 'You wouldn't credit what those ATS girls get up to, in and out of pubs after the soldiers. And I don't suppose the Wrens are much better. Well, the temptation's there all the time, isn't it, with all those sailors about. No, I think your Betty's better off on the land.'

Annie nodded, but she was more worried about Olive. The girl was no better but it was difficult to tell whether she was just moping over her Derek or whether there was some other reason for her pale, miserable face.

There were more children in the city now. Tired of life in the country and believing that Hitler did not, after all, intend to bomb Britain, the evacuees were drifting back home. With only a few schools to go to and nobody to ensure they attended, they formed gangs and roamed the streets. Micky Baxter, from number 10, was leader of one of the gangs and the rest of the community looked on him with disfavour.

'They're up to no good, that lot,' Frank said darkly. 'I reckon it's them been over the allotments, trampling about all over the gardens. Just because there's snow on the ground don't mean there's nothing to worry about underneath. Half my cabbages have been broken down and two black-currant bushes knocked about. I'll knock them about, if I catch them at it!'

'They've got nothing to do, that's their trouble,' Jess commented. 'The authorities ought to open more schools.'

More and more people were demanding that the schools be reopened, as they brought their children home from the country. When their own school at Copnor Road reopened, Jess suggested once again that Rose and the boys should come back, but Frank firmly vetoed the idea.

'I still think we're going to be bombed. This winter's holding everything up – even Hitler seems to have decided against any invasion. But as soon as spring comes – mark my words, there'll be action on all fronts. Anyway, the boys and Rose are getting some schooling at least, where they are. I don't want 'em coming home and getting mixed up with Micky Baxter and his lot.'

Jess had to admit that he was right, especially when they heard that Micky and a gang of other boys, none of them aged over twelve, had marched into a jeweller's shop one day brandishing a gun. It was a pistol left over from the 1914–18 war, kept carelessly lying about by the father of one of the boys, but it was Micky who carried it and waved it in the face of the terrified girl behind the counter. Fortunately, at that moment, the manager came out of the inner room, grabbed Micky by the wrist so that he dropped the gun, and held him while his assistant rang the police. The other boys had fled, but were soon caught and the whole gang brought before the juvenile court.

'Probation!' Frank exclaimed in disgust when he read the report in the *Evening News*. 'They ought to be sent away to an approved school and taught a lesson.'

'There aren't any approved schools now,' Jess said. 'They've all been requisitioned too.'

Frank snorted. 'What sort of world are we building up? We're sending decent young men like Bob Shaw and our Colin off to fight and be killed, and meanwhile the likes of Micky Baxter run wild and turn into criminals. It's crazy.'

'I've always thought so,' she said. 'The whole world's gone crazy.'

By the end of January, everyone was caught up in a new fever. The national waste campaign was under way and as well as exhorting people to 'dig for victory' and reminding them that 'careless talk costs lives' there were posters appealing for all kinds of household waste. Paper and rags were wanted for pulping, bones were needed for fertilizer and kitchen waste for pigswill. One afternoon, Annie came down October Street to find men cutting off the iron railings from the low walls in front of the houses, and was told they were wanted for ships and tanks. Even old saucepans, fire-irons and bedsteads were needed, nothing was too small.

And still there were no bombs. The barrage balloons still floated in quiet skies. And more children came back from the countryside.

Molly Atkinson, who had not seen her children since they went away, was almost at her wits' end.

'I've got to see them,' she said to Dave. 'It's February – they've been away since the beginning of September. Six months! They'll have forgotten us!'

'They won't. Children don't forget their parents.'

'But they'll be missing us so much,' she said, her eyes filling with the tears that came so readily these days. 'They must wonder why we've never been to see them.'

Dave sighed. 'I know. I miss them as much as you do, Molly. But you know how impossible it's been. First you were ill, then you had that fall, then Dad died . . . And the weather's been too bad for travelling. You've never pulled up since the pleurisy you had. You can't go off on a train that might take hours to get there and be freezing cold as well. You know what the railway's been like these past few weeks.'

Molly nodded. There had been numerous complaints to the Railway Executive about train delays, most of which had been excused on the grounds that the blackout had made the loading of goods slow and difficult. There were also frequent unexpected arrivals of fresh food at ports, which must be distributed as quickly as possible, and constant troop movements.

'If only I knew the children were all right,' she said miserably. 'I know we get letters from Wendy, and Miss Woddis wrote thanking us for the groceries and saying the children were well – but I want to see for myself.'

'And so you will,' Dave said. 'As soon as the weather gets better. We'll make a special trip out there, and maybe bring them home for a few days if it's still quiet.'

Molly knew that once the children were home she would never be able to let them go again, but she didn't say so. She stared out of the window at the snow which lay about the streets, piled up in the gutters in huge frozen mounds. It was grey and dirty now, whitened every now and then by a fresh snowfall. Once it did begin to thaw the streets would be running with water.

I wish I'd never sent them away, she thought. There was no need for them to go. They could have been here all the time, perfectly safe. It's not right for little children to be taken away from their mothers.

If only she knew for certain that they were all right . . .

Before the end of February, however, there was cause for celebration in April Grove when the *Exeter* finally arrived home from the South Atlantic. With her sister ship the *Ajax*, she steamed into a harbour still half frozen over, with grey skies threatening yet more snow, but the men aboard her cared nothing for the weather, and neither did the families who thronged the beaches to watch the ships appear and cheered them in. The sailors were fêted again when they marched through the streets of London, smart and proud as the Navy always was, to be given lunch at the Guildhall by the Lord Mayor himself. Headed by a band playing tunes of victory, they strode through crowds of cheering people and as Colin said when he was eventually back in Portsmouth and could toast his toes in front of a roaring fire, it was all a far cry from the Falkland Islands and the River Plate.

'Seems a long time ago now,' Colin said, accepting a cup of tea from his mother. Annie was waiting on him hand and foot, almost unable to let him out of her sight. 'But I'll never forget seeing that ship blow up. I mean, we knew by then what was going to happen – but it was a tremendous sight all the same. And a bit sad, somehow.'

'But what happened?' Jess asked. 'Why did it blow up?'

Colin shrugged. 'What he did, see, he took her out of the main channel into shallow water and just opened the seacocks. That's what people usually do when they scuttle their own ships. But that would've meant we'd raise her and get a good look at her, so he had to destroy her. Blow her up. So he hung torpedoes over the ammunition hatches. They led straight down to the magazines, of course. The last men to leave the ship sloshed petrol all over the decks to set light to it.'

'So the ropes burned through,' Ted said thoughtfully, 'and the torpedoes fell, exploded and blew up the magazines. Just like that.'

Colin nodded. 'That's right. Only the torpedo at the fore end went first and as the ship went nose down, a colossal wave of sea-water flooded up over the aft part and put out the flames! So that torpedo never dropped and never blew up.' He chuckled. 'The first man aboard afterwards was a bloke called Kilroy – a lieutenant-commander. He found the torpedo still hanging there and wrote his name on it – "Kilroy was here". Since then, it's turned into a sort of gag, people have been writing it in all sorts of places.'

'I've seen it!' Frank exclaimed. 'Last week, someone wrote it on one of our boilers. I didn't know what it meant.'

'Probably someone who knew a bloke off the *Exeter* or the *Ajax*,' Colin said. 'Heard the story and thought it would be funny.'

'Wasn't he brave, though?' Betty said admiringly, and Colin nodded. 'He certainly had a nerve, writing his name on a live torpedo hanging over a magazine full of ammo. That rope was pretty charred – it could have gone through at any minute.'

Annie shuddered. 'I hate thinking about it. You could have been blown up, if that ship hadn't been sunk. We thought for a while you had been. Granny Kinch told us the *Exeter* had been sunk.'

'Not us. Takes more than a German battleship to get rid of Colin Chapman.'

'You don't want to listen to rumours,' Frank said. 'There's too many of them about. Someone said German soldiers had landed on the beach over at Gosport the other day – Stokes Bay. Three hundred of them killed, I was told! Absolute rubbish.'

'It might have been true, though,' Betty said, wide-eyed, but Frank shook his head.

'It was just a rumour. I reckon there's a lot of people just putting rumours about to scare us. It's all part of Hitler's propaganda.'

'Well, I don't care about any of that,' Annie said, looking at her son. 'I'm just thankful you're home.'

February drew into March and Jess went back at last to Bridge End, reluctant to leave Frank but anxious to see the children again. She saw Molly Atkinson before she left and promised to go and see Alan and Wendy and take them another parcel.

'The boys have been round, I know,' she comforted the unhappy woman. 'I'm sure your two are all right. They're very respectable ladies.' She thought uneasily of the way she had been rebuffed by the sisters, and made up her mind to do more for the little Atkinsons this time. I should have done more before Christmas, she thought remorsefully, I was just too wrapped up in my own worries about Frank and the baby.

Meat was rationed, not by weight but by price – one shilling and tenpence worth a week. A family of four could buy a six-pound joint of lamb at one and four a pound, an announcement that made Annie laugh. Find one first, she said to Ted – in Hines's shop that morning she had seen lambs that weighed only nine pounds whole. Not much bigger than rabbits, and that's what she'd have taken them for if it hadn't been for their hooves.

'At least our Jess and the children will be getting fed better, out in the country,' she said.

For many of the children, that was true. Rose, who had gone back to the Greenberrys, was learning to cook and although they were subject to rationing like everyone else, there were eggs in plenty and milk with which Mrs Greenberry made her own butter. Bacon too was there at every breakfast-time. All the same, she and Mrs Greenberry experimented with some of the recipes that were being given out over the wireless or in the papers, and were constantly surprising Mr Greenberry with such dishes as passion dock pudding, made with boiled dock leaves and oatmeal, Portman pudding which, with its combination of carrot, potato, sugar and dried fruit, could have been either a vegetable dish or a sweet, and Lord Woolton Pie, which everyone tried.

'A pound each of diced potatoes, cauliflower, carrots and swede, three or four spring onions, or an ordinary one if you haven't got them, a teaspoonful of vegetable extract – what's that?'

'Marmite'll do,' Mrs Greenberry said, getting the jar out of the cupboard.

'—and a tablespoonful of oatmeal.' They gathered the ingredients together and looked at the mound of chopped vegetables. 'Cover with water and cook for ten minutes. Put into a pie dish, sprinkle with chopped parsley – what's parsley?'

'It's that crinkly green plant just outside the kitchen door.'

Rose went to fetch some. 'And cover with a crust of potatoes or wholemeal pastry. Why wholemeal?'

'I suppose it's better for you. We'll just have to make do with ordinary.'

'Bake in a moderate oven until the pastry is brown and serve hot with gravy.'

It was very good, and filling too. The Greenberrys ate it often; so did the Shaws, back in Portsmouth, and even the Chapmans. The Minister of Food was credited with good sense and his recipes and advice regularly followed. There was even a song about him.

> Those who have the will to win
> Cook potatoes in their skin
> Knowing that the sight of peelings
> Deeply hurts Lord Woolton's feelings.

Woolton Pie was not made in the thin Victorian house where the Woddis sisters lived. They were still doing their best to ignore the war, taking each new deprivation as a personal affront, and behaved as if rationing were an impertinence of the local shopkeeper. They snatched the children's ration books as soon as Molly sent them, complaining that as Alan was under six he was allowed only half the meat ration, and gave the children sausages and offal, which were off ration. They liked the sausages but hated the liver, which Miss Millicent cooked to the texture of shoe leather, and never knew that the sisters were sitting down to meat stew or roast after they had gone to bed.

'Children don't appreciate good meat,' Miss Eleanor observed. 'It's not good for them anyway – it makes them aggressive.'

Miss Millicent sniffed. 'The boy's quite aggressive enough already. Do you know, he actually tried to bite my hand yesterday!'

'I hope you smacked him for that, Millicent!'

'Oh, I did. Quite hard. But I don't suppose it will make any difference. There's bad blood there, in my opinion.'

'They obviously had no discipline at home. And we're the ones who have to suffer.'

'It's this dreadul war,' Miss Millicent said. 'It's always the innocent who have to suffer.'

Mostly, however, they kept the war at bay. Except for church and shopping, they rarely left the house and Mrs Cherry's visits were cut to twice a week. Wendy and Alan found themselves being given a list of jobs to do each day, and went to bed each night worn out with sweeping and scrubbing, polishing and washing. The episode of the butter had not been forgotten and they were strictly supervised all the time. In fact, a curious change had come about in the sisters' attitude towards them. From finding their presence a nuisance and an intrusion in the house, they now seemed to look forward to their return from school each day and find positive enjoyment in harrying them about their tasks.

'Why doesn't Mummy come to see us?' Alan asked as they struggled through the snow to school. 'I want her to take us home.'

'She's too poorly.' Wendy too lay awake at night, longing for her mother. She had watched, her heart breaking with misery and yearning, as other children went home for Christmas, and hung around them when they returned, avid for any news of her own family.

Tim and Keith Budd had come to the house again one day, shortly after the snowy morning when they had left her mother's parcel on the step, and she'd stood behind Miss Millicent in the hall and heard them invite her and Alan to the Corners' house, to play snowballs and have tea. But Miss Millicent had refused the invitation. Wendy and Alan both had heavy colds, she said, had stayed in bed all over Christmas and couldn't possibly come out in the snow. And Tim and Keith had gone off down the path, giving Wendy a cheerful wave, and scampered off across the fields, up to their knees in snow, shouting and laughing as they went.

'Why is Mummy poorly?' Alan asked. 'Doesn't she need us to make her better?'

'Daddy says she needs a rest.' Wendy knew that Grandad had died just before Christmas. She had cried for him at night but when Alan asked what was the matter she shook her head. He did not yet understand about death.

'She could have a rest if we went home,' he said now. 'We could do the work and she could sit down.'

They were back at school, sitting like mice at the back of the classroom. The teachers were struggling to teach large groups of children at different stages, all in the same room, and only noticed the noisy ones. Miss Langrish did occasionally glance at Wendy's pale, pinched face and Alan's bruised legs – for Miss Millicent used the strap quite liberally now – but she was too tired and anxious herself to do anything. Her fiancé was in the RAF, flying over Germany most nights, and she slept little as she lay imagining him shot down, his plane spinning in flames and out of control. Besides, her job was teaching, she was not supposed to interfere with the children's home life.

Edna Corner stopped and spoke to them a few times after school. She asked them to tea again, but they shook their heads, knowing that there would be jobs for them back at the house. She looked at them doubtfully and asked if they were all right and Wendy, conscious of Miss Millicent's warnings, said yes thank you, they were quite all right, but they had to go now please as they'd promised to be home early. And with that Edna had had to be satisfied.

It was now a regular occurrence for the children to be shut in the cupboard. Whenever Miss Eleanor and Miss Millicent left the house, for church or shopping, and often when they were indoors, the two children were bundled into the dark space under the stairs and left there. They grew accustomed to it and accustomed to the fear and sick loathing that they experienced inside. Together, unprotesting, they would huddle on the floor, their tears flowing silently, and they would remain silent for a long time after they came out.

In fact, Alan spoke very little these days. His eyes, large and dark, looked out in mute appeal from his white face and if he could not be close to his sister he would find a corner and crouch there, pressing his shoulders against the walls.

'There's something very odd about that boy,' Miss Eleanor said, watching him as he cowered like a frightened animal in a corner of the kitchen. 'I think he's mentally retarded. No, Wendy, leave him alone. If he can't come to the table and eat like a human being he must have his food on the floor like the animal he seems to want to be.' She dropped a few scraps into an old bowl. 'Give him those.'

'He doesn't like liver,' Wendy said timidly, looking at the unappetising collection, and Miss Eleanor snorted with exasperation.

'He'll eat if he's hungry. Here's some bread to go with it – quite enough for a child of his age. If he doesn't like it, all he has to do is sit up at the table and behave like a human being.'

'But he *is* a human being,' Wendy said, and was sent to the cupboard for half an hour for insolence.

'If we're going to be forced to take care of these children for the duration of the war, simply because their own parents are too feckless,' Miss Eleanor said to her sister, 'they must learn to behave as we want them to.' And she carried a tureen of steaming soup, made that morning by Mrs Cherry, into the dining-room, leaving Alan with his bowl of scraps.

Meanwhile, Jess was in Edna Corner's kitchen, also eating soup and catching up on the news. She had been surprised to find herself quite pleased to be renewing acquaintance with the friends she had made at Bridge End, and there was a good deal of gossip to exchange before she came to the subject of the little Atkinsons.

'It's funny you should mention them,' Edna said. 'There's a few of us been wondering just what's going on in that house. I mean, the little ones go to school and that, but they're never out to play with the rest of the children. And I've invited them over to tea a couple of times but there's always been some reason why they can't come.'

'That sounds queer.' Jess wiped the last few drops of soup from the bowl with a piece of Edna's home-made bread. 'It's not as if they're all that fond of children – at least, it didn't strike me that way when I went there. You'd think they'd be glad to let the children out to play so they could get a bit of peace.'

'That's right. I mean, it doesn't matter how much you like children, you're always glad of an hour or two without them.' Edna went to the stove and took out a rice pudding. 'I've been meaning to go round again myself, but you know how time goes by.'

Jess nodded. It had been the same for her before Christmas. She'd really intended to visit the children but somehow there had always been something else that needed doing. But now she was determined not to waste any more time.

'Well, I've got another parcel for them in my pram,' she said. 'I'll go in this afternoon, on my way back to Mrs Greenberry's.'

'And I'll come with you,' Edna said. 'We'll find out just what's going on and maybe I'll bring them back to tea this afternoon. I don't care what those two old tabbies say, it's not good for children to be kept away from their friends.'

'I suppose they think ordinary boys like my Tim and Keith aren't good enough,' Jess said with a sniff. 'Well, they may be little ruffians at times but they're as good as any other child, and a lot better than some.' She told Edna about Micky Baxter and the jeweller's shop. 'And the Atkinsons are little dears. Alan's sweet and Wendy's always ready to help anyone.'

They finished their lunch and Jess fed the baby while Edna put a casserole of brisket and vegetables in the oven for supper. Then, with Maureen once again wrapped up in the white velvet coat and leggings Annie had given her for Christmas, the two women set off along the twisting country lanes for the house at the other side of the village.

On Wednesday afternoons, the two sisters went out to have tea with their old friends Colonel and Mrs Lovel, who lived near the church. If the weather was bad, Colonel Lovel would send his car to collect them, but today, although cold, the sky was clear and they elected to walk.

'Really, we haven't been able to get out much at all this winter,' Miss Eleanor remarked as they put on their galoshes. 'It's been so cold and the paths are so slippery. But now it's thawing we should have some pleasant spring weather.'

As a matter of course, they shut both children in the cupboard. Wendy had been allowed out to go to the lavatory, but pushed back in immediately. She went sulkily but without protest, for by now they both knew that protests were futile. The sisters were adept at turning deaf ears to anything they did not wish to hear and if they became really annoyed were capable of leaving the children shut up for the rest of the day.

Alan and Wendy sat huddled in the darkness. By now it was familiar, but it was no less frightening for all that. There were still spiders and probably worse, the brooms were still half suspected of coming to life when the door was closed, and who knew what other monstrosities might have taken possession since they were last shut in here?

Wendy, more angry than afraid, was less inclined to these imaginings than Alan, but she still hated and feared the long hours of incarceration and spent much of her time planning dreadful revenge on the sisters once she had grown up. But to Alan, the darkness was worse every time, and he crouched in his corner, sobbing with quiet, hopeless despair.

They heard the sisters talking as they put on their coats. Their voices faded as they went down the passage to the front door. The door opened and closed. The house was silent.

'Suppose they never come back?' Alan said, voicing his greatest fear. 'Suppose nobody ever finds us?'

Wendy could not answer. Alan always asked this and she knew that no words of comfort could reassure him. And her own heart echoed his terror. Suppose something *did* happen to the sisters while they were out . . .

It was cold in the cupboard. The only heating in the house came from the solid fuel stove in the kitchen and the fire in the living-room. The passage, which never got any sun, was particularly cold and nobody lingered there. The children huddled close, trying to keep themselves warm, but as the afternoon dragged on their fingers and toes began first to throb and then grow numb.

There was a knock on the door. The children jumped and then sat still, listening.

The bell rang, pealing through the empty house. There was a short silence, then it rang again. Wendy, straining her ears, could just hear faint voices.

'Alan!' she said. 'Bang on the door. Shout. Scream. Come on – we've got to make them hear us. They mustn't go away.'

Together, they began to hammer on the door, yelling at the tops of their voices. 'Help! Help! We're locked in – let us out! Help! Help! *Help!*'

The bell rang once more, drowning their cries. They waited until the jangling stopped and then began again. 'Help! Help!'

'Stop,' Wendy said after a few minutes when both were hoarse and breathless. 'Listen.'

They held their breath. Then they heard the rattle of the letter-box.

'I can't see anyone,' someone murmured faintly. 'The house seems to be empty. But I'm sure I heard . . .' There was a brief silence and then the voice called through more loudly. 'Wendy? Alan? Are you there?'

'We're here!' Wendy screamed. She knew the voice. It was Mrs Budd, who lived in April Grove, Tim and Keith's mum. 'We're locked in the cupboard under the stairs. Let us out! Please, *please* let us out!'

There was another silence. Wendy leaned against the rim of light that showed round the edges of the door. Could she hear voices whispering, or was it her imagination? Perhaps Mrs Budd hadn't heard her at all. Perhaps she had given up and gone away.

'Please,' she shouted again, her voice liquid with tears, 'please don't go away. Please, please help us.'

The letter-box rattled again.

'Wendy,' Mrs Budd's voice said. 'We heard what you said. We're going to try to get in and help you. Don't worry. It might take a little while but we're not going away. We'll be as quick as we can.'

The letterbox rattled once more and there was silence. Wendy sank back, leaning her head on the cobwebby wall. For once, she hardly cared about spiders. She peered through the darkness to where Alan was sitting, silent except for the occasional sobbing breath.

'Alan, it's all right!' she said. 'Mrs Budd's going to save us. She'll get a policeman, I expect, and he'll break down the door and get us out.'

Jess and Edna straightened up and stared at each other.

'Did you hear that? Those two poor little children, locked in a cupboard!'

'And where are the old ladies?' Edna asked. 'Where have they gone?'

'Out to tea, I expect,' Jess said grimly. 'But don't let's waste time worrying about them. We've got to get those children out.' She stepped back, staring up at the house. It stared forbiddingly back, its windows like blind eyes. 'How can we get in?'

'I don't know.' But it was clear Edna was as determined as Jess to rescue the Atkinsons. 'Round the back, perhaps? The door's sure to be unlocked.'

The two women hurried along the narrow, mossy path that led along the side of the house. But the back door was firmly locked. There were two windows in the side wall and they tried them both, but it was probably years since either was open and they stayed firm. They went back round the corner.

'I blame myself,' Jess said. 'I told Molly Atkinson I'd look out for her two and I kept meaning to come round and see how they were and never did. If anything's happened to them—'

'I meant to as well,' Edna said. 'I was a bit worried about them over Christmas. I sent the boys round a couple of times – I ought to have come myself. But you know what it is – I saw them coming out of school, and you don't like to interfere, do you?'

'Maybe we should.' Jess was looking for something to prise a window open with. 'Maybe we should always interfere, just in case – ah!'

'What is it? What've you found?'

'A key,' Jess said triumphantly, holding it up. 'The back-door key – hidden under a flowerpot. Well, if they leave it lying around they can't be surprised if anyone uses it, can they!'

'Hardly anyone round here locks their doors anyway,' Edna observed. 'Trust the Woddises . . . Does it fit?'

For answer, Jess pushed the back door open and they marched inside. The afternoon was growing dark and it was difficult to see across the kitchen, but they found the door to the passage and went quickly to the cupboard. Jess felt for the knob and wrenched the door open, and the two children tumbled out.

'You poor little mites!' Jess and Edna sank to their knees and gathered the crying children into their arms. 'You poor, poor little mites.'

Alan and Wendy leaned against them, sobbing. All the tears they had shed in the past six months, all the other tears they had held back, poured out a hundredfold as they felt, for the first time since leaving home, arms that were warm and comforting. Soft breasts that had become no more than a memory were once again real, and bodies that could wrap around you and keep you safe no longer a dream.

'The bitches,' Jess said in a shaking voice. 'The cruel, disgusting bitches!'

'Let's get them out of here,' Edna said. 'We'll take them back to my house. They can sleep in our bed tonight. They need cuddles – lots of them. And then we'll decide what to do.'

'I've already decided. I'm taking them back to their mother. She's the person they need, and she needs them too. She's been driving herself frantic with worrying about these two. If she had any idea what they've been going through—'

Edna began to straighten up. Alan was clinging to her, his little fingers curled tightly in her clothes, and she lifted him in her arms. Jess gave Wendy a hug and stood up too. They paused for a moment, looking at the dark cavern of the cupboard and the chilly length of the passage.

'Someone's coming,' Edna breathed, and they saw the shape of a person outlined against the stained glass of the front door. 'Let's get out, Jess!'

'No.' Jess stood firm. Her anger was still running high and she wanted to face the Woddis sisters with it, to see their guilt. She took a firm grip of Wendy's hand and stood watching the front door open. 'Let's see what you've got to say about this, you hypocrites,' she muttered.

The sisters entered and stopped dead, staring at the little group in the passage.

'What's this?' Miss Eleanor's voice was high with fear and indignation. 'What are you doing here? And the children – what naughtiness have they been about now?'

'*Naughtiness?*' Jess exclaimed. 'Naughtiness? Why, the poor little scraps hardly know what naughtiness is. What have *you* been about, that's what I want to know, locking them in a cupboard and then going off out and leaving them?'

Miss Eleanor advanced. She was terrifyingly tall in the half light and Jess felt Wendy cringe back against her skirt. She squeezed her hand reassuringly.

'I don't know what nonsense they've been telling you,' Miss Woddis said coldly. 'Of course we didn't lock them in the cupboard. It's one of their games. They're always playing it.'

'It doesn't seem like a game to me. Look at them – filthy dirty and sobbing their poor little hearts out. They were terrified!'

'They frighten themselves with silly stories.' She stared at Jess. 'You're an evacuee woman, aren't you?'

'Yes.' She made it sound like something that had crawled out form under a stone, Jess thought. 'I know these children. I know their mother. They're not naughty and they don't lock themselves into cupboards.'

'I tell you, they were not locked in—'

'And *I* tell *you*, they were.'

'We heard them crying when we knocked at the door,' Edna put in. 'When we came in, it was shut fast.'

Miss Eleanor transferred her gaze to Edna. 'You're not an evacuee. You're one of the village women.'

'Yes, I am,' Edna said boldly. 'And I think the village is going to be very upset to find how you've been treating these poor little children.'

Miss Eleanor brushed that aside. 'How did you get in? What made you think you had the right to walk into my house uninvited?' She glanced round and said to her sister, 'Go and look in the dining-room, Millicent, and see that the silver's all there. And then check the drawing-room.'

Jess gasped. She drew herself up and said angrily, 'We're not thieves. We came in because we heard these children crying. We had every right to come and help them. They could have been hurt – injured. Anybody else would have done the same. And now—'

'And now that you can see they're not, you may leave. Millicent and I will deal with the children.'

Jess felt Wendy press closer. Behind her, she heard Alan begin to cry again, and Edna bent to comfort him.

'We're not going without the children. We couldn't possibly leave them here.' Jess's anger was rising rapidly. How dared these women treat little children so cruelly and then behave as if she and Edna were common criminals? Didn't they have any shame? Didn't they even realise that what they had done was wrong?

'Not hurt?' she said. 'Not injured? Of course they're hurt and injured! They've been away from their mother for months, brought to live in a strange place with strange people – they needed comfort and love, not neglect and cruelty. Look at their little faces! Look at Alan's legs! You've been hitting them, tormenting them, terrifying them and God knows what else. You're not fit to have charge of children for five minutes and I'll not leave them in this house with you a moment longer. Why, you're not even human!'

Millicent gasped and Miss Eleanor took a step forward. Her face was white save for the scarlet patches on her cheeks, and her pale eyes blazed. She put out a hand and grasped Wendy's collar.

'You will not take them away! They're our responsibility—'

'Not any more,' Jess said. 'They're coming with us.'

'They most certainly are *not*. They were brought here to be under our care and—'

'*Your care?* You call this *care?*' Jess stared at the elderly lady. 'Do you know what the police would do if they knew what you'd done to these poor little mites? Do you –?'

'The police!' Eleanor gave a high laugh. 'I wonder you dare to threaten me with the police! After breaking into my house—'

'We did not break in. We used the key you left lying about in the garden. It's still in the door. And any normal person would have done the same.' Jess lifted her chin. 'But if you're not satisfied, why not call them? I'll be happy to tell them what we found here and so will Edna, won't you, Edna?'

'Yes, I will.'

'They'd never believe you,' Miss Eleanor said haughtily, but her voice shook a little. 'Millicent and I have lived here all our lives, and we've known Constable Jenner since he was a child. Why should he take your word against mine?'

'Because we'd be telling him the truth,' Jess said steadily. 'And you know it. And now we're going. Let go of Wendy's collar, please. Wendy, find your coats, it's cold outside.' She watched as the little girl ran into the kitchen, coming back with the coats Molly had sent them at Christmas. 'If you want to send for the police you can do so,' she told Miss Eleanor. 'I'll be happy to tell them whatever they want to know. But they'll have to come and find us, we're not keeping these children in this house a minute longer. Are you ready, Wendy?'

'Yes,' the child whispered.

'Is there anything you need to take at this moment?'

'No.'

'Then let's go.' She half turned, then hesitated and said, 'We may as well use the front door. Excuse me, please,' and stalked past the two speechless ladies. Edna, with Alan once again in her arms, followed her. At the front door, Jess turned.

'I'll call for the children's things tomorrow morning. Please have them ready.'

There was a moment's silence as the four women faced each other. Jess, her anger still high, allowed all her contempt, all her disgust, all her fury, show to its full in her raking gaze. And then she turned away as if the Woddises were worthy of no further consideration and marched down the garden path.

'You were marvellous!' Edna said. 'They won't dare do a thing. But what are we going to do now?'

'We're going to take them to your house,' Jess said. 'There isn't room at the Greenberrys. And then I'm going to take them home to their mother. They need to be at home. After that, it's for her to decide what to do about it.' She looked at the children, at Alan in Edna's arms, his face still stained with dust and tears, his body still heaving with sobs. She looked down at Wendy, at a face that looked too old for eight years, at eyes that had seen depths of misery she could barely comprehend. What had the past few months done to these children? What scars would they bear from this experience?

She stopped in the cold, frozen lane and crouched down beside the little girl, taking her into her arms and holding her close. She felt the too-thin body, the fragile bones, heard the ragged breathing and thought of her own children, so sturdy and cheerful, so well cared for and loved.

'It's all right, Wendy,' she murmured. 'It's all over. You're never going back there again. You're going home.'

11

As the spring weather brought a thaw to frozen Europe, Frank's prediction proved correct and the phoney war came to an end. The map on the wall at number 14 was now covered in pins showing the march of war across the world, and nobody could doubt now that it was real, in all its ruthless brutality.

'They're spreading everywhere,' Jess said as Frank stuck a pin in Holland, where the Germans were now carrying out one of their terrifying *blitzkrieg*, or lightning wars. 'It's like some horrible disease. A cancer.'

'I know. Look at it – Denmark occupied with barely a squeak. Our forces brought out of Norway when we'd only been there a fortnight. Tanks and paratroops all over Holland. Belgium and France expecting to be attacked at any moment.' He shook his head. 'It's a mess.'

Jess stood up, baby Maureen on her hip. Maureen was ten months old now and already walking. She was a smiling, contented child who would sit on the floor for hours playing with a set of old wooden bricks belonging to Tim. She had few other toys – those belonging to the other children had been mostly broken or discarded years ago, and there were none in the shops. A battered teddy-bear that had once been Rose's was her constant companion, and Jess had knitted an elephant from an old cardigan, but apart from these she had to be content with makeshift toys.

'Not that she seems to miss them,' Jess would remark. 'She's happy enough with a cardboard box and a few clothes-pegs, or a couple of saucepan lids to bang together.'

After bringing the Atkinson children home, Jess had stayed at number 14. She'd told Frank firmly that being away from him was bad for her and therefore bad for the baby, and she wouldn't go away again until the bombing started. 'And maybe not then,' she added under her breath. The children were settled and happy in the country – though Rose would have liked to come home too – and she agreed to leave them there, but she'd had enough.

'Mind, Mrs Greenberry couldn't have been kinder and I'm quite happy for Rose to be with her. But my place is here with you, Frank, and I'm not going off and leaving you again, so there's not a bit of use you arguing about it.'

Frank looked at her curiously. 'Something's happened to you out in the country, Jess. You've never spoken like that before. As if – well, as if you'd made up your mind—'

'So I have.'

'—and nothing I can say is going to make any difference.'

'It isn't.' She smiled. 'Perhaps it's standing up to those two old ladies – I've never been one to talk back, as you know. But when I looked at those two poor little children and thought what those two old cats had put them through – well, I saw red.'

'I'm glad you did, Jess. You were right to do what you did. There's times when we have to get up on our hind legs and say what we think, yes and put our own selves at risk for what we think's right, too.' He looked at the map again. 'That's why we're fighting this war. What those two old ladies were doing to Alan and Wendy is what Hitler was doing to the Jews. And we can't let it happen, any more than you could let it go on happening to those children.'

Jess listened thoughtfully. More than once she had railed against this war, bitterly angry with those who had dragged Britain into it. For every young man who went off to fight, for every mother who had to watch him go, her heart had ached anew. The sight of the children in the school playgrounds, waiting for evacuation, of their mothers and fathers who stood outside the railings, had haunted her for months and she had raged inwardly at the injustice of it, at the disruption of so many lives.

It was that rage which had enabled her to stand up to the Woddis sisters on behalf of two helpless children. And it was the same rage, she saw now, that had made Britain go to war on behalf of a helpless nation.

But how long could this terrible destruction last? She looked now at Frank's map, at the pins that represented the German forces, and her heart was cold.

'They're winning,' she said in a low voice. 'Look at it, Frank. They're everywhere. They're driving us back and we don't seem to be able to do a thing about it. They're going to win.'

'It looks bad,' he agreed heavily. 'But they haven't beaten us yet, Jess. We may have pulled out of Norway and we might not have been much help to Denmark or the Low Countries, but we've got plenty of troops in France and it's there that the big battle's going to be fought. The British Expeditionary Force is there now – thousands of soldiers just waiting for the chance to have a go. We're not beaten yet, not by a long way. And now that fool Chamberlain's gone and Churchill's taken over at last . . .'

Jess nodded. Frank had never liked Neville Chamberlain, calling him weak and spineless. It was a view shared by many others, including apparently most of his own government. Only a few days ago, at the end of a debate on the tragic abandonment of Norway, he had been denounced by some of the leading MPs of his own party, and others had chanted at him to resign while the rebellious young Harold Macmillan led a chorus of 'Rule, Britannia!' to jeer him from the House of Commons.

Now Winston Churchill was Prime Minister. As First Lord of the Admiralty, he had claimed his own share of responsibility for what had happened in Norway, but had been told not to allow himself to be 'converted into an air-raid shelter' to 'keep the splinters from his colleagues'. All the same, he had kept Chamberlain on in his War Cabinet and that evening Jess and Frank listened to Chamberlain's final broadcast.

With tears in his voice, he told the nation how he had striven with all his might to maintain peace 'as long as it could be preserved honourably'. And Jess, sensing his emotion, felt a great pity wash over her.

'Poor man,' she said when Frank switched off the wireless. 'He did his best, after all. He never wanted the war.'

'Well, there's plenty more to be sorry for now,' Fank commented. 'And the next time we hear Winnie's voice he'll be Prime Minister. I bet he'll have something to say, and it'll be worth listening to.'

Portsmouth was doing its best for the war effort. As well as collecting kitchen waste for pigswill, the city had been thrown into chaos by the removal of two thousand tons of disused tram rails, half buried under the roads. And at the end of April, the Lord Mayor had inaugurated a National Savings Week, which brought in over twelve hundred pounds and ended with a grand parade in the Guildhall Square by bands of the Royal Navy, the Marines and the Royal Army Service Corps. 'An impressive start to our campaign,' he said from the Guildhall steps, and exhorted the citizens to save even harder.

There was other news too, in the little community around September Street. In March, Heinrich Brunner had been interned, just as he had feared would happen. He had been taken away by the police early one morning while marking up the newspapers.

'They took him to prison,' Alice told Jess when she went into the shop. 'Prison! My Heinrich! Just for being born in the wrong place.' Her red-rimmed eyes stared at Jess and her mouth trembled. 'What did he ever do to deserve that?'

'I don't know, Alice. It's all part of this terrible war. Nobody's safe any more. How long are they going to keep him there?'

Alice shook her head. 'Who knows? As long as the war lasts, I suppose. For the duration. They treated him like a criminal, Jess. Prison! My Heinrich!'

She was struggling now to keep the shop going by herself, with some help from Joy. But a newsagent's shop wasn't easy for a woman on her own to run. It meant early mornings and late evenings, with all the stock of sweets and stationery to keep going as well as the daily papers and the *Evening News*. She also had a small flock of paper-boys to keep in order, though by the end of the first week several of them had stopped work because of her connection with a 'German spy'.

It wasn't fair. But nothing was fair these days, as Olive Chapman, torn with anxiety over Derek, never lost an opportunity of reminding her parents.

'If only we'd been able to get married. D'you realise, he's out there in France and I may never see him again? And if anything happens to him, it won't be me they'll tell, it'll be his mother. I've got to wait for her to tell me,'

'Well, she will,' Annie said, thinking that if anything happened to her son she would want to be first to know, whether he was married or not. 'You work there, after all. She's only got to walk across the yard.'

'It's not the same,' Olive said. 'If I was his wife, it'd be me that'd get the telegram.'

'For goodness sake!' Annie exclaimed. 'You talk as if you *want* a telegram! I should think you'd be thankful there hasn't been one.'

Olive gave her mother a scathing look and flounced out of the room. Of course she didn't want a telegram saying that Derek had been killed or injured. But if there *was* going to be one . . . But it was no use talking to Mum. She didn't understand. All she did was look suspicious and ask if there was any 'reason' why Olive was so upset that they hadn't got married before Derek had gone away.

Well, she must know by now that there wasn't. After a bit of a scare the first month after Derek had gone, Olive's periods had returned to normal and the bag of stained sanitary towels had been in the cupboard waiting to be burnt each month just as usual. It seemed that he'd been right, you didn't get pregnant the first time.

But the days and weeks seemed very long without him. She missed the little red car standing in the road, and she missed his cheerful rat-a-tat knock on the door. She missed his smile and the dark gold of his hair, she missed his voice and his laugh, and most of all she missed his touch and his kisses. At night, she lay in bed remembering the love-making they had shared, the way he would caress her breasts and bury his face in their softness, the way he would straddle her, clasping her tightly in his arms so that she felt completely enclosed by his warmth. She shaped her mouth for his kisses and tried to pretend he was there; she hugged herself with her arms crossed and tried to believe his body was pressed against hers.

But none of her imaginings could convince her and eventually she would drift into sleep, hoping to meet him in her dreams, hoping that in that mysterious country where anything could happen and anything seem real, she would once again lie in his arms and share the love that had grown between them; even though in the morning she must wake again to the cold greyness of reality.

But her dreams refused to co-operate. If she dreamed of Derek at all, it was of some strange, bleak landscape scored with trenches and pitted with deep craters of mud. Barbed wire lay tangled across the stony ground and the roar of gunfire echoed across the monotonous fields, while overhead she could hear the drone of unseen aircraft and the thud and thunder of a rain of bombs. There were people in this landscape, people in grey and brown with hidden faces, who lurked and crouched and skulked. None of them could be trusted; there were no familiar faces, no friendly grins. There was only an air of hatred and menace that glowered down from the sullen clouds and spread like a canker across the grim countryside of nightmare.

I can't bear it, she thought. I can't bear not knowing what's happening to him. And if he gets killed out there, if he's taken away from me . . . what use will it be to stay alive? How will I go on without him?

If only we could have got married . . .

'It wouldn't have made any difference to how bad you feel now,' Betty said when Olive tried to explain these feelings, taking it for granted that Betty felt the same without Graham. 'You'd still be worrying yourself sick.

And it doesn't do any good. It doesn't help Derek and it certainly doesn't help us, seeing you moon about with your face down to your knees.'

Olive stared at her. 'You're callous, that's what you are, Betty Chapman. Your boy's at sea, liable to be torpedoed or blown up by a mine at any minute, and you don't even care! It doesn't even keep you awake at night.'

'Why should it? There's nothing any of us can do.' Betty picked up one of her father's socks and began to darn it. 'We're better off doing something that really does help. There's plenty of war work crying out to be done – learning first aid, helping out with warden work. You could learn to drive – they'll be wanting ambulance drivers once the bombing starts. If you just did some work like that, you'd have other things to think about and something to make you sleep at night instead of grizzling.'

'Like you and your Land Army work, I suppose,' Olive said sarcastically.

Betty flushed. 'It isn't my fault they haven't called me yet. I volunteered.' In fact, she had been to the office several times to ask when she would be going, but had been told that for the moment they were taking no more girls. Bitterly disappointed, she was now looking for something else to do and, without telling her family, had sent for details of the women's Services. But she still hankered after the Land Army.

When Olive had left to take some magazines down to Jess, she thought about Graham. Was Olive right to say that she didn't care? Of course I care, she thought indignantly. But . . . do I feel like Olive seems to feel about Derek?

She wasn't even sure that she *wanted* to feel like that. It was more sensible, surely, to take things calmly, not get in a state over something you couldn't alter. Did she really want to feel that her life would be ruined, just because a certain man wasn't around any more? Was it really possible that the next fifty or sixty years would be miserable because of someone she'd met at eighteen and lost six months later?

And did all this mean she wasn't really in love with Graham?

Of course I'd be upset if anything happened to him, she thought. But I'd be upset if Bob Shaw was killed too. She glanced up at the mantelpiece. A letter from Bob had been waiting there for her this afternoon when she had come in from work. She'd torn it open eagerly, knowing it would be filled with interesting and amusing anecdotes. She looked forward to Graham's letters as well, but he wasn't so good at putting himself on paper as Bob was – all his jokes and mischief seemed to rely on his being there in person. But Bob's personality leapt out of the page as she read, and she laughed, her eyes bright.

That had been wrong too, according to Olive.

'You shouldn't be writing to another boy. It's not fair.'

'Oh, shut up.' Betty had had enough of her sister lately. 'You're always nagging. I'll be glad when I do go into the Land Army, just to get away from you!'

Now, as she sat darning her father's socks, she felt ashamed. She and Olive never used to quarrel like this. It's this war, she thought, this bloody war. It's getting everyone down.

*

On the day that Winston Churchill became Prime Minister, an order came through that all motor vessels must be officially registered.

Ted told Annie about it when he came home from morning shift. 'Right down to the smallest. I mean, what are we supposed to make of that? What use is some creaky little dinghy with an outboard to the government? They must be in a right panic if they think little tubs like that are going to help win the war.'

Annie listened in dismay. 'Even the ferryboats?'

'Well, of course!' Ted's voice was irritable. Although the hours of darkness were shorter now, he still hated taking the boat across the harbour in the pitch-black of night. 'They're not small, are they. Not by these standards, anyway.' He thought of his own boat, the *Ferry King*. She weighed in at fifty-seven tons and was about twenty years old – a fine, sturdy little vessel with another forty or fifty years ahead of her. Like the rest of the boats that plied between Portsmouth and Gosport she was driven by steam and carried her own coal. She needed only three men to run her – himself, the engineer Sam Hardy and the young apprentice Ben. 'What do they want with them all, that's what I want to know?'

A good many other people were wondering the same thing. The latest measures did indeed look like panic. The stormy arguments in Parliament, culminating in the resignation of Mr Chamberlain – the terrible events in Holland, Belgium and Luxembourg – it seemed that every day brought fresh bad news. And in comparison with Hitler's might, the efforts made at fighting back seemed puny.

The registering of the small boats was not the only new measure. A new army was being formed – Dad's Army, some people were calling it, for it was to comprise mostly men too old to be called up, some of them in their seventies. As Local Defence Volunteers, its members had already started parading with broomsticks to simulate guns, provoking almost as much mirth as poor Fred Stokes with his home-made bomb. But the laughter was bitter now. Too many men were dying, at sea, in the air and on the battlefields of Europe, and nobody seriously believed that the coasts could be defended from invasion by a few old men with broomsticks or what Ted scornfully called 'rubber ducks'.

Frank tuned in eagerly to the wireless on 13 May to hear the first broadcast by Winston Churchill as Prime Minister. He had already, as First Lord of the Admiralty, made several broadcasts to the nation and everyone was familiar with his rolling, mellifluous tones. But now he spoke with new authority.

His message was no more cheering. But he had a unique way of making bad news sound like inspiration, and the grim reality of the war that was only just beginning, an opportunity at last to come to grips with the enemy.

'*I have nothing to offer but blood, toil, tears and sweat,*' he declaimed. '*We have before us an ordeal of the most grievous kind . . . our policy is to wage war against a monstrous tyranny, never surpassed in the dark, lamentable catalogue of human crime . . . our aim is victory – victory at all costs, in spite of all terror . . . for without victory there is no survival . . . But I take up my task with buoyancy and hope and I say: Let us go forward together, with our united strength.'*

Frank switched off again. He and Jess looked at each other soberly.

'It sounds bad. But I'll say this for Winnie, he doesn't mince words. He tells you straight. You know just what you're in for with him.'

Jess nodded. 'He's got a way with words. He makes you feel that however bad it is, we're all in it together – and nobody can beat us. If we can win this war at all, he's the man who'll lead us to it. But – oh, Frank—' She reached out her hand. 'How many people are going to die before we're done with it?'

Four days later they heard that Brussels was now occupied by the Germans. The next day Antwerp also capitulated. On the following Wednesday the Emergency Powers Act was passed in Parliament, giving the government full power over almost everybody and everything in the country. Attlee, the new deputy prime minister, urged everyone to keep calm. 'Continue at your jobs until ordered otherwise,' he said, and people realised that their lives could no longer be considered their own. The liberty of the Briton was a thing of the past.

'And the future,' Frank said, 'when we win this war.'

But were the Allies going to win? Grave faces in the streets proclaimed their doubts. News from Europe worsened. German forces were spreading across France, driving the Allies before them. How could the tide be turned? It seemed hopeless, impossible.

Thursday morning brought news closer to home, when Woolworths store in Commercial Road was burned down. There was talk of spies and arson, scornfully discounted by some who declared that Jerry had better things to do than rob the city of its stock of cheap screwdrivers and paper bags. But the thought of treachery in the heart of the city brought a new kind of fear, and with it a suspicion and distrust that were worse.

'At least nobody can say it was Heinrich Brunner,' Jess said as a group of women stood in September Street, discussing the fire. 'He might not like being in prison but it does stop people throwing mud at him.'

She looked at Ethel Glaister as she spoke. The two women had maintained a barbed neutrality since Jess had returned home. Jess had more than a suspicion that Ethel had been setting her cap at Frank while she was away, and Ethel was disgruntled at having been baulked of her prey. Now she tossed her head and looked scornful.

'*He* might be in prison but that doesn't mean he can't give orders to those left outside. Everyone knows about the Fifth Column. Who's to say he doesn't pass messages to his associates?'

'Oh, for goodness sake!' Jess turned away in disgust. 'I've never heard such rubbish. Heinrich Brunner organising a Fifth Column, indeed! You want your head looking at, Ethel Glaister.'

Ethel gasped with indignation but Jess was already walking away. I don't want to be seen talking to her again, she thought. She's mean, spiteful and not worth wasting my breath on.

Granny Kinch was standing at her door as usual. She'd recovered from the shame of having Micky brought up before the Juvenile Court, which had kept her indoors for a whole fortnight, and gave Jess her usual gap-toothed smile.

'They're saying 'Itler's starting his air raids soon.'

'Air raids?' Jess stopped, her heart growing cold. 'How do you know that?'

'My Nancy 'eard it from a friend of 'ers.' She looked over her shoulder. 'Come and tell Mrs Budd what you told me, Nance.'

Nancy Baxter came to the door. As usual, she had a cigarette hanging from her lip but her hair had been set and she looked smarter than usual. She must be making good money these days, Jess thought, and was immediately ashamed of her cynicism. All the same, it was probably true.

'That's right,' Nancy said. 'He's going to start bombing any day. Then we can all look out. If you ask me, this war's all but over. He's going to hammer us into the ground.'

Jess gazed at her. Nancy spoke with a kind of dreary resignation. As if she had lost hope. And perhaps she was right. Everywhere you turned, you met bad news. Britain and her allies were being driven back from Europe, where they had marched so full of hope and determination. Scandinavia and the Low Countries gone – France about to fall. What was happening to the troops that had been sent there, to the thousands of young men who had been torn from their homes to fight what was beginning to seem a useless fight? And what would happen here, once they had been beaten?

As Ted said, how could a few old men with broomsticks and an unruly rabble of small boats prevent invasion from such powerful attack?

'We mustn't think like that,' she said to Nancy. 'We've got to do what Mr Churchill said – we've got to pull together and aim for victory. We can't lose heart now.'

But Nancy just shrugged and turned away.

Granny Kinch looked at Jess and made a rueful face. 'She's worn out. Life's never bin easy for her. And now she's 'aving to watch all 'er friends go off to be mashed to pulp by some ugly Jerry – well, you can't blame 'er for getting a bit low, can you?'

Perhaps you couldn't, Jess thought, making her way back home. It had never occurred to her before that Nancy might actually be fond of her 'friends'. Or even if she had never met them before and would probably never meet them again, that she might still feel pity at knowing what they were going to when when they left her arms. A sudden dim realisation came to her of what life must be like for someone like Nancy: a succession of encounters, empty of love, yet still with enough humanity about them to feel sad that the body you had known so intimately was soon to be no more than dead flesh.

Jess shuddered and went indoors to light the fire and get Frank's supper ready. He was working overtime again, coming home late in the evening worn out from a day's hard toil, with time and strength only to eat his meal, read the newspaper and then go to bed. He was up again at five-thirty and away soon after six, bringing Jess a cup of tea before he left. Yet he still managed to work the allotment at weekends.

'Dig for Victory,' he said to Jess, quoting one of the government exhortations to be seen on posters everywhere. 'It's something I can do. And we're going to need food, Jess. The rationing and shortages are going to get worse.'

Everything was getting worse. In this third week of May 1940, it seemed that the world was holding its breath, waiting for something. The sun shone down from a serene blue sky. The sea rippled gently on the shingle beach of Southsea. Birds who knew nothing of war sang oblivious from their trees, and Henry the cat slumbered contentedly on top of the Anderson shelter, too idle even to stalk the mice who lived behind the shed.

It made the truth of what was happening seem all the more ugly.

Frank stuck pins in his map every day, marking the advance of the German troops through France. It was clear that the Allies were being driven into a trap. The BEF was moving back towards the beaches of Dunkirk. Calais was still held but must surely fall at any moment. And the call came for the motor vessels, registered only a fortnight ago, to make their way to Dover.

'What are they going to do?' Jess asked, and Frank stared at his map and then turned to look at her.

'It's my guess they're going to evacuate,' he said, and the word was like a knell. 'They're bringing them back. We're on the run, Jess.'

'You're going to France?' Annie stared at her husband. 'You're going to France in the *Ferry King*?'

He nodded. 'That's what they tell us.'

'But – you've never been outside the harbour. You've only ever gone to Gosport and back.'

'Think I'll get lost?' He was pacing the room nervously, pausing to look out of the window. 'Think I can't do it?'

Annie lifted her hands helplessly. 'What can I think? I mean, just going over with the ferry in the dark – you hate it. How're you going to manage—'

He turned on her. 'The same way we're all going to manage, Annie. By just getting on and doing it. And not whingeing and whining about it.' He jabbed his finger at the map that he, like Frank, had stuck up on the wall. 'There's men over there, Annie, thousands of them like rats in a trap. If we don't go and fetch 'em, they're going to get killed. Some of them are being killed already. Think of it, Annie – *at this very moment*, men are getting killed on those beaches. We've *got* to get them out. We can't just leave 'em to be massacred because we're scared of the dark!' He paused for a moment, then added quietly, 'I owe it to our Olive, Annie. Her Derek's over there somewhere. I've got to go for her sake. It was me wouldn't let them get married, remember?'

Annie gazed at him, then crossed the room and laid her hands on his arms. She looked up into his face and smiled, her eyes tender.

'I'm proud of you, Ted, you know that? All right, you go. But don't go doing anything foolhardy, will you? I want you back here, safe and sound and all in one piece.'

He grinned at her, but his mouth twisted a little as he took her in his arms and held her close. 'I'll be back, Annie. You don't have to worry about me. The old *Ferry King* will look after us.'

They called it Operation Dynamo, after the generator room deep in the cliffs beneath Dover Castle where it was planned. It was a mission that should never have succeeded – this desperate mobilisation of pleasure steamers, ferries, fishing boats and motor yachts. There were over a thousand of them, requisitioned, voluntarily offered, or in some cases simply taken from their moorings. They came down the Thames, round the coasts and through the Solent to mass at Dover for the crossing to Dunkirk. They were manned by naval reservists and volunteers, often by their owners or skippers like Ted Chapman. But most of them were commanded by Navy personnel, and for this Ted was grateful. As Annie said, crossing the Channel was a far cry from shuttling back and forth across Portsmouth Harbour.

'I hope he'll be all right,' she said to Jess as they sat at the kitchen table with a pot of tea between them. 'I know how it's been preying on his mind, having to take the boat across the harbour in the blackout. And this is going to be a thousand times worse. They're gunning them down from the air.' She twisted her hands in front of her. Her eyes were swollen and tired, and her hair untidy. The normally immaculate kitchen was littered with washing-up from the last meal. 'Jess, I never thought we'd have to face anything like this. I thought this was a young man's war.'

'It's everyone's war,' Jess returned gravely. How could she comfort her sister, how could she tell her that of course Ted would return? The *Ferry King* was a small boat, never intended to cross the Channel, though she had no doubt it was capable of the trip. Small dinghies made it, after all. But under fire, being strafed by enemy warplanes, fired on from the beaches? She shook her head. The whole enterprise seemed crazy. It was like sending mice into the jaws of a tiger. 'We're all going to have to do our bit, Annie, even if it's not what we thought. Like Mr Churchill said, we've got to pull together.'

Annie nodded. She sniffed and blew her nose. 'I know, Jess. And it's not just Ted. It's all the others, all those young men . . . Our Olive is nearly out of her mind over Derek.'

'There's not been any news, then?'

'Not a word. "Somewhere in France",' that's all we know. He could be anywhere. He might even be a prisoner now. Or he might be—'

'He might be dead.'

Both women jumped and turned to see Olive standing in the doorway. She was wearing a summer frock, blue with small white spots and a white collar. She looked fresh and pretty, her dark hair brushed into a long bob, almost touching her shoulders, but her eyes were pools of tragedy.

'That's what you were going to say, wasn't it? He might be dead. He might be lying in some field, forgotten. I might never know what's happened to him.' She came slowly into the kitchen and sank down in the chair Ted normally used. She laid her arms on the table and dropped her head down on them as if she had no more strength to hold it up. 'I'll have nothing to remember him by. No wedding, no baby . . . not even his name.'

'Oh, Olive.' Anne reached out and touched her daughter's shoulder. 'Olive, I'm sorry.'

The girl's head came up at that and there was a flash of the old rebellion in her eyes. 'Sorry? Sorry for what? For not letting us get married?' Then the flame died and her eyes were dull again. 'Oh, it doesn't matter. It wouldn't have made any difference now.' She laid her head once again on her arms. 'If he's dead, it's all over. And if he's not, we'll get married, whatever you and Dad say.'

'I know,' Annie said gently. 'I know. And we won't stand in your way any longer.' She paused and then added very quietly, 'If Dad comes back . . .'

Jess felt the tears burn her own eyes. Already, she thought, there had been too much tragedy in this war, too many tears. Tears for Colin, when they had thought him lost on the *Exeter*. Tears for the children who had been wrenched from their homes and families and sent, bewildered, into the care of strangers – or, like the Atkinsons and Martin Baker, to neglect and cruelty. Tears for Heinrich Brunner, so unfairly torn from his wife and child, and now tears for Derek and Ted.

And if they came home safe, when and for whom would the next tears be shed? For Colin again, back on his ship? For Graham, also at sea? Or for those nearer home, killed in their own beds when the threatened air raids started at last?

Jess had no doubt now that the bombing was going to come. Hitler's success had been too absolute for him to ease off now. Even though he seemed to have paused long enough to enable the evacuation of the BEF to get under way, he could be only drawing breath before launching the next offensive. And with no more troops to be fought on land, he must turn his attention to the air and his final invasion.

By June or July there could be German troops marching the streets of Portsmouth. The streets could ring to the stamp of jackboots and the guttural shouts of '*Heil Hitler!*' The harbour could be filled with the stark shapes of Germans warships and the air throb with the drone of German aircraft.

What will they do with us? she thought. What will they do *to* us? Will we be able to live our normal lives or will we all be turned into slaves? And what about the children?

She raised her eyes and looked around the kitchen. It looked normal enough, though untidy by Annie's standards. She saw the wireless Ted had made in the varnished wooden cabinet he had made for it.

Only a fortnight ago, she and Frank had listened to Winston Churchill's broadcast. And she remembered again the grim message he had passed on – and the inspiration of his final words.

'*I have nothing to offer but blood, toil, tears and sweat . . . Our aim is victory at all costs . . . I take up my task with buoyancy and hope . . . Let us go forward together, with our united strength.*'

Buoyancy and hope. Victory at all costs. Let us go forward together.

Jess got up from her chair. She went to the sink and refilled the kettle. She looked at the bowed heads of her sister and niece and went to lay her hands upon them.

'I'm making another cup of tea,' she said. 'And then we're going over to Ted's allotment. We'll give your Betty a hand and we'll dig for victory, like Frank says. We've got to pull together in this, and sitting here worrying's not going to help anyone.'

Annie smiled ruefully. 'I've been telling our Olive that. And here I am, doing the same thing!'

'We all do it,' Jess said quietly. 'And we all need someone to remind us not to. Of course we can't help worrying – it's human nature. But somehow or other we've got to get over it and carry on, or the whole country's going to fall apart. It's up to us as well, Annie – not just the men, going out to fight and not just those who're bringing them back from France at this moment. It's us women, left at home, who've got to keep things going. Otherwise there's going to be nothing worth bringing them back for.'

It was strange to be on your own ship and yet not in command.

Not that the *Ferry King* was strictly a ship, Ted thought wryly as he stood on the bridge beside the naval reservist who had taken over. But Lieutenant Horner clearly saw it as such and behaved as if he had the wheel of a battleship in his hands. He stared ahead, giving Ted orders in a clipped voice and obviously expecting to be obeyed.

'You're under military authority now,' he said as they steamed out through the harbour mouth on the evening of 26 May. 'I hope that's clearly understood. As far as you and your men are concerned, you're Navy personnel.'

Ted nodded. He'd already accepted this and was glad to do so. He knew that although his expertise in handling the boat was essential, his experience wasn't enough to take the ferryboat across the Channel, and that of his 'men' – Sam Hardy and young Ben! – was even less. It wasn't that they were incapable of handling the boat in rougher waters, it was the navigation involved that might be their undoing. He and Sam had taken their exams of course, but without practical experience and plenty of it, they were sure to have become rusty.

In fact, they were unlikely to get lost, for once out in the Solent they found themselves part of a fleet of assorted ships on their way to Dover to answer the call. From Portsmouth, they recognised the Isle of Wight paddle steamers, *Whippingham* and *Portsdown*, and their own sister ship *Fawley*. The *Bee*, a seventy-five-foot powered barge which normally took cargo between Portsmouth and the Isle of Wight, was in company with four others, and there was a number of ships and small boats from Southampton, Poole, Weymouth and Plymouth. It seemed that the whole of the south coast was involved in the exercise.

If Ted had disliked the journeys across the harbour, that night's steaming east along the coast of England showed him that he had experienced nothing yet. The darkness was absolute. The only relief was from the stars massed above, a brilliant shimmer of needlepoint lights, blotted out to the north by the bulk of the South Downs. Around the boat, the sea lay black and menacing, heaving gently as they pushed their way across it.

Thank God it's not rough, Ted thought, but he did not say so. Everyone was keeping quiet; you never knew who or what might be about this night, and voices carried far over water. The engine ran as softly as Sam Hardy and Ben knew how to make it. Around them, the other ships glided like black-shrouded ghosts, a strange, bizarre navy called to the aid of a country in extremity.

By five they were nearing Dover and daylight was breaking over the harbour. Ben came up from the engineroom with mugs of cocoa for Ted and Lieutenant Horner, and stared.

'Whew! Look at all them boats, Skip!'

The three of them gazed at the scene. With the famous white cliffs as a backdrop, it was difficult to see the water for the craft that covered it. Ships and boats of all sizes, from large ferry steamers from the Isle of Man to small sailing dinghies, rocked gently on the calm blue sea. It looked like the largest regatta ever held, but there was no air of carnival about this flotilla. Instead, there was a grim, determined purpose in the preparations that were going on, and barely had they anchored when the lieutenant ordered Ben to drop overboard the small dinghy intended for use as a lifeboat, should the *Ferry King* ever meet with an accident, and rowed himself ashore.

'We might as well make ourselves useful while he's gone,' Ted remarked, and they cooked breakfast with the stores that had been brought aboard the previous afternoon and set themselves to checking the engine and making sure all was ready for the crossing. But they had not done much before Lieutenant Horner was back.

'We're going to Dunkirk,' he said, confirming the guess they had all made. 'Now look – it's going to be no picnic over there. There's getting on for half a million men stranded and we've got to get them out and bring them back before the Germans shell them all to pieces.'

Ted gaped. 'Half a million? But—' He stared at the fleet of small boats. 'Even this lot'll never get all them out.'

'We're not meant to. Our job's to act as ferries – getting the soldiers from the beach to the ships that are already there, waiting to bring them back. They can't get in close enough, y'see. Now it's not going to be easy. The Germans are strafing them, gunning them and bombing them. They're doing everything bar hold their hands and tell them bedtime stories. And if you don't fancy it, you've only got to say. We can put a couple of sailors on board the vessel and you can go back home, and no hard feelings.' He looked at them hard. 'What do you say?'

There was a small silence. Ted looked at Sam Hardy, nearly sixty years old and a grandfather. He looked at Ben, only sixteen and too young yet for active service. He thought of Annie, sitting at home worrying about him and of Olive, almost frantic about Derek.

'You two can do as you like,' he said. 'I'm staying with the *King*.'

Sam grinned and rubbed his chin, grey with the morning's bristly growth.

'Me too. You don't get rid of me that easy.'

They looked at Ben. He'd been with them for two years now and they'd watched him grow from a skinny boy to a youth in the final stage of his growth towards manhood. His voice was breaking, he had a downy growth where Sam had bristles, he was tall and promised to be well-built. But he was still, Ted thought, really a child.

'You don't have to come,' he said gently. 'Nobody'll think any the worse of you if you leave now. You've done a good job, coming this far.'

'Leave?' Ben said. His voice shook with excitement. 'Leave now? You'll have to tie me up and throw me over the side!'

Sam laughed but Ted felt an unaccustomed ache in his throat. What in God's name am I going to say to his mother if anything happens to him? he thought. He doesn't know what he's saying. He looked at Lieutenant Horner.

The reservist sighed. He wasn't here to play nursemaid, nor make other people's decisions for them. The boy had done well enough to come this far and a sailor could be found to take his place, but the more civilians that were ready to help the better it was. And he was willing enough. The trouble was, he had no idea what he was facing.

'Listen, son,' he said. 'This isn't a pleasure cruise. It's going to be hell over there, and I only use that word because I can't think of a worse one. There's going to be bodies floating in the sea – and bits of bodies. You'll see blood and guts and brains spattered on the decks of your own boat. You'll see men killed in front of your eyes and you might be killed yourself. You could be blown up or shot or drowned, or a bit of all three. You could come home minus an arm or a leg. You'll see sights you'll never forget; sights that will haunt your dreams till your dying day. Do you understand what I'm saying?'

Ben stared at him. His face whitened and green shadows appeared around his mouth and eyes. He bit his lips and swallowed once or twice and Ted thought he was going to vomit, perhaps even faint. He put out a hand to steady the boy, but Ben blinked hard and shook him off. He lifted his chin and looked the officer in the eye.

'Yes, sir,' he said. 'I understand. And I still want to come.' He paused for a moment, then added quietly, 'My brother's over there somewhere.'

They slept the rest of the day, on makeshift bunks in the passengers' cabin below decks. While the sun shone warmly on the idyllic scene, men who had been awake all night rested and small boats shuttled to and fro with supplies. Food and water were brought to craft that normally carried no more than a jug of tea, heated up on the engine. Many of them needed coal, and this must be bagged from dumps ashore and heaved aboard. And blankets and first-aid supplies were stowed in every corner.

'There'll be hospital ships waiting for these,' Lieutenant Horner said, 'but we may have to use them too. Know anything about first aid, Skipper?'

Ted nodded. He had done a course, and so had Sam, but he doubted whether they were up to dealing with the kind of injuries the lieutenant had described to Ben. What did you do with a man who had had a leg blown off? Or a hole punched in his side, or his eyes shot through?

'We'll do our best,' he said, and the naval man nodded.

'Nobody can do more.'

By 7.30 in the evening the fleet was beginning to move. Small boats were wired to larger ones and towed, to give them speed, larger ones went under their own steam. Following the glimmering golden pathway flung down by a setting sun, they left Dover behind and set out for what Lieutenant Horner had described as a 'place worse than hell'.

It was dark when they arrived but there had been no doubt that they were approaching war itself as they steamed slowly towards the glow of the burning city. Dunkirk, the last refuge for half a million soldiers, was being bombarded, its docks on fire and a huge blanket of smoke pouring from a blazing oil container. The acrid sky was spattered with the bitter yellow of flames and burning debris and sliced by the beams of searchlights while overhead could be heard the nasal snarl of German aircraft. Once it became light, the bombardment would increase, and it would not be confined to the town.

We're not going to get out of here, Ted thought, listening to the roar of guns somewhere inland. None of us is going to get out. It's a crazy, mad farce, a last-ditch effort to salvage some of the wreckage of this insane war. And we're all going to die for it. Young or old, soldier, sailor or civilian, we're going to die here in fire and water and the sickening stench of our own blood.

And then he saw the grey light of dawn creep up from the east. He saw the apricot glow of the sun colouring the fringe of the sky, saw it throw its warm, glowing dome of hope above his head. And when he looked at the beaches he knew that they must get back, and that there must be no more thought of defeat.

'Bugger me,' Sam Hardy said quietly. 'Look at 'em. They look as if they've bin standing there for hours.'

The beach was packed with soldiers. Grim and silent, standing as if waiting to witness some great and spectacular event, they stood shoulder to shoulder, their tin hats their only protection from the planes that patrolled overhead. Behind them, the town stood half demolished, hardly a building left undamaged and many of them on fire. A clutter of abandoned vehicles – cars, trucks, tanks – stood at random, as if they were toys thrown down by some petulant giant baby. And the whole scene was darkened, even on this bright spring morning, by the spreading black shadow of filthy, stinking smoke from the burning oil containers.

But most tragic, most pitiful of all, was not the scene on the land, but what was in the sea. Lines of soldiers, queuing up as if waiting at a bus stop, stretching out until they were neck-deep in the water, their packs still on their backs, their rifles held in their arms. Though the sea that swirled about their legs and bodies must be numbingly cold, though their uniforms must be dragging with the weight of the salt water that saturated them, though they were under merciless threat from the planes that droned above their heads, they stood still and patient, waiting for rescue because, in this final extremity, there was nothing else for them to do.

How many hours had they stood there? Ted wondered. Had they been there all night, shuffling in the chilly water, their legs tangled with seaweed and slimy, unseen rocks beneath their feet? He gazed down at them, trying to imagine what had brought them to this point, what battles they had fought, what retreat they had endured to arrive here on the beach at Dunkirk, waiting for rescue.

He looked down at them and the men looked up at the little ships that had come to rescue them, they looked up at the men on the *Ferry King*, and Ted knew that inside they must be feeling the relief of men rescued from the jaws of hell. But their faces were without expression, for even those who were trying to grin had faces too stiff, lips too cold, for the muscles to obey. And perhaps they could not have succeeded anyway, for in their eyes was the dullness of suffering, of fatigue and lost hope.

'Get them up,' Lieutenant Horner snapped. 'Get as many on board as you can. We've got to start getting them away.' He glanced around. The patrolling aircraft were beginning to attack, machine-gunning the beaches and the ships that had come to the rescue, and even as he watched Ted saw men begin to fall. The air that had been quiet, save for the drone of patrolling planes, was now curdled with screams.

And there were other things in the sea too; the dead bodies that Lieutenant Horner had told Ben they would see, some face down, sinking beneath the weight of the packs still strapped to their backs, some floating like corks in life-jackets, with faces that were bloated, burned or mutilated turned up to the sky. And there were the arms and legs that had been blown away, and other parts less readily identifiable, lumps of torn and bloody flesh that had once been human.

Ted heard Ben gag and knew that there was no time to waste. If the boy was to be any use, he must be given something to do. And there was only one task before them now – that of getting the living on board and back to safety. The dead must be left to themselves.

Within five minutes they had the first men aboard. The *Ferry King* had not been built for boarding from a beach and her sides were too high and steep for easy climbing but there were two rope ladders aboard and the mooring ropes at the bow and stern, and the soldiers scrambled up these and fell on the deck, gasping and streaming with water. With rough haste, the crew shoved them aside to make way for the next ones. Their sodden clothes were heavy, their packs and rifles weighing them down, and many of them were too weak with fatigue to lift themselves from the water. It needed the strength of two men, sometimes three, to get them up over the railing and then to move them away. And some were injured and screamed with pain at their rough handling, and the water that ran from their clothes was reddened and thick.

One died in Ben's arms as he lifted him aboard. He stared down at the face so abruptly stilled, at the upturned eyes, and then looked horrified at Ted. But Sam saw the look and pulled the body from his arms, shoving it back over the side.

'It's the living we've got to take, we ain't got time to bother with them as is past help. Give that bloke a hand, Ben, get 'em up as fast as you can and let's have 'em out on the ships quick.'

Ben took one last look at the body that had been cast into the sea and then did as he was told. There was no more time for talk. Together, the four of them worked to heave men out of the water and on the deck, but the ferry was still too high for most of them to scramble aboard and Ted began to rip up the slatted benches where passengers would sit. With the help of Lieutenant Horner, he roped them together to form ladders and dropped them over the side and immediately soldiers began to clamber up.

The planes were directly overheard now, the roar of their engines an almost solid menace, sending a rumble of vibration through the whole boat. The water was spattered with machine-gun bullets. Every time they heard the burst of rattling fire the four men ducked and at first Ted wondered if they ought to take cover. But how could they settle down below, leaving these poor devils on deck and in the sea, at the mercy of the Germans who flew inexorably above? And if they did, how would they ever get their job done?

Ted and Sam had both served in the Great War and had been under fire then. They had seen men break up under the strain and shot by their own officers for cowardice. Others had been sent home, unfit for further service; shuddering, gibbering wrecks unable to string more than two or three words together without stuttering, cowering under the table at the slightest loud noise, shambling about the streets without hope of working or making their own lives again. They were as maimed as the match-seller outside Woolworths, and often became as destitute but were given even less sympathy.

Ted often thought that he could have been one of these wrecks himself. His dislike, amounting to fear, of crossing the harbour in the blackout stemmed from those nights in the trenches with only the stars above for light, when danger lurked in every corner. Now he was reminded even more sharply by the rattle of machine-gun fire and the drone of planes. For a moment, as he stared at the splattered water, he wanted to turn and dive for cover, to hide his head. Why had he come on this crazy mission? Why had any of them come? How could anyone survive this hell, this holocaust? Wasn't it going to mean an even greater waste of lives?

The thoughts ran through his mind like ants whose nest had been suddenly uncovered. And then he turned his head and saw Ben staring at him. The boy looked as if he had been suddenly struck with paralysis. His eyes were wide with fear, his lip trembled and he lifted his hands towards Ted as if begging for help.

With an almost audible snap, Ted's mind came back into focus. He thrust his memories and his fears to the back of his mind and gave Ben the only help possible.

'Come on!' he snapped. 'Don't stand there gawping. There's work to be done – we're not here on our holidays. *Get those men aboard, damn you!*'

His voice was like the harsh scrape of galvanised iron on stone, and it released Ben from his paralysis. He shook his head briefly, then turned and jerked a man bodily into the boat, lifting him by one shoulder. Dropping him on the deck he turned for the next and suddenly soldiers seemed to be almost flying into the boat, pulled up from the makeshift ladders as if they were little more than babies and pushed aside at once to make room for the next.

Within half an hour the *Ferry King* was fully laden. The cabin below was packed with exhausted soldiers, the decks solid with their sprawling bodies. Most of them were too weary to sit up, but as Lieutenant Horner went up on the bridge and signalled to Sam to get the engines going, Ted and Ben went around with bottles of water. The men gulped it down thankfully and began to revive a little.

'Cor, that's better.' They wiped wet hands over grimy faces, leaving streaks of mud and often blood across unshaven skin. 'Now all we needs is a pint o' booze and a packet o' fish an' chips, an' a stroll dahn Lambeth way an' we'll know we're 'ome again.'

'Lambeth! You Cockneys seem tae think that's the centre of the bliddy universe. It's Glasgae Ah'm headin' for, right enough.' The speaker glanced up at Ted. 'Where's your home port, Jimmy?'

'I'm not Jimmy,' Ted began, unravelling the unfamiliar dialect, but the soldier was already leaning back, exhausted, and he passed the water on to the next man. By then the planes were overhead again and machine-guns once more spraying the boat with their deadly rain.

Lieutenant Horner handed the wheel to Ted and he reversed the boat away from the beach. The queue of men looked even longer than when they had begun loading. He took the *Ferry King* well out of her depth before turning to head for the ships that lay outside the harbour. The sky had now lightened to full daylight and although it was still darkened by the pall of smoke from the burning oil containers he could see that the shore was almost black with a solid army of men. They were marching into the water as if intent on some lemming-like mass suicide, and at the head of the beach he could see that the promenade was crowded with more, hundreds of them, thousands . . . How many had Lieutenant Horner said? Half a million?

We'll never do it, he thought. And then: We bloody *will* . . .

The water was thick with boats of all kinds, each of them loading soldiers like some new and valuable cargo. And that's just what they are, he thought. Cannon-fodder one day, ballast the next. But what else could we have done?

Again, there was no time for thought. The men on the beach, the men in the water, were looking to them for hope, for life. Already their faces were blurred as the *King* headed away from the shore and out beyond the ravaged harbour to the ships in deep water.

'Head for that one,' Lieutenant Horner said. 'The destroyer.'

Like all the other ships, it was surrounded by small boats, jostling for places to transfer their cargoes of humanity as quickly as possible. The *Ferry King* joined the crowd and a sailor took the rope Ben threw him and made it fast. A rope ladder was slung down to them and the soldiers began scrambling aboard.

'Thanks, mate. You bin a real toff.' There was no time for more than a word or two, and most of the men were too weary anyway. They clambered aboard the destroyer as if in a dream, their eyes still dark with the horror of all they had seen. And Ted and the lieutenant were anxious only to get away, to get back to the beach and bring off another cargo, to make another small contribution to the gargantuan task that the small boats of a civilian navy had been given in this strange and terrible war.

Oblivious now of time or fatigue, they worked on all day. The stream of soldiers seemed never-ending. One after another, they scrambled or were dragged aboard, one after another they were given water and some food, one after another they were taken to the ships that would carry them home. The destroyer departed, loaded with men, and its place was taken by another, and then another. Nearby, Ted saw the *Gracie Fields*, one of the Isle of Wight boats which had run from Southampton to Cowes before the war had begun. He and Annie and the girls had gone to the Thornycroft shipyard at Woolston to see her launched by the singer herself, warbling 'Sing as We Go' as the ship slid into the River Itchen.

The vessel had been taken off the Isle of Wight run and converted to a minesweeper soon after the war began, but she was still under the command of Captain Larkin, her old master. It was strange and oddly comforting, seeing her here, and Ted gave her a private salute.

The aeroplanes were still overhead but now they had been joined by heavier craft with full bellies who had their own cargo to disgorge. As well as the spray of machine-gun bullets, there were bombs to deal with, and as Ted watched he saw a company of men, grouped on the beach, vanish from sight in a devastating explosion. Sickened, he saw sand and gravel burst in a thunderous detonation, the roar of it obliterating even the cacophony of aircraft, gunfire, engines and shouts and screams that had been the background accompaniment ever since dawn broke. And when the dirt and dust subsided there was only rubble left where, just a few moments before, there had been living men.

Had Derek been one of them? he thought. At every moment, as he worked to save whosoever came first to hand, the thought of his daughter's sweetheart had been at the back of his mind and he had looked briefly into each face in the hope that he might be there. It was foolish, he knew, with so many men waiting for rescue – and who knew that Derek had lived to come this far anyway? – but he could not help it, any more than he could banish from his mind the memory of his daughter's face as she accused him of ruining her life.

'*All we wanted was to be married, and you wouldn't let us. You wouldn't let us!*'

I'll let you now, he promised her silently. If he gets out of this, I'll let you marry the first minute you can . . .

Night fell and still they went on. They were operating on another part of the shore now, in deeper water where the beach shelved suddenly, working with smaller boats which could run further inshore. Some of them were no more than family pleasure cruisers and Ted wondered how they had managed to get across the Channel so quickly. They worked swiftly, running their noses against the shelving shingle so that the soldiers could scramble aboard without risking the deep water. Then they made the short journey back to the larger boats like the *Ferry King*, transferring their loads as the larger boats would transfer them to the ships taking them back across the Channel.

The sea was still calm and although the darkness of the sky was made deeper by the pall of smoke still issuing from the burning oil containers, it was lightened by the fires on shore. Ted and the lieutenant used them as markers as they plied between the larger ships and the shore.

'I hoped the bastards would go home to bed,' Ted said as they listened to the aircraft snarling above them and ducked involuntarily at the sound of each explosion. 'What are they using as targets, for God's sake?'

It was almost impossible to locate the ships in the dark and he knew that they must stop soon to wait for daylight and snatch a few hours' rest. None of them had eaten since morning, nor even realised how time was passing until the sun began to go down. Now he was aware of a gnawing hunger, but there were still thousands of men out there on the beach and he was driven by their own desperate need.

All the same, common sense told him that they could not work on for ever without food or rest, and Horner echoed his thoughts.

'Whether they leave us alone or not, we'll have to heave to after this lot. That lad of yours is almost dead on his feet. You've worked well, all of you, but there'll be more to do tomorrow.'

Ted looked towards the darkened beach. It could have been empty and silent, but he knew that hidden beneath the shroud of night a murmuring mass of defeated and weary soldiers lay huddled on the shore, waiting for rescue. Another trip and they could bring off a hundred or two more. And another . . . and another . . .

But the lieutenant was right. They must rest, to be ready to work even harder when dawn came. For dawn would bring the Messerschmitts again, in greater strength than ever. The last few were flying above them now, dropping their remaining bombs apparently at random but, with so many boats in the sea, almost unable to help scoring hits. And each detonation was accompanied by a searing flash of light that revealed every ship in the vicinity, and each direct hit followed by a blazing fire as yet another ship lurched and wallowed and sank to the bottom.

'They might as well just floodlight the whole bloody place and 'ave done with it,' Sam said as he cooked up a mess of eggs and bacon and fried bread on the fire. ' 'Ere, Ben, you look just about done in. Wrap yerself round this.'

The boy took the plate of food and looked at it as if seeing something else. His face was white, his eyes dark with fatigue. He shook his head slightly but Sam put a knife and fork into his hands, folded his trembling fingers around them and told him to eat.

'You need yer strength. You'll feel more the mark after a coupla bites. And then doss down on one of the benches down below for a bit. The toff's right, there's going to be plenty more where this lot come from.' A nearby explosion deafened them all and rocked the boat violently. They heard debris rain down on the deck above. 'That's another poor bugger hit,' Sam said, and went up the gangway to poke his head out. 'It's that – whatchercallit? That Dutch fisherman, one of them what towed the little 'uns over—'

'*Schuit*,' Lieutenant Horner said.

'That's it, skoot – well, it's just copped a big 'un by the look of it.' He watched for a moment, the flames of the burning ship illuminating his face. 'Ain't nothin' we can do,' he said after a moment. 'There's a coupla boats over there but they're not pickin' anyone up.'

Silent and sober, they finished their meal and found corners to sleep in. Ted and the lieutenant tossed for the first watch and Ted mounted to the bridge and settled himself there with a blanket wrapped about him.

It would be a short night but it would seem long enough, no doubt, with bombs falling about them and the occasional burst of gunfire to splatter the beach. Inland, he could hear the rumble of heavier guns and the thud of shells. Once again, the searchlights were active, sending spears of brilliant light to the stars. What are they looking for? he wondered. Our aircraft? But so far, few British planes had been seen and Horner said they were all inland, fighting off the planes making for the coast. 'It'd be a hell of a sight worse if they weren't,' he said.

After only a few hours' sleep, the four men were up again and back at work, running close into the shore, taking men off from the smallest boats, ferrying them out to the ships. Back and forth they went, back and forth, heaving aboard an endless stream of bodies, almost kicking them aside in their endeavours to rescue yet more, always with one eye on the sky above, always with an ear cocked ready for explosion, always with the knowledge that they might in the next second be blasted from the sea to become nothing more than part of the human flotsam that drifted torn and mangled in the rippling blue water.

'Thanks, mate. Lovely weather for it.' A soldier, unshaven, wet and filthy but still able to manage a twisted grin clambered over the side. 'Don't suppose you got a dry fag, 'ave yer? Mine's a bit damp.'

He had probably been standing in water all night, Ted thought, for the edge of the sea was crowded once again with queues of men. He felt in his pocket and dragged out a crumpled packet of Woodbines. 'Here. There's only a couple left, but you're welcome.' And before the man could thank him, he had turned to help the next aboard.

The sun shone down from a serene blue sky on the calm water. Over and over again, the *Ferry King* chugged out to the waiting ships and back again to the crowded beach for a fresh load. It was the kind of day that should have been set aside for holiday-making, the boats filled with carefree revellers; the waiting passengers could have been any swarm of holiday-makers, eager for a trip round the bay. But they had been waiting too long. Enemy planes droned ceaselessly above. Gunfire crackled and spat about their heads. And bombs fell from the blue sky, blowing sea and ships and men to a cocktail of salt water, blood, debris and mangled flesh that settled at last to become a part of the terrible illusion of calm, sunlit serenity.

The *Ferry King* plied stolidly through the chaos, seemingly immune from attack. Several times she went to supply ships for more fuel, as if in exchange for her human cargo; once the four men went aboard a 'skoot' for a quick meal. The Dutchmen told them of the invasion of Holland only a week or so earlier, of how they had escaped in their boats and fled to England and now found themselves helping with the rescue of their allies.

'We cannot allow this man to take over Europe,' they said in their guttural English. 'He is a terrible man. He is cruel and vicious and if he wins it will be the end of the world.'

Ted listened and agreed, but in his heart there were doubts. This was no victory they were engaged in, but a full-scale retreat. Half a million soldiers were being driven back by the might of an army which had marched unresisted into country after country. How could anyone beat him now? How could anyone think he could be defeated?

But thoughts like that could not – must not – be allowed. His task now was to get as many men off as he could, and he wouldn't do that by sitting in a Dutch fishing-boat quaffing schnapps.

'Come on,' he said, getting to his feet. 'There's blokes out there'd rather be home, and they won't get there if we don't take 'em. Come on, Ben, up off your backside and let's see a smile on your face. Sam? Lieutenant?'

They drained their glasses and went on deck, feeling better. The *Ferry King* cast off from the skoot and chugged away, back towards the beach. Around them, the scene was just as before; the surface of the sea covered with small boats filled with khaki-clad men, the sky loud with enemy aircraft, the air split by the rattle of machine-guns and the roar of exploding bombs.

They were only fifty feet away from the skoot when a German bomber swooped down on her and she was blown out of the water in an explosion that all but sank the *King* as well.

They watched in appalled silence.

'Oh God,' Ben said in a strangled voice. 'Oh *God* . . .'

'Look out,' Sam said, 'he's going!'

The boy was swaying on his feet. His face was green, his eyes wild and unfocused. He reached out both hands, clawing at the air, and sank to his knees. His voice babbled incoherently and he sobbed heart-broken sobs. He covered his face with both hands and wept into them, like a woman mourning.

'Get him on his feet!' Lieutenant Horner ordered harshly. 'We can't afford any backsliding now.'

'He's not backsliding,' Ted retorted angrily, but he knew the lieutenant was right and he bent and grabbed Ben under the arms. 'Come on, Ben, on your feet. We can't give in now. There's men on that beach depending on us. Your own brother's there somewhere, remember? He could be in the next lot.'

The boy stared at him. 'The skoot – those Dutchmen . . .'

'They're out of it now,' Ted said firmly. 'They didn't know a thing about it. It's over for them. But it ain't over for the blokes on the beach, so stop whining and put your back in it, right?'

Night fell again and a third day dawned. It was difficult to remember that there had ever been a different life. Portsmouth, September Street, Annie and the kids, were all but a dream. There had never been anything but this incessant ferrying of broken and exhausted soldiers from shore to ship. Never anything but the rattle of gunfire, the thunder of bombs and the screams and groans of wounded men; never anything but the stench of burning oil and cordite, of blood and guts and shit and fear.

But they must be real, Ted thought, dragging yet another waterlogged body aboard, for when have we had time to dream?

Some of the bigger ships, easier targets, had been sunk. Ted had seen two destroyers go down, one on her way out with a full load of soldiers. The sea was filled with bodies, some alive, others broken and beyond help, and then a different rescue operation was launched by the small boats, and the survivors taken to another ship. It's just one step up and two down, he thought with a wave of hopeless frustration. How many have actually made it to Dover? How many have we really saved?

Sometime on the third day they heard that the *Gracie Fields* had gone. On her way back to Dover, with almost eight hundred soldiers aboard, she had been bombed and hit in the engine room. With her engines impossible to stop and her rudder jammed, the ship had begun to circle, a sitting target for more bombs, until two skoots had managed to come alongside and take off some of the troops. The rest had been transferred to a naval sloop which had then taken the crippled ship in tow. But before the night was over, the slow journey came to an end when the *Gracie Fields* filled with water and sank.

Ted felt a wash of sadness when he heard this. That ship was a part of his life; her launching had been a particularly happy family day. He thought of the jaunt they'd had to Woolston, him and Annie and the girls, and their excitement at seeing the famous singer. And she'd made it a real day out for them, laughing and joking as she cracked a bottle of champagne over the bows and then singing her song. It made you want to follow her anywhere, that song, a real good marching song.

And now, only three years later, her ship was on the bottom. But at least she'd gone heroically, serving a grand cause. And that's what we're all doing, he thought, inspired anew. That's what we're here for. And there's no time for moping – that can come later.

All the same, he couldn't help wondering what had happened to the other ships he knew – his own sister ship, the *Fawley*, the *Whippingham* that had so often towered over him at the Harbour Station jetty, and the *Bee*. Were they still steaming back and forth as he was, or had they too been bombed and sunk? And how many of the little ships, or the big ones either, were going to make it home in the end?

Again, he jerked himself back to the present. But he had been almost four days now with little sleep and erratic meals, working on this never-ending task of dragging men aboard out of the water, ferrying them to one of the big ships, returning to shore for the next load . . . And still they came, and still the beaches were crowded, and still the Messerschmitts flew overhead, battling now with British aircraft but still strafing the waiting soldiers and the ships with gunfire, still hurling death at random, for the whole sea was now one vast and unmissable target. And the planes themselves became bombs as they were shot from the sky by naval guns or by RAF Hurricanes. Ted saw one fall on a motor yacht filled with troops and knew that nobody could survive.

The nightmare went on and on. It was as if they had all died and arrived in hell, a hell that nobody could have imagined. It was as if it would never end, as if they would spend eternity in this blood-soaked chaos, this hopeless yet imperative labour, saving lives only to see them smashed a moment later, throwing dead men back into the water like fish useless in the catch . . . Had someone thrown Derek back like that? Or Bob Shaw, or Ben's older brother?

'Look, Skip,' Ben said suddenly. 'It's the old *Whip*.'

Ted glanced up, startled, at the ship they were approaching with their latest load of soldiers. Its familiar white sides loomed above him, streaked with green, and in gold letters on the bow he read the name *Whippingham*. He grinned, feeling absurdly pleased. It was almost like meeting a member of the family. And once again he felt new heart, and the determination to carry on.

But for both the *Ferry King* and the *Whippingham*, Operation Dynamo was over. As they loaded their last men on to the paddle steamer that was surely already vastly overloaded, they were told that all vessels were being recalled. They could collect one last load from the beach, to take back with them, but then they must return to Dover. The German tanks and troops were at the fringes of Dunkirk and no more men could be saved.

'But what'll happen to them?' Ben asked, staring at the beach. There were fewer men waiting there now, and the still burning town looked empty and deserted compared with the past few days, but it was clear that there must still be many left to face the enemy alone.

'They'll have to do what soldiers always have to do in war,' the lieutenant said tersely. 'Fight or surrender. They'll probably be taken prisoner. But some of them will get away, and then they'll either find some other way home or live wild, fighting on their own account. But they're not our worry. Our job's to get ourselves and as many soldiers as possible back without getting bombed.'

Ted took the boat close in to the shore and the last few men scrambled aboard. There was a subdued air about everyone now, for they knew that when they turned their backs on the beach it was for the last time. Perhaps other boats would come to take those waiting out of danger; perhaps not. And it was no use cursing oneself or the enemy or the fate that had decreed it should be so, for this was war, and war was like a machine that, once started, could not be stopped. Or a disease which must run its course until either it or the body it invaded had been vanquished.

Ted stood on the bridge, watching as the other three hauled the bedraggled soldiers aboard. He felt unutterably weary. Their faces passed before his eyes in a blur, without variation. They could have been one man, passing before him over and over again, for at this stage there was no difference between them, no possibility of recognition.

Except . . . As the last man came aboard, he lifted his eyes for a moment and glanced up at Ted, standing before the funnel. His mouth twitched briefly, then stretched in a travesty of a grin. And Ted saw a lock of hair, still dark gold under the grime and the black, dried blood, and knew that here, at last, was Derek.

There was no time for greetings now. Already there was firing in the town, and the Messerschmitts were renewing their attack. Ted reversed the *King* and took her away from the shore. He turned her for the last time and headed for the open sea.

There would be no towing back to Dover. Only the smallest boats were given that luxury. But the *Whippingham* was still in sight, so heavily laden that the sea was almost on top of her paddles, and he set course to follow her. It felt comfortable and right, and as if they were truly heading for home.

'It's not over yet,' Lieutenant Horner said, coming to his side. 'We're likely to be bombarded still, and there may be minefields. But we're on our way back, Ted, and you and your crew can be proud of yourselves.'

Ted shrugged. 'We've done no more than anyone else. It was a job needed doing, and we did it. But I don't mind admitting I'll be glad enough to be home again.' He glanced at the lieutenant. 'Will you take over now, sir? There's someone I want to see.'

He made his way down from the bridge and through the mass of bodies on deck. Some were sitting up, leaning on each other, some lying exhausted at full length. Many were bandaged, though it was clear that their dressings had not been changed for some time. They looked up at him with dull, hollow eyes that started from haggard faces, and he was sharply reminded of the man who had sold matches outside Woolworths.

Derek was leaning against the roof of the engine-room. He looked up at Ted and again stretched his mouth in a grin.

'Hello, Mr Chapman.' The title sounded strange in these circumstances. 'Bet you thought you'd seen the last of me.'

'Derek,' Ted said. He felt almost as thankful as if it had been his own son sitting there, dirty and unshaven, with blood streaking his face and a bandage round one hand. 'Oh God, Derek . . . Our Olive has been almost out of her mind over you.'

The boy smiled. Like all the other men, he looked tired to death, his face thin and lined below the stubble. But the old glint showed briefly in his eyes and there was a challenge in the way he lifted his chin and looked directly at the man who stood over him.

'Tell her not to worry any more,' he said. 'Tell her I'm on my way home. And tell her mum to buy a new hat, because as soon as I get back Livvy and me are getting married.'

And Ted understood that he was not being asked now, as Derek had asked him a few months ago. He was being told. Because this was no longer the boy from up the road, John Harker's son with his smart job as an accountant and his smart red sports car. That boy had grown up and become a man, and that man would not be put off.

'I'll tell her,' he said. 'I'll tell them both.'

And he bent and shook Derek's hand, and knew that his four days at Dunkirk, saving such men for their families, for their sweethearts and their country, had been time well spent.

By the time Olive and Derek were married, on the sixth of July, France had fallen to the Germans and Mussolini had brought Italy into the war. The Channel Islands had been occupied and the coasts of southern and eastern England were ready for invasion, with a hastily erected barricade of barbed wire, scaffolding and concrete blocks to keep off the might of the invaders. Open ground behind the beaches was littered with old cars, buses, even bedsteads that had escaped the search for scrap-iron. It was now illegal to sound motor-horns or to ring the church bells, for these were the signals of invasion.

'A proper home-made war,' Frank called it, but he was on duty most nights now, watching for the planes that were expected hourly. Air raids had begun in the middle of June though so far there had been no damage. But everyone was on edge, waiting for the devastation they knew must come. Hitler had crushed everything in his path. He had taken almost every country in Europe and he had driven back Britain's own army. There could surely be no stopping him now.

'Well, we'll have a good wedding anyway,' Annie said to Jess as they set the final touches to the long trestle-table in the front room. She stood back, looking at the bowls of salad grown by Frank and Ted, the big plates of tinned salmon and cooked ham. Everyone had helped out with bits from their store-cupboards and it looked as good a spread as they'd had at Christmas. 'They deserve it, the two of them. God knows what they're going to have to face when Derek goes away again.'

'And that could be any day. His unit's on the move again. Peggy Shaw heard from Bob this morning.'

Bob Shaw had escaped from Dunkirk too, so the street had rejoiced for both the young men. But Graham was still away and so was Colin. In almost every house in the street now, there was someone to be anxious for and rejoicing always tempered with fear.

And on the second of July had come the news of the sinking of the *Arandora Star* on her way to Canada. She had been carrying fifteen hundred German and Italian internees, one of them Heinrich Brunner.

'Alice looks terrible,' Jess said sadly. 'It's such a shame. Heinrich was a good man.'

'Well, he might have been saved,' Annie said comfortingly. 'They say there were plenty of survivors. And we can't let it spoil our Olive's day.'

And it seemed that nothing, indeed, could spoil this day. Olive looked radiant in a wedding-dress lent to her by a friend who had got married two years earlier. Derek was handsome in his uniform, his hair gold in the sunshine, his injured hand healed. Rose and Betty were bridesmaids, carrying posies made by Molly Atkinson – for which she refused to charge, in gratitude for what Jess had done for her children. And when they all trooped back from the little church at the top of the street the reception turned into a real party, with singing and laughter late into the night.

'You'd think the war was over, from the row they're making,' Jess said to Frank as they walked home with Maureen fast asleep in her pram. She had celebrated her first birthday only two days earlier and seemed convinced that the party had been held in her honour. 'I wish it was.'

'So do we all.' Frank sighed. 'But there's a long road to travel before that happens, Jess. And a lot more pain and misery to suffer too. We've got away with it light so far, hereabouts. I reckon we're going to see a lot more before we're very much older.'

They stopped at the door of number 14. The stars were bright in the night sky. Soon, it would be filled with enemy bombers and they would all get a taste of what Ted and Derek and thousands of others had suffered at Dunkirk.

Frank opened the front door and went inside, lifting Maureen's pram over the step and manoeuvring it through the narrow space. But Jess paused a moment longer, still looking up at the stars and thinking over all that had happened since the baby had been born.

And she remembered the words of Winston Churchill, spoken to the nation after Dunkirk.

'*We shall go on to the end . . . we shall fight on the beaches, we shall fight on the landing grounds, we shall fight in the streets, we shall fight in the hills; we shall never surrender.*'

And again, after the fall of France:

'*The Battle of France is over. The Battle of Britain is about to begin.*'

The Girls They
Left Behind

For my sister Christine
with love

1

Olive and Derek Harker arrived for the latest possible train on that Sunday evening, but Portsmouth Town Station was as crowded as if it were morning. The carriages were filling with soldiers and airmen going back off leave, and the platform was crowded with the women and children who were bidding them goodbye. Some were smiling bravely, but most were already in tears and few would be dry-eyed as the train steamed out of the station.

'I can't bear it,' Olive wept as Derek held her in his arms. 'You don't seem to have been here five minutes. It's so cruel, taking you away like this. We've only just got married.'

'I know.' He stroked her hair. He was having difficulty with his own feelings. Men didn't cry – especially men who were soldiers, going off to war – but he felt disturbingly as if he might. His throat ached in a way he couldn't remember since he was twelve years old. He swallowed the ache and buried his face in Olive's hair, and she turned her head so that their lips met. She clung to him, her body shaking with sobs, and he wondered how he was ever going to bring himself to break away.

'Livvy, I've got to go,' he whispered despairingly. 'If I miss the train—'

'I know. It'll be jankers.' She tried to smile and it nearly broke his heart. 'It's all right, Derek, I'm not going to make a fuss.' The engine was pouring out steam and it billowed around them, enveloping them in a humid cloud. She stared at his face, her eyes dark and hungry, as if she were trying to memorise each tiny iota. She had made love with the same hunger last night, he remembered, and he had been caught up in her desperation, turning to her again and again as if every moment must be used for loving.

Suppose I didn't go? he thought suddenly. Suppose I just walked away from the train, from the station, from the war itself and said to hell with it, it's not my war, I've got a life to live with my wife and my family – if there is one. And what chance do we have to start one?

Suppose I just refused to go . . .

But he knew what would happen. He was a soldier. He couldn't even plead the excuse of conscience. He'd be posted as a deserter. He'd be caught, court-martialled and imprisoned. Perhaps even shot.

He hadn't been through Dunkirk to end up like that.

The guard blew his whistle. The engine blew its own shrill note. Doors began to slam and one by one the men broke away from their girls, from their sweethearts and wives, and climbed aboard. The women stood, their handkerchiefs at faces that streamed with tears, and watched helplessly. Some of them held children in their arms, children who looked bewildered and lost.

'Derek . . .'

'Livvy, I love you.' He caught her hard against him and kissed her fiercely, then tore himself away and scrambled up into the train. The door slammed and he twisted to stare down at her. 'I love you . . .'

'Derek – Derek.' She could not say the words she knew he longed to hear. She had said them in the night, over and over again, but now her throat closed against them and her lips could only form his name. She gazed up at him, her misery tightening about her like a straitjacket, and heard the slow thump of the pistons as the train began to move. He was going from her, slipping away, leaving, and she could say nothing, only stand mute, shaking her head and feeling the tears like rain upon her face.

'*Livvy* . . .'

'Derek – Derek—' Suddenly her tongue was freed and she ran beside the train as it moved slowly along the platform. 'I love you, Derek. *I love you.*' He had heard, she knew he had heard. He was smiling, an odd, distorted smile, and there was rain on his cheeks too, but it wasn't raining and she knew it must be his own tears. *Derek*, in tears? Her eyes flooded again, blurring her vision, but there was no stopping her now and she ran along the platform, blundering into other women, young girls, mothers with babies, giving them hardly a thought for all her thoughts were with the man who was going back to war and leaving her behind.

'I love you, Derek.' She stood at the end of the platform, waving. The train was pulling away fast and he had gone, but his face was still visible, a pale blur as the train receded, and she could see his hand waving back. And although she knew that he could not possibly hear her now, she called to him one last time, her throat aching with the pain and the tears and the effort of trying to make him understand.

'*I love you* . . .'

In the train, Derek caught the whisper of her love, not through his ears but through some deeper part of him, a part where only Olive dwelt and only Olive could reach him. And the tears ran unchecked down his cheeks as he stood at the window and watched the familiar streets of Portsmouth pass him by.

Soldiers didn't cry. But Derek Harker was crying, and he wasn't going to apologise to any man for that.

Olive went back to work the next morning just as if she hadn't got married on Saturday morning and had a thirty-six hour honeymoon. There didn't seem to be much point in doing anything else, despite her father's disapproval.

Ted Chapman had been stubbornly opposed to his daughter continuing to work at all, even though she was employed by Derek's father in the office of his builder's yard.

'Your mother's never gone out to work and I don't like the idea of my girls doing it, once they're wed,' he said for the dozenth time as Olive came down to breakfast. 'Married women ought to stop at home and look after their men.'

'Chance'd be a fine thing,' Olive retorted, feeling the tears dangerously close again. 'How can I look after Derek when he's living in a Nissen hut down in Devon? And we haven't even *got* a home. What am I supposed to do all day if I haven't got a job?'

'You could give your mum a hand.' But Ted knew his argument was unconvincing. Annie had the housework well under control, and both Olive and Betty did their share. And Annie herself had something to say about that.

'More and more women are having to work these days, what with all the young men being called up for the Forces. If she wasn't doing that, she'd be doing something else. At least Harker's is only a few streets away.' She refilled the big teacup the girls had given him for Christmas a few years ago. 'Anyway, you can't tell her what to do now, she's a married woman.'

It was hard enough to believe that, all the same, and Annie had to keep reminding herself by thinking of Olive and Derek's wedding day only the day before yesterday, with Olive in the white dress she'd borrowed from a friend and her chestnut hair glowing in the sun.

'She's still living under our roof,' Ted muttered, and Annie clicked her tongue in exasperation.

'Honestly, Ted! Anyone would think our Olive was out on the razzle every night and bringing back sailors, like Nancy Baxter. All she's doing is getting married, and it's not her fault she can't start with her own home and her man coming home at nights like a couple should. She's a good girl and you know it, and Derek's a decent chap. You were keen enough for them to get married when you came back from Dunkirk.'

'I never said anything against them getting married. It's her working I don't like. But I suppose you're right. Nothing's the same any more, and you can't tell young people what to do.'

He finished his tea and got up, going out into the back porch to find his bicycle clips. Olive and Betty made a face at each other and Annie sighed.

'I don't know about your dad, I'm sure. He's all on edge these days. He's never properly settled down since he came back from Dunkirk. It upset him a lot, that did.'

'It upset a lot of people,' Olive said, thinking of the things Derek had told her. Young soldiers, no more than kids really, shivering and crying all the way home from Dover in the trains, their uniforms still soaked from having to stand in the water, many of them wounded by the bombing and strafing they'd suffered on the beaches. Her dad had been brave, she knew, taking his ferryboat over to help get them away, but he hadn't had to suffer like they had. And he didn't have to go back. She thought of Derek again, going off on the train with all those others, knowing what they might be going back to.

It was queer to think she was a married woman now. It didn't seem right that her life hadn't changed. Apart from that one day and night with Derek, everything was the same. She got up each morning, helped her mum get breakfast ready, went off to the office and spent the day typing out letters and invoices. A lot of building had stopped because of the war, and business was slack, but John Harker wasn't worried about that. 'It'll pick up soon enough, once the bombing starts,' he said grimly. 'There'll be plenty needs doing then.'

On Thursday evenings Olive usually finished a few minutes early and went to the pictures with Betty. There didn't seem to be any point in changing that, just because she was now a married woman. The men had already gone home and she was shuffling together her papers when her father-in-law came in.

'That's right,' he said. 'You go off and enjoy yourself. A couple of hours at the Odeon'll do you good.'

Olive smiled at him. It already seemed an eternity since Derek had gone away and she missed him more each day. Funny to think that this time last week they hadn't even been married . . .

The air was split by the sudden wail of a siren. Its sound rose and fell like the howl of a banshee. For a full minute it maintained its unearthly shrieking, and then it died slowly away. In the silence left behind, it was as if the whole world held its breath.

Olive stopped what she was doing, a bundle of papers slipping from fingers that had suddenly frozen, and stared at John Harker. For a brief moment, the man and girl stood riveted, their eyes locked. Then John reached out and grabbed Olive's arm.

'The shelter! Quick – leave that.'

'But the invoices—'

'Leave them! This is it, Olive. I can hear the planes already.'

'Maybe it's another false alarm—'

'There've been German planes around all day. They've been all along the coast. They've tried twice already – I heard it on the news. But this lot's got through. Drop the papers, Livvy, and get over to the shelter quick. I'll fetch Florrie.'

He pulled her through the door and they ran across the yard. The Anderson was in the garden, through a tall gate set in the wall that separated the Harkers' home from the business. John Harker put his hand between Olive's shoulder blades and gave her a shove that sent her staggering through the gate and halfway down the garden path. Then he turned and ran into the house.

He and Florrie Harker scrambled down into the dim, musty shelter only seconds before the first explosion.

Olive's cousins, Tim and Keith Budd, were involved in a game of cowboys and Indians. Each armed with a toy pistol, they had scurried out as soon as tea was over to join the children who were, for one reason or another, still at home in Portsmouth, and not evacuated to the country. Some had been evacuated and returned after a few weeks, homesick or even badly treated, some had come to the conclusion that there was, after all, no danger from bombing or gas, and some had never left Portsmouth at all, despite the entreaties of the authorities.

Micky Baxter was one of these. Always the wild boy of April Grove, he had exulted in the sudden freedom of no school and formed a small gang of boys who had nothing to do and all day to do it in. Together, they had roamed the streets, looking for mischief and having no trouble in finding it. Their exploits had come to a head when they had held up an assistant in a jewellery shop with a pistol left over from the 1914–18 war. Micky was still on probation for that, but it didn't seem to make much difference.

Jess Budd didn't like her boys playing with Micky Baxter, but although they were half afraid of his scapegrace nature, they were also fascinated by it. And although a lot of children had come back, their own special friends were still out at Bridge End, where they'd been evacuated.

They gathered at the end of April Grove, near the Budds' house. Tim and Keith were both cowboys, like Micky, and the Indians were Martin Baker, who had come back from evacuation with appendicitis, Jimmy Cross and Cyril Nash, who had a pale, angelic face with large brown eyes and spent most of his time trying to undo the impression that his name and appearance invariably created.

Only those who possessed pistols were allowed to be cowboys, and Micky was undisputed leader because his was reputed to be real. Tim and Keith, who had heard the story of the jeweller's shop, glanced at it with respect, and kept their distance, thankful that they weren't Indians. Suppose it was still loaded? But Jimmy Cross scoffed at them.

'Course it ain't that one. They took it off him, didn't they? Anyway, me and Cyril's got real catapults, better'n any old toy guns, they are.'

He displayed the weapons, made of forked sticks and a wide strip of rubber. Tim watched enviously as he bent, picked up a stone from the road, and sent it zinging down the street. Mrs Seddon, who kept the corner shop, came out of her side gate just as the stone whistled past her and she looked up sharply. The boys skittered hastily into a nearby alley.

I hope she doesn't tell Mum, Tim thought anxiously, but the game was starting now and the three Indians were fleeing up the alley looking for places to hide.

The cowboys turned their backs, as the rules of the game demanded, and scuffed their toes in the dust.

'I s'pose you'll be goin' back to the country soon,' Micky observed. 'Runnin' away from the bombs.'

'We're not running away.' Tim protested, uncomfortably aware that they were. 'We only came back to see our Olive get married. Anyway, it's good in the country. There's all sorts of things to do.'

'Oh yeah?' Micky sneered. 'Pickin' flowers? Countin' sheep? That's girls' stuff.'

'There's plenty of things besides that. Good trees to climb. Birds' nests. And we help on the farm, too. We can milk cows.'

'Milk cows? I'd sooner get it out of a bottle. Catch me goin' to the country. I'd rather stay here – no school or nothing, do what you like. It's good.'

'There are schools,' Keith said. 'Our school's open, I heard Mum say so when she and Dad were talking about us stopping here. But Dad says there's going to be bad bombing soon and he wants us out of it.'

'I 'ope there is,' Micky said. 'I *want* the bombs to come. I ain't scared of 'em. Smash! Crash! Just like Saturday morning pictures, it'll be.'

'But suppose *Germans* come?' Keith asked, speaking the name in a whisper. 'S'pose they invade? That means they'll come and live in our houses, they'll take away everything. What'll you do then?'

'I'll fight 'em, that's what I'll do.' Micky lifted his arm and bent it, clenching his fist to make the biceps stand out. 'Tell you what, they're goin' to come in parachutes. I'll catch one of them, tie him up in his own parachute and take him down the police station.' He frowned, thinking of his last visit to that establishment. 'No, I won't, I'll take him up Hilsea Barracks, let the soldiers have him. They won't get *our* house.'

'You're daft,' Tim said. 'There's going to be hundreds of them – thousands. They'll have guns and bayonets and everything. You'll have to hide and keep out of their way. And I tell you what, it'll be better out in the country then. The people out there, they've taken all the signposts down – the Germans won't be able to find their way anywhere, they'll be lost. *We'll* know where we are, but they won't.'

'They won't want to go out there anyway.' Micky glanced over his shoulder. The alleyway was deserted, the Indians long vanished from sight. 'I reckon they've had long enough to find hideouts now. Anyway, I bet I know where they've gone. They'll be round Carlisle Crescent. Just because Jimmy Cross lives near there, he thinks it's the only place to hide.'

The three boys cocked their pistols and ran up the alley, keeping an eye open as they passed open gateways in case the Indians were skulking in someone's garden. There was no sign of them as they passed along the back of September Street and came to the railway line and level crossing. Carlisle Crescent was on the other side of the track, and Tim and Keith hesitated.

The railway line formed a natural boundary to their normal territory. Although they were allowed to go out to play in the streets, they were not supposed to go beyond certain limits without first letting their mother know. April Grove, March and October Streets, with their maze of alleyways created a small, tight neighbourhood where all the children and adults were known to each other. Cars seldom appeared there, especially in the evenings, and only tradesmen's carts and wagons made regular appearances during the day. Ball games, skipping, hopscotch and marbles could be played unhindered, and although some of the less tolerant residents might object to the constant thud of a ball against the wall of their house, and even forbid the chalking of cricket stumps or goal posts on the bricks, they did little more than make occasional testy appearances, chasing away the offending children. Usually, the children returned after a few days, chalked up their goal posts again and resumed their games.

Children from other streets were less welcome. They were looked upon with suspicion and told to 'Go and play in your own street'. And by the same unwritten rule, if you went to someone else's street you were likely to be sent off with a flea in your ear.

But Jimmy Cross lived in Carlisle Crescent, or near enough, Tim reasoned. So it ought to be all right to go there. And as for letting Mum know, she couldn't expect him to break off from a game of cowboys and

Indians to run home and tell her they might be going over the railway. Specially after what Micky Baxter had been saying about them running away from the bombs.

Anyway, they'd be back long before she came out to call them in for bed, so she'd never know. And as long as they didn't run into Dad, walking home from work, they'd be safe.

The crossing gates were closed and a train approached along the track. The boys scampered up the steps of the bridge and the engine chugged beneath, its roar filling their ears. Steam and smoke billowed around them and they capered about in the cloud, delighted, flapping their hands in front of their faces and grinning at each other through the swirling mist before scuttering down the steps on the other side and into Carlisle Crescent.

The houses here were posher than in April Grove. They weren't in a terrace but were separate, some in twos and some on their own. They were all slightly different and some were bungalows. They had front gardens, big enough for a bit of lawn, and in a few there were bushes and even a tree or two. A couple had greenhouses with tomato plants growing in them. It was almost as good as the country, Tim thought, wishing he could live in such a house. Fancy having grass in your garden, just like a real field!

The three cowboys entered the crescent cautiously, their pistols still held at the ready as they searched for signs of Indians. One of the gardens had a low wall running along beside it and they ran across to it, half-crouching, and peered cautiously over the top, as cowboys did at the cinema.

Tim's hero was Roy Rogers, who had a marvellous horse called Trigger. He modelled himself on Roy Rogers now, imagining himself in cowboy gear, with chaps on his trousers and a holster slung at his waist. He noticed that Keith was limping slightly. Keith's favourite was Hopalong Cassidy.

Zing! A stone whistled past their ears and bounced off the wall beside them. The cowboys jumped, startled, and Tim remembered the catapults. He waved his pistol, regretting the lack of caps. At least he could have made a noise. As it was, he felt helpless.

Another stone whizzed past, almost grazing his cheek, and he was suddenly angry. His mum and dad had always laid down very strict rules about throwing stones. You only threw them into the sea, and even then only when there were no swimmers about. And you never, never threw them at people.

'They're cheating,' he hissed. 'Stones are dangerous. They could hit us in the eye.'

Micky too was feeling disgruntled. The catapults had put the Indians at an advantage, and that was against the rules. The cowboys were supposed to win. He debated introducing a new rule, that only cowboys could have catapults, but knew that the Indians would claim that they were nearer to bows and arrows and should therefore be theirs. Perhaps it would be better if catapults weren't allowed at all. But that would mean he couldn't have one either, and he'd already made up his mind to get himself the best in the street.

If only he hadn't had to give up the old Army pistol. It hadn't actually been his, but he'd been the only one with the nerve to carry it. If he still had that – and could get some ammunition for it – well, there wouldn't be any dispute then. He'd win every time.

He thought of the German parachutist he meant to catch. He'd be armed. Perhaps Micky could get his pistol off him – and some bullets as well. He wouldn't even have to worry about swearing the man to secrecy, since he wouldn't be able to talk English.

Feeling suddenly cheerful, he brought his mind back to the game in hand and nodded.

'You're right,' he said. 'Stones aren't allowed.' He stood up, braving the hail of stones now flying at them from the alleyway across the street, and shouted, 'The game's over. You're cheating, so we've won. Come out or we'll come over and take you prisoner.'

For answer, the biggest stone of all came flying towards him. He ducked, and two things happened very quickly.

From immediately behind him came the sound of splintering glass as the stone smashed into a greenhouse. And from above, from all around, vibrating in the very ground beneath their feet, came the howl of the air-raid siren.

It swelled through the air, filling the sky, spreading over their heads, shrieking its way through the streets, between the houses, along the alleyways and into every narrow passage. It forced its way into houses and woke babies in their cots; it startled old men and women dozing in chairs. It transfixed lovers in quiet corners, and froze women standing at stoves as they cooked their families' suppers. It shrieked at people on the way home from work, leaving them stunned as the unearthly wail rose and fell about them. And as the droning sound died away at last, everyone turned their eyes to the sky to see the approaching aircraft.

There was a moment's silence and then the street erupted into action. Families poured from houses into their gardens, making for the shelters. Firewatchers hurried out, dragging heavy stirrup-pumps and still fastening on tin helmets. An air-raid warden cycled past, intent on reaching his post, never noticing the children. There was a tumult of shouting, of panic, of orders yelled and frightened screams. And then, again, silence as the shelters were reached and closed.

The boys huddled together by the wall. They could hear the faint throb of the planes as they neared the coast. They looked at each other, their faces pale, eyes wide.

'What shall we do?' Tim muttered. 'We ought to be in shelters too.' They all knew what they should be doing. They had rehearsed it often enough. But their rehearsals had always been on the assumption that they would be close to a shelter – either their own, at home, or in their own street or at school. Here, they were on alien territory, in a street where they were not supposed to be playing, and they would as soon have thought of going into someone else's shelter as they would have thought of walking uninvited into the house.

He noticed that somehow the Indians had come across the road and joined them. The catapults dangled from their hands. It didn't seem to matter now that they'd been cheating. Martin Baker was looking white and scared but Cyril Nash's eyes were bright. And Jimmy, although within a hundred yards of his own home, was making no effort to run for shelter.

'They're coming,' he breathed, his voice wobbly with excitement. 'I can hear 'em now. Listen. *Look*!'

The boys craned their necks. Away to the south, where Southsea Common met the sea, they could see a black cloud of aircraft, like starlings gathering for their evening roost. They approached steadily, their engines snarling, and as they came over the city itself, Tim saw the first of the bombs begin to fall.

They dropped like black eggs from the belly of the aircraft and tumbled slowly towards the earth. He stared at them, fascinated. His eyes watched as they descended, falling through the network of balloons that floated above the city, falling towards the ships in the harbour, falling towards the Dockyard where his father worked, falling, falling, falling . . .

The explosion shook the ground under his feet and thundered through the air in great waves of brutal sound that battered against his ears and tore at his body. Almost before it hit him, he flung himself to the ground, and the six boys huddled together on the pavement while the first air-raid of the war stormed over Portsmouth.

Jess Budd stood at the front door of number 14, April Grove, holding her baby daughter Maureen in her arms, and watched her sons scamper along the street. She looked up at the blue sky and shivered. For a moment, she was almost inclined to call them back, but before she could raise her voice Peggy Shaw opened her front door and came out to stand beside her.

'Making the most of the fine evenings,' she remarked. 'What're you going to do about your kids, Jess? Are they going back to the country?'

'Oh, yes. We only had them home for the wedding. Rose wanted to be bridesmaid, and we had to give our Olive a day to remember – she's got precious little else. But Frank says there's going to be bad raids soon and the children have got to be out of it.'

'And are you going too?'

Jess shook her head firmly. 'I'm stopping here. I had enough of being away all through the winter. And Frank needs his wife to look after him.' She looked down at Maureen, who was wriggling in an effort to get down, and set her down to toddle on the pavement. 'I know it means keeping the baby at home too, but there's nothing we can do about that.'

'Well, I won't say I shan't be glad to have you back next door,' Peggy commented. 'It felt really queer all those months, without you about. And the street's like a morgue without Tim and Keith and the other kids playing out there. I'll be sorry to see them go. Mind, I wouldn't moan if it was Micky Baxter. The mischief that boy gets up to, you wouldn't believe.'

'Maybe when the raids start Nancy'll change her mind and send him off after all.' Jess looked up again at the evening sky. It was still blue, with only a faint flush of apricot to show that the sun was beginning to go down. It was good that the weather had been fine these past few weeks, so that Frank could get over to the allotment and work in the fresh air. It blew all the dust of the Dockyard boiler-shop out of his lungs and he always looked a bit happier when he came home with a basket full of gooseberries or blackcurrants or vegetables that he'd grown himself. 'You just can't believe there's people out there killing each other,' she said. 'Bits of boys like your Bob and our Colin, climbing into aeroplanes and coming over to drop bombs on people they've never ever seen. And our lads—'

Her words were drowned by the shriek of the siren. Maureen began to scream in panic and Jess bent and scooped her up in her arms, holding her close. She looked at Peggy Shaw, her face white.

'Is it another false alarm?'

'I don't know.' Peggy stared at her. 'We ought to go down the shelter, just in case . . .'

'But the boys – Tim and Keith. They're out playing somewhere. And Rose – she went up to the Brunners—'

'She'll go in their shelter then.'

Jess bit her lip in a torment of indecision. 'I'll have to go out and find the boys. Can you take the baby for me, Peg?'

People were coming out into the street, looking fearfully at the sky, asking each other if it was real. They heard the throb of aeroplanes.

'That's not our lads!' They had grown used to the sound of British aircraft, but this was different. There was a snarl in the sound, a menace as if a vicious dog was growling deep in its throat. Jess caught her breath.

'That's it! They're here. Oh, *Peg*—'

'Down the air-raid shelter, quick,' Peggy said. 'There's no time to waste. I can hear the guns. Quick, Jess.'

'But the boys – Rose – Frank . . . they're out there somewhere – I can't just—'

'You can't go looking for 'em, either.' Peggy's hand was on her arm, pulling her back through the door. 'Jess, you can't go out in the streets, you'll just have to hope they've got the sense to make for shelter. They know what to do, we've all practised it enough, goodness knows. But you've got Maureen to think of.' She hustled Jess to the back door and they stared at the sky again. It was still clear, still cloudless, but now the blue had taken on a hard, sinister sheen and they could hear the snarl of approaching aircraft. Suddenly, the barrage balloons seemed a weak and flimsy defence against the advancing wave of destruction.

'*Quick*, Jess,' Peggy urged again, but Jess shook her head and broke away.

'You go. Take the baby. But I've got to find the boys. I can't leave them out there . . .'

She hurried back through the house, her breath coming in quick, frightened gasps, and out into the street. The aircraft were visible now, like a cloud of black starlings high above the balloons. Her body ached with terror. She ran across to the corner by Mrs Seddon's shop, staring up October Street.

Peggy was behind her again, Maureen still crying in her arms.

'They're coming,' she panted. 'Jess, you've got to come down the shelter. The boys must have gone in with someone else. They're not here – you can see that. Someone'll be looking after them. Jess, for God's sake, come back . . .'

Jess took one more frantic look up the deserted street. The throb of the planes was closer. In a few seconds they would be overhead. The bombs would begin to fall.

'They must be up the alley.' She dashed to the end of April Grove, where the boys had scampered on their hunt for the Indians, but it was empty. Everyone had run for cover.

Despairing and guilty, she turned and Peggy hustled her through the little house, leaving the doors open as she went. The two women pelted down the garden path and dived into the Anderson shelter. Panting, half sobbing, they squatted on the low benches that Frank had fitted against the walls, and stared at each other. The baby wailed in Peggy's arms, and Jess took her back and cradled her against her breast.

'Oh, Peg—' she began, but the rest of her words were lost in the explosion of the first bombs.

In Portchester Road, Kathy Simmons had just finished giving her children their supper when the siren went.

Stella and Muriel pulled faces. 'Do we *have* to go down the shelter, Mum? It'll only be another false alarm.'

'Yes, we do,' Kathy said sharply, although she would have liked to ignore it herself. 'One of these days it's going to be real, and then what would we do? Anyway, we've got to keep practising, you don't know how quick the planes can—'

She stopped, suddenly aware of a throaty grumble from the sky. Hardly believing her ears, she went to the back door. The sound was closer. She felt a wave of fear, and the baby inside her seemed to jerk as if he felt it too.

'Quick!' she snapped, snatching up the box that contained all the family birth certificates and other papers too important to be lost. 'Come on, Stella – leave that – get down there as fast as you can.'

'But my dolly – I've left her upstairs.' Muriel's voice began to rise in a wail but Kathy grabbed her arm.

'There isn't time for that – she'll be all right – come *on* when I tell you!' The garden path had never seemed so long. She hurried the girls down it and into the Anderson shelter Mike had dug out before he went away. The drone was coming closer, it sounded almost overhead although with her last frightened glance before she ducked through the low doorway, she could see only a cloud of black freckles in the sky, like swarming ants. Oh God, she thought, they're really coming, we're going to be bombed, and Mike not here and our baby boy not even born . . . She folded her arms across her stomach and bowed her head, shutting her eyes tightly as if by doing so she could shut out the terrifying reality.

But reality would not be shut out. She heard the first bomb fall, and was forced to open her eyes and pull her two little girls into her arms, to try to give them the comfort she so desperately needed herself. And as if that first bomb were a signal, others began to fall, sometimes singly, sometimes in clusters, so that the explosions seemed to merge together in one massive blast. As the shock waves ran through the earth, shuddering beneath Kathy's feet, the corrugated iron of the Anderson shelter rattled in her ears. The girls screamed and she clutched them to her convulsively, feeling the unborn baby tremble again in her womb. Be still, she begged it silently, be quiet. You're too small to kick like that, you've only just quickened. But the fluttering movements continued, as if her own fear communicated itself to the tiny, developing life, and would not let it rest.

The detonations continued, deafening her. Surely the planes must be directly overhead. How safe was an Anderson? She'd heard that no shelter could survive a direct hit. The thunder of the bombs threatened to burst her eardrums, shatter her skull. Nobody had ever told her an air-raid would be like this.

In the worst moment of all, it was as if the air inside the dimly-lit Anderson turned into vapour, as if she could see it shimmer all around. The iron of the walls wrinkled, almost as if they cringed in pain. The earth floor split into a thousand tiny cracks. And the noise was no longer noise. It had become something greater, something that took her whole body and shook it without mercy, as a tiger might take and shake its prey until it was senseless.

Dimly, Kathy was aware that she was screaming, although she could hear no sound of her voice. She could feel the vibrations in the children's bodies and knew that they too were crying with terror. She wanted to comfort them, but had no power over her own fear. It swamped her, leaving her no strength for anything else.

For a long time, after the sound of the last plane had faded, the three of them lay still on the splintered floor. The turmoil of the raid still sounded in their ears and it was only gradually that the silence crept back. At last they heard the tentative note of the Raiders Passed signal, and Kathy lifted her head.

'They've gone,' she whispered, and crawled to the steps that led up into the open air.

What she saw then was no surprise. She had known, from that first terrifying explosion, that the bombs were falling dangerously close. She had known that she and the two little girls would have no home to go back to.

But she was still not prepared for the sight of the house she and Mike had loved so much, shattered and gaping like a smashed tooth. Still shaking, she dragged herself out of the shelter and gripped the distorted iron to pull herself upright, staring in misery and despair.

The house was a mess of torn brickwork and splintered wood. There was nothing at all left of the roof, and the upstairs rooms were totally demolished. Downstairs, all she could see was ruin – smashed furniture, ornaments and knick-knacks scattered and broken, a curtain still half hanging from a crooked rail, filthy with dust.

The two girls scrambled out and stood beside her, still sobbing.

'My dolly,' Muriel whispered. 'My dolly . . .'

2

Frank Budd had just left the Dockyard when the siren sounded.

Carrying his leather-bound lunchbox, he walked through Unicorn Gate and turned to go along Flathouse Road towards the Royal Hospital. From there, he would make his way through the maze of narrow side streets towards Kingston and Copnor.

Sometimes he took the bus, but it was too hot this evening to be cooped up on a crowded bus, and it was ten hours since he'd tasted any air other than the steamy heat of the boilershop. With no overtime tonight, for the first time in weeks, he could afford to walk. Jess wouldn't be expecting him till seven and there would still be time to spend a few hours over on his allotment in the fresh air and evening sunshine. There was plenty to be done – hoeing and weeding, and perhaps some soft fruit to pick, if Jess hadn't had time to get over there herself during the afternoon.

The allotment was thriving this year. After the bitter winter and cold spring, he'd been afraid everything would be late, but instead they'd had this glorious summer and the vegetables and fruit had flourished. He'd never seen the beans so high at this time of year before, and the gooseberries and currants were fat and glowing. The row or two of strawberries had done well too, and they'd had them for tea once or twice as well as providing a good bowlful for Olive's wedding last Saturday. Strawberries were, in Frank's opinion, a luxury and he only grew them because Jess liked them so much. They did make a good jam, with a few gooseberries to help them set.

The road was full of men leaving the Dockyard, some on foot like Frank, others cycling. There were buses too, taking them all over the city and down to the Hard, where the ferryboats waited to take those who lived in Gosport on the five-minute trip across the harbour. It was a vast exodus, and other folk kept clear when the Dockyard was coming out.

It was at that moment that the siren sounded.

The wail filled the air. Frank stopped as its shriek hit him, and felt the jolt of shock, followed by a tingling shudder that ran over his whole body. He glanced quickly up and down the street. In that moment, everyone must have done exactly the same – stopped as if frozen. Then there was sudden movement everywhere as people began to run and shout. An old lady who had been creeping slowly along with her hand on the low garden walls to steady herself, stood with confused, frightened eyes, her lips trembling as she clutched her shopping bag close against her.

For a few seconds, Frank stood as uncertain as the rest. Then he remembered that there was a public shelter two streets away. He set off towards it, then turned back and approached the old woman.

'They're coming,' she whispered. 'They're coming to get us.'

'They're not going to, though, are they?' He spoke cheerfully, although already he could hear the snarl of the bombers approaching. Had the warning come too late?

It had certainly come too late for a lot of people to find proper shelter. Especially people like this poor old dear, who was now sobbing helplessly and wetting herself into the bargain. He saw the puddle forming round her feet and tugged her arm gently.

'Come on, missus, let's get you home. You don't want to be out on the street in this.' The planes were very close now and he felt the first shock of explosion as bombs fell in the harbour and the Dockyard. The old woman whimpered and clutched him and he forgot to be gentle and dragged her along the street, ignoring the shopping bag that she had dropped.

'Me rations! Me rations!' she wept as she stumbled along, but Frank was concerned only with getting her indoors. I hope to God she didn't lock the front door, he thought as they reached it, and breathed a sigh of relief as it swung open at his touch. He pushed her inside.

'Have you got a shelter?'

'No. We're a sixer, see, we couldn't have no Anderson, I dunno why. Something to do with the water-pipes in the gardens, they come through every sixth house. My daughter's hubby says we'll have to make do under the stairs, they say that's the safest place, don't they . . .' Her voice faltered as Frank pushed her along the narrow passage. The space beneath the stairs had been boxed in as a big cupboard, with an old mattress shoved inside to sit on. He bent and thrust the old lady inside, then scrambled in beside her as another explosion shook the house.

'Here, that was close.' She seemed to be recovering a little now that she was home. Together, they crouched on the floor in the dimness, listening to the roar of planes overhead and the thunder of the exploding bombs.

'It's bad, innit,' the old woman whispered. 'They're going to bomb us out of our own homes. They're going to keep on bombing till there's none of us left and then they're going to take our homes away and live in 'em and do what they like.' She began to cry again. 'It's not fair. It's not *fair*. Not after what we went through before. I lost my husband in the last lot, killed in action he was, to make England a land fit for heroes to live in, and what good did it do? Tell me that, eh?'

'Ssh.' Frank found her hand and patted it. 'Don't think about it now. It's happening and we've just got to live through it and not let it get us down.' But he spoke absently, for his thoughts were with Jess and the children. For God's sake, he thought, don't let those boys be out roaming the streets in this lot. And he made up his mind that they would be sent back to the safety of the countryside as soon as possible.

The explosions rocked around them. What's happening out there? he wondered. I ought to get out there and help.

He began to crawl out of the cupboard. 'I've got to go now, love. You stay here till they sound the Raiders Passed signal and your daughter gets back, then you have a nice cup of tea. You'll be all right here.' He hoped it was true.

She clutched him with feeble fingers, entreating him to stay, but he gently disentangled her hands. 'You stay here. You're safe here,' he repeated, and stood up, ducking again immediately as an explosion thundered almost overhead and he heard the sound of breaking glass and falling masonry. For a moment, he hesitated. He could have his head blown off the minute he stepped through the front door.

But someone was going to get killed anyway, in this lot. Probably hundreds, maybe thousands of people. And others would be hurt, and buried under collapsed buildings, needing help.

The next explosion was closer still. It sounded as if it were almost next door. The window of the room he was in shattered, glass flying everywhere, and if he hadn't ducked he would have been peppered with it, slashed to pieces perhaps. But this time the thought of scrambling back into the safety of the home-made shelter didn't enter his head. Without another word to the old woman, who was now whimpering with terror, he wrenched open the door and ran along the passage to the street.

Whatever was happening out there, he had to be part of it. He couldn't stay here while his own family and home were in danger, somewhere across the city, and he couldn't take shelter when he had a duty to do.

The front door was still ajar. He pulled it open and stood for a moment looking up and down the street. God knows what I expected, he thought. Complete devastation? Houses knocked down, on fire, bits of bodies lying about all over the place? In fact, his mind had shown him no pictures of what a bombed city might be like. Until now, although he had known the facts, he had been unable to imagine the consequences.

But to his surprise, there was little sign of destruction. At first glance, everything seemed normal. And then he noticed that almost every window in the street was shattered. A few chimneys had fallen or stood askew, ready to topple. And a boy of about twelve – not all that much bigger than his Tim – came by, crying and holding his head. There was blood dripping down through his fingers.

Frank ran out and grabbed his arm. The planes seemed to have passed over now, but more might come at any moment and he could still hear explosions. Smoke rose in black clouds above the rooftops. The danger was by no means over.

'What are you doing out here? You ought to be in a shelter.' His voice was rough with fear and concern, but sounded merely cross and the boy flinched and tried to pull away.

'I wasn't doing nothing wrong, mister. I tried to get 'ome, but the bombs come. I couldn't find nowhere to shelter. And then summat hit me, it hit me head, look. I'm *bleedin'*.'

He began to sob again and Frank felt a flash of rage. He knew now what Jess had meant when she'd railed against the war, saying it wasn't fair that ordinary people who just wanted to live their lives should have to get caught up in such things. Old women like the one he'd left behind in the house, alone and crying with terror, nippers like this one with a wound that could have killed him. And this was just the start.

'Come on,' he said more gently. 'Let's get you to a First Aid post.' He prised the boy's fingers away from his scalp and examined the cut. It was more of a graze, but it had taken off a fair lump of skin and blood was oozing through the matted brown hair. It needed proper attention, from someone who knew what they were doing.

He thought of going back to the Royal Hospital but they'd be too busy with real casualties. There must have been any amount of people killed and hurt in the raid. He could hear the streets coming back to life now as people ventured out, and there were shouts and yells as folk discovered what had happened. There'd be plenty needing help. He felt a stab of fear as he wondered again how Jess and the kids had fared.

But he couldn't just leave the boy. Best get him to a First Aid post, where he could be properly looked after.

Drayton Road Infants' School. It had been taken over by the ARP, they'd have people there who could help. It wasn't too far away. He hoped to God they could get there. There didn't seem to be any bombs falling at the moment, but the sky was filled with black smoke now, split with streaks of orange flame, and he could smell the acrid tang of burning. It looked as if there was a bad fire somewhere, and from the direction he thought it could be the gasholder at Rudmore. If that was on fire, there could be another explosion at any minute, worse than a bomb.

He gripped the boy's arm and began to run. The lad made no more effort to escape and ran along with Frank, still half sobbing. He kept his other hand pressed to his head, the blood still oozing between his fingers. Frank hoped he wouldn't pass out before they got to the First Aid post.

An ARP warden cycled down the road, his wheels wobbling as he avoided glass and broken tiles.

'Get back under shelter!' he shouted. 'There's not bin no Raiders Passed signal yet. There could be another lot coming over any minute. Get inside, all of you.'

Frank took no notice. He had only one thought in his mind, to get this boy to a place where his head could be attended to, and then to get home. His own family might be buried and calling for help, needing him.

He stopped the warden.

'I'm a firewatcher – got to get on duty. But I want this youngster seen to first. Can I get through to Drayton Road?'

The man stared at him. His face was already grimy with dust and smoke. He looked as scared as the rest, and why not? He'd never been bombed either, it was the first time for him same as everyone else.

'Drayton Road?' he said, as if the name were new to him. 'I dunno, mate. There's bin bombs up there, I know that.' He glanced up at the sky, so blue only half an hour ago, now filled with the menacing cloud of fiery black smoke which darkened the streets. 'Summat's burning down near the Yard.'

'I thought it might be Rudmore,' Frank said, and the warden nodded.

'Yeah, it might. And if that goes up we'll cop another packet. This your boy? His head don't look too good.'

Frank shook his head. 'I just want to get him somewhere he can be seen to. Then I'm off up Copnor.'

He set off again. The warden was already turning away to shout at some children who were throwing stones at one of the few unbroken windows left. At the corner of the street a man passed him, his face grey with shock, eyes staring. He looked at Frank and put out a hand.

'The Anchor – you should see what they done to the Anchor.'

'The Anchor?' Frank said. 'The pub, you mean?'

'You should see what they done,' the man repeated. He seemed to be on the verge of tears. 'The bastards. The bastards.' He shook his head blindly and stumbled on, purposelessly, as if he had nowhere to go, nothing in mind but the agony of what he had seen.

'Come on,' Frank said, taking the boy's arm again. 'I can't help it if there are more planes coming, I've got to get back up Copnor.'

They were in Kingston Road now, one of the busiest thoroughfares in the city, leading from the London Road across Portsbridge, and eventually to the beach at Southsea. It was all one long road really, with several different names as it passed through different districts – easy to see from the air, Frank thought, looking up again to see if there were planes. But the sky was still black with smoke. At least that might stop the enemy spotting their targets, he thought grimly.

And it seemed that the danger was, for the moment, over. As he hurried across the main road, aware that a little further along people were shouting and crowding towards Kingston Cross, as if something had happened there, the siren began to wail again. But this time, instead of the fearsome, swelling lament that warned of enemy approach, it was like a long-drawn sigh of relief – the signal that the raid was over.

Kingston Cross. That was where the Blue Anchor Hotel stood. Frank had never been inside, for he was a teetotaller and avoided public houses, but he knew them all by name and used them as landmarks. The family often teased him about his knowledge of local public houses, revealed whenever he gave directions. 'That's just opposite the Coach and Horses.' Or, 'Turn left by the Star and Garter and then keep straight on till you get to the Black Lion.' How did anyone who never touched a drop know so much about pubs, his brother-in-law Ted would ask. But Frank would point out that it was just a matter of knowing the city you'd been born in, knowing it like the back of your hand.

He could see Kingston Cross now, from where he stood at the corner of Powerscourt Road, and it was obvious that something up there had been badly damaged. Already fire engines were appearing, dashing along the roads with bells ringing, but they'd heading for the fire over at Rudmore. He hesitated, wanting to go straight up to the Anchor, but the boy beside him was sobbing again, clearly frightened and in some pain. He'd have to get him seen to first. And he was desperately anxious about Jess and the children.

He turned and made for Drayton Road. Only a few yards now, and he could hand over his burden and go and give whatever help he could.

And then, on the corner of Wymering Road, he stopped dead.

The main part of the school, where the older children went, was still standing, its wide brick façade and narrow tower untouched. But the infant school had received a direct hit. The buildings where five-year-old children had learned to read and write and add two and two together, were little more than a heap of rubble, smashed beyond recognition, and a dense cloud of dust hung over the ruins, swirling in its own breeze, and settling like a miasma of despair over the wreckage.

Frank stared at it, his mouth moving in silent expostulation.

Some of the walls were still partially standing, the rooms inside chaotically exposed, children's drawings and maps of Europe still pinned to the walls along with posters giving instructions about the war and diagrams of bandages and slings. Tables, desks and chairs were tossed and jumbled amongst the wreckage of collapsed ceilings and partitions. First-aid boxes and equipment, stacked ready for the first emergency, were broken and torn, smothered with dust, half buried under wooden laths and plaster. Sandbags, piled outside as an extra protection, had been torn and split open, their contents blown in all directions to add to the gritty cloud of filth.

And amongst it all, bewildered and dazed, staggered the survivors and less badly injured of the people who had manned the post and been there when the sound of the siren first ruptured the air.

'My God,' Frank said in a whisper. And then, more loudly, 'My God. Oh, my *God* . . .'

'It's bad, innit, mister,' the boy beside him said in a frightened voice.

'It is. It's bad.' Frank glanced down at him. The seeping of blood seemed to have stopped and where it had run down his face and neck it was now darkening against the grimy skin. 'Look, you'd better get off home. It don't look as if there'll be any bandages for you here. D'you reckon you can make it by yourself? I'll have to stop here now.'

The boy shook his head a little and flinched as if it still hurt. But his eyes were on the devastation before them. 'I can stop and help too, mister. I ain't hurt that bad.'

Frank hesitated. It didn't seem right, a nipper like this seeing the sights he felt sure they would see. But if there were people buried under that rubble, they'd need all the help they could get. And the kid was looking better, though the shock of seeing the bombed school had turned him a shade or two paler under all the dirt.

'All right, then,' he said. 'But you get off home the minute you want to, see? Your mum'll be half out of her mind worrying about you.' Half an hour ago, he would have given that priority, just as he'd been first anxious to see the old lady into safety and then determined to get home to Jess. But now it was different. There were people here who needed help this minute, if they were to be saved, and they had to be put first. Old ladies who were frightened and mothers worrying about kids – even Jess, his own wife, came second.

He ran across the road towards the school. Other people were flocking round too, appalled, staring at the ruin of the buildings they knew so well. The playground, where children had run and shouted and laughed, was a mass of rubble, the little row of lavatories knocked almost flat. And from the wreckage came a sound that chilled the hearts of all those who heard it – the first, wailing cry for help.

It rose from the broken earth where the bomb had struck. And it seemed to Frank Budd that it was the cry, not of one person, not of one man or woman or child, but a cry that expressed the anguish of all those who were to be a part of the war that was now storming its way over the world.

The war that had begun for Portsmouth on this warm and sunny evening in July 1940.

Jess did not wait for the Raiders Passed signal. As soon as the thunder of the explosions and the roar of the aircraft began to fade, she was at the door of the shelter, gazing out at the sky. She stared in dismay at the dark smoke billowing overhead, and turned to her neighbour.

'God knows what they've done, Peg! The whole place is alight. I've got to find the boys!'

Peggy came to crouch beside her. Together, they watched as the smoke was slashed by orange flame. She twisted her head to look at the row of terraced houses, dreading what she might see.

'Well, they haven't hit April Grove,' she said with relief. 'That's something to be thankful for. We've still got homes to go to.'

'The children . . .' Jess said again. 'I've got to go and look for them.' She turned her eyes up to the blackened sky. 'I can't hear any planes now. They've gone.'

'We're supposed to wait,' Peggy began doubtfully, but she knew that Jess would not be able to rest until she had her family safe at home again. 'Well, I daresay it's all right to go out now. I'll keep Maureen with me.'

'Thanks, Peg.' Jess scrambled out of the shelter and ran up the path. The house stood just as she had left it, all the doors wide open, and she went straight through to the front and out into April Grove. As she came out on to the pavement, the siren sounded again and she gasped, then realised that it meant safety. The raiders really had passed.

Granny Kinch and her daughter Nancy emerged from number 10, Granny Kinch swathed as usual in a grubby flowered pinafore with her grey hair tightly bound in metal curlers. They looked up at the smoke-filled sky.

'Somewhere's caught it, look. I bet that's Rudmore. It'll go up like a torch any minute, see if it doesn't.'

Jess paused. 'Have you seen my boys? They're not with you, are they?'

Nancy Baxter shook her head. 'No, love, they're not here. Nor's our Micky, come to that. Didn't they go off up the street somewhere?'

'I don't know where they are.' Jess stared at the two women. 'You mean your Micky's out somewhere too?'

Nancy shrugged. 'Went out straight after tea. I saw him with that Nash boy and little Martin Baker. Playing cowboys'n'Indians, they were.'

'But they must have been scared to death!'

'Our Micky?' Nancy laughed. 'He'll be all right, he'll have found somewhere to hide, and your two with him. Takes a lot to frighten our Micky.'

'They could have been killed,' Jess said. 'I've been half out of my mind—' She gazed desperately up October Street. People were beginning to come out now, looking up at the sky and turning to each other, needing the reassurance of contact.

Jess's sister Annie appeared, hurrying down from the house at the top of April Grove. She too had an apron on, though it was a good deal cleaner than Granny Kinch's, and her face was anxious.

'Jess! Are you all right? I had to leave the supper half-cooked, ruined it is, and where we're supposed to get more when everything's on ration, I don't—'

'I've lost the boys!' Jess burst out, and saw Annie's face whiten. 'They went out to play and never came back. I don't know where they are.'

'Oh, my goodness.' Annie leaned against the wall, her hand over her heart. 'I thought for a minute . . . You mean they were out in all that lot?'

Jess nodded miserably. 'I've got to find them, Annie. If anything's happened to them – and Frank's not home yet either—'

'I'll come with you.' The two sisters set off up October Street, asking everyone they met if they had seen Tim and Keith. But nobody had, and everybody wanted to talk about the raid. Fred and Ada Brown stopped them as they hurried past. They were both trembling with agitation.

'I thought the bombs were coming right through our ceiling,' Fred Brown said, his old voice quavering. 'Me and our Ada, we got under the stairs, and the whole house was shaking round us.'

'I bet there's hundreds dead. Thousands.' Ada Brown shuddered and stared at Jess. 'You mean your two were out in it? That's terrible.'

'Someone must have seen them,' Jess said. 'There was five or six of them, playing cowboys and Indians. They must be somewhere.'

Her voice was ragged and jerky. Annie gave her a quick look and took her arm. 'Come on. We'll try September Street.'

'They're not supposed to go on the main road.'

'What boys are supposed to do and what they do are two different things,' Annie said. 'What about Rose? Is she all right?'

'She went up to see Joy Brunner.' Jess's steps quickened. 'Peg said she'd have gone in their shelter.'

'Well, that's what she did, then. Maybe the boys are there too.' They turned the corner of September Street. There were one or two cars and vans parked near the shops, and a bus was coming over the level crossing. You'd hardly know there'd been a raid on, except for the acrid smoke overhead and the people standing about in knots talking.

'Oh, my God, look at that.' Mr Hines, the butcher was out in front of his shop. 'Looks like they were trying for the Dockyard.'

'And looks like they missed,' old Mr Clogg said sourly. He ran a tiny hardware shop over the road. He had no shelter and had shuffled over to the Hines's when the warning sounded, still wearing the old carpet slippers he always wore in the shop. 'That fire's not in the Yard.'

'It's not just one fire. I reckon half the city's going up in flames.'

'I thought we were going to as well,' Mrs Hines said. 'Those bombs sounded right overhead. I didn't think we'd see a thing left standing . . .' She shook her head. Her lips trembling, her face white.

'I don't suppose they're all that interested in Copnor,' Mrs Marsh from the dairy said. 'There's nothing here they'd want to bomb.' But no one looked convinced.

Mr Hines was first to make a move. He shrugged his shoulders, glanced at his wife and said, 'Well, we'd better carry on, I suppose. I was halfway through chopping up some ox-liver. I hope you turned the gas off, Freda.'

'So do I,' Mrs Hines said, with an attempt at a smile. 'Else we'll have burnt potatoes for supper.' She looked at the sky again, at the smoke and the flames, and her mouth quivered. 'It's horrible,' she whispered, and Jess saw the tears in her eyes. 'Horrible . . .' She turned and almost ran into the house.

Mr Hines looked embarrassed and gave Jess and Annie a twisted half-grin. 'Freda gets upset,' he said unnecessarily. 'She was in London during the last lot, y'see.' He shrugged helplessly and followed his wife into the shop, and Mr Clogg shuffled back across the road.

Jess heard a sound on the other side and turned to see Alice Brunner and her daughter Joy emerging from their shelter. Rose was close behind them. She saw her mother and ran to her, burying her face against Jess's breast.

'Thank goodness you're all right,' Jess said, her voice choked. She held Rose close against her. 'I've been worried stiff. D'you know where the boys are?'

Rose shook her head. 'Oh, Mum, it was awful . . .'

'I know, love, I know.' Jess stroked the dark hair but her eyes were searching the street. 'But it's over now. It's the boys I'm worried about.' She looked at Alice Brunner. 'Did you see them before it started? Were they up this way?'

Alice was white-faced and Joy's eyes huge with fear. Like everyone else, they looked around them and then stared at the smoke. Alice began to cry.

'They'll be all right,' Mrs Marsh said. 'It doesn't seem to have hit anything round here.'

'And you think that's all right?' Alice's voice was high and shrill. Ever since the war began, she had been living on her nerves. The arrest of her German-born husband Heinrich had brought her close to breaking-point, and since news had come last week of the torpedoing of the *Arandora Star* she had been trembling on the brink of collapse. 'People are being killed, and you think it's *all right*?'

'No, of course I don't.' Jess saw Mrs Marsh bite her lip. 'None of it's all right, Alice. But we've got to carry on, haven't we? We can't just go to pieces. That's the only way we'll win this war – by carrying on, by not *letting* them beat us.' She turned to go indoors. 'I was just going to clean out my big fridge when it started, and that's what I'm going to do now, Germans or no Germans. If Hitler *is* going to invade, I'm not having him say I keep a dirty dairy! And if I were you, Alice Brunner, I'd do the same. Keep your shop tidy and everything as it should be. Your husband would have wanted you to do that, wouldn't he?'

Alice nodded. Her mousy hair was hanging loose about her pale face. 'There wasn't a neater man in Pompey than my Heinrich.'

'Well, then. What'd he say if he walked in and found it in a mess, and you looking like that?'

Joy took her mother's arm. 'Come on in, Mum. I'll make you a cup of tea.'

Jess was still holding Rose. In her imagination, she saw Tim and Keith lying dead in some alleyway, their toy pistols still clutched in their hands.

'I'll never forgive myself if anything's happened to those two,' she said, beginning to run again. 'Frank *said* they should never have come back, he said there'd be bad raids, but I would have them home and now – oh, those Germans, those wicked, *wicked* Germans!'

'They'll be all right.' Annie and Rose kept pace with her, Rose still hiccuping. 'Mrs Marsh was right, you can see there's been no bombing round here. They've just taken shelter somewhere, that's all, and – look!' She quickened her steps further. 'That's them now! Just coming over the railway.'

Jess felt as if her legs were stuck in treacle. They wouldn't move fast enough. She saw Tim and Keith hurtling towards her, their faces wreathed in grins, and she felt the sobs rise in her throat.

The smiles were of embarrassment, appeasement and a half awareness of relief at having survived the bombing. But to Jess they were an affront. Her fear turned to anger, and her relief, so enormous that it demanded instant expression, merged with her anger. A moment ago, her fury had been directed against the Germans; now it was focused for a few moments upon her sons.

'You naughty, naughty boys!' she exclaimed, catching them roughly by the shoulders. 'Whatever do you think you've been doing, staying out in the streets in that lot? Where have you been? I looked for you everywhere when the sirens sounded. Don't you realise you could have been killed? D'you think it's something to laugh at, worrying me like that?'

Tim and Keith stared at her, shocked by her outburst. Jess rarely shouted at them. She could tell them off, and frequently did, and they were well aware of the limits they had better not cross, but she hardly ever shook them like this, with rough hands, and raised her voice. And she was *crying*. Their grins faded and they glanced sideways at each other and ducked their heads.

'We only went over to Carlisle Crescent,' Tim said, trying to sound aggrieved. 'We were playing cowboys and Indians—'

'Carlisle Crescent? That's over the railway. You know you're not supposed to go down there.' Jess shook them both again. 'If you don't stop in your own street, you won't be allowed out to play at all.' Frank was right, they were better off in the country. You couldn't keep track of boys like this, and you couldn't keep them indoors all the time either, they needed to be out playing, letting off steam.

She saw that Keith had begun to cry, large tears creeping down his cheeks, and even Tim's lips were wobbling, and she felt suddenly guilty at the way she had yelled at them. Her hands more gentle now, she pulled them close and hugged them tightly.

'There, it's all right,' she muttered. 'I was just so worried, not knowing where you were and hearing the bombs falling. You mustn't go so far away again. You must always be close enough to get home, see? Come on now, let's go back indoors before they come back.'

Subdued now, the three children walked back down the street beside her. Peggy Shaw was still in number 14, making cocoa. She had fed Maureen and put her to bed, and now she went back next door to her own family.

'And now you two can go to bed as well,' Jess told the boys. 'I don't care if it is before your usual bedtime. Drink your cocoa and scrub that dirt of your faces and then get upstairs.'

Rose, still white-faced and shaking, crept into Frank's armchair and curled up there. She looked at her mother.

'I don't have to go yet, do I? Can't I stop up till Dad comes home?'

Jess's heart gave a lurch. Until now, she'd been too worried about the children to give way to her fears about her husband. Now terror flooded back into her heart and she felt sick all over again.

But there was nothing she could do. She couldn't even go out to look for him.

'Yes,' she said, not wanting to wait on her own. 'You can stop up for a bit. But not too long mind. Your dad might be a bit late tonight.'

The boys went to bed without a word. But Jess and Rose sat together, watching the smoke drift slowly across the sky and worrying about Frank.

It was almost ten o'clock when Frank finally arrived home. For three hours he worked in Drayton Road, helping to pull away the rubble that had buried so many of the ARP wardens and helpers who had been preparing to give aid to others. With his bare hands, he dragged at bricks and laths and plaster, tugging frantically because under all this, somewhere, he could hear a woman's cries or a man shouting for help. Or perhaps there was someone who couldn't cry or shout, who was unconscious but still alive, choking in the dust, crushed by a beam of timber or a pile of broken bricks.

Frank was a big man, powerfully built. He took charge of a little group of men who could lift heavy weights, and they moved from place to place over the ruins, shifting what other people couldn't budge. They needed to take special care because sometimes it was clear that a beam which must be shifted could bring down a whole wall, or a portion of roof that was still hanging as if by a thread above their heads. And sometimes, although they knew that the person who lay buried beneath could only be saved if the beam was moved, they dared not touch it, for fear of its killing others.

As well as moving rubble, there were bodies to be shifted. The bodies of first-aid workers, men and women who had attended classes since the war was declared, determined to be of use, but had had their lives slashed away before they could attend so much as a cut finger. And they were not neatly laid-out, covered with white sheets, as if they had died in hospital or been tidied up by others more accustomed to such things. Instead, they lay like broken dolls amongst the wreckage, their bodies crushed, their limbs smashed, their eyes open and staring from the mess of raw flesh and blackened blood and bone that had been their faces.

Some of them were not even whole. Their legs had been torn from their bodies, their arms lay draped across upturned tables or tangled with chairs, there was even a head that had been wrenched from its neck and rolled by itself to lie perched on a tottering pile of bloodstained bandages. When Frank first caught sight of it, it seemed to be watching him and he turned away and vomited. And I've been in a war before, he thought. How is this going to affect these other people, who never dreamed of such things? How about the boy with the grazed head, that I brought here?

All these fragments must be collected and put together, like some gruesome jigsaw puzzle, and you couldn't turn your back and say it wasn't your job. It was everyone's job.

At last the terrible work was over. Firemen had come and gone, ambulances had taken the injured away to the hospital. The rubble still filled the playground where small children had played hopscotch and fivestones, and would have to be left until there was time to deal with it. But as far as anyone could tell, there was no one left under the chaos of smashed masonry and torn beams. No one alive, anyway.

Eleven dead. Eleven people who had been fit and healthy but for one reason or another not expected to fight – men too old or too young, women who had been glad to offer their time. Eleven people who had left their homes that afternoon expecting to be home in time for supper and would never go home again.

'One of them was the Superintendent,' Frank told Jess when he finally came in through the front door to find her sitting doing nothing, with Rose now asleep in his chair. 'And there was others hurt, some of 'em aren't going to live, you could tell that.' He shuddered a little, thinking of the injuries, things that ought never to happen to human bodies. 'And all the time I was thinking about you and the kids and wondering what was going on up here. I couldn't tell where all the explosions were coming from, and no one seemed to know anything. It seemed as if the whole city had been smashed to bits. And the sky was so full of smoke and flames, I thought they'd set light to whatever was left anyway.'

'I know.' Jess held him tightly, not caring that his clothes were filthy, that his hair was full of dust and plaster. 'We could see it from here. Whatever was it? Someone said it was one of the ships in the Yard on fire.'

Frank shook his head. 'There might've been some ships hit, I dunno. But the fire came from the gasholder at Rudmore. A bomb fell right inside. It wasn't full, one of the firemen who came to Drayton told me that. It could've been nasty, all the same, if they hadn't got it under control so quick.' He sat down wearily at the table and leant his head on his hands. 'Thank God you're all right, Jess. All the way home, I was thinking what it'd be like to turn the corner and see number 14 just a mass of rubble. There's a whole row in Portchester Road, with hardly a slate left and all their windows out. And houses in Farlington Road they'll never be able to patch up, almost nothing left of them, bricks and stuff all over the place. And the Blue Anchor's gone, and half a dozen houses and a garage in Gamble Road. And that's just around this part of Pompey. God knows what the rest of the city's like.'

Henry, the big tabby cat, got up from the rag rug and came over to lay a paw on Frank's knee. Frank reached down and pulled the cat on to his lap and Henry purred and rubbed his head against the dirty shirt. He had spent the raid crouched against the wall of the coalshed and had hardly left Jess's side since she had come back to the house.

'Poor old chap,' Frank said, scratching the hard, furry head. 'You can't understand it at all, can you.'

Jess went out to the scullery to make some more cocoa. As she came back into the room, she saw Rose stir and open her eyes. She saw her father and scrambled out of the chair to run to him and bury her face against his chest.

'Rose!' Jess remonstrated. 'Your father's all dirty still.'

But Frank held his daughter's head and his big hands stroked her straight black hair. He looked down at her trembling body and Jess felt her own heart soften at the expression on his face.

Frank wasn't a man who was demonstrative towards his children. He hadn't had enough of that kind of loving in his own childhood to be able to pass it on. But she knew his heart was tender and that he longed to be able to cuddle them, or even to give them a casual pat, without feeling awkward. And, just occasionally, there were moments when his emotions overcame his reticence and he was able to express them freely and without embarrassment.

This was one of those moments, and Jess felt her eyes fill with tears as she watched her husband and eldest child hold each other closely. And she felt a sharp poignancy and a deep sadness that it took a war, sometimes, to bring people as close as they ought to be to one another. That eleven people had to die before Frank's eyes before he could hold his daughter in his arms and stroke her hair.

3

'Mind you don't go too far away, now. I don't want to have to go looking for you again if there's another raid.'

Jess looked at her sons with some misgivings. After last night, she was half afraid to let them out, but it was impossible to keep them indoors on such a fine morning.

'We'll be all right, Mum.'

Tim and Keith hopped from foot to foot. They had been awake early, gazing out of their bedroom window over the allotments, talking about the raid. It was nothing but a game to them. They hadn't seen what Frank had seen, nor did Jess want them to see such things.

'I want them back out in the country,' she'd said to Frank last night, after Rose had gone to bed. 'Back out at Bridge End, where they'll be safe.'

'We'll take them on Saturday,' he agreed. 'And you can stay there too, at Mrs Greenberry's.' But Jess had shaken her head. She'd liked Mrs Greenberry well enough, and loved being in the country, but she'd hated the months away from Frank when she'd gone with the first evacuation. A wife's place was with her man, and she didn't intend to leave him again.

Tim and Keith raced up the street, as excited as puppies let off the leash. They stopped near the end of April Grove, where the road widened and there was space for a game of cricket. Someone had chalked stumps on the blank wall of the end house of March Street.

'Shall I go back for the bat?' Keith suggested, but Tim shrugged.

'Don't feel like cricket. I want to go exploring.'

Keith looked around. They were near their Auntie Annie's house here and knew every inch of the three streets. He looked through the fence at the allotments. There were footpaths across them, but the boys weren't supposed to go there unless they were going to Frank's allotment, to take him a jug of tea or tell him dinner was ready.

'There's Micky,' he said. 'And Jimmy Cross and Cyril.'

The three boys came through a hole in the fence and joined them. Micky was grinning.

'What happened to you last night? Mummy make you go to bed early?'

Tim flushed. 'We wanted to listen to the wireless.' They hadn't been allowed to, but Micky didn't have to know that. 'D'you want a game of cricket? We could get our bat.'

'Cricket!' Micky said scornfully. 'We've got better things to do than play cricket. We're going down to look at the bombs.'

'Bombs? You mean there's still bombs? Ones that haven't gone off? Bet there's not.'

'Bet there are, then. Bet we'll find some.' Micky strutted cockily. 'We'll get 'em for souvenirs. My mum says she'll put 'em on the mantelpiece if we find any.'

'Not *unexploded* bombs. That'd be dangerous.'

'Well, ones that have gone off, anyway. And shells and bullets and that. There'll be all sorts down Drayton Road way. The school got bombed and hundreds of people were killed. We might find bodies.'

Tim wasn't sure he wanted to find bodies, but the idea of shells and bomb cases was alluring. He hesitated and looked at Keith.

'We're not allowed to go right down Drayton Road.'

'Mummy's boys,' Micky sneered. 'Well, we're going, ain't we?' Cyril and Jimmy nodded. 'Don't suppose we'll have to go that far anyway. There was bombing nearer than that. Bet we'll find all sorts of stuff.'

He turned away, and the other two boys followed him. Tim and Keith stared after them enviously.

'I wouldn't mind finding a few bombs,' Tim said. 'That'd be something to take back to Bridge End. Give that Brian Collins something to think about!'

'But we're not supposed to go out of the street,' Keith said wistfully.

Tim thought for a moment. 'We only promised not to go over the railway. Drayton Road's not over the railway – it's in the opposite direction. And we don't have to go all the way. We can always come back if we get fed up.'

Keith hesitated. He glanced back down the street towards number 14. Their mother had gone back indoors and the only person in sight was Mrs Glaister next door, scrubbing her step. She wouldn't take any notice of them, she never did.

'Come on,' Tim said, setting off up March Street. 'The Germans won't come this early in the morning. And if we go back to Bridge End tomorrow we'll never get another chance to find a bomb of our own.'

Filled with fresh excitement, the two boys scurried up the street and caught up with Micky and his henchmen as they turned the corner into September Street. There were plenty of people about now, opening up their shops or walking to work. A few stood at bus stops, but there weren't many buses about. Perhaps they couldn't get through the bombed streets.

'There's whole rows of houses smashed to bits,' Micky said with relish. 'I bet some of 'em are still burning. We could help put 'em out. We might find a parachute. That's how they're going to invade, by parachute. They'll all come down from the sky, with guns and hand grenades.'

'They won't,' Tim said. 'They'll come in ships.'

They crossed over Copnor Road. The two Budds had never been so far away from April Grove without permission. At first they'd been nervous, half expecting to be called back or spotted by someone who knew them and might tell Mum or Dad. But now there was less chance of that and they relaxed and look round eagerly for signs of bomb damage.

By the time they reached Chichester Road, Keith's short legs were tiring and he was finding it difficult to keep up with the others. But at the first sight of broken windows and debris littering the streets, he forgot his weariness.

'Coo-er! Look at that . . .'

They gazed at the windows, already being boarded up. There were people up on roofs too, putting back slates. A woman with a scarf wound over her head like a turban swept broken glass out of her front door.

'Come on,' Micky urged as they slowed down, 'there's better'n this to see. I want to see some real smashed houses.'

But when they reached Portchester Road, even Micky stopped in awe. They stared at the ruined street, at the piles of debris that still blocked the road, at the shattered roofs and torn walls. Some of the houses had been completely destroyed. Others had whole rooms exposed, with pictures still hanging on the walls and teacups still on the tables.

'There's someone's lav, stuck out in the middle of nowhere.' Micky pointed to a bathroom that had been partially demolished. He sniggered. 'Wonder if they were sittin' on it . . .'

'I could do with a pee,' Cyril said, and ran over to the lavatory bowl which hung at a drunken angle at the top of a splintered staircase. The other boys giggled and someone shouted at them. Cyril came back grinning and they went on down the street, kicking at loose bricks and clambering over piles of rubble.

'There's all sorts of stuff just bin left,' Micky said. 'Look. Tins of peas, beans, all bent and twisted. And kids' toys. I bet some of it's still all right.' He bent and scrabbled through a pile of objects that had been heaped in the gutter. 'There's a Dinky car here, nothing wrong with it at all.'

The other boys began to do the same, turning over broken dolls and mangled train sets. Most of it was beyond repair, but there were a few bits and pieces that could be slipped into pockets. They moved slowly along the pavement, pushing the muddled heaps with their toes, keeping out of the way of the people who were clearing up.

'You can get right into these houses,' Jimmy Cross said. 'I wonder what it's like.'

The nearest house was partly destroyed, with the upper walls torn away to expose its upstairs rooms, while downstairs remained closed and mysterious. Through the broken window, they could see tumbled furniture and doors hanging at crazy angles.

'I wonder if anyone got killed in there,' Tim said in a hushed voice.

Micky's eyes lit up. 'Let's go and see.'

Keith hung back a little. 'Will there be blood? I don't like blood much, it makes me feel funny.'

'Stop out here then.' The bigger boys were already pushing open the front door. It swung back, revealing a mess of broken laths and torn wallpaper. The stairs were covered with broken plaster, with bits of blue carpet showing here and there. Micky glanced up and down the street. 'Quick – no one's watching.'

Tim looked at his brother. He was uneasily aware that they ought not to be here, that this was something that would definitely be forbidden. If Dad ever got to hear about it . . . but the temptation was too strong to be resisted. Yet he couldn't leave Keith out here all by himself.

'Come on,' he said. 'There won't be any blood. They've taken away all the people who got hurt.' He turned to go after the others. Keith, his lips trembling a little, followed him unhappily.

Micky was in the front room, rummaging through a cupboard that had once had a glass front. Most of its contents were broken, but there were a couple of glasses that were only slightly chipped, and he took them out and stood them on the windowsill.

'They'll do for our mum. She likes a glass of port and lemon. So does my gran.' He looked round the filthy room and his eyes gleamed. 'Here, this'd make a smashing den.'

Jimmy Cross was sifting through another heap of rubble. 'It's all girls' stuff,' he said in disgust. 'Look at this – a china doll with its face all smashed. And a teddy-bear with all its stuffing coming out. We're not going to find anything worth having here.'

'This is all right.' Tim had found something else. He wiped the dust off with his sleeve and held it up. 'It's a donkey.'

The other boys crowded round to look. The donkey was made of twisted and woven cane. It carried panniers on its sides and wore a straw sombrero with its ears poking through.

'It's just a kid's toy,' Micky said, but Tim shook his head.

'It's not, it's from Gibraltar. Our Auntie Annie's got one just like it. Her Colin brought it home once – he's a sailor. He helped sink the *Graf Spee*.' He looked at the donkey again. 'I'll take it home for Mum.'

'Oy! What you doing in there?' They jumped as an ARP warden pushed his way into the room and grabbed their shoulders. 'Don'tcher think things is bad enough without looters and sightseers? Clear off, before I calls a copper.'

Micky turned indignantly. 'We're not looting! My auntie lives here. Least, she did till yesterday.' He looked around him at the ruined house. 'We just come over to get a few things for her.'

The warden stared at him. His face was tired and grey, and he looked as if he had neither slept nor shaved for the past two days. The harsh lines softened and he laid his hand on the boy's arm.

'I'm sorry, son,' he said more quietly. 'I wouldn't have bawled at you, only we had a lot of nosy parkers round here today, snooping round to see what they could see – and take away, too, some of 'em. I dunno what they want to come gawping for, they'll see plenty more of it before they're much older. But you didn't ought to be poking round inside, all the same, it ain't safe. The whole lot could come crashing down any minute.'

He led them back on to the littered pavement, and they stood looking up at the ruins of the house. Tim looked at Micky.

'We'd better go home,' he muttered. 'Our mum'll be looking for us again.'

'I was just goin' anyway,' Micky said loudly. 'There's nothin' else worth takin'. Our auntie'll be ever so upset.' He turned and swaggered away up the street.

The rest of the boys trailed after him. Tim felt uncomfortable. He wasn't above telling the odd fib himself, but he felt that there was something wrong about Micky's lie about an auntie living in that house. Only yesterday, someone *had* lived there – someone real, who didn't have a home any more, who might even have been killed. It didn't seem right to take things out of their house and then tell lies about them.

He was still carrying the donkey. He wondered what to do with it. He could drop it in the road, but somehow he didn't like to do that. He wiped some of the dust from its head. Perhaps Maureen would like it.

But by the time he arrived home, he knew that he would never be able to produce it without a lot of explanations about where he had found it. He went up the back garden path, relieved to find that his mother was out shopping, and hid it in the coalshed.

Kathy Simmons woke that morning to find herself sharing a large school hall with a crowd of other people who had been bombed out of their homes or evacuated because of the danger of explosion. She lay for a moment on the hastily made-up camp bed, staring miserably at the sunshine filtering dustily through the tall windows.

For a few moments, before opening her eyes, she had tried to convince herself that the raid had been no more than a nightmare, that she was still at home and had never spent the evening and half the night being pushed from pillar to post, sent first to this rescue centre, then to that, until at last she and the girls had finished up here. But it was no use. Already she could hear the voices of the helpers as they prepared breakfast, the weeping of other people around her and the sobs of her own little girls.

Dragging herself back to reality, she sat up and brushed back her hair with fingers that still trembled. She didn't seem able to stop shaking, even though she'd slept, on and off, for the past three or four hours. Last night it had been worse – great shudders that seemed to tear her body apart. She'd felt so guilty, being unable to control them when Stella and Muriel needed all the comfort she could give them, but someone had given her a cup of tea with a lot of sugar in it and that had helped. For a bit.

Muriel was crying again now in her little nest of blankets. There hadn't been enough beds for everyone, and she and Stella had been put to bed on a heap of old cushions. Kathy hadn't been at all happy about those cushions, they were stained and tattered and she wouldn't have given them house room, but there was nothing else and she'd been too worn out to argue. She bent over and touched Muriel's shoulder, drawing her into her arms.

'Don't cry, pet. It's all over now, we're quite safe. Come into my bed for a minute.'

The child allowed herself to be pulled into bed and lay there in Kathy's arms, sobbing bitterly. Kathy felt her heart wrench. It wasn't fair, bombing little children out of their homes. It wasn't Christian. She stroked the fair hair, wondering if Muriel would ever get over it. She was only six and didn't understand. Stella was nine and had a bit more idea, but she'd never expected the sort of horror that had happened last night. Kathy hadn't expected it herself.

Muriel was trying to say something now, the words choked by sobs. Kathy held her tightly, crooning and smoothing her hair. 'Don't try to talk. It's all over now. Everything's all right now.' She wished she could believe it.

Stella was awake too, sitting up and watching them. Her face was white but she wasn't crying. She looked as if she'd buttoned up everything tightly inside her.

'She wants her dolly,' she said. 'She wants Princess Marcia.'

Kathy's heart sank. They had found the doll last night, during that first unbelieving survey of the bombed house. Almost everything had been smashed. The doll's china face had been broken beyond repair, its arms and legs crushed. Kathy had wept herself at the sight of it. She remembered the day Mike had brought it home, when he'd come back from one of his Mediterranean trips. He'd brought her a little basketwork donkey at the same time . . . She'd turned away, too sick at heart to look for anything else. There wasn't any point.

'I'm sorry about Princess Marcia,' she said, rocking Muriel in her arms. 'We'll get you another dolly.' But she knew it wouldn't be the same.

After that, there wasn't time for crying. The helpers had poured out cups of tea on a trestle table at the end of the hall and everyone was crowding round trying to grab the sugar. There was bread and marge too, but nothing else. Some of the children picked at theirs and left it, others stuffed it into their mouths as though they hadn't seen food for a month. Kathy put the pieces Stella and Muriel couldn't eat into her pocket. There was no knowing where the next meal might come from.

'What are we supposed to do now?' she asked one of the helpers, a woman with grey hair and a tired face. She'd probably been up most of the night, trying to sort out the endless stream of people who'd been bombed out. 'Where can we go?'

The woman shook her head. 'Don't ask me, love. I'm just here to pour out tea and make sandwiches. There'll be someone come in from the council later on to sort all that out for you.'

Kathy went back to the corner where she and the girls had spent the night. It was the only home they had now, that rickety little camp bed and the pile of old cushions. She wondered how long they would have to live here, and what they would do for clothes and food. They had nothing but what they had been wearing when the siren had sounded.

The morning wore on. Nobody seemed to know quite what to do with themselves. People sat on their beds or gathered in small groups to talk about how awful the raid had been. A couple of women started an argument. Most of them were still feeling shaken, and one girl kept being sick.

Helpers came and went, and two or three women carrying briefcases came in and set up a sort of office on the trestle tables. One of them called for attention and asked all those whose names began with A to form a queue to be interviewed.

'That's us at the back as usual,' Kathy commented ruefully. Muriel had stopped her bitter crying now and was sitting miserably on the camp bed.

Stella, still white-faced and subdued, had asked if she could go outside to play, but Kathy had shaken her head. 'I'd rather you stopped here, under my eye. We might have to go somewhere else and I don't want to have to go looking for you.'

There were quite a few children, who had either not been evacuated or had been brought back when it seemed as if there was going to be no bombing. A few had toys they'd managed to salvage, but most of them were growing bored and restless. The smaller ones clung to their mothers, whining and grizzling, and some of the bigger boys started to chase round the hall, jumping on and off beds and shouting.

'I 'opes to Gawd we don't 'ave to stop 'ere long,' said a woman near Kathy. 'You'd think they'd 'ave summat better than this ready. I mean, what're they going to do if there's another lot like last night? We'll be crowded out.'

'I suppose they're trying to get something organised now.' The queue of people had now reached those whose names began with D. The As, Bs and Cs had already returned to their little spaces and gathered up what belongings they still possessed. 'What does your name start with?'

'W,' the woman said gloomily. 'Wilson. It'll be the middle of next week before they gets round to me.'

'Well, I don't see why we got to wait,' someone else chipped in. She had frizzled ginger hair and the end of a cigarette drooping from her lip. 'I'll be going to stop with my sister at Farlington. I don't see as that's their business. They never took no interest in us before.'

'Yes, but they'll give you money, won't they,' Mrs Wilson said. 'To buy new clothes and furniture and stuff. And they wants to know just who's bin bombed out, for their records.'

The ginger woman looked as if she didn't give tuppence for the records, but the possibility of being given money didn't seem to have struck her before. She sat down again and lit another cigarette.

At midday the tables were cleared again and urns of soup and tea brought in. There was more bread and marge, and this time most people ate it. There was milk for the children, but it was obvious that supplies were scarce. Presumably the bombing had made it difficult to get fresh food through, though there seemed to be a good store of tins and packets in the school.

At last the queue reached S, and Kathy found herself sitting in front of the trestle table with the girls one on each side of her. The woman behind the table was wearing a floral dress and looked hot and sticky. She was rather fat, with wavy grey hair that looked as if it had been polished.

'Name?' She had a scratchy pen and an inkpot. 'Address? And how many in your family?'

'Just the two girls,' Kathy said, and the woman looked at her sharply.

'Husband away?'

'He's in the Merchant Navy.'

'I see.' The woman wrote down all the details. 'You've managed to save your documents, that's a good thing. Some people have got nothing, just nothing. What else is salvageable?'

Kathy stared at her.

'What else did you bring with you? Can you get much out of the house? Furniture, clothes, utensils?'

Kathy shook her head numbly. 'Nothing.' She felt the ache in her throat, the hot threat of tears in her eyes. All day she'd been trying to keep them back for the sake of the children, but now her control was slipping.

'Nothing at all?'

'We couldn't even get Princess Marcia,' Muriel said suddenly. 'And Stella's donkey that Daddy brought home.'

The woman looked at the children, then back at Kathy. All day she had been interviewing people who had been bombed out of their houses and now had nothing at all, and she had begun to harden herself towards the tragedy of it all. It was the only way to get through. But the sight of Muriel's face, mourning her lost doll, touched her heart and brought her own tears perilously close.

'Well, there'll be other dolls,' she said briskly, forcing them back. 'The main thing now is to find you somewhere to live and give you some money. Now, you can be housed for a short while in a reception centre about half a mile away – a church hall. This one is being kept for immediate emergencies. You'll be allowed enough money for your immediate needs such as soap and a change of clothes, and when a house is found for you, you'll be given money for furniture.' She opened a tin box and gave Kathy a pound note and a tenshilling one, entering the figure in a column beside Kathy's name. She signed the sheet of paper, then tore it off and handed it over. 'Keep that safe. It tells us what you've had. You're allowed a total of five pounds but it's not to be frittered away, mind. And if you're evacuated the sum will be different, of course, since you won't be requiring furniture.'

'I shan't be evacuated,' Kathy said. 'I want to be in Portsmouth for when my husband gets home.'

The woman pursed her lips. 'You'll be sending the children away, though.'

Kathy shook her head. 'I'd rather we stayed together.'

'They'd be a lot safer out in the country.'

'We'd rather be together.' She tried a shaky smile. 'Anyway, they say lightning never strikes twice in the same place.'

The woman sighed and shrugged. 'Well, it's up to you.' She looked past Kathy at the queue behind her. 'Next.'

Kathy folded the blankets they'd used and piled them neatly at the end of the bed, wondering if they would be used that night by some other bomb victim. With the two little girls, she walked through the streets to the church hall, where she found another camp bed, another pile of blankets, and another pile of battered cushions. Here she was told that she was on high priority for a house and could go to look at one at once.

She sat down on the bed and cuddled Stella and Muriel against her. She had done nothing all day, yet she was exhausted. Tomorrow they'd have to go out and find some cheap clothes, maybe in a second-hand shop. The grey-haired woman was right. Five pounds – even one pound ten – seemed a lot of money. But it would have to be spent carefully to buy all the things they would need.

'Will I be able to have a new dolly?' Muriel asked, and Kathy cuddled her closer, feeling the hard ache once again in her throat.

'Yes,' she said, 'we'll find you a dolly.'

Betty Chapman spent the morning cleaning the windows of the dairy where she worked. Even though they were criss-crossed with brown paper strips, Mrs Marsh insisted that they must be kept clean. A dairy had to be hygienic.

'She'll have me dusting and polishing the sandbags next,' Betty grumbled to her sister Olive as they ate the sausages and chips their mother had prepared for their midday meal. 'I'm sick of frittering my time away in the dairy. Any old woman could do that job. There's better things for people like me.'

Olive sniffed and Betty felt exasperated. Although she had been married for less than a week, she seemed to think she'd gone up in the world, somehow. As if being a 'married woman' as she now liked to call herself, made her better than her younger sister. As if she knew more.

Well, maybe she does, but I bet it's not all that much, Betty thought. I reckon I know as much about the facts of life as she does – except that she knows what it *feels* like. She gazed at Olive's face, trying to see whether there was any difference. Her sister was certainly apt to go off in a dream these days, staring into space with her fork halfway to her mouth. Was she thinking about it then? Was she remembering her wedding night, she and Derek in bed together, thinking about what they'd done?

'I don't think you've heard a word I said,' she exclaimed crossly. 'If you're not going to be a bit more chatty than this, I might as well read *Tit-Bits* while I have my dinner.'

'You'll do no such thing,' Annie said sharply. 'I'll have no reading at table in this house. And it's lunch, not dinner.'

Betty made a face. All her friends called the midday meal 'dinner' and thought her stuck-up when she called it 'lunch'. But Mum had picked up these ideas when she'd been in service in a big house, and you couldn't argue with her.

'Well, it's like a morgue,' she grumbled. 'Our Olive sitting there with a face as long as a wet weekend and nothing cheerful on the wireless. And there's been nothing but the air-raid in the shop this morning. Everyone was either in it or knows someone else who was in it. They can't talk about anything else.'

'And can you blame them? There's been people killed here, in Portsmouth, only half a mile away from this house. It could be us next time, don't you realise that?'

Annie's voice trembled a little. The raid had frightened her badly. All the time she'd been worrying about Olive and Ted. Olive was at Harker's and would almost certainly get into their shelter, but Ted was on evening shift, taking the *Ferry King* across the harbour to Gosport, and she knew how much he hated it, especially since Dunkirk.

'And how d'you think I feel?' Olive demanded suddenly. 'I was married last Saturday, remember? Two days married life I had, and now my Derek's miles away down in Devon, and God knows when I'll see him again.' She glowered at her sister and Betty shrugged.

'That's not my fault is it? I didn't tell you to get married.' She bit her lip. She and Olive had always been good friends, never squabbled much, yet these days it seemed they were always bickering. She said more quietly, 'I'm sorry, Livvy. I know you miss him. Same as I missed Graham when he was away. And he'll be off again soon, once they get the ship sorted out, and I don't know what might happen to him, do I. But that's just what I'm saying. They're both doing something and we're just *stuck* here. I want to be doing something too. Something really important. Don't you?'

'I reckon it's important to keep on going same as always,' Olive said. 'The men have got to have homes to come back to and it's up to us women to make sure they do. Look at that raid last night. Dozens of houses smashed. People have been coming into the office all morning trying to get Mr Harker to do their repairs. How d'you think he'd manage without someone to run his office?'

'Oh, I daresay he needs someone to do all his paperwork for him,' Betty agreed. 'But it doesn't have to be you, does it? Mrs Harker could do that. Anyway—' as she saw her sister's face darken again '—I wasn't talking about you, I was talking about me. I want to do something more than count bags of eggs and make up pats of butter. Not that there's much butter to pat these days, nor eggs to count neither.' She laid her knife and fork together on her plate as Annie had always taught her, and sighed, 'I wish they'd call me up into the Land Army. It's ages since I put my name down.'

'I don't reckon they're going to,' Olive said. 'They've got too many girls registering. I tell you what's happened, with people not using their cars any more, and farmers going back to horses, all the blokes who worked as village garage mechanics have gone on the land. That's why they don't want the girls after all. And there's plenty of old men, farm labourers who know what they're doing and pleased enough to earn themselves a bit of money. I shouldn't think you'll ever get called up.'

'Well, I'll go into one of the other Services then. The Wrens. Or the WAAFs.' She got up and looked into the mirror that hung over the fireplace, pulling with her fingers at the golden-brown curls clustering over her head. 'Which uniform d'you think would suit me best?'

Annie clucked with irritation. 'Honestly, our Betty, you make me so cross at times. You don't go into the Services just because of a pretty uniform. Anyway, I don't expect your Dad would let you go. He's never said yes to you joining the Land Army, you know that.'

Betty pouted. 'He's an old stick-in-the-mud. Why shouldn't I join the Land Army? Or anything else? It's for my country, isn't it? To help win the war? What's wrong with that?'

'Yes, why shouldn't Bet do what she wants?' Olive joined in. She was well aware that her father had been against her marrying Derek before she was twenty-one, until Derek had come back from Dunkirk and made it clear he wasn't waiting any longer. Now she was a married woman and therefore outside her father's jurisdiction, even though she was still living at home with her parents, and she could afford to stick up for her sister. 'If she wants to go and milk cows and dig potatoes, why not?'

Annie sighed and fetched the pudding. It was stewed apple tart with some custard made more with water than milk. The custard was thin, and a year ago she'd have felt like throwing it away, but things had changed since then. You couldn't get the ingredients to make decent puddings and you couldn't afford to waste what there was. You had to make do – she'd already tried making 'banana pudding' with parsnips and a bit of flavouring, and some of the other economy wartime recipes they'd started putting in newspapers and giving out on the wireless, and she had to admit that some of them weren't bad at all.

She set the tart down on the table and cut it into portions, leaving one for Ted when he came home.

'I don't know, I'm sure,' she said. 'Everything's so different these days, I can't keep up with it all. I thought we had our lives all nice and settled, with our Colin in the Navy and you girls growing up and getting nice jobs for a few years before you got married. Now there's you with your man miles away, and our Bet talking about uniforms, and Colin goodness knows where . . .' She shook her head. 'It's like you can't be sure of anything. And then the air-raids—' Her voice broke and she sank into her chair and put her hand up to her quivering mouth. A moment later the tears were pouring down her cheeks, and Olive and Betty stared at her and simultaneously reached out to lay their hands on her arms.

'Mum, don't.' Olive got up and went to her mother, drawing the greying head against her breast. 'Don't cry. It's over now, the air-raid, and we're all safe.'

'Over? It's not over. It's only just started.' Annie looked up at her. 'It's going to be like that all the time now – sirens going off when you don't expect them, bombs exploding in the next street, perhaps on our own house. Never knowing where you all are when it happens, never knowing if you'll walk out of here one morning and not come back. And if our Betty goes off, how'll I know she's safe then, eh? She might be ill or hurt and it'd be days before we heard anything, *days* . . .'

'But that's no different from being evacuated,' Betty said. 'And I'd be safer out in the country—'

'Shut up,' Olive snapped. 'Can't you see she's upset? It's the shock, that's what it is, it's enough to upset anyone. It's all right, Mum,' she murmured, bending her head down to her mother's. 'It's all right. None of us got hurt in the raid, and we won't neither, as long as we make sure and get in the shelter every time. And I don't reckon they'll get through so easy again. Our lads'll be on the watch for 'em now, you see. They won't let those dratted German planes in again.'

Maybe they wouldn't, Betty thought, but she remembered seeing the planes high in the sky, flying steadily, as if determined that nothing would stop them. She looked up and saw the fear in her sister's eyes.

The war had been brought right to their doorstep.

4

'Come on,' Jess said as soon as dinner was finished and the washing-up done. 'We're going down North End to see Grandma and Grandpa.'

She'd half expected an objection from the boys, but none came. They'd been unusually quiet ever since she'd arrived home from the shops to find them already back, and Tim was wearing his guilty look. She wondered what they'd been up to.

Perhaps they'd let it out on the way to North End. Annie had already been last night, to make sure that they were all right after the raid, but Jess was anxious to see them herself.

Rose pushed Maureen's pram. Since coming back from Bridge End she had almost taken over the baby, playing with her, feeding her, washing her – though she still refused to have anything to do with nappies – and taking her for walks. Sometimes Joy Brunner came with her, but Joy was more often busy in the shop, helping her own mother.

The boys wandered alongside, still rather quiet. No, they hadn't been playing cricket, Tim had said when Jess asked him. No, nor cowboys and Indians.

'So what were you doing all morning?' she inquired, as they walked through the streets. 'Hide and seek?'

'Yes,' Tim began, but Keith, speaking at the same moment, said a little more brightly, 'No. We've been exploring.'

'Exploring?' Jess repeated, noticing Tim's scowl. 'Where were you exploring? You haven't been too far away, I hope.'

Keith too had seen his brother's frown and dropped his eyes, saying nothing. His ears had turned red. Jess kept her gaze fixed on Tim's face and he glanced up and reddened as well.

'Where were you exploring?' she asked again.

'Nowhere much,' Tim said, with a shrug, and she was convinced that they had been doing something they shouldn't.

'Where?'

Tim looked at her. He knew that if he told her the truth he and Keith would be in serious trouble. Worse still, they'd be in trouble with Dad. It was bad enough having Mum cross with them, but if it was something she thought Dad should know about, it meant real punishment. A lot of shouting. Probably the cane.

'Africa,' he said, with sudden inspiration. 'And Australia. That's where we explored, wasn't it, Keith?'

Jess looked at them. She knew perfectly well that Tim was evading the truth, and she knew why. She considered insisting, then decided against it. The boys were going away again tomorrow – she didn't want their last day to be a miserable one.

All the same, she had to try to satisfy her need to know.

'You haven't been going down any of the bombed streets, I hope,' she said. 'You know what your father would say if you did. It's dangerous.'

Tim met her eyes so guilelessly that she knew at once that this was just what they had done.

'The bombed streets?' he said. 'But they're miles away. We're not allowed right down there.'

Jess looked into the hazel eyes and sighed. She knew, and Tim knew she knew, that he was lying. I suppose he went down there with that Micky Baxter, she thought, and was glad all over again that her boys would be out in the country again tomorrow, safe from Hitler's bombs, and away from the influence of the bad boy of April Grove.

Arthur and Mary were just finishing their dinner. They got up, glad to see Jess and the children, and Mary went out to the scullery to put the kettle on.

'I'll do that, Mum,' Jess said. 'You sit down and have a rest. You must have had a nasty shock last night.'

Her mother fetched a tin of broken biscuits and handed it to the children. Tim and Keith ran out into the back garden, where Arthur had fixed up a swing from the old apple tree, and Rose went and sat on the step, rocking the pram with one hand.

'We were a bit shook up', Mary confessed. 'But we got ourselves in the shelter and stopped there till it was safe to come out. We were glad to get our gas masks off, I can tell you!'

Jess couldn't help smiling at the thought of the two old people, sitting there in their gas masks, but her amusement was only fleeting. She hadn't even thought of putting on her and Maureen's gas masks, and the boys had gone out to play without theirs.

'They 'ad gas in the first lot,' Arthur said in his thin reedy voice. 'Mustard gas, it was. Cruel stuff. I seen men with their lungs burnt right through their chests with it.'

'Don't, Dad,' Jess begged him, glancing towards the open door. She could hear Tim and Keith calling to each other, and Rose singing softly to the baby. But she knew that he would not be stopped. He seemed to need to go over it all, over and over again, as if by doing so he could make some sense of what was happening now.

But there wasn't any sense to be made, not when you were almost eighty and had already lived through two or three wars, including one that was supposed to end all wars and had failed dismally.

'So what are you going to do about the children?' Mary asked. 'You can't keep them under your eye the whole time.'

'Oh, they're going back straightaway,' Jess said firmly. 'Me and Frank have settled that. Tomorrow, we're taking them. Mr and Mrs Corner wrote saying they're looking forward to having the boys back and I know that nice Mrs Greenberry'll take care of Rose. We're going on the train. I asked Ethel Glaister if she'd like us to take her Shirley along too but no, Bridge End isn't good enough for her. She's decided to send Shirley off to America, or Canada.' Jess sniffed. 'It's one extreme or the other with that one. Wouldn't let her go off with the others last year, thinking nothing was going to happen, then gets scared silly.'

'Ethel Glaister was silly already,' Mary said caustically. She had known Ethel ever since she and Jess had been neighbours. 'Still, I'm glad she's letting Shirley go. It's daft, keeping kiddies at home these days. There was nowhere for the child to go to school, nobody much to play with. But there, I suppose that's how Ethel liked it, she always did think she was a cut above the rest of us.'

Tim came racing in.

'Grandpa, show us your bullets. The ones you got in the last lot.'

Jess flinched. She hated hearing the children use such terms. It seemed so casual, as if the Great War hadn't mattered. And she didn't much like her father showing them souvenirs he'd brought back, either – the cartridge cases and empty shells that he'd polished lovingly and set up on the mantelpiece. It was like keeping bones.

'Come on,' she said abruptly, getting up. 'It's time we went back. I've got a lot to do at home. They're asking us to do half as many sailors' collars again, and I don't know where I'm going to find the time, I'm sure I don't.'

Back in September Street, she let the two boys run on ahead while she and Rose did their own shopping. She went into Atkinson's, the green-grocer, where Molly Atkinson was weighing out potatoes.

People were still talking about the raid. Some of them were frightened, doing their shopping hastily in order to get home as quickly as possible in case there was another. Some were angry, cursing Hitler and using language that caused Molly to speak sharply, telling them to leave her shop if they couldn't keep their mouths clean. One or two were in real distress, for they had lost friends or relatives in the raid and were finding it hard to take in.

'That Mrs Jenkins that used to clean at Drayton Road School, she's gone,' old Mrs Stokes was saying over and over again as Molly made up her order. 'I saw her only Tuesday afternoon. Bright as a button, she was, laughing and joking, doing a bit of a dance because her chap had come home unexpected. And now she's gone. It don't seem possible.'

'My Jack always called in at the Anchor for a pint on his way home,' Carrie Barnes, from Carlisle Crescent, chipped in evidently forgetting this had been a habit she had strongly disapproved. 'He'll never be able to go there again now. Flat as a pancake, and all the beer running away like drainwater.'

'There's one or two would say that's all it was anyway,' someone else remarked caustically, and the other customers laughed, though there was a nervous edge to their laughter. They went out, leaving Molly and Jess alone.

Molly went on sorting the few boxes of potatoes into a display, with her five-year-old son Alan and his sister Wendy helping her. She gave Jess a rueful smile. She looked tired and thin, and no wonder, Jess thought, seeing what she'd been through already in this war.

'Not too good last night, was it, love?' she said. 'Still, I expect you got the children into the shelter, didn't you?'

'We were down there even before the siren had stopped. I know some people didn't bother, thought it was another false alarm, but I wouldn't take the risk.' She laid her hand briefly on Alan's head. 'I've been through enough worry over these two already.'

'I know,' Jess hesitated. 'You won't think of sending them away again, then?'

Molly Atkinson shook her head firmly. 'I'll never let 'em out of my sight again. I know some kids have found good places in the country, but I'd rather have 'em home with me. If we go, we go together, but I couldn't go through all that again, not knowing what's happening to them.'

Jess could understand that, for she knew that Alan and Wendy's experience of evacuation had not been a happy one, but she still felt anxious for these two little ones, kept at home to face bombing such as Portsmouth had known last night. Still, it was Molly's decision and she couldn't blame the young mother. And she'd heard that Alan still hadn't got over it, he was as clinging as a baby, terrified of the dark and screamed in the night as if he were having the most dreadful nightmares.

She went into the newsagent's shop and found young Joy, Rose's friend, serving. Alice Brunner came out from the back, her face pale and her eyes red-rimmed. It was only ten days since news had come of the sinking of the *Arandora Star*, on her way to Canada with fifteen hundred internees, and Alice's German-born husband Heinrich had been amongst them. Reports were still slowly filtering through about survivors, but when Jess asked Alice if there had been any news, the woman shook her head.

'He shouldn't never have been on the ship in the first place,' she said with weary indignation. 'Calling him an alien! He'd lived here over twenty years, we went to Deniston Road church together every Sunday. He was a better Christian than a lot of people I could mention around here, saving present company, of course. He wanted to join the LDV, didn't he? He wanted to help, and instead of that, they take him off in handcuffs and put him in prison like a common criminal, and then send him off to be torpedoed.' She pushed a straggle of hair back from her forehead. 'It's not fair.'

It wasn't fair, but then war never is, Jess thought as she tried to give Alice some comfort. But what could you say? Heinrich might be amongst the survivors but he might have gone down with the ship. And until poor Alice knew for sure, she was going to be tortured by her imaginings, seeing him struggle in the oily water, perhaps badly injured, crying for help, crying for her . . .

It didn't bear thinking about. But you had to think about it. You couldn't just walk away and forget. And there was going to be more of it, more every day until the whole terrible business was over.

'Well, at least you've got Joy,' Jess said lamely, wondering uneasily if this was the right thing to say. 'Maybe it'd be better if . . .' Her voice trailed away but Alice picked up the words sharply.

'Better if what? Better if I let her go off to the country, where she'd be safe?' Her face twisted and crumpled, as if she were trying not to cry. 'I suppose you think I'm selfish, keeping her here. But I can't let her go off too. I'd have nobody then.'

And Alice wasn't a person who could manage with nobody, Jess thought, gazing at the misery in her friend's face. She'd always had someone to depend on – her own mother, when she'd been a child, and then Heinrich. Now it was Joy.

'Anyway, she wouldn't go,' Alice went on, looking at the two girls who were now marking up the *Evening News.* 'She didn't want to go last September, when all the other children went, she just wanted to stay home with us. It was almost like she knew something like this was going to happen.'

Jess collected her newspaper and walked down October Street, her heart heavy. So many lives being disrupted . . . As she came nearer to Mrs Seddon's corner shop, she noticed a young woman with two little girls on the other side of the road, standing outside number 16. At the same moment, Tim came running up to her.

'There's someone who's been bombed out. She's going to live in that house.'

'Ssh,' Jess said sharply. 'People don't want their business shouted up and down the street for all to hear. How do you know, anyway?'

'She told Granny Kinch,' Tim said in an injured tone, and Jess thought that in that case the young woman might just as well let the town crier know her news. Granny Kinch was a grapevine all on her own. She looked across the road again, and saw that the woman was pregnant.

She hesitated, then went across. The young woman was fitting a key into the lock.

'D'you need any help? I don't want to seem nosy, but my boy's just told me you were bombed out last night. If there's anything I can do . . .'

The woman turned. Why, she's not much more than a girl, Jess thought, for all she's got a couple of kiddies of eight or nine. And expecting another one, too!

She was reminded of herself a few years ago, coming down this same street with two children and another on the way. Only in her case there hadn't been a war on, and she and Frank had been coming from rooms to their own house.

'Thanks,' the girl said. 'I don't really know what I've got to do. It's been a bit of a shock.'

'I should think it has. Where d'you live?'

The girl's face twisted. 'We *did* live down Portchester Road, but there's not much left of it now. We got a proper bashing, I can tell you.'

'Portchester Road!' That was where Frank had been yesterday evening. 'D'you mean your house was—'

'Smashed to bits,' the girl said bitterly. 'Had it looking like a little palace too, we did, and then along comes Hitler and smashes it to pieces. Everything we've scrimped and saved for. They say they'll get it rebuilt, or pay compensation or something, but they never will.' She shrugged. 'How can they, the amount that's being bombed? Anyway, if the Germans come and take away the whole lot, *they* won't be paying out no compensation. So now we've got to start again.' She turned and looked at the front of the little house, its windows smeared with dust and grime. 'We're lucky, really, they've put us up the list on account of the children.' Her hand touched her stomach lightly. 'And the one coming. There's some people'll be in those emergency centres for weeks.'

'You poor soul.' Jess gazed at her, wondering what she could say next. 'So what have you got to do?'

'Look at this house, say if we want it or not.' The girl laughed shortly. 'If we want it! What choice have we got? We're lucky to get anywhere.'

'Would you like me to come in with you?' Jess offered diffidently. 'I mean, there might be quite a lot needs to be done. I wouldn't mind giving you a hand.'

The girl's eyes warmed a little. 'Would you really? But you must have a lot to do – those two boys are yours, aren't they? And you've got a baby, too.'

'The boys'll be away tomorrow. We're sending them back to the country.' Jess looked at the two little girls, wondering why they hadn't been evacuated too. Of course, a lot of children had come back, thinking there weren't going to be any bombs. 'And Maureen's no trouble.'

'Well, if you'd just come in with me.' The girl laughed again, a little nervously. 'It's silly, but I've got a sort of funny feeling about going in. Almost like it might be haunted. Daft!'

'It's not. It's reaction.' Jess parked the pram in the tiny scrap of yard in front of the house. 'My name's Jess Budd, by the way. I live just over the corner, in April Grove – number 14.'

'I'm Kathy Simmons.' Kathy turned the key and pushed open the door. 'Well, let's see what they've given us, shall we?' She went into the dark, narrow little passage and sniffed. 'Phew! What a pong. Who lived here before?'

'An old woman. She'd been on her own for years, except for her cats. She had quite a few – just let them breed.' Jess surveyed the discoloured walls. 'You can see nothing's been done to the place since she died. Her family came and took away what bits of furniture were any use and Mr Carter – he's the landlord, owns four or five houses in this street – he cleared out the rest and got a shilling or two for it from the rag-and-bone man.'

Kathy opened the door into the front room and looked in at the bare floorboards and grubby walls. 'Ugh! How could anyone live like this?' Her mouth twisted. 'Well, it looks as if I'm going to find out, doesn't it, me and the girls.'

Jess gazed at her in dismay. Kathy had said that her house was smashed to bits. She must have almost no furniture, clothes or anything. How was she going to manage?

'Do they give you anything to help out?' she asked, wondering if she sounded nosy. 'I mean, surely they give you a bed or something.'

'Five pounds. That's all. Five pounds, for everything you possess. After that, you're left to yourself.' Kathy shut the door and walked through to the tiny back room and scullery. There was nothing in the scullery but an old earthenware sink with a cold tap. The smell of cats was everywhere.

Five pounds to buy furniture seemed like a fortune to Jess, but when you thought about having to get enough beds for a family of four, with another one on the way, and buy all the things you needed for your kitchen, and chairs to sit on and clothes for everyone, well, you could see that it wouldn't go far at all.

'We've got nothing of our own,' Kathy said. 'Just the clothes we were stood up in. And they weren't nothing special, not on a Thursday afternoon.' She grinned suddenly. 'You'd think he could at least bomb us on a Sunday, when we'd got our best clothes on, wouldn't you!'

'If you need any help—' Jess began awkwardly. She couldn't imagine what help she could give – there was no spare money in the Budd household, let alone spare clothes or furniture – but it seemed wrong not to offer. 'I mean, I'll help you scrub out a bit if you like. And when the baby comes, I'd be glad to come over and give you a hand. I've got a few of Maureen's baby things too, you're welcome to them if you'd like them.'

'Oh, I *would*. That's really nice of you.' Kathy smiled at her and Jess thought how brave she was. Fancy being able to make jokes about being bombed out of your own house!

They stood for a moment in silence, surveying the dirty room. Kathy went across to the back door and opened it, letting the afternoon sunlight straggle in. It made the dirt look even worse. She took a deep breath and managed a watery grin.

'Well, I suppose there's no use just looking at it. I'll have to start getting straight. I'll go round the second-hand shops for a few bits and pieces of furniture and some clothes to get us started.' She looked around at the house she must turn into a home for her family. 'You don't realise how much you've got till you lose it. And you've got to get the blackout done before you can even think of anything else.'

'I know,' Jess said. She followed Kathy to the front door and they went out into the fresh air with some relief. Kathy's two little girls were standing by Maureen's pram, holding up a woolly rabbit that Frank's sister-in-law had knitted for her. The street was quiet. 'Do you think the Germans are really going to invade?'

'Do you?' Kathy asked.

It was the question on everyone's lips. Some people didn't want to think about it, they shrugged it away. Others brooded about it the whole time. All through the previous year, when so little had seemed to be happening, although the news had been unremittingly bad about what was going on in other countries, no one had really been able to believe that Hitler would forget Great Britain.

Jess shook her head.

'I don't reckon the Germans are going to come,' she said stoutly. 'Our boys are fighting them off. Look at the way they've gone up after the raiders, day after day. The bombing would have been a lot worse without the RAF to look after us.'

'And it'll get worse yet,' Kathy said darkly. 'Aren't we one of the biggest powers in the world? Stands to reason he wants to take us over! Same as he's taken everyone else over.' She laid her hand over her abdomen and looked at the two girls. 'It's the little ones I worry about. Them, and him in here.'

'I know,' Jess said quietly. 'And maybe if we'd thought there was going to be a war, we'd never have had this little one.' She bent forward and prodded Maureen in the stomach. The baby squealed and chortled. 'But we wouldn't be without you now, would we? Specially with the other three evacuated.' She looked at Kathy. 'Didn't you want to be evacuated? Is your husband in the Forces?'

'In the Merchant Navy. He doesn't believe in evacuation. Nor do I, really. I think everyone ought to stay where they are.' Kathy's face flushed a little. 'Anyway, I never know when he's going to get home for a night or two and I'd rather be here.'

Jess nodded. She knew how Kathy felt, for she hated the idea of leaving Frank. But if he weren't here . . . Still, everyone had to make up their own mind.

'D'you want another girl?' she asked, changing the subject. 'Or would you rather have a boy this time?'

'Oh, a boy,' Kathy said, with a passion that startled her. 'I only want a boy. I only *ever* wanted boys. Well, I don't mean I don't love Muriel and Stella now they're here – and I wouldn't change them, not for the world – but I really do want a boy this time.' She looked at Jess. 'You've got a nice family, haven't you. Three others, is it?'

'Two boys and a girl. They're a bit older than Maureen – she was our afterthought!' She laughed self-consciously. 'Rose is thirteen now and the boys are nine and eleven.'

'Oh, you'll miss them,' Kathy said. 'I don't think I could bear to let my kids go away without me.'

'I will miss them,' Jess said. 'But it's war, isn't it. You just have to do the best you can. And I don't want to go through another experience like last night, not knowing where the boys were and then finding they'd been out in the street the whole time. It still makes me feel sick to think of that.' She shook her head. 'You can't keep them in all the time. Specially boys. They're better off in the country, where they can roam about and play. And we go out to see them whenever we can. My husband goes out on his bike if we haven't got enough for the fare.'

'Well, if I get a boy this time I'm never going to let him out of my sight,' Kathy said. She shut the front door. 'Well, it looks as if we're going to be neighbours. It's a poky little place but it's better than a corner of the church hall.' She looked at Jess and gave her a wavery smile; it was clear she wasn't far from tears. 'Thanks ever so much for coming in with me. I think if I'd been on my own . . .'

'That's all right.' Jess felt her own eyes sting. 'And don't forget, as soon as you want a bit of help you come over and say. I'll be glad to give you a hand – take my mind off other things.' She knew she was going to miss the boys and Rose dreadfully. But at least she had Maureen to think of, and Frank at home. She felt sorry for Kathy Simmons. Being bombed out of her home with a baby due in a couple of months and no husband at home, she needed a friend or two. And the two little girls seemed nice enough. They seemed to enjoy playing with Maureen.

She pushed the pram across the road and round the corner to number 14. Kathy was the first real casualty of the war that she had met, but there would be plenty more. She might even be one herself, before long.

The boys were playing leapfrog on the pavement outside the house. She went indoors to get their tea. This time tomorrow, they'd be back out in the country and Maureen the only child she had at home.

The quiet of the afternoon was split by the sudden wail of the siren. It rose and fell, filling Jess's ears with its shriek, filling her heart with fear. She ran to the door but the boys came tumbling in before she could reach it, and she gathered up the baby and pushed them before her down the garden path.

Back at Bridge End the following week, the Budds found themselves centres of attention as their friends gathered round them to ask what it had been like to be in an air-raid.

'It was smashing,' Tim declared, swaggering along the country lane. 'Planes flying over the top of us, dropping bombs all over the place. Terrific explosions. And a huge great fire, the sky was all full of flames. We thought the whole of Pompey was going to catch fire.'

'Go on,' Brian Collins sneered. 'It couldn't've been that bad. There wasn't that many houses burnt down.'

'It was the gasholder. It could've gone up like a bomb itself. They had every fire engine in Pompey there trying to put it out.'

'Weren't you scared?' a little girl asked, awed, and Brian Collins sniggered again.

'Course he was. That's why he's come back, ain't it? Scared out of his wits, not that he had many to start with.'

Tim scowled. He and Brian Collins had always been enemies. 'I wasn't scared,' he said hotly. 'It was my Dad said we had to come back. Anyway, I like being in the country. After the war we're all going to come and live here, Mum and Dad and our baby, all of us.'

'You're welcome to it,' Brian said. 'I'm fed up with the country. Old man Callaway treats me like a slave. I'd sooner be back in Pompey, going mudlarking.'

'You're not allowed to do that now,' Tim said. 'The harbour's full of unexploded bombs. You'd get blown up.'

Brian made a face at him and Tim turned away. His Dad had told him often enough not to let Brian Collins goad him into a fight. 'You should always stand up for yourself,' he said, 'but you shouldn't start it. Anyway, it's not worth bothering with people like that. Just take no notice.'

Tim tried to follow his father's advice, but it wasn't easy when he saw the sneer on Brian's face. He wanted to wipe it off with a good hard punch. But that would mean he'd hit out first and put himself into the wrong, which Dad had told him was just what Brian wanted.

Rose was less eager to recount her air-raid experiences. She told her foster-mother Mrs Greenberry about it, and the countrywoman's face grew pale.

'You mean you weren't even at home with your Mum? And the boys were out in the streets? That poor soul, she must have been worried sick.'

'Dad wasn't home either,' Rose said. 'He was on his way home from work. He had to stop and help. There was people killed, bodies everywhere.' Frank hadn't told her that, but her own imagination told her it must have been so. She had lain awake, wondering what it had been like. It would have been better if he had told her, she thought, then she wouldn't have to keep imagining it, but she hadn't dared ask him. Even Mum had been cross when she'd mentioned it.

'Little girls don't have to worry about things like that,' she'd told her. 'That's why you're going back to Bridge End. You just help Mrs Greenberry like you help me, and forget about the war.'

Rose hadn't wanted to come back to Bridge End. She liked the Greenberrys and she'd been frightened during the raid, but she'd still rather be at home with Mum. Especially when they knew that Southampton was being bombed and heard on the news that there'd been more raids over Portsmouth.

Suppose something happened to number 14. Suppose Mum and Dad were hurt – killed even – and Rose wasn't there to help. Suppose someone forgot to let her know.

'Of course they won't forget,' Mrs Greenberry said. 'Anyway, nothing's going to happen to your mum and dad. Now, you stop thinking about it and go down the garden and pick us a few peas. Mr Greenberry's brought home a nice rabbit for our supper, and you know you like rabbit.'

But rabbit wasn't enough to stop Rose worrying. And she picked at her dinner that evening, and went to bed with her stomach filled with the leaden lump of fear instead of Mr Greenberry's homegrown vegetables and the rabbit he'd brought from the farm.

Reg and Edna Corner had their worries too. They waited until Tim and Keith were in bed before discussing them.

'I just don't see how we're to manage,' Edna said. 'You're bound to get called up soon, and with a baby coming as well . . .'

'I'm sure Mr Callaway will let you stop on in the cottage,' Reg said. 'I mean, he's not going to get another worker, is he? He'll get one or two of the older men – Simon Barrow, he's still pretty spry, he'll be glad to earn himself a bob or two. Or maybe he'll get a Land Girl.'

'And where's she going to live?' Edna demanded. 'He's already got young Brian billeted on him at the farmhouse. He'll want this cottage, that's what, and he'll probably put up two or three more as well. No, the minute you're called up he'll have me out. I'll have to go and stop with Mum.'

Reg gazed at her. It wasn't what he wanted, starting a family this way, with him away in the Forces and Edna having to go back to her mother's cramped little cottage. He looked round the little room. They'd got it so nice. Even though it wasn't theirs, it was still their home for as long as he worked on the farm, and he'd expected that to be for a good few years, if not for life. What reason was there to move, if you were happy? And he and Edna had been happy, there was no doubt at all about that.

'So what are we going to do about Tim and Keith?' he asked.

Edna shrugged. 'What can we do? You know how I feel about them, they're smashing boys, I feel like they're almost our own. But we can't keep them here once the baby's born. I don't think I could manage it all, specially if you're going to be away. And anyway—'

'Mr Callaway won't let you stop on,' Reg finished for her. 'Well, I daresay you're right. I suppose we'd better let the billeting officer know.'

Edna looked miserable. 'Not too soon, Reg. I don't want to lose them yet.'

'But it's not fair on them, letting them settle in again and then get pushed on somewhere else. We ought to tell their mum and dad at least.' He looked at her. He knew how fond of the two boys she had become. 'Tell you what we'll do, Edna. We'll look out for somewhere for them ourselves. Somewhere we know they'll be happy. And then we'll tell Mrs Budd and the billeting officer.' He put his arm round her and drew her close. 'And now you've got to start thinking about yourself and our own little one. I'm fond of the boys too, but you're more important to me. You and our own baby. That's what you've got to be thinking about.'

Edna smiled. But her heart was sore. Like Reg, she felt bitterly disappointed that things had turned out this way – that their first baby should be coming into such a world, with its father about to be sent off to war and their home taken from them.

It wasn't fair. But the past year had taught everyone that you could no longer expect fairness.

Micky Baxter did not go to Bridge End. He had no wish to leave Portsmouth, and his mother Nancy didn't bother to insist. She hardly looked on Micky as a child anyway; from an early age he had been allowed to fend for himself, running the streets, living by his fists, pinching the odd apple or orange from greengrocers' displays, pocketing all sorts of oddments that it was best not to enquire about.

'It was just left lyin' about,' he would explain. 'There wasn't no sense in just leavin' it, was there?'

'Funny,' Nancy said, 'last time I saw something like that it was lying on a counter in Woolies. You'd better watch yourself, Micky.'

'Oh, leave the boy alone,' Granny Kinch said. 'All boys gets up to a bit o' mischief. There ain't no real harm in him.'

But even she had been shaken when Micky was taken to court for the jeweller's shop incident. At first, she'd refused to believe it had been Micky at all, and then she had tried to blame the boy who had given him the gun. Now she looked on it as a prank that had gone too far. 'He's learnt his lesson,' she said. 'He won't do nothing like that again.'

Micky had no intention of doing anything like that again. He had learned that it was best not to let yourself be seen. Then no one could identify you. Instead of marching into small shops where twelve-year-old boys stood out like sore thumbs, he and the others skulked around Woolworths and British Home Stores. They filched things from barrows in Charlotte Street and slid purses off the top of careless women's shopping baskets. There was never much in the purses but a few coppers soon mounted up.

Not that there was much to spend money on, not when you could pinch most of what you wanted. Even fags could be nicked when the tobacconist was looking for something you'd asked for and he hadn't got. And you could get into the pictures, three for the price of one, by sending one in on a ticket and then waiting by the fire exit.

'We oughter have somewhere to keep the cash,' Micky said. He knew that if he kept it at home his mother or grandmother was likely to find it, and that would be the last he saw of it. And he wasn't prepared to let either of the other boys be treasurer. 'We needs a den.'

'We got a den,' Cyril said. 'Our garden shed. Nobody ever goes in it now Dad's away.'

Micky shook his head. 'Nah. There's better'n that. You come with me.'

Jimmy had a tin money-box with a key that nearly always worked. They put their loot into it – three and sevenpence three-farthings – and set off through the streets.

'Are we going down the bomb sites?' Cyril asked. 'There'd be some good places there.'

Micky nodded but said nothing. He had been exploring the bombed houses several times since the raid and looked on them as his territory. There'd been other boys about too, but he was fairly confident that the place he had discovered was safe.

'Here,' he said, as they turned into the derelict street, 'this is the place.'

The boys looked around them, still awed by the extent of the damage. Only a few houses were left standing, down at the other end, and most of those were damaged. Piles of bricks and rubble still filled gardens, and shattered rooms stood open to the weather.

'These places'll make smashing dens,' Cyril said.

'You wait.' Micky led them into the third house of the row. The front walls were still standing, though badly damaged, and the front door hung crookedly on its hinges. He pushed it open and a sour smell of food gone bad, excreta and cats, hit their faces. Cyril wrinkled his nose.

'Eugh! Something's died in here.'

'Nah. It's just cats' muck.' Micky scrambled over the fallen bricks and plaster. There was a cupboard under the stairs, its door propped shut with a brick. He moved the brick and the door fell open.

'Coo!'

'It's a cellar,' Micky said unnecessarily. 'It's just right for a den. Nobody else knows about it, I bin testing.'

Jimmy and Cyril gazed down into the black abyss. The steps were black and slimy, and the walls green with mould. The air was dank.

'It's smashing,' Cyril said. 'It's the best place we ever found.'

Micky nodded. He produced a box of matches and a stub of candle and led the way down the grimy steps. By the flickering light, they could see that this had been a coal-cellar. There was no coal here now, except for a few lumps piled in one corner, but someone had brought down a rickety table and a couple of broken chairs. Micky touched them proudly.

'See, we even got furniture. I fetched these down. And I left this, just to see if anyone else was nosin' round.' He picked up a battered Dinky car from the table. 'They'd've took this, so that means no one's bin here. It's safe as houses.'

'S'pose it gets bombed again?' Jimmy suggested, glancing at the crumbling walls.

Micky shook his head derisively. 'Nah. They never hits the same place twice.' He sat down in one of the chairs and put his feet on the table. 'Better'n an old garden shed, eh?'

Jimmy put his tin money-box on the table. 'Where we going to hide it?'

'Over here.' Micky swung his feet down and went over to the wall. The guttering candle threw deep shadows but he felt along until one of the bricks came out in his hand. 'See, there's a space here. We can put the tin there. No one'll ever find it and we can come down here whenever we like and get some money, have a fag, whatever we want.'

'We could bring some grub,' Cyril said, his imagination taking flight. 'We could light a fire – cook meals.'

'We can do better'n that.' Micky paused while the other two gazed expectantly at him, then said slowly and dramatically, 'We can keep a parachutist here.'

Jimmy and Cyril drew in their breath. They looked about them at the dark, clammy walls. 'A parachutist? You mean a *German*?'

'Well, we wouldn't keep a British one down here, would we?' Micky said impatiently. 'But we could keep a Jerry for as long as we liked. Pile up stuff against the door so he couldn't get out. Nobody'd hear him shout. He'd be our prisoner.'

Jimmy had a practical question. 'Isn't there a hatch, where they used to deliver coal? He could get out through that.'

'Nah. It's all blocked up with bricks and stuff. I've looked.'

The candle was almost burnt out. Micky put the tin box into the hole and replaced the brick. He picked up the Dinky toy, hesitated, then put it back on the table.

'I'll leave that, just so we always know if anyone's bin pokin' about. And mind you don't come down here without me.'

Jimmy and Cyril shook their heads. They went back up the steps, replaced the door and heaped rubbish against it. Then they went back outside and looked up at the sky.

They were almost disappointed not to see it filled with the billowing umbrellas of German parachutes.

5

Betty Chapman was beginning to think that her application to join the Land Army had been lost for ever, when she found herself opening a brown envelope one morning to find that she had been ordered 'over the hill' to Bishop's Waltham, to work on a farm.

'Bishop's Waltham!' she said in some disappointment. 'Why, that's no distance at all. I thought I'd be sent miles out into the country.'

'There's as good countryside at Bishop's Waltham as you'd find anywhere in England,' her mother said with some asperity. 'Were you looking forward to getting away from us, then?'

'No, of course not.' Betty bit her lip. Nobody in the family had been keen on this idea of her going to work on the land and her father had been downright suspicious about it. Just as if she'd suggested doing something immoral, she thought indignantly. 'I just thought I might get the chance to see a bit more of England, that's all.'

'I've told you before,' Ted Chapman told her curtly, 'this war ain't no holiday camp. If you go and work on a farm you'll have to *work*. It won't be doing the odd bit of weeding and picking a few blackberries for a pie. It'll be getting up at five in the morning, summer and winter, to milk cows, spending all day slaving at some other job and then milking half the evening as well. If you ask me, they're mad to take you on, a bit of a thing like you, and that doctor who gave you your certificate wants his head looking at.'

'Well, it's either that or the Services. They're going to want all us girls, Dad. I might as well start now as wait to be called up and find myself somewhere I don't want to be.'

Ted grunted and didn't answer. He felt increasingly bewildered these days, as if his head was full of cotton-wool, and he no longer felt in control of his own life, let alone those of his family. He was dismayed by the way his daughters had so suddenly grown up. There was Olive, married before she was twenty-one, which was something he'd always declared he wouldn't allow. And now Betty leaving home to go and live out in the wilds. Well, Bishop's Waltham wasn't exactly the *wilds*, but it was country, wasn't it, and there was nobody there he knew. In Pompey he knew hundreds of people, people he'd grown up with, people he'd known since they were nippers. And country folk could be funny, there was no saying they couldn't. Look at some of the tales you heard about the way evacuees got treated.

But parents were the last people to be consulted about their children these days. Girls could do whatever they pleased now and treated their mums and dads as if they were something out of the Ark, as if they knew nothing. And the Government was aiding and abetting them.

'She ought to have gone and got a job at Airspeed,' he said to Annie. 'She'd have been in a reserved occupation then and earned good money too. They're making planes hand over fist up there, and can't get 'em out fast enough.'

'And no wonder, the way they're being shot out of the sky,' Annie observed. 'And she wouldn't be any safer there, would she? Airspeed got hit themselves the other day, and if it hadn't been after working hours any amount of people would've been killed.' But she didn't argue back too much. She knew how Ted's nights were filled with bad dreams, how the things he had seen at Dunkirk still haunted his mind.

There were still plenty of air-raid warnings, though no more bombs had fallen on Portsmouth in the weeks that followed the July attack. And the city was fighting back – two days later, the *Evening News* had launched a 'Buy a Spitfire' appeal, and they had collected the six thousand pounds needed in only a fortnight.

And they certainly needed planes. Every day now, aircraft could be seen in the sky, dodging and swooping crazily as they fired at each other. You could stand and watch the 'dogfights' as they were called, almost as if they were some kind of aerial circus, a spectacle laid on for entertainment.

But the entertainment was a deadly one. The newspapers were full now of reports of the battle which was being waged in the skies. *Twenty-Eight Raiders Shot Down*, the headlines announced on 26 July and, a few days later, *Fighters' Fine Work Over Portsmouth* with a detailed report of the Spitfires which had met a hundred and fifty enemy bombers coming in from the south. Aided by Hurricanes and Defiants, they drove off the German Heinkels and Messerschmitts, shooting down several which fell either into the sea or in open countryside.

One was reported as having dived nose-first down a disused well on the Isle of Wight, only its tail sticking up above the ground with the swastika to prove its nationality. Another crashed into a field, its pilot and navigator captured by a local milkman. A third, flying over in the early hours of the morning, managed to penetrate the barrage and dropped three bombs on a farm, with a total casualty rate of fifty chickens and a rabbit.

'And you reckon our Betty'll be safer, out at Bishop's Waltham!' Ted commented sarcastically, but Annie just shook her head at him. She was beginning to come round to the idea of Betty's going away. Always more down-to-earth than her husband, she accepted the fact that the war had changed everything and you couldn't expect anything to turn out the way you'd thought it would. The best you could hope for was that everyone would get through it alive, however long it lasted – and how long would that be? A year? Two years? – and that the German invasion would be kept at bay. The thought of enemy soldiers marching down September Street made her shudder.

She looked at the photographs in *Picture Post*. Millions of French people, fleeing from Paris and other big cities, carrying whatever possessions they had been able to snatch up in their panic as their Government capitulated. Old men and women, small children and babies in prams, trudging bewildered along endless roads, with no idea of where they were going. Derek Harker had seen them as he came through Dunkirk, and spoke of an old woman who had told him this was the second time she had had to leave her home. The first time was twenty-five years ago in the Great War, and when she had returned it was to find her home razed to the ground. 'I thought I had suffered enough,' she said, picking up the pathetic bundle, wrapped in a tattered blanket, that was all she could carry. 'But it seems one has never suffered too much in this world.'

Annie and Jess had agreed that the only way to carry on was to keep busy. Constant activity would keep your mind off it. And heaven knew there was always plenty to do.

The arrival of Betty's uniform a day or two later helped. Together she, Betty and Olive unpacked the parcel and turned over the garments inside, holding them up for inspection. Olive gave a snort of laughter.

'Look at these gum-boots! Imagine them, all caked in mud. You'll never be able to lift up your feet. And what about this overcoat, it must weigh a ton. They've sent you a soldier's uniform by mistake.'

'And this hat,' Annie said. 'It looks like Roy Roger's, caught in a rain-storm. Mind, these long socks look all right. They'll keep your feet warm.'

'Well, they'll help fill up the boots, anyway. And how about these?' Olive pulled out a pair of fawn trousers. 'You're never going to wear these, our Bet! They look like riding-breeches.'

'You don't expect me to wear my best skirt for milking cows, do you?' Betty retorted. 'Anyway, I think they're rather smart.' She held her head to one side and examined the corduroy breeches. 'And they go well with the green jumper.'

'Go on, you'll look just like a patch of muddy field,' Olive jeered. 'Here, try 'em on, I want to see what they look like.'

Betty slipped off her skirt and blouse. There were three short-sleeved shirts in the parcel as well and she pulled one over her head.

'Well, that's not bad.' Annie said. 'Quite nice, for summer.'

'It's aertex. See all these tiny holes, they help keep you warm or cool, like a string vest.' Betty struggled into the breeches and fastened them up. 'Not a bad fit. I was expecting to have to tie them up with string.' She climbed on to a chair to see herself in the mirror. 'What d'you think of that, then?'

'I don't know what your dad'll say, seeing you in trousers. You know he don't like it for women.'

'Well, he can't tell me not to, can he,' Betty said, exasperated. 'I mean, I've got to wear 'em. I suppose he'd rather have me climbing up on a haycart in a skirt and all the blokes looking up my knickers.'

'Betty! There's no call for talk like that. That's just the sort of thing that worries me, hearing you get so coarse. If that's the kind of thing you'll say at home, what's it going to be like when you're on a farm?' Annie shook her head. 'I think you're dad's right, you ought to have stopped at home. You could easy have got a job round here. You're too young to be going away.'

'I'm nineteen,' Betty said. 'In two years I'll be able to do what I like anyway. If you can't trust me now—'

'It isn't a matter of trusting you—' Annie began, but she was interrupted by the shrill peal of the doorbell. Sighing, she went off to answer it, while Betty looked into the mirror again and twisted herself this way and that.

'I want a nice belt to go round my waist,' she said to Olive. 'That brown leather one of yours would do, you never wear it. Don't you think these breeches make me look slim?'

'Skinny, I'd say,' Olive said, but there was no malice in her voice. She looked at her sister, pivoting on the chair. 'Aren't you going to try on the jumper? And look, here's a tie, you ought to put that on too. And the hat.'

Betty took the tie and tied it rapidly round her neck. She put her hands on her waist and posed again. The two girls looked in the mirror and giggled.

'Ride him cowboy!' Olive said, plonking the hat on her sister's head. 'Well, if the farmer sends you home you can always get a job in films. Here comes Mum, give her a surprise.'

Betty struck another pose but the chair overbalanced and she shrieked and grabbed Olive's shoulders. The two girls staggered and collapsed on the floor in a tumbled heap. Olive's skirt rucked up around her waist and Betty's breeches half unbuttoned. They lay giggling and Annie, coming back into the room, stopped abruptly.

'Whatever are you two doing? Get up at once, and make yourselves decent, for goodness' sake. Here's Graham to see you Betty, he doesn't want to find you making a fool of yourself, and as for you Olive, you're a married woman now, you ought to know better. Whatever would Derek think if he could see you?'

Hastily, Olive smoothed down her skirt and scrambled to her feet. She turned away, scowling slightly. There were times when being a 'married woman' could be a disadvantage. Did it mean you couldn't have fun any more, even with your own sister? And it wasn't fair of Mum, reminding her that Derek was miles away. Anyway, she knew very well what he'd think if he could see her lying on the floor with her skirt up round her waist. Her lips quivered a little at the thought.

Betty fastened her breeches quickly, hoping that Graham didn't notice what she was doing. She definitely needed that belt. She pushed back her curls and grinned at him.

'Hullo, Gray. What d'you think of my new uniform, then?'

There was a hint of defiance in her tone. Graham had never liked the idea of her joining the Land Army. He seemed to think she ought to stay at home, ready to be there whenever his ship happened to come in. But Betty wasn't prepared to stay at home darning socks just because her boy was away at sea. It was her life too, wasn't it? And if she wanted to spend her time digging potatoes, why shouldn't she?

All the same, she was disappointed when he gave her new clothes no more than a brief glance and then said tersely, 'I've got something to tell you, Bet. We're sailing tomorrow.'

'Tomorrow?'

307

She looked at him in dismay. Of course, she'd known he'd be going soon. They'd only stayed in harbour so long because the repairs had taken longer than expected, and there'd been so many other damaged ships coming into the Dockyard. And the battle – the Battle of Britain, they were calling it, as Winston Churchill had foretold – was getting fiercer every day. Only yesterday, there had been the biggest fight yet, with four hundred German aircraft seen off the Island, and sixty shot down, which made four hundred in less than four weeks. And although the battle was taking place in the air, the RAF still needed the support of the Navy.

Betty had known that Graham couldn't be in Portsmouth for long. But she had hoped they'd have this last week together, before she went off to Bishop's Waltham.

Still, maybe it was just as well. Graham wouldn't have taken kindly to her going away first, even if it was only just over the hill.

'You two'd better go in the front room and have a talk,' Annie said. 'Olive, you can help me get supper ready. Your Dad'll be in soon and he'll want it on the table.'

Betty and Graham went into the front room and sat down on the settee. Graham sat upright, saying nothing. His ginger hair was tousled, his bright blue eyes staring straight ahead. Betty glanced sideways at him and took his hand.

'Aren't you going to give me a kiss, then?'

'Didn't know you wanted me to,' he said stiffly. 'You seemed to be having a pretty good time without me. Nobody'd think, to hear you and Olive laughing and joking, that me and Derek Harker might be going to get killed any day. You don't seem a bit worried about me going away.'

'Graham! That's an awful thing to say.' She put her arms round his neck and kissed him. 'Of course I don't want you to go away,' she whispered. 'But we both knew it was going to happen, didn't we? And we've had a lovely time while you've been here.'

'Maybe you have,' he said sullenly. 'It hasn't been much fun for me, I can tell you. Bloody welding going on night and day, the bulkheads half torn off, dockyard workers crawling all over the ship like ants . . .'

'I know,' she said. 'But when you've been ashore, when we've been together, that's been nice, hasn't it?'

'It could've been nicer,' Graham muttered, not looking at her.

There was a moment's silence. Then Betty said, 'I've told you, Graham, I won't give way. I don't want to be left with a baby on my hands. And I don't think you ought to keep on about it.'

'Why not? We're supposed to be engaged, aren't we? I've given you a ring.'

'That's not official, you know it isn't. I only wear it like an engagement ring when there's no one else around.'

'It still means we're engaged. You said it still meant that.'

'It doesn't mean we're married, though, does it? And that's the sort of ring I want on my finger before we go any further.' She gazed at him, wishing that he would leave the subject alone. 'Graham, you know what could happen.'

'It wouldn't. I'd make sure it wouldn't. Look, what's the point of talking about getting married, you've told me time and time again your dad'll never agree—'

'I'm *not* talking about getting married!' she exclaimed, and bit her lip.

Graham stared at her. 'What d'you mean? Are you telling me you want to break it off? You're giving me back my ring, the day before I go away? Well, I think that's—'

'Graham, no!' She wrapped her arms around him again, holding him tightly. 'I didn't say that, I didn't. I just said – oh, I don't know what I did say now. I just don't want to think about getting married yet, that's all. I don't see the point, not with things as they are. Look at our Olive, been married a month and she hasn't seen Derek since. And if she wasn't working for his dad, she'd just as likely lose her job. You know what people are like about married women working. Where's the point? I don't want to be stuck at home with nothing to do.'

'It wasn't me brought up the subject,' he said. 'All I want—'

'I know what you want,' Betty broke in, 'and the answer's no.'

'Betty. It's my last night.' He pulled her close and slipped his hand up under the green jersey. He fumbled with the buttons on the shirt and put his hand over her breast. 'Bet, you don't know what it'd mean to me . . .'

'I know what it might mean to me,' she said, a little breathlessly. Graham had always had more effect on her than she allowed him to see. If he just knew what her body was doing when he kissed her like that, when he squeezed her breasts . . . I shouldn't ever have let him go this far, she thought. One of these days I'm just not going to be able to say no . . .

'I told you, I'll look after you.' His hand was on her knee now, sliding up her thigh. He stroked the crotch of her breeches and she gasped and squirmed. Even through the thick corduroy, there was no doubt as to her response. He slipped his hand up over her stomach and started to fumble with her waistband.

'Graham, don't! Mum and Olive are in the next room and Dad'll be home any minute, he could easy put his head in the door. Graham, please—'

'I love you, Betty.' His lips were covering hers, moving over her face, nibbling at her ears. 'You're the first real girl I've ever had. I just want to love you properly, just once, before I go away.' He managed to undo the top button of her breeches. 'Betty, I'm going to sea tomorrow, we don't know when we'll see each other again, I might get killed . . . You can't say no. You've got to let me, you've *got* to . . .' He pulled her suddenly so that she was half-lying on the settee. He leaned over her, then laid his body on hers and pushed himself hard against her. 'You've got to,' he panted.

Betty's thoughts were in panic. When Graham kissed her, when he stroked her breast or let his hands stray down over her bottom, she found it exciting. She enjoyed his touch and wanted him to go on doing it, and sometimes she knew she'd like him to go further. But she never wanted him to go 'all the way'. All her upbringing was against it, and always in her mind was the thought of her parents' disapproval, a disapproval that would amount to disgust and anger if she ever brought 'trouble' to the house.

Until now, she had always managed to keep the situation under control. But since Graham had come home a month ago and they'd had this unexpected time together, it had been much more difficult. He was restless, demanding, less ready to accept the lines she drew. And she had known that if she wasn't careful, this moment would come, when he would demand too much. The question in her mind had been, would she be able to resist him?

Not if he'd approached her more gradually, perhaps, in some dark, secluded spot where no one was likely to interrupt them. Not if he'd started with some of those lingering kisses that left her weak and melting, if he'd stroked her body gently, not hurrying, just slowly increasing the intimacy with every caress. If he'd taken his time, whispering to her all the time about how he loved her, what a beautiful body she had. If he'd pressed himself more gently against her, letting her feel the firmness of his body and holding her close, even tightly, but without crushing the breath out of her in this sudden almost frantic assault.

She knew that she might have had difficulty in stopping him then, difficulty in stopping herself. But this was worse. She sensed in Graham a desperation he had never shown before, a desperation that would not take 'no' for an answer. And she was suddenly, frighteningly, aware of his strength. She looked up at his face, trying to see his eyes, but they were half-closed, glazed, and she knew he did not see her. She wriggled her arms up and grasped his shoulders, trying to push him away, but he was like a rock.

'These bloody breeches!' he muttered, struggling with the buttons. 'Why did you have to put these on?'

'I didn't know you were coming . . . Graham, please don't—'

Should she call out, shout for Mum? That would stop him, but the thought of her mother coming into the room and finding them like this, struggling on the settee half undressed, was too awful. She'd tell Dad and they'd both blame her, say she'd led Graham on, probably insist they get married. And if they couldn't get married because he was going away, they'd be watching her for the first sign of a baby and it would be the end of the Land Army for her, they'd never let her go. And they'd never trust her again.

'Can't you pull 'em down, Bet?' he muttered, and groaned. 'I don't think I can wait much longer.'

She gave him an agonised look. Wouldn't it be better just to do as he wanted, and get it over with? It seemed as if that was the only way of stopping him now. Let him do it and do it quick, before Mum thumped on the door or Dad came in.

But Mum would know, she thought, the minute she looked at them she'd know. And suppose there was a baby?

Olive had told her it didn't always happen the first time. But Betty knew one or two girls who'd got caught, and they'd sworn it had only happened once.

She gave Graham's shoulders a hard push.

'*No*. Stop it, Graham. I don't want to – and you're hurting my leg. Get off me.'

He stared at her. He had been fumbling with his own trousers and she saw the paleness of his flesh against the dark blue serge. His face was flushed and he was breathing hard.

His ginger brows came together in a frown. 'Take 'em off, Bet. This is my last night—'

'Graham, I *can't*. You know I can't.' To her relief, she heard footsteps on the pavement outside and the click of the front gate. 'There's Dad! He'll be in any minute.' Panic lent her strength and she wriggled clear of Graham's arms and started frantically to do up her clothes. 'Make yourself decent, Graham, for goodness' sake!'

'He doesn't come in this way, does he? He goes round the side, to the back door.'

'I know, but sometimes he comes in the front.' In fact, he hardly ever did, but Betty wasn't going to tell Graham that. 'Anyway, if he's home supper'll be on the table and Mum'll be knocking on the door for us to go back.' She sat up and straightened her jersey, then looked at him. 'I'm sorry, Gray. But I can't do it, not like that. And I'm scared of what might happen.'

'I told you, I wouldn't let anything happen.' He finished tidying himself and looked away from her, still breathing quickly. 'You ought to trust me, Bet. You would, if you really loved me.'

'I do love you.'

'Well, prove it, then,' he challenged her. 'Show me you love me. After supper – we'll come in here again. No one'll disturb us, they know it's my last night. And you can take those daft breeches off and put on a skirt.'

Betty said nothing. She felt miserable and heavy inside. Graham was going away tomorrow, she didn't know when she would see him again, and she felt that he was right, that if she really loved him she'd let him have what he wanted, she wouldn't deny him. So *did* she love him? She thought she did – and she wanted it too, she couldn't deny that. But not like this, she cried out inside, not struggling on a settee in her mother's front room, trying not to be heard and then having to pretend afterwards. And spending the next two or three weeks waiting in terror, and maybe the next nine months in despair.

'Please, Graham,' she said in a low voice, 'don't keep on.'

He gave her a steady look. His blue eyes were hard, the skin taut around them, and his lips were tight. The flush had died from his face, leaving the freckles standing out against the pale skin.

He said, 'All right, Bet. It's all off, then. You can give me back my ring and I'll go. Say goodbye to your mum and dad for me, and tell 'em I'm sorry I won't be seeing them again.' He stood up.

Betty caught at his white summer shirt. The cotton was cool under her fingers. She remembered the day when he had first come here in the matelot's uniform, how proud she had been.

'No, Graham, don't go! Not like that. I do love you, I do, it's just that—' The tears came to her eyes and her voice broke '—I'm scared, that's all. I've never – it's my first time, I – I don't know what it's like – I'm *scared*.' She looked up at him appealingly. 'Graham?' And then she took a deep breath and said shakily, 'All right. I'll do it. After supper.' And felt almost as if she'd signed her life away.

Graham's face cleared and broke into a huge grin. 'You will? You'll let me love you properly? Oh, Bet—' He pulled her up against him and held her tightly. 'Bet, I promise I'll look after you. I won't let anything happen.' He kissed her and squeezed her breast, and she stiffened, terrified that his passion would overtake him again. But at that moment there was a thump on the door and they heard Annie's voice calling that supper was ready. Reluctantly, Graham let Betty go, and she stepped away, conscious of a huge wave of relief.

'Later,' he whispered in her ear. 'I'll be looking forward to it, all through supper.'

Betty gave him a wavering smile. But the feeling of heaviness still persisted inside her, and she knew that she would be unable to eat a thing.

Graham sat at the Chapmans' supper table, conscious of a simmering excitement. He was slightly ashamed of the way he'd behaved in the front room earlier. He hadn't meant to be rough with Betty, but his feelings had overwhelmed him. And he'd been upset by the sight of her in those cowboy breeches and hat. They seemed to take her away, as if she was going to have a new life that he couldn't share.

Graham didn't want Betty going away or having a life he didn't know about. He wanted her at home, where he could picture her when he was away at sea. He wanted to be able to wake up in the morning knowing exactly what she was doing – having her breakfast, walking up March Street to work in the dairy, going down town to do a bit of shopping or helping her mum around the house on Saturday afternoon. Going to church and maybe for a walk with her sister on Sunday. He'd been pleased when Olive got married, that meant there'd be no more chaps coming to the house, less chance of Betty getting off with someone else. And he was glad Bob Shaw was away in Devon, with Derek. He knew Bob was sweet on Betty and he had an idea she'd got a soft spot for him too.

But if Betty went off to the country, to some farm, there was no knowing who she might meet. Not all these country chaps would get called up. And some of them were big, beefy blokes, the sort who might easily sweep a girl off her feet and make her forget she'd got a boy in the Navy.

Still, he'd got her to promise to give herself to him tonight, and that would keep her true, he was sure of that. What's more, and perhaps even more important, he'd find out at last just what this sex business was all about.

At twenty, Graham had never experienced sex with a girl. He'd been thinking about it since he was seventeen or eighteen – before that, really – but although he'd had two or three girlfriends before Betty, he'd never got much further than kissing and the occasional more daring fumble, with his hands quickly slapped away. There had been one girl who'd let him feel her body more intimately, and who had done her own exploring too, through a hole in his trouser pocket, but he'd only been fifteen or sixteen then and a bit scared of the peculiar excitement it had caused. Usually, it had ended with tickling and giggles and, now he came to think of it, they hadn't even kissed very much.

But for the last year or so he'd been feeling increasingly restless. He wanted to know what it was all about. He wanted to know what this feeling was that other blokes talked about, usually with sniggers and dirty jokes, but still as if it was somehow the whole purpose of living, of being a man. And since he'd joined the Navy, it had been worse. You weren't a man until you'd 'done it', yet who were you to 'do it' with?

'You've got a girl, haven't you?' one of his shipmates asked him. 'Well, what's she for?'

But girls like Betty didn't 'do it'. They'd been brought up to save themselves for marriage, and they were pretty sharp when a boy tried to go too far. And the other option, the tarts who stood at the Dockyard gate and walked up and down Queen Street, carried their own risks. During his training on Whale Island, in Portsmouth Harbour, Graham had been subjected to several lectures on venereal disease, with horrific pictures to accompany them, and already on the ship he'd seen a couple of men who were getting regular, and not very sympathetic, treatment from the ship's doctor, and whose eating utensils were marked with red paint and kept separate from everyone else's.

So how was a bloke to find out? And now that he knew that the ship would be sailing, to stay at sea perhaps for weeks or months, and almost sure to be involved in action, perhaps even sunk, he was desperate to experience it, if only once. I can't die without knowing, he thought. I can't. It's not fair.

Betty had to let him. She had to. She was his girl, she'd got him to give her a ring which she wore on her left hand whenever they were out on their own, she'd said she loved him. All he was asking was to do it once, just once, just so that he knew what it was like. It was all right for her, it didn't mean so much to girls, she wouldn't sit at home wondering about it, wishing she could get the chance. And if she did, she could find a bloke easily enough – though she'd better not. But for him, away at sea, there would be no more chances. Perhaps never.

Just now, in the front room, he'd been overwhelmed by the desperation of his need. He looked at Ted Chapman, sitting at the head of the table, and silently cursed him. If he hadn't come in when he did . . . But maybe it'd be better later anyway. Betty had changed those horrible breeches for a skirt and she'd promised she wouldn't stop him, and her mum always let them go in the front room to say goodnight. And this being his last night, she'd be sure to let them have a bit longer, she wouldn't come bursting in. They'd be as safe there as if they were out in the country, with the stars overhead and nobody else around for miles.

'I had a few words with the new people in October Street, where the old lady lived with all the cats,' Annie was saying. 'A mother and two girls about eight or nine. Expecting too – it put me in mind of our Jess, moving into number 14 with Rose and Tim just little ones and Keith on the way.'

'Rose and Tim were only two or three,' Ted objected. 'You said these two were eight or nine.'

'Well, I know. I didn't say they were identical, just that they put me in mind.' Annie spoke with some impatience. Ted always had to be so literal. And couldn't he see she was just talking for something to say? Couldn't he see what was going on right in front of his eyes?

Annie had no illusions about young Graham Philpotts. She had a pretty good idea what was in his mind now, as he sat beside Betty at the supper table. He couldn't keep his eyes off her and was having a job keeping his hands off her too, if she was any judge. She'd given them both a sharp look when they came in from the front room, and seen Betty's over-bright eyes and flushed face, and Graham's smirk. She didn't think they'd actually done anything they shouldn't – well, not too much, and not yet – but Graham looked too much like the cat who'd got the cream for her peace of mind, and there was only one reason for a chap to look like that, the night before he went away to war.

If he hadn't already had the cream, he was expecting to get it.

Well, it was up to her to see that he didn't. It wasn't that she didn't trust Betty, but any girl could get carried away at times like this. That was why Ted was so against her leaving home. But Annie knew that a girl didn't have to leave home to get into trouble. It could happen in her own front room. And even a good girl could be forced into it, if the boy was persistent.

Graham had that persistent look tonight. And Betty was looking upset, as if she was half excited, half scared. She's ripe to fall, Annie thought, and she needs help to see she doesn't.

'Simmons, their name is, the people who are in number 16,' she went on. 'Jess told me she stopped and had a word. The husband's in the Merchant Navy and hasn't been home since March.'

'Where do they come from?' Olive asked. She seemed to have heard all this before, and wasn't particularly interested anyway, but there was something up with Mum, she looked anxious, and Betty and Graham had looked almost as if they'd had a row when they came in. She caught her sister's eye and was startled by the expression, almost of appeal, in her face.

'They were bombed out in that air-raid last month, down in Portchester Road. Their house is wrecked, so they've come to October Street.'

'Where've they been living till now?' Betty was trying desperately to control her juddering feelings, but her voice came out shrilly, as if she'd been crying. She could feel Graham beside her. Why did I promise? she thought. What am I going to do?

'Oh, she's been moved in a couple of weeks – took her a while to get the place fit to live in.' Annie sniffed. Jess had told her about the state the place was in. She wondered what it was like now. Annie cleaned her kitchen – and indeed her whole house – thoroughly each morning. Just as if the King and Queen were coming to visit, Ted sometimes remarked. And suppose they did? Annie would retort. Wouldn't you be thankful that someone cared enough about the place to keep it fit for visitors? And when he observed, as he had been increasingly wont to do just lately, that it was more likely to be Hitler who came walking in the door, she spoke even more sharply.

'I'll not have any German making remarks about *my* front step, nor how clean my net curtains are. And take those dirty boots off before you come in here, Ted Chapman. War or no war, I've still got my floors to keep clean, and I didn't spend half the winter making those rag rugs for you to leave muddy footprints all over them.'

She felt sorry for young Mrs Simmons, being bombed out of a home that was like a little palace and having to start again in something that was no better than a slum.

It had been a good enough start to the conversation, after all. Ted started to talk about other people who had been bombed out in that raid. He knew a couple from the ferry, men who'd gone over to Gosport to work. You got to know the regulars, they always went to the same places on the boat, some favouring the warmth of the funnel, some standing up in the bow with the piles of bikes. There were a couple of others who had never appeared again after that raid, he thought.

'Didn't one of your friends come from Portchester Road?' Betty asked Graham, grateful to be able to ask him something more ordinary. Not that air-raids were ordinary, though her dad and Uncle Frank both reckoned they were going to be. But there hadn't been another one since 11 July after all, though there'd been plenty of fighter planes coming over, and having dogfights with the RAF up there in the sky.

Graham nodded. 'Knocker White. He didn't actually come from there – his auntie lived there. But his mum always went round on a Thursday and we came up that way the next day and found the house bombed flat.'

The family had already heard the story. Graham had told them on the evening he had arrived. Later on, he'd told them that Knocker and his oppo Arnie had gone on to his mother's house and found the two women there, safe enough but a bit battered by the explosion. They had sheltered under the stairs when the raid started, too frightened to make the dash down the garden for the shelter, and had been found half buried in plaster and rubble, scratched and bruised but otherwise unhurt. The auntie had moved in with her sister now and was sleeping in Knocker's room.

Supper was over at last. The two girls washed up while Annie made Ted's sandwiches for next day and wrapped them in greaseproof paper. Ted and Graham read the newspaper and discussed the war, and then they all sat down together again. There was a moment's silence and Graham glanced at Betty. Perhaps now they'd be able to go back to the front room for the rest of the evening.

Annie caught the look and saw the blush on Betty's cheek. She sat up and said brightly, 'How about a game of cards?'

'Cards?' Ted said. 'On a Friday?' The family often played cards, but it was usually on a Sunday evening, and more often in winter than in summer. He looked out of the window. 'I was thinking of walking over to the allotment for an hour.'

'What, on Graham's last evening?' Annie saw his look of astonishment and almost laughed at herself. Why ever should Ted want to stay at home, just because it was Graham's last evening here? He didn't even like the boy all that much. And that's as good a reason as any, she thought grimly. If he doesn't want Graham Philpotts as part of the family, he'd better play his part. 'I'm sure there's nothing wants doing over there that can't wait till tomorrow.'

'It's all right, Mrs Chapman,' Graham said. 'I'm not all that keen on cards myself. I'd just as soon sit and talk for a bit.' In the front room with Betty, preferably, he thought, by ourselves and not doing all that much talking either.

'Oh, I'd like a game,' Betty said quickly. 'It'll be something to remember when you're away, Gray. A nice family evening together.' She avoided his eye. She could feel his disappointment and felt sorry about it, but she knew now that she would do almost anything to avoid being alone with him. Oh, Graham, she thought, I do love you – I'm *sure* I love you – but I'm just not ready . . .

Annie was already getting out the cards and in a few minutes the family found themselves sitting back at the table, sorting out their hands. They'd play Rummy, Annie declared, that was a nice game for five people since you couldn't play whist or solo. And after that they played Sevens, and then a game that Olive knew but couldn't remember the name of and then some silly game that involved putting a handful of farthings in the middle of the table and grabbing them. It made them laugh a lot, especially Betty and Annie, but the laughter was forced somehow and when the game was over they were all quiet, as if there was nothing left to say.

'Look at the time!' Annie said. 'I suppose you'll have to be getting back to the ship, Graham. Lucky it's not dark yet, or you might get lost!'

'I expect I'll find my way all right,' Graham said. His voice was flat. He knew, they all knew, that he'd have to leave in half an hour, not because he had to get back to his ship – he didn't have to be on board until six in the morning, an hour before sailing time – but because at ten o'clock the family would be starting to go to bed and the Chapmans would insist he was out of the house before then. And that didn't leave enough time for anything bar a few kisses. By now, he wasn't even sure that he wanted to kiss Betty anyway.

He refused Annie's offer of a cup of cocoa and she finally allowed them to go into the front room for their last goodnights. He shook hands with her and Ted, gave Olive an awkward peck on the cheek, and then followed Betty through the door. They stood in the front room, as ill at ease as if they had only just met, and then Betty looked up at his face and said, 'I'm sorry, Gray.'

'Yeah, I reckon you are.' He couldn't help his voice sounding bitter. 'I didn't notice you saying no to a game of cards.'

'I couldn't, could I? Mum knew what was up, she was set on us not being in here too long together. She'd have found some other way. We ought to have gone out for a walk.'

'And taken the whole family with us,' he sneered. 'Be honest, Bet, you were glad. You never did want us to do it, did you? You said as much. I just wish you'd said before, that's all—'

'I did, Graham! You know I did.'

'You been leading me on,' he continued as if she had not spoken. 'You wanted to get engaged, not me, you wanted a ring. What does all that mean, eh? What was it all about?'

'It was because I loved you,' she said, her voice quivering. The tears welled up in her eyes and trembled on her lashes. 'I do love you, Graham. It's just—'

'So why don't you prove it? Why don't you *show* me you love me?'

'But I do! Didn't I knit you a Fair Isle pullover? Didn't I make you a chocolate cake? Didn't I—'

'Cake!' he exlaimed. 'A *pullover*! Bet, I'm not talking about cakes and pullovers, I'm talking about—'

'I know what you're talking about,' she said, casting an anxious glance towards the wall that separated the front room from the room where the rest of the family were sitting. 'Please, Gray, don't shout, you'll have our Dad in here wanting to know what's going on. I've told you, I can't. I'm not ready for it. And I'm scared.'

'You don't trust me,' he muttered. 'And you don't love me. I've got to go away to sea tomorrow and I might be killed, never knowing what it's like. D'you realise that, Bet? I might never, never know what it's like.'

'Oh, Graham,' she said, and the tears poured down her cheeks. 'Oh, Graham, I'm sorry. I'm really, really sorry.'

She moved closer and put her arms around his body. She could feel his warmth through the white cotton shirt. She pressed her face against his chest and felt his heart beating under her cheek.

'If only there was time,' she said miserably. 'I'd do it now. I really would, Gray.'

But there was no more time. Already they could hear Olive's footsteps on the stairs and the movements in the next room as Annie and her husband prepared to go to bed. In a few minutes one of them would knock on the wall, and Betty would have to go back.

'I love you, Gray,' she whispered, and lifted her face. 'I really love you.'

He bent and kissed her lips. 'You'll write to me, won't you, Bet?'

'Every day.'

'And you won't get off with some farmer's boy?'

'I hate farmers' boys!' she declared, and they both laughed shakily.

Annie's knock sounded on the wall and they held each other tightly, with sudden passion. Graham groaned and kissed her hard. He felt his frustration well up inside him and clenched his teeth with the despair of it. Betty burst into fresh sobs and dug her fingers into his shoulders.

'Oh, Graham, I don't want you to go. I don't want you to go.'

'I know. I know.' He almost tore himself from her arms. Annie's knock sounded again, a little louder. 'But if I don't go, your Dad'll be in here with a horsewhip.' He held her away from him, gave her a crooked grin and then one last fierce kiss. He wrenched open the door and blundered out into the street.

Betty followed him to the front door. It was still light and she watched through her tears as he strode away up March Street. At the top, he turned and waved, and she lifted her own hand and blew him a kiss. And then he was gone.

She stood for a moment, feeling the emptiness around her where only a few moments before Graham had been. She looked at her hands, still able to feel the warmth and shape of his body on their skin. She wrapped her arms about her own body, trying to imagine that she was holding him still.

He'd been here, close to her, alive and warm and real. And now he was gone, and she didn't know when she'd see him again, when she would be able to touch him.

If she ran to the top of March Street she would still be able to see him, walking along September, tall and proud in his matelot uniform. But it would only be a few more seconds before he was once again lost to sight. It was as if she would never be able to catch up with him again.

The door behind her opened and Annie came out on to the step. She slipped her arm around Betty's waist.

'Don't stand out here fretting, love,' she said gently. 'He's gone. And you did the right thing.'

Betty didn't have to ask her what she meant. And she knew that without her mother's help, or interference, depending on how you looked at it, she might very easily have done the wrong thing.

I suppose I'll be glad about it after a while, she thought drearily as she followed Annie back into the house. But just at that moment I wish I'd been doing the wrong thing all this past month, and given Graham something better than a game of cards to remember when he's at sea.

Graham walked swiftly until he had turned the corner into September Street, and then his footsteps slowed.

Bugger Betty's mum! If it hadn't been for her, he and Betty could have spent a couple of hours in the front room, snug as you like behind the net curtains, and she'd have given him everything he wanted. He knew she would. She'd promised, and Betty wasn't one to go back on a promise. But Mrs Chapman was too sharp, she never had trusted him, and she'd made sure they had no chance. And now he might never know . . .

'Hullo, it's young Ginger Philpotts, isn't it? What's the matter with you, lost a shilling and found sixpence?'

Graham looked up, startled, and recognised Tommy Vickers. He was a smallish man with wavy fair hair and a cheeky grin, who lived at the top of April Grove, by the allotments not far from the Chapmans' house, and always had something to say about whatever was going on. Graham knew him from the days when the Philpotts family had lived in September Street, before they went to live 'over the water' in Gosport. Tommy Vickers had been a popular figure with the children, always ready with a pocketful of toffees to scatter amongst them or a joke to tell.

'Hullo, Mr Vickers,' he said. 'I'm all right, just said goodbye to Betty, that's all. We're sailing in the morning.'

'Oh, so that's it. And you're feeling a bit chocker.' Tommy had been in the Navy – the 'Andrew', he always called it – in the last war. 'Well, if you're not in a hurry, why not come and have a drink?'

'A drink?' Graham said stupidly, and Tommy grinned.

'You're a sailor, aren't you? Don't tell me you don't know what pubs are for. Come on.' It was a Brickwoods house, and he pulled Graham through the door. The smell of beer came to meet them. There was sawdust on the floor and raucous laughter in the air. Graham started to feel better.

'What'll it be? Can't offer you pusser's rum.' Tommy chuckled and Graham grinned back. Naval rum was stronger than any other kind and he had his tot every day in the mess.

'Best thing about the Andrew, the daily tot of rum,' Tommy said, 'but you can't get it outside. Well, you can—' he laid his finger against his nose and winked '—but you got to know the right people. So what is it? Pint of bitter?'

Graham nodded. Beer was another thing he might not get for a long time. The Navy gave you rum, but any other booze was absolutely forbidden, at least for the lower deck. Officers just about swam in pink gin, so he'd heard, but none of it ever filtered down to Jolly Jack.

Tommy brought the glasses over to a small table and they sat down. There was a short silence while they downed the first half. Graham had been half afraid that Tommy would suggest 'oncers' and expect him to drain the whole lot in a go, but he said nothing. Not that Graham couldn't have done it, but it would have meant he'd have to buy the next round and he was painfully conscious that he had very little money in his pocket. He set down his glass and wondered what to say.

Tommy Vickers was never at a loss for words. He cocked a bright blue eye at Graham and said, 'So you're off to sea tomorrow. How d'you like the idea? This is your first ship, isn't it?'

'That's right. I'm a writer.' When he told people that, they thought it meant he wrote books but he didn't have to explain to Tommy that all it meant was a clerk. Even ships had offices and paperwork, even when they went to war, perhaps more so, he thought.

Tommy nodded. 'I was a cook. A good one too. Nobody went hungry on my ship. Fed 'em like fighting cocks, I did. Been to sea yet?'

'Yes.' Graham told him about their attempt to thwart the air-raid a month ago, and how they'd been damaged and had to limp back to Portsmouth. 'We only got just past the Needles. They didn't warn us in time, that's what it was.'

'They didn't warn anyone in time,' Tommy said. 'There'd been two attacks already that day, down Portland, and they got there too late for those too. Caught with their pants right down. And they reckon they spotted our lot coming over the French coast, plenty of time to get everyone into shelters.'

'That's right,' Graham said. 'We saw 'em at a quarter to six. Heinkels, they were, with ME110s holding their hands. Our lads were in Hurricanes but while they were attacking the MEs, the Heinkels just went on and bombed Pompey.' His face was angry, but he gave a sudden reminiscent grin. 'Mind you, we saw two of 'em off – a couple of Hurricanes got round the Heinkels and started driving 'em just like sheep. Two of 'em collided in mid-air and fell straight into the drink. But they couldn't do nothing about the rest.'

'It was a bad do,' Tommy said, and they fell silent. He drank the rest of his beer. 'Well, we won't be caught napping again. I reckon they must've learnt their lesson, up at Bomber Command. Drink up, son. There's time for another one before they close.'

Graham flushed scarlet and felt in his pocket. 'I – I haven't got much dosh,' he stammered, but Tommy waved a hand at him.

'Did I ask you to pay? I was in the last lot, y'know. I came through it all right, but there were a lot of blokes, good mates of mine, who didn't. This one's on me. Call it one for them if you like.'

He went back to the bar and Graham glanced around the room. It was filled with smoke and there were a couple of other sailors there and a few women, but no one he knew. Unless that face was familiar? He stared hard and then realised who it was.

Nancy Baxter from April Grove. She was sitting with a couple of other women, drinking port and lemon by the look of it. She looked much the same as he'd always known her, thin and scraggy, her dark hair cut in a short, ragged bob. She had on a summer frock, the sort women wore when it was hot and sunny, with straps instead of sleeves, and her shoulders looked brown. The front was cut low and he could see the tops of her breasts. They didn't look all that much, but he couldn't help staring all the same.

Nancy Baxter was a tart, the whole street knew that. She was supposed to work nights in a hotel somewhere, but nobody had ever managed to find out which one and it was anyone's guess what kind of hotel it was. The two women with her were probably tarts too, dressed flashily and showing more leg than his Betty ever would. One of them caught his eye and gave him an enquiring smile. She crossed her legs and swung the foot towards him and he heard her laugh as he flushed and turned away.

He was still feeling hot when Tommy came back with the drinks, and his body was behaving in an embarrassing way. He picked up the glass and gulped down some beer.

'Ta. That's good.'

Tommy nodded and gave Graham a shrewd glance. 'Still feeling fed-up?'

'Yeah.' Graham hesitated, then said, 'What did you do when you went to sea, Mr Vickers? About – you know—' he blushed again '—girls, that sort of thing.'

'So that's it, is it?' The older man gave a short laugh. He was about fifty, Graham thought, and must be past it long ago. What was he doing, asking an old man's advice?

'Oh, forget I asked,' he said quickly, picking up his drink again to cover his embarrassment. 'It doesn't matter.'

'Doesn't matter? Of course it matters. It matters a helluva lot. And drop this Mr Vickers nonsense, my name's Tommy as well you know.' He leaned forwards. 'Look, I'll tell you this, sex *never* stops mattering. Well, not till you're a lot older than I am, anyway!' He grinned. 'And there's all the time in the world to find out about it – or ought to be.' He looked more sober. 'That's what's biting you, isn't it? You're off to sea tomorrow and you're scared you're never going to know what it's all about.'

Graham looked down at the table. Some of the beer had slopped over when Tommy set down the glasses, and he made patterns in it with one finger.

'Well . . .'

'Course you are. You're a healthy young man, it'd be a funny thing if you didn't have women on your mind. Been there for a few years too, I should think, eh?' He paused. 'You've been calling round Betty Chapman's place quite a bit lately.'

'Betty and me haven't done anything,' Graham said quickly. 'She's a decent girl. We—' He broke off. He wanted to tell Tommy that he and Betty were secretly engaged, but Tommy Vickers knew the Chapmans well, he lived only a stone's throw away from them and what's more he was the same generation, he'd be just as likely to pass it on. 'We're just friends,' he said lamely.

Tommy laughed. 'Tell that to the marines! Well, I can tell she hasn't given you any goodbye presents, anyway. And you might think yourself lucky, at that. You might've left her with one neither of you wanted.' He drank some of his beer. 'Are you telling me you've never done it at all?'

Graham shook his head miserably.

'What would you do, Mr Vickers? I know there's girls – women—' he couldn't help his eyes straying in the direction of Nancy Baxter and her two friends '—I mean, I know you can get it, but—'

'But you've heard all the horror stories.' Tommy too glanced across the room. 'Well, if I were you, I'd listen to 'em. There's more than one kind of present you can get from girls, and some are worse than others. I've always steered clear, myself. Once you're at sea, you're safe, that's always been my motto, and don't drink too much on shore runs.' He gave Graham a shrewd but kindly glance with his blue eyes. 'I know it seems hard, as the bishop said to the actress, but you're better off wondering than collecting a packet of what those sluts could hand you. But you're a big boy, as the actress said to the bishop, and you've got to make up your own mind.'

Nancy Baxter had got up and was moving in their direction. She leaned over them and said, 'That's right, Tommy. He's got to decide for himself.' She winked at Graham. 'Bet I know what you're talking about!'

Graham felt his skin colour yet again and Tommy said warningly, 'You leave the kid alone, Nance. He don't need your attentions.'

'Oh, don't worry,' she said, 'this is my night off.' She picked up the glass she had set down on the table. 'Just out for a bit of fun with me pals, what's wrong with that?' She winked at Graham again and moved away, swaying her thin hips.

Tommy snorted. 'Beats me how she gets the business. She's nothing to look at. Well, it's coming up to drinking up time and my missus'll be wondering where I've got to. Very handy with the rolling pin, is my missus!'

He winked at Graham and finished his beer. The landlord had rung the bell and more people were beginning to leave. The three tarts were on their way to the door.

'Okay, Mr Vickers – I mean, Tommy,' Graham said, still feeling awkward at using the first name of a man he'd known when he was little. 'I'll remember. And thanks for the drink.'

They walked outside. The twilight of midsummer was deepening to a shadowed blue. The sky was cloudless, with just a few stars prickling its indigo dome. Tommy stood still, looking upwards as everyone did these days. He turned to Graham and stuck out his hand.

'Good luck, Ginger. You're going to need it, I reckon, but someone always gets through, and there's no reason why it shouldn't be you. I did, after all, always reckoned I was lucky, so I'll pass my luck on to you. You remind me of myself a bit, when I was your age.' He grinned. 'Look us up next time you're in Pompey, eh?'

'Thanks. I will.' Graham shook the hand, feeling a sudden urge to hold on to it. 'Cheerio, then.'

He turned and walked away along September Street. The encounter hadn't eased his frustration, but he did feel a bit better for it. At least he'd been able to tell someone how he felt, someone who understood. Maybe Tommy Vickers wasn't past it after all. Or perhaps it was just that his memory was good!

He grinned at the thought, and then jumped as a voice spoke in his ear.

'Ginger? It is little Ginger, ain't it?'

Graham looked round, startled. Nancy Baxter was beside him, her bare shoulder almost touching his. She gave him a smile.

'Didn't you used to live in September Street? I knew your ma, Elsie. And Charlie, your dad. Course, I was only a kiddy then, but I remember 'em well.'

Some kiddy, thought Graham. Nancy Baxter had a boy of around eleven, she must have been at least twenty when he was born. Nobody knew who his father was, supposed to be a soldier, or was it a sailor, someone high-up anyway. So what were Nancy and her mum and Micky doing, living in a two-up, two-down terraced house in a backstreet in Pompey? And didn't she have another kid now? Still, it wasn't worth arguing about, and maybe she really had known his parents when she was young.

'Do they still call you Ginger?' she asked. 'I bet they do, with those carrots! So what're you doing now, then? Off back to your ship? I'd have thought you'd be stopping with Betty Chapman tonight.'

Graham stared at her. 'Stopping with Betty? Why?'

'Well, it's your last night, innit?' She laughed. 'Shouldn't know that, should I! But you'd be surprised what I get to know in my line of business.' She winked and lowered her voice a bit. 'F'r instance, I always know when a bloke's gasping for it. And when it's a nice-looking chap like yourself . . .'

Graham remembered Tommy's warning. 'No thanks. I've got to get back.'

'Why? You ain't sailing till morning.'

'You know more than you ought to,' Graham said. 'And you shouldn't be blabbing it round the streets, either. You know what they say.'

'Oh, I know! Walls have ears, be like Dad and keep Mum, there's a fifth columnist under every bed.' She sniggered again. 'She's had too much to drink, he thought. 'You don't have to worry about me, Ginger. And if there's anything you want, to help speed you on your way, well, you've only got to ask.'

Graham looked at her and turned away quickly, thankful that the twilight hid his blush. 'No thanks.'

'Sure?' She took his arm, turning him back towards her, and searched his face. 'You didn't look too cheerful, back there in the pub with Tommy Vickers. Just said goodbye to young Betty, had you?'

Blimey, Graham thought, everyone knows your bloody business round here. He twisted away again.

'Look, sorry. I've got to get back to the ship . . .'

'What's the hurry?' Nancy held on to his arm. She moved closer and he caught another glimpse of her breasts, where the sundress gaped from her body. 'Look, Ginger, I'm not after business. I've seen too many young chaps going off to sea lately. I know the look – the look you all get. Specially you young 'uns. Never had it and scared you're never going to get it. That's right, innit? Don't try to flannel me, you won't have got much joy out of young Betty, I know, not with a dad like hers hovering outside the door. So what's the hurry? Why not come home with me and go back to your ship in the morning.' She grinned. 'I'll make sure you don't oversleep!'

Graham felt the heat flood over his body, from his neck upwards, from his waist down. He shook his head and stammered.

'I'm not – I don't – I can't – look, I've got to get back. I've got to!'

'Not till morning.' Nancy said calmly. 'And you are, you do and you can. What's more, you want to. Why not come and have a bit of fun while you've got the chance? Where's the harm in it?' She held her head on one side, her eyes like black buttons in the darkness, and reached down to stroke his thigh. 'No one's going to know,' she whispered cajolingly. 'Betty thinks you've gone back ages ago, and Tommy Vickers is home in bed with his own missus by now. And I know how to keep my mouth shut.'

She was thin and a bit scraggy, with bony shoulders. But she was offering him something no other woman had offered, something he badly wanted. He'd wanted it to be Betty, but it couldn't be, wouldn't, for years. And he couldn't wait for years. Nobody had the right to make him wait years.

'I can't,' he stuttered miserably. 'I haven't got any money. I'm skint.'

'Who's talking about money?' she retorted. 'Look, I told Tommy Vickers this was my night off. But that don't mean I can't accommodate a friend, does it? Specially when I knew his mum and dad years ago when I was a nipper. Call it in memory of old times, if you like!' She laughed and hooked his arm into hers. 'Come on, stop looking so worried, we'll go down the back way. And you can be out first thing in the morning, before anyone else is about. Your Betty'll never know, and what she don't know can't hurt her, can it?'

Almost without realising it, Graham had turned and was walking back along September Street, arm in arm in the darkness with Nancy Baxter. His head reeled and his heart thumped. He thought briefly of Betty, then pushed her from his mind.

This was nothing to do with Betty, nor Tommy Vickers, nor his mum and dad. This was between him and Nancy Baxter. In fact, he wasn't even sure it had much to do with Nancy. It was all to do with himself, with the body he had grown into. It was to do with his manhood, with the desperate need he had to know what it felt like to *be* a man, to know what it was all about.

He had a right to it, didn't he? He had a *right*.

Betty heard their footsteps go by as she lay in bed, her pillow wet with tears. She was alone in the bedroom – after her marriage, Olive had moved into Colin's room in the little turret. It didn't seem right, sleeping with her sister now she was a married woman, she'd said, and Betty had been glad enough to have the room to herself, though she missed their whispered conversations and felt less close to her sister now.

She was glad now to have no witness to her tears, although she would have liked the comfort Olive might have given her. And it would have proved to her that Betty did love Graham, just as much as she loved her Derek. Sometimes Olive behaved as if they were the only two who had ever been in love, or missed each other.

At least they're married, Betty thought. They can do what they like. Not like me and Graham. She thought again of his lips on hers, of his searching hands. She'd wanted to give him what he wanted, she'd wanted it herself, but she just couldn't. And she'd hated sending him off like that, miserable.

Maybe next time he comes home, she thought. I'll ask Olive about it, how to make sure nothing goes wrong. Graham's right, it's not fair, not when he has to go off to sea not knowing whether he'll ever come back.

She knew that he was afraid he would lose her to some other boy. She knew that he wanted to know she belonged to him, that he was the first man ever to make love to her. And I want to be his first girl, she thought.

And I will – next time he comes home. I'll write and tell him. It'll be a promise.

The footsteps had faded now. She turned over and fell asleep.

6

It was midday on the Monday after Graham's departure, and Betty Chapman had just handed Mrs Marsh her notice, when the sirens sounded their long-drawn, eerie lament.

'Oh no,' Mrs Marsh said with a cluck of exasperation. 'There it goes again. I suppose we'll have to shut the shop and go down the shelter. You never know but what it might be real.'

Outside, the sun was at its height, glittering on the balloons. The raiders were not yet in sight, but as she went to lock the shop door the low mutter of their approach could be heard over the dying wail of the siren. Suddenly fearful, the two went quickly to the back door and as they came out into the yard the mutter developed into a snarl, and then a low, ominous roar.

Mrs Marsh gave a gasp of fright and ran for the shelter. She had hung her washing on the line earlier and she snatched at it as she ran, pulling it with her. One of the white sheets trailed on the ground and almost tripped her up. She cried out with fear and annoyance, and gathered it up in a bundle, dragging it through the little doorway.

Next door, Alice and Joy Brunner were sorting through a bundle of women's magazines. The siren caught and froze them. Alice's pale face grew even whiter and she began to shake.

Joy dropped the magazines and grabbed her mother's arm.

'Come on, Mum. Down the shelter, quick.'

'It's a false alarm,' Alice said, shuddering. 'It's bound to be. They aren't really coming.'

'They might be.' There had been false alarms day after day, but you could never be sure it wasn't real until the other siren sounded, the one that meant it was safe again. 'We ought to go down the shelter just in case.' Joy let go of her mother's arm and locked the shop door. They'd left it unlocked once and come back to find half the sweets gone from the boxes behind the counter. She had a good idea who it was had taken them too. 'Come on, quick. Where's your gas mask?'

'It's no use, Joy. Even if it is them, it's no use. If we're meant to be killed, we'll be killed, just like your poor father.'

'*Mum!*' The snarl of planes approaching could be heard quite clearly now. Joy pulled again at her mother's arm, dragging her through the shop and out of the back of the house. She glanced up and caught her first sight of an enemy formation, like a cloud of black flies coming directly out of the sun. For a few seconds she stood frozen. Only her head and eyes moved, following the path of the aircraft as they came slowly onwards, flying in a straight, remorseless line over the city.

'Oh-h-h,' Alice moaned, covering her face with her hands. 'Oh, Joy . . . Heinrich . . . Heinrich, where are you . . .?' She broke away from Joy's hand and scuttled like a crab towards the Anderson shelter.

Joy saw the bombs, falling like a bundle of firewood from the belly of the first plane, scattering in the air, falling on Portsmouth . . .

'Joy! *Joy!*'

Alice was screaming at her, her head poking out of the Anderson. With a startled jump, Joy came to her senses and hurled herself down the garden.

'They're right on top of us!' She flung herself in behind her mother. 'They're *diving* on us!' The first explosion shook the ground and was followed by another, another and another. She crouched on the floor and Alice clutched her, gabbling with fear.

'They're not giving us a *chance*. There's people still out in the streets.' The harsh rattle of guns drowned her voice. 'Oh, Joy, what's that?'

'It's anti-aircraft fire,' Joy said. Her voice was trembling and she made a huge effort to control it. 'We're shooting at them. They won't get away as easy as that.'

'What difference does it make whether it's a bomb or an aeroplane that drops on you? You're just as dead.' Alice crouched on the floor, her hands over her ears. 'Oh, it's so *loud*. They must be right overhead. They'll kill us all.'

The planes were roaring overhead. It sounded as if they were simply circling over the city, quite undisturbed by the anti-aircraft guns. Every minute was punctuated by a fresh explosion. Alice and Joy huddled together on the damp earth floor, their arms covering their heads, their bodies jarred by the vibrations that tore through them through both earth and air.

'There'll be nothing left,' Alice whimpered. 'Nothing left . . .'

It seemed as if half a lifetime had passed, yet it was barely twelve-thirty when the Raiders Passed signal sounded. Cautiously, only half believing it, Joy and Alice looked at each other.

The sky was silent again. There was no snarl of approaching Heinkels, no 'crump' of a falling bomb. The last explosion had been several minutes ago.

'D'you think it's really safe?' Alice whispered.

'They've got ways of telling,' Joy said uneasily. 'People looking with telescopes, and that sort of thing. And it's broad daylight. They must be able to see they've gone.'

They scrambled to their feet, stretched their cramped and stiffened limbs and crawled slowly out of the shelter, blinking in the bright sunlight and almost afraid to look about them. It seemed uncannily quiet after the pandemonium of the previous half-hour, but as the thunder died from their ears they became aware of voices from nearby gardens, and then of a shadow passing beneath the sun as black smoke billowed into the sky, with flames of cruel orange and red showing like glimpses of silk lining in a torn black cloak. The Devil's cloak, Joy thought, flung over the city of Portsmouth to stifle it to death . . .

She saw Mrs Marsh and Betty Chapman looking over the fence. Alice was crying again, staring at the black and orange smoke and shaking her head like a doll that had been wound up and couldn't stop.

'It isn't that Mum wants to give in,' she said defensively. 'But she misses Dad so much. And not even knowing what's happened to him.' Her eyes filled with tears. 'We don't even know why they had to take him away. He never did anything wrong.' Her arms were round her mother's thin body, comforting her as if she were the mother and Alice her child.

Mrs Marsh nodded. 'I know, love. It's all too much for her. You take her in and make her a cup of tea, and I'll come round and see if there's anything I can do. It's hard on us all, but we've just got to help each other as best we can.' She looked down at the washing still clutched in her arms. 'I don't know why I took this down with me, I'm sure.'

She went back into the dairy and Betty Chapman followed her. The excitement of being called up into the Land Army had faded. There wasn't much glamour after all in a war that took innocent men away from their homes as if they were criminals, and left women like Alice Brunner frightened and alone.

Ted Chapman was bringing the *Ferry King* alongside the Portsmouth pontoon when the sirens sounded.

He felt the now familiar chill of fear run down his spine. It didn't matter how many false alarms there were, you never lost that little cold shudder or the sickness in your stomach. He looked at Ben, who had just jumped ashore to wind the mooring rope to the stanchion. The other member of the crew, old Sam Hardy, was unfastening the chain to let the passengers off.

'Get up to the shelters, quick!'

Sam shook his head. 'I'll stay aboard.'

Ted drew a ragged breath of exasperation. They had this argument every bloody time. Whichever side of the harbour they were on, the men were supposed to make for the shelters at the top of the Hard. And they never would. The two of them, Sam and young Ben, always insisted on staying with the *King*.

'When you go up to the shelter, so will I,' Sam said flatly, and Ben nodded. But Ted could not bring himself to leave his boat. The *King* had been his life, his pride and joy, for years. He'd crossed the harbour thousands of times, in all weathers, tossing in winter gales, creeping almost blindfold in thick fog. And he'd taken her across to Dunkirk, where she'd worked under heavy shelling and gunfire.

The *King* had stood by him then, and he had a superstitious dread of leaving her.

'For crying out loud!' he shouted, his voice cracking with fear. 'The Jerries are coming – can't you see them?' They were coming in over the Isle of Wight, black as a flock of starlings. 'Get into shelter, for God's sake!'

The passengers were running hell for leather up the sloping pontoon. Above them on the railway station, they could see people leaping off the trains, scuttling along the platforms in a frantic search for safety. Ted looked at the sky. The flock of black planes held a horrible fascination.

Terror ran through his body like a flame at white heat. He screamed again at his crew.

'*The shelters! For God's sake – the shelters!*'

'You come too.' Sam ran up the few steps to the bridge and grabbed his arm. 'Ted, don't be daft – you get bombed here an' you won't know whether to burn or drown. Look at 'em! They're making straight for the Yard. They'll blow the whole bloody lot to smithereens, and us with 'em. What good'll that do anyone?' He dragged Ted down to the deck and thrust him on to the pontoon. 'Look, any more trouble from you and I'll knock you out and *carry* you to the shelter!'

Ted felt his legs begin to run. He was still gibbering a protest, but Sam and Ben were on either side of him, yanking him up the wooden slope. By the time they reached the top and began to run along the bridge, the air was filled with the drone of the aeroplanes. Panic tore at his body. It was Dunkirk all over again, and this time they wouldn't survive.

The first bombs fell as they pushed their way through the shelter door.

Tommy Vickers was working in Old Portsmouth, near Whitewoods, the furniture depository. His job as general handyman with the Council took him all over the city. That was how he liked it. He enjoyed knowing Pompey like the back of his hand, hearing all the gossip, being a familiar figure around the place. Mending pipes, painting street signs, sweeping gutters, he didn't care what he did, so long as he was out and always had time for a cheery word or a joke.

When the siren sounded, he made for the nearest shelter and settled himself on one of the benches. Some kids had been in and pinched the paraffin lamps, but someone had a torch and flashed it around in the darkness. Most of the people were resigned to another false alarm, but the sound of the aeroplanes changed the atmosphere to one of dismay.

'Oh God, not again. It was bad enough last time.'

'What'll they hit this time? Our Fred's house had all its windows blowed out. He's only just got 'em patched up.'

A woman beside Tommy began to cry. He patted her arm.

'It's all right, love, we're safe enough in here. Look, let's have a bit of a singsong. It'll cheer us up.'

'What's there to feel cheerful about?' someone asked out of the darkness, and Tommy shrugged.

'Well, it'll help pass the time. And if we sing loud enough we won't hear the planes. Come on, I'll start and you all join in.'

He cast about in his mind for a song. *Little Brown Jug* had been popular lately. Glenn Miller had been playing it on the wireless.

> 'My wife and I lived all alone,
> In a little log hut we called our own,
> She loved whisky, I loved rum,
> I tell you what, we'd lots of fun.'

He paused. One or two voices joined in, rather feebly.

'Ha-ha-ha,
He-he-he,
Little brown jug, don't I love thee . . .'

A bomb crashed down outside. It drowned their voices, shook the earth beneath their feet, sent a wave of vibration through their bones. The woman near Tommy screamed and began to cry more loudly.

Tommy put his arm around her shoulders and gripped her tightly against him. He started again.

'Dear old pals, jolly old pals,
Clinging together in all sorts of weather,
Dear old pals, jolly old pals,
Give me the friendship of dear old pals.'

Now others were joining in. As Tommy finished his song, another one started in a far corner. More people were singing, their voices wavery and self-conscious at first, rising to a shout of defiance as the noise increased outside.

'*Daisy, Daisy, give me your answer do,*' someone sang, and the response came from a dozen throats.

'I'm half crazy, all for the love of you.'

Another explosion rocked the shelter. The noise of aircraft, ack-ack guns and the screaming whistle of the falling bombs created a pounding cacophony that threatened to burst the eardrums of the people huddled in the shelter, but they kept singing. In every momentary lull, the voices could be heard, straggling on.

'It won't be a stylish marriage,
I can't afford a carriage . . .'

'Bloody hell,' a man near the door said, 'that was a close one. Something's copped it.'

'But you'll look sweet
Upon the seat
Of a bicycle made for two.'

'We 'ad a tandem once,' the woman in Tommy's arms snuffled, and he held her closer. 'But it ain't safe to go out no more.'

'Them days'll come back again, you'll see.'

The raid continued. The same dread was in every heart – what would they see when it was over and they went out into the street? But the songs went on, defiance tempered with desperation and a need to do something together, a communication and reassurance. By the time it was over, those who had dashed into the shelter as strangers were held by a bond of both fear and comfort.

At last the noise diminished. The Raiders Passed signal sounded and those nearest the door peered cautiously out.

'Blimey.'

'What is it? What've the bastards done?'

'Only just about flattened us, that's all.'

Tommy let go of the woman and emerged into the sunlight. It was misted over now, almost obscured by the smoke of flaming buildings. The pungent smell of burning was in the air.

'That's Whitewoods bin hit. Goin' up like a torch.'

'There's a big fire down by the ferry, too. And more in the Yard.'

'It's all over the shop. I don't reckon there's a building left standing.'

Tommy left them and ran down the street. The furniture warehouse was well alight, flames leaping from the roof. The whole façade was a mass of orange fire and as he watched a great section of wall toppled slowly outwards into the road. People were screaming and running about, futilely directing stirrup pumps at the blaze, yelling orders to each other. Others wandered in a daze or slumped against walls.

Tommy did what he could, helping those who were hurt or just plain terrified out of their wits. A fire engine arrived and one of the ARP men who had been rushing about giving orders began to berate the chief.

'One bloody engine ain't enough! You can see what it's like. The whole bloody building's afire. We needs every engine in Pompey to fight this lot.'

The fire chief shook his hand off angrily. 'You go on up round Bonfire Corner and tell 'em that. It's proper livin' up to its name, that is. And Queen Street's nothing but rubble, they've got half the engines trying to put that out. And Brickwoods is smashed – that's next week's beer down the drain.'

'Well, what're we supposed to do 'ere, then?' the ARP man demanded pugnaciously. 'That fire's goin' ter spread if it ain't checked.'

The fire chief turned on him. 'We do whatever we bloody can, don't we? It ain't our fault we ain't got the appliances.' He rubbed a blackened hand over his face. His eyes were desperate. 'The Harbour Station's going up in flames too. We 'aven't got the men, the streets are blocked, and when we do get there, the bloody mains are burst and we can't get no water. Oh, what a bleedin' mess . . .'

'The station?' Tommy stared at him. Portsmouth Harbour Station was a landmark. Everyone who ever went near the ferry knew it. It was built out over the water, so that you could look down from the platforms and see the sea lapping beneath. People came down from London on the train and walked down the platform and straight on to a boat for the Isle of Wight.

'Incendiary,' the fireman said, and turned away again. The warehouse was past saving but sparks and flames were settling on the roofs of other buildings. He ran over to the men who were struggling with the hoses.

Down by the harbour, Ted Chapman also was emerging from the blackness of an air-raid shelter. He stared at the salty blue flames and black smoke billowing from the Harbour Station, and broke into a run.

'Bloody hell, look at that! The whole station's going up. The *King*—'

'They'll never let us near.' Sam and Ben stood behind him, staring.

Already people were running about like ants at the top of the pontoon, by the station entrance. A couple of makeshift fire engines converted from dustcarts were pulling up and blue-uniformed men leaping off them and unreeling long hoses.

'It would be low tide,' Sam said in disgust. There was nothing but mud below the slipway. The pontoon, which floated almost level with the road at high tide, was at the bottom of a steep wooden slope.

Which was probably what had saved the *Ferry King*. Moored to the pontoon, she was well below the station and out of the reach of the flames which had spread so quickly along the structure, turning the trains into a heap of twisted, melting metal.

She was not out of danger. Shards of burning fabric were falling on her and Ted watched in agony, certain that she would burst into flames at any moment. But the water which was being sprayed now over the burning structure of the station was turned upon the ferry-boat too, and the flames sizzled and went out.

The *Ferry King* had survived to cross the harbour another day.

Gosport had been hit as well. Frank's brother Howard lived in Gosport and he cycled the twelve miles round the top of the harbour that evening to tell them he and his family were all right. Jess opened the door to him in relief.

'Thank goodness you weren't bombed, Howard. Frank wanted to come over to you but the ferry's not running and I wouldn't let him go out again without his tea. Was there any damage round you?'

Howard nodded. 'Chap called Herbert Gadsby, killed. He lived down Oval Gardens. I used to pass the time of day with him.'

Jess gazed at him solemnly. It was the first time any of them had actually known someone who had been killed.

Howard worked at Supermarine, near Southampton. They built Spitfires there and his work was secret, he wouldn't even talk to Frank about it. But there was still a lot he didn't know, and the war was as bewildering to him as to anyone else.

'We don't know where we are with Stokes Bay these days,' he said. 'One day we can go down there, the next they're putting up barbed wire, old bedsteads, anything to keep it fenced off. And last week they told us we can go there again! They don't seem to know what's what at all. The Admiralty even requisitioned Lee swimming pool a few weeks ago. What are they going to do with that, teach sailors to sail model yachts?'

It took some time for the details of the raid to reach the people of Portsmouth, and the next day's issue of the *Evening News* was snapped up the moment it appeared on the streets. Frank came home from work to find Jess reading it with tears in her eyes. He took it from her and spread it on the table, and they read it together.

'We've done well,' he said. 'Look at those headlines. *Too Hot for Raiders*. It was one of the German pilots said that. And here's another one. *English Too Good*. They're almost begging to be taken prisoner, look, this one even brought his hair-oil and shaving tackle with him!'

'And one of them was a boy of fifteen,' Jess said. 'Fifteen! That's not much older than our Rose. How can they send children like that to war?'

'Maybe he pretended to be older. Plenty of lads have done that.' Frank looked at the paper again. 'We shot down sixty-one planes. Sixty-one. They've lost over five hundred now. It can't go on much longer, Jess.'

'Why not? Last air-raid we had, you said it was only the beginning.' Jess shook her head. 'Look what they're doing to us. Have you heard about the Eye and Ear Hospital? Look, it says here, well, it doesn't say it was the Eye and Ear, they don't print the names, but everyone knows that's where it was, it says they were just starting a mastoid operation and they went on, right through the raid, even though it was hit. The nurses had to get the patients out to places of safety. Fancy having to drag people out of their hospital beds to go to a shelter! I mean, suppose someone was in traction.'

'They don't put you in traction for eyes and ears,' Frank pointed out, but Jess snapped at him uncharacteristically.

'It doesn't have to be the Eye and Ear gets bombed, does it! It could as easy be the Royal or St Mary's next time. All I'm saying is Hitler's got the whole of Europe now to build his planes in, he's not going to run out in the first five minutes.' She looked at Frank. 'He wants to invade us, doesn't he? He wants us under his heel along with the rest.'

Frank was silent for a moment. He wanted to offer some comfort, but could think of none. Jess was right – Portsmouth had taken a bad knock.

'Oh, Frank,' Jess said, and now the tears were on her cheeks. 'Look at this. That man, the one without any legs, you know, he used to be outside Woolworths selling matches, till it burned down in May. He's been killed. Sitting in the park in his wheelchair, he was, and got killed by flying fragments.' She laid down the paper. 'He lost his legs in the first war. I suppose he couldn't get into a shelter, not in a wheelchair.'

She stood by the gas stove, waiting for the kettle to boil, thinking of the man with no legs. What sort of a life had he had? Blown up in the first war, probably gassed as well for all she knew, scratching a living by sitting on a little wooden cart on the pavement outside Woolworths, selling matches. He hadn't been all that old, probably in his fifties. Just a young man when he lost his legs.

It wasn't only his legs he'd lost, either, she thought. Bert Shaw next door had told her he always bought matches from him and he'd spoken to him quite a few times. The man had told him he'd been engaged to be married when the Great War had broken out, but his sweetheart hadn't been able to face marrying a man with no legs. He'd had to find somewhere to live, a place in Charlotte Street, not much more than a storage room. It had a low washbasin and a lavatory and someone had fixed him up with an old stove to do his bit of cooking, and the other traders had given him some bits of old carpet to put on the stone floor and a few sticks of furniture, and that was about it. That was how he'd lived for the past twenty years or so.

'I can't stop thinking about that poor man,' Jess said, taking Frank's tea through to him. 'His legs, his dreams, his whole life, all just smashed to pieces. And what for? Just so he could crawl about like a beetle all those years and wait to be killed after all.'

'We've been through all this, Jess,' Frank said. 'We had to go in and help Poland. You know we did. Just like you had to go and help those evacuee kiddies, remember? You knew it wasn't right, what was happening to them, and we knew it wasn't right what Hitler was doing. We didn't have any choice.'

Maureen, who had been fast asleep in her pram in the front room, began to cry. Jess went in and picked her up. She brought her into the back room and sat at the table, holding her on her knee. Frank looked at her and frowned.

'It still don't seem right, you and her being in Portsmouth with all this bombing. I wish you'd go back out to Bridge End.'

'We've been through that, too. I won't leave you, Frank, and that's flat. Anyway, I'm not letting Ethel Glaister get her nose through the door again. I know what'd happen, I'd hardly be up the top of the street before she'd be in here with her perm and her smarmy ways and a bit of fruit cake for you to eat. She never has a word to say to me, but I've seen her when you're out in the garden, leaning on the fence and fluttering her eyelashes.'

'I don't give her any encouragement,' Frank protested, and Jess laughed.

'I know that! But that sort doesn't need encouragement. Thinks she's God's gift to mankind, that one does, and she's got worse since George went. I wonder if he knows how she carries on when he's away.'

'She doesn't carry on. Not really. I mean, I've never seen her *with* anyone, and nobody comes to the house.'

'Well, no, I don't mean she carries on in that sense – thinks too much of herself. But she'd like to think all the men are after her.' Jess sniffed. 'And the way she dresses up, you'd never think she had a husband in the Territorials.'

Frank smiled. He knew just what Jess meant, but it sounded funny all the same. He looked at the baby, who was chewing a crust Jess had given her, and reached out awkwardly to touch her cheek. It felt like a peach under his rough finger.

Frank was never entirely at ease with babies, not even his own. He liked the children better when they got old enough to talk to sensibly and to do things with. He liked showing the boys how to make things with wood or mend broken cups and such. But his life revolved around his family, all the same, and he would have died fighting if anyone had tried to harm them.

That's what we're doing, he thought. Fighting for our families. And if Hitler does invade us, I'll fight to the death for this little scrap, yes, and for the boys and Rose as well. And Jess. Especially for Jess.

They had been married for seventeen years and she had brought into his life the first real love he had ever known. It was not something he would give up easily.

7

Ethel Glaister put down her book and glanced restlessly about the room. She was fed up with being on her own. She wanted someone to talk to.

Ethel's older children, Joe and Carol, were out at work all day, and her husband George was away in the Army. And although Ethel was house-proud and liked to keep her home 'nice', her real pleasure lay in showing off her home to envious neighbours. Otherwise, she occupied herself with reading romantic novels or going to the cinema.

But it was nicer to have someone to go to the pictures with, so that you could talk about the film on the way home.

Ethel had no friends in the streets nearby. But she had noticed Kathy Simmons and her two little girls going up and down October Street and heard how they'd been bombed out. Kathy had come from Portchester Road, where the houses were a bit bigger than those in October Street and had bay windows, so she was obviously used to something better, and the girls might make nice friends for her Shirley.

She went out into the scullery, took off her blouse and had a wash at the sink. Upstairs, she put on her second-best blouse, the one with the frilly collar. Her best blouse had frills all the way down the front, but that was too much for an afternoon call. Her powder-blue jacket would be nice, though, and her grey skirt. A lot smarter than that old herringbone jacket and brown skirt Jess Budd always wore to the shops, and it would show Mrs Simmons that although April Grove might be a backstreet it was no slum.

Carefully, she polished her black high-heeled shoes, and minced across to the corner and over to number 16.

Kathy Simmons had been trying once again to rid the Anderson shelter of the smell of cats.

It had been hard work moving in. Nobody had thought to give the house a clean and Kathy, arriving from a home in which nothing had ever been out of place until Hitler got his hands on it, had found herself spending the first part of her five pounds on brooms and scrubbing brushes, just to get it fit to live in. The old lady didn't seem to have decorated for years, and the rooms were dark and dingy. There was no electricity, and only the two downstairs rooms and lean-to scullery were lit with gas. Upstairs, you had to use candles, and you had to take a candle with you to the outside lavatory. How romantic, she thought. That'd get Mike in the mood when he came home!

She had spent the morning scrubbing the scullery, and felt proud of her efforts. The walls were still brown, but at least it was a lighter shade of brown, and the old linoleum on the floor had turned out to be yellow. There were still a few stains she couldn't shift, but on the whole it looked much better. Almost cheerful, in fact. And although she'd felt tired from her efforts and knew she ought to rest in the afternoon, she'd been unable to forget the smell in the shelter, and determined to have another go at it. If they were going to have to keep on going down there, it might as well be as homely as it could be, and she didn't want to have to take her baby down there with it smelling the way it did.

Besides, she had found that it was only by keeping busy that she could keep the memories at bay. The siren wailing just as she was giving the girls their supper. The planes roaring overhead, the whistling of the bombs as they fell and the explosions all around. And then coming out of the shelter to find her home destroyed, with only a few fragments left whole. And Muriel's doll like a baby amongst the rubble, its face smashed, its body torn and broken. A baby, abandoned to the fury of the enemy . . .

Only constant work, a determined effort to put the memories behind her and a smile on her face, could keep such horrors out of her mind.

She gave the shelter another thorough scrub and had come back into the house for more hot water when she heard the doorbell ring.

Drat! She stood for a moment, hesitating, the kettle in her hand. Could she ignore it? No, better not. The girls had gone out to have some lessons in a house up in Deniston Street, and it might be something to do with them. She'd never forgive herself if anything had happened to them and she'd refused to answer the door.

She set the kettle back on the stove. It was still whistling gently as she answered the door and found Ethel Glaister standing on the step.

For a moment or two, she thought that it must be to do with the girls. Or perhaps with the house in Portchester Street. The woman standing on her step was too smart to be anything but an official of some sort. Maybe she was from the Assistance Board, come to see what Kathy had spent the five pounds on. Or perhaps – her mind flicked to Mike. Had anything happened to his ship? The baby inside her gave a sudden kick and she covered it with her hand as if to protect it from shock.

Ethel Glaister stared at Kathy, her eyes moving from the dirty working skirt to the old blouse which was covered by what looked like a man's shirt. She looked doubtfully along the dingy passage. Mrs Simmons had seemed a clean, respectable sort of woman in the street, but this looked no better than a slum after all!

'I'm sorry,' she said, backing away. 'Perhaps you're too busy, I'll come back another day.'

Kathy smiled. Now that the first surprise had passed, she was beginning to recognise her visitor. She lived nearby, somewhere in April Grove. Kathy had seen her walking up and down the street, always smartly dressed, her yellow hair waved and her face made up. Perhaps she'd come to collect for something, war savings, perhaps, or another Spitfire fund. In any case, it would be nice to have someone to talk to for a bit.

'It's all right,' she said. 'I'd nearly finished. To tell the truth, I shouldn't have been doing it anyway. I'm supposed to put my feet up in the afternoons, but I couldn't put up with the stink any longer . . . Did you want something?'

Ethel cast a nervous glance along the passage and then up and down the street, as if afraid to be seen. 'No – oh no,' she said hastily. 'I just called, you know, out of friendliness. You being new here, as it were. I thought you might be pleased to meet one of your neighbours.'

'That's nice of you,' Kathy said cheerfully. 'Come in and have a cup of tea.'

She brushed a hand down her front and grimaced. 'Sorry I'm in such a state. I've been scrubbing out the Anderson. You wouldn't believe the state it was in, I reckon every cat in the street's had a pee in there. Cost me a fortune in Dettol, it has.'

Ethel opened her mouth to protest but Kathy was already disappearing into the back room. Distastefully, she followed, trying not to let her powder-blue jacket brush against the walls. It looked as if they could do with a scrub too, she thought, but it was clear that young Mrs Simmons had been doing her best with the back room and scullery, which both smelt strongly of yellow soap.

All the same, she was swiftly revising her ideas about making a friend of the new neighbour. And as for letting her Shirley come over here to play . . .

'Sit down.' Kathy waved at the sagging armchair. 'Not much of a place, is it, but I'm thankful for anything, I can tell you. Goodness knows where the furniture came from – I stand it out in the back yard when the sun's shining and give it a good beating, you'd be surprised what comes out! Still, it's better than nothing.' She went out into the scullery and Ethel could hear her putting tea into the pot and pouring in boiling water.

'Did you lose everything?' Ethel asked. She moved away from the armchair and perched on the edge of an old kitchen chair, hoping that Mrs Simmons had at least wiped off the grime.

'The lot. Everything we owned. Well, except for a few bits and bobs that we managed to salvage next day. The place just collapsed, you see, got a direct hit.' Kathy rattled cups and saucers together. 'Sorry I can't offer you sugar, I keep it for the kids. They need it, poor little mites.' She came into the room with two cups of tea and handed one to Ethel. 'People don't realise that kids lose everything too, in air-raids. All their clothes, their toys and books, all their little bits and pieces. You don't get any money to replace them. My Muriel had a baby doll, thought the world of it she did, and she'd just put it in its little cradle when the siren went. I wouldn't let her go back for it and it got smashed to smithereens.' Her eyes filled with tears. 'I'll never really forgive myself for that. We found it, you see, its face all broken. Muriel cries for it every night.'

'Better a doll than her, though,' Ethel said. 'Dolls don't matter. What about your hubby, then? Someone told me he's at sea.'

'That's right, in the Merchant Navy.' Deliberately, Kathy forced her mind away from Muriel's broken doll. It haunted her dreams too. It had looked so much like a baby . . . 'He doesn't get home much now. I was hoping he'd be around when the baby's born.' Unconsciously, she caressed her rounded stomach. 'I don't suppose he will, though.'

'There's not many men round here now,' Ethel remarked. 'Only Frank Budd and Tommy Vickers and people like that who're too old to be called up. My George is in the Army, of course. He went straightaway, he was in the Territorials, you see, and they had to report for duty the minute war was declared.' She touched her hair. 'Well, we were on holiday in Devonshire when it was actually declared but naturally we came home at once. We knew our duty.'

Kathy wasn't quite sure what to say. She picked up her cup and said, 'It seems quite nice round here. Quiet.'

'Well, it isn't bad, I suppose,' Ethel said grudgingly. 'Of course, if it hadn't been for the war, we'd have moved. I want a three-bedroomed house with a proper bathroom. Semi-detached, you know. And with George doing so well at his job, we'd have been able to afford it. But now that all this has started—' She shrugged, looking irritated. 'I told him, there wasn't any need for him to go dashing off, but he would go and now we're on Army pay, and *that's* not much, I can tell you!'

Her voice had taken on a querulous note. She sipped her tea, holding her little finger out daintily. Kathy looked at her, at the powder-blue jacket and the frilly blouse and the carefully waved golden hair. What was she doing here? Why had she come?

'You've got two little girls, haven't you?' Ethel said. 'I see you've not sent them away, then.'

'No, I'd rather we were all together. And I want to be in Pompey in case Mike comes home unexpectedly.' Kathy spoke with a touch of defiance in her tone. People treated you like a bad mother, not sending your children to the country. But from some of the stories she'd heard about evacuees, it sounded as if they had a worse time out there than if they'd stayed in the city. She hated to think of Stella and Muriel, far from home, with strangers who didn't understand or care about them. Better here. And hadn't she already proved that if you got into a shelter in time, you were safe?

'I'm thinking of sending my Shirley to Canada,' Ethel said. 'You don't know who they're mixing with out in these villages, do you? They're taking a whole shipload of kiddies to Canada on a liner. I think it'll be a good experience for her.'

Kathy stared at her. Canada! It was on the other side of the world. And they might be gone for years. Why, they'd be strangers when they came back.

'Of course, you'll be used to something better than this,' Ethel remarked, glancing disparagingly round the bare little room. 'I mean, the houses in Portchester Street are quite a bit bigger, aren't they? You must miss it, coming to a place like this.'

'It's no good thinking like that. I'm just glad to have a house. And I can soon get it looking nice, once I get hold of a pot of paint and a bit of wallpaper. And then I can ask people in without apologising for the state of it!' She laughed.

'Oh, I'd be careful who you asked in,' Ethel said quickly. 'I mean, some of the people round here are very nice – in their way – but there are a few I wouldn't want across *my* doorstep, I can tell you.'

'Well, I daresay I'll soon find out who suits me,' Kathy said. 'Jess Budd's nice.'

'Oh, Jess is all right, if you like that type of person,' Ethel said dismissively. 'Rather a mousy little woman, I've never been able to see what her husband sees in her, myself. Now *there's* a fine figure of a man, Frank Budd, you'll have seen him walking home from work, I daresay. A big, tall man. He works in the Dockyard. And there's the Shaws, in number 13, on the other side of the Budds, I don't have much to do with them. Peggy Shaw and Jess Budd are very thick. And Vi Redding, next door to Mrs Shaw, well, the less said about *her* the better. Have you seen the state of her front step? But the person you really want to be careful of is Mrs Kinch – Granny Kinch, they call her. She sits on a chair at her front door all day, keeping an eye on everything that goes on. Used to stand there for hours, till her varicose veins got the better of her.'

'I've seen her. She gave the girls some toffees one day.'

'Oh yes, she does that, always likes to get the kiddies round her. A real nosy old so-and-so, she is. I wouldn't let mine get round her door. And you know what they say about Nancy, of course.'

Kathy shook her head. 'Nancy?'

'Nancy Baxter, so-called. Her daughter. Supposed to be married to some high-up, only sometimes they say he's a soldier, sometimes he's in the Navy, they don't seem to be too sure themselves, and you know what *that* means. Anyway, whatever he is – if he exists at all, which I take leave to doubt – you never see him down April Grove, though you might see plenty of other men.'

Kathy gazed at her. There was a peculiar, avid excitement in Ethel's eyes and now and then she licked her thin lips. I don't want to hear this, she thought. This is what she came for, to pass on her own spiteful gossip. I wish she'd go.

But Ethel was now into her stride. She leaned forward and spoke in an exaggeratedly low whisper, mouthing the words as if they might be overheard. Kathy drew back a little, feeling the same distaste as Ethel had felt as she walked along the dingy passage. She had the same senstion of not wanting her clothes to brush against the other woman, of not wanting to be contaminated.

'. . . a *tart*,' Ethel mouthed. 'Ever since they came here . . . bringing sailors back from the pub . . . supposed to be working in a hotel at nights. Hotel! We all know what *that* means . . . disgusting, it is . . . got a baby now, and not a clue who its father is, I'll be bound. . . And that Micky, just left to run wild . . . ought to be a law . . .'

Her whisper slunk about the room like a dank miasma, feeling its way into corners, hanging in the air. It was like a web, Kathy thought, a dirty cobweb that clung to her face and that she wanted to brush away.

'I'm sorry,' she said, getting up. 'I'll have to go soon. The girls are having lessons up Deniston Street and I'll have to go and fetch them.'

'I'll go with you,' Ethel offered. 'I'd like a nice walk. And we can arrange for you to come over to me one afternoon. Or the pictures. We could go to the pictures together. Henry Fonda's on at the Odeon this week, in *The Grapes of Wrath*, we could go and see that. Or there's Bing Crosby at the Rex. What d'you fancy?'

'I don't think I'll be able to go to the pictures,' Kathy said shortly. 'I don't have time. And it's uncomfortable sitting in the seats, the way I am.'

'Oh, well, yes, I suppose it is. Well, shopping, then. We could go shopping down North End. Or Commercial Road. C&A are advertising some lovely new coats for autumn, all in the newest colours. There's a nice alpaca for four and a half guineas. I'm looking for a new coat, before they put clothes on ration – they're talking about it, you know. You could help me choose.'

'No, thanks,' Kathy said. 'And I'll have to get ready to go now. I can't go up to fetch the kids looking like this. She ushered Ethel to the door. 'It was nice of you to come. I daresay I'll see you in the street, to say hello.'

'Oh,' Ethel began as she was pushed gently out on to the step again. 'But we haven't arranged—' There was a decisive click and she turned in astonishment to find the door closed firmly behind her. 'But – but—' She stared at it for a moment, as if expecting it to open again and Kathy appear, all smiles, in her best clothes, but there was silence from within. And when she rattled at the letter-box and pushed it open to peer inside, there was no sign that there was anyone at home at all.

'*Well!*' Ethel exclaimed. 'Well, did you ever see anything so *rude!* And after I'd been so *nice* to her, too. Telling her things, inviting her to tea, suggesting she might like to come to the pictures with me or do some shopping!' She turned and saw Granny Kinch sitting in her doorway, watching her with beady black eyes. Oh, it was just too much!

With a toss of her head, she marched away up October Street. Where she was going, she had no idea, but she wasn't going to walk past Granny Kinch and give her the satisfaction of knowing she'd been as good as turned out of number 16.

And she certainly wouldn't be calling on Kathy Simmons again. Say hello in the street? she thought furiously. Why, I wouldn't say hello to her in my *grave!*

For boys like Micky Baxter, Jimmy Cross and Cyril Nash, the raids were a huge adventure. Out in the streets from early morning until dark, they seldom went into a shelter when the siren sounded. Instead, they crouched beside a wall, gazing up at the sky, watching the planes zoom low over the city and cheering whenever one was shot down.

'Dirty Jerry bastards,' Micky said with relish as they watched a Heinkel spinning out of control into Langstone Harbour. It seemed to screw itself a hole in the water with its nose and a great spray of flame and water rose like a volcanic eruption into the air. 'Serves 'im right. I 'ope 'e was burnt alive.'

'Well, he's dead anyway.' They flinched and shut their eyes as a bomb fell a few streets away. The crash ricocheted around them. 'Coo, look at that smoke. Once they're gone we'll go an' look for souvenirs again, shall we?'

'Souvenirs!' Micky sneered. 'We can get better'n that. Let's go round the shops. You know people don't lock up proper when the siren goes. We can get some good stuff.'

Jimmy and Cyril looked at each other. Micky was already on probation for walking into a jeweller's shop brandishing a gun left over from the last war. Jimmy's dad said he'd been lucky not to get sent to Borstal.

'Come on,' Micky urged. 'Who's going to see us? They're all down the shelters like rabbits in a burrow. I bet that wireless shop along Copnor Road's open. He's got some good torches in there.' He set off, keeping close to the wall as the bombs rained down on the city.

One of Cyril's dreams was to own a really good torch. A black rubber one. They could go out at night then – it was all right as long as you kept out of the air-raid warden's way. And explore some more of the cellars they'd found in bombed houses.

They came to the wireless shop. To their disgust, the door was locked. Cyril gazed through the window and saw that there were indeed two rubber torches on display.

'I bet if you broke the window nobody'd hear us,' he said. 'Not with all this noise going on.' The bombs were exploding further down in the city, but the noise reverberated around the streets. 'Anyway, they'd just think it was blast.'

Jimmy hesitated, but Micky nodded eagerly.

'You're right. We don't have to worry about locks. Come on.' He picked up a stone, glanced quickly up and down the street, and smashed it against the glass. The dusty display inside was showered with fragments, and Cyril reached through and grabbed one of the torches.

'It's a smasher.' He moved the switch. 'Shit! There's no batteries.'

Micky had his hand on the other torch, but as he closed his fingers around it they heard a yell from the street and turned sharply. Micky, jerking his hand out of the broken window, gave a yelp of pain.

'Oy! You boys! What you up to?' An air-raid warden was advancing on them, waving threateningly. 'You oughter be in the shelter.'

'Run,' Micky muttered, but the other two were already away. Micky raced after them and they dodged round a corner and into the maze of alleyways that ran between the side streets. Half scared, half giggling, they came to a halt against a garden wall, crouching as a bomb exploded closer at hand.

'Fat old fool,' Micky jeered. 'He'll never catch us.'

'He might know us, though,' Jimmy said a little anxiously.

'Nah. He's not from round our street. So long as we don't go down that way for a bit. Anyway, they got more to think about than a broken window.' He gazed up at the sky, at the aircraft still swooping overhead, some German, some British. He could see gunfire spattering against the sides of the planes, the flare as shells burst in the air. Flames and smoke were rising from several places in Portsmouth, and the sound of explosions and the rattle of guns were deafening.

'Smashing,' he breathed, thinking scornfully of all the people who were cowering in their shelters and missing the glory of it all. 'Smashing . . .'

The Germans had named Tuesday, 13 August, *Adlertag*. It meant Eagle Day and was to have been the day when the Luftwaffe would blow the RAF from the skies and the invasion begin. But the British had other ideas.

For the rest of the week, the sirens sounded daily, sometimes more than once, as wave after wave of German bombers flew across the sky. Bad weather gave some respite on Wednesday, but there were still thirty-one German planes reported destroyed in Saturday's *Evening News*, and the resumption of heavy bombing on Thursday brought the Germans a hundred and eighty losses. The total for the week was estimated at four hundred and ninety-two, bringing the total for the war so far at almost a thousand.

A thousand planes, and each with two or three young men inside, either killed or captured. Several came down in fields north of Portsdown Hill, and there were photographs in the paper showing pub landlords or farmers who had been first on the scene, grinning over their prize.

The following week the newspapers carried a report of Mr Churchill's speech in the House of Commons. Standing with his head slightly lowered, looking as always like a bull about to charge, he had praised the RAF for its heroism.

'*The gratitude of every home in our island . . . goes out to the British airmen who are turning the tide of the war*,' he declared, his mellifluous tones rolling around the chamber. '*Never in the field of human conflict was so much owed by so many to so few. All hearts go out to the fighter pilots whose brilliant actions we see with our own eyes, day after day . . . Our people are united and resolved as they have never been before. Death and ruin have become small things, compared with shame and defeat.*'

Four days later, the raiders came again. It was a Saturday afternoon and Betty Chapman and her sister Olive had decided to go to the pictures with the two Shaw sisters. Robert Preston and Dorothy Lamour were in *Typhoon* at the Odeon and Diane Shaw, who was just sixteen, declared herself to be in love with Robert Preston.

'I've seen it twice already,' she said as the four girls walked down Stubbington Avenue together. 'He's gorgeous! I wish I could meet him.'

'He'd never even look at you,' Gladys told her with sisterly bluntness. 'I like Dorothy Lamour, I think she's really glamorous. I reckon I could look a bit like her, if I did my hair the same way.'

'Go on,' Diane said, getting her own back, 'you've been trying to look like Norma Shearer for the past twelve months. I haven't noticed it's got you any more boyfriends.'

'Who says I want boyfriends?' Gladys tossed her head. 'I can get plenty, if I want them. I just haven't fancied anyone lately. Too much bother.'

'I bet she wouldn't say that if your brother was home on leave,' Diane said to Betty, and Gladys blushed.

'Shut up, Di. Colin and me are just friends.'

'Is that why you write to him practically every day?'

'I don't! Not every day. But a boy wants a bit of news from home when he's away at sea. It doesn't mean anything.'

Betty gave Gladys's arm a squeeze. She knew that Gladys had been carrying a torch for Colin for the past couple of years. But just writing to a boy didn't have to mean you were his girlfriend. Didn't she write regularly to Gladys's brother Bob, even though she was secretly engaged to Graham?

'Are you looking forward to being a Land Girl?' Gladys asked her now.

Betty nodded. 'I think it'll be smashing. Specially in this weather. Just imagine being out in the fields, hay-making, while all the rest of you are slaving away in offices and shops.'

'And just imagine it in freezing rain, when all the rest of us are cosy and warm indoors,' Olive said. 'Rather you than me!'

'Well, at least you'll be away from the bombs,' Diane observed. 'I'm getting fed up with these raids. Down the shelter half the time – boring.'

'Boring! I'm too scared to be bored,' Olive said. 'It makes me shudder every time I hear that awful siren, the noise seems to go right down my back. And listening to the planes coming over, and the bombs, ugh, it's horrible.'

'Well, let's forget the war for this afternoon.' They were almost at the cinema now, and Gladys began to fish in her bag for money. 'Which seats shall we go in?'

'Upstairs,' Betty suggested, but Diane shook her head.

'I haven't got enough money. It's the ninepennies for me.'

They bought their tickets and went in. The lights had not yet been lowered and they stood for a moment by the first few rows of seats, debating which to go into. The audience was small – there would be more at the evening show – and there was plenty of room.

'Go on, our Di,' Gladys urged. 'Make up your mind, they'll be starting any minute.'

Diane led the way into the fourth row and immediately passed round a bag of toffees. Chewing comfortably, the four girls looked up at the screen and sighed in happy anticipation as the heavy curtains changed colour under the dimming lights and then slowly drew apart.

The advertisements came first, then the News. They watched as a clipped voice described the scenes that were being shown – news of the war, with pictures of soldiers setting up camp, grinning and waving at the camera, smiling and busy women setting up canteens, evacuated children playing in fields. There were also a few shots of soldiers who had come back from Dunkirk in June, looking tired but cheerful. It was extolled as a victorious rescue.

'Victorious!' Olive muttered. 'We were chased off the beaches, that's what. I wish they wouldn't show this. I came here to forget about the war for a couple of hours.'

The News was over at last and the big film began. Diane passed her toffees along again and they settled down to enjoy the story. Once or twice Gladys touched her hair, imagining it done the way Dorothy Lamour did hers, and Diane dreamed that she was in Robert Preston's arms. Olive wondered if Derek might get some leave soon, the 698 had been moved to

Wiltshire, to stand by when repairs were needed to the runways at Boscombe Down, and Betty thought about Graham and wondered yet again if she should have let him make love to her that last night. If Mum hadn't insisted on playing cards all evening, she might easily have done so. But then if she had, she might have been sitting here now worrying about a baby, and that was something she could do without.

There was Bob Shaw too. Olive told her she was wrong to write to another boy when she was going steady with Graham, but she and Bob had known each other all their lives, they'd played in the street together and learned to swim in Langstone Harbour. It didn't do any harm to write to him, surely, but did it mean she wasn't really in love with Graham after all?

The film continued. Dorothy Lamour swayed seductively on screen and was adored by every man in the audience. The women sighed over Robert Preston and for a little while the war was, indeed, forgotten.

And then, at just twenty minutes past four, the siren began to sound.

There was a general groan. People began to get up, hesitated, half sat down again. A few scrambled along to the ends of the rows of seats and hurried up the aisle. On screen, Dorothy Lamour and Robert Preston drifted into each other's arms and the four girls looked at each other.

'I suppose we ought to go,' Olive said reluctantly.

'Oh, bother it!' Diane had dropped her toffees. She bent and felt about on the floor. 'Well, *I'm* not going. We're just getting to the best bit.'

'But the bombs—'

'They won't be coming up here. It's the Dockyard they're aiming at. Look, they haven't stopped showing the film, have they? So they can't think it's anything much.'

The film stopped suddenly and the lights came on. They looked at each other again and Olive started to get to her feet.

'Wait a minute.' Betty grabbed her arm. 'Someone's coming on the stage.'

Fascinated and half afraid, they watched. Perhaps the Germans had actually invaded. Perhaps this *was* a German, come to tell them what to do. Doubtfully, Betty wondered if an invading German would be likely to be dressed in a dark suit, and then realised that it was the cinema manager. She stifled a nervous giggle.

'I'm very sorry, ladies and gentlemen. Hitler's signature tune is on the air again.' There was a ripple of laughter from the audience. 'You are of course free to leave if you wish to, but the show is going on and you're welcome to stay with us.' He paused, then added, 'Good luck, and thank you for coming this afternoon.'

There was a buzz of chatter. Everyone was asking each other the same question – shall we go or shall we stay? The wail of the siren had died away again and nothing could be heard outside. Perhaps Diane was right, Betty thought, and it was going to be just another false alarm.

'I'm staying too,' she said suddenly. 'This is my last chance to come to the pictures here. I'm not letting Hitler spoil it for me.'

The two older girls hesitated. Gladys shrugged. 'Might as well. If we went outside now we'd never get into a shelter anyway. There was hundreds of people shopping. I reckon we're as safe here as anywhere else.'

'That's right,' Olive agreed. 'And if they're going to keep the film going, I think we *ought* to stay. That'll show Hitler we're not afraid of him. *I'm* not going to run down a hole like a rabbit diving down its burrow just because he starts playing his music.'

The others laughed. The film had started again and Dorothy Lamour and Robert Preston were now involved in the typhoon of the title. The wind howled and shrieked from the screen, and the building suddenly shook with the crash of thunder.

'That was guns!' Olive gasped, and grabbed at Betty's hand.

They could hear the throb of the planes now, and their roar as they passed above. There was an explosion somewhere close by and a splintering sound from overhead. The audience looked up at the darkened roof and saw gaps of daylight appear. As one person, they scrambled towards the sides of the cinema and crouched down as the gaps widened and shrapnel rained down on to the seats they had just vacated.

'Oh, my God,' Gladys gasped. 'They're bombing us, Olive – Betty – they're bombing *us*!'

Another explosion sounded from the car park outside, and the screen trembled and shook. Their laughter forgotten, the girls huddled together, staring with terrified eyes at the film, as if by watching the tumult on the screen they could somehow reduce the reality of what was happening.

'We ought to have gone,' Olive whispered. 'We ought to have got into a shelter.'

'We'd never have made it.' Betty remembered the sight of the enemy flying like a black cloud overhead, as she had stood on Mrs Marsh's garden path. 'We'd have been caught out in the street.'

'And if this place gets hit we'll be buried alive. I'd rather take my chance out in the open.'

But the other girls shook their heads. They knew there was no escape now. Outside, they would be in even more danger than in here. They just had to sit it out and hope that the cinema would make a good shelter.

'Well, at least we can see the end of the film,' Diane observed as Preston and Lamour melted into an embrace. 'I wanted to see him kiss her.'

A bubble of hysterical giggles rose into Betty's throat and she heard Gladys snort. The cinema rocked again, and the music was drowned by a shattering thud. The audience was now pressed into a tight crowd at each side of the auditorium, but the film kept running and all eyes were fixed on the screen.

'I wish we'd never come,' Olive moaned, covering her head with her arms. Betty squeezed her shoulders.

'It doesn't matter where you are. You know what they say – if a bomb's got your name on it, it'll find you. Look – the picture's finished. At least we saw it all!'

Olive smiled weakly. The explosions seemed to have stopped now and she lifted her head and watched the last few shots. The music swelled and throbbed through the cinema and the last scene faded. There was a moment of silence.

The aircraft noise had died away. It was only five minutes since the first thunderous crash. The girls looked at each other uncertainly. They looked at the holes in the roof, at the fragments of shrapnel and the torn seats. Was it safe anywhere?

'Maybe it wasn't so bad after all,' Betty said hopefully. 'Well, we might as well see the programme to the end.'

'Yes, we might,' Gladys said. 'D'you know what the little film's called?'

They shook their heads. And then the title came up on the screen and everyone in the cinema laughed.

'*Though Shalt Not Kill . . .*'

It seemed funny when they were inside the cinema, with the manager declaring that the show must go on and a spirit of defiant bravado holding them together. It was less funny when they came out to bright sunshine and saw a crater in the car park, less funny when they realised that the houses behind the cinema had been demolished, not funny at all when they heard that the Princes Theatre in Lake Road had received a direct hit and eight people been killed. The thousand-pound bomb had crashed through the roof and exploded high above the auditorium, completely wrecking the interior and blowing seats out through the roof into the street.

'That could have been you,' Annie scolded her daughters when they arrived home. 'It's all very well saying Hitler's not going to stop you enjoying yourselves – he *can* stop you. He can stop you living. Next time, get yourselves into a shelter.'

'But I don't suppose we could have done,' Betty argued. 'The shops were full of people – it was really busy down North End. The shelters would have been full before we got anywhere near them. Anyway, the bombs started almost as soon as the siren had gone off, we wouldn't have had time.'

Annie sighed. She knew this was true – she'd barely got into her own shelter when the planes had come overhead. And the whole thing had been over in five minutes.

Gladys Shaw had refused to hurry home with the other girls. Instead, she stopped to give a hand in the street behind the cinema. People had been killed and injured there and, like Frank Budd, she had been shocked and sickened by sights she hadn't dreamed of.

She saw an old man sitting on the kerb, his arms folded over his head as he rocked to and fro. He was crying, his mouth loose and slobbery, his scant grey hair matted with blood. Gladys crouched down beside him, taking out her handkerchief to wipe gently at his head. He must have a very nasty cut.

'No,' he said, 'it ain't me what got hurt. That's my Edie's blood, that is.' He looked at Gladys, his faded eyes as bewildered as a child's. 'We was just having a cup of tea when the siren went, and now she's dead. She's still in there, all crumpled up in her chair.' Gladys followed his gaze to a small house. People were moving about inside, shifting debris, trying to ease something out from under a fallen beam. 'It ain't no good,' he said with the flatness of despair. 'She went straightaway, they might as well leave her at rest.' He told Gladys this through hiccuping sobs, and then he told her again, and a third time when a stout woman in a tweed jacket brought him a mug of tea. He was still repeating it when they led him gently away.

There had been a children's tea-party in the house next door. It had been to celebrate little Doreen's seventh birthday, from the card Gladys found lying in the middle of the littered road outside. She helped one of the First Aid workers gather the survivors together and put her arms round them while they had cuts and bruises washed and bandaged. Some of them were taken to hospital in an ambulance. She didn't ask how many had been killed, nor whether one of them was Doreen herself.

She watched the ambulances drive away and turned back to see what else she could do. A woman was sobbing in a shattered doorway across the street. Gladys stepped off the pavement to go to her and felt something soft against her foot. She looked down, and felt the gorge rise in her throat.

It was a baby, no more than three or four weeks old. The tiny body had been split like a paper bag. It lay soaking in its own blood, its contents spilling out like those of a carelessly wrapped parcel.

Gladys stared at it. It shifted suddenly, horrifyingly, then blurred before her eyes. Her ears roared and she shook her head and turned away, her hands over her mouth. As she swayed, arms caught and held her, and the First Aider she had been helping spoke in her ear.

'Come and have a cuppa,' she said. 'You're not used to it, are you?'

'Who is?' Gladys asked, sitting down on a broken bit of wall. 'Have *you* ever seen things like that before?'

The woman shrugged. 'I was a nurse. I worked in Casualty. There's plenty happens in street accidents and such . . . But it's never easy to take, specially not with kiddies.' She handed Gladys a mug of tea. 'Sip that, it's good and sweet, it'll make you feel better.' The ambulances were beginning to return, and people were searching under the rubble for more survivors. 'Get off home if you like. I'll have to stay and help.'

'I'll stay too.' Gladys gulped down the hot liquid. 'But I don't know that I'm much help. I don't know any First Aid or anything.'

It didn't seem to matter. There was still plenty to do, helping shift debris and giving what comfort she could to the people they did manage to dig out, some of them miraculously unhurt. But it was clear to Gladys that she could have been a lot more help, and by the time she reached home at last, she had made up her mind what to do.

'I'm coming to Red Cross classes with you,' she told her mother as she sank into a chair with a cup of tea. 'I ought to have done it before. And I'm going to learn to drive.'

'Drive?' Peggy echoed. 'What, drive a car, you mean?'

'Well, I'm not going to drive a train,' Gladys said with a weary attempt at humour.

'But what will you drive? I mean, you're not thinking of going on the buses, are you? Your dad'll never—'

'I don't know what I'll do. Nobody knows what they'll have to do in this war.' Glady set down the empty cup and dragged herself out of the chair.

She felt dirty and dog-tired and would have liked nothing better than to sink into a hot bath. But that meant getting in the tin bath from the yard and turning on the geyser to fill it up, and then dragging it out again, and she didn't have the energy. Besides, the family had had their weekly bathing session last night. 'I just think driving'll be a useful thing to be able to do. Oh, I'm so *tired*.' It seemed a lifetime since she and the others had been sitting in the cinema watching Robert Preston.

'You have a good wash, love.' Peggy had been out during the raid too, and was almost as weary as her daughter, but she recognised the signs of shock and knew that Gladys needed comfort and warmth. 'I'll heat you up some of that pea soup that was left over from dinner. And then I reckon you'd be best off to get to bed early.'

Early? To Gladys, it felt as if the day had lasted for ever. She went out into the scullery, took off her top clothes and ran some hot water into the enamel bowl. She stared at it and then, very slowly, washed herself.

The pictures of the typhoon that had seemed so dramatic on screen had faded from her mind. Instead, all she could see were an old man sitting on the pavement, a child's birthday card fluttering in a shattered street and a baby's body lying in the gutter.

I've got to do something about it, she thought. I've got to do my bit.

8

As soon as the Chapmans had finished their Sunday lunch of roast lamb – a smaller joint than they were used to, but Annie refused to lower her standards and have sausages instead – Betty set out to visit Graham's parents in Gosport.

Charlie and Elsie Philpotts lived about a mile from the harbour. Betty caught a bus and got off by the Gipsy Queen, then walked up Carnarvon Road. There were several short cul-de-sacs running off the road on both sides, and the Philpotts' lived in one of these. Charlie was pruning roses in his front garden when Betty arrived. He looked up at the sound of her voice and straightened his thin body, rubbing the small of his back with one hand.

'Every picture tells a story . . . Come over to see the missus, have you? She's somewhere indoors, or else out the back.' He called out in his dry, sandpapery voice, 'Elsie! We've got a visitor.'

Elsie Philpotts appeared, big and blowsy, her mauve satin blouse already parting company with her tight green skirt. Her ginger hair had recently been permed, and clustered round her head in curls so tight they seemed afraid to leave go of each other. She had no stockings on, but had painted her legs with something brown and streaky. On her feet, she wore pink slippers.

'Betty! Well, this is nice.' She enveloped Betty in a hug. It was like being assaulted by two feather pillows. 'Come over to see us on your last day, have you? I call that really nice, don't you, Charlie?'

Her husband blinked at her. His blue eyes always looked half dreamy, as if he was living in another world. 'What d'you mean, her last day? She's not being took off to prison, is she?'

Elsie Philpotts let out a shriek of laughter.

'Took off to prison! What an idea! As if our Betty would do anything to be sent to prison for. *You* know what she's doing, Charlie. I told you. Going for a Land Girl, she is, milking cows and feeding chickens and all that.' She regarded Betty fondly. 'Just think, this time next week you'll be a farmer's girl. Think you're going to like it?'

'I hope so,' Betty said, and Elsie dug her in the ribs with a surprisingly sharp elbow and gave another chortle.

'You'll have to watch out for the farmer, mind! I know what these country bumpkins are like when they get behind a haystack. Eh, Charlie?'

'You'd know more about that than me,' he responded dryly. 'I never went out in the country as much as you did.'

'Well, I had an auntie out at Titchfield, didn't I. I used to go over on me bike,' she told Betty. 'My cousin Jean and me, we used to go all over the place. Oh, we had a few games, I'll tell you. But not with Charlie listening, eh?' She squawked and dug Betty in the ribs again. 'Still, *you* won't be getting up to no hanky-panky, not with Graham to think about.'

'No.' Not much chance of that, Betty thought, with all the young men being called up anyway. There would be nothing but old men left, same as in the towns. But Mrs Philpotts was right, she wouldn't let Graham down any more than he'd be unfaithful to her.

All the same, it didn't mean she couldn't have other friends. Same as she kept on writing to Bob, just as a friend. You couldn't shut yourself away from everything, just because you had a boyfriend in the Navy.

'Here, come and talk to me while I put the kettle on,' Elsie said. 'We'll take a cup of tea out in the back garden and you can tell me all about the Land Army. Have you got your uniform yet? It's trousers, innit? What do your mum and dad think of that, then?'

They went into the house, along the passage with its dark red anaglypta walls and Charlie's bike, and through to the kitchen. It was smallish and distempered in cream, with green woodwork and a green oilcloth on the table. An Ascot water heater was fixed to the wall with a long tap over the sink. Washing-up was piled on the wooden drainer, and there was a smell of cabbage.

'Sunday dinner,' Elsie said cheerfully, opening the back door to put a plate of scraps into the meatsafe just outside. 'We used to have enough meat left over to have it cold on Monday and a nice shepherd's pie on Tuesday. Now we're lucky if we got enough to give the cat a few scraps. Still, Charlie says it won't do me no harm to starve off a bit of me fat!' She laughed and her bosom shook. 'I tell him I'll need it in the winter, the way things are going I won't be able to get a new winter coat. They're talking about rationing clothes, did you know that? Clothes! They'll be rationing fresh air next.'

She filled the kettle and set it on the gas stove. Betty described her uniform and Elsie listened, raising her eyebrows, nodding and pursing her lips at all the right moments.

'I'm doing war work too,' she said. 'I've joined the WVS. Women's Voluntary Service, that is. I'm helping with canteens for people who've been bombed out of their homes.' She shook her head. 'You heard what happened over here the other day? We had fifty of the poor sods down in the Central School. Nowhere to go, no money, lost everything, they had. Well, we'd got crockery and stuff together, and food, and we were going to give 'em a hot meal. They've got good kitchens at the Central School, they used to cook the dinners for the kiddies at Leesland as well. And do you know what?' Her chins quivered with indignation. 'That old so-and-so in charge wouldn't let us cook it! There was a proper up-and-downer about it, I can tell you. I thought there was going to be a riot. Well—' she grinned suddenly '—I *hoped* there'd be a riot. Mean old skinflint, he wanted lynching.'

'What happened?' Betty asked. She knew that there had been several people made homeless by the raids on Gosport. What had it been like for them, their homes destroyed and then refused a hot dinner?

'Oh, in the end he said we could give it to the kids. Well, that was something, but what were their poor mums and dads to do, starve? So Mrs Green, she went down to the Town Hall and the Town Clerk himself came up the school and told him off proper. And he said in future we're to give them a good hot dinner whenever we want to, and never mind the high-and-mighty Public Assistance Officer.' She snorted. 'Public Assistance! Public Interference, that's what I call him.'

The kettle boiled and she made the tea, collected a bottle of milk from the safe and carried them out into the garden, leaving Betty to follow with an assortment of cups and saucers.

'We don't have a matching teaset in the house,' Elsie said, setting the tea down on a rickety table. 'It's not that we've never had one – we've had half a dozen. I just can't keep them, somehow, they break to bits in my hands. Mostly it's when I'm washing up – Charlie reckons I'm too clumsy, but I think it's the hot water.' The milk bottle tipped over and Betty caught it just before it spilled. 'But you can't get the grease off things if you don't use it really hot, can you?'

She took the milk bottle and slopped milk into the three cups. Tea followed, making little brown trails between the cups as she poured, and then she lifted her voice.

'Char-*lie*! Tea up. Sit yourself down, Betty, love, and tell me how you've got on in the raids over there. Haven't they been terrible! I heard there's been Andersons just blown apart, and trench shelters collapsed. And didn't one get a direct hit?'

'That was in the second raid,' Betty said. 'Nearly a hundred and fifty people in it, there were, but there was only one killed. A little boy.'

'Oh, that's sad,' Elsie Philpotts said, her eyes filling with tears. 'A little boy. Think of his poor ma. Mind, we've had a bit over here too – a whole team of young RAF lads looking after a balloon were killed in their shelter last week.' She looked at Betty. 'I don't know whether to be thankful that my Graham's not training to be a pilot or worried about him at sea.'

Betty didn't know what to say. It didn't seem to make any difference which Service he was in, they were all as dangerous as each other. She saw the pallor under Elsie Philpotts' makeup, the tremble of her lips, and realised that under the jollity Graham's mother was badly frightened.

She felt suddenly ashamed. She'd been thinking of Graham almost as if he was away on holiday and would soon be back. But his mother knew that he might never come back. And for her, he was the only boy in the world.

It's worse for mothers, Betty thought. They're losing their children, the only ones they've got. Girls like me, we'll go on even if our sweethearts or husbands get killed, we'll still go on living and we might find someone else. But for a mother, he's gone for ever and there's nobody else.

It didn't matter whether your child was a baby in a pram, a little boy in an air-raid shelter or a grown man fighting for his country. He was your child, and always would be, and nobody could take the place of a child.

Throughout the following week, the sirens continued to sound. Monday afternoon brought a hundred and fifty enemy planes and, amidst the fierce battle that was fought over the heads of the citizens, a direct hit was scored on the gas works at Hilsea and more than seventy properties damaged. This time warning was given sooner and the shelters reached in good time, with the result that only two civilians were hurt. The Royal Marine Barracks of Fort Cumberland, one of the Victorian 'Palmerston's Follies' that ringed Portsmouth, was less fortunate and was hit by more than fifty bombs.

By this time, Betty was out on the farm. She had left home that morning, straight after breakfast, marching self-consciously up the street in her new uniform. The whole family were standing at the gate to see her off – Annie, Ted, Olive, and even Jess with baby Maureen in her arms. Betty turned at the top of the street and waved, feeling suddenly panicky. Suppose she hated it after all! Suppose she couldn't do the work. Suppose . . .

But there was no time for 'supposing'. The bus came along and she climbed aboard, trying not to notice the stares of the passengers. She found a seat and gazed out of the window.

There was a lump in her throat as she passed the familiar landmarks – the school where she had first learnt to read and write, the 'rec' where she'd played cricket with her brother and Bob Shaw. She'd had a letter from Bob last week, but anything interesting had been crossed out by the censor.

She'd heard from Graham too, but Graham wasn't such a good letter-writer as Bob. Nothing got crossed out in his scrawled notes! And he was still sulking a bit over her going away. He hadn't asked a single question about where she was going, and although he wished her luck at the end, it didn't seem as if he meant it.

Oh well, that was men all over, thought women ought to be there at their beck and call whenever they wanted them. This war would teach them different, she thought. Already women were doing a lot of the jobs men generally kept to themselves – why, there was a woman conductor, a conductress, Betty supposed she ought to be called, on this very bus, clipping the tickets as good as any man. And why not? It didn't exactly need big muscles.

'Off to the farm, then, love?'

Betty turned quickly. Tommy Vickers had sat down next to her and was looking at her with bright blue eyes. She smiled and nodded. She liked Mr Vickers. He had often tossed her and the boys a few toffees when they were out playing in the street, and sometimes he would even join in and bowl a few balls at the stumps chalked on the end house. Mrs Vickers had come out once and told him he'd never grow up, and Tommy had laughed and slapped her bottom and told her to be glad of it.

'I heard you were going on the land,' he continued. 'Well, you'll have a better time hoeing turnips than slaving away in some factory making munitions. And the uniform looks very fetching!'

Betty blushed. 'Dad doesn't really like me wearing trousers.'

'Well, not for pleasure, maybe, but it's different when it's work,' Tommy said. 'You can't do farm work in a posh frock. Where are you going?'

'Bishop's Waltham. There's quite a few going. We're getting a coach at the station.'

Tommy nodded. 'Well, you take care of yourself and look out for the farmer's boy.' He winked. 'I've heard a lot of tales about what they get up to behind haystacks – and if they're anything like I was when I was a lad, you'd better stay round the front. I know I wouldn't have wanted to miss a chance of kissing a pretty girl like you!'

Betty felt her blush deepen. 'Oh, I shan't be kissing anyone,' she said hurriedly. 'I've got a boy.'

'Young Ginger Philpotts. Yes.' Tommy gave her a considering look. 'Well, he's not a bad youngster, puts me in mind of myself a bit. I was in the Navy, you know, in the last lot.' He glanced out of the window. 'But it's not serious with him, is it. I mean, you'll have a good few romances before you're ready to settle down.'

'Oh, but—' Betty bit her lip. It had been on the tip of her tongue to tell Mr Vickers that she and Graham were secretly engaged. Why was she talking to him like this? 'I don't think it's fair to go out with other boys,' she said a little stiffly. 'Not when you've got someone away.'

'No, maybe not.' But he still sounded thoughtful. 'Well, I wish you both luck, Betty. I hope it all works out for you. Just don't be surprised if – well, you're both young, you can change your minds and no hard feelings. Anyway, this is my stop.' He grinned at her, suddenly cheerful again. 'Remember what I said now, take care and stand well clear of haystacks!'

He jumped off the bus and Betty looked out and saw him laughing at her from the pavement. She smiled and waved, feeling better. He always had that effect, she thought, people always walked away from Tommy with a smile on their faces.

The bus was nearly at the town station now, and the coach would be waiting. The adventure was about to begin.

The coach was filled with girls like herself or a few years older. They all looked self-conscious in their new uniforms and avoided each other's eyes as they lugged their kitbags on to the bus and found seats. A thin woman with spectacles and a clipboard counted them all on, checking their names on her list, and then checked them at least twice more before allowing the bus to move off.

Betty scrambled aboard and got a window-seat. It had taken nearly two hours to get everyone organised but it looked as if they were off at last. She stared at the crowd of girls, all dressed in their breeches and pullovers. They were from all over Portsmouth, some of them from Gosport, and mostly strangers to each other. One or two knew each other and talked in hushed whispers, as if they were in church.

'Whew! It's hot isn't it?' A tall, lanky girl with untidy brown hair had plonked herself down in the next seat. 'I hope it doesn't take too long now. I thought they'd never get us sorted out, didn't you? Where are you going?'

'Somewhere near Bishop's Waltham,' Betty said. 'What about you?'

'Same place. My Dad says it's hardly worth getting on a bus for.' She laughed, showing a row of square white teeth. 'I told him, they need someone to milk cows just as much in Bishop's Waltham as they do fifty miles away.' She brushed back a loose curl and gave Betty a friendly grin. 'P'raps we'll be seeing a bit of each other. What's your name? I'm Yvonne, Yvonne Hayter.'

The two girls talked as the coach made its way out of Portsmouth and into the countryside. It did not go directly to Bishop's Waltham, but meandered around the lanes, calling at different villages and farms. Several times the driver lost his way and Miss Andrews grew more and more exasperated.

'You'd think they'd send someone who knew the area,' she said sarcastically. 'Don't you have a map?'

'Look, lady, if you think you can do any better, I'll get out of this seat and you can drive instead,' the man retorted. 'I reckon I could do the grumbling as well as you.' He poked his finger at the map he had spread out beside him. 'They've took all the signposts down, haven't they, so Jerry won't be able to find his way about. Well, he's not the only one! And half these farms and places aren't even mentioned on this map.'

'Well, ask someone,' she said impatiently, and he groaned and rolled up his eyes.

'Who? The local cow? Can *you* see anyone to ask?' The lanes were deserted. The girls, who had found the situation funny to begin with, sighed and shifted uncomfortably. The seats were covered with oilcloth which had grown hot and sticky, and their breeches and long socks were too thick for a summer's day. The uniform included dungarees made of strong cotton, but they weren't so smart and it hadn't seemed right to wear them.

Not that many of the girls looked smart as it was, Betty thought. The clothes had been allocated as small, medium and large, and within each category there was quite a range of sizes. She had been lucky, but some of the girls looked half swamped by baggy breeches and socks that had been folded over half a dozen times at the top, and others looked as if they might burst all the seams at any minute.

Eventually, the coach driver managed to find all the places on the list, dropping girls off at each one. Miss Andrews checked and counted them all again each time – 'as if someone might have slipped through the floorboards,' Yvonne muttered in Betty's ear – and at last there were only three left, Betty, Yvonne and a slender girl with china-blue eyes and fair hair curled in ringlets. She looked more like a fairy off a Christmas tree than a land girl, even in her uniform, Betty thought, and wondered if she would be able to do the work. She caught the girl's glance and gave her a smile, but the china-blue eyes were cold and the fair head turned away. Betty felt irritated. I was only trying to be friendly, she thought.

The coach rounded a last corner and stopped in the narrow main street of Bishop's Waltham. The girls looked out with interest. There were a number of people about, all staring at the bus, and Miss Andrews poked out her head and asked for directions to the farm.

'It's another mile down that lane,' she reported. 'And we can't get the coach all the way – the last bit's too narrow. Mr Spencer's going to meet us there.'

Once more they set off, coming to a halt at a little crossroads. The coach driver stopped again.

'I'm not going any further. I'll have a job to turn round here as it is.'

'It's all right,' Miss Andrews said stiffly. 'This is as far as we have to go.' She looked out. The hedges were thick with blackberries but there was no sign of a farmer. 'Where *is* he?'

'Well, this is it,' Yvonne remarked, standing up and bumping her head on the overhead rack. 'Ouch! Why do I have to be so tall?' She glanced at the fair-haired girl. 'I bet they'll put us together. We'll get called Lofty and Titch!'

'They'd better not try,' the girl said grimly. She picked up her kitbag and pushed past them to the front of the bus where Miss Andrews was once again consulting her clipboard. 'My name's Erica Jones and I must have a bedroom to myself.'

'Coo-er,' Yvonne murmured, not too quietly. 'Someone thinks a lot of herself.' A flush touched the fair girl's neck and it was clear she had heard the penetrating whisper. She lifted her head a little higher and said coldly, 'I enquired at the recruiting office and was told it would be arranged.'

'Well, I don't know anything about that,' the woman said in a harassed voice. 'You'll have to see what Mr Spencer says about it.' She looked down the lane and tutted. 'He ought to be here now. I said we'd be here about two, and now it's gone three.'

'Maybe he thought you'd stood him up,' the driver suggested.

Erica Jones sighed impatiently and tapped her foot on the floor of the bus. Betty thought she was probably about twenty-one or two. Her golden curls shone and she wore make-up, though not so much that she looked what Betty's dad would call 'cheap'. Her uniform fitted beautifully, as if it had been made to measure, and she wore small gold earrings. Pierced ears, Betty thought enviously. Neither Annie nor Ted would have allowed her to get her ears pierced. It was obvious that she came from a home with more money than the Chapmans had.

Yvonne looked as though she had been wearing her uniform for the past three months. Her aertex shirt was crumpled and damp, her breeches as creased as if they had been rolled into a ball. Her shoes were already scuffed, her hat battered and her green pullover unravelling at one sleeve. She winked at Betty.

'Are we all going to the same place?' she asked. 'Is Mr Spencer the farmer?'

'What? Oh – yes, that's right.' The clipboard woman had been talking to the driver. She came back looking distracted. 'You're all three down for his farm. But there seems to be some hold-up. I don't know why he isn't here.'

'Because it's milking time.'

The voice made them all jump. They peered out of the bus at the young man who stood smiling up at them. He was tall, lean without being skinny, and had a mop of brown, curly hair. He glanced at the three girls and then smiled again at Miss Andrews. 'I'm Dennis Verney. I work for Mr Spencer. He told me to come down here and meet the young ladies. I'm to take them to their billet.' His gaze travelled slowly over the three staring faces, and

Betty felt a tiny shock as his eyes rested upon her face. 'Why don't you all come with me now?' he suggested, and there was a hint of laughter in his voice, as if Dennis Verney found quite a lot of things funny. 'I reckon Mrs Spencer'll have the kettle on by now and I bet you could all do with a cup of tea.'

'A cup of tea!' Yvonne exclaimed. 'Could I ever!' She jumped down from the bus and linked her arm with Dennis's. They were almost exactly the same height, Betty noticed, and she felt left out and a bit annoyed with Yvonne. Was she a flirt?

Erica too was looking annoyed. She climbed down into the lane, dragging her kitbag behind her, and made a great show of hoisting it on to her back. She looked back at Miss Andrews, who was fussing helplessly, obviously wondering if she should allow her three remaining chicks to go off with this unknown man.

'I still expect a room to myself, you know,' she said accusingly, but the woman shook her head.

'I'm sorry. We can't get the bus down the lane and I have to go back. If there's anything you're not happy about, you'll have to get in touch with the Office.' She stood back to allow Betty to dismount from the bus. 'Someone will call round in a day or two to see that everything's all right. And remember that you're here to work!'

Betty heaved her kitbag on to her shoulder and marched away down the lane after the others. For a moment, she caught herself wishing that she was the one to be swinging along with her arm through Dennis Verney's. Then she frowned and scolded herself.

Didn't she already have a boy, away at sea? Wasn't she wearing his ring this very minute, even if it was on her right hand? And what about Tommy Vickers' warning to be careful of the farmer's boys?

Anyway, a tall, strong young chap like Dennis Verney wasn't going to be around for long. He'd be called up himself in a week or two. And then there'd be three of them – him, Graham and Bob Shaw – to worry about.

I won't get too friendly with him, she decided. It's not worth it.

Dennis Verney led the three girls down the lane. It wound away from the main road and over a little bridge with a watercress-filled stream running lazily beneath it. On either side were broad, sloping fields and the lane twisted between tall hedges to climb a steep hill.

The farm lay at the bottom of the hill, set back off the road, with a large farmyard. The girls looked about with interest.

'My, that's a big house,' Yvonne said with awe. 'It's like a mansion!'

'It's the farmhouse,' Dennis said. 'It's not as big as it looks – all that part on the end is a barn. The hay's kept there for the animals.'

The house was built of grey flints. It had several windows and to Betty looked as big as three of the little terraced houses in April Grove. She shared Yvonne's awe, but Erica sniffed.

'This yard's mucky.'

Dennis grinned.

'It's a farmyard. The cows come through here to be milked. That's the milking shed, over there. The poultry are kept in that other shed and let out during the day.'

The yard was full of hens, picking at the earth. At the far side there was a pond, half covered in green, with a few ducks paddling about at its edge. There was a patch of grass with an apple tree hanging over it and someone had left a chair and a basket in the shade. Two large horses were grazing in a small paddock.

'It's lovely,' Betty said. 'It's real country.'

'It's a farm,' Dennis said again, and smiled at her.

Betty looked at him. He had warm hazel eyes, full of laughter. She felt suddenly confused, but before she could say anything the farmhouse door opened and a woman bustled out. She was about Betty's height and rather plump, with grey hair. She was smiling but looked anxious, and her eyes moved quickly over the three girls.

'So you're our land girls.' Her voice had a soft burr to it, quite different from the sharper accents of Portsmouth. 'Well, I'm pleased to see you. You'll find things a bit different here from what you're used to, I daresay, but we'll all shake down together. Now come in and tell me your names and I'll show you where you're to sleep.'

Betty glanced sideways at Erica, expecting her to claim her own room again, but for once the fair-haired girl was silent. She had put down her kitbag as they stood in front of the house, and now she moved to pick it up.

'Here, little 'un, let me carry that for you,' Dennis said. 'Good lord, it's nearly as tall as you are. How—'

Whatever he had been going to ask was lost as Erica whirled round, fists clenched and eyes blazing, and stamped her foot at him. He backed away, an almost comical expression of amazement on his face, as she let fly.

'Don't call me that! Don't call me "little 'un" or "Titch" or "Shorty" or anything else you might think's funny – I don't like it. It's bad enough *being* short, without everybody else treating it like a joke. So just keep your funny remarks to yourself, see?' She hoisted up her kitbag and swung it on to her shoulder, then looked at Mrs Spencer. 'I'd like to see my room now, please.'

'Whew! She's a star turn and no mistake,' Yvonne muttered in Betty's ear. 'Talk about Lady Muck.'

Mrs Spencer looked taken aback. She tightened her lips and turned to Dennis. 'You'd better go and help with the milking. I can see to these girls.' She waited while he disappeared across the yard, then went back into the house, leaving the girls to follow her.

Erica went first, explaining that she had only agreed to come on condition that she was given her own room. The other two followed, more interested in the farmhouse than in the other girl's demands, and gazed about them at the big kitchen.

It was large and untidy, with a dresser taking up most of one wall and an assortment of cupboards and drawers around the others. The dresser was piled with papers, bills, invoices, numerous forms, letters and old newspapers. A rough-topped table stood in one corner, with what looked like an old church pew with a high back on each of the long sides, and chairs at the end. There was a wide range, with its fire lit in spite of the hot weather, and a door leading into a long sitting-room with two sagging sofas and a couple of armchairs. Each held a pile of washing, evidently waiting to be ironed.

It didn't look as if the Spencers had much more money than the Chapmans, Betty thought in some surprise. Her own mother would have been ashamed to let visitors come in and see the house looking as untidy as this, in fact, it never *did* look as untidy as this. And the furniture looked old-fashioned and not at all up to date.

'Fancy living in a lovely big house like this and not keeping it nice,' she whispered to Yvonne, but the lanky girl gave her a puzzled look.

'It looks all right to me. Hell of a lot better than down Rudmore Alley, that's where I live. Five of us to a bedroom and *she* wants one all to herself!' She gazed around the room, her eye wide. 'I reckon we could get our whole house in this kitchen.'

Betty said nothing. She knew where Rudmore Alley was, over near Stamshaw, where the gas-holder had got hit during the first raid. But she had never been there. It wasn't much better than a slum, her mother said, with narrow passageways of tiny houses, and too many people living too close together. They were all poor down there, working either at the timberyard or on the wharves, and a lot of the children went to school with no shoes on their feet. She wondered what her mother would say if she knew that Betty would be sharing a room with a girl from Rudmore Alley.

'But I *told* them in the office,' Erica was saying. 'I told them, I have to have my own room. I'm not *used* to sharing with other people. I won't be able to *sleep*.'

'You'll sleep all right, after you've done a good day's work.' Erica gasped and they all turned quickly and saw the doorway blocked by a large man. He stood surveying them, his hands on his hips, face shadowed. He moved forwards, his eyes narrowed. 'It's hard work on a farm, aye and mucky too. You'll be no good if you're afraid of mucking out the pigs or milking a cow. I hope you don't think you've come out here on holiday, to get away from the bombs.'

'Of course we don't,' Betty said indignantly. 'We want to help win the war. At least, I do.' She glanced at the other girls. Yvonne, thin but tall, looked ready to do her bit, but what about Erica? She didn't look as if she'd ever got her hands dirty in her life.

'So do I,' Yvonne said warmly. 'And I'm not afraid of pigs, or cows. I'll do whatever you want me to.'

The farmer looked at her, his eyes moving over her lanky body. He's looking at us just as if we were cattle in a market, Betty thought, suppressing a nervous giggle.

'Well, maybe you'll be some use when you've got a bit of flesh on you,' he remarked. 'It's soft living in the city, so they tell me. A couple of weeks harvesting'll soon build you up.'

'It's good food that'll build them up,' his wife said. 'A few eggs and a bit of butter. And proper milk, not like that thin stuff they get out of bottles.' Her voice was warm and motherly as she looked at the three girls. 'We still have to take what rations they give us, but there's always a bit extra being on a farm – a drop of milk in the pail, a cracked egg now and then. And you'll need it, with the work you'll be doing – my husband's right there.'

Erica had recovered herself. She stepped forward, tilting her head to look up at the big farmer, but before she could speak Mrs Spencer said hastily, 'I was just telling you about the sleeping arrangements. I'll take you upstairs now and then Mr Spencer can show you the farm before tea.' She turned and opened a door which Betty had thought to be a cupboard but now saw to lead to a narrow flight of stairs. Bumping their kitbags on the wall, the three girls followed her, Erica looking annoyed.

'I daresay you're hungry after your journey,' Mrs Spencer said. 'I always cook a meal at tea-time. The men need it. My husband's always had a good appetite, and Dennis eats whatever's put in front of him. Oh, you'll need to give me your ration books, I'll have to register you in the shops.' She was leading them along a narrow passage and then set off again, up a further flight of stairs. 'Here. This is your room.'

The three girls crowded into the room behind her. It was long and narrow, with sloping walls, and the windows were so low that you would have to kneel on the floor to look out of them. There were three folding camp beds, close together, and three small chests of drawers.

'Coo,' Yvonne said, 'the ceiling's a bit low. I can't stand up straight, except in the middle.'

Betty stared at the room. She felt a twinge of excitement. It was bigger than her room at home, even if she did have to share it, and the sun was slanting in through the low windows and making striped patterns on the floorboards. The curtains were old but pretty, with patterns of flowers faded to a soft blur. It was like a room out of an Enid Blyton story.

'You're expecting us to sleep *here*?' Erica said, her voice high with disbelief.

Mrs Spencer looked at her. 'What's the matter with it?'

'What's the *matter*? It's an *attic*.'

'It's the only room we've got that's big enough.'

Erica sighed impatiently. 'I've told you, I'm to have my own room. I've never shared a room. I'm afraid there's been some mistake. You'll have to do something about it.'

Mrs Spencer shook her head. 'I can't do anything about it. Nobody said anything to me about a separate room. Anyway, it'll have to do, there's nowhere else for you to go. All the rest of the rooms in the house are occupied.'

'How many people live here?' Yvonne asked curiously. 'Have you got evacuees?'

'No, but there's me and my husband, and Dennis, and old Jonas – he's been with us for years. And we've got my sister and her two children staying with us. They've got Dick and Gerald's rooms.' She looked at them again. 'You'll have to sleep here.'

Yvonne picked up her kitbag and marched into the room. She dumped it on one of the camp beds and said cheerfully, 'Suits me. Which bed d'you want, Bet? The one by the window?'

Betty agreed eagerly. She thought of lying close to that window at night, gazing out at the stars, waking in the morning to see the apple tree outside, its leaves dancing against the sky – why, it was as good as a holiday. She dropped her bag on the bed and grinned at Yvonne, then looked at Erica.

'That leaves you the bed at the end. Come on – it won't be that bad, sharing with us. We haven't got fleas. Anyway, it's that or walk back to Pompey on your own, take your choice.' She lay back on the bed and laughed. 'I think it's a smashing room. I've never slept in an attic before.'

'We haven't even got an attic,' Yvonne remarked, and pulled open the neck of her kitbag.

Erica stared at them both. She turned to look at their hostess, but Mrs Spencer had disappeared down the stairs. She hesitated for a moment, then walked to the end of the room, her back stiff.

'It's only for tonight,' she said haughtily. 'I'll get something done about it first thing in the morning, see if I don't. I'd never have come if I'd thought I was going to be treated like this.' She dumped her kitbag on the bed and sniffed. 'Not that I'm going to be here for long anyway.'

'What d'you mean?' Yvonne was fishing out all her belongings and strewing them about her bed. It looked as if she was turning out a ragbag, Betty thought. The Land Army uniform must have been the first new clothes Yvonne had ever had. 'Where are you going?'

'Oh, I'm getting married.' Erica held up her left hand and they saw the tiny diamond glinting on her finger. 'My fiancé's in the RAF and as soon as he gets leave we'll be having a big wedding. And then I'll go with him, wherever he's stationed.'

'So why did you join the Land Army?'

'It was either that or one of the Services and I wasn't going to join *them*. In any case, we'll be having a baby straightaway so there was no point starting anything important. And then I shan't have to work at all.'

'Having a baby?' Betty said incredulously. 'But why?'

'Why d'you think? I might not get another chance. If Geoffrey gets killed . . .' she shrugged. 'At least I'd have something to remember him by. And I won't have to go into the Services.' Her red lips wrinkled in distaste.

Yvonne stared at her. 'You talk as if a baby's a – a fancy photo or something. It's a person. You can't have a baby just to get out of doing war work.'

'I can if I like,' Erica said coolly. She glanced disparagingly around the attic. 'I suppose these hooks and nails on the wall are their idea of somewhere to hang our clothes. Honestly! Not even a wardrobe. It's disgusting.'

'It's clean.' Betty didn't feel like talking to Erica any more. She opened one of the chests of drawers and began to put away her clothes. 'And Mrs Spencer seems quite nice, though I'm not so sure about the old man.'

'What about the *young* one, though?' Yvonne's eyes sparkled. 'He's a bit of all right, isn't he? Dennis, I think that's a lovely name.' She rolled her eyes. 'Who d'you suppose he is? He doesn't seem to be their son.'

'No, both their boys are away in the war.' Betty remembered Dennis's warm hazel eyes and felt the colour rise in her cheeks. She turned her head away quickly. 'Maybe he just works here. He'll probably be called up any time. Or he might even be on leave.'

'I don't think he is.' For the first time, Erica joined in a conversation that was not centred upon herself. 'If you ask me, there's something funny about him.'

'Funny? What d'you mean?'

'I don't know,' she said slowly. She sat on her bed, unrolling a pair of thick socks, and gazed at them. 'But I don't believe he's in the Forces and I don't believe he's been working on the farm for long. He's not the kind of person who works on a farm. You can tell by his voice. And there's something about him, something I can't quite put my finger on. But I don't trust him.'

The other two girls stared at her. Betty felt a twinge of unease. Something not quite right? Something not to be trusted? She thought of the laughing eyes, the ready grin, and shook her head.

He'd seemed such a nice sort of chap. But it was funny that he was working on the farm instead of being in the Forces. And he didn't seem like the sort of chap you'd expect to find doing the milking and things like that. And his voice *was* too posh, almost as posh as one of the announcers on the wireless.

Maybe Erica was right. There were spies everywhere. And you had to be careful these days about who you trusted.

The three girls looked at each other, suddenly solemn. And somewhere in the distance, so faint that it was little more than a prickle along their spines, they heard the wail of the siren, and then the muffled thud of bombs as they began once more to fall on the city of Portsmouth.

9

The working day started early on a farm, and the three girls were up by six o'clock next morning and drinking tea at the kitchen table. And that was the last lie-in they'd get, Mr Spencer told them when they went out to the byre where the three men were already milking.

'Lie-in!' Erica exclaimed. 'I don't get up till eight o'clock at home.'

Dennis chuckled and the old farmhand, Jonas, snorted. He was sitting on a milking stool, his head pressed against the flank of a large brown cow, his hands squeezing her udder with rhythmic ease. He had already expressed his opinion of the new Land Girls when Mr Spencer had shown them the farm the evening before.

'So you're what they've sent to replace our Dick and Gerald, are you?' He hadn't even bothered to take the straw out of his mouth as he stared at them. 'Well, I suppose the three of you together might be able do the work of one of 'em, but I must say you don't look up to much. Specially you,' he said to Erica, who quivered with fury. 'Why, you're no bigger than a threepenny bit.' Yvonne stifled a giggle and he turned his rheumy eyes on her. 'And you're just a couple of yards of bloody tapwater, but at least you'll be able to reach things. As for you – he turned to Betty – you'll not be able to keep that perm, not when you're out in all weathers, so you might as well forget it.'

'My hair's not permed,' Betty said indignantly. 'It's naturally curly.'

He gave a cackle of laughter. '"Naturally curly", is it! Well, that's a load off my mind, I must say. Hear that, boss? That's one of 'em won't be bothered about setting her hair every bloody Friday night.'

And how much work could *he* do in a day? Betty had wondered as Mr Spencer led them on around the yard. He wasn't much bigger than Erica himself and was as bent as a hairpin. But he looked as tough and scrawny as an old hen, as if he was nothing but bone and sinew. And he'd been on the farm all his life, Mrs Spencer had told them, worked for Mr Spencer's father when he was alive and knew all that there was to know about the job.

Now he finished the cow he was milking and the farmer suggested that each man should show one of the girls how to milk. Betty bit her lip, trying not to giggle again as Jonas gave Erica a look of pure disgust and rose to let her take his place at the next stall.

'Here's the stool. Three-legged – it's steadier that way. You don't want it toppling over every time the beast shifts her weight.' He sat Erica down on it and guided her hands to the udder. 'I 'ope you're not too dainty to touch her teats. Put your fingers round 'em good and hard. You got to squeeze – no good bloody stroking 'em. You ain't doin' it for her delight.'

Betty and Yvonne watched as the blonde girl settled herself gingerly beside the cow. She looked even smaller beside the huge brown beast, and her fingers barely closed around the teat. She looked with some trepidation at the smooth brown flank and gave a tentative squeeze.

'That ain't no good,' Jonas said disgustedly. 'Lean into 'er. Never mind yer pretty hair. Press yerself against 'er belly and give them tits a proper squeeze. You're milkin' er, not askin' 'er to purr. She ain't a pussy-cat.'

Erica bit her lip. Betty could see the frustration on her face. She squeezed again, and nothing happened. The cow shifted as if in irritation, and Erica flinched.

'She doesn't like it. I don't believe there's any milk there.'

'So what's that in 'er bag, bloody champagne? Mebbe you'd get it out quicker if it was.' The old man elbowed her aside and set his own hands on the udder. Immediately, two streams of milk gushed into the pail. 'Looks like milk to me.'

Erica made a sound of exasperation, and Mr Spencer laughed.

'Have another go. Nobody gets it right first time, even Jonas, only he's so old he doesn't remember learning. Just keep trying, little 'un.' He didn't seem to know that Erica hated reference to be made to her smallness. 'Now you other two try. You – Yvonne – come here with me, and Betty, you go with Dennis.' He led the way into another stall and Betty and Dennis looked at each other.

'A case of the blind leading the blind, I'm afraid,' he said cheerfully. 'I've only been doing it a few weeks myself. But I reckon I've just about got the hang of it now. Come and try Buttercup, she's usually pretty generous.'

Betty sat down on the little stool. The cow looked bigger than ever. She laid her face against its side and gave a little exclamation of surprise.

'Isn't she warm!'

Dennis chuckled. 'Of course she is. And I'll tell you something, Betty, this'll be one of the best jobs on the farm in winter. Imagine it in here on a cold, frosty morning, with all the cows breathing out nice warm air and heating the place up with their bodies. The best excuse in the world to spend a couple of hours all cosy against a warm body, better than a teddy-bear any day. What d'you think?'

Betty laughed. 'I think you could be right.' Tentatively, she touched the udder. It felt smooth and firm. Remembering what Jonas had said, she took experimental hold of two opposite teats and began to squeeze.

'No, not quite like that.' Dennis squatted beside her and reached in to cover her hands with his own. 'More like this.' His fingers tightened over hers. His face was very close. She could feel his breath on her cheek. 'That's better,' he said, and there was an odd note in his voice as he drew quickly away. 'Look . . .'

Betty opened her eyes, surprised to find that she had closed them. Her heart was beating quickly and she could feel a warmth in her face that was nothing to do with the cow. She looked into the pail and saw the milk already covering the bottom.

'Am *I* doing that?' Her momentary embarrassment was forgotten as she stared in delight at the jets of milk still issuing from the teats as she squeezed. 'Hey, look, I'm really milking!'

Dennis laughed. He had moved away now and she could no longer feel the warmth of his body close to hers. She blushed again, feeling her heart skitter, then called to the other girls. 'I'm really getting milk out. How are you getting on?'

By the time milking was over each girl had managed to draw off about half a pailful from their respective cows and even Jonas admitted that it wasn't bad for beginners – 'and bloody townies, at that'. But their fingers were stiff and aching and they wondered if they would ever be able to milk the whole herd, as the men were accustomed to do.

'You'll get used to it,' Mrs Spencer assured them, serving everyone with a hearty breakfast of fried potatoes. 'Come next month and you'll be experts.'

'Experts!' Jonas said with a snort. 'Takes longer'n a few months to make experts. Takes a bloody lifetime.'

'Well, you'll have to make do without experts then,' Betty retorted. She was getting tired of Jonas. 'We can't go back to the beginning and get ourselves born on a farm just to please you.'

'Now look you here,' he began, lifting a gnarled finger to point at her. 'I don't 'ave to sit 'ere and be spoke to like that by a chit of a bloody girl—'

'You don't have to sit here at all,' the farmer's wife said sharply. 'I'll have no squabbling at this table, Jonas, and well you know it. The girls have come to help us and they've got to learn, and it's up to you to teach them and look pleasant about it, so mind your manners. *And* your language. If you don't want to share your meals with the rest of us, you can have 'em out in the barn, it's all one to me.'

The old man stared at her, his jaw dropping open so that Betty wanted to giggle again. But the look on Mrs Spencer's face warned her that it would not be welcome and she looked down at her plate instead.

Breakfast was always served after milking, and the kitchen table was crowded, with Mrs Spencer's sister Iris Blake and her two children hurrying through their meal as well. Mrs Blake was married to an Army captain and had come to stay at the beginning of the war. It was already apparent to the girls that the two sisters didn't really see eye to eye, especially over the behaviour of the children. But these days there were plenty of people having to live together who didn't get on, and if you had the room you had to take in someone. It might as well be family as strangers. And at least the children went to school each day in Bishop's Waltham.

The meal was soon over – no time to hang about, Mr Spencer said as he led them outside again. There was a harvest to be gathered, and more things to learn. And learning made everyone slow, so the sooner they got down to it the better.

'It's all the harder because the tractor can't be used now,' Dennis told them as they left the house. 'It takes too much fuel so the horses have come back into their own. And some farmers who don't have horses use oxen, or even cows.'

The girls looked at him blankly until he explained that the farmers were using self-binders, dragged round the fields by a team of horses, which cut the crop and bound it into heavy sheaves. 'Then we come along and prop them up against each other in stooks,' he said. 'Given good weather, it'll dry out and then we can stack it up ready for the threshers.'

'What are the threshers?' Betty asked, and old Jonas raised his eyes to the heavens. 'Well, it's not our fault we don't know,' she told him indignantly. 'I daresay there's quite a few things about towns and ships that *you* don't know!'

'Don't need to, neither,' Jonas said, and spat out a piece of straw. Erica gave him a glance of disgust.

Dennis grinned. 'The threshers aren't a "what", they're a "who". They go round all the farms in turn with a machine and thresh the stacks. Nobody's allowed to have them for more than a few days, so they can only do a part of the crop each time they come. It could be March before they've finished.'

'And meantime all my money stays tied up in the stacks,' Mr Spencer said, joining them. 'And I don't want to see any of you smoking near them, understand? One of those stacks goes up in flames, and it's my livelihood gone for a burton. Now, are we going to harvest this corn or are we just going to let it stand there and rot?'

Dennis led the way over to the paddock and called to the two big horses. They ambled over and rubbed their noses against his sleeve. He fastened the head collars on and handed one to Betty to lead.

'Will he come with me?' She looked a little nervously up at the big head. She was quite accustomed to horses, for many of the tradesmen who called around the streets of Portsmouth still used them, but she had always been warned not to go too close in case they bit or kicked. This one had long yellow teeth and hooves as big as dinner-plates.

'He'll follow his mate.' Dennis turned to go out of the paddock. 'He's called Boxer, and this one's Shandy. They're quiet as lambs, the pair of them.'

He harnessed them to the binder and the work began. At first, the girls watched and then, gradually, they began to join in.

The self-binder had a sharp reciprocating knife which cut the corn as the horses dragged it round the field. It was then guided on to the canvas bed by the 'sails' which prevented it from falling loose, and transported into the box where it was bunched and tied automatically with sisal string. Finally, the sheaves were cast out into rows, the whole procedure taking place continuously as the horses plodded round and round.

Jonas led the horses. It looked the easiest job, Betty thought, but probably it wasn't – Jonas had been doing these jobs for so long that he could make anything look easy. And he was very particular about the knife, checking that it was razor-sharp. 'Makes it easier to cut the corn, and easier to work the horses,' he said, giving away the information as reluctantly as if it were a precious jewel. He hadn't forgiven them for their blundering attempts at milking, Betty realised, nor for her answering back at the breakfast table. His look as Mrs Spencer had told him to mind his manners had been murderous.

She sighed and followed the others. Dennis and Mr Spencer were now following the binder and building the sheaves into stooks, six or eight of them, propped together like a wigwam, with a couple more laid over the top like a roof.

'That's to let the rain run off,' Mr Spencer explained. 'Come the time they're dry, we'll load 'em on to the cart and stack 'em, like Dennis told you.' He surveyed them. 'Well, I reckon I'll leave you to it now. You ought to be able to manage a simple job like that. I daresay Jonas'll tell you when it's time to knock off for half an hour.'

Half an hour! Betty thought as she laboured in the hot sun for the rest of the morning. Was that all the break they were going to get? Already, it seemed as if they had done a full day's work. She thought of the dairy in September Street and how she'd grumbled if Mrs Marsh told her to clean out the big fridge. And Mr Spencer had thought they'd look on this as a holiday!

Still, exhausted as she was when she lay on her bed at the end of that first day, she felt a warm glow of satisfaction at what she had accomplished. Building stooks hadn't been as easy as it looked, but she'd managed to get several standing unaided, although rather drunken-looking, and at afternoon milking she'd managed to draw off all the milk Buttercup had to give, and most of Daisy's as well. Not bad for a beginner, however much old Jonas might look down his battered nose. And tomorrow, she'd do better still.

But the next day the girls' muscles were stiff and sore, and their fingers painful to use. There was no respite from their work, however; cows would be in a worse case if they weren't milked, Mr Spencer told them shortly, and the country the worse off for lack of milk. And the harvest must be got in. Sun wouldn't shine for ever.

Mrs Spencer was slightly more sympathetic, but Betty could tell that she was wondering if city girls could ever be up to the demands of farm work. Perhaps old Jonas was right, she thought, and you had to be bred to it. But Dennis hadn't been, and he could tackle most jobs with a fair amount of efficiency.

'It was just as bad for me when I started,' he told them as they sat at the edge of the cornfield one day, taking what shade they could from the hedge for their midday break. 'I found muscles I didn't know I'd got and ached in places where I didn't know I had places! But it all sorted itself out after two or three weeks and I've never felt fitter than I do now.'

'Two or three weeks?' Yvonne exclaimed. 'I'll be dead by then!'

He laughed. 'No, you won't.'

'Well, I'll probably wish I was,' she retorted. 'Don't you reckon so, Betty?'

Betty smiled and shrugged. 'I think Dennis is right. I'm feeling better already. My fingers hardly ached at all when I was milking this morning.'

'That's because you did hardly any milking,' Yvonne grinned. She looked at Erica, who was sitting a little apart from them reading her latest letter from Geoffrey. 'What d'you reckon, Eric? Think we'll have snuffed it by the end of next week?'

The blonde girl glanced up. Her china-blue eyes were cold and as they moved over Dennis her lip curled slightly. Her voice was stony and bitter.

'I don't suppose so. I expect we'll all be just as alive as we are now, even those who don't deserve to be.' She glanced down at the letter still held between her fingers. 'But there'll be plenty who *will* be dead, men like my Geoffrey, who're ready to risk their lives to save other people's skins. Even the yellow ones who aren't worth saving at all.' With a sudden movement, she crumpled up the letter and stuffed it into her pocket, then scrambled to her feet. 'Come on, let's get on with the stooking. Let's show what *girls* can do to help win the war. It'll make up for some of the company we have to keep.'

She strode away towards Jonas, who was removing the horses' nosebags. Dennis gave them a rueful glance and followed her and Betty and Yvonne stared at each other.

'Well!' Betty exclaimed. 'What d'you make of that? What did she mean about yellow skins? We're not fighting to save Chinamen, are we?'

'Not that I know of,' Yvonne said quietly. 'But I don't reckon she meant that sort of yellow skin, anyway. She was talking about our Dennis. Didn't you see the look she gave him – or the way he looked at us?'

'Dennis? But why? He's not a coward. He's just doing farm work, same as we are.' Betty frowned. 'Ever since we arrived here, Erica's had it in for Dennis. And I don't understand why, do you?'

'I'm not sure,' Yvonne said slowly. She rose to her feet and dusted breadcrumbs off her dungarees. 'But I think Erica knows a bit more about Dennis Verney than we do. And tonight I'm going to ask her just what it is.'

She walked away to join the others, and Betty collected up the grease-proof paper Mrs Spencer had wrapped their sandwiches in and smoothed it out carefully to be used again next day. She thought over the past week, trying to pick out things Dennis had done which could make Erica dislike him so bitterly.

There was nothing. All she could think of were his hazel eyes, so often laughing. His ready smile. The way he was always ready to help or encourage any of them who needed it. The way he had folded his hands over hers as he showed her how to milk Buttercup . . .

I don't think there's anything suspicious about him, she thought, pulling herself to her feet. I don't think there's anything at all.

'He's a conchie.'

The word echoed around the attic bedroom and seemed to hang in the air as if waiting for someone to pick it up. Yvonne was the one.

'A conchie? What's that?'

Erica looked at her contemptuously.

'Don't you know what a conchie is? A CO. A *conscientious objector*. He won't fight.'

Yvonne's brow furrowed. 'What do you mean, won't fight? Won't fight who?'

'The *Germans*, of course. He won't go in the Forces. He probably won't even help make aeroplanes or munitions, or anything to do with the war. He'd rather leave it to someone else. People like my Geoffrey.'

By now the girls had heard a good deal about Geoffrey. He was a pilot stationed at Tangmere and would be coming to the farm soon to see her, Erica promised. But at present, like all the other airmen, he was too busy fighting.

'They have to be ready all the time. When the German planes are seen coming, they have to scramble—'

'Scramble?'

'Run for their planes. It's like a race, Geoffrey says, to see who can get into the air first. He flies a Spitfire, and they have to get right up above the Germans and shoot them down.' Erica stopped abruptly, obviously wondering if she had said too much.

'It's all right,' Betty said. 'We're not fifth columnists. We won't tell anyone what Geoffrey does.'

'It's not you. It's that Dennis. I still don't trust him.'

That was just before she had discovered what he was. Now she despised him even more.

'He's a coward. He pretends he won't fight because he's got principles against it, but it's really because he's too frightened. Principles! Does he think he's the only one with principles?'

'What sort of principles?' Betty asked. In the week that they had been at the farm, she had grown to like Dennis more and more. Her dad would have approved of him, she thought. But if he was a CO . . .

'I thought you *had* to go into the Services if you were called up,' Yvonne said before Erica could answer. 'I didn't think there was any choice.'

'There isn't, unless you can prove you've got principles. But some of these people will go to prison rather than fight for their king and country.' Erica's voice was bitter. She stared out of the window. 'I'm going to apply to be moved. There's still no sign of me having a room of my own, and I'm not stopping where there's a conchie. I don't see that anyone can force me to do that.'

Yvonne shrugged. 'Suits us. We might get someone who's not too toffee-nosed to speak to us. And I think Dennis is nice.'

'You would.' Erica turned her back and went back to the letter she was writing. She wrote long epistles to her Geoffrey and the other two wondered when he got time to read them, if he was so busy. And what could she be saying? It must be one long grumble.

Betty too was writing a letter. She wrote to Graham every day, and to Bob Shaw at least once a week. Now she had to write to her parents and Olive as well. But at least there was plenty to write about.

By the end of that first week, any romantic notions that the girls might have had about country life had been firmly dispelled. The weather was still fine, but there was little time to bask in the sunshine. Apart from the harvest there were cows to be milked twice a day, pigs to be fed and sheep to be dipped. Betty, who had been so eager on that first morning to learn to milk a cow, began to feel as if she had only to finish with one animal to turn and find a line of others awaiting her attention, and her dreams were a turmoil of milking, feeding and dipping.

'I thought I was dipping Roger last night,' she told Yvonne. Roger was the bull and lived by himself in a pen close to the farmyard. He was black and white, and the girls had been told not to go anywhere near him.

Yvonne laughed. 'I bet he put up a fight.' She looked ruefully at her hands. 'How are your blisters, Bet?'

All the girls had blisters on their hands from using unfamiliar implements, and sore muscles all over their bodies. They were scratched and bruised, and the sun had burnt their faces and arms. Betty's nose was peeling and Erica was frantic about her red face.

'Geoffrey said he'd come this weekend. I can't let him see me like this.'

'Go on, he'll see you looking a lot worse than that when you're married,' Yvonne retorted. 'How are you going to manage about your curls then?'

Erica twisted bandages into her hair every night to keep the ringlets in. Tight-lipped, she would turn her back on the other two and work in front of a small mirror which she propped on her bed. She applied a thick layer of cold cream to her face as well, and caused Yvonne to hoot with laughter the first time she saw her.

'You look like one of those pictures of Hottentots! Only they've got black spiky hair and black faces. Doesn't she, Bet?'

'She looks like a negative of one,' Betty said. 'My brother Colin develops his own photos when he's home and she looks just like the negatives.'

Erica scowled. But she continued to bandage her hair every night and to cream her face, and Betty had to admit that the fair girl's skin was standing up to the ravages of long days in the sun better than hers or Yvonne's. It was red, but it wasn't peeling.

Erica didn't answer Yvonne's jibe about her curls. She peered at herself in the mirror and rubbed in a little more cold cream. Then she took Geoffrey's photograph from the wooden box which served as a bedside table and gazed at it.

'I hope he'll be able to come over,' she said. 'It's nearly three weeks since I saw him. And they got bombed there too, you know. He could be killed any day.'

Betty felt sorry for her. She was right, Tangmere had been bombed. And Geoffrey was in danger every time he took to the air in his Spitfire. Every night the evening paper had carried reports of the battle that was going on overhead, the number of Germans shot down, the number of RAF planes lost. The Germans had always suffered more, but that didn't make any difference. There were still British pilots being killed every day.

The sirens could be heard even here, out in the country. Every day the girls could see the planes coming and watch the dogfights going on overhead. They heard the dull thud of the bombs in the distance. Sometimes the bombers came further inland and turned to fly back over Portsmouth in an endeavour to escape the harrying of the RAF, and once or twice they jettisoned their bombs over open country. One fell at Fort

Southwick, on top of Portsdown Hill, and a plume of smoke rose into the air.

The corn was dry now and ready to be brought into the yard and stacked. This time Boxer and Shandy were harnessed to a wain, which was taken out to the field and moved slowly round while Dennis and the three girls loaded it with sheaves. Jonas came with them, shaking his head at their efforts.

'My sainted aunt, you're about as handy as a cow with a musket,' he said as Erica struggled to lift an unwieldy sheaf and pass it up to Dennis, who was acting as loader on the cart. 'Don't tell me that's too heavy for you.'

'It doesn't have to be,' Yvonne said. 'It's nearly as tall as she is. P'raps you'd be better on the cart, Eric.'

'On the cart? That's bloody skilled work, that is.' Jonas passed a disparaging glance over the sheaves Dennis had piled on top. 'Here, let a man have a go, show you how it's done.'

Dennis pulled a comical face and jumped down while Betty took the horses' heads and Jonas clambered up to take Dennis's place. He stood bent-legged on top of the untidy pile and swiftly dragged them around until they were arranged round and round the cart, butt outwards. Then he looked down at the ring of expectant faces.

'That's what they got to look like, see. Tidy. Always remember that everything oughter be tidy – it'll work right then, see. And keep the middle full – you let that get hollow and it'll tip, sure as ninepence, soon's you start moving. Right, now start pitching.'

Dennis took the pitchfork Betty had left leaning against the cart and stabbed it into a sheaf. He swung it into the air and thrust it towards Jonas, who lifted it expertly from the prongs and laid it in position, then turned for the next. Dennis was just lifting it into the air.

'Well, get a move on,' the old man snapped. 'Keep 'em coming. It wastes time to keep the loader standing around with nothing to do. You girls, you oughter be pitchin' in as well, not standing idle. It's not a bloody 'oliday camp.'

Hastily, the three girls began to do as he told them, stabbing the sheaves with their pitchforks and trying to swing them up as Dennis had done. But like everything else, it was harder than it looked. The sheaves slipped off the prongs and when Betty caught on to the idea of twisting the fork to keep them on, she could barely lift it to shoulder-height, never mind up to Jonas on the cart. And when she did manage to heave one into the air, it refused to come off the prongs again. Exasperated and annoyed, sweat running down into her eyes, and irritated almost beyond bearing by the flies which had appeared from nowhere and begun to bite her neck and arms, she dropped the sheaf and stared at it helplessly.

'It's worse than stooking! I just can't lift it.' To her dismay, she felt the tears pricking her eyes and heard the tremor in her voice.

Dennis turned aside from the sheaf he had been about to lift and took her fork from her hands. 'It's not really that hard. It's just that there's a knack to it. Look.' He stood slightly behind her and held her hands over the fork, as he had done with the cow's udder. 'Hold it like this, twist it a bit –

not too much – and then swing round. See?' The sheaf rose in a graceful arc straight into Jonas's arms. 'Poetry in motion.'

Betty laughed despite herself. It was a comfort just to have Dennis's arms around her, and his voice murmuring soothingly in her ear. 'Maybe we should work together all the time,' she said, and blushed. 'I mean – I didn't mean—'

'It's all right,' he said with a grin. 'But I don't think the boss'd like it. Anyway, you'll be able to do it yourself with a bit more practice.' He stepped away and thrust his fork into another sheaf.

The work went on. Gradually, the girls became accustomed to the rhythm and although Jonas still complained that they were slow they kept up a steady pace and the cart made several trips back to the yard, where it was unloaded and the sheaves built into a stack to await the thresher.

This was even harder work. The stack was to be built on a frame of poles laid between four rounded rickstones, like stone mushrooms standing about two feet high, taking up an area of about sixteen feet square. The first time that the wain, loaded almost twenty feet high with sheaves, drew up beside the framework, the girls gazed at it in bewilderment.

'How on earth are we going to get them on?' Yvonne asked. 'Does the wain tip over, or something?'

Jonas snorted. 'Course it don't! Stack has to be built proper.' He glanced at Mr Spencer. 'I dunno why the bloody 'ell you 'ad to ask for Land Girls. This lot'd be better off pickin' flowers.'

'Give them a chance, Jonas,' the farmer said. He turned to the girls. 'It's a fairly simple job, but like everything else there's a knack to it. You have two men on the stack, see, one at each end, and two or three up on top of the load pitching down to them. The stack's built from the outside into the middle, with the heads inside so they're protected, and that's all there is to it.'

'All there is to it?' Yvonne stared up at the sheaves towering above their heads on the cart. 'You mean we have to stand right up there, on top? With nothing to stop us from falling?'

'Don't have time to fall,' Jonas said with what they suspected might be an attempt at humour. Yvonne gave him a withering glance.

'But how do we get up there in the first place?'

'You climb up,' the farmer said tersely, and indicated the ropes that had been slung across the cart, dangling down at each end. 'I suppose you *can* climb?'

'Should've asked for bloody monkeys,' Jonas remarked, and for once Yvonne seemed inclined to agree with him. She looked at Betty and hesitated. And what about Erica? She was so small and dainty, she'd never manage a job like this.

'I think I can manage,' Betty said, remembering how she had always liked climbing trees when she'd been a child, playing with the boys. And once someone had produced a long rope which he said had been given him by his father, who was captain of the bellringers at St Mary's. They had found a tall tree to hang it from and used it as a swing until it snapped, dropping one of the boys in a pile of leaves. She'd often tried climbing that.

'Well, come on,' Mr Spencer said. 'Someone's got to be first.'

Betty stepped forwards. But to her surprise, Erica was there before her, her small hands already clasping the rope.

'We used to do this sort of thing in gym at school,' she said in her clear voice, and began to climb.

'Look at that!' Yvonne said. 'I reckon she went to a different sort of school from what we did, Bet. We never had nothing like that down Rudmore.'

'Nor at Copnor.' They watched with admiration as Erica scrambled swiftly up the side of the load, bracing herself outwards with her feet and hauling herself up on the rope. She had some difficulty in negotiating the overhang at the top, where the load was wider, but eventually she clawed her way over the top and looked down at them triumphantly.

'Well, who'd 'ave thought it?' Jonas said grudgingly. 'Reckon you did get bloody monkeys after all!'

'Thanks for nothing.' Betty grasped the rope and began to climb, copying Erica. But the rope was not like the thin, smooth bellrope she had used years ago. It was thick and rough, scratching her hands. And as she got closer to the top, it was pulled tight by her weight and almost buried in the straw, so that she had difficulty in getting her fingers round it.

The overhang was much harder to climb over than it had looked, too. From below, it hadn't looked all that large, but when you were underneath it and trying to figure out how to swing yourself out and over the top, it looked immense. It's like climbing Everest, she thought. However did Erica manage it?

'That's it,' the clear voice came from above her. 'Pull yourself away – well, not like that.' She heard Erica giggle.

I'm glad you're enjoying it, Betty thought crossly. In swinging herself away from the lower part of the load, she had lost contact with it entirely and was now swinging helplessly in mid-air. Jonas was cackling below, and even Mr Spencer and Dennis were chuckling. She had a sudden picture of what she must look like, and felt her own giggles begin.

Giving up, she let herself cautiously down the rope and stood getting her breath back before having another go. This time, she managed to clamber out under the overhang and scrabble her way over the top. She plonked herself down beside Erica and looked over the side.

'We're as high as a house!'

'I know.' Erica grinned at her. 'It's rather fun, isn't it?'

Fun! Betty looked down at the others. Their faces were upturned and they looked small and distant. 'Do we really have to stand on this thing and pitch sheaves?' she asked dubiously.

It was soon apparent that this was exactly what they did have to do. As soon as Yvonne, looking rather green, had managed to clamber up beside them, Dennis came up with the pitchforks and they stood up rather shakily, trying not to get too close to the edge as they pitched their first sheaves down to Jonas and Mr Spencer on the frame. Once again, as the farmer had warned them, there was a knack to be discovered. Pitch the sheaf wrong and you felt the rough edge of Jonas's tongue. Pitch it just right, and the two men could be kept busy, working rhythmically to arrange the bundles of corn neatly on the poles, rapidly building up the stack.

'At least it gets easier as we go,' Betty remarked, for the load was lessening in height all the time and the stack growing bigger. But it didn't stay easy for long. All too soon, they found themselves lower than Jonas and Mr Spencer, pitching upwards, and their arms and shoulders ached.

In the middle of the afternoon, Mrs Spencer came out with a jug of tea and then Jonas went back for afternoon milking. The girls and Dennis continued to work, with Dennis now back in place on top of the cart. They were out in the field, loading up the last few sheaves, when the siren sounded, and a few minutes later a dogfight began a mile or two away.

They looked at each other and hesitated. It was safe enough out here, surely? They'd heard of people being strafed by enemy aircraft, but these weren't interested in a few farmworkers down on the ground, they were too intent on shooting at each other, and saving their own lives. And then Yvonne gasped, grabbed Betty's arm and pointed.

One of the planes was out of control. It was spinning crazily and diving towards the earth – towards the very field in which they stood. Its engine screamed and little puffs of smoke were appearing in its sides. It was low enough to see the swastika painted on its wings, and above it, harrying it like dogs after a hare, were three RAF planes.

'It's going to crash,' Yvonne whispered as they stared.

The plane's engine stuttered, almost failed, then stuttered again. Betty could see the cockpit, see the movements of people inside it. She lifted both hands to her face, staring in horror. There was fire there – fire in the cockpit, where the people were. She saw the hood lift, saw a man struggling to climb out, saw the flames.

The horses were going wild. They reared in their harness, almost turning the cart over. Dennis rushed to their heads and began to unfasten the straps, shouting for help as he did so. Trembling with fear, Betty went to the other horse, terrified of his hooves as he plunged. His eyes were rolling with panic. She knew that if they were left in harness, they could easily kill themselves. Sobbing with frustration, she fumbled with buckles and collars, thankful when Dennis came round to her side and loosened the last strap. The horses bolted from between the shafts and galloped madly round the field, neighing with terror.

Overhead, the plane was still veering crazily about the sky, the three Spitfires still firing at it. She could see the rips in the sides as the bullets struck. The man who was trying to climb from the cockpit suddenly stopped and hung helpless, half in and half out. The plane's engines stuttered again, then suddenly appeared to come back to life, jerking the aircraft out of its downward spin so that for a few seconds it looked almost as if it might recover and level out of its twisting descent.

But it was too late. It was roaring towards them now, pursued by the Spitfires, and from close by they could hear the violent rattle of fire from the anti-aircraft gun emplacement. Almost mesmerised, they stood staring as the aircraft swooped across the fields, little higher than the hedgerows, with the crew clearly visible, their mouths wide open and their fists pounding at the hood of the cockpit.

'It's coming down!' Erica screamed, and they dived for cover under the haywain and crouched together on the rough, prickly stubble. Betty could feel Dennis's arms around her. She turned and buried her head against his chest.

The plane's engines had stopped. They could hear only the rush of air as it hurtled by directly overhead. Then a tremendous explosion blasted their eardrums, and the ground shook.

There was a moment's silence.

'He did crash, didn't he?' Yvonne whispered.

'It must be almost in the next field,' Dennis said. 'We'd better go and look.'

Betty's ears were still ringing. She didn't want Dennis to let her go. She looked up at him and he met her eyes. His own were grave.

'We'll have to go,' he said. 'The crew might be needing help.'

'They need capturing,' Erica said sharply. She crawled out from under the cart and brushed herself down. 'They're the enemy. They'll have to be handed over to the authorities.'

Dennis let go of Betty and they followed Erica. Yvonne too had scrambled out and was already halfway across the field. Beyond the hedge they could see the tail fin of the plane, sticking up into the air. Suddenly excited, they broke into a run. The stubble cracked and broke beneath their feet and Betty felt it scratch her legs. It was difficult to run on and she felt as if she were in a dream, urgently needing to get somewhere yet unable to make it.

'It's got the swastika on it,' she exclaimed as they reached the gate. They could see the machine now, a crumpled heap of broken wreckage strewn across the stubble of the corn they had gathered yesterday. Its back was broken, its tail torn away and its fuselage a mass of twisted metal. One of its wings was crumpled. The men inside were dragging back the hood. Only two of them were moving; the other still hung over the side, limp as a rag doll.

'Of course it has,' Erica said scathingly. 'It's a Jerry, isn't it?' She scrambled over the gate. 'I'd just like to get my hands on them—'

'No!' Dennis reached out and grabbed her arm. 'Don't go near it.'

'Why not? They won't shoot now. They'll be too scared—'

'Stay here,' he commanded, and at the note in his voice Erica stopped and stared. But Dennis had let go of her arm and was running towards the plane. The three girls started after him, but he turned his head and yelled at them again to stay where they were. They hesitated.

'Who does he think he is?' Erica demanded, obeying him nevertheless. 'Ordering us about like that.'

'He doesn't want us to get hurt.' Betty's hands were at her mouth again, watching as Dennis approached the aircraft.

'They're not doing anything. I bet they're injured,' Yvonne said suddenly. 'He's going to try and help them out.'

'He ought to leave them where they are.'

'That one who tried to get out – he looks as if he's dead.'

'Good thing too. The only good German's a dead German,' Erica said spitefully. But they're *people*, Betty thought.

She began to run forward again. Dennis was now almost there. And then, appalled, she saw its outlines blur in a haze of blue vapour. Before anyone could speak again, the whole plane seemed to shiver slightly, as if it were a mirage seen on a hot day, and then with a roar it was enveloped in a burst of orange flame.

'Oh, *no*.'

Yvonne turned away, her hands over her face, but Erica stared as if transfixed. Slowly, she lifted both fists to her mouth, biting on the knuckles. Her eyes widened and glittered, almost as if in elation.

Betty screamed and raced towards the flames, only to find their searing heat too much for her. She tripped and fell, screaming again as she felt them reach towards her as if eager to devour her too. Desperately, she clawed at the stubble, trying uselessly to get up, and then felt strong arms around her, lifting her to her feet and dragging her across the field.

'Get back,' Dennis said tersely. 'The whole of the field's going to be alight in a few minutes. This stubble's like tinder.'

She turned to him and said frantically, 'There are people in there. I saw them. We've got to help them.'

'We can't,' he said, still pulling her along. 'We'd never get near it.' And when she turned to look again, she knew that he was right. Even at this distance, the heat was scorching their faces. Dennis's skin was black with smoke, his eyebrows and hair singed. There was no possibility of rescue for the men they had seen staring out of the cockpit as the plane flew towards them.

'It's horrible,' she whispered. 'Horrible . . . There were men in there. I saw them move, Dennis, they were *alive*.'

'I know,' he said quietly. 'But they aren't now. And there was no chance of getting any of them out. It must have been over very quickly.'

They could hear shouts now, as other people ran across the fields towards the plane. Jonas and Mr Spencer came through the gate and stood beside them, staring.

'Bloody *'ell*,' the old man whispered. 'Bloody, bloody *'ell* . . .'

'There's nothing we can do,' Dennis said. 'It'll burn itself out pretty soon. And then I suppose the souvenir-hunters will be around.'

Jack Spencer nodded. He looked at the three girls, at Yvonne's white face, at Betty's tears, at Erica's glittering eyes.

'Well,' he said sharply, 'what are you all hanging about here for? The Army'll deal with this. We've got a harvest to be brought in. Let's get on with it, before some joker lands on a field full of stooks. We can't afford to lose the crop just because of Hitler.'

The girls stared at each other. Yvonne looked shocked. 'But someone's just been killed. Don't you *care*? There's men died in that plane – burnt to death. And you want us to just go back and stack corn as if – as if nothing had happened! Don't you have any feelings at all?'

Mr Spencer opened his mouth, but Jonas butted in first.

'Feelings? Those were bloody Jerries in that plane! They'd've bombed us flat without even thinking about it. Why should we 'ave feelings for that sort o' filth, eh?' He glowered at Yvonne. 'You want to be careful, saying things like that – people'll be taking you for a bloody fifth columnist, that's what. Like *'im!*' He jerked his head at Dennis, whose skin flushed under its layer of soot.

'That's enough!' Jack Spencer said quickly. 'Leave the girl alone, Jonas. She's upset, and no wonder. And you'd better watch your own tongue, too.' He turned back to Yvonne, and spoke more quietly. 'Of course I've got feelings, girl. I don't like seeing men burnt to death any more than you do. But like Dennis said, there's nothing more we can do. It's not going to help if we sit about crying over it. And stacking corn's important. You want your families to have food to eat, don't you?'

Yvonne bit her lip. Betty remembered Mrs Marsh saying that whatever Hitler threw at you, you just had to get on with it. And Uncle Frank saying that life had to go on as normal. There was still corn to be harvested, animals to be fed. She took Yvonne's arm and said gently, 'He's right. That's what we're here for. Land Army, remember – we're soldiers too!'

Yvonne's mouth trembled into a watery grin. She nodded, and let Betty lead her back through the gate. But they were silent as they walked across the field. And Betty glanced at Dennis and wondered what he was thinking.

Erica had said he was too frightened to fight. But he hadn't seemed frightened when the plane crashed, and he hadn't run the other way when they'd thought there might be Germans still alive in it. He'd gone to help. They might have turned the plane's guns on him as he ran across the field, they might have fired at him with pistols, but he'd still gone to help.

To *help* – not to fight.

One day, she thought, I'll ask him about this conscientious objector business. I'll ask him to explain why he feels like that and what it all means.

But for now, there were stooks to be loaded, cows to be milked and pigs to be fed. And no time at all for conversation.

10

'Derek Harker! Whatever are you doing here?'

Derek grinned a little self-consciously. With the rest of 698 Unit, he had been working on Salisbury Plain, building an aerodrome. He was in uniform, tanned and fit, and Ethel Glaister looked him up and down admiringly.

'Hello, Mrs Glaister. We've got a forty-eight-hour pass. I've come home for a bit more of my honeymoon.'

Ethel Glaister bridled, as if he had said something offensive. Maybe she'd forgotten what honeymoons were for, Derek thought with a private grin. Looking at poor old George, he wouldn't be a bit surprised.

'Honeymoon!' Ethel said. 'I wonder you haven't got better things to think of, with a war on. Does that mean my George is going to be home too?'

'That's right. He stopped at the newsagent's. Buying you a nice box of chocolates, I wouldn't wonder.' He winked.

'If he is, it'll be the first time,' Ethel retorted. 'And if he's getting them from that spy's wife I shan't take them anyway. I'd rather die!'

Derek stared at her. 'Spy's wife? Mrs Brunner? What d'you mean?'

'You know perfectly well what I mean. Heinrich Brunner was a German, an alien, he was interned. Speaks for itself, doesn't it? What I don't understand is why they never took Alice as well.'

Derek felt suddenly sickened. He looked at Ethel's carefully made-up face, at her permed hair and smart blue suit. He thought of George Glaister, more like a mouse than a man. It wasn't surprising he was so nervy, with a wife like this. No wonder he hadn't seemed all that thrilled when they'd got their leave passes.

'Well, I daresay he'll be pleased to see you,' he said uncertainly. 'And I know Olive'll be pleased to see me. So if you don't mind, Mrs Glaister, I'll be getting along – forty-eight hours isn't long, when you've only had two days' married life!'

He strode on quickly. It seemed a lifetime since he and Olive had got married, and he hadn't been able to get home since. Olive would be at his father's yard now, working in the office, and with any luck he could get the old man to let her off early. We'll have a spree tonight, he thought. Wonder if I can get her mum and dad to go out somewhere this evening.

Or maybe he'd take Olive out himself. There might be something good on at the flicks. At least they'd be able to sit and have a cuddle – spending the evening in polite conversation with his in-laws was not at all what he had in mind!

He turned the last familiar corner and went straight into the yard. The little office was there, looking the same as always, he'd had a brief fear that it might have been hit in a raid and no one told him, and he could see Olive inside, her head bent over her desk. He stood for a moment, gazing in at her.

Derek had had several girlfriends before he had started going out with Olive. They had known each other slightly since childhood, for the streets where they lived were only a few hundred yards apart, but they had not gone to school together. Derek had been sent to a primary school in the opposite direction and then to the boys' Grammar School. He had stayed at school until he was sixteen and then gone to work for an accountant. His friends had moved in a different social circle from Olive, and although he was aware of the pretty, chestnut-haired girl from the bottom of March Street, it wasn't until they both went to the same church dance that he'd ever spoken to her.

From then on, they had spent every spare moment together and when the war had broken out had wanted desperately to get married. But Ted Chapman didn't approve of girls marrying before they were twenty-one, and it had taken Dunkirk to change his mind.

Unable to wait any longer, Derek pushed open the office door. Olive turned, and stared at him. For a moment there was total silence, and then she leapt to her feet, knocking over a pile of invoices, and flung her arms around him. He held her close against his rough khaki tunic, hardly able to believe that she was in his arms again at last, and bent his head to kiss her. He could taste the salt of tears on his tongue, and laughed shakily.

'What are you crying for? Aren't you pleased to see me?'

'Pleased? Oh, Derek – Derek!' She clung to him, lifting her face to his, half crying, half laughing. 'Why didn't you say you were coming? Why didn't you let me know? Oh Derek, *Derek.*'

'Ssh, ssh.' He stroked her back, disconcerted to find that his own eyes were wet. There was a lump in his throat and his lips were quivering. Surely he couldn't be going to cry. He'd hardly cried at all since he was a kid. 'Livvy, I've missed you so much.'

'Oh, Derek, it's been awful without you. Hearing about the raids, never knowing if they were getting through to you. They've been going for the airfields, haven't they? Every day I've woken up and thought, have they bombed my Derek? I couldn't bear it if anything happened to you, I just couldn't bear it . . .' She was crying now, the tears pouring down her cheeks. 'Derek, don't go away again.'

'I'll have to, Livvy. You know that. I'll have to go.' He held her away from him and looked down into her eyes, forcing a tremulous smile to his face. 'But not till the day after tomorrow. I've got forty-eight hours, Livvy, two days. And *two nights,*' he whispered wickedly, making her laugh through her tears. 'So let's make the most of it, eh? And not think about the war at all.'

Olive laughed and sniffed. She felt in her pockets and Derek took out a large handkerchief and mopped her face with it.

'Forget the war!' she said. 'Chance'd be a fine thing, with the siren going off two or three times a day. Still, at least it's mostly in daylight, they don't seem to come over at night much. Frightened of being seen in the searchlights and shot down.'

They heard footsteps running across the yard and Florrie Harker burst in. She threw herself into Derek's arms.

'I couldn't believe it, I couldn't believe it was really you, but Fred Stokes just came in, he said he'd seen you walking up the street. Oh, Derek, why didn't you let us know? I'd have got something special in for supper. And your room's all untidy, it's all piled up with wedding presents and stuff. And what I'm going to give you for your breakfast, I can't think, we haven't seen bacon for weeks and as for eggs—'

'You don't have to give me anything for breakfast, Mum,' Derek said gently. 'I'll be staying with Olive, won't I?' He kissed her. 'Remember, we arranged that we'd be stopping with her parents until all this is over?'

Florrie stared at him. 'Well, yes, of course Olive's stopping with her mum and dad. But when you're home—'

'You don't expect me to say goodnight to Livvy and come back here to sleep, do you?' he said with a grin. 'We're married now. And we've got a double bed at her house.'

His mother looked flustered. 'Well, you'll be in for supper, though, won't you? You'll let us see something of you. And I know Auntie Jane and Uncle Bill will want to come round once they know you're home.'

Derek glanced at Olive. There was a querulous note in Florrie's voice. He thought of his plans for the evening, indoors alone together, if it could be managed, or else at the pictures. Not a family supper, with relatives popping in and out and everyone wanting to know what Army life was like. And there was Olive's family too, they'd want him there part of the time.

Olive said firmly, 'That's kind of you, Mrs – Mum' – she stumbled over the word, still embarrassed by having to call Mrs Harker by the intimate title – 'but I'll be cooking Derek's supper myself tonight. My mum and dad are going out for the evening, to see Charlie Kunz and Elsie and Doris Waters at the Hippodrome, so we'll be able to have the place to ourselves.' She smiled at Derek. 'That's if you'd like that.'

'Need you ask!' he said, grinning, and then turned back to his mother. 'You don't really mind, do you, Mum? Tell you what – we'll have a bit of a do tomorrow night. Ask Auntie Jane and Uncle Bill, and anyone else you want. And maybe Olive's mum and dad can come up too. We'll have a proper party before I have to go back again.'

'Mock Duck, it's called,' Olive said. 'Mum says it's just meatloaf. But the butcher's got nothing in but sausages today, so it's all I can do for tonight. And there's Mock Apricot Flan for afters. It's carrots really, but they look like apricots and they do taste like them, a bit.' She gave him a wry smile.

'It's all pretend, isn't it? Mock this and mock that, it's like playing make-believe when I was a kid.'

'It'll be grand,' Derek said. 'Anyway, I don't want you spending all your time cooking.' He came behind her as she stood at the kitchen table, and slipped his arms around her waist. 'How long's it going to take?'

Olive spooned the mixture of sausage-meat, onion, breadcrumbs and herbs into a loaf tin and pressed it down. 'An hour in the oven. And I've already put in two big potatoes.' She turned into his arms and stood with her eyes closed while he kissed her. 'Oh, Derek . . .'

'So we've got an hour to ourselves while we wait for it to cook?' He moved his hands over her body. 'Let's go upstairs.'

'Derek! It's only six o'clock.'

'So what? I've got two nights, Livvy, that's all. And God knows when I'll get home again.' His hands were urgent now. 'And your mum and dad'll be back – what time's the show finish?'

'Well, it must finish around eight, there's another show at twenty-five past. But I heard Dad say they might go for a drink afterwards. That's if old Hitler lets us off!' The warnings were continuing to sound, sometimes several times in a day, although Portsmouth had had no major raids since Monday. People were learning to live with the 'music' playing so often in their ears. They ran for shelter when the siren's wail rose, but came out again and got on with whatever they had been doing as soon as the Raiders Passed sounded. And even Annie had been persuaded to go to the theatre when she heard that 'Gert and Daisy' were appearing.

'They're her favourites,' Olive said. 'Uncle Frank wanted to go – he thinks they're really funny – but the baby's got a cold and Auntie Jess didn't want to leave her. I told her I'd look after her, but she was a bit worried it might be a fever.'

'Well, I'm glad you didn't,' Derek declared. 'The only baby I want you looking after when I'm at home is ours.' There was a sudden silence and they looked at each other uncertainly.

'Our baby?' Olive said. 'D'you really mean that, Derek? D'you want us to have a baby?'

'I don't know,' he said slowly. 'I've never thought much about it. I mean, we've only been married a couple of months – and we've only had two nights together out of that. And what with the war, and not having our own place, and everything . . .'

'It'd be daft,' Olive said, her voice trembling a little. She stood within the circle of his arms, holding him close. 'It'd be really daft. But, oh Derek, to have our own little baby, to have something of you while you were away. We'd be a family. Our own proper family.'

Derek's eyes darkened as he looked down into her face. A baby, he thought. Our baby. Ours.

Olive, pregnant with our baby.

'Let's go upstairs,' he said with a sudden roughness in his tone. 'Oh, Livvy, I've waited so long to make love to you. Don't make me wait any longer, please . . .'

Derek's leave was short-lived. He was recalled the next day and on 7 September, a year and four days since war had been declared, the full fury of the Luftwaffe was unleashed on London. The East End lay helpless beneath a deluge of high explosive and incendiary bombs, and the sky was lurid with the fires that raged through the docks. In that one raid, nearly five hundred people died and three times as many were injured. It was almost impossible to count the homeless.

Even the Thames was alight as rum, sugar and paint from bonded warehouses drifted on the water and caught fire. Hundreds of people had to be evacuated, some through streets where buildings threatened to collapse on them at any moment, others by boat down the blazing river. And the blitz was not soon over, as the earlier raids had been. Instead, a thousand aircraft droned overhead, wave after wave of them. And as night fell and the city burned, they came again, bombarding people who had barely begun to put out the fires of their first attack.

In Portsmouth, people listened to the news each day and shuddered. It was clear that London was the main target now but nevertheless, the fact that Portsmouth lay on one of the Luftwaffe's flight paths to the capital, and was the home of one of the nation's most important dockyards, brought the sound of the siren several times a day and disrupted the daily lives of even the most phlegmatic.

The raids were now taking place at night as much as during the day, and families would sometimes find themselves incarcerated in their shelters for the entire night. For hours they sat on benches or lay on bunks, perhaps with only the dim flicker of a paraffin lamp to give them comfort, often in pitch darkness. Occasionally, during a lull, a brave – and desperate – soul would dash up the garden to go to the lavatory or even into the house to make some cocoa. And outside, the planes could be heard roaming overhead, and every few minutes the harsh rattle of anti-aircraft fire would break out as they were spotted in the beam of the searchlights which swept the sky.

'Night after night,' Annie said to Jess. 'I don't know how we can stand it. I'm so tired, I can hardly stand up, but the shopping's still got to be done and Ted must have his dinner.' She looked at the dish she was about to place in the oven. 'Toad in the hole we're having today, but it's more hole than toad. I managed to get a few sausages from Mr Hines, but they're poor things, disappear to nothing when you put them in the pan. And you can't make much of a batter when you have to treat eggs as if they came off the Crown Jewels.'

'How are Ted's nerves these days?' Jess too looked exhausted. Frank had to leave home at six each morning for work, and although they tried to sleep in the shelter there was little rest to be had with the roar of planes in their ears. In any case, he was usually on duty as a firewatcher too, which meant standing outside the shelter looking out for incendiaries. Jess hated to think of him out there, exposed to danger, but she knew that someone had to do these jobs, and Frank had said more than once that he felt guilty at not going to fight. He had to do his bit.

'Poor Ted,' Annie said, shaking her head. 'He looks like a man who's walking in Hell. To be quite honest, I don't know how he's going to get through. It's the blackout, you see, he just hates taking the ferryboat over in the pitch dark. And with bombs likely to drop on the harbour at any time, I don't blame him. But what can I do? I can't skipper the boat for him.'

Jess sighed. 'It's awful. It's like the whole world's gone mad. Look at what's happening to those poor souls in London. There's whole streets bombed to bits, and some of those big shops in Oxford Street are completely burnt out.'

'I don't know how they can put up with it.' Annie drew off four cupfuls of water and poured it into the kettle. Ted had worked out that she could save a shillingsworth of gas a week just by doing that. 'They're going down into the Underground stations to sleep.'

'I know. It must be terrible, never knowing what you're going to come out to in the morning.'

'Still, we're giving as good as we get,' Annie declared. 'Our boys have been over to Germany, giving them a taste of what it's like too. That might make them think twice.'

It might have done, but there was little sign of it. The blitz continued unabated, and other cities were attacked as well. Merseyside and South Wales were badly hit, and bombs fell on Buckingham Palace itself. It was said that Mr Churchill wanted the King and Queen to leave the country, or at least to move out of London, but they refused and it was reported that the Queen herself had commented that she was glad that the Palace had been bombed because 'now I can look the East End in the face'.

Portsmouth was not left undisturbed. One evening, after the Raiders Passed signal, a solitary bomber scored a direct hit on a house not many streets away from April Grove, killing a couple who had just returned to bed. Jess and Frank looked at each other, appalled, when they heard the news.

'But they ought to have been safe,' Jess kept saying, though she knew that it meant nothing. 'The all clear had gone. They ought to have been all right. It's not *fair*.'

Frank didn't bother to tell her that this was war and you couldn't expect fairness any more. She knew that as well as he did. But you couldn't just jettison all your old values in the way that the Germans jettisoned their bombs. You had to cling to something when the world was going mad.

'Thank God we're all right, anyway,' he said, holding her against his broad chest. 'And thank God the children are safe out at Bridge End.'

But that was another worry. Edna Corner had written to say that she didn't think she could look after the boys for much longer, as she wasn't at all well.

'What are we going to do?' Jess asked. 'I'd ask Mrs Greenberry, so they could be with Rose, but I know she's got another family billeted on her now. Oh, it's such a pity, the Corners are good to the boys and they love being there.'

'Well, they can stay there a few more weeks,' Frank said. 'Edna says they're welcome until Reg has to go. And she might be feeling a bit better then herself.'

'Yes.' But Jess was unconvinced. Morning sickness might wear off after the first few weeks but there were plenty of other inconveniences to take its place. Perhaps she ought to go out to Bridge End herself and see if she could find somewhere for Tim and Keith to stay. She didn't want them billeted somewhere where they'd be unhappy – better to have them back home than that, bombs or no bombs.

Tim and Keith received the news that they might have to move with equanimity. They enjoyed living with the Corners, but since life had not yet dealt them any harsh knocks they did not expect them. It had been an adventure coming to Bridge End, and it would be another adventure to go somewhere else. Maybe they'd stay on the farm itself next time and be able to put all their new skills to good use.

'Edna says she's having a baby,' Keith said as they walked across the field to the schoolroom which they shared, turn and turn about, with the local children. 'D'you think it's true? She hasn't got fat.'

'I expect she will. It's not going to be until next May, so there's plenty of time.'

'May?' Keith echoed. 'But that's next year! Does it take *that* long to grow a baby?'

Tim shrugged. 'S'pose it must.' The two boys had learned about babies soon after their sister Maureen had been born. The procedure of getting them had seemed far-fetched and unlikely then, but during the past year they had seen cows being serviced by the bull, and rams with the ewes, and Edna had called them early one morning to come downstairs and see Tibby having kittens by the kitchen fire, so they had come to the conclusion that it was probably true.

'I wonder how many Edna will have,' Keith remarked. 'Tibby had six.'

'Don't be daft. People don't have kittens. And they only have one.'

'Sometimes they have more,' Keith argued. 'There's twins. And triplets. And – and—' he searched his mind for the word '—squads. I bet they could have six if they wanted.'

'Well, I bet they couldn't.' Tim was bored with the subject. He began to run across the grass, his arms held out sideways. 'Yaaaaaaarh! You're a German plane and I'm a Spitfire coming to fight you off. Whee! Whee! Yaaaaaarh! I've shot you down, you'll have to bale out or you'll get burned alive.'

'That's not fair! You didn't give me a chance.' Keith zoomed after him, and they zig-zagged across the field, making nasal noises of aircraft engines, gunfire and explosions. By the time they reached the hedge, they had forgotten all about Edna Corner and her baby, and were totally caught up in their own version of the battle that was going on over their heads each day. They clambered over the stile and tumbled into the lane almost at the feet of the Woddis sisters.

Miss Millicent and Miss Eleanor glanced at them with disgust and walked round them. The hairs growing from the mole on Miss Eleanor's chin quivered dangerously and the two boys pressed themselves against the hedge almost as if they were hoping to become invisible.

'Coo,' Tim breathed when the two elderly ladies had passed. 'That was a near thing. They could've caught us easy.'

'D'you think it's true? About them eating evacuees?' Keith whispered nervously.

'Nah. They didn't eat Wendy and Alan, did they? They didn't even fatten them up.' But Tim's voice was less sure than he would have liked. There was something funny about Wendy and Alan Atkinson and the time they'd spent with the Woddis sisters. Something his mother and Edna knew about but wouldn't tell them. And he remembered the day he and Keith had gone to the house, when the snow was deep on the ground, and seen what they thought was a ghost at the window.

The feeling of terror that had gripped them that day had never quite departed and since then the brothers had taken care not to go down the narrow little lane where the tall, thin Victorian house stood isolated. And although Tim was *fairly* sure that the evacuee-eating story was no more than a myth, he wasn't prepared to take chances. Nothing was quite the same these days, after all. If people could start wars and make happy, cheerful men like Reg Corner go off and kill people, how were you to know what else might be true?

'Yaaaaaaaarh!' he screeched suddenly, and zoomed away down the lane, arms outspread once more. 'I'm a Spitfire. You can't catch me. *Nobody* can catch a Spitfire!' And he turned suddenly and dived at Keith, his head down and a rapid gunfire spattering from his lips. 'Bi-bi-bi-bi-bi-bi-bi-bip! I've got you. You're dead.'

'I'm not. I baled out.' Keith was a quick learner. 'I'm in the sea and you've got to rescue me. You've got to take me prisoner.'

Tim made a face. Taking prisoners was no fun at all. He wanted a dogfight, with aircraft swooping through the sky, guns blazing and parachutes opening like flowers overhead. He shrugged and turned away. It was time for school.

Erica Jones did not see much of her airman fiancé during the Battle of Britain. Although Tangmere was near enough for him to be able to visit her, the war gave him little time off, and when the airfield was bombed and almost destroyed he was moved to another a little further away.

'I hate not knowing when I'm going to see him again,' Erica grumbled. It was a Sunday afternoon, and she was lounging on an old blanket flung on the grass with a magazine open on her knee. Betty and Yvonne were up ladders picking a few plums and early apples for Mrs Spencer.

'None of us know when we're going to see our chaps again,' Betty said a little sharply. 'My boy's in the Navy, somewhere at sea, I don't suppose he'll be back for months. At least your Geoff's in England, he can pop over when he's got a few hours off.'

'That's just it, he doesn't *get* time off. They're on standby all the time. They have to fly at a moment's notice. And when they are off-duty they're so exhausted all they can do is sleep.'

Betty shrugged. She still found Erica difficult to get along with, although the three girls had settled down to an uneasy kind of friendship. You had to, living as close as they did. But Erica always seemed to have the idea she was special, somehow. As if what was all right for other people didn't apply to her.

For a while, they were silent. The only sounds were the quacking of Mrs Spencer's ducks on the pond and the clucking of a few hens in the orchard. A soft breeze rustled the leaves. There had been just a touch of autumn in the air that morning, but now the sun was hot again and Erica moved her blanket into the shade.

'Do you realise,' Betty observed, succumbing to the temptation of a ripe Victoria plum, 'there hasn't been a single plane over today? It's just like peacetime.'

'Perhaps it's all over,' Yvonne said. 'Perhaps we've won and they haven't told us yet.' She climbed down her ladder, shifted it and climbed up again. 'Maybe by this time next week we'll all be home again. Not that I'm in any hurry,' she added, thinking of Rudmore Alley. 'I like it here.'

The sound of an engine came from along the narrow lane leading to the farm. Dennis and Mr Spencer were bringing in the cows for milking, and they heard a few indignant moos as the approaching vehicle was brought to a halt. Erica glanced up without much interest.

'What's going on?'

'Dunno.' Betty craned round a branch to see. 'Looks like a sports car. It's full of men – pilots, I should think, they're all wearing flying helmets. I say, d'you suppose—'

'*Pilots*?' Erica was on her feet. 'It's Geoffrey, it must be. Oh good heavens, I look such a sight! He mustn't see me like this. Oh, what shall I do? What shall I *do*?'

'Go in through the back door,' Yvonne said. 'We'll keep them here. But don't take too long making yourself beautiful, they might only have a few hours.' She watched Erica's hasty departure and giggled. 'Wonder what she'll do to herself? She looked all right to me as she was.'

'Oh, she'll dress herself up like a doll.' Betty climbed down her ladder. The cows were now pushing their way into the milking shed, and the little green open sports car was standing in the yard. Three young men were leaping out without bothering to open the doors, each wearing a sheepskin jacket and flying helmet. They looked about them, grinning, and the tallest one accosted Dennis.

'Hey! Have you got a Land Girl called Erica Jones working here?'

Dennis nodded. 'She's about somewhere. Probably over in the orchard.' He waved across the yard to the gate where Betty and Yvonne were standing, then turned to urge the last cow into the shed. The young man looked at the girls and grinned again. He took off his flying helmet and Betty saw that he had thick fair hair and very blue eyes.

'Well, your luck's in, boys. Erica told me there were two other girls here but she never said they were beauties. I like the dungarees!' He strolled across the yard, followed by his two friends. 'I'm Geoff Martin. Is Erica around?'

'She – er – just popped indoors for a minute.' Yvonne returned his look frankly. 'I'm Yvonne and this is Betty. We came at the same time as Erica.'

'Yvonne and Betty, eh? Well, Yvonne and Betty, I've brought you a boyfriend for the afternoon. Thought we'd go for a jaunt round the lanes, didn't we, lads? These two characters are idiots but the best I could rustle up. The short one with a nose like a frog is called Duff and the ginger twerp is Sandy. They'll behave themselves as long as we tie their hands behind their backs.' He took a long look around the farmyard and orchard. 'So this is where she's doing her muck-spreading is it? Well, I never thought she'd stick it.'

'Nor did we,' Betty muttered to Yvonne. Aloud, she said, 'Erica says you'll be getting married soon.'

Geoff shrugged. 'When this lot's over. I'd say next week, but she wants a big wedding and we can't fix it with old Hitler liable to send his guests to the reception. I must say it'd be a lot easier to have her nearer the station. We could get married quarters.'

'That'd be a loss to the mess,' the ginger-headed airman commented. He gave Betty a grin and said, 'Geoff's our star performer.' He had rather a nice grin, she thought. And even more freckles than she had herself.

Betty smiled doubtfully, not sure what he meant. Was Geoff an actor or singer, or something? But before she could ask Erica emerged from the farmhouse door and the three men turned and whistled in unison.

'Wowee! You're a lucky chap, Geoff.'

'So this is what the smart dairymaid's wearing in 1940!'

'Doesn't the skirt get caught up in the machinery?'

Erica gave the other two a withering look and swept up to Geoff, holding out her arms. She looked like Ginger Rogers, about to dance with Fred Astaire, Betty thought. She was wearing a white dress with a heart-shaped neckline and tight, fitted bodice, billowing out from the waist in a full, swirling skirt. Her golden hair was pulled back into a pleat at the nape of her neck, and she had smudged blue shadow on her eyelids and smeared Vaseline on her lashes. Her lips were painted bright red.

'Talk about a glamour queen,' Yvonne whispered. 'She looks like Gloria Swanson.'

'After a bad night,' Betty giggled, but she felt envious of Erica all the same. To have a frock like that and the figure and looks to go with it! She pulled discontentedly at her own short curls and found Sandy watching her.

'You'll come with us, won't you?' he said. 'We know a little tea-place about fifteen miles away from here. We thought we'd have a run out. It's not often we get the chance nowadays.'

Betty looked down at her dungarees. 'We haven't got anything to wear. We've only got our working things and a few other bits and pieces. Nothing posh like Erica's.'

He laughed. 'You don't have to look posh. Actually, I think you look very nice as you are. I like girls in slacks and things. Anyway, there's only room for one frock like that in Geoff's old crate.'

'Yes, come on,' Duff joined in. 'We'll need a bit of company to take our minds of these two canoodling!'

Geoff looked up. His face was now liberally daubed with Erica's lipstick and Betty felt half embarrassed, half envious. Fancy being bold enough to kiss her young man like that, in full view of everyone. Well, full view of herself and Yvonne and twenty cows, anyway. She thought of Graham and felt suddenly lonely. What would he say if he knew she was going out with airmen?

Yvonne saw her hesitation. 'Come on, Bet. It's only a run in a car and a cup of tea. You're not being asked to spend a weekend in Paris.'

'Chance'd be a fine thing,' Sandy laughed. 'Not that I'd fancy a weekend there myself just now. But who knows, when the war's over . . .?' He gave Betty a friendly smile and crooked his arm. 'Come on, you sit with me and we'll leave your friend – Yvonne, is it? – to fight off Duff's advances. You'll have to watch him, mind,' he warned Yvonne. 'Last girl he took to the pictures said it was like going out with an octopus. He might be only five foot nothing, but he's got a good reach!'

They crammed themselves into the little car. Erica sat in the front with Geoffrey and the other four scrambled into the back. Betty found herself beside Sandy, while Duff and Yvonne perched on the top of the seat behind them. There was a good deal of laughter and squeals from the girls, and Betty decided to take Yvonne's advice and enjoy herself. After all, what was the point of moping around by yourself when you could have some fun? And they deserved it, didn't they? They'd worked hard enough on the farm all week.

The little tea-shop was in a pretty village in Sussex. It was part of a flint-built house and had tables set out in a pleasant garden, with a tiny pond. Betty and Yvonne crouched down to exclaim over the goldfish that swam amongst the waterlilies and Erica draped herself gracefully on a garden seat beneath a cherry tree. A waitress in a gingham dress took their orders for tea and sandwiches.

'Plenty of 'em,' Geoffrey demanded. 'And a plate of cakes. And scones with lots of jam. I suppose you haven't got any cream?' he asked with an appealing smile.

The waitress shook her head and went back into the house, and Betty looked around at the peaceful scene.

'You wouldn't think there was a war on, would you? They don't seem to know a thing about it here.'

'Well, it's not on the flight-path, you see. They'd take either a western or an eastern route from here.' Sandy stretched and yawned. 'It's good to have a few hours off.'

Betty looked at him. All the way here, the young airmen had been laughing and joking, but they looked as tired as small boys who have stayed up too late. Their eyes were smudged with fatigue and there were lines that ought not to be on such young faces.

'What's it like?' she asked. 'Flying a plane. Fighting in the sky.'

'Oh, it's wizard fun. There's nothing to beat flying, is there, chaps?' The others shook their heads and suddenly they were all talking together, describing their exploits in the air.

'Bandits everywhere,' Geoff said, waving his hands. 'They just came out of a clear blue sky. No warning at all.'

'That was the day old Snowy came back with half his wing dropping off. He was livid. He loved that crate, darned near took it to bed with him.'

Geoff nodded, still intent on his own tale. 'There was nothing in sight, I was absolutely alone up there, and suddenly I saw it, a vicious-looking brute with a black swastika on its tail. Well, I knew then it was going to be him or me, and I was sure as hell not going to let it be me. Of course, he tried to get behind me, but I wasn't having that, I stalled and dropped below him so that I was behind, and then I started firing. He didn't know what to do. Must've been his first time out, I reckon. Pranged in a field somewhere near Brighton.'

'Was he killed?' Betty asked, and he laughed.

'What do you think? Look, you don't have to feel sorry for 'em. It's us or them. One of our chaps, a gunner he was, was caught in ack-ack over Belgium. The plane caught fire, he knew it could blow up any second, went for his 'chute and found that in flames too. The whole caboodle was ablaze, and all his ammo was going off as well. What could he do?'

'What did he do?' Betty asked, her imagination showing her the young airman, trying desperately to save his life in a blazing aeroplane while anti-aircraft guns fired from below.

'Chucked it all overboard, of course. There was a crew of four, two of them had already baled out. The pilot was still aboard and this gunner managed to get the fire out and the plane limped home. Both pretty badly burned, of course. They say he's in line for a VC. Not bad for a kid of eighteen.'

Eighteen years old! Younger than me, Betty thought. She looked at the three faces again. 'How old are you?'

Geoff grinned. 'Oh, we're ancient. I'm twenty-three, Duff here's twenty-one – got the key of the door last week, didn't you, old man? – and Sandy's the baby. He's nineteen.'

'That's not ancient,' Betty said.

'It is in our line of business,' Geoff replied, and there was a sudden uneasy silence.

Sandy stirred abruptly. 'Where the hell's our tea got to?' He jumped up and went towards the house. His uniform looked too big for him, as if he'd got thinner since it had been issued. The girl in gingham came out, carrying a large tray, and he took it from her and carried it back to the table.

'How about that, then? A teapot they must have pinched from the NAAFI, enough sandwiches to feed an army and a dirty great pile of rock cakes. *And* scones, and a pot of real live strawberry jam. I told you this was a wizard place to come.'

They spread the feast out on the table and fell to with much noisy laughter. How did the café manage to provide such a tea? Betty wondered. But it was true that in the country there didn't seem to be the shortages there were in towns, even though stocks were supposed to be shared fairly round everyone. Still, you could get food off-ration in restaurants and teashops, and if you could have a tea like this every day – or even once a week – it would certainly help the rations go round the rest of the time.

The girl came out three times to replenish their teapot, bringing them more milk and a fresh plate of scones and cakes as well. Betty looked at her face to thank her and glimpsed a strange expression as she gazed at the airmen. A mixture of pain and pity, as if she could see further than the sunny afternoon, into a darkness that lay beyond. She caught Betty's eye and her mouth twisted a little as she turned hurriedly away.

The noisy banter went on, with Yvonne joining in with gusto. But Erica sat silent, her slender body in the white dress pressed close against Geoffrey's side. And for the first time Betty felt some compassion for the girl.

We're all in this together, after all, she thought. And it's as bad for her, saying goodbye to her chap, even though he's only stationed a few miles away, as it is for me seeing Graham off to his ship. And all that daft talk of babies and big weddings doesn't mean she doesn't love him just as much.

She got up to go into the teashop and find a lavatory. The waitress met her at the door. She looked older than Betty had first thought her, about twenty-seven or twenty-eight, perhaps. She nodded her head towards the noisy group on the lawn.

'It's awful, isn't it? They're just kids. They come here a lot, them and their pals, some of 'em haven't even started to shave . . . And then there's a raid and next day there's one or two missing. They never come again. And you know what the rest say if you ask?'

Betty shook her head.

'They say "Old Buster? Oh, he bought it last night." Or he "copped a packet", or "pranged", or something like that. And then one of 'em'll make a joke and they all roar with laughter and never mention his name again.' She looked at Betty, her eyes bright with tears. 'It's not that they don't care. It's that they can't let themselves care. Otherwise it'd break 'em up. And they wouldn't be able to fly. They're all tired out as it is. They're seeing their mates die all around them, all the time. They just wouldn't be able to take it.'

Betty stared at her, appalled. Like everyone else, she had known the facts, known that pilots were being killed. She had never wondered what it was like for those who remained alive, who knew that their chances of being next were greater every time they took to the skies.

'That's why we give 'em a good tea,' the girl said. 'You never know but what it might be their last.'

Their last. Betty came slowly out of the teashop. She looked at the little tableau across the lawn, the table set under the cherry tree, the three young men still laughing and joking around it. Geoffrey was sitting back on the garden seat, his arm around Erica, smoking a cigarette. Duff had shifted his chair closer to Yvonne's and was playing with her hand. Sandy was lying on his back on the grass, his arms behind his head, gazing up into the sky. The sky that was so strangely peaceful today, but which could at any moment turn into a bedlam of fury and killing.

I don't understand it, Betty thought. And she remembered Dennis, the strange young man who had turned his back on the fighting and refused to go to war. Maybe he can explain, she thought. Maybe he's the one who can help me.

11

Jess and Peggy Shaw had been in the habit of sharing an afternoon cup of tea together, often with Annie as well. Now they included Kathy Simmons in their little group. They were over at Kathy's one afternoon when they heard a knock on the door.

Kathy heaved herself to her feet and went to answer it. Jess heard her give a cry, almost a scream, and ran to see what was the matter.

'Mike! *Mike*! Oh God, tell me it's you, tell me it's really you, tell me it's not a dream!'

'It's not a dream. It's really me.' He was holding her in his arms, a tall, rather skinny man with straight brown hair and blue eyes. His face had a rubbery look about it, as if he could pull it into any shape he wanted, and as he caught sight of Jess over his wife's shoulder he twisted his mouth into a grin that must have been meant to be comical, but instead brought the tears to Jess's eyes. 'I had to ask my way to find out where I lived,' he said wryly. 'Last time I looked, it was in Portchester Road.'

'Oh, Mike,' Kathy said again. She drew herself away slightly and laughed a little self-consciously. 'This is Jess Budd, from April Grove. She just came in for a bit of a chat. Her sister and Mrs Shaw are here too.'

He nodded, but his eyes were already on Kathy again and Jess knew she and the others must make themselves scarce. They gathered together their bags of knitting and sewing and slipped out of the room and through the front door. It had closed before they were on the pavement.

Inside, Kathy and Mike Simmons were once again in each other's arms. Kathy was trembling, the tears streaming down her face, and Mike held her close, comforting her.

'It was so awful,' she wept. 'Hearing the bombs, *knowing* they were falling on our house – knowing there'd be nothing left when we came out. And there wasn't, not a thing. And our Muriel's baby doll, the one you brought back for her – oh, Mike, its face, its poor little face!'

'There,' he said softly, moving his hands over her back. 'There, it's all right now, Kathy love. It's over. It's been over a long time.'

But for Kathy, it had not been over. Unable to share her experience, having no one she could talk it over with, and having to keep a bright face for the children, she had bottled it all up inside her. Every night she had relived it, until there were times when she had thought she was going mad. And whenever the sirens sounded, the terror slid down her spine once more, sending her scurrying for the shelter where she would crouch with Stella and Muriel close in her arms, praying that the same thing would not happen again.

'Why don't you go out to the country?' Mike asked as he ate the supper she cooked for him. Her first storm of weeping over, she had pulled herself together and made rissoles from a recipe she had heard on the *Kitchen Front* programme on the wireless. There were just enough potatoes, if she didn't have any herself, and a tin of peas. There was no pudding, but Mike declared himself quite satisfied with bread and margarine and a tiny pot of blackberry and apple jam.

'Jess Budd gave it to me. She makes it. It was nice of her, wasn't it, when you think how scarce sugar is now.'

'It's good jam.' He spread it thinly on his bread. The girls, having come in full of excitement to find their father at home, had gone out to play again, with strict instructions not to go beyond the end of the street and to come back at once if the warning sounded. 'I still think you ought to be out in the country.'

'But I want to be here for you. In any case, I thought you didn't believe in it.'

'I've changed my mind.' He looked at her seriously. 'This war's not going to be over quick, Kathy. I've seen some of it, and it isn't pretty. I'd rather you and the girls were out of it.'

'I've seen it too,' she said obstinately. 'But where would you have gone tonight if I hadn't been here? What would you have done?'

'I'd have stayed aboard ship, like I do other times.' He pushed his plate aside and took her hands in his. 'Kathy, I went and had a look at Portchester Road. They've patched it up a bit now, but I could see what it must've been like. And our house, there's nothing left of it, Kath.'

'I know,' she said, her voice trembling. 'I know.'

He came round the table and put his arms around her shoulders. 'I can't stop thinking of you and the kids in there,' he said. 'Having to manage by yourself and look after them and everything. And what about when the baby comes?' He laid his hand on her stomach and felt the kicking of unborn feet, the punch of unborn fists. 'That's three of them you've got to get down the shelter in the middle of the night. What sort of a life is that? And suppose you get bombed out again?'

'We'd have to move again, I suppose.' She shrugged, then collapsed against him. 'Oh, Mike, I know you're right, I know we ought to go away. Every time the siren goes it's like a knife slicing through me. And I'm scared stiff the girls will be out in the street and won't be able to get back. There was a woman strafed in the street the other day, just going home with her shopping she was, and a plane came right down low and fired a machine-gun at her. In the street! If they did that to our girls . . . But I just can't face it, somehow. Going away, living with strangers. And you know I'm scared of cows!'

Mike burst out laughing. 'Cows? You're scared of *cows*?' But there was more pain than mirth in his laughter. 'Kathy, if that's what it'd take to make you move I'll write to Hitler personally and ask him to send cows instead of bombs.' He held her against him again. 'Let's get the washing-up done now, love, and talk about it again later on. I want to have a bit of time with the girls.'

As he spoke, the air-raid warning sounded for the third time that day, and Kathy flew to the door to call the children from their game. Mike got his wish to spend some time with the girls, for they were in the shelter for the rest of the night after that, not coming out until after the All-Clear at six in the morning. But there was no more time to talk, for by eight he had to be back on board his ship and although Kathy waited all the next evening in the hope that he would be able to come ashore, he never arrived. The ship had sailed, and there was no knowing when she would see him again.

She touched her swollen stomach. By the time Mike came home, the baby might be born. Might be sitting up, walking, talking. Might be out at work, earning a living, she thought bitterly, and cursed the madman over the Channel who had taken her husband away from her.

She thought again about asking to be evacuated. If only Mike had been home a bit longer, if only he could have helped her, she might have agreed to go. But now that she was on her own again, she knew that she had spoken the truth. She really couldn't face it.

And still they came. That one day of peace, when no bombers approached the south coast, when no air-raid warnings sounded, when Betty and Yvonne and Erica spent the afternoon having tea on a sunny lawn, proved to be no more than a flicker of bright light; a brief, teasing reminder of what life could be, and once had been. The next day the raiders returned in force and continued their bombardment of the city of London, paying attention to other towns and cities while they did so. The sound of the sirens became commonplace and while some people remained terrified, others began to develop a defiant, almost blasé attitude towards them. Peggy and Bert Shaw, playing whist with their daughters, finished the hand before gathering up their belongings to run down the garden to the shelter. Jess's mother Mary refused to budge until she had completed a row of her knitting. 'You never pick it up at the same tension again,' she said when Arthur urged her to hurry. And Granny Kinch flatly refused to go to the shelter at all. 'I'm too old to go gallivanting at night,' she told Tommy Vickers with a wink. 'I leave that to the younger ones.'

'Like your Nancy,' he said, and then wished he could bite his tongue. Who was to say Nancy Baxter wasn't doing a service to the young soldiers and sailors who were facing death every day? He thought of Graham Philpotts, desperate to know what sex was like before he went to sea, and of Graham's sweetheart Betty, too 'respectable' and too inhibited to share it with him. Well, you couldn't blame the girl, but neither could you blame Graham for going home with Nancy, as Tommy was certain he had. What else could a young feller do?

Granny Kinch said nothing. She knew Tommy of old, and she wasn't going to apologise to him for what her Nancy did. Of all the people in April Grove, he was the only one who might understand and make allowances.

After all, he'd been in the Navy, he must have met other Nancies in his time, yes and made use of them too. He knew what their lives were like, even if he didn't know what drove them to it.

The old woman turned and hobbled back indoors. Nancy was making a cup of tea, a cigarette hanging from her lip. She had the baby Vera balanced on one hip, grizzling.

'This hot weather plays hell with my feet,' Granny Kinch said, sinking into her sagging armchair. 'Look 'ow swollen my ankles are. And there's flea-bites all up my legs. It's that cat of yours, mangy thing, it must be riddled with vermin.'

'Go on, Ma, we always has fleas in summer.'

'Only because of your cat. It ain't healthy, Nance, having it around with a baby just starting to crawl. You don't know what she's putting in her mouth. There was a dead mouse under the chair for days last week, she could've ate it any time.'

'What, our Vera?' Nancy gave a short laugh. 'It's hard enough getting her dinner down her, let alone dead mice. She wouldn't eat a Christmas dinner if she found it on the floor.'

Granny Kinch sniffed and said nothing. Nancy passed her a cup of tea and she sucked at it.

'Where's young Micky?'

'I dunno. Out somewhere. He's bin running errands for people for a bit of pocket-money.'

'Is that where this come from?' Mrs Kinch picked up a china ashtray. It had a picture of a beach on it and the words 'A Present from Brighton' printed round the edge. 'Run as far as Brighton, did 'e?'

'Oh, that's just something someone give him. Didn't have no money, see, so they give him that instead.' Nancy glanced out of the back window. 'Here he comes now. Looks as if he's got a bag full of groceries.'

Micky came in, swaggering. He dumped a large paper bag on the table and tipped it over. Several tins of fruit rolled out and his mother and grandmother stared at them in astonishment.

'That's peaches!' Granny Kinch said. 'I ain't seen a tin of peaches in a year. Where d'you get those, Micky?'

He shrugged and grinned. 'That's for me to know.'

'Micky!' Nancy said sharply. 'Don't cheek your gran. Tell us where you got the peaches. Runnin' errands, were you?'

'That's right.' He glanced at them sideways. 'Got meself a job. Errand boy at a shop. The boss said I could take whatever I liked.'

'He said you could take *peaches*?'

'Yeah. Whatever I like, I can 'ave.' He struck a nonchalant pose. 'He'll pay me too.'

'What shop's this?' Nancy asked suspiciously. 'Is it far away?' Nobody around September Street was likely to employ Micky.

'Down past Kingston Cross. You wouldn't know it.' He stood the tins upright, balancing them in a tower. 'I can go down there whenever I like. An' I got another job too, choppin' wood for a bloke down Charlotte Street. He gives me fruit an' stuff. I can get all sorts.'

He turned away and they heard him clatter up the stairs. Nancy and her mother looked at each other.

'I s'pose it's all right,' Granny Kinch said. 'So long as he gets in a shelter when the siren goes.'

'Oh, he always does that. I made him promise.'

They looked at the tins again.

'Peaches . . .' Granny Kinch said.

Micky had his little gang well organised now. As soon as the siren sounded, they were out in the back alleys, keeping a wary eye open for air-raid wardens, watching to see people run for their shelters. Nine times out of ten the back door was left open and the boys could slip inside, grab whatever was left lying about, and be gone before the Raiders Passed signal.

You had to be careful, of course – sometimes there was someone left in the house, someone too slow or stubborn to run down the garden. Jimmy Cross once had the fright of his life when he nipped through a back door and suddenly caught sight of a pair of eyes watching him as he rifled through a sideboard drawer. 'I thought it was just a pile of old clothes,' he said indignantly to the others, 'an' it was this old bloke, all huddled up in blankets and stuff. He never said a word, just looked at me, like he was a ghost or something. Didn't 'alf make me jump.'

'Too old to take down the shelter, I s'pose,' Micky said. He sorted through the day's collection. 'We got some good stuff here. Cyril found this wallet with nearly three pound in it, and Jimmy got a pot of jam and a bag of sausages, and I got this.' He held up his own booty with pride and the other boys whistled.

'Cor! A model Spitfire. That's smashing.'

'Someone's made it, see.' Micky set the aeroplane on a box they were using as a table. It was about two feet long, made from wood which had been smoothed and polished, and its wings were made of parchment. 'I bet it was a real pilot made that,' he said, touching it lovingly. 'You can see it's a proper one.'

Making model aeroplanes was a craze amongst all the boys. Comics like *Wizard* and *Beano* carried instructions almost every week, and nearly everyone had a cat's cradle of cotton and string festooned across their bedroom ceilings, with aircraft arranged as if in flight.

This one had not been made by any boy, though. It was clear, as Micky said, that an adult hand had fashioned the wood and shaped the wings; an adult who knew aeroplanes, too. The boys gazed at it with awe.

'That's our best thing.'

'It's my best thing,' Micky corrected them, pushing away their hands. 'I found it.'

'I thought we were going to share everything we found.'

'Stuff like food and money, yeah. But not this. Unless you want me to cut it up into bits?' He picked it up again and held it on his lap, stroking the polished wood. 'Here, how about making a fire and cooking those sausages? I could do with summat to eat.'

Willingly, the other two boys set about gathering wood from the debris which still littered the bombed house. They lit the fire in the middle of the basement floor – they had already tried using the fireplaces, but found the chimneys blocked – and cooked the sausages on an old tin coal shovel they had found. They were burnt on the outside and raw halfway through, but to the boys they were the best sausages they had ever eaten.

'We could live in a place like this,' Micky said, stretching back on his broken chair. 'When the Germans come, we'll hide down here and creep out at night and sabotage 'em. We could murder 'em and they'd never know who it was.'

Replete with half-raw sausages, they sat in the dank gloom of the ruined basement, gazing at the model aeroplane and contemplating a future filled with adventure and excitement. Micky's mind drifted back to the days before the war, days when he had been expected to go to school every day and sit at a desk, bored and frustrated.

'It's good, this war is,' he said with satisfaction. 'I 'ope it goes on for ever 'n' ever.'

In London, people were changing their entire day in order to accommodate the timetable of Goering's bombers.

Shops and offices closed an hour earlier to allow workers to reach home in time for a meal before taking to the shelters. There was no need for a warning – everyone was in place by eight o'clock, women with their bags full of knitting and magazines, men with their newspapers and pipes. After some efforts to prevent it, the Underground stations were now an accepted place of shelter. There was quite a party atmosphere down there, it was reported, with singing and dancing, and even a few impromptu bands composed of mouth organs, concertinas and, if all else failed, the good old comb and lavatory-paper.

The daily newspapers carried pictures of devastation. Huge piles of rubble were all that were left of the great Oxford Street stores, wrecked houses stood open to the sky, vast craters swallowed entire streets. Shops had their stocks burned or ruined by water, and people who were suffering the deprivation of rationing were galled to see molten butter flooding from a storehouse and running down the drains, or precious sugar burning like coal.

There was another rush for safety. Children who had come home from the country during the 'phoney war' were sent back again. True to her word, Ethel Glaister sent her daughter Shirley to Canada, going to Southampton to see her off on a big liner.

In Portsmouth, people found themselves spending long hours in their air-raid shelters. And even worse than the frustration and annoyance of such disruption and wasted time, they found themselves more and more often returning to their homes to find that they had been looted. The newspapers were full of such cases; even a few policemen were found guilty.

'It's kids that's the worst, though,' Frank said, sitting at the table with the *Evening News* spread out in front of him. 'And I bet I know who's one of the ringleaders. Probation! A young hooligan like Micky Baxter's not going to take notice of probation.'

'You don't know it's him, Frank.' Jess took the paper from him and studied it. 'You shouldn't paint people black without knowing the truth.'

'Paint him black! I don't need to – he already is black.'

'We haven't heard he's been in any trouble since that business with the jeweller's shop. Perhaps he's learnt his lesson.' Her eyes moved down the columns. 'Oh, listen to this. One little boy told the magistrate he'd got no school to go to and no friends to play with. "I just took things to play with," he said. "I thought the people weren't coming back." Poor little chap.' She laid the paper down. 'He was just lonely. And frightened too, I daresay.'

But Frank looked stern and shook his head. 'Stealing's stealing. If they don't make an example of boys like him, all the little scamps'll be at it. People have got enough to put up with, without having to reckon with burglars every time the warning goes.'

A sudden violent knocking at the door startled them both. Jess gasped and reached down to pull the baby on to her lap. She looked wide-eyed at Frank.

'D'you think it's them?' The fear of invasion was a menace in everyone's minds. Already there had been reports of German landings at Stokes Bay and other south coast beaches. Nobody knew if it was true that hundreds had been killed, or if it was just rumour, but every unexpected knock on the door brought the same thrill of terror as the wail of the siren. 'Oh, Frank . . .'

'Of course it's not. They wouldn't knock.' But he went down the passage and opened the door with some caution before he looked out.

Ethel Glaister stood there, her cheeks running with tears. Before he could speak, she was in his arms, her face pressed against his shirt. She clutched him, sobbing, and he staggered slightly then held her, patting her shoulder and looking round for Jess.

'What's the matter?' Jess was at the end of the passage, staring at them. 'Who is it?'

'It's Ethel, Mrs Glaister.' He gestured helplessly. 'She's upset. You'd better come in,' he said to the weeping woman. 'Tell us what's happened. Is it George?'

Ethel shook her head. Even in her distress, she managed to convey the impression that she wouldn't have been in this state if it had just been George . . . She sank down on a chair at the table and leaned her head on her hands. Her weeping was almost hysterical.

Jess pushed Frank aside. She viewed Ethel Glaister's woe with concern but she wasn't going to have the woman weeping in Frank's arms. She put her hand on Ethel's shoulder and spoke gently.

'What is it, Ethel? What's happened? Try to tell us.'

'It's Shirley. Our Shirl.' Ethel broke into a fresh gust of sobs. 'Oh, I shouldn't never have done it, I shouldn't never have sent her off . . .'

'Shirley? But she's gone to Canada, she's gone to be safe. What's happened to her?'

Ethel raised her head. Her face distorted like a child's. The make-up she habitually wore was streaked and blotchy. Her eyes were puffed with tears.

'Safe!' she echoed bitterly. 'Safe! They've only torpedoed the bloody ship, that's all. Torpedoed a ship loaded with kids. I mean, what good does that do them, eh? Why should they do a thing like that? Little children!'

Jess and Frank stared at her.

'They've torpedoed the ship? Are you sure?'

'It was on the wireless,' she said drearily. 'They reckon there's hardly any survivors.'

'Oh, *Ethel*,' Jess said, and put her arms around Ethel's shoulders, drawing her close. 'Ethel, that's terrible. I really am sorry.'

Frank stood hesitantly beside her. He was as appalled as Jess, but had no words to express his horror. He caught Jess's eye and realised she wanted him to make Ethel a cup of tea. Thankful to have something to do, he hurried out to the scullery and put the kettle on.

Little Shirley Glaister! She was such a sunny little thing, always smiling and skipping on the garden path. She used to talk to him when he was out in the garden, chattering away nineteen to the dozen, telling him what she'd been doing at school and asking endless questions. What are you doing, Mr Budd? Why? Why is the sky blue, why is grass green, why, why, why?

It made his head buzz at times but he liked her questions. He thought they showed a bright little mind. And now that little mind had been snuffed out, the bright smile wiped away for ever, the chatter silenced.

He went back with three cups of tea. After a shock like that, they could all do with one. He looked at Jess, still standing with her arms around Ethel, and he knew that there was no need to search for the right words, for there were none. At times like this, there was nothing that anyone could say.

The report of the torpedoing reached the newspapers a day or so later. Jess went into the newsagent's and looked at the headlines with Alice Brunner.

'Poor little mite,' Alice Brunner said. 'I don't wish her any harm, she was a nice enough little scrap. But maybe that cat of a mother of hers has got some idea now of what I've been going through all these months.'

'Oh, Alice.' Jess hated to hear the bitterness in her friend's voice. But she couldn't blame Alice. She had suffered more than enough from the cruel remarks made by Ethel at the outbreak of war, when she had called Heinrich an enemy and a spy and tried to prevent customers from using the Brunners' shop. And she had still not heard officially whether Heinrich had died when the *Arandora Star* had been sunk. That, too, had been on the way to Canada.

'We don't even know for sure that Shirley was on that ship,' she said. 'It doesn't give its name here. I suppose they want to let the families know before they read about it in the paper. But you're bound to think it's that one, aren't you?'

'I don't know why she ever wanted to send the child that far away,' Alice observed. 'She's got relations in Devon, hasn't she? She was always on about them and talking about her holidays with them. Why not send the kiddy there? She just wanted to be better than the rest of us, that's what it was. Wanted something to be stuck up about.'

Jess didn't answer. She was growing more and more worried about Alice these days. There was a brittle nervousness about her, a sense that she was hovering on the brink of disaster. She's going to break up completely if something isn't done, Jess thought, gazing at the white face with its flushed cheeks and over-bright eyes. But what could anyone do? It was Heinrich she needed.

'I don't think it does any good to say that sort of thing,' she said at last. 'It's help Ethel needs now. There can't be anything worse than losing a child.'

Alice turned away and started to mark up the pile of evening papers. Joy came in from the back room to help her and they worked in silence for a few minutes. Jess, seeing that Alice didn't want to talk any more, picked up her own paper and went out.

'What difference does it make anyway?' Alice burst out suddenly. 'I mean, I'm sorry for little Shirley Glaister, of course I am, but it don't make any difference whether you're a little child or a grown man when you've been torpedoed. The water was just as cold for your father as it was for Shirley Glaister. It was just as bad for him, floating in hundreds of feet of water, knowing nobody was going to save him. It's as bad for everyone that gets killed.'

Joy gazed at her. 'Mum . . .'

'Everyone tells me to be brave. Everyone says we don't know for certain he's been killed, he could still turn up, stranger things have happened. D'you know something, Joy? I wish we *did* know for certain. I'd rather – I'd rather know he's been drowned than go through this – not knowing, wondering every day whether I might get a telegram, whether he might even walk through the door.' She dropped her pencil on the heap of papers and burst into tears. 'I just can't stand much more of it! I can't *stand* it . . .'

'Mum,' Joy repeated helplessly, but Alice pushed past her and ran through the door to the back room. A moment later, Joy heard her feet on the stairs.

She stood for a moment, struggling with her own tears. A few dropped on to the newspapers and smudged the print.

Alice would not come downstairs again that day, she knew. She would lie on her bed and Joy would hear her sobbing. She would refuse anything to eat and if Joy took her a cup of tea it was as likely to go cold as to be drunk. And there didn't seem to be anything anyone could do for her.

And meanwhile there would be people coming in for their papers, the delivery boys would want their satchels filled and the shop would have to be kept open until six o'clock.

Joy brushed her hand across her eyes and picked up the pencil.

12

'I wonder that Dennis has got the nerve to show his face when my Geoffrey comes here,' Erica said one day after they had waved the little sports car down the lane. 'I don't know how he can stand there, knowing they're risking their lives to save his yellow skin.'

'It's not easy being a CO,' Betty said. 'He's had to go to prison, you know.'

'Good thing too. Pity they ever let him out.'

The atmosphere on the farm was strained. Mr and Mrs Spencer had accepted Dennis for what he was, and provided he did his job well took the view that his principles were none of their business. Yvonne treated him, as she did everyone, with casual friendliness. But Erica made no secret of her contempt and loathing, and Mrs Spencer's sister Iris, who was married to an army captain, sided with Erica and did her best to pretend that Dennis did not exist.

'He's smarmy,' she said. 'He knows when he's well off! It's all wrong, employing men like him when there's good patriotic farmworkers being called up.'

'We've got to get the work done,' Mrs Spencer said mildly. 'Dennis is a good worker.'

'Conchie-petting!' Iris Blake said disgustedly. 'Do you know, they get *paid* when they go for their interview? *And* get a luncheon for three-and-six. I read it in the paper. And then they get a nice soft life on a farm when my husband and Erica's fiancé are risking their lives fighting for their country.' She gave her brother-in-law a defiant look. 'There's plenty of farmers who'd refuse to take 'em.'

'Look,' Mr Spencer said with some force, 'I'm not a politician, I don't know the rights and wrongs of all this, I'm just a farmer trying to do my job. I'm producing food for my country, which I love just as much as anyone else, and I'll take what labour I can get to help me do it. Aye, prisoners of war if it comes to it. Why not? And Ada's right, Dennis is a good worker and he's no trouble about the place. As far as I'm concerned, his reasons are his own affair.'

'They ought to be ours as well—'

'No!' Mr Spencer thumped his fist on the table. 'The man's been to a tribunal, he's been to prison. He's proved himself, and that's good enough for me. I thought this country believed in free speech. I thought that was

399

what this war was all about, letting people live the way they want to live and believe the things they want to believe. And that's the way it'll be on this farm and in this house.' He glowered at his sister-in-law. 'And anyone who doesn't like that can always find themselves somewhere else to live.'

The two stared at each other and then Iris Blake got up and flounced out of the room. There was a small, embarrassed pause and then Mr Spencer glanced at his wife.

'I'm sorry, Ada, but it had to be said. We can't have her making trouble. You know what she's like once she takes against someone.'

'Oh, I know. Our Iris always did set herself a cut above the rest of us. But this is our place, and if she wants to sit at our table she has to put up with our ways.'

'And that goes for us too,' Yvonne said later, as the three girls walked across the yard to the milking shed. 'No more snide remarks about Dennis, see, Erica? Mr and Mrs Spencer don't like it.'

Erica tossed her head.

'I'll say what I like. Free speech counts all ways. And I think Mrs Blake's right – he is smarmy.'

However, there was little time for the situation to develop any further, for there was more than enough work to do and the girls found themselves up at six every morning in order to get it all finished during the diminishing hours of daylight. By the evening, they were usually too exhausted to do anything other than flop on the sagging sofas in the untidy living-room, or on their beds in the narrow attic.

'I'm growing out of all my clothes,' Betty wailed one day as she went through her chest of drawers. She had been home for the weekend to collect her winter skirts and jumpers. 'Everything's too tight.'

'Mine too,' Yvonne said. 'My mum says I'm getting fat, but I don't see how we can be, working the way we do.'

'It's muscle. We're getting stronger, that's what it is.'

Erica gave a shriek. '*Muscle*? But I don't want to get muscles. Girls don't have muscles.'

'Land Girls do,' Betty said, and rolled up her sleeve to look at her arm. It was smooth and firm. 'I couldn't have lifted a bale of hay when we came here and now I can shift 'em all day without noticing. I don't mind getting strong, if it makes the work easier.' She looked out of the attic window. Autumn was beginning to tint the trees with red and brown, and the recently harvested fields were a carpet of golden stubble. The cows were grazing peacefully and she could see Dennis walking across one of the meadows to look at the sheep.

What was he thinking? He was always friendly and good-humoured, but mostly fairly quiet, keeping his thoughts to himself. He must know what people like Erica and Mrs Blake thought of him. Did he care?

She thought of the day the aeroplane had crashed. He hadn't behaved like a coward then. But neither had he shown any hatred for the German pilot and crew. It seemed that, to him, they were just people. Young men like himself, caught up in someone else's war.

The sky was a soft haze, half blue and half gold, fading towards a pearly horizon. A creamy mist drifted between the trees. And as she watched she saw, appearing out of a glow of apricot, a formation of aircraft flying steadily north from the coast.

'Look,' she whispered, and the other two girls came over and knelt beside her, staring out.

'They're Jerries,' Yvonne said in a low voice. 'They're heading for London.'

The planes came nearer. Their shapes were clearly discernible now. They were like a menacing cloud in the golden sky, like a dark cloak which grew larger with every second and would soon be thrown over the shimmering landscape.

'Oh, no . . .' Betty breathed. 'Oh, no . . .'

The planes were almost overhead. Dennis, walking in the meadow, was standing quite still, watching them. The cows were restless, showing signs of alarm, tossing their heads and flicking their tails. The sheep had huddled together, bleating. And then, from high in the sky, there was a sudden swoop of smaller aircraft, like wasps buzzing around the relentless advance, and the girls saw the spattering of the guns and the little bursts of fire, only seconds before they heard the sounds.

In another moment the formation had broken up and the battle was on. The girls ran downstairs and out into the yard, ignoring all the advice they had ever been given to find places of safety while such fights were taking place. They stood staring up at the turmoil, watching the Spitfires dart like mosquitoes around the marauders, watching the more ponderous Hurricanes as they marked their victim and went in for the kill.

Betty lifted her hand to her mouth, biting her knuckles. She saw the flash of fire as one of the German planes was hit. For a second or two it seemed to hesitate, hanging in the sky, and then the flames burst all around it, enveloping it in a brilliant sheet of orange light and thick, billowing black smoke as it spiralled towards the earth.

Betty gasped and shut her eyes tightly. When she opened them again, the plane had gone, but there were others filling the space where it had been, RAF and Luftwaffe all mixed up together, swooping and darting about the sky, the air streaked with flame as more aircraft were hit, some to follow the first to earth, others to lurch away in an effort to escape. And, here and there, the white puffing umbrella of a parachute as the airmen baled out.

Yvonne screamed and turned to clutch Betty's arm and bury her head in her shoulder. They clung together, staring at the sky, half crying, half laughing as the planes of the RAF finally routed the invaders, and sent them scattering and making for the coast from where they had come.

'Hurray!' Erica cried, leaping up and down in her dungarees. 'That gave 'em what for! That taught 'em a lesson! They won't come over here again in a hurry.' She caught Betty's hands and danced her round the yard. 'I bet that was my Geoffrey up there. I bet he scored some hits. He sent them home with a flea in their ears!'

Betty laughed with her, but there was a feeling of unease in her heart. Some of those planes had been shot down, and some of them had been

British planes. Suppose Geoff's had been one of them? So far he seemed to have led a charmed life, but how long could anyone's luck last?

She saw Dennis come into the yard. His face was sober, his eyes veiled. He looked at the dancing girls, and for a moment she thought he was about to say something. And then he seemed to change his mind. He walked slowly past, without speaking, and went into the house.

Betty felt a sudden chill, as if another shadow had passed across the sky. She withdrew her hands from Erica's and moved away. Suddenly, laughter and dancing seemed out of place.

They were sitting round the table in the farmhouse kitchen having their meal later that evening when they heard the sound of the little car buzzing down the lane like a bee. Erica jumped up, her eyes alight. She ran out into the yard, but when she returned a few moments later the light had died from her eyes and she looked pale and frightened.

'It's Duff and Sandy,' she said, and then stopped as if her voice had stuck. She opened her mouth but nothing emerged but a queer strangling sound. She reached out blindly and gripped the back of a chair.

'They – they say—' She shook her head, and tried again. 'They—'

Betty stared at her. Her face was paper-white, her blue eyes enormous. Her whole body was quivering.

The two young men were standing miserably behind her. Betty sought Sandy's eyes but they were downcast. She felt horror brush cold across her skin and spread like a chill web over her body.

Mrs Spencer came swiftly to her feet. She put her hand on Erica's arm and looked at the two airmen.

'Geoff?' All the questions that needed to be asked were in that one syllable. Betty wanted to turn her head away; she didn't want to hear the answer. But her eyes were riveted on Erica's white face.

'Was Geoff – is he –?' She couldn't bring herself to say the words. She shook her own head and tried again. 'Sandy?'

'His plane was shot down this afternoon,' Sandy said in a dull, flat voice. 'I saw it go. He didn't bale out.'

Erica's knees buckled suddenly. Her tears burst from her in great sobs and she collapsed against the chair. Sandy caught her in his arms and held her against him, then carried her through to the sofa in the living room. He laid her down and knelt beside her, stroking her hair. The others followed, Mrs Spencer settling the cushions around her and covering her with a crochet rug, Mr Spencer going straight to the cupboard where he kept a small stock of bottles. Betty and Yvonne knelt beside Sandy, stroking Erica's hands, and Duff hovered uneasily in the background. Even the Blake children were momentarily silenced, their mother's mouth a thin bitter line, while Dennis stood grim-faced beside the door.

'Here, girl, sip this.' Mr Spencer poured some brandy into a glass and held it to Erica's lips. She turned her head away. 'Come on, it'll do you good. You've had a bad shock.'

Erica sipped and coughed. 'I don't want it.'

'Another sip. Come on.'

'I don't want it, I tell you. I want Geoff – my Geoff.' She stared up at them. Her eyes were like black pits in her white face. 'Get my Geoff for me. Get him! I want him, I want him *now*!'

Mrs Spencer spoke soothingly, her voice dry with pity. 'Oh, my poor lamb, we can't get Geoff for you. He – he's—'

'He's *not*!' she cried before Mrs Spencer could utter the dreadful words. 'He's not, he's not. He can't be. He's my Geoff. It's all a horrible lie, it's a joke.' She turned her desperate eyes on the other two young airmen. 'That's what it is, isn't it? It's a joke. You've cooked it up between you, the three of you, and Geoff's outside now. He'll come in any minute and tell me it's all a joke. He *will*.' She paused, staring from face to face while they all gazed unhappily back at her, not knowing what to say. 'He will, won't he?' she whispered, and her voice sounded very thin and small and lonely in the silent room.

'Oh, Erica,' Betty said, and pushed past Sandy to pull the other girl against her. 'Oh, poor, poor Erica.'

Geoff, shot down. Geoff, killed. Was it his plane they had seen, spiralling towards the earth with smoke and flame billowing from the cockpit? Had they actually seen Geoff's last moments, had he looked down and seen them, staring up towards him, known that they were there?

Her own tears were flowing fast now. They ran down her cheeks and into Erica's hair. The fair girl felt their wetness against her neck and drew back her head.

'You're crying,' she said in a tone of surprise, and then her sobs began again, sobs of fury as well as grief, a wild and useless raging against the war that had taken her Geoff away.

At the back of the room, Iris Blake turned on Dennis, her face contorted with fury. 'Well, I just hope you're satisfied!' she blazed. 'I just hope you're enjoying yourself, watching this poor girl suffer. It ought to have been *you* up there today, getting killed. It ought to be you, giving your life to save your country. Why should you and your yellow friends be allowed to stay safe at home in the country, when better men are getting blown to pieces? What's so bloody marvellous about *you* that you get let off? Prison! You ought to have been kept there for the rest of your life. If I had my way, you'd be *shot*!'

There was a moment's silence. Erica was still sobbing. Betty knelt beside her, holding her close, sharing her tears, but at Mrs Blake's words she lifted her head.

Jack Spencer moved forwards.

'Now look, Iris—'

'Oh yes,' she retorted, 'you'll take his part, won't you. You'll stand up for him. And you with two sons of your own away fighting, risking their lives. I don't know how you can, Jack, I really don't, no, nor you, Ada. Don't you care? Doesn't it mean a thing to you, what they're going through? And this girl, her young man's been shot out of the sky, burnt to death as like as not and crying for his mother – I don't know how you can give this lily-livered milksop house-room. You ought to turn him out this minute.'

'I've told you before, Iris—'

Dennis stepped forwards. 'No. Don't argue with her, Mr Spencer. She's got a right to her opinion.' He turned to Mrs Blake. 'I know you can't understand. Not many people can. But believe me, it's not because I'm a coward that I won't fight. It's not because I'm afraid.' He paused for a moment. 'Or maybe it is. Because I *am* afraid. I'm afraid of having to do what some German did to Geoff this afternoon. I'm afraid to have to shoot another man out of the sky. I'm afraid of having to kill people I don't know and have no reason to hate. I'm even afraid of killing people I do hate. Because to me, that's the worst possible thing I could do. Because I don't believe another man's life is mine to take.' He paused again. His face was pale and there was a strange fervour in his eyes, a passion taut in his voice. 'If it came to a straight choice between doing that and being shot, I'd choose to be shot.'

He turned and walked quietly out of the room. But Betty had seen the set of his shoulders. She knew that he was deeply upset.

Erica was still weeping. Betty tightened her arms about her, rocking her gently as if she were a small child. She felt Erica's pain mingle with Dennis's passion in her own body, and her mind reeled with the confusion of it all.

Iris Blake looked around at the shocked faces. She tilted her chin in defiance.

'Excuses!' she said scornfully. 'Just nothing but excuses!'

13

The city of London exploded and burned about its inhabitants' ears. There was no doubt now that the war would not be easily won. There was doubt that it might be won at all.

'Why don't we just give in?' Kathy Simmons said miserably. She crossed her arms over her bulging stomach, as if to keep her growing baby safe. Jess remembered feeling the same when she had been expecting Maureen. But a baby wasn't any safer inside its mother than out. A mother's body was as likely to be blown up as a baby's . . . 'Why don't we just let him come and take over? We could just go back to living normal, without all this killing.'

'Could we?' It was tempting to think so, but Frank said that people who thought that way didn't realise what life would be like under Hitler. They'd already forgotten what he'd done to the Jews. Making them wear yellow stars, not letting them do decent jobs, forcing them to live like rats . . . And there had been those horrible stories about camps like Auschwitz, reported in the papers last year. And the terrible things that had happened in Poland . . . Would he let anyone live a normal life?

'We can't give up now,' she said. 'We're in it too deep.' She looked compassionately at Kathy. 'I suppose there's no chance of your husband getting home?'

'Not this side of heaven.' Kathy flinched. 'I didn't mean that! It didn't come out the way I meant. I just meant, it'll be heaven when he *does* come home, not—'

'I know. It's all right.' It was all too easy to make a casual remark and then realise what it sounded like. 'Look, you know you can come over to Frank and me any time you want anything, don't you? Day or night, it doesn't matter.' She thought of Kathy in her air-raid shelter at night, alone with two little girls. Suppose the baby started to come then? 'If you want to be with us at night anyway, when the time comes – well, you know you're welcome.'

Kathy shook her head. 'There's not room, is there? These little dugouts aren't meant to have parties in. I'll be all right. I don't have babies quick anyway, the girls both took over twelve hours. But I'll be glad of your help just to give an eye to them while I'm laid up.'

Laid up! Why, she wouldn't even be able to go to the shelter after the birth. She ought to be in hospital, Jess thought, where she can be properly looked after.

'Haven't you got any relations? Isn't there anyone you can go to?'

'Not a soul,' Kathy said with a cheerfulness that didn't fool Jess for a minute. 'I'm not a Pompey girl, you see. Mike and me, we both come from Basingstoke. My mum and dad died when I was a kiddy, I was brought up by my gran. She's over ninety now and lives with my aunty, and she hasn't got room for me as well, anyway, we never did get on very well. And Mike's mum's in a home. She don't hardly know what time of day it is.'

Jess gazed at her. How lonely it sounded. She thought of her own family, of her sister Annie who lived at the end of the street and whose family had been in and out of Jess's house ever since they'd moved to April Grove. And Frank's brother Howard, over in Gosport. She and Annie still had their mum and dad, living down North End, and she and Frank had their own four children, close as a family could be even though the war had parted them for the time being. She felt a sudden savage longing for them. Families shouldn't be apart, she thought. They ought to be together, no matter what . . .

'You come over to us any time you like,' she said warmly. 'And I'll come over and stop with you when the baby's born, if you want me to. I know our Annie'll say the same – and Peggy Shaw, and half a dozen other women round here. We won't let you be on your own.'

She went up the street, pushing Maureen's pram. *We won't let you be on your own.* But Kathy Simmons *was* on her own, wasn't she? And so were thousands more like her, young wives and mothers left to manage by themselves, with no idea when their men might be back again. And more and more of them, as time went on, having to manage for the rest of their lives, as widows.

She went into the butcher's shop. There was little enough on the slab these days, but Mr Hines was a kindly man and often had a few sausages or a bit of liver for her. He'd taken a fancy to Maureen too, and liked Jess to take the toddler into the shop with her. Jess lifted her from the pram and let her stagger in on her own legs.

'Well, if it isn't my best girl!' The butcher wiped his big red hands down his blue striped apron and bent to pick Maureen up. He was wearing his straw hat and the baby reached up and grabbed it. 'D'you want my hat, then?' He took it off and plonked it on Maureen's head. It came down over her eyes and she gurgled with laughter.

He stood Maureen on the counter and leaned across to Jess. His face was serious. 'Are you popping in to see Alice Brunner today?'

'I always do. She's been looking worse than ever lately.'

He nodded. 'The wife's proper worried about her. Seems to be losing her grip on things. It's young Joy does all the work there now. Gets up early, marks up the papers, sorts out the paper-boys. Same again in the evenings. And keeps the shop going too. It's not right for a young girl.'

'Joy's a good girl though,' Jess said uneasily. 'She's always been a help.'

'Yes, but to run the place more or less single-handed . . . She's not fourteen yet, you know, she ought to be at school by rights. And she needs her mum to be a mum to her, not lay about all day feeling sorry for herself.'

Jess sighed. It was easy enough to say that Alice ought to pull herself together, but who knew what it felt like to have had your husband torn away from you, thrust into prison and then sent overseas all because he was an 'alien' – even though he'd lived in England almost all his adult life? And worst of all, to hear that his ship had been torpedoed and not even to know whether he was dead or alive . . . Some days, Alice had told Jess, she was certain he was dead. Other times she was equally sure he was alive. And for much of the time, she could only torment herself by wondering.

'I don't know what we can do,' she said miserably. 'Except keep popping in, let her know she's got friends all around who'll help her.'

'Well, she's got those all right,' Mr Hines said warmly. 'Trouble is, she's also got a few of the other sort. Naming no names.'

He didn't need to. Both of them knew that Ethel Glaister was one of the most vociferous of Alice's enemies, never averse to making loud remarks about Germans and aliens in her hearing. Both Jess and Peggy Shaw had had sharp words with Ethel over that, but you couldn't stop spite and Ethel wasn't the only one.

'Well, I'll go in and see her,' she said. 'Come on, Maureen, say goodbye to Larry and give Mr Hines his hat back.'

Maureen had crawled along to the end of the counter, where Mr Hines kept his model lamb. It was life-size and made of *papier-mâché*, and it had been fashioned as if it were in mid-leap, with a comical expression on its face. Maureen loved it and Mr Hines had named it Larry especially for her.

'She's a cheery little soul,' Mr Hines said, giving her a smacking kiss as he handed her back over the counter. 'Keeps us all happy with her sunny smile.'

'She don't know a thing about the war, that's why,' Jess said. 'Thinks it's all a game, going down the shelter at night. Well, it's just as well. It's nice to have someone around who still thinks life's wonderful.'

She took Maureen outside and held her for a moment before putting her back into the pram. Just let's hope it goes on being good for you, she thought. Just so long as nothing happens to you. I couldn't bear it if anything happened to you.

Alice Brunner lay in bed, staring at the net curtain over the window. Her bedroom was over the shop and she could hear the sounds of the street outside, the clop-clop of the baker's horse, the rattle of the little electric milk-float. There were voices and footsteps too as folk did their shopping, and she could hear the chirpy voice of little Maureen Budd calling goodbye to Mr Hines.

That meant Jess was in the street and would be coming into the shop. She'd be asking after her, wondering why Joy was on her own at this time of day. And she'd probably been talking to Mr Hines already, discussing how she left Joy to do nearly all the work these days. Letting the girl get up at crack of dawn – after a night in the shelter, as likely as not – to heave great bundles of newspapers about and sort them all out for delivery. It wasn't right. She knew that. But she just couldn't face it.

She turned over, her face to the wall. Footsteps were coming up the stairs now, not Joy's quick, light tread, but heavier ones, coming more slowly.

And the sound of scrambling which meant that a small child was coming too, heaving herself up step by step.

The door opened and Jess poked her head round it. Alice looked up at her, half ashamed, half defiant but without the energy to express either.

'There you are,' Jess said, as if she thought Alice might have climbed out of the window. 'Well, what's the matter?'

'What d'you think's the matter?' Alice's voice was bitter. Wasn't it enough that she'd lost Heinrich, her rock? Did there have to be something else the matter as well? 'I just felt like a lie-in, that's all.'

'On a weekday?' Lie-ins were unheard of in the Budd home. Even on Sundays she and Frank were up before eight, and *that* was a lie-in, for him. 'Alice—'

'I know what you're going to say. What about Joy? I'm leaving her to do all the work. Well, she's young and strong, she's got nothing else to do. The school's no good to her now, there's only a few kids there and a couple of old teachers they've dragged out of retirement. She's better off learning the trade. Anyway, she likes being in charge.'

Jess sat down on the bed, Maureen standing at her knee. Alice's voice was truculent but there was a bitter pain behind it. Poor woman, Jess thought, she doesn't know what to do with herself. She misses Heinrich like losing her right arm, and she doesn't even know whether to grieve for him or not.

'I know how you're feeling,' she said in a low voice. 'But it can't be good for you, laying in bed like this. You'd be better to get up and carry on, you really would.'

'How do you know? How do you know what'd make me feel better? You can't know how I feel, nobody could who's not going through it.' Alice stared at Jess. Her eyes were dark and hollow, rimmed with red. They looked as if they were set deeper in her head than usual. Her face was like one of her own newspapers, grey and lined. Her hair hung in rat's tails.

'It's all right for you,' she went on. 'You've got your husband at home, and past call-up age. Nobody's going to take him away and send him off in a ship to be blown up. Or die struggling in the water, hurt perhaps and not able to keep his head up.' Her voice shook. 'Heinrich never liked the water. He'd come out to Southsea with Joy and me because we liked it, but he never went into the water himself, not even to paddle. Can you imagine what it must have been like, drowning in the sea, in pitch darkness, choking on oil, maybe burning . . .' The tears came again and she turned her face into the pillow.

Jess stood up. She felt helpless, pitying and angry all at once. It seemed as if Alice was intent on wallowing in her misery, as if she'd *rather* be miserable.

'You're not the only one in this sort of trouble,' she said gently. 'There's Ethel Glaister, half out of her mind over her Shirley. It must be just as bad for her, thinking of her little girl ending like that.' Her voice broke a little. 'Alice, I know it's horrible. I can hardly bear to think of it myself. But it's no good torturing yourself. Whatever happened to Heinrich, it's over now. If – if he died, it must have been quick. You've got to think of yourself now. And Joy. She shouldn't be working all those hours in the shop, she ought to be having a bit of fun with her friends. She's getting old before her time.'

'She's always been a helpful girl. She's always liked being with me and helping.'

'But she's not with you, is she? She's down there all by herself. And you're up here moping. Look, why don't you let me make you a cup of tea while you get up? Have a wash and put on something fresh. Put the wireless on and listen to *Music While You Work*.'

'A cup of tea,' Alice said in a droning voice. 'A wash and a clean blouse. That's all it needs, is it, to make me feel better? To make up for not having Heinrich?' She turned away again.

Jess stared down at her friend and felt like shaking her by the shoulders. It might help. But it might also turn Alice against her, and that would only make things worse. She gave a little sigh of frustration and removed Maureen's hand from a silver brush that lay on Alice's dressing-table.

'I'll go and make a cup of tea,' she said quietly. 'It'll be downstairs if you want it.'

Ethel Glaister looked through her back window and saw Frank Budd out in his garden, looking at the runner beans. She went outside, walking slowly down the garden path. Out of the corner of her eye, she saw Frank hesitate then come over to the fence.

'Hullo, Ethel.' His voice was gruff and awkward. 'How're you feeling now?'

She gave him a wan smile. 'Oh, all right, you know. Bearing up. Not much else to do, is there? Someone's got to keep the home together, what with George being away.' She moved closer, looking up at him. 'I'm glad to see you. It's proper lonely with no one to talk to – *you* know.'

Frank looked embarrassed. 'I thought Jess had been popping in to see you.' Jess had told him that she'd spoken to Ethel several times, meaning to offer her sympathy or ask if there was anything she could do. But after her first desperate cry for help, Ethel hadn't seemed to want sympathy. She had withdrawn even further into herself, answering tersely as if Jess had no right to be speaking to her, making Jess feel guilty that she still had all her children safe.

'Oh, she has. But there's times, you know, when a woman wants a *man* to talk to.' Her voice trembled a little. 'I suppose my trouble is, I'm not really a woman's woman. I need a man to lean on. And with George away . . .'

Frank shifted his big body uncomfortably. 'I don't know what I can do to help, Ethel. I mean, if there's anything you can't manage round the house or garden, you know you've only got to ask, but Jess is better than me at, well, at anything else. I know she feels really sorry about Shirley.'

Ethel drew back slightly. Frank irritated and excited her both at once. He didn't seem to have any idea how to talk to a woman, how to offer a bit of comfort. Surely it wouldn't do him any harm to unbend a bit, just once in a while! And it would help her no end. She was starving to have a man take care of her, take a bit of interest in her. It didn't have to go any further than that. She just wanted to know that they were interested, that's all. Just to make her feel a bit better about things.

'Jess has just gone up the road to see her sister,' Frank said, moving towards his shed again. 'Shall I ask her to pop in when she comes back?'

Ethel shook her head. 'No. Don't bother.' She watched him wistfully for a moment, then went back indoors.

She looked in the mirror again, trying not to see the lines between her brows, the discontented splay of wrinkles around her lips. Her eyes moved to the snap of Shirley on Southsea beach, that George had pinned up on the wall so that he could look at it while he shaved.

The sudden wave of misery struck her, just as the waves at sea must have struck her little girl. She turned away abruptly, went into the back room and switched on the wireless. Glenn Miller's music swelled through the room and she turned it up as loud as it would go, remembering how George had switched it on last time he'd been home and wanted her to dance.

Bugger George, being away just when she needed him. Bugger Frank Budd, who could have taken her mind off all her misery if he'd had a mind to. Bugger the swines who'd torpedoed the ship her Shirley was on, and left her to drown in the middle of the cold Atlantic.

Ethel stood in the middle of the room, letting the music swirl about her. Then she twisted the knob of the wireless to silence it, and stalked out of the room and up the stairs. She put on her powder-blue jacket and the little hat with the veil, found her best high-heeled shoes, and marched downstairs and out through the front door.

People didn't wait for the siren to sound now. They went to the shelters as a matter of course, taking rugs and cushions, books and knitting. Many people 'trekked' out of the city each evening, going to the countryside north of Portsdown Hill for safety. There they would stay with relatives or sleep in tents or barns.

'They ought to dig tunnels in the hill,' Tommy Vickers remarked. 'That'd be the best thing. Hide us in caves, like they're doing round Dover. Like they're doing in London, really.'

But tunnelling into the hill, even though it had already been extensively quarried for chalk, would be a major undertaking, and surely the war wasn't going to last that long?

'No,' Bert Shaw said lugubriously, 'but we might need 'em to hide from Hitler when he invades.'

'You don't have to talk like that,' Peggy said sharply. 'We want to keep cheerful, not make ourselves more miserable. Hitler's not going to invade, our boys won't let him.'

'So why are there all those notices up about what to do when German soldiers come marching down the streets?' Bert demanded. 'Shut the door in their faces? That's what one of them says, just as if a Jerry with a machine-gun's going to be put off by the likes of you and Jess Budd with a broomstick in your hands. And what about all those instructions about ignoring "false alarms and rumours" and "only obeying the orders given by the British Government"? How can you do that if the country's occupied, like France? There won't *be* any British Government, will there!'

Peggy turned on the wireless.

'I'm not listening to any more of that sort of talk, Bert Shaw. Defeatist talk, that's what that is. I'd sooner listen to Tommy Handley and Mrs Mopp. Or those Americans in *Hi Gang*. It's a laugh we want, not gloom and doom.'

It was almost the end of September when Ethel Glaister accosted Frank out in the garden again. Her face was pink and glowing, and she was waving a newspaper and half laughing, half crying.

Frank stared at her. 'What is it? What's happened?'

'It's the ship! The kiddies – they're safe. A lifeboat – they found a lifeboat.' The words cascaded from her lips. 'The *City of Benares*, that's the ship my Shirley was on. They've found a lifeboat full of kiddies, they've got them safe and *my Shirley's one of them*! She's safe, she's *safe*!'

'Your Shirley? Are you sure?' Frank snatched the paper and read it quickly.

'Well, that *is* good news.' He smiled at Ethel. Why, she looked really nice with no make-up on and her face happy and laughing. Why couldn't she be like that all the time? It was her bitterness that put him off, pulling her lips into tight folds and cutting lines between her brows, and putting a hard edge to her voice. Like this, she was altogether different. 'I'm really pleased. I know Jess will be too. She was proper upset about your Shirley.'

'Eight days they were in the lifeboat,' Ethel said, taking the newspaper back and reading it again. 'There was a woman with them, she kept on massaging them to keep them from getting cold and stiff, and she told them a story. They'd nearly run out of food when one of the boys saw a flying-boat and waved to attract its attention. When a ship finally came to rescue them, the poor little devils were too weak to climb aboard.' She looked up at Frank. 'They will be all right, won't they? My Shirley—'

'She'll be all right,' Frank said gently. He reached across the fence and patted her awkwardly on the shoulder. 'You'll get her back safe and sound now, you'll see.'

Ethel nodded. She went back indoors and wept over the newspaper, thinking of her Shirley tossing about at sea in a lifeboat wondering if she would ever see her home again.

Well, at least Jess Budd wouldn't be able to look at her now as if she'd done something wrong. Shirley had had a narrow escape, but she was still alive and just because the Germans had torpedoed the ship it didn't make Ethel a bad mother like some of the women round here would like to make out – Alice Brunner, for instance, and Peggy Shaw who was so thick with Jess. She could stand up and look *them* in the eye again, any day!

Jess had been down to North End to see her parents. Frank told her the news when she came in and she hurried out into the garden first thing next morning to see Ethel.

'I'm so glad. I bet you can't wait to have her back again. You won't want her out of your sight now.'

Ethel Glaister looked at her over the garden fence.

'Oh no, I shan't have her back here,' she said. 'I'll send her straight down to Devonshire. I won't take any more chances with her.'

'Well, I can understand that,' Jess said. 'But surely you'll want to be with her? I know how I'd feel if it was one of mine.'

'And how can I go to Devon?' Ethel demanded. 'I've got Joe and Carol to think of too, haven't I? And George likely to be back home again at all hours. You know they're sending the unit back to Pompey, don't you, to clear up some of the bomb damage. You'd think they'd at least let them spend a bit of time at home, there's enough jobs piling up, for God's sake, but no, he says they'll be too busy, he'll just have to get home whenever he can. Drop in for a meal when he feels like it, that's what he means. Sometimes I think I'm running one of those British Restaurants.'

'You should think yourself lucky he'll be able to come home at all,' Jess retorted. She'd bitten her lip with Alice but she didn't have the patience to listen to Ethel's grumbles. 'Specially now you've heard about Shirley. Think of poor Alice Brunner, still worrying about Heinrich. You've got a lot to be thankful for, Ethel Glaister.'

'Oh yes,' her neighbour sneered. 'Bombs dropping all round night after night, and the street going downhill. That Nancy Baxter's getting worse – she's bringing sailors home quite openly now, the brazen slut. And I wouldn't be surprised if that Mrs Simmons is another of the same sort. Husband in the Merchant Navy! We've only got her word for it.'

'Ethel, how can you say such things? Kathy's husband came home last month, I was there when he arrived.'

'And how d'you know that was her husband? Show you their wedding certificate, did they? You mark my words, once she's had that baby she'll be back on the game same as Nancy, see if I'm not right.'

Jess stared at her in disgust. 'I'm not listening to any more of this. You're a spiteful woman, Ethel, and one day that tongue of yours is going to get you into real trouble. I came out to tell you I was glad about your Shirley, and so I am, but I don't have to stand here and listen to filth. Kathy Simmons is a decent little body and she's having a bad time. And if I hear you saying things like that about her again, you'll be sorry.'

She turned and went back into the house, her blood seething. But she had too much to do to worry about Ethel Glaister. It was washing day, and the copper was just coming to the boil. There were Frank's working shirts to scrub and Maureen's few nappies to wash, though there weren't so many now that she was getting so good on the pot. And then there would be all the mangling to do before she could even hang the things up to dry.

Washing took almost the whole day, and if it wasn't good drying weather there would be wet clothes hung round the fire indoors all evening and even draped over pictures on the wall. Sometimes it was Wednesday before she could do her ironing, and that meant the whole week was put out of joint.

She sighed and bent to take the big yellow bar of Sunlight soap from the cupboard Frank had built under the kitchen sink. Arguing with Ethel had put her in a bad mood. It would be a long time before she went out to give *her* a pleasant word again!

For Alice Brunner, there was no good news.

Each morning she woke knowing that she must go through another day without Heinrich. And without knowing even whether he was alive or dead, for she had still heard nothing of him. Many of the men on board the *Arandora Star* had died, many others been saved, and yet there had been no word of Heinrich. No word of whether he was one of those taken on to Canada, no word of whether he had been deported instead to the Isle of Man. It was as if he had vanished into thin air.

He must have drowned.

There were times when Alice wished he had died before the war had even begun. At least then she could have been a widow, and respected as such by her neighbours. At least she wouldn't have had to suffer the spite of people like Ethel Glaister, who had sneered at her for being married to a Jerry and refused to buy her newspapers from a Hun. And she would have known what had happened to him. She could have shared his last moments.

But no sooner had she let these thoughts travel through her mind than they would be followed by a searing guilt. How could she wish her beloved Heinrich dead? He had been her rock. Her lover, her husband, her friend. Never strong, she had clung to him through all her periods of despondency, through the depression that had so inexplicably followed Joy's birth and which had struck her, usually without apparent reason, at intervals since.

And there was Heinrich's own family too. As soon as war was declared, all communication from Berlin had stopped. It was terrible that a man could be split apart from both his families, the German one and the British. His mother and sister in one country, his wife and daughter in the other.

It's not knowing that's the worst, Alice thought. Not knowing whether *Mutter* has been bombed by our planes, perhaps buried or burned alive like so many of our people. Not knowing whether Heinrich . . .

And there she was, back to the beginning again, in the ceaseless circle of her anguish, on a road that had no end.

As Ethel Glaister had said, in early October the 698 Royal Engineers Unit was brought back from its wanderings to Portsmouth in order to clear some of the bomb damage and demolish the shattered buildings, and Derek was able to spend time at home.

'I never thought you'd be back so soon,' Olive said, hugging Derek in the double bed that had been squeezed into her room. 'Will you be able to get home every night?'

He shook his head. 'They'll want us in the barracks. But most of the blokes are Pompey chaps so they'll have to let us off some of the time, or there'll be a riot! I'll be here every minute I can be, you can bet on that.'

'It'll be like being properly married,' Olive said blissfully, and he laughed.

'We *are* properly married! At least, I hope so, I wouldn't want to think of you carrying on this way with a man you're not married to.'

'Oh, you know what I mean,' she said, punching him. 'With you coming home every day, just like it ought to be. I'll be able to cook your supper and mend your clothes and everything. I'll feel more like your wife.'

'You don't have to worry about cooking and mending,' he said, pulling her closer. 'There's a better way than that of feeling like my wife.'

Olive laughed and nuzzled close. Her heart was alight with happiness. She and Derek had had so little time together, and although he had warned her that the Unit would probably not stay long in Portsmouth, she refused to look ahead to a time when it might move away again. There was plenty to do here, wasn't there? And more damage being done with every raid. Why should it ever be moved away?

She wondered if she should tell Derek that she thought she might be pregnant. It was a bit soon really, only a few weeks since that night he'd had at home in the first week of September. But she'd missed once since then, and been feeling a bit queasy in the mornings. It wasn't enough to be sure, but if she missed again she'd tell him, and they could go and see the doctor together.

We'll be a real family then, she thought. Mum and Dad and baby. A real family.

The Shaws were pleased with 698's return too, for they had missed Bob. They sat around the supper table on the first evening, eating rabbit pie and listening as he told them about Devon and Wiltshire, and about the aerodromes they had been servicing. Before the evacuation of Dunkirk, the Unit had been on active service in France, building advanced landing strips at somewhere called Thelus, and since their return they had been employed in repairing RAF Bomber Command runways damaged by bombs. Bob, who had been unemployed before the war, had found himself enjoying the strenuous work, and his body had filled out as a result.

'Just look at you,' marvelled his sister Gladys. 'You were just a weed when you went away.'

'Thanks for nothing, sis.' But he was grinning as he gave her shoulder a gentle thump. 'I could always rely on you for a kind word.'

'I think you look smashing,' Diane declared. 'Like Mr Universe. I think I'll join the WAACs when I'm old enough. Or maybe the Wrens.'

'Why, what d'you want muscles for?' Bob asked, and Gladys snorted.

'She doesn't. She's more interested in the blokes' muscles than her own.'

'That's enough of that kind of talk,' their father said sharply. 'Tell us a bit more about the building you're doing, Bob. Sounds as if it'll set you up in a good trade for after the war.'

The two men plunged into a discussion of different kinds of bricks and mortar and the girls made a face at each other. They looked at their mother, but Peggy shook her head.

'Let them natter. It's the first time your dad's ever talked to Bob man-to-man. It's good for 'em. Come and help me get a pot of tea.'

It didn't take three women to make a pot of tea, but when they came back into the room with the tray Bob and his father were sitting back looking pleased with themselves, and there was a new confidence in Bob's face as he took his cup. He gave Diane a wink and then turned to Gladys.

'So what've you been getting up to, then? Still learning to drive?'

This was the chance Gladys had been waiting for. She put her nose into the air and said airily, 'No, not any more. I've passed.'

'Passed? What, passed your test? Your *driving* test?'

'Well, it's not a spelling test!' she retorted, and then let her grin break out. 'I passed last week. Last Wednesday. First time.'

'Well, that's a turn-up,' he said admiringly. 'So what are you going to do? Get a job as a bus-driver?'

'She'd better not try,' Bert said disapprovingly. 'And don't you encourage her, Bob. It's a man's job, that is. I don't approve of women driving as it is.'

'And what if there's no men to drive the buses?' Gladys demanded. 'Have we all got to walk everywhere? Anyway, I don't want to drive buses. I'm going to drive ambulances.'

'*Ambulances?*'

'Yes, ambulances. I've joined the Red Cross, along with Mum. We go to the First Aid post whenever there's a raid and look after casualties. And some of 'em need taking to hospital, so that's what I'm going to do.'

Bert looked annoyed. 'I've heard nothing of this.'

'What's the point of telling you?' Gladys said. 'You'd only tell me I couldn't. And I'm going to, so there's no point in arguing.'

Bert's face reddened. He leaned forward, laying his arms on the table, and raised one hand to jab his finger at Gladys. 'Now, you listen to me, my girl—'

'No,' Gladys said. 'You listen to me. There's a war on, isn't there? They're crying out for people to help, and that means *people*, not just men. They're sending all the men away to fight, aren't they? So who's going to run things here? We've all got to look after ourselves in this lot and it's time you men realised that you're not the only ones capable of doing a job of work. There's not much a woman can't turn her hand to, just as good as a man. We proved that in the last war, that's why they had to give in and give us the vote.'

'More's the pity too,' her father retorted. 'It gave you all big ideas, that's what that did. Women doctors! Women drivers! Women this, women that. Who's looking after their homes, that's what I'd like to know, who's getting their husbands' dinners for them? Well, I'll not have such goings-on in *my* house.' He glared at his wife. 'I'm still master here, even if *your daughters* don't seem to think so, and you needn't think *you're* going to go gallivanting off at all hours driving ambulances and such capers!'

'Oh, for God's sake,' Gladys began, but her mother cut in sharply.

'That's enough of that kind of language, our Glad. And you don't have to annoy your father more than you already have done, specially not on our Bob's first night home.' She turned to her husband. 'As for you, Bert, you're just getting silly. I've never said a word about driving ambulances, nor anything like it. All I do down the First Aid Post is put a few bandages on, as well you know. And Gladys is quite right, we all have to pull together in this war and if that means changing our ideas a bit about what we do, well, that's all there is to it. D'you think our Bob *wanted* to go off and and risk getting killed being a soldier? But he's had to do it all the same, and—'

'Get away,' Bert said, 'it's done him the world of good. Given him a trade and made a man of him. Hasn't it, Bob?'

They looked at the young man sitting there, his skin tanned with fresh air, his body filled out and strong. He looked awkward and self-conscious, as though not certain which parent to support, then shrugged and said, 'Well, it's a pretty good life, but I wouldn't say it was much fun in France.'

'No,' Peggy said, 'you were lucky to get back alive from that. So don't try to make it out to be better than it is, Bert. It's a muddle, the whole thing, and we just have to do our best and not start quarrelling amongst ourselves, all right?'

Bert Shaw pushed out his lower lip. He had grown up believing in certain traditions, and every day it seemed that a new one was upset. And he was alarmed by the rate at which his children were growing up – especially the girls. It seemed only yesterday that they had been in pigtails, running to him with their dolls, climbing up on his knee and, most important of all, behaving as he wanted them to behave. Being seen and not heard. Keeping their opinions – if they had any – to themselves. Playing quietly in a corner, and not arguing with their elders and betters.

Now, it seemed as if they wanted to rule the roost, as if they thought they could do as they liked, and they were altogether too free with their opinions. Learning to drive, indeed – and driving *ambulances*, of all things! Why, his Gladys would be in the thick of any bombing if she did that, just when he wanted her safe in a shelter. He'd rather she was driving buses after all.

'All right, Bert?' Peggy repeated, and he scowled.

'I suppose it's as all right as anything is these days. I don't pretend to understand anything. But there, I'm getting old and old men aren't wanted these days, not when there's bits of girls can do their jobs better than they can.'

'Oh, Dad!' Gladys jumped up and came round the table. She put her arms round her father's neck and pulled his head back against her. 'You're just being silly. Of course you're not old! And if there were more men like you, well, maybe girls wouldn't have to do the jobs. But we're *needed*. And we can do them – some of them, anyway. And anyway, why should we have to spend our time in shops and offices when there's so many more interesting things to do—'

'Because men are the ones who have to work!' For a few moments, Bert had seemed to be mollified by her words, but her last question had touched a nerve that many men, and women too, were still finding raw. 'It's *men* who have to provide homes for their families, men who have to earn the money. Women should stay at home and look after their families, not take away the jobs men need just because they're "more interesting". That's the way it is and it's the way it always has been. And the way it always will be, if there's anyone left with any sense after all this is over.'

'Oh yes,' Gladys said, moving away. 'And it's the men who start wars, isn't it, and land us in messes like the one we're in now.'

There was an uncomfortable silence. Bert was breathing heavily, his face suffused with anger. Peggy looked exasperated and anxious. Diane was watching with suppressed enjoyment and Bob was staring at the tablecloth. Gladys stood by the fireplace, her expression sulky but her eyes full of tears.

'Let's drop it,' Peggy said at last. 'You're both getting overheated, and all over nothing. I don't know what you wanted to say that for, Gladys, setting him off all over again. You ought to have known better. And Bert, you've got to realise the girls are growing up. They know their own minds. And things are different from when we were young.'

'You don't have to tell me that,' he returned sullenly. 'I can see it for myself. It doesn't mean to say I have to like it.'

'No, but you've got to put up with it,' she said sharply. 'Same as we all have. And just remember that it's men and women younger than our Bob and Gladys, no more than boys and girls really, who are fighting this war, and getting killed or maimed for life doing it. And if they're old enough to do that, we can't turn round and tell our Glad she can't drive an ambulance, now can we?'

There was another silence. Then Bob lifted his head. He glanced around the table. It's always been like this, he thought. Dad claiming to be 'head of the family' and 'master in his own house', laying down the law and getting us all in a knot. And then Mum, only half his size, putting us all right with a few sharp words. And the girls in tears and me wishing the earth would open . . .

But it didn't have to be like that now. As Mum had said, they were growing up. They didn't have to be treated like kids, and they didn't have to behave like them either.

'Well,' he said with a grin, 'I must say it's good to be home again and find nothing's changed. D'you know, for a while I was afraid you were going to treat me like a visitor. It don't seem like home when you're all on your best behaviour!'

They all turned and stared at him. For a moment, he was afraid that his joke had fallen on stony ground or, worse still, caused even more offence. Then Diane began to giggle and Gladys's face relaxed into an unwilling grin. Peggy gave him a wry smile and they all looked at Bert.

'Come on, Bert,' Peggy said cajolingly. 'Don't let's have a row on Bob's first night home in months.'

'I didn't want to have a row,' he muttered righteously, but he picked up his cup and looked at it. 'I suppose this has gone cold after all that shenanigan.'

'Maybe it has,' Peggy said equably, 'but we can soon make another pot. I don't think the rationing's that bad we can't afford another spoonful of tea to celebrate. And then I suppose Bob'll have to be getting back to the barracks and we'll be off down the shelter for the night. It's nearly time for the warning to go, isn't it?'

Bert nodded. He didn't want upset in the family any more than the rest of them, but he felt scared and uncertain by the way things were changing so fast. The whole world was upside down, he reflected as Peggy filled his cup with fresh tea. And maybe he was just too old to keep up with it all.

I just wish I could go and fight too, he thought, and clenched his big fist on the table. I'm as fit and healthy as any of these youngsters, and got the experience too – yet because I'm over forty, I'm chucked on the scrap heap and left to do the jobs that young girls like our Gladys think they can do better! Why, me and Frank Budd, we've already been through a war – we know what it's like. Why can't *we* go and sort 'em all out?

Instead, they were reduced to being firewatchers. Or members of the Home Guard – parading with broomsticks instead of guns, playing games like kids in the street.

Broomsticks instead of guns! Aeroplanes made out of old saucepans – ships from iron park railings. And now they were even asking for people to hand in their old binoculars because they didn't have enough to give sailors at sea.

A proper home-made war this is, he thought in disgust. How can we ever win it this way?

14

Tim and Keith were building themselves a cart with a set of old pram wheels and a couple of planks of wood that Reg Corner had given them.

'It'll be smashing,' Tim declared, tying the wheels on with bits of string. They were all short bits, collected over a period of some weeks and forming a tangle of ends and knots in his pocket. 'We'll be able to go all over the place on it.'

'Not up hills,' Keith pointed out. 'We'll have to pull it up hills.'

'Well, I know that. But there's lots of hills to go *down*. None of the others have got a cart as good as this.'

'Brian Collins says he's making one.'

'Well, he would, wouldn't he? He's always got to be best.' Tim looked up as Reg came down the garden path and stopped beside them. 'Look, isn't it a smasher? We'll be able to help you on the farm with this.'

Reg squatted down beside them. His face was grave. He looked at the cart and nodded.

'It's a good one. You've done well. But you won't be able to help me on the farm. Not for much longer.'

The boys stared at him.

'Why not?'

'Because I'm not going to be there. I've got my papers.'

Tim and Keith knew what that meant. Reg had been called up. He'd be going away, to fight in the war. They sat back on their heels, the cart momentarily forgotten.

'What are you going to be? Will you be a pilot?'

'No, I'm going in the Navy.'

'Oh.' Tim was momentarily disappointed. 'I'd rather be a pilot. That's what I'm going to be, when I'm old enough, if the war lasts long enough.'

'Let's hope it doesn't,' Reg said soberly. 'We just want it to be over as soon as possible.'

'Don't you want to go and fight?' Keith asked curiously. He and the other boys talked about the war incessantly, discussing aeroplanes, ships and tanks. They were all convinced that if the enemy invaded and penetrated as far as Bridge End, he would meet his match in the children who were prepared to defend it. They had built dens in the woods, ready to go into hiding if the need arose, and were constantly on the lookout for spies.

'I'm no fighter,' Reg answered. 'I'm a farmer. But it seems you can't be what you want to be, these days.' He stopped. He and Edna had always tried never to grumble in front of the boys. As they saw it, they had a duty to make their disrupted childhood as normal as possible. But now it looked as if they weren't going to be able to do that either.

Keith looked at him and saw something of his feeling in his face. He got up and leaned against Reg's big body.

'Don't worry,' he said. 'We'll look after Edna.'

'And the baby,' Tim added. Keith wasn't so sure about the baby, but he nodded anyway.

Reg grinned but the grin faded quickly, leaving his face more serious than ever.

'That's just it, kids. You can't. You see, if I'm not working on the farm any more, we can't stay in the cottage. It belongs to Mr Callaway, and he'll want it for someone else.'

'But what about Edna?'

'She's going to go and stay with her mum.'

The boys digested this in silence. They knew Edna's mum. She was all right, but they didn't think they wanted to go and live in her little cottage. There wasn't really room, not like where Reg and Edna lived now.

'What will we do?' Keith asked at last. His voice was slightly wobbly and Reg put his arm round him.

'We'll have to find you somewhere else, won't we? Somewhere you'll like just as much as being with us.'

Tim frowned. 'There isn't anyone else in the village who could take us.' A sudden fear gripped him. 'We won't have to go and live with Miss Woddis, will we?'

Reg shook his head firmly. 'You won't have to go there, don't worry. I'm sure we'll find someone.'

'I'd rather stay with you,' Keith said, his voice rising a little.

'I know, son. But you can't. Not if I'm going away and Edna goes to her mum's. And with a new baby, too . . .' He looked at them. He and Edna had talked it over night after night, trying to see how they could keep the boys, but there was no solution to the problem.

What he was really worried about was that they might not be able to find Tim and Keith a billet together. Most of the houses in the village were already taken up, with one or two children, and he couldn't think of anyone with enough room.

'It's no use,' he'd said to Edna at last, the previous evening. 'You'll have to write to Mrs Budd. It's for her to decide what to do, not us.' And Edna had agreed and got out the writing pad, her tears dripping on to the pages as she wrote.

Jess read the letter next day and saw the marks of the tears smudging the ink.

'Not many people want two lively boys,' she said as she read the letter to Frank when he came home from work that evening. 'And most of those who've got space for evacuees are already full. I don't like to think of them being split up, Frank.'

'Well, they're not coming home,' he said firmly. 'Not with all these raids. And it's not just the raids – you know what boys are, they'd be wanting to go and look at all the bomb sites. I've seen young Micky Baxter and his gang, clambering about all over ruined houses, collecting shrapnel and bomb cases. One of them's going to pick up something live one day and get blown to pieces. Or get buried by a wall falling on top of them. It's not safe, but you wouldn't be able to get those two young scallywags to see that.'

Jess nodded. She remembered the first raid, when the boys had been out playing cowboys and Indians. There was the problem of school, too. A few schools were open again because so many children had come back, but since the bombing had started a lot of them had been re-evacuated and it was difficult to know which schools were working and which weren't. And nobody seemed to be checking that the children were actually attending.

'I know they're better off in the country,' she said. 'But I want them to be happy there. And I do miss them so much.'

Frank nodded and put his hand on her shoulder. 'I know you do, love. So do I. Look, we'll go out to Bridge End on Sunday and see them. We'll have a talk with Mrs Corner and see what she's got to suggest. And perhaps Mrs Greenberry will know of somewhere they can go.'

Perhaps she would. But Jess wasn't too hopeful. Tim and Keith had fallen on their feet with the Corners, and you couldn't expect that sort of luck twice. And when she remembered what had happened to some of the other children who had been evacuated, it made her shiver.

Better to have the boys at home, facing the dangers with their own parents, than living miserably miles away. But it wouldn't be easy to get Frank to see that.

Mr Churchill had changed his War Cabinet and Mr Chamberlain, whom so many blamed for getting Britain into the war, had resigned. Egypt was demanding the abdication of the King of Greece, and Japan had attacked the Burma Road. Portsmouth set itself to raise a million pounds for weapons in one week, and people began to talk of rebuilding the city when the war was over. But when would that be?

The raiders were still coming, and still being fought off by the RAF. But the pretence that it was no more than a game had been replaced now by a brittle, feverish lightheartedness that was very near hysteria.

Duff and Sandy missed Geoff desperately. As long as the three of them had been flying together, it had seemed as if their luck would hold. Now the leader of the trio had gone, and each time they flew the other two strapped themselves into their seats with a sick fear that they would be next.

Duff had taken over Geoff's little sports car, and they continued to visit the farm whenever they could manage a few hours away from the station. But without Geoff they seemed incomplete. The group of six which had careered so gaily around the countryside was now unbalanced.

'Why not ask Dennis to come with us?' Betty suggested one evening. There was a village hop in the church hall and the girls had dashed up to their room as soon as milking was over to get ready. Erica was standing on a chair where the sloping ceiling was highest, while Betty drew a line down the back of each leg with eye pencil to make it look as if Erica was wearing stockings. 'I bet he can dance all right.'

Erica moved so abruptly that the pencil jerked across her calf and drew a zigzag from knee to ankle. She jumped down, inspecting the damage crossly.

'Now look what you've done! It'll never rub off. I shall look a proper fool.'

'Well, you shouldn't have moved. Just because I said we might ask Dennis—'

'I've told you before, I wouldn't walk to the end of the street with that conchie!' Erica exclaimed. 'I'd rather stay here. I never wanted to go to the dance anyway, not really.' Her face twisted suddenly and she turned away, clenching her arms across her body. 'I know what it'll be like. Stupid girls wrapping themselves round any man they can get hold of, kissing and slobbering all over each other – it'll be disgusting. Well, you can do that if you want to, but I—' She sat down suddenly on her bed and stared at the photograph of Geoffrey that she kept on the little chest of drawers '—I'd rather stay here.'

Her voice broke on the last words and Betty bit her lip. Since her first outburst of grief when Geoffrey had died, Erica had refused to talk about her feelings. She had gone home for a few days and visited his parents, returning with tight lips and glittering eyes, apparently determined to get back to her normal life as quickly as possible. It had been her idea that the girls should go to the village dance.

'I thought she was getting over it,' Betty said as she and Yvonne went out to meet the two young airmen. 'She hasn't said a word against Dennis since she came back.'

'She hasn't said a word *to* him, either,' Yvonne pointed out. They climbed into the little sports car and gave Sandy and Duff a quick rundown on what had happened. 'She hates him more than ever.'

'He seems a decent enough bloke,' Sandy remarked later, when he and Betty had stepped outside the hall for a breath of fresh air. 'He's entitled to have his own ideas.'

'Erica doesn't think so. She thinks he ought to be in prison if he's not going to fight. I tell her he's helping his country more by working on the farm than picking oakum in jail, but she doesn't see it that way.'

'Erica's still in a state. You can't blame her.' Sandy climbed up to sit on top of a gate and threw away his cigarette butt. 'I shouldn't tell you this, but we're going on a big raid over Germany tomorrow.'

'*You* are?' Betty turned her head to look at him. He was staring into the darkness and frowning. 'You mean – bombing?'

'That's right.'

'But I thought you and Duff flew Spitfires.'

'We do. We're going as escort. We've done it before.' He was scowling. 'Look, Betty, there's something I want to ask you.'

She gazed at him, feeling uncomfortable. There was something odd in his manner, something she hadn't encountered before. If it had been Graham, she'd have thought he was about to make a pass at her. But Sandy wasn't like that. He'd never touched her, never even tried to kiss her. He and Duff had just started coming over as company for Geoff, and then the six of them had had fun together. There had never been any more to it than that.

'Don't look so scared,' he said. 'Look, I know you're engaged to this sailor bloke. But – well, I think a lot of you, Betty. And I'd just like to know if – well, if ever things – you know, went wrong or something between you and him – well, if you might think of me a bit, that's all.'

He finished with a rush, his face scarlet, looking away from her into the trees. Betty gazed at him, feeling suddenly touched. She reached out and laid her fingers gently against his sleeve.

'I do think of you, Sandy,' she said in a low voice. 'You're one of the best friends I've ever had. But I can't break faith with Graham, not when he's away at sea. It wouldn't be fair.'

'Oh, I'm not asking you to do that,' he said quickly. 'It's just – well, I'd like to know there was a chance – you know?'

Betty looked at his open face. He wasn't as ginger as Graham, but his fair hair had a definite reddish shine to it. Funny that she should pick up with two boys with red hair. Maybe that was why she liked Sandy, because he reminded her a bit of Graham.

Immediately, she knew that was wrong. Sandy wasn't a bit like Graham. He was shy where Graham was cheeky, reserved where Graham was bold. He'd never once tried to go 'too far', he'd never even tried to kiss her, except for a quick peck on the cheek when he arrived and one when he left. Well, no more should he when she wasn't his girlfriend, but Betty knew very well that that wouldn't have stopped Graham in similar circumstances. Taking a girl out to tea, or just for a run in a car, would have seemed to him quite sufficient excuse to ask for, and expect, a few kisses in return.

She thought of Graham on that last evening, demanding that she let him make love to her, almost trying to force her. As if the fact that he was going to sea tomorrow, and might never know what it felt like, gave him a *right*. But Sandy went flying every day, fighting in the sky, risking his life with every minute he was in the air. And he had never so much as suggested . . .

If she had met Sandy first, would she have fallen in love with him? And what about Bob Shaw? And Dennis . . .?

Sandy climbed down from the gate. His frown was gone and he grinned, put both hands on her waist and swung her high in the air.

'Well, it's back to the 'drome now. See you next weekend, eh? And then I can tell you all about the raid.'

'Oh, I can't,' Betty said in dismay. 'I'm going home next weekend. But I'll see you the week after that. That's if you want to come,' she added, feeling suddenly shy.

'Oh, I'll want to come. You don't know what it's meant to me and the others – I mean, me and Duff – coming over here to see you girls. It's been a lifeline.' He looked at her, his eyes serious again. 'It's pretty lonely up there in the sky, Betty.'

He took her hand to lead her back into the hall for the last dance. But Betty lingered for a moment to look up at the empty sky.

For once, there were no aircraft to be seen. It rose overhead like a smooth blue dome of glass, unmarked, impregnable.

It's pretty lonely up there in the sky.

For Sandy, the loneliness was the worst part of flying. He hadn't minded it at first. It had been a joy, the first time he flew solo, to have the sky to himself, the eternal blue all his own, the clouds to play with. But there had been no marauders then, no vicious black Heinkels or Dorniers to appear suddenly from the sun, no Messerschmitts on his tail.

Like all the young airmen, Sandy tried not to think about death. He ignored the possibility that he might be shot down, that he might not return from the next mission. When other airmen failed to return, he said they'd 'bought it' and turned away from the knowledge of what had really happened. One day, he would have time to let himself feel, but not now, not yet. Now, it was vital to remain cool, not to feel, to be as much a machine as his aircraft.

But now he had seen too many of his friends and colleagues nose-dive to their doom to be able to ignore it any longer, and when he had watched Geoff's plane spiral out of control into the sea, his coolness had departed and he had felt the shock and horror of it throb like a knell through his body. He had relived it a hundred times a day, feeling himself there with Geoff in the cockpit, injured and in pain, struggling with a harness that wouldn't unfasten, watching the flames leap around him, feeling his skin scorch, his eyeballs swell and burst, his lungs on fire.

It wasn't a joke. It wasn't something to dismiss casually with a flippant remark. It was real and it was unbearable, and it had happened to his friend and could happen to him.

Would happen to him . . .

He had never spoken of it to anyone except Betty. Nobody in the mess talked of such feelings, although you could sometimes see the same fear in another man's eyes, before he turned hastily away. Anyone who showed the slightest trace of fear was suspect, a danger to the others. You could be taken off ops, grounded, the ultimate shame. You would be treated as a pariah, as a leper who might spread the deadly virus of panic amongst the others.

The loneliness would follow you down from the sky and be with you all the time.

It was a greater fear than the fear of being shot down, and its effect was to produce an addiction in Sandy. The greater his fear, the more he wanted to be in the sky, shooting down enemy planes, wiping them out of existence. Every one shot down was one less threat. Every one destroyed brought the end of the war a fraction closer. He longed to be up there all the time, destroying, destroying, destroying.

His dreams that night were a turmoil of burning aircraft, of the sharp rattle of machine-guns, of screams and yells, of explosions. Through it all, Betty's face floated like a talisman, but he could never quite see her clearly, never quite hold her expression in his mind. She drifted past and away from him, elusive and unattainable.

He strapped himself into his cockpit the next day in a daze. Duff and the others were noisily exuberant. They ate a huge breakfast, clapped each other on the back, sat about playing cards until it was time to set off. The squadron set off across the Channel, in neat formation.

Nobody was surprised when they were intercepted. Somewhere over Belgium, the expected cloud of enemy fighters appeared before them. And behind them. Above and below; all around. The squadron was suddenly on the defensive, breaking away to tackle them, to force a path for the bombers.

Sandy was still half in a dream. He thought of Geoff in a nose-dive. He thought of his friend, of all his friends who had died, whose lives had been shorn by these very planes, by these men who were shooting now at him. His hatred swelled and burst like a red flame inside his skull and he attacked savagely, blasting about him in the sky, swooping and diving, gunning the planes that swarmed about him, yelling with triumph as one by one they fell away, their sides ripped by his bullets, their engines ablaze.

He never felt the bullets that hit him. He scarcely understood the meaning of the sudden sheet of scorching orange that exploded around him. His brain was lit by white light, as searingly brilliant as if he had flown straight into the eye of the sun. His ears were filled with the screaming of his own blood.

The plane turned slowly over in the air. In his last few dying moments, he knew that he was experiencing what Geoff had experienced, Geoff and a thousand others. But he could not care now, about Geoff, or about anyone other than himself.

He knew the ultimate terror, the awareness of imminent and agonising death. Amongst the crackling of the flames around him, through the frying of his own skin and the boiling of his welling blood, he heard his voice screaming, screaming for the mother who had once kept him safe and who was now too far away ever to hear his voice again.

And then his eardrums burst and he heard no more. He could only feel. And the plane tumbled slowly, too slowly, out of the sky.

Betty knew the moment she saw two strange young airmen drive the little sports car into the yard that Sandy and Duff were dead.

She came out of the cowshed with Yvonne. They looked at the two pilots in silence. For a moment, it was as if time had run backwards and Geoff was arriving again on that first Sunday afternoon when they had all gone out to tea together. But Geoff had been killed, and there was no merriment in these two young faces. They were white and haggard, old before their time.

'You don't have to tell us,' she said to the misery in their eyes. 'It's over, isn't it? Sandy. And Duff. They're—'

'No!' Yvonne gripped her arm so tightly that the nails dug into Betty's skin. 'Don't say it! It's not true. It's not true.'

The young men looked at her wretchedly. Betty felt the tears in her eyes. *It's pretty lonely up there in the sky.* She looked upwards, as if to see him above, and when she lowered her head the tears ran over and down her cheeks like rain. Sandy dead. Sandy, dead.

'It was pretty quick,' one of the boys said. 'They couldn't have known much about it, either of them.'

They'd said that when Geoff was killed. But how could anyone know?

Erica came out of the house. She was looking pale, her mouth taut. She glanced at the car and the two men.

'So that's another two bought it,' she said, her voice hard. 'Well, I daresay there's plenty more where they came from. That's all that matters, isn't it?' Her gaze moved across to the cowshed, and Betty saw through her tears that Dennis was standing there, grave and still. Erica's voice rose suddenly to a shout, harsh with pain. 'You see? There's another two gone, gone to save your yellow skin. I hope you're pleased with yourself. I hope you're bloody *pleased* with yourself.'

She turned on her heel and stalked back into the farmhouse and, through the open door, they heard her voice again.

'I won't stay here another minute with that bloody conchie! I *won't . . .*'

Erica wasn't the only one to take her grief out on Dennis. Iris Blake, too, issued her brother-in-law with an ultimatum.

'Either he goes or we do. It's bad for the children, being influenced that way. He was talking to them again yesterday. I told you, I won't have it.'

'He was helping them thread their conkers,' Mr Spencer said wearily. 'Look, Iris, I've talked it over with him and I don't think he is a bad influence. He's promised me he won't mention the war or his ideas to them. He's a decent chap and a good worker—'

'And that's all that matters to you, isn't it!'

'Well, what else is there, for God's sake? I've got to keep this farm going, haven't I? I've got to have help to get the food produced. I reckon I'm lucky to have a strong young chap about the place, especially one as willing as Dennis. And he's quiet and decent, and not off down the pub every night.'

'They wouldn't have him. They know better.'

'The man's entitled to his ideas,' Mr Spencer repeated. 'They're none of our business.'

'Of course they're our business! He's a traitor and a coward. He ought to be shot.'

'It's the law, Iris.'

'Then the law's daft,' she said. 'Well, if you won't listen to reason, we'll pack our bags and go. Our Primrose has offered to have me and the kids for the winter and I think we'll go there. I reckon we'll be a bit safer up north anyway.'

She gave her brother-in-law a defiant glare, as if expecting him to change his mind and beg her to stay, but Jack Spencer said nothing. He put on his wire-rimmed glasses and began to sort through the pile of papers on the dresser, and after a few minutes Mrs Blake made an exasperated noise and flounced out.

Mr Spencer sighed with relief. Neither he nor his wife had welcomed the intrusion of Mrs Blake and her two badly-behaved children, but they were family so what could you do? But if his other sister-in-law, who lived in Lancashire, was willing to do a turn having them, that would be fine by him. He was more worried about the Land Girl, Erica, wanting to leave. He hadn't thought all that much of her to start with, with her yellow hair and toffee-nosed ways, but she'd settled down and turned into quite a good little worker. If she left, he'd have to get someone else, and that meant an upheaval. Jack Spencer didn't like upheavals.

Dennis had his own solution to the problem.

'Look, maybe I ought to be the one to go,' he said as he and Betty finished the milking one evening. 'It's because of me Mrs Blake and Erica are leaving. It'd be better if I asked for a transfer somewhere else, where I won't cause any trouble.'

'You don't cause trouble,' Betty said. 'They're the ones who cause trouble. We'll be better off without them, specially that Mrs Blake. Just because her husband's an army captain, she thinks we're dirt.'

'Well, I've been thinking I ought to do something else anyway,' Dennis said. 'It's too safe on the farm. Plenty of COs do other jobs, medical orderlies, Red Cross, things like that. I'm not a coward, Betty.'

'I know you're not,' she said soberly, thinking of the day the aircraft had crashed. She hesitated, then said, 'Why did you decide to be a CO, Dennis? I've never really understood what it's all about.'

He smiled slightly. 'Not many people do. That's the trouble.' They walked down the lane towards the little river. He pulled a piece of dry grass from the hedgerow and swished it back and forth as they strolled along. 'I don't think I ever actually decided. It was always there, a part of me. My dad was a CO in the last war and he went through hell for it. But I always thought he was right. He said it was wrong to kill other human beings, whatever the reason, and I agree.'

He looked at her with the hazel eyes she had always liked. They were often merry and laughing, but now they were serious.

'That plane that crashed in the field – the men in it were just like me, and Geoff and Sandy and Duff. They'd been called up and sent to fight and maybe they enjoyed it, because it must be fun to fly a plane and exciting to dodge about in the sky with other blokes in planes – like a game of tag. But it's not fun when you're burning to death or falling to earth without a parachute. It's not fun when you're being bombed or machine-gunned or stabbed through with a bayonet. How can you do that to other people, people you've never even met? How can anyone justify it?'

'But Hitler was taking over the whole of Europe,' Betty said. 'He'd take us over too.'

'I know. I can't tell you the answers to that. All I can say is, to me it's wrong to kill. It's not that I'm not prepared to die for my country, Betty, I am. But I won't kill for it. Nor for anything else.'

Betty sighed. It was difficult to understand. 'But if everyone did the same thing—'

'There'd be no wars,' he said.

She hadn't been going to say that. She'd been going to say *We'd all be overrun.* But in her mind, 'everyone' had meant simply the British. In Dennis's, it had meant everyone in the world.

And he was right. There *would* be no wars. But how could you persuade a whole world to think that way?

'So what happened?' she asked. 'When you decided to register?'

'I had to go to a tribunal. I had to explain why I felt the way I did. Sometimes they accept that and give you exemption, without any condition. Sometimes they say you've got to do something, stay in the job you're in, or work on the land, or go as a stretcher-bearer or something. And sometimes they won't exempt you at all, and they say you have to join up. If you refuse, you go to prison.'

'Is that what happened to you?'

'I was given conditional exemption. I was working in the City Council offices in Portsmouth and I was exempted on condition I stayed in my job.' His mouth twisted a little wryly. 'Actually, I wasn't all that keen on conditional exemption, I thought if the law said COs should have exemption for matters of conscience, there shouldn't be any conditions at all. But as it happened, the City Council decided that for me, they made their own rule that any COs on the staff would be sacked. So I was out anyway.'

'But they were going against the law,' Betty said indignantly.

'That's right. There was quite a rumpus about it, the Free Churches had a lot to say. But it didn't make any difference. So I couldn't fulfil my condition and I refused to accept any other.'

'And was that when they sent you to prison?'

He nodded. 'Yes. Not a lot of fun, prison, especially when the warders treat you worse than the criminals. I was put to sewing uniforms the first day, army uniforms. Well, that was against the law too, they weren't supposed to force us to do anything towards the war effort. So I refused, and that didn't help me much. They gave me other jobs instead.'

Betty wanted to ask what jobs, but the look on Dennis's face warned her to leave the subject alone. Clearly, prison had been a painful experience. He was silent for a moment, then grinned at her.

'Cheer up. It's over now. I was only in for a few months anyway. And I spent the last couple in Wormwood Scrubs, they had a better attitude there. It wasn't too bad, not when you think what my old man went through in his time. And when I came out, I volunteered to work on the land.' He smiled again. 'Daft, I know, but I don't mind volunteering, I just won't be forced. And now I think maybe it's time I volunteered to do something more. I don't like being safe here, when there's people being bombed back in Pompey.'

They had reached the little river. It wasn't much more than a stream really, running through the fields with willow trees hanging over its banks. Dennis sat down on the trunk of a fallen tree and looked down into the water.

'There's only one thing bothers me about going away,' he said quietly. 'I'd miss you, Betty.'

There was a little silence. A few rooks cawed as they made their way home across the chilly fields. A cloud of gnats danced above the surface of the stream.

She looked at him, sitting there on the fallen trunk. He had had his curly brown hair cut short and his face and neck were tanned. His body was lean and hard. Suddenly, Betty felt a powerful urge to hold herself against that body, to feel his warmth on her skin.

'I'd miss you too,' she said wonderingly. 'I don't want you to go away, Dennis.'

There was a catch in her voice. She heard it with surprise, and felt another flood of emotion. What was the matter with her?

Dennis lifted his head. His hazel eyes looked straight into hers and he reached out his hands.

'Betty . . .'

'Oh, *Dennis*,' she said, and moved blindly into his arms.

His body was warm and hard, just as she had known it would be. She could feel his heart beating against her breast. His cheek was slightly rough against hers, and his lips were firm as he kissed her. He held her closely but not tightly, and she felt safe and secure within the circle of his embrace.

For a few moments they stayed close together, and then he let her go.

'I'm sorry. I shouldn't have—'

'No. It's all right. Please, Dennis—'

'You've already got a boy. You're engaged—'

'Not properly,' she said. 'It's just a game really. To make him feel better while he's away.'

Dennis stared at her. 'What d'you mean?'

Betty reddened. 'It wasn't serious at all at first. We just went out together a few times. And then he got called up and he wanted me to – to wait for him. He wanted to know I wouldn't go out with anyone else. So that he could think of me when he was away, you see, knowing I'd be there when he got back. And I sort of thought it would be nice to be engaged, only I knew my mum and dad would never agree, so he gave me this little ring – she fished it out of her collar, where it hung round her neck on a thin chain – and when we're by ourselves I wear it on my engagement finger. But it doesn't mean anything, not really.'

'Doesn't it?' Dennis asked gently. 'Are you sure?'

Betty's blush deepened. 'I don't really know,' she said honestly. 'I thought it did, for a while. But since I've been here . . . I'm not sure, Dennis. And the last time I saw Graham—'

'Yes?' he prompted, and she looked away from him.

'Well, maybe I shouldn't tell you this, but he wanted – he wanted—' She shook her head. 'I can't say it.'

'All right,' Dennis said. 'You don't have to. I can guess what Graham wanted.' He sighed. 'I can understand it. Having a girl like you, and going off to sea, not knowing whether he'd ever see you again. How did you feel about it?'

Betty looked at him. Her face was still scarlet, but suddenly it was easy to talk to him. His eyes were calm and warm, full of understanding. She said, 'I wanted to a bit, but it was wrong. I knew it was wrong. In the end, he kept on so much that I promised I would after supper, and then Mum made us all play cards till it was time for him to go.' She glanced at him sidelong, still a little embarrassed. 'She knew perfectly well what was going on, she did it deliberately. And Graham knew too. He was furious but there was nothing I could do about it.'

Dennis laughed. 'So a game of whist saved you from a fate worse than death!'

'Actually, it was rummy,' she said seriously, and then laughed with him. 'Would it have been worse than death?'

'I don't suppose so,' he said, 'but you might have been in a difficult situation now.'

'I know,' she said with a shiver. 'That's what scared me. Well, partly. But it just didn't seem right.'

'Perhaps Graham wasn't the right one,' he said lightly. 'It has to be the right one, Betty. And you have to really want it. It's no good giving in just because a chap keeps on. That's not love.'

'No,' she said. 'I know.'

She looked at him again. His eyes were grave. He reached out a hand and she took it and let him draw her close. The warmth of his skin radiated and enfolded her, and she rested against him, her head against his chest, his cheek against her hair.

'I'd like to think I might be the right one, Betty,' he said quietly. 'But I won't keep on at you. I want you to be sure. I want us both to be sure.'

Betty looked down at the stream, flowing gently at their feet. She and Dennis seemed to have come a long way this afternoon. Or perhaps they had been moving slowly towards each other for a long time – ever since that first afternoon, when she had stepped off the bus and looked into his hazel eyes for the first time.

I love you, Dennis, she thought experimentally, as if tasting the words. And then, more strongly, with a power that surged through her body: *I love you.*

The words tasted right. They sounded true and honest in her heart. She knew now that what she had felt for Sandy was friendship. Now, with Dennis, she felt a flowering of joy within her, an opening and blossoming that she had never experienced before, with either Sandy or Graham.

Graham . . .

Her heart sank. What in heaven's name was she going to do about Graham?

15

Graham was back in Portsmouth. His ship was in dock again and its crew employed in helping to clear up the devastation in the city. He spent his days shovelling debris and helping to demolish buildings that were considered dangerous.

'It's a respite,' Elsie Philpotts told her son when he went to Gosport for some home cooking. 'I'm thankful to know you're safe here and not at sea. The longer it takes, the better, as far as I'm concerned.'

Graham pushed away his plate. He had packed away a huge mound of fried potatoes and his parents' entire week's ration of bacon. He was accustomed to eating large amounts on the ship, but it wasn't like Mum's cooking. He gave a sigh of satisfaction.

'That was smashing . . . It's all right, I suppose, but I wish Betty was home. There's not much to do when you haven't got a girl to go with.'

'Not much to do? In *Pompey*?' Elsie gave a little scream of laughter. 'And you a sailor? Still, I suppose you're right. It's all right going to pubs with your mates in strange places, but when you're home you want something different. You want your own sweetheart. And with Betty out on that farm, you're bound to feel lonely.'

Graham nodded. He'd been annoyed to come home and find Betty away, even though he'd known it would happen. It was what he'd foreseen when she'd first announced her intention of volunteering for the Land Army, and he'd told her then he didn't approve. Her father hadn't liked it either, but she'd gone ahead and done it just the same.

Maybe we ought to get married, he thought, remembering how she'd let him down that last evening he was home. She'd have to do what I say then, and she'd have to let me make love to her as well. There'd be none of this 'mummy wouldn't like it' nonsense then.

She'd been wearing his ring long enough, after all. Last Christmas, he'd given it to her. It was nearly Christmas again now. That was plenty of time to be engaged. They *ought* to be thinking about getting married.

'She's coming home this weekend,' he told his mother. 'I'll talk to her then. It's time we got things sorted out.'

He went to Betty's house at the weekend, filled with determination. This time, there would be no games of cards, no hiding behind her mother's skirts. Betty was his girl, and if she wouldn't give him what a man needed, they'd just have to have a showdown. They were getting married, he'd tell her, never mind her dad's objections. There were ways of getting round that.

'What d'you mean, ways?' she asked when he said this. They were in the front room as usual, holding hands after their first reunion. He'd have gone straight ahead then, he was ready enough for it, but Betty had held back, as he might have known she would. In fact, her kisses weren't as enthusiastic as he'd expected and he already felt annoyed. He wished they'd gone out for a walk, so that they could talk properly, without her family in the next room, but it was pitch dark out there in the blackout, and raining too, and there was no chance her mum would let her go out with planes liable to come over at any moment.

'We could fix it so he had to let us get married,' he said. 'Plenty of people do.'

She stared at him. 'Get me in the family way, you mean? Deliberately?'

'Better'n doing it by accident,' he said flippantly.

Betty snatched her hand away. 'I don't know what you think you're suggesting, Graham Philpotts. I'm a decent girl—'

'Oh, for crying out loud!' he broke in. 'I'm not asking you to do anything unnatural. I'm asking you to get married. Don't you know a proposal when it hits you on the nose?'

'It'll be you that gets hit on the nose if you go on talking like that,' she retorted. 'My mum would die of shame if I had to get married. She's always told me what would happen if I got into trouble.'

'I'm not talking about getting into trouble. I'm talking about a wedding. You know? White dresses, bridesmaids, a cake? Isn't that what you want, Betty?'

She looked at him. They seemed to have had this conversation before, but last time she had been the one dreaming of the day that was supposed to be the best day in a girl's life. Now, the glitter seemed to have faded. There was more to life than that one day.

'I don't want it all in a rush,' she said quietly. 'Getting married – it's serious. It's not just an excuse for a pretty frock and a party. Anyway, how could I get married in white if – if—'

'Well, that's all right – *I* don't want to wear a pretty frock, and it doesn't matter a tinker's cuss what colour yours is. It can be sky-blue-pink for all I care. And I couldn't care less about the party. We'll just keep it simple, all right? A quick dash into the church, or the registry office, it's all the same to me, and then a pint or two up the pub and home to bed.' His face was flushed and he grabbed her hand again. 'How does that sound, Bet?'

'It sounds horrible!' Again, she pulled away. 'Graham, what's all this about? Why are you so keen to get married all of a sudden? What's the point, when you'll be going away again?'

'That *is* the point! Don't you understand? I'm fed up with going away and not knowing you'll be here waiting for me when I get back. I'm fed up with coming back to Pompey and finding you're out grubbing about on some farm miles away. I'm fed up with taking second place to a spud!' He glared at her, his blue eyes hard and angry. 'You were keen enough before.

You wanted to get engaged. Well, now I want to get married, and I want to know why you don't.' His eyes narrowed with suspicion. 'Is there some other bloke, is that what it is? Some country yokel you've gone and fallen for?'

'No!' The word was out before Betty could stop it, and she turned scarlet. Oh dear, she thought despairingly, what can I say? I ought to tell him things are different now, I don't feel the same. But I didn't want to tell him like this. And I don't even know if I do want them to be different, not really. I don't know *what* I want!

I only know I don't want to hurt him. But he's hurt anyway. And now I've gone and told him a lie, and I don't even know how much of a lie it is.

'All right, then,' Graham demanded, 'so tell me why you *don't* want to get married, all of a sudden.'

'But we never did say we wanted to get married,' Betty said, trying to remember if this was true. Her mind was so confused, she could hardly recall what had happened. 'We just wanted to get engaged, so you'd know I was here waiting for you.'

'Right. And you're not, are you? You're cavorting round the countryside with a lot of farmers—'

'Graham, I'm not! I'm not cavorting. I'm working, working hard.' She showed him her hands, the skin roughened and calloused by toil. 'I'm working as hard as you.'

'Yes, and I don't like it. I don't want my girl slaving away in all weathers, spoiling her looks. You've got hands like a navvy's. What sort of a welcome is that for a bloke when he comes home, to find his girl's got hands like sandpaper? If we were married, you'd come back and act like a woman again instead of trying to pretend you're a man. You'd have my supper on the table and you wouldn't be too tired or too strait-laced to give me what a man wants.'

'Yes, that's it, isn't it,' Betty flashed. 'That's what it's all about. You just want me here, ready to wait on you hand and foot the minute you step through the door. And ready to go to bed with you. It's all for you, isn't it – never mind what *I* want to do. Never mind that it's *my* life we're talking about.'

'I thought it was *our* life—'

'So did I. But you want it all your own way.'

'And don't *you*?' he shouted. 'Don't you want everything *your* own way? First you want to get engaged, so I've got to buy you a ring. Then you want to go off and work on a farm so I never know where you are and you can't be around when my ship comes back to Pompey. God knows what you're doing out there or who you're going with, you could have a different bloke every night for all I know—'

'Graham! That's disgusting!'

'Well, and how do I know it's not true?' he demanded. 'You don't tell me everything in your letters. Do you?'

His eyes were on her face and Betty looked away, biting her lip. It was true that she'd never mentioned the outings in Geoff's car, the walks with Sandy and the others. She hadn't even said much about Dennis. Most of her letters had described her work on the farm. It wasn't surprising Graham had found them boring.

'Do you tell me everything?' she asked, and was surprised to see him flush in his turn.

There was a brief silence. Then Betty touched his sleeve gently.

'Don't let's quarrel, Graham. It's the first time we've seen each other for weeks. We ought to be happy.'

'That's what I want.' He pulled her roughly against him. 'That's what I thought it'd be like. But you seem different. You're harder. You've got more selfish—'

She sighed. 'I haven't got more selfish, Graham. I've just had to grow up a bit, that's all. Life's changed for me. I've been living away from home, I've had to make up my own mind about things. I'm bound to seem a bit different. You're different, too.'

'I'm a man,' he said. 'I've got to go away. But you're a woman, you're supposed to stop at home.'

'It's wartime. That sort of thing isn't true any more.'

'Well, it bloody ought to be!' he exclaimed, losing his temper again. 'For Christ's sake, Betty, isn't there anything you could do at home? Knit balaclava helmets, or work in the canteen like my mum does, or something like that? Do you *have* to go miles away and wallow about in the mud?'

'No, I don't have to. But I want to.' She looked at him, her head on one side, trying to make him smile. 'Can you see me knitting balaclava helmets or making cauldrons of soup, Graham? Can you honestly?'

'I don't see why not. Plenty of other people do. Oh hell, you can do what you like, so long as you're *here*. Don't you understand?'

Betty moved her eyes slowly over his face, taking in the ginger hair, the sandy eyebrows and freckled face. The merriment she had once found so attractive had vanished, leaving his mouth petulant and his eyes sulky. She thought of his mother, jolly and untidy, letting the whole house revolve around her son.

'The trouble with you, Graham, is you're spoilt,' she said. 'You think everything's got to be arranged to suit you. You don't seem to think I'm entitled to a life of my own at all, it's all got to be organised so that I'm here when *you* want me, doing the things *you* want me to do. You think you own me, and you want to get married so that you can own me all the more.'

'That's stupid. I don't want to own you. I just want to know you're my wife.'

'And if I was?' she said. 'Would you let me go on working on the farm?'

'Well, of course not! I'd want you back here, behaving like a wife should. Haven't I already said so?'

'Yes, you have,' Betty said. 'I just wanted to make sure I'd heard you properly. I'm sorry, Graham, but I don't want to give up my life like that. I'm enjoying being on the farm. I'm doing something worthwhile there. I'm not prepared to give it all up and come back here and knit.'

'You don't have to knit. You could go back to the dairy.'

'Thank you very much. I left the dairy, remember?' She looked at him.

She hadn't wanted to hurt him, but she was wondering now just how much he really did love her. Wasn't it just his own idea of himself he loved? 'Graham, I'm sorry, but I don't think this is going to work.' She pulled the chain which held her ring from inside her blouse. 'You'd better have this back.'

He stared at the ring, with its tiny glittering stone. 'What are you talking about?'

'Us being engaged. It isn't working.'

'It isn't getting a chance to work!' he shouted. 'You're not giving it a chance. Look, I've been back five minutes, all I wanted to do was hold you in my arms and kiss you and love you, all the things a bloke wants to do when he gets back home with his girl. But you don't seem to care any more.' He was holding her tightly, rubbing his cheek against hers, covering her face with kisses. He put his hand over her breast and squeezed it. 'Last time I was home, you said you'd let me love you properly, and then you never did. Don't you realise how I've been feeling? Don't you realise what it's been like? And all I wanted, all I've ever wanted—'

'Graham, stop it! You'll have Mum in here, making all that noise.' Betty pulled away and sat panting, her hair dishevelled, her blouse half out of her skirt. 'I'm sorry it doesn't seem the same. I'm sorry. But I can't help it. I can't let you do what you want. I don't want to get caught—'

'I've told you it doesn't matter. We'll get married. They'll have to let us get married.'

'And I've told you it *does* matter! I won't do it that way, Graham, and the way you've been going on tonight I don't think I want to do it at all.'

He stared at her, bewildered. 'What way I've been going on? All I've wanted—'

'All you want is to get me tied down,' she said. 'You don't give a damn what *I* want. I'm to live my life the way you want me to live it, which is sitting at home night after night doing sweet Fanny Adams, just on the off-chance that you'll show up. Well, I won't. I'd be bored stiff.'

'Not if you had a baby,' he said. 'You'd have plenty to do if you had a baby to look after.'

'But I don't *want* a baby! Not yet. Not for years. And I'm certainly not having one just so my mum and dad'll have to let us get married. They'd never forgive me. They probably wouldn't ever speak to me again.'

'Well, that's all right,' he said. 'There needn't be one, not really. We can tell 'em it was all a mistake, or you could say you'd had a miss—'

'Tell *lies* about it?' Betty stared at him. 'You'd want me to tell lies, just so we could get married and you could make me stay at home and knit woolly hats? Is that really what you want me to do? Never mind that it'd break my mum's heart and Dad would probably turn me out.'

'You could go and stay with my mum. In fact, it'd probably be better that way. I wouldn't have to—'

'You wouldn't have to come up this way at all when the ship was in Pompey,' she finished for him. 'You don't understand anything at all, do you? You just want the whole world to revolve around you.'

'Oh, for Christ's sake, Betty—'

'And you needn't bring your language here!' she shouted. 'Just because you're in sailor's uniform you needn't think you can come here laying down the law and swearing—'

'Look, I'm asking you to *marry* me, that's all! What's so bloody wrong with that? Most girls *want* to get married, don't they? They *want* to have kids. You're bloody unnatural, you are. I just want to love you, like any bloke wants to love his girl, I don't see anything so criminal about that. And you'd want it too, if you really loved me. You'd *want* to marry me and be my wife.'

'Well, I don't want to,' she said flatly. 'I don't want to be anyone's wife, if that's what it's all about. I'd rather live an old maid.'

'And that's what you'll be,' he sneered. 'Because I can tell you this, Betty, nobody else is going to want you, with your face getting all lined and weatherbeaten, and your hands like sandpaper, and muscles like a brickie's. Shall I tell you something else? You don't know *how* to be a proper woman. You never did. You always wanted to be a boy, out in the street playing football and cricket. And you're no different now. That's why you won't let me touch you, you've got no proper feelings at all. I reckon there's something wrong with you!'

He came to his feet and stood glowering down at her. Betty sat quite still, shaken by his words, wanting to refute them but too overcome by her own guilt to hurl back any more accusations. Her eyes filled with tears and Graham saw and seized upon them.

'That's right, start piping your eye. Isn't that what girls always do, when they start to lose an argument? Well, cry all you like, Betty, it won't bring me back. I've had enough of your prim and prissy ways and I've had enough of waiting for you to finish the milking before you can spare me a minute or two of your precious time. I'm off!'

'Graham, don't go like that—'

'And how do you want me to go?' he demanded, wrenching open the door. 'In a Rolls-Royce? Or maybe on a carthorse, like you're used to?'

'I didn't mean that. You know I didn't. I just—' She gazed helplessly at him, unable to express what she was feeling. 'Graham, we've had some good times together. Can't we still be friends?'

'Oh yes,' he said bitterly, 'that's the next line, isn't it? Let's stay friends. They all say that, in the "Dear Johns". *I can't love you any more, there's this other man who's the love of my life, but let's stay friends.* Friends! Who wants to be friends? Being friends doesn't get you anywhere.'

'If you think that,' Betty said, 'I'm sorry for you. Really sorry.' She stood up. Her knees were shaking but she tilted her chin and looked him in the eye. 'I didn't mean it to be this way, Graham. But I don't see what else we can do. Thanks for the good times, anyway.'

He stared at her, baffled. Then he swung on his heel and wrenched open the door. In another moment, he was out on the street, the front door crashing behind him.

Betty stood quite still. She put her hands up to cover her face, feeling the tears overflow from her eyes to fill her palms and squeeze slowly out through her fingers.

I really didn't mean it to be like that, she thought. I meant it to be gentle. I didn't want all that argument and bitterness.

But perhaps she'd been fooling herself. Perhaps you couldn't, after all, break up with someone without pain and bitterness. Perhaps Graham was right, and it was impossible to stay 'friends'.

From the other room, she could hear the voices of Olive and her parents. It was almost supper-time. They'd be expecting her and Graham to come through at any minute.

She heard her mother knock on the door and took a deep breath, preparing herself to go through and tell them that Graham wasn't, after all, staying to supper.

16

The news from London was worse each day. It became a dreadful commonplace to pass dead bodies in the street, and even small children developed a casual indifference.

'That's our baker. He's lost his hat.'

'I wonder who'll get his horse . . .'

Huge craters appeared in the roads, and cars, taxis and trolley buses were reduced to smashed wrecks of twisted metal. So many London buses were destroyed that the city appealed for help from other towns, and the streets were suddenly brightened by buses of all colours, taking the place of the familiar red.

The blitz was spreading to other cities. In November the Germans attacked some of Britain's most famous cathedral cities. Nine days later they tore the heart from Coventry in one of the worst raids yet, nearly five hundred bombers, dropping over five hundred tons of high-explosive bombs and nearly a thousand incendiaries. And before the nation could draw breath, they were back again, hurling an apparently inexhaustible supply of red-hot fury at the capital city.

'It's coming closer,' Jess said, sitting in the air-raid shelter and listening to the planes passing overhead. 'It'll be our turn soon.'

Southampton was next. Only three days after the crushing of Coventry, the planes were thundering up the Solent and over the docks which had sheltered some of Britain's most famous ocean liners. A week later they came again, and then again. The flames could be seen for miles around, lighting the sky all night.

They could be seen from Bridge End, where the Budd children and their friends were evacuated. Tim and Keith watched from their bedroom window, excited and only half afraid, while their sister Rose stared in panic, imagining it happening to Portsmouth, imagining her parents and baby sister Maureen, burning alive in the holocaust.

'It's all right, love. It's not Portsmouth. Your mum and dad are all right,' Mrs Greenberry tried to comfort her. But Rose shook her head, her eyes fixed on the brilliant glow.

'They'll go to Portsmouth as well. I know they will. They keep on getting raids there.'

Mrs Greenberry held her against her bosom and sighed. What could she say to the girl? Rose wasn't a child any more, she was thirteen years old and intelligent enough to know what was happening. You couldn't tell her everything would be all right, when you knew it wasn't true. Nothing was all right.

'We'll just have to trust God to look after them,' she said. 'He knows they're there, Rose. He'll take care of them.'

But the girl looked up at her, her brown eyes dark with despair.

'Why should he? He's letting other people be killed. He's not looking after *them*.'

And there wasn't anything you could say to that either. She could only go on holding Rose tight and stay with her, watching the fires that raged over Southampton, thinking of London and of Coventry and waiting for the same thing to happen to Portsmouth.

It began only a few days later, when Portsmouth suffered what was described as 'the most violent attack yet carried out by the Luftwaffe'. Hospitals and cinemas were damaged, property destroyed and fires started all over the city. Gladys, still nervously learning to handle an ambulance, found herself racing along crumbling streets, her way lit by flames, while her mother crouched in the back trying to staunch the bleeding of terrified victims.

'Oh God, it's awful, it's awful,' she kept repeating to herself. 'I can't stand it. I'll go mad. I can't stand it.' But there was no time to give in, and it had to be withstood, for there were people dying and only she and Peggy and a few others to help them in a world that had gone sickeningly mad.

For many, there was no help. They lay buried beneath huge heaps of shattered brick and plaster, pinned down by heavy beams of wood and concrete, blood and breath slowly crushed from their smashed bodies, and they died with the taste of the dust and smoke filling their lungs, and the screams of other victims in their ears.

And in the midst of it all, Kathy Simmons, huddling in the damp little Anderson shelter with her two small daughters, went into labour.

She had been feeling strange all day. Yesterday the baby, which had been riding high, had begun a frenzied burst of activity. It seemed to be kicking itself down her body, like a swimmer diving energetically to the bottom of the sea. Her shape changed by the hour, until the bulge was lying low on her thighs and she felt exhausted.

She called the midwife, but after an examination Mrs Frame told her that she didn't think there was any hurry. 'You say the other two took a long time. I don't reckon this un'll be born for a day or two yet. Head's not properly engaged, see, and nothing can happen till it is. You just get some rest and I'll look in again tomorrow.'

Kathy watched her go, feeling uneasy. Mrs Frame wasn't the best midwife in the district, but she was all Kathy could afford until some more money came through from Mike. And she couldn't ask the baby to wait! She wondered whether to go over to Jess Budd and ask if she could stop the night in their shelter. She looked at her daughters, who had finished their tea and were playing by the fire.

'Put your coats and shoes on. We're just going round the corner to see Mrs Budd.'

Muriel looked up. 'Mrs Budd's out. I saw her with Mrs Chapman, pushing Maureen's pram up the street.'

Kathy felt blank. 'She might have been just going shopping. I expect she'll be back by now.'

Stella shook her head. 'No, she said they were going to tea with her auntie.'

Her auntie. That must be the one who lived half a dozen streets away, the one Jess and Frank had lived with for a while when they first got married. That meant Frank would go there too, straight from work, and they might stop on for supper.

Kathy chewed her lip, wondering what to do. She knew most of the other women in the street now, by sight if no more, and she knew that most of them would help if she needed it, but she was reluctant to bother them for what might be only a false alarm. After all, Mrs Frame had said the baby couldn't be born until the head was engaged, and if that hadn't happened yet she ought to be safe enough. Why not wait till morning, and then ask Jess if she could go over to them at night until the baby was born?

She tried to settle down to some knitting, but she felt heavy and uncomfortable. The baby's head was like a hard rock pressing against her pelvis. The girls were uneasy too, looking at her and whispering to each other. Kathy had told them a baby was on the way – she knew most mothers wouldn't have done, thinking they were too young to know about such things, but you had to take a different view when you were on your own.

She went to the front door and peered out, careful to ensure that no light was showing. The street was very dark. The worst of the air raids had taken place during the full moons which had occurred during the middle of October and November – Bombers' Moon, they'd called them. Tonight, there was no moon at all, but the air was clear and the sky prickling with stars. Was that enough to show German aircraft the route to England? For the first time, Kathy wondered how they found their way through the night skies. During the day, they could follow roads and railway lines, but what did they do at night? She gazed up, thinking how peaceful it looked, and how false.

Footsteps sounded on the pavement and she drew back a little. Her eyes had grown accustomed to the darkness and she could see the figure of a man walking down from September Street.

He caught a glimpse of her movement and stopped.

'Is that Mrs Simmons?'

'Yes. It's Mr Vickers, isn't it?'

'Tommy,' he said cheerfully. 'I've never liked being called "mister". It makes me want to look round to see who's standing behind me.'

Kathy smiled. She had heard a good deal about Tommy Vickers. He was well known for his cheekiness and good humour. He'd do anything to help anyone too, Jess had told her, and didn't make a lot of fuss or noise about it either, like some people did. He'd leave bundles of kindling on the doorsteps of old people, for instance, or go round collecting odd bits of shopping for anyone who found it difficult to get out. He wasn't above a bit of fiddling – he always seemed to know where to lay his hands on a few eggs or a pound or two of potatoes – but he wouldn't have anything to do with real black marketeering, and he'd never do anyone down.

She supposed he was on his rounds now. He'd become an Air Raid Warden soon after the war broke out, but he wasn't one to go around yelling 'Put that light out!' Instead, he'd be more likely to knock on the door where a light was showing and chaff the offender into being more careful.

'What are you doing out here?' he asked. 'It's a bit cold to be standing admiring the view.' He stood gazing up at the glistening sky. 'Not but what it's not a view worth admiring. Look at all those stars. You can see the Milky Way as plain as a main road tonight.'

Kathy nodded. 'It doesn't seem possible it could be full of planes, dropping bombs on us. It's like a – a—' she searched for the right word and remembered something the vicar had said in church once '—a desecration. What's it all about, Mr Vickers? What are they doing it for?'

He shrugged. 'I know why *we're* doing it. So people like you and me can stand at their front doors of an evening and look at the stars without being afraid of being bombed out. But don't ask me why Hitler started it all. I wonder if anyone knows now. It's like a stupid kids' quarrel that's got out of hand, and they've all been home and fetched their dads to fight it out for them.'

Kathy knew exactly what he meant. She had often heard the boys in the street threatening each other. *I'll get my dad to fight your dad . . . Well, my dad's bigger than your dad . . .* The difference was that the fathers usually had more sense than to get involved, and the boys couldn't do that much damage anyway. With the countries of Europe, it was a different matter.

And it wasn't just Europe. It was spreading like a canker, all over the world. Japan and China at each other's throats. Italy, Egypt, Greece. Only America was holding herself aloof and, like most people, Kathy wished they would join in too. Surely with a mighty nation like that on their side, the Allies could finish off Hitler and his cronies for once and for all . . .

The baby gave a sudden violent squirm and she gasped and put her hand on her stomach. Tommy turned his head sharply; she could see the gleam of his eyes in the starlight.

'You all right, love?'

'Yes. It's just the baby – been restless all day.' She gave an embarrassed little laugh, but Tommy didn't seem bothered.

'It must be due around now, surely?'

'Yes, I wondered if it might be on its way but Mrs Frame says not for another day or two.' She sighed and crossed her arms over her chest. 'I wish it'd come and get it over with. I get scared at night, what with all these bombs and wondering when it's going to get born . . . And I'm so *tired*.'

'I know, love.' Everyone was tired, bone tired. Night after night in the shelter, hearing the planes pass overhead, listening for explosions and wondering what had been hit now. And still you had to get up in the morning and go to work. Or see to the kids, get breakfast, do the shopping and housework. Sleep came in snatches these days, like a precious jewel that was handed to you only to be plucked away again just when you thought you had it in your grasp.

'I just want to lean against the wall,' Tommy's wife had said to him a few days ago, and he'd smiled and pulled her close.

'Lean against me instead, love.' But he couldn't be there for her all day, and sometimes he needed to lean on something too.

Now it was Kathy Simmons who needed someone to lean on, and her need couldn't be ignored.

'Look,' he said, 'it's a fine night and I reckon there'll be raiders over any minute. Why don't you get yourself settled down in your shelter with the kids? I'll see you settled and then I'll look in again later on to make sure you're all right.'

'That's good of you, Mr Vickers,' Kathy said gratefully and he gave her arm a little shake.

'I told you, it's Tommy. Now, what d'you usually take down there with you?'

He came into the house and helped her collect together the nightly bundle – blankets, pillows, the mattresses of the two camp beds Kathy had managed to buy. You couldn't leave things there during the day because of damp. He made a big pot of tea and brought that down too, covering it with cushions to keep it warm as long as possible. He made sure the hurricane lamp had enough fuel and that no light showed through the thick curtain Kathy had hung over the door.

'There, that's you all serene.' He'd kept the two little girls laughing as they paraded up and down the garden path with all their belongings. 'Now, I don't want to hear a peep out of any of you till morning.'

'You can't hear peeps,' Stella said cheekily. 'You can only see peeps.'

'You'd be surprised what I can see and hear. I'm like Father Christmas, I am, I know everything.' He pretended to growl and the girls shrieked and scuttled into the corner of the shelter. 'And what I know now is that you're both going to go fast asleep till morning.'

'Even if the bombs come?'

'Even if the bombs come,' he said firmly. He looked at the two little faces and felt a spasm of anger, sharp and hot inside him. Why should little scraps like these two have to worry about bombs? And Kathy, sitting there white-faced and obviously uncomfortable. She ought to be tucked up in bed, with someone to look after her, not facing the night all alone.

He wished he could get Freda to come and give an eye to her. But Freda had developed flu yesterday and he didn't even like the idea of her having to go down to their own shelter, let alone come round to Kathy's. And it wouldn't help the young woman to catch flu at a time like this.

Well, it was only a few hours till morning. He'd poke his head in now and then to reassure her, and –

The wail of the siren splintered his thoughts. He gave a swift look round the dank little cave, and said, 'I'll have to go. You sit tight and don't worry. And you two little uns, remember what I said. Look after your mum and go to sleep.'

How they were to do both at once wasn't clear, but Stella and Muriel nodded, their faces suddenly fearful. They were old enough to be frightened of the bombs, old enough to see and understand the destruction around them even if they couldn't understand its causes. And they still had nightmares about the day their own house was bombed. As Tommy ducked out through the curtain, they drew together on their camp bed, staring up at the flickering shadows on the corrugated iron roof.

'It's all right,' Kathy said, pressing them gently down on the mattress and tucking the blankets around them. 'It's all right. You know we're safe in the shelter.'

She looked at them, huddled together, their eyes huge in white faces. Why don't I just give in and take them out into the country? she thought. They've been through enough. They deserve to sleep safe in their beds at night.

But if she gave up this house and went out to the countryside, there would be no home at all for Mike to come back to. There would be nothing for him to picture as he worked at sea, no family base to give his thoughts security. No roots for any of them.

Kathy hardly knew how to express these feelings. All she knew was that without a home of their own, their marriage would no longer have its firm foundation, a foundation to which they both – *all* of them – needed desperately to cling. In a world that was teetering on its axis, some things just had to remain secure, however dangerous it might seem.

It was less than half an hour after Tommy had gone that she felt the first savage pain.

There had been no possibility of sleep. The raid was a fierce one, beaten off at first by a heavy barrage of anti-aircraft fire, and then followed by a wave of planes that burst through the defences, flying low overhead and scattering bombs all over the city. Kathy and the girls crouched together, feeling the earth shake, remembering that terrible afternoon when their own house had been bombed, wondering if it was about to happen again. The explosions sounded closer, louder – was that one their home, gone again? Or that one, or that?

Kathy felt ill. Pain had been circling round her back and pelvis for hours, pushed away until it became too bad to ignore. The baby could not be born tonight. Not in an air raid shelter, in the middle of a raid, with no one to help her. It could not. It would have to wait till tomorrow. She set her jaw and concentrated, as if by ignoring the steadily increasing contractions, by trying to pretend they weren't happening, she could postpone it till morning. Why not? Why shouldn't it be possible? It *had* to be possible.

It was not possible. As the agony gripped her, starting in the small of her back and spreading like an iron band around her swollen stomach, she knew that nothing now could delay the forces of nature. She could feel the body of the baby, forcing itself along the canal, punching at the walls that had sheltered it for nine months, thrusting its head against the muscles whose strength had carried it and now made their own protesting stand against its assault. Her whole abdomen was clenched in the vice of the most severe contraction she had ever experienced, wave after wave of pain grinding through her until she could hold back the groan no longer and it burst from her lips and swelled like the pain to a scream. And then that was all she was, a scream, a white-hot, searing shriek of anguish that pulsed with the frenzy of flesh and blood and bone that was trying so desperately to escape from the prison of her womb.

Slowly, the waves of pain receded. Kathy opened her eyes, her head swimming, and saw the two little girls sitting bolt upright on their camp bed, staring at her in terror. Shaken, dreading the next contraction, she held out her hands and tried to smile.

'It's all right. It's just the baby, wanting to be born. It'll be all – oh!'

It was coming again, starting low in her back, spreading its grip like a web over her whole body, tightening and strengthening its grasp until she was once more helpless and could only lie on the flimsy bed, the blood roaring in her ears as the enemy aircraft roared overhead and Portsmouth exploded about her.

Tommy Vickers hurried along the darkened streets. The stars above were dimmed now by the brilliance of the searchlights. The unearthly light filtered down into the city, but he was too anxious about Kathy to be either grateful for its help or anxious about the bombs that would follow.

What a time to be having a baby! What a *place*. And all on her own too, with two other kiddies scared out of their wits. It wasn't right that women should have to put up with such things. And it was dangerous.

Tommy didn't know a lot about childbirth. Freda had told him a bit but mostly it was something women talked about between themselves, in hushed voices. But he did know that women could die if they weren't properly looked after. Kathy Simmons needed someone to look after her. And it ought to be someone who knew what they were about.

Who could he ask? He racked his brains. If only Freda wasn't laid up with flu, he would have fetched her. Jess Budd or her sister Annie were the next who came to mind, but he'd seen them going out earlier on. They'd probably be stuck now in someone's shelter. What about Peggy Shaw? No, she'd have gone to the First Aid post, and her daughter Gladys with her.

There must be other neighbours who'd help. But Mrs Minns who lived next door to Kathy was old and frail, and anyway she'd never had any babies. Vi Redding from number 12 had had plenty of kids but she wasn't all that bright. And a lot of the others had started 'trekking' every night, going over the hill to Denmead or Cowplain to escape the bombs.

The snarl of approaching planes could be heard quite clearly now. He stood irresolute for a moment, and then caught a glimpse of light, flickering momentarily from a front door. Ethel Glaister.

'Here!' he shouted. 'Mrs Glaister! I want you.'

The light disappeared. He heard the click of the door and ran down the pavement. There was no sign of life now in the house and he guessed that she was probably going down to the shelter in the back garden. He lifted his fist and pounded on the door, found the letter-box and shouted through it.

'Mrs Glaister! Ethel! Open the door.'

The blackout curtain hung heavily against the letter box. He tried to thrust it aside with his hand. The planes were almost overhead.

'Ethel! It's Tommy Vickers. There's an emergency – for God's sake, open the door.'

'Go away,' a voice called from inside. 'We're going down the shelter.'

'No – open up Ethel, please!'

'There's a raid on—'

'I know that, for crying out loud!' He tried to force the exasperation from his voice. Ethel Glaister was too touchy to offend now. 'Look, I need your help. Open the door a minute.'

There was a pause, then he heard the click of a light being switched off and the door opened slightly. He could see the pale oval of Ethel's face peering out.

'What is it? Has someone been bombed?'

'No, it's—'

'If you got me out here,' she said, beginning to sound haughty, 'just so you could tell me off for showing a light for about half a second—'

'It's nothing to do with that.' He was beginning to feel desperate. 'I just want to ask your help.'

'Help?' Her voice was suspicious. 'What sort of help?'

'It's young Mrs Simmons. The woman who got bombed out – lives in number 16, October—'

'I know who she is. What's the matter with her?'

Her tone wasn't encouraging but Tommy plunged on. 'She's having a baby—'

'Well, anyone can see that, too. What's it got to do with me?'

'She's over there all by herself.' The sky was filled now with the roar of enemy aircraft. 'I'm worried about her – I think the baby might be on its way.' His words were drowned by the whistle of a bomb and the crash of its explosion. He ducked involuntarily. The first explosion was always the worst – after that, you were expecting it. 'I said, I think the baby—'

Ethel had jumped back inside the house. She looked up nervously at the sky and said, 'I'm going down the shelter. I ought to have been there already. You'll get us all killed, Tommy Vickers, standing here gossiping when there's a raid on.'

'I'm not gossiping. I'm worried about young Mrs Simmons. She needs someone with her.' There was another explosion somewhere in the city, and another. 'She shouldn't be there on her own—'

'Look,' Ethel Glaister said sharply, 'we're all having to manage on our own. All us women. Isn't my George away, in the Army? Ask someone who's got her husband at home, someone like Jess Budd next door or Peggy Shaw. I've got my own children to think of. I can't go out gallivanting about having tea with the neighbours in the middle of an air-raid.' Another *crump* sounded, nearer at hand this time. 'Anyway, Kathy Simmons wouldn't want *me* popping over to pass the time of day, as good as turned me out last time, she did, when I tried to be friendly. And now I'm going down our shelter, where I ought to have been ten minutes ago.'

She drew back and slammed the door in Tommy's face. He stared at it for a moment, feeling helpless. Then he thrust his hand through the letter-box again and put his mouth close against it.

'Ethel, she needs your help. She's having her baby, she might be having it this very minute. Ethel, she could *die* over there, with no one who knows what to do . . .'

But there was no reply. And as the bombs fell thick and fast all over Portsmouth, Tommy Vickers knew that there was only one thing he could do.

'My God!'

Kathy scarcely heard Tommy's voice as he ducked back into the shelter, hardly knew he was there, only knew that suddenly a hand was in hers and she was clutching it with all the desperation of a woman drowning and almost beyond help. He slipped his arm under her shoulders and held her hard against him, sharing the anguish with her, waiting until it receded. At the same time, he reached out his other arm and the two frightened children slid across their bed and pressed themselves against the warmth of his body.

'Is Mummy dying?' Stella asked in a small voice as Kathy relaxed again and lay panting, her eyes closed, in the circle of his arm.

'No, of course she isn't. She's just having a baby. You knew you were going to have a baby brother or sister, didn't you?'

'Brother,' Muriel stated firmly.

'Well, we'll soon see. It's going to be born tonight. That's what's happening now, see, it's been living in your mum's tummy all this time and now it's coming out, that's all.'

'But it's hurting her,' Muriel whispered as Kathy began to tense again. 'Why is it hurting her so much?'

'It just does sometimes.' Tommy sought for words to explain but Kathy was groaning again, and her body was thrashing about on the bed. He caught her against him, letting her clutch his hands until he feared she would break all his fingers, and rode the storm with her. His mind echoed the little girl's words. Why was it hurting so much? Why did it have to be like this?

'Does the baby have to make a hole to come out of?' Stella looked fearfully at her mother's body as if expecting it to rip like a paper bag. 'Is that what it's doing now?'

'No, there's a place for it come out.' He looked doubtfully at the swollen body. Should he get some of her clothes off? Surely it would be easier for her. If only there were another woman here. Surely one of the neighbours would help, if he could only let them know they were needed . . . Even that bitch Ethel Glaister . . . He glanced towards the doorway, then swore under his breath and hesitated. Kathy was resting again, but the contractions were coming too quickly for him to go for help. And he couldn't send the children out into the bomb-spattered streets, not even to hop over the fence to next-door's shelter. No, he would have to stay and just do the best he could.

Hot water. Wasn't that what was needed, lots of hot water? He'd never known exactly why. Perhaps it was just to make tea. He looked at the teapot, covered with cushions to keep it hot. Well, at least Kathy could have a drink when she needed it.

Kathy's body bucked and twisted in his arms. He held her tightly, feeling the waves of pain shudder through her body. How long would it go on like this? How long could she *stand* it like this?

'Listen, love,' he said when the contraction had passed, leaving her weak and trembling against him. 'I think we ought to get some of your clothes off. Don't worry – I won't look at you. But the baby's got to have room.'

'It's all right. I don't care what you do.' She managed a twisted grin. 'There's no modesty when you have a baby, Mr Vickers. Just – don't go away.' Her face contorted and she grabbed his hand again and screamed through gritted teeth. 'Oh God! Oh God, oh God, oh *God*!'

The two girls began to cry. 'Mummy, Mummy. It's hurting her, she's going to die, oh Mummy, Mummy, *Mummy* . . .'

'It's all right,' Tommy panted, himself far from sure. 'It'll be over soon and you'll have a lovely brother. Or sister.' It didn't matter a row of buttons which it was, he thought, so long as it didn't take too long. But Freda had been over eighteen hours in labour with their Eunice. Had it been like this all through every one of those eighteen hours? No wonder she'd never wanted any more.

What were you supposed to do? Was it enough just to hold her, or was there something else he ought to be doing? He pulled the blanket down and undid the laces on Kathy's maternity skirt. It fell away, a big rectangle of material. If he could get it out from underneath her, he could lay it over her body. She had knickers on too, huge bloomers with elasticated legs. Blimey, he thought, they're like a ruddy barrage balloon. He tried to ease them down but they were trapped beneath her heavy body. They were soaking wet and sticking to her skin.

'Kathy, you'll have to help me. We've got to get your knickers off.' I hope to God nobody's outside listening, he thought with grim humour. Not that anyone would hear anything, over the cacophony that was going on out there, with planes still droning overhead, ack-ack guns firing and bombs whistling and crashing to the ground. What a time to be having a bloody baby!

'I can't – oh God, no. *No!*' Her head twisted in useless rebuttal. She clutched his hands, her nails digging into his skin. 'It wasn't like this with the other two. Oh God, Mr Vickers, it's killing me!'

'It's not. It's not.' He tried to keep the fear from his voice. Suppose it *was* killing her? Suppose she died here in the shelter, in his arms, in front of her two little girls? 'It's going to be all right, Kathy. Your baby's being born and everything's all right. Just don't panic.' And you're a fine one to talk, Tommy Vickers, he thought. You're on the verge of panic yourself. What in hell's name should I *do*?

Between them, and between the contractions, they managed to get her knickers off. Stella helped, once he'd told her that this was where the baby would come out. She looked at him with some doubt at first, but her mother nodded weakly and said, 'It's right, Stell. You do what Mr Vickers tells you,' and she put her small hands to the waist of the garment and tugged when Kathy, panting hard, lifted her body an inch or two to allow it to be pulled down.

'That's better.' Tommy felt relieved. He pulled the blanket quickly back over the distorted body. If only it wasn't so cold down here. But it was December and the shelter was half underground and damp. Not that Kathy seemed to feel it. She was streaming with sweat.

The labour went on, and overhead the roar of planes and the reverberations of the bombs continued in accompaniment. I ought to be out there doing my rounds, Tommy thought. I ought to be making sure everyone's in shelter and not showing any lights, and I ought to be looking out for fires and parachutes and giving a hand wherever it's needed. But that's what I'm doing, isn't it? You can't say it's not needed here. If only I knew what to do.

'Kathy, love,' he said urgently, 'you're going to have to help me. Tell me what I should be doing. I mean, I've never done this before. You've had babies, you must know . . .'

'Just stay here. Don't go away – for Christ's sake, don't go away.' She was clutching him again. The contractions were coming almost in one long wave now, wrenching at her body, twisting her to and fro. Her heavings had tossed off the blankets and he could see the rippling of the muscles, actually see the pain that threatened to split her in half. Bloody hell, he thought, if this is what women go through it's a wonder any of them ever has more than one kid. But then he remembered his Freda saying that you forgot, somehow, once it was all over. You'd need to, he thought.

The shape of Kathy's body had changed. The bulge was much lower now, right down to her thighs. She was lying with her legs splayed and he could see a gaping black cavern between them, with red lips stretched far apart in a parody of a grin. And just inside the cavern, just visible, something else. Something smooth and dark that approached the mouth of the cavern and then receded, and then, as Kathy gave a shout of pain and her whole body contorted, came almost to the entrance and almost, *almost*, pushed its way out.

'The baby!' he shouted in sudden realisation. 'Kathy, it's the baby! I can see it. Look – Stella, Muriel, look – there's the baby, it's almost born.'

As the contraction passed, it slithered back in again. Once again, Tommy was racked by doubt. Should he help? Put his fingers in and give a bit of a tug? Almost as soon as the thought had entered his mind, he dismissed it. He stared, fascinated, as the space widened and the head emerged a little more. He could see it pulsating. He could almost see its face. Surely it had got to be born now. He remembered the term Freda had used when talking about Eunice's birth.

'Bear down, Kathy! You've got to bear down.' He gripped her hand and lifted his arm so that she could brace her feet against it. 'That's it. Now – next time it starts, bear down. Hard. That's it. That's it. A bit more. A bit harder. Don't stop now – give it all you've got. *Now!*'

'I can't!' Kathy shrieked, kicking so hard that he almost toppled over as her body shot along the bed. 'I can't, I can't, I *can't!*'

'You can! You *have!*' The baby was thrusting from her body, virtually elbowing its way out, in a gush of blood and water and God knew what else. Tommy grabbed it as it came, and almost dropped it on the cold earthen floor. It was covered in grey slime, as slippery as a fish squirming in his grasp, tiny arms and legs flailing, face screwed up and mouth wide open in a yell of fury. He held it in both hands, staring down at it. It's born, he thought dazedly. It's born. A baby. A new baby. No one's ever seen it before, no one. I'm the very first . . .

Kathy had subsided. She lay suddenly flat and exhausted. He looked at the baby and then at her. What did you do next? Weren't you supposed to hold newborn babies up by their feet and smack their bottoms or something? He stared again at the slippery, grey little being who was glowering back at him. It seemed cruel. And what about the cord, which was quite different from anything he had ever imagined – a thick, purple rope leading from the baby's navel back into Kathy's body? What were you meant to do about that?

'What is it?' she whispered. She sounded drained, as if every ounce of strength had been beaten out of her. And no wonder, he thought. 'Is it a boy?'

'A –?' He looked hurriedly, feeling guilty that he hadn't noticed at once. 'Yes. Yes, it's a boy. What – what should I do next?'

'Give him to me.' Her voice was soft. She held out her arms and he laid the baby in them, across her breast. In the tumult, her smock had got rucked up around her neck, and her heavy breasts were bare. She cuddled the naked, slimy little body against them and to Tommy's amazement the small head turned as if already seeking milk.

'Blimey, he's a hungry little bugger,' he said. 'Look at that!'

Kathy smiled at him and he marvelled at the sudden luminous quality of her smile. It was as if the agony of the past hour was already forgotten, just as Freda had said. Then she said, urgently, 'You've got to cut the cord, Tommy. Have you got scissors? And some string or something?'

He shook his head helplessly. The situation was once more desperate. Babies could die – mothers too – if their cords weren't treated properly. Freda had said so. She'd known someone who'd died because of that. He glanced anxiously around the little shelter, lit so dimly by the hurricane lamp. What could you find here to tie and cut a baby's cord with?

'Here, Mr Vickers, I've got a ribbon.' Stella was already untying it, a blue ribbon that held a hank of hair on one side of her head. She handed it to him and he thanked God that she'd been here after all. Sensible kiddy.

'Tie it in two places,' Kathy instructed. 'Near the baby, and then nearer me. Tie it tightly. I don't think it matters about cutting it straightaway, so long as it's tied.' Her voice began to fade. 'Oh God, here comes the afterbirth. Here – take him, quick.'

'The what?' Tommy stared in dismay as her body began to contort again. He snatched the baby and handed him to Stella. 'Kathy, what's happening now, for God's sake? Don't tell me you've got another one in there!'

She laughed in spite of her discomfort. 'I hope not! It's the afterbirth – it's what the cord's attached to. It's a bit mucky, I'm afraid . . .' Again, her body contracted and she closed her eyes and tensed herself. And then it came, gushing out between her legs as the baby himself had come. An almost black mass of flesh and mucus, like a grossly deformed liver, which squirmed as if it had a life of its own and lay on the bed, pulsing like a slowly dying creature.

'Ugh!' Muriel exclaimed. 'It's horrible!'

Tommy thought so too, and he would rather that the little girls had not seen it. But children were seeing a good many things these days that it would be better they didn't see, and birth had to be better than death. He wondered what to do with the squidgy-looking mass. Was having a baby always as mucky as this?

Suddenly, he became aware of a change. He looked up at the roof, almost puzzled, and then grinned.

'Here,' he said, 'the planes have stopped.'

Kathy lifted her head. The baby was back on her breast now and the two girls were close to her, gazing down at their new brother. They all listened for a moment, scarcely able to believe the sudden silence.

'D'you think it's over?' she whispered.

Tommy made up his mind.

'Over or not, I'm going to get you some help. Annie Chapman's girl Olive, she might be home, she'll come across. And I'll go for Mrs Frame as well.' He hesitated. 'There's – er, there's nothing else likely to – er – well, you know . . .?'

Kathy laughed weakly. 'No, the afterbirth's the only thing. But it ought to be attended to.' She smiled down at the baby lying across her bosom. 'And so should this little chap. He badly needs a bath!'

So that's what the hot water was always wanted for. There was certainly a lot of clearing up to do. Tommy surveyed the mess on the floor, the blood-soaked bed. It looked as if there'd been a murder in here rather than a baby being born.

'I'll go and get someone to come and look after you,' he said, and turned towards the doorway.

Kathy reached out a hand and brushed his leg with her fingers. He looked down at her.

'Thanks, Tommy,' she said quietly. 'Thanks a lot.'

Tommy nodded, suddenly unable to speak. He pushed aside the curtain, taking care not to let the slightest glimmer of light escape, and climbed out into fresh, cold air. He gazed up at the stars.

A few minutes ago, death had been raining down from that dark, star-pricked sky. But all the death the Germans hurled down couldn't stop new life being born. Kathy's baby had been determined to live, determined to survive. And if a newborn baby could be that tough . . .

You'll never beat us, he told Hitler silently. You'll never, never win.

17

Christmas was coming. The second Christmas of the war. Last year, they had all been waiting, wondering if anything was ever going to happen. Now, they were in the thick of it and nobody could pretend it would soon be over.

Micky Baxter and his gang were still running wild. There were a few teachers in Portsmouth, mostly retired, who were attempting to run a school of sorts. They gathered children together in front rooms, giving them lessons one or two days a week and setting them homework to do the rest of the time. Some of the children bothered, some didn't. Some rarely attended.

'He ought to come to lessons,' an elderly schoolmaster said, knocking on Nancy Baxter's door one day. 'When this war's over, it's people with education who'll be needed to get the country back on its feet. Your Micky's bright enough to do well if he puts his mind to it.'

'Go on,' Nancy said cynically, 'education won't do my Micky no good. Teachers've always had a down on him. He'll have to look out for 'imself, same as I've 'ad to. That's what it's like for people like us.'

The teacher looked past her along the narrow passage with its dark brown, peeling wallpaper and cracked linoleum. A stale, sour smell wafted through from the back room. He sighed.

'But it doesn't have to be like that. He could pass exams, get a good job. He could better himself, don't you see?'

'Better himself?' Nancy echoed. She removed the cigarette end that hung from her lip and sneered. 'Yes, that's just it, ain't it? We're not good enough as we are, we've got to *better* ourselves. An' we've got to do it your way. My Micky's got to waste his time sitting in school listening to a lot of fat-arsed teachers with posh voices tellin' 'im he's got to learn bits of poetry and draw maps of China. What good's that sort of thing to a boy like my Micky, eh? What good's it ever done you to learn poetry and draw China? It didn't stop a war startin', did it? It didn't stop Hitler tryin' to take over the world.'

The schoolmaster gazed at her blankly and Nancy put the cigarette back between her lips.

'My Micky's 'elpin' me at 'ome,' she said dismissively. ''E's got a job workin' in a shop, errand boy. 'E's doin' more good there than 'e'll ever do in school. Anyway, 'e's not far off fourteen, so you might as well save your breath and your shoe leather.'

She slammed the door and went back inside. Her mother was sitting by the fire, holding out her hands to the small pile of smouldering coal. The baby Vera was playing with a couple of battered saucepan lids.

'Silly old fool,' Nancy said scornfully. 'Comin' round 'ere trying to get our Micky to go for lessons. 'Tain't natural, tyin' a boy like 'im down to a desk all day. Stands to reason 'e won't do it.'

'Still, 'e does have a point, Nance,' Granny Kinch said. 'People do get on better now with a bit of education. You couldn't get it when I was young. I learned to read but your dad never did, and 'e always wished 'e 'ad.'

'Micky can read, and add up too. That's all a boy like 'im wants. The rest is just rubbish.'

'It'd keep 'im off the streets a bit,' Mrs Kinch said. 'We never know where 'e is these days.'

'I don't need to know where 'e is,' Nancy replied, lighting another cigarette. 'Not so long as 'e keeps bringin' stuff 'ome the way 'e does.'

The three of them kept up the fiction of Micky's job as errand boy, although he came home less frequently now with food or ornaments and clothing. People were becoming more careful, keeping their doors locked when the siren sent them running for the shelter. But there were still enough careless ones to bring in a steady supply, and the store-room in the basement of the bombed house was filling with things the boys kept for themselves.

Shrapnel was the latest treasure to be salvaged from the air-raids. They vied with each other to find the largest, most jagged pieces and arranged them around the cellar. Cyril found a large shell case and stood it in the middle of the ramshackle table, where Micky gazed at it enviously.

'I'll get a better one than that,' he said. 'I'll get a proper bomb. An unexploded one. There's plenty around after a raid.'

'What, and blow us all up?' Jimmy jeered. 'Fat lot of good that'd be.'

'A dud one, then. Or I'd take out its fuse. That's easy. I saw a bit about it in my comic. I bet I could do that.'

'Bet you couldn't. Proper soldiers get blown up doing that.'

Micky leaned back and out his feet up on the table. He was smoking a fag-end he'd found in the gutter. Sometimes he pinched cigarettes from his mother's bag, but she kept a sharp eye on them and gave him a good clout if she thought there were any missing.

'I'm goin' to be a proper soldier one day. A Commando. That's what I'm goin' to be – creepin' about round the enemy's camps, layin' mines and blowin' things up and that. And killin' sentries with one blow.'

'I'd rather be a bomber pilot,' Jimmy said. 'Fancy dropping a bomb and seeing a whole city go up in flames. I bet that's really good.'

Micky said nothing. His mind had drifted away to a fantasy of dark woods surrounding the perimeter of a German army camp. He was crawling on his belly, wirecutters in his hand. He had already killed two sentries when he was accosted by a third. One chopping movement with the side of his hand, and the third lay dead as well. From there, it was a simple matter to slice his way through the wire fence and stalk silently to the hut where Hitler, Goebbels and all the rest sat in conference. He took a grenade from his pocket, tugged out the pin with his teeth and lobbed it through the window . . .

Micky Baxter, world hero.

Jess and Frank could not decide whether to bring the children home for Christmas. Frank was against it. The bombing was getting worse, he said, and it was crazy to bring kids back from safety just for the sake of a few days' celebrations. What was there to celebrate anyway? There was almost no food in the shops, nothing much to give them for presents, and any party games they might be playing would probably have to be played in the air-raid shelter.

They were better off where they were. And the Government agreed with him, he pointed out. They were urging parents to leave the children where they were.

'But we're losing their childhood,' Jess argued miserably. 'We hardly know what the boys are doing now. They'll never be this age again. And Rose is making herself ill.'

Frank sighed. He knew Jess was becoming really anxious about Rose. Mrs Greenberry had written twice to say that the girl was worrying herself sick over the bombing. She woke each morning, terrified that her home and parents had been blown up in the night, and listened desperately to the News on the wireless, avid for any mention of Portsmouth.

'I still think they're better off where they are,' he said. 'I'd rather they were alive and miserable than dead.'

'But they wouldn't be. It's safe enough in the shelter. We're still alive. We haven't even had any bombs round here.'

'What about St Alban's church? What about the railway? Look, you don't know where the next bomb's going to fall – nobody does. They just drop 'em wherever they feel like it. And even Anderson shelters can't survive a direct hit. Look at that one in St Mary's Road, a whole family killed.'

Jess knew he was right. But she longed for her boys and her daughter. It wasn't natural, families being split up. Sometimes she thought Kathy Simmons was right and you ought to stay together and keep the home going no matter what happened.

She went over to Kathy's every day to give a hand, feeling guilty that she hadn't been on hand when the baby was born. Fancy the poor young woman having to go through that with no woman beside her! But the baby was thriving despite his dramatic arrival, and didn't even seem to notice the noise of the bombs, Kathy said. Hardly any wonder, when they'd been the first things he'd heard in this world.

Everyone in the street knew now the story of how Tommy Vickers had delivered the baby, and he was a bit of a hero, though he shrugged it off with his usual grin and a joke. All the same, he'd obviously been proud as Punch when Kathy had said she was going to name the baby Thomas after him.

'He was going to be George, after the King,' she said, 'but it wasn't the King who came into the air-raid shelter and brought him into the world, was it!'

Kathy seemed to have recovered well enough too, though Jess knew she was worried about Mike, facing danger at sea every day in the Merchant Navy convoys.

But everyone had someone to worry about. There was Annie, fretting over her Colin, and Alice Brunner still creeping about like a shadow and leaving almost all the work of the shop to Joy.

At least some of the other men were at home now. Derek Harker and Bob Shaw, both in Portsmouth's own 698 Unit, were able to come home at weekends, and so was George Glaister. Not that that seemed to give either him or Ethel much pleasure! Jess could hear them arguing sometimes, through the adjoining wall of the little terraced houses.

'I suppose you think just because you're a soldier now, you can rule the roost at home,' Ethel remarked sarcastically. 'Well, that khaki uniform doesn't cut any ice with me. I know it's still George Glaister inside it, just as much of a mouse as he's ever been.'

George didn't answer. He didn't want to argue with Ethel, and tried to keep silent when she started nagging, but somehow that seemed to make her worse. She'd go on and on, her voice rising all the time, and if he didn't give her any answers she'd provide them for herself, just to give herself something to argue about.

'I know what you're thinking. You think being trained to kill people makes you better than the rest of us. Well, it doesn't as far as I'm concerned, it just makes you a worse brute than ever.' But just now I was a mouse, he thought, staring at the fireplace where a few coals lay sullenly glowing. 'You think you're God's gift to the Army. You think you can win the war with one arm tied behind your back. Well, why not? You do everything else as if you'd got one arm tied behind your back!'

'Oh, for goodness' sake, Ethel, shut up,' he said, goaded at last. 'The way you go on, I wonder why I bother to come home at all. Aren't you a bit pleased to see me?'

'Not much. It's been nice and peaceful here these past few months. And it's a change to have a bit of room in bed and not have to listen to you driving pigs to market.'

'Look,' he said, 'I know you've had a lot on your plate lately, specially with all the worry over our Shirley. But she's safe now and down in Devon with her auntie. Why not relax a bit, Ethel? Let's go out somewhere. The pictures. Or maybe dancing at Kimball's. You used to enjoy a spot of dancing.' He moved over to her and put his arm round her waist. 'You were good at it, too. The belle of the ball, I always said, didn't I?'

Ethel shrugged, but she didn't bite his head off. She let him take hold of her hand, as if they were about to waltz. George reached past her and switched on the wireless. It gurgled and spluttered a bit, then warmed up and they heard the liquid notes of Louis Armstrong's trumpet.

'Hear that?' George said, delighted. 'That used to be one of our favourites. Remember?' He pulled her closer and rubbed his cheek against hers. 'A few smoochy dances and then a bit of a cuddle outside before I walked you home. And then a bit more of a cuddle at your front door. You were a lovely little armful then, Ethel. Still are.' His hand slid down to her bottom. 'How about slipping upstairs for half an hour before our Joe gets home from work?'

Ethel snatched his hand away and jerked herself out of his arms. 'George Glaister! Oh, you men are all the same. It's all you think about. In the middle of the afternoon, too. If that's what being in the Army does for you, you can go right back to your barracks this minute!'

George stood quite still. He felt as if he'd been doused with icy water. He'd been looking forward to coming home – not because he'd expected any special welcome, but because it was his home and he'd had enough of living in a barracks. He wasn't a real soldier after all, only a Territorial. He liked a quiet life, looking after his garden and doing a bit of woodwork in the shed. And somehow he'd forgotten what Ethel had become, and remembered her as she used to be, full of life, thrilled with their home, always ready for a bit of kissing and cuddling even if she'd never been all that keen on what went with it. Somehow, he'd expected to find the old Ethel waiting for him.

Ethel had flounced out to the scullery and he heard her run the tap. Perhaps she was making a cup of tea. He'd been home an hour and not had one yet. He sat down heavily in his armchair and picked up the paper. Joe and Carol would be home soon. Perhaps it would be better when they came in.

The day after the big raid when Kathy Simmons' baby was born, the *Evening News* carried advertisements for Christmas presents alongside its reports of the damage done. The Landport Drapery Bazaar was going to town on silk stockings, thousands of pairs, at prices from three shillings and sixpence up to six-and-three. That was a lot of money when you could get cardigans and jumpers for the same price, but it would be almost impossible to get stockings at all soon and many women would be pleased to receive them amongst their Christmas presents.

There were also notices about Christmas rations. Lord Woolton, the Minister for Food, had announced a 'Christmas box' of an extra four ounces of sugar and two ounces of tea for each person during the week before Christmas. But there was little other festive fare. No cargoes of fresh or tinned fruit were coming into the country, except for a small number of oranges, and although bananas were supposed to be available until Christmas, when their import would be banned, none had been seen around September Street for months. Molly Atkinson shook her head when anyone asked for them, and there were a few mutters about 'black market' and suggestions that the Atkinson children didn't go short of a banana or two. To such comments, Jess Budd was very sharp indeed. She didn't believe Molly was keeping anything back, but if she did give her own children first choice of anything special, who could blame her? They hadn't had much of a Christmas last year, after all.

Turkeys too were in short supply, not that most of the inhabitants of April Grove and its surrounding streets normally bought such grand fare. A big chicken did most of them for Christmas dinner. Annie Chapman usually had one, but Jess and Frank chipped in with the cost of that and it fed both families, together with Jess and Annie's parents. The advice of the Ministry was not to pay any more than two shillings and tenpence a pound for birds up to eighteen pounds in weight, and two and sixpence a pound for bigger ones. (What sort of ovens did people have? Jess wondered.)

Milk was another problem. In order to keep up the supply to those who needed it most – nursing mothers, babies and young children – the rest of the population had to accept a reduction. There was talk of re-introducing the half-pint bottle, but there were difficulties enough in getting people to return their pint bottles for refilling. Unless they did, a number of areas would have to go back to the churn and bucket method, taking their jugs out to the roundsman to have them filled as he came round the streets.

'We don't want that,' Jess said to Kathy. 'It's not nearly so clean. People ought to wash their bottles out and give them back every day.'

'They must lose a lot through the bombing,' Kathy said. 'People put them at their front doors at night, and by morning there's no front door, let alone any milk bottles.' She grinned. 'Someone wrote No Milk Today on one of the doors in Portchester Road. There was practically no house left! I had to laugh.'

Jess smiled. She was feeling better today, for a letter had come from Edna Corner to say that the billet she'd found for Tim and Keith wouldn't be able to take them after all. The woman's son was in the Army and he'd been wounded and sent home for her to look after, so the room was needed. And Edna herself was definitely going to her mother and would be there for Christmas, so the boys would have to come home.

Jess was sorry they wouldn't be able to be with the Corners any more, but she'd known that was going to happen, and she was too pleased at the idea of having them home to worry about what was going to happen next. She'd told Frank she wanted Rose home too, and to her relief he had agreed.

'We can't leave her out there by herself when the rest of the family's all together,' he said. 'But the minute Christmas is over, back they go.'

'Of course. As soon as we find somewhere for them to stay.'

'The billeting officer will do that,' he said, but Jess made a face.

'I've seen some of the places they send the kids to. I want to be sure my boys are going to be looked after properly.'

Frank sighed. 'You can't even be sure they'd go to the same village again. With half the schools back in Pompey, they're sending youngsters all over the place. They might finish up in Yorkshire – we can't go all the way up there to look at billets as if we were the king and queen of England!'

'I wouldn't let them go that far,' Jess said obstinately. 'I want them near enough to be able to go and visit, like we do now.'

Frank looked at her. He knew she still wept for the children every night, and especially for Rose, who was really unhappy despite Mrs Greenberry's kindness. Rose had always been close to her mother, following her about the house as a toddler, pretending to sweep and dust, rolling out bits of grey dough and stamping out biscuits with a teacup, standing up beside her at the sink with a tiny washboard Frank had made her. And as she'd got older, she'd turned into a real mother's help, especially with baby Maureen. He knew Jess missed her a lot.

She missed the boys too, of course. You didn't have a family around underfoot all the time, especially in a house as small as number 14, without noticing the difference when they weren't there. And Tim and Keith were so lively, always up to something but not a scrap of real mischief in them. They might scrump a couple of apples from the orchard in Carlisle Crescent, though if Frank caught them at it, he'd give them a walloping, but they wouldn't go tramping about on other people's allotments or out-and-out stealing like young Micky Baxter. And of course Jess wanted them at home. He did, too. He wanted to see them growing up, to watch them change from babies to boys, to young men.

And that was just it. He wanted to see them grow up. And he was desperately afraid that if they came back to Portsmouth they might be killed.

Frank had still not really recovered from that first raid, when he had come round the corner of Farlington Road and seen the mess the bombers had made of Drayton Road School. He couldn't forget the pall of dust and smoke, the acrid smell that hung over the still trembling streets. He couldn't forget the sight of the smashed buildings, the debris of brick and wood and concrete that had been hurled everywhere as if by some mad giant. Worst of all, he couldn't forget the bodies, ripped to pieces by the blast. The foot he had tried to match up with its mate. The head, gazing at him from a pile of blood-soaked bandages.

Sometimes in his dreams, it was Tim's head, or Keith's. He couldn't bear it when the faces of his sons stared at him like that, in nightmare. And he couldn't tell Jess about such horrors. They were things he had to bear alone.

Well, there were plenty of people having to suffer worse for this war. It wasn't what they'd wanted from life, but life had a way of only giving you part of what you wanted. And you just had to be thankful for that part.

He went down the garden path to his shed. He was making Keith a toy fort for Christmas, with bits of hardboard cut with jagged edges to look like a palisade, and little wooden turrets. Luckily, the boys already had some model cowboys and Indians, and Tim even had a couple of Mounties of which he was very proud. You couldn't get much of that sort of thing now.

Making things for his children was something Frank had little time for these days. But he'd started in good time and he enjoyed tinkering with something that, for once, had nothing at all to do with the war. With so much of his time and attention taken up with it, from his work in the Yard to his firewatching and warden's duties, he didn't get much relaxation at all these days.

He wished there was something he could make for Jess too. She was a wife in a million, his Jess, and she deserved the best. But he knew there was only one present she really wanted this Christmas.

And that was to have her children home around her once more, and to know that this time it was for good.

Jess too was thinking about Christmas presents.

There were a few bits and pieces she could make for Keith's fort, flags sewn from scraps of material, wigwams for the Indian camp, and she had managed to buy a second-hand football for Tim. For Rose, she was knitting a jumper out of an old cardigan of her own that she had unravelled. It was just the shade of green that Rose liked best, and it suited her dark hair and brown eyes.

Maureen, at eighteen months old, was still happy with simple toys. She would play for hours with a few cardboard boxes or some newspaper, and Tim's old building blocks were still her favourites. Her grandmother and various aunts had all made or knitted her things, she had an assortment of woollen animals and dolls in the most unlikely colours, including a fair isle cat knitted by Howard's wife, Nora, who fancied herself with the needles. But it was difficult to know what else to give her.

She went up the street to do her shopping. Kathy Simmons' pram was outside number 16, with little Thomas fast asleep inside. His eyes were fringed with long, dark lashes that curled at the ends and seemed to have been tipped with gold-dust. It's not fair, Jess thought. Boys always get the most gorgeous lashes. And when he opened his eyes, she knew they'd be a dark blue, as if they were going to stay that colour, not the milky colour new babies' eyes often were before they changed to brown or hazel. He was a lovely baby, and Kathy was quite rightly thrilled with him.

'I don't know why I bother to do the shopping every day,' Jess remarked to Mr Hines. 'There's almost nothing about. But you have to keep coming, on the offchance that someone's actually had a delivery.'

Mr Hines stood Maureen on the counter. He winked at Jess and laid his finger alongside his nose.

'Don't tell anyone, and I'll let you have a pound of liver. Came in just this morning. I thought you might be in.'

'Oh, that's good of you.' She watched as Mr Hines weighed it out. There was nothing underhand, or under-the-counter about the transaction – liver wasn't rationed anyway – but there were still enough spiteful people around to make comments if they saw you getting something they didn't. 'I don't know why they don't ration liver. It's so good for you, and there's only one in each animal, isn't there?'

Mr Hines smiled. 'That's right. And kidneys too, twice as many of them, of course, but they're much smaller, they make a real tasty pie or stew. But people don't seem to make the use of 'em.'

'Well, I do, and I make sure this little one eats her share. It's good for her blood.' Jess went to scoop Maureen from the counter. The little girl was kneeling by the *papier-mâché* lamb, her arms around its neck. 'Say goodbye to Larry now, Maureen. She really loves that lamb,' she said to the butcher. 'I wish I could get her something like that for Christmas. But there's just nothing in the shops for kiddies now.'

'I know,' he said. 'The toymakers are all working for the war effort. God knows what they're making, soldiers never took teddy bears to war with them in my day, but there it is. It's like furniture makers, they're all doing different things now. Nothing's the same as it was.'

Jess lifted Maureen off the counter and took her outside. She was getting almost too big for her pram now, but she'd go on using it till she was past two, for you couldn't expect a toddler to walk all the way up the street and round the shops. Besides, it made carrying the shopping so much easier. Jess would miss it when she finally stopped using it.

Alice Brunner was looking whiter than ever. Jess tried to persuade her to come down to number 14 for a cup of tea in the afternoon, but she shook her head. It was as if she were afraid to leave the house.

'She won't go out in case there's a telegram from Daddy,' Joy told her afterwards, coming out on to the pavement on the pretext of cleaning the windows. 'She's got really superstitious about it, as if it would bring bad luck. She's certain that the minute she steps out of doors, they'll tell us he's dead.' The girl rubbed her face tiredly. 'Sometimes I wish they would, then it would all be over. That's an awful thing to say, isn't it?'

'It's an awful thing to feel,' Jess said gently. 'It's been hard on you too.'

The girl's face crumpled. 'I miss Daddy too. But we can't go on as if he's only just died. We've got to carry on, haven't we? That's what everybody says.'

'Yes,' Jess said, 'we've got to carry on.' She hesitated, then said on impulse, 'What are you and your mum doing for Christmas?'

Joy made a face. 'Christmas! We don't even talk about it. We'll only know it's happening because there won't be any papers that day. At least we'll get a lie-in, that'll be our only Christmas present, I reckon.' She bent and swilled her rag about in the bucket of water. 'I got Mum some of those chocolates she likes, and a book. I can't afford any more than that.'

'I'm sure she'll be pleased. But what I was going to say was, why don't you both come down to us for your Christmas dinner? We'll probably be at my sister's, but there's room for another two at the table. We can always squeeze round a bit. It might be better than being on your own.'

Joy paused in her polishing and stared at her. 'Oh, Mrs Budd. Could we really? Will Rose be there too?'

Poor kid, she's lonely, Jess thought. Stuck in this shop all day and all by herself with her mum in the evenings, no time to have fun with her own friends. And she's missing Rose. She's always asking how she is, out at Bridge End.

'You tell your mum that's what you're doing,' she said firmly. 'And as soon as Rose gets home, I'll send her up to see you. It's time you had a bit of companionship of your own age.'

She looked at Joy's face. There were lines that shouldn't be there, a frown of worry on her brow. The girl was growing old before her time.

There were more ways than one of being injured in the war.

18

'Will you be going home for Christmas, Bet?'

Yvonne was sitting on her bed, cutting her toenails. The girls had had their weekly bath and Erica was drying her hair. She had had it all cut off the week after Geoffrey had died, almost as short as a boy's and it had curled just like Betty's. It clustered like a golden halo all over her head and created much envy in Yvonne's breast.

'Look at her. She doesn't even *care* what she looks like now, and she still manages to look like a film star! I thought having all her hair cut off would make her look – well, not ugly, but more ordinary. What chance have you and me got, Bet?'

'I don't know that I want any chances,' Betty said with a sigh. 'Seems to me you've only got to put a skirt on and it causes trouble.'

'It causes even more when you take it off!' Yvonne said with a giggle. 'But you never answered me. Are you going home?'

'I don't know.' The arrangement was that two of the four farm workers – the girls and Dennis – should have Christmas, while the other two had the New Year. Betty wanted to go home, of course, she'd had a letter from Olive only yesterday which hinted at some news she and Derek would be breaking to the family, but she also wanted to be on the farm while Dennis was here. And she hadn't plucked up courage to ask him. 'What are you doing, Yvonne?'

'Oh, I'll go home. Mum's got enough on her plate as it is, with all the kids round her feet.' There were five younger than Yvonne, and her sister Clarice's two who were looked after by their grandmother while Clarrie worked in the Dockyard. 'And Mrs Spencer told me she'd give me a few bits and pieces to take home with me. That'll make a lot of difference in our house.'

'What are you doing, Erica?'

'What?' The blonde girl turned from the photograph she was gazing at. She looked at it every night for hours, as if trying to memorise every line of Geoffrey's face. In fact, she was trying to remember it. In her memory, his face had blurred and become indistinct and it was only when staring at his photograph that she could recall clearly what he looked like. She was bewildered and upset by this, thinking that it meant she hadn't loved Geoffrey after all – and I did, I *did*, she thought despairingly.

'I asked what you're doing at Christmas? Staying here or going home?'

'Oh, I don't know. It doesn't really matter, anyway. My parents don't even know I'm there, half the time.'

'Oh go on, they must do.'

'No, they don't. It was all right while I was little, my mother could dress me up like a little doll and show me off to her friends. But now, she doesn't want me around. It doesn't matter how nice I look – sometimes, I think that makes it worse.'

The other two stared at her, fascinated.

'How could looking nice make her worse?'

Erica shrugged. 'She doesn't want me around when she's got her friends in the house. Her men friends,' she added with slight emphasis.

Betty felt her cheeks turn scarlet. Yvonne smothered a giggle of embarrassment.

'You mean she has – has – you know, lovers?'

'I don't know what they are,' Erica said. 'All I know is, there are always people at our house, men and women. It's like one long party. And if one of the men takes a fancy to me, she doesn't like it. All the same, when I took Geoff home, well, you'd have thought he was *her* boyfriend, not mine!'

She turned back to the photograph. Betty picked up the sock she was darning. Erica's home life sounded so different from her own, she could scarcely believe it. She tried to picture her mother having men friends at home, and failed. Nor could she imagine her father treating life as 'one long party'. As for Annie behaving as if Graham was *her* boyfriend – well, Betty's mind couldn't take that in at all!

Not that Graham was her boyfriend now. She hadn't heard from him since the night he'd walked out and didn't really expect to. She felt sorry that they'd parted bitterly, but relieved to be free of his possessiveness.

She hadn't told Dennis yet about that last quarrel. She wasn't ready yet to start a new relationship. She wanted to get to know him slowly, to try to understand the way he thought about things, the different attitudes he seemed to possess. She asked him about them as they worked together.

Dennis was willing enough to talk.

'I've always believed in peace,' he told Betty. 'It's all any of us want. Well, except for a few madmen who've got the power to send other men to die for what *they* believe in. I think that's what I've got against it mostly. Why should anyone have that sort of power? Why should anyone have the power to send thousands – millions – of people to fight other people they haven't even met?'

Dennis was a Quaker too. He explained this to Betty as they worked together, milking the cows. It was warm and cosy in the byre in the early mornings, with the cows breathing steamily and the lamp flickering gently. Betty pressed her head against the solid flank and squeezed the teats between her fingers. The milk squirted into the bucket and made a white froth.

'We don't really call ourselves Quakers,' he said. 'We're Friends. The Society of Friends.'

'That sounds nice.'

'I think so, too. We believe that every man has the seed of God within him.' Betty blushed, feeling almost as embarrassed by the reference to God as she felt about sex. 'That means Germans and Japanese and Russians, you and me – everyone. And you can't kill someone who's partly God, can you?'

'No. But . . . even Hitler?'

'Even Hitler,' Dennis said firmly. 'And Rommel and Goering and Mussolini and all the rest of them. Not that I mightn't forget about being a Friend and a pacifist if I had *them* there in front of me,' he added thoughtfully, eyeing a pitchfork that was leaning against the wall.

Betty laughed soberly. 'I can see what you meant about the pilots, the ones who crashed in our field. They were just young chaps, like Sandy and the others. But Hitler and those people, they've got to be stopped.'

'Oh yes. But killing young men and girls and children and old people, and people who've got nothing to do with the war, isn't going to stop them.' Dennis finished milking Bluebell and came round the other side to start on Dewdrop. 'Look at what they're doing. They're just getting together as many soldiers and sailors and airmen as they can and setting them against each other, like spiders in a jar. In the end, it'll all come down to who's got most men and most bombs. Why not just count them all in the first place? Or better still, why not just sit down and talk about it?'

Betty shook her head. It sounded so simple when Dennis said that, but could it really be so easy? If it was, why hadn't people tried it?

'Because they're not reasonable people,' he said. 'They're mad. But that doesn't mean everyone else has to go mad as well.'

'But if there's one man like Hitler who goes mad, what can you do about him? He's got so much power, he controls everything. How can people go against him? And if they did – if the whole army rose up against him – he'd still have enough people to take his side. There'd still be a war.' She gazed at Dennis with troubled eyes. 'D'you really think there'll ever be enough people to stand up and say war's wrong, and refuse to fight?'

'I'd like to think so,' Dennis said. 'But I don't suppose there ever will be. But that doesn't mean that those of us who do think that way should be forced to go against our beliefs. And more in this war than ever before, because this is supposed to be a war for free speech. The Archbishop of Canterbury himself said so.'

He finished Dewdrop and stood up. Betty gave Buttercup a pat on the flank and the cow turned large, mild brown eyes on her and blew softly. Dennis came to stand beside her.

'You never told me, Betty. What happened when you went home the other weekend?'

'About Graham and me, you mean?' She looked down at her hands. She still missed Graham's little ring, even though she'd rarely worn it on her left hand. She had felt as though she was wearing it. 'We've broken up. He wanted us to get married so that I'd be there waiting for him whenever he came home. And I didn't want to, so we called it a day.' She looked up into Dennis's eyes. 'I'm not sorry, not really. We shouldn't ever have let it get that far. He wanted to own me, that's why he wanted to get married. That and—' she blushed. 'He never did like the idea of me working on a farm.'

'I see.' Dennis said nothing for a few minutes. Then he said quietly, 'I won't rush you, Betty. You need a bit of time when you've just broken up with someone. But when you feel ready to think about someone else, well, you know I'll be here.'

Betty turned her head to look up at him. He was tall, an inch or two taller than Graham, and his body was lean and strong. Graham had filled out since joining the Navy but there had always been a hint of flabbiness about him, as if he had muscles he didn't bother to use much. He had cheeky eyes and a grin that had caught at her heart for a while, but he didn't really have much sense of humour. He got most of his fun out of teasing, or even taunting, other people.

She remembered the day she had first met him, walking down Queen Street with Bob Shaw. Bob had been friendly but a bit shy and Graham had seized his opportunity to ask her out. If he hadn't, she'd have gone out with Bob, because he'd asked her too, on the bus on their way home, but by then she'd promised Graham.

Well, it was all over and no harm done. And now Bob was in the Army, though he was back in Pompey now, and she'd met Dennis instead.

He was looking down at her, his eyes smiling and serious all at once, and his mouth was slightly curved. Suddenly, she wanted nothing more than to put her arms around him; to feel those smiling lips touch hers.

'I feel ready now,' she said quietly. 'That's if you are too.'

'Oh yes,' Dennis said, 'I've been ready for a long time.'

He slid his arms around her and drew her close. Betty went willingly, feeling the excitement leap like a flame in her body. She closed her eyes, savouring his warmth, the steady beat of his heart. She felt a strength flow from him, a strength that had to do with more than mere physical muscle. There was a power in Dennis that Graham hadn't had, a stamina and courage that she hadn't known before.

Dennis bent his head and laid his lips gently upon hers. She felt their tension, an emotion that quivered very slightly against her mouth. It drew from her an instant response and she tightened her arms about him and opened her mouth to his.

'Betty, I love you.'

The words came from his lips as if they had been born there. She heard them with wonder, heard the truth in each syllable, and felt her answer like a warmth inside, like a flower opening to the sun.

'I love you, Dennis.'

It was like a vow, spoken there in the byre with the cows shifting gently around them and the smell of warm milk in the air. They looked into each other's eyes and smiled gravely, and Dennis lifted one hand and traced the contours of her face with his fingertips.

'You're beautiful, d'you know that? Has anyone told you before?'

Graham had, at least, he'd told her she was a 'smasher'. But it hadn't been the same. Dennis was talking about a beauty that was more than skin deep, a beauty that arose from the love they had just expressed for each other. It was a beauty that shone only for him, and had nothing to do with perms and make-up and silk stockings.

'So are you,' she said, and he laughed.

'Nobody's ever said it to *me* before!'

'No, but you know what I mean.' She gazed at him, noting the straight brows, the golden flecks in his eyes, the firmness of his mouth. 'When I first saw you, I thought how good-looking you were. But I don't mean that. It's not looks, it's something else. Something in your eyes, in the way you look. Oh, I don't know how to explain it but—'

'It's all right. I know what you mean.' He kissed her again. 'And I'm glad you see what I see. It's something between us, isn't it? Something important.'

'Yes.'

They stood quietly for a while, holding each other close. Then Dennis gave a little sigh and said, 'We'd better get on with our work, Betty. Mrs Spencer'll have breakfast ready soon.'

'I know.' She remembered what she had been meaning to ask him. 'Dennis, what are you doing at Christmas? Will you be going home?'

He grinned a little. 'I thought I'd wait and see what you were doing.'

'I was waiting for you!' They both laughed, and she said seriously, 'I suppose we'd both like to be with our own families at Christmas. But Yvonne wants to go home then too, so one of us'll have to stay.'

'What about Erica?'

'She doesn't care much. It doesn't seem as though she's very happy at home.'

Dennis was silent for a moment, then he said, 'Well, suppose we both stay here at Christmas, and then Erica and Yvonne can be here at New Year. I can't see Erica wanting to be here on her own with me. She can barely tolerate being in the same room these days.'

'Oh, Dennis.' Betty held him close again. 'I can't understand why she hates you so much. Anyone can see what sort of person you are, but she treats you like a criminal.'

'No,' he said, 'like a traitor. Don't blame her, Betty. A lot of people feel like that. And when she's lost her own fiancé . . .'

'I know.' Betty thought of the young pilots, so carefree and light-hearted, buzzing around the lanes in their little car, singing at the tops of their voices. But they hadn't been carefree at all, had they? Every day they'd seen more of their comrades killed, shot down, burned to death, drowned. Every day they'd seen their own doom approach a little closer. *It's pretty lonely, up there in the sky.* Every time they'd scrambled for their planes, they'd known this might be the last.

No, it wasn't surprising that Erica and others like her should hate the young men who had refused to fight.

She held Dennis a little tighter. I'll never hate them, she thought, never. And aloud, she said, 'I love you, Dennis.'

'I love you . . .'

At the beginning of Christmas week, families began to arrive home to spend Christmas together.

The Budd children had arrived on Sunday, fetched home by their father who had cycled out to Bridge End and brought them back by train. After Christmas, he would take them back and then ride his bike home again.

'Let's hope there isn't a blizzard like there was last year,' he commented, but at the moment the weather was quiet enough, though cold.

The boys came in with bright eyes and glowing cheeks. Jess had a fire burning in the grate ready for them, and some lentil soup simmering on the stove. Maureen was sitting on the floor, playing with Tim's coloured blocks, and he immediately got down to play with her, showing her how to build a castle. Maureen watched and chuckled, hitting the edifice with her fist the moment he had completed it.

Rose went straight to her mother and buried her face against Jess's breast. Jess held her warmly, feeling the ache in her throat. She had missed Rose's company, for the girl was growing up as a friend as well as daughter and they'd begun to share a good many interests. She held out her hand to Keith and looked at Tim, still kneeling on the rug playing with Maureen.

'Oh, it's good to have you all back,' she said shakily, and looked at Frank. 'This is how things ought to be. The six of us, all together at home. *Nothing* should come between families, Frank, nothing.'

He nodded. He knew what Jess meant and he agreed with her. But even as he agreed, he saw again in his mind the vision of a head, torn from its body, resting on a pile of stained bandages and looking at him with his son's eyes, and he knew that he would have no peace of mind until Christmas was over and he could take them back.

At Annie's house, just up the street, the celebrations were slightly muted by Betty's absence.

Derek was in the front room with Olive, helping to hang up paper-chains and trying to find out why one of the Christmas tree lights didn't work. There was no tree of course, but the lights could be hung round the wall and look just as good. He traced the faulty bulb at last, then arranged them in the pattern of a tree and stood back to admire the effect.

'That's lovely, Derek. Really artistic.' Olive came over and gave him a kiss. 'I like the way you've put those coloured balls round the lights. It makes them really glitter.'

'Maybe I'll set up in business when the war's over,' he said. 'Your room decorated by Harker and Son.'

Olive caught her breath and they looked at each other, smiling with excitement.

'It's really true, isn't it,' she said wonderingly. 'We're having a baby. You and me. A baby all of our own. Oh, Derek . . .'

He kissed her again. 'I can still hardly believe it. I thought when it didn't happen in September—'

'Well, it didn't have much of a chance then, did it?' Olive remembered the day she had waved goodbye to Derek at the station, running along the platform, wondering when she would see him again. Their time together had been so brief. And then he'd been back only a month later! The Unit had stayed in Portsmouth then and looked likely to be here for a while. The longer the better, she thought, laying her head against his chest. Long enough, she hoped, for Derek to be home when their baby was born and hold it in his arms. But perhaps the war would be over by then anyway.

'July,' she said. 'It's due on July the fifteenth. That's St Swithin's Day. If it rains then, it'll rain for forty days, and if the sun shines it's going to shine for forty days.'

'Gosh,' he said, 'I hope that doesn't apply to babies too. I don't know that I want forty kids!'

Olive giggled. 'Neither do I. One'll be enough for the time being.' She hugged him again. 'I hope it's a boy and looks like you.'

'I don't. I hope it's a girl and looks like you.'

'One of each, then. Only not both at once, though I wouldn't mind twins, really. It'd be fun if they were identical and no one could tell them apart. I like seeing twins dressed the same, they're cute.'

'They wouldn't be identical if they were one of each,' he pointed out, and Olive laughed again.

'Well, we'll settle for one, and take whatever we get. I don't care, so long as it's all right. And so long as it's not born in an air-raid shelter, like poor Kathy Simmons'.' She shuddered. 'That must have been awful. She had just Tommy Vickers with her, no woman at all, and those two poor little girls seeing it all.'

'She was lucky to have Tommy.'

'I know. She says he was marvellous. I wouldn't want it to happen to me, all the same.'

They went back to their decorating. Derek had managed to get some holly, and they stuck it behind the mirror and pictures.

'D'you think your mum's got any idea?' he asked.

'About the baby? I don't know, I've caught her looking at me a bit funny once or twice. But there's nothing to show yet, it's only just eight weeks, after all. The doctor said I might get some morning-sickness but I haven't so far. I think she suspected before, I missed after you'd been here in September. But then I came on again, so it was a false alarm.' She sighed contentedly. 'It isn't this time, though. This time it's real.'

'But we'll tell 'em, won't we? At Christmas dinner?'

'Oh yes,' she said. 'We'll tell them then.'

Christmas dinner was going to be different this year, she thought. Me and Derek married – last year, we'd only just got engaged. And our Betty away on the farm. And Alice Brunner and Joy, invited because Auntie Jess was so sorry for them.

It would be different. But for Olive it would be perfect, because Derek would be with her and because they would tell the family that their first baby was on its way.

And next Christmas will be different again, she thought. The baby will be here – six months old. And Derek?

A shiver passed across her skin and she turned towards him and then laughed, forgetting everything as he held up a tiny sprig in his hand.

'Mistletoe! Oh, Derek!'

The Germans had promised a truce over Christmas, although it was not official and nobody could be certain they would keep their word. On Monday, the day before Christmas Eve, everyone went about their preparations with one eye on the sky and one ear ready for the alert. It was quiet, but tense. Nobody knew if it would last.

'If they can call a truce for Christmas, why not call it for the rest of the year? The rest of our lives?' Jess asked, but nobody could answer her and she did not expect them to try. The war had turned into a machine that, once set in motion, could not be stopped. It must, like some terrible disease, run its course.

'Let's be thankful for small mercies,' Annie advised. 'Enjoy our Christmas, with the kids around us.' She sighed, thinking of Betty. The first Christmas in nineteen years without her bright face at the table. But next year, if her suspicions were correct, there'd be another kiddy sitting up in a high chair and banging a spoon on the table. As Kathy Simmons had proved, life must go on.

Jess went up to September Street to do her shopping, accompanied by the whole family. She was proud of them as she watched the boys running ahead and felt Rose's fingers on the handle of the pram. Four lovely children. Two bright, lively boys, a daughter who was all any mother could wish for, and a baby who never stopped smiling. She was spoken to half a dozen times by neighbours who wanted to look at them, to ask them about their life in the country, to talk about Christmas. And there were other mothers with their children too, boys and girls who had been out at Bridge End with Rose and Tim and Keith, and some who had been sent to the Isle of Wight or Salisbury.

'It's good to hear the children's voices in the street again,' Peggy Shaw said. 'You forget what it's like. I've only just realised how quiet it's been all these months.'

'It's going to be harder than ever to let them go again,' Jess remarked wistfully. 'Specially as we don't even know where the boys'll be going. The billeting people have got to find them somewhere else.'

'That's a shame. They were all right where they were, weren't they? It's a pity to move them.'

'So long as they don't split them up,' Jess said. 'It won't be so bad if they can be together. And near Rose.' In fact, the boys saw very little of Rose. Edna Corner invited her to tea once a week and Mrs Greenberry had the brothers over, but apart from that they didn't bother much. She was only their sister, after all. They could see her any time.

Rose went into the newsagent's and Jess left the boys on the pavement with Jimmy Cross and Cyril Nash while she went into the butcher's. Mr Hines was waiting for her, a broad smile on his face.

'I've got something for you.'

'Liver? Sausages?' She smiled back. There wasn't much else a butcher could have for you these days. But to her astonishment, he handed her a large, oddly-shaped brown paper parcel.

'What on earth—?'

'Sssh.' He winked and put his finger to his lips. 'It's for the nipper.' He looked significantly at Maureen.

'For Maureen? But—' Jess looked at the parcel again. 'Whatever – oh . . . Of course. It's L—'

'*Sssh*,' he said again. 'We don't want her knowing before Santa, do we? I thought it might keep her amused a bit over the holiday.'

'Keep her amused! She'll love it.' Jess looked at him, her eyes bright. For goodness' sake, she scolded herself, fancy wanting to cry because a butcher gives you his *papier-mâché* lamb! 'It's very nice of you, Mr Hines. I'm really touched.'

He waved a hand. 'It's all right. I was getting a bit fed up with it on the counter anyway. And the kiddy's fond of it. Like you say, there's not much about in the way of toys just now.'

'Well, I still think it's really nice of you. And the baby'll be thrilled.'

She went next door to the newsagent's. Alice was there, serving behind the counter. Her face was pale but she managed to summon up a wan smile and nodded as Jess asked if she and Joy were still coming down to Annie's on Christmas Day.

'So long as you don't mind looking at my long face,' she said. 'I can't feel much like Christmas, Jess, and that's the truth of it. But you're right, I've got to make an effort for Joy's sake. She deserves a bit of fun, and I know she won't come without me.'

'I should think not. Families ought to be together at Christmas,' Jess said, and closed her mouth abruptly. There she went again, saying exactly the wrong thing! It was so easy. But there was one thing you could say for Alice, she never took offence where there was none meant. And she really did seem to be pulling herself together. Look at her now, smiling at the boys and giving them a toffee each out of a jar. And Joy looked happier too, with Rose to talk to again.

It really seemed as if there had been a truce declared. No bombers came over all day that Monday, the day before Christmas Eve, and there were no warning sirens. The short December afternoon drew into evening and blackout curtains went up. Fires were lit and families who had been parted for months clustered about them. They made toast and ate scones and doughnuts and lardy cake. They played games and listened to the wireless. They almost forgot to listen, to wait, to be afraid.

But the Luftwaffe had not forgotten them. At ten minutes to seven, one bomber came unannounced. It flew over Portsmouth, a single droning note in the empty sky and, before anyone could lift a finger, dropped a bomb packed with two and a half thousand pounds of high explosive. The detonation shook the whole city, and in every home families stared at each other and then raced for their shelters.

'Blimey!' Frank exclaimed. 'That sounded like the whole Yard going up.'

'What about the truce?' Jess was clutching the baby, who was screaming in terror. 'What about Christmas?'

They snatched up the things they kept ready to take to the shelter, the old blankets, the cushions, the biscuits and bottle of water, the tin box that contained all the insurance policies and family photographs. Rose was in a panic, urging them to hurry, the boys were pale, half scared, half excited.

They crammed through the half-sunken doorway and found themselves places on the bunks, staring up at the corrugated iron roof and waiting for the next explosion.

'Coo,' Tim breathed. 'That was a whopper. But I can't hear any more planes.'

'Well, there's no need to sound disappointed,' Jess said sharply. 'We don't want any more. And stop trying to peep out through the curtain, Keith, we'll have Mr Vickers down here telling us off for showing a light.'

'I only wanted to see the searchlights.'

'And the Germans'll see you.'

Frank looked at them and thought again of the head. They ought to have stayed at Bridge End. Christmas or not, they ought to have stayed there.

Even Granny Kinch had been scared into taking cover with her daughter Nancy and the two kids. Ethel Glaister was in her Anderson with Joe and Carol, furiously berating the absent George for not being there to take care of them. Annie, at the top of the street, was thinking anxiously about Ted, skippering his ferryboat across the harbour. But in number 13 Peggy Shaw and her daughter Gladys were setting off for their First Aid Post, ready to deal with whatever casualties the raid might bring.

But there were no more raids that night. The plane had come alone, dropped its bomb and departed.

'It was Conway Street caught it,' Peggy told them later, when the All-Clear had sounded and everyone was back indoors. 'We got the message at the Post. They reckon there was at least a dozen killed. All the houses in the street smashed to rubble, with everyone inside. They're still trying to get 'em out. That young Dr Mulvaney's there of course – she's a marvel, always in the thick of it all, brave as a lion, and only a slip of a thing too. They reckon it was a plane loaded with bombs that got shot down.'

The stories of what had happened in Conway Street abounded. A plane – two planes – three or more, crashed on the houses with their full cargo of explosive. A land-mine. One huge bomb, of a kind never used before. Whatever it was, it shattered the flimsy old houses packed up against the Dockyard wall and left a scene of devastation yet unrivalled by any of the raids.

'There's a crater big enough to get Portsmouth Cathedral into.' 'It blew out every window for miles around.' 'They'll never repair all the damage, never.' 'They'll never get all the bodies out.'

The stories started Christmas Eve off on a sombre note. Nobody could have any faith now in the 'truce'.

It was as if one man had decided to bring terror instead of peace to their Christmas truce. *This is what we can do. This is what you can expect as soon as the truce is over.*

19

'We can't let it spoil the children's Christmas,' Jess said. 'I know it's terrible, all those people killed and others with no homes. But we've got to think of the children.'

She set Rose to peeling vegetables, making jellies and helping to decorate the cake. She had saved enough dried fruit during the past few months to make a reasonable fruit cake, and had carefully hoarded a bag of icing sugar for the top. And on Christmas morning she took all the children except Maureen to church. Indeed, it would have been impossible to take Maureen anywhere that morning without taking Larry along too.

Alice was there, in the Deniston Road church where she and Heinrich had so often worshipped. She looked pale but determined, as if she'd made up her mind to cope. That's better, Jess thought, seeing that Joy too looked brighter, and she was glad she'd invited them to Annie's. As soon as the service was over, they walked down the street to the house with the little turret and arrived to a scene of rejoicing.

'We were going to tell you all at dinner,' Olive said, her cheeks flushed. 'But I couldn't keep it back any longer. I just had to tell Mum first.'

'And so you should.' Jess gave her niece a hug. 'A new baby! Well, that's really lovely. And our Annie a grandma! How d'you feel about that, Annie?'

'I daresay I'll get used to the idea.' But Annie's eyes were bright and her cheeks wet. Her smile broke through and she gave both Olive and Derek a kiss. 'Mind, I still think you ought to have waited. It's no time to be bringing a baby into the world. But since it's on its way, there's not much we can do but give it a welcome.'

'Go on, our Annie, you're as pleased as Punch.' Jess glanced through the window at the children, who were out in the garden playing with Tim's new football. 'We won't say anything to *them* yet, of course. They don't need to know. We don't want any awkward questions.' She knew nothing of Reg Corner's sex education lessons to the two boys, nor of Tibby's kittens. Even Rose hadn't mentioned that she now knew 'all about' babies from helping Mr Greenberry with the sheep.

'Well, let's drink to it anyway,' Ted said, producing a bottle of sherry and filling Annie's best glasses. 'To Olive and Derek's baby, and to a happy Christmas for everyone!'

'To the baby – and a Happy Christmas,' they repeated, and held up their glasses and drank.

Jess looked across the room and caught her husband's eye. Sherry was the one alcoholic drink he would take, and Christmas Day the one day he would take it. She toasted him silently with her eyes, trying to tell him all that she was feeling about this day, like a precious jewel with all her family about her. And she knew from the softening of his gaze that he understood.

And then her glance moved slowly over the rest of the people in the room. Her sister Annie, still defiantly scrubbing her step every morning, still keeping up the 'standards' her time in domestic service had instilled into her. Olive and Derek, starting their family after such a short married life, deserving so much more. Alice Brunner, who looked shy and as if she felt out of place in this family gathering.

Poor Alice. She must be missing Heinrich more than ever this morning. And there were others who were absent too – Colin, still at sea. Betty, away on the farm.

She looked at Frank again, and he must have seen the message in her eyes, for he cleared his throat, so that everyone stopped talking and listened to him.

'Another toast,' he said quietly, and lifted his glass. 'To absent friends.'

And again, they all echoed the toast, in voices that trembled with the emotions they shared.

'To absent friends . . .'

With Iris Blake and her children gone, and Erica away at home, the antagonism that had prevailed towards Dennis evaporated. Mr and Mrs Spencer had never been hostile towards him and old Jonas cared about very little provided his beer and tobacco came regularly and his plate was full at mealtimes. He did his work and spent his evenings in the village pub, sitting in a corner by the fire and making a pint last all evening. He had been more hostile towards the girls than to Dennis, but now that they had proved themselves able to do whatever was asked of them, he had relented far enough to give them a grunt of a morning and even, occasionally, a gap-toothed travesty of a smile.

'He's all right really,' Dennis said. 'He's just like a lot of old people, can't take the changes so he pretends they aren't happening. You can't blame him, he's been through one war already, why should he have to suffer another?'

'He must have been through more than one,' Betty said. 'He's seventy if he's a day. He's seen a lot.'

Erica and Yvonne departed on Christmas Eve, just before afternoon milking and, without them and the Blakes, the farm seemed very quiet. Betty wondered what it would be like to sleep by herself in the long, narrow attic. Dennis too had moved into the house; until now, he had slept in a sectioned-off part of the barn but now that there was more room indoors Mrs Spencer had decided he ought to be offered a proper bed. Betty thought of him, lying in the room below hers, and felt a quiver of excitement. It seemed almost indecently intimate, somehow, even though there would be a floor and several walls between them.

Christmas was to be a real holiday. Only essential chores such as milking and feeding were to be done, and the rest of the time was free. On Christmas morning, the Spencers would be going to church, and Dennis and Betty decided to go along too.

'I'd go to Meeting at home,' he said. 'But there isn't one near enough here. We don't have hymns or prayers or anything like that, but I like the carols.'

'What do you have, then? Bible readings and sermons?'

He laughed. 'No, not unless someone feels like it. We just sit quietly together and wait.'

Betty stared at him. 'What d'you wait for?'

'For God to speak through one of us. Then whoever it is gets up and says what he feels he should say, and sits down again.'

'And that's all?'

'Unless anyone else feels called upon to speak, yes. Sometimes several do, sometimes no one at all. It doesn't matter. It's a very peaceful, happy feeling to be sitting there all together, meeting in God.'

Betty tried to imagine it. She was accustomed to the Church of England services, busy all the way through with prayers and hymns and catechists and psalms. There wasn't a moment of quiet, except at the beginning, when you arrived and knelt to say your own private prayer, or at the end. Never a moment when God might 'speak' through an ordinary member of the congregation. In fact, when she came to think of it, he would have been hard put to it to get a word in anywhere.

'Isn't it boring?' she asked doubtfully.

Dennis smiled. 'Depends what sort of mood you're in. Sometimes I've had a job to sit still at all. But usually I find it very soothing, and afterwards I feel as if I've been, well, sort of re-created. It's not often you can sit with a lot of other people and not be overwhelmed with chatter. It's as if we give each other strength, even if nobody says a word.'

But this Christmas he came to church with Betty and the Spencers, and as they entered to the strains of the little organ Betty felt her own peace and joy in the warmth of companionship. She sat in the pew, looking about her at the faces which had become familiar to her over the past few months; the little woman with white hair, pinned into a bun, who ran the post office, the stout butcher, the greengrocer and the publicans. There were farmers and their wives who were friends and neighbours of the Spencers, and there were a few families who had been evacuated from Portsmouth and Southampton and were slowly becoming a part of the village themselves.

The note of the organ changed and stopped. There was a hushed silence and then the high, clear treble of a boy soprano began to sing. And Betty felt her throat ache with the beauty of his singing.

> 'Once in Royal David's city, stood a lowly cattle shed
> Where a mother laid her baby, in a manger for his bed.'

She turned and looked up at the man who stood at her side. And Dennis returned her look. He laid his hand over hers and clasped it tightly, and they stood together, lost in the tremulous joy of simply being together, and in the joy and peace that was being expressed all over Britain at that very moment in village churches, in great cathedrals, in tranquil villages and even amidst scenes of utter devastation.

It was Christmas, and Christmas could not be ignored.

Later that afternoon, when they had finished the milking, they strolled together down the lane and leant over a gate, watching the twilight steal gently over the sleeping fields.

'Everything seems so much quieter on Christmas Day,' Betty said softly. 'Even the animals are gentler, as if they know it's special. And it really does seem as if there's been a truce. A whole day with no bombs.'

'And if there can be one, why not two? Why start again at all?' Dennis sighed. 'If only they'd get together and talk. But Hitler will never see reason. He'll go on and on.' He stirred restlessly. 'Betty, I've been thinking about what I should do—'

'Oh, Dennis, no, not now!' she exclaimed impulsively. 'Don't let's talk about the war now. It's Christmas Day. Let's just think of happy things.'

He nodded and laid his arm across her shoulders. 'All right, sweetheart. We'll leave it for now. But we've got to talk seriously, you and me. You know that, don't you?'

She nodded, feeling suddenly shy. Her relationship with Dennis, which had grown and ripened so slowly, seemed to have shifted into a faster gear and she was half excited, half afraid, and totally unsure as to what should happen next.

In some ways, it had been easier with Graham. Their romance had followed a set of rules. Their meeting had been flirtatious, with Betty responding saucily to Graham's boldness, and when he'd asked her out it had been to the pictures, which was the accepted venue for any first date. He'd kissed her goodnight that time, after a faint-hearted struggle from Betty, and on subsequent evenings out the goodnight kiss had been taken for granted, lasting a little longer each time and accompanied by caresses which grew ever more daring. It had been all part of the game that Graham should attempt what Betty would forbid, and until the night of the card-game there had never been any serious risk of his demanding more.

Perhaps it was part of the game too that they should be possessive of each other. Betty would have been furious if she had seen Graham looking at another girl, and he was sulky when she announced her intention of joining the Land Army. But war made everything different, and Betty had always been an independent spirit. In the past few months, she had learned a different set of values, and the naive boy-and-girl games she had played with Graham no longer held any appeal.

With Dennis, nothing was the same. There was no place for sauciness, none for teasing. There was a seriousness about Dennis that brought response from a part of Betty she had never known existed. And there was a depth to the love she felt for him and the love she sensed in him for her, that had never been present when she was with Graham.

Yes, she knew they would have to talk seriously, and soon. But this was Christmas. A time for peace. A time for standing still.

Dennis pulled her a little closer and she leant her head on his shoulder. The moon was a sliver of brightness in the sky, rolled on its back amongst the stars. The trees were dark shapes above the huddled hedges. No lights showed from neighbouring farms or villages, but despite the truce – for it was only unofficial and could not be wholly trusted – the thin pencil beams of searchlights played in the sky over Portsmouth. They moved across the heavens like a web of silky light, tracing a silver lattice in space. Closer at hand, an owl hooted and Betty felt the velvet brush of its wings as it flew past her head.

'There are some things we have to talk about,' Dennis said quietly. 'You know what it's like, Betty. Tomorrow might not come. I can't risk leaving it. I've waited a long time to tell you I love you.'

'Dennis, I love you too.' She turned in his arms, seeking his lips with her own. They clung together, their bodies pressed close, feeling their warmth in the cold night air. She felt the firmness of his arms about her and knew that his strength came from deep in his heart, that he would always keep her safe. Her heart spoke to him, making its own vows, but she knew that Dennis needed to hear her voice. With more time, the heart could be given its chance, but did they have that time? She imagined the sound of a bomber droning through the silence of the night and her arms tightened around him.

Dennis pressed his lips against her hair, against her temple, against her cheek and her neck. He found her lips and laid his own gently upon them, but the gentleness turned swiftly to passion and he caught her hard against him, his mouth suddenly fierce. Betty gasped, swung momentarily into terror, for she had never been kissed in this way before, and then her whole body responded, melting against him, her lips soft and yielding, her breasts swelling against his chest. Briefly, she glimpsed the stars wheeling above, and then her eyes closed as Dennis lifted her in his arms and then laid her gently on the icy ground.

'No. It's too cold here.' She felt his strength as he drew her up again into his arms and looked down into her eyes. She could see the stars reflected in his wide, dark pupils, shimmering through the tears that lay bright on her lashes. Gently, he kissed each eyelid, and traced a line of tenderness down her neck to the hollow of her throat. His hand curved about her breast, his palm shaping itself to her softness, and she felt the leap of her heart beneath his touch. 'Betty,' he whispered, 'Betty . . . I want to love you . . .'

Betty clung to him. Her body was surging with desire. She had barely noticed the iciness of the ground, would willingly have opened herself to him there and then. She was shaken with a torrent of feeling more powerful than any she had known before. Graham's fumblings and her own half excited, half irritated response were no more than a pale shadow in comparison with this almost violent rush of emotion. It was like stepping from a familiar room into a jungle, where everything was new and nothing certain.

'Love me now, Dennis,' she whispered, pressing her body against his. 'Oh please, please, love me . . .'

He held her tightly and groaned. Then he lifted his head and pushed her away from him. His arms were strong but she could sense the reluctance in him, the desire to pull her close again, and she laid her hands on his shoulders and tried to draw him back. But Dennis shook his head.

'Not now. Not here. This isn't how it should be between us. We should think, be sensible—'

'*Sensible!*' The word was jerked out of her body. 'Dennis, there's nothing sensible about the way I feel – sense doesn't come into it. Not that sort of sense, anyway.' In fact, all her senses were reeling and she knew it, knew that he was right, but refused to acknowledge it. 'We love each other. What else matters?'

'You know what else.' His voice was ragged. 'Betty, I love you, and because I love you I want to take care of you. I don't want to do anything that might hurt you. Do you know what I mean?'

A little subdued, recognising his emotion, she said, 'Yes.'

'I can't take any risks,' he said. 'I want to marry you, but it's got to be done right. I don't want any shotgun weddings.'

She thought of Graham. He'd said he loved her, but he'd been talking about a different kind of love, or perhaps it wasn't love at all. What sort of love was it that would use a baby to get him what he wanted?

'I don't mind what happens,' she said, 'as long as we can be together.'

He looked down at her gravely and she saw the shine of his eyes in the starlight.

'There's a war on, Betty,' he said. 'We might not be able to be together.'

'So love me! Let's love each other while we can, while we've got this chance. It's Christmas night, Dennis.' She looked up at him, pleadingly. 'There doesn't have to be a risk, does there? Aren't there things you can use? Or – or are Quakers like Roman Catholics and don't believe in it?'

She saw him smile. 'No, we're not at all like Roman Catholics. But there aren't many places open on Christmas night to buy those kind of things, Betty, and I don't keep them in my pockets.' He kissed her again and held her close. 'Besides, you haven't had time to think about it. I told you, I won't rush you. You've got to be sure.'

'I am sure,' she said quietly, but he turned away from the gate and took her hand.

'Let's go back now, my darling. Let's go back, and have our tea, and spend the evening by the fire with Mr and Mrs Spencer and that old grump Jonas. Let's be just like a married couple, sitting on the settee and holding hands and knowing that all our loving is there to be taken later on, a part of us. It won't be any the less for waiting.' He kissed her once more, his lips lingering on hers, his cheek cold against her skin. 'Let's make this Christmas a Christmas we'll always treasure, one we'll look back on when we're old and grey, one that will always shine in our memories because it was the Christmas we fell in love.'

Betty could not answer. With her hand in his, she walked back towards the darkened farmhouse. Inside, she knew, it would be warm and bright, filled with good smells and cheerfulness. Outside, it was black with the shadows of war.

A Christmas to be treasured. To shine in their memories for the rest of their lives.

Would it be really be any more treasured because we didn't make love, because we took no risks? she thought. Wouldn't it shine even more brightly if we had the memory of a sweet loving to carry with us through the years? Perhaps even a child, not used to get them their way as Graham had wanted, but conceived of their tenderness for each other, born of their passion. And shouldn't such a conception be left to the God in whom Dennis believed so steadfastly?

Tea was ready when they went back indoors, a spread of sandwiches and salad, cakes and jelly. Betty thought of the family at home. They would all be there, except herself and Colin. Olive and Derek would have told their news, which had been conveyed to Betty in a slip of paper included with her present (a pair of mittens knitted by Olive). They would have eaten their Christmas dinner and had a walk in the afternoon and after tea they would be making a party of the evening, with games like Family Coach and the Jelly Race and Alibis. By now they would be singing, all the old songs like *Tavern in the Town* and *Molly Malone*, and some of the newer ones too – *A Nightingale Sang in Berkeley Square*, and the one the popular young singer Vera Lynn had made so famous, which brought tears to everyone's eyes, *We'll Meet Again*.

There were tears in Betty's eyes too as she thought of them, enjoying the first family Christmas she had ever missed. Did they notice the empty chair at the table, or had it been filled by someone else? Her mother had told her Mrs Brunner and Joy were coming to spend the day. They had never had 'strangers' in the house at Christmas before. Had it made a difference?

'What sort of Christmas do you usually have?' she asked Mrs Spencer, realising that she and Dennis were 'strangers' at the farm. 'You must be missing your Gerald and Dick.'

'I am.' The older woman looked sadly into the fire. 'It don't seem right without them, and that's the truth of it. And when I think of where they are and what might be happening to them . . .' The Spencer boys were in the Army, fighting the Italians in the Libyan desert. 'I know they say we're winning there, but our boys are still getting killed, aren't they? Perhaps at this very minute . . .' Her eyes filled.

'Now then, Ada,' Mr Spencer said. 'This is Christmas night, remember? There's a truce on. Nobody's getting killed now and our two aren't going to be anyway. They've got hides like crocodiles, the pair of 'em.' He refilled her glass with ginger wine. 'Drink up now. Dennis wants to hear about the old days on the farm, when we were young.'

'Ah, it were different then,' Jonas said in his gravelly voice. 'We 'ad to *work* in them days. None o' this lazin' around 'alf the day suppin' tea. And never did us a mite of 'arm, either. 'Ard work never killed no one.'

Dennis smiled at Betty and squeezed her hand. And for the rest of the evening, they listened to tales of life in the country, of Christmases past, of summers when the sun never stopped shining, and of a time that was almost forgotten, when families were together and peace ruled the land.

It was a Christmas that was different, she thought after she had said goodnight and gone to bed, but it had been a happy one after all. Happiest of all because Dennis had said he loved her. But now, alone in the empty attic, she felt a great desolation wash over her. And she knew that she could not sleep without feeling his arms around her.

This is our Christmas, she thought. Our first. We ought to be together.

Quietly, she slipped out of bed. She found the old coat she used as a dressing-gown and pushed her feet into the slippers her mother had sent her for Christmas. Cautiously, she lifted the latch on the attic door and crept down the stairs to Gerald Spencer's room, where Dennis was now sleeping.

The door opened without a creak. She pushed it gently and slid through the narrow gap. The room was uncurtained and lit faintly by the stars, and she could see the bed and the shape that was Dennis lying in it.

Betty stood for a moment with beating heart. What if he should send her away? What if he were angry, or rejected her? What if he despised her for being so brazen?

Dennis moved. He lifted his head from the pillow and whispered, 'Who's there?'

'It's me. Betty.' Her voice was strained, almost inaudible. 'I – I couldn't sleep.' She came forwards and dropped on her knees beside the bed, her hands reaching out for him. 'Dennis, let me stay. You don't have to do anything. Just let me stay here with you. Just let's be together, please.'

'Betty—'

'You said it yourself,' she whispered. 'Tomorrow might not come. We have to take what chances we have. Hold me in your arms, Dennis, and love me. Let's have this Christmas to remember.' She lifted her face to his and touched his lips with her own. 'I love you, Dennis. I love you so much.'

His arms slipped around her body and she felt the warmth of his skin beneath the thin fabric of her nightdress. Her blood surged and she felt the answering leap of his heart. He drew back the bedclothes and she shrugged the coat from her shoulders and lay beside him.

'You're sure about this?' he whispered. 'I don't want to do anything you'd be sorry for.'

'I'll never be sorry for loving you.'

'Betty,' he breathed. 'Betty . . .'

His lips were gentle on hers. Slowly, delicately, as if uncovering the most fragile of spun glass, he pushed aside the folds of her nightdress. Betty shivered as his fingers touched her skin and a tremor of desire shook her body. She touched his bare chest and felt the warmth of his heart. With a sudden need to feel closer, she pressed her body against his and then drew away to sit up and drag her nightdress over her head.

Dennis watched the movement of her arms as she lifted them, saw the shape of her breasts silhouetted against the window. He lifted one hand and traced the shape, and Betty slid down again and allowed him to twine his arms about her. She felt his legs hard against hers, and the trembling desire deepened to a burning excitement.

Dennis caressed her body slowly, covering her breasts first with his hands, then with his lips. With the tip of one finger, he drew a line between her breasts and a curve in the crease beneath each one. He slid his fingers down her arm, lingering in the crook of her elbow where he planted another kiss. He stroked her waist, her navel and the crease of her thighs.

Betty felt the tenderness of his hands spread like a warm flame, enveloping her body. She was weak with desire and helpless in his arms. She lay soft in his embrace, as dizzy as if she were falling, and felt his touch slide from thigh to knee and back again, into the deepest crease of all.

She felt a sudden flare of sensation and twisted against him. With a gasp, Dennis came into her and suddenly Betty's languor departed and she moved with him, responding to his sudden force with a strength she had not known she possessed. She lay beneath him, her hands on his shoulders, and then Dennis rose high above her, bracing himself on his hands, and threw back his head. In the pale shimmer of starlight, she could see his face, taut and concentrated in the shadows. She felt her own desire tingle through her body, felt the tremor reach to each outflung fingertip, felt the shudder of fulfilment lift her to a momentary peak of delight.

The few seconds were an eternity. And then eternity came to an end and Dennis lowered himself to lie close to her, once again enfolding her with his warmth and whispering his love in Betty's ear.

20

It was a strange Christmas for many that year.

For Gerald and Dick Spencer, it was blisteringly hot. From the gentle scenery of a Hampshire farm, they had come thousands of miles to North African desert sand. From ploughing and harrowing, from milking and shearing, they had come to a battle to the death, with the roar of guns and mines and tanks in their ears. From rain storms they came to desert storms, with sand driving merciless needles against their faces and into their eyes and throats, so that they almost preferred the threat of bombshells and the menace of the hidden mines.

For Colin Chapman, it was a Christmas at sea. His ship, the *Exeter*, had been active ever since the outbreak of war, and was still in the forefront of the battles of the oceans. But Mike Simmons was home. To Kathy's almost unbelieving joy, his ship had docked in Southampton on Christmas Eve and would be there for at least a week, perhaps more. In the bare little house at number 16 October Street, furnished with other people's cast-offs, there was rejoicing and a happy Christmas, with the new baby Thomas the centre of everyone's attention.

Graham was home too, and made much of by his mother, though he was still smarting over the split with Betty. By now, he had expected a letter of apology and a humble request to 'start again'. But no such letter had arrived – not even a Christmas card – and he sat glowering at the fire. What was the use of Christmas without a girl? And you couldn't even go out and find one, everyone was stuck indoors with their families. He didn't even think there would be a welcome for him at Nancy Baxter's.

'Come on, Gray,' his mother urged him. 'There's plenty more fish in the sea. She wasn't never good enough for you, anyway.'

'I liked the girl, myself,' her husband said in his dry, papery voice. 'Always had a smile and a pleasant word, not like some young people these days.'

'Oh, you're just a pushover.' But Elsie was sorry that Betty wouldn't be coming over any more. She'd liked the girl too, in spite of what she said to Graham, and she'd hoped they'd stick together. Chances are it was his fault, she thought, trying it on when he ought to have known Betty wasn't that sort. But men were all the same in that department.

The men of 698 Unit had a peaceful Christmas too. The victims of the latest raid, in battered Conway Street, had all been found homes with relatives or taken away to rest centres or hospital, and the soldiers who were helping to demolish unsafe buildings or repair those less damaged had been given time to be at home with their families. Derek Harker, George Glaister and Bob Shaw were among them.

For the thousands now homeless, it was a time of confusion. Their houses had been bombed, often relatives killed. There were men without wives, women without husbands, children without parents. There were old people who scarcely knew what had happened, babies who knew nothing but turmoil and saw no face for long enough to recognise the features. There were children who had no home and no relatives and who did not know where life would take them next.

And amidst all these were the people who were trying to help them, the Red Cross, the WVS, the Civil Defence, the Salvation Army, the volunteers, the foster parents and the nurses. For all of them, the problem was so immense that they could do nothing but live from day to day, nothing but lend a hand wherever it seemed needed most. 'Carrying on' was the order of the day, and 'smiling through'. And the bulldog tenacity of Churchill, exhorting them to greater efforts. *'We shall never surrender.'*

The spirit took root and grew. From fear and despair, from the misery of loss, rose a determination that the bombed cities would live on. Buildings could be destroyed, cities razed and people killed, but Britain would never be beaten.

The truce had given the country a short respite. But the peace did not last. Two days were all that Hitler allowed. On 27 December the Luftwaffe was back in force, with a hundred bombers attacking London and leaving over six hundred people dead. And two days later the city suffered its worst raid yet, with nearly a hundred and fifty bombers forcing their way past the barrages to drop more than twenty thousand firebombs and something like a hundred and twenty tons of high explosives.

The ensuing blaze was said to be worse than the Great Fire of London. It raged all night, destroying the Old Bailey, the Guildhall and eight of the historic churches of Christopher Wren. Thousands of homes were in ruins, thousands of people homeless. Yet still the spirit of 'carrying on' prevailed. Those who still had homes, left them to go to work. They left early, knowing that they would have to find a new way through the devastation of the streets. They left knowing that they might have no place of work to go to, that everything familiar to them might have been blown away in the night. And as they made their way they gazed at the destruction that had been wrought by the bombs and the fires, and lifted their eyes to see the dome of St Paul's Cathedral still proudly dominating the scarred skyline. And once again the words echoed in their hearts. *We shall never surrender . . .*

In Portsmouth the respite continued, though the nightly warnings still sounded and the removal to the shelters persisted. And the uneasy dread still filled people's hearts as they looked at the wintry sky, hung with barrage balloons like heavy clouds of foreboding.

Annie Chapman was growing more and more worried about Ted. Ever since Dunkirk, he'd been getting more and more jumpy. He picked at his meals and he couldn't sleep. When the siren sounded, he went straight up the stairs to the top of the little turret and stood there, watching for fires, and only Annie knew what an effort it was.

'You feel like everyone can see you up there,' he told her. 'You feel like every Jerry's looking down from his plane and aiming his bombs straight at you. Same as when I'm on the ferry, the old *King* feels as big as the *Ark Royal*.'

'You don't have to go up there, Ted. Let me take a turn. I can watch for fires as well as you.'

But he shook his head. 'I've got to go, Annie. I've been to Dunkirk, remember. I've seen things I don't want to talk about, never. There's men living through worse every day than you and I can even imagine. I can't hide meself while all that's going on.'

There was no more for Annie to say. She could only do whatever she could to give him comfort, the warmth of a mug of cocoa to take up with him, or when he came back down, white and shrammed with cold. The warmth of her arms on the rare nights when they dared sleep in their own bed.

She was more thankful than ever now that Betty at least was safe in the country. The girl had seemed happier when she was home last, though it had been a shock to her when the young Air Force boys had been killed. Annie had wondered a few times whether she wasn't fonder of one of them than she'd admitted. But there'd been a sort of glow about her when she came back for her weekend after Christmas.

Betty hadn't mentioned Dennis to her parents, but Mr and Mrs Spencer had soon realised the situation. They said nothing, simply accepted it as a natural development. The other two Land Girls reacted differently.

'You seem to get plenty of boys,' Yvonne said with envy. 'That sailor, and then Sandy and now Dennis. I wish I could be easy-come, easy-go like that.'

'I'm not easy-come, easy-go,' Betty said sharply. 'It was never really serious between Graham and me. And Sandy was just a friend.' Her voice trembled a little as she remembered him on that last evening, asking if there might be a chance for him. Poor, poor Sandy . . . 'It's different with Dennis and me.'

'Well, I don't know how you can do it,' Erica said. 'Going with a traitor. I'd be ashamed.'

'He's not a traitor,' Betty said, but her voice was quiet. Dennis had already taught her to react without aggression to such taunts. And she felt genuinely sorry for the blonde girl. Suppose she lost Dennis now . . . The pain was unthinkable. But it was the pain Erica was suffering. Betty touched her arm.

'Don't be angry,' she said. 'I know how you feel about Dennis, but he really isn't a traitor, or a coward. He wants to help his country just as much as the rest of us, he just wants to do it a different way. He's just as upset as we are about Geoff and the others.'

'Nobody's as upset about Geoff as me,' Erica said, but she allowed Betty to put her arms around her, and she turned her face into Betty's shoulder as the tears came. And they sat, the three of them close and unspeaking; trying, failing, to understand, yet mourning together.

Tim and Keith Budd were back in the country too. Jess had been reluctant to let them go without knowing where they would be sent, but at the last minute she had heard from Edna Corner that the vicar had room for them. Would she like them to go to him? Jess had agreed at once, though the boys had made faces, protesting that Mr Beckett was an old man, that they'd have to go to church twice every Sunday, that they'd have to say Grace at every meal and never be allowed to play games.

'You'll be safe,' she said firmly. 'And I'm sure it can't be that bad. Mr Beckett's a very nice man.'

'But he's a *vicar*,' Tim said in outraged tones, and Jess snapped at him in irritation.

'For goodness' sake, Tim! You're behaving as if he's a man from Mars. He's no different from anyone else, and if he makes you behave and teaches you the manners you seem to have forgotten, I'll be grateful to him. I know Mr and Mrs Corner were good to you but you seem to have changed since you went out to Bridge End, and not for the better.'

Tim pushed out his lower lip and went to sit on the floor and stroke Henry the cat. He would have preferred it if Mr Beckett had been a man from Mars. That would have been fun. But a vicar . . .

Rose flatly refused to return to Bridge End.

'I don't want to go back. I'm worried all the time about what's happening here. I'm frightened you'll get killed and no one will tell me. I'd rather be here with you and help with the cooking and the baby and everything.' She clung to her mother. 'Don't make me go back, Mum. Please don't make me go back.'

Jess held her and looked helplessly at Frank. They had both known Rose was unhappy, but had been shocked by her appearance when she came home. She was pale and thin, and not developing as she should. At almost thirteen, she ought to have been beginning to round out, but instead she was hollow-chested and gaunt. Jess had been convinced she was ill and wanted to take her to the doctor, but had agreed to wait until after Christmas.

'She's pining,' Annie had said. 'That's all that's wrong with her. She's always been your girl, Jess, and she's missing you.'

Jess repeated her words to Frank after Rose had gone to bed. 'Girls do pine at her age, Frank. They can just stop eating and fade away, what my mother used to call a "decline". We can't let that happen to our Rose.'

'You'd rather she was killed, is that it?'

'Of course not! Don't say such things. But who knows what will happen to any of us? And if she's as miserable as that, she might as well be back here with us. We can look after her. She's not like the boys'd be, wanting to get out and play, and messing about on bomb-sites. Anyway, she's nearly the age you were when you left school. She can make up her own mind.'

'Make up her own mind? She's under my authority till she's twenty-one, that's another seven years. And I don't want her leaving school yet. I want my kids to have an education.'

'Well, they're not getting much of that, wherever they are. I reckon Rose would do as well at home, having lessons with Joy Brunner. And that's another thing. Joy and her have always been friends, and it'd be good for them to be near each other. Joy hasn't got anyone else round here.'

'Joy's a nice enough girl,' Frank acknowledged. 'But I don't see why our Rose has got to be brought home just because there isn't anyone else for Joy.'

'I'm not saying that.' Jess sighed. 'Look, if you want my opinion, our Rose'll be ill if we make her go away again. She's worrying herself half out of her mind. And I tell you straight, I wouldn't be a bit surprised if Mrs Greenberry refused to take her back. She won't want the responsibility.'

In the end, she won. Frank was never easy to persuade but he would, eventually, see reason. And even he could not withstand Rose's distress at the idea of leaving home again.

'All right. She can stay. But not the boys. They go back to Bridge End and they stay there till there's no chance of any more bombing, all right?'

No chance of any more bombing.

December drew to a close. For the second year running, there were no bells rung to mark the passing of another year, no sirens sounded or ships' hooters blown. New Year's Day came in silently, slinking through the storms as if afraid to be seen, and 1941 began with an air of apology for not promising better things.

In bitter cold, Cardiff was raided and Bristol attacked on three separate nights. Manchester too was blitzed. Fires raged everywhere, buildings toppled, families were buried. Fire engines raced through the streets, sometimes never reaching the fire they had set out to deal with. Ambulances were driven by young women like Gladys Shaw through streets lit by flames, while bombs and shrapnel rained about them, to hospitals that were themselves destroyed before they could get there. There were fear and panic, lawlessness and looting, never reported in the newspapers for fear of lowering the already fragile morale, and later buried in people's memories as so many of the injured and dead were buried beneath the ruins of the shattered cities. It could not be acknowledged that the war of terror might be having its effect. It could not be admitted that the bulldog tenacity, the will to carry on, the determination that this was a people who would never surrender, might be faltering at last.

Portsmouth had not been raided again, but nobody could dismiss the possibility that their turn would come. They went into the new year with trepidation, spending each night in the shelters just in case. Each day without bombing brought relief that they had still escaped, and a greater fear that it must come soon.

On 8 January a huge party was held for the children in the Guildhall. Tim and Keith were already back at Bridge End, but Rose went to it with Joy Brunner, though neither of them now thought of themselves as children. Joy had barely attended school since the war began, and had been virtually running the shop for months as well as looking after her mother for much of the time. Rose, out in the country, had been receiving only half-day schooling, and not much of that, for the older girls were expected to help with the younger children and she had spent a lot of her time reading to the little ones and assisting them with their sums.

It seemed strange to them to go into the big, grand building down in the main square of the city, up the wide steps and between the two majestic lions, to attend a children's party. Strange to sit at long tables with a thousand other children, eating jelly from small cardboard bowls, with coloured lamps and balloons festooned above their heads. At one end of the room was a platform, piled high with wrapped gifts, and in front of the platform stood a tall Christmas tree, glittering with tinsel and twinkling fairy lights.

The presents came, the Lady Mayoress explained, from British people who lived in a country called Uruguay, six thousand miles away. They had sent a hundred and fifty pounds to give the children of Portsmouth a treat, and this was it. For three hours, they could forget the war and enjoy themselves.

For three hours, they did. Led by the Lady Mayoress, they marched around the hall, roaring out songs like *Pack Up Your Troubles in Your Old Kit Bag and Smile – Smile – Smile* and *There'll Always Be An England*, accompanied on the big Guildhall organ by the city organist. They played games. They watched a dancing display and a conjurer and were commended for their courage by the Commander-in-Chief himself, a real Admiral in full uniform, who told them they were helping England in her task of winning the war.

'You deserve a prize,' he said, and the children cheered. 'And I shall give you one. A pound note to the first boy or girl of school age who puts out an incendiary bomb. What do you think of that?'

'Hooray!' the children cheered again. 'Hooray! Hooray! Hooray!'

They cheered again as the Lady Mayoress announced that the presents so enticingly displayed on the platform would be handed out, and waited in line, some more patiently than others, as the gifts were handed out. It took an hour, but at last they were all provided for, and when their parents came to take them home each child was well supplied with a stick of rock, a present and a balloon.

Rose and Joy took their leave of the Guildhall in silence. Neither had ever been in such a grand place before, and they looked around the glittering walls with awe. The high ceiling, the white paint, the gold leaf and the gleaming, polished floor – it was like a royal palace to the girls who had known only terraced houses. They looked at the Christmas tree, decorated just for them, at the glowing colours of the Christmas lights. They looked at the walls where portraits of previous Lord Mayors and dignitaries, clothed in rich, fur-trimmed robes, gazed down at them, and wondered if they would ever come here again.

They would not, and nor would many others. For only two nights later, the Luftwaffe's attention turned once again to Portsmouth and the blitz began. The proud Guildhall was almost totally destroyed.

21

It began at seven o'clock in the evening. It was a Friday.

Jess had just put Maureen to bed. She slept in her cot in the back bedroom, where Rose also slept now that the boys were away. She tucked the baby in and was halfway downstairs when the siren began.

Instantly, she was back upstairs and lifting Maureen from the cot, blankets and all. Holding her close, she ran down the stairs. Rose was already gathering together the things they would need, the cushions and old blankets, the thermos flask Frank had bought for Christmas, which was filled with hot water every night, the basket which held packets of cocoa and sugar, a small bottle of milk, a tin of biscuits. They might be in the shelter for only half an hour, they might be there all night. You had to be prepared.

'Quick, Mum, oh, please be quick.' Rose was crouching under the stairs, her face white as Jess quickly thrust Maureen's feet back into the socks she had taken off only twenty minutes earlier. 'Put them on when we get down there. The planes'll be here, oh hurry, hurry.'

Frank was still at work, or more likely on his way home. Jess thought of the first raid, last July, when he'd got caught in the streets. He'd never said much about it, but he'd changed that night, as if he'd seen sights that couldn't be talked of. She prayed that he would come home safely tonight. Frank, Frank . . .

He was right, she thought, looking at Rose's ashen face. The girl would have been better off out in the country. She was terrified. But she'd been just as frightened out there, so Mrs Greenberry had said, and at least if she was here she knew what was going on, knew that her mother and baby sister were safe. As they would be, as soon as they reached the shelter.

The planes could be heard now, droning overhead. It was high time they were in the shelter. Jess wound Maureen up again in her blankets and grabbed the tin box that held all the papers. She made for the back door and, with Rose at her heels, scurried down the garden path.

They had just ducked through the low doorway and scrambled down the steps when the sky turned suddenly red.

Olive Harker had been cooking Derek's supper when the warning went.

'Oh, drat!' she exclaimed. 'I was just looking forward to a nice cosy evening listening to the wireless.'

Her mother came into the kitchen and turned out the gas. 'Down the shelter, quick!'

'But the supper—'

'It don't matter about the supper. You can finish that later on. Derek won't be home anyway, not till it's over.'

'Oh, they do it deliberately,' Olive wailed. 'Just to spoil things!'

'D'you expect them to send us a timetable?' Annie grabbed the bundle of cushions and rugs they kept by the back door and hustled her out. 'Look at those flares. They're going to hammer us tonight, mark my words. Why, it's bright as day out here.'

Olive hung back. 'I promised to look in on Kathy—'

'Kathy'll be going to her own shelter.' The two young women had become friends since Kathy's baby was born. Olive, suddenly passionately interested in babies now that she was expecting her own, had been a daily visitor to admire little Thomas. She spent hours stroking his firm little limbs and trying to make him smile. Yesterday, he had done so for the first time and she had been enchanted.

'But she's there all on her own with those two little girls and the baby.'

'It's what she chooses,' Annie said. 'I don't want to be unkind, Livvy, but she could have been evacuated if she'd wanted.' She pulled Olive's arm. 'Come on, for goodness' sake, do you want us to be bombed on our own doorstep? Look at the way they're lighting us up.'

Olive glanced up. The sky was now almost entirely red, the glow of the flares stretching from sunrise to sunset. The roar of the planes was directly overhead. It could be no more than moments before the first bombs began to drop.

In sudden fear, she ran down the garden path after her mother and scrambled into the shed. Together, they ducked through the doorway and dragged the old woollen curtain across. Annie found the blackout frame and pushed it into place, and then groped for the matches.

'Not that it matters if we show every lamp we've got, the way they're lighting up the whole city,' she said. 'But we don't want Tommy Vickers round here shouting the odds.'

The hurricane lamp flickered into life and they sat back on the bunks and looked at each other.

'Maybe it's just a false alarm,' Olive said, without much hope. 'Maybe they're just passing over, like other nights.'

Annie shook her head. 'I don't reckon so, love. I reckon this is something worse. We've never had flares like that before. They're lighting up their targets, that's what they're doing.' She paused for a moment, then said quietly, 'Tonight they're going to smash Pompey right down into the ground . . .'

Kathy Simmons acted calmly enough. The things they needed to take down to the shelter were kept in a basket close to the back door, blankets and cushions, an old cot mattress for the baby, a thermos flask and cups. There were a couple of books for the girls and one for herself, from the library. There was a hurricane lamp, though she didn't like to use it for too long in case the paraffin ran out. You never knew how long an alert might last, it might be only half an hour before the All-Clear sounded, it might be hours, even though nothing seemed to be happening.

Tonight, as she ran down the path in the red glow of the flares, it looked as if it might be a long time.

Frank Budd and Ted Chapman were on a trolley-bus together, coming up to North End. Both had finished work for the day and were anxious to get home. Frank had boarded the bus to find his brother-in-law sitting in the seat by the door, and he'd nodded and sat down beside him. The bus was dark and gloomy inside, with only the lowest possible lights to show passengers their way, and it crept slowly along the unlit streets.

The two men said nothing for a while. Both were tired from the week's work and from the alerts that sounded night after night. Both were fire-watchers and had to stand outside, looking at the sky, waiting for incendiaries to drop and set Portsmouth ablaze. Both were suffering from broken nights and the dread that hung over the whole country.

'They're doing it to scare people,' Ted said at last, breaking the silence. 'They're trying to wear us down. Bombing London, night after night . . . Hitting places like Bristol and Manchester . . . They think if they keep on hammering us, we'll give in and let Hitler walk all over us.'

'They've got another think coming, then,' Frank said grimly, and they relapsed into silence again.

When the siren sounded, they did no more than sigh and wait for the bus to reach their destination. But when the flares began to light the streets, they looked at each other in dismay. And when the trolley-bus came to a halt, they rose from their seats in real alarm.

'That's as far as we're going,' the conductress called out, her face reddened by the glow. 'You'd better get yourselves to a shelter. There'll be no more service tonight, by the looks of it.'

No more service tonight! 'But I've got miles to go,' one woman exclaimed in despair. 'I live right up Cosham.'

The conductress shrugged. 'Sorry, love.' She was already gathering up her bag and coat, ready to get off the bus. 'You'd better forget about getting home tonight. There won't be no more buses running.' She turned her face up to the sky, and Frank followed her gaze and saw the mass of flares drifting from the sky. 'That's incendiaries comin' down, that is,' she said tersely, and leapt to the pavement and ran.

The street was filled now with hurrying figures. People running for the shelters, people running for home. People just running, with no real idea of where to go. Sheltering in doorways, pressing themselves against walls. Looking up, up at the crimson lights, up towards the ominous drone of the planes. Calling to each other, to lost children, to elderly parents, calling with fear in their voices, whimpering, crying.

Where had they all come from? Frank wondered. It was well after dark, surely most people were safe at home by now. But it seemed that there were plenty who weren't. Or maybe they'd been driven from their homes by the siren, driven out to seek shelter. Not everyone had an Anderson; there were plenty who must go to the public shelters, and if there wasn't room in the first must look for another.

'What're we going to do?' Ted asked, and Frank turned to look at him. His brother-in-law's eyes were scared.

'What *can* we do?' Frank replied. 'Go home, of course. We're on duty there, aren't we? At least we can see to find our way.'

He set off up Stubbington Avenue, striding fast. They could, he knew, have sought shelter. They could have gone to a public one, overcrowded though it might have been, or they could have gone to Jess and Annie's parents who lived nearby. Perhaps they should do that. Nobody would expect them to walk halfway across Portsmouth in the middle of a raid.

But he couldn't do that. He didn't want to spend another night searching through rubble for bodies and bits of bodies, when Jess was there by herself with Rose and the baby, when she didn't know whether or not he was safe. If a bomb fell before he got home, if people needed help, he'd do what he could. Of course he would. But he'd do his damnedest to get home first, and so would Ted.

He looked up again at the sky, listening to the drone of the aircraft, watching the fearsome descent of the parachutes. In God's name, what was going on? Could there possibly be men on the end of those parachutes?

The first stick of bombs, falling on the electricity station, shook the ground with their explosion. And Frank knew that this was no invasion. This was the blitz over Portsmouth.

'There it goes!' Gladys said, and reached for the bag she always kept near the door, containing her First Aid kit and gas mask. 'I'm off.'

'Wait for me.' Peggy too caught up her bag. 'Blimey, they don't give you much warning, do they? I can hear the planes already.'

Diane stared at them, her eyes almost black in her white face. 'What about me? You're not going to leave me here by myself.'

'Oh lor',' Peggy said, stopping, 'she's right, Glad. We can't leave her on her own.'

'Where's Dad?'

'I don't know, up the pub, I suppose. He'll go to the street shelter.'

'Well, he shouldn't,' Gladys said crossly. 'He knows we've got to go when the siren sounds.'

'He knows, and he doesn't like it. He'll expect you or me to stop behind.'

'For God's sake! Don't he know there's a war on? Anyway, he ought to be on duty himself, he's a firewatcher, isn't he?'

Peggy shrugged helplessly. 'That won't help our Diane. There still won't be anyone to stay with her in the shelter.'

'Well, she'd better come with us, then,' Gladys said. 'She can help at the First Aid post. She's helped us practise our bandaging often enough, she must know what to do.'

Peggy opened her mouth to protest. The girl would be in the way, she'd see things she shouldn't. There'd be blood, broken limbs, people crying and shocked. And then she looked at Diane and thought again. She was sixteen, no longer a child. There were plenty of youngsters her age doing war work already – Boy Scouts acting as messengers in raids, girls helping in canteens, lads too young for call-up joining the Home Guard. Diane could easily make herself useful, keeping the kettle and teapot on the go if the rest were busy, and it would be better for her than staying here on her own.

'All right,' she said. 'Get your coat on, Diane. We'll leave a note on the table for your dad.' She found a scrap of paper and scribbled on it while Gladys waited impatiently. 'Here they come.'

The drone was directly overhead. It sounded as if there were planes all over the sky. They looked at each other in sudden fear. They had suffered raids before, they all knew the sound of the planes, but this sounded different, louder, more menacing, as if Hitler had sent the whole of the Luftwaffe to obliterate their city and all within it.

Gladys thought of the blitz on London, of the merciless raids on Coventry, on Bristol, on Plymouth.

She jammed her tin hat on her head, switched off the light and opened the front door. Cautiously, they looked up at the sky, criss-crossed with its web of searchlight beams. The planes could be heard snarling high above, but now they could hear the different note of RAF night fighters flying to intercept them, and the sharp rattle of ack-ack fire. Maybe we're fighting them off, she thought. Maybe it won't be a bad raid after all.

Suddenly, high above her head, she saw a red light. It dropped silently through the darkness, falling like the red balloon young Rose next door had brought home from the Guildhall party. And then, as she stared, it opened out like a flower, like a blood-red rose or a poppy, blossoming as it fell and lighting up the sky around it, and the city beneath.

Before she had realised what it was, she saw another and another, until the sky was full of them. A shower of poppies, scattering over the darkened streets of Portsmouth, casting a warm glow as they descended. A bouquet of death.

'Flares,' Peggy muttered. 'Parachute flares. They're making sure they can see us before they drop their bombs.'

'Gosh,' Diane said, her voice awed. 'It's like firework night.' Her voice quivered a little. 'It's like the biggest rockets you ever saw.'

Gladys gave her arm a shake. 'It's no good being frightened. If you're coming with us you've got to make yourself useful. Otherwise, you'd better go back home.'

'Frightened?' Diane said. 'Who said anything about being frightened? I wouldn't miss this for the world. Look at it! Look at that one!'

Gladys stared at her sister. Her face was reddened by the glow of the flares, her eyes glittering with excitement. She had been drying her hair in front of the fire when the siren sounded, and now it flew loose and tangled about her head. She looked as wild as a gypsy.

'What's got into you?' Gladys said. 'This is a raid – and it looks as if it's going to be a bad one. It's not a bonfire night party.'

'I know. I can't help it, I think it's marvellous. Look at the sky. Look at the colour. It's better than a sunset. Better than a rainbow. *Look*!'

Gladys turned her face to the sky. The flares were dropping thick and fast now, and in their light you could see that each was on its own parachute,

drifting slowly down on the city. All around them were the silver searchlights, like a spider's web woven against the velvet darkness. And between
the blossoming blood-red of the flares and the shimmering filigree of the
lights could be seen the brilliant white sparkle of bursting shells from the
anti-aircraft guns. She watched them, bemused. How many did they
actually hit? Weren't they just firing at random, hoping to strike something
up there in the limitless black sky? But even as she wondered she saw,
here and there, a sudden spiralling orange flare as a plane was hit and
corkscrewed downwards to the earth.

'Look at that,' Diane whispered, and as she spoke there was a tremendous explosion from somewhere deep in Portsmouth. The ground shook
and a huge, billowing cloud of black and red and orange filled the sky.

Gladys was filled with sudden fury. For a moment or two she had been
swayed into something very like wonder as she stared at the strange
kaleidoscope of colour drifting above her. Now she was reminded forcibly
of what it all meant. Her fear flooded back and she shook her sister's arm
savagely.

'Marvellous? There's nothing *marvellous* about bombs and people getting killed. If you think it's so bloody marvellous, you'd better come with
us and see what it really means. And do something to help. You'll soon see
how *marvellous* it is. Well?' Another shake. 'What's it to be? Make up your
mind, quick.'

'I'll come with you. I don't want to be home on my own.'

'You could go in with Mrs Budd—' Gladys began, but her voice was
drowned in the sudden burst of another explosion. The sky flared with
searing white light and another great cloud of smoke and debris rose into
the air, turning rapidly red as the flames began. It was followed immediately by a third, and then a fourth, and then it was as if all hell had
been let loose on the city as bombs were hurled one after another into the
tortured abyss, exploding on every side so that it seemed that there could
be no escape.

The sky was brilliant now with the burnished glow of flames, the
brightness of new fires added at every minute to those already burning.
The stark white beams of the searchlights turned to red as the enemy
showered bombs like deadly rain upon their target. And all the time, in a
chorus of menace, the drone of the planes overhead sounded in their ears
and the sharp rattle of the ack-ack guns gave a bitter commentary on the
enemy's progress.

'Well, we don't have to worry about not finding our way.' They had
paused, cowering back against a wall as the first explosions shook the
ground, but now Gladys was off again, running. So far, it seemed that no
bombs had been dropped on this part of Portsmouth but the streets were lit
by the orange glow that was now spread over the whole sky. It seemed as if
the supply was inexhaustible.

They reached the school which was serving as a First Aid post. It was in
semi-darkness, lit only by a few hurricane lamps. Casualties were already
coming in and the superintendent looked relieved to see Peggy and her
daughters.

'Thank God you're here. This looks like being the big one. We think they've hit the electricity station, all the lights went out with the first bomb. Who's this?'

'My other daughter, Diane. She's come to give a hand.'

'We can do with all the help we can get. Can you put a bandage on? Go over to Mrs Jenkins, she'll tell you what to do.'

Diane nodded. Her strange exhilaration had passed and her face was pale, but she set her mouth firmly. She went over to one of the long tables which was piled high with bandages and dressings. A big, florid woman in a brown coat was already attending to a man with a bleeding head and Diane picked up a roll of bandage and held it out to her.

'She'll be all right,' Peggy said. 'Old mother Jenkins is a bit of a tartar but she won't give her a chance to get frightened. Now what d'you want us to do?'

'Get in the ambulance on stand-by. The way they're hammering us, it won't be long before you know where to go. Anyone not too badly hurt, take 'em to the nearest post, if it's too bad for us to deal with, get 'em to the hospital and then come back. Just do whatever you've got to do.' The superintendent looked up as another bomb whistled above their heads. 'They all sound so near. God knows what it's like when they're really on top of you.'

'They say you never hear the one that hits you,' Peggy remarked, intending to sound cheerful. But it didn't come out like that, somehow. She followed Gladys to the old van that had been converted to an ambulance. Bunks had been fitted inside so that it could carry several casualties, and there were benches for Peggy and less badly hurt people to sit on. A locker had been screwed inside the door and was filled with bandages and bottles of iodine and Dettol.

The explosions were coming thick and fast. Every second, the ground shook with fresh detonations and it seemed impossible that any part of the city could survive unscathed. Gladys sat in the driving seat of the ambulance, her fingers twitching with impatience. There must be people out there needing help.

A figure suddenly skidded into the playground and Gladys realised it was a boy on a bicycle. He was wearing Boy Scout uniform. His face was ruddy in the glow and there was a smear of black across his forehead. He gave her a quick, slightly wavering grin, and ran through the door, leaving it ajar. It hardly mattered about blackout now, she thought, with all this blazing light showing everything up. You could see to read a newspaper in this.

The super ran out and she leaned from the window. 'Where do they want us?'

'Palmerston Road. It's going up like a torch. The whole place is alight, there's buildings collapsed, people buried, it's chaos down there. They need all the help they can get.' Gladys was already starting the engine. She jammed it into gear. 'Take this kid with you and drop him off at the ARP Control Centre.'

The scout scrambled into the back with Peggy, dragging his bike in after him. Gladys drove the van out through the wide gates and on to Copnor

Road. Palmerston Road! That was right out at Southsea. Surely there must be people nearer at hand needing help. She sped through the reddened streets. They looked as if they were already running with blood, she thought. And, with a flash of wry gratitude, at least you could see where you were going . . . She had always been terrified of running someone over in the blackout.

The blitz was still going on. There were explosions on every side, and long before she was anywhere near Palmerston Road Gladys was flagged down by a warden and sent down a side street. She pulled the van into the side of the road and jumped out.

'Over here!' A bomb had fallen on a row of houses, demolishing at least two and leaving the others badly damaged. Two more were on fire and a crowd of people were trying to douse them with stirrup pumps and buckets of water. The flames were already flickering through the roof and, as Gladys watched, a huge orange tongue bellied out through a window and licked up the wall. The roof collapsed amidst a gush of fire.

'There's people in there!' Someone was screaming loudly near her. 'There's my Gramp and Granny in there. They wouldn't come down the shelter – they're burning alive in there.'

'Oh, my God.' Peggy was beside her. 'They'll never get them out . . .'

'Where's the fire engines? Where *are* they? Why don't they come, oh God, why don't they come?' The woman was in a frenzy. 'Gramp and Granny, they're in there, burning alive, they're burning alive, oh God, oh God . . .'

'Where's our Joan?' An elderly woman, her hair in curlers, staggered along the pavement. 'Where's our Joan? 'Ave you seen 'er?' She peered into Peggy's face. 'Our Joan, 'ave you seen 'er?'

'Gramp, Gramp . . .'

'Over 'ere.' A man tugged at Gladys's sleeve. 'You're the doctor, ain'tcher? Over 'ere, there's people buried, we can't get 'em out. They're hurt.'

'Our Joan, Joan . . .'

'Oh, Grampy, poor old Grampy . . . Why don't they come, why don't they come?'

'Over 'ere,' the man urged, pulling Gladys's arm.

'I'm not a doctor,' Gladys began, but he was dragging her across the road. She reached into the van as she passed and grabbed her First Aid satchel. She wasn't a doctor, but she had trained for this and would have to do what she could. But suppose there was nothing . . .? She thought of the other raids in which she had worked and bit her lip.

'Down 'ere, look, we've got a tunnel through. They're in the cellar.'

The man pushed her down and Gladys saw a huge pile of debris. Splintered wooden beams, shattered bricks, plaster, laths, all were stirred together and heaped high in what had once been someone's sitting room. Only half an hour ago, people had been sitting here, having a cup of tea, listening to the wireless. But there was no time to think of that. The warning had gone and they'd dived down the cellar steps. And now they were buried.

'We can 'ear someone calling,' the man said urgently. 'A kiddy. We've managed to get through so far but we don't dare go any further, it might bring the whole lot down. If you could just get through, see if she's hurt, like . . .'

Gladys stared in terror. I'm not a doctor, she wanted to say, I'm just supposed to drive an ambulance. I can't go down there. I won't know what to do. I might make it worse . . .

'Give me a torch,' she said, and lay down flat on her stomach.

The ground was covered with broken bricks and other rubbish. She could feel something sharp digging into her thigh. She pointed the torch down the hole and crawled forwards, praying that the structure would hold up, praying that no more bombs would fall.

'That's it, love. Keep goin' . . .'

I can't, she thought, I can't . . .

She was inside the rough tunnel now, pushing herself forwards with her toes, dragging herself with both hands. She clawed at rough stone, at bricks and mortar, feeling their sharp dust under her nails. Something sliced along her arm and she felt a sudden warmth on her skin. She was halfway along the tunnel now and the light of her torch showed a small, dark cellar just beneath her.

It was only two or three feet away, but it might as well have been a hundred miles. In the torchlight she could see the dankness of it, the water running down the walls, the blackness of the floor. One corner was piled with coal. She squirmed a little further, heard an ominous creak from above, felt the whole of one side of the tunnel shift a little. Oh God, if it collapsed now . . .

I can't be buried alive, Gladys thought, I can't. I'm not ready to die yet. I'm too young. I haven't done anything, I haven't had any life yet, I haven't even had a proper boy . . . Please God, don't let me be buried alive, not before I've done anything . . .

But other people got buried alive. Other people got blown up and burned to death and shot. And maybe most of them hadn't done anything either . . .

She found that her hands were working, as if they had decided to go ahead without the rest of her. They were pulling at the bricks, dragging at bits of wood. They were making the hole larger, carefully, almost tenderly. She watched as if they belonged to someone else and admired their sureness of touch. What a good job she'd brought them with her.

Blimey Glad, she thought, you're going barmy. Talking to your hands like that. You're going off your head and no wonder. It's enough to send anyone round the bend, down here.

She could hear voices. The man from above, encouraging her, urging her on. Her mother, asking anxiously if she were all right. And another voice. That of a small child, a girl probably, calling for help, calling for her mummy.

'It's all right, love,' she said, watching her hands as they scraped busily away at the debris. They didn't seem to care about getting hurt, about being grazed or tearing the fingernails Gladys had been so proud of. 'It's all right, I'm coming, I'll get you out.'

'Mummy,' the child said. 'Where's Mummy?'

'She's all right.' Gladys could see further into the cellar now. There was a bench along one wall, with three people sitting on it, unmoving. 'She'll be here soon.' Her hands went on scrabbling, lifting out bricks, scraping at the thick dust.

The ground was shaking with the unceasing roar of explosions as bombs continued to fall. With every one, a shuddering rumble went through the foundations of the houses and the walls shook. Part of the cellar roof fell in and a shower of brick dust pervaded the air, filling Gladys's lungs and prickling in her eyes. She coughed and retched, and her eyes streamed. She wanted to rub them but could not bend her arms back to do so and the irritation grew worse. I'm not going to get out of here, she thought. I'm going to die here, choked with brick dust, buried in muck and dirt.

But if she died, so would the little girl. And she'd done even less than Gladys. She hadn't even had a chance to grow up.

'What's your name, love? Tell me what your name is.' There was silence. The three figures were still motionless. She tried again, her voice shaking. 'What do they call you?'

'Ruth.'

Thank God. 'Ruth. That's a nice name. I've never known anyone called Ruth before.' The walls shook again and she heard a rumble as something heavy fell not far away. Very carefully, afraid that it might bring everything crashing about her ears, she pulled out a brick and dropped it into the cellar, then knew a different fear. 'That didn't hit you, did it? You're not sitting just underneath?'

'No. I'm in the corner. I can't get out.' A querulous note entered the voice. 'Why doesn't Mummy come and get me out?'

'I expect she's got caught somewhere else. She'll come as soon as she can.' Gladys pulled out another brick. The hole was getting wider. 'I'll come and get you, Ruth, and then we can find Mummy.'

'But I can *see* her. She's sitting there, just *looking* at me.' The voice began to rise in fear. 'Why doesn't she say something? Why doesn't she *come*?'

Gladys looked at the three on the bench. She could see them more clearly now. They were slumped against the wall, their bodies toppled together.

Don't let them be dead, she prayed. Oh God, please don't let them be dead . . .

'How're you doing, love?' She became aware of voices calling down the tunnel. For a moment or two, she had been conscious of nothing but the cellar, nobody but herself and Ruth and the three silent bodies. She answered briefly, almost irritably.

'I'm all right. I'm getting into the cellar now.' She had made the hole wide enough to scramble through. She pushed her head and shoulders into it and found herself about two feet above the cellar floor. She squirmed a little further, reached down with both hands and took the weight of her body, pushing with her feet, clawing with her hands. I'm going to bring the whole lot down with me, she thought, hearing the creaks and crashes, feeling the shudder of each new explosion. I'm going to bring down the whole bloody lot.

The edge of the tunnel gave way and she fell forwards on to the floor. It was littered with debris, and she lay still for a moment, her whole body shrieking in protest. But there was no time for pain. Within less than a minute, she was pulling herself together, looking around for the little girl.

'Oh, *Ruth* . . .'

The child was about eight or nine years old, and she was almost completely covered in dust, plaster, coal and bricks. From her shoulders down, she had been buried as the corner of the cellar had collapsed. Her face was scratched and smeared with blood, her eyes wide and frightened. She stared at Gladys and her mouth trembled.

'It's all right, love,' Gladys said quickly. 'We'll have you out of there in no time.' She looked round at the other three occupants of the cellar, still huddled together as if fast asleep.

'I can't breathe properly,' the little girl said. 'There's all bricks and stuff on me.'

'I know. I'll get it off.'

'Mummy . . .'

Gladys hesitated. The girl was frightened, in pain and might be hurt. The debris that had fallen on top of her was crushing her. She had to be released. But the others might need help even more badly. They might be unconscious, bleeding to death. There were pools of dark liquid at their feet. It was impossible to tell whether it was water or blood.

She looked up at the mouth of the tunnel. I can't do this on my own, she thought. I need help.

Another crash shook the little cellar and she dropped her torch. It went out and the hole was plunged into darkness. The little girl screamed and Gladys gasped with fright and groped frantically for the torch. If the house came down on top of them now . . . But the walls held and after a moment her fingers found the torch and pressed the switch. The beam of light shone out again and she sighed with relief.

'Stay still, Ruthie.' As if the poor little mite could do anything else! 'I'm just going to look at the others. Is – is this your mummy?'

The child nodded. Her eyes were enormous. Gladys crawled across the floor, the thin liquid mud like ice about her legs. She peered at the three huddled bodies. An old man – Ruth's grandfather? – and two women. Their eyes were open, fixed and staring.

Without any hope, she felt the limp wrists and touched the lolling necks. No pulses. No sign of breathing. No heartbeat.

She crawled back to the child. Voices were calling down the narrow shaft and she shouted back. 'The little girl's half buried. I'm going to try to get her out. The others . . .' Her voice trembled and failed. How could you yell the news that a child's family were dead, when she was listening and watching you with those huge, terrified eyes?

'It's all right, Ruthie.' How could she sound so calm? Inside, her heart was like thunder and her nerves were jumping like jags of lightning. Every few moments there was another crash, sometimes at a distance, sometimes almost overhead. The earth trembled and the walls of the cellar shook.

'It's all right,' she said again, and she lifted one hand to the child's head and stroked the matted hair. 'It's all right. We'll have you out of here soon. You'll be safe . . .'

Over the Hill, Betty and Dennis heard the noise and looked from the farmhouse windows to see the glow. Yvonne had gone home for the weekend and Erica was in bed with a heavy cold, but Mr and Mrs Spencer joined them, staring out at the red and orange sky. They could hear the planes roaming overhead, see the web of the searchlights, the flash of ack-ack. They could hear the dull thud-thud-thud of the explosions, their eyes were scorched by the searing blaze of the fires.

'The whole bloody city's in flames,' Jack Spencer said, his voice thick and slow with horror. 'The whole bloody city's going up in smoke . . .'

Betty covered her face with her hands, and Dennis put his arms around her. 'Oh, Mum,' she whispered. 'Dad . . . What's happening to them? And our Livvy, she's going to have a baby. Oh God, what's happening to them?'

'Ssh, ssh,' Dennis said, holding her close. 'They'll be all right. They've got a shelter, haven't they? They'll have gone into that. They'll be safe.'

'They might not. They might be out somewhere. Dad could be at work, on the ferry. Livvy might – Mum might—' She shook her head, staring at the flame-lit sky. Dennis hugged her close and looked helplessly at Mrs Spencer.

'Come on downstairs, love,' the farmer's wife said briskly, though her own voice was trembling too. 'We'll make some cocoa. It don't do no good, standing here watching it. There's nothing we can do. Come with me.'

Betty shook her head, her eyes fixed in terrible fascination on the glowing sky. Gently, Dennis urged her towards the stairs. 'Go on, darling. Mrs Spencer's right. We can't do anything to help by standing here on the landing getting cold.'

Again Betty shook her head, but this time she allowed them to shepherd her down the stairs. In the kitchen, she sat at the big table in one of the settles while Mrs Spencer moved the kettle on to the hottest part of the range to bring it to the boil, and busied herself spooning cocoa into large cups. She mixed it with sugar and a little milk, then filled the cups with boiling water and set one in front of Betty.

'There. That'll warm you up. You're shivering, girl, come a bit nearer the fire. I'll take one up to Erica too, she never got warm all day.'

Betty shook her head. 'I'm not cold.'

'It's shock,' Mrs Spencer said to Dennis. 'Look at her shivering there. And no wonder, poor duck, seeing that out there and thinking of her mum and dad.'

Dennis pushed Betty's cup a little nearer to her. 'Drink your cocoa, sweetheart. It'll do you good.'

'Drop of brandy in it'll do her more good,' Mr Spencer said suddenly and went to the cupboard in the corner. He brought over the bottle, kept for 'medicinal purposes' and poured a generous measure into Betty's cup. 'Do us all good,' he added, treating each cup the same.

Dennis lifted Betty's cup to her lips. 'Come on, darling. It'll warm you up.'

'I'm not cold. I'm not cold. It's Mum who's cold, down there in that shelter. And Dad, on the ferry. And Yvonne, at Rudmore. Oh, what's happening to them?' She lifted her head, looking at them with desperate eyes. 'The whole of Pompey's burning, you can see it. They're being burnt alive, all of them, and me not there. I ought to be there, with them. I shouldn't never have come out here to the farm. Dad never wanted me to.' The words poured from her in a torrent, as the tears streamed down her cheeks. 'He always said I ought to stay at home. Graham did too. None of them wanted me to come out here, and now they're all getting bombed and burnt and killed and I'm – I'm *safe*. And I *shouldn't* be!'

'Betty, Betty. You're talking crazy. D'you think they'd *want* you to be bombed?' Dennis shook her shoulders gently. 'They must be thankful you're safe. They must be glad you came here. They didn't want you to stay at home just so you could be in danger, you know they didn't.'

'Dennis is right,' Mrs Spencer said, coming back down the stairs. 'Why, your mum's probably thanking God on her bended knees at this very moment, knowing no harm's going to come to you. And none's coming to them either,' she added staunchly. 'They'll have got into their shelters at the first peep of the warning, and there they'll stop till the All-Clear. And as soon as one of them can get out to the phone box, they'll be ringing us up to let you know they're all all right, you see if they don't.'

Betty sniffed and nodded. She sipped her cocoa and choked a little. Mrs Spencer did the same and wiped her eyes, looking at her husband.

'You put enough brandy in there to get a regiment drunk! Now, let's get the cards out and have a game of something. It's not a bit of use sitting here worrying ourselves silly, but I can see none of us is going to get any sleep till it's over. And we're not going to sit up all night waiting for a phone call either. There's cows to be seen to in the morning, they won't stop making milk just because Hitler decides to call.'

'Cards!' Betty exclaimed with a flash of hysteria. 'It's always cards. Whenever something happens that shouldn't, we get out the cards. Your boy wants to make love to you, the Germans send their bombers over and set fire to everyone you love, and what do we do? We play cards!'

She turned again into Dennis's arms and buried her face against his chest. He held her close, his hands moving slowly over her shoulders, his voice murmuring in her ear, and after a while her sobs diminished and she lifted her face.

'I'm sorry,' she said shakily. 'I know you're right. Crying doesn't help anyone. Maybe a game of cards would be the best thing.'

She thought of the great historical figures she had been told about at school – Drake, playing bowls on Plymouth Hoe as the Spanish Armada sailed up the Channel. Nero, fiddling while Rome burned.

Perhaps it wasn't so very different, playing cards.

'Why doesn't Mummy speak to me?' The little girl's eyes were fixed on the huddled bodies on the other side of the cellar, only a few feet away. 'Why won't she wake up?'

'She's been hurt, love.' Gladys worked steadily, pulling the rubbish away from the little body. There was no point in hiding the truth. The child would have to know, and sooner rather than later. But Gladys could not quite bring herself to break it so baldly. 'We'll get her to hospital as soon as we've got you out. She won't mind waiting.' She would never mind waiting again. 'Don't worry, Ruthie. Everything's going to be all right.'

She heard her own words with a bitter cynicism. Everything was not going to be all right. It would never again be 'all right' for this little scrap for, no matter what her life might become, she would never be able to escape from the memory of this dreadful night, and the knowledge that her mother had been killed before her eyes. She would never lose the picture of that staring face with the blood congealing to a black scab on the white skin. If she lived to be a hundred, it would still be with her. She would take it with her to her own death.

Everything was very far from 'all right'.

22

There was no time for grief. No time for pain. As one casualty was freed from the smoking, dust-clouded ruins, so a hundred more were in desperate need. As one fire was doused, so another ten broke out.

And the water was never in the right place. Fractured water mains gushed uselessly in the roads and the fire brigade could do nothing but simply let the fires burn until the mains could be hastily repaired and water pumped through.

Sometimes the flames were put out by local firewatchers and neighbours. As soon as the bombs began to fall, people rushed out of their shelters and on to the streets, ready at the risk of their lives to give whatever help might be needed. With buckets of earth and sand, with pumps attached to their own kitchen taps, with blankets and old mats, heedless of shrapnel raining about them, they donned tin hats and battled together to save their city. As buildings crumbled and fell, they fought to tear away the rubble and release those who had been buried.

In all too many cases, there was nothing to find but a few bloody fragments. But in others, there were people, injured but alive, waiting to be released and some of them were even able to joke with their rescuers.

'I'm really sorry about this,' one young man, buried almost to his neck, whispered faintly to Gladys. 'I bet you were going out with your boyfriend tonight, weren't you?'

'Haven't got one,' she said cheerfully, scraping mud away from his mouth. It would be a nice smile when he got himself cleaned up a bit. 'So I wasn't going anywhere, see? Glad to have something to do.'

'No boyfriend? A pretty girl like you?' His voice was slurred, almost as if he were drunk, but Gladys knew that it was really the effect of the morphia injection the young woman doctor had just given him. 'Well, why don't we make a date? A night at the flicks, how would that suit you?' His voice faded, as though speaking was becoming too much of an effort, as if he needed all his energy just to keep breathing.

'It'd do me fine.' She looked at him with pity. A few moments ago, before the injection, his face had been contorted with agony, his voice a thin scream. Goodness only knew what injuries he had sustained when the building had crashed about him. They would find out soon enough, but the doctor had shaken her head. Some of them die as soon as the weight's taken off them, she'd said, and Gladys knew that she half expected it to happen to this boy.

'You can take me out the first day you get out of hospital,' she said. 'And don't think you can get out of it, I'm the one who'll be driving you there, so I'll know just what ward you're in and everything.' That's if you ever get that far, she thought, and felt the tears come to her eyes.

No time for crying. Casualties were being loaded into her ambulance all the time and she must leave this boy for others to dig out, and drive to the hospital again. By now, the Royal had been bombed and the Eye and Ear, their own patients being rescued by the nurses and doctors. That meant a long drive through the streets and over Portsbridge to the Queen Alexandra, right out at Cosham and on the flanks of Portsdown Hill. And suppose the bridge got bombed? Apart from the railway line, it was Portsmouth's only link with the mainland.

Once at the hospital Gladys saw nurses, some of them hardly any older than her sister Diane, dealing frantically with one patient after another. Staunching blood, cleaning off the incredible dirt that flying dust and grit had poured into every wound, bandaging, splinting broken limbs . . . And all by the light of hurricane lamps, emergency lighting or the red glare of fire which permeated every street in the city that night and would burn for ever in the memories of its people.

After two hours of consistent bombing, the sky fell silent and the bombers seemed to depart. People who had spent the time cowering in their shelters crept out and gazed on the destruction of their homes.

'Stay down in the shelter, Jess,' Frank ordered. 'The All-Clear's not gone yet.'

Frank and Ted had arrived home half an hour after the raid had begun. Running along the streets, ignoring the harried bellows of wardens who were as scared as the rest of the populace, they had dived into their shelters to comfort their wives, and to reassure themselves that their families were safe, and then had strapped on their helmets and taken up their own firewatching duties. And firewatching was the right word for it tonight, Frank thought, standing up on top of his own Anderson, staring at the blazing sky. There was nothing to watch *but* fire. God knew what was burning down there, it might be easier to say what *wasn't* burning. And although most of it couldn't be nearer than Commercial Road, you could smell it from here, that all too familiar stench of burning dust, of oil and soot, of metal and stone – could stone burn? – of bricks and mortar and roasting flesh. The smell of death.

'The whole place is going up,' he said in awe. 'There's not going to be anything left . . .'

Along the street, Ted was saying much the same to Annie and Olive. But Olive had ignored his injunction to stay under cover. She scrambled out and stood beside him, a tin helmet jammed over her head, gazing in horror at the billowing clouds of black smoke, their swirling bellies lit with orange flame. Unconsciously, her hands moved over her stomach in the age-old gesture of a pregnant mother protecting her unborn young, and the movement reminded her of Kathy Simmons.

'I'll just pop over and see if she's all right,' she said, turning swiftly. Her father grabbed for her arm, but caught only her sleeve and Olive darted up the garden path. 'I won't be long.'

'Livvy! Come back, the All-Clear's not gone, they could be back any minute, they could be up there now.' There was too much noise from the city to be able to tell if the planes were still above. The *crump* of explosions was still going on, if not bombs, it could be gas-mains, oil tanks, anything. Cars could explode, buses, lorries, anything with oil or petrol, anything with pressure, could go off. Smoke itself made a noise as it billowed about, carrying with it the crackle of flames, the rush of air in a storm of its own making. In such conditions, fire could spread from one end of the city to the other in a matter of minutes, it wasn't safe anywhere. 'Livvy!' he shouted again. 'Livvy! Come back, for God's sake, come back!'

But she was gone, running away from him down the bright-lit street, and he could only stare helplessly after her.

It took Olive no more than two minutes to reach Kathy Simmons' back garden and dive into the damp little shelter. She found her friend as she had expected, huddled in the dark on a flimsy camp bed, cradling her baby against her, with a little girl crouching against her on either side.

'Kathy! Kath, are you all right? I came as soon as I could—'

'Olive? Oh, Olive, is that you?' The young mother reached out a hand. 'Oh God, I've been so frightened. What's been happening out there? It sounds as though the whole of Portsmouth's going sky high.'

'It looks like it too,' Olive said soberly. 'Look.' She held back the old curtain Kathy used as a door. 'Never mind the lamp. That little bit of light won't show anyone the way in this lot.'

Kathy stared out at the crimson sky. 'What is it?'

'What d'you think? Fire. Fires all over Pompey.' Olive's voice shook and she let the curtain fall again. 'They've been dropping flares, bombs, incendiaries, God knows what, and Dad reckons they've not stopped yet. Just gone home for another lot, he says. The All-Clear's not gone and he don't reckon it will. I just slipped over while there's a lull.' She turned the lamp up and studied her friend's face. 'You look done in, Kath. Have you got anything to eat or drink down here?'

Kathy shook her head. 'I had a flask, but the girls needed some cocoa. And I have to save some water for Thomas. Poor little mite, he's slept through it all, can you believe that?' They looked down at the peacefully slumbering baby. One fist was curled like a bud under his chin, and his lashes lay like dark fans on his creamy cheeks. Olive touched him gently with the tip of her finger and again laid her other hand over her stomach. Soon, her own baby would quicken and she would feel its tiny feet pressing against the walls of her womb. A boy like Derek, or a girl like herself? It didn't matter. All that mattered was that it should be born safe and kept safe, away from bombs, away from war and terror.

'I wish I'd brought you something,' she said. 'We've got two or three flasks, we could've spared you one. Or you could come over to us.' Her voice brightened. 'Why don't you do that, Kath? Come over to us and stop the rest of the night. It'd be better for you to be with company, and better for the girls too. We could have a sing-song like they do in the big shelters.'

Kathy hesitated, then shook her head. 'There's not enough room. It's cramped enough as it is.'

'Don't be daft. There's only Mum and me, and Dad when he pops in for a few minutes off firewatching. We'll keep each other warm.' The spatter of ack-ack fire broke into her words. 'It looks as if they might be coming again. Come on, Kath.'

Kathy bit her lip and looked at the girls. They were pale and frightened. Olive watched her, seeing the thoughts chase each other across her face. *Perhaps it would be best. Better for the children. And better for me.* She saw Kathy make up her mind, as clearly as if a light had been switched on, and gripped her hand.

'You are coming, aren't you? Only I think we ought to be quick.'

'Yes. I'm coming. Only – will you take the girls first? I just want to pop indoors and boil a kettle to fill up the flask again. It won't take more'n a minute. I'll come across straightaway then.'

Olive looked at her doubtfully. 'D'you think you ought to? Go indoors, I mean? Suppose they come back . . . ?'

'I'll be quick as a flash,' Kathy promised. She drew back the curtain and looked out. 'It's quiet enough now, look. And they've never dropped anything round these streets yet . . .'

They never had. And Kathy had been bombed once, and ought to have been immune from further disaster. After all, they said lightning never struck twice in the same place, didn't they?

But Kathy wasn't in the same place. And the Luftwaffe did not follow the rules laid down for lightning. The bomb fell in the gardens of October Street, close to the shelter where she had been taking cover. It fractured the gas main at the moment when Kathy had just lit a match in the kitchen to boil her kettle. The gas gushed out and exploded, throwing her and the baby son she had wanted so much clear through the shattering wall.

Olive and the girls were halfway back to the turret house at the end of March Street when it happened. They too were knocked over by the blast, and when Ted Chapman came racing across to help them, found to their dismay that every stitch of clothing was ripped from their bodies. The girls scrambled up, crying and terrified, shuddering with the sudden rush of cold air on their skin. But Olive lay still, racked with sudden agony, and the blood spread in a pool around her body.

There was not a bruise on her body. The blast had torn away her clothes as cleanly as if she had taken them off herself, yet she was quite unhurt.

But there would be no baby for her in July. No baby son who resembled Derek, no daughter who looked like her.

And for Kathy Simmons, no babies ever again. Nothing, ever again.

Twice on that terrible night, the raiders returned. For seven hours they bombarded Portsmouth without relief, until it seemed that the city must have been totally destroyed by their frenzy. And when daylight finally came, to show what could not be seen even by the light of the flames which had consumed so much, so greedily, during the hours of darkness, it revealed just what havoc had been wrought.

The main shopping centres – Palmerston Road, which Gladys had never reached, Commercial Road and King's Road – lay in ruins. At Southsea, Handley's and Knight & Lee's, two of the grandest department stores in the city, were burned, and other buildings dynamited to prevent the flames from spreading. In Commercial Road, the Landport Drapery Bazaar, which was not a bazaar at all but another large department store, was burned down and Woolworths, which had only just been rebuilt after the previous year's fire, C & A and the Royal Sailor's Rest destroyed. At Fratton the big Co-op was little more than a crater.

Six churches and the Salvation Army Citadel had been destroyed. The Eye and Ear Hospital had gone, so had part of the Royal. Clarence Pier, at Southsea, had been reduced to rubble. Gone too were three more cinemas, and the Hippodrome, where Annie and Ted had gone to laugh at Elsie and Doris Waters, was in tatters.

Houses had been smashed by the street, craters left gaping in roadways, roofs torn off and walls blasted away. In one front bedroom, the passer-by could see nothing but destruction, yet still hear the tick of an alarm clock balanced precariously on the remains of a mantelpiece. In another, the ceiling had collapsed on a double bed, killing the occupants who had refused to go to the shelter, but leaving the cot containing their baby son unscathed. In a third, there was no damage at all, only a wall removed as neatly as if it were the front of a doll's house, lifted away for display.

But worst of all for the city and its pride, was the destruction of the Guildhall, that great and gracious building so dear and familiar to them all. Standing at the edge of its square at the end of Commercial Road, it had symbolised the heart of Portsmouth; the deep tones of its bell, ringing out the hours before it was silenced by war, had echoed in the breast of every man and woman who had lived with its sound. And now the bell tower was ablaze, burning like a great torch as if in defiance of the enemy, with flames surging into the sky like crimson plumage. The copper plates of the cupola shimmered in the heat and fell away, the flames spread through the interior and the great hall where only two days earlier a thousand children had eaten jelly and marched to the tune of *There'll Always Be an England* was destroyed for ever. The organ would never play again.

'I don't want to see anything like that again, ever,' Peggy Shaw said to Jess next afternoon. She and Gladys had arrived home late in the morning, filthy and dog-tired. They had had a quick wash and then, weary as she was, Gladys had gone off to Commercial Road to report for work at the ruined shop. Diane too had come back exhausted, her brief exhilaration crushed by a night at the First Aid post. But she had not given way, Mrs Jenkins had remarked to Peggy as they left. She'd been a real help and would be welcome any time to give a hand.

'Our Glad's been a real heroine,' Peggy went on. 'Took her an hour to get that kiddy out from the cellar, and there was bombs falling round our heads all the time. But she never give way. The little un wouldn't hardly let her go when they brought her up. Broken leg, she had, poor little mite, scratched and grazed all over, and her mum killed in front of her eyes. We put her straight in the ambulance and Glad drove round to the Royal. I didn't think she ought to, she was shaking like a leaf when she come up, but she wouldn't hear of letting someone else take the van. That's my ambulance, she said, and I'm responsible for it. So they had to let her do it.'

'She's a good girl. They both are.' That hadn't always been Jess's opinion, privately, she'd thought Peggy a bit too lax with her daughters, though Bert was strict enough. But you couldn't complain about youngsters who'd worked like Gladys and Diane had, even if they were a bit flighty. 'Did she go on driving after that?'

Peggy rolled her eyes. 'Jess, we went everywhere with that van last night! You didn't have to ask where to go – you just left the hospital and there was another street afire or someone flagging you down for help. It was bedlam. I thought we were going to have an accident, I did straight, the times we nearly crashed into fire engines and such. They had the lot there, City firemen, auxiliaries, soldiers, sailors, Marines. There must've been thousands of fires burning. And half the time, they had no water, the water mains were hit, see. What could they do?'

Jess knew all too well that the water mains had been hit. Parts of the city were still cut off, and even those who still had some were asked to be extra sparing with it. And there was still no electricity. When darkness fell, you had to use candles, and there weren't all that many of them, either. What with the coal shortage and problems with the gas supply as well, there was precious little comfort to be had anywhere this bitter January.

'*I don't want to see anything like that ever again . . .*'

She and thousands of others echoed Peggy's words that morning, as they stared at the ruins of their city, as they picked disconsolately through the rubble to salvage what few belongings they could, as they trudged away along the littered streets carrying a few pathetic bundles to find shelter with friends and relatives, or in the emergency centres that had been set up by the council.

What was left for them, now that so much had been taken away? For some, there was still a family; others had lost everyone they loved. For some, there was still a job; others had lost even that. For some, there was comfort; for others, nothing but despair.

The *Evening News* printed a special edition, with a message from the Lord Mayor set squarely in its front page. He himself had been bombed out, for he had moved into the Guildhall some months previously, declaring that since he spent all his waking hours there he might as well be on hand at night as well. He had left the building only minutes before the incendiaries struck. Now he paid tribute to the people of his city.

'At last the blow has fallen. Our proud City has been hit and hit very hard by the enemy. Our Guildhall and many of our cherished buildings now lie a heap of smoking ruins . . . We are bruised but we are not daunted . . . we shall persevere with an unflagging spirit to a decisive victory . . .'

'It's as good as Churchill,' Jess said, when Frank read it out to her. 'It gives people heart when they read things like that. And they need it, too.' Her eyes filled with tears. 'Poor Kathy Simmons. And those two poor little girls. I wonder what'll happen to them now, with no mother and their father away at sea.'

'They've had a bad time of it,' he agreed. But you know, they shouldn't ever have been here. They ought all to have been evacuated, the lot of 'em. And—'

'I know what you're going to say,' she interrupted. 'So should I and Rose and the baby. Well, maybe we *should*. But how can we? You need me here to look after you, you know that. And I couldn't bear to think of being away, not knowing what was happening to you. Annie said she tried to telephone to Betty this morning but she couldn't get through, if there are any phones working, the authorities have got 'em all. She sent a telegram instead, but that poor girl must have been going through agonies wondering how we all were. And if you want Rose to go back, you can be the one to tell her, *I'm* not going to.'

Frank sighed and tightened his lips but he knew there was no point in further argument. They'd had all this out before. Jess saw her duty plainly as being by his side, and beyond that, she *wanted* to be here. She really had been miserable when she'd gone away at the beginning of the war.

'Well, if you can stand stopping here after last night, you can stand anything,' he said. 'And don't think I don't appreciate it, Jess. I want you here, I won't deny it, but I wouldn't make you stop if you didn't want to. And talking of Annie, how's Olive?'

Jess pulled down the corners of her mouth.

'Well enough, considering. She's really cut up about losing the baby. Derek's not been told yet, he's still out helping with demolition and so on. She'll be better when he can be with her.' She sighed. 'I feel sorry for her, but like Annie says, it could be a blessing in disguise. At least the poor little mite won't be blown to bits like little Thomas Simmons.'

Blown to bits, she thought. Babies in their mothers' arms, blown to bits.

23

Betty opened her telegram with shaking fingers. The disruption of Portsmouth had delayed it, so that it was past afternoon milking when it finally arrived. She stared at the orange envelope with dread.

'Shall I open it for you?' Dennis asked, but she shook her head.

'I've got to do it myself.'

Her hand shook so much that the paper tore half across before she could get it out of the envelope. Dennis watched her anxiously. Her face was as white as the milk she had just squeezed from the udders, and her lips quivered. Suddenly, her face distorted, her mouth squaring like a child's, and she dropped the telegram and swayed. He caught her just before she fell.

'Betty, what's happened?'

She shook her head. The tears were pouring down her cheeks and she was making a strange, choking sound, half laughing, half crying. She let the telegram fall and it fluttered to the ground as she clung to his shoulders with both hands, beating her forehead against his chest. He gathered her close, holding her hard, rocking her and making soft little soothing sounds.

'Tell me, Betty. Tell me. What's happened?' His own voice trembled. 'Who – who's gone? Is it your mum? Your dad? Your—'

'No! No! It's none of them – none.' She gripped his collar and leaned back in his arms, gazing up at him. 'They're all right, that's what it says, all of them, Mum, Dad, Livvy, Auntie Jess, Uncle Frank, everyone.' A sudden fear darkened her eyes and sounded sharply in her voice. 'That *is* what it says, isn't it? I haven't read it wrong?'

Dennis loosened his arms and bent to retrieve the scrap of paper. He stared at the hastily-printed words. *All safe. Love, Mum, Dad, Livvy.* He took a deep breath of relief and caught her close again.

'No, sweetheart, you haven't read it wrong. They're all right. And you'll find out any more there is to know soon enough. So now you can stop worrying and give me a hand mucking out these cows. They'll be up to their udders in it soon, and *that* won't make the milk taste very good, now will it!'

Betty laughed shakily and picked up her fork. 'I'm sorry, Dennis,' she said. 'I've been a real misery today, I know.'

'You haven't been a misery at all. You've been worried stiff, and quite right too. Anyone'd be worried about their family, after watching the fires they had in Pompey all night long.' He glanced towards the door of the byre. The smoke had been visible all day, still shot through with red and gold. 'I hope Yvonne's all right too.'

'Oh, Dennis!' Betty stopped raking and stared at him in dismay. 'I forgot all about poor Yvonne. Oh, how could I be so selfish!'

'And you're not selfish either. Yvonne's your friend, but your family's your family.' He worked for a few minutes in silence and then said, 'There's something I ought to tell you. And now that you know your family's all right . . .'

'What?' She stared at him in sudden terror. 'Dennis, what is it?'

'It's all right,' he said. 'Nothing to be scared of. It's just that, well, I've decided I can't go on working on the farm. I've got to do something more.'

Betty felt the blood drain from her face.

'You're joining up.'

He shook his head. 'Not exactly. Well, in a way. I'm going to join the Pioneer Corps.'

'But that's the Army! You'll have to kill people.'

'No. I'll be a non-combatant. I won't be killing anyone. I won't be fighting at all.'

She looked at him. There was something more, she could see it in his face. But at the moment, all she could think of was that he would be leaving the farm.

'You're going away,' she said in a hopeless voice, and he nodded.

'I'm sorry, Betty. I don't want to leave you. I don't want to leave the farm and Mr and Mrs Spencer. It's been like a home to me.' He grinned suddenly. 'I don't even want to leave these cows, bless 'em! But it's something I've been thinking about for a long time. And after last night . . .' He moved restlessly. 'I know what people like Erica think of me, and I don't really mind about that. There's enough like you and the Spencers who can see that a man has to be able to think and decide these things for himself.'

'It's a pity there's not more of them on the City Council,' Betty said with a flash of spirit. 'I mean, they're going right against the Government aren't they, turning you off your job. They're not supposed to do that.'

'No, they're not. But there's not much I can do about that, not without making a lot of fuss.' He paused and she knew that he was trying to decide how to tell her the rest of his decision. Her heart sank.

'You're going to tell me it's all over between us, aren't you? It was good while it lasted—' her voice trembled '—but once you've gone away . . . Don't tell me that, please don't tell me that . . . I'll wait for you.' She remembered Graham, furious because she wouldn't marry him. 'I'll do whatever you want . . .'

'But of course I'm not going to tell you that,' Dennis said, staring at her in amazement. He saw her tears and crossed the space between them with two long strides, pulling her roughly into his arms. 'Betty, my darling, I'll never tell you that, never. I love you. I don't want to leave you, not for a minute. But I can't stay here with an easy conscience. I've got to do something more to help, you see that, don't you?'

She nodded speechlessly, her tears soaking his shirt. 'But you said you never would, you wouldn't even make uniforms in prison, and now you're going in the Army—'

'Non-combatant,' he said quietly. 'I won't fight. I won't even help by making it easier for others to fight. But I will help *save* lives. I'm going to be in the bomb disposal squad.'

There was a moment of silence. The cows shifted in their stalls. Somewhere out in the yard, Jonas called to his dog. In the shed next door the hens burst into noisy, excited clucking as Mrs Spencer fed them.

'The bomb disposal squad?' Betty repeated slowly. 'But that's *dangerous*.' Dennis grinned wryly. 'War *is* dangerous. Think of last night.'

'I know, but that, Dennis, it means defusing unexploded bombs, doesn't it? Poking about looking for buried mines? Going down in craters and making sure there's nothing left to go off? It's more dangerous than *anything*.'

'Not really. There's plenty of other people—'

'I'm not interested in *them*!' she cried. 'I'm interested in you. *You're* the one who's going to be taking unexploded bombs to bits to stop them going off. Dennis, you'll be killed, I know you will. You only have to *touch* some of these bombs – and mines, they go off as soon as someone lays a finger on them. I've seen them on the news at the pictures. And in papers.'

'But the ones I'll be dealing with will be the ones that haven't gone off so easily. They're duds. Look, a bomb that falls hundreds of feet from an aeroplane and hits the ground and doesn't explode isn't going to go off just because I touch it with one finger, is it?'

'Isn't it?' she retorted. 'Don't treat me like a kid, Dennis. I'm not a fool. Bombs do go off after they've fallen. Some of them are *time* bombs – they're not meant to go off straightaway. You can't tell me you won't be taking risks.'

He shrugged. 'A few, yes. Not that many. I'm not treating you like a fool, Betty. It's honestly not that dangerous. Not if you know what you're doing.'

'And do you know what you're doing?'

'No, not yet, but I will. I'll be trained. And I've always been good with mechanical things. One of the first things I remember my dad being cross with me about was when I took his alarm clock to bits to see how it worked.' He laughed. 'I put it together again, but I had two or three bits left over that I didn't tell him about, and it never worked properly after that.'

'And is that supposed to cheer me up?' Betty said. 'How d'you think I'm going to feel when they come and tell me there's only two or three bits of you left over?' Her face crumpled and she clung to him again. 'Dennis, please don't go. Please stay here with me. Or do something else, something that's not so dangerous. Bomb disposal – you couldn't have picked anything worse!'

'Perhaps that's why I'm doing it,' he said slowly. 'Perhaps I want to show people that COs aren't a bunch of lily-livered cowards. The trouble is, most of the jobs they give us are too safe. They make us look like skivers, hiding away on farms, or just carrying on with our peace-time jobs. It's no wonder people turn their noses up. But I can't do it any longer,' he exclaimed with sudden passion. 'I can't stay here, looking out of windows while cities burn and people get killed. I want to be in there, helping save lives that should never be in danger. I won't fight, I won't kill, but I won't stand by and see other people killed when I could be doing something to prevent it.'

He was silent for a moment, then he said quietly, 'You're right, Betty. It is dangerous, and I shouldn't pretend it's not, especially to you. If those bombs weren't expected to go off, I wouldn't be bothered about them. If they were that safe, they could be left there or picked up by anyone who happened to be passing. But they're not. They can explode. And that's why I want to work with them, so that I take the same risks as everyone else.' He looked gravely down into her face. 'I love you, Betty. That's why there's got to be truth between us. It will be dangerous, but I've got to do it. Can you understand that?'

She met his eyes. During the past few weeks, as their love had ripened and their understanding deepened, she had come to respect Dennis's conscience and beliefs. They were not the same as hers, though she felt that with time they might come to mean more to her than the values she had grown up with. But she knew that he had already paid dearly enough to hold them. He had lost his job and many of his friends. He had served in prison. He was now working on hard and menial tasks on a farm. All these prices had been paid with cheerfulness and honesty. He had never shirked a task, but neither had he ever compromised his principles.

Now his conscience was taking him further. It would take him right to the front line, wherever that might be, into dangers and perils as extreme as any faced by a fighting man. It could take him to his death.

'Yes,' she said quietly. 'I understand.' But even while her mind said yes, she felt her heart cry out against it and she wanted to beg him to stay.

But she knew she could not say the words. She could not have said them to Graham, to Bob Shaw, to Derek Harker or her brother Colin. Nor could any woman say them to the man she loved, for this was war and the country had first hold on its men and could take them from their hearths and homes, sending them far across the world to fight battles they did not understand and did not want. They could not choose to stay at home.

And even for Dennis and those like him, who claimed the right to set conscience above the requirements of the country, there was no choice. For the demands of such a conscience were greater even than the demands of the heart, and would drive many of them into greater peril even than those who were prepared to fight. For they could not accept 'safety' and looked instead for ways to use their own brand of courage in the service of their fellow men.

Some, Betty knew, had become stretcher-bearers, ready to go unarmed into the front line of the battlefield. Some had joined the Red Cross or went with the Friends' own field hospitals to those same areas of conflict. And some, like Dennis, went to the very heart of danger and took their lives in their hands as many times a day as it was asked of them.

She held him closely and let her tears run. He was driven by something too powerful for her to do more than glimpse. But that power contained also his love for her, and this she could understand, for her love matched his own, and she would send it with him wherever he might go.

They stood close in the warmth of the cattle byre where they had first fallen in love, and she felt the cold, black shadow of war drift slowly around them.

The work of recovery and rebuilding started at once.

Water had been the biggest problem. With nearly three thousand fires burning in a single night, the fire services had been helped by the Navy, the military and by ordinary civilians, trained and untrained, who worked throughout the bombing to try to keep the flames under control.

But the water supply had never been intended for such a conflagration, and when the mains themselves were fractured people were forced to watch it gushing out and flowing uselessly away where no fire was burning. Tenders were diverted to fill their tanks, people ran hoses down the streets and through their homes to bring them where they were needed, but many of the fires could only be contained and men and women alike wept as they watched their homes burn unchecked to ashes.

Four miles of steel piping was purchased to provide an overland main and huge water tanks were built on cleared bomb sites, ready for the next attack, for nobody believed that Jerry had finished with them. They were still alive, weren't they? Still defiant. The Germans wouldn't like that. They'd come again.

The work took a long time, some of it not begun until after the heaviest of the raids were over. But no one could know whether there was not worse to come, and the City Council, sharply criticised for being unprepared, was not going to repeat its mistakes. It even began to look again at the plans for tunnels into the hills, and the proposal for the Kearney tunnel, to be built beneath the harbour, linking Portsmouth with Gosport.

But before all this, the victims of the first blitz must be buried, and many went together to a communal grave a hundred feet long, lined with Union Jacks, their coffins borne by a long procession of hearses and accompanied by the band of the Royal Marines. Soldiers and sailors marched slowly alongside and the pavements were crowded by those who wanted to pay their last respects to friends and neighbours, those who knew nothing of the ones who had died save that they were fellow Portmuthians, and even some who were there simply from curiosity.

'You don't get many chances to see summat like this,' Jess heard a man say. 'Try and get near the front, we might get a look at the grave.'

She wanted to turn and slap his face. There are people we knew in those coffins, she wanted to cry, there's a young mother there who died with her five-week-old baby in her arms. There's another woman, with her little girl only nine years old, their lives snatched away from them, and an old man of ninety-two who ought to have died peacefully in his own bed. It's not an entertainment!

But there was no point in saying anything and, suddenly sickened, she turned and pushed her way through the crowd. She had paid her respects to Kathy in a different way, by taking in her two little girls until they could be found a billet out in the country where they would be safe. That was better than standing here, watching the sombre procession go by and living through the misery all over again.

In any case, the war had not retreated. Although there were no more raids for almost three weeks, the siren still sounded nightly, and now the All-Clear rarely went until early morning. Enemy aircraft were active in the skies whenever the weather was favourable, and even sometimes when it was not. You could hear them passing overhead, on their way to London or other cities. The south coast was permanently a potential target for those aircraft who had been turned back still loaded with bombs, and you never knew when the target might again be Portsmouth.

More people now had joined the nightly 'trekkers'. Every afternoon, a crowd of mothers with children who had not been evacuated would catch buses to trek 'over the hill' and shelter with relatives in outlying villages. Fathers would cycle to join them after work, or even take their cars, using precious petrol and causing much bitterness amongst those who must queue for a bus, or trudge through the cold and dark to safety. And even those were resented by many who stayed behind to face whatever danger there was.

'They go off for a good night's sleep and expect us to look after their houses,' Peggy Shaw said caustically. She glanced disparagingly at number 15, now left empty each night when Ethel Glaister and her two children departed for her sister's house at Denmead. 'I'd leave it to burn, but you can't let the fire spread just because it's *her* house.'

'Well, we all have to do whatever we think's right.' Jess had been feeling increasingly unhappy about keeping Rose and Maureen at home. She could not get the picture of Kathy Simmons' baby from her mind. She had been the one to find him, still clutched in his mother's arms, the firm little body torn like a rag doll. She had thought of 'trekking' from the city herself, just to keep them safe, but she knew no one out in the villages and couldn't afford to pay for a room. For her, it was either proper evacuation or face it out at home, and she knew which it had to be.

The *Evening News* kept the people together. Each day, its headlines kept them informed of the progress of the war. On the big map which Frank had pinned on the living-room wall, he could see how the RAF had bombed Berlin and Wilhelmshaven, how the British Imperial Forces were closing an 'iron ring' around Tobruk, how the RAF was bombing Naples, Benghasi and Messina. Places he had scarcely heard of were suddenly important strategic points, and he spent as much time as he could studying the newspaper and the map in turn, collecting together enough information to give himself a picture of what was happening.

The map of Europe was no longer enough. He needed a map of the whole world.

But it was local news for which the Portsmouth paper was most eagerly scanned, and in those days after the first blitz the city could hardly have functioned without it. As shops and offices dragged themselves out of the ruins, the paper was filled with notices telling people where to find them.

'It's like a mystery tour, trying to find places these days,' Peggy Shaw commented. 'Bits of the Co-op in Fratton Road, other bits in Kingston. As for trying to find a newsagent or a butcher, it'd be like a needle in a haystack if it wasn't for the *News*. It's a marvel there's places for them all to go.'

'There's not, for some of 'em.' Annie Chapman touched her hair. She had it set every Friday, bombs or no bombs. 'I had an awful job to find Rene's. She's had to set up in her own front room.'

It was like living in a huge board game, where pieces might be moved at random and the player's task was to seek them out, while still living a life as near to normal as possible and snatching some sleep between the sound of the sirens and the nightly journey down the garden to the shelter or 'over the hill'.

The wireless was another lifeline. At nine o'clock every evening, Frank and Jess switched on the set and listened. *'This is the Nine o'clock News and this is Alvar Liddell reading it.'* News was like a drug, you had to have it, good or bad. And, later in the evening, the homely north-country tones of J B Priestley's *Postscripts* would roll into the room, or the quickfire jokes of Tommy Handley in *ITMA*.

'A good laugh,' Jess said, 'that's what we need most. And some nice singing. Those girls, Vera Lynn and Anne Shelton, they're lovely. They give you heart, somehow.'

It was heart that was needed most in these cold and dismal days after the first blitz. Heart and warmth, and courage of a sort that most people had never dreamed they would need, had never believed it possible to find. In the back streets of Copnor and Fratton, in the slums of Rudmore, in the tiny alleyways of Old Portsmouth, those who had been bombed out of their homes, who had lost all that they held most dear, must face whatever came next.

For many, it was too hard a task, for they were already exhausted and became more so as the winter wore on. For many, it seemed that it was a winter that would never end.

For some, it was an adventure.

'We ain't scared,' Micky Baxter boasted. 'We likes watching the planes. I'm waitin' for that parachutist. We're doin' war work, we are.'

The three boys made it their business to investigate all the bombed areas. They roamed through the littered streets and clambered about in ruined houses, keeping a sharp eye open for wardens who would chase them off. They salvaged whatever was worth taking away and filled their basement den with treasures, broken ornaments, crockery, clocks with shattered faces. But they were more interested now in finding shell cases and shrapnel.

'Look at this.' Jimmy Cross was holding up a stubby metal object. Micky and Cyril crowded round to examine it.

'What is it?' Cyril's large brown eyes were even bigger with excitement. 'Is it a bomb?'

'I reckon it is.' Micky touched it with awe. 'It's an unexploded bomb.'

'Will it go off?' Cyril retreated a few steps.

'It might. If it does, we'll all be blown to bits.' Micky gave a sudden yell, then laughed. 'Don't drop it, Jim!'

Jimmy jumped and clutched the object tightly. It had a blunt nose and fins along its side. Gingerly, he held it up to his ear.

'It's not ticking.'

'Well, that's all right then. It's a dud. Let's take it back to the den. it's our best thing yet.' Micky looked at it enviously, wishing he could have been the one to find it. Jimmy Cross had been getting too cocky as it was. He'd be wanting to be leader of the gang soon, just because he'd been lucky enough to find a bomb.

'Our best thing until I gets a parachutist,' he corrected himself, and led the way through the ruined streets.

Tim and Keith were aggrieved that they had missed the big raid. They described the attack of Christmas Eve to anyone who would listen, but a good many of the children had been in Portsmouth themselves and had their own stories to tell.

'I wish we were still in Pompey,' Tim said disconsolately as they sat in the vicarage kitchen listening to the News on the wireless. 'They're getting all the fun.' It had snowed during the night, but even that wasn't enough to make up for what he was missing.

Mrs Mudge, the housekeeper, was making breakfast. She put a bowl of porridge in front of each of them.

'You think yourself lucky you're here, out of it all. There's no fun in being bombed out of your home. It's no place for kiddies, Pompey's not. I feel sorry for the poor souls who have to stay there.'

'Our sister's there,' Keith observed. 'She didn't want to come back and Mum and Dad let her stay. And she doesn't even like it!'

'Nobody likes it. I daresay she wanted to be with your mum and help with the baby.' Mrs Mudge had known Jess when the whole family, except for Frank, had been in Bridge End during the early days of the war. She also knew, from Mrs Greenberry, just how miserable Rose had been after her mother had gone back. 'That doesn't mean you're not better off here.'

Tim made a face and started to eat his porridge. He was still disgruntled at having to stay in the vicarage. Brian Collins already called him 'choirboy' and kept making sneering remarks about saying his prayers at night. And Tim knew that many of the children laughed at old Mr Beckett for his eccentric ways. He knew, because he'd done it himself.

The vicar came into the kitchen and sat down. He'd been to church already that morning and his pyjama trousers could be seen poking out from under his cassock.

'Well, and how are you two faring this morning? I see we had some precipitation in the night. Do you intend to build a snowman?'

Keith looked at him doubtfully. Mr Beckett didn't talk like anyone else he knew. He sounded as if he was on the wireless all the time.

'Are we allowed?' he asked.

'Allowed? My dear child, I shall be mortally offended if you do not. The front lawn, I think, don't you? We can then appoint him our guardian.' For a moment, Keith had a wild idea that he meant 'guardian angel', and imagined a snowman with wings and harp. 'We shall start as soon as breakfast is over.'

'You mean you're going to help?' Tim said in astonishment.

'Help? I shall be in charge! I've wanted to build a snowman every winter but Mrs Mudge here has never allowed it. Now that we have real boys in the house, she will not be able to object. Everyone knows that boys need to build snowmen. And have snowball fights,' he added as an afterthought. 'That's if you'll allow me.'

The two boys gazed at him. They tried to imagine his spidery figure racing about the garden, hurling snowballs. They glanced at each other.

'You're not allowed to put stones in snowballs,' Keith said at last.

'Perish the thought! My snowballs will be as pure as – as – as the driven snow.' He beamed at them. 'Do you drink tea?'

'Tea?'

Mrs Mudge said firmly, 'They drink milk while they're in this house. Growing boys need it.'

'I daresay you don't use all your sugar ration, then,' the vicar said hopefully.

Tim and Keith looked uncertainly at the housekeeper. Their mother had given her their ration books and they took no further interest in them. Food appeared on the table and they ate it (unless it was cabbage). They put sugar on their porridge and in their cocoa, but that was all.

'I wondered, you see,' Mr Beckett said delicately, 'whether we might come to some arrangement.'

'Arrangement?'

'Over sugar. It's a failing of mine, you see. A very sweet tooth. I do like plenty of sugar in my tea, and Mrs Mudge says my ration won't stretch to it. So if you don't use all of yours . . .'

'You'll not take the children's sugar,' Mrs Mudge said at once. 'The idea!'

'Oh, but I'd be happy to buy it,' the vicar said at once. 'A halfpenny a spoonful, I thought.' He looked appealingly at the boys. 'You might like to discuss it and let me know later what you decide.'

'They'll do nothing of the sort—' Mrs Mudge began, but Keith was already nodding.

'I'll sell you mine. I don't mind not having any.'

'It's unpatriotic,' Mrs Mudge said. 'Why, it's almost Black Market.'

'You can have mine too,' Tim said. 'We can buy a present for Mum. And our baby.'

'I never *heard* of such a thing—'

'You can have our tea as well if you like.'

'Such an example to set—'

'That's settled, then,' the vicar said, beaming. 'And now we'll go and make a start on the snowman, shall we?'

'That you will *not*!' Mrs Mudge said, putting her foot down at last. 'Not until you've all cleaned your teeth and put on warm clothes. You,' she said, fixing Mr Beckett with a stern eye, 'are still in your pyjamas.'

Tim and Keith scrambled down from their chairs and made for the door. The vicar followed them. He turned and gave his housekeeper a wink.

Mrs Mudge watched him go with a feeling partly of exasperation, partly of tenderness. She knew quite well what he was doing. She also knew that he was thoroughly enjoying it.

'Boys!' she said, and started on the washing-up.

24

The weather was still bitterly cold. Snow had fallen after the terrible raid of the early weeks, and now it melted into icy floods. The second blitz of Portsmouth was its thirty-seventh raid, but the sirens had sounded many more times than that and people were by now accustomed to whatever arrangements they had made for sheltering.

Frank and Jess had made their Anderson as comfortable as possible. With a concrete floor and plywood fitted against the corrugated iron walls, it was dry and draught-proof. Frank had covered the plywood with cream distemper and Jess had pinned pictures from old Christmas and birthday cards all over it. They brightened up the shelter and gave the baby something to look at and, because Maureen was fond of a comic strip which featured a baby called Henry, she included some of these and added more magazine and newspaper cuttings, pictures of Mr Chad, peering over a wall and asking 'Wot – no bananas?' or 'Wot – no coal?' and photographs of the King and Queen on their visit to Portsmouth.

Winston Churchill came to Portsmouth too, and toured the bombed areas. He picked his way over streets still littered with collapsed houses and pitted with deep craters, and grunted, looking like an angry baby with a cigar stuck in his mouth.

The Royal visit had been a fillip for the city, and especially for Olive Harker, for Derek had actually been presented to them when they came down Commercial Road. 698 Unit were there with a mechanical caterpillar and hawser, pulling down a dangerous wall. Actually, it didn't really need to be pulled down at all, Derek said, and the soldiers weren't best pleased at having to do it just for 'show'. But they'd put their backs into it all the same and the Royal party, with the Lord Mayor and his wife and a crowd of VIPs, had watched until the dust had settled and then come over to speak to the commanding officer.

'O'Rorke was like a dog with two tails,' Derek told Olive when he came in that evening for the hour or two that was all that was allowed for time off. 'He puffed out his chest like a cockerel and told 'em all about how he formed the Unit single-handed and took us over to France. Pity he couldn't claim to have beaten the Germans on their own ground, but he had to admit we'd got evacuated from Dunkirk.'

'Well, that's something to be proud of, it seems,' Olive said. She was still pale after the loss of her baby, and had lost much of her old zest. But the memory of Kathy Simmons, whose baby had been born only to be killed a few weeks later, and who had herself died at the same moment, served to remind her that she was still one of the lucky ones. 'Better to have been evacuated than killed on the beach, or taken prisoner.' She rested her head on his chest. 'I'm so thankful you're still here . . . And did the Queen actually talk to you?'

'She did.' Derek looked as proud as Colonel O'Rorke. 'She asked me my name and whether I was a Pompey chap.'

'Derek! She never said "Pompey"!'

'She did. Well, I thought she did, anyway. Honest, Livvy, she was just like anyone else, only she spoke a bit posher. And she asked about you—'

'About *me*?' Olive sat up and stared at him. 'How on earth did she know about me?'

'Well, she didn't, I suppose. She just asked if I was married and what your name was, so she knows about you now, anyway. And—' he looked away, as if half uncertain as to what to say '—she asked if we had any children.'

'Did you tell her?' Olive asked quietly, and he nodded.

'I said we'd been expecting, *you'd* been expecting, but when the blitz came . . . well, I just told her what happened, that's all.' He glanced at her face and added as if in justification, 'There didn't seem to be anything else to say, Livvy. She was really interested.'

'It's all right.' She took his hand and stroked it. 'It just seems funny, telling the Queen of England about us. Did she say anything else?'

'She said to tell you she was very sorry. And not to be disheartened. She said, "There *will* be a time when we're no longer at war, and you'll raise your family in peace." That's what she said, Livvy.'

'She said that to you?' Olive gazed at him, marvelling. 'The Queen said that to you? And told you to tell me she was sorry – about *our* baby? Oh, Derek.'

'I know.' He grinned. 'It makes it seem different, somehow, doesn't it.'

'It makes it seem easier to carry on.' Olive rested her head on his chest again. 'There's been times these past weeks, Derek, when I've felt, well, that it just wasn't worth the effort. All the struggle to get up every morning and get through the day. Never knowing what's going to happen next. Waiting for the next raid, waiting for the bombs. Sometimes I almost wished Hitler would come himself, and bomb us out of it all, because there don't seem any other way. I can't see that it's ever going to stop, not until there's just nothing left anywhere.'

'Livvy—'

'And then you come and say the Queen's been talking to you, and told you to tell me she's sorry. About our baby! And says that there *will* be peace, and we *will* be able to have our family and bring them up without having bombs dropping on us. Well, somehow it seems possible again. After all, she ought to know. It's not as if they haven't been bombed themselves. They know what it's like.'

Privately, Derek wondered if they did. Buckingham Palace was rather different from the houses in April Grove and March Street, and the King and Queen did not spend their nights in an Anderson, or in a damp, overcrowded street shelter. But he did not say so. It had been a real pleasure – a 'tonic', as more than one man had called it – to see the King and Queen at such close quarters, and to talk to them just as if they were ordinary people. And if it made Olive feel so much better, then it was worth any amount of red tape and show.

Yvonne had come back from that first blitz on Portsmouth subdued and anxious, her careless gaiety dimmed. Her own home had not been bombed but many others had, and she had seen the waves of destruction and heard the screams of the injured. The memory haunted her dreams and she worked with a forlorn doggedness where before she had danced laughing through the days.

'I know we're doing good work out here,' she said to Betty, 'but it don't seem enough, somehow. When I saw what other people are having to put up with, what they're having to do, I ought to be doing more.'

'I know what you mean,' Betty said. 'It doesn't seem right to be safe and comfortable when all the people we know are having such an awful time.' She looked around the fields. Spring was coming rapidly and the trees were beginning to unfurl their buds. One corner of the orchard had been white with snowdrops all through February, and now primroses were beginning to star the banks, and violets throw down a velvet cloak. She had never seen so many birds, nor heard so much liquid song, and would have spent hours watching their busy nest-building. Soon the sheep would begin to lamb.

There was plenty of work on the farm, and it was hard. The girls were fitter now and could keep up with all that Jonas and Mr Spencer asked of them, but there was still a lot to learn and they fell into bed dog-tired at night.

'You don't have to be in danger to be helping the war,' Mr Spencer said. 'People have got to have food. We're feeding Servicemen as well as civilians. If it wasn't for us, the country would starve and Hitler would walk in and take the lot.'

'Anyway, they won't let us change now,' Erica observed. 'The Land Army's a service just like the WAAFs and the rest. We're in it and we've got to stay in it, unless we can give a good reason for getting out.' She thought for a moment and then added, 'Not that I want to get out, as it happens.'

The attic room had become home to the three girls. They pinned up snaps of their families and pictures cut from magazines. Erica had brought a bright quilt from home for her bed, and had given Betty and Yvonne cushions. When Dennis left the farm, Mrs Spencer offered her his bedroom, but she shook her head. 'I'd rather stay here.'

'She's nicer than I thought,' Yvonne said, and Betty heard her creep across the attic floor in the night to comfort Erica as she lay weeping for Geoffrey.

The three girls had drawn closer together, and Betty knew that the deaths of the three airmen had forged a bond between them. She knew that their work was valuable. But it was still hard to stand at the window and watch the glow of fires blazing in Portsmouth. It was hard to wait for the telephone call or telegram that would tell her everyone was safe.

I ought to be there, sharing it, she thought. It doesn't seem right to be safe, these days.

Graham was polishing his shoes and brushing his hair before going ashore for a jaunt round Portsmouth's pubs with Arnie and Knocker White. They'd done this quite a few times now and found plenty of girls who weren't actually tarts yet were more than willing to accommodate a lonely sailor for the price of a few drinks. And why not? 'It's my bit of war work,' one fluffy little blonde had giggled as she squirmed suggestively on Graham's knee. 'And I can tell you're a nice boy, just a bit lonely so far away from home.'

Graham had hidden a grin at that. Gosport wasn't exactly a million miles away! But he'd let her believe he came from London, and she'd listened wide-eyed to his tales of the blitz there, and made no objection afterwards when he took her into a dark shop doorway. Why did I want to waste so much time with Betty? he thought, swaggering back to the ship afterwards. Why bother about little prudes like that, when there's fun and games to be had for the cost of a port and lemon, and no worries afterwards?

All the same, he couldn't help wondering how Betty was, out on the farm. And he missed her bright chatter and the way she would look at him so adoringly with those big hazel eyes of hers. And he missed sitting in her mum's front room with her, holding hands and listening to *ITMA* or *Band Waggon*. It hadn't really mattered all that much that she would never give in to him, it was all part of the game. And now he'd never know what it was like with her.

With Betty, it would really have been making love. With these other girls, the fluffy blonde, the toffee-nosed brunette, the dozens of others who haunted the pubs ready to go walking off arm-in-arm with any man who would buy them a drink, it was no more than sex.

Well, there was nothing to be done about that. Sex was pretty good after all, and who wanted a steady girlfriend worrying about whether she'd got 'caught'? Time enough for that when the war was over. For now, best to enjoy yourself, make the most of what was on offer and get yourself a few pin-ups to look at while you were at sea.

The siren went just as he had finished slicking Brylcreem on his hair.

Everyone in the mess groaned. Most of them had been looking forward to a few jars, and now their evening was gone, unless the raid proved to be a short one. They had to be ready, on stand-by, to go wherever help was needed in the city. They might have to man stirrup pumps or hoses, render First Aid, dig through piles of newly-fallen masonry to find people buried by exploding bombs. They might have to save their own ship, for the bombers would surely aim for the Dockyard, or go to the help of one of the others tied up at jetties or moored in the harbour. Any of these and more they might be called upon to do. And until they were called, all they could do was wait.

'*Bugger* it!' Graham said in disgust. 'Bugger, bugger, *bugger* it!'

For Derek, Bob Shaw and George Glaister, the raid signalled action.

All three had been preparing for an evening of relaxation. Unless there was a raid, the men of 698 Unit were allowed to go home for a few hours at weekends and Derek had been looking forward to eating supper with Olive while her parents went down April Grove to spend the evening with Jess and Frank. Bob had no wife or girlfriend to occupy his evening, but had been cheerfully anticipating an hour or two in a chair by the fire, and the ministrations of his mother and sisters. And even George Glaister had been hoping for a few home comforts at number 15.

But for 698 Unit, the orders were constant. If a raid was expected, all leave was cancelled and they must stand ready to go out into the city. From that point, there was a difference between the part they must play and that demanded of the Navy. The sailors could give real help. The Army's duty was to stand guard.

'Guard against *looters*!' Derek had exploded when he first heard the command. 'Pompey folk don't loot!'

'They're not getting the chance,' the sergeant-major said. 'We'll be at every doorway, armed and with fixed bayonets. It's no good looking at me. I didn't issue the order.'

'Well, who did?' Derek wasn't the only one disgusted. George Glaister was equally annoyed and less frightened of saying so to his sergeant-major than he would have been to his wife. 'We want to be out there *doin*' summat. We're soldiers, aren't we? Fighters. Well, that's what we oughter be doin', tannin' the Huns' backsides for 'em. Standing guard! *Looting*. It's a bloody shame.'

But there was nothing to be done about it. Orders had come from somewhere on high, and such orders must be obeyed. The Unit would be sent out as soon as it was known what damage had been done and where. And yes, they could give a hand to people who'd been injured and dig out any who were buried, and do whatever else they thought necessary. But their prime function was to prevent looting, and they'd better remember it.

The first stick of bombs landed and in the barracks of 698 Unit, as in every home in Portsmouth, the lights went out.

'They'll kill us all,' a woman moaned as Gladys Shaw worked to free her from the rubble of her home. 'Oh, why don't they do it and get it over with? I can't stand this any longer, I just can't.' A bomb whistled as it fell in the next street, and everyone cringed as the explosion brought more debris raining about them. 'Oh no, no, no . . .'

'Here, love, shift out of the way and let me do it.' A navy-clad arm pushed Gladys as she struggled with a heavy beam. 'Little scrap like you can't move that.' The sailor thrust his shoulder under the wooden shaft and heaved. 'There she goes. *The-e-ere* she goes . . .' The beam groaned and creaked, then rose just enough for Gladys to pull the woman free. 'There you are. Takes a man to do a man's job, eh?'

Gladys was half grateful, half annoyed. She said sharply, 'I'd have got it up in a couple more minutes.'

'Daresay you might, but a couple of minutes saved means a couple of minutes to use somewhere else.' The sailor grinned cheekily and reached out to ruffle her hair. Gladys jerked her head away and he stared. 'Here, don't I know you?'

'I dunno. Do you?' she retorted waspishly, already turning away. It was no place to start making up to a girl, in the middle of an air-raid. Trust a sailor! But his next words brought her turning back, startled.

'Yes, I do. You're Gladys Shaw, old Bob's sister. You live down April Grove.'

Gladys stared at him. His cap was gone, his hair covered in dust and soot, but she could see traces of ginger. 'Graham Philpotts! What are you doing here?'

'Having tea with her Majesty, of course,' he retorted, grinning, and ducked as another bomb whistled and crashed a few streets away. 'See you later, Gladdie.'

Gladdie. Ginger Philpotts had been the only person ever to call her that, she thought as she slammed the door of her ambulance and set off once again. They had patched up the Royal Hospital and casualties were being taken there again, but she'd been told to take this lot to the Queen Alexandra. It was a longer drive, and all the way Gladys found auxiliary fire engines passing her on their way from other districts into the city. They must be bringing in thousands, she thought. What in God's name were they expecting?

They were expecting bombs. And bombs they got. All that night and the next, the incendiaries and high explosives rained from the sky. For Gladys, there seemed to be no respite from the ceaseless journeying to and fro through streets that rained with shrapnel and roared on every side with flame. She could feel the heat of it through the sides of the van, her eyes were seared by the blaze that billowed from the houses she passed. Sometimes every house in an entire street was on fire, sometimes a huge building created an inferno. She saw walls, great panels of flaming masonry with each window a scorching glimpse of the fury within, topple slowly outwards across a road she had just been about to enter, and jammed on her brakes violently, swerving to avoid the scattered gobbets of burning debris.

She set her bell ringing, with little hope that it would be heard in all the turmoil, desperate to get her load of injured bodies to the hospital, despairing at having to ignore the pleas of those who flagged her to stop.

There must have been times when she slept, times when she ate and drank and rested. But she could never recall them afterwards, or if she did saw them too as a blur, a vague memory of sandwiches and mugs of tea thrust into her hand, a faint recollection of an hour or so of oblivion on a camp bed, somewhere in a corner of a noisy room.

From time to time, she thought of Ginger Philpotts. She'd known him at school before his parents moved over to Gosport. He'd been in her brother Bob's class and had come round to their house a time or two. Now he was mucking in with the rest of them, giving a hand wherever it was needed, shifting rubbish, crawling into burning buildings, facing danger every minute. And so was Bob, working with the 698s. And so were Betty's brother Colin, somewhere at sea, and George Glaister, and Uncle Tom Cobleigh and all.

She wondered if she would see Graham again. He'd been working in Peterborough Road when she'd come across him, where a bomb had scored a direct hit on an Anderson. Eight bodies there'd been in there, all dead when they'd got the rubble off them. Eight dead, when they'd thought themselves safe. It just showed . . . And where was Graham now, with his ginger hair and his cheeky grin? You couldn't keep track of anyone in this mess.

Graham had been one of the rescuers who had found the Anderson with the family killed inside it. He'd gone at the rubble like a madman, scraping away at torn and jagged corrugated iron until his hands had bled and an ARP man had dragged him off. 'You won't help nobody by getting yourself hurt as well, son.'

Graham knew he was right, but the sight of those poor broken bodies huddled together in the damp little dugout had touched him on the raw. A whole family wiped out, just like that. And what sort of a shelter had they had? A pathetic little hole in the ground. What had the Government been thinking of, to get them all into a mess like this?

The past few weeks had shaken Graham more than he had realised. From being a bit of a game, the war had turned into something serious. At first, he'd felt the same kind of exalted patriotism that many young men had felt as they queued outside the recruitment offices to volunteer. When he'd swaggered down the street in his uniform and gone straight round to Betty's house to show it off, he'd felt important, a sort of hero even though he hadn't done anything yet. Perhaps that was why he'd got so annoyed when she wouldn't do what he wanted. She'd made him feel ordinary again, a chap who wasn't anything special after all, trying to take advantage of his girl.

He went back to the shelter, working more carefully now, but it wasn't long before he was needed to help where someone was buried alive. And then there was another, and another . . . It wasn't until dawn was breaking that he was able to walk slowly back to the ship, through the littered and still burning streets, and remember Gladys.

Gladdie Shaw. He'd known her when they were kids, of course, but he hadn't seen her for years now. She was a bit of all right, though – not very tall, and even though her hair had been covered up with some sort of hat or scarf, he'd been able to see that it was yellow. He liked small girls. They made him feel protective. And he liked yellow hair too.

Mind, Gladdie Shaw didn't seem to need much protecting. She looked as if she knew just what she was doing, helping to get people into the old van she was driving as an ambulance. And she'd been pretty cool with that too, backing it away and then tearing off up the road like a bat out of hell . . . She was quite a girl, was Gladdie Shaw.

I wouldn't mind seeing her again, he thought as he reached the ship and reported aboard before going below to crash out on his bunk. Maybe I'll go up Copnor one day and see how she got on last night . . .

Micky Baxter and his gang had given up searching ruined houses for whatever broken oddments might have been left behind, and looked for bombs instead. Their first one was kept carefully in the basement den. None of them was quite sure whether it was a dud or not and they were half scared, half thrilled to possess it.

They had almost managed to retrieve another from a crater a few streets away, but a policeman caught them just as they were scrambling down the rubble and jerked them roughly back to the road. He banged Micky's and Jimmy's heads together.

'You stupid little twerps! D'you want to get killed? Dragging a little 'un into it, as well.' He looked at Cyril's angelic face. 'You shouldn't be running around with these boys, sonny. Get off home to your mum.'

'Mum's at work.' Cyril watched as a truck arrived and several soldiers jumped out. 'Are they going to explode it?'

'Never you mind about that. You get off home like I said, and you two go with him, see he gets there all right.' The policeman released Micky and Jimmy and gave them a parting cuff. 'And don't get playing round bomb craters any more, it ain't safe.'

The three boys scuttled down an alleyway and then doubled back, flattening themselves against the wall to peer round the corner. The crater had already been roped off and the soldiers were climbing carefully into it. One or two stayed on the rim, peering down. The policeman had retreated to another corner.

'They're going to blow it up,' Cyril breathed. 'We'll be able to get bits for souvenirs.'

'I'd rather have a bomb.' Micky was disgruntled. Jimmy was beginning to challenge his position. Possessing a bomb gave a boy automatic rights and Micky still hadn't found one of his own. If he didn't look out, Jimmy would be trying to take over.

The soldiers scrambled out of the crater. They were moving more easily now and one of them was carrying the bomb. The policeman came out of his shelter and the boys stared in disgust.

'They didn't even blow it up.'

'It musta bin a dud.'

'They defused it, that's what they did.'

They wandered away, feeling let down.

I've got to get a bomb, Micky thought. I've got to.

Betty worked her way slowly down the field, setting the seed potatoes in their rows.

The days on the farm seemed long and hard now that Dennis was away. He had been accepted immediately for bomb disposal work in the Pioneer Corps and had been shifted somewhere up in the Midlands for training. He wrote every other day, and Betty spent hours writing back, but the farm was lonely without him and she lay awake night after night, longing for his touch, for the feel of his arms about her, for the warmth of his body.

She knew that she was not, as she had been with Graham, in love with love. Engagement rings and outward symbols had never figured in their conversation. And Dennis had made no demands, had never assumed that he had rights over her in any way. She was free – free to love him as she wished, free to give her body or to withhold it.

But that freedom brought its own price, and the price she must pay to love Dennis was to give him his own freedom, the freedom to walk into danger, knowing that he might not walk away.

Night after night, Betty lay awake listening to the bombers passing overhead. Nobody was really safe. In the darkness, you could see fires burning, often over the hill in Portsmouth or Gosport, occasionally in another direction.

'We're giving as good as we get,' Mr Spencer said, reading the newspaper reports of RAF attacks on German cities. 'Our lads are flattening them, just like they're trying to flatten us.'

'Good job too,' Erica said. 'The sooner we wipe every German off the face of the earth, the sooner we can get back to normal.' Her lips quivered.

'And how many more of our boys are getting killed while we do it?' Betty demanded. 'I'm sorry, Erica, but what's the point of boys like Geoff and Sandy being killed? They're gone for ever—'

'You don't have to tell me that!'

'Betty, don't,' Mrs Spencer interposed.

'Why not? She's not the only person who's lost someone. We're all going to lose if this goes on.' Betty stared at them. 'You've got two boys out in Libya. I've got a brother in the Navy. And Dennis, you know what he's doing. You can't call him a coward now. But what good is it going to do if they all get killed? What sort of "normal" is there going to be when it's all over?'

'It's not for us to think about. We've just got to do our bit.'

'And let other people drag us into an even worse mess? Look, it's right what Dennis says. We're just killing by numbers. Why can't they sit down and *talk* about it? Or kill the ones who're causing all the trouble? Hitler and Goering and all them.'

'It's not as simple as that,' Jack Spencer said. 'There are more and more countries joining in all the time. The whole world's in a muddle.'

Betty sighed. It was like a tangle of differently-coloured wools that must be sorted out before they could be made into something useful. And perhaps the tangle was so bad that some parts would just have to be cut out . . . But that would spoil the rest, leaving some colours too short to be used at all . . .

It had to be left to the people at the top, even if they were the ones that had got the world into it in the first place. And meanwhile, men were fighting each other on land, sea and air and Dennis was training for one of the most dangerous jobs of all, so dangerous that even the training could kill him.

Erica touched her arm and Betty turned. Her blue eyes were serious.

'I'm sorry, Bet. I know I'm not the only one. We're all worried half out of our minds. And I'm sorry for the things I said about Dennis, too. I never did think he was a traitor, not really.' She smiled waveringly. 'Don't let's fall out. We've all got to pull together now, whatever we really think.'

25

'I'm thankful our Betty's out in the country, anyway,' Annie Chapman said. 'At least I know she's safe.'

Soon after the first blitz she had volunteered to work in an Emergency Centre for those who had been bombed out. Like Elsie Philpotts, she worked day and night, serving out cocoa and hot soup to those who no longer had a home.

'There's hardly space for them all in those schoolrooms, but we have to cram them in somehow. And at least there's a good store of clothes in Pompey now, since the Lady Mayoress set up that collection. But what most of 'em wants first off is just a shoulder to cry on. And a bit of a joke to cheer 'em up.'

She sat back in Frank's armchair and sighed. She had called in for a cup of tea, worn out after a morning at the Centre, cleaning floors on which children had been sick and washing sheets from beds that had been wet or soiled. Yet, exhausted as she was, her own house was kept as spotless as always, for Annie refused to let her standards slip 'just because of Hitler'.

Jess could not help in Emergency Centres or canteens because of Maureen. But she had her own war work, making sailors' square rig collars and stitching on the rows of tapes whenever she had time to spare from her housework.

'It's just as well I've got this to do,' she observed. 'There's precious little dressmaking to be done these days, what with hardly any materials in the shops. And they're talking about putting clothes on ration too. I reckon we're going to have worn out every frock in the England by the time this lot's finished. I'm already cutting down my old jacket to make a winter coat for Rose, and some of Rose's things are going to have to do for the baby. I don't know how women who can't sew are going to manage.'

Annie went back to get Ted's supper ready. She had been gone only ten minutes when a knock brought Jess to the front door. Mike Simmons was there, looking grey and tired. He had come home a few days ago, not that there was a home for him to come to, and had called over to see his two little girls, who were staying with Jess.

Jess brought him into the back room and sat him down in her own armchair. She could sense the shock he'd had in seeing the ruins of his house. She still felt it herself, every time she went up October Street and saw the gap, like the hole left by a rotten tooth.

'I'm ever so sorry, Mr Simmons,' she said. 'It's a terrible thing to have happened. But she couldn't have known anything about it, you know.'

He shook his head. 'I know. Everyone's told me how quick it was. But – she *shouldn't* have died, Mrs Budd. She was too young. And the baby, little Tom, I only saw him the once, at Christmas.' His face twisted and the tears ran down his cheeks. 'I'm sorry,' he mumbled, wiping them uselessly with his hands. 'Letting myself blubber like a kid. I don't seem able to stop, somehow.'

'Don't try. If you can't cry when you lose your wife and baby, when can you? It'll do you good.' She gave him one of Frank's handkerchiefs. 'Stay there and I'll make you a cup of tea.'

He did as he was told. Jess could see he was just about at the end of his tether, all his strength gone, like a little boy again. Well, perhaps the best thing was to treat him like one, be a mum to him for a little while, give him something hot and sweet to drink and let him have his cry out. He'd have enough to face from now on, what with two little girls to think about, and being away at sea most of the time. It was a miracle he'd been able to get home now.

'What am I going to do?' he asked later, when he'd drunk two cups of tea liberally laced with Jess's sugar ration. 'I'm really grateful to you for looking after the girls, but I'll have to do something about them. I suppose they'll have to go out to the country somewhere, but the ship's only in for a day, I'm not going to have time—'

He was sounding desperate again and Jess spoke quickly.

'You needn't worry about the girls, Mr Simmons. I know somewhere they can go, that's if you'd like them to. My boys are out in the country, at Bridge End. It's a nice village and they've been there nearly eighteen months.' She bit her lip, thinking how much she had missed of their boyhoods. 'They're really enjoying themselves,' she went on determinedly, 'and the place they're staying at has got room for some more children. Your Stella and Muriel could stop with them.'

'With your boys?'

'That's right. Tim and Keith, they're eleven and nine. Just a bit older than your two, so they'd be able to look after them a bit. They're good boys,' she added, thinking that he might be doubtful about his daughters staying in the same house with the two young Budds. 'I mean, they get into a bit of mischief now and then but they wouldn't do anything, well, anything you wouldn't like.'

'I reckon any kid of yours'd be a good friend to my girls,' he said. 'But what sort of place is it? A farm? A big house? I don't know as they'd like anywhere too posh.'

Jess smiled. 'I suppose you could call it posh, but not the way you mean. At least, I don't think so. It's a vicarage.'

'A *vicarage*?'

Jess laughed. 'That's right. There's just the vicar there, he's quite old, and a housekeeper. She looks after the boys mostly, sees to their meals and their clothes and that. But Mr Beckett takes quite an interest. He's never had any children of his own, you see, and I think he quite enjoys having youngsters about.'

Mike looked worried. 'But, well, we've never been much of a family for church. I don't know if the girls—'

'Oh, that doesn't matter,' Jess said cheerfully. 'He likes the boys to go to the morning service on a Sunday, but he always lets them out before the sermon. And then Mrs Mudge cooks them a proper Sunday dinner. They have their supper with him every night, and their breakfast in the mornings.' She laughed again. 'The last time I saw them, Tim told me they sold him their sugar!'

'Sold him their sugar?'

'That's right. He's got a sweet tooth, you see, and they don't drink much tea or anything like that, they've always liked plain water best, and a cup of cocoa at bedtime, so they sell him their sugar ration at a halfpenny a spoonful. Mind, I think myself he does it just out of kindness, but it did my heart good to see them measuring it out and adding it all up. It was a sort of *family* thing, if you can understand what I mean.'

Mike found that he could. He listened while Jess told him more about Bridge End and its vicar. Mr Beckett was in his sixties and had always lived alone, it seemed. He was as thin as a spider, in spite of all the sugar, and went everywhere on an old sit-up-and-beg bicycle. He was forgetful and more than a little eccentric, but he was kind and although it was very different at the vicarage from the Corners' house, Tim and Keith were happy with him.

'I was a bit worried when the boys first went there,' Jess confessed. 'I thought they'd hate it. I thought he'd be strict and make them read the Bible all the time – not that there's any harm in that, I read the Bible myself when I'm in church, but boys wouldn't like it. But he seems more like a boy himself. Second childhood, Frank calls it.'

'And you think he'd have room for the girls? You think he'd take them?'

'I know he would. The last time I was there Mrs Mudge said they would probably have to take more children anyway – people are sending them away again, after the blitz. If I were you, I'd take them out there straightaway.' She hesitated, then said diffidently. 'As a matter of fact, they're almost expecting you. I wrote last week and said you might be looking for somewhere for the girls.'

She left Mike to think about it for a few minutes while she went out to the coalshed to fill up the scuttle. Coal was scarce again and the pile she'd got in during the summer had almost gone. She scraped about with her shovel and lifted out something that wasn't coal at all.

Puzzled, Jess carried it out to daylight. It was black with coal dust and a bit damaged, but she brushed it off and saw that it was a donkey, made of wickerwork. She stared at it.

Mike came out through the back door.

'Let me get the coal in for you. And I was thinking, I'd like the girls—' He stopped, his eyes on the wickerwork donkey. 'Where did that come from?'

'I don't know. I've just found it in the coal. I've never seen it before in my life.'

Mike Simmons reached out and touched the dirty, broken ornament.

His fingers traced it gently. They began to shake and Jess looked at him in surprise. His eyes were full of tears.

'Mr Simmons, Mike, what's the matter? What is it?'

'We had a donkey just like this,' he said, his voice cracking. 'I brought it home from Gib one time. Kathy kept it in the front room, on the mantelpiece. It got lost in the bombing.'

Jess looked at it again. 'Our Annie's got one too. I thought for a minute it might be hers, but I know she's still got it. I don't know where this one came from.'

'I could swear it's the one I gave Kathy,' Mike said. 'One of its feet was a bit broken, just like this one. But I know it can't be, not really. How could it have got into your coalshed?'

He took the donkey and held it, his hands trembling. Jess saw his shoulders begin to shake and knew that he was on the verge of breaking down again. She took his arm and led him back indoors.

'Sit down there,' she said gently, and he sank back into the chair with the donkey on his knee. Jess sat with him, listening to the voices of the children outside, thinking of Kathy and the baby Thomas, thinking of her own children at Bridge End and of all the friends and neighbours who were facing pain as Mike was facing it now, a pain that ate into their hearts and would never go away.

Would anyone ever be able to forget the things that were happening in this terrible war?

Gladys had begun, almost without knowing why, to see more of Graham Philpotts. She hardly looked upon him as a boyfriend – she was still writing to Colin Chapman, still hankering after something more than friendship there, and in any case Graham was a year or two younger than she was, and had always been her brother Bob's mate. But she liked his cheery, freckled face, and the way he always had a joke on his lips, and it was nice to have a boy to go about with a bit, when there was time, which wasn't often these days.

All the same, she probably wouldn't have given him much more thought if he hadn't arrived on the doorstep one Sunday afternoon. Peggy had answered the door, surprised to see him there, but had let him in without comment thinking he had called to see Bob. But although the two lads had looked pleased enough to see each other and had chatted for a few minutes, it was only when Gladys had come downstairs that she'd seen his face light up and realised why he had really come.

'Hullo, Gladdie,' Graham said, rather self-consciously. 'I just thought I'd look in to see how you got on in the raid the other night.'

Gladys shrugged. She was blushing to the roots of her hair, Peggy noticed with some surprise, and wasn't that lipstick on her mouth? Had she heard Graham's voice from upstairs and hastily done herself up a bit before coming down?

'I was all right. Bit tired, that's all. And I wish they'd give me a better van.'

'It looked a bit past it,' Graham agreed. 'Still, you drove it pretty well. I didn't know you could drive, Gladdie.'

'No reason why you should, is there?' She sounded a bit sharp – didn't know quite how to take it. Obviously she hadn't expected him to come. Still, Peggy thought, there was no harm in it. Why not encourage them a bit, let 'em have a bit of fun? Gladys hadn't had a boyfriend for a while now, not since she'd started carrying a torch for young Colin Chapman. It'd do her good to have a boy who wasn't always away at sea.

'Why don't you two go in the front room and have a talk?' she suggested. 'I lit the fire in there after dinner, seeing as it's a Sunday. And then you can stop and have a bit of tea with us, Graham, if you'd like to.'

Gladys sat down on the settee and patted the cushion beside her. 'Well, don't just stand there, Graham, you make the place look untidy. Tell us what's been happening.'

Graham sat down awkwardly. Now that he was here, he wasn't sure what to do. He hadn't sat in a girl's front room since the night he'd walked out on Betty. He'd almost forgotten what you did with a girl who wasn't a tart.

'Not much,' he said. 'Been working on bombed houses, mostly. You wouldn't think I'd joined the Navy, more like a flipping builder's yard.'

'That's what our Bob says. He's down in Wiltshire or Dorset or somewhere, putting up huts for the RAF. Why can't the RAF build their own huts?'

Graham shook his head. 'I dunno. Seems a daft way to run a war to me. I don't reckon any of them know what they're doing.' He glanced sideways at her. 'You – you don't mind me coming to see you like this, do you, Gladdie?'

'Mind? Why should I mind? You were lucky to catch me in, that's all.'

'I suppose you get plenty of boyfriends,' he said wistfully.

'As many as I want, I s'pose,' she answered. 'Don't have much time for that sort of thing these days, what with the ambulance and First Aid classes and all that. Why d'you want to know?'

Graham shrugged. 'No reason, really. Well—' he hesitated, then blurted out, 'I just wondered if you might go to the pictures with me one night. I mean, ever since me and Betty broke up, I've been a bit, well, you know. I won't try anything on,' he added anxiously. 'I know you're a decent girl. I just thought – well, if you hadn't got anyone to go with . . .'

He stopped, feeling the blush run up his neck and flood his cheeks. He had never felt so awkward with Betty. He'd always been sure of himself with her, taking every opportunity to kiss her or let his hands rove over her body. Maybe that was why he was in such a state now, because in the end she'd turned him down. Since then, he'd not been with any girl who wasn't a whore, and whores never turned you down.

But whores didn't go to the pictures with you either and sit holding hands, and when you left them they forgot you. They didn't write to you and wait for you and talk about getting married. They didn't care.

'It doesn't matter,' he said, starting to get up. 'Perhaps I shouldn't have come round here. I'd better go. Tell your mum thanks but—'

'Here, hold on,' Gladys said. She grasped his sleeve and pulled him down beside her again. 'You asked me a question. Don't you want to know my answer?' She looked into his flushed, freckled face and smiled. 'I'll come to the pictures with you, Ginger Philpotts,' she said. 'And you can forget all that malarkey about not trying anything on. I might be a decent girl, but I'm not made of stone!'

Graham turned to look at her in surprise, and she laughed, leaned towards him and kissed him full on the mouth.

'There,' she said. 'Thanks for asking me. No—' as he moved to slide his arms around her – 'that's all for now. It's teatime.'

She felt in his pocket and found a handkerchief. She wiped his lips with it and handed it back to him. It was red with lipstick.

'There,' she said. 'Sleep with it under your pillow tonight, Ginger. Shall I tell you what I think?'

He nodded, still dazed, uncertain but elated.

'This war's going to get worse,' Gladys said, her voice suddenly serious. 'You've seen the raids just like I have. People getting buried, blown up, killed. It could be us next time. We've got to take every chance we can of having a bit of fun. That's what I think.'

Derek and Olive Harker had not been able to be together much more after the momentous day when the King and Queen had come to Portsmouth. Once again the Unit had been moved, this time to Warminster where they were to build hutted camps. It seemed that their brief period of action in France was to be their only journey abroad. Olive was deeply thankful, but for Derek and Bob Shaw it was frustrating. They were soldiers. They ought to be fighting.

Even George Glaister, who was glad enough not to have to go and fight, was irked by the mundane jobs he had to do. He had enough trouble with Ethel as it was, without having to confess that his Army career was turning out to be not much different from being a plumber's mate. He'd been looking forward to writing home letters that spoke of gunfire and trenches and 'going over the top', without stopping to think that these were images he had gleaned from stories about the Great War of 1914–18, and that those conditions were far more cruel and savage than any he was likely to endure on the plains of Wiltshire.

'It's just a rest cure, that's all that is,' Ethel said scornfully. 'Going for a soldier! They saw you coming, knew you wouldn't be any good with a gun in your hands, so they gave you a bloody monkey-wrench instead. Just the right tool for you, and all.'

'Well, at least it gets me out of your way,' George retorted. 'The way your face drops every time I come home, you'd obviously rather I never came at all. I suppose you'd be happy if I was sent overseas and got blown up.'

'Don't be stupid! I don't want to be a widow, do I?' Ethel tossed her head. 'If you can't talk better sense than that, you'd be better off not talking at all.'

She stalked out to the greenhouse George had built by roofing in the yard outside the kitchen. Through the door, she could see Frank Budd working in his garden. She watched as Jess came down to say something to him and saw Frank put his hand on her shoulder.

What he saw in that mouse of a woman, Ethel had no idea. Irritated and jealous, she turned and went back into the house to harangue George again.

'I've found one! I've found a bomb!'

The boys were in the cellar, eating cold sausages which Micky had filched from his grandmother's larder. The dimness was lit by a paraffin lamp they had stolen from an air-raid shelter. It stood on the rickety table, close to Jimmy's bomb. Around them, on the floor, was scattered the booty they had gleaned from their forays into other bombed houses, or from their own swift raids when the siren had sounded.

Micky looked up from his sausage. He and Jimmy had arrived first and when Cyril tumbled in ten minutes later, his normally pale face was flushed with excitement.

'Where? Where is it? You sure it's a bomb? I bet it's not.'

'It is.' Cyril stopped his capering and stared with shining eyes at Micky. He had never dreamed that he would be the lucky one. The other two boys were older than he, and Micky was the leader, it had been taken for granted that the next bomb would be his. 'It's a whopper. It's *huge*.'

'Where is it?' Jimmy was playing with an old mouth organ. It had been rusty and full of dust when he found it, but he'd cleaned it out and oiled it and now he could play tunes on it. He was practising *Run, Rabbit, Run*.

'Down Powerscourt Road. Where the first bombs fell last July.'

'Last *July*! Go on, there can't be no more bombs there, they cleared all them houses out.'

'There are,' Cyril said stubbornly. 'I found one. It's down in a cellar, like this one, only it's all full of dirt and stuff. I went down to see if there was anything there and I saw it sticking out. It just wants digging out, that's all. I'm going to take my mum's coal-shovel down.'

'Well, it can't be a time bomb,' Micky said. 'It'd have gone off by now. It must be a dud.'

'It's a good bomb, anyway. It's bigger'n Jimmy's.'

'How much bigger?' Jimmy demanded jealously.

'Twice as big. Three times as big.'

Micky scowled. The other two were arguing now over the sizes of their bombs and the likelihood of their exploding. He felt his leadership slipping away and spoke loudly.

'We'll go down and look at it. We're not digging it out this morning.'

'Why not?' There was a belligerence in Cyril's voice that had never been there before. His large brown eyes met Micky's challengingly. He grabbed a sausage and stuffed it into his mouth.

'Because we'd be seen, stupid. There's people all over the place, they'd never let us carry a bomb through the streets in broad daylight. It'll have to be at night.'

'I'm not allowed out at night,' Cyril objected through a mouthful of sausage.

'You'll have to get out. Or it won't be your bomb.'

'It *is* my bomb. I found it.'

'Finding ain't everything,' Micky said grandly. 'It's gettin' it out and gettin' it back to the den that counts.'

'It's my bomb. You don't know where it is.'

'We can find it. You told us.'

'You don't know exactly. You'll never find it without me. And I won't tell you unless you say it's my bomb. I can dig it out on my own. Or I'll keep it there and have that for my den.'

The three boys stared at each other. Cyril stopped chewing. Jimmy laid down his mouth organ. Micky glowered.

'This is my gang. If you go off, Jimmy'll stay with me. You can't have a den without a gang. You won't be able to come back here. An' if we catch you, we'll torture you.' He put on his most fearsome expression, and Cyril flinched. 'We don't even know for sure it *is* a bomb. I bet it's not really. Anyway, it's only a tiddler, I bet.'

'All right, we'll go and look at it now.' Cyril got up and made for the steps, then turned back and snatched up another sausage. 'You'll see.'

They ran through the streets. Some were untouched by the raids, others ruined. Boarded up windows had graffiti chalked on them, or the new addresses of their occupants. One had a sign that read 'We still live here'. But mostly, the only occupants were a few scrawny cats or stray dogs with their ribs showing.

Cyril led them along the back alleys and through a broken fence into a scruffy garden. There had once been a lawn and flowerbeds, but all were overgrown now with weeds and scrub grass. The house had been bombed. The roof was torn away and every window had been smashed.

Under the back window there was a hole. Cyril ducked into it and scrambled down. He flashed the torch he had stolen around the walls.

'Coo,' Jimmy breathed, gazing at the damp walls and slimy floor. 'It's smashing.'

'Go on,' Micky said disparagingly, 'there's loads of places like this. It ain't nothing special.'

'They don't all have bombs, though.' Cyril shone his torch into a corner. 'See?'

The bomb had fallen nose-down, slicing a path for itself through the rubble wall, and come to rest a foot or so above the basement floor. It was about two feet long. Its sides were half buried and streaked with rust.

'It *is* a bomb,' Jimmy whispered in awe.

'It's a beauty, isn't it,' Cyril said proudly. He reached out a finger and touched it tentatively, then stroked it as gently as if it were a kitten. Jimmy backed away slightly, his eyes goggling.

'It looks live to me.'

'Don't be daft,' Micky said loudly. 'How can a bomb *look* live? Anyway, it can't be, it'd have gone off by now. It musta bin there months.'

'Why don't we tell the warden?' Jimmy suggested. 'They're giving rewards for bombs. The Mayor said so at that party in the Guildhall.'

'That was for putting out incendiaries, and they only give it to the first one. Catch them paying out for every one! Anyway, if we told a warden he'd just pretend he'd found it hisself. This is our bomb.'

'My bomb,' Cyril corrected him.

'It's ours if we dig it out and take it back to the den. It's ours if you want to stay in our gang.' But it was time to give Cyril a little praise. 'It's a smasher. You done well.'

Cyril looked pleased. 'Shall we dig it out then?'

'Yeah, but not now. We'll come back tonight. We'll bring the paraffin lamp and torches and spades or shovels. We'd better bring some grub as well.' He gazed at the bomb, wishing again that he had been the one to find it. 'We'd better be careful in case it is still live.'

They turned to go, creeping warily out of the hole in case anyone saw them. But there was no one about in the trampled gardens or the smelly alleyway and they ran swiftly home through the streets.

'Tonight,' Micky said as they parted. 'We'll go and get it out tonight.'

26

That night, the exhausted city suffered its third heavy blitz.

Thrusting away his fears, Ted Chapman went straight up to the little turret from which his son Colin had fired arrows at the neighbours' cats, and which was now so good a lookout post, while Annie hurried up the road to the school. Frank Budd saw his wife and daughters into the shelter and then climbed over the fence on to the allotment with his stirrup pump. Tommy Vickers started on his rounds, looking into each Anderson shelter in the three streets to make sure that everyone was present, or accounted for. And Peggy, Gladys and Diane Shaw ran to join Annie Chapman.

'Looks like another bad 'un,' Annie commented as they arrived panting at the school gates. Already bombs were whistling down and could be heard exploding in different parts of the city. 'I can tell you, I'm sick of this. If I had Hitler here I'd knock his block off.'

'Not till after I'd finished with him, you wouldn't.' Peggy marched in to register with the superintendent. 'You get that urn on the go, Annie – we'll be glad of summat hot later on. It's going to be a long night.'

Gladys had been hoping to see Graham that evening. She signed her name in the book and went out to her ambulance. It was looking battle-scarred and weary, almost leaning against the school wall, and seemed to heave itself to its feet with a sigh as she started to swing the crank handle. It's as tired as I am, she thought, and no wonder. We've been on duty together through half a dozen raids in the past fortnight. It's had punctures by the score from broken glass and nails and God knows what lying about in the road, it's had its headlamps smashed, not that you can see much with most of the glass blacked out, it's lost its horn that nobody can hear for the noise of bombs and ack-ack, and I'm tired of having to scrub it clean of blood every morning. And Mum's just as exhausted, riding in the back with the casualties night after bloody night when she ought to be sitting safe at home by the fire, listening to Arthur Askey and Tommy Handley, or down the Hippodrome laughing at Elsie and Doris Waters.

But there wasn't a Hippodrome any more. And at this rate there wouldn't be much of a Portsmouth. And as long as Hitler kept sending his planes over, so they'd have to turn out to fight him with whatever weapons they had. And if a battered old van, done up as an ambulance, was her way of fighting, she'd bloody well *fight*. So put that in your pipe and smoke it, Adolf!

Back and forth she drove, from one raging fire to another, from the town railway station and the main post office, both damaged by the blast which destroyed the big Maddens Hotel, to the inferno of McIlroys, yet another of Portsmouth's big department stores. She'd been shopping there herself only a few hours ago . . . All along the way there were bombs falling all about her, debris flying from their blasts, shrapnel raining from the sky. The pitted sides of the van were dented further by red-hot metal, sharp and jagged as a saw, and half a brick came through her windscreen like a cannonball, landing on the seat only inches from her thigh. Swearing, she snatched up the cushion Peggy sat on when she rode in the front, and thrust it through the shattered glass, brushing the fragments impatiently away. The night air blew cold on her face and she shrugged angrily when a warden waved at her to stop. She could still see to drive, couldn't she?

Anger drove her that night. She had been angry from the beginning, when she was torn away from the fireside to go out yet again. She had been angry to see the flares, as red as the fury which consumed her. She'd even been angry to see her poor little van, looking so woebegone and weary, and the destruction of its windscreen was the last straw. From now on, her feelings about the war and Hitler had condensed into one intense spot of white-hot fury. He was hurting her van! Well, *she* would show him.

'Gladys,' her mother remonstrated. 'Let up a bit, girl. You're like a mad thing. Take a coupla minutes off for a cupper tea.'

'Tea? I haven't got time for tea.' Gladys was fidgeting, impatient to be off again. 'There's bombs coming down everywhere. People are getting hurt. We've got to be out there, helping—'

'It won't be no help if you pass out yourself. You've got to get something hot inside you. You're out on your feet.'

'I'm not. I'm all right.' She grabbed the mug Peggy was holding out and gulped down its contents, hardly knowing whether it was tea, cocoa or cabbage-water, and well beyond caring. 'There, I've drunk it, now can we go?'

Peggy sighed and climbed back into the van. 'Look, I want to help as much as you do—'

'Right, let's go then.' They were off once more, tearing through the chaotic streets. It was worse than ever, she thought. It wasn't just tonight's damage, it was all the houses that had been knocked down in the past weeks, through raid after raid, all the holes in the road, not yet patched up, all the streets you couldn't go down, all the blackened and burned-out buildings. Even with the Navy and the Army helping too, there hadn't been time to fence them all off, to make them safe. Something ought to be done, but there wasn't time, there weren't the people to do it, not when other jobs had to be done too, not when the city was struggling simply to keep going.

A bitter despair rose inside her. When would there *ever* be time? Did Hitler know what he was doing, was he keeping up this relentless barrage deliberately so that they would be worn down by the hopelessness of it all, by the impossibility of simply staying awake? She'd seen her father going off to work in the morning, scarcely able to keep his eyes open, and her uncle

Frank stumbling down the street half-dead after a hard day's labouring in the Yard. How long could they keep going? How long could it last?

I *will* keep going, she swore to herself as she battled through the streets on the way back from yet another trip to the hospital. I *won't* let him beat me.

She braked sharply as a bomb screamed down from the sky and scored a direct hit on a house less than a hundred yards away. She ducked her head and, through the gap in her windscreen, felt the hot, choking blast. The ambulance shuddered as the tremor raced outwards through the earth like ripples on a pond, and Gladys clung to the steering-wheel.

'My God,' Peggy called out from behind her, 'that was a big un.'

'It's hit a house just down the road.' Miraculously, the engine was still running. Gladys slammed it into gear and moved forwards. The air was still full of dust but already people were running about near the site of the explosion, and a fire engine had appeared from nowhere. 'There'll be injuries. We'll have to go and see.'

'But we're supposed to be going back to the post—'

'We can't. You know we can't.' She drove as near to the bombed house as she could get and dragged the van to a halt. The air was filled with thick, choking dust, but there didn't appear to be any smoke yet. As soon as the van stopped, she was out, thrusting her way through the little crowd that was already gathering.

'I'm a First Aid worker. Are there people inside?'

One of the women turned to her. She was enormously fat and wrapped in an old coat. Her grey hair was scraped back from her big, coarse face and her eyes were like buttons. But there was real anxiety in her gravelly voice.

'It's Marge Jennings' house.' She turned to another woman who had just run across the pavement. 'Was she inside?'

'Well, she never goes down the shelter, not since her mum was killed in one. She always gets under the stairs, reckons it's safer.'

The fat woman looked at Gladys. There was a small cluster of people around them now, mostly women with one or two old men hobbling on sticks.

'Well, we'd better look for 'er then, 'adn't we? 'I ain't no good standin' 'ere talkin' about it.' She glanced around at the neighbours. 'An' it's not much use you lot standin' 'ere, makin' a target for the next one. Get back in yer own shelters.' She looked impatiently up and down the street. 'Where's old Bertie Hicks, he's supposed to be warden round 'ere, ain't 'e? Just like coppers, never around when you want 'em, but you just let a glimmer of light get out round the blackout and 'e's on the spot right away . . .' Her button eyes came back to Gladys. 'Well, get on with it, poor old Marge could be dyin' in there for all you know.'

Gladys was already jamming on her tin helmet and reaching for her First Aid kit. With Peggy beside her, she made for the front door. There was no problem in getting into the house – the door had been blown off its hinges. Every window was blown out, and when they shone their torches inside they could see that the ceilings had collapsed, turning each of the downstairs rooms into a pile of rubble.

'Think she's got a chance?' Peggy muttered.

'I don't know. I'll see if I can get through. If she's under the stairs, she might be all right.' Gladys peered through the darkness. It was never easy to know exactly where the stairs were in a house. Even in two-up, two-down terraces, there were half a dozen different designs. Sometimes the stairs went straight up from the front door, sometimes they led from the scullery, right at the back of the house, sometimes from one of the rooms. And when a bomb had hit the house and virtually demolished it, it was almost impossible to tell. She stared at the piles of debris. Could anyone have survived a hit like that?

'Mrs Jennings?' she called. 'Marge? Are you there?'

There was no answer. Her heart sank. It didn't look as if she'd survived. Or maybe she'd gone to the shelter after all.

'She might be unconscious,' Peggy said. 'She might be buried.'

'I know. I'll have to go in, Mum.'

Peggy looked at her. 'Glad, you've been working all night. You're just about done in. Why don't you let the warden or someone do it?'

'The warden's not here, is he. Or anyone else. Only a few women and a couple of old men. And the only one who seems to have any sense is that fat one, can you see her crawling through this lot? I'll have to do it.'

'But—' They heard the fat woman's voice again. Peggy went back and then returned to Gladys's side. 'Someone's looked in her shelter. She's not there. And – they told me summat else.' She looked miserably at Gladys. 'There's a baby. Six months old. Her hubby's in the Navy and she lives here by herself.'

'Well, that settles it. I'll have to go in. You stop here, Mum, and be ready if I shout.' Gladys settled her tin helmet more firmly on her head and stepped gingerly on a broken plank. It tilted. She waited a moment, then edged her way along it, supporting herself with her hands on the wall.

Somewhere else in the house she heard a rumble and then a crash. Something had given way. There was still no sound of people. Was Marge Jennings alive or dead? And what about her baby?

Something wet dropped on her cheek and she wiped it away. A water-pipe burst, probably. Or maybe a bottle broken, or a teapot smashed. Or the upstairs lav cracked . . .

I hate this, she thought, I just want to go away somewhere, somewhere nice and peaceful where there's no war and the sun shines and people can do what they want with their lives. I don't want to be crawling through a bombed house, with more bombs falling all over the place, looking for a woman and her baby who are probably dead. I don't want to find them. Why do *I* have to be the one? I never asked to do this.

She flashed her torch. She could get an idea of the layout of the house now. It must have three bedrooms, and there was a long passage from the front door to the stairs. To get to the space underneath it, you had to go through both downstairs rooms to the little kitchen at the back. There'd be a door there, leading to the cupboard that had been made in the space, but when she edged gingerly through she found that the kitchen had collapsed entirely under the weight of the bedroom above, and the door was blocked by piles of masonry and broken furniture.

I can't move all that, Gladys thought, gazing at it in despair. I can't possibly move all that.

She shifted what she could, tearing nails and skin as she wrenched at splintered wood and jagged bricks. A piece of broken glass cut a thin line down her arm but she scarcely noticed it. She propped her torch up on a shelf that was hanging precariously from one wall, and worked on, heaving and pulling, trying to make a way through to the cupboard door.

'Here, love. Let me do that.'

There was a man beside her, a burly man who also wore a tin helmet. He had big hands with big, strong fingers, and he pushed Gladys out of the way and shifted a beam with which she had been struggling. He was wearing a dark blue uniform. A warden, she thought dully, they're never about when you want one. But there was one here now, and they worked together, heaving the rubbish away, staggering as they pulled at beams which were wedged under piles of smashed bricks and mortar, coughing as fresh clouds of dust rose around them.

There were other people too. She was aware of them as a dimly lit crowd, moving in the shadows. Bodies, voices, faces, hands. They came and went before her vision, blurred and reeling. She was grateful for their help. But it was her task really . . .

They seemed to understand this, and when the door was at last free, they drew back, letting her set her hand to the knob, letting her be the one to turn it.

She opened the door and looked inside. Nothing.

'They're not here,' she said, and her voice rose and wavered. 'There's nobody here.'

For a few seconds, there was complete silence. It was as if even the bombs had ceased to fall. From somewhere in the shattered house, she could hear a dripping sound, slow and measured. And then there was a crash from somewhere else in the city and, as if it had touched a button to set them moving again, the rest of the neighbours gathered round, staring into the dusty space.

'Not here?'

'Where is she, then? Where's Marge?'

'She never said she was goin' away. I saw her yest'day and she never said.'

'They must be there.'

Peggy was at Gladys's side.

'Come on, Glad. There's nothing more we can do here. If there's no one hurt we ought to be getting back to the post—'

'No.' Gladys shook her head. She could not believe it. Marge Jennings should have been here with her baby, Gladys should have found them. It was her job. It was what she was supposed to do. 'They've got to be here.'

'Glad, you can see they're not. Come on. There's other people—'

'Listen!'

'Glad—'

'*Listen.*' Gladys turned to her mother and shook her arm, she turned to the others and blazed at them. 'Can't you hear it? Listen. It's the baby!' She dived forwards into the deepest recess of the cupboard, the part where the stairs came right down to the floor. 'Give us a torch, quick.'

She could hear it clearly now, a muffled whimpering, no louder than the mew of a newborn kitten. She scrabbled with her hand, finding the usual kind of rubbish – few old boxes, a rag-bag, a broom . . . A rag-bag! Was that really what it was? She felt Peggy thrust the torch into her hands and shone it on the soft pile under her hands. It cried again and she flashed the light and saw the face screw up, the eyes closing in protest at the sudden brightness.

'I've got it! The baby – it's here!' Cradling it in one arm, she scrambled backwards through the space, hearing the exclamations. 'Look, it's safe, it's alive, it's the baby.' She was out now, in the place that had once been the kitchen. 'I've got the baby, I've got the baby.'

'Oh, *Glad*—'

'The baby! She's got the baby. But where's Marge?' The neighbours passed the word back into the street and Gladys could hear the cheer that went up. But the warden was beside her, urging her out. 'It's not safe in here, love. The whole place could come crashing down round our ears. Get out of it, quick.'

Gladys stumbled out into the street, the baby still held in her arms. It was yelling with rage and fear. She stopped and looked at it more carefully. There seemed to be no injury at all. No blood on its little face, none seeping through its clothing. It had survived unhurt. But where was its mother?

Gladys looked around. She saw the warden go back into the house. She saw the other neighbours gather round, waiting until he came out, and she saw the look on his face when he emerged again at last.

He came over to where she stood, still holding the baby, and touched the little cheek with a dirty forefinger.

'Poor little bugger. Poor little sod.'

'Have – have you found her?'

His mouth twisted and he looked away. 'There wasn't much left to find. Just enough – enough to know it was her.' He drew in a ragged breath. 'She musta put the baby in the cupboard before the raid ever started – did it every night, most like. And she was upstairs. The bomb blew everything apart. Everything.' His whole body shuddered with the memory of what he had seen. 'We'll 'ave to go in and get 'er out, but not tonight. Not tonight.'

Gladys thought of the dripping sound she had heard. She remembered the drop of wetness that had touched her cheek. She put her hand up to her face and saw the stain on her fingers.

She looked at the baby in her arms. He had stopped screaming and was gazing peacefully at the reddened sky. She wondered how soon he would begin to miss his mother.

Burdened with shovels, spades and paraffin lamp, the three boys were halfway down Powerscourt Road when the siren sounded. They stopped and looked at each other.

'I'll have to go back,' Cyril said. 'I'm not supposed to be out.'

'What's the point? They'll know by now. You can't pretend you was in the lav all the time.'

Cyril considered. If he stayed out and went on with their plan, his father would take the strap to him when he got home. But he'd do that anyway, so Micky was right, there was no point in going back now. Besides, he had never been out in a night raid.

The planes were already overhead. The boys watched the shifting white beams of the searchlights criss-crossing the sky and stared at the bursting orange flowers. The sudden riot of noise and colour was like a gigantic firework display. They jumped and capered whenever a bomb exploded somewhere in Portsmouth, looking like demons from hell as they waved their shovels in the gory light, their yells drowned in the shattering blast of bombs and the rattle of gunfire.

'Come on!' Micky shouted. 'Let's get over to the den. No one'll take any notice of us in all this, an' if they see us with the bomb they'll think we're heroes!'

Fired by this new idea, they scurried through the streets. Some were empty as their inhabitants sheltered, others were a noisy confusion of people and vehicles. The fire engines were already out, followed by the vans and old buses that were being used as ambulances. Buildings were already in flames, their walls tottering and collapsing. The boys slid like shadows amongst it all, caught up in the excitement, only half aware that it was real.

'It's better'n the pictures,' Micky breathed as he slunk along a wall, watching a house opposite suddenly burst into flames as the roof was torn away by the inferno within. 'It's like being *in* the pictures . . .'

He was totally enraptured. Like the others, he had never been out in a night raid, and this was the best yet. He felt like a film star, running unscathed through streets that rained with bombs. Anything might happen, but nothing could touch him. He waved his shovel at the sky, yelling at the Germans, sneering and challenging. He was invincible.

They were in Powerscourt Road, climbing through the back fence. The house still stood in ruins, jagged walls in spectral silhouette against the flaming sky. The hole was a black shadow against the wall.

Cyril switched on his torch and climbed down the broken steps.

'It's still here.'

'What d'you expect?' Micky jeered. 'Think it might've walked away by itself?' He scrambled down to stand beside Cyril, gazing at the bomb. The rotting wall in which it was embedded shook with each explosion. Jimmy retreated.

'It could go off any minute.'

'Go on, it's a dud. It must be.' Micky set the paraffin lamp on a pile of bricks. 'Let's get it out.' He looked at Cyril. 'You start.'

Cyril hesitated. He glanced at his shovel, then at the bomb. It looked bigger in the flickering light, more menacing. There was quite a lot of rust along its side.

'You can if you like.'

'It's your bomb,' Micky said with a shrug, and leant his own shovel against the wall. Cyril looked at him again and bit his lip. He advanced slowly upon the bomb.

'I thought you said it was only his if he got it out,' Jimmy said craftily, and Micky scowled. He saw his leadership slipping again.

'All right, then, I'll do it if you're scared.' He pushed Cyril aside and approached the bomb himself. There was another explosion close by, and a few stones and some earth were dislodged around it. They rattled down the wall and the boys jumped back.

'Bombs don't have to be duds just because they haven't gone off,' Jimmy said. 'There was one down Fratton the other day, bin there weeks, suddenly exploded.'

Micky scraped some more rubble away, exposing the bomb's smooth, rounded sides. 'It won't take much more before we can lift it out.' He scraped again.

There was another explosion outside, even nearer. The blast shook the little cellar, bringing down a shower of bricks and plaster over the entrance. The bomb seemed to shiver and Micky leapt back.

'I'm getting out of here!' Jimmy's voice rose in panic. 'We'll get buried alive. Or blown to bits.' He scrabbled at the mound of broken bricks and earth on the steps. 'I can't get out . . .'

The bomb was forgotten. Gripped by sudden terror, the three boys clawed at the debris blocking their exit. Behind them, the paraffin lamp guttered and flared. Outside, through the narrow gap, they could still see a glimmer of fiery light. Desperate now to reach it, to be away from the hole, they pushed and shoved each other aside, each intent only on his own survival.

Another explosion. The ground shook. More debris collapsed above them. Cyril cried out, a gargling scream that sounded as if he were being sick. Micky and Jimmy tore at the bricks and earth, forcing their bodies up the steps. Hair, eyes and mouths were filled with dust and they choked and retched.

Another explosion. There was a roar from above as the entire house began to collapse. Floorboards shattered and plaster rained down into the basement. There was nothing in Micky's mind now but the sheer desperate need to breathe. Jimmy, Cyril, the bomb, all were forgotten in the frantic necessity to fill his choked lungs with air instead of dust, to relieve the intolerable pressure, to silence the roaring of blood in his ears and the terrified screaming of his mind.

He thrust his way through a pile of splintered laths, fell over a heap of bricks, knew without feeling it that he had sliced his arm across a jagged shard of glass. He half rose to his feet, tried to force his trembling legs to run, could manage no more than a crawl. Behind him, the house was toppling; all around, the sky was glaring red, and fire lit the wrecked garden with its angry flicker.

Another explosion. And this time it was the bomb itself, the bomb they had thought to be a dud, the bomb that had lain unexploded for months, awaiting its time. Its rusted sides gave way, the unstable contents stirred into life and it tore a hole in the collapsing house, sending bricks and wood and plaster flying into the sky. The blast shook every house left standing, shattering several more windows and bringing down a hundred or more slates. Like all bomb blasts, its effects were strangely erratic. A plaster gnome in a nearby garden was unaffected. A chimney-pot two streets distant toppled and fell.

It cleared the steps of their debris and blew it away in a fine dust, which became a part of the heavy, choking cloud that shifted and hung over the shattered houses.

There was no movement from the boys. They lay quite still, Micky on top of a pile of bricks and plaster, Jimmy half buried. Of Cyril, there was no sign at all.

Ted Chapman leaned against the low wall of the turret, his hands clutching the rough stone. His body shook with each blast as a bomb whistled down from the sky and burst into a shower of flame somewhere in Portsmouth. He stared at the orange glow that lit up the sky, at the white pencil beams of searchlights. He heard the rattle of anti-aircraft fire, the wild clanging of firebells, the shouts of wardens in the streets, and it was as if he could hear every cry, every scream, that sounded in the city of Portsmouth that night. They shrilled in his ears and battered at his skull; they stabbed into his body, and his head whirled and sickened with the sheer terrible force of it.

He sank to his knees. He had been at Dunkirk and had seen the men standing neck-deep in the water, waiting for rescue. Thousands of them had died there on the beaches before he and the other boats could get them away.

Thousands were dying now, in Portsmouth, in London, in every major city, in towns and villages, at sea and in the sky.

The screams echoed in his head.

By dawn, Gladys was moving in a daze. She scarcely knew what patients were being loaded into her van, scarcely registered the journeys along the chaotic streets. It was as if the ambulance knew its own way, as if something outside her own mind directed the functioning of her body. Down this street, along that – no, you can't, it's blocked. Try the next one – fire engines – well then, the next – yes, this one's clear – no, there's a crater at the end, reverse, watch out for that old woman – this way's OK – which way is the hospital now – down that way – no – yes, there it is at last, drive to the door, stop, get out, see the casualties in, get back in the van, start again . . .

'You ought to give it up,' Peggy said. 'You're done in. We both are.' But she knew they could not give up. As long as the bombs kept falling, as long as there were people to get out of shattered buildings, so the ambulances must keep going, and so their drivers and their attendants. People like Gladys and Peggy, all equally worn out, all forcing themselves to keep going, operating in a dream.

They'll win, Gladys thought, driving to yet another bombed building. If they keep this up, they'll win. We just can't go on for ever.

She pulled up and looked hopelessly at the familiar sight, the cloud of dust, the smoke and flames, the firemen with their hoses, the people huddled on the pavement. Another family homeless.

'*Gladdie!*'

She turned, her heart leaping. Only one person had ever called her that. She saw his face, smeared with dirt but grinning the same as always, his ginger hair almost black with soot under the cap that was still somehow perched at a rakish angle.

'Graham! Oh, Graham . . .'

'So this is where you've got to,' he said cheerfully. 'I thought we had a date tonight.' He looked at her with concern. 'Here, are you all right?'

'Me? Yes, I'm all right. I'm always all right.' Gladys frowned slightly, then swayed a little and Graham caught her in his arms. 'I'm just a bit tired, that's all, a bit fed-up. All these planes coming over all the time, all the bombs . . . I just wish they'd stop, don't you?'

'We all do.' Graham held her up and looked closely into her face. 'You're all in, Gladdie. You ought to have a rest.'

'Can't,' she mumbled. 'Can't rest, got to drive the van, keep going. Too many people, too many bombs . . .' Her knees buckled and Graham tightened his arms and looked round for help.

'Here, what's up with our Glad?' Peggy was at his side, staring anxiously at Gladys's white face. 'Passed out, has she? I'm not surprised, bin driving that van like a mad thing tonight, I told her time and time again she oughter have a rest. Trouble is, there's no one else can drive the bloody thing, they've all got their own jobs to do and *I* can't drive it.' She chewed her lip. 'There's a bloke here hurt bad, we oughter be getting him to hospital. I dunno what to do.'

'I do,' Graham said firmly. 'Get him in the back, Mrs Shaw, and I'll see to Gladys. She can ride with you for a change. I'll drive the van.'

'You?' Peggy stared at him and felt suddenly reassured. He looked tall and capable in his matelot's uniform. She wondered irrelevantly whether Jess Budd had sewn that square collar . . . 'Can you drive?'

'Well enough. I've been learning anyway.'

Gladys moaned and struggled a little in Graham's arms. She put her hand to her head. 'What's happening? The ambulance – I've got to drive the ambulance—'

'You're not driving anywhere,' Peggy said firmly. 'You're coming in the back with me. Graham's going to drive.'

Gladys stared at him. 'You? Ginger? But you can't – it's my job—'

'That's all right,' Graham said. 'You just get in the back with your mum.'

'But—'

The local warden appeared beside them, his arm supporting a man who was hobbling and clutching an obviously broken arm. There was blood oozing from a jagged cut on his head. His clothes were badly torn and there were dark wet stains, as if he was bleeding in several places. His face was grey under its coating of dust.

'This bloke needs to get to the hospital. What's going on here? What's up with her? She's the driver, ain't she?'

'She's not fit to drive,' Peggy said. 'This sailor's taking over. We'll get him there.'

'There's another coupla women ought to go too.' The warden stared at them doubtfully. 'Think you can manage? Perhaps I oughter—'

'It's all right. I know him,' Peggy said, omitting to mention that she had known Graham Philpotts best when he was eight years old, a mischievous small boy who knocked on respectable folk's doors and then ran away . . . 'He'll get us there.'

Another bomb shrieked to a crash a street or two away and the warden looked harassed. 'All right, then. Take 'em, and then come back, we'll have a few more for you by the looks of it. I've gotta go—' He turned and hurried off along the street, shouting for help as he went.

Gladys was standing now, still looking dazed. She turned and made for the ambulance, pulling open the driver's door. 'We've got to get these people to hospital—'

'In the back.' Graham grabbed her arm and led her to the back door, where Peggy was already helping the injured man inside. Two women were leaning against a broken lamp post, one crying weakly. 'You get in too. Come on, Gladdie. You're going to ride in style this time.'

He slammed the back doors and clambered into the driver's seat. In fact, he had never driven anything other than his boss's old van, just up the street and back when the old man wasn't looking. And there was an old car someone had abandoned once on a bit of waste ground in Gosport. He and a few other boys had got hold of a can of petrol and managed to get it going. It had accomplished a few hundred yards in kangaroo hops before finally spluttering to a halt, and that had been that.

But there wasn't really anything to driving, if you knew the principles and after a couple of false starts and a startled leap or two the van set off up the road with Graham holding tightly to the steering wheel. All right so far, he thought, now let's try turning the corner . . .

Fortunately, the street was only half a mile from the Royal Hospital and by the time they reached the building Graham was feeling more confident. The ambulance lurched up to the casualty entrance and came to a juddering halt.

'I thought you said you could drive!' Peggy was out of the van at once. The sky was still roaring with the sound of bombers and night-fighters, the anti-aircraft fire was rattling on all sides and as Graham looked up he saw the red flares of parachute mines dropping steadily through the darkness. It looked too near for comfort . . . He ran to the back of the van and shouted urgently.

'Get 'em out, Gladdie. There's something big coming. Get 'em out and into shelter, for God's sake!'

Gladys dragged her thoughts together. She was feeling slightly better now and aware that the people in the ambulance with her had all been injured. I'm not hurt at all, she thought. I'm just making a lot of fuss over nothing. *Tired!* How can I say I'm tired, when there's people getting killed . . .

'Out, quick,' she said, and together she and Peggy helped the man out.

He looked bad. He ought to have been on a stretcher, she thought, and helped him as gently as she could.

'I can't . . .' the man said, and began to crumple. Instantly, Graham was at his side. He swung the man's good arm over his shoulders and gripped him about the waist.

'Come on, mate. It's not healthy out here.'

The two women climbed out by themselves and staggered in through the casualty entrance. Peggy went with them, handed them over to a nurse and then hurried out again. There were other people about too. A doctor, some nurses, porters, another sailor on his way out. One of the porters came out with Peggy and gave Gladys a nod.

'Good girl. There's some char inside if you want it.'

Gladys shook her head. 'There isn't time—'

'There is,' Peggy said. 'You need it. We all do. We've—'

Whatever else she had been about to say was lost for ever as one of the mines struck the roof of the casualty department and blew the building apart. At the same moment, another bomb fell in the main courtyard and destroyed the main entrance. Fire broke out at once and the blaze spread across the whole of the front of the building. To the pilots high above, it must have seemed then that all Portsmouth was afire and that no more need be done to bring this ancient city to its knees.

Neither Gladys nor Peggy saw the sight.

Gladys was saved by her battered old ambulance, which had protected her from the main blast. She was knocked unconscious by a piece of flying debris, and when she came round later she found herself in St James's Hospital with a broken arm.

Her mother was in the next bed. She had been thrown over thirty feet across the yard and landed in a flowerbed. She was covered in scratches – 'from one of those dratted rosebushes', she said – but otherwise, miraculously, she was uninjured. She was kept in for a few hours for observation and then allowed to go home.

Graham Philpotts, along with the doctor and everyone else who had been in the casualty department at that moment, was killed at once.

27

They had a funeral for little Cyril Nash, though there was little left to put in the coffin. Sometimes, it seemed as if they just buried a coffin, for the sake of it. As if you couldn't feel properly finished without a funeral.

Cyril was buried a few days after the big raid. What he'd been doing down Powerscourt Road, nobody could make out, and they wouldn't even have known he was there if Micky and Jimmy hadn't told them. The boys had lain in the garden, on the edge of the crater, all through the night, drifting in and out of consciousness, and only been found next morning by accident, by some other boys who were climbing about in the wreckage. The boys had dragged Micky out and got him to a First Aid post, where he was given hot tea and wrapped in blankets, but they hadn't been able to do anything for Jimmy. He'd had to wait until a proper rescue team arrived, headed by the young woman doctor, Una Mulvaney, and when he had finally been lifted clear he had lost a leg.

'Poor little bugger,' Granny Kinch said when Micky was brought home in an ambulance van. He'd been kept at the First Aid post for most of the day, until Dr Mulvaney was sure he was fit to be moved. 'That'll put paid to 'is footballing. 'Ave to 'ave a nartificial leg now, 'e will. Thank Gawd it wasn't you, our Mick.'

'Oh, my Micky's got a charmed life,' Nancy remarked. She hadn't even known Micky was missing, for she hadn't been at home when the raid had started and had made the most of it in a dark corner with a sailor. No point in losing good money, after all. 'Knows 'ow to look after 'imself, Micky, does.'

'All the same, 'e didn't oughter bin out in it,' her mother said. 'Worried sick, I was, 'ere all by meself listenin' ter the bombs. It coulda bin you, blowed to bits,' she told Micky severely. 'Then where would you've bin, eh?'

'All over Pompey, I s'pose,' Micky answered, but the cheekiness in his voice was more wavery than usual. His memories of the raid were garbled now, but he could feel with his body the terror of being trapped in the cellar, the panic as the house collapsed about them. He could still taste the dust and smoke, and his eyes were sore from grit and the red flare of the sky. It had seemed an eternity that he had lain there, with bricks digging into his ribs and a sharp spike of wood scratching deeply into his thigh and the cacophony of planes, bombs and guns resounding all about him. He did not know for sure whether it had been real, or a dream. He had a feeling that it had been totally real, but that from now on it would be a recurring nightmare.

'That Micky Baxter ought to be locked up somewhere,' Frank said. 'He's a holy terror. He leads other boys into trouble and gets off scot-free.'

'He had concussion. He nearly died,' Jess said, but in her heart she agreed with Frank. It was terrible to think of little Cyril Nash, killed for the sake of a bit of boyish mischief, and Jimmy Cross with only one leg. It didn't seem right that Micky, who had been the ringleader, should be able to strut about the streets, looking cocky again.

May brought more furious attacks on Portsmouth, Liverpool and London. Dawn scarcely penetrated to the capital city through the smoke that hung like a funeral pall over thousands of stricken buildings, and the firefighters battled through three days and nights to control the flames that threatened to sweep away the rest.

In Portsmouth, nine high explosive bombs fell near the Hilsea Gas Works and on the main railway line to London. Houses were damaged in all the nearby streets and several people killed. One of them was Jess Budd's aunt Nell, who had let Frank and Jess live in two rooms of her house when they had first got married. Jess heard the news with sorrow and went to look at the house where she had started her married life.

'Poor auntie Nell. She had a sharp tongue, but she was good-hearted, she'd never see anyone go in want. We had some good times in that house.'

'Well, she never knew a thing about it, there's that to be thankful for.' Frank held his wife close. 'And she had a good life. As good as anyone can expect, these days.'

'I know.' Jess sighed and straightened her shoulders. She wiped her eyes. There was never time for proper grieving. The blows came thick and fast, as fast as the bombs, and all you could do was take a deep breath and carry on. Carry on, carry on. Keep smiling through. Don't let Hitler win. Are we downhearted? *No* – let 'em all come!

'We're giving as good as we get,' people said, but did that really help? As far as Jess could see, it just meant more and more people killed or homeless. More and more misery.

She went up to Annie's to tell her about Frank's auntie. Her sister was in the kitchen, baking an eggless sponge. She looked tired and there were lines of worry etched on her face.

'Ted's still bad,' she said as she put the kettle on for a cup of tea. 'It's hit him real hard this time. The doctor don't know what to do with him.'

Jess sat down at the kitchen table. Ted had been found on the turret roof, curled up in a corner and sobbing like a child. Annie had had to call Frank to come and help her, and together they'd unwrapped his arms from about his head and led him down the stairs. Bed had seemed the best place and they'd given him some sweet tea and waited for the shock to wear off, but Ted was still there, staring dry-eyed now at the ceiling and refusing to move. It was almost as if he'd had a stroke.

'The doctor says it's nothing like that. Just shock. He says that last raid was too much for him.' Annie glanced at the ceiling and lowered her voice.

'If you ask me, it all comes from Dunkirk. He would go, and you know how scared he was of even going across the harbour at night. Seeing all them poor soldiers being shelled and machine-gunned where they stood – well, he's never got over it, never. He has awful nightmares.' She poured the tea and sat down opposite Jess. 'I don't think he'll ever be the same again.'

'Oh, Annie! He'll get better, I'm sure he will.' Jess reached across and touched her sister's hand. 'It's all been too much for him, but he'll get over it. People always do.'

'Do they?' Annie gave a short laugh. 'What about old Herbie up the road? He was shellshocked in the last war and he's never got over it. I can remember him going off, a fine figure of a man he was, and always laughing. Half the girls in Copnor were in love with him. And a year or so later he was back, a wreck, frightened to crawl along the pavement, jumping half out of his skin if a door slammed. He's hardly been across the doorstep since and they say his poor old mother still has to cut up his food as if he was a baby.'

'Ted won't be like that,' Jess said uncomfortably, but she knew that Annie was right. Some people never did recover.

But it was no use letting it get you down. Like the old song said, there was a silver lining to every dark cloud, and you just had to look for it. *Turn the dark cloud inside out . . .* And there *were* spots of brightness in the gloom, and if you tried you could raise a smile, on even the worst of days.

One of the brightest spots was Maureen. Now fast approaching two years old, she was toddling everywhere, always with a smile on her face. She could talk well and had begun to ask questions. Her favourite word was 'why'.

'Why does the sun shine? Why is it dark? Why is that flower red? Why is the leaf green? Why does Henry scratch his ears? Why – why – why?'

She never asked why a war was being fought, why she must spend every night in an air-raid shelter, why the darkness was filled with the noise of aircraft and bombs. But, standing at her mother's knee one day and hearing the adults talk about 'peace' she furrowed her brow and asked, 'What's peace?' And could not understand the expressions this brought to their faces, nor the reason for the sudden tears in her mother's eyes.

Another bright spot was the letter written each week by Tim and Keith. Jess could imagine them, sitting down together to try to think of things to say. She was amused by the large handwriting, straggling over two or three sheets of paper, on both sides, to make the letter look longer. The letters were singularly uninformative – 'We went to church on Sunday. We went to school. We played' – but she treasured them all the same. Usually, they finished up 'How is our Baby?' and she would write back and tell them all the things Maureen had said and done, and what Henry the cat was doing, mostly sleep, in front of the fire if he could get there, and about the garden and allotment. She kept talk of the bombs and the war out of her letters, unaware of the fact that this was what the boys most wanted to hear.

'Children shouldn't have to think about such things,' she said, but Tim and Keith were avid for news. To them, war was still exciting and such protection kept it so. They knew little of the destruction, the misery, the injured and the homeless. They saw the planes fighting overhead and danced in ecstasy, recreating them as they zoomed along country lanes with arms held wide, pretending to be Spitfires and Hurricanes. They watched the glow in the sky as Portsmouth or Southampton burned and never thought that their own families might be in danger. For the next few days they played firemen, dousing the flames. They longed for an enemy aircraft to be shot down somewhere near the village so that they could take its crew prisoner and be awarded medals by the King himself.

All through the bombing, people tried their best to live normal lives. They went to the pictures and saw films like *Spring Parade*, with Deanna Durbin, to bring a little glamour into their lives, or *Spare a Copper*, with George Formby to bring fun. They saw Laurence Olivier and Vivien Leigh in *21 Days*, and Bette Davis and Charles Boyer in *All This and Heaven Too*. They went dancing and watched football matches, they visited each other for Sunday afternoon tea and played cards and Ludo and Snakes and Ladders. They listened to *In Town Tonight* on Saturday evenings and Gert and Daisy handing out household tips in *The Kitchen Front* on weekday mornings. They coped with ever-tightening rations, with milkless days, with baking cakes with no eggs. They dug their gardens and grew vegetables and made clothes for themselves and their children.

In other places too, the war went on. Turning her attention to nation after nation, Germany threatened Yugoslavia with total destruction. Rommel arrived in Libya and launched his African offensive. The Allies were evacuated from Greece and, a few weeks later, from Crete. Rudolf Hess, Hitler's deputy, parachuted into Scotland and was imprisoned in the Tower of London. The Italian army surrendered in North Africa, and Britain rejoiced as the *Bismarck* was sunk, a fitting vengeance for the sinking of the *Hood*.

'It's not over,' Frank said. 'Not by a long chalk. He's just drawing breath.' He tapped the newspaper in front of him. 'Look at this. They're starting on the plans to make tunnel shelters in the hill. They wouldn't be doing that if they didn't think we were going to need them. They reckon they could get five thousand people in them.'

On the first of June, another announcement appeared in the paper and Jess read it with dismay. She showed it to Peggy Shaw when her neighbour came in for a cup of tea.

'Clothes on ration! We can't buy anything now without coupons.'

'But we haven't got ration books for clothes.'

'No, we're to use our margarine coupons instead. See, there's a list here of all the things we can get. An overcoat or mac'll be sixteen coupons, a pair of trousers six, a skirt seven, a pair of boots or shoes five. We've got sixty-six to last us the year.' She frowned thoughtfully. 'I suppose it's not that bad. I mean, we've got stuff already, it's only whatever we need new. Mind, wool's rationed as well, you have to think of that, and material – three coupons a yard. It says you can get clothes for children under four without coupons though, that'll help with the baby.'

'That's if they've got the stuff in the shops,' Peggy remarked. She was still pale and shaken after the night when the Royal Hospital had been bombed, and had not regained her usual brisk energy. Both she and Gladys had been relieved of their duties with the ambulance for the time being, though they both went to the First Aid post anyway, to help in whatever way they could. Peggy had tried to dissuade Gladys at first, but had soon given up. 'I don't need two hands to pour tea,' the girl had declared. It was as if she couldn't rest, as if she wanted to win the war all by herself, to make up for losing Graham.

Jess looked at her neighbour with sympathy. 'How're you feeling now, Peg?'

'Oh, all right. I mean, I'm all right in meself, I just can't get it out of my mind, that's all. That mine, landing right on the hospital, it seems criminal. I was talking to the doctor only a minute before, ever so nice he was, and you could see he was dead beat but he was still looking after people. That man we took there, and the two women all blown to kingdom come.' She shuddered. 'And Graham Philpotts. That's what I can't get over. Young Ginger. Him and our Bob knocked about together quite a bit when they were little. I remember him tying a string to my door-knocker one day and hiding round the corner.'

'He was a terror,' Jess agreed. 'But there was no harm to him, you know. Our Betty thought a lot of him for a while, till they split up.'

Peggy nodded. The whole street had known that Betty Chapman had been going out with Graham Philpotts. And just because they'd parted brass rags didn't mean she couldn't be sorry he was dead. 'How's she taken it? Our Gladys is proper upset.'

'Well, she's cut up about it, who wouldn't be? But she don't say much these days. She's changed since she went out to the farm.'

'They're all changing,' Peggy said 'My Gladys and Diane, your Annie's two girls. They're all changing, Jess. Maybe for the better, maybe not. But there ain't a blind thing anyone can do about it. All we can do is hang on – and try to give each other a bit of strength.'

Strength.

It was the one thing that Alice Brunner needed most desperately, and the one thing it seemed impossible for her to have.

It was over a year now since Heinrich had been taken away, and would soon be a year since the *Arandora Star* had been sunk. Slowly, she was beginning to face the fact that he must be dead.

And so unnecessarily. Since the sinking of the *Arandora Star*, there had been a change of heart over the treatment of 'aliens'. So many had, like Heinrich, lived in Britain for many years, had made their homes here and adopted it as their own country. Their families were British. Many of them had suffered in Germany and wanted nothing more than to see Hitler beaten and sanity returned to their homeland. And yet, they had been treated as undesirables, and deported as if they had been criminals.

Ordinary people, like Jess Budd and her husband, had respected Heinrich Brunner and men like him. And for once, ordinary people's voices were heard. They reached Parliament itself and caused a bitter debate in which the whole system was denounced as a 'bespattered page in our history'. The interned 'aliens' began to be freed.

They were coming home. Alice had read about it in the newspaper. Over fifteen thousand of the twenty-seven thousand who had been snatched away, were being allowed home. And Heinrich could have been one of them.

He should never have been taken away, she thought bitterly.

She got out of bed, on that first morning of June, and looked out of the window. There had been a raid during the night, but it had been short-lived and she had not bothered to go to the shelter. What was the point, when Heinrich was dead?

In the garden, there was an old apple tree. Heinrich had loved that tree. He would watch it blossom in April, and talk of how it reminded him of an apple tree in the garden where he had spent his boyhood. His mother would sit under it, sewing clothes for her family or shelling peas. He would look for the first pale green leaf to unfurl, and the first tiny apple to form. He would touch the deep creases of its bark, almost as if he were fondling it.

Alice stared at it and realised that it must have blossomed this spring without her noticing. It was in full leaf, the creamy white flowers gone, and she knew that if she looked more closely she would see the small green apples hanging on its boughs.

All this had happened, and she had never noticed.

Alice felt a sharp pang of guilt. It was as if she had betrayed her husband, who had loved the apple tree. She had neglected it, one of the things he loved; because he was not here, she had brushed it aside as if it were of no value, and let its beauty go by unrecognised.

And how much else have I neglected? she thought.

The back door opened and she saw Joy come out into the garden. She carried an old shopping basket, filled with washing – her own and Alice's underclothes and stockings. She must have been up for an hour or more, marking up the newspapers which the paper-boys must by now be delivering, and doing these bits of washing. Alice watched as she hung them out on the line Heinrich had fixed up between the apple tree and the kitchen wall, and felt another stab of guilt.

I've neglected her too, she thought. Our daughter, Heinrich's daughter, I've let her do the work I should have been doing. I've let her shoulder all the responsibility of the shop. And now I'm even letting her wash my knickers. A girl not yet fourteen years old, losing the last days of her childhood because of my selfishness.

She turned away, overwhelmed by the extent of her neglect, neglect her friends, like Jess Budd, had tried to warn her about, and which she had not understood but now saw clearly, as if a veil had been stripped from her eyes. I've been living in a fog, she thought.

She looked into the mirror and was shocked by what she saw. A woman looking older than her years, her face grey and lined, her hair coarse and unkempt. The blue eyes, which Heinrich used to say were the colour of robins' eggs, had faded and there were anxious lines around them. Her mouth looked pinched and her cheeks hollow, as if she had false teeth and had forgotten to wear them. Her neck was gaunt and lined.

If Heinrich came back now, he would not recognise her.

'What have you done to yourself, Alice Brunner?' she asked aloud. 'What have you let happen?'

A surge of feeling flooded through her and she was so unused to it that for a moment she scarcely recognised it for what it was. For almost a year she had struggled with grief and hope, the two blurring into despair. She had turned away from pleasure, thinking it disloyal to Heinrich, and in the same way had brushed aside any emotion other than bitter misery. Now, for a few seconds, she could not identify the emotion that swept through her body like a clean, sharp wind.

Anger. It was anger. Anger with the system that had taken Heinrich from her, anger with the enemy who had sunk his ship and brought about his death – for she was certain now that he must be dead. His own countrymen! But most of all, her anger was directed at herself.

'You're a mess, Alice Brunner. A selfish, self-pitying mess. And it's time you pulled yourself together and started to do what Heinrich wanted you to do, what he *trusted* you to do. Be a proper mother to his daughter.' She thrust her hands through the greying hair, lifting it away from her neck, piling it loosely on top of her head in the style she knew he liked. 'And if you have to be his widow, be a widow he'd be proud of.'

For Gladys, the night of the third blitz brought more than a broken arm and the loss of someone she'd begun to grow fond of. As soon as she was out of hospital, she began collecting leaflets on the women's Services.

'I don't know whether to join the Wrens or the WAAFs,' she said to Olive Harker, who had come down the street to see how she was. 'Or even the ATS.' She smiled, but it was a twisted smile and without merriment. 'One thing I do know, it won't be the Land Army like your Betty.'

'I wouldn't join that either,' Olive said. 'She seems to have spent the whole winter trying to pull up frozen vegetables. You should see her hands – they're as rough as a navvy's and I don't reckon she'll ever get the dirt out. Mind, she says it's not so bad now spring's come. The lambs are sweet.'

'Well, I want to be in an armed Service,' Gladys said. 'I want to feel I'm fighting.'

'But they don't arm women, do they?'

'They don't yet. Who's to say what they'll do if the war carries on?'

The two girls were silent for a few minutes. Then Olive said quietly, 'I was ever so sorry to hear about Graham. I quite liked him when he was coming to our house for Betty. He always had a joke.'

'I know. Mind, I hadn't seen much of him since he moved over to Gosport, and he used to get on my nerves when he came round to play with Bob when they were little. I thought he was a bit of a nuisance. And if it hadn't been for him, our Bob could have been going out with your Betty. But he'd changed, Livvy. Grown up, I suppose. That last night – I could see he'd been working like a slave to get people out of bombed houses. And he drove my ambulance . . .' Her voice shook. 'It should've been *me* in the hospital that night, Livvy. They were *my* casualties – I should've taken them in. Graham shouldn't ever have been there . . .'

Olive gazed at her in pity, unable think of anything to say that would comfort her friend. Dimly, she could understand the feelings that were churning through Gladys's breast. Guilt that Graham had been killed 'in her place'. Relief that she was still alive, and further guilt that she felt such relief. They coiled round inside her like a bitter snake chasing its own tail.

'He wouldn't have wanted you to think that way,' she said. 'He liked being in the Navy. He enjoyed it. He thought it was fun – all of it. He knew he might be killed, but he could still find something to laugh at, even in the raids. He wouldn't have wanted you to be miserable over him.'

'I know. But I can't help it. He's dead, and I'm alive. I feel that if I could just do something – something to make up for it . . .' Gladys shook her head and Olive sighed. Perhaps she was right. Perhaps Service life would be the best thing for her. Perhaps the only way she could find true relief was by taking Graham's place, by offering herself to serve in his stead.

'I should think the Wrens would be best for you,' she said, thinking of Graham in his matelot's uniform. 'The Navy, that's what you'd be good at.'

'D'you really think so?' Gladys looked again at the leaflet she had obtained. It showed a girl in dark blue uniform, saluting, and across it were the words '*Join the Wrens . . . and free a man for the Fleet.*'

The girl had blonde hair. It was almost ginger. Almost the same colour as Graham's.

'It seems right to join the Navy,' she said thoughtfully. 'Being in Pompey.'

'Well, it's up to you,' Olive said, feeling slightly alarmed. She was fairly sure that the prospect of Gladys in the Wrens would not be at all welcome to Gladys's parents – especially to her father. He hadn't yet stopped reminding them all that he'd never been in favour of her learning to drive, but nobody'd taken any notice of him and now look what had happened. He wouldn't stop, either, as long as Gladys's arm was in plaster, and probably not even when it was out.

Gladys looked at her. 'What about you, Livvy? D'you ever think of joining up?'

'I don't think it's going to be a matter of *thinking* about it,' Olive said. 'I think we're going to have to. We've already had to sign on for war work. It can't be long before we're conscripted, if we're not already in a job.'

'We've both got jobs,' Gladys said, 'but I suppose they don't count those as war work.' She looked at the leaflet again. 'I'm going to join the Wrens,' she said decisively. 'I'll apply now and I'll go in as soon as my arm's better. "*Free a man for the Fleet.*" Well, maybe I'll be able to give 'em one back for the one I took.'

'Gladys, you didn't *take* him,' Olive said. 'He was working in the raids. All the sailors were. He could've been killed anywhere that night.'

'But he wasn't. He was killed doing my job. Anyway, it's done now, nothing can bring him back.' Her eyes filled with tears as she thought of the merry-eyed sailor who had knocked her mother's door and run away when he was a small boy, who had grown into a flippant, irresponsible lad, who had become a man during the blitz and come to her aid when she needed it. 'All I can do is try to make up for it.'

Olive was silent. Then she said, 'I'll talk to my Derek. I think you're right, Glad, we ought to join up. But I can't do something like that without talking it over with him first.'

'Don't you think he'll want you to?'

'I think he'll say if I want to do it, I should. But I still can't do it without talking to him. It's different when you're married.'

'I suppose it is.' Gladys looked at the leaflet again. Then she moved her shoulders as if a heavy burden had just slipped away from them. She raised her head and gave Olive a grin. 'D'you know what? I feel better already! I know what I want to do and nobody's going to stop me.' She lifted her right arm in a copy of the salute being given by the girl on the leaflet. 'I'm going to join the Navy. I'm going to be a Wren. I'm going to fight for my country and I'm going to *enjoy* it – just like Graham did!'

For Betty, Graham's death had come as yet another blow.

Safety in the countryside seemed to have a bitter twist when almost everyone you knew was in danger. Since coming out here she had known three young airmen, all shot down; her great-auntie Nell, bombed in her own home; her sister, suffering the loss of her first baby; Kathy Simmons, killed with her little one in her arms; her friend Gladys, injured; and now Graham – who had said he loved her, who had wanted to marry her, who had begged her to let him make love to her – wiped out in the space of a second.

How could she expect Dennis to survive? She folded the telegram that her mother had sent to tell her of Graham's death, and stuffed it into the pocket of her dungarees. It was happening to everyone, everywhere.

How long before she received another yellow envelope, another telegram telling her that someone she loved was dead?

Erica came out of the cowshed and saw her leaning over the orchard gate. It was a fine morning, the June sunshine turning the dew to a pearly film over the gossamer grass. A few late lambs were under the trees with their mothers, clustered together in a corner as they plotted a new game.

'Come on, Betty. It's no good standing there mooning over the lambs.'

'I know. It just seems so strange, us out here, safe, and everyone we know in danger. I'm just wondering whether I did the right thing, joining the Land Army.'

'Of course you did. You like it. You're good at it.'

'That's not the most important thing,' Betty said. 'The most important thing is helping the country. Liking things and being good at them are things for peacetime.'

'And war too,' Erica said staunchly. 'Look, Betty, I've learnt a lot since I came out here. Remember what I was like to start with, insisting on my own room, saying I wouldn't stay where there was a CO?'

Betty smiled and nodded. 'Yvonne and me thought you were a proper toffee-nosed little squirt.'

'Well, so I was,' Erica said. 'And I was worse after Geoff was killed. But since then, well, I've thought about things a lot.' She bit her lip and looked down at a small, newborn lamb which had come up to the gate to stare at them inquisitively. 'Geoff used to tell me off, you know. About the way I treated Dennis. He said everyone had a right to their opinions and Dennis wasn't a coward. I wouldn't listen to him, I didn't *want* to listen to him, but now I know it's true. There's not many men would go and do what Dennis is doing.'

'I wish he wouldn't,' Betty said. 'He's not a coward, but I am. I'm imagining him getting blown up all the time. I just don't see how he'll get through alive. I just can't believe he will.'

Her voice broke and Erica moved to lay a small, roughened hand on her sleeve. Her own voice was ragged as she answered.

'I know how you feel, Betty. I really do. Every day, I thought of Geoff going up in his plane and never coming back. And one day, that's just what happened.' She paused, gathering strength to continue. 'Maybe it will be the same with Dennis. But there's nothing we can do about it, Betty. We just have to take whatever we can, and make the best of it. We just have to love them while they're here.'

The newborn lamb called to its mates and they came over in a small, bleating throng. They pressed against the gate, gazing up at the two girls. Betty reached down a hand to scratch the top of a hard woolly head and the lamb jumped, startled.

'I suppose you're right,' she said. 'I *know* you're right. But – it's so hard, Erica. The waiting – being brave – just getting through the days. It's so hard.'

'I know,' the blonde girl said, and she moved a little closer and put her arm round Betty's shoulders. 'I know . . . But we can do it, Betty. We're all stronger than we thought. And Dennis is still alive, and let's hope he'll stay that way.' She paused, then added, 'At least you do have hope.'

Yes, Betty thought, I do have hope. I can hope that Dennis will survive. I can hope that the war will soon be over. I can hope that Olive and Derek will be able to be together and have a family, and that Colin will come home one day. And I can hope that Erica will find someone else to love, even though she'll never forget Geoff.

She turned from the gate and felt the telegram crinkle in her pocket. She had parted from Graham before he had died, recognising that their love had never been more than a brief infatuation, that in other times would have fizzled out with no hurt feelings on either side. But he would always have a special place, deep in the corner of her heart, for he had been the first boy to kiss her, to tell her that he loved her, and the first for whom she had felt a tremor of emotion. Despite their arguments, there had been a sweetness about it that she could not forget.

And had no reason to forget. For her love for Dennis was of a different kind, an enduring kind. And as Erica said, she could have hope. She could love him while he was here.

That was all that any of them could do – the girls who were left behind.

Keep Smiling Through

For my brother Roy,
with very much love

1

May 1941. The war that had begun in September 1939 between Britain and Germany was throwing its dark shadow over the entire world. The war that was to have been over by Christmas, was beginning to seem as if it would have no end.

The families who lived in April Grove, in the city of Portsmouth, were learning together to face the fears, the privations and the day-to-day drudgery of a war which had stormed its way to their own doorsteps. There was little history to guide them. Never before had war brought death from the skies to the ordinary homes of people who were making no attack, who had no defence. Never before had the population of the entire country been forced to burrow like moles into the earth itself for safety. Never before had a country that had not been invaded woken day after day to find its homes destroyed, its schools and churches ablaze, its workplaces gone.

It was like finding your way through unknown territory, making your own map with each painful step.

'You wouldn't know it was Pompey,' Jess Budd said sadly, when she went down to the Guildhall Square and saw the burned-out shell of her favourite store, McIlroys, the battered railway station, the gutted Guildhall. 'You wouldn't believe it had ever been a lovely city, with happy people, a place it was a pleasure to come to. It's no more than a ruin now — a horrible, dying ruin.'

It was as if the Germans had tried to blast the heart out of the city by devastating its centre, the part that everyone knew and loved. All around the whole area, streets had been bombed, houses flattened, roads obliterated by vast craters. The Madden Hotel was blown apart by a mine, Kingston Prison damaged, the main railway blocked by debris, and even the Royal Hospital struck by a mine. The Dockyard, so vital to the country's defence, was bombed again and again, and fires raged there day and night as the weary firefighters struggled to control them.

But even as she stared, her heart breaking at the sight of so much destruction, Jess felt the stirring of a determination that had been born and and was growing in the heart of every Briton during those dark months of the blitz. We *won't* be beaten, she thought. We *won't* give in. And somewhere deep inside her, like the tolling of a bell, she heard the words of Winston Churchill, spoken to hearten a nation that might otherwise have been brought to its knees.

'We will never surrender . . .'

'I don't know,' Gladys Shaw said restlessly. 'I don't reckon I did all that much. Not when you think about other people, people what died. They're the ones who deserve medals, not me.'

Olive Harker and her sister Betty Chapman looked at the shining silver disc in its little case. Gladys had brought it up the street to the Chapmans' house to show it to them specially. The whole of April Grove had been proud of her when they'd heard the news, and everyone would be wanting a look, but somehow Gladys didn't seem all that thrilled.

I would be if it was me, Betty thought. Or Dennis. And she knew her sister was thinking the same. Suppose she or her husband Derek had won a medal for serving their country in the war. Why, they'd be like a dog with two tails.

She looked at it again. The British Empire Medal, presented by King George the Sixth himself. Well, not handed to Gladys by him personally – she'd had to go to the Chief Constable of Hampshire to get it, and she said that she'd been more nervous about that than she'd been in any of the air-raids of the Portsmouth blitz. But the King had signed the paper, that's what mattered. He *knew* about her.

Betty shook her head, marvelling. 'It's queer to think that the King knows about people like us,' she said. 'Living in little two-up, two-down terraced houses in April Grove in Portsmouth. I mean, you wouldn't think him and the Queen knew we existed, would you?'

'They do, though,' Olive said. 'Look at the way the Queen talked to my Derek when she came last year. Asking him about me and whether we had any kids, and all that—' She fell silent and Betty squeezed her hand. She knew that Olive still grieved over the baby she had lost during one of those terrible air-raids. The words the Queen had spoken to Olive's soldier husband then had given her a lot of comfort, and she treasured them still.

'Well, that's what I mean,' Gladys said. 'There's people like you and Derek – and poor Kathy Simmons, she got *killed* that night – and all those others who did just as much as I did during the blitz, fighting fires and putting out incendiaries and getting rid of bombs, and ending up hurt or dead themselves. Why should *I* get a medal, and not them? It don't seem right.'

'Don't talk so daft,' Olive Harker said stoutly. 'You drove that old van all through the blitz, you went down that bombed cellar and saved that little girl, you went in that house that could've fallen down round your ears at any minute and fetched out that little baby, you did all sorts of things. You were lucky to get away with a broken arm. Of course you deserve a medal. You're a heroine.'

'I'm not!' Gladys said sharply. 'I'm no different to all the others. I just happened to get noticed, that's all. And don't forget there's a lot of people I didn't save.' She fell silent, biting her lip as she remembered the family of little Ruth in the cellar, staring with sightless eyes as she struggled to free the child from the rubble. The tiny baby she'd found wrapped in blankets under the stairs, its mother blown to fragments in the room above. The men and women and children she had taken in her rickety ambulance through streets of flames, to hospitals that might not even exist by the time she reached them.

And Graham Philpotts, the young sailor with the red hair and cheeky grin, who had died from the blast of a land-mine in the doorway of Portsmouth's Royal Hospital, on the night of 17 April 1941.

Betty watched her friend. She saw the tears in Gladys's eyes and knew what she was thinking. She was sad about Graham too – he'd been her boyfriend for a while, they'd even talked about getting married. But she knew it must be much worse for Gladys to feel she was responsible for his death.

'It wasn't your fault,' she said gently, as she'd already said a hundred times. 'You weren't to know what was going to happen. And you'd had enough that night. You were out on your feet. Someone had to drive the van.'

'It should have been me.' Gladys looked again at the medal. 'It was Graham should have got this, not me.'

The girls were silent for a few moments. Betty glanced around the room. It was the family living room, with the furniture her mother and father had collected over the years – a square dining-table with four chairs, a couple of armchairs for Ted and Annie, a dresser which showed off their best tea-set. In one corner was the cabinet that Betty's brother Colin had built before he joined the Navy, to house the gramophone. He'd been mad about Joe Loss and Glenn Miller, and his records were stored in the cupboard underneath the speaker.

It seemed a long time since he'd sat in this room and listened to them, winding the gramophone up after every fourth tune. A long time since he'd swung in through the door in his bell-bottoms, his face wreathed in a cheery grin. Betty missed him badly.

She missed Dennis too, and once again she wished she could bring him here. So far, she'd not said much to her family about the young man she had met on the farm where she worked as a Land Girl. Once you brought a chap home, it was considered 'serious', and although Betty and Dennis had always been very serious about each other, she knew that it would take time for her family to accept him. And the way her father was now, he might never come round to it.

'Have you made up your mind about the Wrens?' she asked Gladys.

Gladys nodded. 'I'm going down the recruiting office as soon as I can. I went before, but they wouldn't have me till me arm was better. Dad don't like the idea much but I can't help that. He's living in the Dark Ages if he thinks he can tell me to stay at home. We've all got to do our bit.'

'I know.' Olive sighed. 'I've almost decided to go for the ATS, but I still haven't talked to Derek about it. He was home on a weekend pass a couple of weeks ago, but you know how it is – we never seemed to get round to talking about things. Anyway, it didn't seem right to spoil his time at home going on about the war. All he wanted to do was – well, *you* know' – she blushed '—and go to the pictures and things like that.' She smiled. 'We went to the Regent to see Arthur Askey and Richard Murdoch in *The Ghost*

Train – it was ever so funny. We nearly fell out of our seats laughing. And they've got George Formby coming to the Odeon next week, in person, to raise funds for air-raid victims. I reckon I might go – why don't you come as well? It'd do you good to have a bit of a laugh.'

'I don't know, I might.' Gladys spoke without enthusiasm. She really did seem down, Betty thought. Perhaps she'd be better once she was doing something again – either back at the First Aid Post, or in the Wrens.

The front doorbell rang shrilly and Betty got up to answer it. She came back into the room a minute or two later with Gladys's younger sister Diane behind her. Diane's face was pink and excited.

'I thought you'd be here. Guess what! I've got a job.'

'What sort of a job?' Gladys stared at her. 'You've already got a job, at the laundry. I didn't know you'd got the sack.'

'I didn't.' Diane tossed her head. She'd had her fair hair cut short lately and it clustered in tight curls round her small face. She was wearing a summer frock with short sleeves and her arms were sunburnt. 'I'm fed up with the laundry. I've got a job at Airspeed.'

'Airspeed? What, making aeroplanes?'

'That's right. I daresay I'll learn to fly them too.' Her tone was casual but the three older girls could tell that she was smouldering with excitement. 'I think that's the best thing anyone could do, don't you? Fly in a plane, up there in the sky.' She glanced towards the window, at the blue square that could be seen through the top of the pane. 'Better'n driving an old van round the streets.'

'Now just you look here, Diane Shaw—' Gladys began, but Olive stopped her with a hand on her arm.

'She don't mean anything, Glad.' She looked at Diane. 'You don't really think you'll be allowed to fly, do you? I mean, everyone knows about Amy Johnson, but they won't let ordinary girls like us fly in the war.'

'Won't they? I bet they will. Women are going to do everything in this war.' Diane's blue eyes glittered. 'There aren't going to be enough men to do the jobs, are there? We'll be doing it all, so that men can go off and join the Forces. And we'll be joining alongside 'em soon, and fighting as well. I tell you what, if we don't make up our own minds what to do they'll make them up for us. And I'm not waiting to be told – I know what *I* want to do.'

There was a moment's silence. Then Gladys laughed uneasily and said, 'Hark at you!' She turned to the other two. 'Our Di always did think she knew it all. I can just guess what our Dad'll have to say about it.'

'He's not getting the chance,' Diane declared, much as Gladys herself had done only ten minutes earlier. 'He can't stop me going to work at Airspeed, and once I'm there he won't be able to do a thing about it. Anyway, I'll probably join the WAAF in a year or so. That's where I'll get the best chance of learning to fly.'

'Learn to fly!' Gladys said scornfully. 'You've got as much chance as I have of steering the *Ark Royal*. The nearest you'll get to flying is walking past an airman in the street.'

'All the same, she's right about some of it,' Olive said. 'Women *are* starting to do all the jobs that men have been doing. And the papers are full of advertisements asking girls to join up. How do we know what we'll be having to do in a few months' time? After all, you'd never have guessed this time last year that you'd be driving an ambulance through air-raids and winning medals, would you?' She thought for a few minutes. 'I'll tell you something else. I reckon she's right about us not having the choice if we wait much longer. We're just the age to get called up, and if I've got to go I want to go into the Army, like my Derek. He'll be home again this weekend – I'll talk to him about it the minute he gets here.'

'But you're a married woman,' Gladys said. 'Surely they won't—'

'Married!' Olive said bitterly. 'You'd hardly know it, would you. You could count the nights Derek and me have had together on your fingers, and still have a few left over to mash the potatoes. I don't reckon that counts for anything these days.'

'Not even if you had a baby?'

'I'm not going to have a baby,' Olive said shortly. 'Not until the war's good and over, anyway.' She got up abruptly. 'I've got to go now, Glad. Mum and Dad are down North End with Granny and Grandpa and I promised to go and meet them so that Mum could go straight to the First Aid Post and I could walk back with Dad. He's still poorly, you know. I wonder sometimes if he'll ever get over that turn he had during the bombing.'

She walked out, and Gladys gave Betty a rueful look.

'I'm a twerp, I really am. I don't know how I could have said that to Olive about babies. One of these days I'm going to open my mouth and shove my foot so far down it I'll swallow my toes.'

'I know. I say things without meaning to as well. But you can't keep on remembering, can you – not when there's so many other things to think about all the time. And we've all got our own worries.'

'Well, we'll have to be going too,' Gladys said, getting up. She looked at her sister, who had opened the gramophone door and started to look through the records. She was humming one of the Glenn Miller tunes, and Betty felt a lump in her throat as she remembered Colin again. *String of Pearls* had been one of his favourites. 'Come on, Di. Tell us a bit more about this job of yours. You're not really going to be helping to build planes, are you?'

Betty went back to the farm next day. She'd been hoping to see Dennis while she was home, but as usual he'd been called out to help deal with some unexploded bombs that had been discovered out at Southsea. You never knew when they were going to turn up, and they always had to be disposed of straight away. The fact that they might have lain there for months didn't mean they weren't going to go off.

'A lot of them are timed,' he'd told Betty. 'Some have delaying mechanisms and their timing doesn't start until they're disturbed, or they might be set like an alarm clock, to go off after a few days – or even months. We can't take any risks with them.'

Betty shuddered. She hated thinking about what Dennis did, even though she admired and loved him for doing it.

'I don't know anyone as brave as you,' she said, and Dennis laughed and hugged her.

'Everybody's brave in this war. We just have different ways of showing it.'

He came out to the farm to see her a couple of days later and she told him about Gladys's medal.

'She doesn't seem to want it at all. I mean, she's thrilled in a way, of course she is, but she doesn't think she deserves it any more than anyone else. It's like you said – *everyone's* brave. Why should just a few be picked out?'

'Because that's the only way you can do it,' Dennis said. 'You can't give everyone a medal just for being alive now – it wouldn't mean anything. I suppose in a way, it isn't Gladys who's getting the medal, but all the ambulance drivers who do the sort of work she does. She's a sort of representative.'

'I reckon you deserve a medal,' Betty said. 'Doing what you do.'

'But I couldn't do it without the Pioneers digging the shafts and the rest of the crew. So if I did get a medal – which I hope I won't – it'll belong to them as much as to me.' He was silent for a moment, then said, 'I'm sorry I couldn't get to see you in Pompey. I wanted to see where you live – and meet your family.'

Betty bit her lip. She met his eyes. They were serious, their hazel light darkened. She sighed.

'You know what I think, Dennis. I *want* you to meet them. I really do. I want them to meet you, to know what a smashing chap I've got. But – I don't think it's a good idea. Not just yet.'

'Is it your dad still?' he asked quietly.

'Yes. He's not getting any better, you see. He's a bag of nerves. And anything that upsets him – well, the doctor says we've got to be really careful or it'll just set him back.'

'And meeting me would upset him.'

'It's not you,' she said quickly. 'I mean, it's not you as a person. It's – it's—'

'It's me as a CO,' he said. 'A conscientious objector. That's what would upset him, isn't it? Someone who refused to fight in the war.'

'You have to understand him,' Betty said. 'I mean, people like us – like him – well, we don't think that way. We think what we've been brought up to think, I suppose. Same as you.'

'No. I was brought up to think for myself.'

'Well, so was I!' she said quickly, then shook her head. 'No, maybe I wasn't. Not in the same way. But you still think the same as your dad, don't you? He was a CO in the last war. And you're one in this. So how d'you know you *are* thinking for yourself?'

Dennis smiled. 'Well, perhaps I might not have known at first. But a few months in prison would soon have told me if I wasn't. And they didn't make any difference to what I thought, did they? No, Betty, I'm pretty convinced about what I'm doing. And I feel a lot better for it now I'm in bomb disposal.' He glanced at her. 'Wouldn't that make your dad feel any different?'

'It might. Well, I'm sure it would. But – he's been through a lot, you know. The first war – and then Dunkirk. And that really was brave. He used to hate even taking the ferryboat across the harbour at night during the raids. Going all that way – and being bombed – and seeing other ships go down, and all those soldiers . . .' She shuddered. 'The doctor said it was all too much for him even though it didn't come out for months, not until that night he was firewatching on top of our turret. It was building up inside him all that time and he just couldn't take any more, and broke down. We've just got to wait till he gets better.'

Dennis nodded. 'I know. I do understand, Betty. And I'd be happy to wait, if only . . .' He took her hand and stroked it gently. '. . . If only we knew things were going to turn out all right for us. If only we could look ahead.'

Betty met his eyes and felt a deep quiver of fear. She knew what Dennis meant. If he didn't meet her family soon, he might never meet them. Life was uncertain for everyone these days, but for no one was it less certain than the members of the bomb disposal crews.

The next bomb might be his last.

'I want to marry you, Betty,' he said softly, drawing her close into his arms. 'But I want it to be with your family's blessing. I don't want anything coming between you and them – just in case . . .'

Betty stared at him, then flung herself hard against him, gripping his body against hers, burrowing her face into his chest.

'Don't say things like that, Dennis! Don't. It frightens me too much. I want to hold you tight and never let go of you. I want you to stay with me, and not go back to those horrible bombs. I don't care about my family, I don't care about anyone else – I just want *you.*'

But it wasn't true, and they both knew it. Families were important. Families, friends, strangers, people they would never even meet – all were important. That was why Betty was working on the farm, toiling until her back was almost breaking, freezing in winter, almost melting in summer. That was why Dennis spent his days at the bottom of a deep shaft, often knee-deep in mud, working painstakingly on a bomb that might explode and shatter his body at any second.

That was what the war was all about.

'So what would you be doing in the ATS?' Derek Harker asked his wife.

They were sitting in the Chapmans' front room. It was understood that when Derek was home on one of his short leaves this room belonged to him and Olive. They'd put out a few of their wedding presents, to make it feel a bit more like their own home, and even Annie wouldn't come in without knocking. Tonight, Derek had brought Olive a bunch of flowers – big coloured daisies and a few Sweet Williams – from Atkinson's, the greengrocer's at the top of March Street, and she'd arranged them in the glass vase Jess and Frank had given them.

Olive sat down and snuggled into the curve of his arm.

'I don't know. But there was a bit in the paper about it last week.' She sat up and reached for a sheet of newspaper on the shelf. It was from the

Evening News, dated 11 June, and the headline read: *War Work With A Punch In It For Girls*. Olive began to read aloud, stopping to make her own comments.

'There's ever so many different things you can do. Some of the girls are trained as gunner girls.'

'What, firing guns?' Derek interrupted. 'I didn't think they let girls do that.'

'I don't think they actually fire them.' Olive read on. 'No, it says the girls spot the raiders and direct the fire. The actual laying and firing – what's laying, I wonder? – is done by men. But it's just as important, the paper says. The girls wear battledress and work under the same conditions as the men, and share their mess and all that.' She gave Derek a mischievous grin. 'It's all right, they do sleep separate! Or I could work in Signals. That sounds interesting. It says here you're right in the "nerve centre" of the Army, replacing signals officers all over the country. I might go anywhere!' She saw his face and added hurriedly, 'Mind, being married I expect they'd try and keep me around here. Or I might get sent down to Wiltshire. That'd be the ticket, wouldn't it, if we were in the same camp.'

'I'll believe that when I see it,' Derek said cynically, but he added, 'Go on, Livvy. What else does it say?'

'They're looking for women with a bit more schooling too,' she said, her finger on the small print. 'They train you for whatever you're going to do, of course, but they don't need any standard of education for those jobs. Just as well!' She laughed. 'But anyone who stayed on and got School Certificate or anything like that, they'll get put with the Royal Artillery on anti-aircraft and searchlight batteries, or even in gunnery research. If you're on that you have to go to a "famous army school of research" – it doesn't say where, of course – and you have a special uniform. It's a white skirt and dark blue jacket and a forage cap in pale and dark blue. Doesn't that sound nice! Better than khaki.'

'Sounds a bit conspicuous to me,' Derek said. 'You'd be seen miles away.'

'It's meant to be. It was designed in 1600. They didn't do camouflage then, they wanted to make sure everyone knew which side they were on.'

'They never had women soldiers then!'

Olive read it again. 'Well, perhaps not. It's been designed to match the men's uniforms, but they were designed then, so it comes to the same thing. Still, I don't suppose I'll be doing that. We never did science at school.'

'Is that all? What about office jobs? That's what you're good at.'

Olive didn't hear him. She was still reading the article.

'Here's something that'd suit Gladys Shaw. They have drivers too, for convoy driving. They take trucks and lorries and all sorts – even tanks, I wouldn't be surprised – all over Britain. Sometimes they're away from headquarters for four or five nights.' She lifted her head and gazed at her husband, her eyes shining. 'Think of it. Cornwall this week, the Highlands of Scotland the next. I've always wanted to go to those places. Oh, I *wish* I'd learnt to drive when Gladys did!'

'Well, I'm not sorry you didn't,' Derek declared. 'Look, Livvy, I don't want to stand in your light, but how d'you think I'd feel, never knowing where you were? I mean, it's bad enough now when we hear there's been a raid on Pompey and I don't know if you were in it. But if you were driving all over the country, I'd be scared all the time that you'd been in some place that had got hit. And Army camps aren't the safest places to be in, you know. The Germans aim for them more than anything.'

'I know.' She laid the newspaper down and sighed. 'Don't you want me to go and register, Derek? Only I just can't stand seeing Gladys with her broken arm and her medal and thinking I'm not doing anything at all. And I think girls like me are going to be called up soon anyway.'

Derek didn't answer at once. Then he said slowly, 'I wish you didn't *have* to do it, Livvy. I don't like the idea that girls have to get mixed up in this war. But there it is, and if you've got to join up I'd rather you were doing something you enjoyed.' He repeated his previous question. 'What about office jobs? There must be plenty of those, and you've got good experience.'

Olive wrinkled her nose. 'To tell you the truth, Derek, I'd be glad to get out of the office. I've never really liked being stuck behind a desk messing about with invoices and such. Some of these jobs sound really interesting. And I'd feel I was *doing* something.' Her eyes strayed again to the headline and the photograph of ATS girls in their uniforms, lining up for parade.

'You'd be doing something in an office,' Derek pointed out, but his voice sounded half-hearted, as if he knew that she really didn't want to be persuaded. 'Well, what sort of pay will you get? I've heard it's pretty low. D'you think you'll be able to manage? I'll send you mine of course, same as I've been doing,'

Olive shook her head. 'Oh, I shan't need to use any of that, Derek. We'll put it away. I want to save up for our home, when all this is over.' She looked back at the newspaper. 'There's a bit here about the pay. Some girls only start at two shillings a day – mind, that's for Sundays as well, so that's fourteen shillings a week – but if you get promoted you can be getting nearly thirty-five bob a week. And all found. No rent or bills to pay, all your food provided, *and* all your clothes. Even your toothbrush! And they keep up the National Insurance, so there's really nothing to come out of that, it's all pocket-money. I should be able to save quite a bit.'

'You know you're going to get promoted then?' he said with a grin.

'I'm going to try my best to be,' Olive declared. She looked at him again. 'Derek, I'm sorry if you don't like it. I could always see if I can get out of it, if you really want me to. I mean, I'm working for your dad in his office – they might let me off.'

'How long for? They'd be calling you up soon anyway.' He shook his head. 'No, I reckon we've got to make the best of it, Livvy, and like I said before, I'd rather you were happy.' He reached out and drew her close again. 'Matter of fact, I think I'll be rather proud of you when you're in uniform. And I'll tell you what—' his face was very close to hers now, his lips brushing her cheek in the way that made her stomach quiver '—I've never kissed a soldier before. It'll be a new experience for me!'

'Derek Harker!' Olive pulled away, pretending to be shocked, and then laughed and let him pull her close again. 'I should just hope you haven't,' she murmured into his neck. 'So you'd better start getting some practice in now, hadn't you, for when I come home in khaki.'

With a swift movement, Derek slid her into a lying position on the settee. He lay above her, resting on his elbows, and looked down into her face. She stared back at him, her heart beating quickly, a teasing, provocative smile on her lips.

'Oh, Livvy,' he said, and his voice came out like a groan. 'Why do we have to be apart? Why can't we be together like this all the time? This bloody, *bloody* war . . .'

2

At first, Jess Budd hardly noticed the old man, shuffling slowly along September Street on that bright June morning of 1941. There were too many like him these days – homeless victims of the blitz that had torn their city to shreds during the past few months. They were housed in church halls or schools, anywhere where a few mattresses could be spread out and people fed while the authorities tried to find them somewhere else to live. And with their workplaces destroyed too, as often as not, there was nothing else to do but wander the streets.

Jess felt sorry for him. He might have only just been bombed out, she thought, glancing at the face behind the straggling grey whiskers, the eyes peering through thick glasses. There had been a raid on Portsmouth the night before, and a huge bomb had dropped in Torrington Road. It had burrowed its way beneath the houses and failed to explode, and there were cordons around it now while they decided what to do about it.

Two nights before that, there had been a bigger raid, which had hit this part of Portsmouth badly. The Germans had dropped a number of high explosive bombs and several oil bombs which had killed some of the soldiers in the RAOC camp nearby. A few houses had caught fire, others had lost their windows. Some of the side streets were still impassable, and the dust of the blast still hung in the warm June air, the peculiarly acrid smell of explosives tingling in the nostrils.

Jess looked at the old man again, hesitating, uncertain whether she knew him. There was something familiar, a half-memory . . . And he was looking at her too, with that same tentative expression.

But no, she had never seen him before, she was sure of it. And he looked so vague and bewildered – why, he probably hardly remembered his own family, the people he lived with, let alone strangers in the street.

She could feel little Maureen tugging at her hand. Jess had let her walk up the street this morning rather than make her get into the pram, and now the little girl was looking frightened, wanting to get away from this strange, whiskery old man. Poor old chap, she thought, giving him an apologetic smile. It isn't his fault. It's this cruel war. It destroys everyone, from the tiniest baby to the oldest person. People who don't even know what it's all about.

She turned and went into the newsagent's shop. Alice Brunner and her daughter Joy were marking up newspapers. Alice smiled at Maureen and gave her a piece of string off the bales, and Joy tickled her to make her laugh.

'We're all behind like a donkey's tail this morning,' Alice said, brushing back her wispy hair. 'All the trains were late, so of course that means all the papers were too, and Joy's got to do the deliveries herself, or else people will have to come and get their own. It's always the same after a raid.'

'But what's happened to the boys?' Jess asked. 'You've still got a few doing deliveries, haven't you?'

'Oh, there's three or four who haven't been evacuated, yes. But Jacky Watson and Gerald Bone, they're both Boy Scouts and they're on message duty during raids, so they won't be fit for much, and young Curly Brown's got himself a job now and if the papers aren't here by eight he can't do it. And there's not many more boys about.' She flipped over a pile of *Daily Mirrors*. 'That Micky Baxter keeps on at me to give him a round, but I wouldn't employ him if he was the last boy on earth. Why, I daren't even turn my back when he's in the shop. You don't know what might be missing.'

Jess sighed and nodded. 'He's a real little scamp. That's about the only good thing about my Tim and Keith being out in the country – it keeps them away from him. When I think it could have been them, playing around the bombed houses and getting themselves blown up like poor little Cyril Nash, and Jimmy Cross . . .'

'And Micky Baxter gets away with it,' Alice nodded. 'It don't seem fair, does it. But then there's plenty in this war that isn't fair.'

She turned away quickly, and Jess knew that she was thinking of her husband Heinrich, interned at the beginning of the war simply because he was a German, even though he'd lived in Portsmouth for twenty years.

She glanced anxiously at Alice's back. For a long time, she and the rest of the people around September Street who knew and liked the Brunners had been afraid that Alice was going to have a complete breakdown after Heinrich had been taken away and then posted missing after the sinking of the *Arandora Star*. Other internees on the torpedoed ship were known to have died, the luckier ones had been rescued and either taken on to Canada or brought back to the Isle of Man, but there had never been any word of Heinrich. Alice had spent her days watching for him, sometimes convinced he must be still alive, sometimes miserably certain he had died, and all the time growing greyer, thinner and more bitter.

She was looking better now, Jess thought as she paid for her newspaper. And her manner was brighter too, as if she'd come to some decision. Perhaps she'd come to terms with the fact that Heinrich must be dead, and made up her mind to go on living, if only for her daughter Joy's sake.

Alice marked up the last *Daily Express* and put down her pencil with a sigh of relief. 'There, that's all done. You can start doing the deliveries now, Joy. Take the ones furthest away, anyone nearby can pop in. I'll have a cup of tea ready when you get back.' She looked at Jess. 'I don't know what I'd do without my Joy. She's a real help – a proper little godsend. Joy by name and joy by nature, that's her. Off you go, now.'

Joy nodded and shoved a stack of papers into the delivery sack. She went out to the back of the shop to fetch her bike. As she did so, the shop door opened with a little 'ping' from the bell and an old man shuffled in.

Jess glanced round. It was the old man she had seen outside. He stood at the door, staring in as if he weren't quite sure why he had come, and she looked at Alice.

There was an odd expression on her friend's face. The same feeling that Jess had experienced – that she knew the man, that he had once been familiar to her. And a growing excitement, followed swiftly by disbelief – as if she were determined not to give way to it, not to be disappointed.

'Yes?' she said, and her voice shook a little. 'What can I get for you?'

The old man gazed at her. His face was thick with grey whiskers, ragged and dirty as though they hadn't been attended to for some time. He wore an old cap that came down over his forehead, and his eyes were hidden behind the pebble-lensed glasses. But he didn't seem to be able to see very well all the same, for he took them off and Jess saw the mild brown eyes beneath, fixed on Alice, intent, as if begging her to understand.

'Alice?' he said at last, and his voice sounded rusty, as if it hadn't been used much lately. 'Alice? Don't you know me?'

Jess stared at him. She felt her heart turn over, very slowly, and her blood seemed to stand still in her veins. Then she saw Alice sway, and stepped forward quickly to catch her in her arms.

'It's me, Alice,' she heard him say, as she held her friend's quivering body. 'It's Heinrich. I've come home . . .'

'Now, that really *is* a bit of good news,' Annie Chapman said. 'Isn't it, Ted? And about time too. I bet Alice Brunner doesn't know where to put herself. She's been really down ever since Heinrich was took away.'

'I know. Mind, she's been picking up a bit lately.' Jess had come straight down from September Street to tell her sister about Heinrich's return. 'But you should have seen her face. It was like watching someone arrive at the gates of Heaven.' She stopped, blushing a little. She didn't normally talk like that, especially to Annie who was so practical and down to earth. But that *was* what Alice's face had looked like. As if the sun had come out for her again.

'Well, I couldn't be more pleased,' Annie declared. She looked at the clock on the mantelpiece. 'I thought our Olive would have been home by now. She promised she'd be back in time for me to go down the Post.' She refilled her sister Jess's teacup and looked enquiringly at her husband. Ted shook his head morosely.

'You know I can't drink it if it's not sweet. And I can't stand those saccharin things.'

'Well, you can't have any more sugar. That's your ration gone for this week. It's either get used to the saccharin or go without.' Annie's voice had a sharp edge to it and she stopped abruptly and bit her lip. She bent and picked up Maureen, who was playing on the floor with a few clothes pegs. 'D'you want a sip of my tea, pet, before you and your mum have to go home?'

'I'll stop on for a bit if you like, till Olive gets back,' Jess offered. She knew that Annie didn't like to leave Ted on his own these days. Mind, this afternoon there didn't seem to be all that much wrong with him, but he was that changeable, it sometimes only needed a sudden noise from outside to set him off. And if there was a raid, like last night . . .

'It's all right,' Ted said suddenly, almost as if he could read her thoughts. 'I'm not a babe in arms. I won't start playing with the gas taps or setting fire to the house the minute you turn your back.'

Jess felt her cheeks turn scarlet. She glanced quickly at her sister and saw that Annie had gone white. *Playing with the gas taps* . . . Was that what she was afraid of – that Ted would do something really daft if he was left alone?

'I never meant—' she began, but Annie interrupted her.

'Don't be a bigger fool than you can help, Ted Chapman. Nobody's suggesting any such thing. You know you don't like being by yourself these days, and all we're trying to do is make sure you've got a bit of company. There's no need to be objectionable about it.' She tipped a tiny saccharin tablet into her tea and stirred fiercely. 'You just say, the minute you want to go back to work and I'm sure we'll all be only too pleased.'

There was a brief, embarrassed silence. Jess hadn't heard her sister speak so sharply to Ted since the night she'd come home from one of the big raids and found him curled up on the top of the little turret roof, crying like a baby. He'd been ordered to bed by the doctor and stayed there, apparently helpless, for a week or more. And when he got up, he'd been like an old man, shuffling downstairs, unable to do anything more for himself than get dressed and take himself to the lavatory.

He'd improved a bit since then, but he still spent most of the time sitting in his chair, doing nothing and hardly speaking. It was shock, the doctor had said, shock from the raids and having to ferry his boat across the harbour between Portsmouth and Gosport day in, day out, and most of all shock from the experience of Dunkirk, when he'd taken the little *Ferry King* across the Channel to rescue the battered soldiers of the BEF.

'But that was months ago,' Annie had expostulated, but the doctor had shaken her head.

'It happens that way sometimes. It must have been building up inside all the time, and that last raid was just too much for him.' She sighed. 'It was too much for a lot of people.'

'But what are we going to do? Is he ever going to get better?'

'I hope so. But it'll take time, and a lot of patience. You can't hurry these things along.'

'And what are we going to do for money?' Annie had said to Jess after the doctor had gone. 'I mean, we're all right for a while, the Friendly Society will pay out. But that only goes on for so long. Suppose he can never go back to work?'

She didn't say those things to Ted. The doctor had impressed upon her the need to be gentle with him, not to reproach him or make him feel guilty. And that was difficult for Annie, for although she was a good nurse, she was also inclined to be a sharp-tongued one, and she had never had any time for malingerers. And although she knew really that Ted wasn't swinging the lead, sometimes when she looked at him, sitting in his chair staring at nothing when other people were working all the hours God sent to help in the war effort – and when their own daughter Betty was working in the Land Army, and their son Colin risking his life at sea aboard HMS *Exeter* – well, it was hard not to say anything.

Now and then, her control snapped. She was always sorry the minute the words were out, but that wouldn't call them back. But he'd scared her, talking about gas taps like that.

'I can't think where Olive's got to,' she said at last, more for something to say than because she was really worried. 'She knew I'd be waiting.'

'She's probably gassing with Gladys Shaw,' Jess said, and turned scarlet again. She could have picked a better word! 'Or maybe she's popped up to see Florrie Harker.'

'I doubt it. She and Florrie don't see eye to eye these days. Mother-in-law trouble. Florrie seems to think our Livvy's stolen her little boy away. Well, It stands to reason he'd want to spend his time with his wife when he gets a couple of days' leave, but Florrie don't seem to see it that way.'

'Derek does go to see her when he's here, though, doesn't he?'

'Oh yes, he pops in, and he and Olive go up there for tea. But that's not enough for Mrs Harker, she wants him spending the evening there. She'd like to have him stopping the night too, but of course he won't, not when there's a nice double bed here.'

The gate clicked and Olive appeared in the open doorway. She was flushed from the sun and her eyes were bright. She looked at her parents and her aunt, and gave a queer little laugh.

'Hello! You look as if you're waiting for someone famous. Is the Queen dropping in for tea?'

'You're the most famous person we're waiting for,' Annie said tartly. 'I was expecting you half an hour ago. Where've you been?' She was already on her feet, gathering together the things she needed to take to the First Aid Post. 'And what have you been up to? You've got a funny look about you.'

'It'll be even funnier when I get into uniform,' Olive said, rather breathlessly. 'I've joined up, Mum. I've volunteered for the ATS. I couldn't sit around any longer, messing about with invoices and worksheets for Mr Harker. *She* can do that. I'm going to do my bit to help my country. And don't say I can't,' she added quickly. 'I've done it, and that's that.'

'You've joined up? Oh, *Olive.*' Annie sat down quickly, as if she were afraid that her legs would fold beneath her. Her face was white. 'But – you're a married woman. What's your Derek going to say?'

'A married woman! I reckon we can forget all about that, as long as this war's on,' Olive said sarcastically. 'What sort of a married life have me and Derek got to look forward to? A day here, a night there – and that's if he stays in England. If he goes abroad, that's it for the duration. I'm not going to sit at home twiddling my thumbs while other people win the war for me. I want to do my bit as well. And Derek agrees. We talked about it last weekend. Anyway, even if he didn't—' She shrugged. 'I'd just go and do it anyway.'

'And that's what this bloody war's doing for us,' Ted said suddenly. 'Killing all our best men, taking husbands away from their wives and sons away from their mothers, and now it's making respectable young women forget what their place really is. *Go and do it anyway!*' He glared at Olive. 'I'd like to hear your mother dare speak to me like that. A man should be master in his own house, and it seems to me you haven't even asked your husband's permission.'

'No, and nor am I asking your permission to go and do First Aid,' Annie said curtly. 'Olive's right. We've all got to do our bit, and we've got to make up our own minds about it. If Livvy thinks she ought to go, it's not for me or you to stop her.' She looked at her daughter. 'If you'd asked me, I'd have said no,' she said quietly. 'I don't want you to go, any more than I wanted our Betty to go off and join the Land Army. But everything's different now, and you've made your choice. I'll help you all I can.'

Olive's eyes filled with tears. She got up and went to her mother, laying her bright, chestnut head against the greying hair.

'I don't know if I'm right or wrong. I just felt I had to do it. We *can't* stop at home and do nothing – not girls like me. We've got to do whatever we can.' She looked pleadingly at her father. 'Can't you understand that, Dad?'

'I don't understand nothing these days,' he grumbled. 'The whole world's turned upside down, if you ask me. Young girls driving buses, talking about going in the Forces just as if they was men. Married women out at work when they ought to be home minding their babies—' He caught Annie's eye and scowled. 'All right, then, minding their own business. But ain't that just what I'm saying? Girls like our Olive, they ought to be thinking about nappies, not worrying about uniforms. Nothing's what it oughter be, these days.'

'You don't have to tell me that, Dad,' Olive said. 'Don't you think that's what I'd rather be doing?'

There was a brief silence. Annie looked at Jess and then sighed and said, 'Well, it seems there's no more to be said. Olive's joined up and that's all there is to it. And I've got to get off down to the Post. We've been busy enough lately, Lord knows what they'll send us tonight. Now, will you be all right, Ted? You know, you could always come and give us a hand.'

Once again, just as she was about to depart, the gate clicked. This time it was Rose, Jess's elder daughter, who stood in the doorway. Her dark hair was untidy, her face pale and upset.

'I've just been up to Joy's,' she said. 'I've seen her dad.'

'I know,' Jess said quickly. 'I was there when he came in. It's the best news we've had for weeks. Isn't it nice for Joy to have her dad home again?'

'I don't know,' Rose said, coming in. 'He doesn't look the same as he used to. He's grown a beard, it doesn't look a bit nice, and he's dressed in some horrible dirty old clothes. His feet were all blisters, Mum. And he looks hungry.' Her voice shook. 'He's changed, Mum. He used to smile at me, he used to be nice. He used to be so clean and tidy, and now he just looks like a dirty old tramp and he didn't want me there, he wouldn't look at me properly and his eyes were all sort of angry. He used to call me his Rosebud. What's happened to him, Mum? What have they done to him?'

Jess drew her close and looked at her sister. 'She's right,' she said quietly. 'He *is* different. I saw it too.' Her voice quickened with anger. 'They promised they'd look after the people they interned,' she said. 'What *have* they been doing to him? Where's he been, all this past year? And why have they sent him home like that now, in dirty clothes, making him walk with blisters on his feet?'

'I told you,' Ted said bitterly. 'It's this bloody war. It's turned the whole world upside down.'

The news of Heinrich's return spread fast. It was the first bit of good news for some time and was the main subject of conversation for several days. The only person not to be pleased was Ethel Glaister, from number 15 April Grove.

'They're daft, letting that lot loose again,' she said to Jess and Peggy Shaw, on the pavement. 'I mean, it's obvious they took them away for a reason. They're all foreigners – Jerries, Eyeties, they're all the enemy. They had 'em safe behind bars. Why let 'em out to roam the streets again, spying and causing trouble?'

'Heinrich Brunner's never caused trouble in his life,' Jess retorted. 'And I don't suppose the others did either. Otherwise they wouldn't be letting them go, would they? It stands to reason.'

'Stands to reason?' Ethel repeated scornfully. 'Huh! Nothing stands to reason these days. If you ask me, there's not one of 'em knows what they're doing. All running round like headless chickens, they are, not knowing what to do next. And that Churchill's no better than the rest. Sticking his fingers up in the air and trying to pretend everything's all right. Who does he think he's fooling?'

'He doesn't try to pretend it's all right,' Peggy said. 'He tells us plain – blood, sweat, toil and tears. But he puts heart into us all the same, somehow or other. I reckon we'd be in a worse state without him.'

Ethel sniffed. It wasn't often she deigned to talk to her neighbours, and even less often that they wanted her to, but she had to pass on her opinions to someone. She sought for something crushing to say, but just at that moment Bert Shaw came out of his house. He'd not been long home from work and had taken his shirt off to wash in the scullery. His braces dangled round his waist.

'I just heard on the wireless,' he said. 'They've got that Hess up at Aldershot. Tried to throw hisself down a staircase to commit suicide.'

'He never!' Peggy said. 'What happened? Is he dead?'

Bert snorted. 'No, worse luck – just broke his leg, that's all. Poor sort of a leader he's turned out to be – can't even make a job of killing hisself. I reckon old Adolf's washed his hands of him.'

'He did that in the first place,' Jess remarked, 'when Hess parachuted into Scotland on his peace mission.'

'*If* that's what it was,' Bert said. 'I wouldn't trust any of those Jerries further than I could throw 'em.'

'And that's just what I'm saying,' Ethel Glaister cut in eagerly. 'I wouldn't, either. That's why I think they're mad, letting all these aliens out again. Ought to keep 'em locked up for the duration, that's what, and I don't care who hears me say so.'

'Oh, for goodness sake,' Jess said disgustedly. 'This is where we came in. Heinrich Brunner isn't an *alien*, he's as good as you or me – a sight *better* than you, if you want my opinion – and I'm glad he's back. And I reckon everyone else round here is too – everyone with any sense, that is.' She glared at Ethel, daring her to answer. 'And I wouldn't advise you to go saying those sorts of things up round the shop, either. You'll have Alice after you. *She* won't take no nasty remarks about Heinrich.'

Ethel sniffed again and put her nose into the air. Her yellow hair had been permed again and lay in the metallic ridges of Marcel waves against her head. It looked as if she'd got a brass cap on.

'Pardon me for breathing,' she said haughtily. 'I was only trying to be neighbourly, after all – expressing an opinion. I thought we were supposed to be allowed to do that in this country, I thought that was what this war was all about, but it seems I'm wrong. And I'm sure I'd never dream of saying anything at all near Alice Brunner, or her shop. I never go in there. I don't even walk past it if I can help it.'

She turned and stalked on her high heels past Jess's front door and into her own house. The door slammed behind her.

'Nasty little cat,' Peggy said. 'I reckon the war was the best thing that ever happened to poor George. He must thank God on his knees every day for being able to join the Army and get away from her.'

'It's right, what she says,' Jess said. 'She crosses the road now, rather than walk past Alice's. I've seen her do it.'

'Oh, she's just plain stupid,' Peggy said dismissively. 'Not worth bothering about.'

'Tell you what else I heard on the wireless,' Bert said. 'They reckon Hitler's just about ready to invade Russia.'

The two women stared at him.

'But Russia's enormous. How can he ever hope to take over a big country like that?'

'Yes, but it's mostly empty,' Bert said. 'All the people are clustered up this end, see. So once he's got places like Moscow and Leningrad, he can take the rest of it easy. It'll be handed over on a plate.'

'But can't anyone stop him?' Jess asked.

Bert shrugged. 'I daresay we'll try. But Finland'll go in with him, see. That'll give him a bigger army. And he's got thousands already. The Russians'll have a fight on their hands, and *we* can't get over there, not with Jerry in the way.'

'But Finland was fighting against Germany before. It don't make sense.'

'Finland'll help anyone what fights Russia,' Bert said. 'They hate their guts.'

Jess went indoors, wishing that people could talk about something else for a change. It was war, war, war all the time, and it had been going on for two years now. Ever since before little Maureen was born. She looked at the toddler, playing on the floor with Henry the cat, and remembered the day she'd been born. Jess had had a bad time and had lain upstairs in the front room, wanting nothing more than just to go to sleep for a few hours, and they'd started delivering the corrugated iron for the Anderson shelters. The clatter had gone on for hours. And it didn't seem to have been quiet since.

She got out her writing pad and started to write to Tim and Keith. They seemed settled enough now at the vicarage at Bridge End, even though Tim had screwed up his face at first and protested that they'd have to say prayers all the time. But Mr Beckett, the thin, spidery vicar, had come as a surprise to him. The last time Jess and Frank had been there, he'd organised a tiddlywinks championship, with a pot of home-made jam as the prize. And they had company now, with the two Simmons girls staying there too. A nice little family – two boys and two girls.

Our sort of family, Jess thought, gazing at Maureen. But we're all split up. Maureen hardly knows her brothers, and Muriel and Stella Simmons are more like sisters to them now. And Rose is growing up so fast, she won't be a child much longer. We'll never have been a real family, all together.

But there was no use in thinking like that. It only made her miserable, and you couldn't afford to let yourself get miserable these days. You had to keep cheerful, or everything would seem hopeless, like it seemed to poor Ted, who seemed to be sinking into a black pit he couldn't climb out of.

Jess opened the writing pad and began to write in the copperplate handwriting she had learned at school.

'*Dear Tim and Keith . . .*'

'I didn't know who I was,' Heinrich said. He was drinking his seventh cup of tea of the day – never mind the rations, Alice said – and he was sitting in his accustomed chair by the fireplace. He still looked dirty and unkempt, but she didn't have the heart to tell him so. And she didn't care anyway. It was enough to have him there, in his own chair. It was enough to be able to reach out her hand and touch him and know that he was real.

'How d'you mean, you didn't know who you were?' she asked.

'I'd lost my memory. After the torpedo hit us, I couldn't remember anything. I didn't know my name or where I lived or how old I was – nothing.' The mild brown eyes were liquid with tears. 'I couldn't remember you, or our little Joy, or even my own *Mutter* and *Vater*.'

'None of us?' Alice said, wonderingly. 'Couldn't you even remember us getting married?'

'I did not know if I was married. I *felt* that I was – but I could remember nothing.'

'Oh, *Heinrich*,' she said softly, taking his hand in both of hers and cradling it against her.

'But you must have been saved from the ship,' Joy said. She was sitting on the rag rug at their feet, gazing up at her father. She had scarcely left his side all day, and the newspapers had never been delivered. But nobody had seemed to mind, when they discovered the reason. 'Didn't anyone else know?'

He shook his head. 'It was a very big ship. There were a great many of us aboard. When we sank, we had to take to whatever lifeboat we could find.'

His shudder racked his whole body and Alice remembered how he had always disliked the water, never even paddling at Southsea beach on a summer afternoon. 'I was in the water for a long time. It seemed like many hours. I thought I would drown.' Another convulsive shudder. 'I have heard people say that when you drown your whole life flashes before your eyes. But mine just disappeared.'

They were silent for a moment, Heinrich gathering his strength to go on, Alice and Joy trying to picture the scene. Both had been to sea, across the Channel when they had visited Heinrich's family in Berlin before the war had begun. They tried to imagine being alone in the water, clinging to a bit of wreckage, feeling the waves slap against their faces and waiting for the one that would finally overwhelm them.

'But a lifeboat came along in the end,' Joy said.

'Yes, but there was on it nobody that I knew. And I had no clothes on, no papers, nothing to say who I was. They asked me questions, but I couldn't answer. I was too cold, too tired. I just lay in the bottom of the boat and waited to die.'

'What happened then?' Joy asked, but Alice shook her head.

'Don't pester your father. You don't have to talk now if you don't want to,' she said to Heinrich. 'There's all the time in the world for you to tell us about it. The main thing is, you're back and all you have to do now is get strong again.' She stroked his arm and winced at the thinness and fragility of it. Heinrich had always been so sturdy, even a little stout. 'I don't know what they did to you,' she said angrily. 'They were supposed to look after you, not starve you to death.'

He shook his head. 'We weren't starved. The food wasn't good, but we weren't starved.'

'Well, you've been ill,' she said, 'and it doesn't seem to me that they looked after you at all.'

'I don't think they thought I was ill. Just that I couldn't remember.' He thought for a minute. 'They did bring a doctor to see me a few times. An Austrian. He was what used to be called an *alienist*.' He smiled suddenly, a smile spoiled by a strange twist to his lips, and by the stained teeth showing through the straggling whiskers. 'An appropriate name, don't you think?'

'Oh, Heinrich,' Alice said again, her voice full of pity, but Joy frowned and asked, 'What's an alienist? Is it a doctor specially for aliens?'

'Joy!' her mother expostulated, but Heinrich shook his head and smiled the strange, twisted smile again.

'No, not that. It's a doctor for the mind.'

'For mad people, you mean? But—'

'I think that's enough talk for now,' Alice said in a hard, strained voice. 'Your father needs a rest. Find yourself something else to do for a while, there's a good girl.'

Joy pouted but got up from the rug and picked up a copy of *Girls' Crystal*. She glanced at the clock. 'Can we have the wireless on? It's *ITMA* tonight.'

Alice looked at Heinrich. He was staring at the empty fireplace. He said nothing, but he seemed to shrink even further into the ill-fitting clothes.

Suddenly, she longed for the Heinrich she had known, stocky and cheerful, always ready with a gentle smile and a kind word. She could not find him in this neglected figure with its matted hair and stained smile. She felt suddenly frightened.

'Let's heat up the water for a bath,' she said. 'I'll cut your hair while we're waiting. And you could have a shave. You'll feel better when you're back in your own clothes.'

'Have I still some clothes?' he asked wonderingly. 'I thought they were all lost on the ship.'

'You didn't take them all. There are still some upstairs. Your best suit and your gardening clothes.' She gave a shaky laugh. 'One extreme to the other!'

'But the air-raid warning'll be going soon,' Joy objected. The siren went nightly now, whether aircraft had been sighted or not. 'There isn't time for a bath.'

'There's time for whatever we want,' Alice said with unaccustomed sharpness. 'Your father needs to feel comfortable. He needs to feel he's at home.'

Joy said nothing, but glanced longingly at the wireless set standing on its shelf in the corner. Alice got up and went into the kitchen. She switched on the Ascot water-heater and went outside to drag in the tin bath.

Heinrich looked at his daughter. She had grown in the past year. Her figure had changed from the flat chest of a child to the rounded curves of a young woman. Her face had altered too. It was less round, a little thinner. But nearly everyone he'd seen seemed to be thinner.

'Your mother has told me what a help to her you've been,' he said gently. 'It has not been easy for you, this past year.'

Joy shrugged. 'It's been all right.' She felt oddly uneasy with her father, as if he were a stranger. He'd been through so much, so much that he hadn't yet told them, that she couldn't begin to imagine. And he looked so different. Like Alice, she felt that he had returned in a strange body, that somewhere inside her real father was lurking and she hadn't yet been able to find him.

She thought of how, in the old days before the war began, he would take her on his knee and cuddle her against him. How warm and secure his body had seemed, how strong his short, stubby fingers. Now, she looked at his mottled hands and shuddered.

At that moment, she was more aware than she had ever been of how much she had missed her father. And she was still missing him. She wanted her *father* back. Not this strange, nervous creature who stared pleadingly at her from red-rimmed eyes almost hidden in a mass of tangled whiskers. She wanted the father who had gone away.

And Heinrich, gazing at her, felt the same yearning, for the affectionate, confiding daughter he had known. He wanted to reach out to her, to make contact, but he could not do it, could not bear the thought of her recoil. And so they sat in silence, looking at each other yet avoiding each other's eyes; sharing the same memories, the same longings, yet both locked fast in their separated hearts.

3

'I never thought you'd be a bad loser, Tim,' Mr Beckett observed. They were in the vicarage garden, playing French cricket on the overgrown tennis court, and Stella Simmons had just caught him out for the third time. Tim handed over the bat as if he'd like to throw it and walked away, a murderous scowl on his face. 'As umpire, I have to say that you were out quite fairly.'

'I can't help it if you bat good catches,' Stella agreed smugly. She placed the vicar's old cricket bat in front of her legs and stood square, waiting for the ball to be thrown. Keith tossed it at her and she sent it flying high, past the edge of the court and into a clump of nettles. 'Ooh – look at *that*!'

Tim, who was nearest the clump, looked at it in disgust. 'I can't get it out of there,' he complained. 'I've only got short sleeves on – I'll get my arm all stung. I think we ought to have a new rule, anyone who hits it into the nettles has to get it out themselves.'

'Don't be a twerp,' Stella said. 'How can I get it out? I'm in.'

'Well, you ought to be out, for hitting it so far.' Tim walked over and kicked at the nettles. 'It's right in the middle.'

Muriel ran over with a stick and poked the ball out on to the grass. She handed it to Tim, who shrugged and looked towards Stella. He threw it carelessly towards her and it fell about six feet away, bounced once or twice and then stopped.

Keith picked it up and threw it again, aiming at Stella's legs. It rolled past her and she gave it a tap as it went by, then turned to protect her legs from the new direction.

'She shouldn't have hit it then,' Tim objected. 'It didn't go anywhere near her legs. She ought to have let it go.'

Muriel immediately came to her sister's defence. 'No, she shouldn't. She can hit it if she likes. There's no rule says it's got to be near your legs.'

'There is.'

'Isn't.'

'Is,' Tim said, and caught the vicar's eye. 'Well, that's the way we always play it, anyway.'

'Is it?' Keith asked innocently. 'I don't *remember* that rule.'

Mr Beckett stalked into the middle of the hot, angry little circle. He was wearing ancient khaki shorts and looked like a spider or a stick insect, his thin, knobbly arms and legs so long and gawky that they seemed as if they must have more joints than most people's. He laid one hand on top of Tim's head and one on Stella's.

'I think it's time we all had a drink of cold water,' he said. 'Perhaps you'd like to get it for us, Tim. Muriel will help you. And then I've a little job for you in the greenhouse.'

Tim opened his mouth to argue, then caught the glint in Mr Beckett's eye. He set off towards the house with Muriel tagging along beside him. They went into the cool, dim kitchen and drew five cups of water from the tap. Mrs Mudge, the housekeeper, was nowhere in sight. She usually took her chair outside on sunny afternoons and dozed under the apple tree.

'I don't see how we're going to carry these,' Tim said in disgruntled tones.

'Use a tray, silly.' Muriel opened a cupboard door and brought out a battered tin tray. 'It's the one we used as a sledge when it snowed, remember?'

Tim looked at it. He remembered the day they'd all gone sledging, not long after the girls had joined him and Keith at the vicarage. Stella and Muriel had been open-mouthed, but Tim and Keith were just getting used to the vicar then. He was, as Mrs Mudge said, just like another child. In fact, he'd fallen off the tray three times and arrived home wet through from melted snow, and Mrs Mudge had told him off just as if he really was a little boy.

'It was funny, wasn't it,' Muriel said, and Tim felt his mouth pull itself into a grin. But he didn't want to smile. He didn't want to go out into the garden again laughing, just as if everything was all right. He drew his lips back tight and pursed them up and pulled his eyebrows down as far as he could.

'It was all right,' he said grudgingly.

'Coo, you are a bear-head,' Muriel said, loading the cups on to the tray. 'Come on. I wonder what Becky's got for you to do in the greenhouse. Will you let me come and help?'

Tim had a very good idea what the vicar had in mind for the greenhouse. He was going to be Talked To. It wouldn't be any more than that – Mr Beckett never touched any of them in anger – but whenever one of them strayed beyond the lines he had drawn, he would take them aside and Talk To them. And it wasn't even that he seemed particularly angry – just sad, and disappointed. But somehow that made it worse.

'Can I?' Muriel asked again. 'Can I come and help?'

Tim turned on her. 'No, you can't! He won't want you there. *I* don't want you there. It's private business. *Boys'* business,' he added cruelly, and they went back to the lawn, Tim marching ahead and Muriel trailing behind, slightly weighed down by the tin tray.

By the time they reached the others, Mr Beckett had organised them into a caterpillar party in the vegetable patch. White butterflies had laid their eggs on the undersides of the cabbage leaves, and these must be removed so that the caterpillars wouldn't hatch out and eat the leaves. In Tim's opinion, it would be a very good thing if they were allowed to do just that, but neither Mr Beckett nor Mrs Mudge seemed to agree with him.

Neither, he knew, would his mother, who seemed to have some strange way of communicating with Mrs Mudge and had told her – before the two women had even met, as far as he could tell – that Tim was to be made to sit at the table until he had eaten every scrap of the disgusting green leaves. Even making himself sick wasn't going to be allowed to work.

He was thankful not to have to be one of those wiping the eggs off the leaves. Even if it did mean being Talked To in the greenhouse.

Keith and the two girls settled, Mr Beckett led Tim across the garden. The greenhouse was a ramshackle construction, probably as old as Mr Beckett himself, which stood in a corner of the garden. It had once been kept in apple-pie order by Mrs Mudge's husband, but Mr Mudge had died a few years ago and nobody had looked after it for years. The vicar, encouraged by all the exhortations to 'Dig for Victory' had decided to grow tomatoes in it and it had rapidly become a wild tangle of growth.

'This is what you do,' Mr Beckett said, showing Tim the plants. 'You pinch out the tops so that they'll bush out and have a lot of flowers. Or is it cut off the side shoots so that the tops will grow?' He thought for a few moments. 'Do you know, I'm not quite sure after all. I shall have to consult my mentor.'

'I know what to do,' Tim said. 'You pinch out above the fourth truss. My Dad told me.'

'Did he, indeed? He grows tomatoes, does he?'

'My Dad can grow anything,' Tim said. 'He's got an allotment. He hasn't got a mentor, though,' he added. 'Do they cost much? I could get him one for Christmas.'

The vicar smiled. 'I don't think he needs one. Tell me, Tim, do you miss your father a great deal?'

Tim considered this. It was so long since he and Keith had first been evacuated – almost two years now – that he'd got used to being away from home. And they'd enjoyed being at the Corners' house, with Reg and Edna. They would probably have stayed there for the rest of the war if Reg hadn't been called up and Edna gone to stay with her mum and have a baby. He'd thought when Mum had first told him that she'd arranged for them to stay at the vicarage that they'd hate it, but it had turned out all right. Mr Beckett wasn't nearly so impatient as Dad. You had to do what Dad said, and do it straight away, if you didn't want the rough edge of his tongue. And he kept a thin cane hanging beside the fireplace, by his razor-strop. He wasn't above using it if he thought the boys deserved it.

Mr Beckett didn't have a cane. Only that sad face, when you'd done something he didn't like.

'I don't mind,' Tim said at last. 'I miss going to the beach, though. Dad used to take us out there every Sunday in the summer.'

'And he taught you about gardening.'

'Well, we had to do that. We had to help.'

'And what about your mother and sisters?' Mr Beckett asked. 'You must think about them sometimes and wonder what they're doing.'

'Not really,' Tim said. 'I know what they're doing. Mum does the washing and cooking and sweeps the floors, and Rose goes up the street with Joy Brunner. Mr Brunner's come home,' he added more eagerly. 'It was in Mum's letter this morning. He just walked in without anyone knowing he was coming, and he had all whiskers, and Mrs Brunner didn't hardly know who he was. He got torpedoed and lost his memory and he's just been wandering about all this time, not knowing who he was or where he lived or *anything*. It must be ever so funny, losing your memory,' he added thoughtfully. 'Have you ever lost your memory, Mr Beckett? Mrs Mudge says you have.'

'*Does* she?' the vicar asked in genuine surprise.

'Yes, she told us you'd lose your head if it wasn't sewn on.' Tim glanced up under his lashes and saw the vicar's lips twitch. 'How d'you think Mr Brunner lost his memory?' he asked innocently.

'I haven't the least idea,' Mr Beckett said firmly, refusing to be diverted. 'And I didn't come here to discuss poor Mr Brunner, pleased though I am to hear that he's returned to the bosom of his family.' At the mention of bosoms, Tim turned pink. 'But surely, Tim, you must sometimes wish you were at home?'

'Well, I'd like to see our baby again. She's different every time we see her. She can talk quite a lot now, Mum says, and she can sing a bit too. I'd like to be able to teach her songs.'

'Yes,' Mr Beckett said, 'it's sad that you have to miss her baby years. And she's missing you, as well.' He paused, nipping off bits of tomato plant, and then said casually, 'But it's not making you too miserable, being here?'

'Miserable?' Tim said. 'No. I like being here.'

The vicar looked pleased. But there was still a small frown creasing his brow and after he had pinched a few more tomatoes, he said, 'You would tell me if there was anything the matter, Tim, wouldn't you? Anything worrying you or making you feel cross. Anything at all. I wouldn't want you to keep such things to yourself, especially if there were something I could do to help.'

There was a moment's silence. The vicar kept his eyes steadily on the tomatoes.

'No,' Tim said. 'I mean, yes. I mean—' He stopped, looking confused, and Mr Beckett laughed.

'I didn't put it very clearly, did I. But I think we understand each other. So – what's making you so bad-tempered lately, hmm? You're usually such a cheerful, merry little lad. But for the past week or so we've hardly had a smile out of you. It's not like you, and I don't like to see it.'

Tim pursed his lips. He'd known there was going to be a Talking To, and he'd done his best to divert it, but Mr Beckett had got there just the same.

'Don't have to smile if I don't feel like it,' he muttered.

'Of course you don't. But what's worrying me is *why* you don't feel like it. There's something wrong, Tim, and I want to know what it is.' Mr Beckett's voice was unusually firm, as if he meant to keep Tim in the greenhouse until he had got at the truth. Like a teacher keeping the class in after school. 'I want to help,' he added more gently. 'You're not in trouble, Tim. Just tell me what it is that's bothering you, and we'll try to sort it out together.'

Tim was silent. He rolled a tomato leaf between his fingers, turning it into a narrow green tube, then crushing it to a pungently smelling pulp. The anger that had been simmering inside him for more than a week seemed to gather itself into a hard lump inside his chest. He felt as if he might cry. He looked up at Mr Beckett, standing like a big, disjointed spider amongst the jungle of tomato plants, and felt the tears sting his eyes.

'It's not fair,' he said at last, the words bursting out of him. 'I ought to have been in the other class. I ought to have been there all the time, only no one said, no one *cared*, and now I can't take the scholarship, it's too late, and everyone else will go up without me. And I'll have to stay behind with the infants. It's not *fair*.'

He threw down the mess of tomato leaf and glared at Mr Beckett. His hazel eyes had lost their mischievous gleam, his mouth was pulled into a sullen tremble. He half turned, as if about to run, and Mr Beckett reached out a long, spidery arm and caught his shoulder.

'All right, Tim,' he said quietly. 'Now let's sit down for a minute and talk about this, shall we? What do you mean, you ought to have been in the other class? And why can't you sit the scholarship? It's not till next January, surely.'

'It was *last* January,' Tim sniffed, sitting down on an upturned bucket beside him. 'The one I ought to have taken was last January. And nobody said. All the others took it and I was left out.'

'But why? Are you sure you should have taken it?'

'Yes. All the boys in my class did. *Brian Collins* took it,' Tim said indignantly, referring to his arch-rival. 'But I was in the other class, only nobody knew because we're all mixed up together and we only go afternoons anyway. I've been doing the same work as them. I'm as old as them. I'm *older* than Brian Collins – his birthday's not till March. Just because he's bigger than me . . .' In fact, most of the boys were bigger than Tim, who was small for his age, smaller even than Keith.

Mr Beckett sighed and rubbed his hand over his face. 'Tim, I don't understand. Are you telling me that you should have sat the scholarship for the secondary school last January, and didn't? And that nobody ever explained to you why you didn't?'

'Nobody ever said anything.'

'But why didn't you ask?'

'I just thought perhaps I didn't need to.'

'But, for heaven's sake—'

'Teachers don't like being asked,' Tim said. 'They're grown-ups. My dad always told me that you do what grown-ups say and don't ask questions. And now everyone else is going up to the big school and I've got to stay with the little kids.' His voice began to rise again. 'It isn't fair. I could have passed the exam, I know I could. I could've passed it better than Brian Collins.'

'I'm sure you could,' the vicar said absently. He was feeling uncomfortably guilty. 'Listen, Tim, would you like me to find out what happened? Why you got left out? There may be some quite reasonable explanation—'

'I've always been in that class,' Tim said. 'I ought to be going up with them. It's not my fault I didn't sit the scholarship.'

'No.' Mr Beckett scratched his head. 'Well, I do think I'd better ask your teacher, don't you? We really ought to find out. And your parents ought to know, as well. Do they think you'll be going up next term?'

Tim shrugged. 'Don't know.'

'Well, we must get it sorted out. Who's your teacher?'

'Mr Hodges. He's old. He's not from our school – Miss Langrish was my teacher, only she's gone now. *She* wouldn't have let me get left out.'

'I'll talk to Mr Hodges,' the vicar said, getting up from his bucket. 'And Mr Wain. He's headmaster, he ought to know what's happened. We'll find out just what happened and what we can do about it. Though I'm very much afraid you'll have to wait now, and sit the exam next year.'

'But it's not *fair*,' Tim said. 'I've *always* been in that class.'

'I know.' Mr Beckett looked down at him from his spidery height. 'All the same, Tim, it's not fair to take it out on people around you, is it? People like Stella and Muriel, I mean. It's not their fault, is it?'

Tim looked at the ground. The tears were beginning to sting again. Reluctantly, he shook his head.

'And Stella did catch you out quite fairly, you know.'

'She's a girl,' Tim muttered. 'Girls aren't any good at games.'

'And that's nonsense,' the vicar said warmly. 'You know perfectly well it is. Anyway, you've always been quite happy to play games with Stella and Muriel.' He paused. 'Does it really make you feel any better to be nasty to them? Really and truly?'

Tim looked up and opened his mouth indignantly, then saw the vicar's face and closed it. He couldn't bear to turn that gentle, inquiring look into one of disappointment. He felt his cheeks flush and said, 'No. Not really.'

'It just makes things worse, doesn't it?' Mr Beckett said. 'It makes them all go hard inside you, like a ball of lead, and you can't get rid of it. Isn't that what it's like?'

'Yes,' Tim said, astonished. 'But how do you—'

'Oh, I've felt like that too,' the vicar said, laughing. 'We all do, at some time or another, Tim. You're not the only one. And now, before we go back to the others, I've got something here you might like. Come and see.'

He went over to a corner of the greenhouse and rummaged amongst the foliage. Tim got up and followed him. After a moment, the vicar exclaimed with pleasure and withdrew his hand. There were two large, juicy strawberries in it.

'I thought they might be starting to ripen,' he said. 'Only these two so far, I'm afraid – and it's not a very big plant, so there won't be more than a few each anyway. But these are for you, Tim. Just to help melt away that horrid ball inside.'

Tim took them. He held one to his lips and bit into it. The sweet fruit was crushed between his teeth and he felt the warm, red juice fill his mouth.

The vicar was right. It did help melt away the ball of nastiness.

He looked longingly at the second one and then turned towards the greenhouse door. 'I'll give this to Stella,' he said offhandedly. 'Girls like strawberries.'

'It's horrible,' Jess said, watching Frank stick yet more pins in the map that stretched across the wall of the back room, above the piano. 'The whole world's getting swept in. They're talking about Japan coming in against us now. How can we ever win, a tiny country like us?'

It was 4 July, and Maureen Budd was celebrating her second birthday with a rag doll Annie had made her, two new pinafores cut down from one of Jess's old frocks and a bag of coloured wooden bricks that had belonged to Keith. Jess had scoured the shops for toys, but there was almost nothing to be had and in the end she'd settled for two or three rag books instead. The colours weren't very good, but Maureen seemed pleased with them.

Two weeks earlier, the Germans had carried out their threatened invasion of Russia, surprising Stalin despite the warnings he had been given by Winston Churchill. Hitler had boasted that the German army's movements were the greatest the world had ever seen, and three million troops, with thousands of tanks, guns and aircraft, were on their way to crush the people of the USSR.

'We've got allies,' Frank said, studying the map. It was covered with pins, from North Africa almost to the Arctic Circle. He had dipped the heads of some in red sealing wax to make them represent the Allies, and they stood out like brave little flames against the black plasticine he had used for the enemy. 'And we've got the British Empire behind us. We're not tiny at all.'

'Well, I know. But if Japan attacks Australia, they'll have too much to do there to bother about coming all this way to help us.' She sighed. 'If only America would help. I mean, I know they're doing a lot, what with Lease-Lend and sending us aid and food parcels and all that, but if they'd just send some soldiers . . .'

'I thought you didn't want the whole world getting involved,' Frank said, and then shook his head. 'I'm sorry, Jess. But that's what it amounts to. Everyone getting drawn in. There won't be a safe place anywhere on earth.'

There was dismaying home news in the papers too. A shortage of tobacco – 'at least *that* doesn't worry us,' Frank commented – and a new issue of ration books coming soon. And coal was to be rationed – only one ton a month available for domestic use, and perhaps not even that much.

'One ton for the entire country? They'll be asking if we want one lump or two,' Tommy Vickers said, calling in with a present for the baby. It was a small bar of chocolate – 'and *they're* about as common as hens' teeth these days,' Tommy remarked – and because it was her birthday they let her have it there and then, sitting on the rag rug and smearing it all over her face as she chewed. She grinned up at them and pushed chocolate-covered hands into her curly fair hair.

'Look at you!' Jess said. 'And in your new pinny, too. I reckon it'll take half our soap ration to get you clean again.' She smiled, feeling the sudden burning sensation of tears in her eyes. 'I just wish the boys could be here as well.'

'Are they coming home for their holiday this summer?' Tommy asked.

He was an air-raid warden and had been in the Royal Navy during the Great War. He looked a bit like the comedian Arthur Askey, and always had a joke on his lips. He liked children and missed the ones who had been evacuated. There was nobody to toss a few toffees to as he walked up and down the street. Nobody except Micky Baxter anyway, and even Tommy never thought to give him a toffee.

'I don't know. I'd like to have them home, if only for a week or two, but it depends.' Jess glanced at her husband. 'I mean, we could always send them back quick if it got bad again. Bridge End's not so far away.'

'Not as long as we're still getting the raids,' Frank said firmly. 'Look at that one we had last week. Thousands of incendiaries there were, showering down all over Portsdown Hill. The whole place was afire.'

'That was gorse, mostly,' Tommy said. 'But you're right, Frank, it could as easily have been in the town, and we'd never have been able to put that lot out. It makes you wonder about these tunnel shelters they're digging under the Hill, too. I mean, how safe are they going to be?'

'Oh, they'll be all right.' Jess had an uncle on the Council. She didn't see much of him but news occasionally came through other members of the family, and the tunnels had been a great topic of conversation. 'They're going to be deep. Too deep for any bombs. There's going to be bunks and everything down there, and people will have tickets for their own places. Not that we'll go, mind. With Frank on firewatch, I like to be here and we're safe enough in the Anderson.'

Tommy opened his mouth and then closed it again. There'd been direct hits on Anderson shelters, whole families wiped out. But it didn't do to think about that. People had to take what shelter they could, and mostly the corrugated iron huts, half buried at the bottom of the gardens, were safe enough. And none of the houses around April Grove had large enough rooms for the newer Morrison shelters, built like big iron tables indoors.

'Well,' he said, getting to his feet, 'I'd better be getting back. Freda's not so good again – keeps getting indigestion. And our Eunice is talking about going in the Wrens, and that's not helping. Any upset, and it goes straight to Freda's chest.'

'Heartburn,' Jess nodded. 'She was telling me about it the other day. I know what it's like – I was a martyr to it while I was expecting Maureen. But at least I knew it would be better once she's born.'

'Gawd,' Tommy said with mock horror, 'I hope that's not what's wrong with my Freda. I don't fancy starting sleepless nights again, not at my age!'

Jess laughed. 'You're a star turn, you are. You and Freda, starting a family again! And as for sleepless nights . . . I don't know when we last had one that wasn't.'

Tommy grinned, winked at Frank, tickled Maureen under her chocolatey chin and went out. They heard him whistling as he went off up the street.

Jess took Maureen into the scullery to wash her. She stood the little girl on the wooden draining-board and stripped off her clothes, then poured some warm water from the Ascot. Maureen stood in the enamel bowl, playing with her mother's hair as Jess wiped off the chocolate.

'That means it's all over me now,' Jess said. 'I ought to have washed your hands first, you dirty little Arab. Well, never mind, you've had a good birthday.' She sighed. 'I wish we could have got you some really nice presents, though. It seems such a shame you're missing so much.'

Frank came through to the scullery and leaned against the door-jamb. 'Did I tell you we're getting women in the Yard?'

For a moment, Jess was tempted to make some saucy reply. That's Tommy Vickers' influence, she thought, trying to repress a smile as she imagined what he would say. *All home comforts provided now, Frank?* Or – *Don't they have to hang about at the gates any more, then?* But Frank wouldn't like to hear her talk like that. He had very definite ideas about the sort of jokes that were suitable for women. Sometimes, she thought he was a bit too strait-laced.

'What d'you mean, women?'

'To help do the work,' he said. 'There's some in the canteens already, but they're putting them in the workshops now. We're having some in the boiler-shop.'

Jess stared at him. 'But that's heavy work. Women can't do that.'

'They can't do what I do, work the steam hammer, no. But there's plenty of jobs they can do.' He sighed. 'I dunno, Jess. It don't seem right, women having to come and work in places like our boiler-shop. It's too rough in the Yard. Not that some of 'em seem to mind that!'

Jess gazed at him, trying to imagine Frank working alongside women. He had never found it very easy to make friends with women, apart from the ones they knew in the family, and he certainly found it difficult to cope with women who were too forward and made up to him, like Jess suspected Ethel Glaister had tried to do once or twice when Jess was away.

Frank was too shy and reserved, that was his trouble. Not like Tommy Vickers. And he liked women to be in their place, running a home and looking after children. He didn't even talk about his work much – he didn't think Jess ought to be bothered with what went on behind the Dockyard gates. It was another world. Now that world was to be disrupted too, and he could never again feel quite so safe behind the big walls.

'I daresay it'll be all right,' Jess said. 'You probably won't have too much to do with them.'

'No, but they're *there*, aren't they,' he said, and she almost laughed. Sometimes he sounded just like Tim in one of his peevish moods.

'Well, what if they are? They're just about everywhere else, too. And you don't need to talk as if women are some sort of strange animal,' she added, remembering that they were discussing her own sex. 'We're human beings too, you know.'

'Well, of course I know that. Don't be daft, Jess.' He watched as she dried Maureen with an old towel and slipped her nightie over her head before lifting her from the draining-board. The nightie was a new one, cut down from one of Jess's, and he'd always liked the silky material. He was sorry Jess wouldn't be wearing it any more, but it was nice that Maureen could enjoy it.

'Two years old,' he said softly. 'It don't seem possible, does it. We've been at war practically all the time since that little scrap was born. She's growing up to the sound of the air-raid sirens, and planes coming over, and bombs falling. It's not right. It's not how a baby should see the world.'

Jess said nothing. Frank's words chimed exactly with her own feelings, and she was sorry she'd laughed at him over the women. She turned, still holding Maureen against her hip, and put her free arm round him, resting her head against his broad chest.

Frank held them both close. He felt Jess's hair against his chin, and the baby's cheek nuzzling his neck. It was the colour of a peach just beginning to ripen, and there was a soft, almost invisible fuzz on it, just like the bloom on the fruit.

He hadn't seen a peach for over two years. Maureen had never seen one.

All the same, they were better off in Britain than millions of others were. He thought of Russia, even now being invaded by the Germans. The poor wretches there didn't have a chance. He thought of mothers like Jess and babies like Maureen, and what would happen to them when the Nazis went marching in.

Suddenly, it didn't seem to matter so much that Maureen didn't have a teddy bear or had never tasted a peach. Nor that he was going to have to work alongside women in the Yard.

Frank wasn't the only one who didn't feel too pleased about women coming to work in Portsmouth Dockyard. Nancy Baxter, a few doors along from the Budds, was grumbling to her mother about it before setting off for her own night's work.

'You can tell just what sort of trollops they'll get in there,' she said, adjusting the neckline of her frock. It was already cut quite low, showing the tops of her breasts – not that there was much to show – but she undid another button and stared critically into the fly-blown mirror that hung over the scullery sink. 'I mean, who's going to want to work in the Yard unless they're after something else? The money's not that good – they'll be looking to make it up a bit, and they'll have all the chances too. It's not fair on the rest of us.' She fished in the scruffy handbag that lay on the table and took out a packet of Woodbines. She lit one and inhaled deeply, then broke into a hacking cough.

'I don't suppose they bothered about that,' Granny Kinch remarked from the back room. 'When's anything been fair to the likes of you and me? We just have to struggle on the best we can. Anyway, you got your regulars, and there's always plenty of sailors about.'

'Yeah, I suppose so.' Nancy smoked for a few minutes in silence, then stubbed out her cigarette in a saucer and got to her feet. 'Well, I'd better get on. Our Vera's gone to sleep all right. I dunno where Micky is.'

'Out earning a few bob, I hope,' Mrs Kinch said. 'He's making hisself quite useful these days, working down Charlotte Street. He brought home a nice bit of shin at dinner-time. I'll make a stew for tomorrow.' She followed Nancy to the door and settled herself on the chair that stood there all day. 'I'll just enjoy the sunset for a bit. It's a lovely colour tonight.'

Nancy walked up the street. She passed a few people who nodded and muttered something, but nobody stopped to chat. At the top, she met Ethel

Glaister coming along September Street and said hello just for devilment, but Ethel put her nose in the air and stalked past, pretending that Nancy didn't exist.

Nancy shrugged. She'd stopped caring a long time ago what people thought of her, especially people like Ethel Glaister. What was so special about Ethel Glaister, anyway? Nancy had seen her, with her permed yellow hair and frilly blouse, trying to flirt with Frank Budd. Especially when Jess had been evacuated at the beginning of the war, leaving Frank on his own. Ethel Glaister had been sniffing round him then like a bitch on heat, until poor old Frank had hardly dared go out in his own garden.

So what made her so different from Nancy, who had to earn a living to keep her mother and her children, and didn't have any other way of doing it?

At that moment, Nancy saw her son, tearing along Copnor Road towards her on an old bike. She waved at him and he skidded to a halt.

'Where d'you get that bike? I hope you never pinched it.'

'Course I didn't,' Micky said indignantly. 'Old man Grover said I could bring it home. I can get down there quicker in the morning and do a few errands too.' He looked proudly at the big basket fixed to the handlebars. 'I'm a proper delivery boy now.'

'You'd better not let the teachers see you. You're not old enough to leave school yet.'

Micky sneered. 'I'm not going back to school. They don't teach you nothing useful. Anyway, they don't hardly know who's there and who isn't these days. If they come round again, you say I bin evacuated after all.'

Nancy laughed. 'I don't suppose they'll bother. I give that teacher the sharp side of my tongue last time. What's in them paper bags?'

'Bit of lettuce and stuff. A few veg. And I managed to pick up a pound of sausages too.' He gave her a sly glance and Nancy, who had opened her mouth to ask how he had managed to persuade a butcher to give him sausages, closed it again. What you didn't know, you couldn't grieve over, that was what Ma always said, though there was probably someone in Pompey now grieving over that pound of sausages. Still, people shouldn't leave sausages lying around where sticky-fingered boys like Micky were skulking about. 'Pick them up' was probably exactly what he'd done.

'Well, I gotta go,' she said. 'You go straight home, mind. If there's a raid tonight I want you with your gran, not roaming the streets. I'll see you in the morning, and save a couple of them sausages for me, all right?'

Micky grinned and pedalled off down the road. Nancy watched for a few moments and then turned away. She wondered if the stallholder in Charlotte Street really had said he could use the bike. Come to that, did stallholders have bikes anyway? You didn't get deliveries from Charlotte Street market. Anyway, there were never more than two or three stalls down there these days.

One of these days, Micky was going to get in trouble again, there was no doubt about it. He'd already been up in front of the magistrates twice. He was that sort of boy – the sort who got picked on and blamed for everything that went wrong. It wasn't surprising if he cocked a snook and did it anyway. But it was a shame, when Nancy knew that he was really a good boy at heart.

Like Ma said, nothing was ever fair to the likes of them.

At that moment, Micky wasn't bothered about fairness. He whistled as his feet pushed the heavy pedals round, thinking how useful it was to have wheels of his own.

Since the night when Cyril Nash had been killed and Jimmy Cross lost a leg, Micky hadn't had anyone to knock about with. Jimmy was still in hospital, and they wouldn't let Micky go to see him. Anyway, he wouldn't have known what to say, and he was scared of hospitals. And Martin Baker, who had played cowboys and Indians with them sometimes, was just a kid; besides, his mum hardly let him out of her sight now.

It was a pity Tim and Keith Budd, from number 14, had been evacuated. They were a bit goody-goody, but Tim was usually ready for some fun and where he went, Keith would follow. They'd probably have joined him in making dens in bombed houses and collecting weapons, even if they drew the line at pinching things.

Until a few weeks ago, Micky had enjoyed the war. It had been a huge game, and a boy with his wits about him could have a good time and get his mum and gran all that they wanted in the way of extra rations and stuff. But now it was different. One of Micky's own mates had been killed and another badly injured, and now he wanted to fight his own war. Drive the Jerries out. Kill the lot of 'em. He could do it, too, if he was just a few years older.

People had lied about their age before, and got into the Army or Navy. But a glance in his mum's cracked mirror in the scullery at home told Micky that he couldn't get away with it. At twelve years old, he hadn't started to shave yet and he wasn't very tall, either. But he could still do something.

He could start his own army.

The thought had struck him this morning, just as he turned the corner into April Grove. He'd stood quite still, staring down the cul-de-sac towards the wall at the end and the backs of the houses in May Street, that ran beside the railway.

His gran was sitting as usual on her chair at the door of number 10, having a yarn with Mr Slattery, who was delivering milk with his electric milk wagon. The greengrocer's cart was standing outside number 6 with Nobby, his old horse, drooping his head into his nosebag. But Micky saw none of this.

Instead, his head was filled with visions of a new army. An army of boys, gathered from all over Pompey, boys who weren't afraid of staying in the city during the raids, boys who would go into bombed buildings and down craters and collect shrapnel and bullets and guns. Boys who would fight the Germans when they invaded.

And if they didn't invade? Micky saw himself at the head of his army – his secret army. Stealing boats to take them across the Channel. Sneaking under cover of darkness into occupied France. Working like commandos, sabotaging the Germans. Winning the war.

And he, Micky Baxter, would be at the head of it. *He* would be the hero then.

That was why he'd been so pleased to find the bike, leaning against an alley wall near Charlotte Street. An army needed transport.

It also needed men. So far Micky hadn't recruited anyone to his secret army. The boys he knew were all either younger than him or older, the sort who'd want to take over. Micky wasn't going to let anyone take over. This was his army, and he meant to be in charge.

As he came to the corner of October Street, he caught sight of Desmond Cook coming along the road.

Desmond was a big boy, older than Micky, but there was something wrong with him – he had a loose, slack mouth and queer eyes, and he was slow and couldn't even read or write yet. He worked as an errand boy for his widowed mother, who had a greengrocer's shop in Copnor Road, and took his work very seriously, knowing exactly which customer preferred cabbage to cauliflower, or who had received oranges the last time they were available.

Most of the time he was amiable enough, but sometimes he seemed to retreat into a world of his own, refusing to speak to anyone else, sometimes hardly seeming to know that they were there, and now and then he was overtaken by sudden terrifying rages. The other children called him barmy and would follow him in the street, taunting him until he flew into a temper and rushed at them, snarling and flailing his fists about, but he wasn't a bad bloke if you took him the right way. Micky had befriended him sometimes in a casual sort of way, and he knew Desmond would follow him anywhere.

Micky stopped the bike and sat back on the saddle as Desmond admired it.

'Give us a ride on the crossbar?' the bigger boy asked enviously.

'All right.' Micky helped him get on and pedalled off, rather more slowly with Desmond's weight added, the front wheel wavering.

'See the raid the other night?' he asked. 'I went up the Lines to watch. It was smashing – better'n Guy Fawkes Night.'

'You're not allowed up the Lines.' Hilsea Lines was an old fort, built like the big ones on top of Portsdown Hill and around Gosport. It consisted of a long earth embankment, tunnelled inside like a rabbit warren with rooms and corridors and just a few heavily barred windows. It was grown over with brambles and trees and had been a popular picnic spot before the war, but now the military were in there and you couldn't go near without a permit.

'There's places you can get in, if you know them.' Micky had been practising for when he invaded France. He would need all the commando's tricks then of hiding from the enemy, sneaking behind their lines to spy on them, keeping out of sight. And although the soldiers in the Lines were British, they were as much enemy to Micky as Germans were. He knew very well what would happen if they caught him.

'I go up there a lot,' he boasted. 'I know the Lines like the back of me hand.'

'We used to go blackberrying there,' Desmond said wistfully. 'Before my dad went away. My mum says the soldiers'll get all the blackberries now.'

Micky shrugged and the bike wobbled. He wasn't much interested in blackberries, though he liked them all right when his gran baked them in a pie with some apple. He was more interested in watching the soldiers doing their drill, and finding out where the ammunition was stored. It was inside somewhere, but getting into the underground fort was a different matter from just wriggling through a hole in the wire. It needed someone really small to get through those barred windows.

'This bike's smashing,' Desmond said, clinging to the handlebars as they swerved their way along the road. 'Is it really yours?'

'Yeah, I can use it whenever I want,' Micky replied, but he spoke absently. For a moment, he was silent and then he said, 'D'you want to be in my gang, Des?'

The bigger boy twisted his head round to look at him. 'You ain't got a gang. You got bombed up.'

'I'm getting another one up. You could be my First Lieutenant if you wanted.'

'First Lieutenant?' Desmond repeated slowly. 'What's a First Lieutenant do?'

'Well, take charge when I'm not there, that sort of thing.' With only two of them in the gang, Micky wasn't giving much away, but he spoke as grandly as if Desmond were to be in command of thousands. 'We'll have to get a few more in,' he added. 'But we won't have just anybody, mind. This is going to be a special gang. It's going to be an army. A secret army.'

'An *army*?' Desmond's voice was awed. 'You mean we're going to fight?'

'We're going to be commandos. We're going to follow people and spy on them and do sabotage and stuff.' The front wheel wobbled again, more wildly. Micky tried to control it, failed and the cycle veered across the road, jack-knifed and deposited them both in the gutter. Desmond gave a yelp.

'Ow! The pedal's gone right into my leg.'

Micky untangled himself and dragged the bicycle off his first lieutenant, who lay with tears in his eyes, biting his lip with the pain. The pedal had dug into his calf and left a red, angry mark, but there didn't seem to be any real damage. Micky looked down at him.

'It won't be no good crying when you're being tortured by the enemy. You can't be in the army if you're going to give our secrets away.'

Desmond sniffed hard and wiped his sleeve across his eyes and nose. 'I'm not crying.' He moved his leg gingerly. 'And I don't want to be tortured.'

'Well, don't get caught then.' Micky surveyed the delivery bike. It was much more heavily built than a normal cycle and had stood up to the crash with no more than a bit more paint being chipped off. 'Are you going to be in my army or not?'

Desmond didn't hesitate. Because of his slowness, and his unattractive looks, he had no friends and was accustomed to being left out of the games the other children played. To be invited to be in Micky Baxter's gang – in his secret army – and to be First Lieutenant, was more than he would ever have dared hope for. Maybe he could even be like Micky himself, bold and cheeky and daring.

'I don't mind.' He got up and rubbed his leg.

'Actually,' Micky said, remembering something he had seen on Saturday morning pictures, 'if you aren't I shall probably have to take you prisoner anyway. You know too much now.'

'I'll be in,' Desmond said. 'And I can be First Lieutenant, can't I? You promised I could.'

'Yeah, that's all right. You got to do what I say, though.' Micky mounted the bike again. 'I'll meet you here tomorrow morning, all right? I'll give you your first orders then. And we'll decide who else to recruit.' He pedalled away. It was nearly time for the siren and he wanted to get the sausages home for Gran to cook them for supper.

He felt pleased with the evening's work. He'd got started with the army, and he had transport – a bike could substitute very well for a tank until they could lay their hands on the real thing. And even if Desmond was only ninepence in the shilling, he was big and strong and he'd do whatever Micky told him.

Micky whistled and tore down October Street and along the back alley of April Grove, narrowly missing running over the Budds' tabby cat who was watching a hole under the fence.

'Sausages for supper, Gran,' he said, bursting through the back door. 'But we got to save a few for Mum, see?'

His grandmother came through from her own sentry duty at the front door, her metal curlers warm from the evening sun. She grinned, showing the gaps in her teeth, as Micky slapped the sausages down on the table.

'Sausages! That's a good boy, Micky. You done well. We don't 'ave much to worry about in this house with you to look after us, do we?'

The frying-pan was already on the stove, still greasy from the last fry-up they had had. Granny Kinch struck a match and turned on the gas. At the moment she did so, the siren began to sound.

'Bugger you,' she said to the approaching aircraft. 'I bin all week waiting for a few bangers. And I reckon our Micky's are going to taste a sight better'n the ones *you're* planning to drop, so just carry on past us, will you? We ain't interested.'

Micky laughed and sat down at the table. But there was a strained note to his laughter and a tightness in his face. It cost him all the strength he possessed to pretend that the drone of the aircraft didn't scare him.

The memory of that other raid, the one in which Cyril had been killed and Jimmy lost his leg, was something he tried to push from his mind. But it still came back to him with the wail of the siren, with the rattle of the anti-aircraft guns and the fury of the explosions. It came back to him in his dreams, when he could do nothing to keep it at bay.

It drove him in his desire to fight the Germans. It drove his desire for an army of his own.

4

'Who is this bloke, anyway?' Ted Chapman asked grumblingly. 'I haven't heard our Betty mention him before.'

Annie was making a special meal. She had stood over half an hour in the queue at the butcher's that morning, hoping that Mr Hines would still have some meat when she reached the counter, but to her dismay he only had a tiny bit of beef when she got there, and that looked scraggy. She'd refused it and gone over the road to the fishmonger. After another half-hour's queueing, with no idea what might be available when she reached the counter, Annie had bought some fresh-salted cod to make a fish pie. It had been soaking in cold water in the fishmonger's big sink for almost two days and Mr Jennings had told her it should be cooked that day.

'Not bad for ninepence a pound,' Annie said now, topping it with mashed potato. 'Mind, I never think fish is as substantial as meat, but the Radio Doctor says it's good for you, and you've got to take what you can get these days. A bit of salad's not enough for a Land Girl. Our Betty's used to hard work and country food now.'

The meal was special for two reasons. Olive was leaving on Monday to join the ATS, and Betty was coming home for the day, and bringing her new young man with her.

'His name's Dennis,' Annie told Ted, 'and she's talked about him before, you know she has, only I never realised there was anything special between them. He was working at Spencers' farm when she first went there, but now he's volunteered for bomb disposal and they've sent him back to Pompey.'

'There's something queer about that,' Ted said. 'I mean, why didn't he volunteer before? Why was he working on a farm? They've got boys of their own, haven't they, the Spencers? Why send them off and then take on another bloke?'

'Couldn't say, I'm sure,' Annie shrugged. 'But he sounds a decent sort of chap and our Betty seems to like him. Anyway, I'm glad she's got someone to think about, after what happened to young Graham.'

'What's that got to do with it? They'd stopped courting months before.'

Annie sighed. Whatever you said these days, Ted seemed to have some objection to it. The doctor said it was all part of his condition – she called it an illness – but to Annie it often seemed more like sheer bad temper. And yet she had to admit he'd never been like it before the war.

'Just let's make it nice for her to come home for a couple of days,' she said. 'She doesn't get much time off, specially at this time of year.' She went out into the garden, before Ted could say that he'd never wanted Betty to go away in the first place.

Olive was picking peas to go with the fish pie. At least Ted had started to take an interest in the garden again, chivvied out there by Annie's constant remarks about digging for Victory and getting the right amount of exercise. The peas were doing well and he'd planted some runner beans and got the sticks ready for them to climb up. It was nice to have your own fresh vegetables, and even more important now there was a war on. Annie didn't think she could have borne to have to queue at the greengrocer's as well.

'I wonder when we'll all be together again,' Olive said, dropping peas in the trug. 'With our Betty out on the farm and me going in the ATS, you and Dad are going to be all on your own.'

'I had noticed that,' Annie said tartly. She wasn't looking forward to the house with no family in it. 'And we're not all together now. I'll thank you to remember you've got a brother too.'

'I know.' Olive flushed. 'I didn't mean I'd forgotten Colin. Only, it's so long since he was home . . . And Derek's not here either, come to that. But after this weekend – well, it'll be just you and our Dad.'

'Yes.' Annie picked a handful of peas and dropped them in Olive's basket. 'That'll be enough for now. I expect this new young man of Betty's has got a good appetite, though they get fed well enough in the Army by all accounts.'

Olive looked at her mother, surprised by the faint note of hostility in her voice. 'I thought you were pleased Betty'd got another young man.'

'So I am. But – well, it's something your father was saying just now. Why hasn't he joined up before? Why was he working on a farm when the Spencers' own boys are in the Army? They've got three Land Girls, they could've got another one. It seems a bit funny, that's all.'

'Maybe he'd been ill or something,' Olive said. 'Anyway, we'll find out soon enough. They'll be here any minute. I'll walk up the road and see if I can meet them, shall I?'

She went out of the gate and, after a moment's hesitation, up March Street. The trouble with living at the bottom, where it joined April Grove, was that there were two ways of getting there from September Street, where the shops and bus stops were. You could walk straight down March Street to the corner where the house with the little turret stood, or you could go down October Street and then turn right along April Grove. Mostly, the family used March Street, unless they wanted to drop in on Auntie Jess and Uncle Frank on the way.

Betty and Dennis would probably come on the green Hants & Dorset bus and get off in Copnor Road. Olive walked as far as the railway line and then stopped, looking up and down the road and debating whether to go any further. She was just making up her mind to go home after all, when she saw two figures come round the bend in the road and recognised her sister Betty, swinging along in corduroy breeches and a yellow blouse. With her was a tall young man with a mop of curly brown hair, and they were holding hands.

Olive advanced, smiling rather shyly. Betty had said nothing about Dennis until quite recently, and nobody had been sure whether they were just friends, or if there was more to it than that. When she'd asked to bring him home for the day it had been obvious that there was something special about him. But even so, to be walking along holding hands, for everyone to see . . .

'Hullo, Livvy,' Betty said. Her eyes sparkled in her tanned face and her short brown curls had gone fair with the sun. Her figure had developed a bit too; she was more rounded, though her waist was as slim as ever.

She looks gorgeous, Olive thought. She looks as though she's in love.

'This is Dennis,' Betty said, keeping her hand on the young soldier's arm. 'This is my sister Olive. You're not to believe a word she says about me.'

'Go on,' he said, smiling. He was very good-looking, Olive decided – nearly as good-looking as her Derek, in a different way. He was tall but not thin, with plenty of muscle under that khaki uniform, and he had a wide, friendly smile with strong, white teeth. His hazel eyes were almost the same colour as Betty's and sparkled in just the same way. In fact, there was quite a lot of likeness between him and Betty, with the same colouring, the same curly hair and the same air of suppressed humour lurking behind their faces. Probably that was why they got on so well.

'Tell me something about Betty,' he said to Olive, 'and I'll tell you if I believe it.'

'Oh, Betty's marvellous,' Olive said. 'She's the best sister anyone could have. She does all my washing for me when she's home, she does the housework and cooks meals for our Mum, she digs the garden for Dad. And she's quite right,' she added, grinning at Betty's open-mouthed astonishment. 'I tell the most enormous lies.'

Dennis roared with laughter. 'So what am I to believe out of that? It's like the story of the black men, one who always tells lies, the other who always tells the truth. I could never work that one out either.' He tucked Olive's hand through the arm Betty wasn't already clasping. 'Well, let's go and see what your Mum and Dad say about you both. I bet they'll tell me what's what.'

The three of them swung along the road, talking and laughing. Olive's brief moment of awkwardness had disappeared. Dennis was nice, she thought. He was really nice. She was looking forward to getting to know him better.

'So you're in bomb disposal,' Ted said as they sat round the table eating Annie's fish pie. 'What d'you have to do, exactly?'

'Well, what d'you think, Dad?' Betty said pertly. 'He disposes of bombs, of course.'

Ted gave her a look and turned back to Dennis. Betty made a face at Olive and rolled her eyes.

'I'm asking a sensible question,' he said. 'Though I daresay a lot of it's secret, isn't it? I mean, you probably can't talk about it too much.'

'Not too much, no, Mr Chapman,' Dennis said easily. 'Seems a bit daft here, I know you don't have any fifth columnists hiding behind the furniture—'

'They'd have to be pretty small ones,' Betty put in, looking round the crowded room.

'But it's best not to say too much all the same,' Dennis went on, giving her hand a squeeze under the table. 'What you don't know, you can't pass on.'

'I hope I'd not pass on anything I was told anyway,' Ted said stiffly. 'But you're right, the girls might say something they didn't mean to. And with our Olive going in the ATS—'

'Our Olive will get to know her own secrets,' Olive said sharply. 'And keep them, too. We're not all tittle-tattlers, Dad.'

'All right, all right.' Ted looked at Dennis again. 'What I'm curious to know is why you didn't get called up sooner? Why were you working on a farm? I thought all your age group would've gone by now.'

'I was given exemption,' Dennis said quietly.

There was a sudden tension in the room. Betty found his hand again and held it tightly. She had dreaded this moment and knew that the dread had made her act differently, making silly jokes and being cheeky to Dad. And that had made the others uneasy – Mum and Olive had both kept looking at her as if wondering what was wrong, and she knew Mum thought she was going to tell them something they wouldn't like – that Dennis had got her 'into trouble', or they wanted to get married. Or both!

She wished it was true. But Dad would never allow them to marry, not until he knew Dennis a lot better – he'd only given in to Olive and Derek because of Dunkirk, and they'd known Derek and his family all their lives.

'Exemption?' Ted repeated, frowning. 'What, because of farm work being a reserved occupation? But the Spencers have got two lads of their own, haven't they?'

'That's right. They're in the Army. That's why I was drafted to the land.' Dennis paused for a moment. Betty might have thought he was nervous, but she knew that he was proud of his beliefs. He could only be uncertain because it was her dad he was talking to, and he didn't know how Ted might react.

'I was given conditional exemption as a conscientious objector,' he said at last, quite calmly.

The room was suddenly silent. Betty sat very still, only her eyes moving as she looked at each face in turn. Dennis looked composed enough, but a tiny muscle ticked in his cheek. Olive was staring at him as if he had suddenly changed into some kind of alien being. Her mother's hand moved slowly to her mouth, as shocked as if he had announced that he was Hitler's brother. And her father had drawn his brows together in a heavy frown.

Oh dear, she thought, he's going to take this really bad. 'A *conchie*?' Ted said at last, spitting out the word as if it were something evil. 'You're a *conchie*?' He turned on Betty, his fury erupting. 'You've had the brass neck to bring home a bloody—'

'Ted!' Annie was on her feet, moving quickly round the table to lay her hand on her husband's arm. 'Now, don't get yourself all excited, you know what the doctor—'

'*Bugger* the doctor!' Ted shook her off. The shock of the word he had used, so seldom heard in this house, struck them all into silence. 'If I want to get excited, I'll *get* bloody excited. I reckon there's something to get excited about.' He turned on Betty again. 'You'd better take this – this *filth* out of my house, before I throw him out myself. I warn you, I'll do it if I have to – and I might not be a young man any more,' he added, his eyes raking Dennis's lean, muscular body, 'but I can still give a good account of meself, same as when I took my ferryboat to Dunkirk, to fetch home better men than you'll ever be!'

'Dad, listen—'

'I'll not listen to nothing while that dirty conchie's in the house,' Ted snarled. 'Look, my girl, I've *seen* it – I've seen what war's about. I've seen men standing up to their necks in the sea, waiting for boats to take 'em off the beaches – and all the time there were German planes flying overhead, backwards and forwards up the beach, dropping bombs on 'em, strafing 'em with machine-guns, mowing 'em down like you been mowing hay in the meadows. Think of that, girl – think, for every blade of grass you cut, that's a soldier's life slashed away while the poor bugger's stood there in the water, helpless. And stood there for *hours*, for a *whole night*, a *day* and a night, some of 'em *three* days, with nowhere else to go – Germans at the back of 'em, Germans overhead, and only our little boats to fetch 'em off, packing 'em in as best we could, pulling 'em on board out of water that wasn't much more than running blood, and them covered in their own blood, and shit, and other blokes' guts and brains what had been sprayed over them when the bombs and bullets got 'em . . . And all the time we was doing that, blokes like *him* – he jerked a contemptuous thumb towards Dennis '—were sitting safe at home, cutting a bit of grass, milking the cows, collecting the eggs from under the hens . . . Real dangerous work *that* is – I don't think! And you've got the cheek to bring him here, with our Olive sitting at the same table and knowing her man was one of the last out from Dunkirk, and could've been left there to rot and moulder on the beach . . .' He spluttered and floundered into silence, his face crimson, his eyes no more than reddened slits.

'Ted . . .' Annie whispered, appalled. She laid her hands on his shoulders again and gripped them hard, and this time he did not shrug her away. Instead, he sat breathing hard, and his big hands, clenched into fists, trembled on the table in front of him.

Annie looked at her daughters. Olive was sitting like stone, her fingers twisted together in her lap. Her face was white and her eyes bright with tears. Until now, Annie knew, Olive had understood little of what went on at Dunkirk. Neither Ted nor Derek had told anyone much. She herself hadn't realised the full horror until Ted's outburst.

Betty, too, was pale and shocked, but there was anger in the tight compression of her lips and her eyes were defiant. She jumped to her feet, facing her father.

'That's not fair! None of it's fair. You're calling Dennis a coward, and he's not. He never was. D'you know what it takes to be a conscientious objector? It takes a lot of thought and a lot of guts. You have to go to a tribunal and have people pull you to pieces for what you believe in. You have to go to *prison*. Dennis spent months in jail, just because he doesn't think it's right to kill people, because he doesn't agree with what went on at Dunkirk or what's going on anywhere else in this horrible war—'

'Pity he didn't stay there,' Ted said brutally. 'Then we wouldn't have to sit and listen to filth at our own dinner-table.'

'You're the one talking filth, not me,' Betty flashed. 'Anyway, what does it matter now? Dennis isn't working on the farm. He's not milking cows and collecting eggs – he's working in bomb disposal. Going down holes where bombs have landed and making sure they won't blow up. And that's a bloody sight more than most people are doing.' She turned to Olive. 'I'm sorry, Livvy, but it's more than your Derek's doing just now. *He's* only building huts down in Wiltshire. Dennis is putting his life at risk every day.' And, looking again at Ted, 'Anyway, since when have you had room to talk? It takes you all your time these days to go out in the garden and plant a few beans. D'you know how many of Dennis's mates got killed last week? *Do* you?'

Ted flushed and started to get to his feet, while Annie glared at her daughter and tried to hold him in his chair.

'There's no call for that, Betty. Your father's been ill—'

'Ill,' Betty sneered. 'He's not ill. He's just plain terrified. He always has been. And he talks about *Dennis* being a coward!'

'That's enough!' Ted tore himself from his wife's grasp. 'It's all right, Annie – I'm not so ill I can't chastise my own daughter when she's saucing me. And you're not too big to be chastised either,' he said to Betty, 'for all you think you're so independent in your trousers and cowboy hat.'

'Go on, then,' she said, standing her ground. 'Go on and hit me. I warn you, if you do I'll walk out of this house and never come back again.'

'*Betty!*' Annie's cry was agonised. She caught again at Ted's sleeve, imploring him to stop. 'Don't let's argue, Ted, for God's sake. Isn't there enough fighting going on in the world, without us adding to it? Look, why don't I make us all a cup of tea and let's sit down and talk about it quietly. And let's listen to what Dennis has to say. We've all been shouting so loud the poor chap hasn't had room to get a word in edgeways.'

Ted hesitated. He was still breathing hard, as if he had run all the way down March Street, and his face was suffused with blood. His eyes, when he looked at Betty, were murderous. He did not look at Dennis at all.

'I won't sit at a table with him,' he said belligerently.

'All right then, you sit in your chair.' That hadn't been what he meant and Annie knew it, but she had been badly frightened by the row and was determined not to let it go any further. 'Betty, you take Dennis out in the garden for a few minutes and Livvy, you can help me make the tea.' She watched as the three younger people got up and left the room, then turned to Ted and laid her hand on his arm again. 'Sit down for a few minutes, Ted, and get your breath back. You've got yourself all upset, but it won't do no good getting yourself at odds with our Betty. You know what she's like.

If she walks out of here in a temper, she's just stubborn enough to stay out.' Her voice trembled for the first time. 'We don't want to lose her, now, do we?'

Ted set his jaw and pushed out his lip, but after a moment or two he glanced at Annie's face and gave in. He sat down in his armchair by the fireplace.

'All right, Annie. I won't do nothing to upset the applecart. But she oughter know better than to bring a bloke like that here. With our Olive and all—'

Olive poked her head round the kitchen door. 'Don't you drag me into it, Dad. I've got nothing against Dennis. He seems a decent chap and he's fond of our Betty, anyone can see that with half an eye, and he is in bomb disposal now. She's right, you can't get much more dangerous than that.'

'Maybe so,' Ted said grudgingly. 'But he didn't volunteer, did he? He tried to get off.'

'I'm not so sure about that,' Annie said. 'I thought once people like that had got exemption it carried on.'

'All the same,' he said, changing tack, 'I still think she oughter've had more sense than to bring him here, after what our Olive's been through. And she might have known *I* wouldn't want him under my roof.'

'You've always told us we could bring our friends home, Dad. You said you wanted us to, so you could see what they were like.'

'I didn't need to see *him* to know what he's like,' Ted declared obstinately. He sat down in his chair and shook out the pages of the *Daily Express.* Annie gave him an exasperated glance and went out into the kitchen, where the kettle was just coming to the boil. She swished a drop of water into the teapot and rinsed it out, then added four spoonfuls of tea from the caddy. Lord Woolton had been encouraging everyone to drink weaker tea – 'one per person and *none* for the pot' – but Annie had taken this a step further. If anyone objected, she said that it was her spoonful she'd left out, so it was her business, and none of the family had the courage to suggest that she kept her hot water separate too.

'Call Betty and Dennis in,' she said to Olive. 'We ought to give that young man a chance to speak for himself. Betty wouldn't have brought him home if she didn't think a lot of him.'

The family gathered again round the square dining-table. Ted remained stubbornly in his chair. Betty was looking pink and there was still a flash of anger in her hazel eyes, and even Dennis's calmness seemed more fragile. Annie glanced from one to the other and then spoke quietly.

'All right. Let's get things straight.' She addressed herself to Dennis. 'I think my husband's right. Betty ought to have told us about you before she brought you here. Not that we'd have refused to let you in,' she added with a warning glance at her husband, 'but we would at least have known where we were right from the start.'

'I don't see as that would have made any difference,' Betty objected. 'It's Dennis I wanted you to meet, not a military rank or a uniform. Though he's got both those now,' she added, 'so I don't see what you've got to complain about.'

Dennis laid his hand on hers. Annie looked at it. It was a strong hand, with long fingers that looked as if they had a firm grip, and his wrist was well muscled. And his nails were clean. Annie did like clean nails, and Ted never managed to keep the oil and grease out of his for long, somehow.

'I think it's time I said something,' Dennis said quietly. 'I didn't butt in before because – well, you all seemed to have plenty to say.' His eyes crinkled with a smile that Annie was hard put to it not to return. 'And I don't like rowing any more than I like fighting. But that doesn't mean I won't stand up for my opinions,' he said to Ted. 'I just do it in a different way, perhaps.'

Ted said nothing. He picked up his teacup and sipped noisily. Dennis waited for a moment and then went on.

'I didn't refuse to fight because I was afraid of being killed. We all have to die some time and that doesn't worry me at all. I believe in God, you see, and I believe in his justice and love, so why should I be afraid of dying?' He looked at them with calm eyes and Annie felt embarrassed. Talking about God like that was almost as bad as talking about death and sex. She cleared her throat and offered Olive the sugar, forgetting that they had all given it up in favour of saccharin.

'What I was afraid of was killing other people,' Dennis continued. 'I just don't believe we have the right to do it. We're told *Thou shall not kill*. I believe that. And I won't do it.'

He made his statement very quietly, but there was a quality in his voice that left no one in any doubt that he meant it. Almost unwillingly, they lifted their heads and gazed at him.

'But that doesn't stop me wanting to help my country. Or my fellow-men.' He paused, and added even more quietly, '*All* my fellow-men.'

'You mean you'd help a Jerry?' Olive asked incredulously.

'In some circumstances, yes. If I found a parachutist, say, hurt, I'd do what I could for him. I wouldn't help him escape, or anything like that – but I wouldn't leave him to bleed to death, either.'

'Well, nor would I,' Annie exclaimed. 'I mean, that's just common humanity, isn't it.'

'I think so, yes.' Dennis smiled at her. 'And I can't see the sense of shooting a man down if you're going to do your best to save his life afterwards. Anyway, that's what I believe in. So I refused to join up and was sent before a tribunal. And as I've already told Betty, they gave me exemption on condition I stayed in my job – the only snag was, my employer, who happened to be Portsmouth City Council, refused to employ me.'

'First bit of sense I've heard all day,' Ted muttered.

'Now look, Dad—'

'All right,' Annie said, raising her voice above Betty's. 'All *right*. We won't start that again, if you don't mind. So that's why you went to work on the farm.'

'After a few months,' Dennis said. 'As Betty told you, I had to serve a while in prison first.'

There was another brief silence. Annie could feel what Ted was thinking.

So she's brought a jailbird into the house as well as a conchie. Swiftly, before he could utter his thoughts, she said, 'But how is it you're in the Army now? Did you change your mind after the blitz?'

'Not exactly,' Dennis said. 'The blitz helped, of course. Seeing the fires over the hill, hearing the explosions, knowing what you were all going through here . . . But I'd been worrying about it long before that. And when people I knew started getting killed – those airmen that used to come out to the farm and see the girls – specially Geoff, the pilot poor Erica was engaged to – well, I knew it wasn't right to stay safe. So I volunteered for a non-combatant role.'

'There you are,' Annie said to her husband. 'He did volunteer.'

'Did you actually choose bomb disposal?' Olive asked. 'I mean, that's really dangerous, like Betty says. Or did they say that's what you had to do?'

'Oh no, I volunteered.' He smiled faintly. 'We're all volunteers. It's no use having men who aren't keen on the work.'

Betty shuddered. 'I don't see how anyone can be keen on work like that. Knowing it could blow you to smithereens any minute.' She moved closer, her eyes challenging her father to object. 'I don't care what anyone says, I'd rather you stayed safe on the farm.'

There was a short silence. Then Annie said, 'Well, I reckon that clears that up. It don't seem to me that Dennis has got anything to be ashamed about, and as far as I'm concerned he's welcome in this house any time he cares to come.' She looked at Ted. 'You can always go out if you feel like it.'

Ted opened his mouth, then closed it again. Like many of his mates, he liked to believe that he was master in his own house, but when it came to the point it was more often Annie who had the final say. He glanced at Olive and then at Betty, and knew that he was beaten.

'Pity our Colin ain't here,' he muttered. 'Chap could do with another bloke around with all these women ruling the roost.'

Dennis laughed. 'My father says just the same. I've got three sisters – against them and Mum, we don't have a chance.'

Ted looked at him. Dennis was smiling, his face open and friendly. But Ted could not respond. He still could not forget the men standing up to their necks in blood and salt water at Dunkirk. He could not forget his own son, Colin, at sea aboard HMS *Exeter*. He could not forget the bombs raining down upon Portsmouth during the blitz, and his own shame as he crumpled on top of the turret where he had been firewatching, his nerve broken at last, leaving him sobbing like a baby under the blazing sky.

Betty and Dennis left that evening. Dennis had to go back to Fort Widley, on the Hill, but he took Betty to Bishop's Waltham on the bus first. They had to walk from the middle of the village out to the Spencers' farm near Stephen Castle Down, and twilight was falling as they strolled through the quiet lanes and beside the watercress-filled stream, their arms around each other's waists.

Despite her defiance, Betty had been shaken by the row with her father. The Chapmans were a close family, not given to rowing, although there had been inevitable grumbles from the girls as they grew up and Ted tried in vain to exert the authority he thought a father should have. They'd won a series of small battles, over lipstick and what time to come in at night – well, that was more a compromise than a victory, for Ted had steadfastly refused to allow either of his daughters to stay out later than ten o'clock, with eleven as an occasional and reluctant concession. But they'd never come as close as this to a real showdown.

It had been sunny and warm all day, and the heat hadn't yet died away. It seemed to rise up from the road and burn her face. She touched her cheek and felt tears against her fingertips. She had hardly known until then that she was crying.

Dennis noticed the movement and stopped. He drew her into his arms and they stood close to the hedge as he kissed her and tasted her tears.

'Sweetheart, don't. He'll come round.'

'It's not just that,' she said, letting the tears come more freely now. 'It's you. When he was talking about Dunkirk – it made it all so real. And when I think of what could happen to you, any day . . .' She looked up at him. 'I feel so scared, Dennis. It's like living in a nightmare.'

'Everyone lives in a nightmare these days,' he said soberly, his hand stroking the back of her neck. 'It's no different for anyone else.'

'I know. And I know what it's like to have that nightmare come true. Think of last summer – first it was poor Erica's Geoff getting shot down, and then Sandy and Duff. And that girl from October Street, Kathy Simmons, and her baby getting blown up, and Olive having a miscarriage. And God knows how many others . . .' For a moment the tears over-whelmed her, and she put her fists against her cheeks and took a deep, shuddering breath.

Dennis held her close. There was no easy comfort to offer her. No platitudes, no murmured 'there, there, it'll all be all right'. It wasn't all right. People were being killed, all the time. Sailors, soldiers, airmen like the ones she had mentioned, who had been such regular and welcome visitors to the farm. Old people, young children, mothers and babies, fathers who had been forced to fight when all they really wanted was to be at home . . . The pain was there all the time, an ache with no cure.

And it wasn't any the less because you'd felt it before, or because everyone else was feeling it too. It made it all the worse, because you couldn't let it out. You could grieve for a while, but then you had to pull yourself out of it and go on with your life. Hardest of all, you had to keep a smile on your lips while you did so.

Dennis hadn't talked much about his work. A lot of it was secret, but Betty knew that as a Pioneer his job had been to dig down to the bombs that had torn their way into the ground, sometimes twenty feet or more down, and lay there unexploded. Nobody knew whether they were still live, and the men had to work with as much care as archaeologists sifting for fragile remains, excavating cautiously and shoring up the walls of the pit as they did so; knowing all the time that the bomb somewhere beneath their feet might even now have begun to tick and so started its progress to explosion.

And nobody ever knew how long the delay might be. It could be a matter of seconds from the moment when the timing mechanism began, or it could be days. It might be even longer than that. And the bombs were changing all the time. You never knew whether this one might be different – and even more deadly.

It was bad enough, Betty thought, when Dennis had been one of those digging down through the ground. But it was even worse now that he had been transferred from Pioneers to Bomb Disposal itself.

'Oh, Dennis,' she said brokenly. 'How long have we got to go on like this? Only seeing each other once or twice a week – wasting so much time. I want to be with you every minute I can. I want to be *married* to you.'

'I know. I want that too, you know I do. But we've got to think of others, Betty. Your dad—'

'I'm not letting him spoil my life!' she broke in. 'He just doesn't want me to do *anything* I want to do. I wouldn't be in the Land Army if he'd had his way. I wouldn't have gone to dances or had any boyfriends or nice clothes, or *anything*. I'd have been still in ankle socks, sitting at home with my knitting and learning to cook. He just doesn't want me to grow up, that's what it is.'

'He's ill,' Dennis said quietly. 'You can tell what Dunkirk did to him. I can understand the way he feels about me, after going through something like that. And all the bombing—'

'There's plenty of people been through the bombing. They don't use it as an excuse to ruin other people's lives.'

Dennis sighed. Gently, he pulled her hands away from her face and held them against his shoulders. He kissed her lips.

'Let's be patient, Betty. We love each other, and nothing can stop that. But I don't want to do anything that'll cause trouble with your family. Your dad thinks the world of you, anyone can see that. It'd break his heart if you stopped going home. And your mum – she's got enough on her plate. She doesn't deserve more worry.'

'But I don't *want* to cause them worry,' Betty said. 'I just want to get married to you. And it'd be all *right* – you're just the sort of chap they'd want for me – if only – if—'

'If only I weren't a CO,' he said as she stumbled into silence.

'Oh, Dennis,' Betty said, in tears again, 'why does everything have to be so *complicated*?'

He laughed. 'Life *is* complicated, sweetheart. And it's usually unfair as well. It's just something we have to put up with. And it helps if we can keep cheerful about it. Don't let it get us down, eh?' He kissed her again and turned to walk on, keeping her hand firmly tucked into his arm. 'Just remember, Betty, we've got each other. That's a lot more than plenty of other people have. And I don't even have to go away. We can be together a lot of the time. Your Olive doesn't see Derek once or twice a week, now does she?'

Betty shook her head, feeling ashamed. Dennis was right. Everyone had something to put up with, and at least they could be together out here on the farm, where everyone knew and liked Dennis. Even Erica, who'd been so much against him to begin with.

If Erica could come round, perhaps Dad would too, when he was better. Perhaps Dennis's way was the right one after all – just waiting, just giving him time.

They were almost at the farm. The flint walls of the long, low building stood before them, shadowy in the gathering darkness. The warm scent of roses wafted across the yard from the thick, tangled bush that climbed beside the front porch to the bedroom windows. Over in the orchard they could hear the murmurings of a mother hen settling her brood.

Betty stopped, her hand on the gate, gazing at the dark bulk of the farmhouse. Even here, the blackout was strictly observed and it was impossible to tell whether there were any lights on indoors. Most likely, everyone was in bed and fast asleep, gathering their energy for the next day's toil.

She and Dennis had met here, they had grown to know and love each other in the fields and meadows that surrounded the farm. They had worked side by side, cutting corn, bringing in the hay, milking the cows and a hundred other jobs. She would have been content to have gone on like that for ever.

But Dennis possessed a conscience that would not allow him to rest while others fought and died. A conscience that might very easily take him to his own death.

'Let's say goodnight now,' Dennis said quietly. 'No use brooding. There's work to do tomorrow.'

'I know.' Betty took one last look at the stars and the moon above. It struck her suddenly that there had been no raid tonight, not even a warning. It was one of those rare nights when it was possible to remember peace.

Peace.

She took a deep breath, drawing in the scent of the roses, and offered her lips to Dennis for his kiss.

5

Annie told Jess about the scene with Betty as they walked up March Street together on Monday morning, after Olive's departure for her new life in the ATS. They'd had a cup of tea in Annie's kitchen before setting out, to give Annie time to get over Olive leaving, but the daily work still had to be done. Shopping took so long these days, with all the queues, and you had to get out early or there'd be nothing left. Often enough, Jess had come home after nearly two hours' queueing in different shops, with barely half a shopping-bag to show for it.

'And it takes as long to queue for two people as for three or four,' Annie remarked. 'It'll seem funny just cooking for Ted and me after all these years.' Her lip trembled a little. 'I dunno – I thought with our Olive married, she'd be stopping at home. But they don't seem to take much account of that these days.'

'It's a pity she lost the baby,' Jess agreed. 'I mean, it was a shame anyway, but it would have kept her at home too. I wouldn't like the idea of our Rose going in the Forces. You don't know who they're going to meet, do you? There's a lot of rough girls going in now they're conscripting.'

'Well, we done our best to bring 'em up decent, we just have to hope they'll remember all they've been taught.'

They came to the top of March Street and made their way along to the shops. Ethel Glaister was waiting at the bus stop. She nodded at them and said, 'There's not a thing worth having round here. I'm going down to Fratton. Smarts have got some lovely autumn coats at their shop.'

'I didn't know Smarts had a shop at Fratton,' Jess said, and Ethel looked impatient.

'Well, it's their blitz address, of course. And I know a really nice greengrocer there, he always keeps something special for me. Not *black market*, of course,' she added, lowering her voice to a whisper, 'but very good value.'

'Well, you're welcome,' Annie said. 'I'd rather support local shops myself. I think we all ought to do what the Government says and not travel any more than we've got to, even if it is only down Fratton.'

Ethel sniffed, but the bus came along and she said no more. She climbed aboard, her tight skirt showing a lot of leg.

'I know we're supposed to save material when we have anything new,' Annie remarked, watching her, 'but Ethel's had that blue costume since well before the war and the skirt never used to be that short. I wonder what George would say if he saw her flaunting herself like that.'

'I sometimes wonder where she goes of an afternoon,' Jess said. 'She's always out, you know, in her best clothes and those high heels. She likes to pretend she's better than the rest of us – too good to shop round here. And that hair! My Frank would kill me if I dyed mine yellow like that. Well, here are the queues. I wonder what we'll be able to get today.'

Desmond had not arrived at the corner when Micky cycled up October Street, so he shrugged and pedalled away. That was the trouble with Desmond, you couldn't rely on him. He probably couldn't even tell the time. It wasn't much use having a First Lieutenant who couldn't tell the time.

However, by the time Micky had reached the point where September Street joined Copnor Road, he had almost forgotten Desmond. His mind was racing ahead to Charlotte Street, the market in the city centre where he could usually manage to pick up an odd job or two.

He'd have to hide the bike somewhere nearby, so that it would be handy for later. Nancy had been quite right to suspect that he hadn't been given permission to use it; he'd noticed it in the alley for two or three days and since nobody seemed to be using it, he'd decided he might as well borrow it. It was a long way to Copnor, unless you could jump a ride on a bus without the conductor noticing. And the basket was useful for bringing home all the bits and pieces he was either given or could help himself to as he scurried between the shops and stalls, running errands.

Some of Micky's wealth was come by honestly enough. More of it was collected by what Nancy called his 'sticky fingers'. But the traders in Charlotte Street weren't like the shopkeepers in September Street. They knew a boy was going to take advantage of any opportunity that came his way, and they just made sure there weren't too many opportunities. And for the most part, they were willing enough to chuck him a halfpenny to run an errand, or give him an apple or a couple of spuds.

Micky parked the bike in an alleyway, hoping it would still be there when he came back, and strolled round to Alf Reckitt, the stallholder who usually had a job or two for him to do. It wasn't really a stall, just a big barrow filled with odds and ends of vegetables and whatever the man could pick up cheap. Before the war, the narrow street had been crammed with barrows like this, or bigger carts with horses still in harness, their heads buried in nosebags. But now there were only a few, selling local produce or stuff they had grown themselves. Once, Alf had brought in a load of cherries and the queue had stretched right out into Commercial Road.

This morning, to Micky's surprise, the road was running with dank, smelly water. Alf Reckitt was staring at it, his long face even more melancholy than usual.

'Look at that,' he said to Micky. 'Bleedin' drain's blocked. And will anyone do anythin' about it? In a pig's eye, they will!'

'Why's the drain blocked?' Micky asked. 'D'you think there's something down there?'

'Well, of *course* there's summat down there,' Alf said irritably. 'Gawd knows what it is. Bleedin' body, I wooden be surprised.'

'A body? *Bleeding?*' Micky gazed at the murky water with awe. 'You mean someone's got bombed, and they're all in bits, and the bits—'

Alf raised his eyes to the sky. 'Gawd give me strength! *Course* I don't mean that. I dunno *what's* down there. Jus' muck, thassall. It wants clearin' out, it does, but *they* won't do nothin' about it. Got too many more important things to worry about than us poor bleeders down Charlotte Street.'

'I'll clear it,' Micky offered. 'I don't mind. You'll have to give me summat for it, though.'

Alf looked at him. 'I'll give yer a penny.'

'Not on your nellie. That's worth a bob any day, that is.'

'A shillin'?' Alf repeated. 'You'll be lucky, mate! I could get a mudlark ter do that for tuppence.'

'You got me,' Micky said, grinning, 'an' I used ter go mudlarking at low tide every Saturday, picking up pennies what folks chucked off the ferry pontoon. But I wouldn't walk down the Hard just for tuppence.'

'Thruppence,' Alf said, making to turn away. He stepped in a wet, soggy mess and swore as it soaked through his shoes.

'Ninepence.'

'You gotta nope. Thruppence, an that's my last word.'

'Tanner, and that's mine,' Micky declared.

There was a moment of silence as their eyes met and locked. Micky held the gaze for about ten full seconds and then let his eyes slide sideways. The water was almost surrounding Alf's barrow now. It had an evil smell which rose and seemed to hang over the collection of battered vegetables like an acrid cloud. Micky wouldn't have been at all surprised if it was oozing from a dead body.

'I'll do it for thruppence and a bag of spuds,' he offered at last.

'You know I can't sell potatoes off ration.'

'I'm not askin' you to sell 'em to me.'

'You know what'd 'appen if a copper caught me,' Alf said, but his voice was wavering.

'Okay,' Micky said, turning away with a swagger. 'I'll go an' see who else needs a bitta help. If I see any mudlarks, I'll tell 'em you've got a job for them.'

'Oh, all right,' Alf said with exasperation. 'But mind you do it proper, see? I don't want it floodin' again. It's losin' me a lotta custom.'

He handed Micky a galvanised bucket, and Micky got down on his knees. The draincover was choked with rubbish and it was easy to see why the drain was flooding. There was certainly something down there, stopping the flow of water. The funny thing was, it hadn't rained for days. Probably a burst waterpipe somewhere, he thought, flooding into it.

The draincover was hard to remove. It probably hadn't been touched for years – Alf was right about the Council, who never seemed to bother themselves about Charlotte Street. Micky got his fingers round the bars and tugged. It didn't move. He tugged again and again, without result.

Breathing hard, he sat back on his heels, then leaned forward and gave another mighty heave.

The draincover came away as if it had just been lying there all the time. Micky fell over backwards and heard Alf laughing.

'Gawd, look at you! Covered in muck from 'ead ter foot. I wooden wanna be in your shoes when you gets 'ome, I reckon your gran'll skin yer.'

Micky scowled at him. 'She won't, not if I got a bag of spuds to give her. You stick to your part of the bargain an' I'll stick to mine.'

'Awright, awright,' Alf said, turning away. 'I won't say another dickybird. You just get on with it an' let me know when you're finished. An' keep an eye on the barrer while I goes an' sees a man about a dog.'

He walked off in the direction of the shack that was used by stallholders and barrow-boys as a lavatory. Micky turned back to the drain and started to fish out the muck that was choking it, piling it up beside the hole. It was impossible to tell just what was in the stinking mass, but some of it looked and smelt like rotting meat.

Bodies . . .

'Oy! Ain't there no one servin'? Or is it all free today?'

Micky looked up. The voice came from a fat woman standing by the barrow. She was dressed in a cotton frock that had seen better days and a man's jacket. Her hair was covered with a grubby scarf, wound into a turban, and underneath it he caught a glimpse of metal curlers like the ones his gran wore.

'Where's Alf?' she demanded. 'I ain't got all day.'

'Gone for a pee,' Micky said, turning back to the drain. 'I 'spect he'll be back soon.'

'Well, it'll be too late for me,' she said irritably. 'My old man'll be 'ome at twelve and he don't 'alf create if 'is dinner ain't ready. Can't you take me money?'

Micky hesitated. He glanced at the few piles of vegetables on the barrow, most of them close to rotting. The barrow-boys in Charlotte Street only ever got the worst these days, especially with so much food being controlled, but it was cheap and all that some people could afford. This old woman probably came from Rudmore or somewhere like that, where they lived ten or fifteen to a two-roomed hovel.

All the same, she had money in her hand and who was to know just how much she handed over?

'All right,' he said. He stood up, wiping his filthy hands down his grey shorts. 'What d'yer want?'

The fat woman had a shopping bag with her. He filled it with potatoes and carrots and took the coins she held out. She turned away and he dropped threepence in Alf's tin and a penny in his own pocket.

Well, that would buy him a bag of chips for his dinner. And as soon as Alf came back he'd –

The air was split by a sudden scream, and Micky whirled round. At his feet, sprawled in the pile of debris he had dragged out of the drain, was a woman in a pale blue suit. Her hair was yellow and carefully waved, her face artificial with make-up. She was screeching and clutching the leg that she had caught in the hole that Micky had left uncovered.

It was Ethel Glaister, from number 15 April Grove.

'I'm taking him to court,' Ethel declared as she gave her children their tea. 'I'm getting him prosecuted. Leaving a drain all uncovered like that. My leg's proper bruised. And all that muck! My blue costume's ruined, and my last pair of silk stockings are torn to shreds.'

'I don't suppose he meant it as a booby-trap,' Joe said, reaching for the dish the shepherd's pie had been in. He scraped at the crispy bits of potato around the edge. 'Anyway, what were you doing down Charlotte Street? I never knew you went down there shopping.'

'That's because you never take an interest,' Ethel said sharply. 'And you might leave a bit of enamel on that dish, Joe, if you don't mind. As it happens, I spend most of my day shopping, cooking and running around after you two, not that I expect any thanks for what I do.'

Joe and Carol glanced at each other. Mum was off again, their looks said, going down the same old track like a train that didn't have anywhere else to go. It had been bad enough when Dad was home and she nagged him all the time, but now that he was away she turned all her attention to them.

'They're calling up all the nineteen-year-old men now,' Joe said, trying to change the subject. 'I reckon it won't be much longer before my lot go.'

'You're not nineteen!'

'I know,' he said patiently, 'but I'll be eighteen in September and the rate we're going there just aren't going to be enough men. They're saying Japan'll be in soon. They're going for China already.'

'I wish you wouldn't talk about it at the table,' Ethel said crossly. 'You know I like mealtimes to be nice.'

Joe and Carol glanced at each other again and Joe lifted his eyes briefly to the ceiling. Carol stifled a sudden giggle and her mother glared at her.

'I don't know what you find so funny about that. Someone has to keep up standards.' She frowned. 'Here, what have you done to your ears? Push back your hair.'

She reached across the table and Carol leaned back, but Ethel was too quick for her. One hand thrust back the roll of hair that hung down fashionably over Carol's right ear, and Ethel stared.

'You've had your ears pierced. Who said you could do that?'

'I didn't ask,' Carol said defiantly. 'They're my ears.'

'And you're my daughter! You're not sixteen yet – you ask permission before you start acting like a grown-up. I suppose you got it done in your dinner-hour.'

'Yes, I did. *Last Friday's* dinner-hour.' Carol stared back at her mother. 'And this is the first day you've noticed it.' She jabbed her fork into the shepherd's pie and Ethel flushed.

'Are you trying to make out I'm a bad mother? Haven't I just told you I went all down Charlotte Street to get a few extra potatoes and things for you two? I don't know why I bother, I really don't. *You* could be bringing me back a bit of shopping to save my legs, but no, you're off with the rest of the trollops from Littlewoods, prancing round the shops and making yourselves up like tarts and getting your ears pierced.' She was breathing quickly, her pale blue eyes snapping with rage. 'Well, I'll tell you something now, my girl, and we'll see how you like this. If you can afford to do that sort of thing, you've got more money in your pocket than's good for you, and you're not giving enough to help here. I'll have another two shillings a week out of your pay packet, and you'll hand it over to me before you open it, so there's no temptation for you to spend on the way home, is that understood?'

'Another two bob! But that'll only leave me enough for my fares and lunches—'

'You'll have as much spending money as a girl your age needs,' Ethel stated. 'There'll still be enough for a few sweets and your Saturday night pictures, and that's all you want.'

'It's not. I want to be able to buy things. I want to be able to get my own clothes.'

'*I'll* see to your clothes. Just because you're out at work, doesn't mean you can start acting like a young woman.' Ethel snatched the dish away from Joe. 'I told you not to scrape that dish bare! D'you think I'm made of money?' She stormed out to the scullery and they heard her clatter the bowl into the earthenware sink.

'I bet that's chipped another inch of enamel off,' Joe muttered, and winked at his sister. 'Cheer up, kid. When I go in the Forces I'll see you right for an extra bob or two. And you might be able to volunteer yourself before long, the way this war's going.'

'She'll never let me,' Carol grumbled. 'Anyway, why shouldn't I get my ears pierced and wear make-up? *She* does.'

'Maybe that's why,' her brother said shrewdly. 'She tries to look young, but when people see you they know she's not, any more. But she can't keep you in ankle socks for ever.'

Carol looked gloomy. For ever was a long time away, and she wanted to wear lipstick and earrings now. She'd been experimenting with her mother's make-up and jewellery for weeks, and was looking forward to trying on her earrings as soon as she could take the sleepers out. There was one pair she specially liked, dangly ones with stones in that looked like real diamonds.

'I wish I was old enough to leave home,' she said. 'I'm fed up with being treated like a kid.'

Ethel came back with the pudding. It was made from custard poured over stale breadcrumbs with a couple of spoonsful of jam stirred in. On top, she'd put a dollop or two of mock cream, made from sugar and marge and dried 'household' milk powder.

Carol stared at it and made a face. But she was still hungry, and it was all there was to eat. She took the bowl her mother gave her and swallowed the mixture, grimacing at the feel of the breadcrumbs mixed with the thin custard.

The sudden hammering at the front door came as a welcome respite.

'I'll get my own back, see if I don't,' Micky raged. 'Doin' a good turn, I was – clearing out that mucky drain, serving at the barrow – and she has to come along and fall in! I mean, she just wasn't looking where she was going. The drain had to be cleared, there was muck pouring out of it, the road was stinking. I reckon that's why she slipped in the first place, in them daft shoes she had on.'

'She was all right, though, wasn't she?' Nancy asked. 'I mean, she wasn't hurt or nothing.'

'Scraped her leg a bit, that's all, and tore her fancy stockings. Alf offered her the money for 'em, but she wouldn't have it. Just stood there screeching at him. And then a copper come along, of course, just like they always do when you don't want 'em, and she told 'im she wanted me charged.' He stared indignantly at his mother and grandmother. 'All I was doing was trying to help! It ain't fair.'

'It ain't,' Granny Kinch declared. 'And I'm going down there to tell 'em so. First thing tomorrow morning, I'm going down the police station, and you can come with me, Micky. And you, our Nance.'

Nancy looked dubious. She had been to the police station more than once on what she termed 'official business', and liked to stay clear as much as possible. Most of the regular bobbies knew her anyway. 'I dunno as that's a good idea, Ma,' she said.

'Well, *I'm* going anyway. And I'll tell you what I'm going to do this minute.' Granny Kinch thrust her misshapen feet into the pair of broken-down old shoes that stood by the door. 'I'm going down to give that Ethel Glaister a piece of my mind. Taking her bad cess out on our Micky when he was doing an honest job.' She didn't add 'for once', but the words seemed to hang in the air. 'I'll make her sorry.'

She shuffled to the door and they heard it slam behind her. Nancy glanced at her son.

'She's not worth bothering with, that Mrs Glaister. I seen her down Charlotte Street a time or two now. I don't reckon it's the shopping she goes for, neither.'

Micky turned away. He wasn't interested in why Ethel Glaister went to Charlotte Street. He wasn't even all that bothered about being taken to court, except that it would probably mean a fine. But he was filled with all the righteous indignation of a young ruffian who has got away with more misdemeanours than he can count and is then arraigned for something he either didn't do, or intended as an honest job. His grandmother's unspoken 'for once' still hung in the air.

I'll get my own back, he swore again vengefully. See if I don't.

The whole street heard the row as Granny Kinch stood at Ethel Glaister's front door, shouting and haranguing. Twice Ethel tried to shut the door but the old woman's foot was firmly stuck in the way. In any case, Ethel couldn't resist yelling back, and Jess, who happened to be outside talking to Peggy Shaw, hustled Rose inside quickly, afraid of the language she might hear.

'You've always had it in for our Micky,' Granny Kinch raged. 'You're just like the rest of 'em – never give 'im a chance. Don't matter what goes wrong round 'ere, it's always our Micky what gets the blame. What d'you 'ave to go down Charlotte Street for, eh, lookin' for trouble? Why did it 'ave to be *you* what fell down the drain?'

'D'you think I did it on purpose, or something?' Ethel screeched. 'D'you think I *want* to go all that way to do a bit of shopping, just so I won't meet any of you lot, and then run into '*im*? Isn't nowhere safe? That was my best stockings ruined this afternoon, and my nice skirt all covered in muck. And what d'you think I felt like, coming home looking like a scarecrow? I could've died of shame.'

'Pity you didn't. I reckon the whole street would've put our Micky up for a medal if he'd rid us of your sour face.'

'*Oh!* You old *bitch*! That's incitement to murder, that's what that is. I could have the law on you, saying things like that.' Ethel glanced around for witnesses, but everyone had disappeared behind their front doors, though she had no doubt that every ear in the street was flapping to catch every word. 'It's no wonder your Micky's turned out the way he has,' she said haughtily to Granny Kinch. 'With a grandmother like you it's a wonder he hasn't finished up in prison before this.'

'With neighbours like you, he'd probably be better off,' the old woman retorted. 'Anyway, you're doin' your best to see he gets there, aincher? Gettin' 'im charged over a simple accident. He was only doin' a good turn, too. It was your fault you fell down that drain, not his. You oughter bin lookin' where you were goin', instead of struttin' along with yer nose in the air.' Her lip curled with scorn. 'One of them stallholders is goin' to take you for a chicken one of these days, the way you walks about.'

'Well, at least they'll never take me for a common *tart*,' Ethel flashed.

There was a tiny silence. Then Granny Kinch said with quiet venom, 'You'll be sorry you said that, Ethel Glaister. You'll be really sorry. Don't forget, I knew you when you lived down Fratton. I knew your ma and I knew about all the dance you led 'er. It wasn't till George Glaister come along that—'

'Shut up!' Ethel screamed, stamping her feet on the doorstep. Her face was scarlet with fury. 'Shut up, shut up *shut up!*'

'No, I won't. I won't shut up. It's time people knew the truth about you and your fancy ways. Settin' yourself up to be Someone when all the time you're nothin' but a dirty little—'

'I won't listen to you. I won't.' Ethel turned and addressed Joe, who was lurking behind her in the passage. 'Go and fetch a policeman this minute, Joe, and tell him this old faggot's causing a breach of the peace. Slandering me, she is. You can go to prison for that, you know,' she added to Granny Kinch. 'And a good job too. Good riddance to bad rubbish, that's what that'll be.'

'That's enough!' Tommy Vickers was on the scene, dressed in his ARP uniform and brandishing a truncheon for all the world as if he were a copper himself. He put a hand on each woman's shoulder, holding them apart. 'Stop that screeching, you two. You're like a pair of alleycats tied to a clothes-line. This is a decent street—' he glanced at Granny Kinch '—well, as decent as we can make it anyway, and we don't want none of your caterwauling here. If I hear any more of it *I'll* be the one fetching a policeman. And I'll be charging you *both* with a breach of the peace.'

'You get out and mind your own business, Tommy Vickers,' Ethel retorted. Her face was scarlet. 'This old cow hasn't got a leg to stand on and she knows it—'

'I thought it was you didn't have a leg to stand on, down Charlotte Street this morning,' Granny Kinch cut in swiftly, and Ethel's face turned even redder. 'All this is just because my Micky was doing someone a good turn and Lady Muck here come along with her nose in the air and fell down the drain.' She sniggered. 'Lady Muck! I reckon that was a good name for you this afternoon, an' all!'

Ethel quivered with fury but before she could retort, Tommy spoke again. He gripped each woman's shoulder firmly and shook them a little.

'I meant what I said. Any more noise and I'll call the police. And it won't be just a court case in front of the magistrate – it'll be a night in cells for both of you, to give you time to cool off.'

Ethel stared at him for a moment, then jerked away and flounced back into the house. She slammed the door so hard that the entire terrace seemed to shake. Granny Kinch shrugged.

'Good job my foot wasn't still in that doorway, I'd have had her up for damages. All right, young Tommy, you can let go now. I ain't goin' ter smash the windows in. Not that it ain't what she deserves, stuck-up bitch.' She turned and shuffled away up the street, back to number 10.

Frank had been working overtime as usual, and had missed the excitement. It wasn't until they were in the shelter that Jess had a chance to tell him. The siren had gone off as usual soon after dark, and they were huddled on the benches with Rose and Maureen. Rose was pressed close against Jess, flinching at every explosion, while Maureen played unconcernedly with her rag doll.

'She never said anything about Charlotte Street when Annie and me saw her, she said she was going to Fratton to look at new coats.'

'I don't reckon you want to believe too much of what Ethel Glaister says,' Frank remarked. 'She's always putting it on. She probably does all the shopping she can in Charlotte Street to save a few coppers for more make-up.'

Rose looked up. The bombing had stopped for a while and they were beginning to think the raiders might have gone.

'Joy Brunner's got a lipstick,' she said. 'I had a go with it. It looked nice.'

'Rose—' Jess began in dismay, but Frank cut angrily across her voice and Rose shrank back, surprised by his sudden sharpness.

'Well, you'd better not have another go with it, my girl. Dolling yourself up at your age! If I catch you wearing lipstick I'll put you over my knee, big as you are.'

'Joy's allowed to wear it,' Rose said in an injured tone. 'I'm fourteen, Dad.'

'Fourteen's fourteen,' Frank said unarguably. 'You're still a child. And what Joy Brunner does is up to her parents. It doesn't mean you can do the same.'

There was a brief silence. Rose glanced at Jess, who tried to make her eyes convey that she sympathised but nevertheless sided with Frank. After a moment, Rose spoke again.

'Joy's leaving school. She's going to work properly in the shop.'

'Joy's hardly been to school since the war started, from what I can make out,' Frank said. 'Why, she practically ran that shop till Mr Brunner came back.'

'Yes, but she's leaving properly now,' Rose persisted. 'I wish I could leave too.'

'Well, you can't.'

'But what's the use of it? I mean, we hardly ever do any proper lessons, just those in people's houses a couple of times a week. I could get a job—'

'You'll get a better job if you stay on at school and do a typing and shorthand course,' Frank said firmly. 'They're starting them after the summer. You can do a year, and then leave and get a decent job in an office like your cousin Olive had.'

'Or even better,' Jess added. 'You might even get into the Civil Service.'

'And what if the war's still on?' Rose asked. 'I'll be getting called up. What use is typing and shorthand going to be then?'

'Qualifications are always useful,' Frank stated. 'There's office work to be done in the Forces same as everywhere else. I wish I'd had your chances when I was a boy . . . Mind, it's more important for a boy – that's why I'm so annoyed over our Tim getting left out of the scholarship. It's put him a year behind, that has.'

'I can't understand why he never said anything,' Jess said wonderingly. 'I mean, he's a bright enough little boy, he ought to have realised. Now he's just fed up. I wouldn't be surprised if he gave up working properly at school.'

She stopped as the drone of enemy aircraft sounded overhead again, and they all crouched and bent their heads in an effort to protect themselves from the detonations. But tonight it didn't seem so bad. Most of the bombs seemed to be dropping with a dull thud in the harbour. It was low tide and they were falling mostly in mud. For some reason, they didn't always seem to go off then, or perhaps you just didn't hear it so much.

Maureen had fallen asleep and Rose's eyelids were drooping. Jess settled the two of them on the other bunk and cuddled up against Frank. Normally, he would have been firewatching, but Bert Shaw and Tommy Vickers and some of the other men were taking their turn tonight, and he was allowed a rest.

'How are those women getting on in the Yard, Frank?' Jess asked after a while.

'Oh, they're all right. There's a few I wouldn't give you tuppence for, but what d'you expect? And some are no more than bits of girls anyway. But most of 'em seem decent enough.' He spoke in a tone of some surprise, as if he had had the same expectations as Nancy concerning the women who were being employed in Portsmouth Dockyard. 'We've got a few in the boiler-shop.'

'I don't suppose you have much to do with them, do you?'

'Oh, I've got a couple working alongside me,' he said, surprising her. 'Doing riveting and things like that. One of 'em's quite a character. Her name's Cherry. Got an answer for everything.'

'Cherry?' Jess imagined a fluffy young girl with yellow hair. Or maybe red. She'd have saucy eyes and a flirty way with her. 'Doesn't sound your sort.'

'Well, they're not there for my entertainment. But we get a few laughs. It helps the work along.'

'I suppose it does.' Jess spoke a little doubtfully. She had never thought of Frank having 'laughs' in the boiler-shop. Still, if it made his day easier . . . She knew that his work was very strenuous and the conditions unpleasant in the hot, steamy atmosphere. She couldn't begrudge him a few moments of relief during the long days.

Frank seemed to have accepted the fact that women were now working in his once all-men domain, more easily than she'd expected. She wondered how much this was due to a saucy little 'character' called Cherry.

6

The heat continued throughout August. A few years ago, the people of Portsmouth would have spent their spare time on Southsea beach, or swimming in whichever parts of either Portsmouth or Langstone harbours were nearest their homes. Now most of the coastal strip was surrounded by barbed wire, and there were rumours that mines had been laid beneath the shingle.

The war was spreading like a black, evil wave over the whole world.

Japan had invaded Indochina, and as a result America and Britain had both imposed trade embargoes. Japan must either yield or go to war. And it seemed that their preference was for war, because their next action was to begin bombing China.

The situation in Russia was going from bad to worse, despite Mr Churchill's promises of aid. A Second Front was being called for, but where were the men to come from to hold it? Already the Forces were being sent all over the globe to answer one threat after another. There just weren't enough, unless the Americans came into the war or the Government started calling up old men and little boys.

The sirens were still sounding every night, and by mid-August there was talk of opening the tunnel shelters which had been dug deep into Portsdown Hill. Admission was to be by ticket, with priority given to mothers with children and those who had no shelter of their own. There was to be room for at least three thousand people.

'They're talking about that tunnel under the harbour again too,' Jess said. She had heard this on the family grapevine, through her parents Arthur and Mary, at North End. Arthur was getting more forgetful and difficult these days, but Mary's mind was as sharp as ever and she relayed all the news. Her cousin John Bellinger, who was on the City Council, still visited her regularly and had told her about the Kearney tunnel.

'It's a sort of tube,' Jess told Frank. 'It'll go to Gosport. It's going to be paid for by America and our people won't have to pay a penny. They'll be able to use it as a railway tunnel after the war.'

'That'll please the ferry,' Frank remarked. 'They get a lot of custom from dockyardmen who live in Gosport.'

But the plan was turned down by the council – by only one vote, it was rumoured – and there were other things to worry about. By the end of August Winston Churchill was accusing the Nazis of the wholesale massacre and 'merciless butchery' of Soviet civilians. Already millions were starving and Leningrad was threatened with a full siege.

'They can't let it go on,' Jess said. Nobody could stand by and let such atrocities happen. But where were the fighting men to come from?

Everyone felt that America must come in soon. Food parcels and Lease Lend were no longer enough. American Navy ships were being attacked too, off Iceland and in other waters. What more must it take to bring them in as Allies?

Accommodation in the tunnel shelters was increased to five thousand.

'They're expecting it to get worse,' Jess said, and made no demur when Frank allowed the boys to come home for only a short summer holiday.

Late in September, one of the Southern Railway paddle steamers which plied across the Solent between Portsmouth and the Isle of Wight, hit a mine and was blown up just off Southsea. It sank at once, losing all eight of the crew. Nobody knew how many passengers were on board.

'That's one of the worst things about this war,' Jess said, reading the newspaper headlines as she walked down the street. 'People go out of the front door in the morning and never come back, and you might never know what happened to them. Got caught in a raid – blown up by an unexploded bomb—'

'Run away from home,' Bert Shaw put in lugubriously. He had had another row with Gladys over going into the Wrens. She'd grown tired of waiting for her papers and gone down to the recruiting office to ask if they were ever going to call her up. 'Seems to me some people can't wait to get away. Look at your Olive. Nothing would do for her but getting married, and now she's off joining the Forces. I mean, what must her bloke be thinking, never knowing where she is or what she's getting up to? What sort of a way is that for a young married woman to behave?'

'That's an awful thing to say,' Jess said sharply. 'The young people just want to do their bit, that's all. They're being patriotic. What's wrong with that?'

Bert snorted. 'They want to cut loose, that's what they want. Get away where no one'll curb them. I know what they're like.'

'You know what *you* were like,' Peggy said, coming out to the doorstep to join them. 'Proper young monkey you were, before you took up with me. My dad went on at me something terrible when he saw us out together.'

'Your dad would've gone on at you if he'd seen you out with the Prince of Wales,' Bert declared, and grinned unwillingly as the women laughed. 'Well, at least I never got a girl into trouble. I had a bit of respect for young women, and they had a bit of respect for themselves. Not like now. Doing men's jobs, getting into all sorts of places a young woman wouldn't have been seen dead in a year or two back – I dunno what the world's coming to.'

Jess was half inclined to agree with him. She knew Annie was anxious about Olive, and she still felt uneasy herself about the women working in the Dockyard, alongside Frank. He'd mentioned that Cherry more than once now, describing things she'd said and done. A proper saucy little piece she sounded, always cheeking the foreman and standing up for her rights – not at all Frank's cup of tea, Jess would have thought. But he sounded as though he admired her, and his serious face broke into a smile when he told Jess of her exploits.

'You can't get anything past her,' he said. 'Sharp as a needle, she is, and got an answer for everything. Don't care what she says or who she says it to.'

She didn't sound a bit the sort of girl Frank would take to, though he'd always admired spirit and told Rose she must always stand up for what she thought was right. But this Cherry seemed to go a lot further than that. Jess imagined her flouncing into the boiler-shop of a morning, all ringlets and hair-ribbons, her mouth red with lipstick, cheeking the men left, right and centre and turning the heads of steady chaps like Frank.

There was something in what Bert Shaw said. You couldn't get away from it. The boys living out in the country, away from her and Frank. Young Betty on a farm, going steady with a man who'd been in prison. Olive joining the Army, just as if she wanted to be a soldier like Derek . . .

The war was turning everything upside down.

It took Olive some time to get used to being in the ATS.

After parting from her family at the bus stop in September Street, it was as if she had simply handed her life over to others. From the moment the conductor had pushed her along to the front seat of the bus, to the orders snapped out by the non-commissioned officers who took charge when she finally arrived at Queen's Camp, just outside Guildford, she had no choices to make, no decisions. Worse still, her most intimate decisions were being made by men.

Still dressed in civilian clothes, the girls were herded into a long shed to be issued with their uniforms. They looked at the tables, piled high with khaki garments, and at the brawny soldiers standing behind like shop assistants, their faces red and surly.

'Strewth,' said the girl behind Olive, 'we ain't going to have to tell them our vital statistics, are we?'

'I hope not,' Olive said, but she knew that her hope was a faint one. The NCOs were already barking out orders to the girls to hurry up, and the first in the queue were being questioned loudly about their sizes.

'*E* cup?' Olive heard a sergeant repeat derisively. 'Blimey, we ain't got anything that big. You'll 'ave ter make do with pillowcases.'

The girl, who was blonde and blowsy, flushed scarlet and swore at him. The sergeant's eyes narrowed.

'Say that again, and you'll be on a charge before you're even in uniform. 'Ere, take this one – a week or two on Army rations and you'll squeeze into it all right.'

'I'll die if he says anything to me,' whispered the girl behind Olive. She was shorter than Olive and rather plump, with tangled black hair. 'I mean, fancy having to tell a man your brassière size. It's not even as if he was your boyfriend!'

The girls passed slowly along the row of tables, collecting their uniform.

Some of the items were men's, and Olive looked at her jacket with some dismay.

'The buttons do up the wrong side. And we can't put our passbooks in the breast pocket, it'll be uncomfortable.'

'Look,' the sergeant said, 'you didn't join the Army to be comfortable. And it ain't my fault if you're built a different shape. That's an Army battledress and if you can't get into it you'll 'ave ter make yer own arrangements. Strap 'em down with elastoplast or summat.' He turned to the man beside him and said, just loudly enough for Olive to hear, 'I dunno what they think they're doin', lettin' this lot in. They might be all right for a bit of snoggin' behind the canteen, but Gawd knows what good they'll be else.'

Worst of all was having to ask the last man in the row for sanitary towels. Every girl who came to his table looked ready to burst into tears. But there was no escape. Nobody could pretend that they wouldn't be needing them, and when they finally emerged from the hut, each clutching a brown paper package along with her uniform, they were all cringing with embarrassment.

'We're going to have to do that *every month*,' the dark girl said. 'I'll never get used to it.'

'Still, at least they've had to get these in specially,' Olive remarked. 'They can't fob us off with men's!' The two girls giggled, feeling the mild hysteria of sudden release from tension. They walked across to the hut where they were to sleep.

'They've even told us what kind of knickers to wear. D'you think they want us to melt away?' she asked as they spread their new acquisitions out on their beds. 'I mean, look at this thick skirt, and this tunic. It's the middle of summer, haven't they noticed? And these awful stockings!'

'Think yourself lucky to have them,' the girl replied. Her name was Brenda Wilson and she came from Gosport. She and Olive had already discovered that they'd both known Graham Philpotts, the young sailor who had been killed while helping Gladys Shaw with her ambulance. 'I ain't seen a pair of stockings in months.'

Her legs were stained brown, with gravy browning or shoe polish, Olive thought. A lot of girls had been doing that, but the summer had been so fine that most of them now had suntanned legs. Drawing the black line down the back of the legs to look like a seam was still tricky, though. Olive had given up trying.

She looked at the rest of the kit she'd been issued with. Everything was khaki – battledress, blouse, trousers, skirt, leather jerkin, anklets, brown boots and tin hat. There were also a gas mask and a water bottle.

'I thought they didn't send women fighting,' she said. 'We've got everything here but guns and bayonets.'

The other girl shrugged. 'Look at these bloomers. Proper passion-killers they are! I wonder the Jerries don't use 'em for parachutes.'

'They probably would,' remarked a fair-haired girl on the other side of Olive. She was called Claudia Stannard and her father was a doctor in Fareham, about five miles west of Portsmouth at the head of the harbour.

'But parachutes have to be made of silk, not this stuff that looks as if it was meant for Army blankets.' She held up a pair of regulation knickers. They were thick and voluminous, and the same drab khaki as the rest of the uniform. 'We can't wear these horrible things in this weather. We'll never stop itching. I've never been able to wear anything but silk next to my skin.'

'I don't suppose you'll go short of volunteers to help you scratch,' Brenda observed. She looked enviously at the other girl. 'I wish I had a figure like yours. You'll look smashing whatever you wear.'

Olive had laid out all her kit on the bed and gazed at it, feeling suddenly depressed. She ought to have been used to uniform, with Derek coming home in his, but the impact of having to wear it herself had not struck her until this moment. She looked regretfully at the summer skirt and blouse she had come in.

'If only we could have had a bit of colour. Or something pretty. It's going to be like wearing mud.'

'You're in the Army now,' Brenda said. 'We're not here to admire each other's outfits. And at least it makes us all equal. I mean, it's bad enough at school or out at work, when some people can afford nice clothes and the rest of us have to make do.' She fingered the battledress jacket. 'I've never had nothing as good as this before.'

Olive felt ashamed. Brenda was right, this wasn't a fashion parade and her own clothes looked worn and old. Claudia, on the other hand, was dressed in a frock that looked brand new and as if it had come from one of the best shops.

Olive came somewhere in between, with the skirt and blouse Auntie Jess had made her last year. Auntie Jess had been a professional dressmaker and the things she made always looked nice. But once in uniform, there would be nothing to tell them all apart.

'I suppose we'd better change,' she said uncertainly, wondering where to go. She looked up and down the hut, which was filled with girls all laying out their uniforms. The beds were only two feet apart and there were no screens or curtains around them. One or two girls had already started to undress.

Claudia unbuttoned her dress and began to pull it over her head. She didn't seem in the least self-conscious. Olive stared at her silky underwear and then turned and caught Brenda's eye. The Gosport girl shrugged and rolled her eyes.

'You might as well forget about being modest,' she said, pulling off her crumpled blouse. 'We're all in this together and there ain't going to be no secrets.'

Her words were proved right over and over again during the four weeks' training at Guildford. Life in the hut was communal; the only privacy was in the lavatories. Baths had a head-high screen between them, but nothing more. As for dressing and undressing, within a few days they had all forgotten their shyness and would sit on their beds or wander about with little or nothing on, chatting while they did their hair or nails.

Homesickness was a greater problem. As Olive lay awake that first night, missing Derek desperately, she heard muffled sobs coming from more than one bed. Almost in tears herself, she pulled the rough blankets over her head to shut out the sound and lay counting the hours until at last she fell into a deep sleep, only to be sharply awoken at 6.30 a.m. by the harsh trumpeting of reveille.

The days passed in a blur. Breakfast was porridge – either lumpy or too slack, with no in-between – followed by parade for inspection and drills. On the first few mornings almost every girl was picked out for having something wrong with her appearance – shoes not shiny enough, buttons dull, collar crooked, hair untidy – and few of them could march in step. Olive, Claudia and a few others had been in the Girl Guides so were a little more practised, but it seemed that nothing would satisfy the drill-sergeant, a hard-faced woman who seemed to take pleasure in keeping them standing for hours under the hot sun.

After lunch, it all began again. More drills, lectures and then 'fatigues' – commonly known, Claudia remarked sourly, as skivvying. Washing dishes, scrubbing floors, cleaning the 'ablutions', preparing vegetables – it all had to be done. And all, it seemed, by the new recruits.

'I don't think much of this as a way of winning the war,' Brenda grumbled as they sat 'spud bashing' in the big kitchen hut. 'Anyway, spuds don't need peeling, we always has them in their jackets at home.'

'My father says they're better for you that way,' Claudia agreed. Different though their backgrounds were, the three girls had drawn together on the first day and stayed friends. Maybe it was the uniform after all, Olive thought, for it was certain that the 'posh' Claudia would never have become friendly with shabby, down-at-heel Brenda in the ordinary way.

'Well, they've got to be done,' she said, dumping yet another peeled potato in the big pan. 'I'll tell you one thing, though, I'm not volunteering to be a cook, not after this.'

Towards the end of the second week, they went on their first route march. Already exhausted by their strenuous new life, they found themselves ordered to pack almost everything they owned into huge rucksacks and carry them on long treks across the countryside. They arrived back at camp tired out, many with blisters, the packs apparently weighing at least twice as much as when they had set out. They flung themselves on to their beds and Brenda dissolved into tears.

'I'm just worn out,' she sobbed as Olive and Claudia tried to comfort her. 'I don't reckon I can take no more. And I've never bin out in fields with cows in – I mean, they're so *big*. And their horns! And the way they follows you around. I was scared stiff.'

'Those weren't cows,' Claudia said. 'They were bullocks.'

'*Bullocks?*' Brenda squealed. 'But they could have gored us to death.' She dropped her head on her arms. 'I tell you, I can't take no more. I've had enough.'

Olive felt much the same way. She was missing Derek more than ever, and lived for his letters. Somehow, living in a Nissen hut on an army camp seemed to have taken her further away from him rather than brought her closer. She had thought that to be living the same kind of life would tighten the bond between them. Instead, because Derek had never been to the camp and because she found it so difficult to write to him about the life, it seemed to have created a gulf.

It had been so much easier to write letters that were filled with the ordinary, familiar things he knew. The office in his father's yard, the men who came in and out, the things his mother had said and done, the life that went on at home in April Grove. All these were things Derek would recognise, things he wanted to know about because they would bring home closer.

Now, Olive too was starved of news from home, and all she could pass on to Derek were the odd scraps of information contained in her mother's short weekly letters. And Annie was no letter-writer. You had to go to Auntie Jess for that.

Claudia came round the bed and put her hand on Brenda's shoulder. 'Come on, Bren. Dry your eyes and have a wash. You're not going to let them get you down, are you?'

Brenda shrugged. 'Why not? It's what they want, isn't it?' She rolled over and stared at them both. 'It wouldn't be so bad if it wasn't for that old cow of a sergeant. She's always on at me. If it's not my shoes it's my hair, and if it's not that it's my belt or my stockings or my fingernails, or anything else she can think of. She picks on me the whole time. She's sent me to the nit-shed three times this week, and she knows they never find any. She just likes being mean.' The tears welled up in her eyes again. 'She's been trying for the past fortnight to make me cry and now she's bloody done it! Why don't you fetch her in to see, give her the satisfaction, then maybe she'll leave off.'

Claudia stared at her and then laughed. 'Picks on *you*? I thought it was me. She never leaves me alone, haven't you noticed? I thought it was because of the way I speak. She's always making some nasty comment about my voice.'

'I think she does it to everyone,' Olive said. '*I* thought it was me, because I'm married!'

They looked at each other and began to laugh. Brenda wiped her eyes and sat up.

'She's just a nasty old bitch who's never been young, never had a bloke and never will. You're right, Claud, we don't have to let the likes of her get us down. Anyway, we'll be out of here in another couple of weeks.'

'And she'll be stuck in Queen's with a new lot of recruits,' Olive said, grinning. 'Maybe we ought to leave them a few notes around the place, warning them.'

At the end of the month, the girls were posted to their units. By this time they had forged bonds of close friendship and were almost as upset to part as they had been to leave their families – more so in the case of some of the girls. They held a party in their hut on the last night, sipping ginger beer and lemonade from the NAAFI and singing the latest songs, and finished up by dancing a conga in a long line through the hut and outside, where they met lines of girls from the other huts doing exactly the same thing.

The officers, who would usually have been on the alert and put a stop to any such goings-on, were conspicuously absent.

'We'll keep in touch, won't we?' Olive said to Brenda and Claudia as they waited in a dejected little group for their transport next morning. 'Write and let us know how you get on, Bren.'

'You write to me too,' Brenda responded. She was looking miserable, although she had got the posting she wanted – she was going as a driver to the RASC Transport Workshop at Camberley. Olive, who had read about the work ATS girls did there, was faintly envious, imagining Brenda driving lorries, Lister platforms and even parts of tanks all over the country. But she remembered Derek saying how he'd never feel safe if he didn't know just where she was. He wouldn't have liked her to be doing that kind of work.

She looked at her own posting, wondering if he'd be any better pleased about that. With Claudia, she'd volunteered for a training course in Wales, learning aircraft recognition and height-finding, and then working along-side soldiers on anti-aircraft guns. There was a good chance she'd be posted back to the Portsmouth area – but what would he say about the danger she'd be in?

I can't help that, she thought. We've all got to face danger these days. I can't hide myself away in an office while girls like Gladys Shaw are out in the raids driving ambulances, and Brenda's driving trucks like a man. Maybe it's not what we wanted – but nobody's getting what they want these days.

The secret, she told herself, is to want what you get and make the most of it. Even if there is a war on.

Micky Baxter's private war continued. He hadn't had much luck with forming his army, but he'd carried out his threat to get his own back on Ethel Glaister. The drain incident had led to a court appearance and a fine of two shillings and sixpence. Nancy had to go to court and pay the fine, and Granny Kinch went too, taking her curlers out for the occasion. She looked unfamiliar with sparse grey curls over her head, wearing a brown felt hat and the shapeless brown coat that did duty during her doorstep vigils in winter. She was incensed by the fine and grumbled all the way home, but Micky said nothing. He was too busy planning his revenge.

Two days later, he forced open the Glaisters' back window, having got in through the unlocked conservatory. He had watched Ethel go out and knew there would be two clear hours before she came back. He was carrying a brown cardboard box under his arm and when he was inside he stood for a moment, looking round the room. Then he grinned, put the box on the table and set to work.

Ethel came home a little later than usual and walked down the road with her son Joe, who had got on the same bus. Joe was an apprentice in the Dockyard. Like Frank Budd, he did a lot of overtime these days, but this afternoon he'd clocked off at the normal time.

'I might go swimming after tea,' he said as they came round the corner of October Street into April Grove. Mrs Seddon had just closed her little shop and the street was quiet and warm in the early evening sun. 'It's been sweltering in the Yard today.'

'Well, you watch out,' Ethel told him. 'You're not supposed to go down the beaches now, you know that.'

'Oh, there's places along Langstone where it's all right.' He waited while his mother fished out her key and unlocked the front door. 'And it's high tide tonight, should be good.'

Ethel went ahead of him into the little passage. She paused and sniffed. 'There's a funny smell.'

'I can't—' Joe came in behind her and stopped abruptly. 'Yes, I can. It's something gone bad somewhere.'

'Don't be daft,' his mother said sharply. 'There's nothing could've gone bad.'

'Something dead, then. A mouse. It must've died in a corner—'

'Are you saying my housework's so scamped I wouldn't notice a dead mouse?' she demanded. 'Anyway, we don't have mice. It's only dirty houses have mice.' She opened the door into the back room. 'I – oh!' Her voice rose to an outraged screech. 'Oh, my *God!*'

'What? What is it?' Joe pressed close behind her, craning to see over her shoulder. His glance took in the scene before them and he drew in an awed breath. 'Coo!'

'Coo?' Ethel repeated wrathfully. '*Coo?* Is that all you can say – coo? Someone's been in here, in *my house*, some *vandal*, chucking the furniture about and smashing things up and leaving *filth* behind – and you know as well as I do just who *that* was – and all you can do is stand there and sound like a bloody *pigeon*? Do something, for God's sake. Go straight up to number 10 and get that Baxter boy down here.' She stared round the room. 'Oh, if only your father was here. I'd give him such an earful! Why couldn't he find us somewhere decent to live? Why do we have to mix with people like that?'

Joe stared over her shoulder. Whoever had been in here had done a thorough job. Every piece of furniture except the heavy sideboard had been turned upside down. The square dining table lay with its legs in the air. The contents of the sideboard and wall cupboards were spread around the room and Ethel's best tea service had been laid out on the underside of the table, as if for a party. In the middle, where a cake might have taken pride of place, was a large meat plate. It was piled with a mass of stinking rubbish, and the rubbish looked as if it might have come out of a drain.

'It's horrible,' Ethel said in a trembling voice. 'Oh, it's horrible. It's *evil.*' She turned on her son, almost beside herself with rage. 'Go and get him! Bring him here. I'll wring his neck. I'll tear him limb from limb, that's what I'll do. Oh, the little devil, the little *devil!*' Tears began to stream down her face, her mascara making black runnels in the heavy make-up.

'You don't know it was him,' Joe said, his lips twitching as he looked at the devastation. 'It could have been someone else.'

'Of course it was him!' Ethel advanced into the chaos. 'Who else would do a thing like this? He ought to be sent away, that's what, he ought to be locked up, and so he will be, if I have anything to do with it.' She turned again, stamping her foot. 'Well, what are you waiting for? Go and fetch him along this minute, and bring that slut of a mother of his as well, *and* that old witch of a grandmother. They were all in it together, likely as not, and they can all give a hand to put it right!'

Joe had been having trouble keeping a straight face ever since he saw the confusion of the room, but the thought of Nancy and Granny Kinch helping Micky turn the furniture upside down and arrange the teacups on the upturned table was too much for him. He broke into a snort of laughter. He tried to smother it at once but Ethel, who had bent to pick up her best teacups, heard and straightened, glaring at him.

'Well, I don't know what you find so funny about this! Don't you realise how serious it is? That little villain's been *in* here, messing about with *my* things and leaving his filth behind to stink us out. I suppose you realise he broke in? And I don't suppose for a minute that he went out empty-handed – oh no, he'll have pinched whatever he could pick up. Why, he's probably been into every room – ransacked the entire house. And it's not just that,' she continued, glowering at her son. 'Now he knows how to get in, he'll be back. I'll never dare go out again!'

'Don't be daft, Mum. Of course he won't be back. That'd be asking for trouble—'

'*Asking for trouble?* Oh, he's going to get trouble, don't you make any mistake about that.' She surveyed the disorder again and then put back the teacup and saucer she was holding. 'I've changed my mind. Don't bring him down here. Go and fetch a policeman instead.'

'A policeman?' Joe echoed. 'But—'

'You heard what I said. Go up the phone box and get one along here at once. Tell 'em there's been a burglary.'

'But we don't know he's taken anything—'

'He's broken in, hasn't he? That's a criminal offence. You can be put in prison for breaking and entering. You don't have to have pinched anything.' Ethel's eyes glittered with angry satisfaction. 'He won't get away with a half-a-crown fine this time. I'll see that young scoundrel in jail yet, you see if I don't.'

The police took Micky's escapade at number 15 April Grove seriously, and the constable who was sent to investigate the 'burglary' looked gravely at the chaos and went straight up to number 10 to interview him.

'Our Micky wouldn't do a thing like that,' declared Granny Kinch, who had been at the door when the policeman cycled down the street and watched with popping eyes as he propped his bike up on the kerb outside number 15. 'He's a good boy. He wouldn't go breaking into people's houses.'

'Go out Eastney and tell it to the Marines,' the constable said wearily. 'You know as well as I do he's bin in and out of trouble since he was five years old. Anyway, who else would have done it, eh? There ain't hardly any other kids around here.'

'So it's got to be our Micky, ain't it. You always got to pick on him. And you'll believe that Ethel Glaister before you believes him. Just because she wasn't looking where she was going and tore her fancy stockings, she has to go and take it out on our Micky. And where she get stockings these days anyway, have you asked her that? There's more'n one sort o' market down Charlotte Street.'

'I'm not here to investigate the black market,' the policeman said. 'Your scallywag of a grandson broke into a house and did damage. That's a serious matter and I'll have to talk to him about it. Mrs Glaister wants to bring charges.'

'I didn't do no damage!' Micky burst out, tumbling into the room from where he had been listening behind the scullery door. 'I never broke nothing and I never pinched nothing either. I just moved it about a bit. There's no law against moving stuff about.'

'There is when it's in someone else's house.' The policeman looked sternly at him. 'So you admit you were there, then.'

Micky opened his mouth to deny it, then realised that he had walked into a trap. He shut his mouth again and glowered sullenly. His grandmother gave him a look of exasperation.

'You little twerp. She couldn't never have proved nothing.'

'She wouldn't need to,' the constable said. 'His fingerprints would have been all over the place. Well, it saves us the trouble of taking them.' He gave Micky another stern look. 'You're in real trouble this time, young man. It's not only Mrs Glaister. We've had complaints from the local cinema manager about you too.'

'The pictures?' Granny Kinch echoed. 'Why, what's he supposed to have done there?'

The policeman consulted his notebook and began to speak in a monotone, as if he were reciting dull poetry. 'According to the manager, a number of his female customers have complained that their handbags have been rifled. They put them under their seats while they were watching the film and when they went outside their purses were empty, even though they knew there was money in them when they went in.' He glanced at Micky again. 'The usherettes were told to keep an eye open and they've noticed this young gentleman several times, on occasions when these thefts have been reported. One of them saw your grandson crawling along empty rows of seats. Obviously, it would be a simple matter for him to reach underneath, pull out the bags, empty them and replace them without being detected.'

'They didn't never actually see him do it, though, did they?' Granny Kinch said sharply. 'There's no proof.'

The policeman sighed. 'Circumstantial evidence—'

'That ain't proof. You needs either proof or a confession. You got no proof and Micky ain't going to confess to summat he never done.' The old woman stared at him with triumphant black eyes. 'Are you, Mick?'

Micky shook his head and the policeman sighed. 'All the same, he's going to have to come down the station about Mrs Glaister's bother. He's admitted he did that.'

It meant another trip to the court for Micky. The cinema manager and usherette came too and made as good a case as they could about the plundered handbags but Micky stuck firmly to his denials and, as his grandmother had said, there was no actual proof. Nevertheless, the magistrate ordered that he should be banned from all the cinemas in the city for a month and Nancy had to promise to send him to Sunday School. Worse still, he was given six strokes of the birch and put on probation.

The sentence was carried out immediately. Micky came home furious, humiliated and crying, one hand rubbing his backside. His grandmother was red-eyed and indignant, hardly knowing whether to stay inside for the next three days or take up her usual position at the front door and accost everyone who went past. Nancy, parting from them outside the court, added to her son's punishment with a cuff on the ear.

'That'll learn you to do daft things,' she said brusquely. 'You'd better keep your nose clean in future, young Mick, or you'll be getting evacuated out to the country with the rest of the kids. I can't be doing with this going to court every five minutes. It's gettin' me a bad name. All them coppers knows our faces now, and they knows just who to pick on every time they wants a scapegoat. I don't want to end up behind bars on account of you.'

'I'm *not* going to Sunday School,' Micky said furiously. 'It's a lot of cissies. I *won't* go.'

'You'll do as you're told for once,' Nancy told him sharply. 'The probation officer'll see to that. And you'll keep out of trouble from now on, see?'

Micky went home with his grandmother. They had baked beans and sausages for dinner – Micky's favourite meal – but he ate them without comment. His heavy dark brows were drawn together as he plotted his next move.

7

For the children at the vicarage, life continued to be sunny. Mr Beckett cycled round the parish like a creaky spider on his old bicycle, and became a sort of honorary child when he was at home. Stella and Muriel Simmons, apparently not too badly affected by the loss of their mother and baby brother, collected rose petals to make scent and strung together immensely long daisy chains which they wore round their necks till the flowers withered. Tim and Keith, scorning these as girls' games, kicked a football around the old lawn and went fishing for sticklebacks in the little stream. For the time being, Tim had stopped worrying about school and given himself over to enjoying life.

Mike Simmons, his ship docking for a few days in Southampton, came out to Bridge End to see his daughters and found them in the shaggy grass, holding a teaparty for two dolls and a battered teddy bear that Mr Beckett had resurrected from the attic.

He stopped at the gate, watching unseen. The sun was warm and the leaves were tinted with autumn. A few dahlias made a patch of bright colour at the edge of the lawn and the gnarled apple tree was heavy with fruit. There was a hum of late bees in the air, a sound as warm as the day itself.

Mike had walked from Eastleigh railway station. He was hot, and wanted a drink of water. But he stood for a few minutes, gazing at the little girls, his heart aching with love and grief.

Only a year ago, his Kathy had been still alive, expecting Thomas. She hadn't wanted to be evacuated – like Mike, she believed that families ought to stay together, and she'd been determined to keep their house in Portchester Street nice for him to come home to. But the house had been destroyed by one of the first bombs to fall on Portsmouth, and she'd had to move to October Street.

Mike had changed his mind about evacuation then. He'd been frightened by the complete demolition of their home and wanted her to come out to the country. He hated the thought of her having to go down to the dank little Anderson shelter night after night, and he'd been horrified when he heard that Thomas was actually born there, in the middle of one of the worst raids of the blitz. But Kathy had steadfastly refused to leave. 'I want to be here when you get home, even if it's just for a few hours,' she'd told him. And then there'd been another raid, another direct hit, and she'd been killed, with the baby in her arms.

Mike had been stunned with grief. If it hadn't been for Jess Budd, he didn't know what he would have done. But Jess had taken in the two girls and looked after them, she'd even arranged for them to come out here to stay with Mr Beckett and her own two boys. And now here they were, playing in the sunshine as if they hadn't a care in the world.

Didn't they miss their mother at all? he wondered, suddenly angry. And then turned his anger on himself. Of course they missed her. And they'd suffered too – they'd been bombed out, endured the raids, been frightened and homeless. But they could still have a bit of pleasure, couldn't they? It was the only childhood they would have – let them enjoy as much of it as they could.

Stella glanced up and saw him leaning on the gate. For a moment, she sat quite still, her eyes huge. Then she jumped up and ran towards him, shrieking at the top of her voice.

'Daddy! It's *Daddy*!'

The others stopped what they were doing. Muriel abandoned her dolls and ran after her sister, hair blowing round her face. The boys stopped kicking their ball and stood a little awkwardly, unsure whether to greet the stranger or melt away. Mrs Mudge appeared at the kitchen door, wiping her hands in her apron, and Mr Beckett popped out from the shed, where he had been mending a puncture in his bicycle.

Mike held out his arms to his daughters and they scrambled up the gate and flung themselves at him. He held them close, half laughing, half crying, and Tim and Keith glanced at each other and turned their backs, studying the grass with sudden attention.

Mrs Mudge watched, her own eyes damp, and the vicar came along the garden path to stand at her side. He smiled and spoke quietly.

'A cup of tea, I think, don't you? And some of your lemonade for the children. It's good to have something to celebrate, for a change.'

For a change! the housekeeper thought as she went indoors to put the kettle on. Celebration was one of the guiding principles of Mr Beckett's life. Few were the days when he did not find something, however small, worth celebrating – the first touch of autumn, the first leaf of spring, the first winter fire, the first warm day. But this was something special.

Mike Simmons came home all too rarely from his Merchant Navy ship, and for the two motherless girls he was their only true family. Hard as she and the vicar might try, they could never really make up for all that Stella and Muriel had lost. Brief though his time might be, it must be made as memorable as they all knew how, to give him and the girls something special to remember.

Mrs Mudge put on the kettle and delved into the back of a large cupboard to find the tin of ham she had put away from the last American food parcel that had arrived at Bridge End. It was supposed to be saved for Christmas. But what better time to have it than now, with a few of the vicar's own tomatoes, to show Mike Simmons just how pleased they all were to see him here?

Mike Simmons' few days at Bridge End were soon over and he went back to sea, feeling an ache in his heart that was even worse than when he'd had to part with Kathy. He took the girls to Southampton to show them his ship, and borrowed an old van to take them for a run in the New Forest. There were still a few places where you could get down to the shore, and they sat on the beach gazing out to sea.

'Are you going away again soon?' Stella asked wistfully, and he nodded.

'Tomorrow.' He felt the tears gather in his throat, thinking of the last time he had said goodbye to his family and feeling a bitter longing for Kathy and their baby son.

The girls said nothing. A convoy was leaving Southampton now, merchant ships surrounded by a protective flotilla of destroyers bristling with guns. They watched as the ships steamed away down the arm of the Solent.

'I expect there's a lot of daddies on those ships,' Muriel observed. 'It's a pity their boys and girls aren't here to wave to them.'

'We could wave for them,' Stella suggested, and stood up, barefoot on the stony beach. 'Let's do that, and perhaps someone will wave for us when our Daddy's sailing away.'

Muriel jumped up beside her sister and together, hand in hand, they made their way down the beach to the edge of the water. They stood, their backs to their father, waving at the ships that were steaming slowly towards the horizon. Stella took a handkerchief from her pocket, and it fluttered in the breeze.

They stood for a long while, watching until the convoy had finally disappeared, and then they turned and came back to where Mike sat, his arms looped around his knees, his eyes dark.

'There,' Stella said in a tone of satisfaction. 'Now they've been waved to, properly.' She wound her arms around her father's neck. 'When you go away, you'll be able to imagine us here waving to you. We thought of you all the time we were waving, didn't we, Mu?'

Muriel nodded. And Mike, looking at them through a sudden blur of tears, knew that he would indeed, as his ship sailed down the Solent next morning, be able to look back and see the figures of his two daughters, waving to him from this small and lonely beach. As if they had left some imprint of themselves in the air; as if their presence here could not be erased.

He shook his head and scrambled to his feet. 'I'll do that,' he said. 'And I'll wave back, all right? And now we'd better get back to Bridge End. Mrs Mudge said she was going to make something special for tea, and I don't want to miss it. And I promised Tim we'd have a game of cricket before bedtime.'

With long, swift strides, he set off up the beach, before the girls could see the tears on his face.

The sirens continued to sound. The blitz was over – for the time being, it appeared, anyway – but there were still minor raids almost every night. One of them dropped its bombs close to the Spencers' farm at Bishop's Waltham. The explosion uprooted trees and flung them into the next field, terrifying the cows and disrupting milk production for the rest of the week. The hens, fastened into their coops for the night, had hysterics and flung themselves at the walls, bruising their wings and feet. In the house, an old grandfather clock which had not worked for years, suddenly chimed twelve and began to tick steadily, keeping perfect time.

One of the cows was badly injured and had to be put down. Betty, Yvonne and Erica mourned her as if she had been a personal friend.

'She was the first cow I ever milked,' Betty said. 'Dennis showed me what to do.' Her eyes filled as she thought of that first morning, with Dennis close to her in the byre. 'It doesn't seem fair,' she said fiercely, dashing the tears away. 'They're making war on *cows* now.'

The aircraft was shot down over Bridge End. It crashed in one of Mr Callaway's fields and the children dashed out to see it. Brian Collins swaggered by the gate, taking a proprietorial attitude because he lived on the farm.

'You can't come into the field,' he said bossily. 'There's a policeman here guarding it till the soldiers get here.'

'Can't we have a bit as a souvenir?' Tim asked longingly. 'I'd like a bit with a swastika on it.'

'I'm having that bit,' Brian said instantly. 'Anyway, I don't suppose they'll let people have bits. It's secret.'

'Why? Why is it secret? It's a German plane. Anyone can see it, anyway.'

'You can only have it if Mr Callaway says so,' Brian said, changing tack. 'It's his field so it's his plane. Anyway, if you come in you're trespassing.'

Tim wandered away. He had never got on with Brian Collins and didn't feel like arguing with him now. He climbed up a wooded slope and sat on a tree-stump, his chin in his hands, staring down at the scene below and imagining the excitement of the chase the night before. He and Keith had heard the planes overhead and longed to be outside, but Mr Beckett had forbidden them. He had made everyone go down into the old cellar, and had sat with his arms around Stella, while Muriel crouched close to Mrs Mudge.

I wish I was old enough to join the Air Force, Tim thought. I could have been up there, flying a Spitfire, shooting down the enemy. I could win medals. I could help win the war.

It didn't seem fair that Brian Collins would get first pick of souvenirs from the wrecked aeroplane.

There were more people in the field now, policemen and soldiers from a nearby camp. They approached the wreckage cautiously, as if expecting someone to open fire on them. But Tim could see that there was no one in the mangled cockpit. The plane must have exploded when it landed, for there was twisted metal everywhere. Probably the pilot had baled out, he thought, and felt a sudden nervous excitement. He might be lurking in these very woods, waiting to pounce.

Tim got up quickly. He felt as though there were eyes on him, watching from the undergrowth. He looked all around, forcing himself to keep still and listen as Reg had taught him when they were looking for birds' nests. His heart was thumping.

Something rustled high in one of the trees. Tim gasped and jumped, feeling as if his heart had leapt right into his throat. He stared upwards, peering through the brown and yellow leaves, and then relaxed as he saw a squirrel gazing down at him. It chattered angrily, and an acorn fell at Tim's feet.

There's no one here, he thought. Any parachutist would have gone by now. He wouldn't have waited to be caught.

But suppose he was injured? Or caught up in a tree? He might be lying somewhere quite close, waiting to be discovered. *Tim* might be the one to find him.

A parachutist. A prisoner. That would be better than any old bit of a plane.

His nervousness only partially replaced by excitement, Tim began to creep cautiously through the trees, his eyes moving from side to side. He kept along the side of the hill, within sight of the field where the wreckage lay, feeling a kind of comfort in the presence of the soldiers down below. They were clustered round the plane now, examining it, picking amongst the bits of wreckage that were flung all over the field. One of them was standing by the gate, keeping out the villagers and children who had gathered to stare.

Tim thought of his triumph as he led his prisoner down the hill towards them. He was convinced now that the pilot had parachuted out of his plane moments before it landed, and was hiding in this very wood. It stood to reason, after all. There was nowhere else for him to hide. He must be here.

Suppose he was armed. Tim hesitated, then shrugged the thought away. Pilots weren't armed, what would be the point? Pistols were no use when you were up in the sky. They had machine-guns in their planes. Besides, once they'd landed in enemy territory they were bound to be caught and taken prisoner. Resistance, he thought grandly, would be useless.

The phrase, gleaned from a Biggles book he had been given one Christmas, struck his imagination and he repeated it several times as he crept through the trees. It would be exactly the right thing to say to the pilot when he discovered him.

Something fluttered from a tree ahead of him, and he stopped, his heart bounding again. It looked like a piece of cloth. He approached cautiously, and stopped about two feet away, staring at it.

It was a bluish grey. The sort of colour a British airman wore, only slightly darker. Tim gazed at it and swallowed. Maybe the pilot really was in these woods. His heart raced and he felt suddenly frightened. Suppose the German wasn't injured after all. He'd be a lot stronger than Tim. He might not *want* to be captured.

Nervously, he glanced again from side to side. The impulse to run was almost too strong to resist. He looked down into the field again, watching the figures of the soldiers as they moved about. They looked very far away.

Suddenly, it didn't seem such a good idea after all to try to take a prisoner.

There was another rustle from the trees and Tim gave a frightened little half-scream and turned to run. Maybe it was just a squirrel, but he wasn't staying to find out. He was going to go straight down to the field, tell the soldiers he was sure the airman was in the woods, let them capture him. Tim would still get the credit for finding him. He could still hold up his head in front of Brian Collins and the others.

He scurried down the slope, his legs shaking, tripped over a twisted tree-root and fell flat on his face in a pile of leaves.

For a few moments he was too winded to move. He shut his eyes tightly, half expecting to feel a heavy hand on his shoulder, convinced that he had been pursued. But nothing happened, and as his breath slowly returned he opened his eyes and turned his head.

There was no one near him. But lying on the ground, quite close to his face, there was a glove.

Tim stared at it. It was a brown leather glove, quite large, the sort a soldier might wear.

Or an airman.

His certainty that the pilot had parachuted into the woods returned. Still lying on the leaves, he reached out a hand and touched the glove. If it really was German, it would be a smashing souvenir. As good as a bit of plane, any day.

With two fingers, he pulled the glove towards him. And then stopped, his heart jittering all over again, a sick bile rising in his throat as he stared at what he had found.

There was no doubt that it was the German pilot's glove. His hand was still inside.

'Poor little chap,' Mrs Mudge said. 'What a thing for a little boy to find. He was sick three times in the night and when he did go to sleep he dreamt that hands were coming after him.'

'The pilot must have been blown to pieces when the plane exploded,' Mr Beckett said. 'The soldiers found most of the remains but there's still a chance that parts will be found by children. They'd better not go near that field for a while.'

For Tim, the war had abruptly stopped being a game, an adventure, and become horribly real. When the other children, their ghoulish imagination protected by not having seen the reality, demanded details, he turned on them in fury and then ran away. He threw Keith's souvenir – a fragment of twisted metal with sharp edges – out of the window, where it landed in the cabbages Mrs Mudge had planted in what had once been a flowerbed. He lay awake at night, listening to the distant wail of sirens over Southampton and Portsmouth, to the *crump* of exploding bombs.

He began to worry about his parents and baby sister. 'How do you *know* they won't get hit?' he asked Mr Beckett, echoing Rose's own tormenting doubts. 'God isn't looking after other people. How do you know he's looking after *my* mum and dad?'

Mr Beckett shook his head. 'We can't know, Tim, I'm afraid. We just have to trust – to have faith.'

Tim stared at him. He thought of all the people who had trusted, and found their trust betrayed. People in Portsmouth who had been bombed out or killed. Stella and Muriel's mother and baby brother. Some of his own friends in the village, who had been called out of class to be told that their fathers had been lost in action.

'I don't see what good faith does,' he said flatly. '*I* don't trust him, not a bit.'

The vicar sighed. He looked at Tim's white face and haunted eyes and longed to give him comfort. Faith in a higher being – call it God, or what you would – could be such a strength at times like this. It kept you bolstered against the terrible things that were happening. But once shattered, it left you very small and defenceless, without hope in a world that was tearing itself to pieces around you. He had to pray hard, night and morning, for strength to keep his own faith. What chance did a boy like Tim have?

'Try to hold on,' he said, putting his hand on Tim's shoulder. 'I know it's hard – but don't turn your face away just yet. You feel as though you're falling in the dark, and the rope you were holding is falling with you. But keep your hands tightly around it, Tim, and you'll find it *will* hold you up, in the end.'

Tim let his eyelids droop, veiling his glance. He did not want Mr Beckett to know that he was right – that Tim felt exactly as if he were falling down a long, dark hole, with nothing to stop him. His fingers moved, as if he were indeed reaching for a rope. But in the darkness of his mind, there was nothing there, and he turned away abruptly.

'I wish I could go home,' he said, his voice angry. 'I'm fed up with being here.'

Mr Beckett sighed again. He watched Tim walk away across the old lawn, his shoulders hunched miserably. He felt the weariness of disappointment and failure weigh down on him.

I'm too old to be in charge of children, he thought. I imagined I could win their trust by becoming one of them, by entering into their world. I imagined I could be a buffer between them and the war, help them to enjoy their precious childhood, and grow strong and healthy in mind and body in my care.

I thought I knew best. And now Tim has shown me the arrogance of my thoughts. How can I, an old man, expect to win the heart of a child? How can I hope to show him the love of God, when every day he sees before him the face of evil?

Tim's sister Rose, too, was feeling restless.

Now that she was back at home, she found life different from what she had expected. Somehow, although she knew that the boys wouldn't be there and baby Maureen would, although she knew very well that there would be air-raids and sirens and nights in the shelter, she hadn't fully realised any of these things. She had come back unconsciously expecting home to be as it had been before the war, before Maureen was born, when it had been just her and the boys and Mum and Dad. She had somehow expected that she herself would be as she had been then, the twelve-year-old Rose still enjoying her childhood. Instead, she was fourteen and had lost interest in dolls and skipping games. And she did not know what to be interested in in their place.

Even her desire to look after the baby was beginning to leave her. Maureen was no longer like a living doll, to be bathed and dressed and pushed in a pram. She was an active toddler, her fingers into everything, and she never stopped talking or asking questions. Rose would play with her for a while, but then she grew irritated, and she resented having to take Maureen about with her.

Worst of all, and making everything harder to bear, her life was overshadowed by the dread of air-raids, of bombing, of invasion.

'They're not coming here,' Jess said. 'We've kept them out so far and we'll go on keeping them out. How could they land? All the beaches are mined. And the RAF won't let them get their planes in.'

But planes did come, night after night. The blitz had abated but there were still plenty of raids. You could never be sure it wasn't going to start again.

School was erratic. There were lessons for Rose and other girls of her age, held in people's front rooms. You went once or twice a week and had homework to do the rest of the time. Rose was bored with them and impatient to leave. Her friend Joy was officially at work now, in her parents' shop, and it had already made a difference. She seemed more grown-up, sure of herself.

'You take that shorthand and typing course,' Frank said to his daughter. 'I don't want you working in a shop. It's all right for Joy, it's her family business, but we've got nothing like that. An office is what'll suit you, the Civil Service.'

The Civil Service would keep her out of the Forces, but he didn't tell her that. Girls of Rose's age were unpredictable and obstinate and if she thought that was what he had in mind she'd be just as likely to fail her exams on purpose.

Still, she enjoyed the typing and sat by the wireless every night taking down the News in shorthand. Perhaps working in an office might not be so bad after all.

There were bright spots amongst all the talk of the Malta convoys, British restaurants, and Russia. There were still cinemas to go to, and Frank allowed his daughter to start attending church dances with Joy, although he still forbade the use of lipstick. And on the last Saturday in September, the famous actress Anna Neagle came, in a drift of silk and perfume, to open the RAOC fete at Hilsea.

'Anna Neagle!' Rose exclaimed when she heard the news. 'She was Queen Victoria in that film we saw. She's gorgeous.'

She and Joy went down to the main railway station and joined the huge throng gathered to see the film star arrive. They tried to get her autograph, but the crowd was too big and they watched instead as the actress drove off in an Army car to have lunch at the officers' mess. By the time she reached the fairground in the afternoon, the girls were there to listen to the speeches and cheer as she told them how pleased she was to be in Portsmouth, and to coax them to spend as much as they could afford that afternoon 'to help get the war over as soon as possible'.

'I'd like to be a film star,' Joy sighed. 'Better than marking up newspapers. I'm fed up with the shop.'

'Well, at least you've got a job,' Rose said. 'My dad hits the roof if I talk about leaving school.'

'My dad hits the roof if I talk. He's an old misery these days and all Mum says is I've got to make allowances because of what he's been through.' Joy scowled. 'I know it was awful, what happened to him, but he's alive, isn't he? He's home again. I'm fed up with making allowances. I've got a life too, haven't I?'

There had been yet another row with her father that morning, when she and Alice had been marking up newspapers. He'd come downstairs, unshaven and bleary-eyed in his pyjamas, to complain that the papers weren't ready, that the boys would be here soon to start their deliveries, that it had never taken so long when *he* had done it. Joy, exasperated and indignant, had turned on him and said he was welcome to do it again, she wouldn't mind staying in bed for a change.

She'd slammed out of the room then and stormed up to her bedroom, trying not to feel guilty at leaving her mother to finish the work, trying not to hear her father's voice as he wept in the room below, trying not to see the pictures his broken words conjured up in her mind.

'What am I to do? How can I find my way back? I feel a part of me is still out there, lost in those black, stinking waters, when all it wants is to be here with you and Joy, happy together as we used to be. Oh, my liebchen, *what is to become of us? Where is it all to end . . . ?'*

Joy had pushed her head under her pillow. She couldn't bear the despair in her father's voice. She couldn't bear the anguish it aroused in her own heart. Instead, she took refuge in anger and disappointment, and found a wilful pleasure in the bright red lipstick she smeared across her mouth, and in marching out of the house that afternoon to go to the fair with Rose.

The two girls wandered amongst the sideshows. The RAOC, which was raising money for its Comforts Fund, had devised a number of ingenious methods of parting them from their money, and the young soldiers called out to invite them to patronise their particular stalls.

'Have a go on the Hoopla, sweetheart?' 'Bowl for a pig, come on, you never know your luck.' 'Try your luck with me, ducky, we've got some smashing prizes today.'

The two girls threw hoopla rings without success but got a bar of chocolate each from the Lucky Dip. At the next stall, they found Carol Glaister rolling pennies. You set the little wooden ramp at the edge of a board marked out in numbered squares and hoped your penny would roll down to land in one. If the penny did not touch the sides of the square, you won that number of pennies back. Most people instantly played them again and lost, but a few canny ones collected up their winnings and went off in triumph to spend them on another attraction.

It didn't really matter. One way or another, all the money was spent at the fair and went into the Comforts Fund. Nobody went home with more money than they'd come with.

'I won sixpence just now,' Carol said. She had a glass vase under one arm. 'And look what I got on the lucky dip. Mum'll be ever so pleased.'

Rose and Joy eyed the vase. It was a virulent shade of green, with crinkly edges. It would just suit Ethel Glaister's front room.

For quite a long time, Carol Glaister and Joy hadn't had much to say to each other. There were almost two years' difference between them, a long time when you were under twelve, but the difference didn't seem so much now. But mostly their constraint was caused by Ethel's antagonism towards the Brunners. It was difficult for the girls to be friends when their mothers were such bitter enemies.

But on this sunny September afternoon, with people milling about all over the field laughing and enjoying themselves, war and bitterness seemed very far away. Carol and Joy looked at each other and smiled, a little uncertainly, and after a moment's hesitation Carol fell in beside them as they sauntered through the fair.

'Have a go at the coconut shy?' a cheeky-eyed young private suggested. 'There's a special prize if you knock one off.'

'Oh, and what's that?' Carol challenged him. She was wearing a pink blouse of her mother's and looked older in it. And she'd rolled her fair hair into a bang at the front. 'Anyway, they're not proper coconuts. They're just balls with bits of matting stuck on them.'

The soldier grinned again. 'Can't help that, darling, the monkeys were on strike. Come on, have a go and I'll give you a special prize anyway.'

Carol gave him a saucy look. 'I want to know what it is first.'

'It comes better as a surprise.'

'Pooh,' she scoffed, 'I can guess just what sort a surprise *you'd* give me! No thanks, we'll spend our money somewhere else. Come on, Rose.' She linked one arm through Rose's and the other through Joy's and stalked off, her nose in the air. The soldier laughed and Rose heard a wolf-whistle float through the air behind them.

'They've got swinging boats over there,' Joy said. 'Real big ones. Only you need two, and Rose says they make her feel sick.'

'I'll come with you,' Carol offered. 'Tell you what – there's going to be a dance tonight. I've got tickets. D'you want to come?'

Joy accepted eagerly. But Rose shook her head. She knew that Frank would never let her go to a dance with soldiers, and in any case she wasn't sure she wanted to go. She was enjoying the fete but felt nervous at the way some of the young men were looking at her. Just lately, her figure had started to develop and she felt embarrassed by it, convinced that everyone was staring.

She watched as Joy and Carol, laughing now like old friends, climbed into the swinging boats. And she felt suddenly lonely, as if she were being left behind.

Ethel Glaister made no demur when Carol announced that she was going to the dance. She simply shrugged and said, 'Don't you go pinching my stockings. Bare legs are good enough for a girl like you. Anyway, I'm going out myself.'

'Where?' Carol asked. She had given her mother the green vase and Ethel had been grudgingly pleased with it and stood it on the little table in the front window so that the neighbours could see. 'Are you going to the dance too?'

'Not likely. And it's none of your business where I'm going. Just out with a friend.' Ethel extracted two pilchards from a tin and laid them on Carol's plate. 'And I shan't be late back, so don't think you can hang around the streets afterwards. I want you back here at ten o'clock on the dot, see?'

'Ten o'clock?' Carol wailed. 'But the dance doesn't finish till eleven.'

'Never mind that. Ten o'clock's your time. It'll be dark by then as it is. Mind you walk home with Joy, and don't let no soldiers bring you back.'

'Why not?' Carol had half made an assignation with the soldier on the penny-rolling stall. The thought of being walked home after the dance had brought a peculiar, tingling excitement.

'Never you mind why not,' Ethel said sharply. 'Just do what I say, or there won't be no dance for you. Do you want some beetroot?'

'No thanks,' Carol said in a sulky tone, but she dared not say any more. Her mother was quite capable of refusing to allow her out, despite the green vase. And she desperately wanted to go to the dance.

She dressed carefully, in a pink crocheted jersey with a frilly neckline and a short, swirling skirt. Her bare legs were tanned and looked better without stockings. Her hair, naturally fair as Ethel's had once been and without the brassiness that her mother's had now, curved in a bob under her ears. She had a stub of lipstick that Ethel no longer used, and she smeared it thickly on her mouth.

'How do I look?' she asked Joy when she reached the newsagent's shop. It was closed now, so she went round to the back door and found the Brunners just finishing their tea.

'Smashing.' Joy had curled her hair again and borrowed one of Alice's blouses. It was made of green satin and looked very sophisticated. Carol gazed at it with envy. Mrs Brunner had probably brought it home from Germany on one of their visits to Mr Brunner's family before the war.

Alice Brunner felt a touch of the same awkwardness that her daughter had experienced with Carol Glaister. She wondered what Ethel had said when she knew that the two girls were going to the dance together. But Carol seemed perfectly natural, and Joy was happy enough about it, especially as Rose Budd couldn't go.

She watched them set off, chattering excitedly, and turned to her husband with a wistful smile, hoping to coax him into a better mood.

'Our Joy's first dance,' she said. 'She's growing up, Heinrich.'

'This war is making everyone grow up,' he replied. 'How can children be children when they are surrounded by hatred and destruction?'

Alice sighed. Heinrich was taking such a long time to get over his experiences. Sometimes, she wondered if he would ever completely recover.

'Well, they enjoyed this afternoon,' she said. 'It seemed like peacetime again, having a fete and someone like Anna Neagle to open it. And then a dance to go to this evening – it's time Joy started to have some fun.'

'And if there's a raid? What then?'

'There's a shelter there,' Alice said firmly, quelling her own fears on that account. 'They'll be looked after all right. It's a properly organised dance, Heinrich. And we can't keep Joy in all the time. She's got to be allowed a bit of independence.'

She got up to clear the table. If there was one thing she'd learned during those difficult months while Heinrich had been lost, it was that you had to keep busy, or your thoughts could drive you mad.

'So what's your name, then?' the young soldier asked, whirling Joy on to the floor.

'Joy.'

'That's a nice name.' He was holding her close, his uniform scratchy against her jersey. 'Mine's Artie. I come from Kent.'

'Kent? Isn't that where they grow hops?' She was feeling slightly breathless, squeezed up against him.

'That's right. Garden of England. Best place in the world.' He grinned down at her. 'Mind you, it's not bad in Portsmouth tonight. Bit hot in here, though. How about going outside for a bit of air?'

'All right,' Joy said, and when they came to the doorway they stopped dancing and he led her through the blackout curtain and outside the hall.

'Over here.'

There were quite a few couples outside the hall in the darkness. Joy could just see their dim outlines and hear their whispers. They were all very close together, and she felt suddenly nervous.

'Look, I don't want—'

'This'll do.' He pulled her into a shadowy corner and put his arms round her. The buttons on his tunic pressed against her breasts. 'How about a little kiss?'

Joy tried to wriggle free. 'I told you, I don't want—'

'Yes, you do.' His face was very close, his breath hot on her cheek. 'It's what you come to dances for, innit? Come on, purse up.'

'No.' She ducked her head. 'Let's go back inside.' One of his hands was moving over her body, feeling the shape of it. 'Don't do that.'

'Like playing hard to get, do you?' He squeezed her breast and Joy gave a little squeak. 'Oh, you like that, don't you.'

'No. No, I don't. It hurts.' Joy's figure had only lately developed and her breasts were tender. 'I don't like you touching me there. I want to go back inside.'

'Now look,' he said, 'you was pleased enough to get the tickets. What did you expect?'

'I came to dance.' She pulled herself out of his arms. 'I'm going back.'

'There's a name for girls like you,' he said angrily, but Joy was already on her way inside. She pushed through the thick curtain, her face hot, and looked around for Carol.

Carol was dancing with a sailor. He had tousled brown hair and looked about eighteen. He had approached her shyly when Joy had gone to dance with the soldier. He had a Scottish accent, which Carol found intriguing.

'I'm no' much of a dancer. You'll have to teach me.'

'Oh, it's easy.' Carol loved dancing. She had been taught several steps by her mother and always went to the church dances, where several of the older men had taken her as a partner. She showed the sailor how to hold her and then explained the steps.

'You have to listen to the music. You're supposed to dance in time with the beat, see? *One*, two, three, *one*, two, three – and you're supposed to guide me so that I don't bump into anyone.' She giggled. 'I haven't got eyes in the back of my head.'

'I havenae got eyes in my feet, either,' he said. 'How'm I supposed to see what they're doing and steer at the same time?' But he was picking up the idea. 'Och, that wasnae bad, was it? We got all the way round!'

'You'll be a second Fred Astaire.' Their feet suddenly became tangled and they tripped and almost fell. 'Whoops – spoke too soon there, didn't we! It's all right. Just stop and wait for the music.'

The tune came to an end just as they reached the seats where Joy and Carol had been sitting. There was no sign of Joy and as the sailor hesitated, Carol sat down and patted the chair beside her. She gave him a friendly smile.

'What's your name? Mine's Carol.'

'Roderick MacPherson. My mates call me Mac but at home I'm called Roddy.'

'Have you been in the Navy long?'

He shook his head. 'I've only just finished my training on Whale Island. I'm waiting for a ship.'

'I bet you can't wait to get to sea,' Carol said. 'My brother wants to go in the Navy. I daresay he'll be called up soon.'

The sailor said nothing. She glanced at him and was surprised to see a look of misery on his face. He was staring at the floor and kicking a scrap of paper about with his toe.

'I didnae want to join up, not really,' he burst out suddenly. 'I was supposed to be going to university. I never wanted to be in the Navy at all.'

'Oh.' Carol felt nonplussed. She remembered her mother talking about Betty Chapman's young man, Dennis. 'You mean you're a CO? A pacifist?'

'No, I'm not. I just don't want to fight. I won't be any good at it. I know I won't.'

'Well, you won't have to. You're not in the Army.'

'I'm a gunner,' he said flatly, and she was silenced. 'I'll be shooting at other ships. And aircraft. Why should I have to do that? I was supposed to go to university.'

'Yes, but everyone's having to help the war effort,' Carol said. 'Lots of people have had to give up their jobs to go into the Forces. They're even calling up women.'

Roddy shrugged. 'And how many of them want to go? Tell me that.'

'Well, probably a lot of them don't, but they haven't got any choice, have they? I mean, even if you are a CO, you still have to go in front of a board, and they don't always—'

'They havenae got any choice,' he repeated. 'That's just it.' He gave her a desperate look. 'I *wanted* a choice, just to live my own life. I want to do something I'd be good at. What's so wrong with that?'

'Nothing. Nothing's wrong with it.' Carol felt a sudden huge sadness and pity for the boy beside her. Until now, she had only known people whose lives were accustomed to adapting to circumstance, who had ordinary jobs and ordinary lives, who had drifted automatically from school into the first job that came along, into the first marriage that came along, and had never had the chance to make choices. They might grumble at the direction their lives were taking now but they wouldn't seriously complain, because they were accustomed to being told what to do.

'And now I've got to go to sea and shoot guns,' he said. 'I never wanted to do that.'

'Why did you become a gunner?' she asked. 'Wasn't there something else you could have done?'

'Och, there were a thousand things I could have done, but they don't ask you that. They give you eye tests and medicals and they look at your records and see what your education is, and then they decide. Or maybe they just pick it out with a pin. And once they've decided, you don't argue. It's lesson number one, that is: never argue. You can forget having a mind of your own.'

The music was beginning again. Carol glanced around, wondering where Joy was. She felt sorry for the sailor but she didn't want to sit here listening to his moans, she wanted to dance.

'Look, I'm sorry,' he said. 'You're fed up with me. I'll go away.'

'No – no, don't do that.' She caught his sleeve. He was wearing a matelot's thin white summer shirt with a square neckline and short sleeves. His arms were brown. 'Let's try this one. It's a rhumba.' The hot South American rhythm was already catching her mind and she grinned at him and jiggled her body. 'Come on.'

Roddy got up. He watched her and watched the other dancers. Then he took a couple of experimental steps.

'That's it! That's right!' Carol laughed and grabbed his hand. 'I thought you said you couldn't dance.'

'I canna. Not this sort, anyway – I can do Scottish dancing.' There was nothing wrong with his sense of rhythm, she thought, letting herself go in the elation of the dance. 'Hey, it's nae so bad, is it?'

'Not so bad at all.' She swung close and then let him catch her in his arms. 'You know, I reckon you're a natural. We could be good partners.'

'Aye,' he said, holding her close and looking down into her face, 'I reckon you're right.'

Carol danced all the way home that night. Hardly noticing Joy's silence, she floated along the moonlit streets, her arms lifted as if the young sailor were still within their embrace. She chattered dreamily.

'I didn't even like him all that much to begin with. I mean, he looked all right but he's only eighteen, just a boy really, and when we got talking he seemed so miserable. Homesick, I reckon. He lives near Edinburgh. I thought he was just sorry for himself. But he turned out really nice. He's got lovely eyes. They're a really dark brown, like velvet.'

Joy said nothing. After coming in from her encounter with the soldier, she had hidden for a while in the ladies' cloakroom, soaking lavatory paper in cold water and pressing it to her eyes. An ATS officer had come in and glanced at her curiously, and Joy had bolted into the cubicle and stayed there until the woman had gone again. After a while, she put on some more lipstick and came out but although Carol had waved and beckoned her over, she hadn't felt like dancing again. She sat on the chair and watched, waiting for the time to pass until they could go home.

'Did you enjoy yourself?' Carol asked, noticing her silence at last. 'I saw you with that soldier. What happened to him?'

Joy shrugged. 'Dunno. Went off.'

'Didn't anyone else ask you?' Carol asked. 'There was plenty of blokes there.'

'I didn't feel like it.'

Carol shook her head. 'What's the matter with you? I thought it was smashing.'

'It was all right,' Joy said, determined not to tell the other girl of her humiliation. 'I just didn't feel like dancing any more, that's all.'

'Oh well,' Carol said, shrugging, 'so long as you enjoyed it. Here, there's another one on in a fortnight. You'll come with me, won't you?'

'I might.' Just at the moment, there was nothing Joy felt less like doing, but having professed to have enjoyed herself, she could think of no excuse not to go again. 'I'll have to see what Mum and Dad say.'

'Roddy says he'll get the tickets,' Carol said. 'And guess what – he's asked me to go to the pictures with him.'

'The pictures?' Joy stared at her friend. She could see her smiling in the moonlight. 'But that's like a – a proper boyfriend.'

'Well, so what? I can have a boyfriend, can't I? I'm nearly sixteen.' Carol lifted her nose, looking suddenly very much like her mother. 'We're going to see *Pimpernel Smith*. It's Leslie Howard – you know, the one who was in *Gone With The Wind*. I think he's smashing.'

'I liked Clark Gable better. When he said "Frankly, I don't give a damn".' Joy shivered and giggled. 'His eyes make me feel all funny.'

'Roddy's eyes make me feel like that,' Carol confided. 'Did that soldier try and kiss you?'

Joy nodded. Her mood, which had begun to lift, was deflated again. Carol eyed her for a moment, then slipped her arm through Joy's.

'You don't want to take no notice of that. They all try it on. It don't mean nothing.'

'I didn't like it,' Joy said. 'He was too rough. I don't want boys pawing me.'

'Well, don't go outside with 'em, then,' Carol said bluntly. 'You don't have to let it stop you having fun. Just say you'd rather dance, and have a good time.' They were almost outside the shop now, and paused. 'You will come to the next one, won't you?'

'I don't know. It's all right for you, you've got a proper boyfriend now. I'll be on my own.'

'No, you won't. I'll ask Roddy to find you a partner. Anyway, you'll never have a boyfriend if you don't go out and find one.'

Joy sighed. For most of the evening she had been wishing that she hadn't dressed up in Alice's blouse and come to the dance. She'd been looking forward to her first time out as a young woman, instead of a girl, but the episode with the soldier had undermined her confidence. She was no longer sure she was ready, and yearned to be indoors with her parents, or playing Ludo with Rose.

But even as she thought of it, she knew that it was no longer enough. Home was no longer the comforting place it had been. And she had crossed some invisible dividing line tonight, had entered a different world. Like it or not, it was the world she would live in from now on, and she could not slip back into childhood.

'Say you'll come,' Carol urged.

But Joy would make no promises. She shook her head and said, 'I'll see', and then slipped down the little side alley to the back door.

Carol looked after her for a moment. Then she tossed her head so that her hair flew round her face, and danced all the way down October Street.

8

Olive returned to Portsmouth in late November, having completed her training as a gunner girl. To her delight, she was posted to the anti-aircraft battery on Southsea Common.

By that time, the war had moved on. In Russia, Leningrad was still under siege and Moscow battling for its life. The onset of the cruel Russian winter seemed to be the city's only hope, for despite Stalin's pleas there was no chance yet of a Second Front. Germany was still too great a threat to Britain and the RAF was fully occupied in attacking the major cities. In one night, nearly four hundred aircraft flew to bomb Berlin, Cologne and Mannheim. One in ten did not return.

There had been a thousand air raids on the island of Malta when the *Ark Royal*, one of the Navy's proudest ships, which carried load after load of Hurricanes there in its defence, was finally sunk off Gibraltar, thus bringing true at last one of Lord Haw-Haw's constant jibes. The only consolation was that almost the whole crew was saved.

The world's attention was turning also to the threat of Japan against America. War between the two countries seemed almost inevitable; it was little more than a matter of when and how it would begin. Winston Churchill announced that such an involvement would be followed 'within the hour' by a British declaration of war against Japan. To many people, it could come only as a relief to have America fighting beside them, even though it meant yet another enemy to be confronted. With the sinking of the first US Navy ship off Iceland, war against Germany too seemed to come closer and the anxiety increased.

The tension spread everywhere. It was like a creeping fog, slithering into the most private places, the most intimate situations, and it cast a deep chill over everyone's lives. Nothing seemed to be the same any more.

But there were still things to be cheerful about, Jess observed. 'Potato Pete' had arrived, easing the shortage of potatoes, and now they were plentiful enough to be used all the time. The price was fixed at a penny a pound and Lord Woolton was recommending that they be used to make pastry, and even mashed potato sandwiches! He also extolled the virtues of carrots and swedes. Carrots were supposed to help you see in the dark, which would help in the blackout, and it was said that they were eaten in huge quantities by night-flying pilots. And tinned food was put on 'points' rationing, and everyone got sixteen points a month, to use as they wanted.

Derek managed to get a weekend pass when Olive came back to Portsmouth, and they had a passionate reunion in Olive's bedroom. But even their lovemaking seemed tainted somehow by fears and anxieties that could not be escaped.

'Oh Derek, I feel as if I've been away for years,' Olive said, pressing herself close against him. It didn't seem possible that he was actually here, in her arms, that she could look into his eyes and run her fingers through his hair. 'I thought the time was never going to pass.'

'North Wales is a hell of a long way away,' he agreed. 'It could have been the North Pole, as far as I was concerned. What was it really like, Livvy?'

Olive had tried to keep her letters as cheerful as possible, but now that she was with him she couldn't pretend any more. She turned down her mouth and wrinkled her nose.

'It was horrible. There's nothing much there, you know – just sea and cliffs and awful black rocks. Might be all right in summer, I suppose, but it's not nice beaches like it is here. And they all speak Welsh, did you know that? It was like being in a foreign country.'

'Didn't they lay on anything for you? Dances and things?' There was a slightly over-casual note to Derek's voice, as if he hoped they hadn't, and Olive felt a faint twinge of resentment. They had dances at the camp in Wiltshire, didn't they? Why shouldn't she have a bit of fun as well? Didn't he trust her?

She shook her head. 'They didn't seem interested. Probably thought we'd attract the Germans and get them all bombed! There were a few dances in the camp but us girls weren't allowed to dance with the officers, even if they asked us, so it wasn't much good. You soon find out who counts for anything in the Army.' She looked at his face and felt ashamed of her sourness. 'Anyway, I didn't want to go, not without you.'

Derek hugged her. 'You poor thing. You've had a miserable time.'

'Well, it was quite interesting, all the same,' Olive said. 'The work, I mean. We did aircraft recognition and we learnt to work out what height the planes were flying at.'

'You did that? I didn't know they trained girls for that sort of thing.'

'Why shouldn't they?' she challenged him. 'We've got brains as well, you know, just the same as the men. We aren't made of cotton-wool.'

'All right, all right, no need to be so touchy. How did you do it then – how did you work out the height?'

'Well, they used to fly across the sea, pulling a big sleeve behind them. You take bearings, see, and work it out with maths. It's not that hard. And once we'd got their height worked out, we'd tell the gunners and they'd fire.'

'Trying to hit the planes?' Derek asked in surprise, and Olive laughed and shook her head.

'Don't be daft! They were aiming at the sleeves. It was awful at first – they didn't hit a single one the whole week. I kept thinking, suppose it was Portsmouth we were defending, and we'd let all those planes get through. It was our fault, you see, the gunner-girls, for not giving them the right directions.'

'But you were all right in the end.'

'Oh yes,' Olive said proudly. 'I passed out top in our group. We hit every one.' Her face grew sober again. 'I just hope we'll be able to do it when it's real.'

'You'll be all right,' Derek said, stroking her neck. 'Just don't expect to be perfect. We all make mistakes, can't help it.'

'That's all right when it's just a matter of burning the dinner or forgetting some shopping. But when it's planes getting through and bombing Portsmouth – perhaps killing your own family—' Olive's face was white. She stared at him with huge brown eyes. 'I don't know how I'll be able to live with myself if anything like that happens.'

Derek was silent for a minute or two. Then he said,'Look, Livvy, some of them are going to get through. They're bound to. You can't shoot down every plane in the sky. And the ones that make it will drop their bombs, we all know that. You don't have to blame yourself for that. You just have to be thankful for the ones you do hit. It's better than nothing. It's lives saved. Just think of that, see?'

'Yes,' Olive said, a little waveringly. She gave him a watery smile. 'I suppose you're right. It just seems – well, such a responsibility.'

'It is,' Derek said, 'but it's not so much responsibility as the people who got us into this. We can't none of us do any more than our best. And now come here and let me do what I do best. I've been starving for you all these weeks, Livvy.'

He began to caress her with more ardour, unbuttoning her pyjama jacket and spreading the cotton fabric aside so that he could bury his face in her breasts. Olive lay back, waiting for the familiar excitement to sweep over her, waiting for her body to be taken over by the sensations she had learned to love so much.

But they were slow to come, and she found herself consumed by anxiety more than by passion. Her thoughts were still circling round the conversation they had had, disturbed by the hint of disapproval in Derek's voice and the touch of resentment she had felt in response.

He never said he didn't want me to go in the ATS, she thought huffily. Maybe it's just dances and things he doesn't want me to go to. And again, she wondered – didn't he trust her?

But that was men all over, wasn't it – one rule for them and another for their wives. And when it looked like this war was going to show them something different, they didn't like it.

'Livvy.' Derek's voice whispered in her ear. 'Livvy, what's wrong? You don't seem to be with me. What's the matter?'

Olive looked up into his face. He was gazing at her with puzzled eyes, as hurt as a puppy who doesn't understand what he's done wrong. She felt a sudden surge of love and caught him hard against her.

'Nothing's the matter,' she said. 'Nothing – only that you're going away again, and I want this horrible war to stop so that we can settle down properly and live our lives the way we wanted to. Oh, *Derek*—' her voice quivered and broke '—oh Derek, make love to me. Make love to me all night and don't ever stop. Don't ever, *ever* stop . . .'

*

Olive returned to camp after Derek had gone back to Wiltshire, feeling as if she had had her right arm torn off. She went into the hut and found Claudia sitting on her bed, painting her toenails.

'So how was married life?' Claudia enquired. 'You know, I'm not sure I like this colour after all. It's too dark for my toes.'

Olive glanced at it. 'I don't see what difference it makes. No one's going to see them.'

'That's not the point. We've got to do something to keep up our morale. They won't let us varnish our fingernails. A girl's got to take a pride in herself.' Claudia frowned. 'All the same, I think I prefer something more *pink*, don't you?'

Olive sat down on her bed. It was hard and narrow, not like the wide bed she shared with Derek in her room at home. She wondered how long it would be before they managed another weekend together, and her eyes filled with tears.

'Now look,' Claudia said, still staring at her feet, 'you're not going to start weeping, I hope. Otherwise I'll have to have a talk with Hatchetface. "We can't have you gels coming back from weekends and flooding out the camp."' Her imitation of the officer's accent was so accurate that Olive had to laugh, despite her tears. 'You must learn to leave your marriage outside the wire fence, Harker. In here, you're a soldier.'

'You're a fool,' Olive said affectionately. 'And I'm not going to flood the camp.' She sighed. 'Heaven knows, I ought to be getting used to saying goodbye to Derek by now.'

'We're all getting used to saying goodbye,' Claudia said soberly, and swung her feet to the floor. 'Well, they'll have to do. I'd rather have pink but since I haven't got it, I'll make do with red.'

'You'll have to take it off the minute Hatchetface spots it. You're not supposed to do your toenails any more than your fingernails.'

'I know. It's because it's inflammable. They're afraid we might burst into flames.' Claudia padded over to the stove. A few girls were sitting round it and there were enamel mugs standing on the top. Claudia reached across to take two and brought them back to the beds.

'Good old Army cocoa, you can't beat it. I bet you've been just longing for this all weekend, haven't you?'

'Haven't I just!' Olive accepted a mug and blew on it before taking a cautious sip. 'Claud, you wouldn't go through my recognition with me again, would you?'

Claudia nodded. All the girls had left their training well able to identify any aircraft in the sky, but they were all terrified that they would let a German go through, to bomb the city. Or, worse still, mistake an Allied one for a German and cause one of their own pilots to be shot down. They went over their recognition again and again.

'Spitfire. Hurricane. Halifax. Lancaster,' Olive recited. 'Boeing B-17 Fortress. Junkers Ju88A, Dornier Do17, Heinkel.'

'Perfect,' Claudia announced at last. 'There won't be a plane in the sky that we can't identify at a glance. We'll be the best gunner-girls the Army's ever had.'

'I hope so.' Olive looked nervously at the pictures again. 'I think I ought to go over them once more, just to make sure.'

'You'll do no such thing.' Claudia removed the booklet and placed it firmly under her pillow. 'You can't know them any better than you do now. Anyway, it's nearly time for lights out.'

Olive washed, undressed and got into her narrow bed. She lay in the darkened hut, listening to the other girls breathing, to the odd snore, and longing for Derek.

She could not forget what had happened during their lovemaking last night. It was the first time in their marriage that anything had gone wrong with the passion that had seemed so secure between them. Now, although in the end they had both cried out in the climax of their loving and had slept with their bodies closely entwined, ready to love each other again with their awakening, there had been a hint of discord which she could not dismiss.

We need to be together, she thought. We need to be together properly, day after day, night after night, like a proper married couple. That's the only way we can build a real marriage, one that'll last us all our lives. You just can't do it with the odd weekend here and there.

It wasn't just her and Derek, either. It was all the girls and men who'd got married only to be torn apart by the war. It was girls like her sister Betty, still waiting, not knowing when they would even be able to get married. Not knowing *if* they ever would . . .

Bugger Hitler, she thought, turning over and thumping her pillow. Bugger, bugger, *bugger* Hitler.

Out at Bishop's Waltham, the Spencers had received a telegram. Gerald, their elder son, had been wounded in the fighting in the Western Desert and was being sent home. Mrs Spencer hardly knew whether to be anxious or relieved.

'They don't say what's happened to him,' she said, scanning the telegram. 'It must be pretty serious if they're sending him home. What d'you think they'll do, Jack?'

'Send him to an Army hospital, I suppose.' The farmer looked almost as anxious as his wife, but he put his big arm round her thin shoulders to comfort her. 'One thing, Ada, he'll be out of the fighting. It's our Dick you ought to be worrying about.'

'D'you think I'm not?' she asked sharply. 'There's not a day goes by when I don't think of 'em both a hundred times. First thing when I opens me eyes in the morning, last thing when I says me prayers at night. And you can't say our Gerald'll be any safer. They've got to get him back to England first, and then you don't know where he'll be in hospital.'

Jack Spencer sighed and nodded. Being brought home was no guarantee of safety, he knew that. But it must be safer than fighting in the African desert.

Jonas, the ancient farmhand who had hobbled out of retirement when the war began and boasted that he could still work any of the 'youngsters' off their feet, said, 'Pity he can't stop at home. Plenty of work on the farm and then we could send these bloody Land Girls back where they come from.'

'Jonas!' Mrs Spencer exclaimed, and Jack Spencer frowned.

'That's enough of that, Jonas. You know as well as I do, the girls do a good job. We'd be in a pretty poor state without 'em.'

'Be in a better one with the men back where they belong,' the old man muttered, and stumped out of the kitchen. The farmer and his wife looked ruefully at the three girls.

'He'll never change,' Mrs Spencer said. 'He don't mean half he says, you know.'

'Oh, we don't take any notice,' Betty said cheerfully. 'We all know Jonas by now. We're all really sorry to hear about Gerald,' she added. 'I hope he isn't too badly wounded.'

'Yes.' The farmer's wife looked down at the telegram again and sighed. 'You think you know all about the war until it hits you in your own family, and then somehow it seems different.' She glanced up at Erica. 'I'm sorry, love – that must sound hard, when you've already lost your young man.'

'It's all right,' the blonde girl said gently. 'I know what you mean. You think you really feel it for all the others, and it's still a terrible shock when it happens to someone you love. But Gerald's going to be all right. They'll bring him home and he'll be as good as new again.' She went over to the sink. 'I'll make you a cup of tea while Betty and Yvonne see to the milking.'

The other two girls went outside. November mist lay like an old grey Army blanket across the yard. The cows had walked through three times already that day and had trampled mud and dung through on their hooves. They were standing in the byre waiting to be milked, their breath steamy.

'Erica's changed a lot since she first came,' Betty remarked as they settled down beside the cows. 'She's nicer, somehow.'

'I know.' Yvonne coiled her lanky legs around her low milking-stool. 'She thinks about other people more. Feels for them, too. She was really good to Mrs Spencer just now.'

Betty giggled suddenly. 'Remember when we first arrived and she wanted a room to herself? I thought she'd have a fit when she saw the attic! We thought she was a right toffee-nosed little squirt.'

'So she was. But I reckon Geoff was good for her. It's a shame he was killed.'

They were silent for a few moments, thinking of the laughing airman and his two friends Duff and Sandy. The milk made a steady hissing sound as it squirted into the pails. One of the cows shifted suddenly and uttered a low moo.

'All the same,' Yvonne said at last, 'I don't reckon Erica would've been so nice now if it hadn't happened. I mean, I know that sounds awful but it was losing him that changed her, somehow. Don't you reckon so?'

'Yes, I think I do,' Betty said thoughtfully. 'Before that, she was against everyone. Especially Dennis. And afterwards too, for quite a while. But then she seemed to gradually change. And she doesn't paint herself up the way she used to. She was a real glamour queen when she first came.'

'Wasn't she just!' Yvonne agreed. 'But it would be a shame if she forgot about being pretty. I mean, she can look gorgeous but she hardly ever bothers now. It's as if she's decided it's not worth bothering.'

'She hasn't got over Geoff yet. Maybe she never will.'

Yvonne shrugged and moved on to the next cow. 'You can't go all through your life hankering after someone who's not there any more. Erica'll find someone else when she's ready. Or someone'll find her.' She glanced across the byre at Betty. 'How's your Dennis, anyway?'

'Oh, he's fine.' Dennis was still at Fort Widley, so he and Betty were able to meet quite frequently. 'He's coming over on Sunday. He's taking me to meet his mum and dad.' She stretched her arms and then shivered. 'I'm scared to death!'

Dennis's parents lived in Portchester, but Betty hadn't met them before because they had been in Somerset, looking after Dennis's grandmother. After a long illness, she had died and now they were back in Portchester where Mr Verney was a librarian.

'I hope they'll like me,' Betty said nervously as she walked beside Dennis along the little road near the old castle. 'They won't think I'm common, will they, because our house doesn't have a bathroom or anything?'

Dennis laughed. 'Of course they won't! We're Friends, remember? Everyone's equal. They won't take any notice of things like that.'

'All the same, they might not think I'm good enough for you.'

Dennis stopped and put his arms round her. He kissed her firmly on the lips.

'Dennis! We're in the middle of the street—'

'I don't care. I love you, Betty, and even if my parents hated you on sight it wouldn't make any difference to that. But they won't. They'll love you, just like I do.' He grinned. 'Well – maybe not *quite* like I do . . .'

'Dennis, you're awful sometimes. Nobody would think you were religious,' Betty said, blushing, and he laughed again.

'What's wrong with liking one of the best things God made for us? Loving's right, Betty, it's good and natural, and we ought to enjoy it.' He let her go and tucked her hand under his arm. 'Come on, they're not ogres. You'll be all right.'

The house was on a corner. It had a semi-circular bay window in front, and a small conservatory behind. The front garden was a square of grass with plants all around it in a border, some green, some purple, some feathery, some with broad, furry leaves. Betty looked at them, puzzled. They weren't flowers but they certainly weren't vegetables.

'They're herbs,' Dennis said. 'Mum grows them for flavouring and medicines. She's a great one for making medicines.'

Betty had never heard of anyone making their own medicines, or using herbs. Her own mother made a lovely mint sauce to have with roast lamb – when she could get lamb – and Aunt Jess mixed up honey and lemon juice for coughs, but any more than that sounded a bit like witchcraft. She looked doubtfully at the little bushes and followed Dennis round the side of the house.

The back garden had been dug up for vegetables. Betty looked at the neat rows of cabbages, turnips and onions and felt happier. A tall man with silver hair was digging potatoes at the end, and Dennis waved at him.

'That's Dad.'

The man came up the garden path, still holding his fork. He was well over six feet tall and looked rather like Betty's idea of Moses coming down from the mountain – except that Moses wouldn't have been carrying a hoe, she thought with a nervous inward giggle – but he was smiling, and he had warm hazel eyes just like Dennis's. He took Betty's hand in his, and she felt the warm, gentle strength in his fingers . . .

'So you're Betty.' His voice was deep and strong. 'Welcome, my dear. We've been waiting a long time to meet you.' He turned and leant the fork against the fence. 'Come in and meet Cicely. She's making a special soup.'

An appetising scent wafted from the kitchen window and Dennis grinned. 'I always know I'm home when I smell one of Mum's soups. Come on, Betty.'

Dennis's mother was as short as his father was tall. She couldn't have been much more than five feet, and she had grey hair, cut short to curl around her face. She was wearing a dark brown skirt and a cream jumper and her face was a mass of wrinkles, all smiling. She had very bright blue eyes that sparkled with energy.

'Dennis! You're looking well. And this is Betty.' She held both Betty's hands, gazing at her with as much pleasure as if Betty were her own daughter. 'Oh, it's so good to see you.' She let go and reached up to kiss her son. 'I've missed you so much while we've been with Granny.'

'I wish I could have come down to Taunton,' he said. 'But they wouldn't give me time off until she'd died. Grandmothers' funerals are allowed – but I told them I'd rather have seen her while she was still alive.'

'She would have liked you to have been there,' his father said quietly. 'But she was proud of you. We all are.'

Cicely Verney turned to the stove and took the lid from a large saucepan. The appetising scent drifted out, more strongly than ever, and Betty felt her saliva begin to flow. She looked around the kitchen.

It was larger than her mother's, with a big, scrubbed wooden table in the middle set for the meal. It was quite plain – just brown soup bowls and plates, with a big platter of bread in the middle. There was a jug of water and four glasses, and at one end Mrs Verney had put a little pottery jug filled with leaves from the herbs Betty had seen in the front garden.

'Sit yourselves down,' Dennis's mother said, taking the pan from the stove and turning off the gas. She tipped the soup into a large bowl and Betty looked at it. It was rich and brown, and thick with vegetables.

'It looks lovely, Mrs Verney. And smells delicious.'

'That's Robert's home-grown vegetables and my herbs,' she said. 'Nothing from the shops at all. And please don't call me Mrs Verney. We like to be addressed by our first names.'

Dennis had already told Betty that Quakers – or Friends, as they preferred to call themselves – disliked the titles Mr and Mrs, but she still felt awkward using the Christian names of people she had only just met – especially when they were her sweetheart's parents. She would have to try to get used to it though – you couldn't go through your whole life addressing your in-laws as 'you'.

The thought of Robert and Cicely Verney being her in-laws gave her a little quiver of excitement. That would mean she was well and truly married to Dennis! She sat quietly beside him, eating her soup and listening to the conversation.

Dennis was talking about his training for bomb disposal work. He made it sound easy, but Betty felt the tremor of fear that she always experienced when she thought of what Dennis did, and wished again that he'd stayed on the farm.

Robert Verney listened gravely.

'I'm thankful that you're treated better than I was,' he said at last. 'The Government has a more civilised attitude these days. The pity is that it doesn't extend to preventing war altogether.'

'But Dennis had an awful time,' Betty exclaimed. 'He went to prison.'

Robert smiled and said nothing, but Cicely said fiercely, 'They nearly tore poor Robert to pieces in 1914. They were barbarians in the Great War, as they like to call it.'

Betty stared at her, then turned to Robert. He was looking serious again and he caught her eye and nodded.

'It's true. Pacifists were very badly treated then. If you weren't in uniform, women – perfect strangers – would come up to you and give you the white feather, for cowardice. And if you refused to join up you were arrested and put into the army anyway.'

'But you – ?' Betty said, and stopped, unable to think of a way of asking how he had been nearly torn to pieces.

'I refused everything. I wouldn't even put on the uniform. So they roped me to a gun-carriage, harnessed the horses and drove them away.' He gave a wry smile. 'It took me quite a long time to recover, and of course I was useless as a soldier. But I was luckier than some of the others.'

'Some people were shot,' Dennis said. 'They had plenty of ways of persuading people to fight. You have to be pretty strong to watch your mates being executed and know it's your turn next if you don't cave in.'

There was a short silence. Betty thought of Erica, who had been so hostile towards Dennis, and of Mrs Spencer's sister Iris, who had hated him with a viciousness that was quite frightening. She looked at Robert Verney, imagining him tied behind a gun-carriage and dragged across the ground. He could have died.

Robert Verney was eating his soup. Betty looked at him, thinking how tall and strong he seemed. And yet she could still sense that gentleness which she had felt when he held her hand. A gentleness and belief in God and man which had compelled him to refuse to fight, coupled with the courage which had given him the will to resist even when tortured.

He looked up suddenly and met her eyes. Betty blushed, certain that he knew exactly what she was thinking, and he smiled again.

'Tell us when we're going to have the pleasure of welcoming you as our daughter,' he said. 'We've longed for a daughter for years. We're both so pleased to have you.'

Betty looked from him to his wife. She thought of her own family and the way her father had reacted to Dennis and the tears came to her eyes.

'I don't know,' she said, feeling suddenly miserable. 'You see, my Mum's all right, but Dad—' She stopped, ashamed to go on, and felt the tears brim over.

Dennis put his arm round her. 'Betty's Dad isn't keen on me being a CO. I keep telling her, he's got a right to his opinion and we'll just wait until he comes around, but it's hard for her.'

Robert nodded. He didn't seem at all embarrassed by Betty's tears, but he didn't ignore them either. He gave her a friendly smile, while Cecily put both her hands over Betty's and held them warmly. 'Dennis is right. Your father deserves his respect. And this is the way Friends work. We don't always agree with one another, you know – we have our problems and our disputes. But when we can't agree, we simply wait. We discuss the matter again. And wait. And slowly, gradually, one by one, those in dispute will begin to change their minds. And when we're all in accord, we act.'

'But that could take years,' Betty said despairingly.

'Years that are well spent. But I know that's hard for you to accept.'

'We're not waiting years,' Dennis said firmly. 'We're going to wait until the summer, or maybe the spring, and if he hasn't come round then . . . At least we'll have given him the chance. But we don't want to wait any longer than that.'

'A spring wedding,' his mother said softly, and took Betty's hand. 'I'm so glad, my dear. So very, very glad.'

Betty's anxiety about the work Dennis was doing had never disappeared, but since nothing had yet happened to him, she tried hard to persuade herself that nothing would. Dennis, however, knew that he was in danger every minute.

He had now finished his training and, having been promoted to Lieutenant, was working full-time on bomb disposal. And there was plenty of work to be done. Of the bombs that had fallen during the blitz, many still lay unexploded at the bottom of craters or beneath buildings. Some were still being reported by people who had not at first realised they had fallen – people who had come back to their homes from evacuation and discovered a strange, sinister cylinder nestling in their coalshed or under an outside wall; people who had re-opened a disused building to find a bomb staring them in the face.

All these must be dealt with as they came to light. And there were still fresh bombs being dropped which might be even more urgent.

The day before he was due to come out to Betty at the farm, Dennis was sent to deal with a bomb which had been discovered in a garden at Cosham. Nobody knew quite when it had fallen, for the occupants had been away since April. It might be from one of the last great raids of the blitz; it might be much more recent, perhaps from one of the swift hit-and-run forays which were often made by lone pilots, perhaps jettisoned by a plane which had been on a mission further up the country and turned back.

'They think it's a five-hundred-pound bastard,' Captain Anderson told him as they drove to Cosham. 'Not all that big, but the sort that the Jerries like to fit with a nice little surprise for us. Wonder what it'll be this time.'

Dennis knew all about the 'surprises' that the enemy liked to attach to their bombs. For some time, the Germans had been using timing devices which could delay a bomb's detonation for days, or even months. And others were booby-trapped, to appear safe until the bomb disposal experts actually began to work on them. Then the slightest vibration could set off the explosion.

The whole street had been evacuated and the Pioneers were already digging the pit when the team arrived. This was the job that Dennis had first volunteered to do – the careful uncovering of a bomb that had buried itself perhaps twelve or twenty feet below the ground. The pit itself must be made safe as it was dug, with a wooden shaft being built to make it possible for the disposal team to climb in and out without risk of crumbling earth and to enable the bomb to be hoisted out after it had been defused.

Every movement must be made with care, for although the bomb had obviously suffered considerable impact when it fell, the devices with which it was fitted might yet mean that the slightest disturbance would trigger its explosion. Or the clock mechanism might have been set to begin on impact, and time even now be running out.

Men were killed every day doing this work, and Dennis knew that his chances of coming unscathed through the war were slim.

He walked to the edge of the pit and looked down. It was about fifteen feet deep. The nose of the bomb was showing and one of the sappers was gently removing the wet earth around the body.

'That's not a five-hundred-pounder,' Dennis said quietly. 'That's a thousand if it's an ounce.'

'Reckon you're right, sir,' the sapper agreed. 'Make a bloody big bang when it goes off.'

'Well, we're not going to let it.' Dennis walked back to Captain Anderson. 'We'd better get the steam steriliser along.'

One of the staff sergeants went off to telephone for the equipment. The sappers continued their work. As well as the wooden shaft, a tripod had to be erected above the pit with pulleys which would drag the bomb up from the depths after it had been made safe. Nearby, a pump was sucking water from the bottom of the shaft. Another staff sergeant was listening from behind a wall on an electrical stethoscope, and Dennis went over to him.

'Any sign of life?'

'No ticking yet, sir. Going to steam it out, are you?'

'If the equipment arrives in time.' Dennis walked back to the pit. The bomb was almost completely exposed now. He stared at it uneasily, then turned to the Captain.

'I'm not sure we ought to wait for the steriliser. I think there are two fuses there. We ought to dismantle them as quickly as possible.'

Anderson nodded. 'I agree. Are you ready to start?'

Dennis nodded. His heart was beating quickly and he felt the familiar tension grip his stomach, but he knew that this initial apprehension, which could if allowed turn into real fear, could be harnessed and channelled into the precise use of skill which gave him such satisfaction.

A quiet excitement flowed in his veins. This was the seventh large bomb he had tackled, and he had never known anything quite like the sense of exhilaration that caught him when he knew that he had succeeded in making them safe.

But he could not allow that excitement to affect him. The job he was about to do demanded total concentration and steadiness of hand and brain. Dennis had already witnessed several incidents in which men had been killed while trying to dismantle unexploded bombs. There were so many things which could go wrong. During his training, he had been watching from a distance when a large UXB was being hoisted with extreme care from its pit to be dealt with at ground level, on the supposition that after a few days the time fuse was no longer dangerous. Just as it reached the surface, one of the men had put a hand on it to stop it swinging. It had exploded at once, killing all eight men in and around the pit.

That was when the Army had begun to realise that timing devices could be set months, rather than days, ahead.

Then there had been the time when a corporal had died at the bottom of the shaft from the effects of ammonia fumes. And the man who had been badly scalded as the explosive was being steamed out of the bomb casing. And the numerous occasions on which an officer, in the act of dismantling a fuse, had set it off by too sudden a movement or by coming across a device not previously encountered. Sometimes, simply turning a screw the wrong way was enough.

For this reason, the officer working on the bomb talked quietly into a telephone headset, narrating every movement he made so that those on the surface knew exactly what was happening. And if his final remark was accompanied by an explosion, the survivors would know what had caused it.

'We'll use the Q-coil,' Captain Anderson said as they prepared to climb down the ladder into the shaft, now vacated by the sappers. 'If there is a clock there, that should stop it and we can get the thing out.'

The Q-coil was a fairly new device, developed to stop the clock by magnetising it. This would deal with the Type-17 fuse. The other – suspected to be a Type-50 – was even more dangerous. This was designed to delay the detonation until the bomb was moved or tapped, and was the one which had killed the eight men during the earlier operation.

To make this fuse safe, a man had to work on the bomb while it was still in its shaft, operating with the utmost care as any slight jarring movement could trigger the explosive.

Dennis and the Captain reached the bottom of the shaft. They studied the bomb, noting every detail. The slightest difference in its construction must be reported, so that the Unit could keep up with the developments and modifications the Germans were constantly making. You could never assume that you knew everything about the deadly weapon facing you.

There might always be some new trick, an innocent-looking button or screw, placed to trap the man working on it.

Bombs did not always fail to go off because they were defective. Many of them were designed to explode later, so that an air-raid of a few hours could extend its powers for many weeks afterwards. And even a 'dud' could never be declared safe until it had been completely dismantled. Deteriorating explosives could be the most unpredictable. Sometimes a clock which had been set in motion would stop, and then re-start. There was no way of knowing how long it had left to run. It might be several days; it might be less than a second.

Dennis began to scrape away the remaining earth from around the bomb. The Type-17 fuse was already partially exposed, but it was also partly underneath the bomb. He dug with his bare hands, trying not to brush against the casing or to let earth fall against it as he scrabbled a little pit under the fuse, large enough to get the clock-stopper over it. The sappers at the top lowered down the device, which weighed about seventy pounds, and Dennis and the Captain manoeuvred it over the fuse.

It was in place and the current switched on. That was the clock made safe, although only for a limited time – to make it permanently safe, a much heavier stopper must be used. But at least they were given some time to work on the even more sensitive Type-50.

'God almighty,' Anderson said in disgust, 'it's right underneath the bloody thing.'

Dennis stared at it. To work on the fuse in the pit was impossible. The bomb must be lifted clear.

He remembered that other bomb, swinging into view. The sergeant's hand, barely touching it. The huge explosion that had blown every man in the team to pieces and shattered every window for half a mile.

'We could dig underneath,' he suggested dubiously.

Anderson shook his head. 'The slightest jarring – just a small stone knocking it – could set it off. You know that as well as I do.'

'So how do we raise it without jarring it?' Dennis asked. 'We've got to get the strops underneath for a start. We're going to have to shift a bit of earth to do that.'

Captain Anderson considered. Dennis watched him, knowing that what he had said was true. But whoever took on the difficult and delicate task of scraping earth and mud from underneath the bomb without giving it the smallest jolt was putting his life at serious risk.

Their lives were already at serious risk, he thought, just standing there. What difference did a little bit more make?

It might make the difference between marrying Betty and living their lives together, and never seeing her again.

'You're right,' the Captain said at last. 'There's not a lot needs shifting. But it's a job only one man can do. You get back up top, Verney, and I'll do it.'

Dennis shook his head. 'I think it should be me, sir. It's my idea.'

Anderson looked faintly exasperated. 'This is no time for grabbing kudos—'

'I'm not interested in kudos. I just think if anything goes wrong, you're more use to the Unit than I am.'

'Nor heroics,' the Captain said sharply. 'A man who wants to be a hero is a dangerous man. You need to be cold steel for this job.'

'And so I am. That's the way I'm looking at it.' Dennis faced his superior steadily. 'I don't want to be a hero, sir, dead or alive. But I'm here to do a job to the best of my ability, and to serve mankind and my God in the best way I can. And I reckon that if only one of us is to come out of this alive, it ought to be you. You're the leader here. I'm not, and never will be.'

Captain Anderson stared at him. Then he said abruptly, 'Very well. We certainly don't have time to stand here arguing about it. That fuse has had five minutes already.' He gave a sharp nod and set his foot on the bottom rung of the ladder. 'Give me three minutes and then start work. And – good luck.'

Dennis nodded back, unsmilingly. The two men's eyes held for a few seconds longer and then the Captain began to climb.

Dennis stood quite still until he had disappeared over the rim of the shaft. He heard the voice above, ordering everyone out of range of the hole. Then he knelt in the damp earth and began, slowly and carefully, to dig away the soil.

9

The shaft was now a tangled cat's cradle. The clock-stopper's wires were straggling down the side of the shaft from its two batteries and switch-box, and there were balloon cables ready to lift the bomb out when it was finally made safe. Dennis crouched at the bottom, trying not to get himself entangled or to catch and jerk one of the wires. He talked quietly into his field telephone as he worked.

'I can see the fuse pretty well now. It's definitely a fifty. I've got it almost clear. I'm scraping away the last few bits of earth.' A tiny pause, and those above held their breath. 'It's been damaged,' he said quietly. 'I don't think we can do anything to it.'

Damaged! Then why hadn't the bomb already exploded? The men above ground looked at each other and shook their heads. Captain Anderson walked back to the top of the shaft.

'You'd better come up right away.'

Dennis looked up. The Captain's face looked odd, hanging above him in the circle of light.

'I think I ought to stay here, sir. I'm safe enough so long as nothing jars it, but if we keep climbing in and out . . .'

'Bugger it, man!' the Captain exploded. 'Don't you *ever* obey orders?'

Dennis grinned. 'All the time, sir. And if you order me to stay here I'll obey willingly.'

The Captain snorted. Then he said, 'So what do you propose to do? Spend the rest of your life down there?'

They both knew that this might well be exactly what Dennis was going to do, and that the rest of his life might be short indeed. But Dennis shook his head and said cheerfully, 'I think we can steam it out, sir. Then we'll detonate both fuses. The steamer ought to be here soon.'

'It's arriving now,' Anderson said, glancing over his shoulder to where an Army truck was pulling in at the end of the street. Soldiers jumped out and one of the officers came down the back alley towards him. He joined the Captain at the rim of the shaft and Anderson gave him a quick briefing on what was happening.

'You reckon it'll steam?' the newcomer said, peering down at Dennis.

'It's our only chance. I can't touch this fuse. But if we can get the TNT out . . .'

The officer nodded. 'Right. Let's get moving. You've had that stopper on it a while already.' He set off back to his truck at a run.

Anderson looked down the shaft again. 'You don't have to do this, Verney.'

'But someone does,' Dennis answered. 'And I'm here.' He paused and added, 'And I won't come up unless you specifically order me to.' He was quite sure that Anderson would not do that now. For one thing, the task they were about to do needed two men and the Captain would probably come down again himself.

He was right. After a few minutes – with the clock-stopper's time steadily running out – Anderson climbed down again and the steamer was lowered into the pit. By now, Dennis had very gently unscrewed the bomb's baseplate. He removed it with a tiny sigh of relief, and Anderson positioned the steam-jenny.

The shaft filled with steam. It billowed about them in a great scalding cloud, hissing in their ears. The humidity soaked into their clothes and filled their nostrils with the smell of hot, wet earth.

TNT began to flow out of the bomb in a wet stream, solidifying as it met the floor of the pit. Even though it was less dangerous in that state, the bomb was far from safe, for even without its explosive the fuses still carried a charge powerful enough to kill them both if they fired. And as more and more steam gushed out, the shaft became hotter and hotter. Dennis found himself taking short, shallow breaths, unable to draw the hot air deep into his lungs. His head reeled but he dared not take his attention from the steam-jenny. Once started, this was a job that had to be finished.

It was two hours before they could declare their task complete. By that time, both were sweating and almost unconscious with the heat, but they channelled every scrap of concentration into what they were doing. Their world narrowed to the inferno of the little pit, and for all they knew time could have become eternity.

'D'you think it's happened?' Anderson muttered once. 'D'you think the whole bloody caboodle's gone sky-high and we've got to Hell?'

Dennis shook his head. 'You haven't got a tail.' He saw the other man's teeth flash briefly in the glimmering light and felt cheered. Not much of a joke, perhaps, but who could be Tommy Handley in a situation like this?

The bomb was empty at last. The floor of the pit was covered in several hundred pounds of solidifying TNT. Three sappers climbed down into the pit and began to carve it into blocks, which were sandbagged and raised to the surface. Nothing more could be done to the bomb until every scrap of explosive had been removed to a safe distance.

It was dark when Dennis and Captain Anderson finally emerged from the hole. They were both filthy, covered in mud, earth and the dank water that had seeped from the walls of the pit or condensed from the steam. They had attached charges to each of the fuse-pockets and timed them to go off after half an hour. There were only a few pounds to detonate, but the restricted area and the steel cases in which the pockets were housed would make a fierce enough explosion.

They climbed wearily out of the pit and went with the rest of the team to take cover.

Twenty minutes later the two charges blew. Every window in the street shattered.

Huddled in their temporary shelter, the men grinned at each other and gave the thumb's-up. Once again, they had challenged death. Once again, they had won.

In early December, the King and Queen made another visit to Portsmouth and lunched in the Dockyard on board HMS *Victory*. Afterwards, the King visited the Gunnery School while Queen Elizabeth toured the city. She visited one of the British Restaurants, St Mary's Hospital and the Dockyard, where Frank Budd saw her. She passed close to the boiler-shop on her way from the *Victory* and they all came out and lined up to be inspected. He told Jess about it that evening.

'She's got the bluest eyes I've ever seen. Cherry said they looked just like robins' eggs.'

'So Cherry was there too?' Jess said.

'Oh yes, men and women alike, we all lined up together.'

Jess sniffed. She'd been hearing a bit more than she wanted to about this Cherry just lately. The girl seemed to worm her way into almost everything Frank said these days. Cherry this, Cherry that – he'd never talked about what went on at work so much before, nor had he ever seemed to find so much to enjoy while he was there. Why, his serious face proper lit up when he was recounting the latest exploit, and made him look quite young again. It's me that ought to be putting that look on his face, Jess thought, me that ought to be making him laugh.

But Frank didn't seem to find much else to laugh about when he got home. He'd come in of an evening – invariably late, because of the overtime – and go straight to the big map on the wall to figure out the latest positions, with the *Daily Express* and the *Evening News* spread out on the dining-table in front of him. Then, having moved all the little pins with their red and black heads, he'd do it all again after the Nine o'Clock News on the wireless. He always looked grave while he was doing this, and no wonder, with the way things were going, but the trouble was that was his evening almost gone. By then it would be time to be out on firewatching duty, or going down to the shelter, or trying to get an early night because he had to be up at five-thirty next morning . . . It didn't give him and Jess any time at all to be together, to be themselves and enjoy each other's company.

It was the people at work who got the best of him, she thought uneasily. And that hadn't worried her when it was chaps like Dick Foster or Harry Banks. But when it came to flighty young girls like this Cherry . . .

I shouldn't worry about him, she thought. I ought to trust him. I do, really – I've never had a moment's doubt over him before, never. I know he loves me, and I know he'd never do anything wrong. But all the same – when a chap's working hard, and worried half out of his mind over what's going to happen next, and he hardly sees his wife and then they stick a saucy little piece like that right under his nose for eight or ten hours a day . . . Well, he's only human, after all.

And so am I. I can't *help* worrying!

Peggy Shaw had seen the Queen too. She told Jess about it next day, full of excitement because Her Majesty had actually visited the First Aid Post where she and Gladys worked as volunteers, and had spoken to them.

'She saw Gladys's BEM. She'd got it pinned on – she didn't want to really, but the Super told her she ought to. The Queen was really pleased – well, it was her hubby what'd give it to our Glad, wasn't it, when you think about it – and she asked what Gladys was going to do and our Glad said she'd volunteered for the Wrens, only they didn't seem to be in any hurry to have her and she was thinking of going for a nurse instead, and the Queen said she thought Glad'd make an *excellent* nurse. That's what she said – excellent.' Peggy stopped for a moment, almost breathless. 'And then she asked me if I had any more children and I said yes, a boy in the Army and another girl working at Airspeed waiting to be old enough for the WAAFs, and guess what she said then, she said I'd done a wonderful job and people like me – and my Bert too, I suppose – were bringing up just the kind of young ones who were going to win the war for us. Me and *Bert*! And she said it was hard for us all but sunshine *would* come again.' Peggy paused again, gazing at Jess with shining eyes. 'Fancy the Queen saying all that to me and Glad. It don't seem possible, does it.'

Jess smiled at her. 'You are lucky, Peg. I wish I'd seen her. It seems as if everyone in the street's talked to the Queen except me. She spoke to Derek Harker last time she came to Portsmouth, you know, after Olive lost the baby. Said much the same to him. It really put heart into Olive.'

Peggy nodded. 'It's made a difference to our Glad too. She's made up her mind she's not waiting any longer for the Wrens to make up their minds. She's going to see about training as a nurse. I think she'll be good at it. She's done really well with her First Aid, driving that ambulance.'

Jess went back indoors. It really was a wonder, the way a few words from someone like the Queen could make such a difference to people who were feeling down. It was as if she had a special, magic touch, as if she knew just what you were feeling and wanted to share it with you. And in a queer sort of way, that made you feel better.

It was a pity she couldn't talk to a few more people. People like Ted, for instance. Poor Annie was nearly at her wits' end over Ted.

'I feel so *ashamed*,' Annie said, brushing tea-leaves up from the carpet, where she had scattered them to pick up the dust. 'I mean, there's all the other men working all the hours God sends to try to win the war, and you just sit there feeling sorry for yourself. There's nothing wrong with you. You're fit and healthy. You've got your strength. But have you gone back to work? No, you haven't – you just whine about what it's like to take the ferryboat across the harbour at night.'

'I've told you time and time again,' Ted said, 'I'll go back to the ferry when I'm ready. The doctor says I've got to take me time. It won't do no good to force it.'

'Well, I don't think you'll feel any better till you *do* go back,' Annie said. 'All this sitting about feeling sorry for yourself isn't doing you no good neither. There's nothing wrong with you. You've never been hurt. There's plenty worse off than you.' She knelt on the floor, her brush in one hand, the sheet of newspaper into which she was sweeping the tea-leaves in the other, and looked up at him. 'Just as if there weren't any others every bit as scared, only *they're* not giving in to it. And then you've got the nerve to sneer at Betty's Dennis and say *he's* a coward!'

'I've told you before, I don't want that chap's name mentioned in my house,' Ted retorted. 'He's not a coward, I'll give him that, and I never said he was, but he still won't fight for his country. That's what sticks in my craw. There's lads like our Colin, and Derek and Bob Shaw and all the others, all doing their bit, and he'd rather go to jail than do what they're doing. *Doesn't think he has the right to kill people!*' he snorted. 'What makes him think he's got the right to decide? World 'ud be in a fine pickle if everyone thought that way.'

'The world's in a pickle as it is,' Annie said sharply. 'Maybe it'd be better if everyone did think his way. It couldn't be any worse, at any rate. But I'm not talking about Dennis, I'm talking about you. What about you getting up off your backside and doing *your* bit?'

'Don't you think I've done my bit?' he demanded. 'Don't you think Dunkirk was enough? I told you, I saw more there in those few days than I ever saw in the first war. More than enough to last me. There's not a day goes by when I don't remember, when I don't see it all again, when I don't hear the screams . . . What I saw at Dunkirk—'

'What you saw at Dunkirk was just the same as what thousands of others saw,' Annie said sharply. 'And a lot of them were wounded, and some still haven't got over *that*. And the rest have gone back to fighting. You done well at Dunkirk, Ted, I'm not denying that, but you've been playing on it ever since.'

'*Playing on it!* Now look here, Annie, I've been up on the roof firewatching more times than you've had hot dinners. I've taken the *King* across the harbour hundreds of times since Dunkirk. I was there the day they bombed the harbour station, thought the boat was going to go up in flames with it. You can't say I've been playing on Dunkirk, because I haven't.'

'And what did you do when we had to call the doctor to you?' Annie demanded. 'You were nothing but a jelly that night, and all you could babble about was Dunkirk and planes and machine guns and bombs.'

'Shock. She said it was delayed shock.'

'All right, all right, I know what she said. You don't need to go over it all again.' She brushed fiercely. 'But there were others at Dunkirk too, Ted, and they haven't just sat back and said they're not doing no more. Soldiers – thousands of them – who've *had* to go back. Sailors who just did it as all part of the day's work and had to go back to sea again. Yes, and men like you, older men who don't have to fight but have still gone on with their own war work – firefighting, ARP and all the rest of it. You weren't the only one there.'

'I know I wasn't,' he muttered. 'And I wish you wouldn't go on about it all the time. It doesn't do any good. I can't help how I feel, don't you understand that? The doctor told you, it's like an illness. I'll get better in me own time, if you'll only leave me alone.'

'Oh, yes?' Annie said sarcastically. 'And just when d'you think that'll be? When the war's over? When there's no more need to worry about bombs dropping? I should think we'll all get better then, Ted Chapman. It'll be easy, won't it. But it's *now* that matters – now, when we all need to pull together. When we all need to pull our own weight.'

'And I'm not, am I,' he said sullenly. 'That's what you're saying, isn't it?'

Annie got stiffly to her feet and stood looking down at him. He was a big man, her Ted, but this morning, sitting in his chair by the empty fireplace, he looked somehow shrunken, as if the heart had gone out of him. She felt a pang of pity, and thrust it away quickly. She'd had enough of feeling sorry for Ted.

'No, you're not,' she said bluntly. 'In fact, if you ask me, you're not pulling any weight at all. What you're doing is more like *pushing.*'

She turned and marched out through the kitchen into the garden. She tipped the contents of the newspaper into the dustbin and then stood there, leaning on the fence, trembling a little.

She hadn't ever spoken to Ted as sharply as that, not since he'd first been taken ill with this nervous trouble of his. The doctor had told her it was depression, brought on by his experiences, and that time was the only cure. But time had passed – it was a year now since Dunkirk – and he seemed to be getting worse, not better. And to Annie, who had always been a believer in getting on with things, it didn't seem right to see a grown man with all his health and strength and a job to do, just sitting there in a chair day after day feeling sorry for himself.

'Fat lot of sympathy I get from you,' he'd said to her one day and she'd answered him sharply.

'You don't need my sympathy. You've got enough of your own.' And immediately she'd bitten her tongue, feeling angry with herself because that was just what the doctor *hadn't* ordered. But maybe the doctor was wrong. Treating Ted like a piece of Dresden china didn't seem to be doing any good at all. Perhaps it was time to start treating him like a sulky child instead. Time to ignore his tantrums and tell him to get on with it. There were plenty worse off in the world, after all, and she had the rest of the family to think of. Betty, out on the farm. Olive, in the ATS. And Colin, somewhere at sea on HMS *Exeter*.

Dennis himself wasn't feeling very brave as he went off duty that night. He'd noticed it before – this reaction that set in after a particularly tricky job. There wasn't so much as a tremor at the time, yet afterwards – hours later, sometimes – he'd start shaking, his body shivering, teeth chattering as if he was freezing cold, and nothing he did seemed able to stop it. He just had to wait for it to pass.

What he'd have most liked to do at such times was go and have a deep hot bath, just lie there and soak the reaction away until his body relaxed. But you couldn't relax much in five inches of water, tepid water at that as often as not. So he usually tried going to bed with a book, or lying there listening to the wireless going in the corner of the hut. A Glenn Miller concert, perhaps, or one of the comedy programmes like *Much Binding in the Marsh*, or *Stand Easy*.

Whatever he did, it wasn't long before his thoughts drifted away to the subject that occupied them most, whenever he wasn't concentrating on dismantling a bomb.

Betty.

At twenty-nine, Dennis knew that he was deeply in love with Betty Chapman, and committed to her in a way in which he had never been committed to any other girl. Brought up as the eldest in a family of devoted Quakers, he had always taken relationships with the opposite sex seriously, and never taken part in the coarse jokes or crude attitudes towards women in which some of his schoolfriends and, later, workmates had indulged. With the example of his gentle father's never-failing courtesy towards his mother always before him, he had grown up believing that marriage should be a haven of loving security, a home for the spirit where none might batter down the door.

He knew, of course, that many marriages were not like that. He had seen his friends' parents spitting at each other like cats, snarling in bitter argument or – worse still, it sometimes seemed – living together in icy silence. One or two had even separated and lived apart, to the shame of their children, and he knew one boy whose parents were divorced and had no more to do with each other.

Divorce was like a dirty word – something you just didn't speak about. You had to go to court to get a divorce, and give evidence about how badly your partner had behaved, with details of what they had done that were reported at length in the newspapers and pored over by strangers. It was almost as bad as committing a crime, and your life afterwards might not be much better than if you'd actually gone to prison.

Dennis did not want a marriage that ended like that, nor one that struggled on with quarrelling or long, cold silences. He wanted a home like the one he had grown up in, with a family whose members loved each other – scrapping from time to time, that was only normal, but never letting their differences get out of hand. Respecting each other as people. Loving both their faults and their virtues.

With Betty, he believed that he could have such a marriage.

Betty wasn't the first girlfriend he had had. There had been a few others, mostly casual affairs that went no further than a Saturday-night outing to the pictures and a goodnight kiss at the front door, and there had been one he'd thought might go deeper. Jean, her name had been, and she'd had long brown hair and slanting eyes. She lived in Fareham and Dennis had met her at Hilsea Lido, where she came swimming on Saturday afternoons. There had been a crowd of them, all in their early twenties, stretching themselves out on the square flagstones to sunbathe or climbing up to the high diving-board that was the best showing-off point in Portsmouth.

Dennis remembered his first sight of Jean, standing like an Amazon against the blue sky. She'd been wearing a scarlet bathing costume which showed off her figure almost as if she'd been naked, and he'd felt his body stir as he gazed at her.

She was the best diver he'd ever seen. He could remember still the shape of her as she spread her arms and floated out in a swallow-dive. He'd almost believed she could really fly.

Looking back, he could see that that was really all there was to his passion for Jean – a desire for that perfect body, a lust he had later been ashamed of. He wasn't ashamed now – it was part of the normal male reaction to a female who offered herself to both his gaze and his touch as readily as Jean had offered herself to him. But after it was over, when he had realised that there was no more between them than an animal attraction, he had been more cautious in his responses. Sex was, he knew now, a powerful driving force that could carry a man into a world he might not want to enter. He was careful not to let it overwhelm him again.

Until Betty. And even then, when he had first known her when she had come to the Spencers' farm as a Land Girl, he had held back. Different though she was from Jean, with her short, naturally curly hair and her laughing eyes, he had felt her attraction at once. But he'd soon discovered that Betty already had a boyfriend, and that they were more or less engaged. It was only later, when their friendship had ripened and he knew that it was more than a sexual attraction that drew him to her, when she'd told him that it was over between herself and Graham, that he'd allowed that deep need in him to begin to surface.

Now, he could not imagine life without Betty and the love they shared. More than anything in the world, he wanted them to be together, to be married and sharing a home as his parents did, bringing up a family in their turn. He longed for the life of 'every day' – the life of an ordinary married couple in a simple home, with a baby or two crawling on the floor and no fears of war to darken their existence.

It would come one day. He was sure of that. Provided he could keep his steady coolness when dealing with bombs that might explode beneath his fingers at any second. Provided he could stay alive.

Richard Murdoch and Kenneth Horne were singing the signing-off tune of *Much Binding in the Marsh*, with their witty commentary on the events of the past week. Dennis hadn't heard a word of it. But his shivering had ceased and he was able to turn over and go to sleep.

In the house with the little turret at the corner of April Grove and March Street, Annie and Ted were also lying in bed. But the closeness they had once shared seemed to have gone and they lay apart, not touching. Since their argument that morning, they had scarcely spoken to each other, and they were too miserable to be able to go to sleep.

Never let the sun go down on your wrath, Annie's mother had always said, and Annie had tried to follow that advice. She remembered it now. I wish I could say I was sorry, she thought. But I can't. I *am* sorry we quarrelled, I'm sorry he's upset, but I still think it's been going on too long. He's got to pull himself together some time, and giving way to it just isn't doing any good. And there *are* people going through worse – much worse – and not complaining about it. And besides –

'Look,' Ted said suddenly, breaking the day-long silence, 'I can't *help* it, Annie. If I could get over it, I would. D'you think I *want* to be like this, old before my time, sitting in a chair and mumbling like a ninety-year-old.' The desperation in his tone was something she had never heard before, and it ran like cold water into her veins. 'I *want* to get back to normal. D'you know something? I hate myself, some days. I look in the mirror and I think, Ted Chapman, what use are you to man or beast? You ought to be out there, doing your bit, helping the war effort like everyone else. And if you can't, you'd be better off making an end of yourself.' His voice sank to a whisper. 'Sometimes, Annie, that's just what I feel like doing. It'd be the best thing all round. You'd all be much better off without me.'

Annie could not reply. She rolled over towards him and felt for his hand. His fingers were stiff and unresponsive. She felt suddenly frightened.

'Don't talk like that, Ted,' she said shakily. 'You mustn't say such things. It's wicked even to think them.'

'It doesn't feel wicked to me,' Ted answered, and the energy had drained from his voice, leaving it flat and hopeless. His hand relaxed suddenly, turning limp and flaccid. 'It feels like the only thing to do.'

'It's not. It's not.' Her fingers tightened around his, trying to find some response, some sign of strength. 'Ted, there's enough tragedy in this world without us adding to it. You've got to think of other people. Think how upset everyone would be if anything happened to you. Think about me. What would I do?'

'You'd be all right. You can cope with anything. I've never known anyone as good at managing as you.'

'Well, I couldn't cope with *that*,' she said vehemently. 'I couldn't manage at all without you, Ted, and don't you forget it. You're all I've got now. Our Colin's at sea, our Betty's on the land, Olive's married and in the ATS – we've got to look after each other, you and me. That's what we got married for in the first place, remember? Not because we wanted kids. Because we wanted *each other*.'

'Oh, Annie,' he said, and she could hear the tears in his voice, the difficult tears of a man who had been unused to weeping for over forty years and was now overwhelmed by the need to cry. 'Annie, I don't know what I'd do without you, I really don't.'

He rolled into her arms and she held him close, letting him weep in great, shuddering sobs against her breast. Her own tears flowed to join his, running down into her neck, pooling in the hollow of her throat, and she felt at last a real compassion – not the pity she had felt until now, which had begun to turn to contempt, but the empathy that was true under-standing of his condition.

He's right, she thought, he can't help it. Dunkirk, the bombing, it's all hurt him somewhere deep down and we've just got to wait for it to heal. And never mind the others, who are going through worse – this is Ted, my Ted, and I can't make him any different from what he is. I've just got to wait, and be strong.

But as his body trembled and shook against hers and his tears soaked her breast, she stared into the darkness, feeling cold and bleak and lonely, and wondering how much longer her strength could last.

10

Since the night of the dance, Carol Glaister and Roddy had spent every spare minute together. At least two nights a week, they went to the cinema and sat in the back row. It took quite a long time on the first evening for Roddy to pluck up courage to slip his arm around Carol's shoulders, even though she was snuggling invitingly against him, but he managed it halfway through the big picture and they sat cuddling close together, watching Leslie Howard in *Pimpernel Smith*. Afterwards, they shared a pennyworth of chips wrapped in newspaper and walked slowly home.

Roddy kissed Carol goodnight just outside her front door and she felt, as she told Joy Brunner afterwards, as if she was drowning. Joy listened, half envious, half unconvinced, and when Carol suggested again that she come to the next dance she shook her head.

'I don't like the soldiers. I don't want to be kissed and pawed about.'

'Go on, it's just a bit of fun. You've got to do it some time.'

'I don't see why.'

'Don't be daft. Everyone's got to do it. You've got to do a lot more than that when you get married.'

Joy wrinkled her nose distastefully. 'I shan't get married, then.'

'You won't have any kids. Not unless they're – you know – *illegitimate*.' Carol lowered her voice to speak the word, glancing over her shoulder as she did so. 'Mind you, you'd still have to do *it*, even then. There's no other way. Your mum and dad did it.'

Joy thought of Alice, with her stringy grey hair, and her father, no longer the neat, dapper little man he had been but carelessly dressed, with stains on his pullover and his moustache turning yellow, and felt revolted. She turned away.

'I don't want to talk about it. And I don't want to know about you and Roddy. I think it's all horrible.'

Carol laughed. 'It's not horrible, it's lovely. Not that we've done anything,' she added quickly. 'Only kissed and held hands in the pictures. There's nothing wrong with that.'

It was at the cinema that they saw most of the war news. *Pathe Pictorial* always came on between the big film and the small one, and a series of images filled the screen, with a commentary told in a hard, hurrying voice. It was much more dramatic than hearing it on the wireless, and they sat staring at film of soldiers out in the deserts of Africa, of Hitler's troops advancing through terrible blizzards on Moscow, or ships like the *Ark Royal* being blown up at sea. Roddy clutched Carol's hand tightly when such pictures appeared and she squeezed back, then lifted her free hand to her mouth and bit her knuckles. When it got too bad she looked down at her lap, trying to shut out the loud, hectoring voice of the commentator.

It wasn't so bad when they showed pictures of people at home. It didn't matter what happened, the film photographers could always find shots of smiling faces, of people 'taking it' as they dug out the rubble of their homes or queued cheerfully for scraps of fish or meat or a handful of sausages. They saw queues of another sort, too – single women in their twenties, being called up to serve in the police, the fire service or the Forces, all women under forty being registered as 'available labour'. That'd give Mum a turn, Carol thought, she was always making out she was still in her thirties when Carol knew for a fact (having come across her marriage certificate in a drawer) that she was forty-two.

'A lot of them women must be fed up at having to go out to work in factories,' she whispered to Roddy. 'But they all look as pleased as if they're going to a party.'

He didn't answer. She glanced at him and saw that even in the darkness his face looked pale. He was still thinking about the pictures of ships being blown up and sunk. They didn't ought to show such things, she thought indignantly. It's not fair.

The next day was a Sunday. Roddy came round after dinner and they went on the ferry to Gosport, just for the ride, and walked up the High Street. There wasn't much there, but it made a change from Pompey and Carol had always liked the short boat trip across the harbour, seeing all the ships, even when the weather wasn't up to much. They walked slowly, pausing to look in some of the shop windows – the little Woolworths and Littlewoods down by the Hard, not a patch on the ones in Pompey, Carol thought, and the sweetshop halfway up, and Nobes, the toyshop in Stoke Road. They passed the Forum cinema and the White Hart.

'I've got something to tell you,' Roddy said at last.

Carol stopped dead in the middle of the pavement. 'You've got a ship.'

He nodded. 'HMS *Cadover*. She's in for repairs. We'll be sailing pretty soon.' He looked at her miserably. 'I'll be going away, Carrie.'

'Oh, Roddy,' she said, and buried her face against the blue serge of his tunic.

He put his arms round her and held her close. Then he turned her face up to his and kissed the tears. 'You know I don't want to go,' he said. 'I canna face leaving you, Carol.'

'I don't want you to go either. But what can we do? Like you said – we don't have any choice.' She drew herself out of his arms and they walked on in silence. They reached Foster Gardens, a little ornamental corner of paths and shrubberies, with a pergola and a round pond in the middle. It was damp and misty, and they were the only people there. They sat on a seat in a small wooden shelter and gazed at the silent pond.

'This is a really pretty place in summer,' Carol said. 'There's roses all over those trellises, and lilies on the pond, and the rockeries are lovely.' Her voice trailed away. 'It's going to be awful without you, Roddy.'

'I know.' He put his arm round her shoulders. 'I don't want to go to sea. I never did, but now I've met you . . . Och, I might never come back, Carrie. I might never see you again.'

'Roddy, don't.' Once again, the tears began to flow. 'I can't bear it.'

They clung together in the quiet garden. A woman came in with a small terrier. She let it off the lead and it rushed up to them and sniffed their ankles. The woman called it away and it gave a yelp, put its head on one side to give them a last, bright-eyed glance, and rushed off.

'I wanted to court you properly,' Roddy said at last. 'I wanted to ask you to marry me, and give you a ring and all that. And now there's nae time.'

Carol lifted her head and stared at him. 'You wanted us to get engaged?'

'I want to be with you all the time. I want you to be my wife.'

'But I'm not old enough! I'm not even sixteen till next month. And Mum would never let us get married.'

'We're never going to get the chance,' Roddy said. 'This war'll finish me, Carrie, I know it. I'm going to be killed, and never have a chance to live my life.' His eyes were desperate. 'I canna go away without loving you just once,' he said. 'I canna just leave you like this.'

'I can't bear you to go.' She felt the roughness of his serge tunic under her fingers, tried to imagine the moment when he walked away from her and she could no longer touch him, see him, hear his voice. The pain of loss filled her already and she gripped his arms convulsively and pulled him hard against her. 'I can't let you go – I can't.'

The short December afternoon was drawing in, the low mist bringing darkness early. The garden was growing dim. The woman with the terrier had gone and there was nothing to be heard but the soft drip of condensation from the leaves of a few evergreen shrubs.

Roddy pressed his face against Carol's cheek. She could feel the faint roughness of his chin against her smooth skin. She turned her face so that their lips met, and stroked her fingers on the back of his neck.

He pulled her coat open and touched her breast. He had done this before, and always Carol felt a surge of excitement at his touch, a need to be closer. She made a tiny, soft whimpering sound and moved her body so that she was half-lying on the bench.

'Oh, Carol,' he whispered in her ear. 'Carol, my sweet, lovely Carol . . . I love you. I love you.'

'I love you too, Roddy.' His lips were warm on hers, on her neck, on her small, growing breasts. Something was fluttering deep inside her, beating butterfly wings against her heart. Her head was spinning. She had forgotten everything except her need to be closer to him, to be somehow merged with him, to keep him with her always. She felt her body become soft and pliable, her bones melt, as his hands touched her and stroked her and caressed her into a daze of need. His fingers brushed her thighs, drawing up her skirt, and she could feel his own skin against hers, his flesh warm and cool, smooth and rough. Her body was liquid. It parted for him and closed around him, and she folded him deep within her and clasped him in a gentle, pulsating rhythm that quickened and soared, sweeping them at last with sudden devastating power to a momentary peak, and holding them there for a breathless instant of eternity before dashing them into the valley below.

They lay in each other's arms, bemused, only half aware of where they were or what had happened.

'Carol . . .' Roddy whispered at last. 'Oh, *Carol* . . .'

'Roddy.' She turned her head. His face was close to hers, his eyes half shut, his lips parted. She kissed them softly. 'Roddy, I love you so much.'

Only a day later, the news came through that the Japanese had attacked Pearl Harbour. America was at war.

Frank added a new section to the big map that now covered the living-room wall. Pearl Harbour was in the islands of Hawaii, deep in the South Pacific. He stared at the unfamiliar territory, fixing in his mind the shapes of China, Japan, Borneo and North Australia. They all looked frighteningly close to each other.

'But Japan's such a little country,' Jess said. 'How can they beat somewhere as big as America?'

'By taking them by surprise,' Frank said soberly. 'It says in the paper they sank nearly twenty warships, destroyed nearly two hundred aircraft and killed two and half thousand men. Just in a couple of hours! And all they lost was five midget submarines, one ordinary one and about thirty planes. They just about wiped out the Pacific Fleet in one go.'

'The aircraft carriers weren't there, though. They didn't get hit.'

'Just as well,' Frank said. 'I bet the Japs were disappointed. If they could have got them as well . . .'

'It's the whole world now, isn't it.' Jess stared at the map with its black and red pins stuck in all over it. 'It's spreading like some horrible disease. Europe, Russia, Africa, Japan, America, Australia – everyone's mixed up in it. I don't see how they can ever sort it all out, Frank.' She bent and picked up Maureen, who was clinging to her skirt and grizzling. 'Poor little mite. What sort of a world have we brought you into?'

A state of emergency had been declared in Singapore and the forces in Malaya stood at battle stations, with the warships *Prince of Wales* and *Repulse* already on their way to give aid. Britain had declared war on Japan, Finland, Hungary and Romania. China also declared war, on Japan, Germany and Italy. It was, as Jess said, like a disease spreading all over the world. And how could anyone keep up with it all? How could you know who was fighting who?

Moscow's torment was eased at last by the bitter winter, which struck at the German troops and forced them to retreat. The Russian army, equipped for the cruel weather that only they understood, drove them across the frozen plains. The Germans announced that they had 'no reason' to expose their troops to the rigours of the Russian winter; they would wait and take Moscow in the spring. But it seemed clear that this offensive had failed and would not be recovered.

Boys and girls of sixteen were now told they must register for service, and the boys encouraged to join the Home Guard. 'We must see that our *boys do not run loose,*' Winston Churchill said as the announcements were made.

'He must be thinking of brats like Micky Baxter,' Frank commented. 'But I wouldn't have thought they'd want his sort in the Home Guard.'

'He's too young, anyway,' Jess said, thankful that the same applied to her own boys. She was still anxious about Tim, who wasn't enjoying the repetition of his last year at junior school. But at least he'd be taking his exam soon. He'd probably feel better then.

Mr Churchill also warned of a *'very hard period'* ahead, but believed that the flow of aid and arms from America would *'vastly exceed anything that could have been expected on a peacetime basis'* and prophesied that together Britain, America and the Soviet Union would teach the *'gangs of wicked men'* a lesson they would not forget in a thousand years.

'He knows what he's doing,' Frank said. 'If anyone can steer us through this mess, he can. And with Roosevelt on our side as well . . . It'll all come out right, Jess, you'll see.'

But for thousands – millions – of people it would not come out all right. They would die, never knowing if their sacrifice was in vain.

The news grew worse. Both *Repulse* and the *Prince of Wales* were sunk by Japanese aircraft as they steamed towards Singapore – another thousand men lost, and each of them some mother's son. It was enough to break your heart.

And there must be thousands of broken hearts, in homes all over the country, as families grieved for these and for others, their lives wasted in a cause that was now irretrievably lost in the muddle of hatred and brutality that the world had become.

Every day the horror grew. Hong Kong, abandoned by the British, Canadian and Indian troops who had been stationed there, lay under siege. More vicious attacks by the Japanese destroyed half the American Far East Air Force, and half the British air strength in northern Malaya. Only a week before Christmas, the British Mediterranean Fleet was torn asunder, with the Malta convoy sailing into a minefield and the battleships *Queen Elizabeth* and *Valiant* destroyed along with several other ships in Alexandria. It began to look as if the Mediterranean would have to be abandoned.

'God knows what would happen then,' Frank said gloomily. 'It's vital, the Med is.'

Frank was gloomy most of the time these days, and Jess hardly dared ask if Tim and Keith could come home for Christmas. There hadn't been so many air-raids lately, but the warnings were still sounding regularly and you never knew when another blitz might start. Why, last year they'd had that terrible raid down in Conway Street on Christmas Eve itself. And the blitz had started not long after the boys had gone back. Who was to say what Hitler had up his sleeve for 1942?

But to her surprise, Frank declared that the boys could come for three days – Christmas Eve, Christmas Day and Boxing Day. Not only that, they'd have Stella and Muriel as well. He would ride his bike over and bring them on the train and take them back.

He hesitated. 'Matter of fact, there's something else I want to talk to you about, Jess.'

'Talk about?' Jess stared at him, feeling a sudden sinking in her heart. 'What's that? Is it about this Cherry?'

'Well, yes.' Frank looked uncomfortable. 'It's just – well, you know I've been talking about her quite a bit—'

'Quite a bit?' Jess said before she could stop herself. 'You haven't stopped these past few weeks.'

'Oh come on, Jess. It's not that bad. You get plenty of chance to put your five eggs in.'

Jess bit her lip. Frank had been touchier lately, answering her sharply and snapping at Rose and even the baby. She'd talked to her sister about it and Annie had given her opinion that everyone was on a short tether these days, what with being up half the night with air-raid warnings and firewatching, and never knowing what was going to happen next. But Jess hadn't been able to suppress an anxious feeling that in Frank's case there might be more to it than that.

Suppose there really was something in her fears about this Cherry. She would never have believed that a steady chap like Frank would ever let a slip of a girl turn his head, but everything was turning upside down these days and you just didn't know. Strain made people do some funny things, and when you got saucy little flirts dancing around a place like a boiler-shop with a lot of men –

'All right, then,' she said, more sharply than she meant to, 'what about this Cherry, then? What's she been up to now?'

'She hasn't been up to anything. I just thought – well, here she is in Pompey with none of her own family around, nothing much to do when she's not at work – I thought we might just ask her over for Christmas dinner or something, that's all.' He looked at Jess, an odd, half pleading expression on his face, and she was reminded suddenly of Tim. 'Only if you want to, mind, but I know she'd like to meet you.'

'She'd like to meet *me*?' Jess stared at him. It was the last thing she'd expected. Not that she knew really just what she did expect, but if anything *was* going on between this Cherry and Frank – not that she'd ever suspect Frank of such a thing, not in a million years, but all the same, men were men, couldn't help it, and some of these young girls these days, nothing but brazen hussies they were, you couldn't get away from it, and . . . She caught up her floundering thoughts and tried to get them into some sort of order. Would Frank be asking to bring this girl home if there was anything – well, not quite right?

'What d'you think?' he asked, a shade anxiously. 'It's for you to say, Jess.'

Suddenly, Jess knew that there was only one thing she could say. Like it or not, she'd have to meet this Cherry, if only so that she could picture her when Frank mentioned her name. And once I see her, I'll know, she thought. I'll know if there's anything to worry about.

She shrugged and spoke offhandedly. 'Tell you what. Ask her for dinner next Sunday, if you want, then if we get on all right we can think about

Christmas. Can't promise anything special, mind, we're on rations, visitors or no visitors.'

'That's all right.' He looked relieved. 'Cherry knows all about rations. I don't reckon she gets more than bread and scrape in her lodgings. Canteen dinner's the only cooked meal she gets. She'll appreciate whatever you provide.'

I just hope she does, Jess thought. And I hope she realises that I'm not going to provide anything apart from a meal. My Frank's not there for the taking.

Perhaps it was a good idea after all to bring her home, so that Jess could size her up and see just what it was about this girl that was fascinating her husband.

Cherry Buckley came to dinner with Frank and Jess the following Sunday. She was coming by bus from her lodgings in Portsea, and Frank walked up the street to meet her.

Jess fussed about the little terraced house, telling herself that it didn't matter two hoots what the girl thought of her home, yet at the same time anxiously determined that there wouldn't be a thing out of place, nor a speck of dirt to be seen. She washed Maureen's face three times in a quarter of an hour and told Rose to dust the ornaments on the mantelpiece half a dozen times before the girl rebelled.

'There isn't any more dust on them, there can't be. Why do we have to do all this anyway? We don't bother when it's Auntie Annie or Mrs Shaw popping in.'

'That's different,' Jess snapped, though she would not have known how to explain the difference if Rose had asked. She glanced at the clock. 'Your father's been gone nearly twenty minutes. Whatever can they be doing?' Her imagination showed her Frank doing something totally uncharacteristic – taking this Cherry into a pub, for instance, which he would never normally dream of. 'I'll walk up the street and see if I can meet them,' she said, removing her pinafore. 'You stay here with Maureen.'

Rose pulled a face, but Jess ignored her and marched out of the front door and over to the corner of October Street. The street was empty, with the quiet of a November Sunday drifting in the mist. There was no sign of Frank, nor of anyone who might be called Cherry.

Jess started to walk up the street. She didn't really want to be introduced to this girl in public, but neither did she want to stay in the house any longer. And she didn't want Rose's sharp eyes observing this first meeting. The girl was getting altogether too knowing just lately. Only the other day, when Jess had told her that a young neighbour had just had a baby, Rose had replied that she'd already known it was on the way, and when asked how had retorted 'Because she got fat, like *you* did.' Jess had been shocked, not least by the resentment in Rose's tone. Maybe we were wrong to keep it from her when Maureen was on the way, she thought. Maybe she would have enjoyed helping to get things ready, sharing it all.

She was halfway up to September Street when two figures came round the corner and approached her. Jess stopped and stared.

One was unmistakably Frank. She could even see the expression on his face – smiling, laughing a bit, walking easily and assured like a man who had nothing to hide, nothing at all to feel uneasy about. But the other . . .

Cherry Buckley – if that was who this was – was no saucy young woman, not long out of school, with flirting eyes and a pert, too obvious figure. Instead, she was almost middle-aged – at least in her late thirties, Jess thought – and short. No more than five feet, probably. And she was plump too – a little round body with a little round head stuck on top, for all the world like a cottage loaf. Her face was round and quite plain, with a distinct resemblance to Winston Churchill, and she had very short, thin hair with almost no colour to it.

This wasn't the sort of person to turn men's heads.

Jess forced herself to step forwards again. They had seen her at once and were approaching quickly. On Frank's face she saw a look of pride and he reached out a hand and laid it on her shoulder, drawing her close.

'This is Jess,' he said, and there was no mistaking the affection in his voice.

Cherry held out her hand. Her round face had split into a thousand beaming creases, her small blue eyes almost disappearing in their folds. Dazed, Jess took her hand and Cherry enveloped it in both of hers.

'Eh, I'm right glad to meet you,' she said in a broad Birmingham accent. 'It's ever so nice of you to ask me over. Frank's told me such a lot about you. Is it all right if I call you Jess? I feel like we're old friends already.'

'Yes – yes, of course it's all right,' Jess stammered. Why hadn't Frank told her Cherry had a strong Birmingham accent? Why hadn't he told her what Cherry *looked* like? 'I'm glad you could come,' she added warmly, feeling relief flood through her body. 'It must be awful being away from your family and having to live in lodgings.'

'Eh, that don't bother me,' Cherry said cheerfully as they started back down October Street. 'I'm used to it. I was a housekeeper when all this lot started, in a big house. Worked me way up from scullerymaid. Went into service when I was fourteen and never lived at home since. The place I've got now isn't much cop, but I've had worse.'

'So you've been in domestic service,' Jess said with interest. 'My sister Annie did that. She was a cook.'

'And a lot of fancy ideas it gave her too,' Frank said from Cherry's other side. 'Jug of water on the table. Rice with meat. Bits of this and bits of that. At least she's had to tone it down a bit since the war started.'

'Oh aye, they likes their bits and pieces, folk with a bit o' money,' Cherry agreed. 'Were you in service too, Jess?'

Her easy use of Jess's first name was slightly startling. Most people gave you your proper title until they knew you really well. But Cherry didn't seem to have any shyness or reserve, she just came straight out with whatever she wanted to say. Perhaps that was why Frank liked her.

'I was apprenticed to a dressmaker,' she said. 'Our mother wanted us to learn things that would always be useful to us. I make nearly all my own clothes, and the girls' too. I can't do so much for the boys now they're bigger, tailoring's not my line.'

'I don't mind a bit of sewing,' Cherry said. 'Or knitting. I knit all me own jumpers and things.'

They reached number 14 and Frank opened the door. Jess led the way in. She'd intended to keep Cherry in the front room, with its three-piece suite and little polished table that Frank had made, but it seemed more natural to take her on into the back, where the fire was burning brightly because it was a Sunday, and Maureen was playing with some coloured wooden bricks on the rag rug.

'Ooh, so you're the baby,' Cherry exclaimed, bending down at once. 'Eh, you're a little beauty an' all.'

Maureen looked up, startled. She was going through a shy phase and Jess wondered if she would burst into tears at this sudden intrusion. But instead, after staring for a moment or two, her face broke into a smile and she reached up a hand and patted Cherry's cheek. Jess noticed the warts on Cherry's skin, but they didn't seem to bother the baby.

'Well, you've scored a hit,' Jess said as Maureen scrambled to her feet and held up her arms. 'And this is Rose. Rose, say hello to Miss Buckley.'

'Eh no, call me Cherry,' the little woman said, beaming at Rose. 'Everyone does. If anyone says "Miss Buckley" I have to look round to see if someone's standing behind me.'

'Sit down,' Frank said, gesturing towards Jess's armchair. 'I daresay the dinner's nearly ready, isn't it, Jess?'

'It won't be long.' Jess watched as the visitor settled herself in the chair and lifted Maureen on to her lap. She had taken off her brown winter coat and was dressed in a grey jumper, obviously handknitted in a rather loose stitch so that it hung baggily on her round little body. Her skirt was a plain, muddy tweed and she wore thick lisle stockings and heavy shoes. Jess had a sudden vision of the Cherry she had expected to see, and felt her lips pull themselves into a smile.

'Well, you are a little duck, and no two ways about it,' Cherry said to Maureen. 'And is this your big sister, then? I bet you did everything for her when she was a little mite, didn't you, Rose?'

'Rose was like a little mother to her,' Jess said warmly. 'No one ever had a better little helper. Mind, she's not always so keen to look after her these days.'

Rose scowled. 'I do a lot to help.'

'Of course you do. She's a lovely little cook,' Jess told Cherry. 'Bake a cake, cook a roast dinner – that's if we ever had such a thing these days – our Rose can turn her hand to anything. She was just learning when the war started – did some lovely little fancy cakes, but now you're not allowed to do icing, she's had to stop. And she does a lot around the house.'

'That's right,' Cherry said. 'It's all good training. Me mum made sure we could all do a bit of cooking and sewing and cleaning before we left school. You can always find a job if you're handy in the house.'

Rose settled down on a stool beside her. 'I'm going to work in an office. I'm learning typing and shorthand.'

'Typing!' Cherry said. 'Eh, that's grand. So you're going to be a secretary, are you?'

'Yes,' Rose said. The idea of being a secretary had never actually occurred to her, but it certainly sounded more impressive than 'working in an office', which her cousin Olive had done in Harker's builder's yard. 'Or a Civil Servant,' she added, remembering what her father had said.

'My godfathers! A Civil Servant. That'll please your dad.'

Frank had gone out to join Jess in the kitchen. The square dining-table that stood in the middle of the room had been laid for four, with Maureen's high chair next to Jess's place. A smell of stew wafted through the door.

Cherry sniffed appreciatively and went on talking to Rose about what she was doing at school and when she would be leaving. She nodded sympathetically when Rose told her that all her friends had already left and got jobs. She was especially interested to hear about Joy Brunner.

'Your dad told me about her. Poor little soul, she's had a rough time. Still, her father's home now and she's working in the shop, she'll be all right.'

'Yes.' But Rose didn't sound too sure. There had been something odd about Joy just lately. She seemed uneasy, sometimes snappy, at others almost in tears as she begged Rose to assure her that they were still 'best friends'. It was as if they had quarrelled, yet Rose couldn't think of anything that had gone wrong between them. It was ever since the day of Hilsea Fair, she thought. The day when they'd met Carol Glaister and Carol had got tickets for the dance.

Rose had asked Joy once how she'd enjoyed the dance, but Joy had just shrugged and said it was 'all right'. But she hadn't gone to any more.

'Dinner's ready,' Jess said, coming back into the room with a large bowl of stew. 'It's not a proper Sunday dinner, we can't often get meat for a roast these days. But I thought on a day like this, a good beef stew with plenty of vegetables would warm us up.'

'Eh,' Cherry said, lifting Maureen into her high chair and settling down beside her, 'that looks right good. Better'n canteen dinners in the Yard, eh, Frank?'

'I should hope so,' he said, bringing in a bowl of mashed potatoes. 'You know I never eat 'em meself, Jess gives me a dinner to heat up. Now, you just have a good plateful, Cherry, it's all homegrown veg and there's some of our own fruit for after. Jess bottles it and we has it stewed all through the winter.'

'That's what I don't make into jam,' Jess said. 'Frank grows a lot of fruit over on the allotment. We wouldn't live half so well if he didn't keep us provided.'

Cherry pointed her fork at Frank. 'I want to see this allotment of yours after. We'll walk over soon as I've helped Jess with the pots.'

Rose gaped at her. She had never heard anyone – not even her mother – talk to Frank like that, as if they were giving him orders. Half afraid of his reaction, she swivelled her eyes round to her father. But he was just helping himself to mashed potatoes and grinning a bit, as if he rather liked being ordered about by Cherry.

During dinner they discussed Jess's methods of bottling fruit and making jam, an argument one of Frank's workmates had had with the foreman and the new tunnel shelters which were being built under Portsdown Hill. They were almost complete and were expected to open after Christmas.

'I don't know that I fancy them much,' Jess said. 'I've never much liked being in caves. I went to Cheddar once and the stalactites were lovely, but I kept thinking about all that rock up on top of us. I mean, what's there to stop it falling in? I knew a little boy once, got buried in a sandpit, he was choked to death before they got him out.'

'Those caves have been there for millions of years,' Frank said. 'They've never fallen in all that time, why should they now?'

'Why shouldn't they?' Cherry asked. 'The world don't stand still. It's all moving a little bit, all the time – you just want one little stone to move and the whole lot'll come tumbling down. Like those bricks your Maureen was playing with just now.'

'Well, anyway, these tunnel shelters aren't the same – they're properly built. There's nothing to worry about there.'

'People are going to have tickets for the shelters,' Rose said. 'There's even going to be bunks with your name on them. It'll be your own special place. And there'll be canteens and First Aid and all sorts down there.'

'I don't know,' Jess said dubiously. 'It sounds all right, but it all depends on the other people, doesn't it? I mean, you can't choose who's going to be in the next bunk. It might be anyone. I think I'd rather stay in our own shelter.'

Frank pushed his pudding bowl over for another helping of stewed gooseberries. Jess might say that she couldn't present such a good table with all this rationing, but today's dinner had been as good as any peacetime meal. Not as much beef as he'd like in the stew, it was true, but plenty of other good things, with the added satisfaction that he'd grown most of it himself.

Later, he and Jess and Cherry walked over to the allotment. Rose had gone up to September Street to spend an hour with Joy and they were able to talk more freely. Jess took the opportunity to mention her worries about their daughter.

'It's nothing you can really put your finger on. She just seems different, somehow. I mean, she's never been one to sulk or answer back, but just lately she's been quite sharp when I've told her to do something. And she seems to be turning against Maureen for no reason at all.'

Maureen was toddling along the narrow paths leading between the allotments. She was wearing a pair of gaiters Jess had made from an old pair of corduroy trousers of Frank's, and she kept stopping to peer down at her legs with a funny little smile of pride crinkling her lips.

'She's growing up too fast,' Frank said. 'They all are these days. Why, I saw that Carol Glaister from next door walking down the street with a sailor the other day, bold as brass, her face all made up and arms round each other's waists. I don't want our Rose getting those ideas.'

'I don't think any of them knows *how* to grow up,' Cherry said. 'I mean, a few years ago it was all plain and easy. Young girls waited till they were sixteen or seventeen before they even thought about walking out with a boy, and then they'd bring him home first for Dad to look over. Now they're getting called up and going away to work on the land or in munitions and all, and they just run riot. We've got a few in the Yard, haven't we, Frank? Saucy little bits of nonsense, wants their bottoms smacked for them.'

And that's the sort of girl I imagined Frank bringing home today, Jess thought. She looked at Cherry's cottage-loaf body, stumping along the path holding Maureen's hand, and wanted to laugh again. But not at Cherry. Her laughter was directed at herself.

Late that night, when Cherry had gone back to her lodgings and she and Frank were in bed, Jess lay in her husband's arms and smiled at him. She knew that her smiles and kisses were different now, just as their lovemaking had been different – lighter, more joyous, more as it used to be. And she knew that this was because a weight had been lifted from her heart that she hadn't even realised was there.

'What are you laughing at?' Frank asked lazily. He too felt more relaxed, his recent tension eased. He did not know why; he only knew that when Jess was happy, he was happy, and when she was miserable, he was worried. 'Tell me the joke.'

'It's not a joke. I was just wondering – why did you make friends with Cherry?'

'Don't you like her?' he asked in surprise. 'I thought the two of you got on really well.'

'Oh, we did. I like her very much. And I'll be glad to have her here for Christmas. But what do *you* like about her, Frank? What made you like her in the first place?'

He considered. 'I dunno, really. I don't think it was so much a matter of *liking* her exactly, not first off. I suppose I felt sorry for her, mostly. I mean, she's no oil-painting, is she, with that funny little face and all those warts and everything. It can't have given her much of a chance in life. But it don't seem to bother her. She's always cheerful, always got something to say, and yet she don't let anyone trample over her. I reckon I just liked her spirit, once I got to know her.'

You felt sorry for her, Jess thought. And she remembered her uneasy suspicions, and felt ashamed.

'Give me another hug,' she said, tightening her arms around him, 'and then we'd better go to sleep.'

On Christmas Day, Hong Kong surrendered to the Japanese. A week later, on January 1st, 1942, the four great powers – Great Britain, the United States, the Soviet Union and China – and 22 other countries signed a solemn agreement, as the 'United Nations', to fight to the utmost against the Axis. They accounted for four-fifths of the world's population.

'That gives us a bit of hope,' Frank said. 'We won't get countries agreeing to peace in dribs and drabs. It's one for all and all for one now.'

But the enemy were still attacking on all fronts, and Japan had embraced war with total dedication. Now they had taken the Malayan capital, Kuala Lumpur, and Singapore itself was under grave threat. They spread across the Pacific like a tidal wave.

Roddy's ship, HMS *Cadover*, had sailed only to be damaged in the North Atlantic by a mine. She wasn't badly damaged and managed to limp back to Portsmouth, where she went into dock again for repairs.

'It was the worst thing I've ever seen,' Roddy told Carol. 'I thought we were a goner. Tore a great hole in the bulkhead and the water just came gushing in. They managed to seal it off but we had a turrible list on all the way back.'

'You could have died,' Carol said, hugging him tightly. 'Oh, Roddy, I don't want you to go away again.'

They were sitting in the front room of number 15. Ethel was out but might come back at any minute and they dared not take the chance to love each other as fully as they longed to do. Roddy slipped his hand inside Carol's blouse and she closed her eyes, ecstatic and yearning.

'I wish we could be married,' she murmured. 'At least we could be together when you came back. We'd have a right.'

'Are you sure you mother wouldnae let you?' Carol had had her sixteenth birthday now and Roddy had given her a tiny pearl pin which she considered her engagement 'ring'.

'Not in a million years. There's no point even asking.'

'If we were in Scotland,' Roddy said, 'we wouldnae have to ask. People can get married there at sixteen without anyone's permission at all.'

'Can they? Really?'

'Aye. There's no harm ever came of it that I've been able to see.'

'If we were in Scotland . . .' Carol repeated dreamily. 'Oh Roddy, just think. If we lived near enough, we could just slip over the Border . . . Isn't there somewhere special you have to go? Gretna Green – I've heard of that.'

'You don't *have* to go there. It's just that it's the nearest place to the Border. There's a tradition that people can get married in the blacksmith's forge.'

'The blacksmith's forge!' Carol giggled. 'What a place to get married. You wouldn't want to wear a white frock, would you.' She thought for a moment. 'All the same, I wish we lived a bit nearer. We could go there and no one could stop us – and once we were married, we could do what we liked.'

'I'd still have to go away,' he pointed out. 'That's the worst of it, Carrie.'

'I know.' She was silent again, then she suddenly drew in a breath and turned to him, her eyes bright. 'Roddy, why don't we do it? Why don't we go to Gretna Green and get married? And then we could just go and live somewhere together, where nobody'd ever find us. You don't have to go back to your ship. You don't have to fight. We could just be together – somewhere nobody will dream of looking. Scotland—'

'That's the first place they'd look. That's where I live.'

'Wales, then. Or London. There are millions of people in London, it'd be like looking for a needle in a haystack. Or *anywhere*.' She gripped his sleeve and gazed at him. 'Let's do it, Roddy. Let's just go away.'

He stared at her, biting his lip, his brows drawn together. His chin had a soft fuzz on it; he had been shaving ever since he joined the Navy, though as yet there was no real need. He'd told Carol he wanted to grow a beard but you had to ask permission and if the growth of hair wasn't very strong they wouldn't let you.

'That's deserting,' he said at last. 'I could get shot.'

'Only if they find you. They'll never find you, Roddy, not if we're careful. We'll change our names. I'll dye my hair. We can get jobs—'

'How? You have to be registered. And what about our ration books?'

'We'll manage somehow.' Carol swept his doubts aside. 'People lose their ration books all the time. We'll say we've been bombed out, got nowhere to go. They'll never check up, they don't have time. We'd be *together*, Roddy.'

'That's all I want,' he said. 'Us to be together, and out of all this fighting.'

'What right do they have to tell us what to do with our lives?' Carol demanded. 'What right do they have to send you away to be killed?'

The sound of Ethel's key in the front door made them spring apart. When she came into the room, wrapped in the astrakhan coat she'd bought in Bulpitt's last winter, they were sitting decorously on the settee, their faces still a little flushed.

Ethel gave them a sharp glance. 'I hope you two haven't been up to anything you shouldn't be.'

Roddy stood up, his flush deepening, but Carol answered pertly, 'We haven't if you haven't.'

'And that's enough of your sauce, miss.' Ethel reddened with anger. She looked at Roddy. 'Time you were out of here, young man. I won't have the neighbours talking about my daughter the way they do about young Diane Shaw.'

'Why, what's Diane been doing?' Carol asked with interest. 'I haven't heard nothing.'

'Never you mind what she's been doing, but when a girl goes out night after night and comes back in the dark with a different bloke every time, it doesn't take many guesses to get it right. She's always been a flighty piece, that Diane, and I'm not having you causing gossip, all right?'

'Let us get married then,' Carol said daringly. 'Doesn't matter what we do then, does it?'

Ethel swung her hand at Carol's cheek, but the girl stepped back quickly and she missed. Roddy stepped forward in dismay.

'Och, there's no need to go hitting her, Mrs Glaister—'

'You mind your own business,' she snapped. 'Carol's my daughter and under my control since her father's gone gallivanting off playing soldiers. I'll discipline her as I see fit. I told you to get out.'

'I was just going to make a cup of cocoa,' Carol said, her voice trembling slightly. 'He can stop for that, can't he?'

'I said *out*,' Ethel repeated, and held back the blackout curtain that hung at the front door.

Roddy gave Carol an agonised glance but she shrugged and turned down the corners of her mouth. 'It's all right,' she said, 'you get back now. I'll see you tomorrow, like we said.'

'We'll see about that,' Ethel began, but Carol met her eyes coolly.

'You can't stop me going to work, Mum. And if I want to see Roddy, I will. He hasn't done anything wrong.' She stepped past her mother and gave Roddy a quick kiss on the lips. ''Night, sweetheart. I'll see you tomorrow and we'll talk about – *you know what*.' And she gave him a quick flicker of a wink and pushed him gently out of the front door.

'And what was all that supposed to mean?' her mother demanded as soon as the door closed. 'What have you two been cooking up between you?'

'Nothing much,' Carol said airily, keeping out of range of Ethel's arm. 'We're just trying to decide which film to go and see, that's all. Roddy wants to see *In Which We Serve* but I'd rather see Leslie Howard again, in *First of the Few*. Which d'you think would be best?'

'I think it'd be best if you stopped going about with sailors,' Ethel said acidly. 'You've been a different girl since you met that young man. I've told you already, I don't like him. There's a look in his eye . . . If he hasn't taken advantage of you already, he'll try soon.' She eyed her daughter. '*Has* he done anything he shouldn't?'

'No, he hasn't,' Carol said emphatically. 'And nor have I. We haven't done anything at all we shouldn't.'

And that was absolutely true, she thought as she climbed the stairs to go to bed. There hadn't been anything happen between her and Roddy that wasn't completely right and natural and good. All they had ever done was love each other.

She undressed and got into the cold bed, longing to feel Roddy's warm body beside her. She lay in the darkness, waiting as everyone always did for the wail of the siren, and thought of him going away, perhaps never to return.

We can't let it happen, she thought. We can't.

11

The tunnel shelters were open now and Granny Kinch went along to have a look, with Nancy and Micky.

There was room for five thousand people in the deep caverns in the chalk. Clutching their tickets, the three entered through the big iron gates and walked down the passages as if they were in church. The walls were lined with corrugated iron, with concrete floors, and in the long dormitories were bunks in tiers of three, stretching away into the hill.

'It ain't a bit like being in a cave,' Micky said, disappointed. 'I thought it'd be all big and dark, with stallywhatsernames hanging down and bats with big wings.'

'Don't be daft,' Nancy said. 'These ain't real caves. They're tunnels what've bin dug down here. Stands to reason they'd make a proper job of it.'

'There's a canteen,' Granny Kinch said, looking at the piece of paper they'd been given. 'And a place for people to have a fag – you're not allowed to smoke in the bunks – and a place for entertainment. I wonder what sort of entertainment there'll be?'

'Tommy Handley,' Micky said gleefully. 'And Arthur Askey, and Enoch and Ramsbottom. It's going to be smashing.'

'They won't have none of them,' Nancy said. 'They'll have Vera Lynn and Anne Shelton. It's singsongs you want in a shelter.'

Micky made a face. Vera Lynn and Anne Shelton sang soppy girls' songs like *White Cliffs of Dover* and *As Time Goes By*. He thought jokes were better any day.

'There's a hospital too,' Granny Kinch said. 'A First Aid room, a sick bay, why there's even an isolation hospital for infectious diseases. You could *live* down here.'

'You could die here too.' Nancy shivered. 'I don't like it. It's not natural, being underground. I mean, suppose they bombed the place where you come in. We'd all be buried alive down here. We'd suffocate, like those poor sods in submarines.'

'Well, I reckon it's smashing,' Micky declared. He looked around the corridors and the long dormitory, his eyes gleaming, and wondered if the tunnels led into the other mysterious places under the Hill, the forts and ammunition dumps that everyone knew must be there.

He thought of all the people here, asleep, their belongings on the floor, the lights dim. And there'd be other boys too, boys he could recruit into his secret army.

He started to go to the tunnel shelters every night. At first, his mother and grandmother came with him, but Nancy soon drifted back to her usual haunts and Granny Kinch began to complain about the conditions down under the Hill. 'I'd rather be in me own place,' she said. 'Have a fag when I feel like it, and nobody around kicking up a din or telling you what to do. It's like being in the army down here. And they've never got Tommy Handley, nor Vera Lynn.'

Micky continued to go alone. He preferred it that way. There was no one to keep an eye on him, no one to question where he went as he roamed the crowded tunnels. People were supposed to stay in their own places, in the bunks that had their name and number on, but for the first few hours at least they were more inclined to go wandering, visiting friends and relatives in different sections, or going to the smoking area or the entertainment room. They brought their knitting and flasks of tea or cocoa and sat nattering, wondering what was going on outside. As often as not, there was no raid, but you could never be sure. Down here, all you'd hear would be the occasional rumble of a really big bomb. The sound of planes going over and the rattle of ack-ack fire was deadened.

And people were careless. They brought in great, sagging bags containing their knitting, magazines, books, newspapers, and strewed them about on the floor. Nagged by the wardens to keep the place tidy, they said there was nowhere else to keep their stuff. They piled it on their narrow bunks and it fell off when they turned over in their sleep. It got pushed and kicked underneath, and all mixed up together.

It was easy for a boy, wandering casually along the aisles as if looking for his own place, or for a mate, to help himself to a few oddments here and there.

So far, Micky hadn't had much luck with his army. He'd managed to gather a few more together, but the trouble was, round Copnor most of the kids at home were quite a bit smaller, like Martin Baker or Alan and Wendy Atkinson – not that he wanted girls in, anyway. There weren't many of about Micky's size. Younger ones were just kids, and bigger boys would want to be in charge.

Desmond, however, had no qualms about recruiting younger children. He felt more at ease with them, as if they were nearer his age than Micky. He had roped in Martin and Alan at once, though even he had had doubts about Wendy.

'You've got to let girls in,' Wendy said. 'Girls are going to be in everything. They're going to be policemen and firemen and soldiers and—'

'Go on,' Martin said derisively. 'How can a girl be a police*man*?'

'Well, they are. My Mum read it out of the paper. Anyway, you can't have Alan without me, he's not allowed out by himself.'

Given a choice between two recruits and no recruit at all, Desmond didn't have much option. He shrugged and hoped Micky wouldn't throw Wendy out straight away. She could climb trees and fight, after all. She was almost as tough as a boy.

'There's Susan Cullen, too,' Wendy said. 'She'll be in it.'

Desmond began to feel dimly alarmed. One girl was bad enough, but two . . . ! However, Martin knew Susan Cullen. He had met her when he was running away from Bridge End, and she'd come with him. They'd been found wandering hand in hand on the Southampton road, lost, hungry and exhausted, and Martin had been taken straight to hospital to have his appendix out. They'd been friends ever since. Desmond knew that he wouldn't be in the army if she was turned out.

Micky was disgusted when he discovered that Desmond had allowed little kids like Alan Atkinson in, and even more when he found out about Wendy and Susan.

'I'm not having girls. Girls can't keep secrets.'

'I can't tell them they're not in now. I've said.'

'Well, say I won't have them. Otherwise you'll have to have an army of your own. A *girls'* army,' Micky sneered.

Wendy, however, was quite amenable to this idea. 'Girls are as good as boys any day. We'll be the Junior ATS. We'll have our own den and if you come round we'll fight you.' She eyed Micky, who was several sizes bigger, and poked out her tongue.

'Garn,' he said, turning his back. 'You'd never be able to get me down.'

For answer, Wendy shot out her foot and placed it between Micky's ankles, tripping him neatly. He lay on the ground, winded, and glared up at her.

'You're asking for it, Wendy Atkinson.'

'Pity you ain't got it,' she retorted, and skipped out of his reach. 'Come on, Alan – Susan. *We'll* show him who's the best army round here.'

'Alan can't be in your army,' Micky called, desperate for the last word. 'Not if it's a girls' army. He's a boy.'

Wendy turned and stuck out her tongue again. 'Think I don't know that? He's my brother, isn't he? He'll be our mascot. Every army has to have a mascot. You can't be a proper army without a mascot, so there, Micky Baxter.'

Micky scowled. The idea of a mascot had never occurred to him. He swore and gave Martin a push to relieve his feelings.

'All right,' he said reluctantly, 'but no more girls, see? This is going to be a fighting army, with real guns and grenades and things, and girls aren't allowed to use them, even in the real army.'

'Where are you going to get guns from?' Wendy asked interestedly, but Micky shook his head.

'That's secret. Only us officers knows that.'

So far, no weapons had been collected. But Micky, walking home from the tunnel shelter, was already turning over a few ideas in his mind. He had a new henchman now, too – Jimmy Cross who had lost his leg but now stumped cheerfully about on a wooden one. Jimmy was scornful of some of the members of the army, especially Desmond.

'I dunno why you want him in,' he said. 'He's barmy.'

'Yeah, but he knows a lot about aeroplanes, and guns and stuff like that,' Micky said. 'He's in the ATC and he goes up the airfield every week, trainin' and learnin' to shoot. You ask him anything about aeroplanes and see.'

Jimmy was sceptical, but the next time the boys met, in the den that Micky had established in the ruins of a bombed house, he listened open-mouthed as Desmond recited a list of the names of Allied aircraft, from the old Sopwith Camels and Tiger Moths that had been famous in the 1914–18 war and were still occasionally used as spotter planes, to the newest Hawker Hurricanes and Typhoons. He knew their weights, their airspeeds, the details of their engine power and their markings. He even knew the different kinds of sound they made.

'I never knew he knew all that,' Jimmy muttered. 'I always thought he was batty.'

'He is,' Micky said. 'He just knows a lot about some things. He don't know nothin' about others. He can't *think*. It's just like people knowin' a lot of poetry, it don't really mean nothin' to him.'

Desmond seemed to think it meant a lot, however. The sight of a home-made model aeroplane with some of the details missing upset him, although he could not explain what was wrong. Jimmy, who had spent a lot of his time in hospital and at home chipping away at bits of wood to make models, slipped the one he had brought back into his pocket. He didn't want to risk one of Desmond's sudden tempers.

As a member of the Air Training Corps, Desmond went to the local airfield on Sunday mornings for drill and rifle practice. He wore a uniform that was modelled on the RAF and although he still looked gangling and awkward in it, he seemed to stand up straighter, as if he was proud of himself. He towered above the other boys.

'It's not fair,' Micky said enviously. 'I ought to be in the ATC. I'd be as good as Des. Better.'

'You're not old enough,' Wendy said unnecessarily. She never missed an opportunity to take a dig at Micky. 'They don't let little boys play with guns.' She dodged expertly out of the way of Micky's foot.

Micky glowered, but said nothing. Wendy was smaller than he was, and a girl, but she could still hold her own in a scrap. And he was surprised to find that he was beginning to develop a grudging sort of liking for her. She didn't kowtow to him like the others did. It made her more interesting. Sometimes he thought it was a pity she couldn't be his Lieutenant instead of Desmond.

But he had other things to think about just now. Watching Desmond shamble away along the street on his way to Sunday morning drill, his mind drifted ahead to the airfield.

Just because of his uniform, Desmond was allowed through the strictly guarded gates. He could wander about amongst the aircraft, see into the hangars. He could use a rifle, handle ammunition.

He knew where everything was and, because of the peculiarity of his mind, he would never forget a single detail of what he had seen. If anyone could help Micky to get weapons for the secret army, Desmond could.

In the middle of January, it began to snow. It covered the ground thickly but soon melted away in the city once daylight came. Out in the country, however, it whipped itself into a blizzard and lay twelve inches deep, with drifts of three or four feet.

Farm work was almost impossible. There was little that could be done other than feed and milk the cows and see to the other animals. Yvonne spent a couple of hours sawing logs for the fires, and Betty and Erica helped Jonas patch up a few weak places in the barn.

Gerald Spencer came out to watch them, his arm in a sling. As well as his injuries, Gerald had been suffering from dysentery and was finding it difficult to regain his strength, so he'd been sent home to rest for a few weeks. After the initial strangeness, he'd slipped easily back into the old life at home and treated the three Land Girls with a teasing familiarity, as if they were his sisters. Though Betty couldn't help noticing, as they all sat round the big kitchen table of an evening playing cards or talking, that he looked at Erica rather a lot. But that was natural enough, seeing how pretty Erica was.

'You don't think he's getting sweet on her, do you?' she asked Yvonne one night as they got ready for bed. Erica was still downstairs, drying her hair in front of the fire. 'It wouldn't be surprising. I mean, he's been away a long time and he doesn't seem to have any girlfriend round here.'

'I dunno, I reckon that Maisie from the pub's got her eye on him.' Yvonne pulled off her vest and wrapped herself swiftly in flannel pyjamas. 'She's been up here three times this week on one excuse or another. Anyway, Erica's not interested in another bloke. She's still got Geoff's picture beside her bed.'

Betty glanced across the attic to the third bed. The face of the young airman laughed out at her from the little wooden frame on the box that served as a bedside table. She bit her lip, feeling the sadness that washed over her every time she thought of the three young men – scarcely more than boys – who had spent all their spare time at the farm almost two years ago. Shot out of the sky, one after another, to plunge to their deaths in flames above the cruel sea. She remembered Sandy's remark – '*It's pretty lonely up there in the sky . . .*' And the day he and Duff had come to tell Erica that Geoff had been killed, with doom in their own haggard young faces.

It almost put you off falling in love, knowing the pain of that sort of loss. It wasn't surprising that girls like Erica refused to take the chance again.

It was bitterly cold in the barn. Gerald sat on a bale of straw, looking as if the walk from the farmhouse door had been almost too much for him.

'You ought to be still in bed,' Betty said. 'You look as white as a sheet.'

'I'm all right. I'm fed up with being in bed. Besides, I'll never get my strength back if I don't exercise.'

'You'll get pneumonia, sitting out here,' Erica said. 'It's freezing. Go back in, Gerald, for heaven's sake.'

'Leave the lad alone,' Jonas growled. 'Fussing over him like a pair of old hens. He's a soldier, he knows how to look after hisself.'

'Matter of fact,' Gerald said, 'I don't think I could walk back at the moment. I feel a bit sort of . . .' His voice trailed off and he slipped sideways on the bale. Erica and Betty rushed to catch him and propped him between them. Erica pressed his head gently down between his knees.

'You shouldn't have come out here,' she scolded. 'It's bitterly cold. You've been in a hot country for months and months, you've been ill and wounded . . .' Her voice shook suddenly and Betty glanced at her in surprise.

Erica was staring down at the bent head, the thin, bony shoulders, as if she had been struck. Her fingers rested on the curling dark hair at the nape of the neck. She moved them very slightly, almost tenderly, and then she withdrew them. Her eyes were filled with sudden tears.

She's thinking of Geoff, Betty thought, and wished the other girl could get over her loss. 'We'd better get him back indoors,' she said. 'Give us a hand, Jonas. You can see he's not fit to be out here.'

Between them, they got Gerald to his feet. He gave them a shaky grin and draped his arm across Betty's shoulders. He glanced round for Erica, but she had moved hastily aside and Jonas took her place.

'Bloody fool,' the old man muttered. 'Shouldn't never have gone for a soldier in the first place. Shoulda stayed on the farm, and then we wouldn't have to have bloody women messing about scared to get their hands dirty. And you wouldn't be in this state.'

Gerald shook his head and tried to speak, but he was clearly exhausted. He gave Betty a glance of apology and she laughed.

'It's all right. We don't take any notice of this old windbag. He knows we can run rings round him any day. Now, you just let us get you back indoors and *stay* there this time, in the warm, see?'

The three of them moved slowly out of the barn and across the snow-covered yard. Erica came to the door to watch them go. She stood just inside, her face shadowed, out of sight of anyone watching.

She looked down at her fingers and tried to understand the sudden tingling they had felt as she stroked the back of Gerald Spencer's neck.

The snow was even deeper out at Bridge End, where Tim was to sit the scholarship examination at last. All around the village, children looked hopefully out of the windows, hoping that the examination would be postponed, but they stumped through the snow to school to find everything laid out ready.

'Sit here, Tim,' Mr Hodges said. 'You've got everything you need – pencil, ruler, a bit of rubber, plenty of paper. If you need to use the pencil-sharpener you'll have to ask, but apart from that you mustn't speak at all. Do you understand?'

Tim nodded a little sulkily. He still hadn't got over his misery at having been left out of the examination a year ago, and he'd spent the intervening months bored and angry. He didn't see why he had to sit in a class with children younger than himself, learning the same things all over again, and he blamed Mr Hodges and the other teachers for missing him out.

'You ought to have said,' Mr Wain, the headmaster, told him, but he knew that the responsibility wasn't really Tim's. But schooling was so difficult these days, with the little village school being shared turn and turn about by the village children, it was a wonder they hadn't got into an even bigger muddle.

A weight of 56 tons is carried 200 miles for £12; how far should 70 tons be carried for the same amount?

Divide £837.19s.4 $\frac{1}{4}$ d by 56.

Divide .04006 by 3.75. Multiply together the same two numbers.

Find the amount of £1520 for 3 $\frac{1}{2}$ years at 4 $\frac{3}{4}$ per cent per annum simple interest.

A bankrupt owes £515.12s.6d to one man, £407 to another, and £293.6s.8d to another; his estate is worth £911.19s.4 $\frac{1}{2}$ d. How much can he pay in the £?

A man leaves £5000 to his wife, and the remainder to be divided equally among his four children. It is found that each of his children has one-seventh of the whole. How much did he leave altogether?

There were sixteen arithmetic questions altogether, although only four of the six most difficult ones had to be answered. Tim did the easy ones and then struggled with the 'problems'. He had never been quite sure what a 'bankrupt' was and had difficulty in understanding how anyone could have the vast sum of £5000 to leave his family. Some of the other questions – about grocers buying huge quantities of sugar or water running into and out of a bath – were equally beyond his comprehension. It wasn't that he couldn't do the arithmetic, it was just that the questions didn't seem to have any relevance to life as he knew it. Water didn't run in and out of baths. You dragged in the tin bath from the yard on Saturday nights and filled it from the tap at the sink, helped out with kettles. Even at the vicarage, they did that. And nobody had thousands of pounds. It would take you a whole lifetime to save up that much.

In the afternoon they had English. A stern warning at the top of the paper said that writing would be taken into account throughout. That meant you had to write slowly and carefully, however little time you had.

Tim started with composition. This was his favourite subject and he had soon covered the requisite page and half with an anecdote about an animal. He chose the big tabby cat, Henry, who was still at number 14 with Mum and Dad and Tim's sisters, and wrote about the time when he was a kitten and had fallen into the lavatory. After that, they'd had to make sure to keep the door closed until he was old enough to know better.

Analysis wasn't nearly so much fun. Tim stared at the rhyme '*In the castle, weak and dying, Was the Norman baron lying.*' Which were the subject and object, and what was the predicate, and what did it matter anyway? He left a space and went on to the next question, which was to parse the words underlined in the rhyme. He left that, too.

The last two questions consisted of several pieces of poetry with long words, to be rewritten so that they meant the same but were easier to understand, and an exchange of conversation between two sailors which had to be punctuated. Tim did the last one but he couldn't make head or tail of the poetry. He always went to sleep or daydreamed during poetry lessons. He chewed his pencil and stared at it, then went back to the analysis, but that made him feel sick. He looked out of the window and wished the exam was over so that he could go and play in the snow.

I bet last year's exam was easier than this, he thought. I could've passed last year, easy as winking. Reg would've helped me with the problems when we got them for homework, and then I'd have known about bankrupts and baths and things. And I bet they used easier poetry then, too. They must have, or Brian Collins wouldn't have passed.

He sat staring at the paper, filled with misery and anger at his wasted year, and when the teacher announced that time was up, he had completed only half the questions. He handed it in, avoiding Mr Hodges' eye, and ran out into the snow, holding his arms straight out sideways and pretending to be a Spitfire.

The next day they had Geography, History and General Knowledge. By now, Tim was almost past caring. He scribbled a page or two about the St Lawrence River and Great Lakes, named several of the chief coalfields in Great Britain, and described a voyage from Southampton to Melbourne. The question about the chief vegetable products of the Punjab, the Sunderbunds and the Deccan completely floored him, as did the chief mountain ranges of South Africa, the difference between the ports of Vancouver and Quebec and a deceptively innocent question about the importance of six of the world's major cities or canals.

History was as bad. Tim knew quite a lot about Julius Caesar but nothing about the Danes. Asked to write a life of Simon de Montfort, he had only the haziest idea of who the man was. He enjoyed telling the story of the Spanish Armada but was stumped by the South Sea Bubble. The Indian Mutiny was exciting but took too long, so that he didn't have time to decide which question to choose last. Dithering between the Crusades and the Wars of the Roses, he had only just written the number of the question when time was called, and then found that he hadn't answered the one question which everyone was supposed to have tried, about Acts of Parliament.

I knew all those things last year, he thought resentfully, handing in the mass of scribblings and crossings-out – he had forgotten all about careful handwriting by this time. I know I'm not going to pass, and it isn't my fault. It's theirs, for forgetting about me.

He plodded slowly home to the vicarage, ignoring the other boys' calls to join a snowball fight, and when he got back Mrs Mudge looked at his face and sat him by the fire with a big mug of cocoa and a slice of cake, which they normally only had on Sundays.

'It's not the end of the world if you don't pass, Tim,' she said. 'There's other things as important as being clever.'

'I *am* clever,' he stated. 'I know I am. I *ought* to be going on to the Grammar School. And I won't be, and it's *not fair*.'

Mrs Mudge sighed. She knew that there was some justice in what he said, but what could you do? You couldn't wind back the clock or make things all right with the wave of a wand.

'Well, you just drink your cocoa and then go out and build a snowman,' she said. 'Or go and talk to Mr Beckett. He's over in the church, looking at the bells.'

Tim liked the bells. They weren't allowed to be rung now, because that was the signal for invasion, but he knew that Mr Beckett and the head bellringer kept them in good condition for the time when they could be rung again, and he was hoping that when that time came he'd be allowed to pull one of the ropes. He finished his cocoa and cake, and pulled on his wellington boots again.

The bells were reached by a spiral staircase, leading up from the ground floor of the tower where the ropes hung with their coloured 'sallies' looped together. There were six of them, hanging in the dim bell-chamber, each in its own frame with a big wheel to make it turn. The ropes came up through the floor and wound round the rim of the wheel. Mr Beckett had told Tim that if the ringer pulled too hard and broke the wooden 'stay' that prevented the bell from turning right over, the whole length of rope would shoot up and wind itself round the wheel, and the ringer would have to let go quickly or be dragged up with it.

The bellringing captain was in the tower with Mr Beckett. They were greasing the bearings and talking about ringing. Words like 'Grandsire', 'Stedman' and 'Treble Bob' floated around the chamber and Tim, his head poking up through the trapdoor from the ladder that led from the top of the spiral staircase, got the impression that the bells were listening and yearning to make their music again.

'The war's spoiling everything,' he said to Mr Beckett when the head bellringer had gone and the two of them were sitting on the top of the frame, gazing down at the big metal bodies. 'I'm fed up with it. Nobody can do what they want to any more.'

'I know. But that's life, Tim. We can't always do what we want to do.' The vicar looked down at the boy's bent head. The fair curls were turning darker. He was still small for his age, but had filled out quite a lot since coming to the country, and his arms and legs were sturdy. How that poor mother must miss her sons, he thought sadly. How all the mothers must be missing their children.

'Shall I tell you a secret?' he asked, and Tim looked up, momentarily bright-eyed, then drooped his head again and shrugged. 'It's the secret of being able to do what you want to do.'

'How?' Tim asked suspiciously. 'I don't see how you can, unless it's magic, and I don't believe in magic any more.'

'There's nothing magic about it. It's just a matter of seeing what you *can* do, and finding something you want in that. And forgetting about the things you know are impossible.'

'But *they're* the things I want,' Tim said, feeling let down. 'I don't think much of that for a secret.'

'It doesn't sound much to start with,' the vicar agreed. 'But if you think about it, you'll see what I mean. For instance, we can't ring the bells now so I can't teach you how to pull the rope and hear the sound. But I could tie up one of the clappers so that it didn't make any sound, and you could learn that way. And you could learn to ring the methods, like Grandsire and Plain Bob, on handbells. Then, when peace comes, you'll be ready to join the team.'

Tim turned his head and stared at him. 'Could I? Could I really learn to ring?'

'If you want to. That's what Mr Enfield and I were talking about just now. That's why we were greasing the bearings. We're going to tie up all the clappers and get the ringers together – those that are still in the village – and start practising again. And teach some new ringers.'

'Reg was a bellringer,' Tim said, thinking of his former foster-home.

'Yes, and a very good one, too. It's a shame he can't be here, he could help teach you. But there are a few old bellringers still in the village, and with you young ones we'll soon have a good team again.'

Tim looked down at the bells. They hung silent in their frames. He thought of them ringing, each one swinging round full circle, its clapper striking against the rim. They wouldn't be doing that, of course, but still . . . The idea of learning something new, something that grown-up people did, made his blood tingle and the misery of the scholarship examination was forgotten.

Brian Collins can't ring the bells, he thought. But Reg could. And I could too. And when peace does come, I'll be here, ready to ring the bells out loud so that everyone can hear them and know we've beaten Hitler.

That's something I can want, he told himself. Something I can want and something I can *do*.

Who cared about silly old school examinations?

12

The bitter weather continued. February was even colder than January, with the temperature never above freezing and often down to 11 degrees of frost. More snow fell, but the newspapers never reported it until at least ten days had passed, by which time everyone knew about it all too well.

Annie was desperately worried about Ted, but even more now about their son Colin on HMS *Exeter* somewhere out in the Far East. The Japanese, entering the war with fresh energy and brand-new equipment, were scoring terrifying victories. Daily reports told of their approach to Singapore, of their dive-bombing of the beleagured island and, finally, of its fall as thirty thousand troops landed and forced back the Australians struggling to hold it. Days later, nearly two hundred aircraft flew in an attack on Darwin, bringing the war into Australia itself.

'If only we knew just where the ship was,' Annie said to Jess. 'But of course they don't tell us. Anyway, I expect she's dodging about all over the place. But when I think of the ships they've already sunk – the *Prince of Wales*, the *Repulse* . . . Even the *Ark Royal*'s gone. All the time old Haw-Haw kept telling us it was sunk and we knew it wasn't, we could laugh at him. But now . . .'

Jess sighed. They were hearing almost every day now of people they knew who had been killed or were missing. The sight of the telegram boy, coming down the street on his red bike, was almost as frightening as the sound of the air raid warning, until you knew where he was going. And if he came to *you* . . .

He hadn't come to Annie yet, but the dread was always in their hearts.

'How's your Betty?' she asked, changing the subject. 'Has she brought that young man of hers home again?'

Annie nodded. 'I must say, he does seem a nice young chap. I'd give 'em my blessing, but Ted just can't seem to accept him. I tell him, the boy's doing a good job now, he's risking his life every day, but Ted can't see past the fact that he's a pacifist and won't fight. Pity there aren't more like him, I said the other day, and you know, I thought Ted was going to hit me, I really did.' She sighed heavily. Ted was still as depressed as ever, and although she could feel for him more sympathetically since his outburst in bed after their quarrel, she found it hard to keep cheerful herself in the face of his continuing gloom. She wondered sometimes if he was ever going to get better.

'Betty must worry about him being on bomb disposal,' Jess was saying now.

'She does. But she don't say much about it. She's changed a lot since she was out on the farm. Grown up, like.'

'Well, she had her twenty-first birthday a couple of weeks ago,' Jess said. 'She can get married if she wants without her father's say-so.'

'I know. But Dennis wants them to start off on the right foot. He says they'll wait till the spring, and if Ted still won't see reason they'll go ahead.'

Wait till the spring. But with a job like Dennis's, would spring ever come for him?

Annie and Jess were on their way to North End to see their parents. They were both anxious about Arthur, who had been growing increasingly forgetful lately. He'd left the gas on twice and one day he'd accused the next-door neighbour, who'd called in with a few potatoes from the garden, of being a burglar.

'He just didn't seem to know who Bill was,' Mary told her daughters. 'He remembered after a few minutes and we passed it off by saying the light was bad, but I don't mind telling you, it frightened me. I mean, he was just like a stranger, not like your Dad at all.'

Arthur was upstairs having a nap. He came down when Mary made a cup of tea and asked for one of the chocolate biscuits they had in the tin.

'Chocolate biscuits!' Mary said. 'I haven't seen a chocolate biscuit for over two years. You're dreaming, Arthur.'

'I'm not. You brought them home yesterday.' He stared at her aggressively. 'You're keeping them all for yourself, that's what it is. You don't want me to have any.'

'Arthur, don't be so daft.' Mary cast a frightened look towards Jess and Annie. 'Of course I wouldn't keep them for myself. We haven't got any. There weren't any.'

'Yesterday,' he repeated. 'You got them in the Co-op. I carried the bag home.'

The three women gazed at him. The Co-op had been bombed and moved to Fratton. Mary never went that far to do her shopping.

'You see what it is,' Mary said in a trembling voice. 'He's in a world of his own half the time.'

Arthur was staring out of the window. He turned back to them and said in a perfectly ordinary, matter-of-fact voice, 'It's a bad job about the Japs. You must be half out of your mind over Colin, Annie.'

The conversation about the chocolate biscuits might never have taken place. Arthur drank his tea and recounted stories of the Boer War – which all of them had heard before – and remained perfectly lucid. For the rest of the afternoon the four of them sat chatting normally about the war, grumbling about the new soap rationing ('How am I ever going to keep Frank's working clothes clean on four ounces of soap a month to go round all of us?') and the bitter weather. Coal was so scarce now that nobody could afford to light a fire before evening, and the house never seemed to get warm, apart from the one room where the whole family gathered.

'It's not right, all the same,' Annie said as she and Jess walked home.

'You could see he wasn't with us over those biscuits. And he nearly drifted away again a couple of times, did you notice?'

Jess nodded. 'Mum told me he sometimes forgets what time of day it is. Says they haven't had their dinner when they have, and sulks if she won't cook again. He accused her of trying to starve him the other day. And when he is all right, he's worrying about the war, fretting because he's not doing his duty to help.'

'Poor Dad,' Annie said. 'And poor Mum.'

They walked on in silence and then stopped as two men, walking the other way, called out their names.

'Mrs Chapman! And Mrs Budd, isn't it?' One of the men was stocky, with grizzled hair and a creased face. The other wasn't much more than a boy – no more than nineteen, Jess guessed. Their faces were vaguely familiar but she couldn't place them. I'm getting as bad as Dad, she though wryly.

Annie knew them, however. 'It's Sam. And Ben.' She smiled at them both. 'I'm pleased to see you. How's the *King* doing these days?'

So that was who they were. The crew of the *Ferry King*, the ferry boat which Ted had skippered across Portsmouth Harbour for years and had taken to Dunkirk. They were working under a new skipper now, but didn't think much of him.

'It's not like being with Ted,' Sam said. 'He let us get on with our own work. This bloke's always breathing down your neck, thinking he can do the job better himself. I nearly gave him a handful of cotton waste the other day and told him to polish up the bilges while I went and steered!'

Annie laughed, but there was a wistful note in her voice as she said, 'I'd be as pleased as you if Ted would go back to work. It'd do him good, instead of moping round the house. It's as if he needs something to jerk him out of himself.'

'Well, we were thinking of calling round one day,' Sam said. 'Young Ben here's got his papers. He's off into the Navy soon. I've been telling him, he ought to go up and say cheerio to Ted.'

'So he should.' Annie looked at the young man. He was tall and thin and lanky. A couple of yards of drainwater, she'd heard Ted describe him as when Ben had first joined the ferry service, but he'd turned out a useful engineer. 'How are you looking forward to going into the Navy?'

'Oh, it'll be all right. I'm going in the engine-rooms – I've finished my apprenticeship now. I'm looking forward to working on really big engines.'

His bony young face had a slight sheen to it, as if he were sweating. But it was too cold for that. Annie looked at the flickering eyes and wondered if he were looking forward to going to sea as much as he said. She wouldn't blame him if he was scared stiff.

He and Sam had both been at Dunkirk with Ted. It might do Ted a bit of good to know that this boy was going off to sea, having been through the same experience.

'Come up and have a cup of tea some time,' she suggested. 'I know he'd like to see you both. And you can tell him all what's been going on down the ferry lately.'

*

'It's going to be this weekend,' Roddy said. 'We're sailing Friday night. I'm not supposed to tell you that. And I cannae tell you where we're going, because we dinnae ken.'

'We're going to have to do it, then,' Carol said. 'We're going to have to run away. Go to Scotland.'

'Och, you know we cannae do that. It's a crazy idea.'

'Crazy? What's crazy about it? We want to be together, don't we? We want to get married? Well, all we have to do is go to Scotland. They'll let us get married there, you said so.'

'No.' He shook his head. 'It's not that easy, Carol. They'll ask for papers – birth certificates and that, to prove who we are. And by then I'll be posted as a deserter and your mother will have set the police after us. We'd be caught right away.'

Carol scowled and thought for a few minutes. Then she looked at him and said, 'All right, then. We won't get married. We don't have to. All we need do is *say* we're married. I'll call myself Mrs MacPherson. No, I wouldn't, we'd have to change our names. I'll be Mrs – Mrs MacGregor. Or Mackintosh. Something Scottish anyway, because of your accent.'

'Och, if only we could,' Roddy sighed. 'It'd be a grand thing, right enough. But we'd need money. We'd need to get right away from Portsmouth and go somewhere where nobody would hear of us, and we'd need money to pay our fares and rent and food and all sorts. All I've got is a few shillings I've managed to save out of my pay.'

'That's all I've got,' Carol said. 'But my mum's got plenty.'

'Your *mum*?'

'Yes. It's in a drawer in her bedroom. I was looking for some earrings and I found it under her jumpers. A big thick envelope full of pound notes.'

'Where did she get that from?' Roddy asked. 'She's always havering on about how hard up she is.'

'I know. I don't know where it came from. But she takes enough off me and Joe, so I reckon I'm entitled to some of it back,' Carol said determinedly.

Roddy shook his head. 'She'll never give it to you. She'll go mad if you ask.'

'I wasn't thinking of asking,' Carol replied, and looked him in the eye.

'But that's stealing,' Roddy said after a moment. 'Stealing from your own mother.'

'Only if it's really her money. And I don't see how it can be. It's money she's had from me and Joe, that's what it is, and she hasn't used it so it's ours. And I know Joe wouldn't mind if I took it.'

'Are you sure that's what it is?'

'What else can it be? There's only the money Dad sends her, and she spends that on the house and stockings and make-up and stuff.'

'Perhaps she's got a wee job. She's out all hours, you told me.'

Carol snorted. 'Mum with a job! She'd never do that – thinks she's too good. Anyway, she obviously doesn't need that money and we do.' She caught his hands and gripped them tightly, gazing into his eyes. 'Roddy, there's enough there to take us anywhere we want to go. Scotland, if you want to. Or London. Anywhere. We can find a room somewhere, get jobs, who's going to know we're not married? If anyone asks, we'll tell them we got bombed out, like I said before, and lost our certificates and everything. And you won't have to go away. You won't have to *fight*.'

Roddy looked at her. He thought of the ship, which still seemed so huge and alien. He knew he would never get used to the grey steel bulkheads, the stark, narrow gangways, the cramped mess, the bare, spartan hardness of it all.The thought of going into action made him feel sick.

'We'd be together,' Carol said. 'We'd have our own little home. You'd come home at night and I'd have your supper cooking and we could listen to the wireless and go to bed whenever we felt like it. We could forget about this horrible war.'

Roddy didn't think it would be possible to forget about the war. But he'd heard that there were places in the country where they hardly knew it was happening. Places where there were still milk and butter and eggs, where people didn't spend night after night in an air-raid shelter.

'I don't like the idea of taking that money, all the same,' he said. 'Suppose your mum told the police? We could go to prison.'

'She won't do that. Not to her own daughter,' Carol said confidently. 'Anyway, we're not going to get caught, are we? We're going to just disappear. We'll be in hiding, like spies.' She looked critically at his matelot's uniform. 'We'll have to get you some different clothes, mind. I wonder if our Joe's things'd fit you.'

'We cannae steal your brother's clothes,' Roddy said, outraged.

'Why not? He's not going to need 'em much longer. He got his own papers this morning. Anyway, it's just to get started. It's only *borrowing*.'

'No. I'll not pinch Joe's clothes. I'll go to a second-hand shop and get fitted out.' At some point, he realised, he seemed to have agreed to this crazy scheme of Carol's. But he couldn't go back now. The thought of going to sea was too hideous. I wouldn't be any good to them as a gunner anyway, he thought. I'd miss everything. They'd be better off without me.

'Will you? Will you really?' Carol's face was alight. She pulled him against her and kissed him enthusiastically. 'Oh Roddy, it'll be all right, I know it will. It'll be lovely. Just think – the two of us in our own little home.' She sighed ecstatically. 'It's better than *Gone With the Wind*.'

'We'll have to make some plans,' Roddy said. 'We'll think about where we're going first. We'd better go on Thursday night – maybe they'll not discover I'm missing till the ship's at sea. And if your mother's out, she won't know you're not there till morning.'

'I'll have everything ready,' Carol promised. 'I'll take my things up to Joy and ask her to look after them for me. Mum never goes into their shop, so no one'll tell her. We can be miles away before anyone realises we've gone!'

She flung her arms around his neck again and he held her tightly. He was scared about what they were doing, but being scared had become a normal part of life for Roddy since he had joined the Navy. And nothing scared him as much as the idea of going to sea.

Friday, he thought. On Friday we'll be away together, starting a new life.

Carrie's right, it doesn't matter that we won't be properly married. It'll feel like that to us, anyway. That's what really matters.

'Och, Carrie,' he said. 'I really do love you.'

Snow and ice turned the roads into skating-rinks, but somehow the buses and trains kept going. The *Evening News* reported stories of dockyardmen having to dig their bus out of a deep snowdrift before it could take them to work early in the morning. One man said the road was so slippery he had been forced to crawl on his hands and knees to reach the stop. Scores of cars were stranded one day on Portsdown Hill, and their drivers had to walk down to Cosham and continue their journey from there. Farmers had to take their milk round by tractor, and in some places they simply left churns at a local pub or accessible house so that their customers could collect it themselves.

On Thursday afternoon, the weather was slightly better and Ethel Glaister went out as usual to have tea with her friend Violet Mitchell, in Kingston. That was the night Carol and Roddy usually chose to go to the pictures, so Ethel wouldn't be surprised when Carol wasn't home that evening. She'd start to worry – or get annoyed – when Carol didn't come in at ten o'clock, but she probably wouldn't go into Carol's room until well after eleven, and by then she and Roddy would be well away. And when she did go in, she'd find the note, pinned to Carol's pillow, telling her not to worry. She might even think Carol was home first and not go in until next morning.

'Have you got everything?' Roddy asked when Carol met him near the railway station. They had agreed it was better not to be seen together where they might be recognised. He had slipped into a public lavatory and changed his uniform for the second-hand clothes he had bought, and he looked strange and unfamiliar in grey flannel trousers and a brown overcoat.

'I've got as many clothes as I could carry.' Carol looked him over and giggled. 'That coat's about three sizes too big for you. We could both get into that.'

'It was all I could find.' He sounded affronted, but inside he was shivering with fear. Suppose someone saw them and reported them? Suppose a redcap were to realise he was a sailor on the run? I've done it now, he thought, looking at the brown sleeve. I've deserted. 'Let's get away from here, Carrie. I feel as if everyone's staring at us.'

They got on the first train that came along and sat in a third-class compartment. It was already dark and there was only a dim blue light showing in the train. Outside, the streets looked dark and gloomy, and when they got out into the countryside the white fields looked hostile.

The train was filled with people. Some of them were going home from work, others were going further afield. The corridor was packed with luggage and there were soldiers sitting on kitbags, smoking. Carol and Roddy were squeezed tightly against each other. They held hands, wishing they could talk.

'Where are we going?' Roddy whispered at last. He had left the buying of tickets to Carol. He knew that she had taken the money from her mother's drawer but he didn't know how much she had. He wasn't really sure if he wanted to know.

'London, of course.' Carol's eyes were bright with excitement. She had had no qualms about taking the big envelope of money. To her mind, it was probably mostly hers anyway, and Joe wouldn't mind her having his share. *Borrowing* it, she corrected herself. She could feel it now in her pocket, a thick wad of paper. She hadn't had time to count it properly but she reckoned there was at least fifty pounds. Fifty pounds! It was a fortune.

'We'll go to an air-raid shelter tonight,' she said. 'And tomorrow we'll find ourselves somewhere to stay. Somewhere cheap but decent. And then we can look for jobs.' She squeezed his arm. 'We could have a couple of days' holiday first, though. See the sights, eh? St Paul's Cathedral, and Westminster, and the Houses of Parliament. I'd like to see the Tower of London too.'

'You cannae go there now. It's all closed.'

'I know, but you can still *see* it, can't you? I've never been to London.' She shivered with excitement. 'It's going to be gorgeous.'

Roddy wasn't sure that blitzed London would be at all 'gorgeous'. But he was too thankful to be away from the ship, and with Carol, to say so. I don't care where I am, he thought, so long as we're together and I don't have to go and fight.

As Carol had hoped, Ethel did not discover her absence until next morning.

She had come home later than usual the evening before and assumed that Carol was already in bed. Joe was asleep on the sofa in the front room downstairs and didn't stir as she passed the door, and there were two cups on the draining-board in the scullery. Ethel washed her face quickly and went straight upstairs to bed.

The next morning, she came down to find Joe already gone to work and no sign of her daughter. It was Carol's job to make tea and start the porridge. Outside, the garden was white again with a fresh fall of snow and she could hear the scrape of a shovel as Jess Budd cleared the pavement in front of the house.

Clicking her tongue with annoyance, Ethel stood at the foot of the stairs. 'Carol! *Carol!* It's time to get up. You've overslept.'

There was no reply. Ethel gave a sharp exclamation and shouted again. Then she stamped quickly up the stairs and flung open Carol's bedroom door.

'Carol! I've called you twice already. When are you going to . . .' Her voice trailed away and she stared, half frightened, half unbelieving, at the empty bed. '*Carol!*'

Jess Budd had just finished scraping away the snow when the door of number 15 burst open and Ethel appeared, her face scarlet and her eyes wild. Jess looked at her in surprise and concern.

'What's the matter? What's happened?'

'It's my Carol. The little slut. The little hussy.' Ethel waved a piece of paper under Jess's nose. 'Look at that. *Look* at it. See what she's done.'

Jess took the note and read it, her eyes widening. 'She says she's run away with Roddy. Is that the sailor she's been going with? But they can't. He's on a ship.'

'Not any more,' Ethel said grimly. 'He's scarpered, that's what he's done. And taken my Carol with him. That's desertion, that is, and he can be shot for it.'

'Oh, no.' Jess gazed at her. 'He's only a boy. And he looks such a nice young chap.'

'So nice he runs away with my daughter. God knows what he's doing to her now.' Ethel clenched her fists and shook them. 'I just wish he'd come walking round the corner now, I'd wring his neck for him, that I would. Oh, I shouldn't never have let her go out with him. I shouldn't never have let her go to that dance up Hilsea. That's what started it all. She hasn't been the same girl since she met him.'

Jess didn't know what to say. She'd never liked Ethel much and there had been quite long periods when they didn't speak to each other, but she was a neighbour all the same and you helped neighbours when they were in trouble. But what could you do when a girl had run off like this? And she couldn't help feeling a sneaking sympathy for Carol. What she'd done was wrong, of course, no two ways about it, but when you looked at her mother and thought what sort of a life she must have had . . .

And youngsters could do some silly things when their heads were turned by being in love, especially the first time. Even more especially these days, when nothing was what it ought to be.

'I'm really sorry,' she said at last. 'What are you going to do about it?'

'What d'you think? I'm going to the police, of course. Carol's only just sixteen, she's under my control, and I want her brought back. I'll tell them what ship that young man's on, too. They'll send the military police after him. I tell you, he's going to find himself in real trouble.'

'Why not wait a day or two?' Jess suggested. 'They'll probably come back of their own accord. Once they run out of money—'

'Money!' Ethel exclaimed. She stared at Jess, then tore the note from her fingers and rushed back indoors. 'If I find that dirty little trollop's been in my drawer – if she's *dared*—'

Jess stood uncertainly on the frozen pavement for a few moments. Then, from the window above, she heard a scream of fury and a stream of swear words that shocked her. And the tone of Ethel's voice turned her cold.

I wouldn't like to be Carol or Roddy when Ethel Glaister catches up with them, she thought. And, feeling shaken and upset, she turned and went indoors to where Rose was giving Maureen her breakfast.

For a few days, Carol's elopement with the young Scottish sailor was the talk of the street. But it was soon overshadowed by greater events.

On the last day of February, Ted came in from the garden to find Annie standing white-faced by the wireless, a duster screwed up into a tight ball in her hand. Quickly, he crossed the room and put his arm round her shoulders while she blurted out the news that had just been given out.

'There's been a big battle in the Java Sea. They said the Dutch had been told they could fight for the East Indies – you know they've got a lot of territory out there – and they've lost any amount of ships, and there've been two British destroyers sunk.' She stared at him. 'They're calling it a major disaster.'

'Destroyers,' Ted said, knowing what was in her mind, almost as frightened as she was. 'Destroyers. The *Exeter*'s a cruiser, Annie. It can't be her.'

But Annie was almost frantic. 'The *Exeter*'s there, though. Our Colin's out there. He could be next. He might even be hurt or dead now. Those awful Japanese, Ted – they're just murdering everybody.'

'It's war,' he said bitterly. 'It doesn't count as murder when it's war. You know what they say – *all's fair.*'

'It's not, though. It's not fair. Why did the Japs have to come in anyway? Nobody was hurting them. The war was nothing to do with them. Why did they have to start?'

'They just saw their chance to grab the Pacific,' Ted said wearily. 'Like a kid, pinching apples when the grocer's back's turned. At least it brought America in on our side.'

'Yes, but it means we've got to send more forces out there, instead of beating Hitler. I don't see how they'll ever sort it out.'

'Look, Annie, there's no use meeting trouble halfway. You know what they say. No news is good news, and there's been nothing said about the *Exeter* yet.'

It was the most positive thing he'd said for months, but before Annie could reply there was a ring on the front doorbell. She went to answer it and came back looking a little more cheerful.

'It's Sam and Ben come to see you, Ted. Ben's got something to tell you. I'll make a cup of tea.'

Sam came in and sat down on one of the chairs round the dining-table. Ben stood just inside the door, looking gawky and self-conscious. Ted looked at them. He felt pleased that they'd taken the trouble to come, but he also felt awkward. He wondered if they thought he was skiving.

'Well, come in properly and sit yourself down, boy,' he said to Ben. 'You make the place untidy standing there . . . How's things on the ferry, then?'

'Oh, much as usual,' Sam answered. 'We'd be better set if you were back. I don't get on with old Len Barber. And what with young Ben here off on his travels—'

'Travels?' Ted said. 'What travels?'

'What d'you think?' Ben asked. 'Been called up, of course. I'm off next week – Royal Navy. Engineer.'

His voice had been late breaking and was still a little squeaky. He looked at Ted with his mouth set, trying to pretend he was pleased to be going. But that boy had seen Dunkirk, Ted thought. He knows what it's going to be like.

'You'll be all right,' he said. 'You know your job. Had a good master.' He glanced at Sam.

'Had a good skipper,' Sam said. 'We made a good team, the three of us.'

And now there would be only one of them on the old *Ferry King*. Ted looked away, unable to meet their eyes. His heart was thumping in his chest. I don't want to do it, he thought. I don't want to go back.

Annie came in with the teapot and a jug of milk. It didn't matter who was there or how urgent it was, she would never bring the milk to the table in a bottle. She poured four cups of tea and handed round the bottle of saccharins.

'It's time for the six o'clock news,' she said. 'Turn on the wireless, Ted, will you?'

They sat drinking their tea and listening, the four of them. And then they heard it.

'*It has just been announced that the British cruiser HMS* Exeter *was sunk in yesterday's fighting in the Java Sea. She was fighting north of Java with four Japanese cruisers. The British destroyer* Encounter *and the US destroyer* Pope *were sunk in the same action. HMS* Exeter *had already been hit in earlier fighting and was facing two enemy ships on the port quarter and two in the starboard beam. She lost all power and sank soon after coming under fire. It is not yet known how many men survived.*

'*The Japanese victories in the Java Sea are presenting a grave danger to Madagascar, at present controlled by the Allies. Enemy control of this island would threaten the western entrance to the Indian Ocean, cutting off the vital supplies of oil from the Persian Gulf and causing a breakdown in communications with the Far East.*

'*Prime Minister Mr Winston Churchill has said—*'

'Turn it off, Ted,' Annie said, her voice trembling. 'Turn it off. I don't want to hear any more. I don't want to hear any more about the war, *ever*.'

Ted snapped the wireless into silence. They sat staring at each other, barely able to take in the news they had just heard.

'*Exeter* sunk,' Ted whispered at last. 'Oh God, Annie . . . the *Exeter*'s been sunk . . .'

'Oh Ted,' she breathed, staring across the table at him. She wanted to be in his arms, feeling his strength, she wanted to hear his voice telling her it wasn't true, it was a dream, a nightmare. 'Ted, what's been happening to our Colin?'

Neither of them could move. They sat rigid, frozen, paralysed. Their need for each other was palpable but neither could stir. Their eyes met, helpless, anguished, and their faces slowly crumbled into despair.

Sam looked slowly from one to the other. He felt their shock as his own. He had known Colin all his life, seen him grow from a lively toddler to a mischievous boy, always up to something – shooting arrows at the neighbours' cats from the top of the turret, coming down to the *Ferry King* and poking about in the engine-room, demanding to be allowed to steer. He'd seen him in his first Naval uniform, swaggering and proud in bell-bottoms.

'They don't know how many's been lost,' he said at last. 'The BBC just said so. There could be a lot saved.' But he knew that this could be of little comfort until they knew that Colin was amongst the survivors.

He poured another cup of tea and pushed it across the table to Annie. She looked at it as if she did not know what it was. He stirred in two saccharins.

'Drink some, Mrs Chapman. It's good for shock.'

Annie shook her head slowly, still gazing at her husband. 'Ted. *Ted* . . .'

With a sudden, violent movement, Ted pushed back his chair. He stumbled to his feet and round the table to his wife. He gripped her in his arms and pulled her out of her chair, hard against his chest, and she burst into sudden, noisy tears. They stood together, clinging, weeping, and Annie clenched her fists and beat them against him.

'Why? Why, Ted, *why*? Why are all these terrible things happening, all over the world – thousands, *millions*, of people being killed, slaughtered like animals, and what's it all for, eh? We went into this to help the Polish – and what have we ever done for them? They're no better off – and now it's spread everywhere, *everywhere*, and nowhere's safe, there's nowhere in the whole world that's safe any more. And where's it all going to end? How *can* it end, until we're all dead, every last one of us, and there's no one left to kill?' Her weeping increased and her words were barely coherent, but each of the men in the room heard her repeat her son's name, over and over again, and heard all the bitter anguish of a mother who has lost her child and knows him to have died in pain.

'Colin. Oh Colin, my little boy, my dear, dear little Colin . . .'

13

Carol and Roddy had been gone for almost a month, and nothing had yet been heard of them.

Ethel was furious, humiliated and bitter. And her temper was not improved by George's arrival home soon after she had sent him the news.

'You mean she's been gone *three weeks* and you never saw fit to let me know!' he shouted. 'What in God's name have you been playing at, Ethel? Didn't it strike you I had a *right* to know? I'm her father, ain't I?'

'I didn't see what you could do about it,' she said sullenly. 'All them miles away. I mean, you're too busy fighting a war to bother about your family, aren't you.'

'And there's no call to get sarky. That ain't going to help. I joined up because I had a duty, as you know perfectly well, and it ain't my fault if they never sent the Unit off to get killed in France or somewhere. That'd please you, wouldn't it – but I daresay we'll go soon enough.' He glared at his wife in a way quite unlike his usual mild manner. 'You oughter got in touch right away.'

'I told the police. And the Navy. There's nothing you can do that they can't.'

'That's not the point. I'm her father. I ought to know what's happening to my kids.' He was angrier than she had ever seen him. 'Seems to me you're not fit to look after 'em on your own, Ethel. Look what's happened since I went away. Our Shirley, torpedoed and nearly drowned because you would have it she was sent off to Canada. And now Carol, getting into God knows what sort of trouble with a sailor. I mean, whatever got into you to let her go about with him? He musta been a bad lot, surely even you could see that.'

Ethel flinched. George had never spoken to her like this before, never shouted at her and laid down the law. It's this Army training, she thought resentfully, it's making a brute out of him.

'You're a fine one to talk,' she retorted. 'You never had a word to say when I was worrying about Shirley being evacuated. Left it all to me, didn't you. *I* make the decisions and *I'm* the one to get blamed when things go wrong. It's always been the same. I have to take all the responsibility and then you can turn round and say it's my fault.' She glowered at him. 'So I'm not fit to look after my own children, am I? Well, maybe *you'd* like to take a turn and I'll go off and fight the war. I'd soon give Hitler a bloody nose, I can tell you!'

'And that's just about all you could give him. There's bloody little else you're prepared to give a bloke!'

Ethel gasped and swung her hand at him. George caught her wrist. She lashed out with her foot, the pointed toe of her high-heeled shoe catching him painfully on the shin, and he gave a howl, let go of her wrist and slapped her hard across the side of the head.

'You bitch! You nasty, spiteful bitch!' Enraged by pain and years of humiliation, he struck her again and she stumbled, tripped over a chair and fell, catching at the tablecloth and bringing all the tea things with her. She lay in an ungainly heap, crying noisily amongst the wreckage.

'You brute, George Glaister. You vicious brute. You've been working up to that, haven't you. You've been working up to it for years.' She sat up, feeling first her elbow, then her head. 'I'm bruised all over. I always knew there was a violent streak in you. My mother warned me. I should have listened to her and taken Bert Spedding. He was after me too.'

'He had a lucky escape, then,' George said. 'I'll remember to congratulate him next time we run into each other.' He looked down at his wife. 'Get up, Ethel.'

'Just so you can knock me down again? No thanks.' But she moved away across the floor and began to gather up the broken cups and saucers. 'Look at all this,' she said, breaking into fresh sobs. 'My second-best teaset, all smashed. And jam all over the rug. And that's all the milk we've got left. I just hope you're proud of yourself.'

George bent to help her. His rage was already evaporating and he was beginning to feel ashamed. He had never touched Ethel in anger before, never been able to understand men who knocked their wives about. He couldn't understand what had got into him. It was as if he'd turned into another person, he thought, just as if someone else had taken charge.

All the same, she ought to have let him know about Carol. How did she think it made him feel, knowing she just hadn't bothered?

'Come on, Ethel. Perhaps I shouldn't have done that. But it just got me on the raw, knowing you didn't think I was worth being told about my own girl. I'm still her dad, after all. And I'm still your husband, too.'

Ethel bit back the retort she wanted to make. She scrambled to her feet and sank into a chair, keeping a wary eye on George in case he suddenly went mad again. She felt scared and bewildered, but she wasn't going to let him get the upper hand, not after all these years.

'Don't you dare do that again,' she said, her voice trembling. 'Don't you dare ever lay a finger on me again. I swear if you do, I'll go to the front door and I'll scream blue murder. I'll get the police round, that's what I'll do, if you ever attack me again like that.'

'I didn't attack you, Ethel. You hit out at me first, and you kicked me. I'm surprised you never broke my leg. Anyway, the police won't interfere between man and wife.'

'More's the pity. There's a lot of women would be a lot happier if they did.'

George sighed. 'This isn't getting us anywhere, Ethel. It's Carol we ought to be thinking about. She's what's important, not bickering like a couple of kids. That's why they've given me a pass, to try and get things sorted out.'

'There's nothing to sort out. They've run off, the pair of them, and haven't even had the common decency to let me know they're all right. The police are looking for them, and so's the Navy. That boy's been posted as a deserter, and serve him right. He'll be for the high jump when they catch him, and no mistake. There's nothing you can do.'

'But what are they living on? Our Carol never had any money, and he wouldn't have been paid much.'

'They took my savings,' Ethel said angrily. 'Searched through my drawer and took out the money I've been putting by for new furniture. I want a new three-piece suite and carpet and some decent curtains when this lot's over. And a new bed for my room. The whole place'll want decorating then, and you can be sure nobody else down April Grove will have thought of that. They'll all be living in hovels while we've got the smartest place in Copnor.'

George stared at her. 'You've been saving up for new furniture?'

'And why not?' she demanded. 'There's nothing wrong with taking a pride in your home, is there?'

'But you always say how hard up you are. You're always complaining about my Army pay. How much d'you manage to save?'

Ethel's eyes shifted. 'A bit. Not that it's any use thinking about it now. That daughter of yours—'

'How much?' George demanded suspiciously.

'Ten pounds. Eleven, something like that.'

'Go on,' he said disbelievingly, 'you've always known to the last penny what money you've got. How much?'

'Fifteen pounds,' she said reluctantly, and then, 'Oh, all right, twenty-one pounds fourteen and a penny, if you must know! Enough to keep those two little thieves comfortable for a few weeks. And my new three-piece gone.' Tears welled up in her eyes again and rolled down her cheeks. 'I'll have to start all over again now, and if they stop this war too soon I'll never be able to get it.'

George sat down on a chair as if his legs had given way beneath him. He felt his anger return and fought to control it.

'Ethel, I just don't understand you. Your daughter's gone missing, run off with a sailor, and all you can think about is your new three-piece suite. Can't you see, none of that matters? It's Carol what matters. What's happening to her, where is she? She might be dead, for all you know – bombed, or strangled. We might never find out. Don't you *care*?'

'Of course I care,' Ethel snapped. 'I'm her mother. I carried her for nine months, I went through hell giving birth to her. Why don't you ask her if she cares about me? Does it look as if she does?'

'I wish I could,' George muttered. 'I only wish I could.'

He got heavily to his feet. 'I'm going down the police station, see what they've got to say about this. I haven't got much time – got to be back Monday morning. And listen to this, Ethel – if you hear *anything*, anything at all, from our Carol, or if she comes back home, you let me know straight away, understand? I'm not going to be kept in the dark again.' He surveyed the mess on the floor. 'You'd better get this lot cleared up. And get something hot on the stove for my supper. I've been travelling all day and had nothing but a bully-beef sandwich. This is still my home, and I'm master in it, whatever you like to think, all right?'

He pulled open the door and stamped out, slamming it behind him. Ethel sat for a moment on the chair, staring at the broken china and shaking with anger and fear.

George had never, in all their marriage, spoken to her like that. He had never dared order her about. She had had the upper hand ever since the day they'd met.

Ethel did not know what to do. But she found herself on her knees, picking up the broken cups and mopping up the spilt milk. And when she had finished, she went out into the kitchen and started to fry some sausages and onions and some leftover potato, for her husband's supper.

Betty shared her family's worries about her sailor cousin, and her anxiety added to her fears for Dennis. There seemed to be more and more unexploded bombs turning up all over Portsmouth, and miles out into the countryside, and they were often reported in the local paper. Sometimes, inevitably, the reports told of people being killed by them.

'It seems as if everyone you know's in danger these days,' she said to the other Land Girls. 'There isn't anyone I can think of who's really safe.'

'We're all in it together,' Yvonne agreed. 'Even out here on the farm – remember that bomb that killed the chickens and started the grandfather clock ticking?'

The clock was still keeping perfect time. The only good thing the Germans ever did, Mr Spencer had commented. Pity they didn't stick to mending clocks.

'A good kick would've got it going just as well,' Betty said. 'It didn't have to be a bomb.'

They were sitting in the barn, having a short break. A shadow loomed up in the doorway and Gerald came in.

Gerald had improved a lot. His arm was still giving him some trouble – chipped elbow bones, the doctor said – but the effects of the dysentery had almost gone and he was slowly building up his strength. It wouldn't be long before he had to go back to his regiment in Africa. Meanwhile, he was able to do some work on the farm, and both Betty and Yvonne had noticed that as often as not, this meant sharing in whatever job Erica was doing.

'Thaw's setting in,' he said. 'We'll be able to get on with that ploughing. Top three fields never got done last autumn, did they?'

The girls shook their heads. Jonas, who had been sitting at a short distance chewing a Marmite sandwich, said, 'Tidden the only job wants doing. We only got half the bloody corn threshed when the team was here. The stack'll be riddled with rats an' mice, an' we're running short of hay to feed the flickin' beasts. Wants someone in there with a couple of terriers, flush out the bloody lot.'

Yvonne shuddered. She wasn't afraid of much, but rats always turned her sick. She glanced appealingly at Betty and Erica.

'I can't stand them. I think it's the way they stare at you with their little eyes. And the way they run – as if they'd got wheels instead of feet. And then having to hit them.'

'Well, someone's got to do it,' Betty said, and glanced mischievously at Jonas. 'You're the one with the terriers.'

'You're the ones with the young legs,' he retorted. 'I can't skip about like you can, don't mind admitting it. Rats needs someone quick an' nimble.'

'So what job d'you want to do, Jonas?' Gerald enquired. 'Seems there's more than enough to go round.'

Jonas glanced at him. 'Ploughing's my job, allus has bin. I'd hev finished them fields last November if I hadn't bin laid up with that flickin' bronchitis. Time I was about again, bloody ground was frozen. I'll carry on with that.'

'Sorry,' Gerald said. 'Dad's already told me to get on with that. I can drive the tractor one-handed—'

'You never can! You need two hands for that job. How d'yer think you can steer the tractor an' pull the levers to lift the plough an' all the rest of it with that gammy arm of yours? Don't talk bloody daft.'

'I'll have one of the girls to help me,' Gerald said. 'They need to learn how to plough anyway. We can't always rely on you being able to do it.'

The old man's face darkened. 'An' what d'yer mean by that? I always bin reliable enough in the past. Over fifty years I worked on this bloody farm, man and boy, worked for your grandad I did when farming *was* farming, none of this fancy modern stuff—'

'Like tractors,' Gerald put in, grinning.

'All right, you can laugh. Yes, we used to plough with horses, *an*' do a damn sight better job'n you young ones ever could. We were using horses till five years back, still do when we needs. I could've done all the lower fields with the horses last autumn if Boxer hadn't gone lame.'

'Seems everything went wrong last autumn,' Gerald observed.

Jonas glared at him. 'So it did. There's a war on here, as well as in bloody Africa.'

Gerald shrugged. He looked at Erica. 'How about it, then? Want to help me on the tractor and learn to plough?'

Erica jumped up and brushed her palms down the seat of her dungarees. 'Yes, *please*.' She blushed, as if surprised by her own enthusiasm, and glanced at the other two. 'Sorry, but I'm not too keen on rats either. I promise I'll take my turn later.'

'You bet you will,' Yvonne said, but she spoke in a resigned tone. The girls had quickly learned that on a farm there was no room for squeamishness. 'I'll be along later to see how straight you've ploughed.'

'It'll be just as if we'd done it with a ruler,' Erica promised, and hurried out of the barn after Gerald.

Betty watched them go and then looked at Yvonne with raised eyebrows. 'Keen, isn't she?'

'Yes,' Yvonne said slowly, 'I reckon she is.'

The two girls smiled at each other. And Jonas snorted.

Gerald and Erica went straight to the tractor-shed. The tractor was a Fordson, bought second-hand and liable to be temperamental. Jonas treated it with as much care as if it had been a living animal, murmuring to it in an unusually gentle voice as he greased and polished.

'He thinks it's his,' Erica said, laying her hand on the mudguard. 'He looks after it like a baby.'

'Or a horse. Jonas was senior horseman when we were still using them for the plough. As soon as the tractor came in, he switched over but secretly I think he still wishes we were using horses.'

'Why does he love it so much, if he'd rather go on in the old way?' Erica asked.

'Because of his position as ploughman. It might sound pretty ordinary to someone from the town, but on the farm the ploughman's top dog. Everything depends on him getting his job right. And he's generally more of a farm foreman for all the other jobs – takes charge.'

'So if Jonas refused to use the tractor and stayed with the horses, your father would have employed someone else as ploughman and Jonas would have taken second place.'

'That's right,' Gerald said, smiling at her. 'Unfortunately for Jonas, that happened anyway because Dick and I ranked higher than him. If we wanted to drive the tractor, we did!'

'Still, he would accept that because you're the farmer's sons. He couldn't grumble about that.'

'Don't you believe it. He might accept it but that wouldn't stop him beefing. He never stopped. If Dick or me did a bit of ploughing, Jonas would be out there walking the furrows, pointing out all the rough bits or the bits we'd missed. Jonas doesn't let anything come between him and his moaning, it's his favourite pastime.'

They laughed. Gerald turned away to reach down to the paraffin can and Erica looked at him affectionately. During the few weeks Gerald had been home, she had grown very fond of him. She wasn't looking forward to his going away again.

Nevertheless, she always tried to keep a little distance between them. The moment when he had almost fainted in the barn, and she had found her fingers stroking the back of his neck, had shaken her. For the first time since Geoffrey's death, she had experienced the tingling of desire, and the feeling left her guilty and disturbed. I shouldn't be feeling like that about another chap, she thought. It's disloyal to Geoff's memory. Yet she could not resist the temptation to spend her time with Gerald whenever possible. So long as it doesn't go any further than that, she thought.

Gerald turned suddenly and caught her glance. They stared at each other and Erica felt her face grow hot.

'Show me what to do,' she said hurriedly. 'What's the paraffin for?'

'To get the engine started. Once it's running, we can switch in to normal fuel.' He gave her a comical look. 'Oh, lor'.'

'What? What's wrong?'

'We're going to have to get old Jonas along after all. You have to crank the engine to get it started, and it's a real brute. I can't do it with one arm, and you certainly haven't got the muscle. We need him to give it a swing.'

'I'll go and fetch him,' Erica offered, and ran across the yard, glad of the cold air on her cheeks. She had seen the darkening of Gerald's eyes as he met her look, and knew that he was talking to cover his own feelings. This is getting serious, she thought. Another couple of minutes in there, and he might have kissed me.

Jonas sneered when she asked him to come over and give a hand with the tractor. 'Two of you on the job, and can't get the bloody thing started! What flickin' use are you going to be out in the field? If the pair of you got no more strength than a couple of kittens, better if you came in here and chased rats.'

'Gerald wants to do the ploughing,' Erica said firmly. 'He wants you to come and give the cranking-handle a swing, that's all. He's not asking you to sell your soul.'

'Always did want to rule the roost, that one,' Jonas grumbled. 'Pair of 'em trying to run before they could walk, and the boss letting 'em.'

Erica stopped in the middle of the yard. She planted her legs apart, put her hands on her hips and faced him.

'Just what's the matter with you, Jonas? Why is it that nothing's ever right? When we first came here, you never stopped grumbling about us taking the boys' places. You never let a day go by without telling us how much better at everything they were. Well, maybe that was true, but it wasn't our fault and we did our best. Now Gerald's back and you grumble just as much about *him*. What is it you're so afraid of? That someone might actually be better than you at something? And why would that be so terrible, anyway? It's the *job* that matters – the *bloody, flickin' job!*'

Jonas stared at her, his eyes narrowing, his mottled lips pushed out. She saw a dark flush rise in his weatherbeaten cheeks and knew that something she had said had scored a hit. For a moment, she wondered if she had gone too far.

The she heard a burst of applause and looked past him to see Betty and Yvonne at the barn door, clapping their hands together. Behind her, Gerald was leaning against the tractor, grinning broadly. And over at the open farmhouse door, Mr and Mrs Spencer were standing open-mouthed.

Jonas saw her glance and followed it. His face reddened deeper yet. He muttered something Erica couldn't hear, and pushed past her.

'All right,' he growled, 'let's get at it. Well, don't just stand there staring! There's bloody work to be done, ain't there?'

Annie had been awake almost all night and then fallen heavily asleep towards dawn. That was how it was now – for hours every night she lay stiff and still in the bed, staring into the darkness and imagining Colin's last hours on the *Exeter*, the ship already damaged and threatened on all sides by the enemy. And then the final attack, guns blazing from every quarter and the brave British ship returning fire, defending herself until those very last minutes when the damage became too great to be borne and she disappeared beneath the waves . . .

They hadn't had a chance, she thought. And still nobody knew how many had really survived.

It was thought that a large number of the men had survived the sinking, that they might even have reached land, but nothing had been heard of them since. They might have wandered off into the jungle and starved to death, or been savaged by wild beasts – though nobody was quite sure what kinds of wild beasts roamed the jungles out there. Anyway, according to the conventions of war, the Japanese should have taken them prisoner and then notified the British of their names. But no such notification had been received. It was as if the men had disappeared off the face of the earth.

'They'll let us know soon,' Ted said when they discussed it. 'They'll have to. It's all a bit of a muddle out there, that's all. They'll get it sorted out.'

'A bit of a muddle! It's blooming chaos,' Annie said. But she knew he was as worried as she, and all they could do was give each other what comfort they could.

Annie turned over in bed and found herself alone. Ted must have got up early. As she realised this, the bedroom door opened and he appeared with two cups of tea. Annie stared at him in astonishment.

'You're in your working clothes—'

'Yes.' He sat down on the bed. 'I'm going down the ferry. I don't know if they'll let me back on the *King* straight away, but whatever they want me to do, I'll do it.' He looked at her gravely. 'I'm ashamed of myself, Annie. The way I've been – well, I dunno how you put up with me, I really don't. Whining and moping round the house all this time when there was work to be done. And young Ben going off to sea. And our Colin . . .' His voice shook a little. 'Well, I been thinking and I reckon it's time I pulled meself together and got back to work. That's all.'

'Oh, Ted.' Annie laid her hand on his arm. 'Ted, I know I've been hard on you these past few weeks—'

'No harder than you should be. You were right to go on at me, Annie.'

'Well,' she said, 'let's not argue about that. But you're not to go back unless you really feel like it, Ted. I mean, there's no use forcing yourself.'

'I'm not forcing myself. I want to.' He set his jaw, looking more determined than she had seen him in months. 'I won't pretend I'm not still scared of the bombs, but I reckon most people must be the same, and if they can carry on, so can I. I'm not letting it beat me again.'

He drank his tea and then gave her a crooked grin. Annie felt the tears in her eyes. She wanted to hug him, but sensed that this was not the moment. Let him stay in charge.

'Right,' he said, putting down his cup and smacking his lips. 'That's it, then. I've had me breakfast, so there's no need for you to get up just yet. I'll get me bike and go.'

He leaned forwards and kissed her. And Annie, unable to restrain herself any longer, threw her arms round his neck and held him tightly. They stayed together for a long moment and then he drew away.

'You're a good wife, Annie. I dunno what I'd have done without you.'

'And you're a good husband. And a good skipper, too. They'll be pleased to see you back on the ferry, I know that.'

She lay back and heard him clump down the stairs and out of the back door. A few minutes later, she heard him wheel his bike along the side of the house and give a cheery ring on the bell.

For a few moments, she had been almost able to forget Colin. Now the remembrance rushed back, almost overwhelming her with fresh pain. But somehow it was just a little easier to bear, now that the worry about Ted was over.

I hope this isn't just a flash in the pan, she thought. I hope he really *is* better.

14

As the spring evenings drew out, Micky's army was able to forage more for weapons. Micky still spent a good deal of time on his own, but he was now often accompanied by Desmond, who followed him like an adoring puppy. He would do anything that Micky asked him, and had brought out several handfuls of live bullets from his Sunday morning firing practice.

'You mean you just carry the boxes of ammo yourselves?' Micky had asked incredulously when he first discovered the routine. Desmond never volunteered information – you had to drag it out of him, though he was willing enough to give it once you asked the right questions. 'They just give you the boxes to carry, and they're full of bullets and not locked or anything?'

Desmond nodded. 'Bullets aren't any good without guns.'

Micky rolled his eyes. No good without guns! 'But they're full of explosive,' he said. 'Gunpowder. We could make bombs.'

'Bombs aren't any good without aeroplanes,' Jimmy Cross said. 'Des is right. Ammo's no use without guns.'

'All right, so we get guns too, don't we. But we can start off by collecting live ammo.' Micky looked at Desmond again. 'You could get some, couldn't you? Take a few out of the box when nobody's looking?'

Desmond's face didn't change. He had very little expression – sometimes he laughed, sometimes he scowled furiously, but mostly he just looked blank. It was difficult to know if he was thinking about Micky's order, picturing himself stealing some bullets, or whether it meant nothing to him. But the following week, after dinner on Sunday afternoon, he turned up at the den with a handful of live bullets.

'Cor, look at that,' Micky breathed rapturously as Desmond dropped them in his hand. 'Just *look* at that.'

The bullets were about two inches long, with shiny caps. They felt smooth and heavy in Micky's palm, and he turned them over and stroked them reverently. He longed for a gun so that he could fire them, and imagined himself lying on his stomach, aiming at the invading Germans. Saving Portsmouth. Saving England.

That would show all those stupid magistrates and the probation officer he had to go and see every week, who just talked to him like a kid.

It wasn't fair that Desmond could be in the ATC and learn to fire guns, and he couldn't.

'Can't you get a gun out?' he asked. 'Stuff it under your jacket? We got to have guns.'

'Have to give the guns back,' Desmond said. 'They always ask for the guns back.'

Well, it stood to reason that they would. Micky looked again at the bullets in his hand and felt his longing increase. There had to be a way.

'Can't you find out where they keep 'em? Are they locked away?' He knew they must be, but people weren't always as careful as they ought to be – look at the way Des had managed to get the bullets. 'Don't they ever leave the guns out anywhere?'

'Not our guns,' Desmond said. He took one of the bullets back and cuddled it in his big hands. 'My bullets.'

'No, they're mine now. You can keep that one but the rest are part of our arsenal. And you got to find a way of getting some guns.' Something Desmond had said struck him. 'You said they didn't leave *your* guns out. Does that mean they leave others around?'

'In the repair shops.' Desmond slipped his bullet back into his pocket. Micky stared at him.

'The repair shops? What d'you mean?'

'Repair shops in the hangars. They've got all old planes in there – Tiger Moths and Camels. They mend them.'

'And they got guns?'

'Yes, they got guns. I seen 'em, on the benches some of them.' He held an imaginary machine-gun in his arms and aimed it around the basement of the bombed house. 'Ratat-at-at-at! You're all dead.'

The others backed away a little. Desmond might be only pretending, but there was something chilling in his blank eyes. They felt glad he hadn't got a real gun.

'But that's just what I bin *asking* you,' Micky said, exasperated. 'Time and time again I asked you if there was guns left out anywhere. You said there wasn't.'

'You asked about *our* guns,' Desmond said, looking hurt, and Micky reminded himself that there was no use in getting annoyed. Desmond answered the questions he was asked, and that was all. It wasn't his fault if you didn't ask the right questions.

Now that Micky knew what to ask him, the information came out quickly enough. Some of the old aircraft that had been used in the Great War were used now for 'spotting' and brought to the airfield for maintenance. Some that were found to be past help were taken to a 'graveyard' at the outer edge of the aerodrome and dumped there, and you could pick up some useful bits and pieces. One boy had a pilot's seat which he'd taken home, and several had smaller souvenirs – bits of engine, scraps of wing, a battered wireless set which might just be able to be mended.

The other aircraft were taken to a big hangar, where repairs and maintenance were carried out, and there they might be partially dismantled. That was when a gun might be removed and put on a bench, out of the way, while the work was being done. Desmond had seen several.

'You mean they just let you wander in and out whenever you like?'

Desmond nodded. 'If we're in uniform we can go in any time. I talk to them. I like looking at the Tiger Moth. They know me.'

Micky could believe that. Desmond would talk to anyone, especially if he could talk about aeroplanes. People were often surprised at how much he knew, yet it was quickly obvious that there were strange, huge gaps in his knowledge and that his actual understanding was very limited. Micky could imagine him wandering in and out of the hangars and maintenance sheds, tolerated by the men working there because they knew that he could never be any threat.

'So you could get a gun,' he said.

Desmond looked uneasy. 'They'd see me. They wouldn't let me.'

'Anyway, how'd he get it out?' Jimmy Cross demanded. 'He'd never get it past the guards. You know their orders – shoot first and ask questions after.'

'Don't want to be shot,' Desmond said, looking frightened.

'You're not going to be.' Micky frowned heavily. 'This is something that's got to be properly planned. We'll have to go in during the night.'

'Don't be daft,' Jimmy said, 'they'd never let you in then. I bet they wouldn't even let Des in. They know the ATC don't go there night-times.'

'There's a way through the fence,' Desmond said suddenly. 'By the graveyard. Nobody else knows it. It's my secret way.' He looked pleased and crafty. 'I could show you. We could go in and I could show you the Tiger Moth.'

'Never mind the Tiger Moth,' Micky said, but his eyes were gleaming. He looked at Desmond speculatively, wondering just how much of what the bigger boy said was true. Last week, Desmond had seen a lion walking down Copnor Road, large as life. He had been present when a barrage balloon collapsed on a house at the end of Tokyo Street. He had helped put out the fire when the Guildhall had been bombed last year. He had jumped from a ferryboat and saved a woman from drowning.

Only one of those incidents – the one with the barrage balloon – had actually happened, though he might have been near the Guildhall during the blitz. But you never knew when he was telling the truth or when he simply thought he was. Lions and acts of bravery on the ferry could be dismissed. But a way into Airspeed? An aeroplane graveyard, where you could pick up real souvenirs? A hangar full of aeroplanes, with machine-guns left lying about on benches?

'Show me,' Micky said decisively. 'Show me where it is.'

The secret army was becoming a real possibility.

Shocked by the damage and the depression they found in London, Carol and Roddy had got on the train again. This time they'd gone to Bournemouth.

'It's a seaside place, there's bound to be lots of cheap places to stay,' Carol said. 'And it hasn't been bombed like London and Pompey. It was horrible up there, wasn't it?'

'Och, it was miserable,' Roddy agreed. 'All those bomb sites. And folk trying to be cheerful but you could see they were feeling awful underneath.

And all crowding into the Underground stations at night, like rats in a hole . . .' He shuddered. 'I cannae stand being in places like that, Carol. It gives me the creeps.'

It wasn't as easy as Carol had expected to find somewhere to live; all the rooms seemed to be taken by soldiers and airmen for their wives to stay in. But at last they found a small backstreet boarding house and asked for a room, telling the thin-faced landlady they'd just got married. She looked at them sceptically but showed them up to a room which looked out on the tiny backyard. There was a small air-raid shelter there, built against the garden wall, and a clothes-line. A weary-looking shrub wilted sadly in an old, broken chimneypot.

Carol and Roddy looked at the room. There was dull green linoleum on the floor and one armchair, covered with worn American cloth. The double bed was iron and pushed into a corner to make enough room. A small kitchen table served as a washstand, and there was a chest of drawers and a cupboard built into the fireplace alcove. The fireplace itself had been removed and a small gas fire put in its place.

'Ten bob a week, with breakfast,' the woman said. 'You'll 'ave to find yer other meals yerselves, but no cookin' up 'ere, mind, I couldn't be responsible. The gas fire's on a meter, shillin' in the slot.'

Ten shillings a week. They could afford that, for a while anyway, till they both got jobs. Carol nodded.

'Do you get many air-raids?'

The woman shrugged. 'We gets a few. Mostly lookin' for the aeroplane factory at Christchurch. There's bin a few bombs.' She looked at them shiftily. 'The shelter's a shillin' a night extra, else you'll 'ave to go to the public.'

She took them downstairs and showed them the lavatory, outside the back door. Carol peered inside the shelter and wrinkled her nose.

'It smells as if something's died in there,' she told Roddy when they were back in the room. 'I wouldn't want to spend the night in it even if it was free.'

'Old skinflint,' Roddy said. 'She'd charge for the air we breathed if she could measure it.' He looked dispiritedly at the little room. 'It's no' the sort of place I wanted to bring you to, Carrie.'

'It doesn't matter.' She hugged him. 'It's our room – our private room. We can do just as we like in here, and nobody to interfere—' She stopped abruptly as the door opened without warning and their landlady came in, staring at the two standing there in each other's arms. They stepped apart quickly, blushing.

'I 'ope everythin's above board with you two,' Mrs Higgs said suspiciously. 'You sure you're married? You look too young to me. This 'as always bin a respectable place, I don't want nothing going on as shouldn't.'

'We told you, we've been married a month,' Carol said coldly. 'Plenty of people are getting married young these days. There's a war on.'

The landlady's sallow face flushed a dull, ugly red. 'And there's no call to be impertinent, miss. Or Mrs, if that's what you call yourself.' She looked pointedly at the ring on Carol's finger. 'Looks more like a curtain ring out o' Woolworths than a proper wedding ring. Still, if that's what you say . . . so long as you pays yer rent on time.' She stood with her hands on her bony hips. 'I come up to tell you about the bath. It's Friday nights, I 'as first turn, and you'll 'ave to 'elp fill it and empty it out after. An' it's an extra shillin' each.'

'A shilling *each*?' Carol said. 'All sharing the same water?'

'Take it or leave it,' Mrs Higgs said, turning to leave the room. 'I'll want 'elp whether you 'as a bath or not, can't manage it on me own. Oh—' She turned to Roddy '—an' you can make it yer business to keep me coal scuttle filled too. It's too 'eavy for me to lift.' Her small, muddy eyes dared him to object. 'My last lodger did it without a murmur. Lovely feller, 'e was. Got called up for the Army. I daresay you'll be goin' off soon too.'

'I've been turned down,' Roddy said, his voice trembling slightly. 'I won't be called up.'

'Turned down? Why? You look all right to me.'

'Flat feet,' Roddy answered, at the same moment as Carol said, 'Short sight.'

There was a long pause as they all looked at each other. Then Carol said, trying to make her voice sound convincing, 'Roddy's got flat feet *and* bad eyesight. That's why they won't have him. But he's really clever. He'll get a good job.'

'Hm,' Mrs Higgs said. She gave them another hard, suspicious stare and turned away, closing the door behind her. They heard her go down the stairs and Roddy sat down heavily on the bed.

'She doesnae believe us. She doesnae believe a word of it.'

'It doesn't matter,' Carol said. She went over to the door and pushed the bolt across, then came back to the bed and sat down beside him. 'It doesn't matter what she thinks. This is our room, our own private room, and we won't let her spoil it. Anyway, I feel just as much married as if we'd been in a church, don't you?' She pulled him close and kissed him. 'I'm your wife, Roderick MacPherson, whatever anyone else thinks, and I love you.'

They lay back on the bed together and, slowly, Roddy relaxed. Carol felt his body tighten against her, felt the hardness and the vigour in him and responded with her own softness. Their passion flared, and they forgot Mrs Higgs and the unlovely room with its cold linoleum and lumpy bed as they swept together into the new world they had discovered, their private world of delight that took them yet again to their own particular mountain peak.

The bed shifted and creaked beneath them. And as they reached the topmost pinnacle, they heard an echoing rhythm from below.

Mrs Higgs was thumping on the ceiling.

Gerald had succeeded in getting Jonas to start the tractor, and he and Erica began on the ploughing. Gerald sat in the seat, steering with his good arm, while Erica rode on the mudguard beside him operating the levers that worked the plough. They finished the first field at sundown and after the tractor had been put away they walked back so that they could admire their work.

'It looks beautiful,' Erica said, letting her gaze run down the rich dark earth of the newly turned furrows. 'Like dark brown corduroy. It's really satisfying to think we've done all that.'

'It'll be just as satisfying when we've sown the corn,' Gerald said, leaning over the gate. 'And when we first see it coming through like tiny green needles, and then when it's standing ripe and golden, waiting to be harvested . . . That's what's so good about farming. You get so much satisfaction out of it – when it all goes right.' He grinned. 'It doesn't always, of course. The weather's wrong or you get pests or blight – there's always something to grumble about. Probably that's why Jonas is the way he is.'

'Your dad's not, though. He generally manages to look on the bright side.'

'Well, there are always two sides to look at, aren't there,' Gerald said thoughtfully. 'For a farmer, especially. I mean, in one field the weather's just right because you need a good downpour of rain, and in the next it's all wrong because you need sunshine and dry. You can choose whether to be pleased or fed up. The thing is to have as many different things on the go as you can, so there's always something to be pleased about.'

'Or grumble at,' Erica said, and he laughed.

'Well, that just depends on the sort of person you are.' He glanced at the girl beside him. 'You seem to take the rough with the smooth pretty well, Erica. I know you've had some pretty hard knocks but you keep smiling just the same.'

'I didn't to start with,' she said. 'I was really bitter. I took it out on everyone – specially Dennis.'

Gerald nodded. He had met Dennis several times, when the young Quaker had come out to the farm to see Betty and give a hand around the farm. Gerald didn't agree with either his politics or his religion, but he admired Dennis's courage.

'It must have been hard for you to understand, when your own fiancé had just been – well—'

'Oh, even before Geoff was killed,' Erica said, surprised that her voice could remain steady while she spoke of him. 'I took against him the minute I saw him. It was as if I knew there was something . . . But you know, I had to work really hard not to like him! Daft, isn't it?'

'I don't think it was daft,' Gerald said gently. 'I don't think you could do anything that was daft.'

There was a brief silence. Erica was still staring at the ploughed furrows. She felt her cheeks grow warm and her heart begin to race. Then, slowly, she turned her head towards him.

Gerald was watching her. His eyes were quite dark. She met their gaze and felt her lips tremble and part.

'Gerald – I—'

'Don't say anything, Erica,' he said quietly. 'Let's just be here together. Just for a few minutes.'

'But—'

'Look,' he said, 'I know I can't be anything to you. You had this marvellous chap you were engaged to, and you wouldn't look twice at a bloke like me – a farmer's son. And I'll be going away again soon, so I won't be around to cause you any trouble – any embarrassment or anything. But – just let me have this, would you? Please? Just a few minutes with you now and then, not talking, not doing anything, just being *with* you. That's all I'm asking.'

Erica gazed at him. He looked much fitter than when he had first come home. His thin body had filled out with muscle and his mother's feeding. His cheeks were no longer gaunt and a dirty yellow, but firm and slightly tanned. He was even beginning, very cautiously, to use his injured arm again.

'Gerald—'

'I've upset you,' he said contritely. 'Oh, blast it. I'm sorry, Erica. I shouldn't have said anything. Now you're fed up – you won't want anything more to do with me.' He straightened up and half turned away. 'Forget I said it, will you? I didn't want to put my foot in it.'

'No. Gerald, don't go—' Impulsively, she put out her hand and touched his arm. 'It's all right,' she said earnestly. 'I don't mind what you said, I don't mind it at all. I – I'm *glad* you said it. I – I like being with you, too.'

Gerald paused. He turned back to face her. The sun was disappearing now, leaving them in dusky twilight. His dark eyes searched her face.

'You don't have to say that, Erica.'

'I'm not just saying it.' She laughed shakily. 'It's true. I like being with you. I feel – sort of comfortable. As if we've known each other a long time.' She shook her head and laughed again. 'Doesn't make sense, does it?'

'Doesn't it?' Gerald asked. 'I think it does. I think it makes a lot of sense.' He moved closer and reached out with his good hand, laying it around her shoulders. 'I feel I've known you all my life, Erica. I feel I've been looking for you for years. It was like a miracle, that first time I saw you. As if a dream had come to life. I couldn't believe it. And all this time—'

'I know,' she said quietly, and moved into his embrace.

Their kiss was tremulous, like the first kiss of a boy and girl experimenting newly with love. Their lips brushed tentatively, parted and then brushed again. Then Gerald gathered her closely against him and his mouth became firmer, and Erica parted her lips for him and closed her eyes.

'Oh, my darling,' he murmured at last. 'My darling, I love you.'

Erica rested her head on his chest. Her thoughts and emotions fluttered together like butterflies, bright and uncatchable. But there was a dark one, too, a shadowy moth that hovered at the edge of the glowing light.

'I didn't think I'd love anyone again after I lost Geoff,' she said at last. 'I never even wanted to. I thought it would be disloyal. But now I feel – I don't know what I feel. Sort of guilty because I don't feel guilty, if you can understand.'

'I can understand. But it's not disloyal. You've got your whole lifetime to live. He wouldn't want you to go on by yourself, never loving anyone. Not if he really cared about you.'

'He did! We cared about each other.' She lifted her face. 'I still do love him, Gerald. But I love you as well.'

'Then that's all right,' he said. 'So long as it's me you marry and live with, and not a ghost.'

Erica gasped. 'Is that a proposal?'

'Well,' he said, 'it certainly sounded like one. Mind you, I didn't plan it. I wasn't going to say anything at all – didn't think there was a chance. But since the subject's come up – well, what d'you think? Could you bear to marry me?'

'It's so quick,' she said, half bemused.

'No quicker than a lot of other people. We don't know how much time we've got these days.'

'But you'll be going back soon – how can we possibly—'

'We'll apply for a licence straight away,' he said. 'I reckon I'm good for another month. We can just fit in a week's honeymoon. Or maybe we can get a special licence. I'll see about it first thing in the morning.'

'You can't. We've got two more fields to plough.'

'Bugger the fields,' he said, and caught her against him again. 'Us getting married's more important than a few fields. We'll let Jonas do them. Then everyone'll be pleased!'

They kissed again, this time with more confidence.

'Just a minute,' Erica said breathlessly, disengaging herself. 'You're forgetting something. I haven't said yes yet.'

'No more you have. And I don't reckon much to that for a proposal anyway.' Dramatically, he went down on one knee, laid his good hand over his heart and held out his other arm, still wrapped in its sling. 'Darling Erica, I love you with all my heart.' His voice had started out as if he were on stage, but as he spoke the words it shook and then became serious, almost imploring. 'Will you – will you *please* – be my wife?'

Erica looked down. His face, upturned, looked suddenly vulnerable. She thought of him going away again, back to the Africa desert. She thought of Geoff, riding the sky to his death.

'Oh, Gerald,' she said, her voice full of tears, 'of course I will.' And she lifted him so that he was standing once again, and put her arms around him to hold him closely against her heart. 'Of *course* I will.'

The moon was at three-quarters, showing a dim light through a haze of cloud on the night Micky and Desmond made their way to the airfield. They had been there twice before and Desmond had shown him the gap in the fence.

It was right on the outer perimeter of the field. You weren't even supposed to go this near without a permit, but there were places where the ground was wild and broken, and you could sneak between the hedges and gorse to the high wire fence. Even then, it looked insurmountable, with several strands of barbed wire stretched at an angle on top of the thick mesh. But to Micky's surprise, he saw that Desmond was right. There was a small place, surrounded by dense, prickly bushes, where the fence had been dragged loose and then roughly replaced. You could pull it up and wriggle underneath.

'Coo-er,' he breathed. 'That's smashing. Did you make it, Des?'

Desmond tilted his head and looked sideways. 'Might have.'

'You're not so daft as you look, sometimes,' Micky said. 'I bet you did, didn't you?'

Desmond looked sly but wouldn't answer. He scraped grass and earth away from the bottom of the fence and bent up the mesh. The gap underneath was just big enough.

'You go first,' he said, but Micky shook his head.

'I want to see how the land lays first. Reconnoitre. It ain't no good rushin' in and gettin' caught first time.'

By now, he had a very good idea of how the factory operated at night and had seen that the guard on the planes was minimal. So long as no unauthorised person came in through the gates, the whole area was deemed sufficiently protected. There were a couple of guards who walked round at night, but it was a good half-hour between each patrol.

The aircraft were on the tarmac ready to be transported to RAF airfields. Sometimes there were none, sometimes there was a whole new batch. That was the time, Micky decided, when he and Desmond should make their raid.

He looked at the gap under the fence, slightly nervous now that the moment had come. He knew that if they were found within the airfield they would be in serious trouble. But the thought of actually being in there – of being able to get near the planes themselves – was too tempting to resist. If he could just get hold of a gun . . .

He lay down and squirmed underneath the wire. Then he held it up so that Desmond could follow him.

Very, very cautiously, still flat on their stomachs, the two of them wriggled through the tussocks of last year's long grass. It seemed a long way, but at last they reached the edge of the apron, and looked out over a wide expanse of tarmac.

The planes were there. A row of them, lined up outside the big, camouflaged hangars. They looked bigger than Micky had expected, like huge, resting birds in the silvery light, and he gazed at them in awe.

'Coo,' he breathed, 'don't they look smashing. I wish I could fly in one.'

They wriggled closer. The guard had walked past five minutes earlier and wouldn't be back for at least another twenty. Sometimes he stopped and had a smoke down at the far end. But you never knew who might be looking out from the buildings, and to get from the grass to the planes they'd have to run across the tarmac, in plain view of anyone watching.

'I don't reckon there's anyone else about,' Micky muttered, more to himself than Desmond. 'When I give the word, we make for the nearest plane, all right? Get right underneath it, so you're in its shadow, and stand still.'

He made sure that Desmond understood, then took one last, careful look around the airfield. It was silent. There was no one in sight. The guard was far away, down at the other end, probably having his cigarette.

'Go,' Micky breathed, and the two boys ran, half crouching, towards the shadow of the nearest aircraft.

Nobody shouted. Nobody ran. Nobody fired at them. They stood in the darkness, panting slightly, half scared by their own daring.

Desmond put up his hand and touched the belly of the aeroplane. 'It's big.'

'Yeah.' Micky craned his neck to stare up at it. He had never been so close to an aircraft before. 'I wonder if you can get inside. You'd have to climb up on the wing. I've seen 'em do it at the pictures.' He thought quickly. 'You stay here and keep a good look-out, tell me if anyone comes.'

Feeling very exposed, he scrambled up on to the wing and felt around the hood of the cockpit. He knew it would slide open, but could not find a catch. A sudden sound made him jump, and he cast a scared glance over his shoulder, but it was only the cry of an animal somewhere in the tangled undergrowth outside the perimeter fence. His fingers shook as he fumbled with the hood. If he couldn't even get *into* the blasted thing . . .

There was a click and the hood gave beneath his fingers. With a surge of triumph, he pushed it back and wriggled inside.

It was astonishingly small. There was just room for the pilot to sit, no more than that. In front of the seat was an array of switches, lights and dials. There was a wireless set, with earphones, and there was a gun, mounted on a turret.

Micky's heart gave a great leap. A wireless and a gun! That would make his army something to be reckoned with. And the RAF would never miss them. There must be heaps more in the stores. It would be far more use for him to have them.

The wireless set came out with a few tugs, leaving wires dangling from the gap where it had been fitted, but the gun was screwed in place. He leaned out of the cockpit and called softly to Desmond.

'I'm going to pass the wireless down to you. Is there anyone around?' He stepped out on to the wing and leaned over. The wireless was heavier than he'd expected and he almost dropped it before Desmond crept out from the shadows and stared up at him, eyes gleaming in the darkness.

'Coo,' Desmond said with awe, 'that's a wireless set.'

'I know that. Take it and get back under the plane.' The moonlight was brighter now and Micky felt as if he were standing in full sunlight, with the eyes of the whole of Portsmouth on him. His hands shook as he handed the heavy wireless to Desmond. 'Don't drop it.'

Desmond disappeared into the shadows. Micky looked after him, longing to jump down into safety, but he couldn't bear to leave without the gun. He turned back and fiddled again with the frame, his fingers trembling.

It was no use. The mounting was firmly fixed in place and refused to budge. And time was running short. Whoever was on patrol would be coming back this way soon, and they'd be sure to look specially at the aeroplanes.

The tarmac was a pool of darkness, lit by the uncertain half-light of the moon, but it was clear enough to see the deeper shadows around the grassy edges. Micky stared into the darkness, wondering if that was a movement he had seen, not too far away. The guard must be on his way back. The question was, how close had he got?

Feeling a sudden panic shake his legs, he scrambled down the wing and half fell under the plane. Desmond was still crouching there, the wireless in his arms.

'That erk must be coming back. You sure no one's seen us?'

Desmond shook his head. He was used to the concept of hide-and-seek. He sniggered, his voice loud in the silence. 'Coming, ready or not!'

'Shut up, you twerp. You want to get us caught?' Micky peered out. The sound of distant footfalls was little more than a disturbance of the air, but he dragged Desmond closer into the shadow. 'We'd better lay low till he's gone past again.'

The waiting seemed endless. They could hear the footsteps clearly now, coming closer. Micky's heart felt as if it were right in his throat, almost choking him. Would the guard look at all the planes? Would he look underneath? Thankful for the blackout, Micky knew that at least he wouldn't be shining any lights. As long as they stayed absolutely quiet in deep shadow, they ought to be safe.

He hoped that Desmond wouldn't do anything stupid. You could never be sure, with Desmond. He was quite capable of forgetting the danger of their position and making some daft noise, or start giggling and larking about. And if he thought the erk was a friend of his – one of the blokes he'd talked to in the hangars . . .

For the first time, Micky considered the consequences of being caught. It would mean prison, at the very least. Maybe even being shot, or hanged, for treason. Nobody would ever believe he was getting together his own army, to fight the Germans. By the time the guard had passed them, without so much as a glance underneath the aircraft, he was almost sick with fright.

The footsteps died away. Desmond drew in a breath, as if to speak, and Micky trod heavily on his foot.

'Shut up. He might still be able to hear us.' He listened. The airfield was silent again. 'Right, we got to get in the hangars, where you seen the planes and stuff. Where's the door?'

Desmond pointed towards the great sheds looming at the edge of the airfield. 'They got big doors. Where the planes go in and out.'

'I know that! But they must have small doors too – they don't open them big ones every time a bloke wants to go for a pee, do they? How d'you get in when you goes there?'

'There's a door in the side.'

'Bet it's locked,' Micky said, following the bigger boy cautiously across the open space, but when they finally reached the shadow of the building and he tried the handle, it gave under his touch. His heart leapt and he pushed the door open and slid inside.

For a few seconds, he stood quite still, gazing about him. The hangar was almost pitch black, but moonlight sloped in through a few gaps in the walls and the high roof. He could see the denser shapes of the aeroplanes, crouching like huge bats in the corners. When he flashed his torch, they shone in the thin light and threw weird, distorted shadows over the empty space.

'I don't like it,' Desmond said. 'Put the lights on.'

'Don't be daft!' Micky's voice was sharp as he fought down his own panic. He wasn't at all sure that all those queer shapes were planes . . .

'You'll get us caught. And don't make a noise. We got to keep quiet, see, like commandos. Where's these planes they're mending?'

'Over there.' Desmond pointed the torch towards a far corner. An aircraft stood half dismantled, with bits and pieces littered around it. Nearby was a wide bench, spread with tools, and as they approached it Micky gave a yelp of excitement.

'A gun! A proper gun! Look – it's just standin' on the bench, for anyone to pick up.'

He reached out and touched the weapon. It was smaller than he had imagined, its barrel not much more than eight inches long, but it was heavy for its size and felt solid in his hands. He put the rest against his shoulder and pretended to aim. 'D'you reckon it's loaded now?'

Desmond shook his head. He had never used any of the guns, only knew their shapes and sizes as he knew the shapes and sizes of aeroplanes and cars and other things that excited his mind. He knew that guns were dangerous, however, and backed away as Micky swung the heavy weapon around.

'You should never point a gun at anyone,' he said in the flat voice he used when reciting facts, or someone else's words. 'It might go off.'

Micky grinned. 'That's the idea, innit?' But he laid the gun down again and looked along the bench. 'Anything else worth pinchin'?'

There were no other guns, nor any ammunition. Micky slipped a few tools into his pockets. The light of the torch began to waver.

'We better get goin'.' He picked up the weapon and stuck it into the front of his jacket, hoping it wasn't loaded. But they wouldn't leave them standing on the benches with bullets in them. 'I'll carry this. You take the wireless.'

He followed Desmond to the small door and they opened it and peered out cautiously. Micky felt his nervousness return. If they were caught now, they'd be for the real high jump. And he had no idea when the patrol would come round again.

'Listen. When I say go, you get over to the fence as quick as you can. We got to get out of here fast.'

'Shall I take the wireless?'

'Of course you take the flippin' wireless! What d'you think we come here for?' Micky listened again. 'Right. *Go.*'

The two boys ran for the fence. There was a moment's panic as they searched for the gap, and then they were flat on their stomachs, wriggling through. Micky felt his jacket catch on the wire and pulled sharply, hearing the material tear. It didn't matter. He was out. He was safe.

'We still got to be quiet,' he said to Desmond. 'We got to stay quiet all the way home. An' we'll go a different way, a long way round, just in case there's anyone followin' us.'

By the time they finally reached home, their arms were aching from their burdens. He shifted the gun carefully, still not sure if it was loaded.

'Shall I take the wireless home with me?' Desmond asked. He was cradling it in his arms like a baby.

'No. I'm keepin' all the stuff. I got a special place for it.' Micky didn't want to risk leaving such valuable possessions in the den, where anyone might find them. He had prised up a couple of floorboards in his bedroom. There was plenty of room there, on the ceiling joists of the room below. 'You can put it down the bottom of our garden. I'll put the gun away first and then fetch it.'

Desmond looked regretful as he pushed the wireless set under a bush, but Micky gave him a friendly pat on the shoulder.

'You're a good soldier, Des. You're my best lieutenant. Tell you what, this is our secret, OK? We won't tell any of the others about it. It's just between the two of us.'

Desmond gave him a wide grin. Then he loped away up the alley, on his way home. Micky wondered how he would explain his absence. But perhaps, being Desmond, he wouldn't need to. His mum must be used to him doing queer things. She wouldn't think anything of it.

Micky hid the gun under the bush with the wireless. Then he went down into the Anderson shelter and curled up on the old mattress they kept down there. Mum would be out and Gran fast asleep in bed. If they wondered where Micky was, they'd just think he was in the tunnel shelters.

He imagined going out to Southsea beach when the Germans invaded, shooting them down with his gun. Using the wireless set to relay orders to his troops. Getting a boat to take him to France, right into the heart of enemy territory.

I might even learn to fly a plane, he thought, remembering the aircraft lined up on the tarmac, ready to be flown away. That'd be better than any old boat. It can't be that hard.

Micky Baxter, world hero. Micky Baxter, air ace. Micky Baxter, *VC*.

15

'When's that *husband* of yours going to get a job?' Mrs Higgs asked, heavily emphasising the word husband, as she always did. She still doesn't believe we're married, Carol thought. Nosy old bat.

'He's been trying,' she said defensively. 'We've both been trying.' It had come as a shock to them both to find that jobs were not as easy to find as they had expected. People wanted to know so much about you. Who you were, where you came from, where you lived. When you were likely to be called up. And Roddy's excuse for not being in the Forces – that he was exempted on the grounds of being unfit – couldn't be used, not when he was looking for work.

'Well, I'd better get a job, then,' Carol had said at last, and they started to look in the local evening paper for jobs a sixteen-year-old girl could do. Serving in a shop, waiting in a restaurant, cleaning in one of Bourne-mouth's hotels. But women – especially young ones – weren't paid as much as men, and the sort of jobs Carol could do paid very little. Certainly not enough to keep two. And no sooner had she started to look than she began to feel ill, and they had a new worry.

'It must be a bilious attack,' she said to Roddy. 'I feel awful.'

He sat on the bed, holding her hand anxiously. She had been sick three times already that morning, running downstairs to the outside lavatory, and the third time she'd only just made it. Roddy had asked Mrs Higgs for a bucket, which she'd handed over with ill grace and a suspicious look, and he'd half expected her to charge extra for it. He brought it upstairs to find Carol back in bed, her face a pale greenish colour.

'It must be something you've eaten,' he said. 'D'you think it was those fish and chips?'

Carol shuddered. 'Don't talk about food. It makes me feel worse. Anyway, I was the same yesterday morning.'

'Well, we had fish and chips the night before too—' he began, but she turned her face away.

'We have them all the time. I'm sick of fish and chips. Ugh!' As if the word itself were enough, she sat up quickly and reached for the bucket. 'Roddy—'

He sat with his arm around her shoulders as she retched. He felt helpless. He had never had to offer comfort to anyone before, had always had it offered to him when he needed it. He wondered if Carol could be really ill, and remembered the time when one of his cousins had had appendicitis and had to be rushed into hospital. Suppose that was what was wrong with Carol?

Carol lay down again. She had brought up nothing but yellow bile but the effort had exhausted her. She groaned and looked up at him miserably.

'I feel as if I'm going to die.'

'No!' he said, panic sharpening his voice. 'No, you're not. You can't. It's just a bilious attack. The fish was off. I thought it tasted a bit funny myself.'

'So why aren't you ill too? Anyway, I was just as bad yesterday, you know I was. And the day before. There's something wrong with me, Roddy, something awful.'

'No,' he said again. 'You were all right in the afternoon. And it was the same the day before, you were only ill in the morning. It must be the fish.'

Carol closed her eyes, as if she hadn't the strength any more to hold the lids open. Roddy sat staring anxiously at her ashen face. He wanted very much to believe it was the fish. He could not even begin to think that it might be something else. He did not know what you did if someone were really ill; in his family, no one ever had been, apart from the cousin, and he hadn't heard about that until it was all over. He wished his mother were here, but his mother was far away in Scotland and did not even know where he was. Since he and Carol had run away, he hadn't written to her for fear of being caught.

'Are you feeling better now?' he asked carefully.

Carol moved her head, very slightly. It could have meant yes or no.

'I'll go and get a doctor if you want one,' Roddy offered, with no idea as to how he should do this. 'Mrs Higgs will know where the surgery is.'

'I don't want her in here. I don't want her knowing I'm ill.'

'But she already does. I had to ask her for the bucket.'

'I don't want her,' Carol said again, wearily.

Roddy didn't want Mrs Higgs in the room either. She took every opportunity to worm her way in as it was, her sharp eyes going everywhere. But she was the only person they knew in Bournemouth, and surely she would help if she knew how ill Carol was.

'Do you still feel sick?' he asked, still not sure what Carol's reply had meant.

'Oh, don't keep talking about it,' Carol said snappily, and turned over on her side.

A faint irritation touched Roddy's helplessness. He had only been trying to help. He did not know what else he could do. He bit his lip and stared out through the grimy window.

'I suppose you're wishing we'd never come here,' Carol said, without opening her eyes.

It was so nearly what Roddy had been thinking that he blushed. 'No! I've never thought that. I love you, Carrie. I just wish you weren't ill. I wish—' He stopped, unable to say all the things he wished, unable even to think them out clearly in his own mind. 'I wish there wasnae a war on,' he said miserably.

'If there wasn't,' Carol said in a small voice, 'we'd never have met each other.' There was a short, unhappy silence and then she sat up and put her arms round his neck. 'I'm sorry, Roddy. I'm sorry I'm such a misery.'

'You're not a misery,' he said, holding her tightly. 'You cannae help being ill. I'm the one who should be sorry, bringing you here.' He looked around the small, mean room with its grimy walls and tattered curtains and the gas fire they couldn't afford to light. 'It's no' what I meant it to be like.'

They sat close together, holding each other, resting their heads each against the other's shoulder, neither of them quite sure whether they were giving comfort or drawing it. Outside, heavy clouds were darkening the April morning to a reminder of winter, and a thin wind whipped a spatter of rain against the streaky window. In the room below, they could hear their landlady clattering with a broom and bucket, and knew that she would soon be on the stairs, making it apparent that they would be better off out of the house.

'What are we going to do, Roddy?' Carol asked at last. 'What's going to happen to us?'

The same April rain was spitting in Jess's face as she pushed Maureen's pram down to North End. Maureen was really getting too big for the pram now, but she couldn't walk all the way there and back, neither could Jess have carried the day's shopping as well as hold her hand. She put up the hood and strapped the waterproof cover over Maureen's legs.

'Want to get out,' Maureen objected. 'Want to walk.'

'You can't. It's raining.'

'Want to walk,' Maureen persisted, turning red. 'Want to walk.'

'I said no.' Jess pushed her hair back under her rainhat. Maureen had been getting very argumentative lately. She also asked incessant questions, driving Rose mad, and although Jess said that the questions must be answered because that was how Maureen learned, even she found them wearisome. And some of them couldn't be answered. Jess doubted if anyone could explain to a two-year-old how the sun stayed up in the sky, or what the sky was made of. But it didn't stop Maureen asking.

Maureen pushed down the front of the cover and started to climb out. 'Walk.'

'You'll get wet.' Jess pushed her back. 'Stop it, Maureen. Do as you're told. We're going to see Granny and Grandpa and I want you to be good.'

Maureen glowered at her. 'I am good. Want to walk.'

Jess sighed. The child was quite right, in a way. There was nothing naughty in wanting to walk. And as a baby, her wants had been attended to at once, without argument. It was difficult for her to accept now that they couldn't be.

Still, she had to learn. Everyone had to learn.

Jess pushed the pram along the road, ignoring Maureen's protests. After a few moments, she scarcely heard them. Her mind was too full of worries about her parents.

Arthur had been growing even more absent-minded lately. He would get up in the morning and dress, then decide that it was evening, undress and go back to bed. Or he would forget that he had just eaten breakfast and demand another one. Sometimes he was so persistent that Mary gave in and sat him down in front of another plate of bread and margarine, but when he had wolfed that down he went no more than a quarter of an hour before asking again.

'He's had three lots this morning,' Mary told Jess when she arrived with Maureen still complaining over not being allowed to walk. 'It don't seem to make a bit of difference. He's still saying he's hungry. I don't see how he can be. It can't be good for him, surely.'

'There must be something wrong with his digestion,' Jess said, lifting Maureen out of the pram. 'It's like he's got worms or something.'

'But he really doesn't remember having any food.' Mary pushed back her wispy grey hair. 'He gobbles it down like he's starving, hasn't seen food for days.' Her lips trembled a little. 'I don't mind telling you, Jess, I'm at me wits' end. I mean, it's bad enough seeing him like it, but when he starts to say I'm trying to starve him – well, it makes me want to weep, it does really. When I think what he used to be like . . .'

'I know, Mum. It's awful.' Jess put her hand on her mother's arm. She would have liked to hug her, to hold her in her arms like a child, but they hadn't held each other for years. 'Where is he now?'

'Out in the back garden. He's digging a hole for an Anderson shelter.'

Jess stared at her. 'But you've already got an Anderson.'

'I know. He's digging right beside it. It's like he doesn't even know it's there.'

Her heart cold, Jess followed her mother through the house and into the long, narrow back garden. It had been dug for vegetables and Ted had been up a week or two ago and sown some seeds. But now the plot was a mess of tumbled earth, and the two women could see Arthur's thin, frail body standing in a rough pit, shovelling earth with all his strength.

'Dad!' Jess approached the edge of the pit. It was almost waist deep. 'What on earth are you doing that for?'

He barely glanced at her. 'I 'aven't got time to stop. There's raids coming. I got to do me bit.'

'But you've already got a shelter. You don't need another one.'

'Bombs. They'll be dropping bombs on us. You'll see. You better get home and dig yourself one.'

'We've got one too. Frank dug it at the beginning of the war. We've had it nearly three years.' Jess stared at him helplessly. 'Dad, you'll make yourself ill, working like that. You'll tire yourself out. Why not come in and have a nice cup of tea?'

'Cup of tea? Ah, that's what she says.' He jerked his head at Mary, who was standing back, trying to keep Maureen away from the pit. 'Keeps on telling me to stop and 'ave some tea, but she won't never give me none, oh no, rather see me starve to death than spare a cup of tea for a poor old man.' He glared up at them, then his glance moved past Jess to Maureen. ''Ere. Who's that kid?'

'It's Maureen, Dad. You know Maureen.'

'Maureen?' His eyes narrowed suspiciously. 'I don't know no Maureen. Tell 'er to get out. I don't want no kids in 'ere, spoilin' things.'

'Dad!' Jess felt close to tears. 'Dad, this is your own grand-daughter. Our little Maureen. You must know her.' She reached behind her and took the toddler's hand. 'Maureen, come and say hello to Grandpa.'

Maureen leaned dangerously over the hole, beaming. 'Hello, G'ndpa. You dug a big hole.'

He stared up at her. 'It's my hole. Go away.'

'Dad!'

Maureen reached out her arms. 'Lift me down,' she commanded.

Her grandfather backed away, clutching his shovel to his chest. 'Get 'er out. I told you, I don't want no kids in 'ere. Take 'er away.'

Maureen stared at him, baffled, then her face screwed up and she began to cry. Jess gathered her up in her arms and turned to her mother in distress.

'Mum—'

'Bring her indoors, love. It's the best thing. He doesn't mean anything. He doesn't know what he's saying.' Mary drew her back into the house and they stood inside the kitchen door, facing each other. 'You see? You see what I've got to put up with?'

'What is it?' Jess whispered. 'What's happening to him?'

'What do you think? It's nothing to do with his digestion, I'm sure of that. It's his mind that's going.' Mary sat down heavily in an old kitchen chair that Arthur had painted green a year or two ago. 'I don't know whether it's this war, or what it is, Jess, but I don't mind telling you it's got me worried stiff. I don't reckon he's ever going to be the same again.'

'Senile dementia,' Jess said later to Frank, after Rose had gone to bed. 'That's what she's afraid of. Oh Frank, it can't be that, can it? I mean, people do go a bit funny sometimes and then they're all right again. Like Ted. A sort of nervous breakdown. It could just be something like that, couldn't it?'

'I suppose it could.' Frank was fastening new heels to a pair of his old shoes. He had cut the shapes carefully from a sheet of rubber and now he was tapping in brads. 'But it don't sound too good to me. Anyway, look how long it took Ted to get better, and he's a lot younger man.'

'I know, but . . . senile dementia! It doesn't bear thinking of.' Jess wiped tears from her cheek with one hand. 'Poor little Maureen, she was really upset. And Mum's worn out with it all. I don't know how long she can go on managing. I mean, she's not that strong herself, and neither of them's getting any younger.'

'None of us are.' Frank finished the shoes and held them side by side, comparing the heels. 'Has she taken him to the doctor?'

'What's the point? They can't do anything, and she can't afford to spend money just to hear them tell her what she already knows.' Jess shook her head. 'It's so awful, seeing him like that. I mean, he used to be such a good father. And a lovely grandad. If you could have seen our Maureen's little face!'

'Better not take her down there any more.'

'But that means Mum won't see her either. And how can I go down, without Maureen? I'll have to leave her with Rose, and you know what she's been like lately.'

'Well, she'll just have to stop being like it,' he said sharply. 'She wants to be at home, she's got to help out. You've got enough to do without pandering to her whims and fancies.'

'Oh, you can't say she don't do anything, Frank. She's ever so good round the house, always ready to give me a hand and loves helping with the cooking. It's just the baby.'

'She liked looking after her all right before.'

'I know. But Maureen was just a baby then, you could pick her up and cuddle her and when you put her down you knew she'd stop there. It's different now, she's into everything. She opened that box Rose keeps her bits and pieces in the other day and upset it all over the floor. You can't blame Rose for getting fed up.'

'Well, she's got to learn. Babies aren't just dolls, to be played with just when you feel like it. You have to take responsibility for them.'

'I know. I tell her that. She says she will when she's got her own babies, but she's not responsible for Maureen.'

Frank put down the shoes. 'She'd better not say that when I'm around! Doesn't matter if it's her baby or not, we're family and families take responsibility for one another. And while she's under our roof and under our authority, she does as we tell her. Or maybe she thinks she's too old for that now she's nearly turned fifteen. They think too much of themselves these days, young girls.'

Jess was silent. She hadn't meant to make Frank angry. She'd come for comfort and support over her own parents. She thought of her father, coming in from the garden that afternoon, dirty and tired after his useless digging. He'd behaved quite normally then, telling her one of his Boer War stories, but all the time she'd been afraid he would turn on Maureen again, and she'd come away as soon as she could, and then felt guilty all the way home for having left her mother to cope.

It seemed all too easy to make Frank cross these days. It was the war, she knew. The constant strain, the work, the weariness. It was getting everyone down. Nobody talked about it much – there was no point, when everyone was in the same boat – but everyone was tired, tired of fear and grief, tired of hearing about death and killing, tired of the whole terrible shambles.

And there still seemed to be no end to it. After almost three long years, the tunnel was still as long, with not even the tiniest spot of light at its end.

She moved closer to Frank and he glanced at her and then put his arm around her shoulders and held her against him. She felt the steady warmth of his big body, like a rock that had been warmed by the sun.

'Don't say anything to Rose,' she said. 'It's as hard for her as it is for the rest of us. And she's growing up too, and there's nothing we can do about that, either.'

'I know.' He bent and gave her a kiss. 'It's all right, Jess. It's just – when I think of the boys, out there in the country, and young Colin's ship being sunk, and Olive working on ack-ack guns – well, I feel as if everything's slipping away from me. I feel frightened, Jess.'

She stared at him. Frank, frightened? She had never thought it possible, never dreamed she would hear him admit it. She bit her lip, trying to stem the tears that stung her eyes.

Frank, frightened. And yet . . . Somehow, it made her feel a bit better, knowing that. As if he was just a bit more like she was, sharing her fears and anxieties. As if it would help him to understand hers just a little bit better.

'I'm glad you don't have to go away,' she said, putting her arms round him. 'I'm glad we can be together.'

Micky Baxter was enjoying the war again. For a time, after Cyril Nash was killed and Jimmy lost his leg, he'd felt fed up with everything. It wasn't his fault that the explosion had happened, it was the Germans', but everyone seemed to blame him, somehow. He couldn't walk down the street without people looking at him as if he was a murderer. And he'd had a lot of bad dreams too, when it all seemed to happen all over again, and sometimes he was the one blown up, or buried under a pile of rubble and knowing no one would ever get him out. For a long time he hadn't wanted to go out much at all, especially at night.

Of course, he never let on that he felt like that. He'd always been the big, bold boy of April Grove, swaggering along as if he was cock of the walk, and he wasn't going to let that go. So he forced himself to go out and march up the street as if nothing had happened, and never let anyone see that he was really quaking inside.

But now he'd got his gang together again and started to dream of winning the war, instead of being buried or blown to pieces, he felt better. And he felt better when he pulled up the floorboard in his bedroom and gloated over his hoard.

As well as the wireless and gun he and Desmond had stolen, he had a small rifle he had filched from a sentry hut near the Lines when Desmond had distracted the soldier's attention one night, and a pistol that young Martin Baker had pinched from an uncle. There was also a hand grenade that someone had found in the street – whether it was still live or not, nobody was sure – and a rusty old bayonet that Wendy had brought in one evening, as proudly as if she were carrying the very latest in tommy-guns.

'It was my grandad's,' she said. 'I found it behind his chest of drawers. It must've been there ever since he got run over.'

Micky stared at it jealously and stretched out his hand, but Wendy snatched the weapon out of his reach.

'It's mine. It's for our army. I only brought it to show you our army's as good as yours.'

'You can't have a bayonet,' Micky said. 'Girls aren't allowed to carry weapons.'

'Nor are boys,' Wendy said smartly. 'Not when they're under sixteen. You're not even old enough to join the Home Guard.'

'I wouldn't want to,' Micky sneered. 'Lot of old men playin' about with broomsticks.'

'They've got proper weapons now,' Martin said. 'Guns and stuff, left over from the big war. I've seen 'em. My uncle's in it.'

Micky gazed at him thoughtfully. 'An' he's got proper weapons?'

Martin nodded. 'He's in charge of them. He's got the key.'

'You mean he can get into the place where they're kept?'

'Any time,' Martin said, a little boastfully.

'So you could too, couldn't you? You could get the key and get in and pinch whatever weapons they've got.'

Martin looked at him nervously. 'I dunno. I dunno where he keeps it.'

'But you could find out,' Micky said. 'You could watch him and find out.'

Martin glanced at Wendy. 'But I'm not in your army. I'm in Wendy's. You said.'

'I can change me mind, can't I?' Micky demanded. 'I can have Wendy in if I want to. And then I'll keep the bayonet and you can get some more weapons off your uncle.'

'I dunno. I mean, suppose we got caught? My uncle can't half hit hard.'

'Anyway, it's stealing,' Wendy said. 'I never stole the bayonet. It was my grandad's.'

'Look,' Micky stated, standing in front of them with his feet planted wide apart, 'this is a war, innit? That means we can do what we like to win it. An' if the Home Guard ain't using the stuff, we got a right to take it. It's our duty to take it, 'cause we're a proper army an' they're just old men.' He gave them a triumphant look. 'We all got to do whatever we can to win this war, an' we'll show 'em we ain't just kids. You get the key to that hut, Martin, an' we'll show 'em!'

By the second week, Carol's sickness was no better and both she and Roddy were beginning to feel frightened.

'It must be something terrible,' she said, lying back after a bout of retching. 'I've never been bad like this before.'

'We'll have to get a doctor,' he said, stroking her forehead. 'You're like this every morning right up till dinner-time. You're getting thinner all the time.'

'It's evenings too.' Her face was the dirty grey of Mrs Higgs' sheets. 'What is it, Roddy? What's the matter with me?'

'I dinnae ken,' he said helplessly. 'I've never known anyone sick like this, only my cousin Moira when she was expecting her Alistair, and—'

'Expecting?' The last shred of colour drained from Carol's face. 'You mean she was expecting a baby?'

'Well, he wasnae a haggis,' Roddy said with a weak attempt at humour. 'Though he looked pretty much like one, the first time I saw him, all puny and whey-faced, but they said there was something wrong with him, jaundice or the like, but he was better in a week or two right enough, and my cousin Moira—'

'Roddy, will you please shut up about your cousin Moira!' Carol struggled to sit up. 'You don't think that's what's the matter with me, do you? You don't think I could be – be expecting?' Her voice dropped to a whisper on the last word. 'Oh, Roddy . . .'

He stared at her. 'I've been careful every time. And we've been using the French letter—'

The first time they had made love, in Foster Gardens, it had taken them both by surprise and neither had known quite what was going to happen. After that, Roddy had asked one of his mates for advice and had pulled himself away from Carol at the crucial moment. But he hadn't been able to time it very well at first, so that sometimes he was too quick and sometimes too slow, and finally he had plucked up his courage and got a French letter from a barber. The rubber wasn't very thin, and neither of them liked it much, but it could be washed and used again and again.

'It doesn't always work, though, does it? If there's a tiny hole in it—'

'There cannae be,' he said. 'I look at it every time, to make sure.'

But Carol knew that Roddy's excitement sometimes overcame his caution. There had been times when he'd put it on almost too late, others when she'd been sure he'd taken it off too quickly.

She laid her hand flat on her stomach. There was no swelling there; she was hollow and empty.

'How soon does a baby start to grow?' she asked. 'How do you know when it'll be born?'

'Doesn't it take nine months?' Roddy said doubtfully. 'My cousin Moira—'

'I know it takes nine months. But nine months from when? How do you know when it started?'

He shrugged helplessly. 'I think the doctor tells you. We'll have to get a doctor, Carol. There'll be all kinds of things to arrange – a midwife, and napkins and a pram and—'

'Roddy, stop it!' The fear in Carol's voice and eyes shrilled into panic. 'I can't have a baby! I can't. How would we manage? What would we do? We're not even married.'

'Carrie, ssh—' Roddy cast a fearful glance towards the door. More than once, they had heard shuffling sounds on the landing and caught Mrs Higgs slinking down the stairs. After the first time, they had never spoken in the room unless it were in a whisper. But this time, their fears had driven all other considerations from their minds.

Roddy's caution was just too late. The door was flung open and their landlady stood there in her grubby flowered apron, arms akimbo, glaring at them triumphantly.

'I thought as much! I knew it, the minute I set eyes on you. There's something shifty about that young man, I said to meself, and that girl's nothing but a trollop. I'd lay a sack of gold they're not wed.' She advanced into the room, pointing her finger at them accusingly. 'You're nothing but a pair of liars, and shirkers too – all this talk about finding jobs, you've no more intention of working than flying to the moon. Parasites, that's what you are, and now you're in the family way and you'll be sucking even more blood out of your country in its hour of need.'

'I'm not,' Carol began desperately. 'I mean, we won't, we want to work, we—' A wave of nausea overcame her and she lay down, and then sat up again quickly and reached for the bucket. Mrs Higgs watched as she retched and heaved over it, with Roddy holding her shoulders, and when Carol had finished and lay back again she curled her lip.

'So you're not in the family way,' she said sardonically. 'Tell me that again when you've got a belly full of arms and legs. You won't be able to hide it when you're walking about like a barrage balloon.'

Carol was too exhausted to argue. Roddy looked at the landlady. Her face was grim, but she was the only possible source of help they had. He said, 'What can we do, Mrs Higgs? Shouldn't we get a doctor?'

'A doctor!' The woman gave an ugly cackle. 'It's not a doctor you oughter be looking for. There's other people can give you the sort of help you need.'

'What d'you mean? What sort of help?'

'Well, you can't tell me you want a brat round your necks,' she said witheringly. 'Couple of kids like you, and living in sin. On the run too, I wouldn't be surprised,' she added, looking at Roddy.

Roddy flushed scarlet and cursed himself as he saw the gleam of triumph in her eyes. They had been so careful not to confirm her suspicions and now he had handed her their guilt on a plate. 'I'm not, not at all,' he said quickly, but he knew it was too late. Mrs Higgs' face had settled into satisfied creases, and she was almost smiling. It was not a nice smile.

'I might be able to help you,' she said unexpectedly. 'I know one or two people. They charge, mind. And I'd need a bit for letting you know their names. It's a risky business and I wouldn't want to see my friends in trouble.'

Roddy and Carol stared at her blankly. Carol had no idea at all what she meant, and Roddy had only a glimmer, gleaned from half-heard stories some of the older sailors had told, and sniggering jokes. There was a song someone had sung once in connection with such jokes, and it came into his mind now.

> 'My uncle's a Harley Street surgeon,
> He uses a knife long and thin.
> He only does one operation
> And oh, how the money rolls in.'

'We're not doing anything illegal,' he said sharply, and laid his hand protectively on Carol's shoulder. 'Naebody's going to do anything to my Carrie.'

Mrs Higgs sneered again. 'Maybe you won't be so high and mighty when she's starting to show and folk start asking questions. It's not so easy having a bastard. But it won't be any good coming to me then, it'll be too late.'

'I don't care,' Roddy said firmly. 'It's dangerous. There was a girl in our street . . . She died.'

Carol gasped and caught at his hand. 'Roddy – you won't let them—'

'Naebody's going to hurt you, Carrie,' he said. 'Not while I'm around to take care of you. Aye, and the bairn too, if there is one.'

'Oh, there's a brat all right,' Mrs Higgs said. 'No doubt about that.' Her small eyes gleamed as she stared at them. 'Well, so what are you going to do?'

'What do you think?' Roddy returned. Before he had known the truth, he'd felt helpless and lost. Now that Mrs Higgs had confirmed their suspicions – and he had no doubt that she was right – he felt suddenly older, more in charge. The thought of becoming a father was both terrifying and uplifting. And it was up to him to take care of the mother of his child. 'We'll go to the doctor and ask him what we should do.'

Mrs Higgs scowled. She did not want Roddy or Carol to make contact with officialdom. Once they did that, questions would be asked – who they were, where they came from, why they had run away – and Mrs Higgs had a fair idea what the answers might be. There would be trouble, she was certain of that – trouble for Roddy as a deserter, trouble because of Carol's age, and – worst of all – trouble for Mrs Higgs for sheltering them. There would be reports in the newspapers, who loved a scandal like this, and her name would be spread all over Bournemouth. The police might even take it into their heads to look a little more closely into certain other matters she'd been at some pains to conceal from them.

'There's no need to do that yet,' she said in a conciliatory tone. 'Only cost you money, that will, and there's nothing he can tell you that I can't. 'Ad four of me own, I 'ave, not that there's one of 'em bothers to come and see me or give me an 'and now, but that's kids for you . . . Anyway, we'll just keep it quiet between ourselves for now, if that's what you want, and then if you changes yer minds about getting rid of it, you can just let me know, see? Only like I say, you'll 'ave to be quick, no one won't take the risk after about four months.'

'But how do we know when that is?' Carol asked. 'How do we know when it started?'

'Well, you must know when you was last *unwell*,' Mrs Higgs said meaningfully, with a glance at Roddy.

'I can't remember.' Carol looked frightened. 'I never even thought – I often miss – I was pleased—'

'Pity you never done something about it straight away,' Mrs Higgs said. 'Castor oil'll often shift it, if you catches it quick. Or you can try jumping off a chair. You could still give it a try.'

'I told you, we'll not do anything of the sort,' Roddy said at once.

The landlady shrugged. 'Please yourself. 'Ow long you bin being sick?'

'A fortnight, I think,' Carol said in a small voice.

'Well, you'd be about eight or nine weeks then. You got seven months to go. That's if you wants to.' She waited a minute. 'Like I say, anything you wants to know, just ask me. There's plenty of girls come to Martha Higgs for a bit of 'elp when they found themselves in trouble.'

'It's very kind of you,' Carol said. 'We didn't know what to do.'

'No, well, you wouldn't, would yer? Never bin told the facts of life proper, I daresay. Most girls ain't, and the boys is just left to find it out from their mates, an' they don't know nothing.' Mrs Higgs sniffed. 'Be a lot less girls in trouble and 'avin' to get married if they was taught a bit more about the birds and the bees, that's what I say. Anyway, that don't 'elp you now.' She gave them a speculative look. ''Ow much can you stretch yerselves to?'

Roddy gazed at her. 'How much? I don't understand—'

'Money,' the landlady snapped. ''Ow much you got?'

'But what do we need money for? There's nothing to buy yet, is there?'

'Rent,' she said succinctly. 'You wants to go on livin' 'ere, you got to pay a bit more. I ain't takin' the chance out of the goodness of me 'eart.'

'But we haven't got any money,' Roddy said. 'Our – our savings have almost gone. We won't have any more until we can get jobs.' He glanced at Carol. 'I mean, till I can get a job.'

'Well, you got to find the cash from somewhere. I ain't keepin' yer. And it'll cost you fifteen bob a week from now on, not ten.'

'Fifteen shillings? But we can't possibly afford that.'

'You wants me to keep quiet, dontcher? I could turn you out this minute if I wasn't so goodhearted. But I won't be taken advantage of. You told me lies already. 'Ow do I know you're on the square now? I could get run in, harbouring a deserter.' She glanced from one to the other, her eyes cruel little pebbles. 'Maybe you ain't found this out yet, but everything you want in this world's got a price, and you can only get it so long as you can pay for it.'

She gave them another swift glance and then marched out, banging the door behind her. Roddy looked down at Carol and then sank on the bed, laying his face on her breast. Carol slipped her arms around him and they stayed close, without speaking, for several minutes.

'She knows,' he said at last, hopelessly. 'She knows everything.'

'She can't. Not our names and where we come from.'

'It doesn't matter. She could go to the police and tell them I'm a deserter. They'd soon find out who I am.' He lifted his head. 'Carrie, they'd send me to prison. They might even shoot me.'

'No!'

'They could. They're allowed to.' He looked at her miserably. 'I don't want to go to prison, Carrie. I want to stay with you.'

'I want you too,' She held him more tightly, staring at the cracked ceiling. 'I wouldn't know what to do without you.'

For a few more moments they were silent, clinging to each other, locked in their desperate thoughts. Then Roddy said, 'D'you think it's true, Carrie? About the bairn? D'you think you're really – you know—'

'Expecting,' she said in a dull voice. 'Oh, I should think so. I mean, it's just the sort of thing that would happen, isn't it?' Her voice was bitter, uncannily like her mother's. 'I haven't never had no luck, not till I met you, and now even that's got to be spoilt.'

'Would it really spoil it?' Roddy asked after a minute or two. 'A bairn's not so bad, Carrie. My cousin Moira's wee one is a lot of fun. His name's Alistair and he—'

'I know all about your cousin Moira,' Carol said peevishly. 'You never stop talking about her.' She sat up. 'Roddy, this is me we're talking about. I don't want a baby – not for a long time. I know what they're like. Mrs Budd, next door to us had one just before the war started, and I could hear her crying every night. It was awful.'

'Mrs Budd was crying? Didnae she want a bairn either?'

'Not Mrs Budd! The baby. They went away to the country when the war started, but they came back at Christmas and the baby cried louder than ever. I could hear it through the walls.'

'Well, all bairns cry,' Roddy said reasonably.

'I know. That's what I'm saying. How would I manage, with a baby crying all night? I wouldn't know what to do. I don't know anything about babies, I don't know how you feed them or anything. It would die.'

Roddy could not think what to say. He remembered the pleasure in his own family when Moira had been expecting Alistair. His mother and his aunts had been busy for months, knitting tiny white garments and talking in hushed voices. And when Alistair had arrived, you'd have thought he was the only baby on earth. There had been no problem in knowing how to look after him – every female member of the family had been round to Moira's with advice.

'Och, you'll be all right once you're a mother,' he said. 'Mothers always know what to do.'

'How do they? How can they know what to do, if no one tells them?'

'It's instinct. We had a sheepdog bitch, and when she had her first litter she knew just—'

'Roddy, I'm not a sheepdog! People aren't like animals. They're humans. Do *you* know what to do?'

'No,' he admitted. 'But—'

'Well, you'll be a father,' Carol said. 'D'you think that's going to make a difference?'

There was a short silence.

'I wish we'd gone to Scotland,' Roddy said at last. 'My mother and father would tell us what to do.'

'Yes. They'd tell you to go back to the Navy. And where would that leave me?'

The door opened again and Mrs Higgs stood there. She glowered down at Roddy, still crouched by the bed, and demanded brusquely, 'Well? What's it to be?'

Roddy looked up at her. 'What d'you mean?'

'What's it to be?' she demanded impatiently. 'Are yer goin' ter pay me the fifteen bob or not?'

'I've already told you. We can't afford it.'

'You can't afford not to,' she said brutally. 'It's pay up or get out. I'm not 'avin' no trouble 'ere, I told yer before.'

'But we're not causing any trouble—'

Mrs Higgs held up her fingers and began to count. 'Livin' under my roof with no weddin' lines. Livin' with a girl what's too young to be away from her mother – that's abduction, young man, in case you don't know it. Puttin' 'er in the family way. *Desertin'.*' The last word was brought out almost with a flourish. 'I reckon they'll chuck the whole bleedin' book at you. They'll march you away so fast your feet won't touch the ground.'

Carol and Roddy stared at her. Then Carol said, 'Please, Mrs Higgs. Give us a bit longer. Roddy'll find a job soon, I know he will. We'll pay you as soon as we can—'

'That we'll not!' Roddy exclaimed. He leapt to his feet and faced the scrawny landlady. 'We'll not pay another penny. You might think you've got us right where you want us, Mrs Higgs, but I'm a Scotsman and proud of it, and I'll no' be browbeaten by the likes of you. It's my bairn Carrie's bearing, my flesh and blood, and I'll no' have it born in this rat-hole. I'll take her back home to Scotland with me, that's what I'll do, and you can whistle for your money!'

'Roddy, no,' Carol begged anxiously, but neither he nor Mrs Higgs took any notice of her. They stood facing each other with furious eyes, their bodies as taut as springs. In another moment, she thought, they would spring at each other like cats.

They did not. Instead, Mrs Higgs suddenly tossed her head, gave a snort like an angry bull and turned on her heel.

'We'll soon see about that,' she said from the doorway. 'Oh, yes, we'll very soon see about that. You're going to regret talking to me like that.'

She slammed out and they heard her feet go heavily down the stairs. There was a short pause and then the front door slammed and the footsteps rapped quickly away up the street.

'What's she going to do?' Carol whispered.

'God knows. She might do anything.' He turned his head and looked at her. 'She might really go to the police.'

'Oh, Roddy.' Carol put her arms around him again and held him tightly. 'Oh, Roddy, what have you done?'

16

During the same week Portsmouth was throwing itself into an orgy of celebration and pageantry such as had not been seen since before the war began.

Warship Week, with a target of one million two hundred thousand pounds to buy a new cruiser, started with a spectacular parade through the streets. It was headed by the band of the Royal Marines – always the smartest of the lot, Frank declared – and included detachments from all the services. Already, the Mayor announced, over half a million pounds had been collected, and more was bound to come as people flooded to the King's Theatre for an all-star entertainment, to the Wessex Drill Hall for exhibitions and to a Tattoo in the Guildhall Square, with the steps being used for the first time since the blitz as grandstand accommodation.

'It's just like in peacetime,' Jess said but Cherry, who had come with them, gave her a comical look.

'What, with the poor old Guildhall standing there a ruin? And planes going over night after night?'

'Well, they are more often British ones than German now,' Frank said. 'We're giving Berlin and Hamburg a taste of what they gave us. Serve 'em right too, when you think what they're doing to poor little Malta.'

Malta was taking the brunt of the Luftwaffe's attention now. The bombing there was almost continuous and it seemed as if the people were almost permanently living in the catacombs and tunnels. But they fought back bravely, refusing to give in. They had been invaded too many times in their long history to allow it to happen again.

At home, news of the war was followed with a kind of eager desperation. For people like Frank, it was imperative to know its progress, to be able to carry a picture of the world as it plunged further and deeper into turmoil. It was as if, once he had let go of the threads, he would never be able to pick them up again and he would be lost in chaos. He listened avidly to the News on the wireless, questioned Jess about what she had seen at the cinema – her one afternoon a week there was her only relaxation – read the *Daily Express* and the *Evening News* from cover to cover, and plotted the changing events on his big wall-map.

For others, the war at home was more than enough. Everything seemed to be affected by the new 'Austerity' measures. The only crockery you could get now was white 'utility', with cups that had no handles, while luxury

742

extras like soup spoons, butter knives and ornamental glassware were no longer made. And there was only one quality of a huge range of goods from sheets, carpets and kitchen utensils to pens, cigarette lighters and umbrellas. Even the few toys still being produced were not permitted to contain such materials as rubber or cork.

'Poor little scrap,' Jess said, watching Maureen playing with Keith's old coloured bricks. 'There's nothing for kiddies now. She's missing such a lot.'

'So am I,' Rose answered, rather sharply. She was getting tired of Maureen and the way everyone was sorry for her because there were no dolls or fluffy animals to be had. She had only ever had one doll herself, and not much more than Maureen had now, but nobody seemed to think of that. 'If it wasn't for the war I'd be able to go out for an evening to the pictures, or a dance. That's what most girls do when they're my age.'

'And look what happens to them,' Jess said. 'Mrs Glaister's half out of her mind with worry over young Carol. You don't think I want that happening to you, do you?'

'I wouldn't be so daft. I wouldn't go running off with a sailor.'

But Jess knew better than Rose how young emotions, coming unexpectedly, could sweep a girl off her feet. And with all these sailors and soldiers about, far from home, you couldn't be too careful. There was talk of Americans coming too, now that they were in the war, and Jess had heard more than she liked about Americans.

'Utility' clothing began to appear too. The hemlines of skirts rose, to save on material, and there was a restriction on pleats or other designs that used more fabric than necessary. Men were forbidden double-breasted coats or turn-ups on their trousers. Already, they had lost pyjama pockets. Sometimes it all seemed so trivial that you had to laugh about it, but it was an aggravation all the same.

'They'll be measuring handkerchiefs next,' Cherry said.

'And what about ties?' Frank agreed. He had always hated wearing a tie. 'Think what we could save if it was against the law to wear ties. And peaked caps, they could save a bit there.'

'And you don't really need lapels on your jackets.' Cherry went on. 'Or—'

'Stop it, you two,' Jess said, laughing. 'You'll have us all in boiler-suits at this rate.'

'Well, why not? Winnie wears 'em all the time. He don't care what he looks like, he just does whatever's most practical. I reckon that's what we should all do, instead of wasting time on all these finicky little rules and regulations.'

'Well, we've all got to do our bit.'

'By handing in pyjama pockets?' Frank said. 'It's going to take more than a few inches of material to win this war, Jess.'

Jess nodded soberly. Like the rest of the family, she was still worried over Colin, who had not been heard of since the *Exeter* had been sunk.

'I can't bear to think of it,' Annie had said only yesterday. 'But I can't stop thinking about it either. Our Colin, drowning thousands of miles away from home. That's not what we had our children for, Jess.'

It wasn't. Jess and Annie had borne their children in times when a Great War had not long ended, a war which was to end all wars. They had hoped to see them grow in peace and prosperity. Instead, they had faced first the Depression and now this. A worldwide quarrel, none of their own choosing, that had got out of hand and looked like destroying everything they had lived for.

It was too much for some people to stand, and the newspapers began to carry more and more reports of suicides. Old men who felt helpless, old women too frightened to go on living, young lovers who were desperate at being parted. Sometimes Jess would look at these reports and think of Carol Glaister and her young sailor. Her heart ached for Ethel, little though she liked the woman, and she tried to express her sympathy.

'The little hussy!' was Ethel's response. 'Running off with all my savings. It just shows, you can't expect no gratitude from youngsters these days. Take all you've got to give and then turn round and stab you in the back. What am I supposed to do for a new summer outfit, with her living the life of Riley on what I've scrimped and saved for?'

Jess stared at her, shocked. She had always thought Ethel a coldhearted woman, but didn't she have any feeling at all for her daughter?

'Aren't you at all worried about her?'

'Why should I be? She'll be all right – always falls on her feet, that one does. Self, self, self, that's all she thinks about, never mind her poor mother.' Ethel looked down at her skirt and smoothed it self-consciously. 'What do you think of this, Jess? I got it in Bulpitt's, the last one they had before the utility stuff. You won't see pleats like this again. And if you'll take my advice, you'll get whatever you want now – there's to be no more lace or appliqué, not even a bit of embroidery. It'll probably be against the law to do anything to brighten yourself up a bit. I think it's a crying shame. Women need a bit of stuff to make them pretty, it gives 'em heart, and the men like it too.'

Jess turned and went indoors. She loved embroidery herself and liked to make Rose's blouses with a flower on the pocket, but she could never have put it before her own daughter's welfare. But perhaps Ethel was more upset than she let on. She'd always been a close one, never one to show her feelings, especially to Jess.

'If Carol was still home, she'd have to register for war service anyway,' she said to Frank. 'Not that they'd take her – they're trying to leave the young ones alone as long as they can – but she might be glad to get away from home. I reckon that's half the reason she's run off.'

'Princess Elizabeth's registered,' Rose said. 'I saw it in the paper. She went in her Girl Guide uniform, as soon as she was sixteen. There's been hundreds and thousands put down their names. Joy says she can't wait to volunteer.'

But however hard people tried to keep up their morale, the increasingly bad news was like a series of hammer blows. A simultaneous battery of raids devastated the cities of Exeter and Bath, closely followed by Norwich and York – all cities with three stars in the Baedeker guidebooks. Malta, awarded the King's own medal, the George Cross, was immediately robbed by the Luftwaffe of thirty of the forty-six Spitfires delivered by the USS *Wasp* and was then abandoned, leaving the shattered island without ships and praying for a miracle. The last ship to leave, bringing back British personnel and their families, was HMS *Penelope*, which was hit so often during her zigzag voyage home that she was nicknamed 'Pepper-pot'.

Yet, despite it all, there were still smiles to be seen on the faces of people in the streets. Still jokes to be cracked and laughter to be heard in even the grimmest of situations. And still bright spots to be found, little sparks of happiness and joy which brightened the days and gave hope that life was, even now, still worth living.

One was the wedding of Erica Jones to Gerald Spencer.

'I never thought I'd love anyone else, after Geoff died,' Erica said to Betty as the girls made themselves ready in the attic room at the farm. 'Sometimes I think I ought to feel guilty – but I can't. I'm too happy. But I did love Geoff, I did really.'

'Of course you did,' Betty said. 'And I bet you still do. But you love Gerald as well. And you're going to marry him and be his wife and live happily ever after. And wherever Geoff is, I bet he's glad!'

'Yes, I think he would be,' Erica said slowly. She held up her arms and Betty slipped the white wedding dress over her head. It had been loaned to Erica by one of Gerald's cousins from Corhampton, who had got married a year or two before the war started, and with a little skilful sewing from Mrs Spencer it fitted Erica's slender figure perfectly. Betty arranged the skirt and stood back to admire the effect.

'It's lovely, Eric.'

Erica turned slowly. The dress was made of white satin and lace, the kind of dress you never saw these days, and it fell like a cascade of foaming water to the floor. The bodice was tight, drawn in to a tiny waist, and there were little pearl buttons down the front. The sleeves came to a narrow point at the wrist, held in place by a satin ribbon which looped around Erica's finger.

The door opened and Yvonne came in. She stopped and whistled.

'Whee-whew! You look a real stunner, Eric. It's like Cinderella – one day a Land Girl in muddy dungarees, the next a fairy princess!' She came forward. 'Let me put on the coronet.'

The coronet was a fragile creation of silver wire and pearls, with a few diamanté stones sparkling as they caught the light. Yvonne lifted it, holding the drift of net clear of Erica's face, and settled it on her pale gold curls. She stepped back to join Betty.

'You look smashing. Gerald won't be able to take his eyes off you.'

Erica grinned a little self-consciously. 'It's all thanks to you. If you hadn't lent me your new lipstick – and Betty didn't have a pair of stockings – and Maisie hadn't let me borrow this dress—'

'You'd have got married just the same, and Gerald would have thought you looked just as lovely in your old dungarees,' Betty said. 'I wish it was me and Dennis walking up the aisle today.'

'You'll have to be next,' Erica said. 'I don't know why you don't. You're mad about each other, anyone can see that.'

'Maybe today'll make him take the plunge,' Yvonne said. 'He is coming, isn't he?'

'If they don't get called out. He's got the leave arranged, but you know how much that means if a bomb's found somewhere.'

There was a knock from the bottom of the stairs and Mrs Spencer called up, 'It's time we were going, girls.'

'Whoops!' Yvonne said, bending to peer into the mirror. 'This is it. Your last chance to back out, Eric.'

'Anyway, you don't have to hurry,' Betty said. 'It's the bride's prerogative to be late.'

'Not likely,' Erica retorted, making for the stairs. 'Gerald's likely to be called back any day now – I don't want to miss a minute of being his wife!'

Laughing, they scrambled down the narrow stairs, Erica going sideways to avoid crushing her dress. They arrived at the bottom and found the Spencers standing there, both arrayed in the best clothes they wore only for going to church on very special occasions. Mrs Spencer looked almost regal in her dark green costume and hat with its tiny veil, while her husband was stiffly upright in a starched collar and black suit. They gazed at Erica for a moment and Mr Spencer cleared his throat gruffly.

'You look beautiful,' Mrs Spencer said at last. She lifted her veil and wiped her eyes with a small handkerchief. 'You look really beautiful.'

Erica laughed a little shakily. 'I feel scared stiff.'

'You'll be all right, my dear.' The farmer's wife shook her head. 'It's such a shame your own mother and father can't see you.'

Erica's parents had left Portsmouth a year ago and were now living in Gloucestershire. They had been invited to the wedding but sent a note saying that they could not possibly travel at such a time. Erica had shrugged and said it didn't matter, but Betty and Yvonne had felt sorry for her and indignant with the parents who showed so little interest in their daughter.

'Her mother's a cat,' said Betty, who had met Mrs Jones once. 'All she thinks about is herself. And our Erica was going the same way when she first came here. I reckon it was the best thing she ever did, joining the Land Army.'

The two girls and Mrs Spencer left to walk up the lane to the village of Bishop's Waltham, its little church already filled with people waiting for the wedding. Gerald had gone ahead with Maisie's husband Jimmy, who was to be best man. Mr Spencer was to give the bride away and the farm cart had been cleaned and scrubbed, and decorated for the occasion with primroses, daffodils, bluebells and all the bits of ribbon that could be found. Even Boxer, the horse, had an early rose tucked behind one ear.

'There you are,' the farmer said, helping Erica climb up into the cart. 'Lucky it's a fine day! Still, we could have used the car if it had rained.'

'I'd rather use this.' Erica sat on the narrow seat, holding a posy of flowers that Betty and Yvonne had picked for her that morning. She thought of the wedding she had planned with Geoff. It was to have been in Portsmouth Cathedral, with the bells and full choir, and the great church would have been filled with her parents' friends and relatives, all vying with each other to look the smartest and most fashionable. There would have been huge sheaves of flowers – exotic lilies, heavily scented freesias, roses like scarlet cabbages. Erica's dress would have been made especially for her and would have been the talk of the city, and after the reception in Southsea's grandest hotel, they would have driven away in Geoff's little sports car for a honeymoon in some romantic hideaway – they might even have gone abroad.

At the time, Erica had thought that was what she wanted. Now she knew that although she could have been happy with Geoff, the pretensions she had learned from her parents would almost certainly have damaged that happiness.

She looked at the primrose-studded banks and the burgeoning green hedgerows, and thought of Gerald, a farmer's son with none of Geoff's advantages, yet a man who would love and honour her through whatever life would bring them. And she felt a great, swelling contentment to be here, seated in a plain farm cart, jogging through the country lanes to her wedding in a little village church.

'I now pronounce you man and wife.'

The vicar's voice echoed softly through the small, crowded church. Almost everyone in the village was there, for the Spencers were known and respected for miles around and the three Land Girls had won the hearts of most of the local inhabitants. Even Jonas was there in the fourth pew, resplendent in a suit that had once been black and was now rusty with age, his ancient hat crushed against his chest as he grated out the hymns. He wore a rose in his lapel, and he glowered at Erica throughout the entire service. Only Betty, glancing at him over her hymn-book, noticed that his rheumy eyes were damp.

Erica was trembling as she made her vows. She looked up and met Gerald's eyes, terrified that she was about to weep, but when she saw the expression in his she hastily cast her glance away, for he looked as near to tears as she. In a shaking voice, she promised to love, honour and obey him, and heard him in turn vow to love, honour and cherish. '*With my body, I thee worship . . .*' Tonight they would lie together for the first time, unrestricted by convention or fear, and bring their love to its full consummation. Tonight, they would be truly married and nothing, not even the war, could part their entwined souls.

The service came to an end. The family party – Erica and her new husband, the Spencers and Betty and Yvonne – crowded into the vestry to witness the signing of the register, and then Gerald took Erica in his arms and kissed her gently on the lips. There was a hubbub of laughter and congratulations, with everyone kissing Erica and Gerald, and the sound of singing in the body of the church. And then out they came, with Erica radiant in the borrowed white dress and Gerald, proud and upright in uniform, his injuries healed and his face once more tanned from working outside.

At the door of the church, they paused. Only one person had a camera –

the local doctor – and he had just one film, with eight exposures to be used. He took two, one of Erica and Gerald alone, one of the family group, and then he folded his camera again.

'I'll let you have the prints when I finish the film.' It might be weeks, months, even a year, for film was so precious he would take no more until another special occasion came along. But one day they would have them to look at, and meanwhile this day would live in their memories as a day of happiness that neither of them had expected.

'Come on,' Gerald said. 'Let's get into the cart and drive away. I want to kiss you properly, where no one else can see us. And – I've got something to tell you.' He looked grave, and a sudden fear clutched at Erica's heart.

'You're going away.'

'Come on,' he said again, and she scrambled into the cart, suddenly careless of the flowing dress, and looked at him with wide eyes.

'Your flowers!' Betty screamed from the crowd, and she turned guiltily, remembering where they were, and tossed the posy towards her friend. Laughing, Betty caught it and held it aloft while the others surged about her like waves. They were all in their best clothes, Erica thought, all arrayed to wish herself and Gerald well on their journey into marriage. But how short was that journey to be?

'When?' she said urgently as the horse trotted away. 'When are you going?'

For a moment or two, he didn't answer. His eyes were fixed on the horse's back and Erica looked at his strong hands, holding the reins, and laid her own on top of them.

'When?'

Gerald turned the cart into a narrow lane. It led nowhere but into one of the Spencers' fields. There had been three haystacks here, built last autumn to feed the animals through the winter, and now there was just part of one left. Gerald drew the cart to a halt by the gate and then turned at last and looked down into Erica's face.

'Today. This afternoon.'

'*This afternoon?*' she echoed unbelievingly. 'But – you can't. We've only just got married. We haven't had a chance—'

'I know. I thought it would be at least another week. But there's something big on in Africa – they're getting back as many men as they can. There's nothing I can do about it.'

'I know.' The demands of the war came before anything else. It could not be escaped. 'But – this afternoon . . . Oh, *Gerald*.'

He held her in his arms, feeling her body tremble against him. His desire for her, which had begun very soon after he had first seen her, was almost overwhelming. He had never seen anyone so perfect as Erica, with her small figure so exactly proportioned, her hair like a golden nimbus about her head, her eyes so clear and blue. And as he had come to know her better, the desire had turned to love, and he had known that he must have her for his wife.

But to be snatched away at the very brink . . . !

'Listen,' he said. 'We've only got a few hours, and we don't have to waste them at a party with a lot of other people. We've got a honeymoon to have.'

Erica lifted her head and stared at him. 'A honeymoon? But how can we—'

'We'll have it here,' he said, and dropped over the side of the cart. 'It's all ready for you, my darling.' He lifted his arms and Erica leaned into them so that he could swing her to the ground. She stood in his embrace, staring in astonishment at the space between the haystack and the hedge, and then she began to laugh.

'Gerald! Behind a haystack!'

'There's not a better place,' he said, and bent to lay his lips upon hers.

He had turned the space into a room, with walls of hay, and furnished it with blankets and a pillow. There were two glasses and a bottle of home-made elderberry wine. There was a small picnic basket, and two plates laid upon the top of it with a silver knife and fork that Erica recognised had come from the Spencers' best service, handed down from Gerald's great-grandparents.

'A haystack honeymoon,' she said, half laughing, half crying as Gerald began to undo the tiny pearl buttons of her bodice. 'Oh Gerald, I love you . . .'

Nobody asked why Gerald and Erica took so long to come back from the church. Word had gone round quickly that Gerald had been recalled, and the reception continued without its central figures. Mr and Mrs Spencer received their guests, gave them each a glass of elderberry wine and sat them down round the long dining-table in the big room for a feast such as had not been seen for years. Betty, helping to serve slices of the huge baked ham and new potatoes she had helped grow herself, wondered what they would say at home if they could see all this. Butter, eggs, flagons of cider – it was like the black market! But this was a farming community and everyone had chipped in with something to help. No one was going to inquire too closely about where the ham had come from – or what had happened to the rest of the pig. The joke was that it was still alive, hobbling about on three legs somewhere.

It seemed queer to have a reception without a bride and groom, but everyone entered into the spirit of it and there were speeches, toasts and a lot of laughter and ribbing just as if Erica and Gerald had indeed been sitting in their chairs at the top of the table. Mr Spencer made a speech about how she had first come to the farm as a haughty townie, expecting her own room. 'She never did get one,' he observed. 'And now she's going to have to share with our Gerald.' There was a roar of laughter and cries of 'Shame!' but Betty, thinking of Erica even now facing the departure of her new husband, felt the tears prick her eyes.

'It's awful,' she said to Dennis. 'Nobody gets a chance these days. How can anyone get a start with all this going on? All the same, I wish it was us. Even if you do have to go away, I'd sooner we were married.'

'So would I,' he said, squeezing her hand. 'I think we ought to fix it up soon. I wanted to wait till all this was over, just so that we could start

properly – but we've waited long enough. We belong to each other, Betty –
I want you to be my wife.'

Betty turned and looked up into his face. Her hazel eyes had deepened to
a burning gold. She felt breathless, as if she had run a long way.

'D'you mean it? D'you really mean it?'

'Would I say it if I didn't?' he asked, smiling.

'Oh. Oh, Dennis.' The tears that had stung her eyes for Erica now welled
up and brimmed over. She brushed them away, but more came and she
gave up and let them stream down her face, laughing at herself, laughing
with happiness. 'When? When shall we do it?'

'Do what?' Jack Spencer was at her elbow, laying his hand on her
shoulder to turn her around. 'Here, Dennis, what are you doing to our
Betty to make her cry?'

Dennis laughed and Betty shook her head. 'He's not doing anything. I
mean, he's going to – we're going to get married, Mr Spencer. We're
engaged – properly engaged. At least—' she turned and looked at Dennis
again '—I suppose we are, aren't we?'

'We've always been engaged,' he said, and he reached out and drew her
close against his side. 'We've always belonged to each other, Betty.'

They gazed into each other's faces, each reading the promise and truth
that now shone out for all to see. And beside them, Jack Spencer banged
loudly on the table and lifted his voice to silence the chatter that filled the
room.

'Quiet, everybody! Quiet! Shut up a minute, will you!'

'Pray silence for his washup the mayor,' somebody called out, and
everyone laughed then fell silent, waiting to hear what Jack Spencer wanted
to say next.

'I've just heard a bit of good news,' the farmer announced. 'A bit of news
we've been waiting for on this farm for a long time now. You all know
young Betty here—' he laid his hand on her shoulder again – 'and you all
know Dennis. Two of the finest young people you could wish to meet, and
if you don't know why, I'll tell you. Betty came here not knowing one end
of a cow from the other and now she can milk the whole herd and still do a
day's ploughing at the end of it. She'll work at anything, any job you care to
give her. And Dennis is the same, only now he's left us to join Bomb
Disposal, and risk his life every day to save the rest of us. He won't fight,
but he's no coward and I wish I could say the same for a lot of other people
I know. We could do with more lads like Dennis.' There was a murmur of
approval from his listeners. 'But that's not what I want to tell you,' Jack
Spencer went on. 'The good news is that these two have decided to follow
the good example set 'em today by our Gerald and young Erica – where've
they got to, by the way—' he paused for the laughter to subside '—and
they're going to get themselves wed, just as soon as it can be arranged. And
I reckon we ought to congratulate 'em – even if it does mean we'll lose
another Land Girl!'

The cheer nearly lifted the farmhouse roof. Betty stood blushing at
Dennis's side, and he held her hand tightly and grinned at everyone. It was
very different from when he had first come here, to face suspicion and

hostility from many of the villagers. He knew that the change was largely because he had joined the Army, but he was also aware that much of the hostility had evaporated even before he'd left the farm. His own cheerful, steady personality had seen to that.

There was a sound at the door and everyone turned.

'Erica!'

She stood there in her white gown, her face radiant yet tragic at the same moment. Behind her, Gerald was sober, but his eyes too held a deep contentment. His hands were on her shoulders, his thumbs stroking her neck, very very slowly, very very gently.

'We just came in to say thank you,' Erica said, her voice trembling. 'Thank you for coming to our wedding. Thank you for all your good wishes and the presents and – and everything. And thank you for having the party without us.' Her lips quivered as she smiled around at them, and Betty's heart ached for her. 'I wish – I wish—' But she could say no more. The tears welled out of her eyes and she turned and laid her head on Gerald's shoulder as he closed his arms around her.

'Another drink, everyone!' Jack Spencer called, and began to move round the table, a bottle in each hand. 'Come on, now – there's got to be a toast to the happy couple. And they are happy, anyone can see that. And they'll go on being happy too, no matter how far apart they've got to be.' He handed a brimming glass to his son, and another to his new daughter-in-law, before planting a smacking kiss on her cheek. 'We're glad to have you in the family. And this lot won't last for ever, you'll see. You'll have years and years of being a farmer's wife.'

17

At last it was time for the scholarship results to be announced. Tim went to school with a tight feeling in his chest that morning, and the whole class was unnaturally quiet and well-behaved. It was almost dinner-time when Mr Wain came in with a sheaf of papers in his hand.

The children stood up at once, as they always did whenever an adult came into the classroom. Tim felt his heart lurch and then seem to climb higher into his throat, beating uncomfortably. His legs trembled.

'You may sit down,' Mr Wain said. He looked at the papers in his hand. 'The following children, stand up when I call your names. These are the ones who have passed the examination for the grammar school.'

The class sat down again. Tim clenched his hands between his knees, pressing them firmly together to try to stop them shaking. It would be awful if he couldn't stand up when his name was called, and it was bound to be one of the first because it began with B.

'Rosemary Andrews,' Mr Wain read out, and a girl with yellow pigtails stood up, red with pleasure. 'John Antrobus. Michael Banks. Jennifer Collins. Robert Cook. Terence Granger. Peter Holliday—'

Tim listened, unbelieving, as the names rolled on. Jennifer *Collins*? Robert *Cook*? Peter *Holliday*? Where was his name? It ought to have been third on the list, straight after Michael Banks. *Tim Budd.* Before the Cs. What had happened?

The list ended. Twelve children were on their feet, looking excited, proud, self-conscious. The rest sat in various degrees of disappointment and resignation. Some had never expected to pass. Some hadn't even wanted to.

Tim stared at his desk. The ink-stained wood blurred and shifted under his gaze. His head seemed to be filled with a roaring noise and he felt sick and dizzy. He swallowed hard to keep from crying.

'As you know,' Mr Wain was saying, 'the grammar school and secondary schools have been evacuated to Winchester. That isn't very far away, but some of you may need to be sent to new billets. We'll be making arrangements during the summer, so there's plenty of time. And of course we'll be contacting your parents, but I expect you'll want to tell them the good news yourselves first, so there are some postcards and stamps here for you to use to write home today.' He smiled round the class. 'And those of you who haven't passed, don't be downhearted, the secondary school is very good and you'll learn lots of interesting things there.'

He nodded to Mr Hodges and went out. The children broke into a buzz of excited chatter. Tim bit his lips hard and dug his fingernails into his palms. It must be a mistake. It had to be a mistake. He must have passed. He was nearly a year older than most of the children in the class and he *ought* to have passed. He ought to have taken the scholarship last year, and passed it then, and he'd already be at the grammar school by now. He couldn't have failed.

Michael Banks was sitting next to him. He turned to Tim, his face glowing, and said, 'Gosh, isn't it smashing! I wish you were coming too, though, Tim. I'll have to sit next to someone else now.'

Tim got up abruptly and pushed his way past the crowded desks to the front of the class. Mr Hodges was talking to Rosemary Andrews and Jennifer Collins, who both sat at the front. Jennifer was the sister of Brian Collins, Tim's old enemy.

'What is it, Tim?' Mr Hodges asked. 'Do you want to be excused?'

Tim shook his head. He knew the tears were not far away, but he couldn't wait to get himself under control. He looked up at him, his lips turned down, his face crumpling.

'Why wasn't my name on the list, sir? Why can't I go to the grammar school?'

Mr Hodges looked embarrassed. 'Well, because you didn't pass the examination, Tim. But the secondary school is nearly as good—'

'But I ought to have passed,' Tim said, his voice turning liquid as the tears welled from his eyes. 'Everyone said I'd pass. *You* said I'd pass.'

'I thought you would. But your work just lately—'

'I did it all last year. I'd have passed then, I know I would.'

'But you didn't take the exam last year,' Mr Hodges said gently. 'You know that. A mistake was made somewhere and you got left off the list. And you know you haven't been doing as well this year.'

'I've had to do everything twice. I'm fed up with it. I'm fed up with school. I don't *want* to go to the secondary school.'

'I'm sorry, Tim,' Mr Hodges said, his voice hardening. 'You just have to accept it. That's where you're going. Now, you can go out to the lavatory and wash your face and then come back for prayers. It's almost time to go home.'

Tim glared at him and then stamped out of the room. He knew that he was likely to get into trouble when he came back, for being rude and slamming the door, but he couldn't help it. It wasn't *fair*. He *ought* to have passed.

He washed his face as instructed and then stood outside the lavatory door, in the little playground. It was the first warm day of spring. The sun was shining and he could see birds flying busily to and fro, building their nests. I'm not going back, he thought. They'll all see I've been crying. I'm not going back.

He turned his back on the school and, with tears once more streaming down his face, ran out of the playground, back to the vicarage and Mr Beckett.

To Tim, there seemed less point than ever in staying at the village primary school. He was only doing the same things over again, he argued, and they hadn't done him any good the first time. And Mr Beckett couldn't help agreeing with him.

'He's got such a lively mind,' he said when Frank and Jess came to visit the boys. He had written to them, asking them to come specially because he was worried about Tim. 'He's getting bored and frustrated, and he's still resentful over what's happened. It's the kind of situation that makes bright little boys like Tim look for mischief.'

'Our Tim's never had to look far to find mischief,' Frank said grimly. 'Being at school's the best thing for him. At least he's under someone's eye.'

'But only for half the day,' Jess pointed out. 'And I think Mr Beckett's right. You know what boys are like when they're fed up. I don't want Tim roaming about getting into trouble. The devil finds work for idle hands, isn't that right, Mr Beckett?'

'It certainly can be,' the vicar agreed. He rubbed his hand across his face. He enjoyed having the children staying with him but there was no doubt it was a responsibility, and neither he nor Mrs Mudge were in their first youth. It was all very well to pretend to be a boy too and build snowmen or play cricket, but when it came to problems like this the parents had to make the decision.

'What do you think we ought to do?' Jess asked him, and he pursed his lips. 'What does Tim himself want?'

'You can't go by that,' Frank said at once. 'He's just a child.'

'It's his life, all the same,' Mr Beckett said. 'And he'll be much more willing to co-operate if he's happy. I'm afraid he hasn't been very happy for the past few months.'

Jess looked distressed. She turned to Frank. 'I don't want him to be miserable.'

'Nor do I. But he's got to learn to take the rough with the smooth, same as the rest of us. And I want him to have a decent education.'

'That's just it, though, isn't it. He ought to have passed that exam. He doesn't want to go to the secondary modern school. And he's just wasting his time at the village school.'

'What do you want me to do, then? Let him leave? He's only twelve years old. I want him to have a better chance than I had.'

'Frank had to leave school when he was twelve,' Jess told Mr Beckett. 'His dad died and he had to help support the rest of the family. They had a hard time – he's always wanted something better for our children.'

'I went to night school,' Frank said. 'For years. I kept my learning up. But there's nothing like that these days, with the war and all. If Tim leaves school now, he'll never be able to catch up. I don't want him doing labouring jobs for the rest of his life.'

'But he needn't,' the vicar said. 'Intelligent boys like Tim will always find a way to use their abilities. But they do need guidance as to the best way to use them.' He paused, then added, 'Suppose you let him leave the village school now and come home for a while? Then he might feel happier about starting at his new school after the summer holiday. He might be able to find some work to do in Portsmouth, to occupy him.'

'Come home?' Jess said. She looked at Frank. 'He could do, couldn't he? The raids aren't anywhere near as bad now.'

Frank shook his head. 'We're still getting 'em, though, and you don't know when they might start again. Look at the way they bombed Exeter and Norwich a few weeks ago. Anyway, even if we did let him leave – and I'm not saying we will, mind – he could still find work out in the country. There's always something to do around farms.' He glanced at Mr Beckett. 'Unless you don't want him here any more. If he's getting to be too much trouble—'

'Indeed not,' the vicar said warmly. 'I'm very fond of both your boys. I enjoy having them about the place. But it's Tim's interests I'm concerned with, and I think he would benefit from a spell at home. He needs something to take his mind off his grievances, and being back at home for a few weeks might be just the thing. Then he can come back fresh to start school again in the autumn.'

'Well, I won't say I wouldn't like to have him home again,' Jess declared. 'Both of them, come to that. But you're right, Mr Beckett, we've got to think what's best for Tim. Anyway, we can't talk any more about it now, I can hear them coming. Frank and me'll have a word and let you know what we decide.'

They discussed it later, on the way home in the train. Frank was still unwilling to consider letting Tim leave the primary school and come home, but the more Jess thought about it, the more she felt it was the answer.

'He's growing up,' she said. 'He's a year older than the boys and girls in his class. He's done all the lessons before, and he's missing his own friends. It's no wonder he's miserable about it.'

'That's all very well, but what's he going to do if he does come home?' Frank demanded. 'I don't want him at a loose end, roaming the streets with youngsters like that Baxter boy. There's going to be trouble there one of these days, you mark my words. That brat's going to end up in prison and I don't want our Tim mixed up with him.'

'Honestly!' Jess said. 'You talk as if Tim hasn't got a mind of his own. Who says he's going to get mixed up with Micky Baxter anyway? Don't you trust your own son? Don't you think we've brought him up to know right from wrong? Our boys might get into a bit of mischief, they wouldn't be boys if they didn't, but they've got their heads screwed on the right way. I think Mr Beckett's right. I think Tim's had a big disappointment, and he needs a bit of help to get over it, and if a spell at home will do that, we ought to let him come back. We're his mum and dad, after all, we're the ones that ought be helping him.'

Frank frowned and stared out of the window, saying nothing. Jess glanced at him and smiled inwardly. It might take a bit of time, but she was pretty sure he'd agree in the end. He'd probably announce it as if it was entirely his own decision – which it would be, of course. Nothing much happened in the Budd family unless Frank decided it would happen, but sometimes Jess had to do a lot of quiet work in the background to get him around to it.

'It'd be nice to be able to teach him a bit of woodwork,' she remarked casually. 'He's always been keen and he's getting to just the right age now.'

Frank gave her a quick look and she smiled innocently and looked out of the window. The train was passing a small wood, misted with green and blue.

'Look at all the bluebells!' she said. 'And the trees, just coming into leaf. They don't know there's a war on, they just go on living their own lives. It's lovely how the countryside just goes on, isn't it, Frank – it gives you heart to carry on somehow.'

Again, Frank said nothing. But he took her hand in his and held it as the train rattled on. And just before they got off at Copnor station, he said gruffly, 'All right. He can come home for a few weeks, till school starts. But that's all, mind. And if we get raids again, back he goes, like it or not. And he's not going to be running around with that Baxter boy. I'll find him a job, he can make himself useful.'

'Oh, he'll be all right,' Jess said. 'He'll be a great help.' But in her heart, she knew that she didn't care a scrap whether Tim was useful or not. It would be joy enough to have him at home, to see his cheeky face looking at her across the meal table, to hear his laugh and the jokes he was forever thinking up.

It was a shame Keith couldn't come home too. But perhaps once Tim had been back for a while and Frank saw that he was all right, she would be able to point out that the boys ought to be together. And then the Budd family would be complete again.

We've never really been a complete family, she thought. Little Maureen was only two months old when the evacuation started, and we've only been together since then at Christmas or for a week or two in summer. And now she's nearly three.

It was such a long time, to be missing your family life.

Roddy had found work. It wasn't regular, but he was paid a few shillings a time for helping to hump boxes at a warehouse. He came home with two pounds at the end of the first week and paid Mrs Higgs a pound for two weeks' rent.

'I told you, it's fifteen bob now,' she said, staring at the handful of coins.

'And I told you we cannae afford that. You know the way we are. I've got to look after Carol and see she's properly fed and that.'

'Not much point, when she's throwing up all the time,' Mrs Higgs said cruelly. She had not yet carried out her threat to report them but they lived in a state of constant dread that she would. Carol was almost afraid to leave the house, even when she felt well enough, and Roddy could feel his back tingling all the time, expecting a heavy hand to land on his shoulder.

'We cannae stay here much longer,' he said when Mrs Higgs had gone muttering downstairs. 'Once the bairn's born the old besom will throw us out, sure as eggs is eggs. Anyway, I'll not have you and our little one living in a place like this.'

'What else can we do?' Carol asked. 'We can't afford anything better.

And if we do leave, she'll report us anyway. She's got us just where she wants us, Roddy.'

'We can just disappear again. Go somewhere else, where they won't find us.' But he spoke without conviction, for they both knew now that it was not so easy to 'disappear'. There were papers that you had to have – ration books, identity cards, references. People were suspicious; you might be a fifth columnist or a spy. Only someone like Mrs Higgs, who was shady herself, would take them in, and then they might find themselves in even worse trouble. Better the devil you knew, Carol thought despondently.

'I'd like to take you home to Scotland,' Roddy said. 'My mother would take care of you right enough. And the bairn.' He touched her stomach gently. There was just a little round swelling there now, not much bigger than a grapefruit and only detectable because Carol had lost so much weight. 'Just think, Carrie, that's our little one in there. A real wee person, made just because we love each other.'

A real wee person they could do without, Carol thought, especially when she couldn't keep her food down. But the tenderness in Roddy's eyes caught at her heart and she could not say so. And when she wasn't feeling sick, there *was* something exciting about it. A real baby. Someone who hadn't existed before, ever, made as Roddy had said, just because they loved each other. It was marvellous and incredible and exciting – and frightening, too. A baby. Her baby. Someone who would depend on her, for everything.

'Roddy, I can't,' she said shakily. 'I won't be able to manage, I know I won't. I don't know anything. I'm not good enough.'

'You're good enough for me,' he said stoutly. 'And you're good enough to have my bairn. We'll manage together, Carrie.'

But they both knew that it couldn't really be like that. They couldn't live for ever on the fringes – one day, they would have to go to a doctor or a hospital, or someone at work would start asking questions about Roddy. Or Mrs Higgs would report them to the authorities.

All they could do was cling together for as long as possible and try to forget what might lie ahead.

Tim came home with mixed feelings. He had enjoyed his time in the country, looking on it as a long holiday and an adventure. Roaming the woods and fields, so different from the streets of Portsmouth, had made him feel like an explorer. I'd like to do that when I grow up, he decided. I'd like to explore the whole world.

Coming back to Portsmouth was an anti-climax. He knew every street around Copnor and many further afield. He was used to the harbour and the long ridge of Portsdown Hill, with the white chalk pits gaping in its side. A lot of the bomb damage, which had ripped the streets apart and turned them into a new kind of playground, had now been patched up and some of the houses demolished. The first excitement of the raids was over and a kind of dreariness had settled over the city.

But it was nice being home again. He hadn't realised how much he'd missed the familiar things, like Dad's armchair that he'd made himself, and the wireless he'd fixed together, and the rag rug Mum had made, which lay in front of the fire with Henry, the cat, curled on it. And he liked being up in the back bedroom with the window looking out over the allotments, which was as near as you could get to being in the country.

'Tim's not having the back bedroom, is he?' Rose demanded when she found him up there the first day. 'Me and Maureen sleep there.'

There were two iron bunks in the back bedroom. Maureen had recently been promoted to the top one, which she loved. She would clamber up the rail and sit there, surrounded by the assortment of animals Cherry had knitted for her – the grey elephant, the mauve donkey, a giraffe in a sort of yellowish tweed mixture – and tell herself stories. It was the only space she had to herself in the tiny house.

'A boy needs a room,' Jess said. 'He needs somewhere to keep his bits and pieces.'

'*I* need somewhere to keep bits and pieces,' Rose said. 'I don't see why I've got to move downstairs just for him.'

'You're not to talk like that. He's your brother. Aren't you glad to have him home?'

'Not much,' Rose said, but she said it under her breath and she made up the bed-settee in the front room with a bad grace. She didn't like sharing a bed with Maureen, who kicked in her sleep, and she didn't like not having a room of her own. But with only two bedrooms upstairs someone had to be down in the front room, and there was no use in arguing about it. And it was nearer to the back door and shelter, if the air-raid warning went.

Maureen was thrilled to have her brother home. Tim had always been ready to play with her and now he was here all the time. She followed him around like a puppy and he enjoyed the attention and let her go everywhere with him, even taking her up to the bedroom and tossing her up on to the top bunk to chat while he changed his clothes or sorted out his possessions.

They sang together. 'You Are My Sunshine, My Only Sunshine' or 'I went to the Animal Fair' were Maureen's favourites and she chanted them all around the house. '. . . *and what became of the monkey, monkey, monkey . . .*' until the rest of the family were sick of them. But Jess was too happy to have her family together again to object. She just wanted Keith home now, and everything would be perfect.

'Perfect!' Frank snorted. 'How can anything be perfect, when the world's tearing itself to bits? I don't reckon there's a country left that's not caught up in this war, one way or another.'

'You know what I mean,' Jess said. 'We're all in it together and we've got to make the best of it. Keep smiling through, like that song says.'

But it was hard for Frank to smile these days. He was up soon after five each morning, ready for the walk down through the battered streets to the Dockyard carrying his lunchbox, and often didn't arrive home, dirty and tired from a long day's heavy labouring, until eight or nine at night. And although there weren't as many raids now, you still had to be on the alert for the siren, and still had to take your turn at firewatching.

Saturday was often as long a working day as the rest, and then there was the garden or allotment to be tended, and jobs to be done around the house. It was only last thing at night, while Jess was putting together his meal for next day, that Frank got a chance to sit back in his armchair and read the paper. And then, as often as not, he'd fall asleep with Henry sprawled on top of him, his snores mingling with the cat's deep purr.

True to his word, once Frank had agreed to Tim's coming home, he had set about finding him a job. At not quite thirteen, there wasn't all that much Tim could do, but the chemist in September Street wanted a delivery boy and agreed to give him a chance. Frank was well known in the area for being steady and reliable, and Mr Driver took it for granted that his son would be the same.

'You can use this bike,' he said, taking Tim out to the shed in the back yard. 'It needs a bit of cleaning up – my last lad went into the Navy six months ago and it hasn't been used since. The wife'll give you some rags and a bit of cotton waste. Then come and see me and I'll show you what to do. I'll pay you five shillings a week.'

Five shillings! It was a fortune to Tim, who had never had more than a shilling at one time in his life. But his delight was soon tempered by Jess, who told him that she would expect him to hand over four shillings to her.

'A shilling's quite enough for a boy like you,' she said firmly. 'That bit extra will be a big help to us. Maureen's forever needing new shoes, and she's growing out of her clothes so fast I can't keep up with her.'

Tim handed the money over, slightly mollified by the thought that he was helping to look after Maureen. He took her out into the garden, jingling the coins that were left in his pocket, and taught her a new song.

> 'I've got sixpence, jolly little sixpence,
> Sixpence to last me all my life.
> I've got tuppence to spend and tuppence to lend
> And tuppence to take home to my wife.'

But he didn't spend all his time with Maureen. As Frank had feared, he wanted friends of his own age, and inevitably he drifted towards Micky Baxter.

'Come 'ome from the country, 'ave you?' Micky jeered when they first met in April Grove. 'Didn't you like being away from Mummy any more? Ain't you scared of the bombs?'

'I'm not scared of anything,' Tim said, pushing away the thought of the crashed aeroplane and the pilot's hand, lying in the undergrowth. 'I've come home to work. I've left school now.'

'You 'aven't! You're not old enough.'

'Nor are you. Anyway, I've got a job, so that proves it.'

'Where d'you work, then?' Micky asked jealously. Nobody had given him a job, except for the few traders left in Charlotte Street, and he wasn't welcome there any more, since Ethel Glaister's accident.

'Up Driver's. The chemist's shop.'

'The chemist's shop?' Micky's eyes gleamed. 'You could get stuff, then. Stuff we need.'

'What sort of stuff?'

Micky debated with himself. To tell Tim what he needed, he'd have to tell him about the secret army and the growing arsenal. That meant trusting him. He wasn't quite sure if Tim could be trusted that much.

'Never you mind,' he said mysteriously, and then realised that he couldn't expect Tim to get 'stuff' if he didn't tell him what he wanted. 'It'd have to be secret.'

'I can keep secrets,' Tim said, immediately intrigued.

'I mean really secret. Not just games.' Micky looked at him speculatively. 'You'd have to swear not to tell a living soul.'

'Can I tell dead ones?' Tim asked, and then bit his lip. It was the sort of remark that nearly always got him into trouble, but he couldn't help making them. 'All right, what d'you want me to swear?'

'No. You'd have to come to our den to swear. And you've got to pass a test first.'

'What sort of test?'

Micky thought again. Here was a way of getting Tim to acquire what the gang wanted, without letting him in on their secret. And once Tim had done that, he wouldn't be able to give them away without getting into trouble himself. He grinned.

'You've got to get stuff to make gunpowder.'

'Gunpowder? What sort of stuff? Why d'you want to make gunpowder?'

'Never you mind. You just get some. And then we'll let you swear.'

'But I don't know what stuff you need,' Tim said. 'And how d'you know Mr Driver'll have any? He's a chemist, not a gunpowder maker.'

'I bet he will. You'll just have to find out, won't you? But you're not to ask him. You've got to get it secretly, so he don't know. That's the test, see? Otherwise it won't count.'

'What're you going to use it for?' Tim stared at him excitedly. 'Are you going to make fireworks?'

'Maybe.' Micky turned away. 'You just get that stuff and we might let you into our gang. But it's gotta be secret, see? Nobody's gotta know.'

Tim mounted his bike again and pedalled away up the road. His heart was racing. Fireworks! He hadn't seen fireworks for years. He thought of the ones his father used to buy before the war, ready for Guy Fawkes night. He'd start in the middle of October, as soon as they came into the shops, and bring home two or three a week – perhaps a roman candle and a rocket, or a catherine wheel, or – Tim's favourite – the zigzag of a jumping jack, which would leap all over the place when lit and make the girls squeal and hop about.

Frank would put the fireworks into a box which was kept at the top of the cupboard, and get it out every Friday evening to add the latest to the collection. Rose and Tim and Keith would gather round, stroking and admiring the coloured paper and longing for November the Fifth to arrive so that they could be set off in the garden. And during the last week, they would make a guy with a few old rags given them by Jess, and build a bonfire to be lit as soon as darkness fell.

There hadn't been any fireworks now since the war started, and nobody knew when they might be available again. Tim might be grown up before they appeared in the shops once more. And Maureen had never seen them at all.

Micky might let me make her some, he thought. If Mr Driver's got the right stuff, and I get some, he'd have to let me. A roman candle, she'd like that. Or one of those golden rod things that looks like a big spray of flowers.

The weather was growing warmer and although Carol was feeling less sick now, she was uncomfortable and almost always tired. The smell of stale cabbage that pervaded the house made her feel queasy, so she went out as much as she could, but there wasn't much to do. There were a lot of Servicemen in the streets and they whistled at her and several tried to pick her up. At one time, she would have answered them back and enjoyed it, but now she was embarrassed and ashamed.

'I saw you trying to get off with them Yanks,' Mrs Higgs told her one afternoon. 'I'd have thought you 'ad enough to think about, without playing the tart. Or maybe you thought you could earn a few bob before you starts to show.' Her small eyes gleamed dully as she stared at Carol's figure, still thin after her sickness. 'Don't you try bringin' men back 'ere, that's all.'

'I'm not,' Carol said furiously. 'I didn't even speak to them. I can't help it if they whistle at me.'

'Don't give me that! Any man knows when a girl's askin' for it. They can see what sort of a hussy you are just by lookin' at yer. They knows, right enough.'

'You're a filthy-minded old woman,' Carol said. 'I wouldn't bring anyone back here anyway. I'd be ashamed to admit I lived here.'

'Oh, would yer? Well, maybe you'd better find somewhere a bit more to yer taste, then. I'm sure I don't want to stand in yer light, Lady Muck. And if that feller of yours can't cough up a bit more rent, you'd better start lookin' for somewhere else anyway.' She turned and slopped downstairs in her down at heel slippers.

'Don't worry,' Carol shouted after her, 'we will. We can't wait to get away from you!'

She banged the door and flung herself on the bed, breathless with rage. She had reached the point now when the mere sight of Mrs Higgs made her angry. And the woman knew just how to taunt her. I'll kill her one of these days, Carol thought, I know I will. I'll push her down the stairs.

Half of her anger was fear. The thought of the baby growing inside her filled her with panic. She wanted to run, to get far away from it, but she knew there was no escape; wherever she went, the baby would be with her, still growing. Once or twice she had thought about trying the landlady's suggestions of taking castor-oil or jumping off a chair. But she couldn't bear the thought of Roddy's disappointment if she did.

He really seems to like the idea of a baby, she thought in wonder. But he's not going to have to look after it, is he?

She couldn't look ahead at all. She and Roddy were fairly sure now that the baby was probably due in November. But November seemed a lifetime away. There was the whole of the summer to get through first.

Roddy too was having problems. The foreman at the warehouse was an old man who had been due to retire when the war started and had already lost his own son in the London blitz and his grandson at Dunkirk. He had been suspicious of Roddy ever since the young sailor had started work, and never tired of trying to catch him out.

'S'pose you're one of them bleedin' conchies,' he mumbled through his sandwich one morning. 'Too lily-livered to fight for your country. Bleedin' collaborator.'

'That I'm not,' Roddy answered angrily. 'It's none of your business anyway.'

'It is. It's everyone's business.' The rheumy eyes stared at him suspiciously. 'Told to look out for fiff columnists, ain't we? People with queer accents and that. I reckon you're about the queerest I've come across, no two ways about it.'

'I'm Scottish. Have you never heard a Scottish accent before?'

'Yes, I have, an' it didn't sound like yours. There was a bloke from Glasgow worked here once. Cut his accent with a knife, you could. Yours ain't anything like that.'

'I should hope not. I live near Edinburgh.'

'Hoity-toity!' the foreman mocked him. 'What's the difference – it's still Scotland, ain't it? You're still a Jock. That's if you really do come from there. Reckon you're a quisling meself. One of them spies.'

'Och, for goodness sake,' Roddy said in disgust. 'You don't know what you're talking about.' He finished his bait and got up. 'I'll get on with that new delivery.'

He started work again, but the old foreman scowled. He didn't like being talked to like that by a bit of a kid and he didn't believe that Roddy was as innocent as he appeared. There was something wrong about a lad of that age, miles from home, doing odd jobs in a warehouse. If he wasn't a 'conchie' he was the next worst thing – a deserter.

The old man thought of his grandson, not much older than Roddy, who had gone off to war as a fresh-faced young soldier and never come back. He thought of what he had heard about Dunkirk – the men standing in the sea, being strafed by German aircraft as they waited for rescue, the bombs, the blood.

'Lily-bleedin'-livered skiver,' he muttered, and shambled off towards the office.

The policeman had been thinking about retirement too. If the war hadn't started, he'd be in that nice little bungalow his missus had always wanted, growing roses and doing a bit of fishing. And his own grandson would be in the Force, instead of being sent out to Africa to fight in the desert. He had a lot of sympathy for the foreman.

'And you reckon there's something funny about this young chap, then?' he asked, leaning on the desk. 'I mean, just because he's Scotch don't mean anything. They're still English, after all, aren't they? They're on our side.'

'If 'e *is* Scotch,' the foreman said. 'Could be anything, couldn't 'e? I mean, 'ow're we supposed to know what 'is accent is? An' if 'e is all above board, why ain't 'e servin'? Whichever way you looks at it, there's summat queer. Any'ow, I thought it was me civic duty to come along and say me piece, so that's what I done. Up to you now.'

'You did quite right,' the sergeant said. 'It's information like this we're on the lookout for. You can't be too careful these days, not when there's a war on.' He drew a pile of forms across the desk and dipped his pen in the inkpot. 'I'd better take down a few details.'

The foreman wasn't the only visitor to the police station that day. Mrs Higgs had been in an hour earlier, complaining about her lodgers. She had spoken to a young constable who was waiting for call-up and his sympathies had been with the young couple she was grumbling about.

'It's not everyone can get into the Services,' he said. 'I bet he's tried hard enough. And if his missus is expecting—'

'Missus!' the landlady said scornfully. 'She's no more his missus than you are. Living in sin, that's what they are, and under my roof what's always been decent. I'd have thrown 'em out weeks ago if I hadn't bin so soft-hearted. But that's always bin my trouble. Fool to meself, that's what I am. "Martha," my late hubby used to tell me, "you're a fool to yourself and it'll get you into trouble one of these days." But there, I couldn't never stand by and see people suffer.'

'So why've you come here now?' the constable asked wearily. 'I mean, d'you want to report them for something or not?'

She stared at him. 'Well, that's for you to say, innit? If they're breakin' the law—'

'Yes, but I don't know that they are, do I? I mean, even if they're not married—'

'The boot'd be on the other foot if you 'ad it in for me,' Mrs Higgs said bitterly. 'Runnin' a house of disrepute, that's what you'd be callin' it. But when I comes all decent and honest and above board to report it, you're not interested. That's typical, that is. And what about 'im bein' a deserter? Ain't that important enough for you?'

'Well, there again, you don't *know* he's on the run.' The constable had recently attended a training course during which it had been impressed upon him that he must be sure of his facts before taking any action. 'Until we've got proof—'

Mrs Higgs' patience snapped. 'Well, ain't that what you're supposed to get, for Gawd's sake? You're the bleedin' police, ain't yer? Can't you investigate? Or are you too busy snoopin' round the shops to see who's getting stuff on the black market?' She glared at the young constable. 'Trouble is, there ain't no proper police these days, just old men and kids barely out of nappies. I dunno what the country's comin' to, I really don't.'

The constable tightened his lips and wrote down the details Mrs Higgs gave him. He left the sheet of paper on top of the pile and the sergeant found it later when he was talking to Roddy's foreman.

'Here,' he said, 'there's another report here. Looks as if it could be the same pair. Scotch lad and a girl he says is his missus. She's in the family way.' He clicked his tongue. 'His landlady reckons they're not married and thinks he's a deserter. What's your chap's name?'

'Macintosh,' the foreman said. 'Some fancy first name – Rodney, would it be? They call him Rod in the warehouse.'

'That's what she says. Roddy, his young woman calls him. It must be the same ones.' The sergeant was beginning to feel excited. It wasn't often something like this happened in his quiet station. 'That's two complaints in the same afternoon. I'd better get round there straight away.'

'Shouldn't you get the authorities?' the foreman suggested. 'The military, I mean. If he is a deserter – he could cut up rough.'

'And if he isn't, I'm going to look a fool. And so will you. No, I'll go round first, ask a few questions.' The sergeant opened the desk to come through and bent to fasten his cycle clips round his ankles. 'You did right to come. I'll deal with it now.'

The foreman hung on, unwilling to miss the action, but he had walked to the police station and the sergeant was already fetching his bike from the passage. He couldn't trot behind him all the way to the street where Roddy lived. And it didn't look as if there was going to be an immediate arrest anyway. You couldn't bring a villain back to the police cells on the back of a pushbike.

'Will there be a reward?' he asked, without much hope. The sergeant gave him a reproving look.

'Helping your country's a reward, innit? Ain't that enough?'

He mounted his bike and pedalled slowly away along the street. The foreman stared after him for a moment or two, then shrugged and turned in the opposite direction. He might as well call in at the Three Bells for a drink. Reporting a deserter was thirsty work.

Roddy had brought fish and chips home for supper. It was what they had most days – without ration books, they could buy little food and had to rely on the chip-shop and the local British restaurant, and they were afraid to go there too much for fear of being recognised. And buying any food at all usually meant standing in a queue for hours, and Carol had almost fainted when she tried that.

'I don't know why anyone ever has babies,' she said miserably, picking at the lukewarm chips. 'I feel like an old woman. And it's going to get worse. What's it going to be like when I'm fat and can't hardly drag myself about?'

Roddy shook his head helplessly. He had no idea what it was like to be pregnant. But women did have babies, lots of them sometimes, and survived. Surely it couldn't be that bad. He couldn't ever remember his cousin Moira being like this.

'Carrie,' he said, 'I think we ought to go to Scotland. My mother'll help us. She'll know what to do. She'll look after you.' He felt in his pocket and produced an envelope. 'I've written to her, see. I've told her all about us and the bairn. We'll save up for the fare and go as soon as we can.'

Carol took the envelope and stared at it. The address was a village a few miles from Edinburgh. She opened her mouth to ask how they could ever afford the fare for such a long journey, but the words were never spoken.

The bedroom door was suddenly flung open. Mrs Higgs stood there, meanly triumphant, and behind her on the landing was the large, portly shape of a police sergeant in uniform.

18

Carol found the letter Roddy had written to his mother much later that night. It had slipped to the floor and got kicked under the bed. She picked it up and stared at the grubby envelope, marked with dust and traces of mud from someone's shoe.

It was too late now to ask Roddy how they could ever afford the fare to Scotland, and she didn't know if they would ever go there together anyway. She didn't know if they would ever go anywhere together again.

Roddy had been arrested. The big policeman had taken him away. It had seemed touch and go for a while whether he might take Carol herself away too, but eventually he'd decided that she hadn't actually committed any crime (thank God he didn't know about her mother's money, Carol thought), and in any case there wasn't any room in the cells. Instead, he had given her a good telling-off before reading out the long list of charges he had against Roddy, and marching him away down the smelly stairs.

'You're not taking him away!' she cried, catching at the dark-blue sleeve. 'It's not true, none of those things are true – Roddy never abducted me, I *wanted* to come with him. We were going to get married. It was *my* idea! And it's not fair to call him a deserter – he shouldn't never have been called up in the first place. He's clever, Roddy is, he was going to university, he didn't ought to be fighting, he—'

'And who are you to say who's to fight and who isn't?' the sergeant demanded. 'It's King and country, not bits of girls like you that we wants young men for. Anyway, that's not all. The whole case has got to be properly investigated. Why, he might be a spy for all we know. So might you, come to that.' He looked at Carol's white face and thin body. 'Here, how old are you anyway?'

'Sixteen,' Carol said wearily, and sat down on the bed. She was beginning to feel sick again.

'Sixteen when?'

'Just after Christmas. It's all right,' she said bitterly, 'I'm old enough to get married. And if we'd managed to get enough money to go to Scotland, I would've been by now.'

'Just after Christmas,' he said, staring at her. 'And how long have you and this young chap been going together, then, eh? Was there anything untoward going on before you was sixteen?'

'I dunno what you mean,' Carol began, and then caught his meaning and flushed scarlet. 'That's none of your business. You keep your dirty mind to yourself.'

'And you be careful of your tongue,' he retorted. 'It'll get you in trouble, it will, talking to a police officer like that. Well, I'll say no more about it now – but there'll be a thorough investigation, you mark my words, a very thorough investigation, and you and this young man might find yourselves in very serious trouble indeed.' He looked at Carol's bewildered face. 'It's rape if a man has carnal knowledge of a girl under the age of sixteen,' he said brutally. 'Statutory rape. And it don't matter if she *did* lead him on. It's a jail sentence.' He shook Roddy's arm. 'You'll be sorry you ever got yourself mixed up with this young woman,' he said. 'Prison's no rest cure, specially in the Services. After a couple of months in the glasshouse, you're going to wish you could be out there in the front line, mark my words.'

'Carol—' Roddy began, agonised.

'Roddy. Oh, *Roddy*—' She reached out both hands, but the sergeant was already shoving him on to the landing. She caught one last glimpse of his terrified face, and then the policeman's bulk filled the doorway.

'Now, you just stop here, young lady, and don't try running off,' he told her sternly. 'Your ma'll be along to fetch you, and if you've got any sense you'll be thankful to go home with nothing worse than a flea in your ear. You've had a lucky escape.'

'Escape!' she echoed bitterly. 'I escaped when I got away and came here.' She reached out again, pleading with him. 'Don't take him away. Please don't take him away. I'll die. I know I will. Please, please, *please*—' The tears were rolling down her cheeks now, and her words came with huge sobs that forced their way up from her chest like great, hard lumps. 'I can't live without Roddy. And I can't go home, I *can't*. It'll be like going back to prison. *Please*—'

Prison. The sergeant was turning away, his face stony. She heard Roddy's voice in her mind. *They'd send me to prison*, he'd said. *They might even shoot me.*

He was gone. All she could hear was the sound of his feet on the stairs, lighter, more stumbling than the sergeant's heavy tread. He was gone, and she might never see him again.

She reached hastily for the bucket and vomited.

The Portsmouth police came to see Ethel that same evening and gave her the fare to Bournemouth to go and fetch Carol herself. She arrived next morning, her immediate relief completely overshadowed by a furious temper, and her first action was to take her daughter by the shoulders and shake her.

'You little hussy! You naughty, *naughty* girl! Have you got any idea how worried I've been? I haven't slept a wink since you ran off, not a wink. I've been imagining all sorts of things – seeing you dead in a ditch, strangled or worse – I don't know how many times I planned your funeral. I thought I was never going to see you again. Don't you realise what I've been through? Don't you care?'

'You didn't care about *me*,' Carol said through her tears. 'You were always telling me off.'

'That's because I'm your mother. I wanted the best for you. I always did my best for you.' Ethel sat down in the battered basket chair and rummaged in her black patent handbag for a handkerchief. 'You don't know what it is to struggle to bring up your children right and then have it all thrown back in your face. You don't know what it is to be a mother.'

'Oh, don't I,' Carol muttered, and felt her face turn scarlet.

Ethel stared at her.

'What's the matter with you? Why've you fired up like that?' She got up again and looked more closely at her daughter. 'There's something funny about you. You're looking peaky. Are you all right?' She grasped Carol's shoulders again and Carol slid her eyes away. 'You're not going to tell me you're—'

'Expecting,' Carol said defiantly, meeting her mother's eyes at last. 'That's what you're going to say, isn't it? Well, I am, so there. I'm expecting a baby, Roddy's baby, and it's due in November, in nice time for Christmas. Won't that be a lovely present for you? You'll be a granny!'

Ethel gasped. She lifted her right hand and struck Carol hard across the face. Carol screamed and stumbled, and Ethel hit her again and then again, raining blows on her daughter's shoulders as the girl half fell, half cringed before her.

'You *filthy* little bitch! You trollop! Bringing shame on the family like this. I'll never be able to hold up my head again, never. I'll never be able to look that Jess Budd in the eye again. Everyone will be staring at us and sneering behind our backs. The whole street'll be talking. Oh, you hussy, you tart, you dirty, filthy little *slut*!'

'Stop it, Mum. Stop it. You'll hurt the baby.' Carol crouched on the floor, her arms held above her head. 'Stop it.'

The bedroom door opened. Mrs Higgs stood there, her arms akimbo, small eyes gleaming maliciously. 'That's right. That's what the little monkey needs. Pity she didn't get it before she got herself into this mess.'

'And you can keep your opinions to yourself,' Ethel snapped, turning on her. 'You ought to be ashamed, letting a bloke bring a decent girl to a place like this. Why, it's nothing but a slum. Filthy dirty windows, grease all over the floor, the stairs in a mess . . . My Carol's been used to something a sight better than this, I can tell you!'

'Well, you wouldn't 'ave known it from the way she's behaved,' the landlady said indignantly. 'Fish and chips every night, being sick in a bucket, stinkin' the place out . . . I'd 'ave thrown the pair of 'em out weeks ago if I 'adn't 'ad such a soft 'eart. They're lucky to 'ave 'ad anywhere at all to live, if you asks me.'

'I wasn't asking you,' Ethel said tartly. 'And I don't recall asking you in here neither, to shove your oar in where it's not wanted.' She turned to Carol. 'Get up and get your things together. We're going home.'

'Home? But—'

'You'll pay off the rent before you do,' Mrs Higgs said, planting herself firmly in the doorway. 'Three weeks behind, they were, and not payin' the full amount then. I give 'em a reduction to start with, to 'elp 'em along a bit, but it was fifteen bob a week after that, and that young scallywag never did give me the full amount. Three pounds they owes me.'

'Well, you'll just have to whistle for it.' Ethel snatched up the few clothes Carol had spread out on the bed and crammed them into her shopping bag. 'I'm not paying no rent.'

'But they *owes* me—' Mrs Higgs began, and then, as Ethel shoved her aside, 'I'll take 'em to court, that's what I'll do. I'll take the whole bleedin' lot of you to court. I'll see you in jail, see if I don't—'

Ethel ignored her. She grabbed Carol's arm and pushed her roughly past the landlady and on to the landing. Together, they stumbled down the dimly-lit stairs and out of the front door.

'Oh, Mum,' Carol said waveringly as Ethel dragged her along the street, 'what are we going to do? Suppose she does take us to court? I don't want to go to prison.'

'Don't be daft. She won't do nothing. I know her sort. She won't want the police nosing round, asking questions. I'm surprised she ever went to them in the first place.' Ethel's fingers were cruelly tight around Carol's arm as she hustled her round the corner, out of earshot of Mrs Higgs' furious yells. 'And now, my lady, we'll get you home and then you can tell me just what's been going on and what you think you're going to do about this baby you're expecting.'

Jess Budd had just come out of her front door when Ethel and Carol came round the corner by Mrs Seddon's shop. She stared at them in surprise and then hurried across the road, smiling with relief.

'Carol! Am I pleased to see you! We wondered whatever had happened to you. Where've you been? Are you all right?'

'Of course she's all right,' Ethel snapped. 'And it's none of your business where she's been. She's home now and that's all you need concern yourself with, and if you don't mind we'll just go indoors and have a cup of tea. We've had a long journey.'

'Hoity-toity,' Jess said as the door of number 15 closed behind the two. 'Well, I'm sure it doesn't matter to us where she's been, does it, Maureen. Wherever it was, if you ask me she didn't look all that glad to be home. I wonder what happened to that young man.' She took Maureen's hand and led her up the street to Annie's house, eager to share the latest scrap of news with her sister. 'Anyway, it's daft of Ethel Glaister to get up on her high horse – it only makes people talk all the more.'

Annie was interested to hear that Carol Glaister had come home, but she didn't have time to pay much attention to Jess's speculations. She had been down to North End that morning to see their parents and was soon telling Jess about Arthur.

'He's getting worse. He got up in the middle of last night and went out. Mum thought he'd gone to the lav – he's gone funny about using the po in front of her lately – but when he didn't come back she went downstairs and found the front door wide open. She went next door and got Mr Barrett out and they found him down near the Odeon in his pyjamas.'

'But that's terrible,' Jess said. 'He could have been run over in the blackout.'

'Well, it was getting light and there wasn't much traffic about, but you're right, anything could have happened.' Annie stirred her tea, frowning. She was looking thinner these days, Jess thought, and no wonder, with the worry over Colin hanging over her. 'I don't know what to suggest. I'd have them up here, we've got the room now, but he won't hear of it.'

'It'd be the best answer, though. We wouldn't have to keep running down to North End, and I could give you a hand with them. Perhaps we could get Frank to talk Dad round.'

'That's a good idea,' Annie said. 'Dad's always thought a lot of Frank. I'll get Ted to chip in too. He might take more notice of the men.' She rubbed her hand across her tired face. 'I dunno, Jess, it seems like this war just piles troubles on you all the time. Whatever would we have thought a few years ago if we could have looked ahead and seen all this happening, eh?'

'Maybe it's a good job we can't,' Jess said. 'I mean, it'd be nice to see into the future if you could be sure it would be good, but I'd be afraid to look now. There don't seem to be any end to it all.'

Together, they turned their heads and looked up at the mantelpiece, where Annie had stood a row of photographs. There were the girls, Betty in her Land Girl's sweater and breeches, Olive in her ATS uniform. And there was Colin, cheeky-faced and grinning, in his sailor's square rig.

There isn't even time to worry about it properly, Jess thought. When something as big as that happens, you need time to take it in, time to consider it all. But instead, there's all these other things – like poor old Dad losing his memory, and Olive risking her life on a gun battery, and Betty getting engaged to young Dennis, that Ted doesn't approve of. And rationing, and shortages, and nothing being the same as it used to be.

And we're supposed to *smile* about it all! Smile and crack a joke, and look for the silver lining. *Turn the dark cloud inside out* . . .

She chuckled suddenly and Annie looked at her enquiringly. 'I never told you what Maureen said to me yesterday. You know how it rained in the morning. Well, I started singing that song, 'Pennies From Heaven', not thinking what her little mind might make of it, and she puzzled right up till dinner-time and then as we were sitting down, she said to me, "Do clouds have pockets, Mummy?" "Pockets?" I said. "No, of course clouds don't have pockets. Whatever makes you think they do?" And you know what she said? She said, "If they don't have pockets, where do they keep their pennies?" I had to think a bit, I can tell you, before I realised what she was on about.' Jess laughed again. 'The things she thinks of! You never know what she's going to come out with next.'

Annie laughed too, and picked up the little girl. 'You're a funny cuts, you are. You keep us all chuckling – I don't know what we'd do without you.' She held her niece close for a moment. 'I just wish they were all this small, so we could keep them safe at home,' she said quietly. 'But there it is, you can't stop the young ones growing up. And you can't stop the old ones getting older, either. You'll get Frank to have a word with Mum and Dad, will you? Perhaps we could all go down together, the four of us. Something's got to be done – they can't go on like this much longer. There's going to be an accident, one way or another.'

Joy heard about Carol's return from her mother. Jess Budd had been in for the *Evening News* and told her about it. Nobody knew much yet, but there was a lot of speculation and whispering in the shop.

'What's it all about?' Joy asked bluntly. 'Why are you all talking behind your hands? I suppose you think Carol's having a baby.'

'Joy! That's not at all a nice thing for a young girl to say. I don't know where you get such ideas.'

'Oh, for goodness sake, Mum. I'm not a little kid. I know how many beans make five.' Joy's restlessness was making her outspoken these days, and she was tired of being treated on the one hand like an adult – expected to do a day's work; and on the other like a child – being seen and not heard. 'Carol went off with a boy, didn't she? Everyone'll be watching her now.'

'I still don't like hearing you talk like that.' Alice frowned. 'And I don't want you seeing a lot of her, either. We don't know what ideas she's come back with. She was always a flighty little piece as it was, and you know what her mother's like.'

'That's right,' Heinrich said. 'Better to stay clear.'

Joy turned away. She had never been particularly friendly with Carol, until Rose had gone away and there hadn't been anyone else, but they'd had a few laughs then. And Roddy'd seemed a nice chap, and really keen on Carol. She wondered what had happened to him.

They all knew, soon enough. Ethel never said a word but it was in the *Evening News* a week or two later, the report of the young sailor who had deserted and run off with a girl who was barely sixteen. As the police sergeant had threatened, there was talk of abduction, and even rape, since Carol had been under age when they first began to go out together, but in the end that was dropped and Carol wasn't even called to give evidence. Roddy faced charges of deception and theft as well as the naval court-martial for desertion. He was dismissed from the Royal Navy and given a term of five years' imprisonment.

'Five years,' Joy said. 'That's awful. He'll be old when he comes out.'

'Twenty-three,' Alice said sharply. 'That might seem old to you, but he'll still be young enough to do plenty of damage. He's ruined that girl's whole life.'

'And at least he'll still have his life,' Heinrich added. 'Plenty of young men will never be twenty-three.' He gave her a hesitant glance, and said more gently, 'Joy, *liebchen*, you know that we only speak to you like this because we care about you. We don't want you to risk the same kind of trouble that Carol has got into. We know what it means, you see.'

Joy looked at him doubtfully. Her father's voice sounded almost as it had done before he was taken away, when he had been the mild, loving father she worshipped. She had not heard him speak like that for over a year. Her eyes stung a little.

Heinrich moved over to her and put his hand on her shoulder. For the first time in many months, she did not flinch away.

'I'm afraid it's true that poor little Carol may be expecting a baby,' he said. 'Her life will never be the same again. If she keeps it – and I cannot see how she can even think of such a thing – she will have a truly terrible time. Everyone will know, everyone will turn away. I am not saying this is right. I am saying it will be so. And how will she manage for money? She will live in poverty, for that mother of hers will never lift a finger to help.'

'And if she gives it away for adoption, she'll never forget it,' Alice added. 'She'll always wonder – every birthday, every Christmas, every *day*. She'll never forget.'

She was looking at her husband almost as if she'd never seen him before. For some weeks now, she had detected a softening in him, an easing in his bitter anger. But that it should take the plight of Ethel Glaister's daughter, of all people, to bring back the man he had been . . . ! She reached out her hand and touched him, feeling the tears in her own eyes, and so the three of them stood for a moment, linked. A family once again.

Joy met Carol in the street a day or two later. They hesitated and looked at each other for a minute, then Carol said, 'I suppose you won't want to talk to me now.'

'I don't mind,' Joy said awkwardly, trying not to look at Carol's waistline. She was wearing a loose frock, which made it difficult to tell if she was looking any fatter. But her face didn't look fat – it looked thin and unhappy. 'It's a shame about Roddy,' she said at last. 'I liked him. He was nice.'

'You needn't talk about him as if he was dead,' Carol said sharply. 'He's still nice.' Her lip quivered suddenly and tears filled her eyes and began to run down her cheeks. 'I hate thinking of him in prison,' she said. 'It must be awful. He never did anything to deserve that, Joy.'

'I know.' Suddenly, the awkwardness between them had gone and Joy could feel nothing but an immense sympathy for the miserable girl. She remembered what her parents had said, the sympathy they had shown. 'Here, I'm going down North End to do a bit of shopping for Mum. Why don't you come with me? I've got enough for the bus fare back.'

'Might as well.' Carol turned and walked beside her. She was silent for a few moments, then she burst out, 'Mum wants me to get rid of the baby. I can't. I've told her I can't. But she says she'll make me.'

Joy stared at her. 'Get rid of it? But – you haven't had it yet, have you?'

'Of course I haven't had it! It's not due till November. You know what I mean. She wants me to go away and have it and then get it adopted so no one round here'll know. She doesn't even want Dad or our Joe to know. It's supposed to be a secret – she'd kill me if she knew I was telling you. But I can't keep it all to myself, and I've got no one else to talk to.'

Joy didn't know what to say. She couldn't imagine Carol with a baby. 'But how would you look after it? I mean, you wouldn't be able to get a job or anything.'

'I don't know,' Carol said hopelessly. 'I don't know what I'd do. But I can't give it away, Joy. It's Roddy's baby. I've got to keep it, for him.'

The whole story poured out now, as the two girls walked along

September Street. All the time in Bournemouth, lying on the creaky bed in Mrs Higgs' room, being sick and thinking she was ill. The search for jobs. The frightening realisation that she was pregnant, and Mrs Higgs' suggestions about an illegal abortion. And Roddy's love, shining steadfast throughout all their anxieties.

'He didn't know what to do. He tried so hard to do his best. And now he's in prison, and he didn't even do the things they said. He never stole any money, Joy – I did that. I took my mum's savings. But he swore it was him, just to keep me out of trouble.'

'He got you into trouble, all the same,' Joy said. 'I mean, you're going to have this baby, aren't you. My mum says he's ruined your life.'

'Well, he hasn't,' Carol said fiercely. 'You can just tell her he hasn't. He's made my life special. Nobody ever loved me till Roddy came along – not really. Even my dad . . . And now I'm going to have his baby, and that'll love me too. And I'll love it and look after it till Roddy comes out of prison and we can get married.'

The determination to have her baby had come almost as soon as she'd arrived home. Until then, she had been terrified, ready to give anything to have the baby magically spirited away. She didn't want an operation, such as Mrs Higgs had suggested, she just wanted it never to have happened. But once home, with Ethel ranting at her, her feelings had changed. She had clasped her hands protectively across her stomach and defied her mother.

'It's my baby! Mine and Roddy's. He wanted me to have it, and I will.' And she had felt a sudden surge of love for the little person growing within her, the person that she and Roddy had made through loving each other. 'You can't force me to give it away.'

'Oh, can't I? And just how do you expect to manage on your own, eh, tell me that. Because you won't get no help from me.'

'I bet Dad'd help me. He wouldn't make me give it away—'

'Your Dad's not going to know nothing about this,' Ethel said sharply. 'Why, it'd break his heart to think his daughter had gone to the bad like this. You're not to tell him, see, nor our Joe, nor no one else. There's no need for anyone to know.'

'Of course they'll know,' Carol said. 'They're not blind.' And she listened in dismay as Ethel outlined her plans. A mother and baby home, full of girls waiting to give birth. Somewhere out in the country – 'far enough away so no one from round here'll know,' Ethel said. And then the baby handed over to strangers, taken away, never to be seen again.

'No,' she said. 'No. Roddy'd never forgive me.'

'*Roddy!* It's nothing to do with him.'

'He's its father,' Carol said. 'He was pleased about it—'

'*Pleased?* The very idea—'

'He wanted us to have it. He'd hate me if I gave it away.'

'He probably hates you anyway,' Ethel said shrewdly, 'for getting him into such a mess. Not that it wasn't all his own fault.'

Carol stared at her. Roddy, hating her? 'It's not true,' she said shakily. 'We love each other.'

'And how long's that going to last?' her mother sneered. 'Five years he's been put away for. Five years. That little bump you've got there'll be at school by then. D'you think he's still going to want you, after he's been in jail for five years? Why, you won't even recognise each other!'

It's not true, Carol thought, squeezing her eyes shut and trying to conjure up Roddy's face. But to her horror, she couldn't do it. She couldn't see him.

She could see his hair and, if she concentrated hard, she could see his hands, long and knobbly, the hands that she'd loved to have caress her. She could catch a glimpse of his eyes – just briefly, for a moment – and then his mouth. But she couldn't put it all together and see *him*.

I can't remember what he looked like, she thought in panic. I've lost him already.

'See?' Ethel said cruelly. 'See?' She waited a moment, then went on, 'We'll have no more argy-bargy about this. You'll do as I say. I'll find out about these homes first thing tomorrow, and we'll see about getting you in one. I'll put it out that you're going down to Devon to be with our Shirley. And then when it's all finished with you can come back here and get yourself another job. It's going to cost me enough as it is, this lot, and I'm not going to keep you in luxury a minute longer than I have to—'

Carol opened her eyes. She stared at her mother and then came abruptly to life. She jumped up from her chair, her hands balled into tight fists, her face scarlet with sudden rage.

'No!' she shouted, so loudly that Jess Budd next door heard her through the wall. 'No, no, *no*! I won't do what you say. I won't go away and have my baby and pretend I'm in Devon. And I won't give it away – I won't. You can't make me. *Nobody* can make me.'

She ran out of the room and up the stairs. Ethel sat quite still, listening to the slam of the bedroom door and the storm of weeping that followed it. Then she shrugged and began to gather up the tea-things.

'Can't I, my lady?' she said to herself. 'We'll see about that. We'll soon see about that.'

19

Babies were more happily in the air out at Bishop's Waltham, where Erica had settled back into life as a Land Girl almost as if she had never married the farmer's son. There were small differences – she had the embarrassment of trying to remember to call Jack and Ada Spencer 'Mum' and 'Dad', and they tried hard to behave as if she were now their daughter rather than a Land Girl. But since they had never had a daughter, and there was still work to be done on the farm, neither of them was quite sure what difference it should make.

'You'll move down into Gerald's room, of course,' Mrs Spencer said. 'I'm sure he'd expect you to.'

Erica hesitated, looking at Betty and Yvonne. 'I don't know – I think I'd rather stop up in the attic now. At least till he comes home – I'll move down then, of course.' She blushed as the others laughed. 'I've got used to the company,' she confessed.

'Well, there's a turn-up,' Betty said. 'First time we came here you looked at us as if we'd got fleas.'

'Mind you, I probably did have,' Yvonne added with a grin. 'We all did, in Rudmore.'

The awkwardnesses soon disappeared. Within a week, Erica had stopped calling her parents-in-law anything at all, and they had returned to their normal behaviour. And up in the attic, it was easy to believe that nothing had changed.

It was about a month after the wedding when Erica first confided her suspicions to the other two girls.

'But we all miss from time to time,' Betty said. 'Specially when something exciting's happening. I never saw my period once, when we went on holiday one summer.'

'I've always been regular as clockwork,' Erica said. 'I'm nearly three weeks over now. And I felt a bit funny yesterday morning, when I bent down to do the milking.'

Betty looked at her. 'But you and Gerald hardly had time. I mean – I never thought you went together before the wedding. I thought—'

'We didn't,' Erica said, blushing. 'But that afternoon – well, we didn't know when we might see each other again. And we *were* married. You couldn't expect us not to—'

'Well, we didn't think you were picking flowers all that time,' Yvonne observed. 'But d'you really mean to say it was only that once?'

Betty remembered her sister Olive, telling her it hardly ever happened the first time. 'How d'you feel about it?' she asked curiously. 'If you really are – you know. Are you pleased?'

Erica looked nonplussed. 'I haven't thought about being pleased or not. I've only just started to wonder if I *am*. But – I don't feel upset. Actually, I think I feel quite excited, really.'

'A baby,' Yvonne said, looking almost as excited as if it were her own. 'That'll be smashing. I bet the guvnor'll be pleased. And Mrs Spencer.' She grinned wickedly. 'Here, you'll be able to call 'em Granny and Grandpa now!'

'You ought to find out if you really are expecting,' Betty said. 'There might be things you shouldn't be doing round the farm. I mean, you want to take care of yourself.' She thought of Olive, losing her baby during an air-raid. 'Isn't there something about not lifting your arms above your head?'

'That's an old wives' tale,' Yvonne said. 'My mum's had six and she never did anything different with any of us. How could she? I mean, she couldn't stop hanging out washing just because there was another one on the way, could she?'

'Well, you ought to see about it anyway,' Betty insisted. 'You're doing a lot of heavy work. You ought to tell Mrs Spencer. She'll know.'

Erica felt shy about telling her mother-in-law the news. For one thing, it made it so obvious what she and Gerald had been doing on the afternoon of their wedding – not, as she had said to Betty, that there was any reason why they shouldn't. But it couldn't be hidden for ever, and Betty was right, there might be things she should be careful of. So one evening, when the other two girls were cutting down some old cotton frocks to make blouses, she went downstairs to where Mrs Spencer was topping and tailing gooseberries in the farm kitchen, and listening to *ITMA* on the wireless.

'I'll do some of those,' she offered, and sat down at the kitchen table with a pair of scissors. The gooseberries were from Mrs Spencer's kitchen garden and would be bottled or made into jam to last the family through the winter. The farmer's wife made other jams and preserves too, with plums and apples from the orchard, and the jars gleamed like precious jewels in the cupboard.

'You'll have to teach me to make jam,' Erica said, when the wireless programme had finished to the music of *It's That Man Again*. 'I want to be ready to be a proper farmer's wife when Gerald comes home.'

'You're doing well enough,' Mrs Spencer answered. 'You can milk a cow as if you'd been brought up to it, and do most of the other jobs around the place as well. But you're right – you ought to be learning a few of the other sorts of skills – they'll be more use to you when you've got a family round your skirts.'

Erica blushed. She'd been wondering how to introduce the subject, yet now that the opportunity had been handed to her she still couldn't find the right words. There was a short silence, and then Mrs Spencer gave her a quick glance and said casually, 'Was there something you wanted to tell me?'

Erica took a deep breath. She knew her face was fiery and she felt almost guilty, as if she were about to confess to some minor sin. We were *married*, she told herself fiercely. There was nothing wrong in what we did, even if it was behind a haystack . . . She looked up and met her mother-in-law's eyes, and then blurted out, 'I'm having a baby. At least, I think I am. But we never – I mean, I don't want you to think . . . It was only that one afternoon . . .'

Mrs Spencer gazed at her. Her eyes were suddenly bright. She blinked and reached across the table for Erica's hand, holding it tightly.

'My dear child! I never thought for one moment – not for one moment that you and Gerald . . . My Gerald wouldn't . . . A *baby*. Oh, that's lovely, that really is lovely. Our first grandchild. Oh, I must tell Jack.' She got up and hurried round the long table to hug Erica. 'I had an idea there might be something – I can always tell, there's something about a girl's skin – but I thought no, it couldn't be, it'd be a miracle . . . Just that one afternoon – oh, I'm so pleased, you can't *think!*'

Erica clung to her, her own tears flowing suddenly. Half laughing, half crying, she said, 'I didn't know how to tell you. I mean, I don't know for certain. And I don't really know what all the signs are. I really wanted to tell Gerald first, but I can't say anything unless I'm sure. I don't want to raise his hopes if it's a false alarm.'

'Of course you don't.' Ada Spencer gazed at her fondly. 'We'd better wait a week or two more before we mention it to anyone else. And then you'd better go and see the doctor. They can tell at about eight weeks.' She hesitated and then said, 'I daresay you'll want to go and see your mum and dad, to tell them.'

Erica looked away. 'Well, some time, I suppose. To tell the truth, I don't think they'd be all that interested.' She glanced down at the bowl of gooseberries. 'I mean, they never came to the wedding, and they've got all their own friends down in Gloucestershire. I don't think they're bothered about me now.'

'Not bothered about their own daughter, not even when she's expecting her first baby? Oh, you poor love.' Mrs Spencer enfolded Erica in her arms again. 'Well, I hope you're wrong about that. I hope you'll find they're as pleased as I am. But if not – well, you know you've me and Jack to look after you. *We're* your mum and dad now, and this is your home for as long as you and our Gerald want it to be.' She let go of Erica to mop her eyes with the corner of her apron. 'And I hope it'll always be your home, and that you'll have a lot more kiddies to bring up here for us to love.'

'So do I,' Erica said shakily. She looked around the big, cluttered kitchen, remembering how scornful she had been when she first walked in two years ago, and how haughtily she'd demanded a room of her own. Now, it appeared comfortable and homely, a place where she could be her true self – the Erica who had almost got lost in the pretensions of society.

She looked at her mother-in-law. Ada Spencer was small and plump, with grey hair that she cut herself, curling in wisps around her plain, round face. Perhaps she had been pretty once, but it was honest kindness that shone from her eyes now and that, Erica knew, was worth more than any surface beauty.

'Oh, Mum,' she said, and the name came as naturally to her tongue as if she had been using it all her life, 'I *am* glad I came here.'

Carol held out for another week, but Ethel's continual haranguing and her own shaky health added up to a misery that she could fight no longer. She was still being sick several times a day – some young mothers-to-be were, the doctor said, examining Carol with some sympathy, and it could last right up till she was delivered – and as she lay on her bed, listening to her mother's diatribes it began to seem as if anything must be better than staying at home.

'All right,' she said at last. 'All right, all right, all *right*. I'll go. I'll go tomorrow if that's what you want. Then I'll be out of your way and you won't have to be ashamed of me. You won't have to keep looking at me to see if my belly's getting fat so that everyone'll know. You can forget all about me.'

'Forget about you!' Ethel said, but her eyes gleamed triumphantly. 'It'll take a long time to forget the dance you've led me these past few months. A proper little madam you've turned out to be, and I hope they make you see sense where you're going. You'll be putting it up for adoption, mind. I'm not having you come back here with a bundle in your arms.'

Carol's eyes filled with tears, but she was too exhausted to argue any more. And she knew that it would be impossible for her to keep her baby if her mother refused to accept it. Impossible for her to manage alone, either. A sixteen-year-old girl couldn't earn enough to keep herself, let alone a baby, and how would she be able to go to work anyway? She had no choice.

'You'll thank me for it in the end,' Ethel told her. 'You'll be grateful when you look back on this. You've got your whole life in front of you – you don't want to start off saddled with a mistake you made when you were barely out of your own pram.'

'Oh yes,' Carol said with a weak attempt at sarcasm, 'and you'll be telling me next you're doing it all for my own good.'

'Well, so I am! I'm your mother, ain't I? Of course I'm doing it for your good.' Ethel prepared to leave the room. 'I'll go and write to the Home straight away. They said they could take you this week. We'll arrange to go on Friday, after my hair appointment – I don't want them thinking you come from a poor home or anything like that.'

She went downstairs. Carol lay for a few minutes staring at the ceiling. Then she felt under her mattress and drew out a grubby, creased envelope. It was the letter Roddy had written to his mother. Carol had never opened it. She'd kept it exactly as it was, the traces of mud still smeared across it, and at night she fell asleep with it clutched between her fingers. It was the only thing of Roddy's she had, the only souvenir by which to remember him.

Since his court-martial and imprisonment, she had heard nothing from him. Ethel had forbidden her to write to him, but in any case Carol did not know which prison he was in. She had thought of writing to the address on the envelope and asking his mother to send on a letter, but she was afraid that such a request would be refused. Roddy's mother must hate her for what had happened to him. Even if she sent the letter he had written, Carol didn't think Mrs MacPherson would take any notice of it. She would simply tear it up. And then her last shred of comfort would be gone.

'It's no good you hanging about waiting to hear from him,' Ethel had told her, noticing that she spent a lot of time waiting for the postman. 'They don't let prisoners write letters. And if anything came to this house with a prison postmark on it, I'd put it straight in the fire.'

Carol pressed the crumpled envelope against her cheek, and then turned her face to the wall and closed her eyes. Oh Roddy, Roddy, she thought, I'm sorry. But what else can I do?

By the end of the week, Carol had gone again. Sent down to relations in Devonshire, Ethel said, to be with her little sister Shirley. It was the best thing for her, after what she'd been through, poor kid. Maybe she'd come home again after a few months.

The other residents of April Grove took this with a pinch of salt, not least because Ethel had never in her life been heard to express sympathy for her daughter.

'She hasn't gone to Devon,' Rose said scornfully. 'She's gone to a Home, where they take girls who're going to have babies.'

'Whatever are you talking about?' Jess demanded, shocked. 'How do *you* know she's expecting a baby?'

Rose gave her an exasperated look. 'Everyone knows, Mum. We're not kids any more. Anyway, she told Joy.'

'Well, I don't want you talking about it all the same. Especially when our Tim's here.'

But Tim wasn't interested in Carol Glaister. He was off on his bike every morning, up to Mr Driver's, where he collected his errands and cycled all over Copnor delivering medicines. He enjoyed being in the open air and getting to know the customers, and he whistled cheerfully as he zoomed round the corners, practising riding with no hands or with his feet on the handlebars.

He had not forgotten his desire to be in Micky Baxter's secret army, however, and when he saw Micky and Jimmy Cross coming along September Street, he rang his bell and skidded to a halt.

'I got that stuff you wanted.'

Micky stared at him. 'What stuff?'

'To make gunpowder with. It's saltpetre.' Tim handed Micky a screw of brown paper. 'That's what you want for gunpowder. I looked it up in a book.'

'You never said nothing to old man Driver, did you?' Micky asked suspiciously.

'Cross my heart I never.' Tim was still feeling guilty over this. He had looked in his father's encyclopaedia first and then in one of the chemist's books when the shop was full of customers. He'd found the saltpetre in a jar under its name of potassium nitrate, and scooped a few teaspoonsful into the brown paper, screwing it up quickly, terrified of discovery. Afterwards, he'd found it difficult to meet Mr Driver's eye and had scurried out of the shop as soon as he could.

Micky unwrapped the brown paper and examined the white crystalline powder. 'You sure it's the right stuff? It looks like sugar to me.'

'I wouldn't put it in your tea,' Tim said. 'It'll blow your head off. It's saltpetre, like I said. And I'm not getting any more. There's enough there to blow up all Pompey.'

'In this little bit?' Micky stared at it unbelievingly. 'Garn! You're having us on.'

'It'd take a bomb as big as a ship to blow up Pompey,' Jimmy Cross chipped in. 'Bigger. The one that blew my leg off, it was six foot long, and that never blew up no more than a couple of old houses.'

'Well, it probably didn't have saltpetre in it,' Tim said. 'There's all sorts of different kinds of gunpowder. I'm not getting any more, anyway.' He looked at Micky. 'I've done what you said, I've passed the test. Now you've got to let me come to your den and tell me your secret.'

'All right. But you've got to swear utter secrecy, mind. Otherwise we tells old man Driver about the saltpetre.'

He took Tim to the den that evening. He had brought his collection of souvenirs with him, and Desmond had added a few more bits and pieces that he'd collected from the wrecked planes in the corner of the aerodrome. Tim stared in fascination at the growing display, lit by the flickering glow of an old paraffin lamp.

'Where d'you get all this? That looks like a proper wireless. And that's a real bayonet.'

Micky gave him a contemptuous glance. 'Course they're real. We're a real army. This ain't a kids' game. And if you want to be in it, you'll 'ave to get your own weapon. A gun'd be best. We got guns too, only I didn't bring them tonight.'

Tim looked at him. It sounded like one of his boasts.

'I don't believe you. Where could you get guns?'

'We got 'em from the Home Guard shed. Martin got the key.' They had gone there late one night, he and Desmond with the key Martin had filched from his uncle's kitchen, and come out with half a dozen assorted weapons, some British, some German, to add to their arsenal. They were all at least twenty-five years old but the Home Guard had cleaned them and they were ready for use. They were special, Martin had said proudly; some of the Home Guards in the country were still using broomsticks, and hardly any had an armoury like this. 'We'll bring 'em along one night and show you. We gotta do some shooting practice, anyway.'

'I bet you don't know how to shoot them,' Tim said jealously, still only half believing him. 'You've got to know what you're doing with guns.'

'Garn!' Micky scoffed. 'What d'you know about it? I bet you ain't never even touched one.'

'I have. Reg Corner used to take me and Keith shooting when we were out at Bridge End. He let me fire it and I shot a rabbit. We had it for supper,' Tim said proudly, but Micky sneered again.

'Rabbits! We're goin' to be shootin' *Germans*. You can 'ave them for supper if you want!' He picked up Wendy's bayonet. 'This is from the last war too. It was Wendy's grandad's. He killed about a hundred Germans with it, didn't he, Wen?' He stroked the rusty blade with some reverence. 'You can still see the blood, dried on.'

'What else have you got?' Tim asked, looking at the pile on the old table.

'Coupla gas masks. A wireless set – we're goin' to get it to work and listen in to the pilots when they're goin' on raids. Three unexploded incendiaries – we're goin' to dismantle them and use the stuff for our own bomb. And two grenades.'

'Aren't you scared they'll go off?'

'Nah. Safe as houses.' Micky waved his hand around the ruined cellar. 'An' look what we got over here.'

He shone the lamp into a dark corner, where almost no light could filter down through the cracked ceiling, and Tim felt the skin lift at the back of his neck.

'Crikey! What's that?'

'It's part of a German plane,' Micky said proudly. 'Des got it. It's a pilot's seat and the lid off the cockpit. We're makin' our own plane, see?'

Tim stared at it. In the dim corner, it looked very much as if a complete aircraft were there, nosing out of the shadows. He could see the dome of the cockpit bubble, a patchwork of cracked Perspex glinting in the unsteady light. And something else, something black and shifting.

'There's someone in it,' he whispered. 'It's not – it's not a *dead pilot*, is it?' The image of a hand, encased in a leather glove, rose in his mind, and he felt his flesh crawl.

'Yaaargh!' The bubble lifted suddenly and the shadowy figure came terrifyingly to life, leaping out with arms outstretched, fingers clawing the air. 'Yaaargh! Got you – yaaargh! You're dead!'

Tim screeched and fell backwards, tipping the lamp out of Micky's hand as he did so. There was immediate panic as the boys scrabbled to save the light. Wendy yelped as someone trod on her hand, and Desmond scrambled down from the cockpit and began to laugh.

'That scared you. You all thought I was a dead pilot. Hooo-hooo-hooo, that scared you.'

'You stupid twerp,' Micky said furiously, steadying the lamp and setting it on the table. 'You coulda got us all blown up. You won't be allowed to be in the army if you can't 'ave a bit more sense.'

'That's right,' Jimmy Cross said. 'I dunno what my mum'd say if I went home without my other leg.'

Tim spluttered, but there was an edge of fear to his laughter. He looked at the heap of bits and pieces on the table, his eyes drawn to the grenades and incendiaries.

'Where d'you keep them? You don't leave them here, do you?'

'Don't be daft. They gotta be locked away. Anyway, never you mind, it ain't none of your business.' Micky planted himself firmly in front of the table. 'It's secret, understand? Everything here's secret.'

'Can I be in your army, then? Can I help make fireworks and things?'

'Fireworks! We ain't makin' fireworks. That's kids' stuff, that is. We're makin' *bombs*. Proper bombs. We're goin' to blow things up. We're an army.' Micky narrowed his eyes and gave Tim a hard look. 'I'll talk it over with the others, all right? We might let you in – and we might not. You can come back tomorrow and we'll tell you then. Now you can scram.'

Tim shrugged. He felt annoyed at being sent away, but he wasn't sorry to scramble up the broken steps and out into the fresh air again. He knew that Micky was just playing with him, pretending that he might not be allowed to join them, when they obviously needed everyone they could get. By tomorrow, he was confident that he would be a member of the secret army, perhaps even a Lieutenant.

They'll have to let me in now, he thought, now that I've seen the den and the bits of plane and everything. And then he remembered that with all the fuss over Desmond's prank, Micky hadn't made him swear to secrecy after all.

Whistling, he climbed on to his bike and pedalled off along the road. It was one of those that had been bombed early on, and some of the ruined houses had been cleared and static water tanks erected in the spaces. Their grey galvanised steel sides were scrawled with messages to Hitler and chalk pictures of him in undignified postures, and children were clambering on piles of bricks to peer in. They made good swimming pools on hot days, though there was trouble if a warden or policeman caught you.

Tim rode down to North End. He had promised Jess he would go to see his grandparents and he was keen to see if Arthur had any relics of the Boer War that he could take with him to tomorrow's meeting. Micky had said that any new member of the gang had to provide his own weapon – he thought of their faces if he turned up with a real rifle, or even a musket. He was fairly sure his grandfather had used a musket.

Arthur had been a little better just lately. Since Frank and Ted, accompanied by their wives, had been to see him and discuss the idea of him and Mary moving into Annie's house, he had been quiet, even a little subdued, and had hardly stirred from the house. He hadn't even gone into the garden to dig the hole for the new shelter, and he hadn't once complained that Mary was starving him. She was relieved but as she'd told Jess, she still wasn't really happy about him.

'It's as if he's not there half the time. He just sits in his armchair, staring at the fireplace, and doesn't seem to hear me, nor the wireless, nor nothing. It's like he's lost all interest. All he keeps on about is that he's not doing his bit for the war. He says he's useless.'

'Poor Dad,' Jess said. 'I still think he's had a sort of breakdown. Like Ted did. And look at Ted now – right as ninepence, except that he drinks a drop too much beer these days. I'll send our Tim down, see if he can cheer him up a bit. He's always had a soft spot for Tim.'

Tim leant his bike against the front wall and knocked on the door. His grandmother opened it, her face anxious.

'Tim! I thought it was your grandad. You haven't seen him, have you?'

Tim shook his head. 'No, I thought he'd be at home. I came down to see him. I wanted to ask him something.'

Mary drew him indoors. She looked up and down the street and then shut the door. 'I'm worried stiff, Tim, I don't mind telling you. He went out after tea, said he was going for a drink up the Star. I didn't want him to go, not the way he's been just lately, but he started to get his dander up a bit and I didn't want to upset him, so I didn't say no more. I had half a mind to walk up there myself after a bit, make sure he was all right. Did you come past that way?'

'Yes, but I never saw Grandad. He must have been inside.'

Mary pulled worriedly at her lip. 'I don't know. He's been gone two hours now, and you know he's not a drinking man, not really. I don't suppose he goes to the pub more than half a dozen times a year. I think I ought to go and have a look, only I'm frightened to go out in case he comes back a different way and wanders off again.'

'I'll go,' Tim offered. 'I can go to the Jug and Bottle and ask if Grandad's there. I'll get him to come home, shall I?'

'Oh, Tim, that would be a help, it really would. Then I can stop here so that if he comes home I won't miss him. I don't know what he'd do if he came in and found the house empty, he might go off anywhere. You go and find him, Tim. He'll come home for you.'

Tim cycled off up Stubbington Avenue again. He wasn't really worried about his grandfather, but he knew that the old man was supposed to have been ill lately and Jess always said you shouldn't stay out late in the evening if you'd been poorly. The night air could give you a cold.

It was light until late in the evening now and there were plenty of people about in the street. The air-raid warnings had been fewer lately and weren't generally expected until after dark anyway. It gave everyone a bit more time to do their gardens, or just visit each other for a talk.

Tim was almost at the top of Stubbington Avenue when he saw his grandfather. He was coming down the street between two young soldiers, each rather red in the face and holding on to his arms.

'Come on, old feller,' one of them said as they drew nearer to Tim. 'Not so far now, and then we'll all sit down for a cuppa, eh? That's the ticket.'

'Cuppa?' Arthur piped. 'Cuppa? You'll be lucky, mate. My missus won't give nobody no cuppas, she never even gives me one. Starves me, she does. I 'aven't 'ad no tea for weeks. Just plain water, that's all I gets.'

'Shame,' the other soldier said. He had red hair and his cap was stuffed into his pocket. 'You'd be better off in barracks along with us.'

'That's where I'd like to be. 'Elpin' with the war, that's what I oughter be doin'. I bin in two wars already, the Boer War and the last lot, what was supposed to be the war to end all wars.' Arthur snorted. 'There'll never be no war to end all wars. But it's blokes like me they wants, blokes who's seen it already, got a bit of experience. I could tell 'em what to do. I could give old Rommel a bloody nose.'

'That's right, old chap. You tell 'em.'

'I would, too. But they won't take no notice. They don't want to listen to blokes like me, what knows a thing or two. Just chuck us on the rubbish heap, that's what they does.' Arthur's face crumpled and he began to sob.

'We ain't fit for nothing else. Rubbish, that's what we are, just useless rubbish.'

Tim could bear no more. He stopped his bike in front of the staggering trio and said, 'That's my Grandad. I've come to take him home.'

The soldiers stopped. 'Your Grandad?' The red-headed one looked at Arthur. 'That right, mate? This kid belong to you?'

Arthur peered blearily and Tim held his breath, wondering if the old man would recognise him. Then he saw the wavering eyes clear a little.

'It's our Tim. My Jess's boy,' he explained to the soldiers. 'Bin out in the country, he has, refugee or whatever they call 'em. I didn't know you'd come back,' he said to Tim.

Tim had seen him three times since his return but he said nothing. He reached out and touched his grandfather's arm. 'Come on home,' he said gently. 'Grandma's waiting for you. She's been worried.'

'Dunno why she should be,' Arthur said resentfully. 'She don't 'ave no time for me nowadays. Won't even give me a cuppa tea for me breakfast.'

The soldiers looked at Tim, who shook his head.

'He doesn't remember. He forgets everything. She gives him everything he wants.'

'Poor old sod,' the red-headed soldier said. 'He's been in the Star and Garter, asking for drinks and carrying on about the war. Only he didn't seem to know whether we were fighting the Germans or the South Africans. The landlord thought we'd better bring him home – if he could remember where that was.'

'Well, I'll take him now,' Tim said. He touched his grandfather's arm again. 'Come on, Grandad.'

Arthur was leaning against a low wall, crying softly, his old face tired and hopeless. Between his sobs, only a few words could be made out, and as he listened Tim felt his heart move oddly, as if it were twisting in his breast.

'Rubbish,' Arthur whimpered. 'Useless rubbish . . . no use to no one . . . nothing but rubbish . . .'

'Come on, Grandad.' Tim was near to tears himself. 'Come on home. Grandma's waiting for you, with a cup of tea.'

But the words seemed to mean nothing to his grandfather. Shrunken now from the man he had once been to a trembling shadow hardly bigger than Tim, Arthur allowed himself to be led down the long street to the house where he and Mary had lived for so many years. Once again, he was lost in his own world. A world where the spectres of war pressed unbearably about him, where fear and misery stalked, and despair cast a fog over his bewildered mind.

The soldiers came all the way to the front door and then slipped away, not waiting for Mary's thanks. Between them, Tim and Mary got Arthur up the stairs and into bed, with a cup of tea which he seemed unable to taste and finally left to go cold on the table beside him.

Tim went home, subdued and miserable. His grandmother got into bed beside her husband and lay wakeful for several hours before finally falling into a deep sleep.

Arthur fell asleep quickly, but woke an hour later. For a while he lay in the darkness, puzzled, unable to remember where he was. His mind was filled with images of war – of war in Africa, in the Crimea, in the trenches and fields of Flanders. He heard the ear-pounding rattle of gunfire, the scream of bombs, the drone of enemy aircraft and the incessant, torment-ing wail of the siren. And at last he got out of bed and went downstairs and out into the back garden. He opened the door of the old washhouse and found a coil of washing line, and hanged himself from the pulley in the ceiling.

20

Arthur was buried a week later, after an inquest which concluded that he had taken his own life 'while the balance of his mind was disturbed'. Mary, who was exhausted, did not attend, and her daughters stayed at home with her while the men saw him to his resting place. Tim and Rose were sent over to Gosport to spend the day with their Uncle Howard, and Keith stayed out at Bridge End with Mr Beckett.

Olive and Betty both got leave for the day and busied themselves unobtrusively about the house, getting a few sandwiches ready for the men when they came back. They took a pot of tea into the front room, where their mother and grandmother and Auntie Jess were sitting, but didn't stay. The atmosphere in the living room, with the table laid with Annie's embroidered tablecloth and the best teacups, was more comfortable.

Like the rest of the family, Olive was very shaken by her grandfather's death, but at least it brought Derek home for a couple of days' leave and they were able to have some time together in their bedroom at Annie's house. They lay close together, reluctant to waste even a moment in sleep, each treasuring the beat of the other's heart.

'Sometimes I think this is all we're ever going to have,' Olive said. 'A day or two here and there, a couple of nights. We never have time to get used to each other.'

'I don't want to get used to you.' Derek moved his hands gently up and down her back. 'I want to feel like this about you for the rest of my life. I don't want to stop feeling excited because we're together.'

Olive laughed softly and nuzzled her face into his neck. 'Nor do I. I don't want to get like a lot of old people, just living in the same house and hardly bothering about each other. But I'd like us to be together all the time. I'd like to know that you'll be home for your tea every night and you'll be in bed with me every morning when I wake up.'

'I'd like to know that too. Specially the bed bit.' He held her hard against him. 'Oh, Livvy, I miss you so much when I'm away. And now you're in the ATS and working on that gun . . . I hate thinking of you there at night, and not in this bed where I can imagine you.'

Olive sighed. 'We've been through all this before, Derek. I told you then, I wouldn't volunteer if you didn't want me to. But even if I didn't, I'd be called up. At least this way I got a bit of choice, and I *am* back in Pompey.'

'I know, I know. It just feels queer, that's all. You doing things I don't know about. I mean, if you were still in Dad's office I'd know where you were every minute, I could picture you walking up the street and sitting down at your desk and doing your typing and invoices and things . . . Now, I just don't know where you might be, and all the time I'm scared you're going to get hurt.'

'I could get hurt just as easy in the office. We don't always get proper warnings – one of these hit-and-run raiders comes over, and half the street's flattened before anyone knows a thing about it. Anyway, don't you think it's the same for me? I don't know what you're doing. I've never even seen the camp, only from outside when I've come down to see you on a few weekends. And you could be bombed just the same.'

'I know. I'm sorry, Livvy. It just takes a bit of getting used to, that's all – knowing you've got a whole life that's nothing to do with me.'

'I tell you about it,' she said, feeling a little hurt. 'Maybe you don't really like me having it – is that what it is? Or maybe it's because I enjoy it. You don't think I should.'

'I never said that.' He held her more closely. 'That makes me sound really selfish. I'm glad you're doing something you enjoy. But – well, a man *likes* to know what his wife's doing. It doesn't seem right, that's all, you doing things I don't know about.'

'You think I'm not telling you things I ought to tell you. You think I'm keeping secrets from you. But they're only war secrets, Derek – things we all have to keep quiet about. There's nothing else.' She looked anxiously into his face. 'You do believe that, don't you? You do trust me?'

'Of course I do.' But they both knew that, in a strange way, she was right, and Olive was silent. It was true that there were things she didn't tell Derek. And the main thing was that, although he knew she enjoyed her work, she was always careful not to let him know just how much she enjoyed it.

She had found something in the Ack-ack team that she had never known before, and she liked it. She liked the sense of urgency, the knowledge that she was doing something real in the war effort, and she liked the company of the rest of the team. She had never before experienced the camaraderie of a group of people who forged special bonds through working closely together. It gave her a special glow that she took pains to conceal from Derek, knowing that he might be hurt by it.

And concealing anything from Derek added to that tiny gulf and made it just a little wider.

She clutched him fiercely against her. 'I love you, Derek. I *love* you. Nothing's going to come between us – nothing. I won't let it. I won't let anything happen to us.'

'Of course it won't.' He spoke gently, comfortingly. 'We're special, Livvy. We'll come through this and we'll be together always, sleeping in the same bed every night. Don't sound so frightened. Everything'll be all right one day.' He ran his hand down her spine and she shivered and pressed closer. 'Everything'll be all right,' he repeated. 'Nothing's going to happen to us.'

Everything will be all right.

Dennis and Betty told each other this too. It was what everyone said – it *won't happen to us, nothing can come between us, we're special.* Yet even as they spoke the words, they knew that it couldn't be true for everybody. It's true for us, they insisted, it's got to be true for us. You couldn't go on, day after day, if you didn't believe that.

'The more experience I get, the safer I am,' Dennis said. 'I know every bomb now like the back of my hand. I could defuse them with my eyes shut.'

'Well, don't try to prove it,' Betty said. 'The Germans are tricky devils. You know they keep changing things so that you'll be taken by surprise.'

'That's what makes the job so interesting,' Dennis said with a grin. 'Never the same from one day to the next. Keeps you on your toes.'

'Stay on them, then, ready to run. Don't forget, we've got a wedding to have.'

They had not yet decided where to have their wedding. At first, Betty had wanted to be married in church, like her sister Olive, but Ted was still against their marriage and she was afraid he would refuse to give her away. And the serene gentleness of the Quaker way was becoming more and more attractive to her.

'Come to Meeting with me,' Dennis said. 'You'll see what it's like then, and you can choose. I'll do whatever makes you feel happiest, Betty.'

They went to Portsmouth and stayed with Dennis's parents. Betty had been there several times now, and grown accustomed to the quiet house and the serenity of the two elderly people who lived there. Robert and Cecily Verney had married in their thirties and Dennis had been born five years later, the only child they were to have. Now Robert was seventy years old, a tall, rather thin man with silver hair and kind grey eyes, and Cecily was a small, bright little wren of a woman, always busy yet never harassed. They welcomed Betty as if she were already their daughter, and she found herself in the kitchen with her sleeves rolled up, making scones as if she'd lived there all her life.

'I love getting my hands into a bowl of flour,' Cecily said, bustling about the old-fashioned kitchen. 'It seems such a natural thing – something women have been doing for thousands of years. Making a home and family, feeding people you love – it's what life is for, isn't it?'

Betty had never thought of it like that. Doing household chores and cooking meals had always seemed to her to be something you had to do but would rather not. Something you got out of the way as soon as possible so that you could go on to more interesting things. And even though her own mother took great pride in the whiteness of her step, the crispness of her curtains and the quality of the food she served, it was more a matter of pride itself than as a service to her family.

Everything Cecily did, from cleaning the lavatory to polishing the furniture, seemed to be done as a gift, either to her family or her God. It didn't matter that it would soon all have to be done again – that simply gave her the chance to renew her gift. And if she didn't have time to complete all the tasks, or if something went wrong, she accepted it as the way of the world, and felt content that she had done all that was possible.

'We're all human beings,' she said to Betty. 'We can't work miracles. Yet we all have the seed of God within us, which can help us to achieve so much more than we think is possible.'

Betty was getting used to these ideas now. At first, she had been embarrassed by Dennis's references to God – although her mother was a churchgoer, there was seldom any 'religious' talk at home – but she was coming to appreciate the certainty they all had of their beliefs, and the tolerance that they had for others.

'Of course we *think* we're right,' Robert Verney said with a smile. 'But nobody can know for certain. And there are many paths to the top of a mountain. The view may be the same for all of us, once we reach it.'

As Dennis had suggested, Betty accompanied them to their Sunday morning Meeting. She felt rather timid about it, knowing that the entire hour might be spent in silence unless someone felt compelled to speak, but the rest of the people there welcomed her smilingly and drew her into their circle. She sat beside Dennis, listening to the silence and slowly feeling herself relax.

There was no form of service, no prayers or hymns. A few children sat on the benches, most holding a toy of some sort, and after twenty minutes they all got up and went out with a dark-haired young woman who was carrying a book. Betty supposed she would read to them, or let them play or draw pictures. The adult members sat on, their eyes closed or fixed on the floor or the ceiling. She wondered what they were thinking of.

You weren't really supposed to think about anything, Dennis had said. You were supposed to empty your mind and let God speak through you, if he wished. You weren't supposed to come with anything prepared, because that would be 'you' speaking and not God. You weren't supposed to know what you were going to say, or even that you were going to speak at all.

'You're just a mouthpiece,' he said.

'Like a sort of loudspeaker, or megaphone?'

'That's right,' Dennis said with a grin, 'but not so loud.'

It seemed to Betty that anything that broke this silence would sound unnaturally loud. She wondered if anyone would dare to get up.

The meeting was almost three-quarters over before anyone stirred. And then Robert Verney rose to his feet and laid his hand lightly on Betty's shoulder.

'Something very good has happened in our family this week. Our son Dennis has told us that he is planning to marry Betty and make her our daughter. It has shown us that even in these dark and terrible days, good may come out of evil, for if it had not been for this war these two might never have met. And how many others are meeting and finding love through the chaos that the world is in today? How much love is growing out of the ruins of our cities and our countries, as plants and flowers are growing on the places where bombs have fallen? Let us all look around us and see the good that is proving triumphant each day, and thank God for the brightness of his love.'

He sat down again. Nobody moved or spoke, but Betty felt a breath of warmth stir the air, as gentle as a sigh. She felt Dennis's hand touch hers and let him fold her fingers in his palm.

After a while, a woman rose to her feet, and then another man, each to give their own example of love coming out of the war. And as they stood chatting afterwards in the little garden that surrounded the Meeting House, Betty felt that she had been touched by the serenity that she had noticed both in Dennis's parents and the other members of the Meeting. It was something like the feeling of 'goodness' that she'd had after church as a child, yet it went deeper than that. As they walked home, she was thoughtful, and later she asked Dennis what happened at a Quaker wedding.

'Well, it's something like a Meeting,' Dennis said. 'But of course everyone knows they're there for the wedding, so there's more preparation. But we all sit quietly until the bridegroom feels that the right moment has come, and then he stands up and says that he wants to marry the bride and she says she wants to marry him, and really that's all there is to it.'

'That's all?' Betty said. 'It doesn't sound much.'

'Well, they do make their vows. But they make them in their own words, not just repeating what someone else is telling them – and it seems to mean more. It's really very moving.'

'But suppose they can't think what to say? I mean, they might miss out something important.'

'Well, they do have the Certificate on the table in front of them, so they can read it if they need to,' Dennis said, 'and don't forget that God is there to help.'

Betty was silent. She wasn't sure that she believed that God was inside her, a part of her, telling her what to say. If he was, the devil must be there too, she thought, because all too often she said the wrong thing.

'I always thought I'd get married in church,' she said. 'With a white dress and veil and everything. You don't have them at Quaker weddings, do you?'

'No, we don't really believe in dressing up. But if that's what you want, Betty, that's what we'll do. Whichever way we choose to get married, it won't make any difference to me because as far as I'm concerned we're married already. This is just a sort of declaration to all our friends. And a legal certificate, of course!'

Betty laid her head against his shoulder. She wanted to say that it didn't matter to her either. But it still did, a little, and she knew that she could not pretend. There had to be real honesty between herself and Dennis.

'Let's think about it a little while longer,' she said. 'Let me have some time to get used to the idea.'

For a few weeks it seemed as though there was a brief respite in the tribulations of the war. Bomber Command was making heavy attacks on Germany – a thousand aircraft at a time were sent to bomb cities like Cologne, Essen and Bremen, reciprocating the blitz on London and other British cities. The fires were seen almost two hundred miles away and although many like Jess thought of the innocent lives – children and old people – that were being lost, the general opinion was that it was a just reprisal and essential in the conduct of the war.

'Serves 'em right,' Ethel Glaister said viciously, and even Tommy Vickers shook his head and said, 'It's got to be done. You can't hold back when you're fighting someone like Hitler.'

In Portsmouth, Stay-at-Home Holidays were the fashion. Few people would have gone away anyway, unless they had relatives to visit, but now the local authorities took some trouble to arrange entertainment for those who had to stay in Portsmouth. A Naval and Military Tattoo was staged at Fratton Park, and the Royal Marine and Naval bands gave performances every week at Hilsea Lido, Milton Park and Southsea Common. Jess and Frank went out to a few, but for the most part Frank worked on the allotment, using his week's holiday to get the ground ready for the next crop of vegetables.

'There were a few funny things in the paper last night,' Cherry remarked as she ate Sunday tea with Jess and Frank. 'It said that since the year 1400 BC, the world's had three thousand, one hundred and twenty years of war and only two hundred and ninety-one years of peace. How do they know that, I wonder? I didn't think history went back that far.'

'I suppose they use the Bible,' Frank said. He was feeding the cat Henry with small triangular pieces of bread, spread with fish paste. 'That's full of wars. I dunno why they have to print that sort of stuff though – supposed to cheer us up, is it?'

'There was another bit. D'you know, the Isle of Man's been in a state of war with Germany for the past twenty-eight years! They forgot to invite them to Versailles after the last war, so they never signed the peace treaty. It's like not inviting one of the fairies to the Princess's christening, isn't it.'

'What fairies?' Frank asked in bewilderment. 'And which Princess? Are you talking about Princess Elizabeth or Margaret Rose?'

'No, of course I'm not, you daft ha'porth. The Sleeping Beauty and that sort of princess. *You* know what I means, don't you, Jess?'

'Of course I do,' Jess said, laughing. 'But Frank's mind doesn't run much on fairy tales.'

'Anyway,' Frank said, trying to redeem himself with his own touch of humour, 'if they've been at war with Germany all that time, it's a pity they didn't do something about Hitler before. They could have saved us all this trouble.'

'Oh, they've always been an independent lot,' Cherry observed. 'It comes of having three legs.' She winked at Rose and Tim. 'Did you know that? About people in the Isle of Man having three legs?'

'Of course I did,' Tim said. 'That's why they turn cartwheels instead of walking. And people from Portland have got tails, I bet you didn't know that. And if you take polar bears to the Antarctic, the penguins kill them.'

The three adults stared at him. 'The penguins kill them? How?'

'They get stuck in their throats,' Tim said, and went off into a peal of laughter while Jess and Frank groaned and Rose rolled her eyes.

'It's just one of his stupid jokes. He's always making jokes.'

'Well, I think it was a right funny one,' Cherry declared, her small, round body shaking. 'You're a star turn, you are, Tim, and no mistake. My godfathers, I wish I could think up jokes like that. The penguins kill them! Eh, I'll have to remember that to tell 'em in the boiler-shop tomorrow.'

'D'you often tell them jokes?' Tim asked curiously.

'Well, we have to do something to pass the time along. No use going around with our faces down to our knees. That's not going to win the war.'

'You mean telling jokes helps win the war? You mean it's patriotic?'

'Don't encourage him,' Jess began, but Cherry was already nodding her head.

'Of course, Anything that keeps a smile on people's faces is patriotic. Look at Tommy Handley and Arthur Askey and Charlie Chester. And George Formby, going out to entertain the troops. And I bet it does people good to see your cheeky face coming round with their medicines.'

Tim strummed an imaginary banjo. '*You should see the things I see, when I'm cleaning windows . . .*' He caught his father's eye and stopped hastily, though not without muttering something about 'being patriotic', and sniggered behind his hand.

'You'll make him worse,' Jess told Cherry. 'He's getting above himself lately. Thinks he's grown up because we've let him have a few weeks off school and he's got a job. You know you've got to go back to Bridge End after the holidays,' she said to Tim.

Tim made a face. 'Do I have to? I like being at work.'

'Yes, you do have to,' Frank said severely. 'You're only just coming up to thirteen. You're not leaving until you've got a good education behind you. I want you to have the chances I should have had.'

'But I don't see what good learning History and stuff like that does. I'm going to be an explorer.'

'You'll need to learn Geography, then,' Frank said smartly. 'Or you won't know where to explore. You don't know much about the world as it is. D'you know where the Galapagos Islands are? Or New Guinea?'

'I know where Japan is,' Tim said. 'And Burma. And Java, and Malta, and the Yangtse River. I bet you didn't know those places when you were thirteen.'

'That's enough, Tim,' Jess began, seeing Frank's face darken, but for once her husband wasn't about to tell Tim off for being cheeky. He looked at her and shook his head.

'All places that are caught up in the war. You're right, Tim. I didn't know about all those places when I was your age. I didn't need to. But all the same, I want you to go back to school and learn as much as you can. Things are going to be different once this lot's over. We're going to need people who've had an education. And I want you to have a better chance than I did.'

'Your dad's right,' Cherry said. 'It's a hard life doing the sort of work he does. I wouldn't like to see you having to slave like he does in that boiler-shop.'

Jess looked at her. It was strange that Cherry knew so much about Frank, things that Jess herself had never known and would never see. It was as if he had two lives and Cherry was allowed into them both, whereas Jess was shut out.

But there were no feelings of jealousy or envy in Jess these days. She felt secure and comfortable in Frank's love, and knew that whatever relationship he might have with Cherry, it could never threaten her. Indeed, she felt now that Cherry was almost as much her friend as his.

She'd been even more her friend since Arthur's terrible death, coming round at once to offer whatever help might be needed, sitting and listening as Jess wept, even managing to offer some comfort to Tim and Rose. It was funny that a little woman without any looks, who'd never been married herself or had children, should seem to know just what to say. And it wasn't empty comfort, either. It was down-to-earth common sense.

Jess knew nothing of the words Dennis's father had spoken at the Quaker meeting. But dimly, she felt the same wonder that, out of a war that had brought about so many terrible things, there were still bright new spots of friendship and love to help them on their way.

Perhaps Tim was right. Making jokes *was* patriotic. Anything that kept a smile on people's faces had to be good.

I just wish we could have Keith at home too, she thought wistfully. Then there really would be something to smile about.

21

The Home Carol Glaister was taken to by her mother was at Godalming, near Guildford. She wasn't likely to run into many Portsmouth people there, and in any case the house was right out in the countryside and it didn't look as if the girls left it very often, especially as their condition began to show.

It wasn't at all what Carol had expected. She'd thought it would be like a hospital, with rows of beds, or perhaps like the boarding schools she'd read about. Instead, it was just a big house with a lot of bedrooms and three or four large rooms downstairs. One of these rooms was private – she and Ethel went in there when they arrived, to be interviewed – and the rest were for the girls' use. There was a dining room with a big table, a sitting room with a lot of rather shabby armchairs, and a sewing room with a few treadle machines and some trestle tables spread with material and half-made baby-clothes.

It was all rather bare, with no carpets on the wooden floors, and the decorations looked as if they'd been done a long time ago and needed renewing. There were some girls, all in different stages of pregnancy, sweeping and dusting in the big rooms and sitting at the machines and tables in the sewing-room. The glanced at Carol with automatic curiosity, running their eyes expertly over her body.

The woman who ran the Home was called Mrs Whiting. She was middle-aged, with a big bust, and wore a tweed suit. She spoke in a posh voice, as if she were just finishing a toffee. She offered Ethel and Carol a cup of tea and told them to sit down.

'Now, let me see, you're expecting delivery some time in November.' Her voice was as brisk and matter-of-fact as if she was talking about a parcel, Carol felt a sudden urge to giggle. 'Well, I don't usually take gels quite this early, but I understand there are special circumstances in this case. A rather unpleasant court case . . . yes, I think you're quite right, Mrs Glaister, it will be a good idea to have Carol away from home. Less to remind her.'

But I want to remember, Carol thought. However, she did not have the energy to say so. Since agreeing to come here, she had been sunk in a state of lethargy and couldn't raise the strength to object to anything. All she could think of now was that at least she'd be free of her mother. Just go away and leave me, she begged Ethel silently. Just leave me alone.

Mrs Whiting was asking a series of questions now, all of which Ethel answered, and again Carol had no energy to make any objection. Roddy didn't 'take me away', she thought, and he didn't take advantage of me. And he never took that money, Mum knows that. But whatever Ethel might say to Carol in private, she was not going to let anyone else think ill of her daughter. That was too much a reflection on herself as a mother.

'Well, I think that's all very satisfactory,' Mrs Whiting said at last. She had been making notes in a folder and now she closed it and gave Ethel a polite smile. 'I think Carol will get along very well with us.'

'I don't want her mixing with any rough girls, mind,' Ethel said. 'She's been brought up nice. Just because she's in this trouble now—'

'I quite understand. And I can assure you we have no "rough" gels here,' Mrs Whiting said coldly. 'I'm very careful who I take, and any gel who doesn't know how to behave is sent home at once.' She gave Ethel a stern glance, as if to say that she would know just who to blame if Carol didn't behave herself. 'Of course, you understand that Carol will have to work while she's here. I don't believe in giving these gels the lap of luxury to live in. Some of them will have to be fending for themselves when they leave here, and some actually choose to keep their babies. I give them all a good grounding in housework and cooking, and they make all their own maternity clothes and a *layette*, whether they're keeping the child or not.'

'Well, that's something,' Ethel said. 'It's costing enough as it is. At least she'll be learning something useful.'

'Most of the costs are met by charity,' Mrs Whiting pointed out with a touch of acid in her voice. 'We're asking only that you pay what it would normally cost you to keep the gel at home. And to provide her with a small sum as pocket money for personal necessities and so on.'

'Pocket money!' Ethel grumbled. 'Ought to be out earning her own living, that's what she ought to be doing. Shouldn't be costing me a penny by now.'

But Mrs Whiting refused to be drawn into any argument. Instead, she pressed a button in the wall beside the fireplace and after a few minutes the door opened and a girl came in. She looked about nineteen, and she was heavily pregnant.

'Show Carol the bedroom, Susan,' Mrs Whiting ordered. 'Carol will be in Room Three with you and Ann and Mary. Then you can take her to the kitchen. I daresay there'll be a job there she can do.'

She stood up and offered her hand to Ethel. 'We think it's best for the girls to feel part of the establishment at once. I expect you'll be wanting to catch your train. I believe there's one soon after two o'clock. It's a pleasant walk back to town, and you've got plenty of time – you'll be able to have a snack lunch in the little cafeteria on the station.'

Ethel stared at her. She opened her mouth and then closed it again. Once more, Carol had the urge to giggle, but she was afraid that if she did she might cry instead. Now that the moment had almost come, she felt an unexpected reluctance to be left here alone.

I wish all this had never happened, she thought miserably, but that would mean that she would never have met Roddy, and that was a thought she couldn't bear. Pushing it from her mind, she followed Susan out of the room, aware of her mother close behind.

'Well!' Ethel said as soon as the door was closed. '*She* won't stand for no nonsense, you can see that. You'll have to mind your p's and q's here, young woman, or you'll be back on the doorstep so fast you won't know what's hit you – and you won't be getting no welcome from *me* if that happens, I can tell you. I'm not going through all this caper again.'

They stood in the hall, looking at each other uncertainly. I suppose we've got to say goodbye now, Carol thought. That Mrs Whiting didn't say anything about Mum coming upstairs. She darted a quick glance at her mother's face and then looked down at the floor.

'Cheerio then, Mum,' she mumbled, and half turned away.

'Well, is that all you can say?' Ethel exclaimed. '*Cheerio?* When we might not see each other for months, and by then you'll – you'll have had—' She seemed unable to say the words. Instead, she reached out both hands and grabbed Carol by the arms, dragging her closer. 'Don't I even get a kiss? I am your mother, after all.'

Carol submitted to the awkward kiss bestowed upon her – the first she could remember for years – and stepped back thankfully when it was over. Ethel produced a small, lace-edged handkerchief from her handbag and touched it to her eyes.

'You be a good girl, mind. Write to me regular. And I won't say but what I might not try and get up to see you some time – before it's all over. But you know how it is these days, I'm so busy, what with your father and Joe and little Shirley . . .' Her eyes flickered sideways and Carol realised that she was keeping one eye on the door to Mrs Whiting's room, and one eye on Susan, who was standing by looking bored. Of course, she thought. Mum wouldn't want to give them the impression she didn't care about me.

'Yeah, all right,' she said, and turned away again. 'Cheerio.'

She didn't wait to see Ethel go out of the front door. She followed Susan up to the large, bare bedroom, nodded silently as she was shown her own iron bed with its brown blankets, and listened as she was told which chest of drawers was hers and where she could hang her clothes. Then she went down to the kitchen.

There were several girls there, all preparing vegetables or making pastry. Carol was given a pile of potatoes to peel. She started to scrape at them with a knife, misery weighing like a lump of lead on her heart.

Roddy doesn't even know where I am now, she thought. And I don't know where he is either. We might as well be in different worlds.

Out at Bridge End, Keith was feeling miserable. He missed Tim and was fed up with being with Stella and Muriel. He resented being the only member of the family who was still evacuated – as if he were a baby, he thought, kicking at stones as he mooched through the country lanes. But Maureen was a baby, and *she* wasn't evacuated, it wasn't fair.

'I think it was a lot better before the war started,' he grumbled to Mrs Mudge. 'We used to go out to the beach at Southsea and stay all day. We'd get the bus from Copnor and take sandwiches and lemonade and Dad would swim right out deep and take us on his back. One at a time,' he added, not wishing Mrs Mudge to imagine a picture of the three of them sitting on Frank's back in a row, like Indians paddling a canoe. 'And there were sweets in the shops, loads and loads of sweets in big jars. Me and Tim used to go and look in the window and choose what to buy.'

'What sort of sweets did you buy?' Mrs Mudge asked, only half attending. She was making a casserole with corned beef and haricot beans. A bowl of dried egg, mixed with water, stood on the table beside her, ready to be used for a cake. 'I used to like a nice toffee myself, with nuts in, but since I had my plate I can't manage them, they get stuck. It's like figs, the pips get right underneath. Not that you see a lot of figs these days,' she added with a sigh.

'We couldn't afford toffees,' Keith said. 'We only got threepence a week. I used to get sherbet balls mostly, the pink and white ones. They go all fizzy in your mouth. Tim used to get mint humbugs – they had little ones, you'd get quite a lot in two ounces. Or liquorice bootlaces.'

'Well, you can still get your sweets,' Mrs Mudge said. 'You're allowed two ounces a week.' But Keith knew it wasn't the same. The few sweets that were still available were rationed now and you had to give up 'points' for them. And there wasn't any fun in choosing any more – Mrs Mudge had the ration book and she did the shopping and just gave the children whatever she'd managed to buy.

'Nothing's any fun any more,' Keith said glumly. 'We're not even getting a proper holiday this summer. School's going on all through August. It's not fair.'

'Well, you'll just have to learn to be thankful for what there is,' the housekeeper said a little sharply. She was sorry for the children, but she was too busy looking after the rambling vicarage and trying to make meals out of almost nothing to be very sympathetic towards Keith – he might miss his brother, but he hadn't lost anyone, after all. And she was anxious about Mr Beckett, who was looking more and more tired. 'Go and play outside. It's too nice a day for you to be sculling about indoors.'

Keith went out, but he was no longer interested in fishing for sticklebacks or picking blackberries. He kicked idly at stones and threw sticks at birds and wished he could go back to Portsmouth too.

'But you've always got along so well with Stella and Muriel,' Mr Beckett said later, when Keith refused to go swimming with them. 'You'll hurt their feelings if you keep behaving like this.'

Keith shrugged. 'So are my feelings hurt. Nobody cares about that.'

'Of course they do,' Mr Beckett was beginning, when the door from the kitchen suddenly burst open and Mrs Mudge erupted into the room, her face scarlet and wet with tears, and her lips working. She was waving an orange telegram envelope and trying to say something, but her words were drowned by sobs.

'My dear Mrs Mudge! What is it? Whatever's happened?' The vicar caught at the envelope and tore the flimsy sheet of paper from inside. 'Is it your son? Has something happened –?' He stared at the sheet, and Keith saw his face go suddenly grey. 'Oh, how dreadful. How perfectly dreadful.'

Keith felt a moment of panic. He knew very well what a telegram meant. They hardly ever brought good news. They came to say when people had been killed, or taken prisoner of war. And everyone stopped what they were doing when they saw the familiar red bike of a telegraph boy come spinning along the street. Everyone had the same moment of fear, dreading that it might be for them, dreading what news it might contain.

Mrs Mudge's son Stanley was in the Army. He'd been away ever since the war began and Keith had never seen him. He stared at her now, trying to imagine what it must be like to hear that your son had been killed thousands of miles away.

But she was shaking her head. 'It's not my Stanley. Thank God, it's not him. But oh, those poor little girls, those poor, dear little girls—'

'Stella and Muriel?' Keith asked, his voice high with fear. 'What's happened to Stella and Muriel? They were all right just now, I saw them in the garden—' He realised that the telegram couldn't possibly concern them and his thoughts flew to the only other two girls he could think of in that moment. 'Is it our Rose and Maureen? What's happened to them? What is it?'

Mr Beckett turned his head and looked down at him. For a moment or two, his eyes were blank, almost as if he didn't know who Keith was. At last he spoke, his voice remote, as if it were coming from a great distance.

'It's not Rose and Maureen,' he said quietly, and laid his hand on Keith's shoulder. 'It's not your sisters.' He paused and then said, 'Keith, I'm going to ask you to be very brave and very kind. You see, we're going to have to help Stella and Muriel quite a lot.' He looked again at the telegram, as if to make sure that it really did say what he thought it said. 'Mr Simmons – their father – has been killed. His ship was on convoy, taking essential supplies to Malta. It was hit by German bombers and sunk.' His voice shook a little. 'This is going to make them very unhappy indeed.'

'You mean he's dead?' Keith repeated. 'He's not coming back? Not ever?'

'Not ever.'

'But they haven't got a mum,' Keith argued, as if the Germans would surely have taken this into account. 'That means they're orphans. Won't they be able to stop here any more?'

'Of course they'll be able to stop here,' Mr Beckett said sharply. 'And you're not to say anything to them to make them think they can't. I told you, we've got to be very kind.' He paused. Keith was only a child, he had no real comprehension of what it all meant. Or had he? Children were forced to grow up so quickly these days . . . He turned to Mrs Mudge. 'Call them in, my dear. I'd better tell them at once. Keith, why don't you go out for a little while. And when you next see the girls, just tell them how sorry you are. There won't be any need to ask a lot of questions.'

The news left the two little girls stunned.

'But we haven't got anybody now,' Muriel said in a bewildered voice. 'We haven't got Mummy, or our baby, *or* Daddy. Who's going to look after us?'

Mr Beckett shook his head. It was almost unbearable to try to imagine what must be in their minds. They'd already been through the blitz, seeing their own home bombed twice and their mother and baby brother killed. They'd had to wave goodbye to their father, knowing he was going into danger, and now they had to face the fact of his death. All this, and they were still at an age which ought to be concerned with nothing more worrying than how to dress their dolls. It was quite inhuman.

And we're doing the same thing, he thought heavily. In Germany, there are little girls just like this, and boys like Tim and Keith, facing just the same tragedies. What *is* the world about, to allow it all to happen?

'Mrs Mudge and I will look after you,' he said gently. 'This is your home – at least until someone says there is another home for you to go to. And try to remember that whatever your father suffered, it must have been very quick—' he hoped that was true '—and it's all over now. He's at peace, with all the other brave men and women who have died in this war.' This cruel and terrible war.

'Daddy . . . ?' Muriel said, still in the same bewildered voice. 'Daddy's not coming home? But we *waved* to him. We waved really hard.'

'No,' Stella said in a hard, unchildlike voice, 'we didn't wave to him, Mu. We waved to some other daddies. We just pretended it was him.' She moved away and stared out of the window, her eyes blank and hopeless. 'I don't suppose there was anybody who waved to him, not really.'

'You mean it was *our fault?*' Muriel said, her voice breaking, and before either Mr Beckett or Mrs Mudge could speak, the tears were pouring down her cheeks. She cried loudly, sitting quite still in her chair, her mouth a square hole in her crimson face. It was almost like an animal in pain, Mr Beckett thought despairingly, like a dog howling at the moon. He looked helplessly at Mrs Mudge, and the housekeeper gathered Muriel against her bosom, stroking her hair and murmuring in her ear. But nothing, it seemed, would stop Muriel's weeping.

'It's natural,' Mrs Mudge said quietly, under cover of the sobs. 'She needs to let it out.' She reached out an arm to Stella. 'Come here, Stell. You need a good cry too. It'll make you feel better.'

'How will it?' the older girl demanded. 'Mum and Dad will still be dead, won't they? And our Tom? Crying's not going to bring them back to life.'

'Nothing's going to bring them back to life,' Mr Beckett said quietly. 'But there isn't anything we can do about that now. We have to think about you and Muriel, and you have to think about yourselves. It's quite right to cry at times like these. Mrs Mudge is right. It helps to mourn.'

'Like when we were bombed out,' Stella said in the same hard voice. 'Like when Mum and our Tom were blown to bits. And now Dad—' She stood up, looking away from Mr Beckett and Mrs Mudge. 'I'm fed up with crying. It doesn't do any good.'

'Stella—' Mr Beckett said, reaching towards her. But she backed away, like an animal afraid to be touched, and looked at him with stony eyes.

'I'm going upstairs,' she said, and was out of the room before anyone could move.

Mrs Mudge looked at the vicar. She was still holding Muriel, who was sobbing now against her chest. 'I suppose we'd better let her go. Perhaps she'll cry when she's alone. But I don't like to think of her, grieving all by herself. She needs some comfort.'

'We all have to grieve in our own way,' Mr Beckett said. 'And I daresay we'll have plenty of chances to help poor Stella. It's been a terrible shock for her – for them both.' He moved across and stroked Muriel's hair. 'Poor little souls. It's a cruel, cruel world.'

'The poor little scraps,' Mrs Mudge said later. Her eyes were red with crying. 'Haven't they got any other relatives at all?'

'Only Mike's mother, and she's in a mental hospital. She doesn't recognise anyone. And poor young Mrs Simmons lost her parents when she was a child. She was brought up by her grandmother and an aunt, but I believe they're both dead now.'

Mr Beckett sighed and reached for his cup of cocoa. It had taken Mrs Mudge all evening to get Muriel to go to sleep, and even now she was likely to cry out and wake again. And Stella was still lying stiffly in her bed, refusing to speak at all.

'What's going to happen to them, then?'

Mr Beckett shook his head. 'It's up to the authorities. I hope they'll leave them with us for the time being – there's no point in taking them away. We're all the family they've got.'

'It's a shame you can't adopt them,' Mrs Mudge said thoughtfully.

'I'd like to. But – I don't know. I'm an old man, Mrs Mudge. I'll be getting on for eighty by the time those two are grown up. What I'd like is to see them settled with some nice family. The Budds would be ideal – Mrs Budd's a motherly little body and Mr Budd's a decent man. And they get along well with the boys and Rose. But all they've got is that tiny terraced house, with two bedrooms. I don't know how they fit their family in as it is.'

'They couldn't afford it, anyway,' Mrs Mudge agreed. 'Two extra children on a dockyardman's wage . . . And I don't suppose there'll be much coming to the girls from their dad.'

'Well, we must just carry on as we are.' The vicar stood up and stretched his thin, spidery body. 'Everyone's so busy these days, I daresay they'll be glad to leave the girls with us.'

It wasn't just the girls, he thought, making his way upstairs. It was Keith as well. He knew the boy had been frightened and unsettled by the news of Mike Simmons' death. He didn't know how to cope with it. He had only met Mr Simmons once, so couldn't feel any grief, and Stella and Muriel's despair frightened and embarrassed him. His mind was mixed up with a blur of reality and fairy-tales – the word 'orphan' came straight out of the Brothers Grimm and conjured up visions of children wandering lost in everlastingly bleak landscapes. He pictured Stella and Muriel, setting off hand in hand on a journey that had no end.

'Where *do* people go when they're dead?' he asked Mr Beckett when the vicar came in to say goodnight. He'd been asking this question for years and nobody had ever been able to answer it satisfactorily, but now it seemed even more urgent to find an answer. 'I mean, there's so many people dying now, Heaven must be getting ever so crowded. Suppose there's not room for them all? What happens then?'

'There's room for everyone,' the vicar said, but even he had begun to wonder lately. 'Heaven is infinite.'

'I don't know what that means,' Keith said a little sulkily. He didn't like it when people used words he couldn't understand.

'Without end,' Mr Beckett said, feeling on surer ground now. 'Like the sky. Think of the stars at night, Keith, going on for ever and ever, further than we can see. Millions and millions of them, stretching out in space for millions and millions of miles.'

'But they must come to an end,' Keith argued. 'Even millions and *millions* of miles have got to come to an end sometime.'

'Not in infinity. And not in Heaven.' The vicar placed his hand on Keith's shoulder. 'Don't worry about it, Keith. Don't even try to understand. None of us can, our minds aren't able to take it in. Just have faith.'

But it wasn't easy to have faith, when you were living with two little girls who had no mother or father, no uncles, aunts or grandparents, and who didn't seem to believe in anything any more.

Stella lay in bed, staring into the darkness. In the garden, under her window, was the shaggy patch of grass where nothing else would grow, the patch where she and Muriel had been playing the day Daddy had come to see them. She could see him now, tall and sunburnt, watching them over the gate. She could feel the joy leap in her breast as she jumped up and ran towards him. And now he would never stand there again, and she would never feel his arms around her or see that broad smile which lit up his eyes and made even his curly hair look as if it were laughing.

Daddy, Daddy . . .

The tears made her throat ache. But she'd cried before, when they'd come out of the Anderson shelter, right back at the beginning of the war when the raids had begun, and seen their house no more than a ruin. She'd cried for her dolls and her toys, for the little bedroom she and Muriel had shared, that Mummy had made so pretty with flowery curtains and pale green wallpaper. She'd cried when she saw the house they were to live in in October Street, bare and damp and stinking of cats' pee.

Daddy . . .

And she'd cried again when the bomb had hit that house, and they'd told her that Mummy had gone for ever, and her baby brother Thomas. Stella had seen Thomas being born, she'd helped look after him, she'd held him and bathed him and changed his nappies. She hadn't been able to believe that he was dead. He'd only been a few months old. What was the use of being born at all, if that was going to happen to you?

The crying had hurt. It had hurt her chest and her throat and made her nose swell and her eyes sore. And it hadn't done any good. It wouldn't do any good now.

She lay with her face to the wall, her hands clenched, her anger building inside her like a hard, jagged lump, refusing to cry, refusing to sleep.

But she could not stay awake for ever. And when she slept at last, the images in her brain grew larger and darker, their shadows looming over her like menacing ghosts. She heard the roar of the aircraft, the thunder of exploding bombs, the crash of falling houses. She heard the screams and the shouts, the panic and the sobs, and she could no longer refuse to cry, no longer refuse to understand that her father was dead, that he had died like her mother and brother, blown apart by a German bomb as he did what his country had required him to do in a quarrel that was not of his own making.

She knew, and she understood, and her understanding welled up in a searing nightmare of grief and anger, of fear and despair.

She sat bolt upright in bed, and her screams rang through the silent house.

'*Daddy! Daddy! Daddy!*'

22

The bombing began again in August, and Portsmouth suffered its first air-raid for over a year – the fifty-eighth raid of the war. Eight high-explosive bombs were dropped around Cosham, on the railway embankment and in the grounds of the mental hospital. Four failed to detonate and Dennis and his team were called out to deal with them.

'The trains have been stopped,' Captain Anderson said. 'One of the bombs is sticking out of the embankment, one's in the hospital grounds, the others have buried themselves. The thing we've got to decide is which one to deal with first.'

They examined each site. The bomb sticking out of the embankment had a clockwork fuse-pocket in plain view on top of it. The Pioneers were already digging carefully down to its mate, at the bottom of a deep crater about twenty yards away. The third had landed much too close for comfort, and the fourth had dug itself a pit in the middle of the hospital gardens. It had been cordoned off, but the hospital windows were crowded with curious faces.

'You'll have to get all those people away from there,' Captain Anderson said sharply to the matron. 'If that goes off, it'll probably shatter every window and they'll be cut to ribbons.'

'It's the patients. They're fascinated by anything different.'

'Well, they'll have to be fascinated somewhere else. Get 'em round the back of the building.' He turned to Dennis. 'Which d'you think we'd better deal with first?'

'This one's nearest to civilians. But the others could cause a lot of damage to the railway, and it's the main line from Portsmouth to the West Country. They'll take longer to deal with, too, the three of them.'

'During which time this little beauty might blow up and take the hospital with it.' The Captain frowned and pulled his lip. 'Get the men over here. They'd be halfway down if they'd started straight away.'

The officer in charge of the Pioneers wasn't too pleased to have his decision countermanded, but he brought his men across and they began to build a shaft down to the bottom of the crater. The bomb could be seen nose-down in the chalk, its tail sticking out – one of the least attractive propositions a bomb disposal team could work on for, until the earth was scraped away from its sides, its type and condition couldn't be assessed, and nobody knew how long any time-fuse might have to run. All those personnel not actively engaged upon the work moved away to what was considered a safe distance.

'Let's have a look at that clockwork toy,' Anderson said, and they walked back to the embankment. 'We could make a start on this one while they're digging.'

Dennis clamped his stethoscope to the side of the bomb. He could hear the steady, measured ticking that meant the bomb was alive and timed to explode. It might be at any time – from the very next minute, to several months.

You always assumed it was due to go off at once. It might lie there ticking until Christmas, but you always acted as though it had only minutes to run.

'Bloody hell,' Anderson said. 'We're not supposed to touch it.'

Dennis raised his head and stared at him.

'That new order from DBD. We're not supposed to deal with clockwork fuses until they've sent one of their bods down to make some experiments. We're supposed to report to them and then wait.'

'*Wait?*' Dennis echoed. 'But that's madness. We don't know how long it's got to run. And once we've started work on it, it's our responsibility.'

'Mine,' the Captain said. 'My sole responsibility. Not yours, Verney.'

Dennis ignored this. He knew Anderson wasn't trying to pull rank, simply stating the facts as laid down by military orders. But they worked so closely together now that he took almost as much part as the Captain in making the decisions.

'We can't leave it now,' he said. 'It'll take at least two hours to get anyone down from London. We'll be lucky if it lasts twenty minutes.' He thought for a moment. 'Anyway, we've started – we've used a stethoscope on it. That makes it our bomb.'

Anderson grinned faintly. 'I doubt if DBD will take that view. But let's go ahead anyway. I agree with you – we can't take the chance. And we've got three other bombs, a railway line and a hospital full of patients to think about too.'

With the bomb in such a convenient position, stopping the clock and removing the fuse was as simple as such a task could ever be, with the menace of an explosion still hanging like a shadow over everyone's head. But Dennis did not allow himself to think of that. He had schooled himself to think of the job as just a job – something that needed the utmost care, but held no danger whatsoever, at least to himself. Yet he never forgot the other men who were compelled to work close to him, listening on their headsets or helping with the delicate work of scraping away mud or keeping the right tools at the ready.

As always, immediately before he began work, he thought for a moment of Betty. She was like both a prayer and a beacon in his mind and his heart, a reminder that he had the world to live for. He held the thought of her and then pushed it gently away. There was no room for distraction in the task he was about to begin.

The fuse was out. The team breathed a sigh of relief and began the work of removing the bomb to the truck for safe disposal. The clock stopped just as they were strapping it down.

'So much for waiting for the boffin from London,' Dennis remarked. He and Captain Anderson looked at each other and grinned, and Dennis wiped the sweat from his brow. 'Well, that's one down. Three to go. Let's go and see how they're getting on with the one at the hospital.'

The shaft was almost completed now, its walls lined with close boarding. It was almost a crime to build so well and then dismantle it all again, Dennis thought. But any of the Pioneers would be able to set up as a builder and joiner after the war – if they survived.

'It's keeping all the pressure equal that's the skill of it, sor,' the Irishman in charge told him. 'There's a whole lot of strain on the sides, don't ye see, especially when ye get down deep, and ye have to be sure that it's properly distributed or ye'll get a collapse. And there's water down there too, so we'll have to be putting the pump on it before ye can start work.'

Flannery was a good workman, an expert on timbering and excavation, and Dennis knew that he took as much pride in his work as if he were building a house for the Queen. He watched as the pumps were installed and the water began to gush up from the depths.

'There's a lot down there. How much will this pump extract?'

'Quarter of a million gallons a day, sor. But we can put another one in if that's not enough.' They looked at the stream of the water that was now finding a channel across the garden. 'They should be gathering that up for the vegetable gardens. It'll be a gift, after the drought we've had.'

With the pit relatively dry at last, Dennis and Captain Anderson climbed down the long ladders to the bottom, their headsets fastened on so that they could talk to the men above. They stared at the bomb, now standing on its nose supported from above by strong webbing straps.

'Looks straightforward enough,' Dennis said.

'Hmm. It *looks* straightforward. But we never take anything for granted in this job.'

Once again, the bomb had begun to tick, and the big clock-stopping magnet was clamped to the side and switched on. Time was now less of a problem, but the bomb was still filled with explosive and in an unstable state. And there was always the chance that the clock would start again, or a second fuse come into operation.

Captain Anderson settled himself at the other end of the bomb with his stethoscope. They took turns at this job, working together as smoothly as a machine. It didn't matter who finally defused the bomb; as Anderson had told Dennis on his first operation, there was no place for heroes in this job.

Dennis inserted his chisel gently into one of the notches on the base-plate. He tapped his hammer against it.

The hammer refused to move away from the chisel.

'Christ,' he said softly, 'the whole lot's stuck to the magnet.'

He pulled and prised, struggling to free the tools, but the magnet was too powerful. The entire bomb had become a magnet. He wondered what that was doing to its electrical fields, and whether there would be any change in the explosive. Was this a new German device, or merely a freak?

The tools came away in his hand. He tried again, jerking the hammer away after a sharp tap, and this time managed to loosen the plate slightly. The bomb seemed to give a tiny sigh, and Dennis felt his flesh crawl.

Betty, he thought. Betty. I'm coming out of this alive and we're getting married. As soon as possible. In a church or a Meeting, or at the back of one of the pigsties, I don't care which.

He pushed the thought of Betty away and concentrated again. The chisel slid in and out of the second notch, then the third and the fourth. The plate came away in his hand.

Now for the fuse-pocket.

Dennis switched on his torch and shone it inside the bomb. It was oddly hollow, and it took him a moment or two to realise why. Instead of being cast-filled, as most of the German bombs were, this one had been filled with powder. The powder had begun to deteriorate and liquefy to pure nitro-glycerine which had settled into the nose of the bomb, leaving the tail end, which was uppermost, empty.

That was why it had magnetised the hammer and chisel, he thought. But the important thing now was to get the fuse-pocket out. And the fuse-pocket was low down in the bomb, half submerged in a pale brown fluid which could detonate at the slightest vibration.

Very gently, Dennis reached down the inside of the casing. The slightest ripple caused by his fingers could cause an explosion, and in the confines of the narrow shaft it would be devastating. But there was no other choice. He felt the touch of liquid against his fingertips and almost physically forced his heart to remain steady. Even an increase in the beat of his pulse could do it . . .

Slowly, gradually, he let his fingertips drift deeper into the syrup. He remembered once, as a boy, being taught to catch trout with his hands by 'tickling' them. You did it almost casually, letting your fingers relax and whisper along their bodies so that they noticed it no more than the flowing of the stream. The slightest suspicion of anything more, and they were off.

Tickling a bomb was a hundred times more delicate than that.

He had his entire hand in the fluid now. His fingers were closing round the fuse-pocket. It was loose, making the bomb even more unstable than they had supposed, and he felt the weight of it – a steel casing which held almost two pounds of picric explosive, itself highly sensitive to movement or disruption. A bomb in miniature, a bomb within a bomb.

Moving with infinite care, he withdrew it from the nitro-glycerine and squatted for a moment holding it in both hands, still trying to quell the thudding of his heart. He had only to breathe a little too fast . . . But with ordinary care, it ought to be safe enough now.

'I'll get it out of here,' he said quietly to Captain Anderson, and began to climb the ladder.

It was a job he had done dozens of times before. It ought, as he had said, to have been straightforward. Safe. But somewhere on his way to the far end of the hospital grounds to destroy the fuse, something went wrong. Perhaps he tripped. Perhaps he stumbled. Perhaps the explosive had simply become so unstable that nothing would have prevented it going off.

Dennis's last thought was of Betty, and the wedding they had been looking forward to so much.

23

'They don't know if he'll pull through or not,' Betty told the Spencers as she sat in the farm kitchen, white and exhausted, after her first visit to the hospital. Mrs Spencer had put a cup of tea in front of her the moment she walked in, but she hadn't touched it and there was a thin scum forming on its surface. 'He's all bandaged up like one of those Egyptian mummies, and they've shaved off his hair and he's got tubes and things sticking into his arms. I don't think he even knew I was there. It's horrible.'

'Poor Dennis,' Erica said soberly. Her waist had begun to thicken now and she had taken out the seams of her breeches until they could be stretched no further. But she had suffered almost no sickness, and her hair and skin glowed with health. 'He's really brave, Betty. I'm sorry I was such a pig to him when we first came here.'

'Don't you insult my pigs,' Yvonne said, but there was no heart in her banter. She took Betty's cup and emptied it down the sink. 'Here, have a fresh one. It'll do you good. And take lots of sugar.'

'I don't like sugar,' Betty said drearily, but she lifted the cup and sipped it, and a little of her colour began to return to her cheeks. 'I wish I could stop in the hospital all the time. I wouldn't be in the way. I'd just sit there beside him, and be there if – if he wakes up. But they won't let anyone stay for more than an hour.'

'They never do,' Mrs Spencer said. 'Goodness knows what they're doing all the time, but it's like a secret world. Especially Army hospitals. They'd keep you out all the time if they could.'

'Oh, they're nice enough, it's just that those are the rules.' Betty set down her teacup and it rattled against the saucer. 'I want to be *with* him. He needs me. And suppose – suppose anything happens. I mean, he might *die* and me not there.'

Her voice rose dangerously, and Mrs Spencer reached out and laid a firm hand on her arm. 'Now, you're not to talk like that. Dennis isn't going to die. He's stayed alive three days, he'll not give up now. I'm sure he knows you were there and he's making up his mind this instant that he's going to get better so you can get wed. In fact, if you ask me it might be a good time now to start sewing yourself a wedding dress. I've got some nice white muslin laid by, we could use that unless you want to borrow the one Erica had.'

Yvonne looked scared. 'I don't think we ought to do anything like that. It might be unlucky. Like buying a pram before the baby's born.'

'Rubbish,' the farmer's wife began robustly, but Betty shook her head.

'I'm not having a wedding dress. We're getting married the Quaker way, without any fuss. We ought to have done it straight away – I'd have been Dennis's wife by now, instead of just his fiancée. It'd be me the doctors talked to, and I'd be allowed to see him more often.'

Erica nodded. 'You can't afford to wait these days. You just don't know what's going to happen. None of us does.'

She looked down at her lap. Gerald knew about the baby now, and had written to express his delight, but it hurt that he'd never been able to tell her to her face how pleased he was, that he'd never been able to take her in his arms and give her that special kiss. She wondered if he would be able to come home before the baby was born, or if it would be sitting up, perhaps even walking and talking, before he saw it. Or if he would ever see it . . .

The fighting in North Africa and the Western Desert was still serious and Churchill himself flew to Cairo to see what was going on. General Auchinleck had done well at El Alamein, he said, but it was imperative to deal with the Germans, who were even now only sixty miles from Alexandria. An offensive was needed. He appointed 'Strafer' Gott as commander of the Eighth Army.

The new leader never had the chance to prove his own capabilities. His transport aircraft was shot down within twenty-four hours by German fighters and he was killed. Someone else had to be found quickly, and that someone was Bernard Law Montgomery.

Montgomery was an unknown quantity. He was small for a soldier, his face as sharp as a ferret's, with bright eyes and an arrogance that suggested not so much that he looked to God for help, as that God looked to him. He had fought in the Great War – now beginning to be called the First World War – and won the DSO, and he had been in France before Dunkirk. Now he strutted into North Africa, under the cynical eyes of an army which had already suffered heavy losses, and declared that only he could defeat the Desert Fox.

'Thinks a lot of himself,' Frank remarked. 'Let's hope it's not another lot of hot air. I'm beginning to wonder if any of them knows what they're up to.'

'They've been having nothing but rows in Parliament,' Ted agreed. 'And by all accounts, Winnie and that General Auchinleck had a stand-up row right there in the desert – the general saying the army was exhausted and had to have better tanks and stuff, and Churchill shouting him down and saying nothing mattered but beating Rommel. How can he say that? They've got to have the right equipment, haven't they? They can't fight a war without guns.'

'That's right. And it was Churchill himself who said "Give us the tools and we'll finish the job". I don't suppose anyone dared remind him about that, though.'

There was a lot of grumbling these days, about the way the war was being managed. All the authorities came in for their own slice of people's disapproval, from the government downwards. Portsmouth City Council received its own barrage of complaints.

'What's the point of having their offices all the way out at Southsea? It's all right for them, in a nice hotel on the front, but it's a day's march to get there. And that new Citizen's Advice Bureau office, it's just snowed under, when you can find it at all. It took Annie hours to track it down when she wanted to find out about clothes for that family down Kendal Street, and there's only two women running it, you know, two sisters, and half the time they can't find out what you wants to know, any more than anyone else, not that it's for want of trying.'

'You can't blame the Council for everything,' Jess said. 'I saw Uncle John the other day and he said they're working all the hours there are to keep things going. I know a lot of people moan about the Mayor, but I reckon he does his best. None of them expected to have to run the city during wartime, after all, when they put up for election, and nobody knew what the war would be like. Nor how long it'd last.'

That was the trouble, really. Nobody had expected the war to last this long, and there was still no end in sight. In fact, it seemed to be going from bad to worse, with the whole world sliding into chaos. Sometimes it seemed that it never *could* end. It was like a huge tangle of wool that could never ever be unravelled.

Betty came home to see her mother one afternoon, before she went to the hospital. She had timed it so that her father would be out, saying she couldn't bear to see him, knowing how he felt about Dennis.

'You ought to give him a chance,' Annie said. 'Your dad's not a monster. He wouldn't have wanted anything like this to happen.'

'That's not the impression he's given me. Struck me he'd think getting blown up was too good for Dennis. Anyway, even if he did change his mind he'd be too bloody obstinate to say so.'

Annie opened her mouth to object to her daughter's language, and then closed it again. Betty was having a bad enough time as it was, without starting a row about something that didn't really matter. She was obviously worried out of her mind about Dennis, sitting there at the kitchen table, her face streaked with tears, fiddling with a cup of tea.

'You can't go in to see Dennis looking like that,' Annie said. 'You wants to look cheerful, put a bit of heart into him. He's got enough to put up with, without seeing you with a face as long as a fiddle.'

'I've told you, he can't see me at all. His face is all bandaged up. And he's still unconscious.' Dennis had made little visible progress, though the doctors told Betty that some of his injuries were beginning to mend. 'Oh, Mum, what am I going to do if he never wakes up? He could stop like that for months – years. People do. I can't bear seeing him like that, lying there so helpless.'

'I know, love.' Annie put her arm around Betty's shoulders. 'It's a dreadful thing. But there's nothing we can do about it except hope for the best. I'm sure he knows when you're there. He must be able to feel you holding his hand and loving him.'

Betty sniffed and rubbed her eyes with the heel of her hand. 'I try to talk to him. I tell him I'm getting ready for our wedding. I'm going to marry him, as soon as he's fit, you know. I don't care what Dad or anyone else thinks. But I never know if he can hear me or not.' Her sobs began again. 'He just *lies* there like a – a statue.' She had almost said 'mummy'. But mummies were dead, and Dennis still had a spark of life in him. She spent her visiting times praying that the spark would ignite again.

The back door opened suddenly and Ted came into the kitchen. He stopped short in the doorway and the two women looked up at him, startled.

'Ted! You're early. I never expected you until six o'clock.'

'We've changed shifts. I forgot to tell you.' His eyes were on Betty. 'I suppose that's why you came round, you thought I wouldn't be here.'

Betty shrugged and didn't answer. Her father sat down heavily opposite her.

'Don't tell me it's not true. I'm not a fool. You've been avoiding me for weeks. Just because you can't have your own way—'

'You've been drinking,' Betty said coldly. 'Spent the rest of your shift in the Keppel's Head, have you?'

'Now, look here, my girl—'

'Stop it,' Annie said loudly. 'Stop it at once, the pair of you. Ted, you know what our Betty's going through. Whether you like Dennis or not, he's been badly hurt and no one knows if he's going to live or die. Just think of that. And if he does die, it'll be because he was trying to save folks like you and me from getting blown up. I can't see what you've got against him, I really can't.'

'Who said I had anything against him?' Ted muttered. 'He's all right. It was only when he was a pacifist—'

'Don't make any mistake, Dad,' Betty said at once. 'He's still a pacifist.'

'Well, all right, but at least he's doing something now, ain't he? Or he was, until—' Ted stopped and scowled, then looked up at Betty from under his brows and reached his hand awkwardly across the table. 'Look, girl, I don't want to make things worse for you. I know you think a lot of the chap. And maybe I was a bit hasty, taking against him the way I did. Anyway, all I want to say is – well, I hope he gets better soon, that's all. He's a decent enough young man, even if he does have some funny ideas, and if you still want to get wed when he's on his feet again – well, I'll not stand in your way.'

He finished gruffly, and Betty's face crumpled as she took his hand. He had not touched her in this way since she was a little girl, and she felt the warmth of his strong fingers with a strange sense of familiarity. The tears blurred her eyes, but she gave him a wavery smile.

'Thanks, Dad. I really do love Dennis, you know. And he loves me.'

'I know. And it's for you to work out your life. You're twenty-one, after all, old enough to make your own decisions. All I'm saying is, me and your mother will back you up, whatever you decide. We just want you to be happy, ain't that right, Annie?'

Annie nodded. She'd suspected for some time that Ted might be changing his mind, but as Betty had said, he would find it difficult to admit it. But now he'd done so, and only she knew what it had cost his pride.

'You're a good man, Ted,' she said. 'A good husband and a good father. Have I ever told you that?'

'Not nearly as often as you should,' he answered with a grin. 'And I'd say you were a good wife too, only I've been in the house ten minutes already and I'm still sitting here at this table without a cup of tea in front of me. Is that the way to treat the head of the household, I ask you?'

'Oh, you . . . !' Annie jumped up and fetched his cup from the dresser. She poured a stream of strong brown tea into it and placed it before him. 'There you are. Head of the household, indeed! I'd just like to know where we'd all be if *you* had the running of the house, with all the rations to sort out and the cooking and washing to do, instead of spending all your time on a boat going backwards and forwards across the harbour!'

Ted lifted his cup. He winked at Betty and she grinned back. Suddenly, the atmosphere in the house was lighter than it had been for many months. And when she set off an hour later to visit Dennis in the hospital, she knew that her gnawing anxiety had been eased by the relief of being on good terms with her father once more.

But all relief fled when she walked into the ward and saw that the screens were standing around Dennis's bed. Her knees shook as she approached and she looked fearfully at the nurse who emerged from behind the screen. The girl gave her a small, sympathetic smile.

'I don't know how long you'll be able to stay,' she murmured. 'He's not at all well. The doctor thinks—' She hesitated, and Betty saw with shock that there were tears in her eyes. She was a very young nurse, no more than eighteen or nineteen, and she hadn't had time to get hardened yet. The ward was full of young soldiers, and every day one or two of them died.

Simultaneously, the two girls put out their hands and touched each other, each wanting both to give and receive comfort. They stood close for a few seconds, and then a patient called out in sudden distress from the far end of the ward and the young nurse disengaged herself and hurried off.

Betty tiptoed quietly through the screens and looked down at the bed. Dennis was lying very still. He was still heavily bandaged and looked thin and flat under the white sheets. He had lost two fingers from one hand, the doctor had told her, but the other was miraculously undamaged. He might easily have lost both.

Tubes emerged from beneath the covers, one attached to a bottle that hung from the bedhead, another disappearing under the bed. His chest rose and fell very slightly with his faint breathing.

'Oh, Dennis . . .' Betty whispered, and sank on to the chair that stood beside him.

Dennis's uninjured arm lay across him, on top of the sheets. She laid her hand on his, very gently. It felt cold.

'Dennis, my darling, don't leave me. Please don't leave me.'

The words were no more than a thread of sound in the tiny oasis of silence. Beyond the screens, she could hear the sounds of the busy ward – people crying out and groaning, visitors walking in and chatting to someone two or three beds along, the brisk clack of the nurses' shoes. They seemed to have nothing to do with this little space where only she and Dennis existed, where two lives that should have been shared were threatened with the final parting.

'Dennis . . .'

Only his mouth and nose were visible amongst the bandages. His lips were pale and slightly parted. There was a tiny bubble of moisture in one corner. If that bubble bursts, he'll die, Betty thought irrationally. In sudden panic, she began to talk to him, her voice a whisper though she wanted to shout through the thick, muffling bandages. She talked to him about Erica and Gerald and the coming baby, about Yvonne and the pig which had pinned her to the wall of the sty, about the weather and the winter mud and the sale of last spring's lambs, about every detail of life on the farm. She talked about herself, how she was missing him, how she longed to feel his arms about her again. She talked about the days when they had begun to fall in love, the first Christmas they had spent together, the night she had slipped down from the attic room to be with him, and the glory and delight of their lovemaking.

'Don't leave me, Dennis,' she begged, stroking his unresponsive hand with trembling fingers. 'Don't go away. I need you. We belong together. We've got to be together. We're getting married, remember? A Quaker wedding, just as you wanted. It's all I want – just to be your wife. To be together for the rest of our lives. Till we're *old*, Dennis – till we're really, really old.'

There was a slight movement behind her and she sensed the nurse's presence at her side. She could not look up. She kept her eyes fixed on the bandaged face, on the pale lips and tiny bubble of moisture. It hadn't burst. It wasn't going to burst. He had to stay alive.

'Dennis, I love you,' she whispered.

The nurse touched her shoulder. Reluctantly, Betty turned her head and glanced up, meeting the tired young eyes. There was sympathy there still, but there was also a resignation, as if already Dennis had slipped away too far to be called back. No, Betty thought, *no.*

'I'm afraid he can't hear you,' the nurse said quietly. 'He's very near the end.'

He's not. He's not. Betty turned back to the bed, her fingers tightening on Dennis's hand. She felt a sudden wave of outrage, a pure, clear anger, like a knife slicing through her breast.

'No,' she said, in the same anguished whisper. 'No, Dennis. You mustn't. I need you. I love you. You're not to die. *You're not to die.*'

'It's no use—' the nurse began, but Betty lifted her free hand in a gesture of restraint. She was staring at Dennis intently, her heart beating fast. There had been a movement. She was certain there had been a movement. An almost imperceptible stirring in the cold, still fingers. A shiver across the parted lips.

'He's different,' she breathed, staring at the muffled face. 'He's breathing differently.'

'They do when—' The nurse's voice was still quiet, but there was a detachment in it now, as if she had accepted the fact of Dennis's death and was already seeing him as just another ex-patient, a bed to be emptied and remade for the next young soldier. Again, Betty felt a wave of anger. He's not a 'they', she thought, he's Dennis and he's mine and he's not going to die.

She bent her head so that her face was close to the swathe of bandages. Very gently, she touched her lips to his, felt their dryness against her skin, let the tip of her tongue move lightly across them. Dennis, Dennis . . . She hardly knew whether she uttered his name or simply thought it. But she knew that the strength of her longing, of her determination, was reaching him. She knew that he could hear her with his mind.

And if he could hear her with his mind, his heart would listen too.

'Please,' the nurse said anxiously. 'Please, you mustn't—'

But Betty did not hear her. For a fraction of a second, she had felt Dennis's lips move in response to hers. For the briefest instant of time, he had shared her kiss.

'He knows I'm here,' she breathed. 'He knows. Oh, Dennis – *Dennis* . . .'

And under her hand she felt his fingers stir, felt a trace of warmth creep back into the chilly flesh. She flashed a swift glance of triumph at the nurse's face and saw her stare as Dennis's hand moved, shakily and unsteadily, and the fingers curled beneath Betty's to turn his palm to hers.

'Look,' she said softly, 'he's smiling.'

It was the faintest of smiles. A mere quiver of the parted lips. But for Betty, it was a sunburst, and she knew that Dennis was going to live.

The bubble of moisture had disappeared. But it didn't matter any more.

24

It seemed as if the Germans had suddenly remembered where Portsmouth was. In the next raid over a hundred buildings were damaged, though nobody was killed.

'We're getting our own back, though,' Frank said with grim satisfaction. All day the wireless had been giving news bulletins of a massive raid on France. The French had been told that it was not the invasion itself, and were advised to keep out of the way for the time being and wait to be told how they could help. 'The biggest air battle since the Battle of Britain, they're calling it. That'll keep 'em busy.'

It did, but the next news was worse. A huge contingent of commandos, mostly Canadian, were killed during an attempt to seize the port of Dieppe. Of the six thousand men who had departed from ports in the South of England – including Portsmouth – only two thousand returned, and of the RAF air cover, over a hundred planes were lost. It was, the newsreader reported in a sober voice, one of the worse disasters since Dunkirk.

'And now the Duke of Kent's been killed,' Jess said sadly a few days later. 'Flying on active service over Scotland. They say a shepherd found the plane on fire. And the baby Prince Michael only two months old – that's awful.'

'It's the same for a lot of other people,' Frank remarked. 'But that doesn't make it any easier for the family, I know. Royal or not, it comes down to the same thing in the end.'

'I saw him when he came to Pompey last year,' Jess said. 'Me and Annie went down to the Guildhall Square. I thought he was lovely. He looked so much like the old King. He said he'd never seen so many cheerful people anywhere. Not that everyone's managing to keep smiling,' she added. 'Ethel Glaister next door's had a face like a wet weekend for the past fortnight.'

It was the sort of remark that made Frank smile and the children giggle. But Jess was right. Ethel Glaister had nothing to smile about these days, nothing at all.

'You're nothing better than a lodger these days,' Ethel said tartly, as she and George finished their supper of fried potatoes with a bit of scrambled dried egg. 'Off playing soldiers for weeks on end, leaving me with all the responsibility, then coming back for a couple of days just when you feel like it. It's been a godsend to you, this war, hasn't it? Given you a taste of freedom. Think you're a single bloke again.'

'For God's sake, Ethel, don't start,' he said wearily. 'It's not my fault I don't get home often. Can't I have a bit of affection?'

'Affection! So that's what you call it. A bit of a fumble in bed and you snoring like a pig straight after. Not much affection in that.'

George looked at her with distaste. Now that she'd mentioned it, he didn't think he wanted that kind of 'affection' either. Once upon a time, when they were young, Ethel had been really attractive with her blonde hair nicely done, a bit of make-up on her face and her neat little figure shown off just right in the smart clothes she wore. He'd only had to look at her to feel the stir of desire, and she'd been as ready as he was, laughing and giggling and egging him on. They'd had a lot of fun together.

But now she looked hard. Her painted fingernails were more like talons and her hair was set in rigid waves, as if it were a metal cap. The colour didn't look so natural either – it was brassy, and sometimes it even looked a queer sort of green when the light shone on it. And her clothes were a bit tight, though they were still very smart – too smart, somehow. She was forever fussing about them and you couldn't touch her for fear of creasing something or leaving fingermarks.

And he didn't want to touch her. When he looked at her now he felt nothing – only this faint repugnance, this little shudder of loathing. And he wasn't even sure he could manage it now, not after the way she talked to him. A man needed to feel his wife looked up to him a bit, after all. He didn't want to feel treated like dirt.

You've gone too far, my girl, he thought. You've pushed just that little bit too far.

It was a sad feeling, but it was also liberating. He felt suddenly free – free of Ethel, free of the hurt she could deal him, free of her nagging tongue and bitter sarcasm. He felt as if he had grown suddenly taller.

'No,' he said, 'there isn't any affection in it. And you don't have to worry, Ethel. You can have your bed to yourself tonight. In fact, you can have it to yourself for the rest of your life.'

Ethel stared at him, her mouth open. He noticed that her teeth were beginning to go yellow with nicotine, and her skin looked coarse under the powder. Her fingertips were yellow too.

'What do you mean? What are you on about?'

'Oh, come off it, Ethel. You've been nagging at me about my snoring and using up half the bed for years. Well, I'm telling you I won't be any more. From now on, it's your bed. I won't be bothering you again.'

'Well, I know you're away most of the time, don't I. There's no need to be nasty about it.'

'I'm not talking about being away,' he said. 'Not like I'm away now. I'm talking about not coming back.'

'Don't be daft. There's nothing happening where you are. You'll be coming back, turning up like a bad penny. After all, you don't fight anyway, you just build a few tin huts.'

George took no notice. Not so long ago, her words would have pricked him with humiliation. Now, they just didn't matter.

'I'm not coming back at all, Ethel. I mean, I'm not coming back to you. To this house.'

Her jaw dropped even further and her face whitened, leaving only the rouge standing out like red blotches on her cheeks. 'You're not coming back? You mean you're *deserting* me?'

'If you want to put it that way, yes.' He pushed back his chair and stood up. 'I've had enough, Ethel. Enough of being treated like an intruder in my own home. I've had enough of listening to you going on and on at me all the time. I've had enough of *you*. More than enough.'

Ethel's mouth closed and then opened again. She looked like a fish, he thought, one of those cods you used to see on fishmongers' slabs, lying there with their cold eyes staring.

'Well, aren't you pleased?' he asked. 'You can't pretend you want me here. You've been making it pretty plain that I'm in the way. And now you've got your house to yourself. I'm off and I'm not coming back.'

Ethel found her voice. 'What about money? How am I going to manage? What about the children? You're not thinking of them.'

'They'll be all right. Our Shirley's in the country, she'll be safe and happy enough there. And Joe's finding his feet in the Navy. As for Carol—' He stopped and gave her a glance of pure loathing. 'Well, you ought to be proper proud of yourself over Carol.'

'What do you mean? Our Carol's all right. She's safe and happy down in Devon. If it wasn't for me going and fetching her back from Bournemouth, she'd be in a fine pickle. As it is—'

'As it is, she's not in Devon at all like you've given out, she's in a home for unmarried mothers up near Guildford,' he broke in, and saw Ethel's face redden. 'For God's sake, Ethel! You didn't really think you were going to keep it a secret from me, did you? I told you before, Carol's my daughter and I've got a right to know what's happening to her.'

'How did you find out? Who told you?'

'Carol did, of course,' he said scornfully. 'She can write, you know. She wrote me a letter and told me all about it. You shouldn't have sent her to that Home, Ethel. She's miserable there.'

'She don't deserve to be anything else. Bringing trouble on the house. And what d'you expect me to do? Keep her here? I'd have died of shame.'

'Well, I don't reckon she'll ever come back, not now she's got away,' George said. 'We'll probably never see her again – and never know our own grandchild.'

'I don't want to talk about Carol,' Ethel said coldly. 'She's no daughter of mine.'

'You're wrong there. She's your daughter through and through. You could have been in the same position as her if I hadn't held back till we were married. You were panting for it. And I don't reckon it was just me, neither. There was plenty of other boys after you, and you didn't do much to put 'em off.' He paused for a moment, then added quietly, 'I always had a bit of a suspicion about our Joe.'

Ethel flushed scarlet. 'That's a filthy thing to say!'

'So it is,' he agreed. 'It's not very nice thinking it, neither. Most of the time I put it out of me head and took him as my son. But there's a look about him at times – puts me in mind of that Will Barlow you used to be pally with.'

'I'm not going to listen to this,' Ethel said, getting up and clattering the plates together. 'I don't know what's got into you, George Glaister, I don't, honest. It must be the strain of going away.'

'It's the strain of being here with you for over eighteen years,' he said. He buttoned up his tunic and looked around for his hat. 'Well, I don't see much point in hanging about here any longer. I've told you I'm leaving you, and that's all there is to it. I might as well go straight back to the camp now and get a good night's sleep.'

'A good night's sleep! And just what d'you suppose *I'm* going to get?' Ethel slammed the plates back on the table. 'I won't be able to sleep a wink, not a wink. My own husband, deserting me – why, I'll never be able to hold up my head again. What are all the neighbours going to say? What's that Jess Budd next door going to say? I'll be a laughing-stock, that's what I'll be, a laughing-stock.'

'Well, that's your business.' George glanced in the mirror that hung over the fireplace. He had grown a moustache since he'd been in the Army, and he looked different – stronger, somehow, more upright. It might have been the square-bashing and the outdoor life, but he felt that it had a good deal to do with his own attitude. His attitude towards himself, and to Ethel. 'I'm not interested any more. And I don't suppose anyone else is, not all that much. They've got their own lives to live. You'll be all right.'

'But how am I going to manage?' Her shrill voice had turned into a whine. 'What about money? How am I going to live? You've got to look after me, George, that's the law, you've got to provide for me.'

'Oh, you'll get your money,' he said. 'You don't have to worry about that. It'll be sent through, same as always. But don't expect it to be as much. I'm allowing a bit to our Carol as well.'

'*Carol?* You're sending money to that little hussy? *My* money?'

'No,' he said, 'my money. I've taken off what I spend on beer. It won't make no difference to you. But it'll make a lot to her, what with the baby coming and all.'

'You can't. If there's any spare money, you ought to be giving it to me. I'll take you to court.'

'You do whatever you want,' he said, turning away. 'I've made up my mind and now I'm off. You won't be seeing me here again, Ethel.' He looked at her and hesitated for a moment. Even now, it didn't seem quite right to walk out without a goodbye kiss. But Ethel hadn't kissed him in years, not properly. Not more than a peck on the cheek. And the way she was looking at him now, she was more likely to bite his ear off.

'Goodbye,' he said quietly, and went out of the door.

Ethel stood quite still. She heard the front door open and close. She heard his footsteps march quickly away up the street. And then she ran after him, jerked the door open and yelled into the darkness.

'George Glaister! Don't you dare walk away like that. You come back here this minute. You're not to go, d'you hear me? You're not to leave me. You're *my husband*, you promised to look after me till death us do part. You're *not* deserting me, you're *not!*'

Her screams grew louder and more frantic, penetrating the closed doors and windows of almost every house in April Grove. Jess Budd heard them as she sat sewing sailors' collars in her back room. The Shaw family heard them as they sat playing cards. Mrs Seddon in the corner shop heard them as she sat at her table with a pile of ration coupons before her, struggling with the everlasting paperwork.

George Glaister heard them as he marched away up October Street. But he never turned his head, and his steps never faltered. He felt as if he were marching away from a dark shadow and into a world that was new, a world that was just for him. He could be himself at last, he thought, and it didn't matter what discomfort or hardship he might have to face, he could face it as himself, standing tall and upright with his head held high.

George Glaister had become a man again.

'It's time we done something,' Micky declared. 'The Jerries are gettin' worse. And we ain't doin' nothing to stop 'em. That raid on Dieppe was stupid. They practically *told* the Jerries they were comin'. What they wants to do is go over secretly, so no one don't know nothing about it, and get at the headquarters. Shoot old Hitler, that's what they wants to do.'

The secret army had gathered in Micky's den. He had brought a few of his trophies – some fragments of shell and shrapnel, Wendy's bayonet, the wireless set, and a handful of Desmond's bullets. He had left the guns he and Desmond had collected in his bedroom, some hidden under the floorboards, the rest in the old fireplace with a bit of plywood fixed over it so that his gran wouldn't go nosing.

'Shoot Hitler,' Desmond said, aiming an imaginary gun. 'Kill Hitler. Kill. Rat-tat-tat-tat tat.'

'Shut up, Des.' Micky looked round the den at the little group. 'What I'm sayin' is, *they* won't do it, so we got to. The war's never goin' to finish otherwise. It's up to us.'

'You'd never get near him,' Tim said. He shared Micky's dream of defeating the enemy single-handed, but couldn't rid himself of the suspicion that it simply wasn't possible. 'I mean, if it was that easy, someone would've done it already.'

Micky shook his head. 'They don't do it that way. They don't kill the leaders. They just sets the soldiers against each other. But it's Hitler what's in charge, and if he was out of the way the rest'd chuck it in. I mean, I've seen him on the pictures, he's barmy.'

It sounded reasonable enough. Most people believed that Hitler was not only evil but mad as well. With him gone, perhaps the others would return to sanity. And soldiers only fought if they were ordered to. With no leader to egg them on, they would probably just put down their guns and go home.

'So what are you going to do?' Tim asked. 'How d'you reckon you're going to get to Hitler?'

'I'll get a boat. We'll row across the Channel and land in France at dead of night. We'll get to Berlin and find out where he is. They won't take no notice of us. That's our advantage, see. Nobody bothers about kids. We can get into his hideout easy and then—' Micky waved his arm '—it'll be curtains for Adolf.'

Tim pursed his lips. It couldn't be that easy.

'Berlin's hundreds of miles away from France,' he said. 'How are you going to get there – walk? It'll take weeks. And you can't speak French, or German. They'd rumble you straight away and you'd finish up in one of those concentration camps.'

Micky scowled. 'Think of a better idea, then.'

Tim shrugged. He had never been convinced that Micky's army would be a success. 'You haven't got any guns.'

Micky gave him a sideways glance. He had been wary of taking Tim into his confidence over the weapons he had collected, suspecting that Tim might draw the line at stealing guns from the airfield. Taking the enemy's weapons as trophies was one thing – stealing them from your own side quite another, even if they weren't using them to good effect. But he couldn't resist the opportunity to boast.

'We have got guns, so there.'

'You haven't. What sort?'

'A Lewis gun,' Micky said proudly, not entirely sure that he was right. He had to go by Desmond's knowledge, after all, and Desmond might easily be wrong. Anyway, it didn't matter . . . 'And a Vickers K. And some tommy guns.' These were the ones they had filched from the Home Guard shed when Martin had managed to 'borrow' the key from his uncle.

'I don't believe you,' Tim said. 'Anyway, you don't even know how to shoot.'

Micky jumped up. 'I do! Desmond's got the ammo, haven't you, Des. And he knows how to load 'em. He's been learning all about it in the ATC on Sunday mornings. He's been on the ranges, shooting. He's a crack shot. And so am I. I'm *better*.'

'Oh, yeah?'

'Yeah.' Micky squared up to Tim, his fists clenched. 'Want me to prove it?'

Tim stared at him. He and Micky had known each other since they were five years old. Each a natural leader, they had vied to be top dog in the street. But Micky had never been tied down by a strict father or anxious mother. He had always been allowed to roam freely in the streets, doing as he pleased and coming home when he felt like it. The other children, made to go to school regularly and called indoors at bedtime, were fascinated by his wildness.

Lately, with his secret army and his den, his power had been absolute.

Tim envied him. It didn't seem fair that Micky should be the one to be able to shoot, to have his own guns, to be leader of the army. It didn't seem fair that he should be able to talk about going to Berlin and shooting Hitler, being a hero.

But being at home with his father and mother had brought home to Tim some of the realities of the war. He listened to the news more than he had out in the country. He heard the bombers flying over every night. He read the newspapers and saw the headlines about the disastrous raid on Dieppe. He saw his cousin Betty with her eyes reddened with weeping over Dennis, and his aunt grey-faced with worry over Colin. He thought of Stella and Muriel, with no mother or father now to love and look after them.

'I don't care whether you're a crack shot or not,' he said to Micky. 'You'd never get anywhere near Berlin. You're just a lot of hot air, like a barrage balloon.'

Micky took a swing at him, but Desmond came out of the shadows and thrust himself between them. Micky's fist caught him a glancing blow on the shoulder, but the bigger boy took no notice. His face was white and there was a pinched look around his nose.

'*We're* real soldiers,' Desmond said pugnaciously, standing in front of Tim. 'We're Micky's army. Kill Hitler.'

'That's right,' the others joined in. 'Kill Hitler!' They leapt up and down, waving their arms and jeering. 'Kill, kill, kill.'

'Oh, for cripes' sake,' Tim said, turning away, 'you're all as barmy as he is. I'm fed up with this army. It's not an army at all. You're just a lot of stupid kids. I'm not going to be in it any more.' He gave Desmond a push. 'Get out of my way.'

Micky started to speak again, but his voice was drowned as Desmond gave a sudden bellow and made a lunge for Tim, his big fists windmilling wildly. His eyes glittered in his white face, and Tim felt suddenly scared. There was something inhuman about Desmond when he got into this mood. He was like a machine running out of control. Tim backed off, looking round for support.

'Get him off. Stop him.' A swinging fist caught him on the ear and he spun back against the wall. 'He's gone mad!'

Desmond was coming after him. His eyes looked red – like a mad bull, Tim thought – and his lips were drawn back so that his teeth were exposed in a snarl. They were dirty, yellow teeth that looked as if they might poison you if they bit you. His hands were enormous.

Another smack caught Tim on the shoulder. He raised his fists and lashed out, hardly knowing where his punches would land. One of Desmond's blows landed on his eye and he let out a yelp of pain, staggering as the cellar walls spun round him in a blur of red and black and bright, jagged white light. Desmond gave a roar of triumph and grabbed his arms, wrestling him to the ground. For a few more moments they flailed at each other and then Tim felt his knuckles connect with something hard. A vicious pain shot up his arm.

'*Ow!*' Desmond hopped backwards, holding his nose. Tim peered up at him. Blood flowed between the bigger boy's fingers and he was starting to cry. Tim felt pleased and triumphant and guilty all at once.

Micky grabbed Desmond's arm. 'Pack it in, Des. *Pack it in.* Or I won't let you be my Lieutenant no more.' The bigger boy hiccuped a couple of times and then stopped crying and stood still, like a chastened dog. Micky gave Tim a contemptuous glance.

'Go on then, if you want to. Get out. I always knew you were a cissy anyway. I only let you in so we could get some saltpetre to make bombs with. And don't come here no more, see?'

'Don't want to,' Tim said defiantly. He scrambled up the cellar steps and stood looking down at them. Micky watched him.

'And don't go blabbin' our secrets round, neither. You've sworn an oath of secrecy, remember.'

'I didn't. I never did. I never swore anything.' The swearing-in ceremony had been forgotten. 'I can tell anyone I like.'

He saw Micky start up the stairs after him, and turned and ran. Within seconds, he could hear the whole gang in hot pursuit – but the derelict street was a jungle of overgrown weeds and garden plants run riot, with broken fences and holes making booby traps everywhere. Soon, he had left them behind and was able to make his way home through the maze of alleyways and back paths without being seen again.

It was a daft thing to do, telling Micky they'd forgotten that oath. Now the captain of the secret army would be on the lookout for him all the time.

And although Tim told himself he wasn't really scared, he still couldn't hide a small quiver of apprehension. Suppose they really did have guns . . .

Betty visited Dennis in hospital as often as she could. Since the day he had turned the corner, he had improved steadily, the wounds caused by the flying fragments of shell as the bomb exploded healing well. Nothing could put back the two missing fingers, of course, and his head was still bandaged, but he could talk and Betty liked to be there even if he was asleep.

'You don't have to keep coming so often,' he said one day. 'You've got enough to do on the farm. You'll wear yourself out.'

'What else would I do with my spare time?' she asked mockingly. 'Just sit about and watch the wheat grow? Oh, Dennis—' her voice broke '—I don't want to be anywhere in the world but with you. You must know that. I can't manage without you.'

'But we have to be able to manage without each other,' he said gently. 'None of us can rely on having the right person with us all the time. We're all alone in the end, you know.'

Betty stared at him. 'What do you mean? I don't like it when you talk like that.'

'It's the truth. One day, however hard we try to be together all the time, one of us is going to leave the other one alone. You know that's true.'

'But not for a long time,' she said on a note of desperation. 'Not till we're really old.'

'Betty, how can you say that? Face the facts, darling. Life is never certain, and it's more uncertain these days than ever.'

'But you won't be going back to bomb disposal. You can't.' She touched his hand, the one with the missing fingers. 'You've done your bit, Dennis. Nobody can call you a coward now.'

'I was never worried about being called a coward,' he said. 'I didn't go into BD because of that.'

'I know . . .'

'I joined because I wanted to save some of the lives that are being wasted. And I know I can't go back. But that doesn't mean I can't do something else.'

'The farm. You could come back to the farm. Mr Spencer would be pleased to have you. He'll need someone soon – Jonas is getting slower every day, only he won't admit it. There's plenty you could do on the farm.'

'Yes,' Dennis said with a little sigh. 'Perhaps.'

Betty looked at him. Only the lower half of his face was visible under the helmet of bandages. She knew that the doctors had been afraid that his head injuries might have affected his brain. They didn't seem to have done, but Dennis had never talked quite like this before, about being alone and uncertain. He had always shown such cheerful optimism – such faith.

'Dennis,' she said timidly, 'you don't feel different about – about, you know, Quakers and – and God – do you?'

His mouth smiled. 'I don't think so. Why d'you ask?'

'Because you seem different. As if you *see* things differently now. I wondered if – well, people do lose their faith when something terrible happens to them.'

'Then it wasn't much of a faith in the first place,' he said. 'How can anyone look around and see the appalling things that happen to others and expect to be immune? If you're a human being, you share in the human condition and you don't expect your God to look after you at the expense of others. No, I haven't lost my faith, Betty.' He paused, his smile wry. 'But perhaps you're right. Perhaps I am seeing things differently.'

The nurse came along the ward then and told Betty she must go. A new doctor was coming to see Dennis. Disturbed and reluctant, Betty laid her cheek against Dennis's and he turned his face to press his lips against hers. She felt a wild desire to hold him fiercely in her arms, to feel the length of his body against her, his limbs entwined with hers in the act of love they had shared so deeply and fully together. But a kiss – hardly more than a peck – was all she was allowed in this public place.

'I'll see you again in a few days,' she said softly. 'Oh Dennis, I love you so much.'

'I love you too, my darling Betty,' he said, but there was a note in his voice that disturbed her even more. If I didn't know better, she thought, I'd think he was saying goodbye.

And as she walked, with slow, dragging steps, out of the ward and through the hospital she felt as if she were leaving a part of herself behind.

It was impossible for Tim to avoid Micky and his henchmen for long. For a few days, he went straight up to the chemist's shop early in the morning and spent an hour or two in the back room, amongst all the bottles and carboys, helping to make up the medicines. This amounted mostly to counting pills and labelling the bottles, but once or twice Mr Driver let him mix some of the coloured fluids and explained to him what was happening.

He was gratified to find a boy so interested in his work, and toyed with the idea of offering Tim a permanent job.

Frank had been angry when he saw Tim's black eye, though somewhat mollified when he heard that it was Micky Baxter's gang he'd been fighting with. At least, he said to Jess, that meant the boy wasn't getting mixed up in any of their scrapes. He decided to teach Tim to box, and gave him several lessons in the back garden.

Tim cycled round the streets doing his deliveries, keeping a sharp eye open for the secret army. Not that he was scared of them, he assured himself, but he didn't want to get into any more fights. In fact, he was rather regretting his action. Micky and the others were the only children around, and he missed the company of the others out in the country more than he'd realised. And even if he hadn't really believed in the secret army, it had been something to think about – something exciting to be part of.

Accordingly, when he saw Martin Baker wandering along September Street, he pulled on the brakes and skidded to a halt beside him. He wasn't scared of Martin anyway. Nobody could be scared of a little kid like Martin.

'Shot any Germans yet?' he asked with a touch of scorn in his voice.

Martin looked at him. 'Micky says you're a traitor to your country.'

'I'm not!'

'You are. He says the secret army was made to win the war, and if you won't be in it you're a traitor.'

'That's daft. It's not a proper army. He can't say I'm a traitor to my country just because I won't be in his stupid gang.'

'It's not stupid,' Martin said. He had been completely won over by Micky's glamour, and would have followed him anywhere. 'It's a proper army.'

'Oh yeah,' Tim sneered. 'With proper guns and all. Only he never shows them, does he. They're all under the floor in his bedroom. Have *you* ever seen them?'

'Yes, I have. And Micky's bringing them tonight so we can learn to shoot.' He paused and glanced at Tim. 'You could come too if you want.'

'I can't. I've left.'

'You could join again. Micky says you could join again.'

'Don't want to,' Tim said, struggling with a desire to see if they really did have guns.

'Go on,' Martin said coaxingly. 'It's a good army. And Micky reckons he knows where he can get a boat, to go to France. With an engine.'

'He couldn't—'

'He knows the boat. It's already been to France. It was at Dunkirk.'

'My uncle went to Dunkirk,' Tim said. He leant on his handlebars. He had finished his deliveries for the day, there was nothing good on the wireless that evening and he'd already read that week's *Hotspur* from cover to cover. The evening stretched ahead of him.

They didn't really have any guns, of course. It was just a pretence. But it wasn't a bad game, pretending to be a secret army. Better than sitting at home playing Ludo with Rose, or listening to her and Joy nattering on about clothes.

'All right,' he said. 'I'll come after tea. But you tell Micky to make sure that Desmond keeps off, see?'

The secret army was in the cellar in full strength, waiting for him – Micky, Martin Baker, Jimmy Cross, Wendy and Alan. And Desmond, skulking sullenly in a corner, fiddling with an old pilot's cap. He stared inimically as Tim came cautiously down the steps, letting his eyes get used to the dimness.

'Well, get an eyeful of this,' Micky said as Tim reached the bottom step. 'The wanderer returns. I s'pose you think we ought to kill a fatted calf or whatever it was.'

'You must have learnt that at Sunday School,' Tim retorted and saw Micky flush. The Sunday afternoons he had been forced to spend in the schoolroom, listening to Bible stories and colouring in pictures of Jesus carrying a small lamb, were still a sore point.

'Look, we don't 'ave to 'ave you in the army,' Micky began, but Tim's eyes were on the table. He stopped, then took a cautious step forward, staring.

'Those are guns. Real guns.'

'Well, I told you we 'ad 'em, didn't I. Now perhaps you'll believe me.'

The guns lay spread out as if on display. The sort of guns Tim had seen illustrated in *Hotspur* They were, quite obviously, not toys.

'Coo,' he breathed. 'They're smashing.'

He reached out and touched one gently with the tip of his finger. The other children were watching him. Beside the guns, he saw a pile of bullets and his eyes widened again. Suddenly touched by panic, he stepped back.

'Where did you get them?'

'Never you mind. We bin issued with 'em, see. We're a proper secret army, and if you don't join in you're a traitor.'

'I'm not. You can't make me join.' His eyes strayed back to the guns.

'We can. It's conscription. You got to be in it. So's anyone else, if I says so. And you got to swear an oath.'

Tim hesitated. It didn't really seem likely that Micky Baxter would have been entrusted with the task of forming a secret army. But it wouldn't have seemed likely a few years ago that girls would be firing Ack-ack guns, like his cousin Olive, or driving ambulances like Gladys Shaw. You didn't know what they'd decide to do next.

A thought struck him. 'You haven't got uniforms. If you're a proper army, you ought to have uniforms.'

Micky rolled his eyes. 'Give me strength! We wouldn't be a secret then, would we? Now look, are you going to be in this army and swear this oath or not?'

Tim stared at him and then looked at the guns again. He made up his mind.

'No. I don't believe you. You've pinched those guns from somewhere.' A memory stirred in his mind, something his father had read out of the *Evening News*. 'I bet they're the ones that got took from the Home Guard shed. You pinched them from there. Didn't you?'

Micky glanced round at the others. His eyes narrowed and he took a step forward.

'I told you, it's none of your business. Anyway, you got to be in the army now. You know too much.' He'd heard the phrase at Saturday morning pictures and kept it ready in his mind. 'You got to swear the oath.'

'No,' Tim said. 'No, I won't.' He turned to go.

Micky grabbed his arm. 'You got to. You got to swear secrecy. We don't want no one else knowing about this.'

Tim shook Micky's arm off angrily. 'Let go.'

Micky grabbed him again. 'You're our prisoner, then. If you're not in the army, you've got to be kept prisoner. We can't take no risks of you telling the coppers. We'll keep you here. We'll torture you.'

'Don't be daft,' Tim said, trying not to feel scared. The cellar was a grim place, with black, damp-streaked walls and dark recesses that might hold anything. 'You can't keep me prisoner.'

'Can't we, then?' Micky sneered at him. 'Who's to stop us, eh?'

'If I don't go home tonight, they'll look for me. My Dad'll get the police out.'

'They wouldn't find you,' Jimmy Cross said. 'This place is secret.'

'They would. They'd look everywhere.'

Micky sneered again. 'Garn! They'd just think you'd got blowed up. Or run off. There's plenty of people disappears these days and no one never finds out where they've gone.'

'Kill him,' Desmond said suddenly. 'He's a traitor. Kill him.'

There was a sudden, cold silence. The other children glanced at each other uneasily. Wendy Atkinson shifted her feet and reached her hand out to her brother, who crept close to her, his eyes big and fearful.

'You can't do that,' Tim said. 'That's murder.'

'It's execution,' Desmond said. 'Kill. Kill Hitler.' He picked up one of the guns.

Micky looked at him, then turned his eyes back to Tim.

'He doesn't know what he's saying,' Tim said. 'You know that. He says things and he doesn't know what they mean. He's round the twist.'

Desmond took a handful of bullets from his pocket and began to load the gun.

'Stop him,' Wendy said in a high, frightened voice. 'Stop him.'

'It's all right,' Micky said. 'They're not the right ammo. It won't work.' But his glance was uneasy. He held out his hand. 'Give us that gun, Des. It ain't yours.'

Desmond held on to it. 'It is mine. I got it. My gun. My bullets.'

'Give it here.' There was an edge to Micky's voice now. 'I'm captain of this army, I give the orders. You give it here.'

Desmond did not answer. He turned away and went on forcing the bullets into the gun.

'He's barmy,' Wendy said. 'He'll kill us. Come on, Alan. We're going home.'

Alan held tightly to her hand. He was whimpering softly, like a puppy which had hurt its paw. Together, they sidled round the wall to the steps. Martin Baker gave Micky a quick look and followed them.

'Stop here,' Micky said. 'Nobody's goin' out till I says so.'

'You can't stop us.'

'I'm the captain. This is my army. You got to do what I say.'

'Not if we don't want to,' Wendy said boldly. 'It's not a real army. It's only pretend. Go on, Alan.' She pushed her brother up the steps.

'No!' Micky said roughly. 'No. Nobody's to go.' He looked at Desmond, still struggling with the gun. 'Give us the gun. Give it here.'

For answer, the older boy hefted the weapon against his shoulder and pointed it at Micky, squinting along the barrel as if taking aim. Wendy gave a scream, and pushed Alan harder up the steps. Martin Baker scrabbled close behind them, sobbing with fright. Tim backed into a corner, thinking of bullets ricocheting around the tiny basement and wishing he'd never got involved with Micky Baxter and his secret army.

'Don't do that, Des,' Jimmy Cross said. 'You know you're not supposed to point guns at people.'

'Kill,' Desmond said in the monotonous voice that meant he was retreating into his own private world, hardly aware of other people. 'Kill Hitler. Kill, kill, kill.'

'I'm not Hitler,' Micky said. His voice had roughened to fear. 'Give us that gun.'

'Kill. Kill. Kill.'

'For Christ bloody Jesus' sake,' Micky said. 'Give us it.'

'He's gone off his rocker,' Tim muttered, and slid along the blackened wall. 'He's gone right round the bend.'

There was a sharp spike of sound as Desmond cocked the gun. Jimmy Cross made a faint noise, almost a gargle, and Tim almost cried out. He knew that the gun was now armed and might go off at any minute. If only Desmond hadn't got his finger on the trigger. *Please*, don't let him have his finger on the trigger . . .

He slid further round the wall, coming close behind Desmond, who was still aiming the gun at Micky. He felt sick with fright. He could hear Wendy's voice, in the ruined rooms of the house above, and wished he could have escaped as well. His hand trembling, he reached out and grabbed Desmond's arm.

'Let go. Let go of the gun, Des. *Let go, or you'll kill us all.*'

Desmond jumped violently and sprang backwards, knocking Tim to the ground. He was screaming and clutching the gun to his body, his hands tightly squeezed around it, and it was pointing at the ceiling and firing, over and over again, the explosions shattering the crumbling walls, the bullets ripping through the lath and plaster above. Tim heard Wendy cry out in terror somewhere overhead. There were shards of brick and splinters of wood flying everywhere, and he felt a sudden searing pain as something stabbed into one of his legs. He screamed at Desmond – '*Let go, let go, let go!*' – but his voice went unheard and Desmond's eyes were shut, his face horribly distorted as he flailed with the gun, clutching it like a lifeline rather than the instrument of death it really was.

He heard Micky yell, and then Desmond crashed to the floor with a long, thin scream that sounded exactly like the rabbit Tim had shot with Reg Corner out at Bridge End.

25

'He's really done it this time,' Frank said grimly. 'I always said that boy'd bring trouble. And I told *you* to keep away from him,' he added to Tim. 'You'll be lucky if you don't end up in prison.'

'He's lucky he's still alive,' Jess said. She had been crying most of the night and her eyes were red and swollen in a pale, puffy face. 'Oh, Tim, how could you be so stupid? Getting mixed up with guns – secret armies – I thought you were a sensible boy. I thought you could be trusted.'

'I can,' Tim said, but he didn't sound too sure about it. 'I never stole anything. I didn't even know they had guns till last night. I thought it was just a game.'

'A *game!*' Frank echoed. 'Funny sort of game, when two boys end up in hospital. You ought to have known that Baxter boy would be up to something. Look at what happened last time – young Cyril Nash blown to bits and the Cross boy with only one leg. You'd have thought he'd have known better than to go back for more.'

'More legs?' Tim said, and immediately wished he hadn't. He knew as well as his father that this was no time for jokes – he just hadn't been able to help it. He saw Frank take a deep breath, his angry face darkening even further, and added quickly, 'I didn't mean that. I didn't even know I was going to say it.'

'Your tongue's going to get you in trouble one of these days,' Frank told him. 'It's about time you learnt to control it. Time you learnt a few other things as well.' He turned to Jess. 'I told you he'd be better off out in the country. If he'd stayed out at Bridge End, this would never have happened.'

'Yes, it would,' Tim said. 'I just wouldn't have been there when it did. *Ow!*'

Exasperated beyond words, Frank had lashed out and cuffed him sharply on the ear. Tim retreated to a corner and sat miserably rubbing his head. His dad was right. He did have too much to say, and usually at the wrong moments. And it wasn't even that he found the situation funny. He was scared and upset, and his legs and arms still shook when he thought of the gun going off and everybody yelling and scrambling to get out of the way. It was a miracle someone hadn't been killed, the policeman had said.

Tim thought of it all again. It was like remembering a nightmare. There were gaps in his memory where he couldn't recall anything clearly, and flashes when everything seemed to be happening at once. And the noises –

Micky's voice, harsh with panic, bawling out orders, Desmond screaming like that shot rabbit, the sharp rattle of the gun, going on and on as if it had taken over and couldn't be stopped . . . It was horrible. He didn't think he would ever be able to forget it.

Mum was right. They were lucky nobody had been killed. As it was, Tim had got away with a big splinter of wood in his leg and a few grazes, but Micky had almost bled to death and they thought Desmond would lose one of his eyes. And the police had been up in number 10 half the night, tearing the place to bits if what Nancy Baxter said was true, and Tim had been told to stay indoors until they came to talk to him too.

'That's a day's work lost,' Frank grumbled. 'I can't go in the Yard till they've been. I just hope you're proud of yourself.'

Tim said nothing. Of course he wasn't proud of himself. He felt humiliated and ashamed and frightened. Suppose he did end up in prison. His father would never want to speak to him again. And Mum wouldn't be able to show her face in the street again. They'd probably have to move, and they might not even tell Tim where they'd gone, for they surely wouldn't want him back at home when he came out.

I might be there for years, he thought, and saw himself sitting alone in a bare cell, living on nothing but bread and water, until he was an old man.

There was a sudden loud knocking on the front door, and Tim almost jumped out of his skin. Jess gasped and put her hand to her mouth, turning to Frank, who got up and stood for a moment in the middle of the room.

'Now you answer his questions properly,' he said sternly to Tim. 'Tell him the truth. It won't help you to go telling lies to try to get out of it.'

He went through the passage and they heard him open the door. There was a murmur of deep voices, and then he came back, followed by a policeman carrying his helmet. If he hadn't taken it off, Tim thought, he wouldn't have been able to get through the door. As it was, he seemed to fill the room with his huge body in its dark blue uniform.

The policeman nodded to Jess. 'I'm sorry about this, missus. It's a bad do. I'll have to ask your boy a few questions.' He glanced at Tim. 'This the young man?'

'Yes, this is Tim. He's our oldest boy.' Jess's voice was quick and nervous. 'He's a good boy, really, he's never been in any trouble before. It's only that he's got into bad company . . .' Her voice trailed away. Mothers always said those things. The policeman must have heard them a hundred times before. Probably Nancy Baxter herself had said exactly the same about Micky.

The policeman nodded. He put his helmet down on the dining table and pulled out a chair. He sat down, his hands on his knees, facing Tim. His big face was serious.

'Now then. You were one of the boys involved in the incident last night in the basement of number 24 Turkey Street, is that right?'

Tim nodded miserably.

'Tell me exactly what happened. In your own words.'

Whose words would I use, Tim thought, but there were no jokes left in him now. In a small, hesitant voice, he described what had taken place in the ruined den.

'I wanted to leave. I was fed up with it – I couldn't see we'd ever do any good. And I was fed up with Micky ordering me about. He just wants to be in charge all the time.' A faint note of indignation crept into his voice. 'He thinks he's boss of the whole street.'

'All right, I know all about Micky Baxter,' the policeman said. 'So you wanted to leave, did you? Why didn't you, then?'

'I tried. I told Micky I was going. He said I couldn't go, I'd sworn an oath of secrecy. I hadn't,' Tim said, turning his eyes towards his father. 'I never swore anything. But Micky said I knew too much and I'd have to be kept prisoner down there. He said nobody would ever know what had happened to me. He said people would just think I'd run off, or – or got blown up or something.' Tim's voice shook and ended in a whisper. He hardly dared look at his mother.

'Oh, that awful boy,' Jess said, almost in tears again. 'He's a wicked, wicked boy. We might never have seen our Tim again.' She covered her face with both hands and Frank put his hand on her shoulder. But he was looking grimmer than ever. He nodded curtly at Tim.

'Go on, then. Tell us what happened after that. How did they come to start shooting?'

'That was Desmond.' Tim strove to be fair. 'I mean, I don't think he really knew what he was doing. He'd gone all funny, you know, like he does – his voice went sort of flat. He said I ought to be killed. But he was talking about Hitler too. That was what Micky wanted to do – get over to Germany and kill Hitler. That was why he was getting the guns. But I think Desmond had got muddled up and maybe he thought we were there, or we'd caught Hitler or something – I don't know.'

'So was it him did the shooting?'

'Yes. He picked up the gun and aimed it at Micky. I tried to get it off him but he must have already had his finger on the trigger.' Tim's voice was thick now, as if he were trying not to be sick. 'It went off and just kept on going. Desmond was sort of jumping about – it was like he couldn't let go – and the bullets were hitting the walls and bouncing . . .' He shook his head, trying to go on, but his voice refused to work and the tears were streaming down his face. 'I thought we were all going to be killed,' he whispered at last.

The three adults stared at him, then turned their eyes to each other. Jess was as white as snow, and even the policeman's face had lost its ruddiness. Frank cleared his throat.

'You're lucky you weren't,' he said gruffly. 'You're all lucky you weren't. You were bloody silly, the whole lot of you.'

Tim nodded. There was a brief silence, then Frank turned to the policeman.

'So what happens now? Are they going to be charged?'

The policeman shrugged. 'That's not up to me, sir. I'll have to go back to the station and make a report. The super will decide what to do about it. It's obvious that the Baxter boy was the ringleader – a proper little arsenal we found, up in his bedroom. Grenades, bullets, a bayonet – you never saw anything like it.' He glanced apologetically towards Jess. 'And I'm sorry, missus, but we'll have to have a look around here too. See if your boy's been hiding anything.'

'Oh, no, he wouldn't—' Jess began, then stopped and looked at Tim. 'You haven't got any – any guns or anything, have you?'

'No. I never had anything, only a couple of bits of shrapnel for souvenirs. Everyone has that.' For a moment, Tim was afraid that it was against the law even to collect shrapnel. He met his mother's eyes and she stared hard at him.

'Tell the truth, now. It won't do you any good to tell lies.'

It was almost the worst moment of all, to know that his mother no longer trusted him. Cheeky and mischievous as Tim had been, he had never lied to Jess – well, only about things like whether he'd cleaned his teeth or eaten the last apple, things that didn't really matter. He gazed at her, trying to find the warmth he had always been used to seeing in her eyes, but all he could see was doubt and disappointment.

'I haven't got anything. I really haven't.' He turned back to the policeman. 'You can look anywhere you like. Under my bed – in the drawers. I haven't got anything at all.' He thought suddenly of the white powder he had slipped out of the jar in Mr Driver's shop and felt his skin scorch with colour. 'I mean—'

'Yes, Tim?' Jess said sharply. 'What? You'd better tell us.'

He wriggled miserably on his chair. 'It's just – well, I thought it was for fireworks. We haven't had fireworks for ages and Maureen's never seen any at all. I was going to make a her a golden shower.'

'Fireworks?' Frank said. 'You were going to make fireworks? How? What with?'

'Saltpetre,' Tim whispered. 'That's what Micky said we needed. He said I had to get it.' His eyes were agonised as he looked round at the three adults. 'I didn't think it was stealing, not really. I mean, there was a whole jarful and I only took a couple of spoons. And hardly anybody ever asks for it.'

'Let's get this straight,' Frank said. 'You took saltpetre from Mr Driver's shop? You took it for Micky Baxter to make fireworks?'

Tim nodded. Frank tightened his jaw and looked at the policeman.

'I can guess what sort of fireworks that young ruffian was going to make. He's a menace, that boy is, always has been. If ever anything went wrong in this street, that Micky Baxter was at the bottom of it – broken windows, stuff pinched off the allotments, you name it . . . Why, look what he did next door in Mrs Glaister's house, practically wrecked the place. And he's been up in court more times than I've had hot dinners.' He glowered at his son. 'If I've told you once to keep clear of him, I've told you a hundred times. And now you're in it as deep as he is. Fireworks! Stealing saltpetre from Mr Driver! And what's *he* going to have to say about it, eh? Tell me that. He gave you that job as a favour to me. How'm I going to go in there and tell him you've been stealing stuff off his shelves?'

Tim shook his head. There was nothing he could say to defend himself. He'd known he was doing wrong, taking the saltpetre without asking. And he *had* known Micky had guns. He'd never actually seen them – he might pretend he'd thought Micky was spinning a yarn – but he'd half-known it was true really.

'I'm sorry,' he said wretchedly. 'I didn't think it'd matter. I never took anything else. I just wanted to make a golden shower for Maureen.' He looked at his mother. 'She's never seen a firework.'

Jess felt her heart move with sudden pity. Poor Tim, she thought. He really didn't mean any harm. He'd got led astray by young Micky, and he'd been silly, but he'd never done anything really serious. He'd just wanted to do something for his baby sister.

'It's hard on boys like Tim,' she said to Frank after the policeman had gone. 'I mean, they've had their childhood taken away from them. Look at fireworks. Tim and Keith used to love Bonfire Night, with you bringing home a couple of fireworks every week and making a bonfire in the back garden. And everyone in the street watching each other's displays, and seeing rockets going up in the sky all over Portsmouth. And then all that stopped, and they weren't allowed to go to the beach any more, or fly their kites, and then they got sent out to the country, away from home. I don't think we realised just how bad it was for them.'

'Bad? It's been like a holiday! They were as happy as sandboys with Mr and Mrs Corner, you know that. Spoilt, they were. And that vicar's not much better, what with playing cricket and building snowmen with them half his time. They've been allowed to run wild, that's the trouble. They haven't been disciplined as they should.'

Jess sighed. Tim had been sent upstairs to tidy his bedroom after the policeman had gone. The room had been thoroughly searched – even the floorboards had been lifted up – but nothing had been found, apart from an old pocket-knife that Frank had lost years ago and a marble that Keith had once forced through a knothole. But the policeman hadn't been able to tell them what would happen next. He would have to go to each boy's house, and then he'd have to go and see the chemist.

'I'll take that young man up to see Mr Driver myself,' Frank decided. 'I know it won't make such difference – we can't ask for special treatment – but at least young Tim can tell him what's happened and apologise. I feel proper ashamed, I do. I always thought we'd brought our boys up to be trusted.'

'We have,' Jess said. 'I honestly don't think he realised how serious it could be.'

'Well, he should have done. He's almost thirteen – quite old enough to know the difference between right and wrong. Anyway, he's old enough to take responsibility for his own actions. I'm not going to apologise for him – he's got to do that for himself.' He went to the door at the foot of the staircase and shouted. 'Tim! Come down here. That's his job finished, anyway,' he went on as they heard Tim's footsteps come slowly down. 'Mr Driver won't want a thief working for him.'

Tim arrived just in time to hear the last words, and Jess saw him turn scarlet. She looked at his tear-filled eyes and once again felt overwhelmingly sorry for him. Poor Tim. He'd been silly, but that was all, and he was certainly getting his punishment now. She was sure he'd never do anything like it again.

She watched as Frank led his son up the street. Even standing at the door, she felt exposed, as if all the neighbours were peering out of their windows and talking about it. And this was only the beginning. If Tim had to go to court, everyone would know about it. It would be in the *Evening News*. She'd never be able to hold up her head again.

Jess shut the door and went back to the kitchen. She dumped a pile of washing on the wooden draining-board beside the sink and started to run some hot water out of the Ascot. The green soap she used to scrub clothes was almost finished; when she'd done this lot the scrap that was left would have to go in the jamjar with the rest, to be melted down into one lump so that none would be wasted. You couldn't afford to waste anything these days – string, greaseproof paper, tiny stubs of pencil, it was all carefully saved so as to get the most use possible.

She worked automatically, carrying out her chores without thinking about them, doing the things she did every day almost without being aware of it, her mind fixed entirely on Tim and what had happened in the bombed house.

She'd been as angry and upset as Frank. But although she'd been hurt by the fact that Tim had taken stuff from Mr Driver, and by his allowing Micky Baxter to lead him into trouble, she knew that a good deal of her anger – and Frank's too – stemmed from their shock at what *could* have happened. It was frightening to think of Micky Baxter, hoarding guns and grenades in his bedroom, carrying them through the streets, letting the other children play about with them. And that Desmond – why, the boy was simple, there was no knowing what he might have done. Almost had done . . .

We might never have seen our Tim again, she thought, and the tears that she'd thought must have all been cried during the night began to flow again. Tim, hopping about on one leg like Jimmy Cross. Tim, torn to pieces in an explosion like Cyril Nash . . .

Jess left the washing and went and sat down at the table. She felt sick and giddy. She laid her head on her arms and wept.

Mr Driver listened with a grave face to what Tim had to say.

At first, it had been hard for Tim to say anything at all. He'd tried frantically to think what words he could use to tell the chemist what he had done. They jangled about in his head, a great tangle of them jostling and bumping into each other, not making any sense at all. Some of them repeated themselves and echoed in the hollowness that seemed to have replaced his brain, hammering against the inside of his skull and making his head ring.

'Just tell me simply what it is, Tim,' Mr Driver said gently, and he put his hands on Tim's arms and shifted him slightly, so that he was looking straight into his face.

The chemist's eyes were brown and mild. Short-sightedness had etched a little frown between his brows, but it didn't make him look cross, only slightly puzzled. Tim had never seen him look angry.

'Just tell me one word,' Mr Driver said. 'And then another one. Let's piece it together gradually, shall we?'

But once Tim had got out one word, the rest came tumbling after it, like the litter of piglets Reg Corner had once shown him at the farm. To Tim's ears, his words seemed just as muddled, but Mr Driver listened patiently and seemed to understand.

'So you thought Micky Baxter wanted to make fireworks, and he asked you to get some saltpetre for them. But why didn't you ask me, Tim?'

'I don't know. Well, you might have thought it was dangerous.'

'So I should hope,' Frank began, but Mr Driver shook his head.

'Boys are bound to want to make experiments, but it's best if they have a little bit of guidance so that they don't take unnecessary risks. If you'd asked me, Tim, I would have told you what saltpetre was and how it should be used. And I would probably have suggested that you bring your friends along here one evening, so that we could experiment together. Then we wouldn't have had any accidents.'

'I'm sorry,' Tim whispered.

'Well, is that all you can say?' Frank exploded. 'The young hooligans had guns and ammunition that they'd stolen from the Home Guard. They had a couple of hand grenades, a bayonet and God knows what else, all stashed away in that Baxter boy's bedroom. And you can't tell me they wanted the saltpetre to make fireworks. It was gunpowder they were after making. Bombs. Why, they could have blown up the entire street!'

Tim was crying now, his shoulders shaking with great, retching sobs that seemed to force their way up from deep inside his chest like hard, rough lumps. He coughed and spluttered, and felt his father's angry disgust trickle down through his fingers.

'No. We wouldn't. It was *Hitler* . . . We wanted to *help* . . .'

'Micky Baxter never wanted to help anybody but himself,' Frank stated grimly.

Mr Driver frowned thoughtfully. 'But you say you thought it was to make fireworks. Did you really believe that, Tim?'

Tim hesitated. He badly wanted to say yes. He wanted to pretend he'd never known anything about the guns or Micky's plans, that he'd thought it was just a game. But he looked up and met Mr Driver's mild brown gaze, and knew that he couldn't do it.

'I tried to,' he said at last, reluctantly.

Mr Driver smiled a little. 'You tried to. I expect you thought you'd succeeded too, didn't you? So long as you didn't think about it too much.' He glanced up at Frank. 'I don't think you need to worry too much about this young man, Mr Budd. He's always struck me as a very honest and open lad. I think he's just got himself into rather a muddle with this secret army and plans to kill Hitler – all very laudable, after all – and lost sight of things a bit. I don't think I shall be taking the matter any further.'

Tim stared at him. He turned his eyes up to Frank. His father was looking bewildered.

'But the matter's already gone further,' Frank said. 'It's a police matter. It's out of our hands.'

Mr Driver shook his head. 'As far as what happened last night, you're right, of course. But nothing can be done about the saltpetre unless I press charges.'

'You mean you'll not tell them he took the stuff? But—'

'Oh, I won't hide anything from them. And I don't advise you to try either, Tim. But they can't charge him with theft without my agreement. And I don't propose to ruin the boy's life because of one foolish error.'

'Well,' Frank said after a moment, 'that's very generous of you, Mr Driver. And a damn sight more than you deserve,' he said to Tim. 'You ought to be very grateful.'

'Yes,' Tim said humbly. 'I am. Thank you, Mr Driver. And – and I really am sorry.'

'Yes, I believe you are,' the chemist said. He gave Tim a kind, rather tired smile and said, 'I haven't forgotten what it is to be a boy. I was always fascinated by chemistry, always mixing substances together to see what happened. One day, perhaps, I'll tell you about some of them. But for now—' he glanced at the Roman numerals on the clock hanging on the wall '—there's work to be done. I've got a lot of deliveries waiting to be made.'

'Yes,' Frank said, 'and I daresay you're looking for a new delivery boy now, to take 'em round. You'll want a boy you can trust.'

'Oh,' Mr Driver said, 'I think I can trust Tim. Can't I, Tim?'

Tim felt as if his heart had leapt into his throat. He gazed at the chemist, scarcely able to believe his ears. He opened his mouth, struggling once again for speech, and finally managed a sort of gargling, 'Yes. Oh, yes—'

'Mind, I shall want your promise that you will never again take anything from any of my jars or boxes without permission,' the chemist said warningly. 'I shall have to have that. But if you can promise me that, then I see no reason why you shouldn't start work again straight away. As I said, there's a lot to be done.'

The door opened and Mrs Driver put her head into the room. 'Old Mrs Brannigan's out here, asking where her medicine is. She says it ought to have been sent round this morning, first thing. And there's a queue halfway down the street with prescriptions to be made up. I'm sorry to interrupt, but I think you'll have to come—'

'It's all right, my dear. I'm coming now.' Mr Driver indicated a pile of packages and bottles standing on the bench. 'There they are, Tim, all ready for you. And it sounds as if there'll be some more when you get back. It's going to be a busy day.'

26

'Well, I don't know as I'd have done it,' Annie said. 'Giving him a responsible job like that. I mean, you don't know what else he might be tempted to do.'

Jess stared at her. 'Annie, this is our *Tim*. He's as honest as the day is long. Of course he wouldn't pinch the medicines.'

'Well, he'd already pinched something,' Annie said reasonably. 'Who's to say? You know what boys are. Once they start—'

'Tim'll never do anything like that again,' Jess said positively. 'He's been silly and he's learnt his lesson. He's not a bad boy, you know he's not – not like that Micky Baxter.'

'Look, he's been away from home for two years,' Annie pointed out. 'He's been out of your care. How d'you know what sort of children he was mixing with out in the country? How d'you know what sort of ideas they have out there?'

'For goodness sake, Annie, he wasn't on the moon!' Jess could not remember ever having felt so exasperated with her sister before. 'And he was staying in a vicarage. I don't suppose Mr Beckett taught him to steal. Or Reg and Edna Corner, where he was before. A more decent couple you couldn't wish to meet.'

'Well, he got it from somewhere,' Annie said and went out to the kitchen in a huff.

Jess walked back down April Grove almost in tears. Her own sister, painting Tim black like that – Tim, the favourite of the family, always smiling and ready with a joke.

'I thought I'd get some sympathy from Annie, of all people,' she said to Frank when he came home from work, bringing Cherry with him for a game of cards. 'But all she seemed to want to do was make it worse. I've never known her like it before.'

'I daresay she's worrying about Colin,' Cherry said. 'She still hasn't heard anything, has she? It must be terrible not to know what's happened to your boy.'

Jess looked at her, feeling ashamed. 'You're right. She must think I'm lucky to have Tim safe. And then to have to listen to me whining about a bit of boys' trouble—'

'You can't help that,' Cherry said. 'You're upset too, and no wonder. It was a bit more than "boys' trouble" after all. Someone could have been killed.'

'I know. That's the awful part. I feel sick every time I think about it. Even if it hadn't been Tim—' She shuddered. 'It doesn't bear thinking about.'

Frank got out the cards and began to shuffle them. Rose, who had been reading in a corner, got up to join them at the table. Tim was upstairs, chipping away at a model aeroplane. He'd been quiet and subdued since the accident, spending a lot of time by himself. Keeping out of Frank's way, Jess thought, knowing her husband was still angry, but she felt sorry for her son all the same. Yet now that Cherry had pointed it out, she knew that Annie needed her sympathy and support just as much.

'There's Mum, too,' she said. 'Annie does much more for her than I do. She goes down North End nearly every day to do a bit of work and cook her some dinner. It'd be a lot easier if Mum would agree to come and live with her, but she won't – says all her memories are in that house and she won't leave it.'

And even that wasn't the extent of Annie's worries. There was Olive as well, and Betty. Ted seemed to have come round about Dennis, but he still wasn't out of hospital and Annie had told her Betty seemed to be worrying about him more than you'd expect, now he was recovering. But people did sometimes act a bit funny after a bad accident. It took time to get over it.

I'll go up and see her first thing in the morning, Jess decided. I'll leave Rose to get the dinner and go down to Mum's with her. She needs a bit of company just as much as I do. We ought to share our worries, not upset each other over them.

She looked across the table at Cherry, who was fanning her cards out in her hand. It never ceased to surprise her, how Cherry could put her finger on things. Funny how she'd so quickly become such a member of the family.

Even funnier, when Jess thought back to her first impression of 'Cherry' – the saucy little flirt, wiggling her bottom round the boiler-shop and turning all the men's heads.

Betty was at the hospital. When she had come into the ward, she'd been pleased to find Dennis sitting up in bed. His eyes were still bandaged but he turned his head and smiled when she came into the ward. He held out his hand.

'I knew it was you. I know your footsteps. And that nice scent you wear.'

'It's Ashes of Roses.' She kissed him and then sat down beside him, holding his hand. 'How're you feeling today, Dennis?' She felt uneasy. There was something different about him today – a tightness in his lips, a brittle hardness in his voice.

'I'm all right,' he said, but he didn't sound all right and Betty looked at him more closely. She saw the creases on his forehead, the lines around mouth and nose. Some of them were scars, but others looked more like bitterness and anger.

Dennis had never been a bitter or angry man. And those lines had not been there the last time she came in.

'What is it, Dennis?' she asked. 'What's happened?'

'Nothing. Nothing I can't deal with myself.'

She was shocked. 'But you don't have to deal with *anything* yourself, Dennis. You've got me. We share things. Everything.'

'There are some things,' he said, 'that nobody can share.'

'I don't understand. What are you talking about?'

He was silent for a moment, playing with her fingers. Then he said quietly, 'I've been thinking, Betty. I think maybe we made a mistake. Well, not a mistake – I know we loved each other—'

'We still do.' Her voice was edged with panic. 'Nothing's changed, Dennis. I haven't changed. I still love you as much as ever. More.'

'I know. But – I can't hold you to the promises we made, Betty. Not any more. Things have changed. I've changed. Nothing will ever be the same again.'

'I don't know what you're saying.'

'I'm trying to tell you—'

'No!' she cried. 'I don't want to hear it! Don't say it, Dennis – please, *please* don't—'

'I have to. I must.'

'No. No. *No*.' She was in tears, clutching his hands, staring into his face. But he couldn't see her, couldn't see her anguish. 'Dennis, no—'

'Betty, don't make this hard for me—'

'What else can I do? I can't let you—'

'And *I* can't let *you*,' he said with sudden strength. 'Betty, do you know what they told me today? Do you know what the doctors say? They say I'm blind.' His voice shivered and dropped. 'I'm never going to see again. I'm going to be like this all my life – useless. How can I marry you? How can I be such a burden?'

Betty stared at him, at the scarred face and the bandaged eyes that would never see again. Blind eyes, that turned Dennis into a different man.

But that wasn't true. He was the same Dennis. Nothing could change the Dennis who lived inside.

'You'd never be a burden,' she said shakily.

'I would. What could I do? What can a blind man do? Tune pianos?' His voice was bitter. 'That's what they do, isn't it. How many pianos are there going to be to tune after the war – and how many blind men to tune them?'

'Dennis, don't talk like that,' she begged. 'There must be other things – people do all kinds of things.'

'What sort of things?'

'I don't know.' Betty had never known anyone who was blind. 'But there must be things. Anyway, what does it matter so long as we're together?'

'I'll tell you how much it matters,' he said. 'I'll tell you what it means. It means I'll never be able to do anything useful again. I won't be able to read or write or even walk down the street. I won't be able to ride a bike or drive a tractor or plough a field. I won't be able to do my job. I won't be able to go back to BD. I'm useless.'

'BD? But of course you can't go back to BD – and I'm thankful for it. D'you think I want you going back to that? You've done quite enough.

You've saved any amount of people from being blown up. You've risked your life over and over again. You were lucky not to be killed that last time. I think you've done as much as anyone could expect.'

'I haven't done as much as *I* expected—'

'You expected too much, then. Who do you think you are, Dennis Verney? Who said you had to do it all by yourself? What is it makes *you* so special?'

'But there's still bombs out there,' he said restlessly. 'They're finding more and more every day. And the raids haven't stopped. They reckon we'll be getting a fresh lot soon. This has just been a lull.'

'Well, I'll be just as glad if you're not out there,' Betty said robustly. She moved closer and put her arms round him. 'It was bad enough before, knowing what you were doing – but seeing you like this, knowing that you were almost killed – I'd never have a minute's peace.'

'Nobody's getting any peace,' he said. 'That's what all this is about.'

Betty was silent. Since Dennis had been in hospital, she had come to realise even more strongly that there was a thread of steel running through him that was unbreakable. It had been there when he refused to abandon his principles and join up, when he had gone to prison, when he had worked on the farm. She had recognised it again when he left the farm and joined BD. When she had first seen him lying in the hospital bed, unconscious, unmoving, his broken body swathed in bandages, she had feared it was gone. But it had been there still, keeping him alive, bringing him back to consciousness, forcing him to recover.

'There are times when you have a choice,' he'd said to her when he'd been able to talk again. 'It's like standing on a high diving-board, trying to decide whether to jump. You can choose whether to live or die. I was tempted to die – but then I heard your voice, telling me about the farm, talking about the times we'd spent together . . . I couldn't leave you, Betty. I had to come back.'

She reminded him of that now. 'It was me you wanted to come back to, Dennis. Not BD. It was *us* – our life together. That's what's important. You've done your bit for the war.'

'I didn't do it for the war,' he said wearily. 'I did it for the peace. Aren't you *ever* going to understand?'

Betty bit her lip. She was acutely hurt by his words, and even more so because he'd spoken to her in a way he'd never done before. And because he was putting a gap between them – a gap in their understanding, their closeness. She felt a sudden panic, as if he were drifting away from her all over again.

'Of course I understand,' she said gently. 'I'm sorry – it was the wrong word to use. But I can't help the way I feel, Dennis. I can't help wanting to keep you safe.'

'And I can't help the way *I* feel.' He sat silent for a moment or two, then burst out, 'I feel so bloody useless, sitting here all day, Betty. It was bad enough when I thought I'd get better and be able to go back. But now—' He shook his head. 'Look, I'm trying not to be sorry for myself. I keep telling myself there must be a reason why I'm still alive – there must be work still for me to do. But I've got to face it myself. I can't hide behind your skirts.'

'You wouldn't be,' Betty said, still hurt. 'It wouldn't be like that.'

'It would. Of course it would.' Dennis shook his head again and let go of her hand to run his fingers through his hair. 'Look, I won't be able to do a *thing*. You'll have to do it all. Everything around the house, every little job – all the things a man ought to be doing. You'll have to do the lot. And how can we have children? What use is a father who can't see? No, you'll be better off without me. Better off finding someone else.'

'No! I couldn't do that. There'll never be anyone but you, Dennis.'

'Yes there will.' He spoke as if he had spent a long time convincing himself. 'You're young, you're pretty – you're everything a man could want. They'll be queueing up for you, Betty.'

'Then they'll be disappointed,' she said sharply. 'The shop's shut. I'm not interested in anyone else, Dennis, nor ever will be.'

But she could not convince him. And in the end, the nurses sent her away and she walked out of the hospital feeling as though she had left her heart behind.

Over the following week, she visited him as often as she could. But he would not change his mind, and on the seventh day she arrived to find a strange young soldier in the bed that had been his. Dennis had been moved to another hospital, they said, a hospital about sixty miles away, where he would be taught to live life as a blind man.

27

The secret army appeared in the Juvenile Court halfway through November. Micky was out of hospital now, but Desmond had been kept in for several operations on his damaged eye. He was also very confused, and there was talk of moving him to St James', the mental hospital, when he was better.

Frank and Jess went to the court with Tim, all dressed in their best clothes. Frank wore the dark suit he'd got married in and Jess had her brown hat and coat with one of Annie's scarves in the neck. She had debated wearing the spray brooch Frank had given her one Christmas, gold wire with coloured stones that looked like flowers, but decided in the end that the magistrates might think it looked too flashy for such a sober occasion.

'Why don't you put a bit of lipstick on?' Rose suggested. 'You look ever so pale.'

But Jess shook her head. She had never worn make-up and knew Frank wouldn't like it. And she didn't want to look common.

The court was a gloomy place, all dark panelled walls and flaking distemper. There was a long table for the magistrates, with three high-backed chairs behind it, and there were seats like church pews lined up in front of them.

The magistrates came in through a side door. There were two men and one woman, all dressed in dark colours. The men looked between sixty and seventy, one with silver hair and rimless spectacles, the other with a short dark beard like Edward the Seventh's. The woman was short and plump, with heavy glasses and dark hair. She looked about fifty and reminded Jess of a schoolmistress.

The boys stood in a row, their parents and the police close behind. Micky's probation officer was there, and Granny Kinch had persuaded Nancy that she had to come too. Nancy wore her red coat, buttoned neatly except where one had come off, and a black scarf wound round her head like a turban. Granny Kinch wore the herringbone tweed she had had ever since Jess had known her. She looked odd with her curlers out, her sparse grey hair sticking out from under a shapeless brown felt beret, and she kept chobbling her mouth at the unfamiliar feeling of having her teeth in.

Mr Beckett had come down from Bridge End. He was at the court when

Jess and Frank arrived, tall and solemn in his dark clerical suit. He shook their hands and murmured a few words of reassurance before the magistrates entered, then sat down beside Mr Driver.

'I never thought we'd have to come to a place like this,' Jess whispered to Frank as they took their seats. 'I mean, our Tim of all children! He's not a bad boy, not really.'

'He got led astray,' Frank allowed. 'And I don't think he ever really believed in those guns. But you can't expect to get into bad company and not be tainted, that's what it boils down to. He's been silly and now he's going to have to pay.'

In fact, Tim hadn't been charged with much at all. Micky bore the brunt of it, and the charges against him – breaking into Home Guard premises, stealing weapons, possessing those weapons – were very serious. Desmond too had been charged with the same offences, but the other children – Jimmy Cross, Tim, Martin Baker and Wendy and Alan – had been accused merely of 'being accessories' which didn't seem so bad. And Martin and Alan were both too young to appear in court, while Wendy had been let off because she hadn't actually been in the house when the gun was fired.

The four boys made a sorry little line in front of the magistrates. Desmond had been allowed out of hospital for the day and stood swaying slightly, his head still bandaged. He had lost weight and his old jacket hung loosely from his bony shoulders. He stared blankly about him with his one eye and didn't acknowledge any of the other boys; most of the time he mumbled to himself in a slurred undertone.

Micky stood cockily with his legs apart, glowering under his heavy brows and trying to look as if he didn't care. His grandmother had forced him into a relatively clean shirt and tried to brush his jacket, but his shoes were scuffed and grimy and one of his socks was already falling down. His hair had been cut last night, with a pudding-basin over his head, but the scissors hadn't been sharp enough and it looked ragged round the edges.

Jimmy Cross stood on his wooden leg, leaning on his crutch. As soon as the magistrates saw him, they called for a chair, and he was allowed to sit down, the false leg sticking out in front of him. He looked a bit pale, as if he was scared of what was going to happen. His mother hadn't let him out of the house since the night of the accident and he was bored, fed up and frightened. He'd decided he wasn't ever going to speak to Micky Baxter again.

Tim stood on the end of the row. His face was white, but he looked clean and tidy. Jess had washed his hair last night and brushed it this morning until the fair curls shone. His face had been scrubbed pink, and he wore a new shirt made from a yard and a half of grey flannel that Jess had been saving, and his best grey jacket and short trousers. Frank had lent him one of his own ties, and his shoes had been polished until he could see his face in them.

The magistrates listened while the policeman read out a report on what had happened, and then they looked severely at the boys and started to ask questions.

'Why did you want to collect the weapons? What was the purpose of this "secret army"? Where did you get the weapons? Who actually broke into the store? What did the rest of you know about this?'

Gradually they got all the truth and heard the story of the shooting. Then they moved closer to each other and talked in low voices for a while. From time to time, they all turned and stared at the boys, examining their faces and looking them up and down.

Thank goodness I smartened Tim up a bit, Jess thought. He looks a nice little boy. That Micky Baxter looks a real little villain, and anyone can see Jimmy Cross has just been led astray. And as for Desmond – well, he doesn't seem to know what's going on. You can't help feeling sorry for him really.

She turned her eyes to the other adults. Mrs Cross was looking pale and frightened, and Desmond's mother looked worn out. Poor soul, she'd had a terrible time, what with her hubby getting killed when Desmond was a baby and having to struggle to bring him up, as well as run the shop all by herself. But you couldn't be sure that the magistrates would take any notice of that. They might just lump all the boys in together and send them off to an approved school as an 'example'. Breaking into Home Guard premises and stealing guns *was* serious, and even though Tim hadn't been involved in that he'd still been there that night. And he had taken the saltpetre, although Mr Driver had been as good as his word and never pressed charges.

At last the magistrates seemed to come to a decision. They drew apart, nodding, and faced the court again. The one who looked like the old King leaned forward and addressed the boys sternly.

'You're all aware that this a very grave matter. Breaking and entering is always serious, and stealing is more serious still. Stealing weapons such as guns and explosives such as hand grenades, even in times of peace, must be dealt with harshly. At the present time, with the country at war and in need of all its defences, it borders on treachery.' He paused and looked at them solemnly. Tim was crying and Jimmy Cross was staring at his feet. Only Micky met his eye with an attempt at bravado, and then gazed at the ceiling.

Jess turned quickly to Frank and grabbed his hand. Treachery! The magistrate was calling them traitors. Her Tim, a *traitor*. She felt the tears, which hadn't been far away all morning, come hot to her eyes.

'We shall take into account the fact that you say you were trying to form your own so-called army in defence of your country and that you had no other purpose in collecting these weapons.' The magistrate stroked his short grey beard. 'It seems that you may have been driven by misguided motives rather than criminal ones. Nevertheless—' his heavy brows drew together in a frown and Tim shrank visibly '—you must realise the seriousness of your actions. Guns are not toys. They're lethal weapons, to be used only by qualified men in very special circumstances. We cannot and will not have gangs of children setting themselves up as soldiers and risking their own and others' lives. The country has troubles enough, without mischievous boys adding to them.'

He paused. The courtroom was silent. All eyes were fixed on his face.

Even Micky had removed his gaze from the ceiling and was watching him. After a few moments, he went on, speaking slowly and impressively.

'The youngest boy, Timothy Budd, has shown that he did not fully understand the actions of the rest of the group. He was unaware that his friends possessed authentic weapons. He had already decided to leave the group. Moreover, he has never been in any kind of trouble and has been vouched for by his employer, neighbours and by those with whom he has been billeted with in the country, as a decent, well-behaved and quiet youngster from a good home.'

The magistrate's eyes rested for a moment on Jess and Frank, and then on Mr Beckett and Mr Driver. Jess tried to meet his gaze without flinching, but felt her colour rise. Frank, still holding Jess's hand, looked steadily back at him.

'James Cross.' The glance moved on to Jimmy, sitting on his chair with his wooden leg stuck out in front of him. 'I must confess I find it difficult to understand why a boy who has already been in danger of his life, and suffered severe injury at the hands of this same gang leader, should want to take further such risks. James, you have already lost a leg. What in heaven's name possessed you to allow yourself to get involved in such danger again?'

Jimmy shrugged and said nothing. There was nothing to say. It would be impossible to explain to this man what it was like to be a boy at home alone in Portsmouth while your friends were mostly out in the country and war raged all over the world. You took what friends there were, and what excitement you could get. And Micky *was* exciting – there was no question about that.

The magistrate sighed and turned his attention to Desmond. 'Desmond Cook. Now this I find a very sad case. A boy who is clearly backward, with very little understanding of what is happening around him, easily led and easily used. Desmond, I understand you are still receiving hospital treatment, is that correct?' He leaned a little closer and looked into Desmond's face, but Desmond looked blankly past him. The magistrate glanced towards Mrs Cook.

'Yes, sir, he is,' she whispered. 'In fact, they think – they think he'll have to stop there all his life.' She lifted a handkerchief to her face and began to cry.

'Yes.' The magistrate looked down at the papers on his desk. 'Yes, I see that here.' He cleared his throat and shuffled the papers about. He looked from under his brows at Micky.

'Michael Baxter.' His voice had deepened. 'Michael Baxter, you've been before this court before, more than once. You've been charged with breaking and entering a neighbour's house, with shoplifting, with a number of petty offences. You are already on probation. Now you come before us on much more serious charges, charges which cannot be overlooked or dealt with by a probation order.'

He's going to send him away, Jess thought. And if he does that, he'll send them all away. Jimmy, and Desmond and my Tim. Oh God, *please* don't let him send my Tim away . . .

'Whatever your motives were – and we'll suppose that they were as good as you claim – you have broken into Government premises and stolen Government property. You've been in illegal possession of dangerous weapons and because of this possession others have been harmed – could easily have been killed. You might have been killed yourself.'

He looked as if he didn't think that would have been such a bad thing, Jess thought. But he didn't say so. He went on, still speaking in that deep, stern voice.

'As it is, Desmond Cook has lost the sight of one eye and may have to spend the rest of his life in hospital care. And all this despite the fact that another of your friends, James Cross, is here with only one leg owing to an earlier escapade, while another young boy, Cyril Nash, lost his life during the same incident.

'It seems to us that you do not have the ability to learn a lesson from events. We have a duty to the rest of the community to ensure that you learn this lesson – and others too which seem to have passed you by. You're a dangerous young man, the clear and self-confessed ringleader in this unhappy affair, and the community is entitled to be protected from you. We therefore have no choice but to send you to an approved school for a term of two years, with a recommendation that you be treated as the criminal you are and given no privileges until you can prove yourself worthy of them. I hope this will have the effect of making you think about where your errors are leading you, and helping you to become a decent and upright citizen.'

There was a snorting sound from further along the pew. Granny Kinch was sobbing noisily, her face smothered by a stained and crumpled handkerchief. Nancy was staring stonily in front of her. Micky shrugged and looked at the ceiling again, but his face was pale and his jaw was clenched.

'As for the other boys,' the magistrate continued, 'we take the view that they were led astray by Michael Baxter and that no useful purpose would be served by sending them away. Desmond Cook has many more months, if not years, of hospital treatment to face anyway, and James Cross must surely have learned his lesson by now. As for Timothy Budd, I'm surprised he was ever brought in front of this court. It's quite clear that he merely strayed into the fringe of Baxter's activities and was withdrawing from them. He strikes me as a child who does know how to learn a lesson, and who has learned this one well. I do not think we shall see him before this court again.' He paused, while Tim stared at him. 'We are therefore sending you, Timothy Budd, from this court without a stain on your character – but we do warn you that if we see you here again, *for whatever reason*, the penalties may be very heavy.' He turned to the other two boys. 'Desmond Cook, you will return to hospital with no further action taken against you. James Cross, you will be put on probation for eighteen months and given the same warning as Timothy Budd. We do not wish to see any of you in this court again.' He stacked his papers together and stood up. The three magistrates filed out.

Tim stood uncertainly for a moment or two, then turned and ran into his mother's arms. She clasped him against her, laying her wet face against his hair, while Frank stood by, one hand on her shoulder, the other gripping his son's arm. His face was tight, almost angry, but Jess knew that he was as near to tears as he was ever likely to come.

'Oh, Tim,' she said. 'Oh, *Tim* . . .'

28

November was a month of both sadness and celebration.

Field-Marshal Montgomery – known by now to all as 'Monty' – had scored an emphatic victory at El Alamein. Rommel's army had fled, defeated, leaving Monty a hero, and in honour of the occasion Churchill declared that the church bells could be rung throughout the land.

They rang in Portsmouth, at the Cathedral and at St Mary's, while the chimes were struck at the Guildhall by four volunteers who climbed ladders into the tower which stood so proudly above the gutted building. Jess and Frank walked down with Rose and Maureen to watch, Jess thinking sadly of the day in October 1938 when they had come to celebrate Mr Chamberlain's announcement of 'peace in our time'. It was then that she and Frank had decided to try for one last baby to complete their family. Later, filled with dread of what was to come, she had regretted that decision, but as she looked at Maureen's rosy face now, she could not wish it any different. I'm glad we've got her, she thought. I'm really glad.

But the world was still at war. The French fleet was scuttled at Toulon, seventy brave ships – which it had been hoped would be able to join the Allied forces – sunk rather than submit to seizure by the Germans. Such a waste, Jess thought, adding to the waste the war had already caused – a waste of ships, a waste of aircraft, of buildings and, most of all, a waste of lives.

'And they tell us not to waste a thing,' she said, thinking of the old biscuit tin with all the bits and pieces – string, buttons, little strips of sticky paper from the edges of stamps – carefully stored there. 'It doesn't seem to make sense.'

Tim and Keith were delighted to have the bells ringing. Tim was back at Bridge End and he went to the church tower to help Mr Beckett untie the clappers, and watch as the ringers raised the bells 'open' for the first time since the war had begun. Their music sounded over the fields and woods of the countryside, bringing people out of their homes to listen with misty eyes to a sound that spoke to their hearts of peace.

'Let the youngster have a pull,' one of the old men said, and Tim took hold of the rope, trembling a little with excitement and praying that he could keep his bell in its place, sounding sweetly amongst the others. He pulled off behind the treble and heard the creak of the ropes, followed immediately by the tumble of notes, from the highest to the lowest, like a cascade above his head. I'm doing that, he thought exultantly, I'm making that noise. And a huge grin broke out over his face as he pulled the rope, catching and releasing the sally, stretching his arms high on the rope's end.

It was the best thing that had happened since he'd come back to Bridge End soon after the court case. He was at the secondary school now, but it was an awkward journey each day on the bus, and when he got there he found all his old resentment returning when he was placed in a class of boys all at least a year younger than himself. And the secondary school didn't do the subjects he'd been looking forward to – French, Latin, the interesting maths. He was bored and irritated, and the shock and misery of the gun episode and the court case were still weighing on his mind.

The atmosphere at the vicarage was depressing these days, too. Stella and Muriel were still suffering from the shock of their father's death. Muriel had constant nightmares and was afraid to go to sleep, so made excuse after excuse not to go to bed. And Stella had completely withdrawn into herself. She had lost interest in schoolwork, in learning to cook with Mrs Mudge, in playing and reading – in everything, it seemed. And she had even drawn away from her sister, which upset Muriel even more.

'Why won't you give your sister a kiss and cuddle?' Mr Beckett asked in despair. 'Don't you see how unkind you're being? You're all she has now.'

Stella gave him a withering look. 'I know that.'

'Then why –?' He gazed at her helplessly. 'Stella, look at me. Look at me properly.'

She turned her head, but her gaze slid past him. He wanted to shake her, but he knew it would do no good. She was as unhappy as Muriel, and no wonder. But he couldn't let her freeze into her misery.

'We have to love each other,' he said gently. 'There isn't any point in life if we don't.'

'There isn't any point anyway,' she said in a small, hard voice. Her eyes met his for the first time, and he was shocked to see the depth of her desolation. 'What's the use? People just get killed if you love them.'

'Stella, you mustn't say that!' He stopped himself, wondering just why she shouldn't say it. In her short experience, that was just what did happen. 'It doesn't happen to everyone,' he went on, praying for the right words. 'And it doesn't happen *because* you love them. We live in dreadful times – nobody can deny that – but we still have to go on loving each other. Whatever happens. In fact, it's more important now than ever before.'

'I can't,' she said, still in the small, desolate voice. 'I can't. I'm afraid that if I love Mu, something will happen to her. It happened to Mummy, and Thomas, and now Daddy, and if it happened to Mu as well . . . It would be my fault.'

'*No!*' He could not let her go on thinking this. 'Nothing's going to happen to Muriel. Nothing. Your family has had enough tragedy. Nothing more will happen to you.'

She looked directly at him. 'You can't promise that.' But there was a very faint note of hope in her voice as she added, almost as if against her will, 'Can you?'

He knew that he could not. He could make no promises. If he did so, and something did happen, Stella would never regain her lost trust . . . But the chances were that nothing would happen to Muriel. Out here in the country, she was as safe as any child. And he couldn't let Stella go on suffering in this way.

'I promise,' he said steadily, lifting his eyes only momentarily towards the ceiling. *If You are really there, hear this prayer* . . . 'Nothing is going to happen to Muriel.'

He watched her carefully. There was only the slightest change in her expression – little more than a minute relaxation of the muscles. But it was a start, he thought. A corner turned.

Already, he prayed every night that nothing would happen to the children in his care. Now he must pray even harder for the two girls. That they would stay safe in his care for as long as they might need. That they should, somehow and however slowly, eventually regain their faith in the life they had been given.

That nothing more would harm their damaged hearts.

Carol Glaister's baby was born in the middle of November. Ethel was notified by telegram. She stared at the orange envelope for a few minutes, wondering what it contained. Telegrams these days were usually the bringers of bad tidings, and she had both a husband and a son serving in the Forces.

Jess Budd was at her front door when the boy came skidding round the corner on his red bicycle, and she hesitated, not wanting to go in and leave Ethel to face bad news on her own.

'What is it?' she asked uncertainly.

'Well, I don't know, do I,' Ethel snapped. 'I haven't got X-ray eyes.' She tore the envelope open with one finger. 'I hope to God it's not my Joe. But I daresay it's just George gone and got himself wounded. I just hope they're not thinking of sending him back here to be looked after.'

The woman doesn't have any feelings at all, Jess thought. She had heard the screeching that had gone on the night George left, and was pretty sure they'd had a bust-up, but that didn't mean Ethel had to be utterly callous. But you never really knew with Ethel. She was the sort who kept her feelings tightly buttoned up. And she really had been upset when she'd thought her little Shirley had been drowned.

She waited while Ethel read the brief message. Then, to her astonishment, she saw her neighbour's face darken with fury. With a swift movement, Ethel screwed the paper up in one hand and flung it into the gutter.

'The nerve! The sheer bloody nerve! How dare she send me a telegram, for those nosey parkers up the Post Office to see and laugh over. Why couldn't she write a letter, decent and private? I never heard such cheek.'

'What is it? What's happened?' Jess asked anxiously. 'Is it your Shirley? Is she ill?'

'Shirley? No, of course it's not Shirley. It's that little hussy Carol, that's who it is. Can't write to me herself, oh no, has to hide behind someone else's skirts. As if I was interested anyway. As if I *cared*.'

But you do care, Jess thought, watching her. You wouldn't be making such a song and dance about it if you didn't. Though I'm not sure whether it's Carol you care about, or yourself.

'Has she had her baby?' she asked tentatively, still not quite sure whether she was supposed to know about Carol's 'trouble'. 'Is she all right?'

'All right? That little madam will always be all right. Fall down a sewer and she'll come up smelling of roses. Not that it's any business of yours, Jess Budd, and I'll thank you not to go discussing our business with the rest of the neighbourhood, if you don't mind.' Ethel turned to go indoors. 'I suppose she'll be expecting me to write and say how pleased I am. Well, she'll just have to wait. Pleased! I've never been so ashamed in all my life.'

The front door slammed behind her and Jess looked at it for a long moment. I hope I never feel like that about my Rose, or Maureen, she thought. I hope I'll be able to bring them up not to get into trouble.

She glanced at the ball of paper lying in the gutter. I shouldn't, she thought. It's private, even if it is a telegram. But Ethel had thrown it down there for anybody to pick up, so she couldn't really care. And after a moment or two's indecision, she bent and picked it up, smoothing it out quickly and guiltily, half afraid that Ethel might be watching her through the window.

It was from someone called Elizabeth Whiting, and it had been sent from Godalming. The message was brief and, to most mothers, would have been an occasion for joy.

17 NOVEMBER CAROL GLAISTER GAVE BIRTH TO BOY 6LB 2 OZ BOTH WELL WRITING.

So that was that, Jess thought, turning to go into her own house. That poor young girl was a mother now, and still not seventeen. And not likely to get any help from her own mother, by the look of it.

I suppose she'll give him up for adoption now. A sad business. They weren't much more than babies themselves, either of them. They'd done wrong, there was no denying that, but who hadn't made a mistake at some time during their life?

Fall down a sewer and come up smelling of roses, she thought with a wry smile, and remembered the day when Ethel herself had fallen down a drain in Charlotte Street and come up smelling of something very different.

For the families in Portsmouth, one of the darkest moments of November was the departure of 698 Unit for North Africa. They came home for a few days' embarkation leave and it was almost like a miniature Christmas, with the pain of separation like a shadow in the background.

'We've done nothing but say goodbye ever since we were married,' Olive said to Derek as they lay in bed on their last night. 'Are we ever going to be able to have a proper married life, d'you think?'

'We'd better,' he said grimly. 'Soon as we've fixed Adolf. It can't be long now, Livvy. We've been at it three years – he's bound to crack soon.'

'I don't know. He's as stubborn as ever, it seems to me. He'll never give in. And he's got all the rest of the world at each other's throats – I mean, it's going to take years to sort it all out.'

Derek didn't reply. Until now, he had managed to keep the worst of his fears at bay. The Unit had been lucky not to be sent overseas again after Dunkirk, and he'd hoped to see the war out without having to go abroad, although there had been times of frustration when he wondered just why he was in the Army at all, if all they were going to do was build tin huts . . . But like most married men, all he really wanted was to get home and live his own life.

'Don't worry about it,' he said at last, kissing her. 'Us worrying about it isn't going to make a scrap of difference. Let's just enjoy what we've got now.'

Olive lay in his arms. The family had given them a real party tonight, just like Christmas, with a meal as good as any Annie had cooked in peacetime – well, almost as good – and games and a sing-song till gone midnight. They'd all given Derek presents – mostly things like bars of chocolate from their own ration, or cigarettes, shampoo or Brylcreem – and he had given them gifts as well. There had been a lot of laughter when it was discovered that his gifts too were mostly bars of chocolate or cigarettes, for the Army received better rations than civilians, and everyone had remarked that it was the thought that counted after all, and the children had unwrapped their chocolate immediately and eaten it as fast as they could.

Olive had given Derek a new mouth-organ. He had grown quite proficient on his old one, but this one was chromatic, with a slider so that he could get double the notes, and he started to play it at once, to accompany the sing-song. He gave his old one to Jess, to pass on to Tim at Christmas.

'It's a shame Betty's not here,' Jess said to Annie. The sisters had patched up their differences, agreeing that everyone was a bit short-tempered these days, and Annie had given Tim a bar of chocolate from her own ration when he'd come home from the court. 'She was looking proper peaky when I saw her last week.'

'I know. But she's working hard on the farm, making up for all the time she had off when Dennis was in hospital. And trying to keep her mind off him, I wouldn't wonder.' Annie sighed. 'Worrying herself stiff, she is, and there don't seem to be anything she can do about it. I don't know how to advise her, I really don't.'

'Is he still saying he doesn't want to marry her?'

'Well, it's not that he doesn't want to, that's the trouble. I mean, if he just didn't feel the same way, she'd have to accept it and look round for someone else. But she says he loves her as much as ever. In a way, that's *why* he won't go on with the wedding – he says he won't burden her with a blind man. He doesn't think he can give her a good life.'

'He's right, in a way,' Ted said. 'I mean, a husband who can't see isn't much of an asset to a young woman.'

'But if they'd already been married when it happened—' Jess began.

'That's what Betty says. She wants to stick by him. She says she doesn't want anyone else, and she doesn't want to live without him.'

'So why doesn't she just go up to this place he's at and tell him?'

Annie sighed. 'Oh, it's this Quaker business. She won't try to persuade him. Says she's just got to wait until he comes around to it of his own accord. I dunno how she's got the patience.'

'Well, I think they want their heads knocking together,' Olive declared. 'I know what I'd do if it was me.' She wound her arm round Derek's. 'I wouldn't want to give up the chance of being married.'

'I don't think Betty wants to give it up either,' Annie said a little sharply. 'But she can't force Dennis to walk up the aisle, can she.'

'Maybe Dad could though,' Olive suggested wickedly. 'You know – shotgun wedding!'

'*Olive!*' Annie was outraged, 'I never thought to hear such things from a daughter of mine. Why, if you were a bit younger I'd send you to the kitchen to wash out your mouth.' She glanced at Jess as Olive and Derek moved away, grinning at each other. 'I don't know what young people are coming to, I'm sure. It's being in the ATS, that's what it is. They mix with all sorts.'

Now, at last, the party was over and everyone had gone home or to bed. The house was quiet. Olive lay in Derek's arms, feeling him stroke her body with an intense concentration, as if trying to memorise every tiny contour, every minute crease. She breathed deeply, inhaling the scent of him – the real scent of him, not the sharp, medicated smell that came off a bar of soap, but the scent that was Derek alone, warm and faintly musky. Sometimes, when he was away, she would go to the cupboard and bury her face in his civvy clothes, just to remind herself of that scent.

'Oh, Derek,' she said, 'we've said goodbye so many times. And now you're really going away. *Africa* – I can't even imagine it.'

'I'll be thinking of you all the time, Livvy.' He didn't say everything would be all right, or that it would all be over soon. People didn't say those things any more. They were so obviously not true. All he could say were the things that were true. 'I love you. There'll never be anyone else for me. And when we get back, we'll do all the things we've always planned to do. Get the car out again. Have our own house. Start a family.'

'If only we hadn't lost the baby,' Olive said sadly. 'It would have been born by now. We'd have been a real family, before you went away.' She looked at him suddenly. 'Derek – shall we try again? For a baby, I mean? It might – it might—' She stopped and turned her face away, the tears brimming in her eyes.

'It might be our last chance,' he said quietly. 'I know, Livvy. I know.'

'I'm sorry,' she whispered. 'I didn't think – I didn't realise I was going to say that.'

'But it's true,' he said. 'And you know what? We've got to face the truth. We can't pretend, not any more. Not tonight.' He stopped his caressing and held her hard against his body. 'It might be the last time we'll ever hold each other like this.'

They lay tightly entwined, as close as if they were trying to merge into one, so that no one, nothing, could ever separate them. Olive buried her face in his neck, feeling the pulse against her lips. She did not know whether the tears that flowed against her cheeks were Derek's or her own.

'There must be thousands of people who feel like this,' she whispered. 'Millions. It's got to be the last time for some of them. Oh, Derek – suppose – suppose—'

'I'm going to do my damnedest to make sure it isn't,' he said forcibly. 'I'm not ready to chuck in the towel yet, Livvy, not by a long way. What, when I've got you to come back to? And maybe our baby as well? I tell you, they'll have a job to kill *me* – I came back from Dunkirk, remember!'

'I just couldn't bear it if anything happened to you,' she whispered, and he put his hands on her shoulders and shook her gently.

'I wouldn't think so much of it myself! Now—' he smiled down into her eyes and brushed the tears away from her face with tender fingers '—how about getting on with the matter in hand, eh? Didn't someone say something about a baby? Well, there's only one way of getting one that I know of.'

He bent to lay his lips on hers, and Olive closed her eyes. She pushed all other thought out of her mind, concentrating entirely on Derek, on his kiss, on the feeling of his body next to hers, his skin touching her skin, on the length and hardness of his thighs, the strength and tenderness in his arms.

In a few hours, he would be back in his rough khaki uniform, swinging his kitbag on to his shoulder and marching away up the street. Marching away from Olive. Marching away for goodness knows how long. But for tonight, he was naked and he was hers.

29

Tim and Keith came home for Christmas, even though only ten days beforehand there had been German hit-and-run raids all over southern England. Twenty houses had been wrecked in Henderson Road and a further two hundred damaged. German aircraft had swooped low over the city, machine-gunning people in the streets. Frank had been all for making the boys stay out in the country, but Jess was adamant.

'We have this argument every year,' she said. 'And the Germans always drop a few bombs just before Christmas. They do it just to spoil things for us, and I'm not having it. In fact, if I had my way the boys would come home for good.'

'You don't have to tell me that,' Frank grunted. 'And I don't have to tell you that they're better off at Bridge End. Look what happened when Tim was here in the summer.'

He'll never let us forget that, Jess thought, but she won the day and Tim and Keith came home on the train two days before Christmas.

'Can't I stop here?' Tim had asked, almost as soon as he came through the door. 'I don't like it at Winchester. It's horrible. I liked working for Mr Driver. He was teaching me science.'

'You do science at school,' Frank said.

'Not proper science, with experiments and things. We don't get all the stuff like Mr Driver has. Anyway, he knows more about it than the teacher does.' Tim looked at his mother with his large, hazel eyes. 'I could help you look after Maureen. I bet she misses me.'

Jess sighed. It was true, the little girl did seem to have been pining for her brother. She roamed the house looking for him and asked for Timmy when she went to bed. And she'd stopped singing 'You Are My Sunshine'.

She was curled up on the floor with him now, leaning against his legs and humming softly to herself. She looked happier than Jess had seen her since he'd gone back to Bridge End.

'You've got to stay at school, Tim,' she said sadly, but to Frank, when the children were in bed, she said, 'Couldn't he come home? He really doesn't seem to be settling. And there *are* schools open in Portsmouth – he could go somewhere, surely.'

'I don't want his education messed about with any more. He's got to get down to it and learn whatever he can.'

Jess said no more. She was pretty sure that Tim was learning very little, but it was no use harping on about it. Frank would only get annoyed. And she'd learned that if you left him to think things through himself, he very often came round in the end.

1943 started wet and windy. It wasn't really cold, but drying clothes was a constant problem and the coal ration was barely enough, even if you only lit the fire at teatime. The Budds' small room was continually festooned with damp washing, either ranged on the wooden clothes-horse in front of the fire, so that no one could see the flames, or draped around the picture-rails. And Frank's coat never did seem to dry out. It was soaking when he came home in the evening and still damp when he put it on next morning.

'It's not healthy,' Jess said worriedly. 'You'll be getting pneumonia.' But there was nothing to be done about it, and he still went to work early every morning, even when he was streaming with a cold.

'There's a war on,' he said. 'You've just got to carry on.'

Most people did, with dogged persistence. They hadn't got this far just to be beaten. Hitler had given them nearly four years of hell and the longer it went on the more determined they were not to give in. And to keep a smile on their faces while they did it, too.

At least there was plenty of entertainment to help them. You could go to the pictures every week, two or three times if you had the time and the money, and see stars like Joan Crawford and Bette Davis in *Stage Door Canteen*, or Ingrid Bergman in *For Whom The Bell Tolls*. Betty Grable was the most popular star of all, and there was a new girl called Veronica Lake, who had lovely rich hair that hung half across her face.

The wireless was good too. All the comedy shows were still running, together with newer ones like Charlie Chester's *Stand Easy*, and there was lots of music. The big bands were popular – Tommy Dorsey, Harry James, Artie Shaw, Woody Herman and, most of all, Glenn Miller. Glenn Miller's music seemed to express the feeling of the war, somehow, especially when he volunteered for military service and started to modernise the American army and air force music with numbers like 'Blues in the Night', 'American Patrol' and 'In the Mood'. And there were crooners like Bing Crosby and Frank Sinatra singing 'You'll Never Know' and 'My Heart and I', and the lovely young Anne Shelton who recorded the German favourite 'Lili Marlene' and made it a British hit.

The raids went on, sometimes during the day, sometimes at night. A church was bombed in the Isle of Wight during a children's service. Planes swooped low over the streets, gunning down people walking or cycling. There was a stream of advice as to what to do – don't run, lie down wherever you are – but it was hard not to run when an enemy aeroplane was roaring overhead and you could hear the spatter of machine-gun bullets all around you.

The *Evening News* said that the war was costing fourteen million pounds a day. Fourteen million pounds! It seemed unbelievable that there could be that much money in the country. And all being spent on killing people.

A pilot from Southsea was awarded the BEM. His bomber had crashed into the sea, and he and the sergeant had swum for over three hours with the injured gunner before being picked up, while the navigator stayed with the broken plane, supporting the wireless operator who had a fractured spine. All three men were rewarded with medals and commended for their courage.

Halfway through the month, a violent gale swept Southern England, accompanied by thunder and vivid lightning. Maureen thought it was an air-raid and asked Jess persistently why they didn't go to the Anderson shelter. In the end, she became so anxious that Jess took her down there until it was over. It wasn't that she was frightened, exactly, she told Annie later, it was just that that was what they always did in an air-raid, and the baby was worried when they didn't. She didn't really know what there was to be frightened of, poor little scrap.

After that the weather turned cold and there was a heavy snowfall, followed by a gale so severe that it was almost classed as a hurricane. Trees were uprooted, roofs torn off, seaside promenades battered almost to pieces and roads subsided in the floods caused by the heavy rain and swollen seas. Buildings that had already been damaged or shaken by the bombing collapsed and strewed rubble across the roads. And in the Dockyard two men were killed when the howling wind smashed the roof they were working on.

'I'm thankful January's over,' Jess said as they surveyed the mess the gale had left behind. 'Perhaps February'll be a bit better.'

'Elsie and Doris Waters are coming to the King's again,' Frank remarked. Elsie and Doris were his favourite radio characters, with their comically wry discussions on wartime life. They seemed like real people, people like himself and Jess with the same kind of lives and problems. 'We'll book up and go. It'll do us good to have an evening out. Rose can stop with Maureen, she can have young Joy down to keep her company if she likes.'

The boys were back in the country, but Mr Beckett had written to say that he still wasn't happy about Tim. It was difficult for him to get to the secondary school and he didn't seem to be settling down there. The lessons didn't suit him and he didn't even seem to be making any friends.

'Our Tim, not making friends! But he's always been a popular boy. Everyone likes Tim,' Jess said with some indignation.

'I'm afraid it's partly due to his own attitude,' Mr Beckett said when they went to see him. 'I don't mean he's being deliberately obstructive, but he really does deeply resent not having taken the scholarship examination at the right time and being forced to stay at the primary school for an extra year. And he seemed so much happier being at home during the summer and having a job – despite the spot of trouble he got into. I'm sure that wouldn't happen again.'

'Are you saying you think Tim ought to come home again?' Frank said bluntly.

'I think it's something we ought to consider. Well – it's your decision, of course, not mine. I don't want to interfere in any way—'

'But you know a lot about Tim,' Jess said. 'You can see what's happening to him. We only see him when he's happy at home.'

'That's quite true. And he *is* happy at home, isn't he? There's no doubt about that.'

'No,' Jess said, glancing at Frank, 'there's not. But he's been happy here too.'

'I know, but that was when it was all a game, an adventure. A lot of things have happened to Tim in the past year. Finding that pilot's hand – seeing his friends shoot each other – realising what the war is all about. Seeing what's happened to Stella and Muriel. It's all had its effect.'

'Those poor little girls,' Jess said, momentarily diverted. 'What's happening about them now, Mr Beckett?'

The vicar sighed and rubbed his tired face. He had been like a boy again when the children first came to the vicarage. But the shocks they had suffered, not to mention the troubles and difficulties of his own parishioners, had taken their toll. A year or two ago, he'd had to remind himself that he was almost seventy. Now, he needed no reminder that he had passed the allotted threescore years and ten and was living on what some would call borrowed time. He was too old at last for snowball games and cricket, but he felt a greater sadness that somehow the children in his care had grown too old too.

'I'm afraid the authorities have decided to take them away. They're no longer official evacuees, you see – they're orphans. They'll be going to a children's home as soon as places can be found for them.' His old eyes blurred. 'I pray that they will at least be able to stay together.'

Jess stared at him in horror. 'They'd never separate them! Why, it would be criminal. They've only got each other.'

'I agree, Mrs Budd, I agree. But the authorities see things rather differently. I doubt if I shall be given any say in the matter at all.'

'I don't see why they can't stop here,' Frank said gruffly. 'You've given 'em a good home, Mr Beckett. None better.'

There was a short silence. Then the vicar shook himself and said, 'But you came here to talk about Tim. He's no longer a little boy, Mrs Budd. He's growing up. He isn't satisfied with games of cricket or building snowmen any more.'

Jess nodded. She felt near to tears. Her Tim, growing up, no longer a little boy. I've missed the last three years of his childhood, she thought, and they'll never come back again. And if this war goes on much longer, he'll be called up himself and have to go right away – and maybe never come back . . .

She thought of Sella and Muriel, being sent to yet another strange place, perhaps even separated. Their childhood had been ruined – perhaps their whole lives. They needed each other. They needed their mother and father. Families ought to be together, she thought again.

'I want him at home,' she said abruptly, turning to Frank. 'I want them both at home. This has gone on long enough.'

'You know what I think about that—' Frank began.

'Yes, I do know. You've told me over and over again. But I've got a right to say what I think, too, and I don't reckon it's doing Tim any good to be here now. You've been good to him,' she said to Mr Beckett, 'and so were

Reg and Edna Corner, but you're right, evacuation is for children, not boys growing into young men, and that's what our Tim is now.'

'He's only thirteen years old—'

'I don't care what he is, he's growing up. This war's making everybody grow up. Don't you realise, he could be in the Army in three years' time. They're making sixteen-year-olds register now, you know that. It could be fifteen-year-olds next – *fourteeen*-year-olds. Who's to say? I want my boys at home. I want to be a family while we've got the chance.'

Frank stared at her. He had seldom heard Jess speak so forcefully, seldom seen that look of determination on her face. He wanted to argue, to tell her that he was head of the family and they'd do what he said, but he couldn't do it. She really meant it this time, he could see that, and she wouldn't let go.

'All right,' he said at last, 'we'll think about it. Perhaps he can come home and go to the secondary school in Pompey. There's still one or two open, like you said. But not Keith. He's still at the village school and he's doing well there. I don't want him unsettled.'

Tim came home a fortnight later. But he didn't start at another school. He didn't want another change, he said, and he hadn't been learning anything anyway. He wanted to go back and work for Mr Driver. He wanted a proper job.

'Well, he could get an apprenticeship in a year or two,' Frank allowed. 'Fitter, or toolmaker, or something like that. He's a bright enough boy and he likes making things. I'll see if there's a chance for him in the Yard.'

'What about the ferry?' Ted suggested. He and Annie had come down for Sunday tea. 'We've got a lad just coming up to his last year. A good engineering apprenticeship'd stand him in good stead. I'll put his name forward if you like, when the time comes.'

That seemed a good idea, and they discussed it for a while. But to Jess, none of it seemed all that important. She had him home again, she could look across the table and see his cheerful face, she could listen to his everlasting jokes. And the main thing was that he was happy again. She had her old Tim back.

I don't know how she's got the patience, Annie had said.

Betty didn't know how she had the patience either. A year or two ago, she thought, I wouldn't have been able to bear it. But she knew now that she had to give Dennis the time and space to work out his own problems. Persuading someone to do what they really felt to be wrong never worked. It would only bring trouble later.

All through January, she worked on the farm in the wind and rain, coming in soaked of an evening to the big, warm kitchen, stripping off her wet clothes in the attic and rubbing herself dry with a towel before coming downstairs in her pyjamas and the old coat she used for a dressing-gown, to sit by the range with Erica and Yvonne. Erica was heavily pregnant by now, for it was almost exactly nine months since her May wedding, and she did no work outside but stayed indoors with Mrs Spencer, learning to cook and sew.

'I never enjoyed sewing at school,' she confessed. 'It didn't seem much use – making silly little aprons and doing patchwork. But I don't mind doing something useful.'

'Oh, I like doing patchwork and embroidery too,' Mrs Spencer declared. 'You get fed up with the everyday stuff. Turning shirt collars and doing sheets sides-to-middle – well, it's something and nothing, isn't it. I mean, you can't really look at it and think you've done something worthwhile, even if you have. But a nice patchwork quilt – why, that's a work of art. I've still got my grandmother's, that she made when she was a girl. It's an heirloom, that is.'

They spent a lot of time making clothes for the baby. Erica learned to knit and made several little matinee coats in fine white wool. Mrs Spencer unravelled an old blue jumper and made leggings and a coat.

'Suppose it's a girl?' Yvonne said when she saw them.

'Well, she'll just have to wear blue, won't she,' Mrs Spencer said tartly. 'Even a baby can't be fussy in wartime.'

But the baby turned out to be a boy and arrived with the minimum of fuss. He was born at the beginning of February in the middle of the night, keeping the whole household awake ('the first time of many' the doctor said wryly). By daylight he was wrapped in a soft white shawl knitted by Mrs Spencer, and lying beside his mother in the bed in Gerald's room. He had a fuzz of golden hair, just like Erica's, and brown eyes like his father.

'He's gorgeous,' Yvonne said, bending over and touching the soft cheek with the back of her finger. 'And he's not even wrinkled! I thought all babies looked as if they'd been badly packed. How d'you do it, Eric?'

'Easy,' Erica murmured, half dozing on her pillows. 'Easy as shelling peas.'

'That's not what I've heard! You're a lucky one, you are.'

'She is,' Mrs Spencer said. She had been hovering by the bed ever since the baby had been born, unable to tear herself away from her first grandchild. 'She's a natural mother. And he's a beautiful baby. Let's hope there'll be plenty more like him.'

Betty gazed down at the small red face. She felt a confusing variety of emotions. Delight that Erica's baby had been born, relief that he and his mother were both well. Sadness that Gerald wasn't here to see his son. And a huge, overwhelming grief for herself and Dennis.

She had not seen Dennis since he had been moved. He had written to her once, telling her that the move had been sudden and there hadn't been time to let her know. But on the whole, he said, he felt it was for the best. Coming to see him had been hurting her more and more each time, and hurting him too. He loved her as much as ever – too much to put her through a life burdened by a blind, helpless husband. He had nothing to offer her now, and he wanted her to be happy with someone else.

Betty knew that he was wrong. But she also knew that once Dennis had made up his mind to take a course of action, nothing would sway him. He had already been to prison for his beliefs. He had risked his life. He would not give in if he really felt he was doing the right thing.

'Wait a while,' Mr Verney had counselled her when she had gone to see him and his wife. 'He may come round, when he's more accustomed to the idea of blindness. It's a very great shock, to lose your sight. He needs time to regain himself.'

'He needs me, too,' Betty said, but there was nothing to be done about it and she kept away from the hospital and restricted her letters to two a week, telling him about the farm and the village doings, but making no effort to persuade him to change his mind. She signed her letters *from your loving Betty* and left it at that.

Now, she looked down at Erica's baby and felt an overwhelming sense of loss, a despair that she would never hold Dennis's baby in her arms like this. Never hold any baby, for if she couldn't have Dennis's she would never have one at all. And, following the despair, there came a rush of furious anger.

You've no right to do this to me, she thought. You've no right to take away everything I want. What's a pair of eyes compared with a lifetime? What does it matter if a father can't see his children, so long as he has them?

'He's gorgeous, Eric,' she said in a shaking voice, and turned swiftly away to walk from the room.

She would go to the hospital straight away. She'd beg the money for her train fare or hitch-hike the sixty miles. She would see Dennis and tell him that she could not, *would not*, accept his decision. He had no right to make it alone. It was her life too. They must at least talk about it, she must make him see that life was possible again, that it was there to be shared whatever the difficulties, that there was still so much to be enjoyed.

She must make him see that their promises, and their love, held as strongly as ever.

There was no need for Betty to hitch-hike to the blind hospital. As soon as she told the Spencers what she meant to do, they gave her their full support and insisted that she take enough money to keep her there for as long as necessary. 'I know you've got your savings,' Mrs Spencer told her, 'but you don't know how long you'll need to stop, and you've got to find somewhere to stay. We can't have you sleeping in a ditch.'

'That's right,' Yvonne chimed in. 'And you'll want warm clothes too. You can borrow my new jersey.'

Yvonne's new jersey had been knitted from two old ones, unpicked and washed and the best bits of wool rewound. ('We threw away the holes,' she said with a grin.) The colours were oddly merged but it was thick and warm, and Yvonne had worn it every day under her old jacket. Betty was reluctant to take it, but her own clothes were wearing thin and she hadn't got enough coupons for new wool.

'I'm leaving you with all the work to do,' she said awkwardly, knowing that to be honest she shouldn't be leaving at all. The Land Army worked under the same conditions as the Armed Services, after all, and you weren't supposed just to march off and leave it. But Mr Spencer shook his head.

'We'll call it compassionate leave, if anyone asks. But I don't suppose they will. Got too much else on their plates. And there's not much we can be doing outside in this weather.'

Betty set off early one morning, taking the train from Winchester to London. The hospital was on the other side of the city, out towards Essex, and she had to cross from Victoria Station to Liverpool Street. She sat on the bus, looking out at the bombed streets.

It was even worse than Pompey. Row after row of shattered houses, some patched up with boards and tarpaulin, others just left to rot. Big shops with gaping windows. Churches with their roofs open to the sky, their interiors filled with rubble. Damage that had obviously been done three years previously, during the worst of the blitz, and fresh damage that must have occurred only weeks or days ago. It was a wonder there was anyone left.

The hospital was on the edge of a quiet village, about ten miles from the centre of the city. It was a big house, surrounded by gardens that had been mostly dug up to grow vegetables, and Betty carried her small suitcase up the long drive, her knees trembling as she wondered what Dennis was going to say when she arrived. I won't let him send me away, no matter how hard he tries, she told herself. I won't give him up. I *know* we belong together.

It was a fine, dry morning and there were a few people walking around the grounds and some working on the vegetable beds. They must have other patients here as well as blind people, she thought, and then noticed that most of them were tapping the paths with white sticks. And others were sitting on benches, chatting as if they'd just met in the park, their heads turned towards each other. Surely they could see.

'Dennis Verney?' the nurse said in the front hall of the big house. 'Yes, he's here. He's out in the garden somewhere. He spends a lot of his time outside. He used to work on a farm, you know.'

'Yes,' Betty's throat felt tight. She wanted to say *He taught me to milk a cow*, but the words wouldn't come and anyway the nurse was already turning away to deal with a man who was fumbling his way down the stairs, his eyes blank and sightless. Betty murmured her thanks and went out again through the front door. She stood for a moment or two, looking across the quiet garden and wondering where to start looking.

She came upon him quite suddenly, at the far corner of the grounds, working on a fence. It had been damaged, probably by animals forcing their way through, and he was painstakingly snipping off lengths of new wire, tacking them to the post and winding them in with the existing mesh.

Betty stood still. He looked much better than when she'd seen him last, in hospital. He had filled out a little, so that he was no longer gaunt, and his skin had regained some of its colour. His hands worked methodically with the wire, and except for the fact that his fingers seemed to stroke the post as he felt for the right place to fix the new strand, it would have been hard to tell that he couldn't see what he was doing.

Dennis, she thought, Dennis, and her whole body seemed to melt and yearn towards him.

She was never sure what made Dennis pause suddenly and turn his head towards her. Perhaps she made a small sound. Perhaps he knew, by a slight alteration, a shift in the atmosphere, that he was no longer alone.

'Hullo?' he said enquiringly. 'Who's there?' And then, as Betty took a tentative step towards him, his nostrils flared a little and he narrowed his blind eyes. 'Who is it?'

Betty could not speak. She took another step, saw the suspicion dawn slowly on his face. He tilted his head slightly, as if trying to identify something, and then he said slowly, 'Ashes of Roses. *Ashes of Roses.* Betty, is it you? *Betty . . . ?*'

Lots of girls wore Ashes of Roses. But Dennis had told her once it smelt different on her than on anyone else. More natural. More true. He had said he would never forget it.

'Dennis,' she whispered, and walked straight into his arms.

'I thought I was never going to see you again,' Betty wept against Dennis's shoulder. 'I thought you were going to go away and forget all about me.'

'I'd never forget you.' He held her tightly. His own tears were soaking into her hair. 'If you knew how I've wanted you, how I've lain awake at night just aching to hold you again—'

'If it's half as much as I've wanted you, I do know,' she whispered. 'Dennis, it's been awful . . . I'm not going away, you know. I'm not leaving you, and if you try to leave me again, I'll – I'll – well, I don't know *what* I'll do!'

He laughed shakily. 'Marry me.'

Betty lifted her head and stared at him. '*What?*'

'Marry me,' he said. 'That's the best way of making sure I don't leave you again.' The shake in his voice deepened to an unsteady throb. 'I mean it, Betty. Marry me, before I can change my mind again. Not that I will. Not now. I want to be with you. I want to be safe.'

She understood what he meant. It wasn't danger he was afraid of, it was loneliness – her loneliness as much as his. And the waste of a precious love.

She felt her strength returning and stood more firmly against him. It didn't matter that he was blind. It didn't matter that life might be difficult for them. What mattered was that they would face it together, that they would be an ordinary couple, man and wife, with an ordinary family.

'I'm not letting you go,' she said. 'Tell me what we have to do to get married.'

30

The last few days of March were blustery as the month went out like a lion, but spring was around the corner and the lighter evenings brought new heart. And at the end of the first week of April, two events brought great pleasure to the residents of April Grove and its surrounding cluster of streets.

'Proper funny do, this is going to be,' Ted Chapman grumbled as he and Annie got off the bus near Fratton Station and walked with Olive and the Budds through the streets to the Meeting House. 'No hymns, no prayers – not that I've ever been one for kneeling down and spouting a lot of mumbo-jumbo – and your mother not even allowed to wear her best frock. Too bright and gaudy, if you please! I thought it was supposed to be a wedding, not a funeral.'

'Well, it's Betty's choice and I think she should have what she wants,' Olive declared. 'Anyway, you ought to be pleased. It's not costing you much!'

'That's not the point,' Annie said. 'The point is every mother wants her girl to have a nice wedding, and this looks as if it's going to be a proper dismal affair. Your dad's right. Them Quakers don't know how to enjoy themselves. No proper invites, no wedding breakfast, no bridesmaids. And our Betty not even wearing white – I thought I'd die of shame when she told me.'

'It doesn't mean anything, Mum,' Olive said, though privately she thought it probably did. 'Not what you think, anyway. They just don't do it that way. They like things to be quiet.'

'Well, a white frock don't make a lot of noise,' Annie said. 'And I do think she could've had little Maureen with a few flowers.' They walked in silence for a few moments and then she added, 'Well, I'm glad I've asked a few people back home after. At least our friends'll know it's not our doing.'

The whole family had been in and out of Annie's house for the past two days, bringing contributions and helping to prepare a spread that was almost as good as pre-war. Tins of spam had been produced, jellies made and piles of sandwiches cut and filled with jam or fish paste. It was too early for much in the way of salad but Annie had opened a jar of beetroot and some of her pickles, and done a big bowl of new potatoes. There were fresh carrots too, from Frank's allotment, and bottles of cider and jugs of lemon squash.

And there was a cake. Everyone had given eggs, butter, sugar and fruit from their rations and Annie had baked it in her biggest tin. You weren't allowed to make icing now, but she'd made a sort of marzipan and put on a few plaster roses, saved from someone else's wedding several years earlier, to decorate it. It didn't look anything really, when she thought of the beautiful cakes she'd made and decorated in the past, but it was the best she could manage and Betty was delighted with it.

'It's the thought that counts,' she said, giving her mother a hug. 'And it'll taste smashing.'

Betty and Dennis were coming together, from his parents' house. That was another thing that seemed wrong to Annie and Ted. A girl ought to be married from her own home, not her bridegroom's. But everything was upside down at this wedding, and there didn't seem to be anything you could do about it. And the Verneys were such nice, kind people – even if they were really a bit above the Chapmans' class – that you couldn't argue. Anyway, Betty said Quakers didn't argue.

'What, never?' Annie had asked sceptically, and Dennis grinned.

'Well, hardly ever! They do sometimes,' he added fairly. 'They're not angels or anything.'

'I still don't know about our Betty marrying that young man,' Ted said to Annie privately. 'When all's said and done, they're different to us. I mean, his father works in the library, doesn't he? That's not our sort of people. And with all these funny ideas – and then to top it all, him being blind – well, I dunno how our Betty's going to settle to it, I really don't.'

'They love each other. You can see that. And our Betty's been a different girl since they fixed the date. They'll be all right, Ted. It isn't easy for anyone these days.' She sighed. 'Look at our Olive.'

Derek had been away for four months now and Olive had lost weight. She looked pale and miserable, and though she tried to keep a smile on her face, Annie could tell that it was hard for her. It was just as well she had her job to keep her mind occupied, and the rest of the gun crew sounded a nice bunch.

The Meeting House was in Claremont Road. The little group reached the door and hesitated.

A number of people were going in. They wore ordinary clothes, mostly in quiet, neutral colours though there was one woman with a bright feather in her hat. They looked at the little party and smiled, and as Annie paused on the step a small man in a dark suit and spectacles came forward and held out his hand.

'Mrs Chapman? You must be Elizabeth's mother. Welcome to our Meeting. Come inside. My name's Oliver Bradshaw. I'm one of the elders.'

'Thank you,' Annie murmured. It had taken her a moment to realise that it was Betty he meant when he said 'Elizabeth'. 'Er – this is my husband – um, Edward.'

Ted's eyebrows shot up, but he put out his hand and shook the other man's. 'Ted, they call me. Pleased to meet you, Mr Bradshaw.'

'Oliver, please,' the little man said, smiling. He had a nice face, Annie decided, a bit ugly but kind. I don't think I could call him Oliver though, not till I knew him a lot better.

He led them into the meeting room. It was a large, square room with seats like church pews all around – not in rows, like in a proper church, but against each wall, in a square. There were three rows on each side, and in the middle was a large, low table with a small jug of primroses on it and a couple of Bibles.

There were already a good many people in the room. Annie looked at them in surprise. It seemed as if the whole congregation had come. Yet Betty had told her that they wouldn't be inviting anyone. 'It'll just be announced at the meeting for a week or two before,' she'd said, 'and people will come if they want to.'

They must have all wanted to. There was hardly a seat left in the place. But Oliver Bradshaw led them to one of the empty pews in the front row and told them to sit there. 'We've been saving these places for you,' he said with his kind smile.

Annie sat down, with Ted on one side of her and Olive on the other. Jess and Frank took the rest of the pew, with the boys and Rose between them. Tim was starting to grow now and his legs looked lanky in his short trousers. He'd started to pester for long ones, but Jess said he'd have to wait till he was fourteen and took no notice of his complaints.

Now that they were settled, Annie could see quite a few familiar faces. The Spencers were here, from Bishop's Waltham, and Yvonne and Erica with the baby. Frank's brother Howard and his wife had come over from Gosport, and there were two or three cousins and their families. Uncle John Bellinger, who was on the City Council, was here in his dark suit and he winked at her. Annie frowned at him. It might not be a proper church, but you ought to behave with a bit of respect all the same.

It was a shame Mum couldn't have come. But ever since Dad had died, she'd seemed to fade away. She hardly went anywhere now, and although Annie had persuaded her at last to come and stop with them, she didn't have the life in her that she used to have. She just sat in a chair all day, shaking her head and grieving. It almost broke Annie's heart to see her.

Mr Bradshaw and three other men came in and closed the door behind them. They sat down on the empty pew opposite Annie and folded their hands in their laps. She realised that one of the men was Mr Verney.

The room was quiet. Annie glanced at Ted, who was looking uneasy. She peeped sideways at Olive, and past her towards Jess. Her sister glanced round and their eyes met, each asking the same question. What was supposed to happen now? Where were Betty and Dennis?

Mrs Verney was sitting behind her husband. She was wearing a brown skirt and jacket, not exactly a costume but looking very neat, with a white blouse underneath. She had a matching brown hat, quite plain, no feather or veil or anything to make it pretty. She caught Annie's eye and gave her a friendly smile.

Doesn't anybody say *anything*, Annie thought. Are we all going to sit here, staring at the floor and not saying a word, for the rest of the morning?

If our Betty was here, she'd be getting the giggles. But our Betty *should* be here. Where on earth has the girl got to?

The silence went on. Annie felt Ted fidget beside her. He was getting impatient, she thought, and besides that he'd never liked being in confined spaces ever since his 'trouble'. If something didn't happen soon he'd be just as likely to drop something, just to make a noise.

There was a soft click as someone turned the handle of the door. Annie looked round and breathed a sigh of relief. They were here at last, Betty and Dennis, standing in the doorway and smiling. Betty had her hand in the crook of Dennis's arm and he was holding his head up high. His scars were almost healed, his eyes were open and you wouldn't have known he was blind.

The Quakers stood up, looking towards the couple and smiling. Annie and Ted and the rest got hastily to their feet, glancing sideways to see what to do next.

Dennis and Betty came forward side by side. Betty turned him gently so that he could sit on the last empty pew. She was wearing a frock Jess had made for her in soft grey wool, some material she'd got in Bulpitt's with coupons from half the street. It wasn't a wedding dress, but at least she'd be able to wear it afterwards. And even though grey was a funny colour for a wedding, Annie had to admit she looked well in it, with her hair brushed into a soft, red-gold halo of curls and her skin healthy from the outdoor life she led.

Betty looked across the little space at her mother, and Annie smiled at her. Now, at last, the wedding could begin.

Betty felt the warmth of Dennis's hand in hers. She'd been afraid she would be nervous, here in this crowd of people who were mostly strangers, for she'd only attended this Meeting about half a dozen times. Instead, she felt wrapped and comforted by their silent peace.

She caught her mother's eye and smiled back. Her father was looking stiff and uncomfortable. Poor Dad. He must wonder what on earth was going on. So must Auntie Jess and Uncle Frank and all the others who had come along to this plain room, so different from the churches they were used to. But she was sure that by the end of the morning they would all be feeling the peace that was in her heart, the peace she had always sensed in this quiet company. Then they would understand.

She sat very still. Her father shuffled his best black shoes and she heard him sigh. Annie touched him reprovingly, but when she glanced at Betty again there was bewilderment in her eyes and Betty knew that she was wondering when something was going to happen. Wasn't anyone going to get up, say a prayer, read a service of some kind? Wasn't there anyone to lead it, as a vicar or priest would have done?

I've tried to explain, Betty thought, but they just couldn't understand. They couldn't really believe how anyone could get married without some stranger in a white frock reading a lot of words over them. They couldn't believe that you could use words you had chosen or even made up yourself, and that you could decide for yourself when and how to say them.

'I've heard people ask each other which priest or minister married them,' Dennis had said. 'We Friends don't say that. We say we marry each other. It's our own business. We don't involve anyone else, except as witnesses.'

'But doesn't there have to be a registrar?' Betty had asked. 'There always has to be a registrar, surely.'

'Not at a Quaker wedding. Quakers and Jews are the only ones allowed to marry without. One of the elders acts as registering officer.'

Quakers and Jews. An odd combination, and yet it seemed peculiarly appropriate for weren't both persecuted, in their different ways, during this war?

'We consider it a privilege,' Dennis added with a smile.

'Well, I'm glad you've got some privileges. And the Jews as well.' There had been increasing concern over the treatment it was said the Nazis were meting out to the Jews. Some people refused to believe rumours of slave labour and death camps; others swore they were only too true.

The silence had grown very deep. It was as if the souls, the spirits, the essential *beings* of all the people in the room, had gathered into one, as if there were just one entity present, a benign and loving presence that enfolded and absorbed everyone here. Betty felt almost as if she had been lifted slightly above her body, as if she had drifted just outside herself to join that unity; and as if the same thing had happened to them all, so that they met and touched in a space that was neither physical nor even of the mind, but of something else entirely.

Dennis's fingers tightened about hers. She felt his movement and rose to her feet alongside him. They turned to face each other and he held her hands closely in his. His voice was deep and steady. The big white certificate lay on the table before them, and Betty glanced at it, prepared to whisper the words, but Dennis had no need of a reminder.

'Friends,' he said, 'I take this my friend Elizabeth Anne Chapman to be my wife, promising, through divine assistance, to be unto her a loving and faithful husband, so long as we both on earth shall live.'

There was a pause. Betty looked up into his face. If she had not known he was blind, she would have believed that his eyes smiled into hers. Then she caught the glint of tears in them, and knew that she was not far from weeping herself.

'Friends,' she said, and her voice was low yet clear, with just a hint of the tears which were building so strongly in her, 'I take this my friend Dennis James Verney to be my husband, promising, through divine assistance, to be unto him a loving and faithful wife, so long as we both on earth shall live.'

They stood very still, facing each other, their fingers entwined. And then Dennis felt in his pocket and took out the golden wedding ring. Betty held out her shaking hand and he slipped it on, pushing it over the knuckle. She stared at it and a tear dropped on to the back of her hand and ran down to touch the gold, magnifying it so that it blazed with sudden light.

Dennis bent and kissed her lips. Then they sat down together, still holding hands very tightly. Betty was shaking.

I'm Mrs Verney, she thought. Just those few words in front of these people, and I'm Mrs Verney. And I don't feel a bit different. Not a scrap.

But that, she realised, was because she had been feeling like Dennis's wife for a very long time. Ever since that Christmas two years ago, when she had crept down to his room and slipped into his waiting arms. Ever since she had first said she loved him.

It was several minutes before anyone else spoke. And then Oliver Bradshaw rose to his feet. He looked at the newly-weds kindly.

'Friends, we have come here today to witness the marriage between these two young people. I know we all wish them well, all the happiness that they deserve. And there will be those amongst us who know these two young people, who will have kind and generous things to say about them. Forgive me if I ask to be the first.'

He paused, then went on quietly, 'I've known Dennis and his father Robert for many, many years. Indeed, I think I can say I've known Dennis all his life, for he first came to this Meeting in his pram as a small baby, only just able to sit up. He would be wheeled into that corner there and allowed to sleep or to play, whichever he preferred. He was not always quiet. I can remember one occasion when his mother took him out, and she might as well have let him stay, for his screams could be heard as clearly through the windows as they could when he were still in the room.'

There was a quiver of laughter in the air. Oliver Bradshaw smiled and waited a moment, then continued.

'Since then, I've watched – many of us have watched – Dennis grow into the fine young man he is today. We've seen his belief and determination match that of his father's as he faced the tribunal as a conscientious objector and quietly accepted their decision. We've seen his strength as he endured a prison sentence and his cheerfulness and willingness as he worked on the land. And we have seen his courage as he took the decision to risk his life in the service of others.'

Not in fighting the war, Betty thought. In the service of others.

'Finally,' Oliver Bradshaw said, 'we see the greatest evidence of all of courage as he faces the future without sight. And we see the fortitude and love of our friend Betty, who stands beside him today as his wife. Friends,' he said, turning to Betty and Dennis, 'this Meeting wishes you great happiness in your union. We are glad to have been here today to witness it.'

He sat down. Again, nobody moved or spoke but the atmosphere in the room was filled with a tender lovingness and after a few moments, someone else got up and spoke of knowing Dennis, recounting a story of Dennis's exploits as a boy that made them all laugh. And then, as if a spring had been released, one after another the members of the Meeting rose and made their own contribution so that the good wishes and the stories went on and on and the gathering began to seem more like a celebration. And at the very last, when it seemed that there was no more to be said, Ted Chapman cleared his throat and came to his feet, twisting his hat in his hands, big and awkward in the crowded room.

'I don't know if it's proper for me to do this,' he began gruffly. 'I never been to one of these sorta weddings before. It ain't what I'm used to, and standing up like this and speechifying in public, that ain't what I'm used to neither. But it gotta be said, and I'm the one that's gotta say it.'

The Quakers listened attentively, and Oliver Bradshaw nodded. Annie, who had been about to tug at Ted's sleeve, glanced anxiously along the pew at her sister, who shrugged. He was on his feet now. There was nothing to be done about it.

Ted lowered his head. It was an almost belligerent movement, like a bull about to charge, and the glowering look he sent about the room added to the impression. But Annie knew that he was simply nervous. Oh Ted, she thought, don't make a fool of yourself.

'When I first met young Dennis here,' he said gruffly, 'he was working on the farm with our Betty. She brought him home to Sunday dinner one weekend. We knew there must be summat special about him, but she hadn't said nothing else. She never told us why he was on the land. Why he wasn't in the Services.'

He's going to put his foot in it, Annie thought. He's going to offend them all. Oh, *Ted*.

'I asked him that dinner-time, straight out. I could see there was summat funny about it. *If* you'll pardon me. And he told me, just as straight. He never tried to hide nothing, I had to give him that.'

He paused again. The Meeting Room was totally silent. You could have heard a hair drop.

'Well, I dunno if you can imagine what I thought about *that*,' Ted said, his tone leaving no room for doubt as to what he'd thought. 'I don't mind telling you, I was proper disgusted. And I said so. Called him a coward and I dunno what else. I told him to get out of my house. And I told my daughter not to bring him back, neither.'

Annie had heard of people wishing that the ground would open up under their feet. She stared at the wooden floorboards, praying to see them suddenly part. She dared not look at Betty.

'Course, he told me he was joining the Pioneers,' Ted said. 'And maybe I oughter've backed down a bit. But I'm a stubborn old devil – pardon my language – and I couldn't forget that I had a lad in the Royal Navy – a lad whose ship's bin sunk off Japan and we've never heard whether he's still alive or not – nor that I'd got a girl in the ATS. And I couldn't forget Dunkirk, neither, and going over in the old *Ferry King* to pick up the poor bug – the poor devils – pardon me again, but me feelings are a bit too strong to watch me words, as anyone who'd been there would understand. Anyway, what I means to say is I thought of all that and I looked at this bloke, fit and healthy and refusing to fight, and I don't mind telling you, it stuck in me craw to have him sitting there at me own table.'

'*Ted*,' Annie whispered agonisedly. 'Ted, for heaven's sake sit down . . .'

He flicked his hand in a gesture of silence. 'I'll sit down when I've had me say, and not before. I haven't finished yet, not by a long chalk.' He surveyed the room again. The Quakers were still sitting with eyes downcast, showing almost no reaction to his words, although one or two were looking flushed. The rest of the guests, the Budds and the Shaws and their other friends and neighbours, were looking as embarrassed as Annie.

'It's all right,' he said. 'You don't need to look so flummoxed. I didn't come here to cause no unpleasantness. What I'm working up to is this. I've come to realise I was wrong. I've watched this lad – well, *heard* about him, more like, through the wife and our Betty – join up and do just about the most dangerous job there is. He still won't fight, and I can't pretend I understand why when you looks at what's going on in the world, but he's no coward. He's proved that, over and over again. He's risked his life and he's lost his sight, and all I want to say is this.' He looked over towards Dennis and then stepped across the little space and held out his hand. 'I'm proud to know you, Dennis, and I'm even prouder to have you for a son-in-law. I hope you and Betty has a long and happy life together. And if you can see your way to overlooking what happened before, I hope you'll come down April Grove and see us as often as you can. You're welcome in the Chapman family.'

Dennis came to his feet. Betty nudged his right arm and he lifted it so that Ted could take his hand. They clasped each other's palms firmly and Ted gripped Dennis's forearm and then clapped him on the shoulder.

'Oh, *Dad*,' Betty said, and flung herself into his arms, tears streaming down her face.

There was a collective sigh of relief and pleasure. Annie got up and hugged Ted's arm, then kissed both Betty and Dennis. The Verneys joined in, followed swiftly by Jess Budd and then Frank. And everyone, Quakers and guests alike, turned to each other, smiling and holding out their hands or kissing. The quiet room was suddenly filled with hubbub and laughter.

The Meeting never did return to order. Dennis had told Betty that after everyone had said all they wanted to, there would be a final period of silence and meditation before the elders shook hands to signify that it was over. But once they were all on their feet, the silence broken, there was no chance of settling down again. They moved to the table to see the registering officer – another of the elders – fill in the big Certificate of Marriage, which set out the words that Dennis and Betty had used, and was then signed by everyone present. While that was being done, he completed the more usual certificate and handed it to Betty.

'Be happy, my dear,' he said, smiling, and she took it and thanked him. But it was the big Quaker certificate, rolled into a long cardboard tube, that she held most tenderly. This was the complete record of the day.

They left the room. In one of the other rooms, someone had made tea and they stood about, drinking and chatting and nibbling biscuits. It wasn't much of a wedding feast, Annie thought, thankful that she'd prepared something more festive at home, but somehow it didn't seem to matter after all. And neither did the fact that there were no bridesmaids, nor that she'd been denied the chance of wearing her best pink frock or that Betty wasn't in white.

What mattered was the radiance on Betty and Dennis's faces. The sheer joy that shone like an aura all around them. The ecstatic happiness that vibrated in the air and filled the room from wall to wall, from corner to corner.

And it didn't matter, either, that they had to go home in a bus. The one that came along had the whole top deck empty and they all climbed up the stairs and sat chattering and laughing, drawing the conductor into the fun. When he heard that they were a wedding party he put away his ticket-machine and went back downstairs.

'I've never seen yer,' he said as his head disappeared. 'Never saw no one up there. Bin the quietest run of the morning, this one 'as.'

'Wasn't that nice,' Annie said to Jess when they were back in April Grove, in the house with the turret. 'You know, I thought it was going to be a bit of a washout, but it was lovely. I mean, there wasn't hardly anything to it, but somehow or other it seemed to mean such a lot. I don't know how to explain it. Everyone seemed to be part of it, in a way, even all them people we didn't know.'

'I know,' Jess said thoughtfully. 'I felt it too. Like as if everyone was together – not just sitting in a room, but in a different sort of way. Close.'

There's only two things missing,' Annie said, glancing through the open door into the other room. Betty and Dennis were there in the middle of a laughing crowd, but Olive was sitting with her grandmother near the window, looking out into the sunlit street. Her face was abstracted and sad.

'I know. Olive must be missing Derek badly today. And we all know who else ought to be here.' Jess reached out, her face filled with concern for Annie's lips were quivering and her eyes were suddenly filled with tears. 'Colin. Oh, Annie, I don't know what to say—'

She stopped abruptly. Olive, sitting by the window, had suddenly leapt to her feet. Pushing past Dennis and Betty, she thrust a way to the door. She jerked open the front door just as the bell began to shrill, and snatched at the orange envelope that was being held out by a boy in dark blue uniform.

'A telegram! She must've seen him coming down the street.' Jess lifted her fingers to her mouth. 'Oh, Annie, if something's happened to Derek, today of all days—'

But Olive, her face as pale as ashes, was staring at the envelope and making no attempt to open it. Moving stiffly, as if in a trance, she turned and looked across the crowd towards her mother.

'It's for you,' she said in a strange, creaky voice. 'Mum – it's for you.'

'For *me*?' Annie gaped at her, then stepped forwards. 'A telegram for me? Oh, my goodness. Oh, Ted—'

He was beside her, taking the envelope from Olive's fingers. While everyone fell silent, he pulled out the sheet of paper and read it. They saw his face whiten. They saw Annie's unbelieving stare, the slow shake of her head as if refuting the news it had brought. They saw her turn her head and gaze up at her husband as if asking him if it were really true.

Jess found Frank beside her, and felt for his hand. 'It's Colin. It must be Colin. Oh, poor Annie.'

But Annie was smiling. Her white face had regained its colour in a rush and she was smiling, even beginning to laugh. It's hysterics, Jess thought, it's shock, reaction. She stepped forward, ready to fold her sister in her arms.

Annie turned to her. 'Look at this, Jess! Look at this! He's *safe* – our

Colin's safe. Look! It says he's in Japanese hands – in a Japanese prisoner-of-war camp. He's been alive, all this time. Oh Jess, Jess, *Jess*!'

The tears were cascading down her cheeks now and she was laughing and crying at the same time. It was hysteria, right enough, but no one had the heart to do anything about it. Let Annie laugh or cry all she liked. She'd kept her feelings to herself long enough.

Jess took the envelope and the sheet of paper and read it carefully. Then she turned to Frank and smiled, and the tears were in her eyes too.

'It's true,' she said. 'Colin's still alive. He's a Japanese prisoner of war. He's going to come home again, Frank. He's *all right*.'

'Thank God for that,' Frank said quietly. 'And let's hope it's not too long before the war's over and he's back again, eh, Jess? Nearly four years it's been going on. That's as long as the First War lasted. It's got to come to an end soon.'

The wedding reception had become a party, the quietness of the Meeting forgotten in a sudden burst of jubilant celebration. And in the midst of it all, Dennis and Betty stood close, their arms wound about each other's waists, unwilling to part even for a moment.

'I love you, Betty,' he whispered in her ear, and she smiled back at him.

'I love you too, Dennis. And everything's going to be all right now. Uncle Frank's right – the war can't last very much longer. Derek'll come home and make Olive happy again. And best of all, our Colin's safe.' She smiled. 'D'you know something? I feel as if today's a turning point for us all. From now on, everything's going to get better. Just you wait and see.'

'Like in the song,' he said with a grin. 'And what's the other one? "Keep Smiling Through"? D'you know, Betty, I can hear your smile when you talk. And it's just as lovely as when I could see it. So you will keep doing it, won't you? Smiling through, I mean. It's what keeps everyone going.'

He was right, Betty thought as they went out for a breath of air a little later and wandered hand in hand across the moonlit path over the allotments. Smiling did keep you going. It had kept Olive going while Derek was away, it had kept her mother going through all the anxiety over Colin. It had kept Betty herself going when Dennis was taking those terrible risks. It had kept them all going through raids and sleepless nights and the grinding despair of the days.

Four years. It *couldn't* be much longer.